HARLEM RENAISSANCE
FOUR NOVELS OF THE 1930s

Harlem Renaissance

FOUR NOVELS OF THE 1930s

Not Without Laughter • Langston Hughes
Black No More • George Schuyler
The Conjure-Man Dies • Rudolph Fisher
Black Thunder • Arna Bontemps

Rafia Zafar, *editor*

THE LIBRARY OF AMERICA

Black Thunder reprinted by arrangement with Beacon Press.

The paper used in this publication meets the
minimum requirements of the American National Standard for
Information Sciences–Permanence of Paper for Printed
Library Materials, ANSI Z39.48–1984.

Distributed to the trade in the United States
by Penguin Group (USA) Inc.
and in Canada by Penguin Books Canada Ltd.

Library of Congress Control Number: 2010942024
ISBN 978-1-59853-101-5

———

First Printing
The Library of America—218

Manufactured in the United States of America

Harlem Renaissance: Four Novels of the 1930s
is published with support from

THE SHELLEY & DONALD RUBIN FOUNDATION

Contents

NOT WITHOUT LAUGHTER by Langston Hughes 1

BLACK NO MORE by George S. Schuyler. 219

THE CONJURE-MAN DIES by Rudolph Fisher 373

BLACK THUNDER by Arna Bontemps 593

Chronology 817

Biographical Notes 827

Note on the Texts 834

Notes 839

NOT WITHOUT LAUGHTER

Langston Hughes

To
J. E. and Amy Spingarn

Contents

I · *Storm* · 5

II · *Conversation* · 14

III · *Jimboy's Letter* · 23

IV · *Thursday Afternoon* · 28

V · *Guitar* · 36

VI · *Work* · 44

VII · *White Folks* · 51

VIII · *Dance* · 60

IX · *Carnival* · 74

X · *Punishment* · 83

XI · *School* · 89

XII · *Hard Winter* · 95

XIII · *Christmas* · 105

XIV · *Return* · 115

XV · *One by One* · 120

XVI · *Nothing but Love* · 128

XVII · *Barber-Shop* · 133

XVIII · *Children's Day* · 139

XIX · *Ten Dollars and Costs* · 146

XX · *Hey, Boy!* · 150

XXI · *Note to Harriett* · 157

XXII · *Beyond the Jordan* · 165

XXIII · *Tempy's House* · 170

XXIV · *A Shelf of Books* · 175

XXV · *Pool Hall* · 179

XXVI · *The Doors of Life* · 185

XXVII · *Beware of Women* · 190

XXVIII · *Chicago* · 198

XXIX · *Elevator* · 208

XXX · *Princess of the Blues* · 212

ONE

Storm

A UNT HAGER WILLIAMS stood in her doorway and looked out at the sun. The western sky was a sulphurous yellow and the sun a red ball dropping slowly behind the trees and house-tops. Its setting left the rest of the heavens grey with clouds.

"Huh! A storm's comin'," said Aunt Hager aloud.

A pullet ran across the back yard and into a square-cut hole in an unpainted piano-box which served as the roosting-house. An old hen clucked her brood together and, with the tiny chicks, went into a small box beside the large one. The air was very still. Not a leaf stirred on the green apple-tree. Not a single closed flower of the morning-glories trembled on the back fence. The air was very still and yellow. Something sultry and oppressive made a small boy in the doorway stand closer to his grandmother, clutching her apron with his brown hands.

"Sho is a storm comin'," said Aunt Hager.

"I hope mama gets home 'fore it rains," remarked the brown child holding to the old woman's apron. "Hope she gets home."

"I does, too," said Aunt Hager. "But I's skeared she won't."

Just then great drops of water began to fall heavily into the back yard, pounding up little clouds of dust where each drop struck the earth. For a few moments they pattered violently on the roof like a series of hammer-strokes; then suddenly they ceased.

"Come in, chile," said Aunt Hager.

She closed the door as the green apple-tree began to sway in the wind and a small hard apple fell, rolling rapidly down the top of the piano-box that sheltered the chickens. Inside the kitchen it was almost dark. While Aunt Hager lighted an oil-lamp, the child climbed to a chair and peered through the square window into the yard. The leaves and flowers of the morning-glory vines on the back fence were bending with the rising wind. And across the alley at the big house, Mrs.

Kennedy's rear screen-door banged to and fro, and Sandy saw her garbage-pail suddenly tip over and roll down into the yard, scattering potato-peelings on the white steps.

"Sho gwine be a terrible storm," said Hager as she turned up the wick of the light and put the chimney on. Then, glancing through the window, she saw a black cloud twisting like a ribbon in the western sky, and the old woman screamed aloud in sudden terror: "It's a cyclone! It's gwine be a cyclone! Sandy, let's get over to Mis' Carter's quick, 'cause we ain't got no cellar here. Come on, chile, let's get! Come on, chile! . . . Come on, chile!"

Hurriedly she blew out the light, grabbed the boy's hand; and together they rushed through the little house towards the front. It was quite dark in the inner rooms, but through the parlor windows came a sort of sooty grey-green light that was rapidly turning to blackness.

"Lawd help us, Jesus!"

Aunt Hager opened the front door, but before she or the child could move, a great roaring sound suddenly shook the world, and, with a deafening division of wood from wood, they saw their front porch rise into the air and go hurtling off into space. Sailing high in the gathering darkness, the porch was soon lost to sight. And the black wind blew with terrific force, numbing the ear-drums.

For a moment the little house trembled and swayed and creaked as though it were about to fall.

"Help me to shut this do'," Aunt Hager screamed; "help me to shut it, Lawd!" as with all her might she struggled against the open door, which the wind held back, but finally it closed and the lock caught. Then she sank to the floor with her back against the wall, while her small grandson trembled like a leaf as she took him in her lap, mumbling: "What a storm! . . . O, Lawdy! . . . O, ma chile, what a storm!"

They could hear the crackling of timbers and the rolling limbs of trees that the wind swept across the roof. Her arms tightened about the boy.

"Dear Jesus!" she said. "I wonder where is yo' mama? S'pose she started out fo' home 'fore this storm come up!" Then in a scream: "Have mercy on ma Annjee! O, Lawd, have mercy on this chile's mamma! Have mercy on all ma chillens! Ma

Harriett, an' ma Tempy, an' ma Annjee, what's maybe all of 'em out in de storm! O, Lawd!"

A dry crack of lightning split the darkness, and the boy began to wail. Then the rain broke. The old woman could not see the crying child she held, nor could the boy hear the broken voice of his grandmother, who had begun to pray as the rain crashed through the inky blackness. For a long while it roared on the roof of the house and pounded at the windows, until finally the two within became silent, hushing their cries. Then only the lashing noise of the water, coupled with the feeling that something terrible was happening, or had already happened, filled the evening air.

After the rain the moon rose clear and bright and the clouds disappeared from the lately troubled sky. The stars sparkled calmly above the havoc of the storm, and it was still early evening as people emerged from their houses and began to investigate the damage brought by the twisting cyclone that had come with the sunset. Through the rubbish-filled streets men drove slowly with horse and buggy or automobile. The fire-engine was out, banging away, and the soft tang-tang-tang of the motor ambulance could be heard in the distance carrying off the injured.

Black Aunt Hager and her brown grandson put their rubbers on and stood in the water-soaked front yard looking at the porchless house where they lived. Platform, steps, pillars, roof, and all had been blown away. Not a semblance of a porch was left and the front door opened bare into the yard. It was grotesque and funny. Hager laughed.

"Cyclone sho did a good job," she said. "Looks like I ain't never had no porch."

Madam de Carter, from next door, came across the grass, her large mouth full of chattering sympathy for her neighbor.

"But praise God for sparing our lives! It might've been worse, Sister Williams! It might've been much more calamitouser! As it is, I lost nothin' more'n a chimney and two wash-tubs which was settin' in the back yard. A few trees broke down don't 'mount to nothin'. We's livin', ain't we? And we's more importanter than trees is any day!" Her gold teeth sparkled in the moonlight.

"'Deed so," agreed Hager emphatically. "Let's move on down de block, Sister, an' see what mo' de Lawd has 'stroyed or spared this evenin'. He's gin us plenty moonlight after de storm so we po' humans can see this lesson o' His'n to a sinful world."

The two elderly colored women picked their way about on the wet walk, littered with twigs and branches of broken foliage. The little brown boy followed, with his eyes wide at the sight of baby-carriages, window-sashes, shingles, and tree-limbs scattered about in the roadway. Large numbers of people were out, some standing on porches, some carrying lanterns, picking up useful articles from the streets, some wringing their hands in a daze.

Near the corner a small crowd had gathered quietly.

"Mis' Gavitt's killed," somebody said.

"Lawd help!" burst from Aunt Hager and Madam de Carter simultaneously.

"Mister and Mis' Gavitt's both dead," added a nervous young white man, bursting with the news. "We live next door to 'em, and their house turned clean over! Came near hitting us and breaking our side-wall in."

"Have mercy!" said the two women, but Sandy slipped away from his grandmother and pushed through the crowd. He ran round the corner to where he could see the overturned house of the unfortunate Gavitts.

Good white folks, the Gavitts, Aunt Hager had often said, and now their large frame dwelling lay on its side like a doll's mansion, with broken furniture strewn carelessly on the wet lawn—and they were dead. Sandy saw a piano flat on its back in the grass. Its ivory keys gleamed in the moonlight like grinning teeth, and the strange sight made his little body shiver, so he hurried back through the crowd looking for his grandmother. As he passed the corner, he heard a woman sobbing hysterically within the wide house there.

His grandmother was no longer standing where he had left her, but he found Madam de Carter and took hold of her hand. She was in the midst of a group of excited white and colored women. One frail old lady was saying in a high determined voice that she had never seen a cyclone like this in her whole life, and she lived here in Kansas, if you please, going on seventy-three years. Madam de Carter, chattering nervously, began to tell them how she had recognized its coming and had rushed to the cellar the minute she saw the sky turn green. She had not come up until the rain stopped, so frightened had she been. She was extravagantly enjoying the telling of her fears as Sandy kept tugging at her hand.

"Where's my grandma?" he demanded. Madam de Carter, however, did not cease talking to answer his question.

"What do you want, sonny?" finally one of the white women asked, bending down when he looked as if he were about to cry. "Aunt Hager? . . . Why, she's inside helping them calm poor Mrs. Gavitt's niece. Your grandmother's good to have around when folks are sick or grieving, you know. Run and set on the steps like a nice boy and wait until she comes out." So Sandy left the women and went to sit in the dark on the steps of the big corner house where the niece of the dead Mrs. Gavitt lived. There were some people on the porch, but they soon passed through the screen-door into the house or went away down the street. The moonlight cast weird shadows across the damp steps where Sandy sat, and it was dark there under the trees in spite of the moon, for the old house was built far back from the street in a yard full of oaks and maples, and Sandy could see the light from an upstairs window reflecting on the wet leaves of their nearest boughs. He heard a girl screaming, too, up there where the light was burning, and he knew that Aunt Hager was putting cold cloths on her head, or rubbing her hands, or driving folks out of the room, and talking kind to her so that she would soon be better.

All the neighborhood, white or colored, called his grandmother when something happened. She was a good nurse, they said, and sick folks liked her around. Aunt Hager always came when they called, too, bringing maybe a little soup that she had made or a jelly. Sometimes they paid her and sometimes they didn't. But Sandy had never had to sit outdoors in the darkness waiting for her before. He leaned his small back against the top step and rested his elbows on the porch behind him. It was growing late and the people in the streets had all disappeared.

There, in the dark, the little fellow began to think about his mother, who worked on the other side of town for a rich white lady named Mrs. J. J. Rice. And suddenly frightful thoughts came into his mind. Suppose she had left for home just as the storm came up! Almost always his mother was home before dark—but she wasn't there tonight when the storm came—and she should have been home! This thought appalled him. She should have been there! But maybe she had been caught by the storm and blown away as she walked down Main Street! Maybe Annjee had been carried off by the great black wind that had overturned the Gavitt's house and taken his grandma's porch flying through the air! Maybe the cyclone had gotten his mother, Sandy thought. He wanted her! Where was she? Had something terrible happened to her? Where was she now?

The big tears began to roll down his cheeks—but the little fellow held back the sobs that wanted to come. He decided he wasn't going to cry and make a racket there by himself on the strange steps of these white folks' house. He wasn't going to cry like a big baby in the dark. So he wiped his eyes, kicked his heels against the cement walk, lay down on the top step, and, by and by, sniffled himself to sleep.

"Wake up, son!" Someone was shaking him. "You'll catch your death o' cold sleeping on the wet steps like this. We're going home now. Don't want me to have to carry a big man like you, do you, boy? . . . Wake up, Sandy!" His mother stooped to lift his long little body from the wide steps. She held him against her soft heavy breasts and let his head rest on one of her shoulders while his feet, in their muddy rubbers, hung down against her dress.

"Where you been, mama?" the boy asked drowsily, tightening his arms about her neck. "I been waiting for you."

"Oh, I been home a long time, worried to death about you and ma till I heard from Madam Carter that you-all was down here nursing the sick. I stopped at your Aunt Tempy's house when I seen the storm coming."

"I was afraid you got blowed away, mama," murmured Sandy sleepily. "Let's go home, mama. I'm glad you ain't got blowed away."

On the porch Aunt Hager was talking to a pale white man and two thin white women standing at the door of the lighted hallway. "Just let Mis' Agnes sleep," she was saying. "She'll be all right now, an' I'll come back in de mawnin' to see 'bout her. . . . Good-night, you-all."

The old colored woman joined her daughter and they started home, walking through the streets filled with debris and puddles of muddy water reflecting the moon.

"You're certainly heavy, boy," remarked Sandy's mother to the child she held, but he didn't answer.

"I'm right glad you come for me, Annjee," Hager said. "I wonder is yo' sister all right out yonder at de country club. . . . An' I was so worried 'bout you I didn't know what to do—skeared you might a got caught in this twister, 'cause it were cert'ly awful!"

"I was at Tempy's!" Annjee replied. "And I was nearly crazy, but I just left everything in the hands o' God. That's all." In silence they walked on, a piece; then hesitantly, to her mother: "There wasn't any mail for me today, was there, ma?"

"Not a speck!" the old woman replied shortly. "Mail-man passed on by."

For a few minutes there was silence again as they walked. Then, "It's goin' on three weeks he's been gone, and he ain't written a line," the younger woman complained, shifting the child to her right arm. "Seems like Jimboy would let a body know where he is, ma, wouldn't it?"

"Huh! That ain't nothin'! He's been gone before this an' he ain't wrote, ain't he? Here you is worryin' 'bout a letter from that good-for-nothing husband o' your'n—an' there's ma house settin' up without a porch to its name! . . . Ain't you seed what de devil's done done on earth this evenin', chile? . . . An' yet de first thing you ask me 'bout is de mail-man! . . . Lawd! Lawd! . . . You an' that Jimboy!"

Aunt Hager lifted her heavy body over fallen tree-trunks and across puddles, but between puffs she managed to voice her indignation, so Annjee said no more concerning letters from her husband. Instead they went back to the subject of the cyclone. "I'm just thankful, ma, it didn't blow the whole house down and you with it, that's all! I was certainly worried! . . . And

then you-all was gone when I got home! Gone on out—
nursing that white woman. . . . It's too bad 'bout poor Mis'
Gavitt, though, and old man Gavitt, ain't it?"

"Yes, indeedy!" said Aunt Hager. "It's sho too bad. They
was certainly good old white folks! An' her married niece is
takin' it mighty hard, po' little soul. I was nigh two hours,
her husband an' me, tryin' to bring her out o' de hysterics.
Tremblin' like a lamb all over, she was." They were turning
into the yard. "Be careful with that chile, Annjee, you don't
trip on none o' them boards nor branches an' fall with him."

"Put me down, 'cause I'm awake," said Sandy.

The old house looked queer without a porch. In the moonlight he could see the long nails that had held the porch roof
to the weather-boarding. His grandmother climbed slowly
over the door-sill, and his mother lifted him to the floor level
as Aunt Hager lit the large oil-lamp on the parlor table. Then
they went back to the bedroom, where the youngster took off
his clothes, said his prayers, and climbed into the high feather
bed where he slept with Annjee. Aunt Hager went to the next
room, but for a long time she talked back and forth through
the doorway to her daughter about the storm.

"We was just startin' out fo' Mis' Carter's cellar, me an' Sandy,"
she said several times. "But de Lawd was with us! He held us
back! Praise His name! We ain't harmed, none of us—'ceptin' I
don't know 'bout ma Harriett at de club. But you's all right.
An' you say Tempy's all right, too. An' I prays that Harriett
ain't been touched out there in de country where she's workin'.
Maybe de storm ain't passed that way."

Then they spoke about the white people where Annjee
worked . . . and about the elder sister Tempy's prosperity.
Then Sandy heard his grandmother climb into bed, and a few
minutes after the springs screaked under her, she had begun to
snore. Annjee closed the door between their rooms and slowly
began to unlace her wet shoes.

"Sandy," she whispered, "we ain't had no word yet from
your father since he left. I know he goes away and stays away
like this and don't write, but I'm sure worried. Hope the cyclone ain't passed nowhere near wherever he is, and I hope
ain't nothin' hurt him. . . . I'm gonna pray for him, Sandy.
I'm gonna ask God right now to take care o' Jimboy. . . . The

Lawd knows, I wants him to come back! . . . I loves him.
. . . We both loves him, don't we, child? And we want him to
come on back!"

She knelt down beside the bed in her night-dress and kept
her head bowed for a long time. Before she got up, Sandy had
gone to sleep.

TWO

Conversation

IT WAS broad daylight in the town of Stanton and had been for a long time.

"Get out o' that bed, boy!" Aunt Hager yelled. "Here's Buster waitin' out in de yard to play with you, an' you still sleepin'!"

"Aw, tell him to cut off his curls," retorted Sandy, but his grandmother was in no mood for fooling.

"Stop talkin' 'bout that chile's haid and put yo' clothes on. Nine o'clock an' you ain't up yet! Shame on you!" She shouted from the kitchen, where Sandy could hear the fire crackling and smell coffee boiling.

He kicked the sheet off with his bare feet and rolled over and over on the soft feather tick. There was plenty of room to roll now, because his mother had long since got up and gone to Mrs. J. J. Rice's to work.

"Tell Bus I'm coming," Sandy yelled, jumping into his trousers and running with bare feet towards the door. "Is he got his marbles?"

"Come back here, sir, an' put them shoes on," cried Hager, stopping him on his way out. "Yo' feet'll get long as yard-sticks and flat as pancakes runnin' round barefooted all de time. An' wash yo' face, sir. Buster ain't got a thing to do but wait. An' eat yo' breakfast."

The air was warm with sunlight, and hundreds of purple and white morning-glories laughed on the back fence. Earth and sky were fresh and clean after the heavy night-rain, and the young corn-shoots stood straight in the garden, and green pea-vines wound themselves around their crooked sticks. There was the mingled scent of wet soil and golden pollen on the breeze that blew carelessly through the clear air.

Buster sat under the green apple-tree with a pile of black mud from the alley in front of him.

"Hey, Sandy, gonna make marbles and put 'em in the sun to dry," he said.

"All right," agreed Sandy, and they began to roll mud balls in the palms of their hands. But instead of putting them in the sun to dry they threw them against the back of the house, where they flattened and stuck beautifully. Then they began to throw them at each other.

Sandy's playmate was a small ivory-white Negro child with straight golden hair, which his mother made him wear in curls. His eyes were blue and doll-like and he in no way resembled a colored youngster; but he was colored. Sandy himself was the shade of a nicely browned piece of toast, with dark, brown-black eyes and a head of rather kinky, sandy hair that would lie smooth only after a rigorous application of vaseline and water. That was why folks called him Annjee's sandy-headed child, and then just—Sandy.

"He takes after his father," Sister Lowry said, "'cept he's not so light. But he's gonna be a mighty good-lookin' boy when he grows up, that's sho!"

"Well, I hopes he does," Aunt Hager said. "But I'd rather he'd be ugly 'fore he turns out anything like that good-for-nothing Jimboy what comes here an' stays a month, goes away an' stays six, an' don't hit a tap o' work 'cept when he feels like it. If it wasn't for Annjee, don't know how we'd eat, 'cause Sandy's father sho don't do nothin' to support him."

All the colored people in Stanton knew that Hager bore no love for Jimboy Rodgers, the tall good-looking yellow fellow whom her second daughter had married.

"First place, I don't like his name," she would say in private. "Who ever heard of a nigger named Jimboy, anyhow? Next place, I ain't never seen a yaller dude yet that meant a dark woman no good—an' Annjee is dark!" Aunt Hager had other objections, too, although she didn't like to talk evil about folks. But what she probably referred to in her mind was the question of his ancestry, for nobody knew who Jimboy's parents were.

"Sandy, look out for the house while I run down an' see how is Mis' Gavitt's niece. An' you-all play outdoors. Don't bring no chillen in, litterin' up de place." About eleven o'clock Aunt Hager pulled a dustcap over her head and put on a clean white apron. "Here, tie it for me, chile," she said, turning her broad back. "An' mind you don't hurt yo'self on no rusty nails and rotten boards left from de storm. I'll be back atter while." And she disappeared around the house, walking proudly, her black face shining in the sunlight.

Presently the two boys under the apple-tree were joined by a coal-colored little girl who lived next door, one Willie-Mae Johnson, and the mud balls under her hands became mud pies carefully rounded and patted and placed in the sun on the small box where the little chickens lived. Willie-Mae was the mama, Sandy the papa, and Buster the baby as the old game of "playing house" began anew.

By and by the mail-man's whistle blew and the three children scampered towards the sidewalk to meet him. The carrier handed Sandy a letter. "Take it in the house," he said. But instead the youngsters sat on the front-door-sill, their feet dangling where the porch had been, and began to examine the envelope.

"I bet that's Lincoln's picture," said Buster.

"No, 'taint," declared Willie-Mae. "It's Rossiefelt!"

"Aw, it's Washington," said Sandy. "And don't you-all touch my mama's letter with your hands all muddy. It might be from my papa, you can't tell, and she wants it kept clean."

" 'Tis from Jimboy," Aunt Hager declared when she returned, accompanied by her old friend, Sister Whiteside, who peddled on foot fresh garden-truck she raised herself. Aunt Hager had met her at the corner.

"I knows his writin'," went on Hager. "An' it's got a post-mark, K-A-N-, Kansas City! That's what 'tis! Niggers sho do love Kansas City! . . . Huh! . . . So that's where he's at. Well, yo' mama'll be glad to get it. If she knowed it was here, she'd quit work an' come home now. . . . Sit down, Whiteside. We gwine eat in a few minutes. You better have a bite with us an' stay an' rest yo'self awhile, 'cause I knows you been walkin' this mawnin'!"

" 'Deed I is," the old sister declared, dropping her basket of lettuce and peas on the floor and taking a chair next to the table in the kitchen. "An' I ain't sold much neither. Seems like folks ain't got no buyin' appetite after all that storm an' wind last night—but de Lawd will provide! I ain't worried."

"That's right," agreed Hager. "Might o' been me blowed away maself, 'stead o' just ma porch, if Jesus hadn't been with us. . . . You Sandy! Make haste and wash yo' hands, sir. Rest o' you chillens go on home, 'cause I know yo' ma's lookin' for you. . . . Huh! This wood fire's mighty low!"

Hager uncovered a pot that had been simmering on the stove all morning and dished up a great bowlful of black-eyed peas and salt pork. There was biscuit bread left from breakfast. A plate of young onions and a pitcher of lemonade stood on the white oilcloth-covered table. Heads were automatically bowed.

"Lawd, make us thankful for this food. For Christ's sake, amen," said Hager; then the two old women and the child began to eat.

"That's Elvira's boy, ain't it—that yaller-headed young-one was here playin' with Sandy?" Sister Whiteside had her mouth full of onions and beans as she asked the question.

"Shsss! . . . That's her child!" said Hager. "But it ain't Eddie's!" She gave her guest a meaning glance across the table, then lowered her voice, pretending all the while that Sandy's ears were too young to hear. "They say she had that chile 'fore she married Eddie. An' black as Eddie is, you knows an' I knows ain't due to be no golden hair in de family!"

"I knowed there must be something funny," whispered the old sister, screwing up her face. "That's some white man's chile!"

"Sho it is!" agreed Hager. . . . "I knowed it all de time. . . . Have some mo' meat, Whiteside. Help yo'self! We ain't got much, but such as 'tis, you're welcome. . . . Yes, sir, Buster's some white man's chile. . . . Stop reachin' cross de table for bread, Sandy. Where's yo' manners, sir? I declare, chillens do try you sometimes. . . . Pass me de onions."

"Truth, they tries you, yit I gits right lonesome since all ma young-ones is gone." Sister Whiteside worked her few good teeth vigorously, took a long swallow of lemonade, and smacked her lips. "Chillen an' grandchillen all in Chicago an' St. Louis an' Wichita, an' nary chick nor child left with me in de house. . . . Pass me de bread, thank yuh. . . . I feels kinder sad an' sorry at times, po' widder-woman that I is. I has

ma garden an' ma hens, but all ma chillens done grown and
married. . . . Where's yo' daughter Harriett at now, Hager?
Is she married, too? I ain't seen her lately."

Hager pulled a meat skin through her teeth; then she answered: "No, chile, she too young to marry yet! Ain't but sixteen, but she's been workin out this summer, waitin' table at
de Stanton County Country Club. Been in de country three
weeks now, since school closed, but she comes in town on
Thursdays, though. It's nigh six miles from here, so de women-
help sleeps there at night. I's glad she's out there, Sister. Course
Harriett's a good girl, but she likes to be frisky—wants to run
de streets 'tendin' parties an' dances, an' I can't do much with
her no mo', though I hates to say it."

"But she's a songster, Hager! An' I hears she's sho one smart
chile, besides. They say she's up with them white folks when it
comes to books. An' de high school where she's goin' ain't
easy. . . . All ma young ones quit 'fore they got through with
it—wouldn't go—ruther have a good time runnin' to Kansas
City an' galavantin' round."

"De Lawd knows it's a hard job, keepin' colored chillens in
school, Sister Whiteside, a mighty hard job. De niggers don't
help 'em, an' de white folks don't care if they stay or not. An'
when they gets along sixteen an' seventeen, they wants this, an'
they wants that, an' t'other—an' when you ain't got it to give
to 'em, they quits school an' goes to work. . . . Harriett say
she ain't goin' back next fall. I feels right hurt over it, but she
'clares she ain't goin' back to school. Says there ain't no use in
learnin' books fo' nothin' but to work in white folks' kitchens
when she's graduated."

"Do she, Hager? I's sho sorry! I's gwine to talk to that gal.
Get Reverend Berry to talk to her, too. . . . You's struggled
to bring up yo' chillens, an' all we Christians in de church
ought to help you! I gwine see Reverend Berry, see can't he
'suade her to stay in school." The old woman reached for the
onions. "But you ain't never raised no boys, though, has you,
Hagar?"

"No, I ain't. My two boy-chillens both died 'fore they was
ten. Just these three girls—Tempy, an' Annjee, an' Harriett—
that's all I got. An' this here grandchile, Sandy. . . . Take yo'
hands off that meat, sir! You had 'nough!"

"Lawd, you's been lucky! I done raised seven grandchillen 'sides eight o' ma own. An' they don't thank me. No, sir! Go off and kick up they heels an' git married an' don't thank me a bit! Don't even write, some of 'em. . . . Waitin' fo' me to die, I reckon, so's they can squabble over de little house I owns an' ma garden." The old visitor pushed back her chair. "Huh! Yo' dinner was sho good! . . . Waitin' fo' me to die."

"Unhuh! . . . That's de way with 'em, Sister Whiteside. Chillens don't care—but I reckon we old ones can't kick much. They's got to get off fo' themselves. It's natural, that's what 'tis. Now, my Tempy, she's married and doin' well. Got a fine house, an' her husband's a mail-clerk in de civil service makin' good money. They don't 'sociate no mo' with none but de high-toned colored folks, like Dr. Mitchell, an' Mis' Ada Walls, an' Madam C. Frances Smith. Course Tempy don't come to see me much 'cause I still earns ma livin' with ma arms in de tub. But Annjee run in their house out o' the storm last night an' she say Tempy's just bought a new pianer, an' de house looks fine. . . . I's glad fo' de chile."

"Sho, sho you is, Sister Williams, you's a good mother an' I knows you's glad. But I hears from Reverend Berry that Tempy's done withdrawed from our church an' joined de Episcopals!"

"That's right! She is. Last time I seed Tempy, she told me she couldn't stand de Baptist no mo'—too many low niggers belonging, she say, so she's gonna join Father Hill's church, where de best people go. . . . I told her I didn't think much o' joinin' a church so far away from God that they didn't want nothin' but yaller niggers for members, an' so full o' forms an' fashions that a good Christian couldn't shout—but she went on an' joined. It's de stylish temple, that's why, so I ain't said no mo'. Tempy's goin' on thirty-five now, she's ma oldest chile, an' I reckon she knows how she wants to act."

"Yes, I reckon she do. . . . But there ain't no church like de Baptist, praise God! Is there, Sister? If you ain't been dipped in that water an' half drowned, you ain't saved. Tempy don't know like we do. No, sir, she don't know!"

There was no fruit or dessert, and the soiled plates were not removed from the table for a long time, for the two old women, talking about their children, had forgotten the dishes. Young flies crawled over the biscuit bread and hummed above the bowl of peas, while the wood fire died in the stove, and Sandy went out into the sunshine to play.

"Now, ma girl, Maggie," said Sister Whiteside; "de man she married done got to be a big lawyer in St. Louis. He's in de politics there, an' Maggie's got a fine job herself—social servin', they calls it. But I don't hear from her once a year. An' she don't send me a dime. Ma boys looks out for me, though, sometimes, round Christmas. There's Lucius, what runs on de railroad, an' then Andrew, what rides de horses, an' John, in Omaha, sends me a little change now an' then—all but Charlie, an' he never was thoughtful 'bout his mother. He ain't never sent me nothin'."

"Well, you sho is lucky," said Hager; "'cause they ain't no money comes in this house, Christmas nor no other time, less'n me an' Annjee brings it here. Jimboy ain't no good, an' what Harriett makes goes for clothes and parties an' powderin'-rags. Course, I takes some from her every week, but I gives it right back for her school things. An' I ain't taken nothin' from her these three weeks she's been workin' at de club. She say she's savin' her money herself. She's past sixteen now, so I lets her have it. . . . Po' little thing! . . . She does need to look purty." Hager's voice softened and her dark old face was half abashed, kind and smiling. "You know, last month I bought her a gold watch—surprise fo' her birthday, de kind you hangs on a little pin on yo' waist. Lawd knows, I couldn't 'ford it— took all de money from three week's o' washin', but I knowed she'd been wantin' a watch. An' this front room—I moved ma bed out last year an' bought that new rug at de second-hand store an' them lace curtains so's she could have a nice place to entertain her comp'ny. . . . But de chile goes with such a kinder wild crowd o' young folks, Sister Whiteside! It worries me! The boys, they cusses, an' the girls, they paints, an' some of 'em live in de Bottoms. I been tried to get her out of it right along, but seems like I can't. That's why I's glad she's in de country fo' de summer an' comes in but only once a week, an' then she's home with me. It's too far to come in town at night, she say, so she gets her rest now, goin' to bed early an' all, with de country air round her. I hopes she calms down from runnin' round when she comes back here to stay in de fall. . . . She's a good chile. She don't lie to me 'bout where she goes, nor nothin' like that, but she's just wild, that's all, just wild."

"Is she a Christian, Sister Williams?"

"No, she ain't. I's sorry to say it of a chile o' mine, but she ain't. She's been on de moaner's bench time after time, Sunday mawnins' an' prayer-meetin' evenin's, but she never would rise. I prays for her."

"Well, when she takes Jesus, she'll see de light! That's what de matter with her, Sister Williams, she ain't felt Him yit. Make her go to church when she comes back here. . . . I reckon you heard 'bout when de big revival's due to come off this year, ain't you?"

"No, I ain't, not yet."

"Great colored tent-meetin' with de Battle-Ax of de Lawd, Reverend Braswell preachin'! Yes, sir! Gwine start August eighteenth in de Hickory Woods yonder by de edge o' town."

"Good news," cried Hager. "Mo' sinners than enough's in need o' savin'. I's gwine to take Sandy an' get him started right with de Lawd. An' if that onery Jimboy's back here, I gwine make him go, too, an' look Jesus in de face. Annjee an' me's saved, chile! . . . You Sandy, bring us some drinkin'-water from de pump." Aunt Hager rapped on the window with her knuckles to the boy playing outside. "An' stop wrastlin' with that gal."

Sandy rose triumphant from the prone body of black little Willie-Mae, lying squalling on the cinder-path near the back gate. "She started it," he yelled, running towards the pump. The girl began a reply, but at that moment a rickety wagon drawn by a white mule and driven by a grey-haired, leather-colored old man came rattling down the alley.

"Hy, there, Hager!" called the old Negro, tightening his reins on the mule, which immediately began to eat corn-tops over the back fence. "How you been treatin' yo'self?"

"Right tolable," cried Hager, for she and Sister Whiteside had both emerged from the kitchen and were approaching the driver. "How you doin', Brother Logan?"

"Why, if here ain't Sis' Whiteside, too!" said the old beau, sitting up straight on his wagon-seat and showing a row of ivory teeth in a wide grin. "I's doin' purty well for a po' widower what ain't got nobody to bake his bread. Doin' purty well. Hee! Hee! None o' you all ain't sorry for me, is you? How de storm treat you, Hager? . . . Says it carried off yo' porch? . . . That's certainly too bad! Well, it did some o' these white folks worse'n that. I got 'nough work to do to last me de next fo' weeks, cleanin' up yards an' haulin' off trash, me an' dis mule here. . . . How's yo' chillen, Sis' Williams?"

"Oh, they all right, thank yuh. Annjee's still at Mis' Rice's, an' Harriet's in de country at de club."

"Is she?" said Brother Logan. "I seed her in town night 'fore last down on Pearl Street 'bout ten o'clock."

"You ain't seed Harriett no night 'fore last," disputed Hager vigorously. "She don't come in town 'ceptin' Thursday afternoons, an' that's tomorrow."

"Sister, I ain't blind," said the old man, hurt that his truth should be doubted. "I—seen—Harriett Williams on Pearl Street . . . with Maudel Smothers an' two boys 'bout ten o'clock day before yestidy night! An' they was gwine to de Waiters' Ball, 'cause I asked Maudel where they was gwine, an' she say so. Then I says to Harriett: 'Does yo' mammy know you's out this late?' an' she laughed an' say: 'Oh, that's all right!' . . . Don't tell me I ain't seen Harriett, Hager."

"Well, Lawd help!" Aunt Hager cried, her mouth open. "You done seed my chile in town an' she ain't come anear home! Stayed all night at Maudel's, I reckon. . . . I tells her 'bout runnin' with that gal from de Bottoms. That's what makes her lie to me—tellin' me she don't come in town o' nights. Maudel's folks don't keep no kind o' house, and mens goes there, an' they sells licker, an' they gambles an' fights. . . . Is you sho that's right, Brother Logan, ma chile done been in town an' ain't come home?"

"It ain't wrong!" said old man Logan, cracking his long whip on the white mule's haunches. "Gittiyap! You ole jinny!" and he drove off.

"Um-uh!" said Sister Whiteside to Hager as the two toil-worn old women walked toward the house. "That's de way they does you!" The peddler gathered up her things. "I better be movin', 'cause I got these greens to sell yit, an' it's gittin' 'long towards evenin'. . . . That's de way chillens does you, Sister Williams! I knows! That's de way they does!"

THREE

Jimboy's Letter

KANSAS CITY, MO.
13 June 1912

DEAR ANNJELICA,
 I been laying off to written you ever since I left home but you know how it is. Work has not been so good here. Am with a section gang of coloreds and greeks and somehow strained my back on the Union Pacific laying ties so I will be home on Saturday. Will do my best to try and finish out weak here. Love my darling wife also kiss my son Sandy for me. Am dying to see you,

affectionately as ever and allways
till the judgment day,
Jimboy Rogers

"Strained his back, has he? Unhuh! An' then comes writin' 'bout till de judgment day!" Hager muttered when she heard it. "Always something wrong with that nigger! He'll be back here now, layin' 'round, doin' nothin' fo' de rest o' de summer, turnin' ma house into a theatre with him an' Harriett singin' their rag-time, an' that guitar o' his'n wangin' ever' evenin'! 'Tween him an' Harriett both it's a wonder I ain't plumb crazy. But Harriett do work fo' her livin'. She ain't no loafer. . . . Huh! . . . Annjee, you was sho a fool when you married that boy, an' you still is! . . . I's gwine next do' to Sister Johnson's!" Aunt Hager went out the back and across the yard, where, next door, Tom and Sarah Johnson, Willie-Mae's grandparents, sat on a bench against the side-wall of an unpainted shanty. They were both quietly smoking their corn-cob pipes in the evening dusk.

Sandy, looking at the back of the letter that his mother held, stood at the kitchen-table rapidly devouring a large piece of fresh lemon pie, which she had brought from Mrs. J. J. Rice's. Annjee had said to save the two cold fried lamb chops until to-morrow, or Sandy would have eaten those, too.

"Wish you'd brought home some more pie," the boy declared, his lips white with meringue, but Annjee, who had just got in from work, paid no attention to her son's appreciative remarks on her cookery.

Instead she said: "Ma certainly ain't got no time for Jimboy, has she?" and then sat down with the open letter still in her hand—a single sheet of white paper pencilled in large awkward letters. She put it on the table, rested her dark face in her hands, and began to read it again. . . . She knew how it was, of course, that her husband hadn't written before. That was all right now. Working all day in the hot sun with a gang of Greeks, a man was tired at night, besides living in a box-car, where there was no place to write a letter anyway. He was a great big kid, that's what Jimboy was, cut out for playing. But when he did work, he tried to outdo everybody else. Annjee could see him in her mind, tall and well-built, his legs apart, muscles bulging as he swung the big hammer above his head, driving steel. No wonder he hurt his back, trying to lay more ties a day than anybody else on the railroad. That was just like Jimboy. But she was kind of pleased he had hurt it, since it would bring him home.

"Ain't you glad he's comin', Sandy?"

"Sure," answered the child, swallowing his last mouthful of pie. "I hope he brings me that gun he promised to buy last Easter." The boy wiped his sticky hands on the dish-cloth and ran out into the back yard, calling: "Willie-Mae! Willie-Mae!"

"Stay right over yonder!" answered his grandmother through the dusk. "Willie-Mae's in de bed, sir, an' we old folks settin' out here tryin' to have a little peace." From the tone of Hager's voice he knew he wasn't wanted in the Johnson's yard, so he went back into the house, looked at his mother reading her letter again, and then lay down on the kitchen-floor.

"Affectionately as ever and allways till the judgment day," she read, "Jimboy Rogers."

He loved her, Annjee was sure of that, and it wasn't another woman that made him go away so often. Eight years they'd been married. No, nine—because Sandy was nine, and he was ready to be born when they had had the wedding. And Jimboy left the week after they were married, to go to Omaha, where he worked all winter. When he came back, Sandy was in the world, sitting up sucking meat skins. It was springtime and they bought a piano for the house—but later the instalment man came and took it back to the store. All that summer her husband stayed home and worked a little, but mostly he fished, played pool, taught Harriett to buck-dance, and quarrelled with Aunt Hager. Then in the winter he went to Jefferson City and got a job at the Capitol.

Jimboy was always going, but Aunt Hager was wrong about his never working. It was just that he couldn't stay in one place all the time. He'd been born running, he said, and had run ever since. Besides, what was there in Stanton anyhow for a young colored fellow to do except dig sewer ditches for a few cents an hour or maybe porter around a store for seven dollars a week. Colored men couldn't get many jobs in Stanton, and foreigners were coming in, taking away what little work they did have. No wonder he didn't stay home. Hadn't Annjee's father been in Stanton forty years and hadn't he died with Aunt Hager still taking in washings to help keep up the house?

There was no well-paid work for Negro men, so Annjee didn't blame Jimboy for going away looking for something better. She'd go with him if it wasn't for her mother. If she went, though, Aunt Hager wouldn't have anybody for company but Harriett, and Harriett was the youngest and wildest of the three children. With Pa Williams dead going on ten years, Hager washing every day, Tempy married, and Annjee herself out working, there had been nobody to take much care of the little sister as she grew up. Harriett had had no raising, even though she was smart and in high school. A female child needed care. But she could sing! Lawdy! And dance, too! That was another reason why Aunt Hager didn't like Jimboy. The devil's musicianer, she called him, straight from hell, teaching Harriett buck-and-winging! But when he took his soft-playing guitar and picked out spirituals and old-time Christian hymns on its sweet strings, Hager forgot she was his enemy, and sang and rocked with the rest of them. When Jimboy was home, you couldn't get lonesome or blue.

"Gee, I'll be glad when he comes!" Annjee said to herself. "But if he goes off again, I'll feel like dying in this dead old town. I ain't never been away from here nohow." She spoke aloud to the dim oil-lamp smoking on the table and the sleeping boy on the floor. "I believe I'll go with him next time. I declare I do!" And then, realizing that Jimboy had never once told her when he was leaving or for what destination, she amended her utterance. "I'll follow him, though, as soon as he writes." Because, almost always after he had been away two or three weeks, he would write. "I'll follow him, sure, if he goes off again. I'll leave Sandy here and send money back to mama. Then Harriett could settle down and take care of ma and stop runnin' the streets so much. . . . Yes, that's what I'll do next time!"

This going away was a new thought, and the dark, strong-bodied young woman at the table suddenly began to dream of the cities she had never seen to which Jimboy would lead her. Why, he had been as far north as Canada and as far south as New Orleans, and it wasn't anything for him to go to Chicago or Denver any time! He was a travelling man—and she, Annjee, was too meek and quiet, that's what she was—too stay-at-homish. Never going nowhere, never saying nothing back to those who scolded her or talked about her, not even sassing white folks when they got beside themselves. And every colored girl in town said that Mrs. J. J. Rice was no easy white woman to work for, yet she had been there now five years, accepting everything without a murmur! Most young folks, girls and boys, left Stanton as soon as they could for the outside world, but here she was, Annjelica Williams, going on twenty-eight, and had never been as far as Kansas City!

"I want to travel," she said to herself. "I want to go places, too."

But that was why Jimboy married her, because she wasn't a runabout. He'd had enough of those kind of women before he struck Stanton, he said. St. Louis was full of them, and Chicago running over. She was the first nice girl he'd ever met who lived at home, so he took her. . . . There were mighty few dark women had a light, strong, good-looking young husband, really a married husband, like Jimboy, and a little brown kid like Sandy.

"I'm mighty lucky," Annjee thought, "even if he ain't here." And two tears of foolish pride fell from the bright eyes in her round black face. They trickled down on the letter, with its blue lines and pencil-scrawled message, and some of the words on the paper began to blur into purple blots because the pencil had been an indelible one. Quickly she fumbled for a handkerchief to wipe the tears away, when a voice made her start.

"You Annjee!" cried Aunt Hager in the open door. "Go to bed, chile! Go on! Settin' up here this late, burnin' de light an' lurin' all sorts o' night-bugs an' creepers into de house!" The old woman came in out of the dark. "Lawd! I might anigh stumbled over this boy in de middle o' de flo'! An' you ain't even took off yo' hat since you got home from work! Is you crazy? Settin' up here at night with yo' hat on, an' lettin' this chile catch his death o' cold sleepin' down on de flo' long after his bedtime!"

Sheepishly Annjee folded her letter and got up. It was true that she still had on her hat and the sweater she had worn to Mrs. Rice's. True, too, the whole room was alive with soft-winged moths fluttering against the hot glass of the light—and on the kitchen floor a small, brown-skin, infinitely lovable edition of Jimboy lay sprawled contentedly in his grandmother's path, asleep!

"He's my baby!" Annjee said gently, stooping to pick him up. "He's my baby—me and Jimboy's baby!"

FOUR

Thursday Afternoon

HAGER had risen at sunrise. On Thursdays she did the Reinharts' washing, on Fridays she ironed it, and on Saturdays she sent it home, clean and beautifully white, and received
as pay the sum of seventy-five cents. During the winter Hager
usually did half a dozen washings a week, but during the hot
season her customers had gone away, and only the Reinharts,
on account of an invalid grandmother with whom they could
not travel, remained in Stanton.

Wednesday afternoon Sandy, with a boy named Jimmy Lane,
called at the back door for their soiled clothes. Each child took
a handle and between them carried the large wicker basket
seven blocks to Aunt Hager's kitchen. For this service Jimmy
Lane received five cents a trip, although Sister Lane had repeatedly said to Hager that he needn't be given anything. She
wanted him to learn his Christian duties by being useful to old
folks. But Jimmy was not inclined to be Christian. On the contrary, he was a very bad little boy of thirteen, who often led
Sandy astray. Sometimes they would run with the basket for no
reason at all, then stumble and spill the clothes out on the
sidewalk—Mrs. Reinhart's summer dresses, and drawers, and
Mr. Reinhart's extra-large B.V.D.'s lying generously exposed to
the public. Sometimes, if occasion offered, the youngsters
would stop to exchange uncouth epithets with strange little
white boys who called them "niggers." Or, again, they might
neglect their job for a game of marbles, or a quarter-hour of
scrub baseball on a vacant lot; or to tease any little colored girl
who might tip timidly by with her hair in tight, well-oiled
braids—while the basket of garments would be left forlornly in
the street without guardian. But when the clothes were safe in
Aunt Hager's kitchen, Jimmy would usually buy candy with
his nickel and share it with Sandy before he went home.

After soaking all night, the garments were rubbed through
the suds in the morning; and in the afternoon the colored arti-

28

cles were on the line while the white pieces were boiling seriously in a large tin boiler on the kitchen-stove.

"They sho had plenty this week," Hager said to her grandson, who sat on the stoop eating a slice of bread and apple butter. "I's mighty late gettin' 'em hung out to dry, too. Had no business stoppin' this mawnin' to go see sick folks, and me here got all I can do maself! Looks like this warm weather old Mis' Reinhart must change ever' piece from her dress to her shimmy three times a day—sendin' me a washin' like this here!" They heard the screen-door at the front of the house open and slam. "It's a good thing they got me to do it fo' 'em! . . . Sandy, see who's that at de do'."

It was Harriett, home from the country club for the afternoon, cool and slender and pretty in her black uniform with its white collar, her smooth black face and neck powdered pearly, and her crinkly hair shining with pomade. She smelled nice and perfumy as Sandy jumped on her like a dog greeting a favorite friend. Harriett kissed him and let him hang to her arm as they went through the bedroom to the kitchen. She carried a brown cardboard suit-case and a wide straw hat in one hand.

"Hello, mama," she said.

Hager poked the boiling clothes with a vigorous splash of her round stick. The steam rose in clouds of soapy vapor.

"I been waitin' for you, madam!" her mother replied in tones that were not calculated to welcome pleasantly an erring daughter. "I wants to know de truth—was you in town last Monday night or not?"

Harriett dropped her suit-case against the wall. "You seem to have the truth," she said carelessly. How'd you get it? . . . Here, Sandy, take this out in the yard and eat it, seed and all." She gave her nephew a plum she had brought in her pocket. "I *was* in town, but I didn't have time to come home. I had to go to Maudel's because she's making me a dress."

"To Maudel's! . . . Unhuh! An' to de Waiters' Ball, besides galavantin' up an' down Pearl Street after ten o'clock! I wouldn't cared so much if you'd told me beforehand, but you said you didn't come in town 'ceptin' Thursday afternoon, an' here I was believing yo' lies."

"It's no lies! I haven't been in town before."

"Who brung you here at night anyhow—an' there ain't no trains runnin'?"

"O, I came in with the cook and some of the boys, mama, that's who! They hired an auto for the dance. What would be the use coming home, when you and Annjee go to bed before dark like chickens?"

"That's all right, madam! Annjee's got sense—savin' her health an' strength!"

Harriett was not impressed. "For what? To spend her life in Mrs. Rice's kitchen?" She shrugged her shoulders.

"What you bring yo' suit-case home fo'?"

"I'm quitting the job Saturday," she said. "I've told them already."

"Quitting!" her mother exclaimed. "What fo'? Lawd, if it ain't one thing, it's another!"

"What for?" Harriett retorted angrily. "There's plenty what for! All that work for five dollars a week with what little tips those pikers give you. And white men insulting you besides, asking you to sleep with 'em. Look at my finger-nails, all broke from scrubbing that dining-room floor." She thrust out her dark slim hands. "Waiting table and cleaning silver, washing and ironing table-linen, and then scrubbing the floor besides —that's too much of a good thing! And only three waitresses on the job. That old steward out there's a regular white folks' nigger. He don't care how hard he works us girls. Well, I'm through with the swell new Stanton County Country Club this coming Saturday—I'm telling everybody!" She shrugged her shoulders again.

"What you gonna do then?"

"Maudel says I can get a job with her."

"Maudel? . . . Where?" The old woman had begun to wring the clothes dry and pile them in a large dish-pan.

"At the Banks Hotel, chambermaid, for pretty good pay."

Hager stopped again and turned decisively towards her daughter. "You ain't gonna work in no hotel. You hear me! They's dives o' sin, that's what they is, an' a child o' mine ain't goin' in one. If you was a boy, I wouldn't let you go, much less a girl! They ain't nothin' but strumpets works in hotels."

"Maudel's no strumpet." Harriett's eyes narrowed.

"I don't know if she is or ain't, but I knows I wants you to stop runnin' with her—I done tole you befo'. . . . Her mammy ain't none too straight neither, raisin' them chillen in sin. Look at Sammy in de reform school 'fore he were fifteen for gamblin'. An' de oldest chile, Essie, done gone to Kansas City with that yaller devil she ain't married. An' Maudel runnin' de streets night an' day, with you tryin' to keep up with her! . . . Lawd a mercy! . . . Here, hang up these clothes!"

Her mother pointed to the tin pan on the table filled with damp, twisted, white underwear. Harriett took the pan in both hands. It was heavy and she trembled with anger as she lifted it to her shoulders.

"You can bark at me if you want to, mama, but don't talk about my friends. I don't care what they are! Maudel'd do anything for me. And her brother's a good kid, whether he's been in reform school or not. They oughtn't to put him there just for shooting dice. What's that? I like him, and I like Mrs. Smothers, too. She's not always scolding people for wanting a good time and for being lively and trying to be happy."

Hot tears raced down each cheek, leaving moist lines in the pink powder. Sandy, playing marbles with Buster under the apple-tree, heard her sniffling as she shook out the clothes and hung them on the line in the yard.

"You Sandy," Aunt Hager called loudly from the kitchen-door. "Come in here an' get me some water an' cut mo' firewood." Her black face was wet with perspiration and drawn from fatigue and worry. "I got to get the rest o' these clothes out yet this evenin'. . . . That chile Harriett's aggravatin' me to death! Help me, Sandy, honey."

They ate supper in silence, for Hager's attempts at conversation with her young daughter were futile. Once the old woman said: "That onery Jimboy's comin' home Saturday," and Harriett's face brightened a moment.

"Gee, I'm glad," she replied, and then her mouth went sullen again. Sandy began uncomfortably to kick the table-leg.

"For Christ's sake!" the girl frowned, and the child stopped, hurt that his favorite aunt should yell at him peevishly for so slight an offense.

"Lawd knows, I wish you'd try an' be mo' like yo' sisters, Annjee an' Tempy," Hager began as she washed the dishes, while Harriett stood near the stove, cloth in hand, waiting to dry them. "Here I is, an old woman, an' you tries ma soul! After all I did to raise you, you don't even hear me when I speak." It was the old theme again, without variation. "Now, there's Annjee, ain't a better chile livin'—if she warn't crazy 'bout Jimboy. An' Tempy married an' doin' well, an' respected ever'where. . . . An' you runnin' wild!"

"Tempy?" Harriett sneered suddenly, pricked by this comparison. "So respectable you can't touch her with a ten-foot pole, that's Tempy! . . . Annjee's all right, working herself to death at Mrs. Rice's, but don't tell me about Tempy. Just because she's married a mail-clerk with a little property, she won't even see her own family any more. When niggers get up in the world, they act just like white folks—don't pay you no mind. And Tempy's that kind of a nigger—she's up in the world now!"

"Close yo' mouth, talking that way 'bout yo' own sister! I ain't asked her to be always comin' home, is I, if she's satisfied in her own house?"

"No, you aren't asking her, mama, but you're always talking about her being so respectable. . . . Well, I don't want to be respectable if I have to be stuck up and dicty like Tempy is. . . . She's colored and I'm colored and I haven't seen her since before Easter. . . . It's not being black that matters with her, though, it's being poor, and that's what we are, you and me and Annjee, working for white folks and washing clothes and going in back doors, and taking tips and insults. I'm tired of it, mama! I want to have a good time once in a while."

"That's 'bout all you does have is a good time," Hager said. "An' it ain't right, an' it ain't Christian, that's what it ain't! An' de Lawd is takin' notes on you!" The old woman picked up the heavy iron skillet and began to wash it inside and out.

"Aw, the church has made a lot of you old Negroes act like Salvation Army people," the girl returned, throwing the dried knives and forks on the table. "Afraid to even laugh on Sundays, afraid for a girl and boy to look at one another, or for people to go to dances. Your old Jesus is white, I guess, that's why! He's white and stiff and don't like niggers!"

Hager gasped while Harriett went on excitedly, disregarding her mother's pain: "Look at Tempy, the highest-class Christian in the family—Episcopal, and so holy she can't even visit her own mother. Seems like all the good-time people are bad, and all the old Uncle Toms and mean, dried-up, long-faced niggers fill the churches. I don't never intend to join a church if I can help it."

"Have mercy on this chile! Help her an' save her from hell-fire! Change her heart, Jesus!" the old woman begged, standing in the middle of the kitchen with uplifted arms. "God have mercy on ma daughter."

Harriett, her brow wrinkled in a steady frown, put the dishes away, wiped the table, and emptied the water with a splash through the kitchen-door. Then she went into the bedroom that she shared with her mother, and began to undress. Sandy saw, beneath her thin white underclothes, the soft black skin of her shapely young body.

"Where you goin'?" Hager asked sharply.

"Out," said the girl.

"Out where?"

"O, to a barbecue at Willow Grove, mama! The boys are coming by in an auto at seven o'clock."

"What boys?"

"Maudel's brother and some fellows."

"You ain't goin' a step!"

A pair of curling-irons swung in the chimney of the lighted lamp on the dresser. Harriett continued to get ready. She was making bangs over her forehead, and the scent of scorching hair-oil drifted by Sandy's nose.

"Up half de night in town Monday, an' de Lawd knows how late ever' night in de country, an' then you comes home to run out agin! . . . You ain't goin'!" continued her mother.

Harriett was pulling on a pair of red silk stockings, bright and shimmering to her hips.

"You quit singin' in de church choir. You say you ain't goin' back to school. You won't keep no job! Now what *is* you gonna do? Yo' pappy said years ago, 'fore he died, you was too purty to 'mount to anything, but I ain't believed him. His last dyin' words was: 'Look out fo' ma baby Harriett.' You was his favourite chile. . . . Now look at you! Runnin' de streets an' wearin' red silk stockings!" Hager trembled. "'Spose yo' pappy was to come back an' see you?"

Harriett powdered her face and neck, pink on ebony, dashed

white talcum at each arm-pit, and rubbed her ears with perfume from a thin bottle. Then she slid a light blue dress of
many ruffles over her head. The skirt ended midway between
the ankle and the knee, and she looked very cute, delicate, and
straight, like a black porcelain doll in a Vienna toy shop.

"Some o' Maudel's makin's, that dress—anybody can tell,"
her mother went on quarrelling. "Short an' shameless as it can
be! Regular bad gal's dress, that's what 'tis. . . . What you
puttin' it on fo' anyhow, an' I done told you you ain't goin'
out? You must think I don't mean ma words. Ain't more'n sixteen last April an' runnin' to barbecues at Willer Grove! De
idee! When I was yo' age, wasn't up after eight o'clock, 'ceptin'
Sundays in de church house, that's all. . . . Lawd knows
where you young ones is headin'. An' me prayin' an' washin'
ma fingers to de bone to keep a roof over yo' head."

The sharp honk of an automobile horn sounded from the
street. A big red car, full of laughing brown girls gaily dressed,
and coatless, slick-headed black boys in green and yellow silk
shirts, drew up at the curb. Somebody squeezed the bulb of
the horn a second time and another loud and saucy honk!
struck the ears.

"You Sandy," Hager commanded. "Run out there an' tell
them niggers to leave here, 'cause Harriett ain't goin' no place."

But Sandy did not move, because his young and slender
aunt had gripped him firmly by the collar while she searched
feverishly in the dresser-drawer for a scarf. She pulled it out,
long and flame-colored, with fiery, silky fringe, before she released the little boy.

"You ain't gwine a step this evenin'!" Hager shouted. "Don't
you hear me?"

"O, no?" said Harriett coolly in a tone that cut like knives.
"You're the one that says I'm not going—*but I am!*"

Then suddenly something happened in the room—the anger
fell like a veil from Hager's face, disclosing aged, helpless eyes
full of fear and pain.

"Harriett, honey, I wants you to be good," the old woman
stammered. The words came pitiful and low—not a command
any longer—as she faced her terribly alive young daughter in
the ruffled blue dress and the red silk stockings. "I just wants you
to grow up decent, chile. I don't want you runnin' to Willer

Grove with them boys. It ain't no place fo' you in the night-time—an' you knows it. You's mammy's baby girl. She wants you to be good, honey, and follow Jesus, that's all."

The baritone giggling of the boys in the auto came across the yard as Hager started to put a timid, restraining hand on her daughter's shoulder—but Harriett backed away.

"You old fool!" she cried. "Lemme go! You old Christian fool!"

She ran through the door and across the sidewalk to the waiting car, where the arms of the young men welcomed her eagerly. The big machine sped swiftly down the street and the rapid sput! sput! sput! of its engine grew fainter and fainter. Finally, the auto was only a red tail-light in the summer dusk. Sandy, standing beside his grandmother in the doorway, watched it until it disappeared.

FIVE

Guitar

> Throw yo' arms around me, baby,
> Like de circle round de sun!
> Baby, throw yo' arms around me
> Like de circle round de sun,
> An' tell yo' pretty papa
> How you want yo' lovin' done!

JIMBOY was home. All the neighborhood could hear his rich low baritone voice giving birth to the blues. On Saturday night he and Annjee went to bed early. On Sunday night Aunt Hager said: "Put that guitar right up, less'n it's hymns you plans on playin'. An' I don't want too much o' them, 'larmin' de white neighbors."

But this was Monday, and the sun had scarcely fallen below the horizon before the music had begun to float down the alley, over back fences and into kitchen-windows where nice white ladies sedately washed their supper dishes.

> Did you ever see peaches
> Growin' on a watermelon vine?
> Says did you ever see peaches
> On a watermelon vine?
> Did you ever see a woman
> That I couldn't get for mine?

Long, lazy length resting on the kitchen-door-sill, back against the jamb, feet in the yard, fingers picking his sweet guitar, left hand holding against its finger-board the back of an old pocket-knife, sliding the knife upward, downward, getting thus weird croons and sighs from the vibrating strings:

> O, I left ma mother
> An' I cert'ly can leave you.
> Indeed I left ma mother
> An' I cert'ly can leave you,

36

> For I'd leave any woman
> That mistreats me like you do.

Jimboy, remembering brown-skin mamas in Natchez, Shreveport, Dallas; remembering Creole women in Baton Rouge, Louisiana:

> O, yo' windin' an' yo' grindin'
> Don't have no effect on me,
> Babe, yo' windin' an' yo' grindin'
> Don't have no 'fect on me,
> 'Cause I can wind an' grind
> Like a monkey round a coconut-tree!

Then Harriett, standing under the ripening apple-tree, in the back yard, chiming in:

> Now I see that you don't want me,
> So it's fare thee, fare thee well!
> Lawd, I see that you don't want me,
> So it's fare—thee—well!
> I can still get plenty lovin',
> An' you can go to—Kansas City!

"O, play it, sweet daddy Jimboy!" She began to dance.

Then Hager, from her seat on the edge of the platform covering the well, broke out: "Here, madam! Stop that prancin'! Bad enough to have all this singin' without turnin' de yard into a show-house." But Harriett kept on, her hands picking imaginary cherries out of the stars, her hips speaking an earthly language quite their own.

"You got it, kid," said Jimboy, stopping suddenly, then fingering his instrument for another tune. "You do it like the stage women does. You'll be takin' Ada Walker's place if you keep on."

"Wha! Wha! . . . You chillen sho can sing!" Tom Johnson shouted his compliments from across the yard. And Sarah, beside him on the bench behind their shack, added: "Minds me o' de ole plantation times, honey! It sho do!"

"Unhuh! Bound straight fo' de devil, that's what they is," Hager returned calmly from her place beside the pump. "You an' Harriett both—singin' an' dancin' this stuff befo' these

chillens here." She pointed to Sandy and Willie-Mae, who sat
on the ground with their backs against the chicken-box. "It's a
shame!"

"I likes it," said Willie-Mae.

"Me too," the little boy agreed.

"Naturally you would—none o' you-all's converted yet,"
countered the old woman to the children as she settled back
against the pump to listen to some more.

The music rose hoarse and wild:

> I wonder where ma easy rider's gone?
> He done left me, put ma new gold watch in pawn.

It was Harriett's voice in plaintive moan to the night sky.
Jimboy had taught her that song, but a slight, clay-colored
brown boy who had hopped bells at the Clinton Hotel for a
couple of months, on his way from Houston to Omaha, discovered its meaning to her. Puppy-love, maybe, but it had hurt
when he went away, saying nothing. And the guitar in Jimboy's
hands echoed that old pain with an even greater throb than
the original ache itself possessed.

Approaching footsteps came from the front yard.

"Lord, I can hear you-all two blocks away!" said Annjee,
coming around the house, home from work, with a bundle of
food under her left arm. "Hello! How are you, daddy? Hello,
ma! Gimme a kiss Sandy. . . . Lord, I'm hot and tired and
most played out. This late just getting from work! . . . Here,
Jimboy, come on in and eat some of these nice things the white
folks had for supper." She stepped across her husband's outstretched legs into the kitchen. "I brought a mighty good
piece of cold ham for you, hon', from Mis' Rice's."

"All right, sure, I'll be there in a minute," the man said, but
he went on playing *Easy Rider*, and Harriett went on singing,
while the food was forgotten on the table until long after
Annjee had come outdoors again and sat down in the cool,
tired of waiting for Jimboy to come in to her.

Off and on for nine years, ever since he had married Annjee,
Jimboy and Harriett had been singing together in the evenings.
When they started, Harriett was a little girl with braided hair,
and each time that her roving brother-in-law stopped in
Stanton, he would amuse himself by teaching her the old

Southern songs, the popular rag-time ditties, and the hundreds of varying verses of the blues that he would pick up in the big dirty cities of the South. The child, with her strong sweet voice (colored folks called it alto) and her racial sense of rhythm, soon learned to sing the songs as well as Jimboy. He taught her the *parse me la*, too, and a few other movements peculiar to Southern Negro dancing, and sometimes together they went through the buck and wing and a few taps. It was all great fun, and innocent fun except when one stopped to think, as white folks did, that some of the blues lines had, not only double, but triple meanings, and some of the dance steps required very definite movements of the hips. But neither Harriett nor Jimboy soiled their minds by thinking. It was music, good exercise—and they loved it.

"Do you know this one, Annjee?" asked Jimboy, calling his wife's name out of sudden politeness because he had forgotten to eat her food, had hardly looked at her, in fact, since she came home. Now he glanced towards her in the darkness where she sat plump on a kitchen-chair in the yard, apart from the others, with her back to the growing corn in the garden. Softly he ran his fingers, light as a breeze, over his guitar strings, imitating the wind rustling through the long leaves of the corn. A rectangle of light from the kitchen-door fell into the yard striking sidewise across the healthy orange-yellow of his skin above the unbuttoned neck of his blue laborer's shirt.

"Come on, sing it with us, Annjee," he said.

"I don't know it," Annjee replied, with a lump in her throat, and her eyes on the silhouette of his long, muscular, animal-hard body. She loved Jimboy too much, that's what was the matter with her! She knew there was nothing between him and her young sister except the love of music, yet he might have dropped the guitar and left Harriett in the yard for a little while to come eat the nice cold slice of ham she had brought him. She hadn't seen him all day long. When she went to work this morning, he was still in bed—and now the blues claimed him.

In the starry blackness the singing notes of the guitar became a plaintive hum, like a breeze in a grove of palmettos; became a low moan, like the wind in a forest of live-oaks strung with long strands of hanging moss. The voice of Annjee's golden, handsome husband on the door-step rang high and far

away, lonely-like, crying with only the guitar, not his wife, to
understand; crying grotesquely, crying absurdly in the summer
night:

> I got a mule to ride.
> I got a mule to ride.
> Down in the South somewhere
> I got a mule to ride.

Then asking the question as an anxious, left-lonesome girl-
sweetheart would ask it:

> You say you goin' North.
> You say you goin' North.
> How 'bout yo' . . . lovin' gal?
> You say you goin' North.

Then sighing in rhythmical despair:

> O, don't you leave me here.
> Babe, don't you leave me here.
> Dog-gone yo' comin' back!
> Said don't you leave me here.

On and on the song complained, man-verses and woman-
verses, to the evening air in stanzas that Jimboy had heard in
the pine-woods of Arkansas from the lumber-camp workers; in
other stanzas that were desperate and dirty like the weary roads
where they were sung; and in still others that the singer created
spontaneously in his own mouth then and there:

> O, I done made ma bed,
> Says I done made ma bed.
> Down in some lonesome grave
> I done made ma bed.

It closed with a sad eerie twang.

"That's right decent," said Hager. "Now I wish you-all'd
play some o' ma pieces like *When de Saints Come Marchin' In*
or *This World Is Not Ma Home*—something Christian from de
church."

"Aw, mama, it's not Sunday yet," said Harriett.

"Sing *Casey Jones*," called old man Tom Johnson. "That's
ma song."

So the ballad of the immortal engineer with another mama in the Promised Land rang out promptly in the starry darkness, while everybody joined in the choruses.

"Aw, pick it, boy," yelled the old man. "Can't nobody play like you."

And Jimboy remembered when he was a lad in Memphis that W. C. Handy had said: "You ought to make your living out of that, son." But he hadn't followed it up—too many things to see, too many places to go, too many other jobs.

"What song do you like, Annjee?" he asked, remembering her presence again.

"O, I don't care. Any ones you like. All of 'em are pretty." She was pleased and petulant and a little startled that he had asked her.

"All right, then," he said. "Listen to me:"

> Here I is in de mean ole jail.
> Ain't got nobody to go ma bail.
> Lonesome an' sad an' chain gang bound—
> Ever' friend I had's done turned me down.

"That's sho it!" shouted Tom Johnson in great sympathy. "Now, when I was in de Turner County Jail . . ."

"Shut up yo' mouth!" squelched Sarah, jabbing her husband in the ribs.

The songs went on, blues, shouts, jingles, old hits: *Bon Bon Buddy, the Chocolate Drop; Wrap Me in Your Big Red Shawl; Under the Old Apple Tree; Turkey in the Straw*—Jimboy and Harriett breaking the silence of the small-town summer night until Aunt Hager interrupted:

"You-all better wind up, chillens, 'cause I wants to go to bed. I ain't used to stayin' 'wake so late, nohow. Play something kinder decent there, son, fo' you stops."

Jimboy, to tease the old woman, began to rock and moan like an elder in the Sanctified Church, patting both feet at the same time as he played a hymn-like, lugubrious tune with a dancing overtone:

> Tell me, sister,
> Tell me, brother,
> Have you heard de latest news?

Then seriously as if he were about to announce the coming of the Judgment:

> A woman down in Georgia
> Got her two sweet-men confused.

How terrible! How sad! moaned the guitar.

> One knocked on de front do',
> One knocked on de back—

Sad, sad . . . sad, sad! said the music.

> Now that woman down in Georgia's
> Door-knob is hung with black.

O, play that funeral march, boy! while the guitar laughed a dirge.

> An' de hearse is comin' easy
> With two rubber-tired hacks!

Followed by a long-drawn-out, churchlike:

> Amen . . . !

Then with rapid glides, groans, and shouts the instrument screamed of a sudden in profane frenzy, and Harriett began to ball-the-jack, her arms flopping like the wings of a headless pigeon, the guitar strings whining in ecstasy, the player rocking gaily to the urgent music, his happy mouth crying: "Tack 'em on down, gal! Tack 'em on down, Harrie!"

But Annjee had risen.

"I wish you'd come in and eat the ham I brought you," she said as she picked up her chair and started towards the house. "And you, Sandy! Get up from under that tree and go to bed." She spoke roughly to the little fellow, whom the songs had set a-dreaming. Then to her husband: "Jimboy, I wish you'd come in."

The man stopped playing, with a deep vibration of the strings that seemed to echo through the whole world. Then he leaned his guitar against the side of the house and lifted straight up in his hairy arms Annjee's plump, brown-black little body while he kissed her as she wriggled like a stubborn child, her soft breasts rubbing his hard body through the coarse blue shirt.

"You don't like my old songs, do you, baby? You don't want to hear me sing 'em," he said, laughing. "Well, that's all right. I like you, anyhow, and I like your ham, and I like your kisses, and I like everything you bring me. Let's go in and chow down." And he carried her into the kitchen, where he sat with her on his knees as he ate the food she so faithfully had brought him from Mrs. J. J. Rice's dinner-table.

Outside, Willie-Mae went running home through the dark. And Harriett pumped a cool drink of water for her mother, then helped her to rise from her low seat, Sandy aiding from behind, with both hands pushing firmly in Aunt Hager's fleshy back. Then the three of them came into the house and glanced, as they passed through the kitchen, at Annjee sitting on Jimboy's lap with both dark arms tight around his neck.

"Looks like you're clinging to the Rock of Ages," said Harriett to her sister. "Be sure you don't slip, old evil gal!"

But at midnight, when the owl that nested in a tree near the corner began to hoot, they were all asleep—Annjee and Jimboy in one room, Harriett and Hager in another, with Sandy on the floor at the foot of his grandmother's bed. Far away on the railroad line a whistle blew, lonesome and long.

SIX

Work

THE sunflowers in Willie-Mae's back yard were taller than Tom Johnson's head, and the hollyhocks in the fence corners were almost as high. The nasturtiums, blood-orange and gold, tumbled over themselves all around Madam de Carter's house. Aunt Hager's sweet-william, her pinks, and her tiger-lilies were abloom and the apples on her single tree would soon be ripe. The adjoining yards of the three neighbors were gay with flowers. "Watch out for them dogs!" his grandmother told Sandy hourly, for the days had come when the bright heat made gentle animals go mad. Bees were heavy with honey, great green flies hummed through the air, yellow-black butterflies suckled at the rambling roses . . . and watermelons were on the market.

The Royal African Knights and Ladies of King Solomon's Scepter were preparing a drill for the September Emancipation celebration, a "Drill of All Nations," in which Annjee was to represent Sweden. It was not to be given for a month or more, but the first rehearsal would take place tonight.

"Sandy," his mother said, shaking him early in the morning as he lay on his pallet at the foot of Aunt Hager's bed, "listen here! I want you to come out to Mis' Rice's this evening and help me get through the dishes so's I can start home early, in time to wash and dress myself to go to the lodge hall. You hears me?"

"Yes'm," said Sandy, keeping his eyes closed to the bright stream of morning sunlight entering the window. But half an hour later, when Jimboy kicked him and said: "Hey, bo! You wanta go fishin'?" he got up at once, slid into his pants; and together they went out in the garden to dig worms. It was seldom that his father took him anywhere, and, of course, he wanted to go. Sandy adored Jimboy, but Jimboy, amiable and indulgent though he was, did not often care to be bothered with his ten-year-old son on his fishing expeditions.

Harriett had gone to her job, and Hager had long been at the tubs under the apple-tree when the two males emerged from the kitchen-door. "Huh! You ain't workin' this mawnin', is you?" the old woman grunted, bending steadily down, then up, over the wash-board.

"Nope," her tall son-in-law answered. "Donahoe laid me off yesterday on account o' the white bricklayers said they couldn't lay bricks with a nigger."

"Always something to keep you from workin'," panted Hager.

"Sure is," agreed Jimboy pleasantly. "But don't worry, me and Sandy's gonna catch you a mess o' fish for supper today. How's that, ma?"

"Don't need no fish," the old woman answered. "An' don't come ma-in' me! Layin' round here fishin' when you ought to be out makin' money to take care o' this house an' that chile o' your'n." The suds rose foamy white about her black arms as the clothes plushed up and down on the zinc wash-board. "Lawd deliver me from a lazy darky!"

But Jimboy and Sandy were already behind the tall corn, digging for bait near the back fence.

"Don't never let no one woman worry you," said the boy's father softly, picking the moist wriggling worms from the up-turned loam. "Treat 'em like chickens, son. Throw 'em a little corn and they'll run after you, but don't give 'em too much. If you do, they'll stop layin' and expect you to wait on 'em."

"Will they?" asked Sandy.

The warm afternoon sun made the river a languid sheet of muddy gold, glittering away towards the bridge and the flour-mills a mile and a half off. Here in the quiet, on the end of a rotting jetty among the reeds, Jimboy and his son sat silently. A long string of small silver fish hung down into the water, keeping fresh, and the fishing-lines were flung far out in the stream, waiting for more bites. Not a breeze on the flat brown-gold river, not a ripple, not a sound. But once the train came by behind them, pouring out a great cloud of smoke and cinders and shaking the jetty.

"That's Number Five," said Jimboy. "Sure is flyin'," as the

train disappeared between rows of empty box-cars far down the track, sending back a hollow clatter as it shot past the flour-mills, whose stacks could be dimly seen through the heat haze. Once the engine's whistle moaned shrilly.

"She's gone now," said Jimboy as the last click of the wheels died away. And, except for the drone of a green fly about the can of bait, there was again no sound to disturb the two fishermen.

Jimboy gazed at his lines. Across the river Sandy could make out, in the brilliant sunlight, the gold of wheat-fields and the green of trees on the hills. He wondered if it would be nice to live over there in the country.

"Man alive!" his father cried suddenly, hauling vigorously at one of the lines. "Sure got a real bite now. . . . Look at this catfish." From the water he pulled a large flopping lead-colored creature, with a fierce white mouth bleeding and gaping over the hook.

"He's on my line!" yelled Sandy. "I caught him!"

"Pshaw!" laughed Jimboy. "You was setting there dreaming."

"No, I wasn't!"

But just then, at the mills, the five-o'clock whistles blew. "Oh, gee, dad!" cried the boy, frightened. "I was s'posed to go to Mis' Rice's to help mama, and I come near forgetting it. She wants to get through early this evenin' to go to lodge meeting. I gotta hurry and go help her."

"Well, you better beat it then, and I'll look out for your line like I been doing and bring the fishes home."

So the little fellow balanced himself across the jetty, scrambled up the bank, and ran down the railroad track towards town. He was quite out of breath when he reached the foot of Penrose Street, with Mrs. Rice's house still ten blocks away, so he walked awhile, then ran again, down the long residential street, with its large houses sitting in green shady lawns far back from the sidewalk. Sometimes a sprinkler attached to a long rubber hose, sprayed fountain-like jets of cold water on the thirsty grass. In one yard three golden-haired little girls were playing under an elm-tree, and in another a man and some children were having a leisurely game of croquet.

Finally Sandy turned into a big yard. The delicious scent of frying beefsteak greeted the sweating youngster as he reached the screen of the white lady's kitchen-door. Inside, Annjee was standing over the hot stove seasoning something in a saucepan, beads of perspiration on her dark face, and large damp spots under the arms of her dress.

"You better get here!" she said. "And me waiting for you for the last hour. Here, take this pick and break some ice for the tea." Sandy climbed up on a stool and raised the ice-box lid while his mother opened the oven and pulled out a pan of golden-brown biscuits. "Made these for your father," she remarked. "The white folks ain't asked for 'em, but they like 'em, too, so they can serve for both. . . . Jimboy's crazy about biscuits. . . . Did he work today?"

"No'm," said Sandy, jabbing at the ice. "We went fishing."

At that moment Mrs. Rice came into the kitchen, tall and blond, in a thin flowered gown. She was a middle-aged white woman with a sharp nasal voice.

"Annjee, I'd like the potatoes served just as they are in the casserole. And make several slices of very thin toast for my father. Now, be sure they *are* thin!"

"Yes, m'am," said Annjee stirring a spoonful of flour into the frying-pan, making a thick brown gravy.

"Old thin toast," muttered Annjee when Mrs. Rice had gone back to the front. "Always bothering round the kitchen! Here 'tis lodge-meeting night—dinner late anyhow—and she coming telling me to stop and make toast for the old man! He ain't too indigestible to eat biscuits like the rest of 'em. . . . White folks sure is a case!" She laid three slices of bread on top of the stove. "So spoiled with colored folks waiting on 'em all their days! Don't know what they'll do in heaven, 'cause I'm gonna sit down up there myself."

Annjee took the biscuits, light and brown, and placed some on a pink plate she had warmed. She carried them, with the butter and jelly, into the dining-room. Then she took the steak from the warmer, dished up the vegetables into gold-rimmed serving-dishes, and poured the gravy, which smelled deliciously onion-flavored.

"Gee, I'm hungry," said the child, with his eyes on the big steak ready to go in to the white people.

"Well, just wait," replied his mother. "You come to work, not to eat. . . . Whee! but it's hot today!" She wiped her wet face and put on a large white bungalow apron that had been hanging behind the door. Then she went with the iced tea and a pitcher of water into the dining-room, struck a Chinese gong, and came back to the kitchen to get the dishes of steaming food, which she carried in to the table.

It was some time before she returned from waiting on the table; so Sandy, to help her, began to scrape out the empty pans and put them to soak in the sink. He ate the stewed corn that had stuck in the bottom of one, and rubbed a piece of bread in the frying-pan where the gravy had been. His mother came out with the water-pitcher, broke some ice for it, and returned to the dining-room where Sandy could hear laughter, and the clinking of spoons in tea-glasses, and women talking. When Annjee came back into the kitchen, she took four custards from the ice-box and placed them on gold-rimmed plates.

"They're about through," she said to her son. "Sit down and I'll fix you up."

Sandy was very hungry and he hoped Mrs. Rice's family hadn't eaten all the steak, which had looked so good with its brown gravy and onions.

Shortly, his mother returned carrying the dishes that had been filled with hot food. She placed them on the kitchen-table in front of Sandy, but they were no longer full and no longer hot. The corn had thickened to a paste, and the potatoes were about gone; but there was still a ragged piece of steak left on the platter.

"Don't eat it all," said Annjee warningly. "I want to take some home to your father."

The bell rang in the dining-room. Annjee went through the swinging door and returned bearing a custard that had been but little touched.

"Here, sonny—the old man says it's too sweet for his stomach, so you can have this." She set the yellow cornstarch before Sandy. "He's seen these ripe peaches out here today and he wants some, that's all. More trouble than he's worth, po' old soul, and me in a hurry!" She began to peel the fruit. "Just like a chile, 'deed he is!" she added, carrying the sliced peaches into the dining-room and leaving Sandy with a plate of food before him, eating slowly. "When you rushing to get out, seems like white folks tries theirselves."

In a moment she returned, ill-tempered, and began to scold Sandy for taking so long with his meal.

"I asked you to help me so's I can get to the lodge on time, and you just set and chew and eat! . . . Here, wipe these dishes, boy!" Annjee began hurriedly to lay plates in a steaming row on the shelf of the sink; so Sandy got up and, between mouthfuls of pudding, wiped them with a large dish-towel.

Soon Mrs. Rice came into the kitchen again, briskly, through the swinging door and glanced about her. Sandy felt ashamed for the white woman to see him eating a left-over pudding from her table, so he put the spoon down.

"Annjee," the mistress said sharply. "I wish you wouldn't put quite so much onion in your sauce for the steak. I've mentioned it to you several times before, and you know very well we don't like it."

"Yes, m'am," said Annjee.

"And do *please* be careful that our drinking water is cold before meals are served. . . . You were certainly careless tonight. You must think more about what you are doing, Annjee."

Mrs. Rice went out again through the swinging door, but Sandy stood near the sink with a burning face and eyes that had suddenly filled with angry tears. He couldn't help it—hearing his sweating mother reprimanded by this tall white woman in the flowered dress. Black, hard-working Annjee answered: "Yes, m'am," and that was all—but Sandy cried.

"Dry up," his mother said crossly when she saw him, thinking he was crying because she had asked him to work. "What's come over you, anyway?—can't even wipe a few plates for me and act nice about it!"

He didn't answer. When the dining-room had been cleared and the kitchen put in order, Annjee told him to empty the garbage while she wrapped in newspapers several little bundles of food to carry to Jimboy. Then they went out the back door, around the big house to the street, and trudged the fourteen blocks to Aunt Hager's, taking short cuts through alleys, passing under arc-lights that sputtered whitely in the deepening twilight, and greeting with an occasional "Howdy" other poor colored folks also coming home from work.

"How are you, Sister Jones?"

"Right smart, I thank yuh!" as they passed.

Once Annjee spoke to her son. "Evening's the only time we niggers have to ourselves!" she said. "Thank God for night . . . 'cause all day you gives to white folks."

SEVEN

White Folks

WHEN they got home, Aunt Hager was sitting in the cool of the evening on her new porch, which had been rebuilt for thirty-five dollars added to the mortgage. The old woman was in her rocking-chair, with Jimboy, one foot on the ground and his back against a pillar, lounging at her feet. The two were quarrelling amicably over nothing as Annjee and Sandy approached.

"Good-evenin', you-all," said Annjee. "I brought you a nice piece o' steak, Jimboy-sugar, and some biscuits to go with it. Come on in and eat while I get dressed to go to the drill practice. I got to hurry."

"We don't want no steak now," Jimboy answered without moving. "Aunt Hager and me had fresh fish for supper and egg-corn-bread and we're full. We don't need nothin' more."

"Oh! . . ." said Annjee disappointedly. "Well, come on in anyhow, honey, and talk while I get dressed." So he rose lazily and followed his wife into the house.

Shortly, Sister Johnson, pursued by the ever-present Willie-Mae, came through the blue-grey darkness from next door. "Good-evenin', Sister Williams; how you been today?"

"Tolable," answered Hager, "'ceptin' I's tired out from washin' an' rinsin'. Have a seat. . . . You Sandy, go in de house an' get Sister Johnson a settin'-chair. . . . Where's Tom?"

"Lawd, chile, he done gone to bed long ago. That there sewer-diggin' job ain't so good fer a man old as Tom. He 'bout played out. . . . I done washed fer Mis' Cohn maself today. . . . Umh! dis cheer feels good! . . . Looked like to me she had near 'bout fifty babies' diddies in de wash. You know she done got twins, 'sides dat young-'un born last year."

The conversation of the two old women rambled on as their grandchildren ran across the front yard laughing, shrieking, wrestling; catching fire-flies and watching them glow in closed fists, then releasing them to twinkle in the sultry night-air.

Harriett came singing out of the house and sat down on the

51

edge of the porch. "Lord, it's hot! . . . How are you, Mis' Johnson? I didn't see you in the dark."

"Jest tolable, chile," said the old woman, "but I can't kick. Honey, when you gits old as I is, you'll be doin' well if you's livin' a-tall, de way you chillens runs round now 'days! How come you ain't out to some party dis evenin'?"

"O, there's no party tonight," said Harriett laughing. "Besides, this new job of mine's a heart-breaker, Mis' Johnson. I got to stay home and rest now. I'm kitchen-girl at that New Albert Restaurant, and time you get through wrestling with pots and arguing with white waitresses and colored cooks, you don't feel much like running out at night. But the shifts aren't bad, though, food's good, and—well, you can't expect everything." She shrugged her shoulders against the two-by-four pillar on which her back rested.

"Long's it keeps you off de streets, I's glad," said Hager, rocking contentedly. "Maybe I can git you goin' to church agin now."

"Aw, I don't like church," the girl replied.

"An', chile, I can't blame you much," said Sister Johnson, fumbling in the pocket of her apron. "De way dese churches done got now'days. . . . Sandy, run in de house an' ask yo' pappy fo' a match to light ma pipe. . . . It ain't 'Come to Jesus' no mo' a-tall. Ministers dese days an' times don't care nothin' 'bout po' Jesus. 'Stead o' dat it's rally dis an' collection dat, an' de aisle wants a new carpet, an' de pastor needs a 'lectric fan fer his red-hot self." The old sister spat into the yard. "Money! That's all 'tis! An' white folkses' religion—Lawd help! 'Taint no use in mentionin' them."

"True," agreed Hager.

"Cause if de gates o' heaven shuts in white folkses' faces like de do's o' dey church in us niggers' faces, it'll be too bad! Yes, sir! One thing sho, de Lawd ain't prejudiced!"

"No," said Hager; "but He don't love ugly, neither in niggers nor in white folks."

"Now, talking about white folks' religion," said Annjee, emerging from the house with a fresh white dress on, "why, Mis' Rice where I work don't think no more about playing bridge on Sunday than she does about praying—and I ain't never seen her pray yet."

"You're nuts," said Jimboy behind her. "People's due to have a little fun on Sundays. That's what's the matter with colored folks now—work all week and then set up in church all day Sunday, and don't even know what's goin' on in the rest of the world."

"Huh!" grunted Hager.

"Well, we won't argue, daddy," Annjee smiled. "Come on and walk a piece with me, sweetness. Here 'tis nearly nine and I should a been at the hall at eight, but colored folks are always behind the clock. Come on, Jimboy."

"Good-bye, mama," yelled Sandy from the lawn as his parents strolled up the street together.

"Jimboy's right," said Harriett. "Darkies do like the church too much, but white folks don't care nothing about it at all. They're too busy getting theirs out of this world, not from God. And I don't blame 'em, except that they're so mean to niggers. They're right, though, looking out for themselves . . . and yet I hate 'em for it. They don't have to mistreat us besides, do they?"

"Honey, don't talk that way," broke in Hager. "It ain't Christian, chile. If you don't like 'em, pray for 'em, but don't feel evil against 'em. I was in slavery, Harrie, an' I been knowin' white folks all ma life, an' they's good as far as they can see—but when it comes to po' niggers, they just can't see far, that's all."

Harriett opened her mouth to reply, but Jimboy, who left Annjee at the corner and had returned to the porch, beat her to it. "We too dark for 'em, ma," he laughed. "How they gonna see in the dark? You colored folks oughta get lighter, that's what!"

"Shut up yo' mouth, you yaller rooster!" said Sister Johnson. "White folks is white folks, an' dey's mean! I can't help what Hager say," the old woman disagreed emphatically with her crony. "Ain't I been knowin' crackers sixty-five years, an' ain't dey de cause o' me bein' here in Stanton 'stead o' in ma home right today? De dirty buzzards! Ain't I nussed t'ree of 'em up from babies like ma own chillens, and ain't dem same t'ree boys done turned round an' helped run me an' Tom out o' town?"

The old sister took a long draw on her corn-cob pipe, and a fiery red spot glowed in its bowl, while Willie-Mae and Sandy stopped playing and sat down on the porch as she began a tale they had all heard at least a dozen times.

"I's tole you 'bout it befo', ain't I?" asked Sister Johnson.

"Not me," lied Jimboy, who was anxious to keep her going.

"No, you haven't," Harriett assured her.

"Well, it were like dis," and the story unwound itself, the preliminary details telling how, as a young freed-girl after the Civil War, Sister Johnson had gone into service for a white planter's family in a Mississippi town near Vicksburg. While attached to this family, she married Tom Johnson, then a field-hand, and raised five children of her own during the years that followed, besides caring for three boys belonging to her white mistress, nursing them at her black breasts and sometimes leaving her own young ones in the cabin to come and stay with her white charges when they were ill. These called her mammy, too, and when they were men and married, she still went to see them and occasionally worked for their families.

"Now, we niggers all lived at de edge o' town in what de whites called Crowville, an' most of us owned little houses an' farms, an' we did right well raisin' cotton an' sweet 'taters an' all. Now, dat's where de trouble started! We was doin' too well, an' de white folks said so! But we ain't paid 'em no 'tention, jest thought dey was talkin' fer de pastime of it. . . . Well, we all started fixin' up our houses an' paintin' our fences, an' Crowville looked kinder decent-like when de white folks 'gin to 'mark, so's we servants could hear 'em, 'bout niggers livin' in painted houses an' dressin' fine like we was somebody! . . . Well, dat went on fer some time wid de whites talkin' an' de coloreds doin' better'n better year by year, sellin' mo' cotton ever' day an' gittin' nice furniture an' buyin' pianers, till by an' by a prosp'rous nigger named John Lowdins up an' bought one o' dese here new autimobiles—an' dat settled it! . . . A white man in town one Sat'day night tole John to git out o' dat damn car 'cause a nigger ain't got no business wid a autimobile nohow! An' John say: 'I ain't gonna git out!' Den de white man, what's been drinkin', jump up on de runnin'-bo'ad an' bust John in de mouth fer talkin' back to him—he a white man, an' Lowdins nothin' but a nigger. 'De very idee!' he say, and hit John in de face six or seven times. Den John drawed his gun! One! two! t'ree! he fiah, hit dis old red-neck cracker in de shoulder, but he ain't dead! Aint nothin' meant to kill a cracker what's drunk. But John think he done kilt this white man, an' so he left him kickin' in de street while he runs that car o' his'n lickety-split out o' town, goes to Vicksburg, an' catches de river boat. . . . Well, sir! Dat night Crowville's plumb full o' white folks wid dogs an' guns an' lanterns, shoutin' an' yellin' an' scarin' de wits out o' us coloreds an' wakin' us up way late in de night-time lookin' fer John, an' dey don't find him. . . . Den dey say dey gwine teach dem Crowville niggers a lesson, all of 'em, paintin' dey houses an' buyin' cars an' livin' like white folks, so dey comes to our do's an' tells us to leave our houses—git de hell out in de fields, 'cause dey don't want to kill nobody there dis evenin'! . . . Well, sir! Niggers in night-gowns an' underwear an' shimmies, half-naked an' barefooted, was runnin' ever' which way in de dark, scratchin' up dey legs in de briah patches, fallin' on dey faces, scared to death! Po' ole Pheeny, what ain't moved from her bed wid de paralytics fo' six years, dey made her daughters carry her out, screamin' an' wall-eyed, an' set her in de middle o' de cotton-patch. An' Brian, what was sleepin' naked, jumps up an' grabs his wife's apron and runs like a rabbit with not another blessed thing on! Chillens squallin' ever'where, an' mens a-pleadin' an' a-cussin', an' womens cryin' 'Lawd 'a' Mercy' wid de whites of dey eyes showin'! . . . Den looked like to me 'bout five hundred white mens took torches an' started burnin' wid fiah ever' last house, an' hen-house, an' shack, an' barn, an' privy, an' shed, an' cow-slant in de place! An' all de niggers, when de fiah blaze up, was moanin' in de fields, callin' on de Lawd fer help! An' de fiah light up de whole country clean back to de woods! You could smell fiah, an' you could see it red, an' taste de smoke, an' feel it stingin' yo' eyes. An' you could hear de bo'ads a-fallin' an' de glass a-poppin', an' po' animals roastin' an' fryin' an' a-tearin' at dey halters. An' one cow run out, fiah all ovah, wid her milk streamin' down. An' de smoke roll up, de cotton-fields were red . . . an' dey ain't been no mo' Crowville after dat night. No, sir! De white folks ain't left nothin' fer de niggers, not nary bo'ad standin' one 'bove another, not even a dog-house. . . . When it were done —nothin' but ashes! . . . De white mens was ever'where wid guns, scarin' de po' blacks an' keepin' 'em off, an' one of 'em

say: 'I got good mind to try yo'-all's hide, see is it bullet
proof—gittin' so prosp'rous, paintin' yo' houses an' runnin
ovah white folks wid yo' damn gasoline buggies! Well, after dis
you'll damn sight have to bend yo' backs an' work a little!'
. . . Dat's what de white man say. . . . But we didn't—not
yit! 'Cause ever' last nigger moved from there dat Sunday
mawnin'. It were right funny to see ole folks what ain't never
been out o' de backwoods pickin' up dey feet an' goin'. Ma
Bailey say: 'De Lawd done let me live eighty years in one place,
but ma next eighty'll be spent in St. Louis.' An' she started out
walkin' wid neither bag nor baggage. . . . An' me an' Tom
took Willie-Mae an' went to Cairo, an' Tom started railroad-
workin' wid a gang; then we come on up here, been five summers ago dis August. We ain't had not even a rag o' clothes
when we left Crowville—so don't tell me 'bout white folks
bein' good, Hager, 'cause I knows 'em. . . . Yes, indeedy, I
really knows 'em. . . . Dey done made us leave our home."

The old woman knocked her pipe against the edge of the
porch, emptying its dead ashes into the yard, and for a moment no one spoke. Sandy, trembling, watched a falling star
drop behind the trees. Then Jimboy's deep voice, like a bitter
rumble in the dark, broke the silence.

"I know white folks, too," he said. "I lived in the South."

"And I ain't never been South," added Harriett hoarsely,
"but I know 'em right here . . . and I hate 'em!"

"De Lawd hears you," said Hager.

"I don't care if He does hear me, mama! You and Annjee are
too easy. You just take whatever white folks give you—*coon* to
your face, and *nigger* behind your backs—and don't say nothing. You run to some white person's back door for every job
you get, and then they pay you one dollar for five dollars'
worth of work, and fire you whenever they get ready."

"They do that all right," said Jimboy. "They don't mind firin'
you. Wasn't I layin' brick on the *Daily Leader* building and the
white union men started sayin' they couldn't work with me because I wasn't in the union? So the boss come up and paid me
off. 'Good man, too,' he says to me, 'but I can't buck the union.'
So I said I'd join, but I knew they wouldn't let me before I
went to the office. Anyhow, I tried. I told the guys there I was
a bricklayer and asked 'em how I was gonna work if I couldn't

be in the union. And the fellow who had the cards, secretary I guess he was, says kinder sharp, like he didn't want to be bothered: 'That's your look-out, big boy, not mine.' So you see how much the union cares if a black man works or not."

"Ain't Tom had de same trouble?" affirmed Sister Johnson. "Got put off de job mo'n once on 'count o' de white unions."

"O, they've got us cornered, all right," said Jimboy. "The white folks are like farmers that own all the cows and let the niggers take care of 'em. Then they make you pay a sweet price for skimmed milk and keep the cream for themselves—but I reckon cream's too rich for rusty-kneed niggers anyhow!"

They laughed.

"That's a good one!" said Harriett. "You know old man Wright, what owns the flour-mill and the new hotel—how he made his start off colored women working in his canning factory? Well, when he built that orphan home for colored and gave it to the city last year, he had the whole place made just about the size of the dining-room at his own house. They got the little niggers in that asylum cooped up like chickens. And the reason he built it was to get the colored babies out of the city home, with its nice playgrounds, because he thinks the two races oughtn't to mix! But he don't care how hard he works his colored help in that canning factory of his, does he? Wasn't I there thirteen hours a day in tomato season? Nine cents an hour and five cents overtime after ten hours—and you better work overtime if you want to keep the job! . . . As for the races mixing—ask some of those high yellow women who work there. They know a mighty lot about the races mixing!"

"Most of 'em lives in de Bottoms, where de sportin' houses are," said Hager. "It's a shame de way de white mens keeps them sinful places goin'."

"It ain't Christian, is it?" mocked Harriett. . . . "White folks!" . . . And she shrugged her shoulders scornfully. Many disagreeable things had happened to her through white folks. Her first surprising and unpleasantly lasting impression of the pale world had come when, at the age of five, she had gone alone one day to play in a friendly white family's yard. Some mischievous small boys there, for the fun of it, had taken hold of her short kinky braids and pulled them, dancing round and round her and yelling: "Blackie! Blackie! Blackie!" while she screamed and tried to run away. But they held her and pulled her hair terribly, and her friends laughed because she *was* black and she *did* look funny. So from that time on, Harriett had been uncomfortable in the presence of whiteness, and that early hurt had grown with each new incident into a rancor that she could not hide and a dislike that had become pain.

Now, because she could sing and dance and was always amusing, many of the white girls in high school were her friends. But when the three-thirty bell rang and it was time to go home, Harriett knew their polite "Good-bye" was really a kind way of saying: "We can't be seen on the streets with a colored girl." To loiter with these same young ladies had been all right during their grade-school years, when they were all younger, but now they had begun to feel the eyes of young white boys staring from the windows of pool halls, or from the tennis-courts near the park—so it was not proper to be seen with Harriett.

But a very unexpected stab at the girl's pride had come only a few weeks ago when she had gone with her class-mates, on tickets issued by the school, to see an educational film of the under-sea world at the Palace Theatre, on Main Street. It was a special performance given for the students, and each class had had seats allotted to them beforehand; so Harriett sat with her class and had begun to enjoy immensely the strange wonders of the ocean depths when an usher touched her on the shoulder.

"The last three rows on the left are for colored," the girl in the uniform said.

"I— But— But I'm with my class," Harriett stammered. "We're all supposed to sit here."

"I can't help it," insisted the usher, pointing towards the rear of the theatre, while her voice carried everywhere. "Them's the house rules. No argument now—you'll have to move."

So Harriett rose and stumbled up the dark aisle and out into the sunlight, her slender body hot with embarrassment and rage. The teacher saw her leave the theatre without a word of protest, and none of her white classmates defended her for being black. They didn't care.

"All white people are alike, in school and out," Harriett concluded bitterly, as she told of her experiences to the folks sitting with her on the porch in the dark.

Once, when she had worked for a Mrs. Leonard Baker on Martin Avenue, she accidentally broke a precious cut-glass pitcher used to serve some out-of-town guests. And when she tried to apologize for the accident, Mrs. Baker screamed in a rage: "Shut up, you impudent little black wench! Talking back to me after breaking up my dishes. All you darkies are alike— careless sluts—and I wouldn't have a one of you in my house if I could get anybody else to work for me without paying a fortune. You're all impossible."

"So that's the way white people feel," Harriett said to Aunt Hager and Sister Johnson and Jimboy, while the two children listened. "They wouldn't have a single one of us around if they could help it. It don't matter to them if we're shut out of a job. It don't matter to them if niggers have only the back row at the movies. It don't matter to them when they hurt our feelings without caring and treat us like slaves down South and like beggars up North. No, it don't matter to them. . . . White folks run the world, and the only thing colored folks are expected to do is work and grin and take off their hats as though it don't matter. . . . O, I hate 'em!" Harriett cried, so fiercely that Sandy was afraid. "I hate white folks!" she said to everybody on the porch in the darkness. "You can pray for 'em if you want to, mama, but I hate 'em! . . . I hate white folks! . . . I hate 'em all!"

EIGHT

Dance

M RS. J. J. RICE and family usually spent ten days during
the August heat at Lake Dale, and thither they had gone
now, giving Annjee a forced vacation with no pay. Jimboy was
not working, and so his wife found ten days of rest without
income not especially agreeable. Nevertheless, she decided that
she might as well enjoy the time; so she and Jimboy went to
the country for a week with Cousin Jessie, who had married
one of the colored farmers of the district. Besides, Annjee
thought that Jimboy might help on the farm and so make a
little money. Anyway, they would get plenty to eat, because
Jessie kept a good table. And since Jessie had eight children of
her own, they did not take Sandy with them—eight were
enough for a woman to be worried with at one time!

Aunt Hager had been ironing all day on the Reinharts'
clothes—it was Friday. At seven o'clock Harriett came home,
but she had already eaten her supper at the restaurant where
she worked.

"Hello, mama! Hy, Sandy!" she said, but that was all, because she and her mother were not on the best of terms. Aunt
Hager was attempting to punish her youngest daughter by not
allowing her to leave the house after dark, since Harriett, on
Tuesday night, had been out until one o'clock in the morning
with no better excuse than a party at Maudel's. Aunt Hager
had threatened to whip her then and there that night.

"You ain't had a switch on yo' hide fo' three years, but don't
think you's gettin' too big fo' me not to fan yo' behind,
madam. 'Spare de rod an' spoil de chile,' that's what de Bible
say, an' Lawd knows you sho is spoiled! De idee of a young gal
yo' age stayin' out till one o'clock in de mawnin', an' me not
knowed where you's at. . . . Don't you talk back to me! . . .
You rests in this house ever' night this week an' don't put yo'
foot out o' this yard after you comes from work, that's what
you do. Lawd knows I don't know what I's gonna do with

you. I works fo' you an' I prays fo' you, an' if you don't mind, I's sho gonna whip you, even if you is goin' on seventeen years old!"

Tonight as soon as she came from work Harriett went into her mother's room and lay across the bed. It was very warm in the little four-room house, and all the windows and doors were open.

"We's got some watermelon here, daughter," Hager called from the kitchen. "Don't you want a nice cool slice?"

"No," the girl replied. She was fanning herself with a palm-leaf fan, her legs in their cheap silk stockings hanging over the side of the bed, and her heels kicking the floor. Benbow's Band played tonight for the dance at Chaver's Hall, and everybody was going—but her. Gee, it was hard to have a Christian mother! Harriett kicked her slippers off with a bang and rolled over on her stomach, burying her powdery face in the pillows. . . . Somebody knocked at the back door.

A boy's voice was speaking excitedly to Hager: "Hemorrhages . . . and papa can't stop 'em . . . she's coughin' something terrible . . . says can't you please come over and help him"— frightened and out of breath.

"Do, Jesus!" cried Hager. "I'll be with you right away, chile. Don't worry." She rushed into the bedroom to change her apron. "You Harriett, listen; Sister Lane's taken awful sick an' Jimmy says she's bleedin' from de mouth. If I ain't back by nine o'clock, see that that chile Sandy's in de bed. An' you know you ain't to leave this yard under no circumstances. . . . Po' Mis' Lane! She sho do have it hard." In a whisper: "I 'spects she's got de T. B., that what I 'spects!" And the old woman hustled out to join the waiting youngster. Jimmy was leaning against the door, looking at Sandy, and neither of the boys knew what to say. Jimmy Lane wore his mother's cast-off shoes to school, and Sandy used to tease him, but tonight he didn't tease his friend about his shoes.

"You go to bed 'fore it gets late," said his grandmother, starting down the alley with Jimmy.

"Yes'm," Sandy called after her. "So long, Jim!" He stood under the apple-tree and watched them disappear.

Aunt Hager had scarcely gotten out of sight when there was

a loud knock at the front door, and Sandy ran around the house to see Harriett's boy friend, Mingo, standing in the dusk outside the screen-door, waiting to be let in.

Mingo was a patent-leather black boy with wide, alive nostrils and a mouth that split into a lighthouse smile on the least provocation. His body was heavy and muscular, resting on bowed legs that curved backward as though the better to brace his chunky torso; and his hands were hard from mixing concrete and digging ditches for the city's new water-mains.

"I know it's tonight, but I can't go," Sandy heard his aunt say at the door. They were speaking of Benbow's dance. "And his band don't come here often, neither. I'm heart-sick having to stay home, dog-gone it all, especially this evening!"

"Aw, come on and go anyway," pleaded Mingo. "After I been savin' up my dough for two weeks to take you, and got my suit cleaned and pressed and all. Heck! If you couldn't go and knew it yesterday, why didn't you tell me? That's a swell way to treat a fellow!"

"Because I wanted to go," said Harriett; "and still want to go. . . . Don't make so much difference about mama, because she's mad anyhow . . . but what could we do with this kid? We can't leave him by himself." She looked at Sandy, who was standing behind Mingo listening to everything.

"You can take me," the child offered anxiously, his eyes dancing at the delightful prospect. "I'll behave, Harrie, if you take me, and I won't tell on you either. . . . Please lemme go, Mingo. I ain't never seen a big dance in my life. I wanta go."

"Should we?" asked Harriett doubtfully, looking at her boy friend standing firmly on his curved legs.

"Sure, if we got to have him . . . damn 'im!" Mingo replied. "Better the kid than no dance. Go git dressed." So Harriett made a dash for the clothes-closet, while Sandy ran to get a clean waist from one of his mother's dresser-drawers, and Mingo helped him put it on, cussing softly to himself all the while. "But it ain't your fault, pal, is it?" he said to the little boy.

"Sure not," Sandy replied. "I didn't tell Aunt Hager to make Harrie stay home. I tried to 'suade grandma to let her go," the child lied, because he liked Mingo. "I guess she won't care about her goin' to just one dance." He wanted to make everything all right so the young man wouldn't be worried. Besides, Sandy very much wanted to go himself.

"Let's beat it," Harriett shrilled excitedly before her dress was fastened, anxious to be gone lest her mother come home. She was powdering her face and neck in the next room, nervous, happy, and afraid all at once. The perfume, the voice, and the pat, pat, pat of the powder-puff came out to the waiting gentleman.

"Yo' car's here, madam," mocked Mingo. "Step right this way and let's be going!"

Wonder where ma easy rider's gone—
He done left me, put ma new gold watch in pawn!

Like a blare from hell the second encore of *Easy Rider* filled every cubic inch of the little hall with hip-rocking notes. Benbow himself was leading and the crowd moved like jellyfish dancing on individual sea-shells, with Mingo and Harriett somewhere among the shakers. But they were not of them, since each couple shook in a world of its own, as, with a weary wail, the music abruptly ceased.

Then, after scarcely a breath of intermission, the band struck up again with a lazy one-step. A tall brown boy in a light tan suit walked his partner straight down the whole length of the floor and, when he reached the corner, turned leisurely in one spot, body riding his hips, eyes on the ceiling, and his girl shaking her full breasts against his pink silk shirt. Then they recrossed the width of the room, turned slowly, repeating themselves, and began again to walk rhythmically down the hall, while the music was like a lazy river flowing between mountains, carving a canyon coolly, calmly, and without insistence. The *Lazy River One-Step* they might have called what the band was playing as the large crowd moved with the greatest ease about the hall. To drum-beats barely audible, the tall boy in the tan suit walked his partner round and round time after time, revolving at each corner with eyes uplifted, while the piano was the water flowing, and the high, thin chords of the banjo were the mountains floating in the clouds. But in sultry tones, alone and always, the brass cornet spoke harshly about the earth.

Sandy sat against the wall in a hard wooden folding chair. There were other children scattered lonesomely about on chairs, too, watching the dancers, but he didn't seem to know any of them. When the music stopped, all the chairs quickly filled with loud-talking women and girls in brightly colored dresses who fanned themselves with handkerchiefs and wiped their sweating brows. Sandy thought maybe he should give his seat to one of the women when he saw Maudel approaching.

"Here, honey," she said. "Take this dime and buy yourself a bottle of something cold to drink. I know Harriett ain't got you on her mind out there dancin'. This music is certainly righteous, chile!" She laughed as she handed Sandy a coin and closed her pocketbook. He liked Maudel, although he knew his grandmother didn't. She was a large good-natured brown-skinned girl who walked hippishly and used too much rouge on her lips. But she always gave Sandy a dime, and she was always laughing.

He went through the crowd towards the soft-drink stand at the end of the hall. "Gimme a bottle o' cream soda," he said to the fat orange-colored man there, who had his sleeves rolled up and a white butcher's-apron covering his barrel-like belly. The man put his hairy arms down into a zinc tub full of ice and water and began pulling out bottles, looking at their caps, and then dropping them back into the cold liquid.

"Don't seem like we got no cream, sonny. How'd a lemon do you?" he asked above the bedlam of talking voices.

"Naw," said Sandy. "It's too sour."

On the improvised counter of boards the wares displayed consisted of cracker-jacks, salted peanuts, a box of gum, and Sen Sens, while behind the counter was a lighted oil-stove holding a tin pan full of spare-ribs, sausage, and fish; and near it an ice-cream freezer covered with a brown sack. Some cases of soda were on the floor beside the zinc tub filled with bottles, in which the man was still searching.

"Nope, no cream," said the fat man.

"Well, gimme a fish sandwich then," Sandy replied, feeling very proud because some kids were standing near, looking at him as he made his purchase like a grown man.

"Buy me one, too," suggested a biscuit-colored little girl in a frilly dirty-white dress.

"I only got a dime," Sandy said. "But you can have half of mine." And he gallantly broke in two parts the double square of thick bread, with its hunk of greasy fish between, and gravely handed a portion to the grinning little girl.

"Thanks," she said, running away with the bread and fish in her hands.

"Shame on you!" teased a small boy, rubbing his forefingers at Sandy. "You got a girl! You got a girl!"

"Go chase yourself!" Sandy replied casually, as he picked out the bones and smacked his lips on the sweet fried fish. The orchestra was playing another one-step, with the dancers going like shuttles across the floor. Sandy saw his Aunt Harriett and a slender yellow boy named Billy Sanderlee doing a series of lazy, intricate steps as they wound through the crowd from one end of the hall to the other. Certain less accomplished couples were watching them with admiration.

Sandy, when he had finished eating, decided to look for the wash-room, where he could rinse his hands, because they were greasy and smelled fishy. It was at the far corner of the hall. As he pushed open the door marked GENTS, a thick grey cloud of cigarette-smoke drifted out. The stench of urine and gin and a crowd of men talking, swearing, and drinking licker surrounded the little boy as he elbowed his way towards the wash-bowls. All the fellows were shouting loudly to one another and making fleshy remarks about the women they had danced with.

"Boy, you ought to try Velma," a mahogany-brown boy yelled. "She sure can go."

"Hell," answered a whisky voice somewhere in the smoke. "That nappy-headed black woman? Gimme a high yaller for mine all de time. I can't use no coal!"

"Well, de blacker de berry, de sweeter de juice," protested a slick-haired ebony youth in the center of the place. . . . "Ain't that right, sport?" he demanded of Sandy, grabbing him jokingly by the neck and picking him up.

"I guess it is," said the child, scared, and the men laughed.

"Here, kid, buy yourself a drink," the slick-headed boy said, slipping Sandy a nickel as he set him down gently at the door. "And be sure it's pop—not gin."

Outside, the youngster dried his wet hands on a handkerchief, blinked his smoky eyes, and immediately bought the soda, a red strawberry liquid in a long, thick bottle.

Suddenly and without warning the cornet blared at the other end of the hall in an ear-splitting wail: "Whaw! . . . Whaw! . . . Whaw! . . . Whaw!" and the snare-drum rolled in answer. A pause . . . then the loud brassy notes were repeated and the banjo came in, "Plinka, plink, plink," like timid drops of rain after a terrific crash of thunder. Then quite casually, as though nothing had happened, the piano lazied into a slow drag, with all the other instruments following. And with the utmost nonchalance the drummer struck into time.

"Ever'body shake!" cried Benbow, as a ribbon of laughter swirled round the hall.

Couples began to sway languidly, melting together like candy in the sun as hips rotated effortlessly to the music. Girls snuggled pomaded heads on men's chests, or rested powdered chins on men's shoulders, while wild young boys put both arms tightly around their partners' waists and let their hands hang down carelessly over female haunches. Bodies moved ever so easily together—ever so easily, as Benbow turned towards his musicians and cried through cupped hands: "Aw, screech it, boys!"

A long, tall, gangling gal stepped back from her partner, adjusted her hips, and did a few easy, gliding steps all her own before her man grabbed her again.

"Eu-o-oo-oooo-oooo!" moaned the cornet titillating with pain, as the banjo cried in stop-time, and the piano sobbed aloud with a rhythmical, secret passion. But the drums kept up their hard steady laughter—like somebody who don't care.

"I see you plowin', Uncle Walt," called a little autumn-leaf brown with switching skirts to a dark-purple man grinding down the center of the floor with a yellow woman. Two short prancing blacks stopped in their tracks to quiver violently. A bushy-headed girl threw out her arms, snapped her fingers, and began to holler: "Hey! . . . Hey!" while her perspiring partner held doggedly to each hip in an effort to keep up with her. All over the hall, people danced their own individual movements to the scream and moan of the music.

"Get low . . . low down . . . down!" cried the drummer, bouncing like a rubber ball in his chair. The banjo scolded in diabolic glee, and the cornet panted as though it were out of breath, and Benbow himself left the band and came out on the floor to dance slowly and ecstatically with a large Indian-brown woman covered with diamonds.

"Aw, do it, Mister Benbow!" one of his admirers shouted frenziedly as the hall itself seemed to tremble.

"High yallers, draw nigh! Brown-skins, come near!" somebody squalled. "But black gals, stay where you are!"

"Whaw! Whaw! Whaw!" mocked the cornet—but the steady tomtom of the drums was no longer laughter now, no longer even pleasant: the drum-beats had become sharp with surly sound, like heavy waves that beat angrily on a granite rock. And under the dissolute spell of its own rhythm the music had got quite beyond itself. The four black men in Benbow's wandering band were exploring depths to which mere sound had no business to go. Cruel, desolate, unadorned was their music now, like the body of a ravished woman on the sun-baked earth; violent and hard, like a giant standing over his bleeding mate in the blazing sun. The odors of bodies, the stings of flesh, and the utter emptiness of soul when all is done—these things the piano and the drums, the cornet and the twanging banjo insisted on hoarsely to a beat that made the dancers move, in that little hall, like pawns on a frenetic checker-board.

"Aw, play it, Mister Benbow!" somebody cried.

The earth rolls relentlessly, and the sun blazes for ever on the earth, breeding, breeding. But why do you insist like the earth, music? Rolling and breeding, earth and sun for ever relentlessly. But why do you insist like the sun? Like the lips of women? Like the bodies of men, relentlessly?

"Aw, play it, Mister Benbow!"

But why do you insist, music?

Who understands the earth? Do you, Mingo? Who understands the sun? Do you, Harriett? Does anybody know—among you high yallers, you jelly-beans, you pinks and pretty daddies, among you sealskin browns, smooth blacks, and chocolates-to-the-bone—does anybody know the answer?

"Aw, play it, Benbow!"

"It's midnight. De clock is strikin' twelve, an' . . ."

"Aw, play it, Mister Benbow!"

*

During intermission, when the members of the band stopped making music to drink gin and talk to women, Harriett and Mingo bought Sandy a box of cracker-jacks and another bottle of soda and left him standing in the middle of the floor holding both. His young aunt had forgotten time, so Sandy decided to go upstairs to the narrow unused balcony that ran the length of one side of the place. It was dusty up there, but a few broken chairs stood near the railing and he sat on one of them. He leaned his arms on the banister, rested his chin in his hands, and when the music started, he looked down on the mass of moving couples crowding the floor. He had a clear view of the energetic little black drummer eagle-rocking with staccato regularity in his chair as his long, thin sticks descended upon the tightly drawn skin of his small drum, while his foot patted the pedal of his big bass-drum, on which was painted in large red letters: "BENBOW'S FAMOUS KANSAS CITY BAND."

As the slow shuffle gained in intensity (and his cracker-jacks gave out), Sandy looked down drowsily on the men and women, the boys and girls, circling and turning beneath him. Dresses and suits of all shades and colors, and a vast confusion of bushy heads on swaying bodies. Faces gleaming like circus balloons—lemon-yellow, coal-black, powder-grey, ebony-black, blue-black faces; chocolate, brown, orange, tan, creamy-gold faces—the room full of floating balloon faces—Sandy's eyes were beginning to blur with sleep—colored balloons with strings, and the music pulling the strings. No! Girls pulling the strings—each boy a balloon by a string. Each face a balloon.

Sandy put his head down on the dusty railing of the gallery. An odor of hair-oil and fish, of women and sweat came up to him as he sat there alone, tired and a little sick. It was very warm and close, and the room was full of chatter during the intervals. Sandy struggled against sleep, but his eyes were just about to close when, with a burst of hopeless sadness, the *St. Louis Blues* spread itself like a bitter syrup over the hall. For a moment the boy opened his eyes to the drowsy flow of sound, long enough to pull two chairs together; then he lay down on them and closed his eyes again. Somebody was singing:

St. Louis woman with her diamond rings . . . .

as the band said very weary things in a loud and brassy manner and the dancers moved in a dream that seemed to have forgotten itself:

Got ma man tied to her apron-strings . . .

Wah! Wah! Wah! . . . The cornet laughed with terrible rudeness. Then the drums began to giggle and the banjo whined an insulting leer. The piano said, over and over again: "St. Louis! That big old dirty town where the Mississippi's deep and wide, deep and wide . . ." and the hips of the dancers rolled.

Man's got a heart like a rock cast in de sea . . .

while the cynical banjo covered unplumbable depths with a plinking surface of staccato gaiety, like the sparkling bubbles that rise on deep water over a man who has just drowned himself:

Or else he never would a gone so far from me . . .

then the band stopped with a long-drawn-out wail from the cornet and a flippant little laugh from the drums.

A great burst of applause swept over the room, and the musicians immediately began to play again. This time just blues, not the *St. Louis*, nor the *Memphis*, nor the *Yellow Dog*—but just the plain old familiar blues, heart-breaking and extravagant, ma-baby's-gone-from-me blues.

Nobody thought about anyone else then. Bodies sweatily close, arms locked, cheek to cheek, breast to breast, couples rocked to the pulse-like beat of the rhythm, yet quite oblivious each person of the other. It was true that men and women were dancing together, but their feet had gone down through the floor into the earth, each dancer's alone—down into the center of things—and their minds had gone off to the heart of loneliness, where they didn't even hear the words, the sometimes lying, sometimes laughing words that Benbow, leaning on the piano, was singing against this background of utterly despondent music:

> When de blues is got you,
> Ain't no use to run away.

> When de blue-blues got you,
> Ain't no use to run away,
> 'Cause de blues is like a woman
> That can turn yo' good hair grey.

Umn-ump! . . . Umn! . . . Umn-ump!

> Well, I tole ma baby,
> Says baby, baby, babe, be mine,
> But ma baby was deceitful.
> She must a thought that I was blind.

De-da! De-da! . . . De da! De da! Dee!

> O, Lawdy, Lawdy, Lawdy,
> Lawdy, Lawdy, Lawd . . . Lawd . . . Lawd!
> She quit me fo' a Texas gambler,
> So I had to git another broad.

Whaw-whaw! . . . Whaw-whaw-whaw! As though the laughter of a cornet could reach the heart of loneliness.

These mean old weary blues coming from a little orchestra of four men who needed no written music because they couldn't have read it. Four men and a leader—Rattle Benbow from Galveston; Benbow's buddy, the drummer, from Houston; his banjoist from Birmingham; his cornetist from Atlanta; and the pianist, long-fingered, sissyfied, a coal-black lad from New Orleans who had brought with him an exaggerated rag-time which he called jazz.

"I'm jazzin' it, creepers!" he sometimes yelled as he rolled his eyes towards the dancers and let his fingers beat the keys to a frenzy. . . . But now the piano was cryin' the blues!

Four homeless, plug-ugly niggers, that's all they were, playing mean old loveless blues in a hot, crowded little dance-hall in a Kansas town on Friday night. Playing the heart out of loneliness with a wide-mouthed leader, who sang everybody's troubles until they became his own. The improvising piano, the whanging banjo, the throbbing bass-drum, the hard-hearted little snare-drum, the brassy cornet that laughed, "Whaw-whaw-whaw. . . . Whaw!" were the waves in this lonesome sea of harmony from which Benbow's melancholy voice rose:

> You gonna wake up some mawnin'
> An' turn yo' smilin' face.
> Wake up some early mawnin',
> Says turn yo' smilin' face,
> Look at yo' sweetie's pillow—
> An' find an' empty place!

Then the music whipped itself into a slow fury, an awkward, elemental, foot-stamping fury, with the banjo running terrifiedly away in a windy moan and then coming back again, with the cornet wailing like a woman who don't know what it's all about:

> Then you gonna call yo' baby,
> Call yo' lovin' baby dear—
> But you can keep on callin',
> 'Cause I won't be here!

And for a moment nothing was heard save the shuf-shuf-shuffle of feet and the immense booming of the bass-drum like a living vein pulsing at the heart of loneliness.

"Sandy! . . . Sandy! . . . My stars! Where is that child? . . . Has anybody seen my little nephew?" All over the hall. . . . "Sandy! . . . Oh-o-o, Lord!" Finally, with a sigh of relief: "You little brat, darn you, hiding up here in the balcony where nobody could find you! . . . Sandy, wake up! It's past four o'clock and I'll get killed."

Harriett vigorously shook the sleeping child, who lay stretched on the dusty chairs; then she began to drag him down the narrow steps before he was scarcely awake. The hall was almost empty and the chubby little black drummer was waddling across the floor carrying his drums in canvas cases. Someone was switching off the lights one by one. A mustard-colored man stood near the door quarrelling with a black woman. She began to cry and he slapped her full in the mouth, then turned his back and left with another girl of maple-sugar brown. Harriett jerked Sandy past this linked couple and pulled the boy down the long flight of stairs into the street, where Mingo stood waiting, with a lighted cigarette making a white line against his black skin.

"You better git a move on," he said. "Daylight ain't holdin' itself back for you!" And he told the truth, for the night had already begun to pale.

Sandy felt sick at the stomach. To be awakened precipitately made him cross and ill-humored, but the fresh, cool air soon caused him to feel less sleepy and not quite so ill. He took a deep breath as he trotted rapidly along on the sidewalk beside his striding aunt and her boy friend. He watched the blue-grey dawn blot out the night in the sky; and then pearl-grey blot out the blue, while the stars faded to points of dying fire. And he listened to the birds chirping and trilling in the trees as though they were calling the sun. Then, as he became fully awake, the child began to feel very proud of himself, for this was the first time he had ever been away from home all night.

Harriett was fussing with Mingo. "You shouldn't 've kept me out like that," she said. "Why didn't you tell me what time it was? . . . I didn't know."

And Mingo came back: "Hey, didn't I try to drag you away at midnight and you wouldn't come? And ain't I called you at one o'clock and you said: 'Wait a minute'—dancin' with some yaller P. I. from St. Joe, with your arms round his neck like a life-preserver? . . . Don't tell me I didn't want to leave, and me got to go to work at eight o'clock this mornin' with a pick and shovel when the whistle blows! What de hell?"

But Harriett did not care to quarrel now when there would be no time to finish it properly. She was out of breath from hurrying and almost in tears. She was afraid to go home.

"Mingo, I'm scared."

"Well, you know what you can do if your ma puts you out," her escort said quickly, forgetting his anger. "I can take care of you. We could get married."

"Could we, Mingo?"

"Sure!"

She slipped her hand in his. "Aw, daddy!" and the pace became much less hurried.

When they reached the corner near which Harriett lived, she lifted her dark little purple-powdered face for a not very lingering kiss and sent Mingo on his way. Then she frowned anxiously and ran on. The sky was a pale pearly color, waiting for the warm gold of the rising sun.

"I'm scared to death!" said Harriett. "Lord, Sandy, I hope ma ain't up! I hope she didn't come home last night from Mis' Lane's. We shouldn't 've gone, Sandy . . . I guess we shouldn't 've gone." She was breathing hard and Sandy had to run fast to keep up with her. "Gee, I'm scared!"

The grass was diamond-like with dew, and the red bricks of the sidewalk were damp, as the small boy and his young aunt hurried under the leafy elms along the walk. They passed Madam de Carter's house and cut through the wet grass into their own yard as the first rays of the morning sun sifted through the trees. Quietly they tiptoed towards the porch; quickly and quietly they crossed it; and softly, ever so softly, they opened the parlor door.

In the early dusk the oil-lamp still burned on the front-room table, and in an old arm-chair, with the open Bible on her lap, sat Aunt Hager Williams, a bundle of switches on the floor at her feet.

NINE

Carnival

BETWEEN the tent of Christ and the tents of sin there stretched scarcely a half-mile. Rivalry reigned: the revival and the carnival held sway in Stanton at the same time. Both were at the south edge of town, and both were loud and musical in their activities. In a dirty white tent in the Hickory Woods the Reverend Duke Braswell conducted the services of the Lord for the annual summer tent-meeting of the First Ethiopian Baptist Church. And in Jed Galoway's meadow lots Swank's Combined Shows, the World's Greatest Midway Carnival, had spread canvas for seven days of bunko games and cheap attractions. The old Negroes went to the revival, and the young Negroes went to the carnival, and after sundown these August evenings the mourning songs of the Christians could be heard rising from the Hickory Woods while the profound syncopation of the minstrel band blared from Galoway's Lots, strangely intermingling their notes of praise and joy.

Aunt Hager with Annjee and Sandy went to the revival every night (Sandy unwillingly), while Jimboy, Harriett, and Maudel went to the carnival. Aunt Hager prayed for her youngest daughter at the meetings, but Harriett had not spoken to her mother, if she could avoid it, since the morning after the dance, when she had been whipped. Since their return from the country Annjee and Jimboy were not so loving towards each other, either, as they had been before. Jimboy tired of Jessie's farm, so he came back to town three days before his wife returned. And now the revival and the carnival widened the breach between the Christians and the sinners in Aunt Hager's little household. And Sandy would rather have been with the sinners—Jimboy and Harriett—but he wasn't old enough; so he had to go to meetings until, on Thursday morning, when he and Buster were climbing over the coal-shed in the back yard, Sandy accidentally jumped down on a rusty nail, which penetrated the heel of his bare foot. He set up a wail, cried until noon over the pain, and refused to eat any dinner; so finally Jimboy said that if he would only hush hollering he'd take him to the carnival that evening.

"Yes, take de rascal," said Aunt Hager. "He ain't doin' no good at de services, wiggling and squirming so's we can't hardly hear de sermon. He ain't got religion in his heart, that chile!"

"I hope he ain't," said his father, yawning.

"All you wants him to be is a good-fo'-nothin' rounder like you is," retorted Hager. And she and Jimboy began their daily quarrel, which lasted for hours, each of them enjoying it immensely. But Sandy kept pulling at his father and saying: "Hurry up and let's go," although he knew well that nothing really started at the carnival until sundown. Nevertheless, about four o'clock, Jimboy said: "All right, come on," and they started out in the hot sun towards Galoway's Lots, the man walking tall and easy while the boy hobbled along on his sore foot, a rag tied about his heel.

At the old cross-bar gate on the edge of town, through which Jed Galoway drove his cows to pasture, there had been erected a portable arch strung with electric lights spelling out "SWANK'S SHOWS" in red and yellow letters, but it was not very impressive in the day-time, with the sun blazing on it, and no people about. And from this gate, extending the whole length of the meadow on either side, like a roadway, were the tents and booths of the carnival: the Galatea illusion, the seal and sea-lion circus, the Broadway musical-comedy show, the freaks, the games of chance, the pop-corn- and lemonade-stands, the colored minstrels, the merry-go-round, the fun house, the hoochie-coochie, the Ferris wheel, and, at the far end, a canvas tank under a tiny platform high in the air from which the World's Most Dangerous and Spectacular High Dive took place nightly at ten-thirty.

"We gonna stay to see that, ain't we, papa?" Sandy asked.

"Sure," said Jimboy. "But didn't I tell you there wouldn't be nothin' runnin' this early in the afternoon? See! Not even the band playin', and ain't a thing open but the freak-show and I'll bet all the freaks asleep." But he bought Sandy a bag of peanuts and planked down twenty cents for two tickets into the sultry tent where a perspiring fat woman and a tame-looking wild-man were the only attractions to be found on the platforms.

The sword-swallower was not yet at work, nor the electric marvel, nor the human glass-eater. The terrific sun beat fiercely through the canvas on this exhibit of two lone human abnormalities, and the few spectators in the tent kept wiping their faces with their handkerchiefs.

Jimboy struck up a conversation with the Fat Woman, a pink and white creature who said she lived in Columbus, Ohio; and when Jimboy said he'd been there, she was interested. She said she had always lived right next door to colored people at home, and she gave Sandy a postcard picture of herself for nothing, although it had "10¢" marked on the back. She kept saying she didn't see how anybody could stay in Kansas and it a dry state where a soul couldn't even get beer except from a bootlegger.

When Sandy and his father came out, they left the row of tents and went across the meadow to a clump of big shade-trees beneath which several colored men who worked with the show were sitting. A blanket had been spread on the grass, and a crap game was going on to the accompaniment of much arguing and good-natured cussing. But most of the men were just sitting around not playing, and one or two were stretched flat on their faces, asleep. Jimboy seemed to know several of the fellows, so he joined in their talk while Sandy watched the dice roll for a while, but since the boy didn't understand the game, he decided to go back to the tents.

"All right, go ahead," said his father. "I'll pick you up later when the lights are lit and things get started; then we can go in the shows."

Sandy limped off, walking on the toe of his injured foot. In front of the sea-lion circus he found Earl James, a little white boy in his grade at school; the two of them went around together for a while, looking at the large painted canvas pictures in front of the shows or else lying on their stomachs on the ground to peep under the tents. When they reached the minstrel-show tent near the end of the midway, they heard a piano tinkling within and the sound of hands clapping as though someone was dancing.

"Jeezus! Let's see this," Earl cried, so the two boys got down on their bellies, wriggled under the flap of the tent on one side, and looked in.

A battered upright piano stood on the ground in front of the stage, and a fat, bald-headed Negro was beating out a rag. A big white man in a checkered vest was leaning against the piano, derby on head, and a long cigar stuck in his mouth. He was watching a slim black girl, with skirts held high and head thrown back, prancing in a mad circle of crazy steps. Two big colored boys in red uniforms were patting time, while another girl sat on a box, her back towards the peeping youngsters staring up from under the edge of the tent. As the girl who was dancing whirled about, Sandy saw that it was Harriett.

"Pretty good, ain't she, boss?" yelled the wrinkle-necked Negro at the piano as he pounded away.

The white man nodded and kept his eyes on Harriett's legs. The two black boys patting time were grinning from ear to ear.

"Do it, Miss Mama!" one of them shouted as Harriett began to sashay gracefully.

Finally she stopped, panting and perspiring, with her lips smiling and her eyes sparkling gaily. Then she went with the white man and the colored piano-player behind the canvas curtains to the stage. One of the show-boys put his arms around the girl sitting on the box and began tentatively to feel her breasts.

"Don't be so fresh, hot papa," she said. And Sandy recognized Maudel's voice, and saw her brown face as she leaned back to look at the showman. The boy in the red suit bent over and kissed her several times, while the other fellow kept imitating the steps he had just seen Harriett performing.

"Let's go," Earl said to Sandy, rolling over on the ground. The two small boys went on to the next tent, where one of the carnival men caught them, kicked their behinds soundly, and sent them away.

The sun was setting in a pink haze, and the show-grounds began to take on an air of activity. The steam calliope gave a few trial hoots, and the merry-go-round circled slowly without passengers. The paddle-wheels and the get-'em-hot men, the lemonade-sellers and the souvenir-venders were opening their booths to the evening trade. A barker began to ballyhoo in front of the freak-show. By and by there would be a crowd. The lights came on along the Midway, the Ferris wheel swept languidly up into the air, and when Sandy found his father, the colored band had begun to play in front of the minstrel show.

"I want to ride on the merry-go-round," Sandy insisted. "And go in the Crazy House." So they did both; then they bought hamburger sandwiches with thick slices of white onion and drank strawberry soda and ate pop-corn with butter on it. They went to the sea-lion circus, tried to win a Kewpie doll at the paddle-wheel booth, and watched men losing money on the hidden pea, then trying to win it back at four-card monte behind the Galatea attraction. And all the while Sandy said nothing to his father about having seen Harriett dancing in the minstrel tent that afternoon.

Sandy had lived too long with three women not to have learned to hold his tongue about the private doings of each of them. When Annjee paid two dollars a week on a blue silk shirt for his father at Cohn's cut-rate credit store, and Sandy saw her make the payments, he knew without being told that the matter was never to be mentioned to Aunt Hager. And if his grandmother sometimes threw Harriett's rouge out in the alley, Sandy saw it with his eyes, but not with his mouth. Because he loved all three of them—Harriett and Annjee and Hager— he didn't carry tales on any one of them to the others. Nobody would know he had watched his Aunt Harrie dancing on the carnival lot today in front of a big fat white man in a checkered vest while a Negro in a red suit played the piano.

"We got a half-dollar left for the minstrel show," said Jimboy. "Come on, let's go." And he pulled his son through the crowd that jammed the long Midway between the booths.

All the bright lights of the carnival were on now, and everything was running full blast. The merry-go-round whirled to the ear-splitting hoots of the calliope; bands blared; the canvas paintings of snakes and dancing-girls, human skeletons, fire-eaters, billowed in the evening breeze; pennants flapped, barkers shouted, acrobats twirled in front of a tent; a huge paddle-wheel clicked out numbers. Folks pushed and shoved and women called to their children not to get lost. In the air one smelled the scent of trampled grass, peanuts, and hot dogs, animals and human bodies.

The large white man in the checkered vest was making the

ballyhoo in front of the minstrel show, his expansive belly turned towards the crowd that had been attracted by the band. One hand pointed towards a tawdry group of hard-looking Negro performers standing on the platform.

"Here we have, ladies and gents, Madam Caledonia Watson, the Dixie song-bird; Dancing Jenkins, the dark strutter from Jacksonville; little Lizzie Roach, champeen coon-shouter of Georgia; and last, but not least, Sambo and Rastus, the world's funniest comedians. Last performance this evening! . . . Strike her up, perfesser! . . . Come along, now, folks!"

The band burst into sound, Madam Watson and Lizzie Roach opened their brass-lined throats, the men dropped into a momentary clog-dance, and then the whole crowd of performers disappeared into the tent. The ticket-purchasing townspeople followed through the public opening beneath a gaudily painted sign picturing a Mississippi steamboat in the moonlight, and two black bucks shooting gigantic dice on a street-corner.

Jimboy and Sandy followed the band inside and took seats, and soon the frayed curtain rose, showing a plantation scene in the South, where three men, blackened up, and two women in bandannas sang longingly about Dixie. Then Sambo and Rastus came out with long wooden razors and began to argue and shoot dice, but presently the lights went out and a ghost appeared and frightened the two men away, causing them to leave all the money on the stage. (The audience thought it screamingly funny—and just like niggers.) After that one of the women sang a ragtime song and did the eagle-rock. Then a man with a banjo in his hands began to play, but until then the show had been lifeless.

"Listen to him," Jimboy said, punching Sandy. "He's good!"

The piece he was picking was full of intricate runs and trills long drawn out, then suddenly slipping into tantalizing rhythms. It ended with a vibrant whang!—and the audience yelled for more. As an encore he played a blues and sang innumerable verses, always ending:

> An' Ah can't be satisfied,
> 'Cause all Ah love has
> Done laid down an' died.

And to Sandy it seemed like the saddest music in the world—
but the white people around him laughed.

Then the stage lights went on, the band blared, and all the
black actors came trooping back, clapping their hands before
the cotton-field curtain as each one in turn danced like fury,
vigorously distorting agile limbs into the most amazing positions, while the scene ended with the fattest mammy and the
oldest uncle shaking jazzily together.

The booths were all putting out their lights as the people
poured through the gate towards town. Sandy hobbled down
the road beside his father, his sore heel, which had been forgotten all evening, paining him terribly until Jimboy picked
him up and carried him on his shoulder. Automobiles and
buggies whirled past them in clouds of gritty dust, and young
boys calling vulgar words hurried after tittering girls. When
Sandy and his father reached home, Aunt Hager and Annjee
had not yet returned from the revival. Jimboy said he thought
maybe they had stopped at Mrs. Lane's to sit up all night with
the sick woman, so Sandy spread his pallet on the floor at the
foot of his grandmother's bed and went to sleep. He did not
hear his Aunt Harriett when she came home, but late in the
night he woke up with his heel throbbing painfully, his throat
dry, and his skin burning, and when he tried to bend his leg, it
hurt him so that he began to cry.

Harriett, awakened by his moans, called drowsily: "What's
the matter, honey?"

"My foot," said Sandy tearfully.

So his young aunt got out of bed, lit the lamp, and helped
him to the kitchen, where she heated a kettle of water, bathed
his heel, and covered the nail-wound with vaseline. Then she
bound it with a fresh white rag.

"Now that ought to feel better," she said as she led him back
to his pallet, and soon they were both asleep again.

The next morning when Hager came from the sickbed of
her friend, she sent to the butcher-shop for a bacon rind, cut
from it a piece of fat meat, and bound it to Sandy's heel as a
cure.

"Don't want you havin' de blood-pisen here," she said. "An'
don't you run round an' play on that heel. Set out on de porch

an' study yo' reader, 'cause school'll be startin' next month."
Then she began Mrs. Reinhart's ironing.

The next day, Saturday, the last day of the carnival, Jimboy
carried the Reinharts' clothes home for Hager, since Sandy
was crippled and Jimmy Lane's mother was down in bed. But
after delivering the clothes Jimboy did not come home for
supper. When Annjee and Hager wanted to leave for the revival
in the early evening, they asked Harriett if she would stay home
with the little boy, for Sandy's heel had swollen purple where
the rusty nail had penetrated and he could hardly walk at all.

"You been gone ever' night this week," Hager said to the
girl. "An' you ain't been anear de holy tents where de Lawd's
word is preached; so you ought to be willin' to stay home one
night with a po' little sick boy."

"Yes'm," Harriett muttered in a noncommittal tone. But
shortly after her mother and Annjee had gone, she said to her
nephew: "You aren't afraid to stay home by yourself, are you?"

And Sandy answered: "Course not, Aunt Harrie."

She gave him a hot bath and put a new piece of fat meat on
his festering heel. Then she told him to climb into Annjee's
bed and go to sleep, but instead he lay for a long time looking
out the window that was beside the bed. He thought about
the carnival—the Ferris wheel sweeping up into the air, and the
minstrel show. Then he remembered Benbow's dance a few
weeks ago and how his Aunt Harriett had stood sullenly the
next morning while Hager whipped her—and hadn't cried at
all, until the welts came under her silk stockings. . . . Then
he wondered what Jimmy Lane would do if his sick mother
died from the T. B. and he were left with nobody to take care
of him, because Jimmy's step-father was no good. . . . Eu-
uuu! His heel hurt! . . . When school began again, he would
be in the fifth grade, but he wished he'd hurry up and get to
high school, like Harriett was. . . . When he got to be a man,
he was going to be a railroad engineer. . . . Gee, he wasn't
sleepy—and his heel throbbed painfully.

In the next room Harriett had lighted the oil-lamp and was
moving swiftly about taking clothes from the dresser-drawers
and spreading them on the bed. She thought Sandy was asleep,
he knew—but he couldn't go to sleep the way his foot hurt
him. He could see her through the doorway folding her dresses

in little piles and he wondered why she was doing that. Then she took an old suit-case from the closet and began to pack it, and when it was full, she pulled a new bag from under the bed, and into it she dumped her toilet-articles, powder, vaseline, nail-polish, straightening comb, and several pairs of old stockings rolled in balls. Then she sat down on the bed between the two closed suit-cases for a long time with her hands in her lap and her eyes staring ahead of her.

Finally she rose and closed the bureau-drawers, tidied up the confusion she had created, and gathered together the discarded things she had thrown on the floor. Then Sandy heard her go out into the back yard towards the trash-pile. When she returned, she put on a tight little hat and went into the kitchen to wash her hands, throwing the water through the back door. Then she tip-toed into the room where Sandy was lying and kissed him gently on the head. Sandy knew that she thought he was asleep, but in spite of himself he suddenly threw his arms tightly around her neck. He couldn't help it.

"Where you going, Aunt Harriett?" he said, sitting up in bed, clutching the girl.

"Honey, you won't tell on me, will you?" Harriett asked.

"No," he answered, and she knew he wouldn't. "But where are you going, Aunt Harrie?"

"You won't be afraid to stay here until grandma comes?"

"No," burying his face on her breast. "I won't be afraid."

"And you won't forget Aunt Harrie?"

"Course not."

"I'm leaving with the carnival," she told him.

For a moment they sat close together on the bed. Then she kissed him, went into the other room and picked up her suit-cases—and the door closed.

TEN

Punishment

OLD white Dr. McDillors, beloved of all the Negroes in
Stanton, came on Sunday morning, swabbed Sandy's festering foot with iodine, bound it up, and gave him a bottle of
green medicine to take, and by the middle of the week the boy
was able to hobble about again without pain; but Hager continued to apply fat meat instead of following the doctor's
directions.

When Harriett didn't come back, Sandy no longer slept on a
pallet on the floor. He slept in the big bed with his grandma
Hager, and the evenings that followed weren't so jolly, with his
young aunt off with the carnival, and Jimboy spending most of
his time at the pool hall or else loafing on the station platform
watching the trains come through—and nobody playing music
in the back yard.

They went to bed early these days, and after that eventful
week of carnival and revival, a sore heel, and a missing Aunt
Harriett, the muscles of Sandy's little body often twitched and
jerked in his sleep and he would awaken suddenly from dreaming that he heard sad raggy music playing while a woman
shouted for Jesus in the Gospel tent, and a girl in red silk stockings cried because the switches were cutting her legs. Sometimes
he would lie staring into the darkness a long time, while Aunt
Hager lay snoring at his side. And sometimes in the next room,
where Annjee and Jimboy were, he could hear the slow rhythmical creaking of the bedsprings and the low moans of his
mother, which he already knew accompanied the grown-up
embraces of bodily love. And sometimes through the window
he could see the moonlight glinting on the tall, tassel-crowned
stalks of corn in the garden. Perhaps he would toss and turn
until he had awakened Aunt Hager and she would say drowsily: "What's de matter with you, chile? I'll put you back on de
flo' if you can't be still!" Then he would go to sleep again, and
before he knew it, the sun would be flooding the room with

83

warm light, and the coffee would be boiling on the stove in
the kitchen, and Annjee would have gone to work.

Summer days were long and drowsy for grown-ups, but for
Sandy they were full of interest. In the mornings he helped
Aunt Hager by feeding the chickens, bringing in the water for
her wash-tubs and filling the buckets from which they drank.
He chopped wood, too, and piled it behind the kitchen-stove;
then he would take the broom and sweep dust-clean the space
around the pump and under the apple-tree where he played.
Perhaps by that time Willie-Mae would come over or Buster
would be there to shoot marbles. Or maybe his grandmother
would send him to the store to get a pound of sugar or ten
cents' worth of meal for dinner, and on the way there was certain to be an adventure. Yesterday he had seen two bad little
boys from the Bottoms, collecting scrap-iron and junk in the
alleys, get angry at each other and pretend to start a fight.

The big one said to the smaller one: "I'm a fast-black and
you know I sho won't run! Jest you pick up that piece o' iron
that belongs to me. Go ahead, jest you try!"

And the short boy replied: "I'm your match, long skinny!
Strike me an' see if you don't get burnt up!" And then they
started to play the dozens, and Sandy, standing by, learned several new and very vulgar words to use when talking about
other peoples' mothers.

The tall kid said finally: "Aw, go on, you little clay-colored
nigger, you looks too much like mustard to me anyhow!"
Picking up the disputed piece of scrap-iron, he proceeded on
his quest for junk, looking into all the trash-piles and garbage-
cans along the alley, but the smaller of the two boys took his
gunnysack and went in the opposite direction alone.

"Be careful, sissy, and don't break your dishes," his late companion called after his retreating buddy, and Sandy carefully
memorized the expression to try on Jimmy Lane some time—
that is, if Jimmy's mother got well, for Mrs. Lane now was in
the last stages of consumption. But if she got better, Sandy was
going to tell her son to be careful and not break his dishes—
always wearing his mother's shoes, like a girl.

By that time he had forgotten what Hager sent him to the
store to buy, and instead of getting meal he bought washing-

powder. When he came home, after nearly an hour's absence, his grandmother threatened to cut an elm switch, but she satisfied herself instead by scolding him for staying so long, and then sending him back to exchange the washing-powder for meal—and she waiting all that time to make corn dumplings to put in the greens!

In the afternoon Sandy played in his back yard or next door at the Johnson's, but Hager never allowed him outside their block. The white children across the street were frequently inclined to say "Nigger," so he was forbidden to play there. Usually Buster, who looked like a white kid, and Willie-Mae, who couldn't have been blacker, were his companions. The three children would run at hide-and-seek, in the tall corn; or they would tag one another in the big yard, or play house under the apple-tree.

Once when they were rummaging in the trash-pile to see what they could find, Sandy came across a pawn ticket which he took into the kitchen to Hager. It was for a watch his Aunt Harriett had pawned the Saturday she ran away.

Sometimes in the late afternoon the children would go next door to Madam de Carter's and she would give them ginger cookies and read to them from the *Bible Story Reader*. Madam de Carter looked very pompous and important in her silk waist as she would put on her *pince-nez* and say: "Now, children, seat yourselves and preserve silence while I read you-all this moralizing history of Samson's treacherous hair. Now, Buster, who were Samson? Willie-Mae, has you ever heard of Delilah?"

Sometimes, if Jimboy was home, he would take down his old guitar and start the children to dancing in the sunlight—but then Hager would always call Sandy to pump water or go to the store as soon as she heard the music.

"Out there dancin' like you ain't got no raisin'!" she would say. "I tells Jimboy 'bout playin' that ole ragtime here! That's what ruint Harriett!"

And on Sundays Sandy went to Sabbath school at the Shiloh Baptist Church, where he was given a colored picture card with a printed text on it. The long, dull lessons were taught by Sister Flora Garden, who had been to Wilberforce College, in Ohio. There were ten little boys in Sandy's class, ranging from nine to fourteen, and they behaved very badly, for Miss Flora Garden, who wore thick-lensed glasses on her roach-colored face, didn't understand little boys.

"Where was Moses when the lights went out?" Gritty Smith asked her every Sunday, and she didn't even know the answer.

Sandy didn't think much of Sunday-school, and frequently instead of putting his nickel in the collection basket he spent it for candy, which he divided with Buster—until one very hot Sunday Hager found it out. He had put a piece of the sticky candy in his shirt-pocket and it melted, stuck, and stained the whole front of his clean clothes. When he came home, with Buster behind him the first thing Hager said was: "What's all this here stuck up in yo' pocket?" and Buster commenced to giggle and said Sandy had bought candy.

"Where'd you get the money, sir?" demanded Aunt Hager searchingly of her grandson.

"I—we—er—Madam Carter gimme a nickel," Sandy replied haltingly, choosing the first name he could think of, which would have been all right had not Madam de Carter herself stopped by the house, almost immediately afterwards, on her way home from church.

"Is you give Sandy a nickel to buy candy this mawnin'?" Hager asked her as soon as she entered the parlor.

"Why, no, Sister Williams, I isn't. I had no coins about me a-tall at services this morning."

"Umn-huh! I thought so!" said Hager. "You Sandy!"

The little boy, guilt written all over his face, came in from the front porch, where he had been sitting with his father after Buster went home.

"Where'd you tell me you got that nickel this mawnin'?" And before he could answer, she spat out: "I'm gonna whip you!"

"Jehovah help us! Children sure is bad these days," said Madam de Carter, shaking her head as she left to go next door to her own house. "They sure *are* bad," she added, self-consciously correcting her English.

"I'm gonna whip you," Hager continued, sitting down amazed in her plush chair. "De idee o' withholdin' yo' Sunday-school money from de Lawd an' buyin' candy."

"I only spent a penny," Sandy lied, wriggling.

"How you gwine get so much candy fo' a penny that you has some left to gum up in yo' pocket? Tell me that, how you gonna do it?"

Sandy, at a loss for an answer, was standing with lowered eyelids, when the screen door opened and Jimboy came in. Sandy looked up at him for aid, but his father's usually amiable face was stern this time.

"Come here!" he said. The man towered very tall above the little fellow who looked up at him helplessly.

"I's gwine whip him!" interposed Hager.

"Is that right, you spent your Sunday-school nickel for candy?" Jimboy demanded gravely.

Sandy nodded his head. He couldn't lie to his father, and had he spoken now, the sobs would have come.

"Then you told a lie to your grandma—and I'm ashamed of you," his father said.

Sandy wanted to turn his head away and escape the slow gaze of Jimboy's eyes, but he couldn't. If Aunt Hager would only whip him, it would be better; then maybe his father wouldn't say any more. But it was awful to stand still and listen to Jimboy talk to him this way—yet there he stood, stiffly holding back the sobs.

"To take money and use it for what it ain't s'posed to be used is the same as stealing," Jimboy went on gravely to his son. "That's what you done today, and then come home and lie about it. Nobody's ugly as a liar, you know that! . . . I'm not much, maybe. Don't mean to say I am. I won't work a lot, but what I do I do honest. White folks gets rich lyin' and stealin'—and some niggers gets rich that way, too—but I don't need money if I got to get it dishonest, with a lot o' lies trailing behind me, and can't look folks in the face. It makes you feel dirty! It's no good! . . . Don't I give you nickels for candy whenever you want 'em?"

The boy nodded silently, with the tears trickling down his chin.

"And don't I go with you to the store and buy you ice-cream and soda-pop any time you ask me?"

The child nodded again.

"And then you go and take the Sunday-school nickel that your grandma's worked hard for all the week, spend it on candy, and come back home and lie about it. So that's what you do! And then lie!"

Jimboy turned his back and went out on the porch, slamming the screen door behind him. Aunt Hager did not whip her grandson, but returned to the kitchen and left him standing disgraced in the parlor. Then Sandy began to cry, with one hand in his mouth so no one could hear him, and when Annjee came home from work in the late afternoon, she found him lying across her bed, head under the pillows, still sobbing because Jimboy had called him a liar.

ELEVEN

School

SOME weeks later the neighbors were treated to an early morning concert:

> I got a high yaller
> An' a little short black,
> But a brown-skin gal
> Can bring me right on back!
> I'm singin' brown-skin!
> Lawdy! . . . Lawd!
> Brown-skin! . . . O, ma Lawd!

"It must be Jimboy," said Hager from the kitchen. "A lazy coon, settin' out there in the cool singin', an' me in here sweatin' and washin' maself to dust!"

> Kansas City Southern!
> I mean de W. & A.!
> I'm gonna ride de first train
> I catch goin' out ma way.
> I'm got de railroad blues—

"I wish to God you'd go on, then!" mumbled Hager over the wash-boilers.

> But I ain't got no railroad fare!
> I'm gwine to pack ma grip an'
> Beat ma way away from here!

"Learn me how to pick a cord, papa," Sandy begged as he sat beside his father under the apple-tree, loaded with ripe fruit.

"All right, look a-here! . . . You put your thumb like this. . . ." Jimboy began to explain. "But, doggone, your fingers ain't long enough yet!"

Still they managed to spend a half-day twanging at the old instrument, with Sandy trying to learn a simple tune.

The sunny August mornings had become September mornings, and most of Aunt Hager's "white folks" had returned from their vacations; her kitchen was once more a daily laundry. Great boilers of clothes steamed on the stove and, beside the clothes, pans of apple juice boiled to jelly, and the peelings of peaches simmered to jam.

There was no news from the runaway Harriett. . . . Mrs. Lane died one sultry night, with Hager at the bedside, and was buried by the lodge with three hacks and a fifty-dollar coffin. . . . The following week the Drill of All Nations, after much practising by the women, was given with great success and Annjee, dressed in white and wrapped in a Scandinavian flag, marched proudly as Sweden. . . . Madam de Carter's house was now locked and barred, as she had departed for Oklahoma to organize branches of the lodge there. . . . Tempy had stopped to see Hager one afternoon, but she didn't stay long. She told her mother she was out collecting rents and that she and her husband were buying another house. . . . Willie-Mae had a new calico dress. . . . Buster had learned to swear better than Sandy. . . . And next Monday was to be the opening of the new school term.

Sandy hated even to think about going back to school. He was having much fun playing, and Jimboy had been teaching him to box. Then the time to go to classes came.

"Wash yo' face good, sir, put on yo' clean waist, an' polish yo' shoes," Aunt Hager said bright and early, " 'cause I don't want none o' them white teachers sayin' I sends you to school dirty as a 'cuse to put you back in de fourth grade. You hear me, sir!"

"Yes'm," Sandy replied.

This morning he was to enter the "white" fifth grade, having passed last June from the "colored" fourth, for in Stanton the Negro children were kept in separate rooms under colored teachers until they had passed the fourth grade. Then, from the fifth grade on, they went with the other children, and the teachers were white.

When Sandy arrived on the school grounds with his face shining, he found the yard already full of shouting kids. On the girls' side he saw Willie-Mae jumping rope. Sandy found Earl and Buster and some boys whom he knew playing mumble-peg on the boys' side, and he joined them. When the bell rang, they all crowded into the building, as the marching-lines had not yet been formed. Miss Abigail Minter, the principal, stood at the entrance, and there were big signs on all the room doors marking the classes. Sandy found the fifth-grade room upstairs and went in shyly. It was full of whispering youngsters huddled in little groups. He saw two colored children among them, both girls whom he didn't know, but there were no colored boys. Soon the teacher rapped briskly on her desk, and silence ensued.

"Take seats, all of you, please," she rasped out. "Anywhere now until we get order." She rapped again impatiently with the ruler. "Take seats at once." So the children each selected a desk and sat down, most of the girls at the front of the room and most of the boys together at the back, where they could play and look out the windows.

Then the teacher, middle-aged and wearing glasses, passed out tiny slips of paper to each child in the front row, with the command that they be handed backwards, so that every student received one slip.

"Now, write your names on the paper, turning it longways," she said. "Nothing but your names, that's all I want today. You will receive forms to fill out later, but I want to get your seats assigned this morning, however."

Amid much confusion and borrowing of pencils, the slips were finally signed in big awkward letters, and collected by the teacher, who passed up and down the aisles. Then she went to her desk, and there was a delightful period of whispering and wriggling as she sorted the slips and placed them in alphabetical order. Finally she finished.

"Now," she said, "each child rise as I call out your names, so I can see who you are."

The teacher stood up with the papers in her hand.

"Mary Atkins . . . Carl Dietrich . . . Josephine Evans," she called slowly glancing up after each name. "Franklin Rhodes . . . James Rodgers." Sandy stood up quickly. "Ethel Shortlidge . . . Roland Thomas." The roll-call continued, each child standing until he had been identified, then sitting down again.

"Now," the teacher said, "everybody rise and make a line around the walls. Quietly! No talking! As I call your names this time, take seats in order, starting with number one in the first row near the window. . . . Mary Atkins . . . Carl Dietrich. . . ." The roll was repeated, each child taking a seat as she had commanded. When all but four of the children were seated, the two colored girls and Sandy still were standing.

"Albert Zwick," she said, and the last white child sat down in his place. "Now," said the teacher, "you three colored children take the seats behind Albert. You girls take the first two, and you," pointing to Sandy, "take the last one. . . . Now I'm going to put on the board the list of books to buy and I want all of you to copy them correctly." And she went on with her details of schoolroom routine.

One of the colored girls turned round to Sandy and whispered: "She just put us in the back cause we're niggers." And Sandy nodded gravely. "My name's Sadie Butler and she's put me behind the Z cause I'm a nigger."

"An old heifer!" said the first little colored girl, whispering loudly. "I'm gonna tell my mama." But Sandy felt like crying. And he was beginning to be ashamed of crying because he was no longer a small boy. But the teacher's putting the colored children in the back of the room made him feel like crying.

At lunch-time he came home with his list of books, and Aunt Hager pulled her wet arms out of the tub, wiped her hands, and held them up in horror.

"Lawdy! Just look! Something else to spend money for. Ever' year more an' more books, an' chillens learn less an' less! Used to didn't have nothin' but a blue-backed speller, and now look ahere—a list as long as ma arm! Go out there in de yard an' see is yo' pappy got any money to give you for 'em, 'cause I ain't."

Sandy found Jimboy sitting dejectedly on the well-stoop in the sunshine, with his head in his hands. "You got any money, papa?" he asked.

Jimboy looked at the list of books written in Sandy's childish scrawl and slowly handed him a dollar and a half.

"You see what I got left, don't you?" said his father as he turned his pants-pockets inside out, showing the little boy a jack-knife, a half-empty sack of Bull Durham, a key, and a dime. But he smiled, and took Sandy awkwardly in his arms and kissed him. "It's all right, kid."

That afternoon at school they had a long drill on the multiplication table, and then they had a spelling-match, because the teacher said that would be a good way to find out what the children knew. For the spelling-bee they were divided into two sides—the boys and the girls, each side lining up against an opposite wall. Then the teacher gave out words that they should have learned in the lower grades. On the boys' side everyone was spelled down except Sandy, but on the girls' side there were three proud little white girls left standing and Sandy came near spelling them down, too, until he put the *e* before *i* in "chief," and the girls' side won, to the disgust of the boys, and the two colored girls, who wanted Sandy to win.

After school Sandy went uptown with Buster to buy books, but there was so large a crowd of children in the bookstore that it was five o'clock before he was waited on and his list filled. When he reached home, Aunt Hager was at the kitchen-stove frying an egg-plant for supper.

"You stayin' out mighty long," she said without taking her attention from the stove.

"Where's papa?" Sandy asked eagerly. He wanted to show Jimboy his new books—a big geography, with pictures of animals in it, and a *Nature Story Reader* that he knew his father would like to see.

"Look in yonder," said Hager, pointing towards Annjee's bedroom.

Sandy rushed in, then stopped, because there was no one there. Suddenly a queer feeling came over him and he put his books down on the bed. Jimboy's clothes were no longer hanging against the wall where his working-shirts and overalls were kept. Then Sandy looked under the bed. His father's old suit-case was not there either, nor his work-shoes, nor his Sunday patent-leathers. And the guitar was missing.

"Where's papa?" he asked again, running back to the kitchen.

"Can't you see he ain't here?" replied his grandmother,

busily turning slices of egg-plant with great care in the skillet. "Gone—that's where he is—a lazy nigger. Told me to tell Annjee he say goodbye, 'cause his travellin' blues done come on . . . ! Huh! Jimboy's yo' pappy, chile, but he sho ain't worth his salt! . . . an' I's right glad he's took his clothes an' left here, maself."

TWELVE
Hard Winter

SEPTEMBER passed and the corn-stalks in the garden were cut. There were no more apples left on the trees, and chilly rains came to beat down the falling leaves from the maples and the elms. Cold and drearily wet October passed, too, with no hint of Indian summer or golden forests. And as yet there was no word from the departed Jimboy. Annjee worried herself sick as usual, hoping every day that a letter would come from this wandering husband whom she loved. And each night she hurried home from Mrs. Rice's, looked on the parlor table for the mail, and found none. Harriett had not written, either, since she went away with the carnival, and Hager never mentioned her youngest daughter's name. Nor did Hager mention Jimboy except when Annjee asked her, after she could hold it no longer: "Are you sure the mail-man ain't left me a letter today?" And then Aunt Hager would reply impatiently: "You think I'd a et it if he did? You know that good-for-nothin', up-settin' scoundrel ain't wrote!"

But in spite of daily disappointments from the postal service Annjee continued to rush from Mrs. Rice's hot kitchen as soon after dinner as she could and to trudge through the chill October rains, anxious to feel in the mail-box outside her door, then hope against hope for a letter inside on the little front-room table—which would always be empty. She caught a terrible cold tramping through the damp streets, forgetting to button her cloak, then sitting down with her wet shoes on when she got home, a look of dumb disappointment in her eyes, too tired and unhappy to remove her clothes.

"You's a fool," said her mother, whose tongue was often much sharper than the meaning behind it. "Mooning after a worthless nigger like Jimboy. I tole you years ago he were no good, when he first come, lookin' like he ought to be wearin' short pants, an' out here courtin' you. Ain't none o' them bell-hoppin', racehoss-followin' kind o' darkies worth havin', an'

that's all Jimboy was when you married him an' he ain't much
mo'n that now. An' you older'n he is, too!"

"But you know why I married, don't you?"

"You Sandy, go outdoors an' get me some wood fo' this
stove. . . . Yes, I knows why, because he were de father o'
that chile you was 'bout to bring here, but I don't see why it
couldn't just well been some o' these steady, hard-workin'
Stanton young men's what was courtin' you at de same
time. . . . But, chile or no chile, I couldn't hear nothin' but
Jimboy, Jimboy, Jimboy! I told you you better stay in de high
school an' get your edication, but no, you had to marry this
Jimboy. Now you see what you got, don't you?"

"Well, he ain't been so bad, ma! And I don't care, I love
him!"

"Umn-huh! Try an' live on love, daughter! Just try an' live
on love. . . . You's made a mistake, that's all, honey. . . . But
I guess there ain't no use talkin' 'bout it now. Take off yo' wet
shoes 'fore you catch yo' death o' cold!"

On Thanksgiving at Mrs. Rice's, so Annjee reported, they
had turkey with chestnut dressing; but at Aunt Hager's she
and Sandy had a nice juicy possum, a present from old man
Logan, parboiled and baked sweet and brown with yams in the
pan. Aunt Hager opened a jar of peach preserves. And she told
Sandy to ask Jimmy Lane in to dinner because, since his mother
died, he wasn't faring so well and the people he was staying
with didn't care much about him. But since Jimmy had quit
school, Sandy didn't see him often; and the day before
Thanksgiving he couldn't find him at all, so they had no company to help them eat the possum.

The week after Thanksgiving Annjee fell ill and had to go to
bed. She had the grippe, Aunt Hager said, and she began to
dose her with quinine and to put hot mustard-plasters on her
back and gave her onion syrup to drink, but it didn't seem to
do much good, and finally she had to send Sandy for Dr.
McDillors.

"System's all run down," said the doctor. "Heavy cold on
the chest—better be careful. And stay in the bed!" But the
warning was unnecessary. Annjee felt too tired and weak ever
to rise, and only the mail-man's whistle blowing at somebody

else's house would cause her to try to lift her head. Then she would demand weakly: "Did he stop here?"

Hager's home now was like a steam laundry. The kitchen was always hung with lines of clothes to dry, and in the late afternoon and evenings the ironing-board was spread from the table to a chair-back in the middle of the floor. All of the old customers were sending their clothes to Hager again during the winter. And since Annjee was sick, bringing no money into the house on Saturdays, the old woman had even taken an extra washing to do. Being the only wage-earner, Hager kept the suds flying—but with the wet weather she had to dry the clothes in the kitchen most of the time, and when Sandy came home from school for lunch, he would eat under dripping lines of white folks' garments while he listened to his mother coughing in the next room.

In the other rooms of the house there were no stoves, so the doors were kept open in order that the heat might pass through from the kitchen. They couldn't afford to keep more than one fire going; therefore the kitchen was living-room, dining-room, and work-room combined. In the mornings Sandy would jump out of bed and run with his clothes in his hands to the kitchen-stove, where his grandmother would have the fire blazing, the coffee-pot on, and a great tub of water heating for the washings. And in the evenings after supper he would open his geography and read about the strange countries far away, the book spread out on the oilcloth-covered kitchen-table. And Aunt Hager, if her ironing was done, would sit beside the stove and doze, while Annjee tossed and groaned in her chilly bedroom. Only in the kitchen was it really bright and warm.

In the afternoons when Sandy came home from school he would usually find Sister Johnson helping Hager with her ironing, and keeping up a steady conversation.

"Dis gonna be a hard winter. De papers say folks is out o' work ever' where, an', wid all dis sleet an' rain, it's a terror fo' de po' peoples, I tells you! Now, ma Tom, he got a good job tendin' de furnace at de Fair Buildin', so I ain't doin' much washin' long as he's workin'—but so many colored men's out o' work here, wid Christmas comin', it sho is too bad! An' you, Sis Williams, wid yo' daughter sick in bed! Any time yo' clothes git kinder heavy fo' you, I ain't mind helpin' you out. Jest send dis chile atter me or holler 'cross de yard if you kin make me hear! . . . How you press dis dress, wid de collar turn up or down? Which way do Mis' Dunset like it?"

"I always presses it down," returned Hager, who was ironing handkerchiefs and towels on the table. "Better let me iron that, an' you take these here towels."

"All right," agreed Sister Johnson, "'cause you knows how yo' white folks likes dey things, an' I don't. Folks have so many different ways!"

"Sho do," said Hager. "I washed for a woman once what even had her sheets starched."

"But you's sure got a fine repertation as a washer, Sis Williams. One o' de white ladies what I washes fo' say you washes beautiful."

"I reckon white folks does think right smart of me," said Hager proudly. "They always likes you when you tries to do right."

"When you tries to do yo' work right, you means. Dey ain't carin' nothin' 'bout you 'yond workin' fo' 'em. Ain't dey got all de little niggers settin' off in one row at dat school whar Sandy an' Willie-Mae go at? I's like Harriett—ain't got no time fo' white folks maself, 'ceptin' what little money dey pays me. You ain't been run out o' yo' home like I is, Hager. . . . Sandy, make haste go fetch my pipe from over to de house, an' don't stay all day playin' wid Willie-Mae! Tote it here quick! . . . An' you oughter hear de way white folks talks 'bout niggers. Says dey's lazy, an' says dey stinks, an' all. Huh! Dey ought to smell deyselves! You's smelled white peoples when dey gets to sweatin' ain't you? Smells jest like sour cream, only worser, kinder sickenin' like. And some o' dese foriners what's been eating garlic—phew! Lawdy!"

When Sandy returned with the pipe, the conversation had shifted to the deaths in the colored community. "Hager, folks dyin' right an' left already dis winter. We's had such a bad fall, dat's de reason why. You know dat no-'count Jack Smears passed away last Sunday. Dey had his funeral yesterday an' I went. Good thing he belonged to de lodge, too, else he'd been buried in de po'-field, 'cause he ain't left even de copper cents to put on his eyes. Lodge beared his funeral bill, but I heard more'n one member talkin' 'bout how dey was puttin' a ten-dollar nigger in a hundred-dollar coffin! . . . An' his wife were at de funeral. Yes, sir! A hussy! After she done left him last year wid de little chillens to take care of, an' she runnin' round de streets showin' off. Dere she sot, big as life, in front wid de moaners, long black veil on her face and done dyed her coat black, an' all de time Reverend Butler been preachin' 'bout how holy Jack were, she turn an' twist an' she coughed an' she whiffled an' blowed an' she wiped—tryin' her best to cry an' couldn't, deceitful as she is! Then she jest broke out to screamin', but warn't a tear in her eye; makin' folks look at her, dat's all, 'cause she ain't cared nothin' 'bout Jack. She been livin' in de Bottoms since last Feb'ary wid a young bell-hop ain't much older'n her own son, Bert!"

"Do Jesus!" said Hager. "Some womens is awful."

"Worse'n dat," said Sister Johnson. . . . "Lawdy! Listen at dat sleet beatin' on dese winders! Sho gwine be a real winter! An' how time do pass. Ain't but t'ree mo' weeks till Christmas!"

"Truth!" said Sandy's grandmother. "An' we ain't gwine have no money a-tall. Ain't no mo'n got through payin' ma taxes good, an' de interest on ma mortgage, when Annjee get sick here! Lawd, I tells you, po' colored womens have it hard!"

"Sho do!" said Sister Johnson, sucking at her pipe as she ironed. "How long you been had this house, Sis Williams?"

"Fo' nigh on forty years, even sence Cudge an' me come here from Montgomery. An' I been washin' fo' white folks ever' week de Lawd sent sence I been here, too. Bought this house washin', and made as many payments myself as Cudge come near; an' raised ma chillens washin'; an' when Cudge taken sick an' laid on his back for mo'n a year, I taken care o' him washin'; an' when he died, paid de funeral bill washin', cause he ain't belonged to no lodge. Sent Tempy through de high school and edicated Annjee till she marry that onery pup of a Jimboy, an' Harriett till she left home. Yes, sir. Washin', an' here I is with me arms still in de tub! . . . But they's one mo' got to go through school yet, an' that's ma little Sandy. If de Lawd lets me live, I's gwine make a edicated man out o' him. He's gwine be another Booker T. Washington." Hager turned a voluminous white petticoat on the ironing-board as she carefully pressed its emroidered hem. "I ain't never raised no boy o' ma own yet, so I wants this one o' Annjee's to 'mount to something. I wants him to know all they is to know, so's he can help this black race o' our'n to come up and see de light and take they places in de world. I wants him to be a Fred Douglass leadin' de people, that's what, an' not followin' in de tracks o' his good-for-nothin' pappy, worthless an' wanderin' like Jimboy is."

"O, don't say that, ma," Annjee cried weakly from her bed in the other room. "Jimboy's all right, but he's just too smart to do this heavy ditch-digging labor, and that's all white folks gives the colored a chance at here in Stanton; so he had to leave."

"There you go excitin' yo'self agin, an' you sick. I thought you was asleep. I ain't meant nothin', honey. Course he's all right," Hager said to quiet her daughter, but she couldn't resist mumbling: "But I ain't seen him doin' you no good."

"Well, he ain't beat her, has he?" asked Sister Johnson, who, for the sake of conversation, often took a contrary view-point. "I's knowed many a man to beat his wife. Tom used to tap me a few times 'fo' I found out a way to stop him, but dat ain't nedder here nor dere!" She folded a towel decisively and gave it a vigorous rub with the hot iron. "Did I ever tell you 'bout de man lived next do' to us in Cairo what cut his wife in de stomach wid a razor an' den stood ovah her when de doctor was sewin' her up moanin': 'I don't see why I cut her in de stomach! O, Lawd! She always told me she ain't want to be cut in de stomach!' . . . An' it warn't two months atter dat dat he done sliced her in de stomach agin when she was tryin' to git away from him! He were a mean nigger, that man were!"

"Annjee, is you taken yo' medicine yet? It's past fo' o'clock," Hager called. "Sandy, here, take this fifteen cents, chile, and run to do store an' get me a soup bone. I gwine try an' make a little broth for yo' mother. An' don't be gone all day neither, 'cause I got to send these clothes back to Mis' Dunset." Hager was pressing out the stockings as she turned her attention to the conversation again. "They tells me, Sister Johnson, that Seth Jones done beat up his wife something terrible."

"He did, an' he oughter! She was always stayin' way from

home an' settin' up in de church, not even cookin' his meals, an' de chillens runnin' ragged in de street."

"She's a religious frantic, ain't she?" asked Hager. . . . "You Sandy, hurry up, sir! an' go get that soup bone!"

"No, chile, 'tain't that," said Sister Johnson. "She ain't carin' so much 'bout religion. It's Reverend Butler she's runnin' atter. Ever' time de church do' opens, there she sets in de preacher's mouth, tryin' to 'tract de shepherd from his sheep. She de one what taken her husband's money an' bought Reverend Butler dat gold-headed walkin'-cane he's got. I ain't blame Seth fer hittin' her bap on de head, an' she takin' his money an' buyin' canes fer ministers!"

"Sadie Butler's in my school," said Sandy, putting on his stocking cap. "Reverend Butler's her step-father."

"Shut up! You hears too much," said Hager. "Ain't I told you to go on an' get that soup bone?"

"Yes'm. I'm going."

"An' I reckon I'll be movin' too," said Sister Johnson, placing the iron on the stove. "It's near 'bout time to be startin' Tom's supper. I done told Willie-Mae to peel de taters 'fo' I come ovah here, but I spects she ain't done it. Dat's de worse black gal to get to work! Soon as she eat, she run outdo's to de privy to keep from washin' de dishes!"

Sandy started to the store, and Sister Johnson, with on old coat over her head, scooted across the back yard to her door. It was a chill December afternoon and the steady sleet stung Sandy in the face as he ran along, but the air smelled good after the muggy kitchen and the stale scent of Annjee's sick-room. Near the corner Sandy met the mail-man, his face red with cold.

"Got anything for us?" asked the little boy.

"No," said the man as he went on without stopping.

Sandy wished his mother would get well soon. She looked so sad lying there in bed. And Aunt Hager was always busy washing and ironing. His grandmother didn't even have time to mend his stockings any more and there were great holes in the heels when he went to school. His shoes were worn out under the bottoms, too. Yesterday his mother had said: "Honey, you better take them high brown shoes of mine from underneath the bed and put 'em on to keep your feet dry this wet weather. I can't afford to buy you none now, and you ain't got no rubbers."

"You want me to wear old women's shoes like Jimmy Lane?" Sandy objected. "I won't catch cold with my feet wet."

But Hager from the kitchen overruled his objections. "Put on them shoes, sir, an' don't argue with yo' mother, an' she sick in de bed! Put 'em on an' hush yo' mouth, till you get something better."

So this morning at recess Sandy had to fight a boy for calling him "sissy" on account of his mother's shoes he was wearing.

But only a week and a half more and the Christmas vacation would come! Uptown the windows were already full of toys, dolls, skates, and sleds. Sandy wanted a Golden Flyer sled for Christmas. That's all he wanted—a Golden Flyer with flexible rudders, so you could guide it easy. Boy! Wouldn't he come shooting down that hill by the Hickory Woods where the fellows coasted every year! They cost only four dollars and ninety-five cents and surely his grandma could afford that for him, even if his mother was sick and she had just paid her taxes. Four ninety-five—but he wouldn't want anything else if Aunt Hager would buy that sled for Santa Claus to bring him! Every day, after school, he passed by the store, where many sleds were displayed, and stood for a long time looking at this Golden Flyer of narrow hard-wood timbers varnished a shiny yellow. It had bright red runners and a beautiful bar with which to steer.

When he told Aunt Hager about it, all she said was: "Boy, is you crazy?" But Annjee smiled from her bed and answered: "Wait and see." Maybe they would get it for him—but Santa Claus was mean to poor kids sometimes, Sandy knew, when their parents had no money.

"Fifteen cents' worth of hamburger," he said absent-mindedly to the butcher when he reached the market. . . . And when Sandy came home, his grandmother whipped him for bringing ground meat instead of the soup bone for which she had sent him.

So the cold days passed, heavy and cloudy, with Annjee still in bed, and the kitchen full of garments hanging on lines to dry because, out of doors, the frozen rain kept falling. Always in Hager's room a great pile of rough-dried clothes eternally waited to be ironed. Sandy helped his grandmother as much as he could, running errands, bringing in coal and wood, pumping water in the mornings before school, and sitting by his mother in the evenings, reading to her from his *Nature Story Reader* when it wasn't too cold in her bedroom.

Annjee was able to sit up now and she said she felt better, but she looked ashen and tired. She wanted to get back to work, so she would have a little money for Christmas and be able to help Hager with the doctor's bill, but she guessed she couldn't. And she was still worrying about Jimboy. Three months had passed since he went away—a longer time than usual that he hadn't written. Maybe something *had* happened to him. Maybe he was out of work and hungry, because this was a hard winter. *Maybe he was dead!*

"O, my God, no!" Annjee cried as the thought struck her.

But one Sunday morning, ten days before Christmas, the door-bell rang violently and a special-delivery boy stood on the front porch. Annjee's heart jumped as she sat up in bed. She had seen the youngster approaching from the window. Word from Jimboy surely—or word about him!

"Ma! Sandy! Go quick and see what it is!"

"Letter for Mrs. Annjelica Rodgers," said the boy, stamping the snow from his feet. "Sign here."

While Sandy held the door open, letting the cold wind blow through the house, Hager haltingly scrawled something on the boy's pink pad. Then, with the child behind her, the old woman hurried to her daughter's bed with the white envelope.

"It's from him!" Annjee cried; "I know it's from Jimboy," as she tore open the letter with trembling fingers.

A scrap of dirty tablet-paper fell on the quilt, and Annjee quickly picked it up. It was written in pencil in a feminine hand.

> Dear Sister,
>   I am stranded in Memphis, Tenn. and the show has gone on to New Orleans. I can't buy anything to eat because I am broke and don't know anybody in this town.

Annjee, please send me my fare to come home and mail it to the Beale Street Colored Hotel. I'm sending my love to you and mama.

Your baby sister,
Harriett

THIRTEEN

Christmas

P O' LITTLE thing," said Hager. "Po' little thing. An' here we ain't got no money."

The night before, on Saturday, Hager had bought a sack of flour, a chunk of salt pork, and some groceries. Old Dr. McDillors had called in the afternoon, and she had paid him, too.

"I reckon it would take mo'n thirty dollars to send fo' Harriett, an' Lawd knows we ain't got three dollars in de house."

Annjee lay limply back on her pillows staring out of the window at the falling snow. She had been crying.

"But never mind," her mother went on, "I's gwine see Mr. John Frank tomorrow an' see can't I borry a little mo' money on this mortgage we's got with him."

So on Monday morning the old lady left her washing and went uptown to the office of the money-lender, but the clerk there said Mr. Frank had gone to Chicago and would not be back for two weeks. There was nothing the clerk could do about it, since he himself could not lend money.

That afternoon Annjee sat up in bed and wrote a long letter to Harriett, telling her of their troubles, and before she sealed it, Sandy saw his mother slip into the envelope the three one-dollar bills that she had been guarding under her pillow.

"There goes your Santa Claus," she said to her son, "but maybe Harriett's hungry. And you don't want Aunt Harrie to be hungry, do you?"

"No'm," Sandy said.

The grey days passed and Annjee was able to get up and sit beside the kitchen-stove while her mother ironed. Every afternoon Sandy went downtown to look at the shop windows, gay with Christmas things. And he would stand and stare at the Golden Flyer sleds in Edmondson's hardware-shop. He could feel himself coasting down a long hill on one of those light, swift, red and yellow coasters, the envy of all the other boys, white and colored, who looked on.

When he went home, he described the sled minutely to Annjee and Aunt Hager and wondered aloud if that might be what he would get for Christmas. But Hager would say: "Santa Claus are just like other folks. He don't work for nothin'!" And his mother would add weakly from her chair: "This is gonna be a slim Christmas, honey, but mama'll see what she can do." She knew his heart was set on a sled, and he could tell that she knew; so maybe he would get it.

One day Annjee gathered her strength together, put a woollen dress over her kimono, wrapped a heavy cloak about herself, and went out into the back yard. Sandy, from the window, watched her picking her way slowly across the frozen ground towards the outhouse. At the trash-pile near the alley fence she stopped and, stooping down, began to pull short pieces of boards and wood from the little pile of lumber that had been left there since last summer by the carpenters who had built the porch. Several times in her labor she rose and leaned weakly against the back fence for support, and once Sandy ran out to see if he could help her, but she told him irritably to get back in the house out of the weather or she would put him to bed without any supper. Then, after placing the boards that she had succeeded in unearthing in a pile by the path, she came wearily back to the kitchen, trembling with cold.

"I'm mighty weak yet," she said to Hager, "but I'm sure much better than I was. I don't want to have the grippe no more. . . . Sandy, look in the mail-box and see has the mail-man come by yet."

As the little boy returned empty-handed, he heard his mother talking about old man Logan, who used to be a carpenter.

"Maybe he can make it," she was saying, but stopped when she heard Sandy behind her. "I guess I'll lay back down now."

Aunt Hager wrung out the last piece of clothes that she had been rinsing. "Yes, chile," she said, "you go on and lay down. I's gwine make you some tea after while." And the old woman went outdoors to take from the line the frozen garments blowing in the sharp north wind.

After supper that night Aunt Hager said casually: "Well, I reckon I'll run down an' see Brother Logan a minute whilst I got nothin' else to do. Sandy, don't you let de fire go out, and take care o' yo' mama."

"Yes'm," said the little boy, drawing pictures on the oilcloth-covered table with a pin. His grandmother went out the back door and he looked through the frosty window to see which way she was going. The old woman picked up the boards that his mother had piled near the alley fence, and with them in her arms she disappeared down the alley in the dark.

After a little, Aunt Hager returned puffing and blowing.

"Can he do it?" Annjee demanded anxiously from the bed-room when she heard her mother enter.

"Yes, chile," Hager answered. "Lawd, it sho is cold out yon-der! Whee! Lemme git here to this stove!"

That night it began to snow again. The great heavy flakes fell with languid gentility over the town and silently the white-ness covered everything. The next morning the snow froze to a hard sparkling crust on roofs and ground, and in the late afternoon when Sandy went to return the Reinharts' clothes, you could walk on top of the snow without sinking.

At the back door of the Reinharts' house a warm smell of plum-pudding and mince pies drifted out as he waited for the cook to bring the money. When she returned with seventy-five cents, she had a nickel for Sandy, too. As he slid along the street, he saw in many windows gay holly wreaths with red berries and big bows of ribbon tied to them. Sandy wished he could buy a holly wreath for their house. It might make his mother's room look cheerful. At home it didn't seem like Christmas with the kitchen full of drying clothes, and no Christmas-tree.

Sandy wondered if, after all, Santa Claus might, by some good fortune, bring him that Golden Flyer sled on Christmas morning. How fine this hard snow would be to coast on, down the long hill past the Hickory Woods! How light and swift he would fly with his new sled! Certainly he had been a good boy, carrying Aunt Hager's clothes for her, waiting on his mother when she was in bed, emptying the slops and cutting wood every day. And at night when he said his prayers:

> Now I lay me down to sleep.
> Pray the Lord my soul to keep.
> If I should die before I wake,
> Pray the Lord my soul to take. . . .

he had added with great earnestness: "And let Santa bring me a Golden Flyer sled, please, Lord. Amen."

But Sandy knew very well that there wasn't really any Santa Claus! He knew in his heart that Hager and his mother were Santa Claus—and that they didn't have any money. They were poor people. He was wearing his mama's shoes, as Jimmy Lane had once done. And his father and Harriett, who used to make the house gay, laughing and singing, were far away somewhere. . . . There wasn't any Santa Claus.

"I don't care," he said, tramping over the snow in the twilight on his way from the Reinharts'.

Christmas Eve. Candles and poinsettia flowers. Wreaths of evergreen. Baby trees hung with long strands of tinsel and fragile ornaments of colored glass. Sandy passed the windows of many white folks' houses where the curtains were up and warm floods of electric light made bright the cozy rooms. In Negro shacks, too, there was the dim warmth of oil-lamps and Christmas candles glowing. But at home there wasn't even a holly wreath. And the snow was whiter and harder than ever on the ground.

Tonight, though, there were no clothes drying in the kitchen when he went in. The ironing-board had been put away behind the door, and the whole place was made tidy and clean. The fire blazed and crackled in the little range; but nothing else said Christmas—no laughter, no tinsel, no tree.

Annjee had been about all day, still weak, but this afternoon she had made a trip to the store for a quarter's worth of mixed candies and nuts and a single orange, which she had hidden away until morning. Hager had baked a little cake, but there was no frosting on it such as there had been in other years, and there were no strange tissue-wrapped packages stuck away in the corners of trunks and drawers days ahead of time.

Although the little kitchen was warm enough, the two bedrooms were chilly, and the front room was freezing-cold because they kept the door there closed all the time. It was hard to afford a fire in one stove, let alone two, Aunt Hager kept saying, with nobody working but herself.

"I's thinking about Harriett," she remarked after their Christmas Eve supper as she rocked before the fire, "and how I's always tried to raise her right."

"And I'm thinking about—well, there ain't no use mentionin' him," Annjee said.

A sleigh slid by with jingling bells and shouts of laughter from the occupants, and a band of young people passed on their way to church singing carols. After a while another sleigh came along with a jolly sound.

"Santa Claus!" said Annjee, smiling at her serious little son. "You better hurry and go to bed, because he'll be coming soon. And be sure to hang up your stocking."

But Sandy was afraid that she was fooling, and, as he pulled off his clothes, he left his stockings on the floor, stuck into the women's shoes he had been wearing. Then, leaving the bedroom door half open so that the heat and a little light from the kitchen would come in, he climbed into his mother's bed. But he wasn't going to close his eyes yet. Sandy had discovered long ago that you could hear and see many things by not going to sleep when the family expected you to; therefore he remained awake tonight.

His mother was talking to Aunt Hager now: "I don't think he'll charge us anything, do you, ma?" And the old woman answered: "No, chile, Brother Logan's been tryin' to be ma beau for twenty years, an' he ain't gonna charge us nothin'."

Annjee came into the half-dark bedroom and looked at Sandy, lying still on the side of the bed towards the window. Then she took down her heavy coat from the wall and, sitting on the edge of a chair, began to pull on her rubbers. In a few moments he heard the front door close softly. His mother had gone out.

Where could she be going, he wondered, this time of night? He heard her footsteps crunching the hard snow and, rolling over close to the window, he pulled aside the shade a little and looked out. In the moonlight he saw Annjee moving slowly down the street past Sister Johnson's house, walking carefully over the snow like a very weak woman.

"Mama's still sick," the child thought, with his nose pressed against the cold window-pane. "I wish I could a bought her a present today."

Soon an occasional snore from the kitchen told Sandy that Hager dozed peacefully in her rocker beside the stove. He sat up in bed, wrapped a quilt about his shoulders, and remained looking out the window, with the shade hanging behind his back.

The white snow sparkled in the moonlight, and the trees made striking black shadows across the yard. Next door at the Johnson's all was dark and quiet, but across the street, where white folks lived, the lights were burning brightly and a big Christmas-tree with all its candles aglow stood in the large bay window while a woman loaded it with toys. Sandy knew that four children lived there, three boys and a girl, whom he had often watched playing on the lawn. Sometimes he wished he had a brother or sister to play with him, too, because it was very quiet in a house with only grown-ups about. And right now it was dismal and lonely to be by himself looking out the window of a cold bedroom on Christmas Eve.

Then a woman's cloaked figure came slowly back past Sister Johnson's house in the moonlight, and Sandy saw that it was his mother returning, her head down and her shadow moving blackly on the snow. You could hear the dry grate of her heels on the frozen whiteness as she walked, leaning forward, dragging something heavy behind her. Sandy prepared to lie down quickly in bed again, but he kept his eyes against the window-pane to see what Annjee was pulling, and, as she came closer to the house, he could distinguish quite clearly behind her a solid, home-made sled bumping rudely over the snow.

Before Anjee's feet touched the porch, he was lying still as though he had been asleep a long time.

The morning sunlight was tumbling brightly into the windows when Sandy opened his eyes and blinked at the white world outside.

"Aren't you ever going to get up?" asked Annjee, smiling timidly above him. "It's Christmas morning, honey. Come see what Santa Claus brought you. Get up quick."

But he didn't want to get up. He knew what Santa Claus had brought him and he wanted to stay in bed with his face to the wall. It wasn't a Golden Flyer sled—and now he couldn't even hope for one any longer. He wanted to pull the covers over his head and cry, but, "Boy! You ain't up yet?" called Aunt Hager cheerily from the kitchen. "De little Lawd Jesus is in His manger fillin' all de world with light. An' old Santa done been here an' gone! Get out from there, chile, an' see!"

"I'm coming, grandma," said Sandy slowly, wiping his tear-filled eyes and rolling out of bed as he forced his mouth to smile wide and steady at the few little presents he saw on the floor—for the child knew he was expected to smile.

"O! A sled!" he cried in a voice of mock surprise that wasn't his own at all; for there it stood, heavy and awkward, against the wall and beside it on the floor lay two picture-books from the ten-cent store and a pair of white cotton gloves. Above the sled his stocking, tacked to the wall, was partly filled with candy, and the single orange peeped out from the top.

But the sled! Home-made by some rough carpenter, with strips of rusty tin nailed along the wooden runners, and a piece of clothes-line to pull it with!

"It's fine," Sandy lied, as he tried to lift it and place it on the floor as you would in coasting; but it was very heavy, and too wide for a boy to run with in his hands. You could never get a swift start. And a board was warped in the middle.

"It's a nice sled, grandma," he lied. "I like it, mama."

"Mr. Logan made it for you," his mother answered proudly, happy that he was pleased. "I knew you wanted a sled all the time."

"It's a nice sled," Sandy repeated, grinning steadily as he held the heavy object in his hands. "It's an awful nice sled."

"Well, make haste and look at de gloves, and de candy, and them pretty books, too," called Hager from the kitchen, where she was frying strips of salt pork. "My, you sho is a slow chile on Christmas mawnin'! Come 'ere and lemme kiss you." She came to the bedroom and picked him up in her arms. "Christmas gift to Hager's baby chile! Come on, Annjee, bring his clothes out here behind de stove an' bring his books, too. . . . This here's Little Red Riding Hood and the Wolf, and this here's Hansee and Gretsle on de cover—but I reckon you can read 'em better'n I can. . . . Daughter, set de table. Breakfast's 'bout ready now. Look in de oven an' see 'bout that corn-bread. . . . Lawd, this here Sandy's just like a baby lettin' ole Hager hold him and dress him. . . . Put yo' foot in that stocking, boy!" And Sandy began to feel happier, sitting on his grandmother's lap behind the stove.

Before noon Buster had come and gone, showing off his new shoes and telling his friend about the train he had gotten that ran on a real track when you wound it up. After dinner Willie-Mae appeared bringing a naked rag doll and a set of china dishes in a blue box. And Sister Johnson sent them a mince pie as a Christmas gift.

Almost all Aunt Hager's callers knocked at the back door, but in the late afternoon the front bell rang and Annjee sent Sandy through the cold parlor to answer it. There on the porch stood his Aunt Tempy, with several gaily wrapped packages in her arms. She was almost a stranger to Sandy, yet she kissed him peremptorily on the forehead as he stood in the doorway. Then she came through the house into the kitchen, with much the air of a mistress of the manor descending to the servants' quarters.

"Land sakes alive!" said Hager, rising to kiss her.

Tempy hugged Annjee, too, before she sat down, stiffly, as though the house she was in had never been her home. To little black Willie-Mae she said nothing.

"I'm sorry I couldn't invite you for Christmas dinner today, but you know how Mr. Siles is," Tempy began to explain to her mother and sister. "My husband is home so infrequently, and he doesn't like a house full of company, but of course Dr. and Mrs. Glenn Mitchell will be in later in the evening. They drop around any time. . . . But I had to run down and bring you a few presents. . . . You haven't seen my new piano yet, have you, mother? I must come and take you home with me some nice afternoon." She smiled appropriately, but her voice was hard.

"How is you an' yo' new church makin' it?" asked Hager, slightly embarrassed in the presence of her finely dressed society daughter.

"Wonderful!" Tempy replied. "Wonderful! Father Hill is so dignified, and the services are absolutely refined! There's never anything niggerish about them—so you know, mother, they suit me."

"I's glad you likes it," said Hager.

There was an awkward silence; then Tempy distributed her gifts, kissed them all as though it were her Christian duty, and went her way, saying that she had calls to make at Lawyer and Mrs. Moore's, and Professor Booth's, and Madam Temple's before she returned home. When she had gone, everybody felt relieved—as though a white person had left the house. Willie-Mae began to play again, and Hager pushed her feet out of her shoes once more, while Annjee went into the bedroom and lay down.

Sandy sat on the floor and untied his present, wrapped in several thicknesses of pink tissue paper, and found, in a bright Christmas box, a big illustrated volume of *Andersen's Fairy Tales* decorated in letters of gold. With its heavy pages and fine pictures, it made the ten-cent-store books that Hager had bought him appear cheap and thin. It made his mother's sled look cheap, too, and shamed all the other gifts the ones he loved had given him.

"I don't want it," he said suddenly, as loud as he could. "I don't want Tempy's old book!" And from where he was sitting, he threw it with all his might underneath the stove.

Hager gasped in astonishment. "Pick that up, sir," she cried amazed. "Yo' Aunt Tempy done bought you a fine purty book an' here you throwin' it un'neath de stove in de ashes! Lawd have mercy! Pick it up, I say, this minute!"

"I won't!" cried Sandy stubbornly. "I won't! I like my sled what you-all gave me, but I don't want no old book from Tempy! I won't pick it up!"

Then the astonished Hager grabbed him by the scruff of the neck and jerked him to his feet.

"Do I have to whip you yet this holy day? . . . Pick up that book, sir!"

"No!" he yelled.

She gave him a startled rap on the head with the back of her hand. "Talkin' sassy to yo' old grandma an' tellin' her no!"

"What is it?" Annjee called from the bedroom, as Sandy began to wail.

"Nothin'," Hager replied, " 'ceptin' this chile's done got beside hisself an' I has to hit him—that's all!"

But Sandy was not hurt by his grandmother's easy rap. He

was used to being struck on the back of the head for misde-
meanors, and this time he welcomed the blow because it gave
him, at last, what he had been looking for all day—a sufficient
excuse to cry. Now his pent-up tears flowed without ceasing
while Willie-Mae sat in a corner clutching her rag doll to her
breast, and Tempy's expensive gift lay in the ashes beneath the
stove.

FOURTEEN
Return

AFTER Christmas there followed a period of cold weather, made bright by the winter sun shining on the hard crusty snow, where children slid and rolled, and over which hay-wagons made into sleighs on great heavy runners drove jingling into town from the country. There was skating on the frozen river and fine sledding on the hills beyond the woods, but Sandy never went out where the crowds were with his sled, because he was ashamed of it.

After New Year's Annjee went back to work at Mrs. Rice's, still coughing a little and still weak. But with bills to pay and Sandy in need of shoes and stockings and clothes to wear to school, she couldn't remain idle any longer. Even with her mother washing and ironing every day except the Sabbath, expenses were difficult to meet, and Aunt Hager was getting pretty old to work so hard. Annjee thought that Tempy ought to help them a little, but she was too proud to ask her. Besides, Tempy had never been very affectionate towards her sisters even when they were all girls together—but she ought to help look out for their mother. Hager, however, when Annjee brought up the subject of Tempy's help, said that she was still able to wash, thank God, and wasn't depending on any of her children for anything—not so long as white folks wore clothes.

At school Sandy passed all of his mid-year tests and, along with Sadie Butler, was advanced to the fifth A, but the other colored child in the class, a little fat girl named Mary Jones, failed and had to stay behind. Mary's mother, a large sulphur-yellow woman who cooked at the Drummer's Hotel, came to the school and told the teacher, before all the children, just what she thought of her for letting Mary fail—and her thoughts were not very complimentary to the stiff, middle-aged white lady who taught the class. The question of color came up, too, during the discussion.

"Look at ma chile settin' back there behind all de white

115

ones," screamed the sulphur-yellow woman. "An' me payin' as much taxes as anybody! You treats us colored folks like we ain't citizerzens—that's what you does!" The argument had to be settled in the principal's office, where the teacher went with the enraged mother, while the white children giggled that a fat, yellow colored lady should come to school to quarrel about her daughter's not being promoted. But the colored children in the class couldn't laugh.

St. Valentine's day came and Sadie Butler sent Sandy a big red heart. But for Annjee, "the mail-man passed and didn't leave no news," because Jimboy hadn't written yet, nor had Harriett thanked her for the three dollars she had mailed to Memphis before Christmas. There were no letters from anybody.

The work at Mrs. Rice's was very heavy, because Mrs. Rice's sister, with two children, had come from Indiana to spend the winter, and Annjee had to cook for them and clean their rooms, too. But she was managing to save a little money every week. She bought Sandy a new blue serge suit with a Norfolk coat and knickerbocker pants. And then he sat up very stiffly in Sterner's studio and had his picture taken.

The freckled-faced white boy, Paul Biggers, who sat across from Sandy in school, delivered the *Daily Leader* to several streets in Sandy's neighborhood, and Sandy sometimes went with him, helping to fold and throw the papers in the various doorways. One night it was almost seven o'clock when he got home.

"I had a great mind not to wait for you," said Aunt Hager, who had long had the table set for supper. "Wash yo' face an' hands, sir! An' brush that snow off yo' coat 'fo' you hang it up."

His grandmother took a pan of hot spoon-bread from the oven and put it on the table, where the little oil-lamp glowed warmly and the plain white dishes looked clean and inviting. On the stove there was a skillet full of fried apples and bacon, and Hager was making a pot of tea.

"Umn-nn! Smells good!" said Sandy, speaking of everything at once as he slid into his chair. "Gimme a lot o' apples, grandma."

"Is that de way you ask fo' 'em, sir? Can't you say please no mo'?"

"Please, ma'am," said the boy, grinning, for Hager's sharpness wasn't serious, and her old eyes were twinkling.

While they were eating, Annjee came in from work with a small bucket of oyster soup in her hands. They heated this and added it to their supper, and Sandy's mother sat down in front of the stove, with her feet propped up on the grate to dry quickly. It was very comfortable in the little kitchen.

"Seems like the snow's melting," said Annjee. "It's kinder sloppy and nasty underfoot. . . . Ain't been no mail today, has they?"

"No, honey," said Hager. "Leastwise, I been washin' so hard ain't had no time to look in de box. Sandy, run there to de front do' an' see. But I knows there ain't nothin', nohow."

"Might be," said Annjee as Sandy took a match and went through the dark bedroom and parlor to the front porch. There was no mail. But Sandy saw, coming across the slushy dirty-white snow towards the house, a slender figure approaching in the gloom. He waited, shivering in the doorway a moment to see who it was; then all at once he yelled at the top of his lungs: "Aunt Harrie's here!"

Pulling her by the hand, after having kissed and hugged and almost choked her, he ran back to the kitchen. "Look, here's Aunt Harrie!" he cried. "Aunt Harrie's home!" And Hager turned from the table, upsetting her tea, and opened wide her arms to take her to her bosom.

"Ma chile!" she shouted. "Done come home again! Ma baby chile come home!"

Annjee hugged and kissed Harriett, too, as her sister sat on Hager's knees—and the kitchen was filled with sound, warm and free and loving, for the prodigal returned.

"Ma chile's come back!" her mother repeated over and over. "Thank de Lawd! Ma chile's back!"

"You want some fried apples, Harrie?" asked Sandy, offering her his plate. "You want some tea?"

"No, thank you, honey," she replied when the excitement had subsided and Aunt Hager had released her, with her little black hat askew and the powder kissed off one side of her face.

She got up, shook herself, and removed her hat to brush down her hair, but she kept her faded coat on as she laid her little purse of metal mesh on the table. Then she sat down on the chair that Annjee offered her near the fire. She was thinner and her hair had been bobbed, giving her a boyish appearance, like the black pages in old Venetian paintings. But her lips were red and there were two little spots of rouge burning on each cheek, although her eyes were dark with heavy shadows as though she had been ill.

Hager was worried. "Has you been sick, chile?" she asked.

"No, mama," Harriett said. "I've been all right—just had a hard time, that's all. I got mad, and quit the show in Memphis, and they wouldn't pay me—so that was that! The minstrels left the carnival for the winter and started playing the theatres, and the new manager was a cheap skate. I couldn't get along with him."

"Did you get my letter and the money?" Annjee asked. "We didn't have no more to send you, and afterwards, when you didn't write, I didn't know if you got it."

"I got it and meant to thank you, sis, but I don't know—just didn't get round to it. But, anyway, I'm out of the South now. It's a hell—I mean it's an awful place if you don't know anybody! And more hungry niggers down there! I wonder who made up that song about *Dear Old Southland*. There's nothing dear about it that I can see. Good God! It's awful! . . . But I'm back." She smiled. "Where's Jimboy? . . . O, that's right, Annjee—you told me in the letter. But I sort-a miss him around here. Lord, I hope he didn't go to Memphis!"

"Did you find a job down there?" Annjee asked, looking at her sister's delicate hands.

"Sure, I found a *job* all right," Harriett replied in a tone that made Annjee ask no more questions. "Jobs are like hen's teeth —try and find 'em." And she shrugged her shoulders as Sandy had so often seen her do, but she no longer seemed to him like a little girl. She was grown-up and hard and strange now, but he still loved her.

"Aunt Harrie, I passed to the fifth A," he announced proudly.

"That's wonderful," she answered. "My, but you're smart! You'll be a great man some day, sure, Sandy."

"Where's yo' suit-case, honey?" Hager interrupted, too happy to touch her food on the table or to take her eyes away from the face of her returned child. "Didn't you bring it back with you? Where is it?"

"Sure, I got it. . . . But I'm gonna live at Maudel's this time, mama. . . . I left it at the station. I didn't think you-all'd want me here." She tried to make the words careless-like, but they were pitifully forced.

"Aw, honey!" Annjee cried, the tears coming.

The shadow of inner pain passed over Hager's black face, but the only reply she made was: "You's growed up now, chile. I reckon you knows what you's doin'. You's been ten thousand miles away from yo' mammy, an' I reckon you knows. . . . Come on, Sandy, let's we eat." Slowly the old woman returned to the cold food on her plate. "Won't you eat something with us, daughter?"

Harriett's eyes lowered and her shoulders drooped. "No, mama, thank you. I'm—not hungry."

Then a long, embarrassing silence followed while Hager gulped at her tea, Sandy tried to swallow a mouthful of bread that seemed to choke him, and Annjee stared stupidly at the stove.

Finally Harriett said: "I got to go now." She stood up to button her coat and put on her hat. Then she took her metal purse from the table.

"Maudel'll be waiting for me, but I'll be seeing you-all again soon, I guess. Good-bye, Sandy honey! I got to go. . . . Annjee, I got to go now. . . . Good-bye, mama!" She was trembling. As she bent down to kiss Hager, her purse slipped out of her hands and fell in a little metal heap on the floor. She stooped to pick it up.

"I got to go now."

A tiny perfume-bottle in the bag had broken from the fall, and as she went through the cold front room towards the door, the odor of cheap and poignant drugstore violets dripped across the house.

FIFTEEN

One by One

YOU could smell the spring.

"'Tain't gwine be warm fo' weeks yet!" Hager said.

Nevertheless, you could smell the spring. Little boys were already running in the streets without their overcoats, and the ground-hog had seen its shadow. Snow remained in the fence corners, but it had melted on the roofs. The yards were wet and muddy, but no longer white.

It was a sunny afternoon in late March that a letter came. On his last delivery the mail-man stopped, dropped it in the box—and Sandy saw him. It was addressed to his mother and he knew it must be from Jimboy.

"Go on an' take it to her," his grandma said, as soon as she saw the boy coming with it in his hand. "I knows that's what you want to do. Go on an' take it." And she bent over her ironing again.

Sandy ran almost all the way to Mrs. Rice's, dropping the letter more than once on the muddy sidewalk, so excited he did not think to put it in his pocket. Into the big yard and around to the white lady's back door he sped—and it was locked! He knocked loudly for a long time, and finally an upper window opened and Annjee, a dust-rag around her head, looked down, squinting in the sunlight.

"Who's there?" she called stridently, thinking of some peddler or belated tradesman for whom she did not wish to stop her cleaning.

Sandy pantingly held up the letter and was about to say something when the window closed with a bang. He could hear his mother almost falling down the back stairs, she was coming so fast. Then the key turned swiftly in the lock, the door opened, and, without closing it, Annjee took the letter from him and tore it open where she stood.

"It's from Jimboy!"

Sandy stood on the steps looking at his mother, her bosom

heaving, her sleeves rolled up, and the white cloth tied about her head, doubly white against her dark-brown face.

"He's in Detroit, it says. . . . Umn! I ain't never seen him write such a long letter. 'I had a hard time this winter till I landed here,' it says, 'but things look pretty good now, and there is lots of building going on and plenty of work opening up in the automobile plants . . . a mighty lot of colored folks here . . . hope you and Sandy been well. Sorry couldn't send you nothing Xmas, but I was in St. Paul broke. . . . Kiss my son for me. . . . Tell ma hello even if she don't want to hear it. Your loving husband, Jimboy Rogers.'"

Annjee did her best to hold the letter with one hand and pick up Sandy with the other, but he had grown considerably during the winter and she was still a little weak from her illness; so she bent down to his level and kissed him several times before she re-read the letter.

"From your daddy!" she said. "Umn-mn. . . . Come on in here and warm yourself. Lemme see what he says again!" . . . She lighted the gas oven in the white kitchen and sat down in front of it with her letter, forgetting the clock and the approaching time for Mrs. Rice's dinner, forgetting everything. "A letter from my daddy! From my far-off sugar-daddy!"

"From *my* daddy," corrected Sandy. . . . "Say, gimme a nickel to buy some marbles, mama. I wanta go play."

Without taking her eyes from the precious note Annjee fumbled in her apron and found a coin. "Take it and go on!" she said.

It was a dime. Sandy skipped around the house and down the street in the chilly sunshine. He decided to stop at Buster's for a while before going home, since he had to pass there anyway, and he found his friend in the house trying to carve boats from clothes-pins with a rusty jack-knife.

Buster's mother was a seamstress, and, after opening the front door and greeting Sandy with a cheery "Hello," she returned to her machine and a friend who was calling on her. She was a tall young light-mulatto woman, with skin like old ivory. Maybe that was why Buster was so white. But her husband was a black man who worked on the city's garbage-trucks and was active politically when election time came, getting colored men to vote Republican. Everybody said he made lots of money, but that he wasn't really Buster's father.

The golden-haired child gave Sandy a butcher-knife and together they whacked at the clothes-pins. You could hear the two women talking plainly in the little sewing-room, where the machine ran between snatches of conversation.

"Yes," Buster's mother was saying, "I have the hardest time keeping that boy colored! He goes on just like he was white. Do you know what he did last week? Cut all the blossoms off my geranium plants here in the house, took them to school, and gave them to Dorothy Marlow, in his grade. And you know who Dorothy is, don't you? Senator Marlow's daughter! . . . I said: 'Buster, if you ever cut my flowers to carry to any little girl again, I'll punish you severely, but if you cut them to carry to little white girls, I don't know what I'll do with you. . . . Don't you know they hang colored boys for things like that?' I wanted to scare him—because you know there might be trouble even among kids in school over such things. . . . But I had to laugh."

Her friend laughed too. "He's a hot one, taking flowers to the women already, and a white girl at that! You've got a fast-working son, Elvira, I must say. . . . But, do you know, when you first moved here and I saw you and the boy going in and out, I thought sure you were both white folks. I didn't know you was colored till my husband said: 'That's Eddie's wife!' You-all sure looked white to me."

The machine started to whir, making the conversation inaudible for a few minutes, and when Sandy caught their words again, they were talking about the Elks' club-house that the colored people were planning to build.

"Can you go out?" Sandy demanded of Buster, since they were making no headway with the tough clothes-pins and dull knives.

"Maybe," said Buster. "I'll go see." And he went into the other room and asked his mother.

"Put on your overcoat," she commanded. "It's not summer yet. And be back in here before dark."

"All right, Vira," the child said.

The two children went to Mrs. Rumford's shop on the corner and bought three cents' worth of candy and seven cents' worth of peewees with which to play marbles when it got warm. Then Sandy walked back past Buster's house with him and they played for a while in the street before Sandy turned to run home.

Aunt Hager was making mush for supper. She sent him to the store for a pint bottle of milk as soon as he arrived, but he forgot to take the bottle and had to come back for it.

"You'd forget yo' head if it wasn't tied to you!" the old woman reminded him.

They were just finishing supper when Annjee got home with two chocolate éclairs in her coat-pocket, mashed together against Jimboy's letter.

"Huh! I'm crazy!" she said, running her hand down into the sticky mess. "But listen, ma! He's got a job and is doing well in Detroit, Jimboy says. . . . And I'm going to him!"

"You what?" Hager gasped, dropping her spoon in her mush-bowl. "What you sayin'?"

"I said I'm going to him, ma! I got to!" Annjee stood with her coat and hat still on, holding the sticky letter. "I'm going where my heart is, ma! . . . Oh, not today." She put her arms around her mother's neck. "I don't mean today, mama, nor next week. I got to save some money first. I only got a little now. But I mean I'm going to him soon's I can. I can't help it, ma—I love him!"

"Lawd, is you foolish?" cried Hager. "What's you gwine do with this chile, trapesin' round after Jimboy? What you gwine do if he leaves you in Detroiter or wherever he are? What you gwine do then? You loves him! Huh!"

"But he ain't gonna leave me in Detroit, 'cause I'm going with him everywhere he goes," she said, her eyes shining. "He ain't gonna leave me no more!"

"An' Sandy?"

"Couldn't he stay with you, mama? And then maybe we'd come back here and live, Jimboy and me, some time, when we get a little money ahead, and could pay off the mortgage on the house. . . . But there ain't no use arguing, mama, I got to go!"

Hager had never seen Annjee so positive before; she sat speechless, looking at the bowl of mush.

"I got to go where it ain't lonesome and where I ain't

unhappy—and that's where Jimboy is! I got to go soon as I can."

Hager rose to put some water on the stove to heat for the dishes.

"One by one you leaves me—Tempy, then Harriett, then you," she said. "But Sandy's gonna stick by me, ain't you, son? He ain't gwine leave his grandma."

The youngster looked at Hager, moving slowly about the kitchen putting away the supper things.

"And I's gwine to make a fine man out o' you, Sandy. I's gwine raise one chile right yet, if de Lawd lets me live—just one chile right!" she murmured.

That night the March wind began to blow and the window-panes rattled. Sandy woke up in the dark, lying close and warm beside his mother. When he went back to sleep again, he dreamed that his Aunt Tempy's Christmas book had been turned into a chariot, and that he was riding through the sky with Tempy standing very dignifiedly beside him as he drove. And he couldn't see anybody down on earth, not even Hager.

When his mother rolled out at six o'clock to go to work, he woke up again, and while she dressed, he lay watching his breath curl mistily upwards in the cold room. Outside the window it was bleak and grey and the March wind, humming through the leafless branches of the trees, blew terrifically. He heard Aunt Hager in the kitchen poking at the stove, making up a blaze to start the coffee boiling. Then the front door closed when his mother went out and, as the door slammed, the wind howled fiercely. It was nice and warm in bed, so he lay under the heavy quilts half dreaming, half thinking, until his grandmother shook him to get up. And many were the queer, dream-drowsy thoughts that floated through his mind —not only that morning, but almost every morning while he lay beneath the warm quilts until Hager had called him three or four times to get ready for school.

He wondered sometimes whether if he washed and washed his face and hands, he would ever be white. Someone had told him once that blackness was only skin-deep. . . . And would he ever have a big house with electric lights in it, like his Aunt Tempy—but it was mostly white people who had such fine

things, and they were mean to colored. . . . Some white folks
were nice, though. Earl was nice at school, but not the little
boys across the street, who called him "nigger" every day . . .
and not Mrs. Rice, who scolded his mother. . . . Aunt Harrie
didn't like any white folks at all. . . . But Jesus was white and
wore a long, white robe, like a woman's, on the Sunday-school
cards. . . . Once Jimmie Lane said: "God damn Jesus" when
the teacher scolded him for not knowing his Bible lesson. He
said it out loud in church, too, and the church didn't fall down
on him, as Sandy thought it might. . . . Grandma said it was
a sin to cuss and swear, but all the fellows at school swore—and
Jimboy did, too. But every time Sandy said "God damn," he
felt bad, because Aunt Hager said God was mighty good and it
was wrong to take His name in vain. But he would like to learn
to say "God damn" without feeling anything like most boys
said it—just "God damn! . . . God damn! . . . God damn!"
without being ashamed of himself. . . . The Lord never
seemed to notice, anyhow. . . . And when he got big, he
wanted to travel like Jimboy. He wanted to be a railroad engineer, but Harriett had said there weren't any colored engineers
on trains. . . . What would he be, then? Maybe a doctor; but
it was more fun being an engineer and travelling far away.

Sandy wished Annjee would take him with her when she
went to join Jimboy—but then Aunt Hager would be all by
herself, and grandma was so nice to him he would hate to leave
her alone. Who would cut wood for her then? . . . But when he
got big, he would go to Detroit. And maybe New York, too,
where his geography said they had the tallest buildings in the
world, and trains that ran under the river. . . . He wondered
if there were any colored people in New York. . . . How ugly
African colored folks looked in the geography—with bushy
heads and wild eyes! Aunt Hager said her mother was an
African, but she wasn't ugly and wild; neither was Aunt Hager;
neither was little dark Willie-Mae, and they were all black like
Africans. . . . And Reverend Braswell was as black as ink, but
he knew God. . . . God didn't care if people were black, did
He? . . . What was God? Was He a man or a lamb or what?
Buster's mother said God was a light, but Aunt Hager said He
was a King and had a throne and wore a crown—she intended
to sit down by His side by and by. . . . Was Buster's father

white? Buster was white and colored both. But he didn't look like he was colored. What made Buster not colored? . . . And what made girls different from boys? . . . Once when they were playing house, Willie-Mae told him how girls were different from boys, but they didn't know why. Now Willie-Mae was in the seventh grade and had hard little breasts that stuck out sharp-like, and Jimmy Lane said dirty things about Willie-Mae. . . . Once he asked his mother what his navel was for and she said, "Layovers to catch meddlers." What did that mean? . . . And how come ladies got sick and stayed in bed when they had babies? Where did babies come from, anyhow? Not from storks—a fairy-story like Santa Claus. . . . Did God love people who told fairy-stories and lied to kids about storks and Santa Claus? . . . Santa Claus was no good, anyhow! God damn Santa Claus for not bringing him the sled he wanted Christmas! It was all a lie about Santa Claus!

The sound of Hager pouring coal on the fire and dragging her wash-tubs across the kitchen-floor to get ready for work broke in on Sandy's drowsy half-dreams, and as he rolled over in bed, his grandmother, hearing the springs creak, called loudly: "You Sandy! Get up from there! It's seven and past! You want to be late gettin' to yo' school?"

"Yes'm, I'm coming, grandma!" he said under the quilts. "But it's cold in here."

"You knows you don't dress in yonder! Bring them clothes on out behind this stove, sir."

"Yes'm." So with a kick of the feet his covers went flying back and Sandy ran to the warmth of the little kitchen, where he dressed, washed, and ate. Then he yelled for Willie-Mae—when he felt like it—or else went on to school without her, joining some of the boys on the way.

So spring was coming and Annjee worked diligently at Mrs. Rice's day after day. Often she did something extra for Mrs. Rice's sister and her children—pressed a shirtwaist or ironed some stockings—and so added a few quarters or maybe even a dollar to her weekly wages, all of which she saved to help carry her to Jimboy in Detroit.

For ten years she had been cooking, washing, ironing, scrubbing—and for what? For only the few weeks in a year, or a half-year, when Jimboy would come home from some strange place and take her in his strong arms and kiss her and murmur: "Annjee, baby!" That's what she had been working for—then the dreary months were as nothing, and the hard years faded away. But now he had been gone all winter, and, from his letter, he might not come back soon, because he said Detroit was a fine place for colored folks. . . . But Stanton—well, Annjee thought there must surely be better towns, where a woman wouldn't have to work so hard to live. . . . And where Jimboy was.

So before the first buds opened on the apple-tree in the back yard, Annjee had gone to Detroit, leaving Sandy behind with his grandmother. And when the apple blossoms came in full bloom, there was no one living in the little house but a grey-headed old woman and her grandchild.

"One by one they leaves you," Hager said slowly. "One by one yo' chillen goes."

SIXTEEN

Nothing but Love

"A YEAR ago tonight was de storm what blowed ma porch away! You 'members, honey? . . . Done seem like this year took more'n ma porch, too. My baby chile's left home an' gone to stay down yonder in de Bottoms with them triflin' Smothers family, where de piano's goin' night an' day. An' yo' mammy's done gone a-trapesin' after Jimboy. . . . Well, I thanks de Lawd you ain't gone too. You's mighty little an' knee-high to a duck, but you's ma stand-by. You's all I got, an' you ain't gwine leave yo' old grandma, is you?"

Hager had turned to Sandy in these lonely days for comfort and companionship. Through the long summer evenings they sat together on the front porch and she told her grandchild stories. Sometimes Sister Johnson came over and sat with them for a while smoking. Sometimes Madam de Carter, full of chatter and big words about the lodge and the race, would be there. But more often the two were alone—the black wash-woman with the grey hair and the little brown boy. Slavery-time stories, myths, folk-tales like the Rabbit and the Tar Baby; the war, Abe Lincoln, freedom; visions of the Lord; years of faith and labor, love and struggle filled Aunt Hager's talk of a summer night, while the lightning-bugs glowed and glimmered and the katydids chirruped, and the stars sparkled in the far-off heavens.

Sandy was getting to be too big a boy to sit in his grandmother's lap and be rocked to sleep as in summers gone by; now he sat on a little stool beside her, leaning his head on her legs when he was tired. Or else he lay flat on the floor of the porch listening, and looking up at the stars. Tonight Hager talked about love.

"These young ones what's comin' up now, they calls us ole fogies, an' handkerchief heads, an' white folks' niggers 'cause we don't get mad an' rar' up in arms like they does 'cause things is kinder hard, but, honey, when you gets old, you knows they

128

ain't no sense in gettin' mad an' sourin' yo' soul with hatin'
peoples. White folks is white folks, an' colored folks is colored,
an' neither one of 'em is bad as t'other make out. For mighty
nigh seventy years I been knowin' both of 'em, an' I ain't never
had no room in ma heart to hate neither white nor colored.
When you starts hatin' people, you gets uglier than they is—an'
I ain't never had no time for ugliness, 'cause that's where de
devil comes in—in ugliness!

"They talks 'bout slavery time an' they makes out now like it
were de most awfullest time what ever was, but don't you
believe it, chile, 'cause it weren't all that bad. Some o' de white
folks was just as nice to their niggers as they could be, nicer
than many of 'em is now, what makes 'em work for less than they
needs to eat. An' in those days they had to feed 'em. An' they
ain't every white man beat his slaves neither! Course I ain't
sayin' 'twas no paradise, but I ain't going to say it were no hell
either. An' maybe I's kinder seein' it on de bestest side 'cause I
worked in de big house an' ain't never went to de fields like
most o' de niggers did. Ma mammy were de big-house cook
an' I grewed up right with her in de kitchen an' played with little
Miss Jeanne. An' Miss Jeanne taught me to read what little I
knowed. An' when she growed up an' I growed up, she kept
me with her like her friend all de time. I loved her an' she loved
me. Miss Jeanne were de mistress' daughter, but warn't no difference 'tween us 'ceptin' she called me Hager an' I called her
Miss Jeanne. But what difference do one word like 'Miss' make
in yo' heart? None, chile, none. De words don't make no difference if de love's there.

"I disremembers what year it were de war broke out, but white
folks was scared, an' niggers, too. Didn't know what might
happen. An' we heard talk o' Abraham Lincoln 'way down
yonder in de South. An' de ole marster, ole man Winfield, took
his gun an' went to war, an' de young son, too, an' de superin-
tender and de overseer—all of 'em gone to follow Lee. Ain't
left nothin' but womens an' niggers on de plantation. De
womens was a-cryin' an' de niggers was, too, 'cause they was
sorry for de po' grievin' white folks.

"Is I ever told you how Miss Jeanne an' Marster Robert was
married in de springtime o' de war, with de magnolias all
a-bloomin' like candles for they weddin'? Is I ever told you,

Sandy? . . . Well, I must some time. An' then Marster Robert had to go right off with his mens, 'cause he's a high officer in de army an' they heard Sherman were comin'. An' he left her a-standin' with her weddin'-clothes on, leanin' 'gainst a pillar o' de big white porch, with nobody but me to dry her eyes—ole Missis done dead an' de men-folks all gone to war. An' nobody in that big whole mansion but black ole deaf Aunt Granny Jones, what kept de house straight, an' me, what was stayin' with ma mistress.

"O, de white folks needed niggers then mo'n they ever did befo', an' they ain't a colored person what didn't stick by 'em when all they men-folks were gone an' de white womens was a-cryin' an' a-faintin' like they did in them days.

"But lemme tell you 'bout Miss Jeanne. She just set in her room an' cry. A-holdin' Marster Bob's pitcher, she set an' cry, an' she ain't come out o' her room to see 'bout nothin'—house, horses, cotton—nothin'. But de niggers, they ain't cheat her nor steal from her. An' come de news dat her brother done got wounded an' died in Virginia, an' her cousins got de yaller fever. Then come de news that Marster Robert, Miss Jeanne's husband, ain't no mo'! Killed in de battle! An' I thought Miss Jeanne would like to go crazy. De news say he died like a soldier, brave an' fightin'. But when she heard it, she went to de drawer an' got out her weddin'-veil an' took her flowers in her hands like she were goin' to de altar to meet de groom. Then she just sink in de flo' an' cry till I pick her up an' hold her like a chile.

"Well, de freedom come, an' all de niggers scatter like buckshot, goin' to live in town. An' de yard niggers say I's a ole fool! I's free now—why don't I come with them? But I say no, I's gwine stay with Miss Jeanne—an' I stayed. I 'lowed ain't nary one o' them colored folks needed me like Miss Jeanne did, so I ain't went with 'em.

"An' de time pass; it pass an' it pass, an' de ole house get rusty for lack o' paint, an' de things, they 'gin to fall to pieces. An' Miss Jeanne say: 'Hager, I ain't got nobody in de world but you.' An' I say: 'Miss Jeanne, I ain't got nobody in de world but you neither.'

"And then she'd start talkin' 'bout her young husband what died so handsome an' brave, what ain't even had time that last

day fo' to 'scort her to de church for de weddin', nor to hold
her in his arms 'fore de orders come to leave. An' we would set
on de big high ole porch, with its tall stone pillars, in de evenin's
twilight till de bats start flyin' overhead an' de sunset glow
done gone, she in her wide white skirts a-billowin' round her
slender waist, an' me in ma apron an' cap an' this here chain
she gimme you see on ma neck all de time an' what's done
wore so thin.

"They was a ole stump of a blasted tree in de yard front o'
de porch 'bout tall as a man, with two black pieces o' branches
raised up like arms in de air. We used to set an' look at it, an'
Miss Jeanne could see it from her bedroom winder upstairs,
an' sometimes this stump, it look like it were movin' right up
de path like a man.

"After she done gone to bed, late one springtime night when
de moon were shinin', I hear Miss Jeanne a-cryin': 'He's come!
. . . Hager, ma Robert's come back to me!' An' I jumped out
o' ma bed in de next room where I were sleepin' an' run in to
her, an' there she was in her long, white night-clothes standin'
out in de moonlight on de little balcony, high up in de middle
o' that big stone porch. She was lookin' down into de yard at
this stump of a tree a-holdin' up its arms. An' she thinks it's
Marster Robert a-callin' her. She thinks he's standin' there in
his uniform, come back from de war, a-callin' her. An' she say:
'I'm comin', Bob, dear'; . . . I can hear her now. . . . She
say: 'I'm comin'!' . . . An' 'fore I think what she's doin', Miss
Jeanne done stepped over de little rail o' de balcony like she
were walkin' on moonlight. An' she say: 'I'm comin', Bob!'

"She ain't left no will, so de house an' all went to de State,
an' I been left with nothin'. But I ain't care 'bout that. I followed her to de grave, an' I been with her all de time, 'cause
she's ma friend. An' I were sorry for her, 'cause I knowed that
love were painin' her soul, an' warn't nobody left to help her
but me.

"An' since then I's met many a white lady an' many a white
gentleman, an' some of 'em's been kind to me an' some of 'em
ain't; some of 'em's cussed me an' wouldn't pay me fo' ma
work; an' some of 'em's hurted me awful. But I's been sorry fo'
white folks, fo' I knows something inside must be aggravatin'
de po' souls. An' I's kept a room in ma heart fo' 'em, 'cause

white folks needs us, honey, even if they don't know it. They's like spoilt chillens what's got too much o' ever'thing—an' they needs us niggers, what ain't got nothin'.

"I's been livin' a long time in yesterday, Sandy chile, an' I knows there ain't no room in de world fo' nothin' mo'n love. I knows, chile! Ever'thing there is but lovin' leaves a rust on yo' soul. An' to love sho 'nough, you got to have a spot in yo' heart fo' ever'body—great an' small, white an' black, an' them what's good an' them what's evil—'cause love ain't got no crowded-out places where de good ones stays an' de bad ones can't come in. When it gets that way, then it ain't love.

"White peoples maybe mistreats you an' hates you, but when you hates 'em back, you's de one what's hurted, 'cause hate makes yo' heart ugly—that's all it does. It closes up de sweet door to life an' makes ever'thing small an' mean an' dirty. Honey, there ain't no room in de world fo' hate, white folks hatin' niggers, an' niggers hatin' white folks. There ain't no room in this world fo' nothin' but love, Sandy chile. That's all they's room fo'—nothin' but love."

SEVENTEEN

Barber-Shop

M R. LOGAN, hearing that Aunt Hager had an empty room since all her daughters were gone, sent her one evening a new-comer in town looking for a place to stay. His name was Wim Dogberry and he was a brickmason and hod-carrier, a tall, quiet, stoop-shouldered black man, neither old nor young. He took, for two dollars and a half a week, the room that had been Annjee's, and Hager gave him a key to the front door.

Wim Dogberry was carrying hod then on a new moving-picture theatre that was being built. He rose early and came in late, face, hands, and overalls covered with mortar dust. He washed in a tin basin by the pump and went to bed, and about all he ever said to Aunt Hager and Sandy was "Good-mornin'" and "Good-evenin'," and maybe a stumbling "How is you?" But on Sunday mornings Hager usually asked him to breakfast if he got up on time—for on Saturday nights Wim drank licker and came home mumbling to himself a little later than on a week-day evenings, so sometimes he would sleep until noon Sundays.

One Saturday night he wet the bed, and when Hager went to make it up on the Sabbath morning, she found a damp yellow spot in the middle. Of this act Dogberry was so ashamed that he did not even say "Good-mornin'" for several days, and if, from the corner, he saw Aunt Hager and her grandson sitting on the porch in the twilight when he came towards home, he would pass his street and walk until he thought they had gone inside to bed. But he was a quiet roomer, he didn't give anyone any trouble, and he paid regularly. And since Hager was in no position to despise two dollars and a half every week, she rather liked Dogberry.

Now Hager kept the growing Sandy close by her all the time to help her while she washed and ironed and to talk to her while she sat on the porch in the evenings. Of course, he played sometimes in his own yard whenever Willie-Mae or Buster or, on Sundays, Jimmie Lane came to the house. But Jimmie Lane was running wild since his mother died, and Hager didn't like him to visit her grandson any more. He was bad.

When Sandy wanted to go to the vacant lot to play baseball with the neighbor boys, his grandmother would usually not allow him to leave her. "Stay here, sir, with Hager. I needs you to pump ma water fo' me an' fill up these tubs," she would say. Or else she would yell: "Ain't I told you you might get hurt down there with them old rough white boys? Stay here in yo' own yard, where you can keep out o' mischief."

So he grew accustomed to remaining near his grandmother, and at night, when the other children would be playing duck-on-the-rock under the arc-light at the corner, he would be sitting on the front porch listening to Aunt Hager telling her tales of slavery and talking of her own far-off youth. When school opened in the fall, the old woman said: "I don't know what I's gwine do all day without you, Sandy. You sho been company to me, with all my own chillens gone." But Sandy was glad to get back to a roomful of boys and girls again.

One Indian-summer afternoon when Aunt Hager was hanging up clothes in the back yard while the boy held the basket of clothes-pins, old man Logan drove past on his rickety trash-wagon and bowed elaborately to Hager. She went to the back fence to joke and gossip with him as usual, while his white mule switched off persistent flies with her tail.

Before the old beau drove away, he said: "Say, Hager, does you want that there young one o' your'n to work? I knows a little job he can have if you does," pointing to Sandy.

"What'll he got to do?" demanded Hager.

"Well, Pete Scott say he need a boy down yonder at de barber-shop on Saturdays to kinder clean up where de kinks fall, an' shine shoes fo' de customers. Ain't nothin' hard 'bout it, an' I was thinkin' it would just 'bout be Sandy's size. He could make a few pennies ever' week to kinder help things 'long."

"True, he sho could," said Hager. "I'll have him go see Pete."

So Sandy went to see Mr. Peter Scott at the colored barber-shop on Pearl Street that evening and was given his first regular job. Every Saturday, which was the barber-shop's only busy day, when the working-men got paid off, Sandy went on the job at noon and worked until eight or nine in the evening. His duties were to keep the place swept clean of the hair that the three barbers sheared and to shine the shoes of any customer who might ask for a shine. Only a few customers permitted themselves that last luxury, for many of them came to the shop in their working-shoes, covered with mud or lime, and most of them shined their own boots at home on Sunday mornings before church. But occasionally Cudge Windsor, who owned a pool hall, or some of the dressed-up bootleggers, might climb on the stand and permit their shoes to be cleaned by the brown youngster, who asked shyly: "Shine, mister?"

The barber-shop was a new world to Sandy, who had lived thus far tied to Aunt Hager's apron-strings. He was a dreamy-eyed boy who had grown to his present age largely under the dominant influence of women—Annjee, Harriett, his grand-mother—because Jimboy had been so seldom home. But the barber-shop then was a man's world, and, on Saturdays, while a dozen or more big laborers awaited their turns, the place was filled with loud man-talk and smoke and laughter. Baseball, Jack Johnson, racehorses, white folks, Teddy Roosevelt, local gossip, Booker Washington, women, labor prospects in Topeka, Kansas City, Omaha, religion, politics, women, God—discussions and arguments all afternoon and far up into the night, while crisp kinks rolled to the floor, cigarette and cigar-butts were thrown on the hearth of the monkey-stove, and Sandy called out: "Shine, mister?"

Sometimes the boy earned one or two dollars from shines, but on damp or snowy days he might not make anything except the fifty cents Pete Scott paid him for sweeping up. Or perhaps one of the barbers, too busy to go out for supper, would send Sandy for a sandwich and a bottle of milk, and thus he would make an extra nickel or dime.

The patrons liked him and often kidded him about his sandy hair. "Boy, you's too dark to have hair like that. Ain't nobody but white folks s'posed to have sandy-colored hair. An' your'n's nappy at that!" Then Sandy would blush with embarrassment —if the change from a dry chocolate to a damp chocolate can be called a blush, as he grew warm and perspired—because he didn't like to be kidded about his hair. And he hadn't been around uncouth fellows long enough to learn the protective art of turning back a joke. He had discovered already, though, that so-called jokes are often not really jokes at all, but rather unpleasant realities that hurt unless you can think of something equally funny and unpleasant to say in return. But the men who patronized Pete Scott's barber-shop seldom grew angry at the hard pleasantries that passed for humor, and they could play the dozens for hours without anger, unless the parties concerned became serious, when they were invited to take it on the outside. And even at that a fight was fun, too.

After a winter of Saturday nights at Pete's shop Sandy himself became pretty adept at "kidding"; but at first he was timid about it and afraid to joke with grown-up people, or to give smart answers to strangers when they teased him about his crinkly, sand-colored head. One day, however, one of the barbers gave him a tin of Madam Walker's and told him: "Lay that hair down an' stop these niggers from laughin' at you." Sandy took his advice.

Madam Walker's—a thick yellow pomade—and a good wetting with water proved most efficacious to the boy's hair, when aided with a stocking cap—the top of a woman's stocking cut off and tied in a knot at one end so as to fit tightly over one's head, pressing the hair smooth. Thereafter Sandy appeared with his hair slick and shiny. And the salve and water together made it seem a dark brown, just the color of his skin, instead of the peculiar sandy tint it possessed in its natural state. Besides he soon advanced far enough in the art of "kidding" to say: "So's your pa's," to people who informed him that his head was nappy.

During the autumn Harriett had been home once to see her mother and had said that she was working as chambermaid with Maudel at the hotel. But in the barber-shop that winter Sandy often heard his aunt's name mentioned in less proper connections. Sometimes the boy pretended not to hear, and if Pete Scott was there, he always stopped the men from talking.

"Tired o' all this nasty talk 'bout women in ma shop," he said one Saturday night. "Some o' you men better look after your own womenfolks if you got any."

"Aw, all de womens in de world ain't worth two cents to me," said a waiter sitting in the middle chair, his face covered with lather. "I don't respect no woman but my mother."

"An' neither do I," answered Greensbury Jones. "All of em's evil, specially if they's black an' got blue gums."

"I's done told you to hush," said Pete Scott behind the first chair, where he was clipping Jap Logan's hair. "Ma wife's black herself, so don't start talkin' 'bout no blue gums! I's tired o' this here female talk anyhow. This is ma shop, an' ma razors sho can cut somethin' else 'sides hair—so now just keep on talkin' 'bout blue gums!"

"I see where Bryant's runnin' for president agin," said Greensbury Jones.

But one Saturday, while the proprietor was out to snatch a bite to eat, a discussion came up as to who was the prettiest colored girl in town. Was she yellow, high-brown, chocolate, or black? Of course, there was no agreement, but names were mentioned and qualities were described. One girl had eyes like Eve herself; another had hips like Miss Cleopatra; one smooth brown-skin had legs like—like—like—

"Aw, man! De Statue of Liberty!" somebody suggested when the name of a famous beauty failed the speaker's memory.

"But, feller, there ain't nothin' in all them rainbow shades," a young teamster argued against Uncle Dan Givens, who preferred high yellows. "Gimme a cool black gal ever' time! They's too dark to fade—and when they are good-looking, I mean they *are* good-looking! I'm talkin' 'bout Harrietta Williams, too! That's who I mean! Now, find a better-looking gal than she is!"

"I admits Harrietta's all right," said the old man; "all right to look at but—sput-t-tsss!" He spat contemptuously at the stove.

"O, I know that!" said the teamster; "but I ain't talkin' 'bout what she is! I'm talkin' 'bout how she looks. An' a songster out o' this world don't care if she is a—!"

"S-s-s-sh! Soft-pedal it brother." One of the men nudged the speaker. "There's one o' the Williamses right here—that kid over yonder shinin' shoes's Harriett's nephew or somethin' 'nother."

"You niggers talks too free, anyhow," one of the barbers added. "Somebody gwine cut your lips off some o' these days. De idee o' ole Uncle Dan Givens' arguin' 'bout women and he done got whiskers all round his head like a wore-out cheese."

"That's all right, you young whip-snapper," squeaked Uncle

Dan heatedly. "Might have whiskers round ma head, but I ain't wore out!"

Laughter and smoke filled the little shop, while the winter wind blew sleet against the big plate-glass window and whistled through the cracks in the doorway, making the gas lights flicker overhead. Sandy smacked his polishing cloth on the toes of a gleaming pair of brown button shoes belonging to a stranger in town, then looked up with a grin and said: "Yes, sir!" as the man handed him a quarter.

"Keep the change," said the new-comer grandly.

"That guy's an actor," one of the barbers said when the man went out. "He's playin' with the *Smart Set* at the Opery House tonight. I bet the top gallery'll be full o' niggers sence it's a jig show, but I ain't goin' anear there myself to be Jim-Crowed, cause I don't believe in goin' nowhere I ain't allowed to set with the rest of the folks. If I can't be the table-cloth, I won't be the dish-rag—that's my motto. And if I can't buy the seats I want at a show, I sure God can keep my change!"

"Yes, and miss all the good shows," countered a little red-eyed porter. "Just as well say if you can't eat in a restaurant where white folks eat, you ain't gonna eat."

"Anybody want a shine?" yelled Sandy above the racket. "And if you don't want a shine, stay out of my chair and do your arguing on the floor!"

A brown-skin chorus girl, on her way to the theatre, stepped into the shop and asked if she could buy a *Chicago Defender* there. The barber directed her to the colored restaurant, while all the men immediately stopped talking to stare at her until she went out.

"Whew! . . . Some legs!" the teamster cried as the door closed on a vision of silk stockings. "How'd you like to shine that long, sweet brown-skin mama's shoes, boy?"

"She wouldn't have to pay me!" said Sandy.

"Whoopee! Gallery or no gallery," shouted Jap Logan, "I'm gonna see that show! Don't care if they do Jim-Crow niggers in the white folks' Opery House!"

"Yes," muttered one of the barbers, "that's just what's the matter now—you ain't got no race-pride! You niggers ain't got no shame!"

EIGHTEEN
Children's Day

WHEN Easter came that spring, Sandy had saved enough money to buy himself a suit and a new cap from his earnings at the barber-shop. He was very proud of this accomplishment and so was Aunt Hager.

"You's a 'dustrious chile, sho is! Gwine make a smart man even if yo' daddy warn't nothin'. Gwine get ahead an' do good fo' yo'self an' de race, yes, sir!"

The spring came early and the clear balmy days found Hager's back yard billowing with clean white clothes on lines in the sun. Her roomer had left her when the theatre was built and had gone to work on a dam somewhere up the river, so Annjee's room was empty again. Sandy had slept with his grandmother during the cold weather, but in summer he slept on a pallet.

The boy did not miss his mother. When she had been home, Annjee had worked out all day, and she was quiet at night because she was always tired. Harriett had been the one to keep the fun and laughter going—Harriett and Jimboy, whenever he was in town. Sandy wished Harrie would live at home instead of staying at Maudel's house, but he never said anything about it to his grandmother. He went to school regularly, went to work at the barber-shop on Saturdays and to Sunday-School on Sundays, and remained with Aunt Hager the rest of his time. She was always worried if she didn't know where he was.

"Colored boys, when they gets round twelve an' thirteen, they gets so bad, Sandy," she would say. "I wants you to stay nice an' make something out o' yo'self. If Hager lives, she ain't gonna see you go down. She's gonna make a fine man out o' you fo' de glory o' God an' de black race. You gwine to 'mount to something in this world. You hear me?"

Sandy did hear her, and he knew what she meant. She meant a man like Booker T. Washington, or Frederick Douglass, or like Paul Lawrence Dunbar, who did poetry-writing. Or maybe

Jack Johnson. But Hager said Jack Johnson was the devil's kind of greatness, not God's.

"That's what you get from workin' round that old barber-shop where all they talks 'bout is prize-fightin' an' hossracin'. Jack Johnson done married a white woman, anyhow! What he care 'bout de race?"

The little boy wondered if Jack Johnson's kids looked like Buster. But maybe he didn't have any kids. He must ask Pete Scott about that when he went back to work on Saturday.

In the summer a new amusement park opened in Stanton, the first of its kind in the city, with a merry-go-round, a shoot-the-shoots, a Ferris wheel, a dance-hall, and a bandstand for week-end concerts. In order to help popularize the park, which was far on the north edge of town, the *Daily Leader* announced, under its auspices, what was called a Free Children's Day Party open to all the readers of that paper who clipped the coupons published in each issue. On July 26 these coupons, presented at the gate, would entitle every child in Stanton to free admittance to the park, free popcorn, free lemonade, and one ride on each of the amusement attractions—the merry-go-round, the shoot-the-shoots, and the Ferris wheel. All you had to do was to be a reader of the *Daily Leader* and present the coupons cut from that paper.

Aunt Hager and Sister Johnson both took the *Leader* regularly, as did almost everybody else in Stanton, so Sandy and Willie-Mae started to clip coupons. All the children in the neighborhood were doing the same thing. The Children's Day would be a big event for all the little people in town. None of them had ever seen a shoot-the-shoots before, a contrivance that pulled little cars full of folks high into the air and then let them come whizzing down an incline into an artificial pond, where the cars would float like boats. Sandy and Willie-Mae looked forward to thrill after thrill.

When the afternoon of the great day came at last, Willie-Mae stopped for Sandy, dressed in her whitest white dress and her new patent-leather shoes, which hurt her feet awfully. Sandy's grandmother was making him wash his ears when she came in.

"You gwine out yonder 'mongst all them white chillens, I wants you to at least look clean!" said Hager.

They started out.

"Here!" called Aunt Hager. "Ain't you gwine to take yo' coupons?" In his rush to get away, Sandy had forgotten them.

It was a long walk to the park, and Willie-Mae stopped and took off her shoes and stockings and carried them in her hands until she got near the gate; then she put them on again and limped bravely along, clutching her precious bits of newspaper. They could hear the band playing and children shouting and squealing as the cars on the shoot-the-shoots shot downward with a splash into the pond. They could see the giant Ferris wheel, larger than the one the carnival had had, circling high in the air.

"I'm gonna ride on that first," said Sandy.

There were crowds of children under the bright red and white wooden shelter at the park entrance. They were lining up at the gate—laughing, merry, clean little white children, pushing and yelling and giggling amiably. Sandy let Willie-Mae go first and he got in line behind her. The band was playing gaily inside. . . . They were almost to the entrance now. . . . There were just two boys in front of them. . . . Willie-Mae held out her black little hand clutching the coupons. They moved forward. The man looked down.

"Sorry," he said. "This party's for white kids."

Willie-Mae did not understand. She stood holding out the coupons, waiting for the tall white man to take them.

"Stand back, you two," he said, looking at Sandy as well. "I told you little darkies this wasn't your party. . . . Come on— next little girl." And the line of white children pushed past Willie-Mae and Sandy, going into the park. Stunned, the two dark ones drew aside. Then they noticed a group of a dozen or more other colored youngsters standing apart in the sun, just without the bright entrance pavilion, and among them was Sadie Butler, Sandy's class-mate. Three or four of the colored children were crying, but most of them looked sullen and angry, and some of them had turned to go home.

"My papa takes the *Leader*," Sadie Butler was saying. "And you see what it says here on the coupons, too—'Free Admittance to Every Child in Stanton.' Can't you read it, Sandy?"

"Sure, I can read it, but I guess they didn't mean colored," he answered, as the boy watched the white children going in the gate. "They wouldn't let us in."

Willie-Mae, between the painful shoes and the hurt of her disappointment, was on the verge of tears. One of the small boys in the crowd, a hard-looking little fellow from Pearl Street, was cursing childishly.

"God damn old sons of biscuit-eaters, that what they are! I wish I was a big man, dog-gone, I'd shoot 'em all, that's what I'd do!"

"I suppose they didn't mean colored kids," said Sandy again.

"Buster went in all right," said Sadie. "I seen him. But they didn't know he was colored, I guess. When I went up to the gate, the man said: 'Whoa! Where you goin'?' just like I was a horse. . . . I'm going home now and tell my papa."

She walked away, followed by five or six other little girls in their Sunday dresses. Willie-Mae was sitting on the ground taking off her shoes again, sweat and tears running down her black cheeks. Sandy saw his white schoolmate, Earl, approaching.

"What's matter, Sandy? Ain't you goin' in?" Earl demanded, looking at his friend's worried face. "Did the little girl hurt her foot?"

"No," said Sandy. "We just ain't going in. . . . Here, Earl, you can have my coupons. If you have extra ones, the papers says you get more lemonade . . . so you take 'em."

The white boy, puzzled, accepted the proffered coupons, stood dumbly for a moment wondering what to say to his brown friend, then went on into the park.

"It's yo' party, white chile!" a little tan-skin girl called after him, mimicking the way the man at the gate had talked. "Whoa! Stay out! You's a nigger!" she said to Sandy.

The other children, in spite of themselves, laughed at the accuracy of her burlesque imitation. Then, with the music of the merry-go-round from beyond the high fence and the laughter of happy children following them, the group of dark-skinned ones started down the dusty road together—and to all the colored boys and girls they met on the way they called out, "Ain't no use, jigaboos! That party's for white folks!"

When Willie-Mae and Sandy got home and told their story, Sister Johnson was angry as a wet hen.

"Crackers is devils," she cried. "I 'spected as much! Dey ain't nary hell hot 'nough to burn ole white folks, 'cause dey's devils deyselves! De dirty hounds!"

But all Hager said was: "They's po' trash owns that park what don't know no better, hurtin' chillens' feelin's, but we'll forgive 'em! Don't fret yo'self, Sister Johnson. What good can frettin' do? Come on here, let's we have a party of our own." She went out in the yard and took a watermelon from a tub of well-water where it had been cooling and cut it into four juicy slices; then they sat down on the grass at the shady side of the house and ate, trying to forget about white folks.

"Don't you mind, Willie-Mae," Hager said to the little black girl, who was still crying. "You's colored, honey, an' you's liable to have a hard time in this life—but don't cry. . . . You Sandy, run round de house an' see didn't I heard de mail-man blowin'."

"Yes'm," said Sandy when he came back. "Was the mail-man, and I got a letter from mama." The boy sat on the grass to read it, anxious to see what Annjee said. And later, when the company had gone, he read it aloud to Hager.

Dear little Son:

How have you all been? how is grandma? I get worried about you when I do not hear. You know Aunt Hager is old and can't write much so you must do it for her because she is not used to adress letters and the last one was two weeks getting here and had went all around everywhere. Your father says tell you hello. I got a job in a boarding house for old white folks what are cranky about how they beds is made. There are white and colored here in the auto business and women to. Tell Madam de Carter I will send my Lodge dues back because I do not want to be transfer as I might come home sometime. I ain't seen you all now for more'n a year. Jimboy he keeps changing jobs from one thing to another but he likes this town pretty well. You know he broke his guitar carrying it in a crowded street car. Ma says you are growing and

have bought yourself a new suit last Easter. Mama certainly does right well to keep on washing and ironing at
her age and worrying with you besides. Tempy ought to
help ma but seem like she don't think so. Do you ever
see your Aunt Harrie? I hope she is settling down in her
ways. If ma wasn't all by herself maybe I could send for
you to come live with us in Detroit but maybe I will be
home to see you if I ever get any money ahead. Rent is so
high here I never wittnessed so many folks in one house,
rooming five and six together, and nobody can save a
dime. Are you still working at the barber shop. I heard
Sister Johnson was under the weather but I couldn't
make out from ma's scribbling what was the matter with
her. Did she have a physicianer? You behave yourself with
Willie-Mae because you are getting to be a big boy now
and she is a girl older then you are. I am going to send
you some pants next time I go down town but I get off
from work so late I don't have a chance to do nothing
and your father eats in the restaurant count of me not
home to fix for him and I don't care where you go colored folks has a hard time. I want you to mind your
grandma and help her work. She is too old to be straining at the pump drawing water to wash clothes with.
Now write to me. Love to you all both and seven kisses
XXXXXXX right here on the paper,

                              Your loving mother,
                              Annjelica Rogers

   Sandy laughed at the clumsy cross-mark kisses. He was glad
to get a letter from his mother, and word in it about Jimboy.
And he was sorry his father had broken his guitar. But not
even watermelon and the long letter could drive away his sick
feeling about the park.
   "I guess Kansas is getting like the South, isn't it, ma?" Sandy
said to his grandmother as they came out on the porch that
evening after supper. "They don't like us here either, do
they?"
   But Aunt Hager gave him no answer. In silence they watched
the sunset fade from the sky. Slowly the evening star grew

bright, and, looking at the stars, Hager began to sing, very softly at first:

> From this world o' trouble free,
> Stars beyond!
> Stars beyond!

And Sandy, as he stood beside his grandmother on the porch, heard a great chorus out of the black past—singing generations of toil-worn Negroes, echoing Hager's voice as it deepened and grew in volume:

> There's a star fo' you an' me,
> Stars beyond!

NINETEEN

Ten Dollars and Costs

I N THE fall Sandy found a job that occupied him after school hours, as well as on Saturday and Sunday. One afternoon at the barber-shop, Charlie Nutter, a bell-hop who had come to have his hair cut, asked Sandy to step outside a minute. Once out of earshot of the barbers and loafers within, Charlie went on: "Say, kid, I got some dope to buzz to yuh 'bout a job. Joe Willis, the white guy what keeps the hotel where I work, is lookin' for a boy to kinder sweep up around the lobby every day, dust off, and sort o' help the bell-boys out sometimes. Ain't nothin' hard attached to it, and yuh can bring 'long your shine-box and rub up shoes in the lobby, too, if yuh wants to. I though maybe yuh might like to have the job. Yuh'd make more'n yuh do here. And more'n that, too, when yuh got on to the ropes. Course yuh'd have to fix me up with a couple o' bucks o' so for gettin' yuh the job, but if yuh want it, just lemme know and I'll fix it with the boss. He tole me to start lookin' for somebody and that's what I'm doin'." Charlie Nutter went on talking, without stopping to wait for an answer. "Course a boy like you don't know nothin' 'bout hotel work, but yuh ain't never too young to learn, and that's a nice easy way to start. Yuh might work up to me some time, yuh never can tell—head bell-hop! 'Cause I ain't gonna stay in this burg all my life; I figger if I can hop bells here, I can hop bells in Chicago or some place worth livin' at. But the tips ain't bad down there at the Drummer's though—lots o' sportin' women and folks like that what don't mind givin' yuh a quarter any time. . . . And yuh can get well yourself once in a while. What yuh say? Do yuh want it?"

Sandy thought quick. With Christmas not far off, his shoes about worn out, and the desire to help Aunt Hager, too—"I guess I better take it," he said. "But do I have to pay you now?"

"Hell, naw, not now! I'll keep my eye on yuh, and yuh can just slip me a little change now and then down to the hotel when you start workin.' Other boy ain't quittin' nohow till next week. S'pose yuh come round there Sunday morning and I'll kinder show yuh what to do. And don't pay no mind to Willis when he hollers at yuh. He's all right—just got a hard way about him with the help, that's all—but he ain't a bad boss. I'll see yuh, then! Drop by Sunday and lemme know for sure. So long!"

But Aunt Hager was not much pleased when Sandy came home that night and she heard the news. "I ain't never wanted none o' my chillens to work in no ole hotels," she said. "They's evil, full o' nastiness, an' you don't learn nothin' good in 'em. I don't want you to go there, chile."

"But grandma," Sandy argued, "I want to send mama a Christmas present. And just look at my shoes, all worn out! I don't make much money any more since that new colored barber-shop opened up. It's all white inside and folks don't have to wait so long 'cause there's five barbers. Jimmy Lane's got the porter's job down there . . . and I have to start working regular some time, don't I?"

"I reckons you does, but I hates to see you workin' in hotels, chile, with all them low-down Bottoms niggers, and bad womens comin' an' goin'. But I reckon you does need de job. Yo' mammy ain't sent no money here fo' de Lawd knows when, an' I ain't able to buy you nice clothes an' all like you needs to go to school in. . . . But don't forget, honey, no matter where you works—you be good an' do right. . . . I reckon you'll get along."

So Sandy found Charlie Nutter on Sunday and told him for sure he would take the job. Then he told Pete Scott he was no longer coming to work at his barber-shop, and Pete got mad and told him to go to hell, quitting when business was bad after all he had done for Sandy, besides letting him shine shoes and keep all his earnings. At other shops he couldn't have done that; besides he had intended to teach Sandy to be a barber when he got big enough.

"But go on!" said Pete Scott. "Go on! I don't need you. Plenty other boys I can find to work for me. But I bet you won't stay at that Drummer's Hotel no time, though—I can tell you that!"

The long Indian summer lingered until almost Thanksgiving, and the weather was sunny and warm. The day before Sandy went to work on his new job, he came home from school, brought in the wood for the stove, and delivered a basket of newly ironed clothes to the white folks. When he returned, he found his grandmother standing on the front porch in the sunset, reading the evening paper, which the boy had recently delivered. Sandy stopped in the twilight beside Hager, breathing in the crisp cool air and wondering what they were going to have for supper.

Suddenly his grandmother gave a deep cry and leaned heavily against the door-jamb, letting the paper fall from her hands. "O, ma Lawd!" she moaned. "O, ma Lawd!" and an expression of the uttermost pain made the old woman's eyes widen in horror. "Is I read de name right?"

Sandy, frightened, picked up the paper from the porch and found on the front page the little four-line item that his grandmother had just read:

NEGRESSES ARRESTED

Harrietta Williams and Maudel Smothers, two young negresses, were arrested last night on Pearl Street for street-walking. They were brought before Judge Brinton and fined ten dollars and costs.

"What does that mean, ma—street-walking?" the child asked, but his grandmother raised her apron to her eyes and stumbled into the house. Sandy stopped, perplexed at the meaning of the article, at his aunt's arrest, at his grandmother's horror. Then he followed Hager, the open newspaper still in his hands, and found her standing at the window in the kitchen, crying. Racking sobs were shaking her body and the boy, who had never seen an old person weep like that before, was terribly afraid. He didn't know that grown-up people cried, except at funerals, where it was the proper thing to do. He didn't know they ever cried alone, by themselves in their own houses.

"I'm gonna get Sister Johnson," he said, dropping the paper on the floor. "I'm gonna get Sister Johnson quick!"

"No, honey, don't get her," stammered the old woman. "She can't help us none, chile. Can't nobody help us . . . but de Lawd."

In the dusk Sandy saw that his grandmother was trying hard to make her lips speak plainly and to control her sobs.

"Let's we pray, son, fo' yo' po' lost Aunt Harriett—fo' ma own baby chile, what's done turned from de light an' is walkin' in darkness."

She dropped on her knees near the kitchen-stove with her arms on the seat of a chair and her head bowed. Sandy got on his knees, too, and while his grandmother prayed aloud for the body and soul of her daughter, the boy repeated over and over in his mind: "I wish you'd come home, Aunt Harrie. It's lonesome around here! Gee, I wish you'd come home."

TWENTY

Hey, Boy!

I N THE lobby of the Drummer's Hotel there were six large
brass spittoons—one in the center of the place, one in each
corner, and one near the clerk's desk. It was Sandy's duty to
clean these spittoons. Every evening that winter after school
he came in the back door of the hotel, put his books in the
closet where he kept his brooms and cleaning rags, swept
the two short upper halls and the two flights of stairs, swept
the lobby and dusted, then took the spittoons, emptied their
slimy contents into the alley, rinsed them out, and polished
them until they shone as brightly as if they were made of gold.
Except for the stench of emptying them, Sandy rather liked
this job. He always felt very proud of himself when, about six
o'clock, he could look around the dingy old lobby and see the
six gleaming brass bowls catching the glow of the electric
lamps on their shining surfaces before they were again covered
with spit. The thought that he himself had created this brightness with his own hands, aided by a can of brass-polish, never
failed to make Sandy happy.

He liked to clean things, to make them beautiful, to make
them shine. Aunt Hager did, too. When she wasn't washing
clothes, she was always cleaning something about the house,
dusting, polishing the range, or scrubbing the kitchen-floor
until it was white enough to eat from. To Hager a clean thing
was beautiful—also to Sandy, proud every evening of his six
unblemished brass spittoons. Yet each day when he came to
work, they were covered anew with tobacco juice, cigarette-
butts, wads of chewing-gum, and phlegm. But to make them
clean was Sandy's job—and they were beautiful when they
were clean.

Charlie Nutter was right—there was nothing very hard
about the work and he liked it for a while. The new kinds of
life which he saw in the hotel interested and puzzled him, but,
being naturally a silent child, he asked no questions, and, beyond the directions for his work, nobody told him anything.

Sandy did his cleaning well and the boss had not yet had occasion to bellow at him, as he often bellowed at the two bellboys.

The Drummer's Hotel was not a large hotel, nor a nice one. A three-story frame structure, dilapidated and run down, it had not been painted for years. In the lobby two large panes of plate glass looked on the street, and in front of these were rows of hard wooden chairs. At the rear of the lobby was the clerk's desk, a case of cigars and cigarettes, a cooler for water, and the door to the men's room. It was Sandy's duty to clean this toilet, too.

Upstairs on the second and third floors were the bedrooms. Only the poorest of travelling salesmen, transient railroad workers, occasionally a few show-people, and the ladies of the streets with their clients rented them. The night trade was always the most brisk at the Drummer's Hotel, but it was only on Saturdays that Sandy worked after six o'clock. That night he would not get home until ten or eleven, but Aunt Hager would always be waiting for him, keeping the fire warm, with the wash-tub full of water for his weekly bath.

There was no dining-room attached to the hotel, and, aside from Sandy, there were only five employees. The boss himself, Joe Willis, was usually at the desk. There were two chambermaids who worked in the mornings, an old man who did the heavy cleaning and scrubbing once or twice a week, and two bell-boys—one night boy and one day boy supposedly, but both bellmen had been there so long that they arranged the hours to suit themselves. Charlie Nutter had started small, like Sandy, and had grown up there. The other bell-boy, really no boy at all, but an old man, had been in the hotel ever since it opened, and Sandy was as much afraid of him as he was of the boss.

This bellman's name was Mr. George Clark. His uniform was frayed and greasy, but he wore it with the air of a major, and he acted as though all the burdens of running the hotel were on his shoulders. He knew how everything was to be done, where everything was kept, what every old guest liked. And he could divine the tastes of each new guest before he had been there a day. Subservient and grinning to white folks, evil and tyrannical to the colored help, George was the chief authority, next to Joe Willis, in the Drummer's Hotel. He it was who found some fault with Sandy's work every day until he learned to like the child because Sandy never answered back or tried to be fly, as George said most young niggers were. After a time the old fellow seldom bothered to inspect Sandy's spittoons or to look in the corners for dust, but, nevertheless, he remained a person to be humored and obeyed if one wished to work at the Drummer's Hotel.

Besides being the boss's right-hand man, George Clark was the official bootlegger for the house, too. In fact, he kept his liquor-supply in the hotel cellar. When he was off duty, Charlie, the other bell-hop, sold it for him if there were any calls from the rooms above. They made no sales other than to guests of the house, but such sales were frequent. Some of the white women who used the rooms collected a commission from George for the sales they helped make to their men visitors.

Sandy was a long time learning the tricks of hotel work. "Yuh sure a dumb little joker," Charlie was constantly informing him. "But just stay around awhile and yuh'll get on to it."

Christmas came and Sandy sent his mother in Detroit a big box of drugstore candy. For Aunt Hager he started to buy a long pair of green ear-rings for fifty cents, but he was afraid she might not like them, so he bought her white handkerchiefs instead. And he sent a pretty card to Harriett, for one snowy December day his aunt had seen him through the windows sweeping out the lobby of the hotel and she had called him to the door to talk to her. She thrust a little piece of paper into his hand with her new address on it.

"Maudel's moved to Kansas City," she said, "so I don't live there any more. You better keep this address yourself and if mama ever needs me, you can know where I am."

Then she went on through the snow, looking very pretty in a cheap fur coat and black, high-heeled slippers, with grey silk stockings. Sandy saw her pass the hotel often with different men. Sometimes she went by with Cudge Windsor, the owner of the pool hall, or Billy Sanderlee. Almost always she was with sporty-looking fellows who wore derbies and had gold teeth. Sandy noticed that she didn't urge him to come to see her at this new house-number she had given him, so he put the paper

in his pocket and went back to his sweeping, glad, anyway, to
have seen his Aunt Harriett.

One Saturday afternoon several white men were sitting in
the lobby smoking and reading the papers. Sandy swept around
their chairs, dusted, and then took the spittoons out to clean.
This work did not require his attention; while he applied the
polish with a handful of soft rags, he could let his mind wander
to other things. He thought about Harriett. Then he thought
about school and what he would do when he was a man; about
Willie-Mae, who had a job washing dinner dishes for a white
family; about Jimmy Lane, who had no mama; and Sandy
wondered what his own mother and father were doing in another town, and if they wanted him with them. He thought
how old and tired and grey-headed Aunt Hager had become;
how she puffed and blowed over the wash-tubs now, but never
complained; how she waited for him on Saturday nights with
the kitchen-stove blazing, so he would be warm after walking
so far in the cold; and how she prayed he would be a great man
some day. . . . Sitting there in the back room of the hotel,
Sandy wondered how people got to be great, as, one by one,
he made the spittoons bright and beautiful. He wondered how
people made themselves great.

That night he would have to work late picking up papers in
the lobby, running errands for the boss, and shining shoes. After
he had put the spittoons around, he would go out and get a
hamburger sandwich and a cup of coffee for supper; then he
would come back and help Charlie if he could. . . . Charlie
was a good old boy. He had taken only a dollar for getting
Sandy his job and he often helped him make tips by allowing
Sandy to run to the telegraph office or do some other little odd
job for a guest upstairs. . . . Sure, Charlie was a nice guy.

Things were pretty busy tonight. Several men had their
shoes shined as they sat tipped back in the lobby chairs while
Sandy with his boot-black box let them put up a foot at a time
to be polished. One tall farmer gave him a quarter tip and a pat
on the head.

"Bright little feller, that," he remarked to the boss.

About ten o'clock the blond Miss Marcia McKay's bell rang,
and, Charlie being engaged, Joe Willis sent Sandy up to see

what she wanted. Miss McKay had just come in out of the snow a short time before with a heavy-set ugly man. Both of them were drunk. Sandy knocked timidly outside her room.

"Come in," growled the man's voice.

Sandy opened the door and saw Miss McKay standing naked in the middle of the floor combing her hair. He stopped on the threshold.

"Aw, come in," said the man. "She won't bite you! Where's that other bell-boy? We want some licker! . . . Damn it! Say, send Charlie up here! He knows what I want!"

Sandy scampered away, and when he found Charlie, he told him about Miss McKay. The child was scared because he had often heard of colored boys' being lynched for looking at white women, even with their clothes on—but the bell-boy only laughed.

"Yuh're a dumb little joker!" he said. "Just stay around here awhile and yuh'll see lots more'n that!" He winked and gave Sandy a nudge in the ribs. "Boy, I done sold ten quarts o' licker tonight," he whispered jubilantly. "And some a it was mine, too!"

Sandy went back to the lobby and the shining of shoes. A big, red-necked stranger smoking and drinking with a crowd of drummers in one corner of the room called to him "Hey, boy! Shine me up here!" So he edged into the center of the group of men with his blacking-box, got down on his knees before the big fellow, took out his cans and his cloths, and went to work.

The white men were telling dirty stories, uglier than any Sandy had heard at the colored barber-shop and not very funny—and some of them made him sick at the stomach.

The big man whose shoes he was shining said: "Now I'm gonna tell one." He talked with a Southern drawl and a soft slurring of word-endings like some old colored folks. He had been drinking, too. "This is 'bout a nigger went to see Aunt Hanner one night. . . ."

A roar of laughter greeted his first effort and he was encouraged to tell another.

"Old darky caught a gal on the levee . . ." he commenced.

Sandy finished polishing the shoes and put the cloths inside his wooden box and stood up waiting for his pay, but the speaker did not notice the colored boy until he had finished his tale and laughed heartily with the other men. Then he looked at Sandy. Suddenly he grinned.

"Say, little coon, let's see you hit a step for the boys! . . . Down where I live, folks, all our niggers can dance! . . . Come on, boy, snap it up!"

"I can't," Sandy said, frowning instead of smiling, and growing warm as he stood there in the smoky circle of grinning white men. "I don't know how to dance."

"O, you're one of them stubborn Kansas coons, heh?" said the red-necked fellow disgustedly, the thickness of whisky on his tongue. "You Northern darkies are dumb as hell, anyhow!" Then, turning to the crowd of amused lobby loungers, he announced: "Now down in Mississippi, whar I come from, if you offer a nigger a dime, he'll dance his can off . . . an' they better dance, what I mean!"

He turned to the men around him for approbation, while Sandy still waited uncomfortably to be paid for the shine. But the man kept him standing there, looking at him drunkenly, then at the amused crowd of Saturday-night loungers.

"Now, a nigger his size down South would no more think o' not dancin' if a white man asked him than he would think o' flyin'. This boy's jest tryin' to be smart, that's all. Up here you-all've got darkies spoilt, believin' they're somebody. Now, in my home we keep 'em in their places." He again turned his attention to Sandy. "Boy! I want to see you dance!" he commanded.

But Sandy picked up his blacking-box and had begun to push through the circle of chairs, not caring any longer about his pay, when the southerner rose and grabbed him roughly by the arm, exhaling alcoholic breath in the boy's face as he jokingly pulled him back.

"Com'ere, you little—" but he got no further, for Sandy, strengthened by the anger that suddenly possessed him at the touch of this white man's hand, uttered a yell that could be heard for blocks.

Everyone in the lobby turned to see what had happened, but before Joe Willis got out from behind the clerk's desk, the boy, wriggling free, had reached the street-door. There Sandy turned, raised his boot-black box furiously above his head, and flung it with all his strength at the group of laughing white men in which the drunken southerner was standing. From one end of the whizzing box a stream of polish-bottles, brushes, and cans fell clattering across the lobby while Sandy disappeared through the door, running as fast as his legs could carry him in the falling snow.

"Hey! You black bastard!" Joe Willis yelled from the hotel entrance, but his voice was blown away in the darkness. As Sandy ran, he felt the snow-flakes falling in his face.

TWENTY-ONE

Note to Harriett

S EVERAL days later, when Sandy took out of his pocket the piece of paper that his Aunt Harriett had given him that day in front of the hotel, he noticed that the address written on it was somewhere in the Bottoms. He felt vaguely worried, so he did not show it to his grandmother, because he had often heard her say that the Bottoms was a bad place. And when he was working at the barber-shop, he had heard the men talking about what went on there—and in a sense he knew what they meant.

It was a gay place—people did what they wanted to, or what they had to do, and didn't care—for in the Bottoms folks ceased to struggle against the boundaries between good and bad, or white and black, and surrendered amiably to immorality. Beyond Pearl Street, across the tracks, people of all colors came together for the sake of joy, the curtains being drawn only between themselves and the opposite side of the railroad, where the churches were and the big white Y.M.C.A.

At night in the Bottoms victrolas moaned and banjos cried ecstatically in the darkness. Summer evenings little yellow and brown and black girls in pink or blue bungalow aprons laughed invitingly in doorways, and dice rattled with the staccato gaiety of jazz music on long tables in rear rooms. Pimps played pool; bootleggers lounged in big red cars; children ran in the streets until midnight, with no voice of parental authority forcing them to an early sleep; young blacks fought like cocks and enjoyed it; white boys walked through the streets winking at colored girls; men came in autos; old women ate pigs' feet and watermelon and drank beer; whisky flowed; gin was like water; soft indolent laughter didn't care about anything; and deep nigger-throated voices that had long ago stopped rebelling against the ways of this world rose in song.

To those who lived on the other side of the railroad and never realized the utter stupidity of the word "sin," the Bottoms was vile and wicked. But to the girls who lived there, and the boys who pimped and fought and sold licker there, "sin" was a silly word that did not enter their heads. They had never looked at life through the spectacles of the Sunday-School. The glasses good people wore wouldn't have fitted their eyes, for they hung no curtain of words between themselves and reality. To them, things were—what they were.

"Ma bed is hard, but I'm layin' in it jest de same!"

sang the raucous-throated blues-singer in her song;

"Hey! . . . Hey! Who wants to lay with me?"

It was to one of these streets in the Bottoms that Sandy came breathlessly one bright morning with a note in his hand. He knocked at the door of a big grey house.

"Is this where Harriett Williams lives?" he panted.

"You means Harrietta?" said a large, sleek yellow woman in a blue silk kimono who opened the door. "Come in, baby, and sit down. I'll see if she's up yet." Then the woman left Sandy in the parlor while she went up the stairs calling his aunt in a clear, lazy voice.

There were heavy velvet draperies at the windows and doors in this front room where Sandy sat, and a thick, well-worn rug on the floor. There was a divan, a davenport covered with pillows, a centre table, and several chairs. Through the curtains at the double door leading into the next room, Sandy saw a piano, more sofas and chairs, and a cleared oiled floor that might be used for dancing. Both rooms were in great disorder, and the air in the house smelled stale and beerish. Licker-bottles and ginger-ale bottles were underneath the center table, underneath the sofas, and on top of the piano. Ash-trays were everywhere, overflowing with cigar-butts and cigarette-ends—on the floor, under chairs, overturned among the sofa-pillows. A small brass tray under one of the sofas held a half-dozen small glasses, some of them still partly full of whisky or gin.

Sandy sat down to wait for his aunt. It was very quiet in the house, although it was almost ten o'clock. A man came down the stairs with his coat on his arm, blinking sleepily. He passed through the hall and out into the street. Bedroom-slippered feet shuffled to the head of the steps on the second floor, and the lazy woman's voice called: "She'll be down in a minute, darling. Just wait there."

Sandy waited. He heard the splash of water above and the hoarse gurgling of a bath-tub being emptied. Presently Harriett appeared in a little pink wash dress such as a child wears, the skirt striking her just above the knees. She smelled like cashmere-bouquet soap, and her face was not yet powdered, nor her hair done up, but she was smiling broadly, happy to see her nephew, as her arms went round his neck.

"My! I'm glad to see you, honey! How'd you happen to come? How'd you find me?"

"Grandma's sick," said Sandy. "She's awful sick and Aunt Tempy sent you this note."

The girl opened the letter. It read:

> Your mother is not expected to live. You better come to see her since she has asked for you. Tempy.

"O! . . . Wait a minute," said Harriett softly. "I'll hurry."

Sandy sat down again in the room full of ash-trays and licker-bottles. Many feet pattered upstairs, and, as doors opened and closed, women's voices were heard: "Can I help you, girlie? Can I lend you anything? Does you need a veil?"

When Harriett came down, she was wearing a tan coat-suit and a white turban, pulled tight on her head. Her face was powdered and her lips rouged ever so slightly. The bag she carried was beaded, blue and gold.

"Come on, Sandy," she said. "I guess I'm ready."

As they went out, they heard a man's voice in a shabby house across the street singing softly to a two-finger piano accompaniment:

> Sugar babe, I'm leavin'
> An' it won't be long. . . .

While outside, on his front door-step, two nappy-headed little yellow kids were solemnly balling-the-jack.

Two days before, Sandy had come home from school and found his grandmother lying across the bed, the full tubs still standing in the kitchen, her clothes not yet hung out to dry.

"What's the matter?" he asked.

"I's washed down, chile," said the old woman, panting. "I feels kinder tired-like, that's all."

But Sandy knew that there must be something else wrong with Aunt Hager, because he had never seen her lying on the bed in broad daylight, with her clothes still in the tubs.

"Does your back ache?" asked the child.

"I does feel a little misery," sighed Aunt Hager. "But seems to be mo' ma side an' not ma back this time. But 'tain't nothin'. I's just tired."

But Sandy was scared. "You want some soda and water, grandma?"

"No, honey." Then, in her usual tones of assumed anger: "Go on away from here an' let a body rest. Ain't I told you they ain't nothin' the matter 'ceptin' I's all washed out an' just got to lay down a minute? Go on an' fetch in yo' wood . . . an' spin yo' top out yonder with Buster and them. Go on!"

It was nearly five o'clock when the boy came in again. Aunt Hager was sitting in the rocker near the stove then, her face drawn and ashy. She had been trying to finish her washing.

"Chile, go get Sister Johnson an' ask her if she can't wring out ma clothes fo' me—Mis' Dunset ain't sent much washin' this week, an' you can help her hang 'em up. I reckon it ain't gonna rain tonight, so's they can dry befo' mawnin'."

Sandy ran towards the door.

"Now, don't butt your brains out!" said the old lady. "Ain't no need o' runnin'."

Not only did Sister Johnson come at once and hang out the washing, but she made Hager get in bed, with a hot-water bottle on her paining side. And she gave her a big dose of peppermint and water.

"I 'spects it's from yo' stomick," she said. "I knows you et cabbage fo' dinner!"

"Maybe 'tis," said Hager.

Sister Johnson took Sandy to her house for supper that evening and he and Willie-Mae ate five sweet potatoes each.

"You-all gwine bust!" said Tom Johnson.

About nine o'clock the boy went to bed with his grandmother, and all that night Hager tossed and groaned, in spite of her efforts to lie quiet and not keep Sandy awake. In the morning she said: "Son, I reckon you better stay home from school, 'cause I's feelin' mighty po'ly. Seems like that cabbage ain't digested yet. Feels like I done et a stone. . . . Go see if you can't make de fire up an' heat me a cup o' hot water."

About eleven o'clock Madam de Carter came over. "I thought I didn't perceive you nowhere in the yard this morning and the sun 'luminating so bright and cheerful. You ain't indispensed, are you? Sandy said you was kinder ill." She chattered away. "You know it don't look natural not to see you hanging out clothes long before the noon comes."

"I ain't well a-tall this mawnin'," said Hager when she got a chance to speak. "I's feelin' right bad. I suffers with a pain in ma side; seems like it ain't gettin' no better. Sister Johnson just left here from rubbin' it, but I still suffers terrible an' can't eat nothin'. . . . You can use de phone, can't you, Sister Carter?"

"Why, yes! Yes indeedy! I oftens phones from over to Mis' Petit's. You think you needs a physicianer?"

In spite of herself a groan came from the old woman's lips as she tried to turn towards her friend. Aunt Hager, who had never moaned for lesser hurts, did not intend to complain over this one—but the pain!

"It's cuttin' me in two." She gasped. "Send fo' old Doc McDillors an' he'll come."

Madam de Carter, proud and important at the prospect of using her white neighbor's phone, rushed away.

"I didn't know you were so sick, grandma!" Sandy's eyes were wide with fright and sympathy. "I'm gonna get Mis' Johnson to come rub you again."

"O! . . . O, ma Lawd, help!" Alone for a moment with no one to hear her, she couldn't hold back the moans any longer. A cold sweat stood on her forehead.

The doctor came—the kind old white man who had known Hager for years and in whom she had faith.

"Well," he said, "It's quite a surprise to see you in bed, Aunty." Then, looking very serious and professional, he took her pulse.

"Go out and close the door," he said gently to Madam de Carter and Sister Johnson, Willie-Mae and Sandy, all of whom had gathered around the bed in the little room. "Somebody heat some water." He turned back the quilts from the woman's body and unbuttoned her gown.

Ten minutes later he said frankly, but with great kindness in his tones: "You're a sick woman, Hager, a very sick woman."

That afternoon Tempy came, like a stranger to the house, and took charge of things. Sandy felt uncomfortable and shy in her presence. This aunt of his had a hard, cold, correct way of talking that resembled Mrs. Rice's manner of speaking to his mother when Annjee used to work there. But Tempy quickly put the house in order, bathed her mother, and spread the bed with clean sheets and a white counterpane. Before evening, members of Hager's Lodge began to drop in bringing soups and custards. White people of the neighborhood stopped, too, to inquire if there was anything they could do for the old woman who had so often waited on them in their illnesses. About six o'clock old man Logan drove up the alley and tied his white mule to the back fence.

The sun was setting when Tempy called Sandy in from the back yard, where he was chopping wood for the stove. She said: "James"—how queerly his correct name struck his ears as it fell from the lips of this cold aunt!—"James, you had better send this telegram to your mother. Now, here is a dollar bill and you can bring back the change. Look on her last letter and get the correct address."

Sandy took the written sheet of paper and the money that his aunt gave him. Then he looked through the various drawers in the house for his mother's last letter. It had been nearly a month since they had heard from her, but finally the boy found the letter in the cupboard, under a jelly-glass full of small coins that his grandmother kept there. He carried the envelope with him to the telegraph office, and there he paid for a message to Annjee in Detroit:

Mother very sick, come at once. Tempy.

As the boy walked home in the gathering dusk, he felt strangely alone in the world, as though Aunt Hager had already gone away, and when he reached the house, it was full of lodge members who had come to keep watch. Tempy went home, but Sister Johnson remained in the sick-room, changing the hot-water bottles and administering, every three hours, the medicine the doctor had left.

There were so many people in the house that Sandy came

out into the back yard and sat down on the edge of the well. It was cool and clear, and a slit of moon rode in a light-blue sky spangled with stars. Soon the apple-trees would bud and the grass would be growing. Sandy was a big boy. When his next birthday came, he would be fourteen, and he had begun to grow tall and heavy. Aunt Hager said she was going to buy him a pair of long pants this coming summer. And his mother would hardly know him when she saw him again, if she ever came home.

Tonight, inside, there were so many old sisters from the lodge that Sandy couldn't even talk to his grandmother while she lay in bed. They were constantly going in and out of the sick-room, drinking coffee in the kitchen, or gossiping in the parlor. He wished they would all go away. He could take care of his grandmother himself until she got well—he and Sister Johnson. They didn't even need Tempy, who, he felt, shouldn't be there, because he didn't like her.

"They callin' you inside," Willie-Mae came out to tell him as he sat by himself in the cold on the edge of the well. She was taller than Sandy now and had a regular job taking care of a white lady's baby. She no longer wore her hair in braids. She did it up, and she had a big leather pocket-book that she carried on her arm like a woman. Boys came to take her to the movies on Saturday nights. "They want you inside."

Sandy got up, his legs stiff and numb, and went into the kitchen. An elderly brown woman, dressed in black silk that swished as she moved, opened the door to Hager's bedroom and whispered to him loudly: "Be quiet, chile."

Sandy entered between a lane of old women. Hager looked up at him and smiled—so grave and solemn he appeared.

"Is they takin' care o' you?" she asked weakly. "Ain't it bed-time, honey? Is you had something to eat? Come on an' kiss yo' old grandma befo' you go to sleep. She'll be better in de mawnin'."

She couldn't seem to lift her head, so Sandy sat down on the bed and kissed her. All he said was: "I'm all right, grandma," because there were so many old women in there that he couldn't talk. Then he went out into the other room.

The air in the house was close and stuffy and the boy soon became groggy with sleep. He fell across the bed that had been

Annjee's, and later Dogberry's, with all his clothes on. One of the lodge women in the room said: "You better take off yo' things, chile, an' go to sleep right." Then she said to the other sisters: "Come on in de kitchen, you-all, an' let this chile go to bed."

In the morning Tempy woke him. "Are you sure you had Annjee's address correct last night?" she demanded. "The telegraph office says she couldn't be found, so the message was not delivered. Let me see the letter."

Sandy found the letter again, and the address was verified.

"Well, that's strange," said Tempy. "I suppose, as careless and irresponsible as Jimboy is, they've got it wrong, or else moved. . . . Do you know where Harriett can be? I don't suppose you do, but mother has been calling for her all night. I suppose we'll have to try to get her, wherever she is."

"I got her address," said Sandy. "She wrote it down for me when I was working at the hotel this winter. I can find her."

"Then I'll give you a note," said Tempy. "Take it to her."

So Sandy went to the big grey house in the Bottoms that morning to deliver Tempy's message, before the girls there had risen from their beds.

TWENTY-TWO

Beyond the Jordan

DURING the day the lodge members went to their work in the various kitchens and restaurants and laundries of the town. And Madam de Carter was ordered to Tulsa, Oklahoma, where a split in her organization was threatened because of the elections of the grand officers. Hager was resting easy, no pain now, but very weak.

"It's only a matter of time," said the doctor. "Give her the medicine so she won't worry, but it does no good. There's nothing we can do."

"She's going to die!" Sandy thought.

Harriett sat by the bedside holding her mother's hand as the afternoon sunlight fell on the white spread. Hager had been glad to see the girl again, and the old woman held nothing against her daughter for no longer living at home.

"Is you happy, chile?" Hager asked. "You looks so nice. Yo' clothes is right purty. I hopes you's findin' what you wants in life. You's young, honey, an' you needs to be happy. . . . Sandy!" She called so weakly that he could hardly hear her, though he was standing at the head of the bed. "Sandy, look in that drawer, chile, under ma night-gowns an' things, an' hand me that there little box you sees down in de corner."

The child found it and gave it to her, a small, white box from a cheap jeweller's. It was wrapped carefully in a soft handkerchief. The old woman took it eagerly and tried to hold it out towards her daughter. Harriett unwound the handkerchief and opened the lid of the box. Then she saw that it contained the tiny gold watch that her mother had given her on her sixteenth birthday, which she had pawned months ago in order to run away with the carnival. Quick tears came to the girl's eyes.

"I got it out o' pawn fo' you," Hager said, "'cause I wanted you to have it fo' yo'self, chile. You know yo' mammy bought it fo' you."

It was such a little watch! Old-timey, with a breast-pin on it.

Harriett quickly put her handkerchief over her wrist to hide the flashy new timepiece she was wearing on a gold bracelet.

That night Hager died. The undertakers came at dawn with their wagon and carried the body away to embalm it. Sandy stood on the front porch looking at the morning star as the clatter of the horses' hoofs echoed in the street. A sleepy young white boy was driving the undertaker's wagon, and the horse that pulled it was white.

The women who had been sitting up all night began to go home now to get their husbands' breakfasts and to prepare to go to work themselves.

"It's Wednesday," Sandy thought. "Today I'm supposed to go get Mrs. Reinhart's clothes, but grandma's dead. I guess I won't get them now. There's nobody to wash them."

Sister Johnson called him to the kitchen to drink a cup of coffee. Harriett was there weeping softly. Tempy was inside busily cleaning the room from which they had removed the body. She had opened all the windows and was airing the house.

Out in the yard a rooster flapped his wings and crowed shrilly at the rising sun. The fire crackled, and the coffee boiling sent up a fragrant aroma. Sister Johnson opened a can of condensed milk by punching it with the butcher-knife. She put some cups and saucers on the table.

"Tempy, won't you have some?"

"No, thank you, Mrs. Johnson," she called from the dead woman's bedroom.

When Aunt Hager was brought back to her house, she was in a long box covered with black plush. They placed it on a folding stand by the window in the front room. There was a crape on the door, and the shades were kept lowered, and people whispered in the house as though someone were asleep. Flowers began to be delivered by boys on bicycles, and the lodge members came to sit up again that night. The time was set for burial, and the *Daily Leader* carried this paragraph in small type on its back page:

> Hager Williams, aged colored laundress of 419 Cypress Street, passed away at her home last night. She was known and respected by many white families in the community. Three daughters and a grandson survive.

They tried again to reach Annjee in Detroit by telegram, but without success. On the afternoon of the funeral it was cold and rainy. The little Baptist Church was packed with people. The sisters of the lodge came in full regalia, with banners and insignia, and the brothers turned out with them. Hager's coffin was banked with flowers. There were many fine pieces from the families for whom she had washed and from the white neighbors she had nursed in sickness. There were offerings, too, from Tempy's high-toned friends and from Harriett's girl companions in the house in the Bottoms. Many of the bell-boys, porters, and bootleggers sent wreaths and crosses with golden letters on them: "At Rest in Jesus," "Beyond the Jordan," or simply: "Gone Home." There was a bouquet of violets from Buster's mother and a blanket of roses from Tempy herself. They were all pretty, but, to Sandy, the perfume was sickening in the close little church.

The Baptist minister preached, but Tempy had Father Hill from her church to say a few words, too. The choir sang *Shall We Meet Beyond the River?* People wept and fainted. The services seemed interminable. Then came the long drive to the cemetery in horse-drawn hacks, with a few automobiles in line behind. In at the wide gates and through a vast expanse of tombstones the procession passed, across the graveyard, towards the far, lonesome corner where most of the Negroes rested. There Sandy saw the open grave. Then he saw the casket going down . . . down . . . down, into the earth.

The boy stood quietly between his Aunt Tempy and his Aunt Harriett at the edge of the grave while Tempy stared straight ahead into the drizzling rain, and Harriett cried, streaking the powder on her cheeks.

"That's all right, mama," Harriett sobbed to the body in the long, black box. "You won't get lonesome out here. Harrie'll come back tomorrow. Harrie'll come back every day and bring you flowers. You won't get lonesome, mama."

They were throwing wet dirt on the coffin as the mourners walked away through the sticky clay towards their carriages. Some old sister at the grave began to sing:

> Dark was the night,
> Cold was the ground . . .

in a high weird monotone. Others took it up, and, as the mourners drove away, the air was filled with the minor wailing of the old women. Harriett was wearing Hager's gift, the little gold watch, pinned beneath her coat.

When they got back to the house where Aunt Hager had lived for so long, Sister Johnson said the mail-man had left a letter under the door that afternoon addressed to the dead woman. Harriett was about to open it when Tempy took it from her. It was from Annjee.

"Dear mama," it began.

> We have moved to Toledo because Jimboy thought he would do better here and the reason I haven't written, we have been so long getting settled. I have been out of work but we both got jobs now and maybe I will be able to send you some money soon. I hope you are well, ma, and all right. Kiss Sandy for me and take care of yourself. With love and God's blessings from your daughter,
>
> Annjee

Tempy immediately turned the letter over and wrote on the back:

> We buried your mother today. I tried to reach you in Detroit, but could not get you, since you were no longer there and neglected to send us your new address. It is too bad you weren't here for the funeral. Your child is going to stay with me until I hear from you.
>
> Tempy

Then she turned to the boy, who stood dazed beside Sister Johnson in the silent, familiar old house. "You will come home with me, James," she said. "We'll see that this place is locked first. You try all the windows and I'll fasten the doors; then we'll go out the front. . . . Mrs. Johnson, it's been good of you to help us in our troubles. Thank you."

Sister Johnson went home, leaving Harriett in the parlor. When Sandy and Tempy returned from locking the back windows and doors, they found the girl still standing there, and for a moment the two sisters looked at one another in silence. Then Tempy said coldly: "We're going."

Harriett went out alone into the drizzling rain. Tempy tried the parlor windows to be sure they were well fastened; then, stepping outside on the porch, she locked the door and put the key in her bag.

"Come on," she said.

Sandy looked up and down the street, but in the thick twilight of fog and rain Harriet had disappeared, so he followed his aunt into the waiting cab. As the hack clattered off, the boy gave an involuntary shiver.

"Do you want to hold my hand," Tempy asked, unbending a little.

"No," Sandy said. So they rode in silence.

TWENTY-THREE

Tempy's House

"JAMES, you must get up on time in this house. Breakfast has been ready twenty minutes. I can't come upstairs every morning to call you. You are old enough now to wake yourself and you must learn to do so—you've too far to walk to school to lie abed."

Sandy tumbled out. Tempy left the room so that he would be free to dress, and soon he came downstairs to breakfast.

He had never had a room of his own before. He had never even slept in a room alone, but here his aunt had given him a small chamber on the second floor which had a window that looked out into a tidy back yard where there was a brick walk running to the back gate. The room, which was very clean, contained only the bed, one chair, and a dresser. There was, too, a little closet in which to hang clothes, but Sandy did not have many to put in it.

The thing that impressed him most about the second floor was the bathroom. He had never lived where there was running water indoors. And in this room, too, everything was so spotlessly clean that Sandy was afraid to move lest he disturb something or splash water on the wall.

When he came downstairs for breakfast, he found the table set for two. Mr. Siles, being in the railway postal service, was out on a trip. The grapefruit was waiting as Sandy slid shyly into his place opposite the ash-brown woman who had become his guardian since his grandma's death. She bowed her head to say a short grace; then they ate.

"Have you been accustomed to drinking milk in the mornings?" Tempy asked as they were finishing the meal. "If you have, the milkman can leave another bottle. Young people should have plenty of milk."

"Yes'm, I'd like it, but we only had coffee at home."

"You needn't say 'yes'm' in this house. We are not used to slavery talk here. If you like milk, I'll get it for you. . . . Now,

170

how are your clothes? I see your stocking has a hole in it, and one pants-leg is hanging."

"It don't stay fastened."

"It *doesn't*, James! I'll buy you some more pants tomorrow. What else do you need?"

Sandy told her, and in a few days she took him to Wertheimer's, the city's largest store, and outfitted him completely. And, as they shopped, she informed him that she was the only colored woman in town who ran a bill there.

"I want white people to know that Negroes have a little taste; that's why I always trade at good shops. . . . And if you're going to live with me, you'll have to learn to do things right, too."

The tearful letter that came from Annjee when she heard of her mother's death said that Toledo was a very difficult place to get work in, and that she had no money to send railroad fare for Sandy, but that she would try to send for him as soon as she could. Jimboy was working on a lake steamer and was seldom home, and she couldn't have Sandy with her anyway until they got a nicer place to stay; so would Tempy please keep him a little while?

By return post Tempy replied that if Annjee had any sense, she would let Sandy remain in Stanton, where he could get a good education, and not be following after his worthless father all over the country. Mr. Siles and she had no children, and Sandy seemed like a quiet, decent child, smart in his classes. Colored people needed to encourage talent so that the white race would realize Negroes weren't all mere guitar-players and housemaids. And Sandy could be a credit if he were raised right. Of course, Tempy knew he hadn't had the correct environment to begin with—living with Jimboy and Harriett and going to a Baptist church, but undoubtedly he could be trained. He was young. "And I think it would be only fair to the boy that you let him stay with us, because, Annjee, you are certainly not the person to bring him up as he should be reared." The letter was signed: "Your sister, Tempy," and written properly with pen and ink.

So it happened that Sandy came to live with Mr. and Mrs.

Arkins Siles, for that was the name by which his aunt and uncle were known in the Negro society of the town. Mr. Siles was a mail-clerk on the railroad—a position that colored people considered a high one because you were working for "Uncle Sam." He was a paste-colored man of forty-eight who had inherited three houses from his father.

Tempy, when she married, had owned houses too, one of which had been willed her by Mrs. Barr-Grant, for whom she had worked for years as personal maid. She had acquired her job while yet in high school, and Mrs. Barr-Grant, who travelled a great deal in the interest of woman suffrage and prohibition, had taken Tempy east with her. On their return to Stanton she allowed the colored maid to take charge of her home, where she also employed a cook and a parlor girl. Thus was the mistress left free to write pamphlets and prepare lectures on the various evils of the world standing in need of correction.

Tempy pleased Mrs. Barr-Grant by being prompt and exact in obeying orders and by appearing to worship her Puritan intelligence. In truth Tempy did worship her mistress, for the colored girl found that by following Mrs. Barr-Grant's early directions she had become an expert housekeeper; by imitating her manner of speech she had acquired a precise flow of language; and by reading her books she had become interested in things that most Negro girls never thought about. Several times the mistress had remarked to her maid: "You're so smart and such a good, clean, quick little worker, Tempy, that it's too bad you aren't white." And Tempy had taken this to heart, not as an insult, but as a compliment.

When the white lady died, she left one of her small houses to her maid as a token of appreciation for faithful services. By dint of saving, and of having resided with her mistress where there had been no living expenses, Tempy had managed to buy another house, too. When Mr. Siles asked her to be his wife, everybody said it was a fine match, for both owned property, both were old enough to know what they wanted, and both were eminently respectable. . . . Now they prospered together.

Tempy no longer worked out, but stayed home, keeping house, except that she went each month to collect her rents and those of her husband. She had a woman to do the laundry and help with the cleaning, but Tempy herself did the cooking, and all her meals were models of economical preparation. Just enough food was prepared each time for three people. Sandy never had a third helping of dessert in her house. No big pots of black-eyed peas and pigtails scented her front hall, either. She got her recipes from *The Ladies' Home Journal*—and she never bought a watermelon.

White people were for ever picturing colored folks with huge slices of watermelon in their hands. Well, she was one colored woman who did not like them! Her favorite fruits were tangerines and grapefruit, for Mrs. Barr-Grant had always eaten those, and Tempy had admired Mrs. Barr-Grant more than anybody else—more, of course, than she had admired Aunt Hager, who spent her days at the wash-tub, and had loved watermelon.

Colored people certainly needed to come up in the world, Tempy thought, up to the level of white people—dress like white people, talk like white people, think like white people— and then they would no longer be called "niggers."

In Tempy this feeling was an emotional reaction, born of white admiration, but in Mr. Siles, who shared his wife's views, the same attitude was born of practical thought. The whites had the money, and if Negroes wanted any, the quicker they learned to be like the whites, the better. Stop being lazy, stop singing all the time, stop attending revivals, and learn to get the dollar—because money buys everything, even the respect of white people.

Blues and spirituals Tempy and her husband hated because they were too Negro. In their house Sandy dared not sing a word of *Swing Low, Sweet Chariot*, for what had darky slave songs to do with respectable people? And rag-time belonged in the Bottoms with the sinners. (It was ironically strange that the Bottoms should be the only section of Stanton where Negroes and whites mingled freely on equal terms.) That part of town, according to Tempy, was lost to God, and the fact that she had a sister living there burned like a hidden cancer in her breast. She never mentioned Harriett to anyone.

Tempy's friends were all people of standing in the darker world—doctors, school-teachers, a dentist, a lawyer, a hair-dresser. And she moved among these friends as importantly as

Mrs. Barr-Grant had moved among a similar group in the white race. Many of them had had washwomen for mothers and day-laborers for fathers; but none ever spoke of that. And while Aunt Hager lived, Tempy, after getting her position with Mrs. Barr-Grant, was seldom seen with the old woman. After her marriage she was even more ashamed of her family connections—a little sister running wild, and another sister married for the sake of love—Tempy could never abide Jimboy, or understand why Annjee had taken up with a rounder from the South. One's family as a topic of conversation, however, was not popular in high circles, for too many of Stanton's dark society folks had sprung from humble family trees and low black bottoms.

"But back in Washington, where I was born," said Mrs. Doctor Mitchell once, "we really have blood! All the best people at the capital come from noted ancestry—Senator Bruce, John M. Langston, Governor Pinchback, Frederick Douglass. Why, one of our colored families on their white side can even trace its lineage back to George Washington! . . . O, yes, we have a background! But, of course, we are too refined to boast about it."

Tempy thought of her mother then and wished that black Aunt Hager had not always worn her apron in the streets, uptown and everywhere! Of course, it was clean and white and seemed to suit the old lady, but aprons weren't worn by the best people. When Tempy was in the hospital for an operation shortly after her marriage, they wouldn't let Hager enter by the front door—and Tempy never knew whether it was on account of her color or the apron! The Presbyterian Hospital was prejudiced against Negroes and didn't like them to use the elevator, but certainly her mother should not have come there in an apron!

Well, Aunt Hager had meant well, Tempy thought, even if she didn't dress right. And now this child, Sandy—James was his correct name! At that first breakfast they ate together, she asked him if he had a comb and brush of his own.

"No'm, I ain't," said Sandy.

"I haven't," she corrected him. "I certainly don't want my white neighbors to hear you saying 'ain't' . . . You've come to live with me now and you must talk like a gentleman."

TWENTY-FOUR

A Shelf of Books

THAT spring, shortly after Sandy went to stay with Tempy, there was an epidemic of mumps among the schoolchildren in Stanton, and, old as he was, he was among its early victims. With jaws swollen to twice their normal size and a red sign, MUMPS, on the house, he was forced to remain at home for three weeks. It was then that the boy began to read books other than the ones he had had to study for his lessons. At Aunt Hager's house there had been no books, anyway, except the Bible and the few fairytales that he had been given at Christmas; but Tempy had a case full of dusty volumes that were used to give dignity to her sitting-room: a row of English classics bound in red, an *Encyclopedia of World Knowledge* in twelve volumes, a book on household medicine full of queer drawings, and some modern novels—*The Rosary, The Little Shepherd of Kingdom Come*, the newest Harold Bell Wright, and all that had ever been written by Gene Stratton Porter, Tempy's favorite author. The Negro was represented by Chestnut's *House Behind the Cedars*, and the *Complete Poems* of Paul Lawrence Dunbar, whom Tempy tolerated on account of his fame, but condemned because he had written so much in dialect and so often of the lower classes of colored people. Tempy subscribed to *Harper's Magazine*, too, because Mrs. Barr-Grant had taken it. And in her sewing-room closet there was also a pile of *The Crisis*, the thin Negro monthly that she had been taking from the beginning of its publication.

Sandy had heard of that magazine, but he had never seen a copy; so he went through them all, looking at the pictures of prominent Negroes and reading about racial activities all over the country, and about racial wrongs in the South. In every issue he found, too, stirring and beautifully written editorials about the frustrated longings of the black race, and the hidden beauties in the Negro soul. A man named Du Bois wrote them.

"Dr. William Edward Burghardt Du Bois," said Tempy, "and he is a great man."

"Great like Booker T. Washington?" asked Sandy.

"Teaching Negroes to be servants, that's all Washington did!" Tempy snorted in so acid a tone that Sandy was silent. "Du Bois wants our rights. He wants us to be real men and women. He believes in social equality. But Washington—huh!" The fact that he had established an industrial school damned Washington in Tempy's eyes, for there were enough colored workers already. But Du Bois was a doctor of philosophy and had studied in Europe! . . . That's what Negroes needed to do, get smart, study books, go to Europe! "Don't talk to me about Washington," Tempy fumed. "Take Du Bois for your model, not some white folks' nigger."

"Well, Aunt Hager said—" then Sandy stopped. His grandmother had thought that Booker T. was the greatest of men, but maybe she had been wrong. Anyway, this Du Bois could write! Gee, it made you burn all over to read what he said about a lynching. But Sandy did not mention Booker Washington again to Tempy, although, months later, at the library he read his book called *Up from Slavery*, and he was sure that Aunt Hager hadn't been wrong. "I guess they are both great men," he thought.

Sandy's range of reading increased, too, when his aunt found a job for him that winter in Mr. Prentiss's gift-card- and printing-shop, where he kept the place clean and acted as delivery boy. This shop kept a shelf of current novels and some volumes of the new poetry—Sandburg, Lindsay, Masters—which the Young Women's Club of Stanton was then studying, to the shocked horror of the older white ladies of the town. Sandy knew of this because Mr. Prentiss's daughter, a student at Goucher College, used to keep shop and she pointed out volumes for the boy to read and told him who their authors were and what the books meant. She said that none of the colored boys they had employed before had ever been interested in reading; so she often lent him, by way of encouragement, shop-worn copies to be taken home at night and returned the next day. Thus Sandy spent much of his first year with Tempy deep in novels too mature for a fourteen-year-old boy. But Tempy was very proud of her studious young nephew. She began to decide that she had made no mistake in keeping him with her, and when he entered the high school, she bought

him his first long-trouser suit as a spur towards further application.

Sandy became taller week by week, and it seemed to Tempy
as if his shirt-sleeves became too short for him overnight. His
voice was changing, too, and he had acquired a liking for foot-
ball, but his after-school job at Prentiss's kept him from playing
much. At night he read, or sometimes went to the movies with
Buster—but Tempy kept him home as much as she could.
Occasionally he saw Willie-Mae, who was keeping company
with the second cook at Wright's Hotel. And sometimes he
saw Jimmy Lane, who was a bell-hop now and hung out with
a sporty crowd in the rear room of Cudge Windsor's pool hall.
But whenever Sandy went into his old neighborhood, he felt
sad, remembering Aunt Hager and his mother, and Jimboy,
and Harriett—for his young aunt had gone away from Stanton,
too, and the last he heard about her rumored that she was on
the stage in Kansas City. Now the little house where Sandy had
lived with his grandmother belonged to Tempy, who kept it
rented to a family of strangers.

In high school Sandy was taking, at his aunt's request, the
classical course, which included Latin, ancient history, and
English, and which required a great deal of reading. His
teacher of English was a large, masculine woman named
Martha Fry, who had once been to Europe and who loved to
talk about the splendors of old England and to read aloud in
a deep, mannish kind of voice, dramatizing the printed words.
It was from her that Sandy received an introduction to
Shakespeare, for in the spring term they studied *The Merchant
of Venice*. In the spring also, under Miss Fry's direction, the
first-year students were required to write an essay for the freshman essay prizes of both money and medals. And in this contest
Sandy won the second prize. It was the first time in the history
of the school that a colored pupil had ever done anything of
the sort, and Tempy was greatly elated. There was a note in the
papers about it, and Sandy brought his five dollars home for
his aunt to put away. But he gave his bronze medal to a girl
named Pansetta Young, who was his class-mate and a new-
found friend.

From the first moment in school that he saw Pansetta, he
knew that he liked her, and he would sit looking at her for

hours in every class that they had together—for she was a little baby-doll kind of girl, with big black eyes and a smooth pinkish-brown skin, and her hair was curly on top of her head. Her widowed mother was a cook at the Goucher College dining-hall; and she was an all-alone little girl, for Pansetta had no brothers or sisters. After Thanksgiving Sandy began to walk part of the way home with her every day. He could not accompany her all the way because he had to go to work at Mr. Prentiss's shop. But on Christmas he bought her a box of candy—and sent it to her by mail. And at Easter-time she gave him a chocolate egg.

"Unh-huh! You got a girl now, ain't you?" teased Buster one April afternoon when he caught Sandy standing in front of the high school waiting for Pansetta to come out.

"Aw, go chase yourself!" said Sandy, for Buster had a way of talking dirty about girls, and Sandy was afraid he would begin that with Pansetta; but today his friend changed the subject instead.

"Say come on round to the pool hall tonight and I'll teach you to play billiards."

"Don't think I'd better, Bus. Aunt Tempy might get sore," Sandy replied, shaking his head. "Besides, I have to study."

"Are you gonna read yourself to death?" Buster demanded indignantly. "You've got to come out some time, man! Tell her you're going to the movies and we'll go down to Cudge's instead."

Sandy thought for a moment.

"All the boys come round there at night."

"Well, I might."

"Little apron-string boy!" teased Buster.

"If I hit you a couple of times, you'll find out I'm not!" Sandy doubled up his fists in pretended anger. "I'll black your blue eyes for you!"

"Ya-a-a-a?" yelled his friend, running up the street. "See you tonight at Cudge's—apron-string boy!"

And that evening Sandy didn't finish reading, as he had planned, *Moby Dick*, which Mr. Prentiss's daughter had lent him. Instead he practised handling a cue-stick under the tute-lage of Buster.

TWENTY-FIVE

Pool Hall

THERE were no community houses in Stanton and no recreation centres for young men except the Y.M.C.A., which was closed to you if you were not a white boy; so, for the Negro youths of the town, Cudge Windsor's pool hall was the evening meeting-place. There one could play billiards, shoot dice in a back room, or sit in summer on the two long benches outside, talking and looking at the girls as they passed. In good weather these benches were crowded all the time.

Next door to the pool hall was Cudge Windsor's lunch-room. Of course, the best colored people did not patronize Cudge's, even though his business was not in the Bottoms. It was located on Pearl Street, some three or four blocks before that thoroughfare plunged across the tracks into the low terrain of tinkling pianos and ladies who loved for cash. But since Cudge catered to what Mr. Siles called "the common element," the best people stayed away.

After months of bookishness and subjection to Tempy's prim plans for his improvement, Sandy found the pool hall an easy and amusing place in which to pass time. It was better than the movies, where people on the screen were only shadows. And it was much better than the Episcopal Church, with its stoop-shouldered rector, for here at Cudge's everybody was alive, and the girls who passed in front swinging their arms and grinning at the men were warm-bodied and gay, while the boys rolling dice in the rear room or playing pool at the tables were loud-mouthed and careless. Life sat easily on their muscular shoulders.

Adventurers and vagabonds who passed through Stanton on the main line would often drop in at Cudge's to play a game or get a bite to eat, and many times on summer nights reckless black boys, a long way from home, kept the natives entertained with tales of the road, or trips on side-door Pullmans, and of far-off cities where things were easy and women generous. They had a song that went:

179

> O, the gals in Texas,
> They never be's unkind.
> They feeds their men an'
> Buys 'em gin an' wine.
> But these women in Stanton,
> Their hearts is hard an' cold.
> When you's out of a job, they
> Denies you jelly roll.

Then, often, arguments would begin—boastings, proving and fending; or telling of exploits with guns, knives, and razors, with cops and detectives, with evil women and wicked men; out-bragging and out-lying one another, all talking at once. Sometimes they would create a racket that could be heard for blocks. To the uninitiated it would seem that a fight was imminent. But underneath, all was good-natured and friendly—and through and above everything went laughter. No matter how belligerent or lewd their talk was, or how sordid the tales they told—of dangerous pleasures and strange perversities—these black men laughed. That must be the reason, thought Sandy, why poverty-stricken old Negroes like Uncle Dan Givens lived so long—because to them, no matter how hard life might be, it was not without laughter.

Uncle Dan was the world's champion liar, Cudge Windsor said, and the jolly old man's unending flow of fabulous reminiscences were entertaining enough to earn him a frequent meal in Cudge's lunch-room or a drink of licker from the patrons of the pool hall, who liked to start the old fellow talking.

One August evening when Tempy was away attending a convention of the Midwest Colored Women's Clubs, Sandy and Buster, Uncle Dan, Jimmy Lane, and Jap Logan sat until late with a big group of youngsters in front of the pool hall watching the girls go by. A particularly pretty high yellow damsel passed in a thin cool dress of flowered voile, trailing the sweetness of powder and perfume behind her.

"Dog-gone my soul!" yelled Jimmy Lane. "Just gimme a bone and lemme be your dog—I mean your salty dog!" But the girl, pretending not to hear, strolled leisurely on, followed by a train of compliments from the pool-hall benches.

"Sweet mama Venus!" cried a tall raw-bony boy, gazing after her longingly.

"If angels come like that, lemme go to heaven—and if they don't, lemme be lost to glory!" Jap exclaimed.

"Shut up, Jap! What you know 'bout women?" asked Uncle Dan, leaning forward on his cane to interrupt the comments. "Here you-all is, ain't knee-high to ducks yit, an' talkin' 'bout womens! Shut up, all o' you! Nary one o' you's past sebenteen, but when I were yo' age—Hee! Hee! You-all want to know what dey called me when I were yo' age?" The old man warmed to his tale. "Dey called me de 'stud nigger'! Yes, dey did! On 'count o' de kind o' slavery-time work I was doin'—I were breedin' babies fo' to sell!"

"Another lie!" said Jap.

"No, 'tain't, boy! You listen here to what I's gwine tell you. I were de onliest real healthy nigger buck ma white folks had on de plantation, an' dese was ole po' white folks what can't 'ford to buy many slaves, so dey figures to raise a heap o' darky babies an' sell 'em later on—dat's why dey made me de breeder. . . . Hee! Hee! . . . An' I sho breeded a gang o' pickaninnies, too! But I were young then, jest like you-all is, an' I ain't had a pint o' sense—laying wid de womens all night, ever' night."

"Yes, we believe you," drawled Jimmy.

"An' it warn't no time befo' little yaller chillens an' black chillens an' red chillens an' all kinds o' chillens was runnin' round de yard eatin' out o' de hog-pen an' a-callin' me pappy. . . . An' here I is today gwine on ninety-three year ole an' I done outlived 'em all. Dat is, I done outlived all I ever were able to keep track on after de war, 'cause we darkies sho scattered once we was free! Yes, sah! But befo' de fightin' ended I done been pappy to forty-nine chillens—an' thirty-three of 'em were boys!"

"Aw, I know you're lying now, Uncle Dan," Jimmy laughed.

"No, I ain't, sah! . . . Hee! Hee! . . . I were a great one when I were young! Yes, sah!" The old man went on undaunted. "I went an' snuck off to a dance one night, me an' nudder boy, went 'way ovah in Macon County at ole man Laird's plantation, who been a bitter enemy to our white folks. Did I ever tell you 'bout it? We took one o' ole massa's best hosses out de barn to ride, after he done gone to his bed. . . . Well, sah! It were late when we got started, an' we rid dat hoss lickety-split uphill an' down holler, ovah de crick an' past de mill, me an' ma buddy both on his back, through de cane-brake an' up anudder hill, till he wobble an' foam at de mouth like he's 'bout to drap. When we git to de dance, long 'bout midnight, we jump off dis hoss an' ties him to a post an' goes in de cabin whar de music were—an' de function were gwine on big. Man! We grabs ourselves a gal an' dance till de moon riz, kickin' up our heels an' callin' figgers, an' jest havin' a scrumptious time. Ay, Lawd! We sho did dance! . . . Well, come 'long 'bout two o'clock in de mawnin', niggers all leavin', an' we goes out in de yard to git on dis hoss what we had left standin' at de post. . . . An' Lawd have mercy—de hoss were dead! Yes, sah! He done fell down right whar he were tied, eyeballs rolled back, mouth a-foamin', an' were stone-dead! . . . Well, we ain't knowed how we gwine git home ner what we gwine do 'bout massa's hoss—an' we was skeered, Lawdy! 'Cause we know he beat us to death if he find out we done rid his best hoss anyhow—let lone ridin' de crittur to death. . . . An' all de low-down Macon niggers what was at de party was whaw-whawin' fit to kill, laughin' cause it were so funny to see us gittin' ready to git on our hoss an' de hoss were dead! . . . Well, sah, me an' ma buddy ain't wasted no time. We took dat animule up by de hind legs an' we drug him all de way home to massa's plantation befo' day! We sho did! Uphill an' down holler, sixteen miles! Yes, sah! An' put dat damn hoss back in massa's barn like he war befo' we left. An' when de sun riz, me an' ma buddy were in de slavery quarters sleepin' sweet an' lowly-like as if we ain't been nowhar. . . . De next day old massa 'maze how dat hoss die all tied up in his stall wid his halter on! An' we niggers 'maze, too, when we heard dat massa's hoss been dead, 'cause we ain't knowed a thing 'bout it. No, sah! Ain't none o' us niggers knowed a thing! Hee! Hee! Not a thing!"

"Weren't you scared?" asked Sandy.

"Sho, we was scared," said Uncle Dan, "but we ain't act like it. Niggers was smart in them days."

"They're still smart," said Jap Logan, "if they can lie like you."

"I mean!" said Buster.

"Uncle Dan's the world's champeen liar," drawled a tall lanky boy. "Come on, let's chip in and buy him a sandwich, 'cause he's lied enough fo' one evening."

They soon crowded into the lunch-room and sat on stools at the counter ordering soda or ice-cream from the fat good-natured waitress. While they were eating, a gambler bolted in from the back room of the pool hall with a handful of coins he had just won.

"Gonna feed ma belly while I got it in ma hand," he shouted. "Can't tell when I might lose, 'cause de dice is runnin' they own way tonight. Say, Mattie," he yelled, "tell chef to gimme a beefsteak all beat up like Jim Jeffries, cup o' coffee strong as Jack Johnson, an' come flyin' like a airship so I can get back in the game. Tell that kitchen buggar sweet-papa Stingaree's out here!"

"All right, keep yo' collar on," said Mattie. "De steak's got to be cooked."

"What you want, Uncle Dan?" yelled the gambler to the old man. "While I's winnin', might as well feed you, too. Take some ham and cabbage or something. That sandwich ain't 'nough to fill you up."

Uncle Dan accepted a plate of spareribs, and Stingaree threw down a pile of nickels on the counter.

"Injuns an' buffaloes," he said loudly. "Two things de white folks done killed, so they puts 'em on de backs o' nickels. . . . Rush up that steak there, gal, I's hongry!"

Sandy finished his drink and bought a copy of the *Chicago Defender*, the World's Greatest Negro Weekly, which was sold at the counter. Across the front in big red letters there was a headline: *Negro Boy Lynched*. There was also an account of a race riot in a Northern industrial city. On the theatrical page a picture of pretty Baby Alice Whitman, the tap-dancer, attracted his attention, and he read a few of the items there concerning colored shows; but as he was about to turn the page, a little article in the bottom corner made him pause and put the paper down on the counter.

ACTRESS MAKES HIT

St. Louis, Mo., Aug. 3: Harrietta Williams, sensational young blues-singer, has been packing the Booker

Washington Theatre to the doors here this week. Jones and Jones are the headliners for the all-colored vaudeville bill, but the singing of Miss Williams has been the outstanding drawing card. She is being held over for a continued engagement, with Billy Sanderlee at the piano.

"Billy Sanderlee," said Buster, who was looking over Sandy's shoulder. "That's that freckled-faced yellow guy who used to play for dances around here, isn't it? He could really beat a piano to death, all right!"

"Sure could," replied Sandy. "Gee, they must make a great team together, 'cause my Aunt Harrie can certainly sing and dance!"

"Ain't the only thing she can do!" bellowed the gambler, swallowing a huge chunk of steak. "Yo' Aunt Harrie's a whang, son!"

"Shut yo' mouth!" said Uncle Dan.

TWENTY-SIX

The Doors of Life

DURING Sandy's second year at high school Tempy was busy sewing for the local Red Cross and organizing Liberty Bond clubs among the colored population of Stanton. She earnestly believed that the world would really become safe for democracy, even in America, when the war ended, and that colored folks would no longer be snubbed in private and discriminated against in public.

"Colored boys are over there fighting," she said. "Our men are buying hundreds of dollars' worth of bonds, colored women are aiding the Red Cross, our clubs are sending boxes to the camps and to the front. White folks will see that the Negro can be trusted in war as well as peace. Times will be better after this for all of us."

One day a letter came from Annjee, who had moved to Chicago. She said that Sandy's father had not long remained in camp, but had been sent to France almost immediately after he enlisted, and she didn't know what she was going to do, she was so worried and alone! There had been but one letter from Jimboy since he left. And now she needed Sandy with her, but she wasn't able to send for him yet. She said she hoped and prayed that nothing would happen to his father at the front, but every day there were colored soldiers' names on the casualty list.

"Good thing he's gone," grunted Tempy when she read the letter as they were seated at the supper-table. Then, suddenly changing the subject, she asked Sandy: "Did you see Dr. Frank Crane's beautiful article this morning?"

"No, I didn't," said the boy.

"You certainly don't read as much as you did last winter," complained his aunt. "And you're staying out entirely too late to suit me. I'm quite sure you're not at the movies all that time, either. I want these late hours stopped, young man. Every night in the week out somewhere until ten and eleven o'clock!"

"Well, boys do have to get around a little, Tempy," Mr. Siles objected. "It's not like when you and I were coming up."

"I'm raising this boy, Mr. Siles," Tempy snapped. "When do you study, James? That's what I want to know."

"When I come in," said Sandy, which was true. His light was on until after twelve almost every night. And when he did not study late, his old habit of lying awake clung to him and he could not go to sleep early.

"You think too much," Buster once said. "Stop being so smart; then you'll sleep better."

"Yep," added Jimmy Lane. "Better be healthy and dumb than smart and sick like some o' these college darkies I see with goggles on their eyes and breath smellin' bad."

"O, I'm not sick," objected Sandy, "but I just get to thinking about things at night—the war, and white folks, and God, and girls, and—O, I don't know—everything in general."

"Sure, keep on thinking," jeered Buster, "and turn right ashy after while and be all stoop-shouldered like Father Hill." (The Episcopalian rector was said to be the smartest colored man in town.) "But I'm not gonna worry about being smart myself. A few more years, boy, and I'll be in some big town passing for white, making money, and getting along swell. And I won't need to be smart, either—I'll be ofay! So if you see me some time in St. Louis or Chi with a little blond on my arm— don't recognize me, hear! I want my kids to be so yellow-headed they won't have to think about a color line."

And Sandy knew that Buster meant what he said, for his light-skinned friend was one of those people who always go directly towards the things they want, as though the road is straight before them and they can see clearly all the way. But to Sandy himself nothing ever seemed quite that clear. Why was his country going stupidly to war? . . . Why were white people and colored people so far apart? Why was it wrong to desire the bodies of women? . . . With his mind a maelstrom of thoughts as he lay in bed night after night unable to go to sleep quickly, Sandy wondered many things and asked himself many questions.

Sometimes he would think about Pansetta Young, his classmate with the soft brown skin, and the pointed and delicate breasts of her doll-like body. He had never been alone with

Pansetta, never even kissed her, yet she was "his girl" and he liked her a great deal. Maybe he loved her! . . . But what did it mean to love a girl? Were you supposed to marry her then and live with her for ever? . . . His father had married his mother—good-natured, guitar-playing Jimboy—but they weren't always together, and Sandy knew that Jimboy was enjoying the war now, just as he had always enjoyed everything else.

"Gee, he must of married early to be my father and still look so young!" he thought. "Suppose I marry Pansetta now!" But what did he really know about marriage other than the dirty fragments he had picked up from Jimmy and Buster and the fellows at the pool hall?

On his fifteenth birthday Tempy had given him a book written for young men on the subject of love and living, called *The Doors of Life*, addressed to all Christian youths in their teens—but it had been written by a white New England minister of the Presbyterian faith who stood aghast before the flesh; so its advice consisted almost entirely in how to pray in the orthodox manner, and in how *not* to love.

"Avoid evil companions lest they be your undoing (see Psalms cxix, 115–20); and beware of lewd women, for their footsteps lead down to hell (see Proverbs vii, 25–7)," said the book, and that was the extent of its instructions on sex, except that it urged everyone to marry early and settle down to a healthy, moral, Christian life. . . . But how could you marry early when you had no money and no home to which to take a wife, Sandy wondered. And who were evil companions. Neither Aunt Hager nor Annjee had ever said anything to Sandy about love in its bodily sense; Jimboy had gone away too soon to talk with him; and Tempy and her husband were too proper to discuss such subjects; so the boy's sex knowledge consisted only in the distorted ideas that youngsters whisper; the dirty stories heard in the hotel lobby where he had worked; and the fact that they sold in drugstores articles that weren't mentioned in the company of nice people.

But who were nice people anyway? Sandy hated the word "nice." His Aunt Tempy was always using it. All of her friends were nice, she said, respectable and refined. They went around with their noses in the air and they didn't speak to porters and washwomen—though they weren't nearly so much fun as the folks they tried to scorn. Sandy liked Cudge Windsor or Jap Logan better than he did Dr. Mitchell, who had been to college—and never forgotten it.

Sandy wondered if Booker T. Washington had been like Tempy's friends? Or if Dr. Du Bois was a snob just because he was a college man? He wondered if those two men had a good time being great. Booker T. was dead, but he had left a living school in the South. Maybe he could teach in the South, too, Sandy thought, if he ever learned enough. Did colored folks need to know the things he was studying in books now? Did French and Latin and Shakespeare make people wise and happy? Jap Logan never went beyond the seventh grade and he was happy. And Jimboy never attended school much either. Maybe school didn't matter. Yet to get a good job you had to be smart—and white, too. That was the trouble, you had to be white!

"But I want to learn!" thought Sandy as he lay awake in the dark after he had gone to bed at night. "I want to go to college. I want to go to Europe and study. 'Work and make ready and maybe your chance will come,' it said under the picture of Lincoln on the calendar given away by the First National Bank, where Earl, his white friend, already had a job promised him when he came out of school. . . . It was not nearly so difficult for white boys. They could work at anything—in stores, on newspapers, in offices. They could become president of the United States if they were clever enough. But a colored boy. . . . No wonder Buster was going to pass for white when he left Stanton.

"I don't blame him," thought Sandy. "Sometimes I hate white people, too, like Aunt Harrie used to say she did. Still, some of them are pretty decent—my English-teacher, and Mr. Prentiss where I work. Yet even Mr. Prentiss wouldn't give me a job clerking in his shop. All I can do there is run errands and scrub the floor when everybody else is gone. There's no advancement for colored fellows. If they start as porters, they stay porters for ever and they can't come up. Being colored is like being born in the basement of life, with the door to the light locked and barred—and the white folks live upstairs. They don't want us up there with them, even when we're respectable like Dr. Mitchell, or smart like Dr. Du Bois. . . . And guys like Jap Logan—well, Jap don't care anyway! Maybe it's best not to care, and stay poor and meek waiting for heaven like Aunt Hager did. . . . But I don't want heaven! I want to live first!" Sandy thought. "I want to live!"

He understood then why many old Negroes said: "Take all this world and give me Jesus!" It was because they couldn't get this world anyway—it belonged to the white folks. They alone had the power to give or withhold at their back doors. Always back doors—even for Tempy and Dr. Mitchell if they chose to go into Wright's Hotel or the New Albert Restaurant. And no door at all for Negroes if they wanted to attend the Rialto Theatre, or join the Stanton Y.M.C.A., or work behind the grilling at the National Bank.

The Doors of Life. . . . God damn that simple-minded book that Tempy had given him! What did an old white minister know about the doors of life for him and Pansetta and Jimmy Lane, for Willie-Mae and Buster and Jap Logan and all the black and brown and yellow youngsters standing on the threshold of the great beginning in a Western town called Stanton? What did an old white minister know about the doors of life anywhere? And, least of all, the doors to a Negro's life? . . . Black youth. . . . Dark hands knocking, knocking! Pansetta's little brown hands knocking on the doors of life! Baby-doll hands, tiny autumn-leaf girl-hands! . . . Gee, Pansetta! . . . The Doors of Life . . . the great big doors. . . . Sandy was asleep . . . of life.

TWENTY-SEVEN

Beware of Women

"I WON'T permit it," said Tempy. "I won't stand for it. You'll have to mend your ways, young man! Spending your evenings in Windsor's pool parlor and running the streets with a gang of common boys that have had no raising, that Jimmy Lane among them. I won't stand for it while you stay in my house. . . . But that's not the worst of it. Mr. Prentiss tells me you've been getting to work late after school three times this week. And what have you been doing? O, don't think I don't know! I saw you with my own eyes yesterday walking home with that girl Pansetta Young! . . . Well, I want you to understand that I won't have it!"

"I didn't walk home with her," said Sandy. "I only go part way with her every day. She's in my class in high school and we have to talk over our lessons. She's the only colored kid in my class I have to talk to."

"Lessons! Yes, I know it's lessons," said Tempy sarcastically. "If she were a girl of our own kind, it would be all right. I don't see why you don't associate more with the young people of the church. Marie Steward or Grace Mitchell are both nice girls and you don't notice them. No, you have to take up with this Pansetta, whose mother works out all day, leaving her daughter to do as she chooses. Well, she's not going to ruin you, after all I've done to try to make something out of you."

"Beware of women, son," said Mr. Siles pontifically from his deep morris-chair. It was one of his few evenings home and Tempy had asked him to talk to her nephew, who had gotten beyond her control, for Sandy no longer remained in at night even when she expressly commanded it; and he no longer attended church regularly, but slept on Sunday mornings instead. He kept up his school-work, it was true, but he seemed to have lost all interest in acquiring the respectable bearing and attitude towards life that Tempy thought he should have. She bought him fine clothes and he went about with ruffians.

"In other words, he has been acting just like a nigger, Mr. Siles!" she told her husband. "And he's taken up with a girl who's not of the best, to say the least, even if she does go to the high school. Mrs. Francis Cannon, who lives near her, tells me that this Pansetta has boys at her house all the time, and her mother is never at home until after dark. She's a cook or something somewhere. . . . A fine person for a nephew of ours to associate with, this Pansy daughter of hers!"

"Pansetta's a nice girl," said Sandy. "And she's smart in school, too. She helps me get my Latin every day, and I might fail if she didn't."

"Huh! It's little help you need with your Latin, young man! Bring it here and I'll help you. I had Latin when I was in school. And certainly you don't need to walk on the streets with her in order to study Latin, do you? First thing you know you'll be getting in trouble with her and she'll be having a baby—I see I have to be plain—and whether it's yours or not, she'll say it is. Common girls like that always want to marry a boy they think is going to amount to something— going to college and be somebody in the world. Besides, you're from the Williams family and you're good-looking! But I'm going to stop this affair right now. . . . From now on you are to leave that girl alone, do you understand me? She's dangerous!"

"Yes," grunted Mr. Siles. "She's dangerous."

Angry and confused, Sandy left the room and went upstairs to bed, but he could not sleep. What right had they to talk that way about his friends? Besides, what did they mean about her being dangerous? About his getting in trouble with her? About her wanting to marry him because her mother was a cook and he was going to college?

A white boy in Sandy's high-school class had "got in trouble" with an Italian girl and they had had to go to the juvenile court to fix it up, but it had been kept quiet. Even now Sandy couldn't quite give an exact explanation of what getting in trouble with a girl meant. Did a girl have to have a baby just because a fellow walked home with her when he didn't even go in? Pansetta had asked him into her house often, but he always had to go back uptown to work. He was due at work at four o'clock—besides he knew it wasn't quite correct to call on a young lady if her mother was not at home. But it wasn't necessarily bad, was it? And how could a girl have a baby and say it was his if it wasn't his? Why couldn't he talk to his Aunt Tempy about such things and get a clear and simple answer instead of being given an old book like *The Doors of Life* that didn't explain anything at all?

Pansetta hadn't said a word to him about babies, or anything like that, but she let him kiss her once and hold her on his lap at Sadie Butler's Christmas party. Gee, but she could kiss—and such a long time! He wouldn't care if she did make him marry her, only he wanted to travel first. If his mother would send for him now, he would like to go to Chicago. His Aunt Tempy was too cranky, and too proper. She didn't like any of his friends, and she hated the pool hall. But where else was there for a fellow to play? Who wanted to go to those high-toned people's houses, like the Mitchells', and look bored all the time while they put Caruso's Italian records on their new victrola? Even if it was the finest victrola owned by a Negro in Stanton, as they always informed you, Sandy got tired of listening to records in a language that none of them understood.

"But this is opera!" they said. Well, maybe it was, but he thought that his father and Harriett used to sing better. And they sang nicer songs. One of them was:

> Love, O love, O careless love—
> Goes to your head like wine!

"And maybe I really am in love with Pansetta. . . . But if she thinks she can fool me into marrying her before I've travelled all around the world, like my father, she's wrong," Sandy thought. "She can't trick me, not this kid!" Then he was immediately sorry that he had allowed Tempy's insinuations to influence his thoughts.

"Pretty, baby-faced Pansetta! Why, she wouldn't try to trick anybody into anything. If she wanted me to love her, she'd let me, but she wouldn't try to trick a fellow. She wouldn't let me love her that way anyhow—like Tempy meant. Gee, that was ugly of Aunt Tempy to say that! . . . But Buster said she would. . . . Aw, he always talked that way about girls! He said no women were any good—as if he knew! And Jimmy

Lane said white women were worse than colored—but all the boys who worked at hotels said that."

Let 'em talk! Sandy liked Pansetta anyhow. . . . But maybe his Aunt Tempy was right! Maybe he had better stop walking home with her. He didn't want to "get in trouble" and not be able to travel to Chicago some time, where his mother was. Maybe he could go to Chicago next summer if he began to save his money now. He wanted to see the big city, where the buildings were like towers, the trains ran overhead, and the lake was like a sea. He didn't want to "get in trouble" with Pansetta even if he did like her. Besides, he had to live with Tempy for awhile yet and he hated to be quarrelling with his aunt all the time. He'd stop going to the pool hall so much and stay home at night and study. . . . But, heck! it was too beautiful out of doors to stay in the house—especially since spring had come!

Through his open window, as he lay in bed after Tempy's ti-rade about the girl, he could see the stars and the tops of the budding maple-trees. A cool earth-smelling breeze lifted the white curtains, scattering the geometry papers that he had left lying on his study table. He got out of bed to pick up the pa-pers and put them away, and stood for a moment in his pyjamas looking out of the window at the roofs of the houses and the tops of the trees under the night sky.

"I wish I had a brother," Sandy thought as he stood there. "Maybe I could talk to him about things and I wouldn't have to think so much. It's no fun being the only kid in the family, and your father never home either. . . . When I get married, I'm gonna have a lot of children; then they won't have to grow up by themselves."

The next day after school he walked nearly home with Pan-setta as usual, although he was still thinking of what Tempy had said, but he hadn't decided to obey his aunt yet. At the corner of the block in which the girl lived, he gave her her books.

"I got to beat it back to the shop now. Old man Prentiss'll have a dozen deliveries waiting for me just because I'm late."

"All right," said Pansetta in her sweet little voice. "I'm sorry you can't come on down to my house awhile. Say, why don't you work at the hotel, anyway? Wouldn't you make more money there?"

"Guess I would," replied the boy. "But my aunt thinks it's better where I am."

"Oh," said Pansetta. "Well, I saw Jimmy Lane last night and he's making lots of money at the hotel. He wanted to meet me around to school this afternoon, but I told him no. I said you took me home."

"I do," said Sandy.

"Yes," laughed Pansetta; "but I didn't tell him you wouldn't ever come in."

During the sunny spring weeks that followed, Sandy did not walk home with her any more after school. Having to go to work earlier was the excuse he gave, but at first Pansetta seemed worried and puzzled. She asked him if he was mad at her, or something, but he said he wasn't. Then in a short time other boys were meeting her on the corner near the school, buying her cones when the ice-cream wagon passed and taking her home in the afternoons. To see other fellows buying her ice-cream and walking home with her made Sandy angry, but it was his own fault, he thought. And he felt lonesome having no one to walk with after classes.

Pansetta, in school, was just as pleasant as before, but in a kind of impersonal way, as though she hadn't been his girl once. And now Sandy was worried, because it had been easy to drop her, but would it be easy to get her back again if he should want her? The hotel boys had money, and once or twice he saw her talking with Jimmy Lane. Gee, but she looked pretty in her thin spring dresses and her wide straw hat.

Why had he listened to Tempy at all? She didn't know Pansetta, and just because her mother worked out in service she wanted him to snub the girl. What was that to be afraid of—her mother not being home after school? Even if Pansetta would let him go in the house with her and put his arms around her and love her, why shouldn't he? Didn't he have a right to have a girl like that, as well as the other fellows? Didn't he have a right to be free with women, too, like all the rest of the young men? . . . But Pansetta wasn't that kind of girl!

. . . What made his mind run away with him? Because of what
Tempy had said? . . . To hell with Tempy!

"She's just an old-fashioned darky Episcopalian, that's what
Tempy is! And she wanted me to drop Pansetta because her
mother doesn't belong to the Dunbar Whist Club. Gee, but
I'm ashamed of myself. I'm a cad and a snob, that's all I am,
and I'm going to apologize." Subconsciously he was living
over a scene from an English novel he had read at the printing-
shop, in which the Lord dropped the Squire's daughter for a
great Lady, but later returned to his first love. Sandy retained
the words "cad" and "snob" in his vocabulary, but he wasn't
thinking of the novel now. He really believed, after three weeks
of seeing Pansetta walking with other boys, that he had done
wrong, and that Tempy was the villainess in the situation. It
was worrying him a great deal; he decided to make up with
Pansetta if he could.

One Friday afternoon she left school with a great armful of
books. They had to write an English composition for Monday
and she had taken some volumes from the school library for
reference. He might have offered to carry them for her, but he
hadn't. Instead he went to work—and there had been no other
colored boys on the corner waiting for her as she went out. Now
he could have kicked himself for his neglect, he thought, as he
cleaned the rear room of Mr. Prentiss's gift-card shop. Suddenly
he dropped the broom with which he was sweeping, grabbed
his cap, and left the place, for the desire to make friends with
Pansetta possessed him more fiercely than ever, and he no
longer cared about his work.

"I'm going to see her right now," he thought, "before I go
home to supper. Gee, but I'm ashamed of the way I've treated
her."

On the way to Pansetta's house the lawns looked fresh and
green and on some of them tulips were blooming. The late afternoon sky was aglow with sunset. Little boys were out in the
streets with marbles and tops, and little girls were jumping
rope on the sidewalks. Workmen were coming home, empty
dinner-pails in their hands, and a band of Negro laborers
passed Sandy, singing softly together.

"I must hurry," the boy thought. "It will soon be our

supper-time." He ran until he was at Pansetta's house—then came the indecision: Should he go in? Or not go in? He was ashamed of his treatment of her and embarrassed. Should he go on by as if he had not meant to call? Suppose she shut the door in his face! Or, worse, suppose she asked him to stay awhile! Should he stay? What Tempy had said didn't matter any more. He wanted to be friends with Pansetta again. He wanted her to know he still liked her and wanted to walk home with her. But how could he say it? Had she seen him from the window? Maybe he could turn around and go back, and see her Monday at school.

"No! I'm not a coward," he declared. "Afraid of a girl! I'll walk right up on the front porch and knock!" But the small house looked very quiet and the lace curtains were tightly drawn together at the windows. . . . He knocked again. Maybe there was no one home. . . . Yes, he heard somebody.

Finally Pansetta peeped through the curtains of the glass in the front door. Then she opened the door and smiled surprisingly, her hair mussed and her creamy-brown skin pink from the warm blood pulsing just under the surface. Her eyes were dark and luminous, and her lips were moist and red.

"It's Sandy!" she said, turning to address someone inside the front room.

"O, come in, old man," a boy's voice called in a tone of forced welcome, and Sandy saw Jimmy Lane sitting on the couch adjusting his collar self-consciously. "How's everything, old scout?"

"All right," Sandy stammered. "Say, Pansy, I—I— Do you know— I mean, what is the subject we're supposed to write on for English Monday? I must of forgotten to take it down."

"Why, 'A Trip to Shakespeare's England.' That's easy to remember, silly. You must have been asleep. . . . Won't you sit down?"

"No, thanks, I've— I guess I got to get back to supper."

"Jesus!" cried Jimmy jumping up from the sofa. "Is it that late? I'm due on bells at six o'clock. Wait a minute, Sandy, and I'll walk up with you as far as the hotel. Boy, I'm behind time!" He picked up his coat from the floor, and Pansetta held it for him while he thrust his arms into the sleeves, glancing around meanwhile for his cap, which lay among the sofa-pillows. Then

he kissed the girl carelessly on the lips as he slid one arm familiarly around her waist.

"So long, baby," he said, and the two boys went out. On the
porch Jimmy lit a cigarette and passed the pack to Sandy.

Jimmy Lane looked and acted as if he were much older than
his companion, but Jimmy had been out of school several
years, and hopping bells taught a fellow a great deal more
about life than books did—and also about women. Besides, he
was supporting himself now, which gave him an air of independence that boys who still lived at home didn't have.

When they had walked about a block, the bell-boy said carelessly: "Pansetta can go! Can't she, man?"

"I don't know," said Sandy.

"Aw, boy, you're lying," Jimmy Lane returned. "Don't try to
hand me that kid stuff! You had her for a year, didn't you?"

"Yes," replied Sandy slowly, "but not like you mean."

"Stop kidding," Jimmy insisted.

"No, honest, I never touched her that way," the boy said. "I
never was at her house before."

Jimmy opened his mouth astonished. "What!" he exclaimed.
"And her old lady out working till eight and nine every night!
Say, Sandy, we're friends, but you're either just a big liar—or
else a God-damn fool!" He threw his cigarette away and put
both hands in his pockets. "Pansetta's easy as hell, man!"

TWENTY-EIGHT

Chicago

DEAR SANDY:
Have just come home from work and am very tired but thought I would write you this letter right now while I had time and wasn't sleepy. You are a big boy and I think you can be of some help to me. I don't want you to stay in Stanton any longer as a burden on your Aunt Tempy. She says in her letters you have begun to stay out late nights and not pay her any mind. You ought to be with your mother now because you are all she has since I do not know what has happened to your father in France. The war is awful and so many mens are getting killed. Have not had no word from Jimboy for 7 months from Over There and am worried till I'm sick. Will try and send you how much money you need for your fare before the end of the month so when school is out in june you can come. Let me know how much you saved and I will send you the rest to come to Chicago because Mr. Harris where I stay is head elevator man at a big hotel in the Loop and he says he can put you on there in July. That will be a good job for you and maybe by saving your money you can go back to school in Sept. I will help you if I can but you will have to help me too because I have not been do-ing so well. Am working for a colored lady in her hair dressing parlor and am learning hairdressing myself, sham-poo and straighten and give massauges on the face and all. But colored folks are hard people to work for. Madam King is from down south somewhere and these southern Negroes are not like us in their ways, but she seems to like me. Mr. Harris is from the south too in a place called Baton Rouge. They eat rice all the time. Well I must close hoping to see you soon once more because it has been five

years since I have looked at my child. With love to you
and Tempy, be a good boy,

Your mother,
Annjelica Rogers.

A week later another letter came to Sandy from his mother.
This time it was a registered special-delivery, which said: "If
you'll come right away you can get your job at once. Mr. Harris
says he will have a vacancy Saturday because one of the elevator boys are quitting." And sufficient bills to cover Sandy's fare
tumbled out.

With a tremendous creaking and grinding and steady clack-
ing of wheels the long train went roaring through the night
towards Chicago as Sandy, in a day coach, took from his pocket
Annjee's two letters and re-read them for the tenth time since
leaving Stanton. He could hardly believe himself actually at
that moment on the way to Chicago!

In the stuffy coach papers littered the floor and the scent of
bananas and human feet filled the car. The lights were dim and
most of the passengers slumbered in the straight-backed green-
plush seats, but Sandy was still awake. The thrill of his first all-
night rail journey and his dream-expectations of the great city
were too much to allow a sixteen-year-old boy to go calmly to
sleep, although the man next to him had long been snoring.

Annjee's special-delivery letter had come that morning.
Sandy had discovered it when he came home for lunch, and
upon his return to the high school for the afternoon classes he
went at once to the principal to inquire if he might be excused
from the remaining days of the spring term.

"Let me see! Your record's pretty good, isn't it, Rogers?"
said Professor Perkins looking over his glasses at the young
colored fellow standing before him. "Going to Chicago, heh?
Well, I guess we can let you transfer and give you full credit for
this year's work without your waiting here for the examinations
—there are only ten days or so of the term remaining. You are
an honor student and would get through your exams all right.
Now, if you'll just send us your address when you get to
Chicago, we'll see that you get your report. . . . Intending
to go to school there, are you? . . . That's right! I like to see

your people get ahead. . . . Well, good luck to you, James."
The old gentleman rose and held out his hand.

"Good old scout," thought Sandy. "Miss Fry was a good
teacher, too! Some white folks *are* nice all right! Not all of
them are mean. . . . Gee, old man Prentiss hated to see me
quit his place. Said I was the best boy he ever had working
there, even if I was late once in awhile. But I don't mind leaving Stanton. Gee, Chicago ought to be great! And I'm sure
glad to get away from Tempy's house. She's too tight!"

But Tempy had not been glad to see her nephew leave. She
had grown fond of the boy in spite of her almost nightly lectures to him recently on his behavior and in spite of his never
having become her model youth. Not that he was bad, but he
might have been so much better! She wanted to show her
white neighbors a perfect colored boy—and such a boy certainly wouldn't be a user of slang, a lover of pool halls and non-
Episcopalian ways. Tempy had given Sandy every opportunity
to move in the best colored society and he had not taken advantage of it. Nevertheless, she cried a little as she packed a
lunch for him to eat on the train. She had done all she could.
He was a good-looking boy, and quite smart. Now, if he
wanted to go to his mother, well—"I can only hope Chicago
won't ruin you," she said. "It's a wicked city! Goodbye, James.
Remember what I've tried to teach you. Stand up straight and
look like you're somebody!"

Stanton, Sandy's Kansas home, was back in the darkness,
and the train sped towards the great center where all the small-
town boys in the whole Middle West wanted to go.

"I'm going now!" thought Sandy. "Chicago now!"

A few weeks past he had gone to see Sister Johnson, who
was quite feeble with the rheumatism. As she sat in the corner
of her kitchen smoking a corn-cob pipe, no longer able to wash
clothes, but still able to keep up a rapid flow of conversation,
she told him all the news.

"Tom, he's still at de bank keepin' de furnace goin' an' sort
o' handy man. . . . Willie-Mae, I 'spects you knows, is figurin'
on gettin' married next month to Mose Jenkins, an' I tells her
she better stay single, young as she is, but she ain't payin' me
no mind. Umn-unh! Jest let her go on! . . . Did you heerd
Sister Whiteside's daughter done brought her third husband

home to stay wid her ma—an' five o' her first husband's chillens
there too? Gals ain't got no regard for de old folks. Sister
Whiteside say if she warn't a Christian in her heart, she don't
believe she could stand it! . . . I tells Willie-Mae she better
not bring no husbands here to stay wid me—do an' I'll run
him out! These mens ought be shame o' demselves comin'
livin' on de womenfolks."

As the old woman talked, Sandy, thinking of his grandmother, gazed out of the window towards the house next
door, where he had lived with Aunt Hager. Some small children were playing in the back yard, running and yelling. They
belonged to the Southern family to whom Tempy had rented
the place. . . . Madam de Carter, who still owned the second
house, had been made a national grand officer in the women's
division of the lodge and many of the members of the order
now had on the walls of their homes a large picture of her
dressed in full regalia, inscribed: "Yours in His Grace," and
signed: "Madam Fannie Rosalie de Carter."

"Used to be just plain old Rose Carter befo' she got so important," said Sister Johnson, explaining her neighbor's lengthy
name. "All these womens dey mammy named Jane an' Mary
an' Cora, soon's dey gets a little somethin', dey changes dey
names to Janette or Mariana or Corina or somethin' mo' flowery then what dey had. Willie-Mae say she gwine change her'n
to Willetta-Mayola, an' I tole her if she do, I'll beat her—don't
care how old she is!"

Sandy liked to listen to the rambling talk of old colored
folks. "I guess there won't be many like that in Chicago," he
thought, as he doubled back his long legs under the green-
plush seat of the day coach. "I better try to get to sleep—there's
a long ways to go until morning."

Although it was not yet June, the heat was terrific when, with
the old bags that Tempy had given him, Sandy got out of the
dusty train in Chicago and walked the length of the sheds into
the station. He caught sight of his mother waiting in the
crowd, a fatter and much older woman than he had remembered her to be; and at first she didn't know him among the
stream of people coming from the train. Perhaps, unconsciously, she was looking for the little boy she left in Stanton;

but Sandy was taller than Annjee now and he looked quite a young man in his blue serge suit with long trousers. His mother threw both plump arms around him and hugged and kissed him for a long time.

They went uptown in the street-cars, Annjee a trifle out of breath from helping with the bags, and both of them perspiring freely from the heat. And they were not very talkative either. A strange and unexpected silence seemed to come between them. Annjee had been away from her son for five growing years and he was no longer her baby boy, small and eager for a kiss. She could see from the little cuts on his face that he had even begun to shave on the chin. And his voice was like a man's, deep and musical as Jimboy's, but not so sure of itself.

But Sandy was not thinking of his mother as they rode uptown on the street-car. He was looking out of the windows at the blocks of dirty grey warehouses lining the streets through which they were passing. He hadn't expected the great city to be monotonous and ugly like this and he was vaguely disappointed. No towers, no dreams come true! Where were the thrilling visions of grandeur he had held? Hidden in the dusty streets? Hidden in the long, hot alleys through which he could see at a distance the tracks of the elevated trains?

"Street-cars are slower, but I ain't got used to them air lines yet," said Annjee, searching her mind for something to say. "I always think maybe them elevated cars'll fall off o' there sometimes. They go so fast!"

"I believe I'd rather ride on them, though," said Sandy, as he looked at the monotonous box-like tenements and dismal alleys on the ground level. No trees, no yards, no grass such as he had known at home, and yet, on the other hand, no bigness or beauty about the bleak warehouses and sorry shops that hugged the sidewalk. Soon, however, the street began to take on a racial aspect and to become more darkly alive. Negroes leaned from windows with heads uncombed, or sat fanning in doorways with legs apart, talking in kimonos and lounging in overalls, and more and more they became a part of the passing panorama.

"This is State Street," said Annjee. "They call it the Black Belt. We have to get off in a minute. You got your suit-case?"

She rang the bell and at Thirty-seventh Street they walked over to Wabash Avenue. The cool shade of the tiny porch that Annjee mounted was more than welcome, and as she took out her key to unlock the front door, Sandy sat on the steps and mopped his forehead with a grimy handkerchief. Inside, there was a dusky gloom in the hallway, that smelled of hair-oil and cabbage steaming.

"Guess Mis' Harris is in the kitchen," said Annjee. "Come on—we'll go upstairs and I'll show you our room. I guess we can both stay together till we can do better. You're still little enough to sleep with your mother, ain't you?"

They went down the completely dark hall on the second floor, and his mother opened a door that led into a rear room with two windows looking out into the alley, giving an extremely near view of the elevated structure on which a downtown train suddenly rushed past with an ear-splitting roar that made the entire house tremble and the window-sashes rattle. There was a wash-stand with a white bowl and pitcher in the room, Annjee's trunk, a chair, and a brass bed, covered with a fresh spread and starched pillow-covers in honor of Sandy's arrival.

"See," said Annjee. "There's room enough for us both, and we'll be saving rent. There's no closet, but we can drive a few extra nails behind the door. And with the two windows we can get plenty of air these hot nights."

"It's nice, mama," Sandy said, but he had to repeat his statement twice, because another L train thundered past so that he couldn't hear his own words as he uttered them. "It's awful nice, mama!"

He took off his coat and sat down on the trunk between the two windows. Annjee came over and kissed him, rubbing her hand across his crinkly brown hair.

"Well, you're a great big boy now. . . . Mama's baby—in long pants. And you're handsome, just like your father!" She had Jimboy's picture stuck in a corner of the wash-stand—a postcard photo in his army uniform, in which he looked very boyish and proud, sent from the training-camp before his company went to France. "But I got no time to be setting here petting you, Sandy, even if you have just come. I got to get on back to the hairdressing-parlor to make some money."

So Annjee went to work again—as she had been off only long enough to meet the train—and Sandy lay down on the bed and slept the hot afternoon away. That evening as a treat they had supper at a restaurant, where Annjee picked carefully from the cheap menu so that their bill wouldn't be high.

"But don't think this is regular. We can't afford it," she said. "I bring things home and fix them on an oil-stove in the room and spread papers on the trunk for a table. A restaurant supper's just in honor of you."

When they came back to the house that evening, Sandy was introduced to Mrs. Harris, their landlady, and to her husband, the elevator-starter, who was to give him the job at the hotel.

"That's a fine-looking boy you got there, Mis' Rogers," he said, appraising Sandy. "He'll do pretty well for one of them main lobby cars, since we don't use nothing but first-class intelligent help down where I am, like I told you. And we has only the best class o' white folks stoppin' there, too. . . . Be up at six in the mornin', buddy, and I'll take you downtown with me."

Annjee was tired, so they went upstairs to the back room and lit the gas over the bed, but the frequent roar of the L trains prevented steady conversation and made Sandy jump each time that the long chain of cars thundered by. He hadn't yet become accustomed to them, or to the vast humming of the city, which was strange to his small-town ears. And he wanted to go out and look around a bit, to walk up and down the streets at night and see what they were like.

"Well, go on if you want to," said his mother, "but don't forget this house number. I'm gonna lie down, but I guess I'll be awake when you come back. Or somebody'll be setting on the porch and the door'll be open."

At the corner Sandy stopped and looked around to be sure of his bearings when he returned. He marked in his mind the sign-board advertising CHESTERFIELDS and the frame-house with the tumbledown stairs on the outside. In the street some kids were playing hopscotch under the arc-light. Somebody stopped beside him.

"Nice evening?" said a small yellow man with a womanish kind of voice, smiling at Sandy.

"Yes," said the boy, starting across the street, but the stranger followed him, offering Pall Malls. He smelled of perfume, and his face looked as though it had been powdered with white tal-cum as he lit a tiny pocket-lighter.

"Stranger?" murmured the soft voice, lighting Sandy's ciga-rette.

"I'm from Stanton," he replied, wishing the man had not cho-sen to walk with him.

"Ah, Kentucky," exclaimed the perfumed fellow. "I been down there. Nice women in that town, heh?"

"But it's not Kentucky," Sandy objected. "It's Kansas."

"Oh, out west where the girls are raring to go! I know! Just like wild horses out there—so passionate, aren't they?"

"I guess so," Sandy ventured. The powdered voice was softly persistent.

"Say, kid," it whispered smoothly, touching the boy's arm, "listen, I got some swell French pictures up in my room— naked women and everything! Want to come up and see them?"

"No," said Sandy quickening his pace. "I got to go some-where."

"But I room right around the corner," the voice insisted. "Come on by. You're a nice kid, you know it? Listen, don't walk so fast. Stop, let me talk to you."

But Sandy was beginning to understand. A warm sweat broke out on his neck and forehead. Sometimes, at the pool hall in Stanton, he had heard the men talk about queer fellows who stopped boys in the streets and tried to coax them to their rooms.

"He thinks I'm dumb," thought Sandy, "but I'm wise to him!" Yet he wondered what such men did with the boys who accompanied them. Curious, he'd like to find out—but he was afraid; so at the next corner he turned and started rapidly to-wards State Street, but the queer fellow kept close beside him, begging.

". . . and we'll have a nice time. . . . I got wine in the room, if you want some, and a vic, too."

"Get away, will you!"

They had reached State Street where the lights were bright and people were passing all the time. Sandy could see the fel-low's anxious face quite clearly now.

"Listen, kid . . . you . . ."

But suddenly the man was no longer beside him—for Sandy commenced to run. On the brightly lighted avenue panic seized him. He had to escape this powdered face at his shoulder. The whining voice made him sick inside—and, almost without knowing it, his legs began swerving swiftly between the crowds along the curb. When he stopped in front of the Monogram Theatre, two blocks away, he was freed of his companion.

"Gee, that's nice," panted Sandy, grinning as he stood looking at the pictures in front of the vaudeville house, while hundreds of dark people passed up and down on the sidewalk behind him. Lots of folks were going into the theatre, laughing and pushing, for one of the great blues-singing Smiths was appearing there. Sandy walked towards the ticket-booth to see what the prices were.

"Buy me a ticket, will you?" said a feminine voice beside him. This time it was a girl—a very ugly, skinny girl, whose smile revealed a row of dirty teeth. She sidled up to the startled boy whom she had accosted and took his hand.

"I'm not going in," Sandy said shortly, as he backed away, wiping the palm of his hand on his coat-sleeve.

"All right then, stingy!" hissed the girl, flouncing her hips and digging into her own purse for the coins to buy a ticket. "I got money."

Some men standing on the edge of the sidewalk laughed as Sandy went up the street. A little black child in front of him toddled along in the crowd, seemingly by itself, licking a big chocolate ice-cream cone that dripped down the front of its dress.

So this was Chicago where the buildings were like towers and the lake was like a sea . . . State Street, the greatest Negro street in the world, where people were always happy, lights for ever bright; and where the prettiest brown-skin women on earth could be found—so the men in Stanton said.

"I guess I didn't walk the right way. But maybe tomorrow I'll see other things," Sandy thought, "the Loop and the lake and the museum and the library. Maybe they'll be better."

He turned into a side street going back towards Wabash Avenue. It was darker there, and near the alley a painted woman called him, stepping out from among the shadows.

"Say, baby, com'ere!" But the boy went on.

Crossing overhead an L train thundered by, flashing its flow of yellow light on the pavement beneath.

Sandy turned into Wabash Avenue and cut across the street. As he approached the colored Y.M.C.A., three boys came out with swimming suits on their arms, and one of them said: "Damn, but it's hot!" They went up the street laughing and talking with friendly voices, and at the corner they turned off.

"I must be nearly home," Sandy thought, as he made out a group of kids still playing under the streetlight. Then he distinguished, among the other shabby buildings, the brick house where he lived. The front porch was still crowded with roomers trying to keep cool, and as the boy came up to the foot of the steps, some of the fellows seated there moved to let him pass.

"Good-evenin', Mr. Rogers," Mrs. Harris called, and as Sandy had never been called Mr. Rogers before, it made him feel very manly and a little embarrassed as he threaded his way through the group on the porch.

Upstairs he found his mother sleeping deeply on one side of the bed. He undressed, keeping on his underwear, and crawled in on the other side, but he lay awake a long while because it was suffocatingly hot, and very close in their room. The bedbugs bit him on the legs. Every time he got half asleep, an L train roared by, shrieking outside their open windows, lighting up the room, and shaking the whole house. Each time the train came, he started and trembled as though a sudden dragon were rushing at the bed. But then, after midnight, when the elevated cars passed less frequently, and he became more used to their passing, he went to sleep.

TWENTY-NINE

Elevator

T HE following day Sandy went to work as elevator-boy at
the hotel in the Loop where Mr. Harris was head bellman,
and during the hot summer months that followed, his life in
Chicago gradually settled into a groove of work and home—
work, and home to Annjee's stuffy little room against the elevated tracks, where at night his mother read the war news and
cried because there had been no letter from Jimboy. Whether
Sandy's father was in Brest or Saint-Lazare with the labor bat-
talions, or at the front, she did not know. The *Chicago De-*
fender said that colored troops were fighting in the Champagne
sector with great distinction, but Annjee cried anew when she
read that.

"No news is good news," Sandy repeated every night to
comfort his mother, for he couldn't imagine Jimboy dead.
"Papa's all right!" But Annjee worried and wept, half sick all
the time, for ever reading the death lists fearfully for her husband's name.

That summer the heat was unbearable. Uptown in the Black
Belt the air was like a steaming blanket around your head. In
the Loop the sky was white-hot metal. Even on the lake front
there was no relief unless you hurried into the crowded water.
And there were long stretches of beach where the whites did
not want Negroes to swim; so it was often dangerous to bathe
if you were colored.

Sandy sweltered as he stood at the door of his box-like, mir-
rored car in the big hotel lobby. He wore a red uniform with
brass buttons and a tight coat that had to be kept fastened no
matter how warm it was. But he felt very proud of himself
holding his first full-time job, helping his mother with the
room rent, and trying to save a little money out of each pay in
order to return to high school in the fall.

The prospects of returning to school, however, were not
bright. Some weeks it was impossible for Sandy to save even a

half-dollar. And Annjee said now that she believed he should stay out of school and work to take care of himself, since he was as large as a man and had more education already than she'd had at his age. Aunt Hager would not have felt that way, though, Sandy thought, remembering his grandmother's great ambition for him. But Annjee was different, less far-seeing than her mother had been, less full of hopes for her son, not ambitious about him—caring only for the war and Jimboy.

At the hotel Sandy's hours on duty were long, and his legs and back ached with weariness from standing straight in one spot all the time, opening and closing the bronze door of the elevator. He had been assigned the last car in a row of six, each manned by a colored youth standing inside his metal box in a red uniform, operating the lever that sent the car up from the basement grill to the roof-garden restaurant on the fifteenth floor and then back down again all day. Repeating up-down—up-down—up-down interminably, carrying white guests.

After two months of this there were times when Sandy felt as though he could stand it no longer. The same flow of people week after week—fashionable women, officers, business men; the fetid air of the elevator-shaft, heavy with breath and the perfume of bodies; the same doors opening at the same unchanging levels hundreds of times each innumerable, monotonous day. The L in the morning; the L again at night. The street or the porch for a few minutes of air. Then bed. And the same thing tomorrow.

"I've got to get out of this," Sandy thought. "It's an awful job." Yet some of the fellows had been there for years. Three of the elevator-men on Sandy's shift were more than forty years old—and had never gotten ahead in life. Mr. Harris had been a bell-hop since his boyhood, doing the same thing day after day—and now he was very proud of being head bell-boy in Chicago.

"I've got to get out of this," Sandy kept repeating. "Or maybe I'll get stuck here, too, like they are, and never get away. I've got to go back to school."

Yet he knew that his mother was making very little money—serving more or less as an apprentice in the hairdressing-shop, trying to learn the trade. And if he quit work, how would he live? Annjee did not favor his returning to school. And could he study if he were hungry? Could he study if he were worried about having no money? Worried about Annjee's displeasure?

"Yes! I can!" he said. "I'm going to study!" He thought about Booker Washington sleeping under the wooden pavements at Richmond—because he had had no place to stay on his way to Hampton in search of an education. He thought about Frederick Douglass—a fugitive slave, owning not even himself, and yet a student. "If they could study, I can, too! When school opens, I'm going to quit this job. Maybe I can get another one at night or in the late afternoon—but it doesn't matter—I'm going back to my classes in September. . . . I'm through with elevators."

Jimboy! Jimboy! Like Jimboy! something inside him warned, quitting work with no money, uncaring.

"Not like Jimboy," Sandy countered against himself. "Not like my father, always wanting to go somewhere. I'd get as tired of travelling all the time, as I do of running this elevator up and down day after day. . . . I'm more like Harriett—not wanting to be a servant at the mercies of white people for ever. . . . I want to do something for myself, by myself. . . . Free. . . . I want a house to live in, too, when I'm older—like Tempy's and Mr. Siles's. . . . But I wouldn't want to be like Tempy's friends—or her husband, dull and colorless, putting all his money away in a white bank, ashamed of colored people."

"A lot of minstrels—that's all niggers are!" Mr. Siles had said once. "Clowns, jazzers, just a band of dancers—that's why they never have anything. Never be anything but servants to the white people."

Clowns! Jazzers! Band of dancers! . . . Harriett! Jimboy! Aunt Hager! . . . A band of dancers! . . . Sandy remembered his grandmother whirling around in front of the altar at revival meetings in the midst of the other sisters, her face shining with light, arms outstretched as though all the cares of the world had been cast away; Harriett in the back yard under the apple-tree, eagle-rocking in the summer evenings to the tunes of the guitar; Jimboy singing. . . . But was that why Negroes were poor, because they were dancers, jazzers, clowns? . . . The other way round would be better: dancers because of their poverty; singers because they suffered; laughing all the time because they must forget. . . . It's more like that, thought Sandy.

A band of dancers. . . . Black dancers—captured in a white world. . . . Dancers of the spirit, too. Each black dreamer a captured dancer of the spirit. . . . Aunt Hager's dreams for Sandy dancing far beyond the limitations of their poverty, of their humble station in life, of their dark skins.

"I wants you to be a great man, son," she often told him, sitting on the porch in the darkness, singing, dreaming, calling up the deep past, creating dreams within the child. "I wants you to be a great man."

"And I won't disappoint you!" Sandy said that hot Chicago summer, just as though Hager were still there, planning for him. "I won't disappoint you!" he said, standing straight in his sweltering red suit in the cage of the hotel elevator. "I won't disappoint you, Aunt Hager," dreaming at night in the stuffy little room in the great Black Belt of Chicago. "I won't disappoint you now," opening his eyes at dawn when Annjee shook him to get up and go to work again.

THIRTY

Princess of the Blues

O NE hot Monday in August Harrietta Williams, billed as
"The Princess of the Blues," opened at the Monogram
Theatre on State Street. The screen had carried a slide of her
act the week previous, so Sandy knew she would be there, and
he and his mother were waiting anxiously for her appearance.
They were unable to find out before the performance where
she would be living, or if she had arrived in town, but early
that Monday evening Sandy hurried home from work, and he
and Annjee managed to get seats in the theatre, although it
was soon crowded to capacity and people stood in the aisles.

It was a typical Black Belt audience, laughing uproariously,
stamping its feet to the music, kidding the actors, and joining
in the performance, too. Rows of shiny black faces, gay white
teeth, bobbing heads. Everybody having a grand time with the
vaudeville, swift and amusing. A young tap-dancer rhymed his
feet across the stage, grinning from ear to ear, stepping to the
tantalizing music, ending with a series of intricate and amazing
contortions that brought down the house. Then a sister act
came on, with a stock of sentimental ballads offered in a wholly
jazzy manner. They sang even a very melancholy mammy song
with their hips moving gaily at every beat.

> O, what would I do
> Without dear you,
> Sweet mammy?

they moaned reverently, with their thighs shaking.

"Aw, step it, sweet gals!" the men and boys in the audience
called approvingly. "We'll be yo' mammy and yo' pappy, too!
Do it, pretty mamas!"

A pair of black-faced comedians tumbled on the stage as the
girls went off, and began the usual line of old jokes and razor
comedy.

"Gee, I wish Aunt Harriett's act would come on," Sandy said
as he and Annjee laughed nervously at the comedians.

Finally the two blacked-up fellows broke into a song called *Walking the Dog*, flopping their long-toed shoes, twirling their middles like egg-beaters, and made their exit to a roar of laughter and applause. Then the canvas street-scene rose, disclosing a gorgeous background of blue velvet, with a piano and a floor-lamp in the centre of the stage.

"This is Harriett's part now," Sandy whispered excitedly as a tall, yellow, slick-headed young man came in and immediately began playing the piano. "And, mama, that's Billy Sanderlee!"

"Sure is!" said Annjee.

Suddenly the footlights were lowered and the spotlight flared, steadied itself at the right of the stage, and waited. Then, stepping out from among the blue curtains, Harriett entered in a dress of glowing orange, flame-like against the ebony of her skin, barbaric, yet beautiful as a jungle princess. She swayed towards the footlights, while Billy teased the keys of the piano into a hesitating delicate jazz. Then she began to croon a new song—a popular version of an old Negro melody, refashioned with words from Broadway.

"Gee, Aunt Harrie's prettier than ever!" Sandy exclaimed to his mother.

"Same old Harriett," said Annjee. "But kinder hoarse."

"Sings good, though," Sandy cried when Harriett began to snap her fingers, putting a slow, rocking pep into the chorus, rolling her bright eyes to the tune of the melody as the piano rippled and cried under Billy Sanderlee's swift fingers.

"She's the same Harrie," murmured Annjee.

When she appeared again, in an apron of blue calico, with a bandanna handkerchief knotted about her head, she walked very slowly. The man at the piano had begun to play blues—the old familiar folk-blues—and the audience settled into a receptive silence broken only by a "Lawdy! . . . Good Lawdy! Lawd!" from some southern lips at the back of the house, as Harriett sang:

> Red sun, red sun, why don't you rise today?
> Red sun, O sun! Why don't you rise today?
> Ma heart is breakin'—ma baby's gone away.

A few rows ahead of Annjee a woman cried out: "True, Lawd!" and swayed her body.

> Little birds, little birds, ain't you gonna sing this morn?
> Says, little chirpin' birds, ain't you gonna sing this morn?
> I cannot sleep—ma lovin' man is gone.

"Whee-ee-e! . . . Hab mercy! . . . Moan it, gal!" exclamations and shouts broke loose in the understanding audience.

"Just like when papa used to play for her," said Sandy. But Annjee was crying, remembering Jimboy, and fumbling in her bag for a handkerchief. On the stage the singer went on—as though singing to herself—her voice sinking to a bitter moan as the listeners rocked and swayed.

> It's a mighty blue mornin' when yo' daddy leaves yo'
>   bed.
> I says a blue, blue mornin' when yo' daddy leaves yo'
>   bed—
> 'Cause if you lose yo' man, you'd just as well be dead!

Her final number was a dance-song which she sang in a sparkling dress of white sequins, ending the act with a mad collection of steps and a swift sudden whirl across the whole stage as the orchestra joined Billy's piano in a triumphant arch of jazz.

The audience yelled and clapped and whistled for more, stamping their feet and turning to one another with shouted comments of enjoyment.

"Gee! She's great," said Sandy. When another act finally had the stage after Harriett's encores, he was anxious to get back to the dressing-room to see her.

"Maybe they won't let us in," Annjee objected timidly.

"Let's try," Sandy insisted, pulling his mother up. "We don't want to hear this fat woman with the flag singing *Over There*. You'll start crying, anyhow. Come on, mama."

When they got backstage, they found Harriett standing in the dressing-room door laughing with one of the black-face comedians, a summer fur over her shoulders, ready for the street. Billy Sanderlee and the tap-dancing boy were drinking gin from a bottle that Billy held, and Harriett was holding her glass, when she saw Sandy coming.

Her furs slipped to the floor. "My Lord!" she cried, enveloping them in kisses. "What are you doing in Chicago, Annjee?

My, I'm mighty glad to see you, Sandy! . . . I'm certainly surprised—and so happy I could cry. . . . Did you catch our act tonight? Can't Billy play the piano, though? . . . Great heavens! Sandy, you're twice as tall as me! When did you leave home? How's that long-faced sister o' mine, Tempy?"

After repeated huggings the new-comers were introduced to everybody around. Sandy noticed a certain harshness in his aunt's voice. "Smoking so much," she explained later. "Drinking, too, I guess. But a blues-singer's supposed to sing deep and hoarse, so it's all right."

Beyond the drop curtain Sandy could hear the audience laughing in the theatre, and occasionally somebody shouting at the performers.

"Come on! Let's go and get a bite to eat," Harriett suggested when they had finally calmed down enough to decide to move on. "Billy and me are always hungry. . . . Where's Jimboy, Annjee? In the war, I suppose! It'd be just like that big jigaboo to go and enlist first thing, whether he had to or not. Billy here was due to go, too, but licker kept him out. This white folk's war for democracy ain't so hot, nohow! . . . Say, how'd you like to have some chop suey instead of going to a regular restaurant?"

In a Chinese café they found a quiet booth, where the two sisters talked until past midnight—with Sandy and Billy silent for the most part. Harriett told Annjee about Aunt Hager's death and the funeral that chill rainy day, and how Tempy had behaved so coldly when it was all over.

"I left Stanton the week after," Harriett said, "and haven't been back since. Had hard times, too, but we're kinder lucky now, Billy and me—got some dates booked over the Orpheum circuit soon. Liable to get wind of us at the Palace on Broadway one o' these days. Can't tell! Things are breakin' pretty good for spade acts—since Jews are not like the rest of the white folks. They will give you a break if you've got some hot numbers to show 'em, whether you're colored or not. And Jews control the theatres."

But the conversation went back to Stanton, when Hager and Jimboy and all of them had lived together, laughing and quarrelling and playing the guitar—while the tea got cold and the chop suey hardened to a sticky mess as the sisters wept.

Billy marked busily on the table-cloth meanwhile with a stubby pencil, explaining to Sandy a new and intricate system he had found for betting on the numbers.

"Harrie and me plays every day. Won a hundred forty dollars last week in Cleveland," he said.

"Gee! I ought to start playing," Sandy exclaimed. "How much do you put on each number?"

"Well, for a nickel you can win . . ."

"No, you oughtn't," checked Harriett, suddenly conscious of Billy's conversation, turning towards Sandy with a handkerchief to her eyes. "Don't you fool with those numbers, honey! . . . What are you trying to do, Billy, start the boy off on your track? . . . You've got to get your education, Sandy, and amount to something. . . . Guess you're in high school now, aren't you, kid?"

"Third year," said Sandy slowly, dreading a new argument with his mother.

"And determined to keep on going here this fall, in spite o' my telling him I don't see how," put in Annjee. "Jimboy's over yonder, Lord knows where, and I certainly can't take care of Sandy and send him to school, too. No need of my trying— since he's big enough and old enough to hold a job and make his own living. He ought to be wanting to help me, anyway. Instead of that, he's determined to go back to school."

"Make his own living!" Harriett exclaimed, looking at Annjee in astonishment. "You mean you want Sandy to stay out of school to help you? What good is his little money to you?"

"Well, he helps with the room rent," his mother said. "And gets his meals where he works. That's better'n we'd be doing with him studying and depending on me to keep things up."

"What do you mean better?" Harriett cried, glaring at her sister excitedly, forgetting they had been weeping together five minutes before. "For crying out loud—better? Why, Aunt Hager'd turn over in her grave if she heard you talking so calmly about Sandy leaving school—the way she wanted to make something out of this kid. . . . How much do you earn a week?" Harriett asked suddenly, looking at her nephew across the table.

"Fourteen dollars."

"Pshaw! Is that all? I can give you that much myself," Harriett said. "We've got straight bookings until Christmas— then cabaret work's good around here. Bill and I can always make the dough—and you go to school."

"I want to, Aunt Harrie," Sandy said, suddenly content.

"Yea, old man," put in Billy. "And I'll shoot you a little change myself—to play the numbers," he added, winking.

"Well," Annjee began, "what about . . ."

But Harriett ignored Billy's interjection as well as her sister's open mouth. "Running an elevator for fourteen dollars a week and losing your education!" she cried. "Good Lord! Annjee, you ought to be ashamed, wanting him to keep that up. This boy's gotta get ahead—all of us niggers are too far back in this white man's country to let any brains go to waste! Don't you realize that? . . . You and me was foolish all right, breaking mama's heart, leaving school, but Sandy can't do like us. He's gotta be what his grandma Hager wanted him to be—able to help the black race, Annjee! You hear me? Help the whole race!"

"I want to," Sandy said.

"Then you'll stay in school!" Harriett affirmed, still looking at Annjee. "You surely wouldn't want him stuck in an elevator for ever—just to help you, would you, sister?"

"I reckon I wouldn't," Annjee murmured, shaking her head.

"You know damn well you wouldn't," Harriett concluded. And, before they parted, she slipped a ten-dollar bill into her nephew's hand.

"For your books," she said.

When Sandy and his mother started home, it was very late, but in a little Southern church in a side street, some old black worshippers were still holding their nightly meeting. High and fervently they were singing:

> By an' by when de mawnin' comes,
> Saints an' sinners all are gathered home. . . .

As the deep volume of sound rolled through the open door, Annjee and her son stopped to listen.

"It's like Stanton," Sandy said, "and the tent in the Hickory Woods."

"Sure is!" his mother exclaimed. "Them old folks are still singing—even in Chicago! . . . Funny how old folks like to sing that way, ain't it?"

"It's beautiful!" Sandy cried—for, vibrant and steady like a stream of living faith, their song filled the whole night:

An' we'll understand it better by an' by!

BLACK NO MORE

BEING AN ACCOUNT OF THE STRANGE
AND WONDERFUL WORKINGS OF
SCIENCE IN THE LAND OF THE
FREE, A.D. 1933–1940

George S. Schuyler

THIS BOOK IS DEDICATED TO ALL
CAUCASIANS IN THE GREAT REPUB-
LIC WHO CAN TRACE THEIR AN-
CESTRY BACK TEN GENERATIONS
AND CONFIDENTLY ASSERT THAT
THERE ARE NO BLACK LEAVES,
TWIGS, LIMBS OR BRANCHES ON
THEIR FAMILY TREES.

PREFACE

OVER twenty years ago a gentleman in Asbury Park, N. J. began manufacturing and advertising a preparation for the immediate and unfailing straightening of the most stubborn Negro hair. This preparation was called Kink-No-More, a name not wholly accurate since users of it were forced to renew the treatment every fortnight.

During the intervening years many chemists, professional and amateur, have been seeking the means of making the down-trodden Aframerican resemble as closely as possible his white fellow citizen. The temporarily effective preparations placed on the market have so far proved exceedingly profitable to manu-facturers, advertising agencies, Negro newspapers and beauty culturists, while millions of users have registered great satisfac-tion at the opportunity to rid themselves of kinky hair and grow several shades lighter in color, if only for a brief time. With America's constant reiteration of the superiority of whiteness, the avid search on the part of the black masses for some key to chromatic perfection is easily understood. Now it would seem that science is on the verge of satisfying them.

Dr. Yusaburo Noguchi, head of the Noguchi Hospital at Beppu, Japan, told American newspaper reporters in October 1929, that as a result of fifteen years of painstaking research and experiment he was able to change a Negro into a white man. While he admitted that this racial metamorphosis could not be effected overnight, he maintained that "Given time, I could change the Japanese into a race of tall blue-eyed blonds." The racial transformation, he asserted, could be brought about by glandular control and electrical nutrition.

Even more positive is the statement of Mr. Bela Gati, an electrical engineer residing in New York City, who, in a letter dated August 18, 1930 and addressed to the National Association for the Advancement of Colored People said, in part:

> "Once I myself was very strongly tanned by the sun and a Eu-ropean rural population thought that I was a Negro, too. I did not suffer much but the situation was disagreeable. Since that time I have studied the problem and I am convinced that the

surplus of the pigment could be removed. In case you are interested and believe that with the aid of your physicians we could carry out the necessary experiments, I am willing to send you the patent specification . . . and my general terms relating to this invention. . . . The expenses are so to say negligible."

I wish to express my sincere thanks and appreciation to Mr. V. F. Calverton for his keen interest and friendly encouragement and to my wife, Josephine Schuyler, whose coöperation and criticism were of great help in completing *Black No More*.

GEORGE S. SCHUYLER

NEW YORK CITY,
September 1, 1930

Chapter One

MAX DISHER stood outside the Honky Tonk Club puffing a panatela and watching the crowds of white and black folk entering the cabaret. Max was tall, dapper and smooth coffee-brown. His negroid features had a slightly satanic cast and there was an insolent nonchalance about his carriage. He wore his hat rakishly and faultless evening clothes underneath his raccoon coat. He was young, he wasn't broke, but he was damnably blue. It was New Year's Eve, 1933, but there was no spirit of gaiety and gladness in his heart. How could he share the hilarity of the crowd when he had no girl? He and Minnie, his high "yallah" flapper, had quarreled that day and everything was over between them.

"Women are mighty funny," he mused to himself, "especially yallah women. You could give them the moon and they wouldn't appreciate it." That was probably the trouble; he'd given Minnie too much. It didn't pay to spend too much on them. As soon as he'd bought her a new outfit and paid the rent on a three-room apartment, she'd grown uppity. Stuck on her color, that's what was the matter with her! He took the cigar out of his mouth and spat disgustedly.

A short, plump, cherubic black fellow, resplendent in a narrow-brimmed brown fedora, camel's hair coat and spats, strolled up and clapped him on the shoulder: "Hello, Max!" greeted the newcomer, extending a hand in a fawn-colored glove, "What's on your mind?"

"Everything, Bunny," answered the debonair Max. "That damn yallah gal o' mine's got all upstage and quit."

"Say not so!" exclaimed the short black fellow. "Why I thought you and her were all forty."

"Were, is right, kid. And after spending my dough, too! It sure makes me hot. Here I go and buy two covers at the Honky Tonk for tonight, thinkin' surely she'd come and she starts a row and quits!"

"Shucks!" exploded Bunny, "I wouldn't let that worry me none. I'd take another skirt. I wouldn't let no dame queer my New Year's."

"So would I, Wise Guy, but all the dames I know are dated up. So here I am all dressed up and no place to go."

"You got two reservations, aint you? Well, let's you and me go in," Bunny suggested. "We may be able to break in on some party."

Max visibly brightened. "That's a good idea," he said. "You never can tell, we might run in on something good."

Swinging their canes, the two joined the throng at the entrance of the Honky Tonk Club and descended to its smoky depths. They wended their way through the maze of tables in the wake of a dancing waiter and sat down close to the dance floor. After ordering ginger ale and plenty of ice, they reared back and looked over the crowd.

Max Disher and Bunny Brown had been pals ever since the war when they soldiered together in the old 15th regiment in France. Max was one of the Aframerican Fire Insurance Company's crack agents, Bunny was a teller in the Douglass Bank and both bore the reputation of gay blades in black Harlem. The two had in common a weakness rather prevalent among Aframerican bucks: they preferred yellow women. Both swore there were three things essential to the happiness of a colored gentleman: yellow money, yellow women and yellow taxis. They had little difficulty in getting the first and none at all in getting the third but the yellow women they found flighty and fickle. It was so hard to hold them. They were so sought after that one almost required a million dollars to keep them out of the clutches of one's rivals.

"No more yallah gals for me!" Max announced with finality, sipping his drink. "I'll grab a black gal first."

"Say not so!" exclaimed Bunny, strengthening his drink from his huge silver flask. "You aint thinkin' o' dealin' in coal, are you?"

"Well," argued his partner, "it might change my luck. You can trust a black gal; she'll stick to you."

"How do you know? You ain't never had one. Ever' gal I ever seen you with looked like an ofay."

"Humph!" grunted Max. "My next one may be an ofay, too! They're less trouble and don't ask you to give 'em the moon."

"I'm right with you, pardner," Bunny agreed, "but I gotta

have one with class. None o' these Woolworth dames for me! Get you in a peck o' trouble. . . Fact is, Big Boy, ain't none o' these women no good. They all get old on the job."

They drank in silence and eyed the motley crowd around them. There were blacks, browns, yellows, and whites chatting, flirting, drinking; rubbing shoulders in the democracy of night life. A fog of tobacco smoke wreathed their heads and the din from the industrious jazz band made all but the loudest shrieks inaudible. In and out among the tables danced the waiters, trays balanced aloft, while the patrons, arrayed in colored paper caps, beat time with the orchestra, threw streamers or grew maudlin on each other's shoulders.

"Looky here! Lawdy Lawd!" exclaimed Bunny, pointing to the doorway. A party of white people had entered. They were all in evening dress and in their midst was a tall, slim, titian-haired girl who had seemingly stepped from heaven or the front cover of a magazine.

"My, my, my!" said Max, sitting up alertly.

The party consisted of two men and four women. They were escorted to a table next to the one occupied by the two colored dandies. Max and Bunny eyed them covertly. The tall girl was certainly a dream.

"Now that's my speed," whispered Bunny.

"Be yourself," said Max. "You couldn't touch her with a forty-foot pole."

"Oh, I don't know, Big Boy," Bunny beamed self-confidently, "You never can tell! You never can tell!"

"Well, I can tell," remarked Disher, "'cause she's a cracker."

"How you know that?"

"Man, I can tell a cracker a block away. I wasn't born and raised in Atlanta, Georgia, for nothin', you know. Just listen to her voice."

Bunny listened. "I believe she is," he agreed.

They kept eyeing the party to the exclusion of everything else. Max was especially fascinated. The girl was the prettiest creature he'd ever seen and he felt irresistibly drawn to her. Unconsciously he adjusted his necktie and passed his well-manicured hand over his rigidly straightened hair.

Suddenly one of the white men rose and came over to their

table. They watched him suspiciously. Was he going to start something? Had he noticed that they were staring at the girl? They both stiffened at his approach.

"Say," he greeted them, leaning over the table, "do you boys know where we can get some decent liquor around here? We've run out of stuff and the waiter says he can't get any for us."

"You can get some pretty good stuff right down the street," Max informed him, somewhat relieved.

"They won't sell none to him," said Bunny. "They might think he was a Prohibition officer."

"Could one of you fellows get me some?" asked the man.

"Sure," said Max, heartily. What luck! Here was the very chance he'd been waiting for. These people might invite them over to their table. The man handed him a ten dollar bill and Max went out bareheaded to get the liquor. In ten minutes he was back. He handed the man the quart and the change. The man gave back the change and thanked him. There was no invitation to join the party. Max returned to his table and eyed the group wistfully.

"Did he invite you in?" asked Bunny.

"I'm back here, aint I?" answered Max, somewhat resentfully.

The floor show came on. A black-faced comedian, a corpulent shouter of mammy songs with a gin-roughened voice, three chocolate soft-shoe dancers and an octette of wriggling, practically nude, mulatto chorines.

Then midnight and pandemonium as the New Year swept in. When the din had subsided, the lights went low and the orchestra moaned the weary blues. The floor filled with couples. The two men and two of the women at the next table rose to dance. The beautiful girl and another were left behind.

"I'm going over and ask her to dance," Max suddenly announced to the surprised Bunny.

"Say not so!" exclaimed that worthy. "You're fixin' to get in dutch, Big Boy."

"Well, I'm gonna take a chance, anyhow," Max persisted, rising.

This fair beauty had hypnotized him. He felt that he would give anything for just one dance with her. Once around the floor with her slim waist in his arm would be like an eternity in heaven. Yes, one could afford to risk repulse for that.

"Don't do it, Max!" pleaded Bunny. "Them fellows are liable to start somethin'."

But Max was not to be restrained. There was no holding him back when he wanted to do a thing, especially where a comely damsel was concerned.

He sauntered over to the table in his most sheikish manner and stood looking down at the shimmering strawberry blond. She was indeed ravishing and her exotic perfume titilated his nostrils despite the clouds of cigarette smoke.

"Would you care to dance?" he asked, after a moment's hesitation.

She looked up at him haughtily with cool green eyes, somewhat astonished at his insolence and yet perhaps secretly intrigued, but her reply lacked nothing in definiteness.

"No," she said icily, "I never dance with niggers!" Then turning to her friend, she remarked: "Can you beat the nerve of these darkies?" She made a little disdainful grimace with her mouth, shrugged daintily and dismissed the unpleasant incident.

Crushed and angry, Max returned to his place without a word. Bunny laughed aloud in high glee.

"You said she was a cracker," he gurgled, "an' now I guess you know it."

"Aw, go to hell," Max grumbled.

Just then Billy Fletcher, the headwaiter passed by. Max stopped him. "Ever see that dame in here before?" he asked.

"Been in here most every night since before Christmas," Billy replied.

"Do you know who she is?"

"Well, I heard she was some rich broad from Atlanta up here for the holidays. Why?"

"Oh, nothin'; I was just wondering."

From Atlanta! His home town. No wonder she had turned him down. Up here trying to get a thrill in the Black Belt but a thrill from observation instead of contact. Gee, but white folks were funny. They didn't want black folks' game and yet they were always frequenting Negro resorts.

*

At three o'clock Max and Bunny paid their check and ascended to the street. Bunny wanted to go to the breakfast dance at the Dahomey Casino but Max was in no mood for it.

"I'm going home," he announced laconically, hailing a taxi. "Good night!"

As the cab whirled up Seventh Avenue, he settled back and thought of the girl from Atlanta. He couldn't get her out of his mind and didn't want to. At his rooming house, he paid the driver, unlocked the door, ascended to his room and undressed, mechanically. His mind was a kaleidoscope: Atlanta, sea-green eyes, slender figure, titian hair, frigid manner. "I never dance with niggers." Then he fell asleep about five o'clock and promptly dreamed of her. Dreamed of dancing with her, dining with her, motoring with her, sitting beside her on a golden throne while millions of manacled white slaves prostrated themselves before him. Then there was a nightmare of grim, gray men with shotguns, baying hounds, a heap of gasoline-soaked faggots and a screeching, fanatical mob.

He awoke covered with perspiration. His telephone was ringing and the late morning sunshine was streaming into his room. He leaped from bed and lifted the receiver.

"Say," shouted Bunny, "did you see this morning's *Times*?"

"Hell no," growled Max, "I just woke up. Why, what's in it?"

"Well, do you remember Dr. Junius Crookman, that colored fellow that went to Germany to study about three years ago? He's just come back and the *Times* claims he's announced a sure way to turn darkies white. Thought you might be interested after the way you fell for that ofay broad last night. They say Crookman's going to open a sanitarium in Harlem right away. There's your chance, Big Boy, and it's your only chance." Bunny chuckled.

"Oh, ring off," growled Max. "That's a lot of hooey."

But he was impressed and a little excited. Suppose there was something to it? He dressed hurriedly, after a cold shower, and went out to the newsstand. He bought a *Times* and scanned its columns. Yes, there it was:

NEGRO ANNOUNCES REMARKABLE
DISCOVERY
Can Change Black to White in Three Days.

Max went into Jimmy Johnson's restaurant and greedily read the account while awaiting his breakfast. Yes, it must be true. To think of old Crookman being able to do that! Only a few years ago he'd been just a hungry medical student around Harlem. Max put down the paper and stared vacantly out of the window. Gee, Crookman would be a millionaire in no time. He'd even be a multi-millionaire. It looked as though science was to succeed where the Civil War had failed. But how could it be possible? He looked at his hands and felt at the back of his head where the straightening lotion had failed to conquer some of the knots. He toyed with his ham and eggs as he envisioned the possibilities of the discovery.

Then a sudden resolution seized him. He looked at the newspaper account again. Yes, Crookman was staying at the Phyllis Wheatley Hotel. Why not go and see what there was to this? Why not be the first Negro to try it out? Sure, it was taking a chance, but think of getting white in three days! No more jim crow. No more insults. As a white man he could go anywhere, be anything he wanted to be, do most anything he wanted to do, be a free man at last . . . and probably be able to meet the girl from Atlanta. What a vision!

He rose hurriedly, paid for his breakfast, rushed out of the door, almost ran into an aged white man carrying a sign advertising a Negro fraternity dance, and strode, almost ran, to the Phyllis Wheatley Hotel.

He tore up the steps two at a time and into the sitting room. It was crowded with white reporters from the daily newspapers and back reporters from the Negro weeklies. In their midst he recognized Dr. Junius Crookman, tall, wiry, ebony black, with a studious and polished manner. Flanking him on either side were Henry ("Hank") Johnson, the "Numbers" banker and Charlie ("Chuck") Foster, the realtor, looking very grave, important and possessive in the midst of all the hullabaloo.

"Yes," Dr. Crookman was telling the reporters while they eagerly took down his statements, "during my first year at college I noticed a black girl on the street one day who had several irregular white patches on her face and hands. That intrigued me. I began to study up on skin diseases and found out that the girl was evidently suffering from a nervous disease known as vitiligo. It is a very rare disease. Both Negroes and

Caucasians occasionally have it, but it is naturally more con-spicuous on blacks than whites. It absolutely removes skin pig-ment and sometimes it turns a Negro completely white but only after a period of thirty or forty years. It occurred to me that if one could discover some means of artificially inducing and stimulating this nervous disease at will, one might possibly solve the American race problem. My sociology teacher had once said that there were but three ways for the Negro to solve his problem in America," he gestured with his long slender fin-gers, "'To either get out, get white or get along.' Since he wouldn't and couldn't get out and was getting along only in-differently, it seemed to me that the only thing for him was to get white." For a moment his teeth gleamed beneath his smartly waxed mustache, then he sobered and went on:

"I began to give a great deal of study to the problem during my spare time. Unfortunately there was very little information on the subject in this country. I decided to go to Germany but I didn't have the money. Just when I despaired of getting the funds to carry out my experiments and studies abroad, Mr. Johnson and Mr. Foster," he indicated the two men with a graceful wave of his hand, "came to my rescue. I naturally at-tribute a great deal of my success to them."

"But how is it done?" asked a reporter.

"Well," smiled Crookman, "I naturally cannot divulge the secret any more than to say that it is accomplished by electrical nutrition and glandular control. Certain gland secretions are greatly stimulated while others are considerably diminished. It is a powerful and dangerous treatment but harmless when properly done."

"How about the hair and features?" asked a Negro reporter.

"They are also changed in the process," answered the biolo-gist. "In three days the Negro becomes to all appearances a Caucasian."

"But is the transformation transferred to the offspring?" persisted the Negro newspaperman.

"As yet," replied Crookman, "I have discovered no way to accomplish anything so revolutionary but I am able to trans-form a black infant to a white one in twenty-four hours."

"Have you tried it on any Negroes yet?" queried a sceptical white journalist.

"Why of course I have," said the Doctor, slightly nettled. "I would not have made my announcement if I had not done so. Come here, Sandol," he called, turning to a pale white youth standing on the outskirts of the crowd, who was the most Nordic looking person in the room. "This man is a Senegalese, a former aviator in the French Army. He is living proof that what I claim is true."

Dr. Crookman then displayed a photograph of a very black man, somewhat resembling Sandol but with bushy Negro hair, flat nose and full lips. "This," he announced proudly, "is Sandol as he looked before taking my treatment. What I have done to him I can do to any Negro. He is in good physical and mental condition as you all can see."

The assemblage was properly awed. After taking a few more notes and a number of photographs of Dr. Crookman, his associates and of Sandol, the newspapermen retired. Only the dapper Max Disher remained.

"Hello, Doc!" he said, coming forward and extending his hand. "Don't you remember me? I'm Max Disher."

"Why certainly I remember you, Max," replied the biologist rising cordially. "Been a long time since we've seen each other but you're looking as sharp as ever. How's things?"

The two men shook hands.

"Oh, pretty good. Say, Doc, how's chances to get you to try that thing on me? You must be looking for volunteers."

"Yes, I am, but not just yet. I've got to get my equipment set up first. I think now I'll be ready for business in a couple of weeks."

Henry Johnson, the beefy, sleek-jowled, mulatto "Numbers" banker, chuckled and nudged Dr. Crookman. "Old Max ain't losin' no time, Doc. When that niggah gits white Ah bet he'll make up fo' los' time with these ofay girls."

Charlie Foster, small, slender, grave, amber-colored, and laconic, finally spoke up: "Seems all right, Junius, but there'll be hell to pay when you whiten up a lot o' these darkies and them mulatto babies start appearing here and there. Watcha gonna do then?"

"Oh, quit singin' th' blues, Chuck," boomed Johnson. "Don't cross bridges 'til yuh come tuh 'em. Doc'll fix that okeh. Besides, we'll have mo' money'n Henry Ford by that time."

"There'll be no difficulties whatever," assured Crookman rather impatiently.

"Let's hope not."

Next day the newspapers carried a long account of the interview with Dr. Junius Crookman interspersed with photographs of him, his backers and of the Senegalese who had been turned white. It was the talk of the town and was soon the talk of the country. Long editorials were written about the discovery, learned societies besieged the Negro biologist with offers of lecture engagements, magazines begged him for articles, but he turned down all offers and refused to explain his treatment. This attitude was decried as unbecoming a scientist and it was insinuated and even openly stated that nothing more could be expected from a Negro.

But Crookman ignored the clamor of the public, and with the financial help of his associates planned the great and lucrative experiment of turning Negroes into Caucasians.

The impatient Max Disher saw him as often as possible and kept track of developments. He yearned to be the first treated and didn't want to be caught napping. Two objects were uppermost in his mind: To get white and to Atlanta. The statuesque and haughty blonde was ever in his thoughts. He was head over heels in love with her and realized there was no hope for him to ever win her as long as he was brown. Each day he would walk past the tall building that was to be the Crookman Sanitarium, watching the workmen and delivery trucks; wondering how much longer he would have to wait before entering upon the great adventure.

At last the sanitarium was ready for business. Huge advertisements appeared in the local Negro weeklies. Black Harlem was on its toes. Curious throngs of Negroes and whites stood in front of the austere six-story building gazing up at its windows.

Inside, Crookman, Johnson and Foster stood nervously about while hustling attendants got everything in readiness. Outside they could hear the murmur of the crowd.

"That means money, Chuck," boomed Johnson, rubbing his beefsteak hands together.

"Yeh," replied the realtor, "but there's one more thing I wanna get straight: How about that darky dialect? You can't change that."

"It isn't necessary, my dear Foster," explained the physician, patiently. "There is no such thing as Negro dialect, except in literature and drama. It is a well-known fact among informed persons that a Negro from a given section speaks the same dialect as his white neighbors. In the South you can't tell over the telephone whether you are talking to a white man or a Negro. The same is true in New York when a Northern Negro speaks into the receiver. I have noticed the same thing in the hills of West Virginia and Tennessee. The educated Haitian speaks the purest French and the Jamaican Negro sounds exactly like an Englishman. There are no racial or color dialects; only sectional dialects."

"Guess you're right," agreed Foster, grudgingly.

"I know I'm right. Moreover, even if my treatment did not change the so-called Negro lips, even that would prove to be no obstacle."

"How come, Doc," asked Johnson.

"Well, there are plenty of Caucasians who have lips quite as thick and noses quite as broad as any of us. As a matter of fact there has been considerable exaggeration about the contrast between Caucasian and Negro features. The cartoonists and minstrel men have been responsible for it very largely. Some Negroes like the Somalis, Filanis, Egyptians, Hausas and Abyssinians have very thin lips and nostrils. So also have the Malagasys of Madagascar. Only in certain small sections of Africa do the Negroes possess extremely pendulous lips and very broad nostrils. On the other hand, many so-called Caucasians, particularly the Latins, Jews and South Irish, and frequently the most Nordic of peoples like the Swedes, show almost Negroid lips and noses. Black up some white folks and they could deceive a resident of Benin. Then when you consider that less than twenty per cent of our Negroes are without Caucasian ancestry and that close to thirty per cent have American Indian ancestry, it is readily seen that there cannot be the wide difference in Caucasian and Afro-American facial characteristics that most people imagine."

"Doc, you sho' knows yo' onions," said Johnson, admiringly. "Doan pay no 'tenshun to that ole Doubtin' Thomas. He'd holler starvation in a pie shop."

There was a commotion outside and an angry voice was heard above the hum of low conversation. Then Max Disher burst in the door with a guard hanging onto his coat tail.

"Let loose o' me, Boy," he quarreled. "I got an engagement here. Doc, tell this man something, will you."

Crookman nodded to the guard to release the insurance man. "Well, I see you're right on time, Max."

"I told you I'd be Johnny-on-the-spot, didn't I?" said Disher, inspecting his clothes to see if they had been wrinkled.

"Well, if you're all ready, go into the receiving room there, sign the register and get into one of those bathrobes. You're first on the list."

The three partners looked at each other and grinned as Max disappeared into a small room at the end of the corridor. Dr. Crookman went into his office to don his white trousers, shoes and smock; Johnson and Foster entered the business office to supervise the clerical staff, while white-coated figures darted back and forth through the corridors. Outside, the murmuring of the vast throng grew more audible.

Johnson showed all of his many gold teeth in a wide grin as he glanced out the window and saw the queue of Negroes already extending around the corner. "Man, man, man!" he chuckled to Foster, "at fifty dollars a th'ow this thing's gonna have th' numbah business beat all hollow."

"Hope so," said Foster, gravely.

Max Disher, arrayed only in a hospital bathrobe and a pair of slippers, was escorted to the elevator by two white-coated attendants. They got off on the sixth floor and walked to the end of the corridor. Max was trembling with excitement and anxiety. Suppose something should go wrong? Suppose Doc should make a mistake? He thought of the Elks' excursion every summer to Bear Mountain, the high yellow Minnie and her colorful apartment, the pleasant evenings at the Dahomey Casino doing the latest dances with the brown belles of Harlem, the prancing choruses at the Lafayette Theater, the hours he had whiled away at Boogie's and the Honky Tonk Club, and he hesitated. Then he envisioned his future as a white man, probably as the husband of the tall blonde from Atlanta, and with firm resolve, he entered the door of the mysterious chamber.

He quailed as he saw the formidable apparatus of sparkling nickel. It resembled a cross between a dentist's chair and an electric chair. Wires and straps, bars and levers protruded from it and a great nickel headpiece, like the helmet of a knight, hung over it. The room had only a skylight and no sound entered it from the outside. Around the walls were cases of instruments and shelves of bottles filled with strangely colored fluids. He gasped with fright and would have made for the door but the two husky attendants held him firmly, stripped off his robe and bound him in the chair. There was no retreat. It was either the beginning or the end.

Chapter Two

SLOWLY, haltingly, Max Disher dragged his way down the hall to the elevator, supported on either side by an attendant. He felt terribly weak, emptied and nauseated; his skin twitched and was dry and feverish; his insides felt very hot and sore. As the trio walked slowly along the corridor, a blue-green light would ever and anon blaze through one of the doorways as a patient was taken in. There was a low hum and throb of machinery and an acrid odor filled the air. Uniformed nurses and attendants hurried back and forth at their tasks. Everything was quiet, swift, efficient, sinister.

He felt so thankful that he had survived the ordeal of that horrible machine so akin to the electric chair. A shudder passed over him at the memory of the hours he had passed in its grip, fed at intervals with revolting concoctions. But when they reached the elevator and he saw himself in the mirror, he was startled, overjoyed. White at last! Gone was the smooth brown complexion. Gone were the slightly full lips and Ethiopian nose. Gone was the nappy hair that he had straightened so meticulously ever since the kink-no-more lotions first wrenched Aframericans from the tyranny and torture of the comb. There would be no more expenditures for skin whiteners; no more discrimination; no more obstacles in his path. He was free! The world was his oyster and he had the open sesame of a pork-colored skin!

The reflection in the mirror gave him new life and strength. He now stood erect, without support and grinned at the two tall, black attendants. "Well, Boys," he crowed, "I'm all set now. That machine of Doc's worked like a charm. Soon's I get a feed under my belt I'll be okeh."

Six hours later, bathed, fed, clean-shaven, spry, blonde and jubilant, he emerged from the out-patient ward and tripped gaily down the corridor to the main entrance. He was through with coons, he resolved, from now on. He glanced in a superior manner at the long line of black and brown folk on one side of the corridor, patiently awaiting treatment. He saw many persons whom he knew but none of them recognized him. It thrilled him to feel that he was now indistinguishable from nine-tenths of the people of the United States; one of the great majority. Ah, it was good not to be a Negro any longer!

As he sought to open the front door, the strong arm of a guard restrained him. "Wait a minute," the man said, "and we'll help you get through the mob."

A moment or two later Max found himself the center of a flying wedge of five or six husky special policemen, cleaving through a milling crowd of colored folk. From the top step of the Sanitarium he had noticed the crowd spread over the sidewalk, into the street and around the corners. Fifty traffic policemen strained and sweated to keep prospective patients in line and out from under the wheels of taxicabs and trucks.

Finally he reached the curb, exhausted from the jostling and squeezing, only to be set upon by a mob of newspaper photographers and reporters. As the first person to take the treatment, he was naturally the center of attraction for about fifteen of these journalistic gnats. They asked a thousand questions seemingly all at once. What was his name? How did he feel? What was he going to do? Would he marry a white woman? Did he intend to continue living in Harlem?

Max would say nothing. In the first place, he thought to himself, if they're so anxious to know all this stuff, they ought to be willing to pay for it. He needed money if he was going to be able to thoroughly enjoy being white; why not get some by selling his story? The reporters, male and female, begged him almost with tears in their eyes for a statement but he was adamant.

While they were wrangling, an empty taxicab drove up. Pushing the inquisitive reporters to one side, Max leaped into it and yelled "Central Park!" It was the only place he could think of at the moment. He wanted to have time to compose his mind, to plan the future in this great world of whiteness. As the cab lurched forward, he turned and was astonished to find another occupant, a pretty girl.

"Don't be scared," she smiled. "I knew you would want to get away from that mob so I went around the corner and got a cab for you. Come along with me and I'll get everything fixed up for you. I'm a reporter from *The Scimitar*. We'll give you a lot of money for your story." She talked rapidly. Max's first impulse had been to jump out of the cab, even at the risk of having to face again the mob of reporters and photographers he had sought to escape, but he changed his mind when he heard mention of money.

"How much?" he asked, eyeing her. She was very comely and he noted that her ankles were well turned.

"Oh, probably a thousand dollars," she replied.

"Well, that sounds good." A thousand dollars! What a time he could have with that! Broadway for him as soon as he got paid off.

As they sped down Seventh Avenue, the newsboys were yelling the latest editions. "Ex—try! Ex—try! Blacks turning white! Blacks turning white! . . . Read all about the gr-r-reat dis—covery! Paper, Mister! Paper! . . . Read all about Dr. Crookman."

He settled back while they drove through the park and glanced frequently at the girl by his side. She looked mighty good; wonder could he talk business with her? Might go to dinner and a cabaret. That would be the best way to start.

"What did you say your name was?" he began.

"I didn't say," she stalled.

"Well, you have a name, haven't you?" he persisted.

"Suppose I have?"

"You're not scared to tell it, are you?"

"Why do you want to know my name?"

"Well, there's nothing wrong about wanting to know a pretty girl's name, is there?"

"Well, my name's Smith, Sybil Smith. Now are you satisfied?"

"Not yet. I want to know something more. How would you like to go to dinner with me tonight?"

"I don't know and I won't know until I've had the experience." She smiled coquettishly. Going out with him, she figured, would make the basis of a rattling good story for tomorrow's paper. "Negro's first night as a Caucasian!" Fine!

"Say, you're a regular fellow," he said, beaming upon her. "I'll get a great kick out of going to dinner with you because you'll be the only one in the place that'll know I'm a Negro."

Down at the office of *The Scimitar*, it didn't take Max long to come to an agreement, tell his story to a stenographer and get a sheaf of crisp, new bills. As he left the building a couple of hours later with Miss Smith on his arm, the newsboys were already crying the extra edition carrying the first installment of his strange tale. A huge photograph of him occupied the entire front page of the tabloid. Lucky for him that he'd given his name as William Small, he thought.

He was annoyed and a little angered. What did they want to put his picture all over the front of the paper for? Now everybody would know who he was. He had undergone the tortures of Doc Crookman's devilish machine in order to escape the conspicuousness of a dark skin and now he was being made conspicuous because he had once had a dark skin! Could one never escape the plagued race problem?

"Don't worry about that," comforted Miss Smith. "Nobody'll recognize you. There are thousands of white people, yes millions, that look like you do." She took his arm and snuggled up closer. She wanted to make him feel at home. It wasn't often a poor, struggling newspaper woman got a chap with a big bankroll to take her out for the evening. Moreover, the description she would write of the experience might win her a promotion.

They walked down Broadway in the blaze of white lights to a dinner-dance place. To Max it was like being in heaven. He had strolled through the Times Square district before but never with such a feeling of absolute freedom and sureness. No one now looked at him curiously because he was with a white girl, as they had when he came down there with Minnie, his former octoroon lady friend. Gee, it was great!

They dined and they danced. Then they went to a cabaret, where, amid smoke, noise and body smells, they drank what was purported to be whiskey and watched a semi-nude chorus do its stuff. Despite his happiness Max found it pretty dull. There was something lacking in these ofay places of amusement or else there was something present that one didn't find in the black-and-tan resorts in Harlem. The joy and abandon here was obviously forced. Patrons went to extremes to show each other they were having a wonderful time. It was all so strained and quite unlike anything to which he had been accustomed. The Negroes, it seemed to him, were much gayer, enjoyed themselves more deeply and yet they were more restrained, actually more refined. Even their dancing was different.

They followed the rhythm accurately, effortlessly and with easy grace; these lumbering couples, out of step half the time and working as strenuously as stevedores emptying the bowels of a freighter, were noisy, awkward, inelegant. At their best they were gymnastic where the Negroes were sensuous. He felt a momentary pang of mingled disgust, disillusionment and nostalgia. But it was only momentary. He looked across at the comely Sybil and then around at the other white women, many of whom were very pretty and expensively gowned, and the sight temporarily drove from his mind the thoughts that had been occupying him.

They parted at three o'clock, after she had given him her telephone number. She pecked him lightly on the cheek in payment, doubtless, for a pleasant evening's entertainment. Somewhat disappointed because she had failed to show any interest in his expressed curiosity about the interior of her apartment, he directed the chauffeur to drive him to Harlem. After all, he argued to himself in defense of his action, he had to get his things.

As the cab turned out of Central Park at 110th Street he felt, curiously enough, a feeling of peace. There were all the old familiar sights: the all-night speakeasies, the frankfurter stands, the loiterers, the late pedestrians, the chop suey joints, the careening taxicabs, the bawdy laughter.

He couldn't resist the temptation to get out at 133rd Street and go down to Boogie's place, the hangout of his gang. He tapped, an eye peered through a hole, appraised him critically, then disappeared and the hole was closed. There was silence.

Max frowned. What was the matter with old Bob? Why didn't he open that door? The cold January breeze swept down into the little court where he stood and made him shiver. He knocked a little louder, more insistently. The eye appeared again.

"Who's 'at?" growled the doorkeeper.

"It's me, Max Disher," replied the ex-Negro.

"Go 'way f'm here, white man. Dis heah place is closed."

"Is Bunny Brown in there?" asked Max in desperation.

"Yeh, he's heah. Does yuh know him? Well, Ah'll call 'im out heah and see if he knows you."

Max waited in the cold for about two or three minutes and

then the door suddenly opened and Bunny Brown, a little unsteady, came out. He peered at Max in the light from the electric bulb over the door.

"Hello Bunny," Max greeted him. "Don't know me do you? It's me, Max Disher. You recognize my voice, don't you?"

Bunny looked again, rubbed his eyes and shook his head. Yes, the voice was Max Disher's, but this man was white. Still, when he smiled his eyes revealed the same sardonic twinkle—so characteristic of his friend.

"Max," he blurted out, "is that you, sure enough? Well, for cryin' out loud! Damned 'f you ain't been up there to Crookman's and got fixed up. Well, hush my mouth! Bob, open that door. This is old Max Disher. Done gone up there to Crookman's and got all white on my hands. He's just too tight, with his blond hair, 'n everything."

Bob opened the door, the two friends entered, sat down at one of the small round tables in the narrow, smoke-filled cellar and were soon surrounded with cronies. They gazed raptly at his colorless skin, commented on the veins showing blue through the epidermis, stroked his ash-blond hair and listened with mouths open to his remarkable story.

"Whatcha gonna do now, Max?" asked Boogie, the rangy, black, bullet-headed proprietor.

"I know just what that joker's gonna do," said Bunny. "He's goin' back to Atlanta. Am I right, Big Boy?"

"You ain't wrong," Max agreed. "I'm goin' right on down there, brother, and make up for lost time."

"Whadayah mean?" asked Boogie.

"Boy, it would take me until tomorrow night to tell you and then you wouldn't understand."

The two friends strolled up the avenue. Both were rather mum. They had been inseparable pals since the stirring days in France. Now they were about to be parted. It wasn't as if Max was going across the ocean to some foreign country; there would be a wider gulf separating them: the great sea of color. They both thought about it.

"I'll be pretty lonesome without you, Bunny."

"It ain't you, Big Boy."

"Well, why don't you go ahead and get white and then we could stay together. I'll give you the money."

"Say not so! Where'd you get so much jack all of a sudden?" asked Bunny.

"Sold my story to *The Scimitar* for a grand."

"Paid in full?"

"Wasn't paid in part!"

"All right, then, I'll take you up, Heavy Sugar." Bunny held out his plump hand and Max handed him a hundred-dollar bill.

They were near the Crookman Sanitarium. Although it was five o'clock on a Sunday morning, the building was brightly lighted from cellar to roof and the hum of electric motors could be heard, low and powerful. A large electric sign hung from the roof to the second floor. It represented a huge arrow outlined in green with the words BLACK-NO-MORE running its full length vertically. A black face was depicted at the lower end of the arrow while at the top shone a white face to which the arrow was pointed. First would appear the outline of the arrow; then, BLACK-NO-MORE would flash on and off. Following that the black face would appear at the bottom and beginning at the lower end the long arrow with its lettering would appear progressively until its tip was reached, when the white face at the top would blazon forth. After that the sign would flash off and on and the process would be repeated.

In front of the sanitarium milled a half-frozen crowd of close to four thousand Negroes. A riot squad armed with rifles, machine guns and tear gas bombs maintained some semblance of order. A steel cable stretched from lamp post to lamp post the entire length of the block kept the struggling mass of humanity on the sidewalk and out of the path of the traffic. It seemed as if all Harlem were there. As the two friends reached the outskirts of the mob, an ambulance from the Harlem Hospital drove up and carried away two women who had been trampled upon.

Lined up from the door to the curb was a gang of tough special guards dredged out of the slums. Grim Irish from Hell's Kitchen, rough Negroes from around 133rd Street and 5th Avenue (New York's "Beale Street") and tough Italians from the lower West Side. They managed with difficulty to keep an aisle cleared for incoming and outgoing patients. Near the curb were stationed the reporters and photographers.

The noise rose and fell. First there would be a low hum of voices. Steadily it would rise and rise in increasing volume as the speakers became more animated and reach its climax in a great animal-like roar as the big front door would open and a whitened Negro would emerge. Then the mass would surge forward to peer at and question the ersatz Nordic. Sometimes the ex-Ethiopian would quail before the mob and jump back into the building. Then the hardboiled guards would form a flying squad and hustle him to a waiting taxicab. Other erstwhile Aframericans issuing from the building would grin broadly, shake hands with friends and relatives and start to graphically describe their experience while the Negroes around them enviously admired their clear white skins.

In between these appearances the hot dog and peanut vendors did a brisk trade, along with the numerous pickpockets of the district. One slender, anemic, ratty-looking mulatto Negro was almost beaten to death by a gigantic black laundress whose purse he had snatched. A Negro selling hot roasted sweet potatoes did a land-office business while the neighboring saloons, that had increased so rapidly in number since the enactment of the Volstead Law that many of their Italian proprietors paid substantial income taxes, sold scores of gallons of incredibly atrocious hootch.

"Well, bye, bye, Max," said Bunny, extending his hand. "I'm goin' in an' try my luck."

"So long, Bunny. See you in Atlanta. Write me general delivery."

"Why, ain't you gonna wait for me, Max?"

"Naw! I'm fed up on this town."

"Oh, you ain't kiddin' me, Big Boy. I know you want to look up that broad you saw in the Honky Tonk New Year's Eve," Bunny beamed.

Max grinned and blushed slightly. They shook hands and parted. Bunny ran up the aisle from the curb, opened the sanitarium door and without turning around, disappeared within.

For a minute or so, Max stood irresolutely in the midst of the gibbering crowd of people. Unaccountably he felt at home here among these black folk. Their jests, scraps of conversation and lusty laughter all seemed like heavenly music. Momentarily he felt a disposition to stay among them, to share again their troubles which they seemed always to bear with a lightness that was yet not indifference. But then, he suddenly realized with just a tiny trace of remorse that the past was forever gone. He must seek other pastures, other pursuits, other playmates, other loves. He was white now. Even if he wished to stay among his folk, they would be either jealous or suspicious of him, as they were of most octoroons and nearly all whites. There was no other alternative than to seek his future among the Caucasians with whom he now rightfully belonged.

And after all, he thought, it was a glorious new adventure. His eyes twinkled and his pulse quickened as he thought of it. Now he could go anywhere, associate with anybody, be anything he wanted to be. He suddenly thought of the comely miss he had seen in the Honky Tonk on New Year's Eve and the greatly enlarged field from which he could select his loves. Yes, indeed there were advantages in being white. He brightened and viewed the tightly-packed black folk around him with a superior air. Then, thinking again of his clothes at Mrs. Blandish's, the money in his pocket and the prospect for the first time of riding into Atlanta in a Pullman car and not as a Pullman porter, he turned and pushed his way through the throng.

He strolled up West 139th Street to his rooming place, stepping lightly and sniffing the early morning air. How good it was to be free, white and to possess a bankroll! He fumbled in his pocket for his little mirror looked at himself again and again from several angles. He stroked his pale blond hair and secretly congratulated himself that he would no longer need to straighten it nor be afraid to wet it. He gazed raptly at his smooth, white hands with the blue veins showing through. What a miracle Dr. Crookman had wrought!

As he entered the hallway, the mountainous form of his landlady loomed up. She jumped back as she saw his face.

"What you doing in here?" she almost shouted. "Where'd you get a key to this house?"

"It's me, Max Disher," he assured her with a grin at her astonishment. "Don't know me, do you?"

She gazed incredulously into his face. "Is that you sure enough, Max? How in the devil did you get so white?"

He explained and showed her a copy of *The Scimitar*

containing his story. She switched on the hall light and read it. Contrasting emotions played over her face, for Mrs. Blandish was known in the business world as Mme. Sisseretta Blandish, the beauty specialist, who owned the swellest hair-straightening parlor in Harlem. Business, she thought to herself, was bad enough, what with all of the competition, without this Dr. Crookman coming along and killing it altogether.

"Well," she sighed, "I suppose you're going down town to live, now. I always said niggers didn't really have any race pride."

Uneasy, Max made no reply. The fat, brown woman turned with a disdainful sniff and disappeared into a room at the end of the hall. He ran lightly upstairs to pack his things.

An hour later, as the taxicab bearing him and his luggage bowled through Central Park, he was in high spirits. He would go down to the Pennsylvania Station and get a Pullman straight into Atlanta. He would stop there at the best hotel. He wouldn't hunt up any of his folks. No, that would be too dangerous. He would just play around, enjoy life and laugh at the white folks up his sleeve. God! What an adventure! What a treat it would be to mingle with white people in places where as a youth he had never dared to enter. At last he felt like an American citizen. He flecked the ash of his panatela out of the open window of the cab and sank back in the seat feeling at peace with the world.

Chapter Three

D R. JUNIUS CROOKMAN, looking tired and worn, poured himself another cup of coffee from the percolator near by and turning to Hank Johnson, asked "What about that new electrical apparatus?"

"On th' way, Doc. On th' way," replied the former Numbers baron. "Just talkin' to th' man this mornin'. He says we'll get it tomorrow, maybe."

"Well, we certainly need it," said Chuck Foster, who sat beside him on the large leather divan. "We can't handle all of the business as it is."

"How about those new places you're buying?" asked the physician.

"Well, I've bought the big private house on Edgecombe Avenue for fifteen thousand and the workmen are getting it in shape now. It ought to be ready in about a week if nothing happens," Foster informed him.

"If nuthin' happens?" echoed Johnson. "Whut's gonna happen? We're settin' on th' world, ain't we? Our racket's within th' law, ain't it? We're makin' money faster'n we can take it in, ain't we? Whut could happen? This here is the best and safest graft I've ever been in."

"Oh, you never can tell," cautioned the quondom realtor. "These white newspapers, especially in the South, are beginning to write some pretty strong editorials against us and we've only been running two weeks. You know how easy it is to stir up the fanatical element. Before we know it they're liable to get a law passed against us."

"Not if I c'n git to th' legislature first," interrupted Johnson. "Yuh know, Ah knows how tuh handle these white folks. If yuh 'Say it with Bucks' you c'n git anything yuh want."

"There is something in what Foster says, though," Dr. Crookman said. "Just look at this bunch of clippings we got in this morning. Listen to these: 'The Viper in Our Midst,' from the Richmond *Blade*; 'The Menace of Science' from the Memphis *Bugle*; 'A Challenge to Every White Man' from the Dallas

Sun; 'Police Battle Black Mob Seeking White Skins,' from the Atlanta *Topic;* 'Negro Doctor Admits Being Taught by Germans,' from the St. Louis *North American.* Here's a line or two from an editorial in the Oklahoma City *Hatchet:* 'There are times when the welfare of our race must take precedence over law. Opposed as we always have been to mob violence as the worst enemy of democratic government, we cannot help but feel that the intelligent white men and women of New York City who are interested in the purity and preservation of their race should not permit the challenge of Crookmanism to go unanswered, even though these black scoundrels may be within the law. There are too many criminals in this country already hiding behind the skirts of the law.'

"And lastly, one from the Tallahassee *Announcer* says: 'While it is the right of every citizen to do what he wants to do with his money, the white people of the United States cannot remain indifferent to this discovery and its horrible potentialities. Hundreds of Negroes with newly-acquired white skins have already entered white society and thousands will follow them. The black race from one end of the country to the other has in two short weeks gone completely crazy over the prospect of getting white. Day by day we see the color line which we have so laboriously established being rapidly destroyed. There would not be so much cause for alarm in this, were it not for the fact that this vitiligo is not hereditary. In other words, THE OFFSPRING OF THESE WHITENED NEGROES WILL BE NEGROES! This means that your daughter, having married a supposed white man, may find herself with a black baby! Will the proud white men of the Southland so far forget their traditions as to remain idle while this devilish work is going on?"

"No use singin' th' blues," counseled Johnson. "We ain' gonna be both'ed heah, even if them crackahs down South do raise a little hell. Jus' lissen to th' sweet music of that mob out theah! Eve'y scream means fifty bucks. On'y reason we ain't makin' mo' money is 'cause we ain't got no mo' room."

"That's right," Dr. Crookman agreed. "We've turned out one hundred a day for fourteen days." He leaned back and lit a cigarette.

"At fifty bucks a th'ow," interrupted Johnson, "that means we've took in seventy thousand dollahs. Great Day in th' mornin'! Didn't know tha was so much jack in Harlem."

"Yes," continued Crookman, "we're taking in thirty-five thousand dollars a week. As soon as you and Foster get that other place fixed up we'll be making twice that much."

From the hallway came the voice of the switchboard operator monotonously droning out her instructions: "No, Dr. Crookman cannot see anyone. . . . Dr. Crookman has nothing to say. . . . Dr. Crookman will issue a statement shortly. . . . Fifty Dollars. . . . No, Dr. Crookman isn't a mulatto. . . . I'm very sorry but I cannot answer that question."

The three friends sat in silence amid the hum of activity around them. Hank Johnson smiled down at the end of his cigar as he thought back over his rather colorful and hectic career. To think that today he was one of the leading Negroes of the world, one who was taking an active and important part in solving the most vexatious problem in American life, and yet only ten years before he had been working on a Carolina chain gang. Two years he had toiled on the roads under the hard eye and ready rifle of a cruel white guard; two years of being beaten, kicked and cursed, of poor food and vermin-infested habitations; two years for participating in a little crap game. Then he had drifted to Charleston, got a job in a pool room, had a stroke of luck with the dice, come to New York and landed right in the midst of the Numbers racket. Becoming a collector or "runner," he had managed his affairs well enough to be able to start out soon as a "banker." Money had poured in from Negroes eager to chance one cent in the hope of winning six dollars. Some won but most lost and he had prospered. He had purchased an apartment house, paid off the police, dabbled in the bail bond game, given a couple of thousand dollars to advance Negro Art and been elected Grand Permanent Shogun of the Ancient and Honorable Order of Crocodiles, Harlem's largest and most prosperous secret society. Then young Crookman had come to him with his proposition. At first he had hesitated about helping him but later was persuaded to do so when the young man bitterly complained that the dicty Negroes would not help to pay for the studies abroad. What a stroke of luck, getting in on the ground floor like this! They'd all be richer than Rockefeller inside of a year. Twelve million Negroes at fifty dollars apiece! Great Day in the morning! Hank spat regally into the brass cuspidor across the office and reared back contentedly on the soft cushion of the divan.

Chuck Foster was also seeing his career in retrospect. His life had not been as colorful as that of Hank Johnson. The son of a Birmingham barber, he had enjoyed such educational advantages as that community afforded the darker brethren; had become a schoolteacher, an insurance agent and a social worker in turn. Then, along with the tide of migration, he had drifted first to Cincinnati, then to Pittsburgh and finally to New York. There the real estate field, unusually lucrative because of the paucity of apartments for the increasing Negro population, had claimed him. Cautious, careful, thrifty and devoid of sentimentality, he had prospered, but not without some ugly rumors being broadcast about his sharp business methods. As he slowly worked his way up to the top of Harlem society, he had sought to live down this reputation for double-dealing and shifty practices, all too true of the bulk of his fellow realtors in the district, by giving large sums to the Young Men's and Young Women's Christian Associations, by offering scholarships to young Negroes, by staging elaborate parties to which dicty Negroes of the community were invited. He had been glad of the opportunity to help subsidize young Crookman's studies abroad when Hank Johnson pointed out the possibilities of the venture. Now, although the results so far exceeded his wildest dreams, his natural conservatism and timidity made him somewhat pessimistic about the future. He supposed a hundred dire results of their activities and only the day before he had increased the amount of his life insurance. His mind was filled with doubts. He didn't like so much publicity. He wanted a sort of genteel popularity but no notoriety.

Despite the coffee and cigarettes, Dr. Junius Crookman was sleepy. The responsibility, the necessity of overseeing the work of his physicians and nurses, the insistence of the newspapers and the medical profession that he reveal the secrets of his treatment and a thousand other vexatious details had kept him from getting proper rest. He had, indeed, spent most of his time in the sanitarium.

This hectic activity was new to him. Up until a month ago his thirty-five years had been peaceful and, in the main, studious ones. The son of an Episcopal clergyman, he had been born and raised in a city in central New York, his associates carefully selected in order to protect him as much as possible from the defeatist psychology so prevalent among American Negroes and given every opportunity and inducement to learn his profession and become a thoroughly cultivated and civilized man. His parents, though poor, were proud and boasted that they belonged to the Negro aristocracy. He had had to work his way through college because of the failure of his father's health but he had come very little in contact with the crudity, coarseness and cruelty of life. He had been monotonously successful but he was sensible enough to believe that a large part of it was due, like most success, to chance. He saw in his great discovery the solution to the most annoying problem in American life. Obviously, he reasoned, if there were no Negroes, there could be no Negro problem. Without a Negro problem, Americans could concentrate their attention on something constructive. Through his efforts and the activities of Black-No-More, Incorporated, it would be possible to do what agitation, education and legislation had failed to do. He was naïvely surprised that there should be opposition to his work. Like most men with a vision, a plan, a program or a remedy, he fondly imagined people to be intelligent enough to accept a good thing when it was offered to them, which was conclusive evidence that he knew little about the human race.

Dr. Crookman prided himself above all on being a great lover of his race. He had studied its history, read of its struggles and kept up with its achievements. He subscribed to six or seven Negro weekly newspapers and two of the magazines. He was so interested in the continued progress of the American Negroes that he wanted to remove all obstacles in their path by depriving them of their racial characteristics. His home and office were filled with African masks and paintings of Negroes by Negroes. He was what was known in Negro society as a Race Man. He was wedded to everything black except the black woman—his wife was a white girl with remote Negro ancestry, of the type that Negroes were wont to describe as being "able to pass for white." While abroad he had spent his spare time ransacking the libraries for facts about the achievements of Negroes and having liaisons with comely and available fraus and fräuleins.

"Well, Doc," said Hank Johnson, suddenly, "you'd bettah go on home 'n git some sleep. Ain' no use killin' you'sef. Eve'thing's gonna be all right heah. You ain' gotta thing tuh worry 'bout."

"How's he gonna get out of here with that mob in front?" Chuck inquired. "A man almost needs a tank to get through that crowd of darkies."

"Oh, Ah've got all that fixed, Calamity Jane," Johnson remarked casually. "All he's gotta do is tuh go on down staihs tuh the basem'nt, go out th' back way an' step into th' alley. My car'll be theah waitin' fo' 'im."

"That's awfully nice of you, Johnson," said the physician. "I am dead tired. I think I'll be a new man if I can get a few hours of sleep."

A black man in white uniform opened the door and announced: "Mrs. Crookman!" He held the door open for the Doctor's petite, stylishly-dressed wife to enter. The three men sprang to their feet. Johnson and Foster eyed the beautiful little octoroon appreciatively as they bowed, thinking how easily she could "pass for white," which would have been something akin to a piece of anthracite coal passing for black.

"Darling!" she exclaimed, turning to her husband. "Why don't you come home and get some rest? You'll be ill if you keep on in this way."

"Jus' whut Ah bin tellin' him, Mrs. Crookman," Johnson hastened to say. "He got eve'ything fixed tuh send 'im off."

"Well, then, Junius, we'd better be going," she said decisively.

Putting on a long overcoat over his white uniform, Dr. Crookman, wearily and meekly followed his spouse out of the door.

"Mighty nice looking girl, Mrs. Crookman," Foster observed.

"Nice lookin'!" echoed Johnson, with mock amazement.

"Why, nigguh, that ooman would make uh rabbit hug uh houn'. Doc sez she's cullud, an' she sez so, but she looks mighty white tuh me."

"Everything that looks white ain't white in this man's country," Foster replied.

Meantime there was feverish activity in Harlem's financial institutions. At the Douglass Bank the tellers were busier than bootleggers on Christmas Eve. Moreover, they were short-handed because of the mysterious absence of Bunny Brown. A long queue of Negroes extended down one side of the bank, out of the front door and around the corner, while bank attendants struggled to keep them in line. Everybody was drawing out money; no one was depositing. In vain the bank officials pleaded with them not to withdraw their funds. The Negroes were adamant: they wanted their money and wanted it quick. Day after day this had gone on ever since Black-No-More, Incorporated, had started turning Negroes white. At first, efforts were made to bulldoze and intimidate the depositors but that didn't succeed. These people were in no mood to be trifled with. A lifetime of being Negroes in the United States had convinced them that there was great advantage in being white.

"Mon, whutcha tahlk ab't?" scoffed a big, black British West Indian woman with whom an official was remonstrating not to draw out her money. "Dis heah's mah mahney, ain't it? Yuh use mah mahney alla time, aintcha? Whutcha mean, Ah shouldn't draw't out? . . . You gimme mah mahney or Ah broke up dis place!"

"Are you closing your account, Mr. Robinson?" a soft-voiced mulatto teller inquired of a big, rusty stevedore.

"Ah ain't openin' it," was the rejoinder. "Ah wants th' whole thing, an' Ah don't mean maybe."

Similar scenes were being enacted at the Wheatley Trust Company and at the local Post Office station.

An observer passing up and down the streets would have noted a general exodus from the locality. Moving vans were backed up to apartment houses on nearly every block.

The "For Rent" signs were appearing in larger number in Harlem than at any time in twenty-five years. Landlords looked on helplessly as apartment after apartment emptied and was not filled. Even the refusal to return deposits did not prevent the tenants from moving out. What, indeed, was fifty, sixty or seventy dollars when one was leaving behind insult, ostracism, segregation and discrimination? Moreover, the whitened Negroes were saving a great deal of money by being able to change localities. The mechanics of race prejudice had forced them into the congested Harlem area where, at the mercy of white and black real estate sharks, they had been compelled to pay exorbitant rentals because the demand for housing far exceeded the supply. As a general rule the Negroes were paying one hundred per cent more than white tenants in other parts of the city for a smaller number of rooms and worse service.

The installment furniture and clothing houses in the area were also beginning to feel the results of the activities of Black-No-More, Incorporated. Collectors were reporting their inability to locate certain families or the articles they had purchased on time. Many of the colored folk, it was said, had sold their furniture to second-hand stores and vanished with the proceeds into the great mass of white citizenry.

At the same time there seemed to be more white people on the streets of Harlem than at any time in the past twenty years. Many of them appeared to be on the most intimate terms with the Negroes, laughing, talking, dining and dancing in a most un-Caucasian way. This sort of association had always gone on at night but seldom in the daylight.

Strange Negroes from the West and South who had heard the good news were to be seen on the streets and in public places, patiently awaiting their turn at the Crookman Institute.

Madame Sisseretta Blandish sat disconsolately in an armchair near the front door of her ornate hair-straightening shop, looking blankly at the pedestrians and traffic passing to and fro. These two weeks had been hard ones for her. Everything was going out and nothing coming in. She had been doing very well at her vocation for years and was acclaimed in the community as one of its business leaders. Because of her prominence as the proprietor of a successful enterprise engaged in making Negroes appear as much like white folks as possible, she had recently been elected for the fourth time a Vice-President of the American Race Pride League. She was also head of the Woman's Committee of the New York Branch of the Social Equality League and held an important place in local Republican politics. But all of these honors brought little or no money with them. They didn't help to pay her rent or purchase the voluminous dresses she required to drape her Amazonian form. Only that day her landlord had brought her the sad news that he either wanted his money or the premises.

Where, she wondered, would she get the money. Like most New Yorkers she put up a big front with very little cash behind it, always looking hopefully forward to the morrow for a lucky break. She had two-thirds of the rent money already, by dint of much borrowing, and if she could "do" a few nappy heads she would be in the clear; but hardly a customer had crossed her threshold in a fortnight, except two or three Jewish girls from downtown who came up regularly to have their hair straightened because it wouldn't stand inspection in the Nordic world. The Negro women had seemingly deserted her. Day after day she saw her old customers pass by hurriedly without even looking in her direction. Verily a revolution was taking place in Negro society.

"Oh, Miss Simpson!" cried the hair-straightener after a passing young lady. "Ain't you going to say hello?"

The young woman halted reluctantly and approached the doorway. Her brown face looked strained. Two weeks before she would have been a rare sight in the Black Belt because her kinky hair was not straightened; it was merely combed, brushed and neatly pinned up. Miss Simpson had vowed that she wasn't going to spend any dollar a week having her hair "done" when she only lacked fifteen dollars of having money enough to quit the Negro race forever.

"Sorry, Mrs. Blandish," she apologized, "but I swear I didn't see you. I've been just that busy that I haven't had eyes for anything or anybody except my job and back home again. You know I'm all alone now. Yes, Charlie went over two weeks ago and I haven't heard a word from him. Just think of that! After all I've done for that nigger. Oh well! I'll soon be over there myself. Another week's work will fix me all right."

"Humph!" snorted Mme. Blandish. "That's all you niggers

are thinking about nowadays. Why don't you come down here and give me some business? If I don't hurry up and make some more money I'll have to close up this place and go to work myself."

"Well, I'm sorry, Mrs. Blandish," the girl mumbled indifferently, moving off toward the corner to catch the approaching street car, "but I guess I can hold out with this here bad hair until Saturday night. You know I've taken too much punishment being dark these twenty-two years to miss this opportunity. . . . Well," she flung over her shoulder, "Goodbye! See you later."

Madame Blandish settled her 250 pounds back into her armchair and sighed heavily. Like all American Negroes she had desired to be white when she was young and before she entered business for herself and became a person of consequence in the community. Now she had lived long enough to have no illusions about the magic of a white skin. She liked her business and she liked her social position in Harlem. As a white woman she would have to start all over again, and she wasn't so sure of herself. Here at least she was somebody. In the great Caucasian world she would be just another white woman, and they were becoming a drug on the market, what with the simultaneous decline of chivalry, the marriage rate and professional prostitution. She had seen too many elderly, white-haired Caucasian females scrubbing floors and toiling in sculleries not to know what being just another white woman meant. Yet she admitted to herself that it would be nice to get over being the butt for jokes and petty prejudice.

The Madame was in a quandary and so also were hundreds of others in the upper stratum of Harlem life. With the Negro masses moving out from under them, what other alternative did they have except to follow. True, only a few hundred Negroes had so far vanished from their wonted haunts, but it was known that thousands, tens of thousands, yes, millions would follow them.

Chapter Four

MATTHEW FISHER, alias Max Disher, joined the Easter Sunday crowds, twirling his malacca stick and ogling the pretty flappers who passed giggling in their Spring finery. For nearly three months he had idled around the Georgia capital hoping to catch a glimpse of the beautiful girl who on New Year's Eve had told him "I never dance with niggers." He had searched diligently in almost every stratum of Atlanta society, but he had failed to find her. There were hundreds of tall, beautiful, blonde maidens in the city; to seek a particular one whose name one did not know was somewhat akin to hunting for a Russian Jew in the Bronx or a particular Italian gunman in Chicago.

For three months he had dreamed of this girl, carefully perused the society columns of the local newspapers on the chance that her picture might appear in them. He was like most men who have been repulsed by a pretty girl, his desire for her grew stronger and stronger.

He was not finding life as a white man the rosy existence he had anticipated. He was forced to conclude that it was pretty dull and that he was bored. As a boy he had been taught to look up to white folks as just a little less than gods; now he found them little different from the Negroes, except that they were uniformly less courteous and less interesting.

Often when the desire for the happy-go-lucky, jovial good-fellowship of the Negroes came upon him strongly, he would go down to Auburn Avenue and stroll around the vicinity, looking at the dark folk and listening to their conversation and banter. But no one down there wanted him around. He was a white man and thus suspect. Only the black women who ran the "Call Houses" on the hill wanted his company. There was nothing left for him except the hard, materialistic, grasping, ill-bred society of the whites. Sometimes a slight feeling of regret that he had left his people forever would cross his mind, but it fled before the painful memories of past experiences in this, his home town.

The unreasoning and illogical color prejudice of most of the people with whom he was forced to associate, infuriated him. He often laughed cynically when some coarse, ignorant white man voiced his opinion concerning the inferior mentality and morality of the Negroes. He was moving in white society now and he could compare it with the society he had known as a Negro in Atlanta and Harlem. What a let-down it was from the good breeding, sophistication, refinement and gentle cynicism to which he had become accustomed as a popular young man about town in New York's Black Belt. He was not able to articulate this feeling but he was conscious of the reaction nevertheless.

For a week, now, he had been thinking seriously of going to work. His thousand dollars had dwindled to less than a hundred. He would have to find some source of income and yet the young white men with whom he talked about work all complained that it was very scarce. Being white, he finally concluded, was no Open Sesame to employment for he sought work in banks and insurance offices without success.

During his period of idleness and soft living, he had followed the news and opinion in the local daily press and confessed himself surprised at the antagonistic attitude of the newspapers toward Black-No-More, Incorporated. From the vantage point of having formerly been a Negro, he was able to see how the newspapers were fanning the color prejudice of the white people. Business men, he found were also bitterly opposed to Dr. Crookman and his efforts to bring about chromatic democracy in the nation.

The attitude of these people puzzled him. Was not Black-No-More getting rid of the Negroes upon whom all of the blame was placed for the backwardness of the South? Then he recalled what a Negro street speaker had said one night on the corner of 138th Street and Seventh Avenue in New York: that unorganized labor meant cheap labor; that the guarantee of cheap labor was an effective means of luring new industries into the South; that so long as the ignorant white masses could be kept thinking of the menace of the Negro to Caucasian race purity and political control, they would give little thought to labor organization. It suddenly dawned upon Matthew Fisher that this Black-No-More treatment was more of a menace to white business than to white labor. And not long afterward he became aware of the money-making possibilities involved in the present situation.

How could he work it? He was not known and he belonged to no organization. Here was a veritable gold mine but how could he reach the ore? He scratched his head over the problem but could think of no solution. Who would be interested in it that he could trust?

He was pondering this question the Monday after Easter while breakfasting in an armchair restaurant when he noticed an advertisement in a newspaper lying in the next chair. He read it and then re-read it

THE KNIGHTS OF NORDICA

Want 10,000 Atlanta White Men and Women to
Join in the Fight for White Race Integrity.

Imperial Klonklave Tonight

The racial integrity of the Caucasian Race is being
threatened by the activities of a scientific
black Beelzebub in New York

Let us Unite Now Before It Is

TOO LATE!

Come to Nordica Hall Tonight
Admission Free.
Rev. Henry Givens,
Imperial Grand Wizard

Here, Matthew figured, was just what he had been looking for. Probably he could get in with this fellow Givens. He finished his cup of coffee, lit a cigar and paying his check, strolled out into the sunshine of Peachtree Street.

He took the trolley out to Nordica Hall. It was a big, unpainted barn-like edifice, with a suite of offices in front and a huge auditorium in the rear. A new oil cloth sign reading "THE KNIGHTS OF NORDICA" was stretched across the front of the building.

Matthew paused for a moment and sized up the edifice.

Givens must have some money, he thought, to keep up such a large place. Might not be a bad idea to get a little dope on him before going inside.

"This fellow Givens is a pretty big guy around here, ain't he?" he asked the young man at the soda fountain across the street.

"Yessah, he's one o' th' bigges' men in this heah town. Used to be a big somethin' or other in th' old Ku Klux Klan 'fore it died. Now he's stahtin' this heah Knights o' Nordica."

"He must have pretty good jack," suggested Matthew.

"He oughtta have," answered the soda jerker. "My paw tells me he was close to th' money when he was in th' Klan."

Here, thought Matthew, was just the place for him. He paid for his soda and walked across the street to the door marked "Office." He felt a slight tremor of uneasiness as he turned the knob and entered. Despite his white skin he still possessed the fear of the Klan and kindred organizations possessed by most Negroes.

A rather pretty young stenographer asked him his business as he walked into the ante room. Better be bold, he thought. This was probably the best chance he would have to keep from working, and his funds were getting lower and lower.

"Please tell Rev. Givens, the Imperial Grand Wizard, that Mr. Matthew Fisher of the New York Anthropological Society is very anxious to have about a half-hour's conversation with him relative to his new venture." Matthew spoke in an impressive, businesslike manner, rocked back on his heels and looked profound.

"Yassah," almost whispered the awed young lady, "I'll tell him." She withdrew into an inner office and Matthew chuckled softly to himself. He wondered if he could impress this old fakir as easily as he had the girl.

Rev. Henry Givens, Imperial Grand Wizard of the Knights of Nordica, was a short, wizened, almost-bald, bull-voiced, ignorant ex-evangelist, who had come originally from the hilly country north of Atlanta. He had helped in the organization of the Ku Klux Klan following the Great War and had worked with a zeal only equalled by his thankfulness to God for escaping from the precarious existence of an itinerant saver of souls.

Not only had the Rev. Givens toiled diligently to increase the prestige, power and membership of the defunct Ku Klux Klan, but he had also been a very hard worker in withdrawing as much money from its treasury as possible. He convinced himself, as did the other officers, that this stealing was not stealing at all but merely appropriation of rightful reward for his valuable services. When the morons finally tired of supporting the show and the stream of ten-dollar memberships declined to a trickle, Givens had been able to retire gracefully and live on the interest of his money.

Then, when the newspapers began to recount the activities of Black-No-More, Incorporated, he saw a vision of work to be done, and founded the Knights of Nordica. So far there were only a hundred members but he had high hopes for the future. Tonight, he felt would tell the story. The prospect of a full treasury to dip into again made his little gray eyes twinkle and the palms of his skinny hands itch.

The stenographer interrupted him to announce the newcomer.

"Hum-n!" said Givens, half to himself. "New York Anthropological Society, eh? This feller must know somethin'. Might be able to use him in this business. . . . All right, show him in!"

The two men shook hands and swiftly appraised each other. Givens waved Matthew to a chair.

"How can I serve you, Mr. Fisher?" he began in sepulchral tone dripping with unction.

"It is rather," countered Matthew in his best salesman's croon, "how I can serve you and your valuable organization. As an anthropologist, I have, of course, been long interested in the work with which you have been identified. It has always seemed to me that there was no question in American life more important than that of preserving the integrity of the white race. We all know what has been the fate of those nations that have permitted their blood to be polluted with that of inferior breeds." (He had read some argument like that in a Sunday supplement not long before, which was the extent of his knowledge of anthropology.) "This latest menace of Black-No-More is the most formidable the white people of America have had to face since the founding of the Republic. As a resident of New York City, I am aware, of course, of the extent of the activities of this Negro Crookman and his two associates. Already thousands of blacks have passed over into the white race. Not satisfied with operating in New York City, they have opened their sanitariums in twenty other cities from Coast to Coast. They open a new one almost every day. In their literature and advertisements in the darky newspapers they boast that they are now turning four thousand Negroes white every day." He knitted his blond eyebrows. "You see how great the menace is? At this rate there will not be a Negro in the country in ten years, for you must remember that the rate is increasing every day as new sanitariums are opened. Don't you see that something must be done about this immediately? Don't you see that Congress must be aroused; that these places must be closed?" The young man glared with belligerent indignation.

Rev. Givens saw. He nodded his head as Matthew, now glorying in his newly-discovered eloquence made point after point, and concluded that this pale, dapper young fellow, with his ready tongue, his sincerity, his scientific training and knowledge of the situation ought to prove a valuable asset to the Knights of Nordica.

"I tried to interest some agencies in New York," Matthew continued, "but they are all blind to this menace and to their duty. Then someone told me of you and your valuable work, and I decided to come down here and have a talk with you. I had intended to suggest the organization of some such militant secret order as you have started, but since you've already seen the necessity for it, I want to hasten to offer my services as a scientific man and one familiar with the facts and able to present them to your members."

"I should be very glad," boomed Givens, "very happy, indeed, Brother Fisher, to have you join us. We need you. I believe you can help us a great deal. Would you, er—ah, be interested in coming out to the mass meeting this evening? It would help us tremendously to get members if you would be willing to get up and tell the audience what you have just related about the progress of this iniquitous nigger corporation in New York."

Matthew pretended to think over the matter for a moment or two and then agreed. If he made a hit at the initial meeting, he would be sure to get on the staff. Once there he could go after the larger game. Unlike Givens, he had no belief in the racial integrity nonsense nor any confidence in the white masses whom he thought were destined to flock to the Knights of Nordica. On the contrary he despised and hated them. He had the average Negro's justifiable fear of the poor whites and only planned to use them as a stepladder to the real money.

When Matthew left, Givens congratulated himself upon the fact that he had been able to attract such talent to the organization in its very infancy. His ideas must be sound, he concluded, if scientists from New York were impressed by them. He reached over, pulled the dictionary stand toward him and opened the big book at A.

"Lemme see, now," he muttered aloud. "Anthropology. Better git that word straight 'fore I go talkin' too much about it. . . . Humn! Humn! . . . That boy must know a hull lot." He read over the definition of the word twice without understanding it, closed the dictionary, pushed it away from him, and then cutting off a large chew of tobacco from his plug, he leaned back in his swivel chair to rest after the unaccustomed mental exertion.

Matthew went gaily back to his hotel. "Man alive!" he chortled to himself. "What a lucky break! Can't keep old Max down long. . . . Will I speak to 'em? Well, I won't stay quiet!" He felt so delighted over the prospect of getting close to some real money that he treated himself to an expensive dinner and a twenty-five-cent cigar. Afterward he inquired further about old man Givens from the house detective, a native Atlantan.

"Oh, he's well heeled—the old crook!" remarked the detective. "Damnify could ever understand how such ignorant people get a-hold of th' money; but there y'are. Owns as pretty a home as you can find around these parts an' damn 'f he ain't stahtin' a new racket."

"Do you think he'll make anything out of it?" inquired Matthew, innocently.

"Say, Brother, you mus' be a stranger in these parts. These damn, ignorant crackers will fall fer anything fer a while. They ain't had no Klan here fer goin' on three years. Leastwise it ain't been functionin'." The old fellow chuckled and spat a

stream of tobacco juice into a nearby cuspidor. Matthew sauntered away. Yes, the pickings ought to be good.

Equally enthusiastic was the Imperial Grand Wizard when
he came home to dinner that night. He entered the house humming one of his favorite hymns and his wife looked up from
the evening paper with surprise on her face. The Rev. Givens
was usually something of a grouch but tonight he was as happy
as a pickpocket at a country fair.

"What's th' mattah with you?" she inquired, sniffing suspiciously.

"Oh, Honey," he gurgled, "I think this here Knights of
Nordica is going over big; going over big! My fame is spreading. Only today I had a long talk with a famous anthropologist
from New York and he's going to address our mass meeting
tonight."

"Whut's an anthropologist?" asked Mrs. Givens, wrinkling
her seamy brow.

"Oh-er, well; he's one of these here scientists what knows all
about this here business what's going on up there in New York
where them niggers is turning each other white," explained
Rev. Givens hastily but firmly. "He's a mighty smaht feller and
I want you and Helen to come out and hear him."

"B'lieve Ah will," declared Mrs. Givens, "if this heah rheumatism'll le' me foh a while. Doan know 'bout Helen, though.
Evah since that gal went away tuh school she ain't bin int'rested
in nuthin' up-liftin'!"

Mrs. Givens spoke in a grieved tone and heaved her narrow
chest in a deep sigh. She didn't like all this newfangled foolishness of these young folks. They were getting away from God,
that's what they were, and she didn't like it. Mrs. Givens was a
Christian. There was no doubt about it because she freely admitted it to everybody, with or without provocation. Of course
she often took the name of the Creator in vain when she got to
quarreling with Henry; she had the reputation among her
friends of not always stating the exact truth; she hated Negroes;
her spouse had made bitter and profane comment concerning
her virginity on their wedding night; and as head of the ladies'
auxiliary of the defunct Klan she had copied her husband's financial methods; but that she was a devout Christion no one

doubted. She believed the Bible from cover to cover, except what it said about people with money, and she read it every evening aloud, greatly to the annoyance of the Imperial Grand Wizard and his modern and comely daughter.

Mrs. Givens had probably once been beautiful but the wear and tear of a long life as the better half of an itinerant evangelist was apparent. Her once flaming red hair was turning gray and roan-like, her hatchet face was a criss-cross of wrinkles and lines, she was round-shouldered, hollow-chested, walked with a stoop and her long, bony, white hands looked like claws. She alternately dipped snuff and smoked an evil-smelling clay pipe, except when there was company at the house. At such times Helen would insist her mother "act like civilized people."

Helen was twenty and quite confident that she herself was civilized. Whether she was or not, she was certainly beautiful. Indeed, she was such a beauty that many of the friends of the family insisted that she must have been adopted. Taller than either of her parents, she was stately, erect, well proportioned, slender, vivid and knew how to wear her clothes. In only one way did she resemble her parents and that was in things intellectual. Any form of mental effort, she complained, made her head ache, and so her parents had always let her have her way about studying.

At the age of eleven she had been taken from the third grade in public school and sent to an exclusive seminary for the double purpose of gaining social prestige and concealing her mental incapacity. At sixteen when her instructors had about despaired of her, they were overjoyed by the decision of her father to send the girl to a "finishing school" in the North. The "finishing school" about finished what intelligence Helen possessed; but she came forth, four years later, more beautiful, with a better knowledge of how to dress and how to act in exclusive society, enough superficialities to enable her to get by in the "best" circles and a great deal of that shallow facetiousness that passes for sophistication in American upper-class life. A winter in Manhattan had rounded out her education. Now she was back home, thoroughly ashamed of her grotesque parents, and, like the other girls of her set, anxious to get a husband who at the same time was handsome, intelligent, educated, refined and rolling in wealth. As she was ignorant of the fact that no such man existed, she looked confidently forward into the future.

"I don't care to go down there among all those gross people," she informed her father at the dinner table when he broached the subject of the meeting. "They're so crude and el-emental, don't you know," she explained, arching her narrow eyebrows.

"The common people are the salt of the earth," boomed Rev. Givens. "If it hadn't been for the common people we wouldn't have been able to get this home and send you off to school. You make me sick with all your modern ideas. You'd do a lot better if you'd try to be more like your Ma."

Both Mrs. Givens and Helen looked quickly at him to see if he was smiling. He wasn't.

"Why don'tcha go, Helen?" pleaded Mrs. Givens. "Yo fathah sez this heah man f'm N'Yawk is uh—uh scientist or somethin' an' knows a whole lot about things. Yuh might l'arn somethin'. Ah'd go mys'f if 'twasn't fo mah rheumatism." She sighed in self-pity and finished gnawing a drumstick.

Helen's curiosity was aroused and although she didn't like the idea of sitting among a lot of mill hands, she was anxious to see and hear this reputedly brilliant young man from the great metropolis where not long before she had lost both her provincialism and chastity.

"Oh, all right," she assented with mock reluctance. "I'll go."

The Knights of Nordica's flag-draped auditorium slowly filled. It was a bare, cavernous structure, with sawdust on the floor, a big platform at one end, row after row of folding wooden chairs and illuminated by large, white lights hanging from the rafters. On the platform was a row of five chairs, the center one being high-backed and gilded. On the lectern downstage was a bulky bible. A huge American flag was stretched across the rear wall.

The audience was composed of the lower stratum of white working people: hard-faced, lantern-jawed, dull-eyed adult children, seeking like all humanity for something permanent in the eternal flux of life. The young girls in their cheap finery with circus makeup on their faces; the young men, aged be-fore their time by child labor and a violent environment; the middle-aged folk with their shiny, shabby garb and beaten countenances; all ready and eager to be organized for any purpose except improvement of their intellects and standard of living.

Rev. Givens opened the meeting with a prayer "for the success, O God, of this thy work, to protect the sisters and wives and daughters of these, thy people, from the filthy pollution of an alien race."

A choir of assorted types of individuals sang "Onward Christian Soldiers" earnestly, vociferously and badly.

They were about to file off the platform when the song leader, a big, beefy, jovial mountain of a man, leaped upon the stage and restrained them.

"Wait a minute, folks, wait a minute," he commanded. Then turning to the assemblage: "Now people let's put some pep into this. We wanna all be happy and get in th' right spirit for this heah meetin'. Ah'm gonna ask the choir to sing th' first and last verses ovah ag'in, and when they come to th' chorus, Ah wantcha to all join in. Doan be 'fraid. Jesus wouldn't be 'fraid to sing 'Onward Christian Soldiers,' now would he? Come on, then. All right, choir, you staht; an' when Ah wave mah han' you'all join in on that theah chorus."

They obediently followed his directions while he marched up and down the platform, red-faced and roaring and waving his arms in time. When the last note had died away, he dismissed the choir and stepping to the edge of the stage he leaned far out over the audience and barked at them again.

"Come on, now, folks! Yuh caint slow up on Jesus now. He won't be satisfied with jus' one ole measly song. Yuh gotta let 'im know that yuh love 'im; that y're happy an' contented; that yuh ain't got no troubles an' ain't gonna have any. Come on, now. Le's sing that ole favorite what yo'all like so well: 'Pack Up Your Troubles in Your Old Kit Bag and Smile, Smile, Smile.'" He bellowed and they followed him. Again the vast hall shook with sound. He made them rise and grasp each other by the hand until the song ended.

Matthew, who sat on the platform alongside old man Givens, viewed the spectacle with amusement mingled with amazement. He was amused because of the similarity of this meeting to the religious orgies of the more ignorant Negroes and amazed that earlier in the evening he should have felt any qualms about lecturing to these folks on anthropology, a subject with which neither he nor his hearers were acquainted. He quickly saw that these people would believe anything that was shouted at them loudly and convincingly enough. He knew what would fetch their applause and bring in their memberships and he intended to repeat it over and over.

The Imperial Grand Wizard spent a half-hour introducing the speaker of the evening, dwelt upon his supposed scholastic attainments, but took pains to inform them that, despite Matthew's vast knowledge, he still believed in the Word of God, the sanctity of womanhood and the purity of the white race.

For an hour Matthew told them at the top of his voice what they believed: i.e., that a white skin was a sure indication of the possession of superior intellectual and moral qualities; that all Negroes were inferior to them; that God had intended for the United States to be a white man's country and that with His help they could keep it so; that their sons and brothers might inadvertently marry Negresses or, worse, their sisters and daughters might marry Negroes, if Black-No-More, Incorporated, was permitted to continue its dangerous activities.

For an hour he spoke, interrupted at intervals by enthusiastic gales of applause, and as he spoke his eye wandered over the females in the audience, noting the comeliest ones. As he wound up with a spirited appeal for eager soldiers to join the Knights of Nordica at five dollars per head and the half-dozen "planted" emissaries led the march of suckers to the platform, he noted for the first time a girl who sat in the front row and gazed up at him raptly.

She was a titian blonde, well-dressed, beautiful and strangely familiar. As he retired amid thunderous applause to make way for Rev. Givens and the money collectors, he wondered where he had seen her before. He studied her from his seat.

Suddenly he knew. It was she! The girl who had spurned him; the girl he had sought so long; the girl he wanted more than anything in the world! Strange that she should be here. He had always thought of her as a refined, educated and wealthy lady, far above associating with such people as these.

He was in a fever to meet her, some way, before she got out of his sight again, and yet he felt just a little disappointed to find her here.

He could hardly wait until Givens seated himself again before questioning him as to the girl's identity. As the beefy song leader led the roaring of the popular closing hymn, he leaned toward the Imperial Grand Wizard and shouted: "Who is that tall golden-haired girl sitting in the front row? Do you know her?"

Rev. Givens looked out over the audience, craning his skinny neck and blinking his eyes. Then he saw the girl, sitting within twenty feet of him.

"You mean that girl sitting right in front, there?" he asked, pointing.

"Yes, that one," said Matthew, impatiently.

"Heh! Heh! Heh!" chuckled the Wizard, rubbing his stubbly chin. "Why that there's my daughter, Helen. Like to meet her?"

Matthew could hardly believe his ears. Givens's daughter! Incredible! What a coincidence! What luck! Would he like to meet her? He leaned over and shouted "Yes."

Chapter Five

A HUGE silver monoplane glided gracefully to the surface of Mines Field in Los Angeles and came to a pretty stop after a short run. A liveried footman stepped out of the forward compartment armed with a stool which he placed under the rear door. Simultaneously a high-powered foreign car swept up close to the airplane and waited. The rear door of the airplane opened, and to the apparent surprise of the nearby mechanics a tall, black, distinguished-looking Negro stepped out and down to the ground, assisted by the hand of the footman. Behind him came a pale young man and woman, evidently secretaries. The three entered the limousine which rapidly drove off.

"Who's that coon?" asked one of the mechanics, round-eyed and respectful, like all Americans, in the presence of great wealth.

"Don't you know who that is?" inquired another, pityingly. "Why that's that Dr. Crookman. You know, the fellow what's turnin' niggers white. See that B N M on the side of his plane? That stands for Black-No-More. Gee, but I wish I had just half the jack he's made in the last six months!"

"Why I thought from readin' th' papers," protested the first speaker, "that th' law had closed up his places and put 'im outta business."

"Oh, that's a lotta hockey," said the other fellow. "Why just yesterday th' newspapers said that Black-No-More was openin' a place on Central Avenue. They already got one in Oakland, so a coon told me yesterday."

"'Sfunny," ventured a third mechanic, as they wheeled the big plane into a nearby hangar, "how he don't have nuthin' but white folks around him. He must not like nigger help. His chauffeur's white, his footman's white an' that young gal and feller what was with him are white."

"How do you know?" challenged the first speaker. "They may be darkies that he's turned into white folks."

"That's right," the other replied. "It's gittin' so yuh can't tell who's who. I think that there Knights of Nordica ought to do something about it. I joined up with 'em two months ago but they ain't done nuthin' but sell me an ole uniform an' hold a coupla meetin's."

They lapsed into silence. Sandol, the erstwhile Senegalese, stepped from the cockpit grinning. "Ah, zese Americains," he muttered to himself as he went over the engine, examining everything minutely.

"Where'd yuh come from, buddy?" asked one of the mechanics.

"Den-vair," Sandol replied.

"Whatcha doin', makin' a trip around th' country?" queried another.

"Yes, we air, what you callem, on ze tour inspectione," the aviator continued. They could think of no more to say and soon strolled off.

Around an oval table on the seventh floor of a building on Central Avenue, sat Dr. Junius Crookman, Hank Johnson, Chuck Foster, Ranford the Doctor's secretary and four other men. At the lower end of the table Miss Bennett, Ranford's stenographer, was taking notes. A soft-treading waiter whose Negro nature was only revealed by his mocking obsequiousness, served each with champagne.

"To our continued success!" cried the physician, lifting his glass high.

"To our continued success!" echoed the others.

They drained their glasses, and returned them to the polished surface of the table.

"Dog bite it, Doc!" blurted Johnson. "Us sho is doin' fine. Ain't had a bad break since we stahted, an' heah 'tis th' fust o' September."

"Don't holler too soon," cautioned Foster. "The opposition is growing keener every day. I had to pay seventy-five thousand dollars more for this building than it's worth."

"Well, yuh got it, didn't yuh?" asked Johnson. "Just like Ah allus say: when yuh got money yuh kin git anything in this man's country. Whenever things look tight jes pull out th' ole check book an' eve'ything's all right."

"Optimist!" grunted Foster.

"I ain't no pess'mist," Johnson accused.

"Now gentlemen," Dr. Crookman interrupted, clearing his throat, "let's get down to business. We have met here, as you know, not only for the purpose of celebrating the opening of this, our fiftieth sanitarium, but also to take stock of our situation. I have before me here a detailed report of our business affairs for the entire period of seven months and a half that we've been in operation.

"During that time we have put into service fifty sanitariums from Coast to Coast, or an average of one every four and one-half days, the average capacity of each sanitarium being one hundred and five patients. Each place has a staff of six physicians and twenty-four nurses, a janitor, four orderlies, two electricians, bookkeeper, cashier, stenographer and record clerk, not counting four guards.

"For the past four months we have had an equipment factory in Pittsburgh in full operation and a chemical plant in Philadelphia. In addition to this we have purchased four airplanes and a radio broadcasting station. Our expenditures for real estate, salaries and chemicals have totaled six million, two hundred and fifty-five thousand, eighty-five dollars and ten cents." . . .

"He! He!" chuckled Johnson. "Dat ten cents mus' be fo' one o' them bad ceegars that Fostah smokes."

"Our total income," continued Dr. Crookman, frowning slightly at the interruption, "has been eighteen million, five hundred thousand, three hundred dollars, or three hundred and seventy thousand and six patients at fifty dollars apiece. I think that vindicates my contention at the beginning that the fee should be but fifty dollars—within the reach of the rank and file of Negroes." He laid aside his report and added:

"In the next four months we'll double our output and by the end of the year we should cut the fee to twenty-five dollars," he lightly twirled his waxed mustache between his long sensitive fingers and smiled with satisfaction.

"Yes," said Foster, "the sooner we get this business over with the better. We're going to run into a whole lot more opposition from now on than we have so far encountered."

"Why man!" growled Johnson, "we ain't even stahted on

dese darkies yet. And when we git thu wi' dese heah, we kin work on them in th' West Indies. Believe me, Ah doan *nevah* want dis graft tuh end."

"Now," continued Dr. Crookman, "I want to say that Mr. Foster deserves great praise for the industry and ingenuity he has shown in purchasing our real estate and Mr. Johnson deserves equally great praise for the efficient manner in which he has kept down the opposition of the various city officials. As you know, he has spent nearly a million dollars in such endeavors and almost as much again in molding legislative sentiment in Washington and the various state capitals. That accounts for the fact that every bill introduced in a legislature or municipal council to put us out of business has died in committee. Moreover, through his corps of secret operatives, who are mostly young women, he has placed numbers of officials and legislators in a position where they cannot openly oppose our efforts."

A smile of appreciation went around the circle.

"We'll have a whole lot to do from now on," commented Foster.

"Yeh, Big Boy," replied the ex-gambler, "an' whut it takes tuh do it Ah ain't got nuthin' else but!"

"Certainly," said the physician, "our friend Hank has not been overburdened with scruples."

"Ah doan know whut dat is, Chief," grinned Johnson, "but Ah knows whut a check book'll do. Even these crackers tone down when Ah talks bucks."

"This afternoon," continued Crookman, "we also have with us our three regional directors, Doctors Henry Dogan, Charles Hinckle and Fred Selden, as well as our chief chemist, Wallace Butts. I thought it would be a good idea to bring you all together for this occasion so we could get better acquainted. We'll just have a word from each of them. They're all good Race men, you know, even if they have, like the rest of our staff, taken the treatment."

For the next three-quarters of an hour the three directors and the chief chemist reported on the progress of their work. At intervals the waiter brought in cold drinks, cigars and cigarettes. Overhead whirred the electric fans. Out of the wide open windows could be seen the panorama of bungalows, pavements, palm trees, trundling street cars and scooting automobiles.

"Lawd! Lawd! Lawd!" Johnson exclaimed at the conclusion of the meeting, going to the window and gazing out over the city. "Jes gimme a coupla yeahs o' dis graft an' Ah'll make Henry Foahd look like a tramp."

Meanwhile, Negro society was in turmoil and chaos. The colored folk in straining every nerve to get the Black-No-More treatment, had forgotten all loyalties, affiliations and responsibilities. No longer did they flock to the churches on Sundays or pay dues in their numerous fraternal organizations. They had stopped giving anything to the Anti-Lynching campaign. Santop Licorice, head of the once-flourishing Back-To-Africa Society, was daily raising his stentorian voice in denunciation of the race for deserting his organization.

Negro business was being no less hard hit. Few people were bothering about getting their hair straightened or skin whitened temporarily when for a couple of weeks' pay they could get both jobs done permanently. The immediate result of this change of mind on the part of the Negro public was to almost bankrupt the firms that made the whitening and straightening chemicals. They were largely controlled by canny Hebrews, but at least a half-dozen were owned by Negroes. The rapid decline in this business greatly decreased the revenue of the Negro weekly newspapers who depended upon such advertising for their sustenance. The actual business of hair straightening that had furnished employment to thousands of colored women who would otherwise have had to go back to washing and ironing, declined to such an extent that "To Rent" signs hung in front of nine-tenths of the shops.

The Negro politicians in the various Black Belts, grown fat and sleek "protecting" vice with the aid of Negro votes which they were able to control by virtue of housing segregation, lectured in vain about black solidarity, race pride and political emancipation; but nothing stopped the exodus to the white race. Gloomily the politicians sat in their offices, wondering whether to throw up the sponge and hunt the nearest Black-No-More sanitarium or hold on a little longer in the hope that

the whites might put a stop to the activities of Dr. Crookman
and his associates. The latter, indeed, was their only hope because the bulk of Negroes, saving their dimes and dollars for
chromatic emancipation, had stopped gambling, patronizing
houses of prostitution or staging Saturday-night brawls. Thus
the usual sources of graft vanished. The black politicians appealed to their white masters for succor, of course, but they
found to their dismay that most of the latter had been safely
bribed by the astute Hank Johnson.

Gone was the almost European atmosphere of every Negro
ghetto: the music, laughter, gaiety, jesting and abandon.
Instead, one noted the same excited bustle, wild looks and
strained faces to be seen in a war time soldier camp, around a
new oil district or before a gold rush. The happy-go-lucky
Negro of song and story was gone forever and in his stead was
a nervous, money-grubbing black, stuffing away coin in socks,
impatiently awaiting a sufficient sum to pay Dr. Crookman's fee.

Up from the South they came in increasing droves, besieg-
ing the Black-No-More sanitariums for treatment. There were
none of these havens in the South because of the hostility of
the bulk of white people but there were many all along the
border between the two sections, at such places as Washington,
D. C., Baltimore, Cincinnati, Louisville, Evansville, Cairo, St.
Louis and Denver. The various Southern communities attempted to stem this, the greatest migration of Negroes in the
history of the country, but without avail. By train, boat, wagon,
bicycle, automobile and foot they trekked to the promised
land; a hopeful procession, filtering through the outposts of
police and Knights of Nordica volunteer bands. Where there
was great opposition to the Negroes' going, there would suddenly appear large quantities of free bootleg liquor and crisp
new currency which would make the most vigilant white
opponent of Black-No-More turn his head the other way.
Hank Johnson seemed to be able to cope with almost every
situation.

The national office of the militant Negro organization, the
National Social Equality League, was agog. Telephone bells
were ringing, mulatto clerks were hustling excitedly back and
forth, messenger boys rushed in and out. Located in the Times

Square district of Manhattan, it had for forty years carried on the fight for full social equality for the Negro citizens and the immediate abolition of lynching as a national sport. While this organization had to depend to a large extent upon the charity of white folk for its existence, since the blacks had always been more or less skeptical about the program for liberty and freedom, the efforts of the society were not entirely unprofitable. Vistas of immaculate offices spread in every direction from the elevator and footfalls were muffled in thick imitation-Persian rugs. While the large staff of officials was eager to end all oppression and persecution of the Negro, they were never so happy and excited as when a Negro was barred from a theater or fried to a crisp. Then they would leap for telephones, grab telegraph pads and yell for stenographers; smiling through their simulated indignation at the spectacle of another reason for their continued existence and appeals for funds.

Ever since the first sanitarium of Black-No-More, Incorporated, started turning Negroes into Caucasians, the National Social Equality League's income had been decreasing. No dues had been collected in months and subscriptions to the national mouthpiece, *The Dilemma*, had dwindled to almost nothing. Officials, long since ensconced in palatial apartments, began to grow panic-stricken as pay days got farther apart. They began to envision the time when they would no longer be able for the sake of the Negro race to suffer the hardships of lunching on canvasback duck at the Urban Club surrounded by the white dilettante, endure the perils of first-class Transatlantic passage to stage Save-Dear-Africa Conferences or undergo the excruciating torture of rolling back and forth across the United States in drawing-rooms to hear each other lecture on the Negro problem. On meager salaries of five thousand dollars a year they had fought strenuously and tirelessly to obtain for the Negroes the constitutional rights which only a few thousand rich white folk possessed. And now they saw the work of a lifetime being rapidly destroyed.

Single-handed they felt incapable of organizing an effective opposition to Black-No-More, Incorporated, so they had called a conference of all of the outstanding Negro leaders of the country to assemble at the League's headquarters on December 1, 1933. Getting the Negro leaders together for any purpose except boasting of each other's accomplishments had previously been impossible. As a usual thing they fought each other with a vigor only surpassed by that of their pleas for racial solidarity and unity of action. This situation, however, was unprecedented, so almost all of the representative gentlemen of color to whom invitations had been sent agreed with alacrity to come. To a man they felt that it was time to bury the hatchet before they became too hungry to do any digging.

In a very private inner office of the N. S. E. L. suite, Dr. Shakespeare Agamemnon Beard, founder of the League and a graduate of Harvard, Yale and Copenhagen (whose haughty bearing never failed to impress both Caucasians and Negroes) sat before a glass-topped desk, rubbing now his curly gray head, and now his full spade beard. For a mere six thousand dollars a year, the learned doctor wrote scholarly and biting editorials in *The Dilemma* denouncing the Caucasians whom he secretly admired and lauding the greatness of the Negroes whom he alternately pitied and despised. In limpid prose he told of the sufferings and privations of the downtrodden black workers with whose lives he was totally and thankfully unfamiliar. Like most Negro leaders, he deified the black woman but abstained from employing aught save octoroons. He talked at white banquets about "we of the black race" and admitted in books that he was part-French, part-Russian, part-Indian and part-Negro. He bitterly denounced the Nordics for debauching Negro women while taking care to hire comely yellow stenographers with weak resistance. In a real way, he loved his people. In time of peace he was a Pink Socialist but when the clouds of war gathered he bivouacked at the feet of Mars.

Before the champion of the darker races lay a neatly typed resolution drawn up by him and his staff the day before and addressed to the Attorney General of the United States. The staff had taken this precaution because no member of it believed that the other Negro leaders possessed sufficient education to word the document effectively and grammatically. Dr. Beard re-read the resolution and then placing it in the drawer of the desk, pressed one of a row of buttons. "Tell them to come in," he directed. The mulattress turned and switched out of the room, followed by the appraising and approving eye of the aged scholar. He heaved a regretful sigh as the door closed and his thoughts dwelt on the vigor of his youth.

In three or four minutes the door opened again and several well-dressed blacks, mulattoes and white men entered the large office and took seats around the wall. They greeted each other and the President of the League with usual cordiality but for the first time in their lives they were sincere about it. If anyone could save the day it was Beard. They all admitted that, as did the Doctor himself. They pulled out fat cigars, long slender cigarettes and London briar pipes, lit them and awaited the opening of the conference.

The venerable lover of his race tapped with his knuckle for order, laid aside his six-inch cigarette and rising, said:

"It were quite unseemly for me who lives such a cloistered life and am spared the bane or benefit of many intimate contacts with those of our struggling race who by sheer courage, tenacity and merit have lifted their heads above the mired mass, to deign to take from a more capable individual the unpleasant task of reviewing the combination of unfortunate circumstances that has brought us together, man to man, within the four walls of the office." He shot a foxy glance around the assembly and then went on suavely. "And so, my friends, I beg your august permission to confer upon my able and cultured secretary and confidant, Dr. Napoleon Wellington Jackson, the office of chairman of this temporary body. I need not introduce Dr. Jackson to you. You know of his scholarship, his high sense of duty and his deep love of the suffering black race. You have doubtless had the pleasure of singing some of the many sorrow songs he has written and popularized in the past twenty years, and you must know of his fame as a translator of Latin poets and his authoritative work on the Greek language.

"Before I gratefully yield the floor to Dr. Jackson, however, I want to tell you that our destiny lies in the stars. Ethiopia's fate is in the balance. The Goddess of the Nile weeps bitter tears at the feet of the Great Sphinx. The lowering clouds gather over the Congo and the lightning flashes o'er Togoland. To your tents, O Israel! The hour is at hand."

The president of the N. S. E. L. sat down and the erudite Dr. Jackson, his tall, lanky secretary got up. There was no fear of Dr. Jackson ever winning a beauty contest. He was a sooty black, very broad shouldered, with long, ape-like arms, a diminutive egg-shaped head that sat on his collar like a hen's egg on a demitasse cup and eyes that protruded so far from his head that they seemed about to fall out. He wore pince-nez that were continually slipping from his very flat and oily nose. His chief business in the organization was to write long and indignant letters to public officials and legislators whenever a Negro was mistreated, demanding justice, fair play and other legal guarantees vouchsafed no whites except bloated plutocrats fallen miraculously afoul of the law, and to speak to audiences of sex-starved matrons who yearned to help the Negro stand erect. During his leisure time, which was naturally considerable, he wrote long and learned articles, bristling with references, for the more intellectual magazines, in which he sought to prove conclusively that the plantation shouts of Southern Negro peons were superior to any of Beethoven's symphonies and that the city of Benin was the original site of the Garden of Eden.

"Hhmm! Hu-umn! Now er—ah, gentlemen," began Dr. Jackson, rocking back on his heels, taking off his eye glasses and beginning to polish them with a silk kerchief, "as you know, the Negro race is face to face with a grave crisis. I-ah-presume it is er-ah unnecessary for me to go into any details concerning the-ah activities of Black-No-More, Incorporated. Suffice er-ah umph! ummmmh! to say-ah that it has thrown our society into rather a-ah bally turmoil. Our people are forgetting shamelessly their-ah duty to the-ah organizations that have fought valiantly for them these-ah many years and are now busily engaged chasing a bally-ah will-o-the wisp. Ahem!

"You-ah probably all fully realize that-ah a continuation of the aforementioned activities will prove disastrous to our-ah organizations. You-ah, like us, must feel-uh that something drastic must be done to preserve the integrity of Negro society. Think, gentlemen, what the future will mean to-uh all those who-uh have toiled so hard for Negro society. What-ah, may I ask, will we do when there are no longer any-ah groups to support us? Of course, Dr. Crookman and-ah his associates have a-uh perfect right to-ah engage in any legitimate business, but-ah their present activities cannot-ah be classed under that head, considering the effect on our endeavors. Before we go any further, however, I-ah would like to introduce our research expert Mr. Walter Williams, who will-ah describe the situation in the South."

Mr. Walter Williams, a tall, heavy-set white man with pale blue eyes, wavy auburn hair and a militant, lantern jaw, rose and bowed to the assemblage and proceeded to paint a heartrending picture of the loss of pride and race solidarity among Negroes North and South. There was, he said, not a single local of the N. S. E. L. functioning, dues had dwindled to nothing, he had not been able to hold a meeting anywhere, while many of the stanchest supporters had gone over into the white race.

"Personally," he concluded, "I am very proud to be a Negro and always have been (his great-grandfather, it seemed, had been a mulatto), and I'm willing to sacrifice for the uplift of my race. I cannot understand what has come over our people that they have so quickly forgotten the ancient glories of Ethiopia, Songhay and Dahomey, and their marvelous record of achievement since emancipation." Mr. Williams was known to be a Negro among his friends and acquaintances, but no one else would have suspected it.

Another white man of remote Negro ancestry, Rev. Herbert Gronne of Dunbar University, followed the research expert with a long discourse in which he expressed fear for the future of his institution whose student body had been reduced to sixty-five persons and deplored the catastrophe "that has befallen us black people."

They all listened with respect to Dr. Gronne. He had been in turn a college professor, a social worker and a minister, had received the approval of the white folks and was thus doubly acceptable to the Negroes. Much of his popularity was due to the fact that he very cleverly knew how to make statements that sounded radical to Negroes but sufficiently conservative to satisfy the white trustees of his school. In addition he possessed the asset of looking perpetually earnest and sincere.

Following him came Colonel Mortimer Roberts, principal of the Dusky River Agricultural Institute, Supreme General of the Knights and Daughters of Kingdom Come and president of the Uncle Tom Memorial Association. Colonel Roberts was the acknowledged leader of the conservative Negroes (most of whom had nothing to conserve) who felt at all times that the white folks were in the lead and that Negroes should be careful to guide themselves accordingly.

He was a great mountain of blackness with a head shaped like an upturned bucket, pierced by two pig-like eyes and a cavernous mouth equipped with large tombstone teeth which he almost continually displayed. His speech was a cross between the woofing of a bloodhound and the explosion of an inner tube. It conveyed to most white people an impression of rugged simplicity and sincerity, which was very fortunate since Colonel Roberts maintained his school through their contributions. He spoke as usual about the cordial relations existing between the two races in his native Georgia, the effrontery of Negroes who dared whiten themselves and thus disturb the minds of white people and insinuated alliance with certain militant organizations in the South to stop this whitening business before it went too far. Having spoken his mind and received scant applause, Colonel (some white man had once called him Colonel and the title stuck) puffing and bowing, sat down.

Mr. Claude Spelling, a scared-looking little brown man with big ears, who held the exalted office of president of the Society of Negro Merchants, added his volume of blues to the discussion. The refrain was that Negro business—always anemic—was about to pass out entirely through lack of patronage. Mr. Spelling had for many years been the leading advocate of the strange doctrine that an underpaid Negro worker should go out of his way to patronize a little dingy Negro store instead of going to a cheaper and cleaner chain store, all for the dubious satisfaction of helping Negro merchants grow wealthy.

The next speaker, Dr. Joseph Bonds, a little rat-faced Negro with protruding teeth stained by countless plugs of chewing tobacco and wearing horn-rimmed spectacles, who headed the Negro Data League, almost cried (which would have been terrible to observe) when he told of the difficulty his workers had encountered in their efforts to persuade retired white capitalists, whose guilty consciences persuaded them to indulge in philanthropy, to give their customary donations to the work. The philanthropists seemed to think, said Dr. Bonds, that since the Negroes were busily solving their difficulties, there was no need for social work among them or any collection of data. He almost sobbed aloud when he described how his collections had fallen from $50,000 a month to less than $1000.

His feeling in the matter could easily be appreciated. He was engaged in a most vital and necessary work: i.e., collecting bales of data to prove satisfactorily to all that more money was needed to collect more data. Most of the data were highly informative, revealing the amazing fact that poor people went to jail oftener than rich ones; that most of the people were not getting enough money for their work; that strangely enough there was some connection between poverty, disease and crime. By establishing these facts with mathematical certitude and illustrating them with elaborate graphs, Dr. Bonds garnered many fat checks. For his people, he said, he wanted work, not charity; but for himself he was always glad to get the charity with as little work as possible. For many years he had succeeded in doing so without any ascertainable benefit accruing to the Negro group.

Dr. Bonds' show of emotion almost brought the others to tears and many of them muttered "Yes, Brother" while he was talking. The conferees were getting stirred up but it took the next speaker to really get them excited.

When he rose an expectant hush fell over the assemblage. They all knew and respected the Right Reverend Bishop Ezekiel Whooper of the Ethiopian True Faith Wash Foot Methodist Church for three reasons: viz., his church was rich (though the parishioners were poor), he had a very loud voice and the white people praised him. He was sixty, corpulent and an expert at the art of making cuckolds.

"Our loyal and devoted clergy," he boomed, "are being forced into manual labor and the Negro church is rapidly dying" and then he launched into a violent tirade against Black-No-More and favored any means to put the corporation out of business. In his excitement he blew saliva, waved his long arms, stamped his feet, pummeled the desk, rolled his eyes, knocked down his chair, almost sat on the rug and generally reverted to the antics of Negro bush preachers.

This exhibition proved contagious. Rev. Herbert Gronne, face flushed and shouting amens, marched from one end of the room to the other; Colonel Roberts, looking like an inebriated black-faced comedian, rocked back and forth clapping his hands; the others began to groan and moan. Dr. Napoleon

Wellington Jackson, sensing his opportunity, began to sing a spiritual in his rich soprano voice. The others immediately joined him. The very air seemed charged with emotion.

Bishop Whooper was about to start up again, when Dr. Beard, who had sat cold and disdainful through this outbreak of revivalism, toying with his gold-rimmed fountain pen and gazing at the exhibition through half-closed eyelids, interrupted in sharp metallic tones.

"Let's get down to earth now," he commanded. "We've had enough of this nonsense. We have a resolution here addressed to the Attorney General of the United States demanding that Dr. Crookman and his associates be arrested and their activities stopped at once for the good of both races. All those in favor of this resolution say aye. Contrary? . . . Very well, the ayes have it. . . Miss Hilton please send off this telegram at once!"

They looked at Dr. Beard and each other in amazement. Several started to meekly protest.

"You gentlemen are all twenty-one, aren't you?" sneered Beard. "Well, then be men enough to stand by your decision."

"But Doctor Beard," objected Rev. Gronne, "isn't this a rather unusual procedure?"

"Rev. Gronne," the great man replied, "it's not near as unusual as Black-No-More. I have probably ruffled your dignity but that's nothing to what Dr. Crookman will do."

"I guess you're right, Beard," the college president agreed.

"I know it," snapped the other.

The Honorable Walter Brybe, who had won his exalted position as Attorney General of the United States because of his long and faithful service helping large corporations to circumvent the federal laws, sat at his desk in Washington, D. C. Before him lay the wired resolution from the conference of Negro leaders. He pursed his lips and reached for his private telephone.

"Gorman?" he inquired softly into the receiver. "Is that you?"

"Nossuh," came the reply, "this heah is Mistah Gay's valet."

"Well, call Mister Gay to the telephone at once."

"Yassuh."

"That you, Gorman," asked the chief legal officer of the nation addressing the National Chairman of his party.

"Yeh, what's up?"

"You heard 'bout this resolution from them niggers in New York, aint you? It's been in all of the papers."

"Yes I read it."

"Well, whaddya think we oughtta do about it?"

"Take it easy, Walter. Give 'em the old run around. You know. They ain't got a thin dime; it's this other crowd that's holding the heavy jack. And 'course you know we gotta clean up our deficit. Just lemme work with that Black-No-More crowd. I can talk business with that Johnson fellow."

"All right, Gorman, I think you're right, but you don't want to forget that there's a whole lot of white sentiment against them coons."

"Needn't worry 'bout that," scoffed Gorman. "There's no money behind it much and besides it's in states we can't carry anyhow. Go ahead; stall them New York niggers off. You're a lawyer, you can always find a reason."

"Thanks for the compliment, Gorman," said the Attorney General, hanging up the receiver.

He pressed a button on his desk and a young girl, armed with pencil and pad, came in.

"Take this letter," he ordered: "To Doctor Shakespeare Agamemnon Beard (what a hell of a name!), Chairman of the Committee for the Preservation of Negro Racial Integrity, 1400 Broadway, New York City.

"My dear Dr. Beard:

The Attorney General has received the resolution signed by yourself and others and given it careful consideration.

Regardless of personal views in the matter (I don't give a damn whether they turn white or not, myself) it is not possible for the Department of Justice to interfere with a legitimate business enterprise so long as its methods are within the law. The corporation in question has violated no federal statute and hence there is not the slightest ground for interfering with its activities.

Very truly yours,

WALTER BRYBE.

"Get that off at once. Give out copies to the press. That's all."

Santop Licorice, founder and leader of the Back-to-Africa Society, read the reply of the Attorney General to the Negro leaders with much malicious satisfaction. He laid aside his morning paper, pulled a fat cigar from a box near by, lit it and blew clouds of smoke above his woolly head. He was always delighted when Dr. Beard met with any sort of rebuff or embarrassment. He was doubly pleased in this instance because he had been overlooked in the sending out of invitations to Negro leaders to join the Committee for the Preservation of Negro Racial Integrity. It was outrageous, after all the talking he had done in favor of Negro racial integrity.

Mr. Licorice for some fifteen years had been very profitably advocating the emigration of all the American Negroes to Africa. He had not, of course, gone there himself and had not the slightest intention of going so far from the fleshpots, but he told the other Negroes to go. Naturally the first step in their going was to join his society by paying five dollars a year for membership, ten dollars for a gold, green and purple robe and silver-colored helmet that together cost two dollars and a half, contributing five dollars to the Santop Licorice Defense Fund (there was a perpetual defense fund because Licorice was perpetually in the courts for fraud of some kind), and buying shares at five dollars each in the Royal Black Steamship Company, for obviously one could not get to Africa without a ship and Negroes ought to travel on Negro-owned and operated ships. The ships were Santop's especial pride. True, they had never been to Africa, had never had but one cargo and that, being gin, was half consumed by the unpaid and thirsty crew before the vessel was saved by the Coast Guard, but they had cost more than anything else the Back-To-Africa Society had purchased even though they were worthless except as scrap iron. Mr. Licorice, who was known by his followers as Provisional President of Africa, Admiral of the African Navy, Field Marshal of the African Army and Knight Commander of the Nile, had a genius for being stuck with junk by crafty salesmen. White men only needed to tell him that he was shrewder than white men and he would immediately reach for a check book.

But there was little reaching for check books in his office nowadays. He had been as hard hit as the other Negroes. Why should anybody in the Negro race want to go back to Africa at a cost of five hundred dollars for passage when they could stay in America and get white for fifty dollars? Mr. Licorice saw the point but instead of scuttling back to Demerara from whence he had come to save his race from oppression, he had hung on in the hope that the activities of Black-No-More, Incorporated, would be stopped. In the meantime, he had continued to attempt to save the Negroes by vigorously attacking all of the other Negro organizations and at the same time preaching racial solidarity and coöperation in his weekly newspaper, *"The African Abroad,"* which was printed by white folks and had until a year ago been full of skin-whitening and hair-straightening advertisements.

"How is our treasury?" he yelled back through the dingy suite of offices to his bookkeeper, a pretty mulatto.

"What treasury?" she asked in mock surprise.

"Why, I thought we had seventy-five dollars," he blurted.

"We did, but the Sheriff got most of it yesterday or we wouldn't be in here today."

"Huumn! Well, that's bad. And tomorrow's pay day, isn't it?"

"Why bring that up?" she sneered. "I'd forgotten all about it."

"Haven't we got enough for me to get to Atlanta?" Licorice inquired, anxiously.

"There is if you're gonna hitch-hike."

"Well, of course, I couldn't do that," he smiled deprecatingly.

"I should say not," she retorted surveying his 250-pound, five-feet-six-inches of black blubber.

"Call Western Union," he commanded.

"What with?"

"Over the telephone, of course, Miss Hall," he explained.

"If you can get anything over that telephone you're a better man than I am, Gunga Din."

"Has the service been discontinued, young lady?"

"Try and get a number," she chirped. He gazed ruefully at the telephone.

"Is there anything we can sell?" asked the bewildered Licorice.

"Yeah, if you can get the Sheriff to take off his attachments."

"That's right, I had forgotten."

"You would."

"Please be more respectful, Miss Hall," he snapped. "Somebody might overhear you and tell my wife."

"Which one?" she mocked.

"Shut up," he blurted, touched in a tender spot, "and try to figure out some way for us to get hold of some money."

"You must think I'm Einstein," she said, coming up and perching herself on the edge of his desk.

"Well, if we don't get some operating expenses I won't be able to obtain money to pay your salary," he warned.

"The old songs are the best songs," she wise-cracked.

"Oh, come now, Violet," he remonstrated, pawing her buttock, "let's be serious."

"After all these years!" she declared, switching away.

In desperation, he eased his bulk out of the creaking swivel chair, reached for his hat and overcoat and shuffled out of the office. He walked to the curb to hail a taxicab but reconsidered when he recalled that a worn half-dollar was the extent of his funds. Sighing heavily, he trudged the two blocks to the telegraph office and sent a long day letter to Henry Givens, Imperial Grand Wizard of the Knights of Nordica—collect.

"Well, have you figured it out?" asked Violet when he barged into his office again.

"Yes, I just sent a wire to Givens," he replied.

"But he's a nigger-hater, isn't he?" was her surprised comment.

"You want your salary, don't you?" he inquired archly.

"I have for the past month."

"Well, then, don't ask foolish questions," he snapped.

Chapter Six

Two important events took place on Easter Sunday, 1934. The first was a huge mass meeting in the brand new reinforced concrete auditorium of the Knights of Nordica for the double purpose of celebrating the first anniversary of the militant secret society and the winning of the millionth member. The second event was the wedding of Helen Givens and Matthew Fisher, Grand Exalted Giraw of the Knights of Nordica.

Rev. Givens, the Imperial Grand Wizard of the order, had never regretted that he had taken Fisher into the order and made him his right-hand man. The membership had grown by leaps and bounds, the treasury was bursting with money in spite of the Wizard's constant misappropriation of funds, the regalia factory was running night and day and the influence of the order was becoming so great that Rev. Givens was beginning to dream of a berth in the White House or near by.

For over six months the order had been publishing *The Warning*, an eight-page newspaper carrying lurid red headlines and poorly-drawn quarter-page cartoons, and edited by Matthew. The noble Southern working people purchased it eagerly, devouring and believing every word in it. Matthew, in 14-point, one-syllable word editorials painted terrifying pictures of the menace confronting white supremacy and the utter necessity of crushing it. Very cleverly he linked up the Pope, the Yellow Peril, the Alien Invasion and Foreign Entanglements with Black-No-More as devices of the Devil. He wrote with such blunt sincerity that sometimes he almost persuaded himself that it was all true.

As the money flowed in, Matthew's fame as a great organizer spread throughout the Southland, and he suddenly became the most desirable catch in the section. Beautiful women literally threw themselves at his feet, and, as a former Negro and thus well versed in the technique of amour, he availed himself of all offerings that caught his fancy.

At the same time he was a frequent visitor to the Givens home, especially when Mrs. Givens, whom he heartily detested, was away. From the very first Helen had been impressed by

Matthew. She had always longed for the companionship of an educated man, a scientist, a man of literary ability. Matthew to her mind embodied all of these. She only hesitated to accept his first offer of marriage two days after they met because she saw no indication that he had much, if any, money. She softened toward him as the Knights of Nordica treasury grew; and when he was able to boast of a million-dollar bank account, she agreed to marriage and accepted his ardent embraces in the meantime.

And so, before the yelling multitude of nightgowned Knights, they were united in holy wedlock on the stage of the new auditorium. Both, being newlyweds, were happy. Helen had secured the kind of husband she wanted, except that she regretted his association with what she called lowbrows; while Matthew had won the girl of his dreams and was thoroughly satisfied, except for a slight regret that her grotesque mother wasn't dead and some disappointment that his spouse was so much more ignorant than she was beautiful.

As soon as Matthew had helped to get the Knights of Nordica well under way with enough money flowing in to satisfy the avaricious Rev. Givens, he had begun to study ways and means of making some money on the side. He had power, influence and prestige and he intended to make good use of them. So he had obtained audiences individually with several of the leading business men of the Georgia capital.

He always prefaced his proposition by pointing out that the working people were never so contented, profits never so high and the erection of new factories in the city never so intensive; that the continued prosperity of Atlanta and of the entire South depended upon keeping labor free from Bolshevism, Socialism, Communism, Anarchism, trade unionism and other subversive movements. Such un-American philosophies, he insisted had ruined European countries and from their outposts in New York and other Northern cities were sending emissaries to seek a foothold in the South and plant the germ of discontent. When this happened, he warned gloomily, then farewell to high profits and contented labor. He showed copies of books and pamphlets which he had ordered from radical book stores in New York but which he asserted were being distributed to the prospect's employees.

He then explained the difference between the defunct Ku Klux Klan and the Knights of Nordica. While both were interested in public morals, racial integrity and the threatened invasion of America by the Pope, his organization glimpsed its larger duty, the perpetuation of Southern prosperity by the stabilization of industrial relations. The Knights of Nordica, favored by increasing membership, was in a position to keep down all radicalism, he said, and then boldly asserted that Black-No-More was subsidized by the Russian Bolsheviks. Would the gentlemen help the work of the Nordicists along with a small contribution? They would and did. Whenever there was a slump in the flow of cash from this source, Matthew merely had his print shop run off a bale of Communistic tracts which his secret operatives distributed around in the mills and factories. Contributions would immediately increase.

Matthew had started this lucrative side enterprise none too soon. There was much unemployment in the city, wages were being cut and work speeded up. There was dissatisfaction and grumbling among the workers and a small percentage of them was in a mood to give ear to the half-dozen timid organizers of the conservative unions who were being paid to unionize the city but had as yet made no headway. A union might not be so bad after all.

The great mass of white workers, however, was afraid to organize and fight for more pay because of a deepset fear that the Negroes would take their jobs. They had heard of black labor taking the work of white labor under the guns of white militia, and they were afraid to risk it. They had first read of the activities of Black-No-More, Incorporated, with a secret feeling akin to relief but after the orators of the Knights of Nordica and the editorials of *The Warning* began to portray the menace confronting them, they forgot about their economic ills and began to yell for the blood of Dr. Crookman and his associates. Why, they began to argue, one couldn't tell who was who! Herein lay the fundamental cause of all their ills. Times were hard, they reasoned, because there were so many white Negroes in their midst taking their jobs and undermining their American standard of living. None of them had ever attained an American standard of living to be sure, but that fact never occurred to any of them. So they flocked to the meetings of the Knights of Nordica and night after night sat spellbound while Rev. Givens, who had finished the eighth grade in a one-room country school, explained the laws of heredity and spoke eloquently of the growing danger of black babies.

Despite his increasing wealth (the money came in so fast he could scarcely keep track of it), Matthew maintained close contact with the merchants and manufacturers. He sent out private letters periodically to prominent men in the Southern business world in which he told of the marked psychological change that had come over the working classes of the South since the birth of the K. of N. He told how they had been discontented and on the brink of revolution when his organization rushed in and saved the South. Unionism and such destructive nostrums had been forgotten, he averred, when *The Warning* had revealed the latest danger to the white race. Of course, he always added, such work required large sums of money and contributions from conservative, substantial and public-spirited citizens were ever acceptable. At the end of each letter there appeared a suggestive paragraph pointing out the extent to which the prosperity of the New South was due to its "peculiar institutions" that made the worker race conscious instead of class conscious, and that with the passing of these "peculiar institutions" would also pass prosperity. This reasoning proved very effective, financially speaking.

Matthew's great success as an organizer and his increasing popularity was not viewed by Rev. Givens with equanimity. The former evangelist knew that everybody of intelligence in the upper circles of the order realized that the growth and prosperity of the Knights of Nordica was largely due to the industry, efficiency and intelligence of Matthew. He had been told that many people were saying that Fisher ought to be Imperial Grand Wizard instead of Grand Exalted Giraw.

Givens had the ignorant man's fear and suspicion of anybody who was supposedly more learned than he. His position, he felt, was threatened, and he was decidedly uneasy. He neither said nor did anything about it, but he fretted a great deal to his wife, much to her annoyance. He was consequently overjoyed when Matthew asked him for Helen's hand, and gave his consent with alacrity. When the marriage was consummated, he saw his cup filled to overflowing and no clouds on the horizon. The Knights of Nordica was safe in the family.

One morning a week or two after his wedding, Matthew was sitting in his private office, when his secretary announced a caller, one B. Brown. After the usual delay staged for the purpose of impressing all visitors, Matthew ordered him in. A short, plump, well-dressed, soft-spoken man entered and greeted him respectfully. The Grand Exalted Giraw waved to a chair and the stranger sat down. Suddenly, leaning over close to Matthew, he whispered, "Don't recognize me, do you Max?"

The Grand Giraw paled and started. "Who are you?" he whispered hoarsely. How in the devil did this man know him? He peered at him sharply.

The newcomer grinned. "Why it's me, Bunny Brown, you big sap!"

"Well, cut my throat!" Matthew exclaimed in amazement. "Boy, is it really you?" Bunny's black face had miraculously bleached. He seemed now more chubby and cherubic than ever.

"It aint my brother," said Bunny with his familiar beam.

"Bunny, where've you been all this time? Why didn't you come on down here when I wrote you? You must've been in jail."

"Mind reader! That's just where I've been," declared the former bank clerk.

"What for? Gambling?"

"No: Rambling."

"What do you mean: Rambling?" asked the puzzled Matthew.

"Just what I said, Big Boy. Got to rambling around with a married woman. Old story: husband came in unexpectedly and I had to crown him. The fire escape was slippery and I slipped. Couldn't run after I hit the ground and the flatfoot nabbed me. Got a lucky break in court or I wouldn't be here."

"Was it a white woman?" asked the Grand Exalted Giraw.

"She wasn't black," said Bunny.

"It's a good thing you weren't black, too!"

"Our minds always ran in the same channels," Bunny commented.

"Got any jack?" asked Matthew.

"Is it likely?"

"Do you want a job?"

"No, I prefer a position."

"Well, I think I can fix you up here for about five grand to begin with," said Matthew.

"Santa Claus! What do I have to do: assassinate the President?"

"No, kidder; just be my right-hand man. You know, follow me through thick and thin."

"All right, Max; but when things get too thick, I'm gonna thin out."

"For Christ's sake don't call me Max," cautioned Matthew.

"That's your name, aint it?"

"No, simp. Them days has gone forever. It's Matthew Fisher now. You go pulling that Max stuff and I'll have to answer more questions than a traffic officer."

"Just think," mused Bunny. "I been reading about you right along in the papers but until I recognized your picture in last Sunday's paper I didn't know who you were. Just how long have you been in on this graft?"

"Ever since it started."

"Say not so! You must have a wad of cash salted away by this time."

"Well, I'm not appealing for charity," Matthew smiled sardonically.

"How many squaws you got now?"

"Only one, Bunny—regular."

"What's matter, did you get too old?" chided his friend.

"No, I got married."

"Well, that's the same thing. Who's the unfortunate woman?"

"Old man Givens' girl."

"Judas Priest! You got in on the ground floor didn't you?"

"I didn't miss. Bunny, old scout, she's the same girl that turned me down that night in the Honky Tonk," Matthew told him with satisfaction.

"Well, hush my mouth! This sounds like a novel," Bunny chuckled.

"Believe it or not, papa, it's what God loves," Matthew grinned.

"Well, you lucky hound! Getting white didn't hurt you none."

"Now listen, Bunny," said Matthew, dropping to a more serious tone, "from now on you're private secretary to the Grand Exalted Giraw; that's me."

"What's a Giraw?"

"I can't tell you; I don't know myself. Ask Givens sometime. He invented it but if he can explain it I'll give you a grand."

"When do I start to work? Or rather, when do I start drawing money?"

"Right now, Old Timer. Here's a century to get you fixed up. You eat dinner with me tonight and report to me in the morning."

"Fathers above!" said Bunny. "Dixie must be heaven."

"It'll be hell for you if these babies find you out; so keep your nose clean."

"Watch me, Mr. Giraw."

"Now listen, Bunny. You know Santop Licorice, don't you?"

"Who doesn't know that hippo?"

"Well, we've had him on our payroll since December. He's fighting Beard, Whooper, Spelling and that crowd. He was on the bricks and we helped him out. Got his paper to appearing regularly, and all that sort of thing."

"So the old crook sold out the race, did he?" cried the amazed Bunny.

"Hold that race stuff, you're not a shine anymore. Are you surprised that he sold out? You're actually becoming innocent," said Matthew.

"Well, what about the African admiral?" Bunny asked.

"This: In a couple of days I want you to run up to New York and look around and see if his retention on the payroll is justified. I got a hunch that nobody is bothering about his paper or what he says, and if that's true we might as well can him; I can use the jack to better advantage."

"Listen here, Boy, this thing is running me nuts. Here you are fighting this Black-No-More, and so is Beard, Whooper, Gronne, Spelling and the rest of the Negro leaders, yet you have Licorice on the payroll to fight the same people that are fighting your enemy. This thing is more complicated than a flapper's past."

"Simple, Bunny, simple. Reason why you can't understand it is because you don't know anything about high strategy."

"High what?" asked Bunny.

"Never mind, look it up at your leisure. Now you can savvy the fact that the sooner these spades are whitened the sooner this graft will fall through, can't you?"

"Righto," said his friend.

"Well, the longer we can make the process, the longer we continue to drag down the jack. Is that clear?"

"As a Spring day."

"You're getting brighter by the minute, old man," jeered Matthew.

"Coming from you, that's no compliment."

"As I was saying, the longer it takes, the longer we last. It's my business to see that it lasts a long time but neither do I want it to stop because that also would be disastrous."

Bunny nodded: "You're a wise egg!"

"Thanks, that makes it unanimous. Well, I don't want my side to get such an upper hand that it will put the other side out of business, or vice versa. What we want is a status quo."

"Gee, you've got educated sincc you've been down here with these crackers."

"You flatter them, Bunny; run along now. I'll have my car come by your hotel to bring you to dinner."

"Thanks for the compliment, old man, but I'm staying at the Y.M.C.A. It's cheaper," laughed Bunny.

"But is it safer?" kidded Matthew, as his friend withdrew.

Two days later Bunny Brown left for New York on a secret mission. Not only was he to spy on Santop Licorice and see how effective his work was, but he was also to approach Dr. Shakespeare Agamemnon Beard, Dr. Napoleon Wellington Jackson, Rev. Herbert Gronne, Col. Mortimer Roberts, Prof. Charles Spelling, and the other Negro leaders with a view to getting them to speak to white audiences for the benefit of the Knights of Nordica. Matthew already knew that they were in a precarious economic situation since they now had no means of income, both the black masses and the philanthropic whites having deserted them. Their white friends, mostly Northern plutocrats, felt that the race problem was being satisfactorily solved by Black-No-More, Incorporated, and so did the Negroes. Bunny's job was to convince them that it was better to lecture for the K. of N. and grow fat than to fail to get chances to lecture to Negroes who weren't interested in what they said anyhow. The Grand Exalted Giraw had a personal interest in these Negro leaders. He realized that they were too old or too incompetent to make a living except by preaching and writing about the race problem, and since they had lost their influence with the black masses, they might be a novelty to introduce to the K. of N. audiences. He felt that their racial integrity talks would click with the crackers. They knew more about it too than any of regular speakers, he realized.

As the train bearing Bunny pulled into the station in Charlotte, he bought an evening paper. The headline almost knocked him down:

WEALTHY WHITE GIRL HAS NEGRO BABY

He whistled softly and muttered to himself, "Business picks up from now on." He thought of Matthew's marriage and whistled again.

From that time on there were frequent reports in the daily press of white women giving birth to black babies. In some cases, of course, the white women had recently become white but the blame for the tar-brushed offspring in the public mind always rested on the shoulders of the father, or rather, of the husband. The number of cases continued to increase. All walks of life were represented. For the first time the prevalence of sexual promiscuity was brought home to the thinking people of America. Hospital authorities and physicians had known about it in a general way but it had been unknown to the public.

The entire nation became alarmed. Hundreds of thousands of people, North and South, flocked into the Knights of Nordica. The real white people were panicstricken, especially in Dixie. There was no way, apparently, of telling a real Caucasian from an imitation one. Every stranger was viewed with suspicion, which had a very salutory effect on the standard of sex morality in the United States. For the first time since 1905, chastity became a virtue. The number of petting parties, greatly augmented by the development of aviation, fell off amazingly. One must play safe, the girls argued.

The holidays of traveling salesmen, business men and fraternal delegates were made less pleasant than of yore. The old orgiastic days in the big cities seemed past for all time. It also suddenly began to dawn upon some men that the pretty young thing they had met at the seashore and wanted to rush to the altar might possibly be a whitened Negress; and young women were almost as suspicious. Rapid-fire courtships and gin marriages declined. Matrimony at last began to be approached with caution. Nothing like this situation had been known since the administration of Grover Cleveland.

Black-No-More, Incorporated, was not slow to seize upon this opportunity to drum up more business. With 100 sanitariums going full blast from Coast to Coast, it now announced in full page advertisements in the daily press that it was establishing lying-in hospitals in the principal cities where all prospective mothers could come to have their babies, and that whenever a baby was born black or mulatto, it would immediately be given the 24-hour treatment that permanently turned black infants white. The country breathed easier, particularly the four million Negroes who had become free because white.

In a fortnight Bunny Brown returned. Over a quart of passable rye, the two friends discussed his mission.

"What about Licorice?" asked Matthew.

"Useless. You ought to give him the gate. He's taking your jack but he isn't doing a thing but getting your checks and eating regularly. His followers are scarcer than Jews in the Vatican."

"Well, were you able to talk business with any of the Negro leaders?"

"Couldn't find any of them. Their offices are all closed and they've moved away from the places where they used to live. Broke, I suppose."

"Did you inquire for them around Harlem?"

"What was the use? All of the Negroes around Harlem nowadays are folks that have just come there to get white; the rest of them left the race a long time ago. Why, Boy, darkies are as hard to find on Lenox Avenue now as they used to be in Tudor City."

"What about the Negro newspapers? Are any of them running still?"

"Nope, they're a thing of the past. Shines are too busy getting white to bother reading about lynching, crime and peon-age," said Bunny.

"Well," said Matthew, "it looks as if old Santop Licorice is the only one of the old gang left."

"Yeah, and he won't be black long, now that you're cutting him off the payroll."

"I think he could make more money staying black."

"How do you figure that out?" asked Bunny.

"Well, the dime museums haven't closed down, you know," said Matthew.

Chapter Seven

ONE June morning in 1934, Grand Exalted Giraw Fisher received a report from one of his secret operatives in the town of Paradise, South Carolina, saying:

"The working people here are talking about going on strike next week unless Blickdoff and Hortzenboff, the owners of the Paradise Mill increase pay and shorten hours. The average wage is around fifteen dollars a week, the work day eleven hours. In the past week the company has speeded up the work so much that the help say they cannot stand the pace.

"The owners are two Germans who came to this country after the war. They employ 1000 hands, own all of the houses in Paradise and operate all of the stores. Most of the hands belong to the Knights of Nordica and they want the organization to help them unionize. Am awaiting instructions."

Matthew turned to Bunny and grinned. "Here's more money," he boasted, shaking the letter in his assistant's face.

"What can you do about it?" that worthy inquired.

"What can I do? Well, Brother, you just watch my smoke. Tell Ruggles to get the plane ready," he ordered. "We'll fly over there at once."

Two hours later Matthew's plane sat down on the broad, close-clipped lawn in front of the Blickdoff-Hortzenboff cotton mill. Bunny and the Grand Giraw entered the building and walked to the office.

"Whom do you wish to see?" asked a clerk.

"Mr. Blickdoff, Mr. Hortzenboff or both; preferably both," Matthew replied.

"And who's calling?"

"The Grand Exalted Giraw of the Ancient and Honorable Order of the Knights of Nordica and his secretary," boomed that gentleman. The awed young lady retired into an inner sanctum.

"That sure is some title," commented Bunny in an under-
tone.

"Yes, Givens knows his stuff when it comes to that. The longer and sillier a title, the better the yaps like it."

The young lady returned and announced that the two owners would be glad to receive the eminent Atlantan. Bunny and
Matthew entered the office marked "Private."

Hands were shaken, greetings exchanged and then Matthew
got right down to business. He had received contributions
from these two mill owners so to a certain extent they understood one another.

"Gentlemen," he queried, "is it true that your employees are
planning to strike next week?"

"So ve haff heardt," puffed the corpulent, under-sized Blickdoff.

"Well, what are you going to do about it?"

"De uszual t'ing, uff coarse," replied Hortzenboff, who resembled a beer barrel on stilts.

"You can't do the usual thing," warned Matthew. "Most of
these people are members of the Knights of Nordica. They are
looking to us for protection and we mean to give it to them."

"Vy ve t'ought you vas favorable," exclaimed Blickdoff.

"Und villing to be reasonable," added Hortzenboff.

"That's true," Matthew agreed, "but you're squeezing these
people too hard."

"But ve can't pay dem any more," protested the squat partner. "Vot ve gonna do?"

"Oh, you fellows can't kid me, I know you're coining the
jack; but if you think its worth ten grand to you, I think I can
adjust matters," the Grand Giraw stated.

"Ten t'ousand dollars?" the two mill men gasped.

"You've got good ears," Matthew assured them. "And if you
don't come across I'll put the whole power of my organization
behind your hands. Then it'll cost you a hundred grand to get
back to normal."

The Germans looked at each other incredulously.

"Are you t'reatening us, Meester Fisher?" whined Blickdoff.

"You've got a good head at figuring out things, Blickdoff,"
Matthew retorted, sarcastically.

"Suppose ve refuse?" queried the heavier Teuton.

"Yeah, suppose you do. Can't you imagine what'll happen when I pull these people off the job?"

"Ve'll call oudt de militia," warned Blickdoff.

"Don't make me laugh," Matthew commented. "Half the militiamen are members of my outfit."

The Germans shrugged their shoulders hopelessly while Matthew and Bunny enjoyed their confusion.

"How mutch you say you wandt?" asked Hortzenboff.

"Fifteen grand," replied the Grand Giraw, winking at Bunny.

"Budt you joost said ten t'ousand a minute ago," screamed Blickdoff, gesticulating.

"Well, it's fifteen now," said Matthew, "and it'll be twenty grand if you babies don't hurry up and make up your mind."

Hortzenboff reached hastily for the big check book and commenced writing. In a moment he handed Matthew the check.

"Take this back to Atlanta in the plane," ordered Matthew, handing the check to Bunny, "and deposit it. Safety first." Bunny went out.

"You don't act like you trust us," Blickdoff accused.

"Why should I?" the ex-Negro retorted. "I'll just stick around for a while and keep you two company. You fellows might change your mind and stop payment on that check."

"Ve are honest men, Meester Fisher," cried Hortzenboff.

"Now I'll tell one," sneered the Grand Giraw, seating himself and taking a handful of cigars out of a box on the desk.

The following evening the drab, skinny, hollow-eyed mill folk trudged to the mass meeting called by Matthew in the only building in Paradise not owned by the company—the Knights of Nordica Hall. They poured into the ramshackle building, seated themselves on the wooden benches and waited for the speaking to begin.

They were a sorry lot, under-nourished, bony, vacant-looking, and yet they had seen a dim light. Without suggestion or agitation from the outside world, from which they were almost as completely cut off as if they had been in Siberia, they had talked among themselves and concluded that there was no hope for them except in organization. What they all felt they needed was wise leadership, and they looked to the Knights of

Nordica for it, since they were all members of it and there was no other agency at hand. They waited now expectantly for the words of wisdom and encouragement which they expected to hear fall from the lips of their beloved Matthew Fisher, who now looked down upon them from the platform with cynical humor mingled with disgust.

They had not long to wait. A tall, gaunt mountaineer, who acted as chairman, after beseeching the mill hands to stand together like men and women, introduced the Grand Exalted Giraw.

Matthew spoke forcefully and to the point. He reminded them that they were men and women; that they were free, white and twenty-one; that they were citizens of the United States; that America was their country as well as Rockefeller's; that they must stand firm in the defense of their rights as working people; that the worker was worthy of his hire; that nothing should be dearer to them than the maintenance of white supremacy. He insinuated that even in their midst there probably were some Negroes who had been turned white by Black-No-More. Such individuals, he insisted made poor union material because they always showed their Negro characteristics and ran away in a crisis. Ending with a fervent plea for liberty, justice and a square deal, he sat down amid tumultuous applause. Eager to take advantage of their enthusiasm, the chairman began to call for members. Happily the people crowded around the little table in front of the platform to give their names and pay dues.

Swanson, the chairman and acknowledged leader of the militant element, was tickled with the results of the meeting. He slapped his thighs mountaineer fashion, shifted his chew of tobacco from the right cheek to the left, his pale blue eyes twinkling, and "allowed" to Matthew that the union would soon bring the Paradise Mill owners to terms. The Grand Exalted Giraw agreed.

Two days later, back in Atlanta, Matthew held a conference with a half-dozen of his secret operatives in his office. "Go to Paradise and do your stuff," he commanded, "and do it right."

The next day the six men stepped from the train in the little South Carolina town, engaged rooms at the local hotel and got busy. They let it be known that they were officials of the

Knights of Nordica sent from Atlanta by the Grand Exalted Giraw to see that the mill workers got a square deal. They busied themselves visiting the three-room cottages of the workers, all of which looked alike, and talking very confidentially.

In a day or so it began to be noised about that Swanson, leader of the radical element, was really a former Negro from Columbia. It happened that a couple of years previously he had lived in that city. Consequently he readily admitted that he had lived there when asked innocently by one of the strangers in the presence of a group of workers. When Swanson wasn't looking, the questioner glanced significantly at those in the group.

That was enough. To the simple-minded workers Swanson's admission was conclusive evidence that the charge of being a Negro was true. When he called another strike meeting, no one came except a few of Fisher's men. The big fellow was almost ready to cry because of the unexplained falling away of his followers. When one of the secret operatives told him the trouble he was furious.

"Ah haint no damn nigger a-tall," he shouted. "Ah'm a white man an' kin prove hit!"

Unfortunately he could not prove to the satisfaction of his fellow workers that he was not a Negro. They were adamant. On the streets they passed him without speaking and they complained to the foremen at the mill that they didn't want to work with a nigger. Broken and disheartened after a week of vain effort, Swanson was glad to accept carfare out of the vicinity from one of Matthew's men who pretended to be sympathetic.

With the departure of Swanson, the cause of the mill workers was dealt a heavy blow, but the three remaining ringleaders sought to carry on. The secret operatives of the Grand Exalted Giraw got busy again. One of the agitators was asked if it was true that his grandfather was a nigger. He strenuously denied the charge but being ignorant of the identity of his father he could not very well be certain about his grandfather. He was doomed. Within a week the other two were similarly discredited. Rumor was wafted abroad that the whole idea of a strike was a trick of smart niggers in the North who were in the pay of the Pope.

The erstwhile class conscious workers became terror-stricken by the specter of black blood. You couldn't, they said, be sure of anybody any more, and it was better to leave things as they were than to take a chance of being led by some nigger. If the colored gentry couldn't sit in the movies and ride in the trains with white folks, it wasn't right for them to be organizing and leading white folks.

The radicals and laborites in New York City had been closely watching developments in Paradise ever since the news of the big mass meeting addressed by Matthew was broadcast by the Knights of Nordica news service. When it seemed that the mill workers were, for some mysterious reason, going to abandon the idea of striking, liberal and radical labor organizers were sent down to the town to see what could be done toward whipping up the spirit of revolt.

The representative of the liberal labor organization arrived first and immediately announced a meeting in the Knights of Nordica Hall, the only obtainable place. Nobody came. The man couldn't understand it. He walked out into the town square, approached a little knot of men and asked what was the trouble.

"Y're from that there Harlem in N'Yawk, haint ye?" asked one of the villagers.

"Why yes, I live in Harlem. What about it?"

"Well, we haint a gonna have no damn nigger leadin' us, an' if ye know whut's healthy fer yuh yo'll git on away f'um here," stated the speaker.

"Where do you get that nigger stuff?" inquired the amazed and insulted organizer. "I'm a white man."

"Yo ain't th' first white nigger whut's bin aroun' these parts," was the reply.

The organizer, puzzled but helpless, stayed around town for a week and then departed. Somebody had told the simple folk that Harlem was the Negro district in New York, after as-certaining that the organizer lived in that district. To them Harlem and Negro became synonymous and the laborite was doomed.

The radical labor organizer, refused permission to use the Knights of Nordica Hall because he was a Jew, was prevented from holding a street meeting when someone started a rumor that he believed in dividing up property, nationalizing women, and was in addition an atheist. He freely admitted the first, laughed at the second and proudly proclaimed the third. That was sufficient to inflame the mill hands, although God had been strangely deaf to their prayers, they owned no property to divide and most of their women were so ugly that they need have had no fears that any outsiders would want to nationalize them. The disciple of Lenin and Trotsky vanished down the road with a crowd of emaciated workers at his heels.

Soon all was quiet and orderly again in Paradise, S. C. On the advice of a conciliator from the United States Labor Department, Blickdoff and Hortzenboff, took immediate steps to make their workers more satisfied with their pay, their jobs and their little home town. They built a swimming pool, a tennis court, shower baths and a playground for their employees but neglected to shorten their work time so these improvements could be enjoyed. They announced that they would give each worker a bonus of a whole day's pay at Christmas time, hereafter, and a week's vacation each year to every employee who had been with them more than ten years. There were no such employees, of course, but the mill hands were overjoyed with their victory.

The local Baptist preacher, who was very thoughtfully paid by the company with the understanding that he would take a practical view of conditions in the community, told his flock their employers were to be commended for adopting a real Christian and American way of settling the difficulties between them and their workers. He suggested it was quite likely that Jesus, placed in the same position, would have done likewise.

"Be thankful for the little things," he mooed. "God works in mysterious ways his wonders to perform. Ye shall know the truth and the truth shall set ye free. The basis of all things is truth. Let us not be led astray by the poison from vipers' tongues. This is America and not Russia. Patrick Henry said 'Give me liberty or give me death' and the true, red-blooded, 100 per cent American citizen says the same thing today. But there are right ways and wrong ways to get liberty. Your employers have gone about it the right way. For what, after all is liberty except the enjoyment of life; and have they not placed within your reach those things that bring happiness and recreation?

"Your employers are interested, just as all true Americans are interested, in the welfare of their fellow citizens, their fellow townsmen. Their hearts beat for you. They are always thinking of you. They are always planning ways to make conditions better for you. They are sincerely doing all in their power. They have very heavy responsibilities.

"So you must be patient. Rome wasn't built in a day. All things turn out well in time. Christ knows what he is doing and he will not permit his children to suffer.

"O, ye of little faith! Let not your hearts store up jealousy, hatred and animosity. Let not your minds be wooed by misunderstanding. Let us try to act and think as God would wish us to, and above all, let us, like those two kindly men yonder, practice Christian tolerance."

Despite this inspiring message, it was apparent to everyone that Paradise would never be the same again. Rumors continued to fill the air. People were always asking each other embarrassing questions about birth and blood. Fights became more frequent. Large numbers of the workers, being of Southern birth, were unable to disprove charges of possessing Negro ancestry, and so were forced to leave the vicinity. The mill hands kept so busy talking about Negro blood that no one thought of discussing wages and hours of labor.

In August, Messrs. Blickdoff and Hortzenboff, being in Atlanta on business, stopped by Matthew's office.

"Well, how's the strike?" asked the Grand Giraw.

"Dot strike!" echoed Blickdoff. "Ach Gott! Dot strike neffer come off. Vat you do, you razscal?"

"That's my secret," replied Matthew, a little proudly. "Every man to his trade, you know."

It had indeed become Matthew's trade and he was quite adept at it. What had happened at Paradise had also happened elsewhere. There were no more rumors of strikes. The working people were far more interested in what they considered, or were told was, the larger issue of race. It did not matter that they had to send their children into the mills to augment the family wage; that they were always sickly and that their death rate was high. What mattered such little things when the very foundation of civilization, white supremacy, was threatened?

Chapter Eight

FOR over two years now had Black-No-More, Incorporated, been carrying on its self-appointed task of turning Negroes into Caucasians. The job was almost complete, except for the black folk in prisons, orphan asylums, insane asylums, homes for the aged, houses of correction and similar institutions. Those who had always maintained that it was impossible to get Negroes together for anything but a revival, a funeral or a frolic, now had to admit that they had coöperated well in getting white. The poor had been helped by the well-to-do, brothers had helped sisters, children had assisted parents. There had been revived some of the same spirit of adventure prevalent in the days of the Underground Railroad. As a result, even in Mississippi, Negroes were quite rare. In the North the only Negroes to be seen were mulatto babies whose mothers, charmed by the beautiful color of their offspring, had defied convention and not turned them white. As there had never been more than two million Negroes in the North, the whitening process had been viewed indifferently by the masses because those who controlled the channels of opinion felt that the country was getting rid of a very vexatious problem at absolutely no cost; but not so in the South.

When one-third of the population of the erstwhile Confederacy had consisted of the much-maligned Sons of Ham, the blacks had really been of economic, social and psychological value to the section. Not only had they done the dirty work and laid the foundation of its wealth, but they had served as a convenient red herring for the upper classes when the white proletariat grew restive under exploitation. The presence of the Negro as an under class had also made of Dixie a unique part of the United States. There, despite the trend to industrialization, life was a little different, a little pleasanter, a little softer. There was contrast and variety, which was rare in a nation where standardization had progressed to such an extent that a traveler didn't know what town he was in until someone informed him. The South had always been identified with the

Negro, and vice versa, and its most pleasant memories trea-
sured in song and story, were built around this pariah class.

The deep concern of the Southern Caucasians with chivalry,
the protection of white womanhood, the exaggerated development of race pride and the studied arrogance of even the poorest half-starved white peon, were all due to the presence of the
black man. Booted and starved by their industrial and agricultural feudal lords, the white masses derived their only consolation and happiness from the fact that they were the same color
as their oppressors and consequently better than the mudsill
blacks.

The economic loss to the South by the ethnic migration was
considerable. Hundreds of wooden railroad coaches, long since
condemned as death traps in all other parts of the country, had
to be scrapped by the railroads when there were no longer any
Negroes to jim crow. Thousands of railroad waiting rooms remained unused because, having been set aside for the use of
Negroes, they were generally too dingy and unattractive for
white folk or were no longer necessary. Thousands of miles of
streets located in the former Black Belts, and thus without
sewers or pavement, were having to be improved at the insistent behest of the rapidly increased white population, real and
imitation. Real estate owners who had never dreamed of making
repairs on their tumble-down property when it was occupied
by the docile Negroes, were having to tear down, rebuild and
alter to suit white tenants. Shacks and drygoods boxes that had
once sufficed as schools for Negro children, had now to be
condemned and abandoned as unsuitable for occupation by
white youth. Whereas thousands of school teachers had received
thirty and forty dollars a month because of their Negro ancestry,
the various cities and counties of the Southland were now
forced to pay the standard salaries prevailing elsewhere.

Naturally taxes increased. Chambers of Commerce were
now unable to send out attractive advertising to Northern
business firms offering no or very low taxation as an inducement to them to move South nor were they able to offer as
many cheap building sites. Only through the efforts of the
Grand Exalted Giraw of the Knights of Nordica were they still
able to point to their large reserves of docile, contented,

Anglo-Saxon labor, and who knew how long that condition would last?

Consequently, the upper classes faced the future with some misgivings. As if being deprived of the pleasure of black mistresses were not enough, there was a feeling that there would shortly be widespread revolt against the existing medieval industrial conditions and resultant reduction of profits and dividends. The mill barons viewed with distaste the prospect of having to do away with child labor. Rearing back in their padded swivel chairs, they leaned fat jowls on well-manicured hands and mourned the passing of the halcyon days of yore.

If the South had lost its Negroes, however, it had certainly not lost its vote, and the political oligarchy that ruled the section was losing its old assurance and complacency. The Republicans had made inroads here and there in the 1934 Congressional elections. The situation politically was changing and if drastic steps were not immediately taken, the Republicans might carry the erstwhile Solid South, thus practically destroying the Democratic Party. Another Presidential election was less than two years off. There would have to be fast work to ward off disaster. Far-sighted people, North and South, even foresaw the laboring people soon forsaking both of the old parties and going Socialist. Politicians and business men shuddered at the thought of such a tragedy and saw horrible visions of old-age pensions, eight-hour laws, unemployment insurance, workingmen's compensation, minimum-wage legislation, abolition of child labor, dissemination of birth-control information, monthly vacations for female workers, two-month vacations for prospective mothers, both with pay, and the probable killing of individual initiative and incentive by taking the ownership of national capital out of the hands of two million people and putting it into the hands of one hundred and twenty million.

Which explains why Senator Rufus Kretin of Georgia, one of the old Democratic war horses, an incomparable Negro-baiter, a faithful servitor of the dominant economic interests of his state and the lusty father of several black famillies since whitened, walked into the office of Imperial Grand Wizard Givens one day in March, 1935.

"Boys," he began, as closeted with Rev. Givens, Matthew and Bunny in the new modernistic Knights of Nordica palace, they quaffed cool and illegal beverages, "we gotta do sumpin and do it quick. These heah damn Yankees ah makin' inroads on ouah preserves, suh. Th' Republican vote is a-growin'. No tellin' what's li'ble tuh happen in this heah nex' 'lection."

"What can we do, Senator?" asked the Imperial Grand Wizard. "How can we serve the cause?"

"That's just it. That's just it, suh; jus' what Ah came heah fo'," replied the Senator. "Naow sum o' us was thinkin' that maybe yo'all might be able to he'p us keep these damn hicks in line. Yo'all are intelligent gent'men; you know what Ah'm gettin' at?"

"Well, that's a pretty big order, Colonel," said Givens.

"Yes," Matthew added. "It'll be a hard proposition. Conditions are no longer what they used to be."

"An'," said Givens, "we can't do much with that nigger business, like we used to do when th' old Klan was runnin'."

"What about one o' them theah Red scares," asked the Senator, hopefully.

"Humph!" the clergyman snorted. "Better leave that there Red business alone. Times ain't like they was, you know. Anyhow, them damn Reds'll be down here soon enough 'thout us encouragin' 'em none."

"Guess that's right, Gen'ral," mused the statesman. Then brightening: "Lookaheah, Givens. This fellah Fisher's gotta good head. Why not let him work out sumpin?"

"Yeah, he sure has," agreed the Wizard, glad to escape any work except minding the treasury of his order. "If he can't do it, ain't nobody can. Him and Bunny here is as shrewd as some o' them old time darkies. He! He! He!" He beamed patronizingly upon his brilliant son-in-law and his plump secretary.

"Well, theah's money in it. We got plenty o' cash; what we want now is votes," the Senator explained. "C'ose yuh caint preach that white supremacy stuff ve'y effectively when they haint no niggahs."

"Leave it to me. I'll work out something," said Matthew. Here was a chance to get more power, more money. Busy as he was, it would not do to let the opportunity slip by.

"Yuh caint lose no time," warned the Senator.

"We won't," crowed Givens.

A few minutes later they took a final drink together, shook

hands and the Senator, bobbing his white head to the young ladies in the outer office, departed.

Matthew and Bunny retired to the private office of the Grand Exalted Giraw.

"What you thinkin' about pullin'?" asked Bunny.

"Plenty. We'll try the old sure fire Negro problem stuff."

"But that's ancient history, Brother," protested Bunny. "These ducks won't fall for that any more."

"Bunny, I've learned something on this job, and that is that hatred and prejudice always go over big. These people have been raised on the Negro problem, they're used to it, they're trained to react to it. Why should I rack my brain to hunt up something else when I can use a dodge that's always delivered the goods?"

"It may go over at that."

"I know it will. Just leave it to me," said Matthew confidently. "That's not worrying me at all. What's got my goat is my wife being in the family way." Matthew stopped bantering a moment, a sincere look of pain erasing his usual ironic expression.

"Congratulations!" burbled Bunny.

"Don't rub it in," Matthew replied. "You know how the kid will look."

"That's right," agreed his pal. "You know, sometimes I forget who we are."

"Well, I don't. I know I'm a darky and I'm always on the alert."

"What do you intend to do?"

"I don't know, Big Boy, I don't know. I would ordinarily send her to one of those Lying-in Hospitals but she'd be suspicious. Yet, if the kid is born it'll sure be black."

"It won't be white," Bunny agreed. "Why not tell her the whole thing and since she's so crazy about you, I don't think she'd hesitate to go."

"Man, you must be losing your mind, or else you've lost it!" Matthew exploded. "She's a worse nigger-hater than her father. She'd holler for a divorce before you could say Jack Robinson."

"You've got too much money for that."

"You're assuming that she has plenty of intelligence."

"Hasn't she?"

"Let's not discuss a painful subject," pleaded Matthew. "Suggest a remedy."

"She don't have to know that she's going to one of Crookman's places, does she?"

"No, but I can't get her to leave home to have the baby."

"Why?"

"Oh, a lot of damn sentiment about having her baby in the old home, and her damned old mother supports her. So what can I do?"

"Then, the dear old homestead is the only thing that's holding up the play?"

"You're a smart boy, Bunny."

"Don't stress the obvious. Seriously, though, I think everything can be fixed okeh."

"How?" cried Matthew, eagerly.

"Is it worth five grand?" countered Bunny.

"Money's no object, you know, but explain your proposition."

"I will not. You get me fifty century notes and I'll explain later."

"It's a deal, old friend."

Bunny Brown was a man of action. That evening he entered the popular Niggerhead Café, rendezvous of the questionable classes, and sat down at a table. The place was crowded with drinkers downing their "white mule" and contorting to the strains issuing from a radio loud speaker. A current popular dance piece, "The Black Man Blues," was filling the room. The songwriters had been making a fortune recently writing sentimental songs about the passing of the Negro. The plaintive voice of a blues singer rushed out of the loudspeaker:

> *"I wonder where my big, black man has gone;*
> *Oh, I wonder where my big, black man has gone.*
> *Has he done got faded an' left me all alone?"*

When the music ceased and the dancers returned to their tables, Bunny began to look around. In a far corner he saw a waiter whose face seemed familiar. He waited until the fellow came close when he hailed him. As the waiter bent over to get his order, he studied him closely. He had seen this fellow somewhere before. Who could he be? Suddenly with a start he remembered. It was Dr. Joseph Bonds, former head of the Negro Data League in New York. What had brought him here and to this condition? The last time he had seen Bonds, the fellow was a power in the Negro world, with a country place in Westchester County and a swell apartment in town. It saddened Bunny to think that catastrophe had overtaken such a man. Even getting white, it seemed, hadn't helped him much. He recalled that Bonds in his heyday had collected from the white philanthropists with the slogan: "Work, Not Charity," and he smiled as he thought that Bonds would be mighty glad now to get a little charity and not so much work.

"Would a century note look good to you right now?" he asked the former Negro leader when he returned with his drink.

"Just show it to me, Mister," said the waiter, licking his lips. "What you want me to do?"

"What will you do for a hundred berries?" pursued Bunny.

"I'd hate to tell you," replied Bonds, grinning and revealing his familiar tobacco-stained teeth.

"Have you got a friend you can trust?"

"Sure, a fellow named Licorice that washes pots in back."

"You don't mean Santop Licorice, do you?"

"Ssh! They don't know who he is here. He's white now, you know."

"Do they know who you are?"

"What do you mean?" gasped the surprised waiter.

"Oh, I won't say anything but I know you're Bonds of New York."

"Who told you?"

"Oh, a little fairy."

"How could that be? I never associate with them."

"It wasn't that kind of a fairy," Bunny reassured him, laughing. "Well, you get Licorice and come to my hotel when this place closes up."

"Where is that?" asked Bonds. Bunny wrote his name and room number down on a piece of paper and handed it to him.

Three hours later Bunny was awakened by a knocking at his door. He admitted Bonds and Licorice, the latter smelling strongly of steam and food.

"Here," said Bunny, holding up a hundred dollar bill, "is a century note. If you boys can lay aside your scruples for a few hours you can have five of them apiece."

"Well," said Bonds, "neither Santop nor I have been over-burdened with them."

"That's what I thought," Bunny murmured. He proceeded to outline the work he wanted them to do.

"But that would be a criminal offense," objected Licorice.

"You too, Brutus?" sneered Bonds.

"Well, we can't afford to take chances unless we're pro-tected," the former President of Africa argued rather weakly. He was money-hungry and was longing for a stake to get back to Demerara where, since there was a large Negro population, a white man, by virtue of his complexion, amounted to some-thing. Yet, he had had enough experience behind the bars to make him wary.

"We run this town and this state, too," Bunny assured him. "We could get a couple of our men to pull this stunt but it wouldn't be good policy."

"How about a thousand bucks apiece?" asked Bonds, his eyes glittering as he viewed the crisp banknotes in Bunny's hand.

"Here," said Bunny. "Take this century note between you, get your material and pull the job. When you've finished I'll give you nineteen more like it between you."

The two cronies looked at each other and nodded.

"It's a go," said Bonds.

They departed and Bunny went back to sleep.

The next night about eleven-thirty the bells began to toll and the mournful sirens of the fire engines awakened the entire neighborhood in the vicinity of Rev. Givens's home. That stately edifice, built by Ku Klux Klan dollars was in flames. Firemen played a score of streams onto the blaze but the house appeared to be doomed.

On a lawn across the street, in the midst of a consoling crowd, stood Rev. and Mrs. Givens, Helen and Matthew. The old couple were taking the catastrophe fatalistically, Matthew was puzzled and suspicious, but Helen was in hysterics. She presented a bedraggled and woebegone appearance with a blanket around her night dress. She wept afresh every time she looked across at the blazing building where she had spent her happy childhood.

"Matthew," she sobbed, "will you build me another one just like it?"

"Why certainly, Honey," he agreed, "but it will take quite a while."

"Oh, I know; I know, but I want it."

"Well, you'll get it, darling," he soothed, "but I think it would be a good idea for you to go away for a while to rest your nerves. We've got to think of the little one that's coming, you know."

"I don't wanna go nowhere," she screamed.

"But you've got to go somewhere," he reasoned. "Don't you think so, Mother?" Old Mrs. Givens agreed it would be a good idea but suggested that she go along. To this Rev. Givens would not listen at first but he finally yielded.

"Guess it's a good idea after all," he remarked. "Women folks is always in th' way when buildin's goin' on."

Matthew was tickled at the turn of affairs. On the way down to the hotel, he sat beside Helen, alternately comforting her and wondering as to the origin of the fire.

Next morning, bright and early, Bunny, grinning broadly walked into the office, threw his hat on a hook and sat down before his desk after the customary salutation.

"Bunny," called Matthew, looking at him hard. "Get me told!"

"What do you mean?" asked Bunny innocently.

"Just as I thought," chuckled Matthew. "You're a nervy guy."

"Why, I don't get you," said Bunny, continuing the pose.

"Come clean, Big Boy. How much did that fire cost?"

"You gave me five grand, didn't you?"

"Just like a nigger: a person can never get a direct answer from you."

"Are you satisfied?"

"I'm not crying my eyes out."

"Is Helen going North for her confinement?"

"Nothing different."

"Well, then, why do you want to know the why and wherefore of that blaze?"

"Just curiosity, Nero, old chap," grinned Matthew.

"Remember," warned Bunny, mischievously, "curiosity killed the cat."

The ringing of the telephone bell interrupted their conversation.

"What's that?" yelled Matthew into the mouthpiece. "The hell you say! All right, I'll be right up." He hung up the receiver, jumped up excitedly and grabbed his hat.

"What's the matter?" shouted Bunny. "Somebody dead?"

"No," answered the agitated Matthew, "Helen's had a miscarriage," and he dashed out of the room.

"Somebody dead right on," murmured Bunny, half aloud.

Joseph Bonds and Santop Licorice, clean shaven and immaculate, followed the Irish red cap into their drawing room on the New York Express.

"It sure feels good to get out of the barrel once more," sighed Bonds, dropping down on the soft cushion and pulling out a huge cigar.

"Ain't it the truth?" agreed the former Admiral of the Royal African Navy.

Chapter Nine

"BUNNY, I've got it all worked out," announced Matthew, several mornings later, as he breezed into the office.

"Got what worked out?"

"The political proposition."

"Spill it."

"Well, here it is: First, we get Givens on the radio; national hookup, you know, once a week for about two months."

"What'll he talk about? Are you going to write it for him?"

"Oh, he knows how to charm the yokels. He'll appeal to the American people to call upon the Republican administration to close up the sanitariums of Dr. Crookman and deport everybody connected with Black-No-More."

"You can't deport citizens, silly," Bunny remonstrated.

"That don't stop you from advocating it. This is politics, Big Boy."

"Well, what else is on the program?"

"Next: We start a campaign of denunciation against the Republicans in *The Warning*, connecting them with the Pope, Black-No-More and anything else we can think of."

"But they were practically anti-Catholic in 1928, weren't they?"

"Seven years ago, Bunny, seven years ago. How often must I tell you that the people never remember anything? Next we pull the old Write-to-your-Congressman- Write-to-your-Senator stuff. We carry the form letter in *The Warning*, the readers do the rest."

"You can't win a campaign on that stuff, alone," said Bunny disdainfully. "Bring me something better than that, Brother."

"Well, the other step is a surprise, old chap. I'm going to keep it under my hat until later on. But when I spring it, old timer, it'll knock everybody for a row of toadstools." Matthew smiled mysteriously and smoothed back his pale blond hair.

"When do we start this radio racket?" yawned Bunny.

"Wait'll I talk it over with the Chief," said Matthew, rising, "and see how he's dated up."

*

The following Thursday evening at 8:15 p.m. millions of
people sat before their loud speakers, expectantly awaiting the
heralded address to the nation by the Imperial Grand Wizard
of the Knights of Nordica. The program started promptly:

"Good evening, ladies and gentlemen of the radio audience.
This is Station W H A T, Atlanta, Ga., Mortimer K. Shanker
announcing. This evening we are offering a program of tremendous interest to every American citizen. The countrywide
hookup over the chain of the Moronia Broadcasting Company
is enabling one hundred million citizens to hear one of the most
significant messages ever delivered to the American public.

"Before introducing the distinguished speaker of the evening, however, I have a little treat in store for you. Mr. Jack
Albert, the well-known Broadway singer and comedian, has
kindly consented to render his favorite among the popular
songs of the day, 'Vanishing Mammy.' Mr. Albert will be accompanied by that incomparable aggregation of musical talent,
Sammy Snort's Bogalusa Babies. . . . Come on, Al, say a word
or two to the ladies and gentlemen of the radio audience before you begin."

"Oh, hello folks. Awfully glad to see so many of you out
there tonight. Well, that is to say, I suppose there are many of
you out there. You know I like to flatter myself, besides I
haven't my glasses so I can't see very well. However, that's not
the pint, as the bootleggers say. I'm terribly pleased to have the
opportunity of starting off a program like this with one of the
songs I have come to love best. You know, I think a whole lot
of this song. I like it because it has feeling and sentiment. It
means something. It carries you back to the good old days that
are dead and gone forever. It was written by Johnny Gulp with
music by the eminent Japanese-American composer, Forkrise
Sake. And, as Mr. Shanker told you, I am being accompanied
by Sammy Snort's Bogalusa Babies through the courtesy of the
Artillery Café, Chicago, Illinois. All right, Sammy, smack it!"

In two seconds the blare of the jazz orchestra smote the
ears of the unseen audience with the weird medley and clash
of sound that had passed for music since the days of the
Panama-Pacific Exposition. Then the sound died to a whisper

and the plaintive voice of America's premier black-faced trou-
badour came over the air:

> *Vanishing Mammy, Mammy! Mammy! of Mi—ne,*
> *You've been away, dear, such an awfully long time*
> *You went away, Sweet Mammy! Mammy! one summer night*
> *I can't help thinkin', Mammy, that you went white.*
> *Of course I can't blame you, Mammy! Mammy! dear*
> *Because you had so many troubles, Mammy, to bear.*
> *But the old homestead hasn't been the same*
> *Since I last heard you, Mammy, call my name.*
> *And so I wait, loving Mammy, it seems in vain,*
> *For you to come waddling back home again*
> *Vanishing Mammy! Mammy! Mammy!*
> *I'm waiting for you to come back home again.*

"Now, radio audience, this is Mr. Mortimer Shanker speaking again. I know you all loved Mr. Albert's soulful rendition
of 'Vanishing Mammy.' We're going to try to get him back
again in the very near future.

"It now gives me great pleasure to introduce to you a man
who hardly needs any introduction. A man who is known
throughout the civilized world. A man of great scholarship,
executive ability and organizing genius. A man who has, practically unassisted, brought five million Americans under the
banner of one of the greatest societies in this country. It affords
me great pleasure, ladies and gentlemen of the radio audience,
to introduce Rev. Henry Givens, Imperial Grand Wizard of
the Knights of Nordica, who will address you on the very
timely topic of 'The Menace of Negro Blood'."

Rev. Givens, fortified with a slug of corn, advanced nervously
to the microphone, fingering his prepared address. He cleared
his throat and talked for upwards of an hour during which
time he successfully avoided saying anything that was true, the
result being that thousands of telegrams and long distance
telephone calls of congratulation came in to the studio. In his
long address he discussed the foundations of the Republic, anthropology, psychology, miscegenation, coöperation with Christ,
getting right with God, curbing Bolshevism, the bane of birth
control, the menace of the Modernists, science versus religion,
and many other subjects of which he was totally ignorant. The

greater part of his time was taken up in a denunciation of Black-No-More, Incorporated, and calling upon the Republican administration of President Harold Goosie to deport the vicious Negroes at the head of it or imprison them in the federal penitentiary. When he had concluded "In the name of our Saviour and Redeemer, Jesus Christ, Amen," he retired hastily to the washroom to finish his half-pint of corn.

The announcer took Rev. Givens's place at the microphone:

"Now friends, this is Mortimer K. Shanker again, announcing from Station W H A T, Atlanta, Ga., with a nationwide hookup over the chain of the Moronia Broadcasting Company. You have just heard a scholarly and inspiring address by Rev. Henry Givens, Imperial Grand Wizard of the Knights of Nordica on 'The Menace of Negro Blood.' Rev. Givens will deliver another address at this station a week from tonight. . . . Now, to end our program for the evening, friends, we are going to have a popular song by the well-known Goyter Sisters, lately of the State Street Follies, entitled 'Why Did the Old Salt Shaker'. . . ."

The agitation of the Knights of Nordica soon brought action from the administration at Washington. About ten days after Rev. Givens had ceased his talks over the radio, President Harold Goosie announced to the assembled newspaper men that he was giving a great deal of study to the questions raised by the Imperial Grand Wizard concerning Black-No-More, Incorporated; that several truckloads of letters condemning the corporation had been received at the White House and were now being answered by a special corps of clerks; that several Senators had talked over the matter with him, and that the country could expect him to take some action within the next fortnight.

At the end of a fortnight, the President announced that he had decided to appoint a commission of leading citizens to study the whole question thoroughly and to make recommendations. He asked Congress for an appropriation of $100,000 to cover the expenses of the commission.

The House of Representatives approved a resolution to that effect a week later. The Senate, which was then engaged in a spirited debate on the World Court and the League of Nations, postponed consideration of the resolution for three weeks. When it came to vote before that august body, it was passed, after long argument, with amendments and returned to the House.

Six weeks after President Goosie had made his request of Congress, the resolution was passed in its final form. He then announced that inside of a week he would name the members of the commission.

The President kept his word. He named the commission, consisting of seven members, five Republicans and two Democrats. They were mostly politicians temporarily out of a job.

In a private car the commission toured the entire country, visiting all of the Black-No-More sanitariums, the Crookman Lying-in Hospitals and the former Black Belts. They took hundreds of depositions, examined hundreds of witnesses and drank large quantities of liquor.

Two months later they issued a preliminary report in which they pointed out that the Black-No-More sanitariums and Lying-in Hospitals were being operated within the law; that only one million Negroes remained in the country; that it was illegal in most of the states for pure whites and persons of Negro ancestry to intermarry but that it was difficult to detect fraud because of collusion. As a remedy the Commission recommended stricter observance of the law, minor changes in the marriage laws, the organization of special matrimonial courts with trained genealogists attached to each, better equipped judges, more competent district attorneys, the strengthening of the Mann Act, the abolition of the road house, the closer supervision of dance halls, a stricter censorship on books and moving pictures and government control of cabarets. The commission promised to publish the complete report of its activities in about six weeks.

Two months later, when practically everyone had forgotten that there had ever been such an investigation, the complete report of the commission, comprising 1789 pages in fine print came off the press. Copies were sent broadcast to prominent citizens and organizations. Exactly nine people in the United States read it: the warden of a county jail, the proofreader at the Government Printing Office, the janitor of the City Hall in Ashtabula, Ohio, the city editor of the Helena (Ark.) *Bugle*, a stenographer in the Department of Health of Spokane, Wash., a dishwasher in a Bowery restaurant, a flunky in the office of the Research Director of Black-No-More, Incorporated, a life termer in Clinton Prison at Dannemora, N. Y., and a gag writer on the staff of a humorous weekly in Chicago.

Matthew received fulsome praise from the members of his organization and the higher-ups in the Southern Democracy. He had, they said, forced the government to take action, and they began to talk of him for public office.

The Grand Exalted Giraw was jubilant. Everything, he told Bunny, had gone as he had planned. Now he was ready to turn the next trick.

"What's that?" asked his assistant, looking up from the morning comic section.

"Ever hear of the Anglo-Saxon Association of America?" Matthew queried.

"No, what's their graft?"

"It isn't a graft, you crook. The Anglo-Saxon Association of America is an organization located in Virginia. The headquarters are in Richmond. It's a group of rich highbrows who can trace their ancestry back almost two hundred years. You see they believe in white supremacy the same as our outfit but they claim that the Anglo-Saxons are the cream of the white race and should maintain the leadership in American social, economic and political life."

"You sound like a college professor," sneered Bunny.

"Don't insult me, you tripe. Listen now: This crowd thinks they're too highbrow to come in with the Knights of Nordica. They say our bunch are morons."

"That about makes it unanimous," commented Bunny, biting off the end of a cigar.

"Well, what I'm trying to do now is to bring these two organizations together. We've got numbers but not enough money to win an election; they have the jack. If I can get them to see the light we'll win the next Presidential election hands down."

"What'll I be: Secretary of the Treasury?" laughed Bunny.

"Over my dead body!" Matthew replied, reaching for his flask. "But seriously, Old Top, if I can succeed in putting this deal over we'll have the White House in a bag. No fooling!"

"When do we get busy?"

"Next week this Anglo-Saxon Association has its annual meeting in Richmond. You and I'll go up there and give them a spiel. We may take Givens along to add weight."

"You don't mean intellectual weight, do you?"

"Will you never stop kidding?"

Mr. Arthur Snobbcraft, President of the Anglo-Saxon Association, an F.F.V. and a man suspiciously swarthy for an Anglo-Saxon, had devoted his entire life to fighting for two things: white racial integrity and Anglo-Saxon supremacy. It had been very largely a losing fight. The farther he got from his goal, the more desperate he became. He had been the genius that thought up the numerous racial integrity laws adopted in Virginia and many of the other Southern states. He was strong for sterilization of the unfit: meaning Negroes, aliens, Jews and other riff raff, and he had an abiding hatred of democracy.

Snobbcraft's pet scheme now was to get a genealogical law passed disfranchising all people of Negro or unknown ancestry. He argued that good citizens could not be made out of such material. His organization had money but it needed popularity—numbers.

His joy then knew no bounds when he received Matthew's communication. While he had no love for the Knights of Nordica which, he held, contained just the sort of people he wanted to legislate into impotency, social, economic and physical, he believed he could use them to gain his point. He wired Matthew at once, saying the Association would be delighted to have him address them, as well as the Imperial Grand Wizard.

The Grand Exalted Giraw had long known of Snobbcraft's obsession, the genealogical law. He also knew that there was no chance of ever getting such a law adopted but in order to even try to pass such a law it would be necessary to win the whole country in a national election. Together, his organization and Snobbcraft's could turn the trick; singly neither one could do it.

In an old pre-Civil War mansion on a broad, tree-shaded boulevard, the directors of the Anglo-Saxon Association gathered in their annual meeting. They listened first to Rev. Givens and next to Matthew. The matter was referred to a committee which in an hour or two reported favorably. Most of these men had dreamed from youth of holding high political office at the national capital as had so many eminent Virginians but none of them was Republican, of course, and the Democrats never won anything nationally. By swallowing their pride for a season and joining with the riff raff of the Knights of Nordica, they saw an opportunity, for the first time in years to get into power; and they took it. They would furnish plenty of money, they said, if the other group would furnish the numbers.

Givens and Matthew returned to Atlanta in high spirits.

"I tell you, Brother Fisher," croaked Givens, "our star is ascending. I can see no way for us to fail, with God's help. We'll surely defeat our enemy. Victory is in the air."

"It sure looks that way," the Grand Giraw agreed. With their money and ours, we can certainly get together a larger campaign fund than the Republicans."

Back in Richmond Mr. Snobbcraft and his friends were in conference with the statistician of a great New York insurance company. This man, Dr. Samuel Buggerie, was highly respected among members of his profession and well known by the reading public. He was the author of several books and wrote frequently for the heavier periodicals. His well-known work, *The Fluctuation of the Sizes of Left Feet among the Assyrians during the Ninth Century before Christ* had been favorably commented upon by several reviewers, one of whom had actually read it. An even more learned work of his was entitled *Putting Wasted Energy to Work*, in which he called attention, by elaborate charts and graphs, to the possibilities of harnessing the power generated by the leaves of trees rubbing together on windy days. In several brilliant monographs he had proved that rich people have smaller families than the poor; that imprisonment does not stop crime; that laborers usually migrate in the wake of high wages. His most recent article in a very intellectual magazine read largely by those who loafed for a living, had proved statistically that unemployment and poverty are principally a state of mind. This contribution was enthusiastically hailed by scholars and especially by business men as an outstanding contribution to contemporary thought.

Dr. Buggerie was a ponderous, nervous, entirely bald, specimen of humanity, with thick moist hands, a receding double chin and very prominent eyes that were constantly shifting about and bearing an expression of seemingly perpetual wonderment behind their big horn-rimmed spectacles. He seemed about to burst out of his clothes and his pockets were always bulging with papers and notes.

Dr. Buggerie, like Mr. Snobbcraft, was a professional Anglo-Saxon as well as a descendant of one of the First Families of Virginia. He held that the only way to tell the pure whites from the imitation whites, was to study their family trees. He claimed that such a nationwide investigation would disclose the various non-Nordic strains in the population. Laws, said he, should then be passed forbidding these strains from mixing or marrying with the pure strains that had produced such fine specimens of mankind as Mr. Snobbcraft and himself.

In high falsetto voice he eagerly related to the directors of the Anglo-Saxon Association the results of some of his preliminary researches. These tended to show, he claimed, that there must be as many as twenty million people in the United States who possessed some slight non-Nordic strain and were thus unfit for both citizenship and procreation. If the organization would put up the money for the research on a national scale, he declared that he could produce statistics before election that would be so shocking that the Republicans would lose the country unless they adopted the Democratic plank on genealogical examinations. After a long and eloquent talk by Mr. Snobbcraft in support of Dr. Buggerie's proposition, the directors voted to appropriate the money, on condition that the work be kept as secret as possible. The statistician agreed although it hurt him to the heart to forego any publicity. The very next morning he began quietly to assemble his staff.

Chapter Ten

HANK JOHNSON, Chuck Foster, Dr. Crookman and Gorman Gay, National Chairman of the Republican National Committee, sat in the physician's hotel suite conversing in low tones.

"We're having a tough time getting ready for the Fall campaign," said Gay. "Unfortunately our friends are not contributing with their accustomed liberality."

"Can't complain about us, can you?" asked Foster.

"No, no," the politician denied quickly. "You have been most liberal in the past two years, but then we have done many favors for you, too."

"Yuh sho right, Gay," Hank remarked. "Dem crackahs mighta put us outa business efen it hadn' bin fo' th' admin'strations suppo't."

"I'm quite sure we deeply appreciate the many favors we've received from the present administration," added Dr. Crookman.

"We won't need it much longer, though," said Chuck Foster.

"How's that?" asked Gay, opening his half-closed eyes.

"Well, we've done about all the business we can do in this country. Practically all of the Negroes are white except a couple of thousand diehards and those in institutions," Chuck informed him.

"Dat's right," said Hank. "An' it sho makes dis heah country lonesome. Ah ain't seen a brown-skin ooman in so long Ah doan know whut Ah'd do if Ah seen one."

"That's right, Gay," added Dr. Crookman. "We've about cleaned up the Negro problem in this country. Next week we're closing all except five of our sanitariums."

"Well, what about your Lying-In hospitals?" asked Gay.

"Of course we'll have to continue operating them," Crookman replied. "The women would be in an awful fix if we didn't."

"Now look here," proposed Gay, drawing closer to them and lowering his voice. "This coming campaign is going to be one of the bitterest in the history of this country. I fear there will be rioting, shooting and killing. Those hospitals cannot be closed without tremendous mental suffering to the womanhood of the country. We want to avoid that and you want to avoid it, too. Yet, these hospitals will constantly be in danger. It ought to be worth something to you to have them especially protected by the forces of the government."

"You would do that anyway, wouldn't you Gay?" asked Crookman.

"Well, it's going to cost us millions of votes to do it, and the members of the National Executive Committee seem to feel that you ought to make a very liberal donation to the campaign fund to make up for the votes we'll lose."

"What would you call a liberal donation?" Crookman inquired.

"A successful campaign cannot be fought this year," Gay replied, "under twenty millions."

"Man," shouted Hank, "yuh ain't talkin' 'bout dollahs, is yuh?"

"You got it right, Hank," answered the National Chairman. "It'll cost that much and maybe more."

"Where do you expect to get all of that money?" queried Foster.

"That's just what's worrying us," Gay replied, "and that's why I'm here. You fellows are rolling in wealth and we need your help. In the past two years you've collected around ninety million dollars from the Negro public. Why not give us a good break? You won't miss five million, and it ought to be worth it to you fellows to defeat the Democrats."

"Five millions! Great Day," Hank exploded. "Man, is you los' yo' min'?"

"Not at all," Gay denied. "Might as well own up that if we don't get a contribution of about that size from you we're liable to lose this election. . . . Come on, fellows, don't be so tight. Of course, you're setting pretty and all you've got to do is change your residence to Europe or some other place if things don't run smoothly in America, but you want to think of those poor women with their black babies. What will they do if you fellows leave the country or if the Democrats win and you have to close all of your places?"

"That's right, Chief," Foster observed. "You can't let the women down."

"Yeah," said Johnson. "Give 'im th' jack."

"Well, suppose we do?" concluded Crookman, smiling.

The National Chairman was delighted. "When can we collect?" he asked, "and how?"

"Tomorrow, if yuh really wants it then," Johnson observed.

"Now remember," warned Gay. We cannot afford to let it be known that we are getting such a large sum from any one person or corporation."

"That's your lookout," said the physician, indifferently. "You know *we* won't say anything."

Mr. Gay, shortly afterward, departed to carry the happy news to the National Executive Committee, then in session right there in New York City.

The Republicans certainly needed plenty of money to re-elect President Goosie. The frequent radio addresses of Rev. Givens, the growing numbers of the Knights of Nordica, the inexplicable affluence of the Democratic Party and the vitriolic articles in *The Warning*, had not failed to rouse much Democratic sentiment. People were not exactly for the Democrats but they were against the Republicans. As early as May it did not seem possible for the Republicans to carry a single Southern state and many of the Northern and Eastern strongholds were in doubt. The Democrats seemed to have everything their way. Indeed, they were so confident of success that they were already counting the spoils.

When the Democratic Convention met in Jackson, Mississippi, on July 1, 1936, political wiseacres claimed that for the first time in history the whole program was cut and dried and would be run off smoothly and swiftly. Such, however, was not the case. The unusually hot sun, coupled with the enormous quantities of liquor vended, besides the many conflicting interests present, soon brought dissension.

Shortly after the keynote speech had been delivered by Senator Kretin, the Anglo-Saxon crowd let it be known that they wanted some distinguished Southerner like Arthur Snobbcraft nominated for the Presidency. The Knights of Nordica were intent on nominating Imperial Grand Wizard Givens. The

Northern faction of the party, now reduced to a small minority in party councils, was holding out for former Governor Grogan of Massachusetts who as head of the League of Catholic voters had a great following.

Through twenty ballots the voting proceeded, and it remained deadlocked. No faction would yield. Leaders saw that there had to be a compromise. They retired to a suite on the top floor of the Judge Lynch Hotel. There, in their shirt sleeves, with collars open, mint juleps on the table and electric fans stirring up the hot air, they got down to business. Twelve hours later they were still there.

Matthew, wilted, worn but determined, fought for his chief. Simeon Dump of the Anglo-Saxon Association swore he would not withdraw the name of Arthur Snobbcraft. Rev. John Whiffle, a power in the party, gulped drink after drink, kept dabbing a damp handkerchief at the shining surface of his skull, and held out for one Bishop Belch. Moses Lejewski of New York argued obstinately for the nomination of Governor Grogan.

In the meantime the delegates, having left the oven-like convention hall, either lay panting and drinking in their rooms, sat in the hotel lobbies discussing the deadlock or cruised the streets in automobiles confidently seeking the dens of iniquity which they had been told were eager to lure them into sin.

When the clock struck three, Matthew rose and suggested that since the Knights of Nordica and the Anglo-Saxon Association were the two most powerful organizations in the party, Givens should get the presidential nomination, Snobbcraft the vice-presidential and the other candidates be assured of cabinet positions. This suggested compromise appealed to no one except Matthew.

"You people forget," said Simeon Dump, "that the Anglo-Saxon Association is putting up half the money to finance this campaign."

"And you forget," declared Moses Lejewski, "that we're supporting your crazy scheme to disfranchise anybody possessing Negro ancestry when we get into office. That's going to cost us millions of votes in the North. You fellows can't expect to hog everything."

"Why not?" challenged Dump. "How could you win without money?"

"And how," added Matthew, "can you get anywhere without the Knights of Nordica behind you?"

"And how," Rev. Whiffle chimed in, "can you get anywhere without the Fundamentalists and the Drys?"

At four o'clock they had got no farther than they had been at three. They tried to pick some one not before mentioned, and went over and over the list of eligibles. None was satisfactory. One was too radical, another was too conservative, a third was an atheist, a fourth had once rifled a city treasury, the fifth was of immigrant extraction once removed, a sixth had married a Jewess, a seventh was an intellectual, an eighth had spent too long at Hot Springs trying to cure the syphilis, a ninth was rumored to be part Mexican and a tenth had at one time in his early youth been a Socialist.

At five o'clock they were desperate, drunk and disgusted. The stuffy room was a litter of discarded collars, cigarette and cigar butts, match stems, heaped ash trays and empty bottles. Matthew drank little and kept insisting on the selection of Rev. Givens. To the sodden and nodding men he painted marvelous pictures of the spoils of office and their excellent chance of getting there, and then suddenly declared that the Knights of Nordica would withdraw unless Givens was nominated. The threat aroused them. They cursed and called it a holdup, but Matthew was adamant. As a last stroke, he rose and pretended to be ready to bolt the caucus. They remonstrated with him and finally gave in to him.

Orders went out to the delegates. They assembled in the convention hall. The shepherds of the various state flocks cracked the whip and the delegates voted accordingly. Late that afternoon the news went out to a waiting world that the Democrats had nominated Henry Givens for President and Arthur Snobbcraft for Vice-President. Mr. Snobbcraft didn't like that at all, but it was better than nothing.

A few days later the Republican convention opened in Chicago. Better disciplined, as usual, than the Democrats, its business proceeded like clockwork. President Goosie was nominated for reëlection on the first ballot and Vice-President Gump was again selected as his running mate. A platform was adopted whose chief characteristic was vagueness. As was customary, it stressed the party's record in office, except that which was criminal; it denounced fanaticism without being specific, and it emphasized the rights of the individual and the trusts in the same paragraph. As the Democratic slogan was White Supremacy and its platform dwelt largely on the necessity of genealogical investigation, the Republicans adopted the slogan: Personal Liberty and Ancestral Sanctity.

Dr. Crookman and his associates, listening in on the radio in his suite in the Robin Hood Hotel in New York City, laughed softly as they heard the President deliver his speech of acceptance which ended in the following original manner:

"And finally, my friends, I can only say that we shall continue in the path of rugged individualism, free from the influence of sinister interests, upholding the finest ideals of honesty, independence and integrity, so that, to quote Abraham Lincoln, 'This nation of the people, for the people and by the people shall not perish from the earth.'"

"That," said Foster, as the President ceased barking, "sounds almost like the speech of acceptance of Brother Givens that we heard the other day."

Dr. Crookman smiled and brushed the ashes off his cigar. "It may even be the same speech," he suggested.

Through the hot days of July and August the campaign slowly got under way. Innumerable photographs appeared in the newspapers depicting the rival candidates among the simple folk of some village, helping youngsters to pick cherries, assisting an old woman up a stairway, bathing in the old swimming hole, eating at a barbecue and posing on the rear platforms of special trains.

Long articles appeared in the Sunday newspapers extolling the simple virtues of the two great men. Both, it seemed, had come from poor but honest families; both were hailed as tried and true friends of the great, common people; both were declared to be ready to give their strength and intellect to America for the next four years. One writer suggested that Givens resembled Lincoln, while another declared that President Goosie's character was not unlike that of Roosevelt, believing he was paying the former a compliment.

Rev. Givens told the reporters: "It is my intention, if elected, to carry out the traditional tariff policy of the Democratic Party" (neither he or anyone else knew what that was).

President Goosie averred again and again, "I intend to make my second term as honest and efficient as my first." Though a dire threat, this statement was supposed to be a fine promise.

Meanwhile, Dr. Samuel Buggerie and his operatives were making great headway examining birth and marriage records throughout the United States. Around the middle of September the Board of Directors held a conference at which the learned man presented a partial report.

"I am now prepared to prove," gloated the obese statistician, "that fully one-quarter of the people of one Virginia county possess non-white ancestry, Indian or Negro; and we can further prove that all of the Indians on the Atlantic Coast are part Negro. In several counties in widely separated parts of the country, we have found that the ancestry of a considerable percentage of the people is in doubt. There is reason to believe that there are countless numbers of people who ought not to be classed with whites and should not mix with Anglo-Saxons."

It was decided that the statistician should get his data in simple form that anyone could read and understand, and have it ready to release just a few days before election. When the people saw how great was the danger from black blood, it was reasoned, they would flock to the Democratic standard and it would be too late for the Republicans to halt the stampede.

No political campaign in the history of the country had ever been so bitter. On one side were those who were fanatically positive of their pure Caucasian ancestry; on the other side were those who knew themselves to be "impure" white or had reason to suspect it. The former were principally Democratic, the latter Republican. There was another group which was Republican because it felt that a victory for the Democrats might cause another Civil War. The campaign roused acrimonious dispute even within families. Often behind these family rifts lurked the knowledge or suspicion of a dark past.

As the campaign grew more bitter, denunciations of Dr. Crookman and his activities grew more violent. A move was started to close all of his hospitals. Some wanted them to be closed for all time; others advised their closing for the duration of the campaign. The majority of thinking people (which wasn't so many) strenuously objected to the proposal.

"No good purpose will be served by closing these hospitals," declared the New York *Morning Earth.* "On the contrary such a step might have tragic results. The Negroes have disappeared into the body of our citizenry, large numbers have intermarried with the whites and the offspring of these marriages are appearing in increasing numbers. Without these hospitals, think how many couples would be estranged; how many homes wrecked! Instead of taking precipitate action, we should be patient and move slowly."

Other Northern newspapers assumed an even more friendly attitude, but the press generally followed the crowd, or led it, and in slightly veiled language urged the opponents of Black-No-More to take the law into their hands.

Finally, emboldened and inflamed by fiery editorials, radio addresses, pamphlets, posters and platform speeches, a mob seeking to protect white womanhood in Cincinnati attacked a Crookman hospital, drove several women into the streets and set fire to the building. A dozen babies were burned to death and others, hastily removed by their mothers, were recognized as mulattoes. The newspapers published names and addresses. Many of the women were very prominent socially either in their own right or because of their husbands.

The nation was shocked as never before. Republican sentiment began to dwindle. The Republican Executive Committee met and discussed ways and means of combating the trend. Gorman Gay was at his wits' end. Nothing, he thought, could save them except a miracle.

Two flights below in a spacious office sat two of the Republican campaigners, Walter Williams and Joseph Bonds, busily engaged in leading the other workers (who knew better) to believe that they were earning the ten dollars a day they were receiving. The former had passed for a Negro for years on the strength of a part-Negro grandparent and then gone back to the white race when the National Social Equality League was forced to cease operations at the insistence of both the sheriff and the landlord. Joseph Bonds, former head of the Negro Data League who had once been a Negro but thanks to Dr. Crookman was now Caucasian and proud of it, had but recently returned to the North from Atlanta, accompanied by Santop Licorice. Both Mr. Williams and Mr. Bonds had been unable to stomach the Democratic crowd and so had fallen in with the Republicans, who were as different from them as one billiard ball from another. The two gentlemen were in low tones discussing the dilemma of the Republicans, while rustling papers to appear busy.

"Jo, if we could figure out something to turn the tables on these Democrats, we wouldn't have to work for the rest of our lives," Williams observed, blowing a cloud of cigarette smoke out of the other corner of his mouth.

"Yes, that's right, Walt, but there ain't a chance in the world. Old Gay is almost crazy, you know. Came in here slamming doors and snapping at everybody this morning," Bonds remarked.

Williams leaned closer to him, lowered his flame-thatched head and then looking to the right and left whispered, "Listen here, do you know where Beard is?"

"No," answered Bonds, starting and looking around to see if anyone was listening. "Where is he?"

"Well, I got a letter from him the other day. He's down there in Richmond doing research work for the Anglo-Saxon Association under that Dr. Buggerie."

"Do they know who he is?"

"Of course they don't. He's been white quite a while now, you know, and of course they'd never connect him with the Dr. Shakespeare A. Beard who used to be one of their most outspoken enemies."

"Well, what about it?" persisted Bonds, eagerly. "Do you think he might know something on the Democrats that might help?"

"He might. We could try him out anyway. If he knows anything he'll spill it because he hates that crowd."

"How will you get in touch with him quickly? Write to him?"

"Certainly not," growled Williams, "I'll get expenses from Gay for the trip. He'll fall for anything now."

He rose and made for the elevator. Five minutes later he was standing before his boss, the National Chairman, a worried, gray little man with an aldermanic paunch and a convict's mouth.

"What is it, Williams?" snapped the Chairman.

"I'd like to get expenses to Richmond," said Williams. "I have a friend down there in Snobbcraft's office and he might have some dope we can use to our advantage."

"Scandal?" asked Mr. Gay, brightening.

"Well, I don't know right now, of course, but this fellow is a very shrewd observer and in six months' time he ought to have grabbed something that'll help us out of this jam."

"Is he a Republican or a Democrat?"

"Neither. He's a highly trained and competent social student. You couldn't expect him to be either," Williams observed. "But I happen to know that he hasn't got any money to speak of, so for a consideration I'm sure he'll spill everything he knows, if anything."

"Well, it's a gamble," said Gay, doubtfully, "but any port in a storm."

Williams left Washington immediately for Richmond. That night he sat in a cramped little room of the former champion of the darker races.

"What are you doing down there, Beard?" asked Williams, referring to the headquarters of the Anglo-Saxon Association.

"Oh, I'm getting, or helping to get, that data of Buggerie's into shape."

"What data? You told me you were doing research work. Now you say you're arranging data. Have they finished collecting it?"

"Yes, we finished that job some time ago. Now we're trying to get the material in shape for easy digestion."

"What do you mean: easy digestion?" queried Williams. "What are you fellows trying to find out and why must it be so easily digested. You fellows usually try to make your stuff unintelligible to the herd."

"This is different," said Beard, lowering his voice to almost a whisper. "We're under a pledge of secrecy. We have been investigating the family trees of the nation and so far, believe me, we certainly have uncovered astounding facts. When I'm finally discharged, which will probably be after election, I'm going to peddle some of that information. Snobbcraft and even Buggerie are not aware of the inflammatory character of the facts we've assembled." He narrowed his foxy eyes greedily.

"Is it because they've been planning to release some of it that they want it in easily digestible form, as you say?" pressed Williams.

"That's it exactly," declared Beard, stroking his now clean-shaven face. "I overheard Buggerie and Snobbcraft chuckling about it only a day or two ago."

"Well, there must be a whole lot of it," insinuated Williams, "if they've had all of you fellows working for six months. Where all did you work?"

"Oh, all over. North as well as South. We've got a whole basement vault full of index cards."

"I guess they're keeping close watch over it, aren't they?" asked Williams.

"Sure. It would take an army to get in that vault."

"Well, I guess they don't want anything to happen to the stuff before they spring it," observed the man from Republican headquarters.

Soon afterward Williams left Dr. Beard, took a stroll around the Anglo-Saxon Association's stately headquarters building, noted the half-dozen tough looking guards about it and then caught the last train for the capital city. The next morning he had a long talk with Gorman Gay.

"It's okeh, Jo," he whispered to Bonds, later, as he passed his desk.

Chapter Eleven

"WHAT'S the matter with you, Matt?" asked Bunny one morning about a month before election. "Ain't everything going okeh? You look as if we'd lost the election and failed to elect that brilliant intellectual, Henry Givens, President of the United States."

"Well, we might just as well lose it as far as I'm concerned," said Matthew, "if I don't find a way out of this jam I'm in."

"What jam?"

"Well, Helen got in the family way last winter again. I sent her to Palm Beach and the other resorts, thinking the travel and exercise might bring on another miscarriage."

"Did it?"

"Not a chance in the world. Then, to make matters worse, she miscalculates. At first she thought she would be confined in December; now she tells me she's only got about three weeks to go."

"Say not so!"

"I'm preaching gospel."

"Well, hush my mouth! Waddya gonna do? You can't send her to one o' Crookman's hospitals, it would be too dangerous right now."

"That's just it. You see, I figured she wouldn't be ready until about a month after election when everything had calmed down, and I could send her then."

"Would she have gone?"

"She couldn't afford not to with her old man the President of the United States."

"Well, whaddya gonna do, Big Boy? Think fast! Think fast! Them three weeks will get away from here in no time."

"Don't I know it?"

"What about an abortion?" suggested Bunny, hopefully.

"Nothing doing. First place, she's too frail, and second place she's got some fool idea about that being a sin."

"About the only thing for you to do, then," said Bunny, "is to get ready to pull out when that kid is born."

"Oh, Bunny, I'd hate to leave Helen. She's really the only

woman I ever loved, you know. Course she's got her prejudices and queer notions like everybody else but she's really a little queen. She's been an inspiration to me, too, Bunny. Every time I talk about pulling out of this game when things don't go just right, she makes me stick it out. I guess I'd have been gone after I cleaned up that first million if it hadn't been for her."

"You'd have been better off if you had," Bunny commented.

"Oh, I don't know. She's hot for me to become Secretary of State or Ambassador to England or something like that; and the way things are going it looks like I will be. That is, if I can get out of this fix."

"If you can get out o' this jam, Matt, I'll sure take my hat off to you. An' I know how you feel about scuttling out and leaving her. I had a broad like that once in Harlem. 'Twas through her I got that job in th' bank. She was crazy about me, Boy, until she caught me two-timin'. Then she tried to shoot me.

"Squaws are funny that way," Bunny continued, philosophically. "Since I've been white I've found out they're all the same, white or black. Kipling was right. They'll fight to get you, fight to keep you and fight you when they catch you playin' around. But th' kinda woman that won't fight for a man ain't worth havin'."

"So you think I ought to pull out, eh Bunny?" asked the worried Matthew, returning to the subject.

"Well, what I'd suggest is this:" his plump friend advised, "about time you think Helen's gonna be confined, get together as much cash as you can and keep your plane ready. Then, when the baby's born, go to her, tell her everything an' offer to take her away with you. If she won't go, you beat it; if she will, why everything's hotsy totsy." Bunny extended his soft pink hands expressively.

"Well, that sounds pretty good, Bunny."

"It's your best bet, Big Boy," said his friend and secretary.

Two days before election the situation was unchanged. There was joy in the Democratic camp, gloom among the Republicans. For the first time in American history it seemed that money was not going to decide an election. The propagandists and publicity men of the Democrats had so played upon the fears

and prejudices of the public that even the bulk of Jews and
Catholics were wavering and many had been won over to the
support of a candidate who had denounced them but a few
months before. In this they were but running true to form,
however, as they had usually been on the side of white supremacy in the old days when there was a Negro population observ-
able to the eye. The Republicans sought to dig up some scandal
against Givens and Snobbcraft but were dissuaded by their
Committee on Strategy which feared to set so dangerous a
precedent. There were also politicians in their ranks who were
guilty of adulteries, drunkenness and grafting.

The Republicans, Goosie and Gump, and the Democrats,
Givens and Snobbcraft had ended their swings around the
country and were resting from their labors. There were parades
in every city and country town. Minor orators beat the lectern
from the Atlantic to the Pacific extolling the imaginary virtues
of the candidates of the party that hired them. Dr. Crookman
was burned a hundred times in effigy. Several Lying-In hospitals were attacked. Two hundred citizens who knew nothing
about either candidate were arrested for fighting over which
was the better man.

The air was electric with expectancy. People stood around in
knots. Small boys scattered leaflets on ten million doorsteps.
Police were on the alert to suppress disorder, except what they
created.

Arthur Snobbcraft, jovial and confident that he would soon assume a position befitting a member of one of the First Families
of Virginia, was holding a brilliant pre-election party in his palatial residence. Strolling in and out amongst his guests, the
master of the house accepted their premature congratulations
in good humor. It was fine to hear oneself already addressed as
Mr. Vice-President.

The tall English butler hastily edged his way through the
throng surrounding the President of the Anglo-Saxon Association and whispered, "Dr. Buggerie is in the study upstairs. He
says he must see you at once; that it is very, very important."

Puzzled, Snobbcraft went up to find out what in the world
could be the trouble. As he entered, the massive statistician
was striding back and forth, mopping his brow, his eyes start-

ing from his head, a sheaf of typewritten sheets trembling in his hand.

"What's wrong, Buggerie?" asked Snobbcraft, perturbed.

"Everything! Everything!" shrilled the statistician.

"Be specific, please."

"Well," shaking the sheaf of papers in Snobbcraft's face, "we can't release any of this stuff! It's too damaging! It's too inclusive! We'll have to suppress it, Snobbcraft. You hear me? We musn't let anyone get hold of it." The big man's flabby jowls worked excitedly.

"What do you mean?" snarled the F. F. V. "Do you mean to tell me that all of that money and work is wasted?"

"That's exactly what I mean," squeaked Buggerie. "It would be suicidal to publish it."

"Why? Get down to brass tacks, man, for God's sake. You get my goat."

"Now listen here, Snobbcraft," replied the statistician soberly, dropping heavily into a chair. "Sit down and listen to me. I started this investigation on the theory that the data gathered would prove that around twenty million people, mostly of the lower classes were of Negro ancestry, recent and remote, while about half that number would be of uncertain or unknown ancestry."

"Well, what have you found?" insisted Snobbcraft, impatiently.

"I have found," continued Buggerie, "that over half the population has no record of its ancestry beyond five generations!"

"That's fine!" chortled Snobbcraft. "I've always maintained that there were only a few people of good blood in this country."

"But those figures include all classes," protested the larger man. "Your class as well as the lower classes."

"Don't insult me, Buggerie!" shouted the head of the Anglo-Saxons, half rising from his seat on the sofa.

"Be calm! Be calm!" cried Buggerie excitedly, "You haven't heard anything yet."

"What else, in the name of God, could be a worse libel on the aristocracy of this state?" Snobbcraft mopped his dark and haughty countenance.

"Well, these statistics we've gathered prove that most of our

social leaders, especially of Anglo-Saxon lineage, are descendants of colonial stock that came here in bondage. They associated with slaves, in many cases worked and slept with them.
They intermixed with the blacks and the women were sexually
exploited by their masters. Then, even more than today, the illegitimate birth rate was very high in America."

Snobbcraft's face was working with suppressed rage. He
started to rise but reconsidered. "Go on," he commanded.

"There was so much of this mixing between whites and
blacks of the various classes that very early the colonies took steps
to put a halt to it. They managed to prevent intermarriage but
they couldn't stop intermixture. You know the old records
don't lie. They're right there for everybody to see. . . .

"A certain percentage of these Negroes," continued Buggerie, quite at ease now and seemingly enjoying his dissertation, "in time lightened sufficiently to be able to pass for white.
They then merged with the general population. Assuming that
there were one thousand such cases fifteen generations ago—
and we have proof that there were more—their descendants
now number close to fifty million souls. Now I maintain that
we dare not risk publishing this information. Too many of our
very first families are touched right here in Richmond!"

"Buggerie!" gasped the F. F. V., "Are you mad?"

"Quite sane, sir," squeaked the ponderous man, somewhat
proudly, "and I know what I know." He winked a watery eye.

"Well, go on. Is there any more?"

"Plenty," proceeded the statistician, amiably. "Take your
own family, for instance. (Now don't get mad, Snobbcraft.)
Take your own family. It is true that your people descended
from King Alfred, but he has scores, perhaps hundreds of
thousands of descendants. Some are, of course, honored and
respected citizens, cultured aristocrats who are a credit to the
country; but most of them, my dear, dear Snobbcraft, are in
what you call the lower orders: that is to say, laboring people,
convicts, prostitutes, and that sort. One of your maternal
ancestors in the late seventeenth century was the offspring of
an English serving maid and a black slave. This woman in turn
had a daughter by the plantation owner. This daughter was
married to a former indentured slave. Their children were all

white and you are one of their direct descendants!" Buggerie beamed.

"Stop!" shouted Snobbcraft, the veins standing out on his narrow forehead and his voice trembling with rage. "You can't sit there and insult my family that way, suh."

"Now that outburst just goes to prove my earlier assertion," the large man continued, blandly. "If you get so excited about the truth, what do you think will be the reaction of other people? There's no use getting angry at me. I'm not responsible for your ancestry! Nor, for that matter, are you. You're no worse off than I am, Snobbcraft. My great, great grandfather had his ears cropped for non-payment of debts and was later jailed for thievery. His illegitimate daughter married a free Negro who fought in the Revolutionary War." Buggerie wagged his head almost gleefully.

"How can you admit it?" asked the scandalized Snobbcraft.

"Why not?" demanded Buggerie. "I have plenty of company. There's Givens, who is quite a fanatic on the race question and white supremacy, and yet he's only four generations removed from a mulatto ancestor."

"Givens too?"

"Yes, and also the proud Senator Kretin. He boasts, you know of being descended from Pocahontas and Captain John Smith, but so are thousands of Negroes. Incidentally, there hasn't been an Indian unmixed with Negro on the Atlantic coastal plain for over a century and a half."

"What about Matthew Fisher?"

"We can find no record whatever of Fisher, which is true of about twenty million others, and so," he lowered his voice dramatically, "I have reason to suspect that he is one of those Negroes who have been whitened."

"And to think that I entertained him in my home!" Snobbcraft muttered to himself. And then aloud: "Well, what are we to do about it?"

"We must destroy the whole shooting match," the big man announced as emphatically as possible for one with a soprano voice, "and we'd better do it at once. The sooner we get through with it the better."

"But I can't leave my guests," protested Snobbcraft. Then

turning angrily upon his friend, he growled, "Why in the devil didn't you find all of this out before?"

"Well," said Buggerie, meekly, "I found out as soon as I could. We had to arrange and correlate the data, you know."

"How do you imagine we're going to get rid of that mountain of paper at this hour?" asked Snobbcraft, as they started down stairs.

"We'll get the guards to help us," said Buggerie, hopefully. "And we'll have the cards burned in the furnace."

"All right, then," snapped the F. F. V., "let's go and get it over with."

In five minutes they were speeding down the broad avenue to the headquarters of the Anglo-Saxon Association of America. They parked the car in front of the gate and walked up the cinder road to the front door. It was a balmy, moonlight night, almost as bright as day. They looked around but saw no one.

"I don't see any of the guards around," Snobbcraft remarked, craning his neck. "I wonder where they are?"

"Probably they're inside," Buggerie suggested, "although I remember telling them to patrol the outside of the building."

"Well, we'll go in, anyhow," remarked Snobbcraft. "Maybe they're down stairs."

He unlocked the door, swung it open and they entered. The hall was pitch dark. Both men felt along the wall for the button for the light. Suddenly there was a thud and Snobbcraft cursed.

"What's the matter?" wailed the frightened Buggerie, frantically feeling for a match.

"Turn on that God damned light!" roared Snobbcraft. "I just stumbled over a man. . . Hurry up, will you?"

Dr. Buggerie finally found a match, struck it, located the wall button and pressed it. The hall was flooded with light. There arranged in a row on the floor and neatly trussed up and gagged were the six special guards.

"What the hell does this mean?" yelled Snobbcraft at the mute men prone before them. Buggerie quickly removed the gags.

They had been suddenly set upon, the head watchman explained, about an hour before, just after Dr. Buggerie left, by a crowd of gunmen who had blackjacked them into unconsciousness and carried them into the building. The watchman displayed the lumps on their heads as evidence and looked quite aggrieved. Not one of them could remember what transpired after the sleep-producing buffet.

"The vault!" shrilled Buggerie. "Let's have a look at the vault."

Down the stairs they rushed, Buggerie wheezing in the lead, Snobbcraft following and the six tousled watchmen bringing up the rear. The lights in the basement were still burning brightly. The doors of the vault were open, sagging on their hinges. There was a litter of trash in front of the vault. They all clustered around the opening and peered inside. The vault was absolutely empty.

"My God!" exclaimed Snobbcraft and Buggerie in unison, turning two shades paler.

For a second or two they just gazed at each other. Then suddenly Buggerie smiled.

"That stuff won't do them any good," he remarked triumphantly.

"Why not?" demanded Snobbcraft, in his tone a mixture of eagerness, hope and doubt.

"Well, it will take them as long to get anything out of that mass of cards as it took our staff, and by that time you and Givens will be elected and no one will dare publish anything like that," the statistician explained. "I have in my possession the only summary—those papers I showed you at your house. As long as I've got that document and they haven't, we're all right!" he grinned in obese joy.

"That sounds good," sighed Snobbcraft, contentedly. "By the way, where is that summary?"

Buggerie jumped as if stuck by a pin and looked first into his empty hands, then into his coat pockets and finally his trousers pockets. He turned and dashed out to the car, followed by the grim-looking Snobbcraft and the six uniformed watchmen with their tousled hair and sore bumps. They searched the car in vain, Snobbcraft loudly cursing Buggerie's stupidity.

"I—I must have left it in your study," wept Buggerie, meekly and hopefully. "In fact I think I remember leaving it right there on the table."

The enraged Snobbcraft ordered him into the car and they

drove off leaving the six uniformed watchmen gaping at the entrance to the grounds, the moonbeams playing through their tousled hair.

The two men hit the ground almost as soon as the car crunched to a stop, dashed up the steps, into the house, through the crowd of bewildered guests, up the winding colonial stairs, down the hallway and into the study.

Buggerie switched on the light and looked wildly, hopefully around. Simultaneously the two men made a grab for a sheaf of white paper lying on the sofa. The statistician reached it first and gazed hungrily, gratefully at it. Then his eyes started from his head and his hand trembled.

"Look!" he shrieked dolefully, thrusting the sheaf of paper under Snobbcraft's eyes.

All of the sheets were blank except the one on top. On that was scribbled:

> Thanks very much for leaving that report where I could get hold of it. Am leaving this paper so you'll have something on which to write another summary.
>
> Happy dreams, Little One.
>
> G. O. P.

"Great God!" gasped Snobbcraft, sinking into a chair.

Chapter Twelve

THE afternoon before election Matthew and Bunny sat in the latter's hotel suite sipping cocktails, smoking and awaiting the inevitable. They had been waiting ever since the day before. Matthew, tall and tense; Bunny, rotund and apprehensive, trying ever so often to cheer up his chief with poor attempts at jocosity. Every time they heard a bell ring both jumped for the telephone, thinking it might be an announcement from Helen's bedside that an heir, and a dark one, had been born. When they could no longer stay around the office, they had come down to the hotel. In just a few moments they were planning to go back to the office again.

The hard campaign and the worry over the outcome of Helen's confinement had left traces on Matthew's face. The satanic lines were accentuated, the eyes seemed sunken farther back in the head, his well-manicured hand trembled a little as he reached for his glass again and again.

He wondered how it would all come out. He hated to leave. He had had such a good time since he'd been white: plenty of money, almost unlimited power, a beautiful wife, good liquor and the pick of damsels within reach. Must he leave all that? Must he cut and run just at the time when he was about to score his greatest victory. Just think: from an underpaid insurance agent to a millionaire commanding millions of people— and then oblivion. He shuddered slightly and reached again for his glass.

"I got everything fixed," Bunny remarked, shifting around in the overstuffed chair. "The plane's all ready with tanks full and I've got Ruggles right there in the hangar. The money's in that little steel box: all in thousand dollar bills."

"You're going with me, aren't you, Bunny?" asked Matthew in almost pleading tones.

"I'm not stayin' here!" his secretary replied.

"Gee, Bunny, you're a brick!" said Matthew leaning over and placing his hand on his plump little friend's knee. "You sure have been a good pal."

"Aw, cut th' comedy," exclaimed Bunny, reddening and turning his head swiftly away.

Suddenly the telephone rang, loud, clear, staccato. Both men sprang for it, eagerly, open-eyed, apprehensive. Matthew was first.

"Hello!" he shouted. "What's that! Yes, I'll be right up."

"Well, it's happened," he announced resignedly, hanging up the receiver. And then, brightening a bit, he boasted, "It's a boy!"

In the midst of her pain Helen was jubilant. What a present to give her Matthew on the eve of his greatest triumph! How good the Lord was to her; to doubly bless her in this way. The nurse wiped the tears of joy away from the young mother's eyes.

"You must stay quiet, Ma'am," she warned.

Outside in the hall, squirming uneasily on the window seat, was Matthew, his fists clenched, his teeth biting into his thin lower lip. At another window stood Bunny looking vacantly out into the street, feeling useless and out of place in such a situation, and yet convinced that it was his duty to stay here by his best friend during this great crisis.

Matthew felt like a young soldier about to leave his trench to face a baptism of machine gun fire or a gambler risking his last dollar on a roll of the dice. It seemed to him that he would go mad if something didn't happen quickly. He rose and paced the hall, hands in pockets, his tall shadow following him on the opposite wall. Why didn't the doctor come out and tell him something? What was the cause of the delay? What would Helen say? What would the baby look like? Maybe it might be miraculously light! Stranger things had happened in this world. But no, nothing like that could happen. Well, he'd had his lucky break; now the vacation was over.

A nurse, immaculate in white uniform, came out of Helen's bedroom, passed them hurriedly, smiling, and entered the bathroom. She returned with a basin of warm water in her hands, smiled again reassuringly and reëntered the natal chamber. Bunny and Matthew, in unison, sighed heavily.

"Boy!" exclaimed Bunny, wiping the perspiration from his brow. "If somethin' don't happen pretty soon, here, I'm gonna do a Brodie out o' that window."

"The both of us," said Matthew. "I never knew it took these doctors so damn long to get through."

Helen's door opened and the physician came out looking quite grave and concerned. Matthew pounced upon him. The man held his finger to his lips and motioned to the room across the hall. Matthew entered.

"Well," said Matthew, guiltily, "what's the news?"

"I'm very sorry to have to tell you, Mr. Fisher, that something terrible has happened. Your son is very, very dark. Either you or Mrs. Fisher must possess some Negro blood. It might be called reversion to type if any such thing had ever been proved. Now I want to know what you want done. If you say so I can get rid of this child and it will save everybody concerned a lot of trouble and disgrace. Nobody except the nurse knows anything about this and she'll keep her mouth shut for a consideration. Of course, it's all in the day's work for me, you know. I've had plenty of cases like this in Atlanta, even before the disappearance of the Negroes. Come now, what shall I do?" he wailed.

"Yes," thought Matthew to himself, "what should he do?" The doctor had suggested an excellent way out of the dilemma. They could just say that the child had died. But what of the future? Must he go on forever in this way? Helen was young and fecund. Surely one couldn't go on murdering one's children, especially when one loved and wanted children. Wouldn't it be better to settle the matter once and for all? Or should he let the doctor murder the boy and then hope for a better situation the next time? An angel of frankness beckoned him to be done with this life of pretense; to take his wife and son and flee far away from everything, but a devil of ambition whispered seductively about wealth, power and prestige.

In almost as many seconds the pageant of the past three years passed in review on the screen of his tortured memory: the New Year's Eve at the Honky Tonk Club, the first glimpse of the marvelously beautiful Helen, the ordeal of getting white, the first, sweet days of freedom from the petty insults and cheap discriminations to which as a black man he had always been subjected, then the search for Helen around Atlanta, the organization of the Knights of Nordica, the stream of successes, the coming of Bunny, the campaign planned and executed by him: and now, the end. Must it be the end?

"Well?" came the insistent voice of the physician.

Matthew opened his mouth to reply when the butler burst into the room waving a newspaper.

"Excuse me, sir," he blurted, excitedly, "but Mister Brown said to bring this right to you."

The lurid headlines seemed to leap from the paper and strike Matthew between the eyes:

DEMOCRATIC LEADERS PROVED OF NEGRO DESCENT

Givens, Snobbcraft, Buggerie, Kretin and Others of Negro Ancestry, According to Old Records Unearthed by Them.

Matthew and the physician, standing side by side, read the long account in awed silence. Bunny entered the door.

"Can I speak to you a minute, Matt?" he asked casually. Almost reluctant to move, Matthew followed him into the hall.

"Keep your shirt on, Big Boy," Bunny advised, almost jovially. "They ain't got nothin' on you yet. That changing your name threw them off. You're not even mentioned."

Matthew braced up, threw back his shoulders and drew a long, deep breath. It seemed as if a mountain had been taken off his shoulders. He actually grinned as his confidence returned. He reached for Bunny's hand and they shook, silently jubilant.

"Well, doctor," said Matthew, arching his left eyebrow in his familiar Mephistophelian manner, "it sort of looks as if there is something to that reversion to type business. I used to think it was all boloney myself. Well, it's as I always say: you never can tell."

"Yes, it seems as if this is a very authentic case," agreed the physician, glancing sharply at the bland and blond countenance of Matthew. "Well, what now?"

"I'll have to see Givens," said Matthew as they turned to leave the room.

"Here he comes now," Bunny announced.

Sure enough, the little gray-faced, bald-headed man, came

leaping up the stairs like a goat, his face haggard, his eyes bulging in mingled rage and terror, his necktie askew. He was waving a newspaper in his hand and opened his mouth without speaking as he shot past them and dashed into Helen's room. The old fellow was evidently out of his head.

They followed him into the room in time to see him with his face buried in the covers of Helen's bed and she, horrified, glancing at the six-inch-tall headline. Matthew rushed to her side as she slumped back on the pillow in a dead faint. The physician and nurse dashed to revive her. The old man on his knees sobbed hoarsely. Mrs. Givens looking fifteen years older appeared in the doorway. Bunny glanced at Matthew who slightly lowered his left eyelid and with difficulty suppressed a smile.

"We've got to get out o' this!" shouted the Imperial Grand Wizard. "We've got to get out o' this, Oh, it's terrible. . . . I never knew it myself, for sure. . . Oh, Matthew, get us out of this, I tell you. They almost mobbed me at the office. . . Came in just as I went out the back way. . . Almost ten thousand of them. . . We can't lose a minute. Quick, I tell you! They'll murder us all."

"I'll look out for everything," Matthew soothed condescendingly. "I'll stick by you." Then turning swiftly to his partner he commanded, "Bunny order both cars out at once. We'll beat it for the airport. . . Doctor Brocker, will you go with us to look out for Helen and the baby? We've got to get out right now. I'll pay you your price."

"Sure I'll go, Mr. Fisher," said the physician, quietly. "I wouldn't leave Mrs. Fisher now."

The nurse had succeeded in bringing Helen to consciousness. She was weeping bitterly, denouncing fate and her father. With that logicality that frequently causes people to accept as truth circumstantial evidence that is not necessarily conclusive, she was assuming that the suspiciously brown color of her new-born son was due to some hidden Negro drop of blood in her veins. She looked up at her husband beseechingly.

"Oh, Matthew, darling," she cried, her long red-gold hair framing her face, "I'm so sorry about all this. If I'd only known, I'd never have let you in for it. I would have spared you this disgrace and humiliation. Oh, Matthew, Honey, please forgive me. I love you, my husband. Please don't leave me, please don't leave me!" She reached out and grasped the tail of his coat as if he were going to leave that very minute.

"Now, now, little girl," said Matthew soothingly, touched by her words, "You haven't disgraced me; you've honored me by presenting me with a beautiful son."

He looked down worshipfully at the chubby ball of brownness in the nurse's arms.

"You needn't worry about me, Helen. I'll stick by you as long as you'll have me and without you life wouldn't be worth a dime. You're not responsible for the color of our baby, my dear. I'm the guilty one."

Dr. Brocker smiled knowingly, Givens rose up indignantly, Bunny opened his mouth in surprise, Mrs. Givens folded her arms and her mouth changed to a slit and the nurse said "Oh!"

"You?" cried Helen in astonishment.

"Yes, me," Matthew repeated, a great load lifting from his soul. Then for a few minutes he poured out his secret to the astonished little audience.

Helen felt a wave of relief go over her. There was no feeling of revulsion at the thought that her husband was a Negro. There once would have been but that was seemingly centuries ago when she had been unaware of her remoter Negro ancestry. She felt proud of her Matthew. She loved him more than ever. They had money and a beautiful, brown baby. What more did they need? To hell with the world! To hell with society! Compared to what she possessed, thought Helen, all talk of race and color was damned foolishness. She would probably have been surprised to learn that countless Americans at that moment were thinking the same thing.

"Well," said Bunny, grinning, "it sure is good to be able to admit that you're a jigwalk once more."

"Yes, Bunny," said old man Givens, "I guess we're all niggers now."

"Negroes, Mr. Givens, Negroes," corrected Dr. Brocker, entering the room. "I'm in the same boat with the rest of you, only my dark ancestors are not so far back. I sure hope the Republicans win."

"Don't worry, Doc," said Bunny. "They'll win all right. And how! Gee whiz! I bet Sherlock Holmes, Nick Carter and all the Pinkertons couldn't find old Senator Kretin and Arthur Snobbcraft now."

"Come on," shouted the apprehensive Givens, "let's get out o' here before that mob comes."

"Whut mob, Daddy?" asked Mrs. Givens.

"You'll find out damn quick if you don't shake it up," replied her husband.

Through the crisp, autumn night air sped Fisher's big tri-motored plane, headed southwest to the safety of Mexico. Reclining in a large, comfortable deck chair was Helen Fisher, calm and at peace with the world. In a hammock near her was her little brown son, Matthew, Junior. Beside her, holding her hand, was Matthew. Up front near the pilot, Bunny and Givens were playing Conquian. Behind them sat the nurse and Dr. Brocker, silently gazing out of the window at the twinkling lights of the Gulf Coast. Old lady Givens snored in the rear of the ship.

"Damn!" muttered Givens, as Bunny threw down his last spread and won the third consecutive game. "I sure wish I'd had time to grab some jack before we pulled out o' Atlanta. Ain't got but five dollars and fifty-three cents to my name."

"Don't worry about that, Old Timer," Bunny laughed. "I don't think we left over a thousand bucks in the treasury. See that steel box over there? Well, that ain't got nothin' in it but bucks and more bucks. Not a bill smaller than a grand."

"Well, I'm a son-of-a-gun," blurted the Imperial Grand Wizard. "That boy thinks o' everything."

But Givens was greatly depressed, much more so than the others. He had really believed all that he had preached about white supremacy, race purity and the menace of the alien, the Catholic, the Modernist and the Jew. He had always been sincere in his prejudices.

When they arrived at the Valbuena Air Field outside Mexico City, a messenger brought Bunny a telegram.

"You better thank your stars you got away from there, Matt," he grinned, handing his friend the telegram. "See what my gal says?"

Matthew glanced over the message and handed it to Givens without comment. It read:

Hope you arrive safely Senator Kretin lynched in Union Station Stop Snobbcraft and Buggerie reported in flight Stop Goosie and Gump almost unanimously reëlected Stop Government has declared martial law until disturbances stop Stop When can I come?

MADELINE SCRANTON.

"Who's this Scranton broad?" queried Matthew in a whisper, cutting a precautionary glance at his wife.

"A sweet Georgia brown," exclaimed Bunny enthusiastically.

"No!" gasped Matthew, incredulous.

"She ain't no Caucasian!" Bunny replied.

"She must be the last black gal in the country," Matthew remarked, glancing enviously at his friend. "How come she didn't get white, too?"

"Well," Bunny replied, a slight hint of pride in his voice. "She's a race patriot. She's funny that way."

"Well, for cryin' out loud!" exclaimed Matthew, scratching his head and sort of half grinning in a bewildered way. "*What* kind o' *sheba* is that?"

Old man Givens came over to where they were standing, the telegram in his hand and an expression of serenity now on his face.

"Boys," he announced, "it looks like it's healthier down here right now than it is back there in Georgia."

"*Looks* like it's healthier?" mocked Bunny. "Brother, you know damn *well* it's healthier!"

Chapter Thirteen

Toward eleven o'clock on the evening before election day, a long, low roadster swept up to the door of a stately country home near Richmond, Va., crunched to a stop, the lights were extinguished and two men, one tall and angular, the other huge and stout, catapulted from the car. Without wasting words, they raced around the house and down a small driveway to a rambling shed in a level field about three hundred yards to the rear. Breathless, they halted before the door and beat upon it excitedly.

"Open up there, Frazier!" ordered Snobbcraft, for it was he. "Open that door." There was no answer. The only reply was the chirping of crickets and the rustle of branches.

"He must not be here," said Dr. Buggerie, glancing fearfully over his shoulder and wiping a perspiring brow with a damp handkerchief.

"The damned rascal had better be here," thundered the Democratic candidate for Vice-President, beating again on the door. "I telephoned him two hours ago to be ready."

As he spoke someone unlocked the door and rolled it aside an inch or two.

"Is that you, Mr. Snobbcraft?" asked a sleepy voice from the darkness within.

"Open that damned door, you fool," barked Snobbcraft. "Didn't I tell you to have that plane ready when we got here? Why don't you do as you're told?" He and Dr. Buggerie helped slide the great doors back. The man Frazier snapped on the lights, revealing within a big, three-motored plane with an automobile nestling under each of its wings.

"I-I kinda fell asleep waitin' for you, Mr. Snobbcraft," Frazier apologized, "but everything's ready."

"All right, man," shouted the president of the Anglo-Saxon Association, "let's get away from here then. This is a matter of life and death. You ought to have had the plane outside and all warmed up to go."

"Yes sir," the man mumbled meekly, busying himself.

"These damned, stupid, poor white trash!" growled Snobb-craft, glaring balefully at the departing aviator.

"D-D-Don't antagonize him," muttered Buggerie. "He's our only chance to get away."

"Shut up, fool! If it hadn't been for you and your damned fool statistics we wouldn't be in this fix."

"You wanted them, didn't you?" whined the statistician in defense.

"Well, I didn't tell you to leave that damned summary where anybody could get hold of it." Snobbcraft replied, reproach-fully. "That was the most stupid thing I ever heard of."

Buggerie opened his mouth to reply but said nothing. He just glared at Snobbcraft who glared back at him. The two men presented a disheveled appearance. The Vice-Presidential candidate was haggard, hatless, collarless and still wore his smok-ing jacket. The eminent statistician and author of *The Incidence of Psittacosis among the Hiphopa Indians of the Amazon Valley and Its Relation to Life Insurance Rates in the United States*, looked far from dignified with no necktie, canvas breeches, no socks and wearing a shooting jacket he had snatched from a closet on his way out of the house. He had forgotten his thick spectacles and his bulging eyes were red and watery. They paced impatiently back and forth, glancing first at the swiftly working Frazier and then down the long driveway toward the glowing city.

Ten minutes they waited while Frazier went over the plane to see that all was well. Then they helped him roll the huge metal bird out of the hangar and on to the field. Gratefully they climbed inside and fell exhausted on the soft-cushioned seats.

"Well, that sure is a relief," gasped the ponderous Buggerie, mopping his brow.

"Wait until we get in the air," growled Snobbcraft. "Any-thing's liable to happen after that mob tonight. I was never so humiliated in my life. The idea of that gang of poor white trash crowding up my steps and yelling nigger. It was disgraceful."

"Yes, it was terrible," agreed Buggerie. "It's a good thing they didn't go in the rear where your car was. We wouldn't have been able to get away."

"I thought there would be a demonstration," said Snobbcraft, some of his old sureness returning, "that's why I 'phoned Frazier to get ready. . . . Oh, it's a damned shame to be run out of your own home in this way!"

He glared balefully at the statistician who averted his gaze.

"All ready, sir," announced Frazier, "where are we headed?"

"To my ranch in Chihuahua, and hurry up," snapped Snobbcraft.

"But—But we ain't got enough gas to go that far," said Frazier. "I-I-You didn't say you wanted to go to Mexico, Boss."

Snobbcraft stared incredulously at the man. His rage was so great that he could not speak for a moment or two. Then he launched into a stream of curses that would have delighted a pirate captain, while the unfortunate aviator gaped indecisively.

In the midst of this diatribe, the sound of automobile horns and klaxons rent the air, punctuated by shouts and pistol shots. The three men in the plane saw coming down the road from the city a bobbing stream of headlights. Already the cavalcade was almost to the gate of the Snobbcraft country estate.

"Come on, get out of here," gasped Snobbcraft. "We'll get some gas farther down the line. Hurry up!"

Dr. Buggerie, speechless and purple with fear, pushed the aviator out of the plane. The fellow gave the propeller a whirl, jumped back into the cabin, took the controls and the great machine rolled out across the field.

They had started none too soon. The automobile cavalcade was already coming up the driveway. The drone of the motor drowned out the sound of the approaching mob but the two fearful men saw several flashes that betokened pistol shots. Several of the automobiles took out across the field in the wake of the plane. They seemed to gain on it. Snobbcraft and Buggerie gazed nervously ahead. They were almost at the end of the field and the plane had not yet taken to the air. The pursuing automobiles drew closer. There were several more flashes from firearms. A bullet tore through the side of the cabin. Simultaneously Snobbcraft and Buggerie fell to the floor.

At last the ship rose, cleared the trees at the end of the field and began to attain altitude. The two men took deep breaths of relief, rose and flung themselves on the richly upholstered seats.

A terrible stench suddenly became noticeable to the two passengers and the aviator. The latter looked inquiringly over his shoulder; Snobbcraft and Buggerie, their noses wrinkled and their foreheads corrugated, glanced suspiciously at each other. Both moved uneasily in their seats and looks of guilt succeeded those of accusation. Snobbcraft retreated precipitously to the rear cabin while the statistician flung open several windows and then followed the Vice-Presidential candidate.

Fifteen minutes later two bundles were tossed out of the window of the rear cabin and the two passengers, looking sheepish but much relieved, resumed their seats. Snobbcraft was wearing a suit of brown dungarees belonging to Frazier while his scientific friend had wedged himself into a pair of white trousers usually worn by Snobbcraft's valet. Frazier turned, saw them, and grinned.

Hour after hour the plane winged its way through the night. Going a hundred miles an hour it passed town after town. About dawn, as they were passing over Meridian, Mississippi, the motor began to miss.

"What's the matter there?" Snobbcraft inquired nervously into the pilot's ear.

"The gas is runnin' low," Frazier replied grimly. "We'll have to land pretty soon."

"No, no, not in Mississippi!" gasped Buggerie, growing purple with apprehension. "They'll lynch us if they find out who we are."

"Well, we can't stay up here much longer," the pilot warned.

Snobbcraft bit his lip and thought furiously. It was true they would be taking a chance by landing anywhere in the South, let alone in Mississippi, but what could they do? The motor was missing more frequently and Frazier had cut down their speed to save gasoline. They were just idling along. The pilot looked back at Snobbcraft inquiringly.

"By God, we're in a fix now," said the president of the Anglo-Saxon Association. Then he brightened with a sudden idea. "We could hide in the rear cabin while Frazier gets gasoline," he suggested.

"Suppose somebody looks in the rear cabin?" queried Buggerie, dolefully, thrusting his hands into the pockets of his white trousers. "There's bound to be a lot of curious people about when a big plane like this lands in a farming district."

As he spoke his left hand encountered something hard in the pocket. It felt like a box of salve. He withdrew it curiously. It was a box of shoe polish which the valet doubtless used on Snobbcraft's footgear. He looked at it aimlessly and was about to thrust it back into the pocket when he had a brilliant idea.

"Look here, Snobbcraft," he cried excitedly, his rheumy eyes popping out of his head farther than usual. "This is just the thing."

"What do you mean?" asked his friend, eyeing the little tin box.

"Well," explained the scientist, "you know real niggers are scarce now and nobody would think of bothering a couple of them, even in Mississippi. They'd probably be a curiosity."

"What are you getting at, man?"

"This: we can put this blacking on our head, face, neck and hands, and no one will take us for Snobbcraft and Buggerie. Frazier can tell anybody that inquires that we're two darkies he's taking out of the country, or something like that. Then, after we get our gas and start off again, we can wash the stuff off with gasoline. It's our only chance, Arthur. If we go down like we are, they'll kill us sure."

Snobbcraft pursed his lips and pondered the proposition for a moment. It was indeed, he saw, their only chance to effectively escape detection.

"All right," he agreed, "let's hurry up. This ship won't stay up much longer."

Industriously they daubed each other's head, neck, face, chest, hands and arms with the shoe polish. In five minutes they closely resembled a brace of mammy singers. Snobbcraft hurriedly instructed Frazier.

The plane slowly circled to the ground. The region was slightly rolling and there was no good landing place. There could be no delay, however, so Frazier did his best. The big ship bumped over logs and through weeds, heading straight for a clump of trees. Quickly the pilot steered it to the left only to send it head first into a ditch. The plane turned completely over, one wing was entirely smashed and Frazier, caught in the wreckage under the engine, cried feebly for help for a few moments and then lay still.

Shaken up and bruised, the two passengers managed to crawl out of the cabin window to safety. Dolefully they stood in the Mississippi sunlight, surveying the wreckage and looking questioningly at each other.

"Well," whined Dr. Buggerie, rubbing one large sore buttock, "what now?"

"Shut up," growled Snobbcraft. "If it hadn't been for you, we wouldn't be here."

Happy Hill, Mississippi, was all aflutter. For some days it had been preparing for the great, open-air revival of the True Faith Christ Lovers' Church. The faithful for miles around were expected to attend the services scheduled for the afternoon of Election Day and which all hoped would last well into the night.

This section of the state had been untouched by the troubles through which the rest of the South had gone as a result of the activities of Black-No-More, Incorporated. The people for miles around were with very few exceptions old residents and thence known to be genuine blue-blooded Caucasians for as far back as any resident could remember which was at least fifty years. The people were proud of this fact. They were more proud, however, of the fact that Happy Hill was the home and birthplace of the True Faith Christ Lovers' Church, which made the prodigious boast of being the most truly Fundamentalist of all the Christian sects in the United States. Other things of which the community might have boasted were its inordinately high illiteracy rate and its lynching record—but these things were seldom mentioned, although no one was ashamed of them. Certain things are taken for granted everywhere.

Long before the United States had rid themselves of their Negroes through the good but unsolicited offices of Dr. Junius Crookman, Happy Hill had not only rid itself of what few Negroes had resided in its vicinity but of all itinerant blackamoors who lucklessly came through the place. Ever since the Civil War when the proud and courageous forefathers of the Caucasian inhabitants had vigorously resisted all efforts to draft them into the Confederate Army, there had been a sign nailed over the general store and post office reading, "NIGER REDE & RUN. IF U CAN'T REDE, RUN ENEYHOWE." The literate denizens of Happy Hill would sometimes stand off and spell out the words with the pride that usually accompanies erudition.

The method by which Happy Hill discouraged blackamoors who sought the hospitality of the place, was simple: the offending Ethiopian was either hung or shot and then broiled. Across from the general store and post office was a large iron post about five feet high. On it all blacks were burned. Down one side of it was a long line of nicks made with hammer and chisel. Each nick stood for a Negro dispatched. This post was one of the landmarks of the community and was pointed out to visitors with pardonable civic pride by local boosters. Sage old fellows frequently remarked between expectorations of tobacco juice that the only Negro problem in Happy Hill was the difficulty of getting hold of a sufficient number of the Sons or Daughters of Ham to lighten the dullness of the place.

Quite naturally the news that all Negroes had disappeared, not only from their state but from the entire country, had been received with sincere regret by the inhabitants of Happy Hill. They envisioned the passing of an old, established custom. Now there was nothing left to stimulate them but the old time religion and the clandestine sex orgies that invariably and immediately followed the great revival meetings.

So the simple country folk had turned to religion with renewed ardor. There were several churches in the county, Methodist, Baptist, Campbellite and, of course, Holy Roller. The latter, indeed, had the largest membership. But the people, eager for something new, found all of the old churches too tame. They wanted a faith with more punch to it; a faith that would fittingly accompany the fierce corn liquor which all consumed, albeit they were all confirmed Prohibitionists.

Whenever and wherever there is a social need, some agency arises to supply it. The needs of Happy Hill were no exception. One day, several weeks previously, there had come to the community one Rev. Alex McPhule who claimed to be the founder of a new faith, a true faith, that would save all from the machinations of the Evil One. The other churches, he averred, had

failed. The other churches had grown soft and were flirting
with atheism and Modernism which, according to Rev. McPhule,
were the same thing. An angel of God had visited him one
summer evening in Meridian, he told them, when he was
down sick in bed as the result of his sinning ways, and had told
him to reform and go forth into the world and preach the true
faith of Christ's love. He had promised to do so, of course, and
then the angel had placed the palm of his right hand on Rev.
McPhule's forehead and all of the sickness and misery had
departed.

The residents of Happy Hill and vicinity listened with rapt
attention and respect. The man was sincere, eloquent and obviously a Nordic. He was tall, thin, slightly knock-kneed, with
a shock of unkempt red hair, wild blue eyes, hollow cheeks,
lantern jaw and long ape-like arms that looked very impressive
when he waved them up and down during a harangue. His
story sounded logical to the country people and they flocked
in droves to his first revival held in a picturesque natural am-
phitheater about a mile from town.

No one had any difficulty in understanding the new faith.
No music was allowed besides singing and thumping the bottom of a wooden tub. There were no chairs. Everybody sat on
the ground in a circle with Rev. McPhule in the center. The
holy man would begin an extemporaneous song and would soon
have the faithful singing it after him and swinging from side to
side in unison. Then he would break off abruptly and launch
into an old fashion hellfire-and-damnation sermon in which demons, brimstone, adultery, rum, and other evils prominently
figured. At the height of his remarks, he would roll his eyes
heavenward, froth at the mouth, run around on all fours and
embrace in turn each member of the congregation, especially
the buxom ladies. This would be the signal for others to follow
his example. The sisters and brothers osculated, embraced
and rolled, shouting meanwhile: "Christ is Love! . . . Love
Christ! . . . Oh, be happy in the arms of Jesus! . . . Oh,
Jesus, my Sweetheart! . . . Heavenly Father!" Frequently
these revivals took place on the darkest nights with the place of
worship dimly illuminated by pine torches. As these torches
always seemed to conveniently burn out about the time the

embracing and rolling started, the new faith rapidly became popular.

In a very short time nothing in Happy Hill was too good for Rev. Alex McPhule. Every latchstring hung out for him. As usual with gentlemen of the cloth, he was especially popular with the ladies. When the men were at work in the fields, the Man of God would visit house after house and comfort the womenfolk with his Christian message. Being a bachelor, he made these professional calls with great frequency.

The Rev. Alex McPhule also held private audiences with the sick, sinful and neurotic in his little cabin. There he had erected an altar covered with the white marble top from an old bureau. Around this altar were painted some grotesque figures, evidently the handiwork of the evangelist, while on the wall in back of the altar hung a large square of white oilcloth upon which was painted a huge eye. The sinner seeking surcease was commanded to gaze upon the eye while making confessions and requests. On the altar reposed a crudely-bound manuscript about three inches thick. This was the "Bible" of the Christ Lovers which the Rev. McPhule declared he had written at the command of Jesus Christ Himself. The majority of his visitors were middle-aged wives and adenoidal and neurotic young girls. None departed unsatisfied.

With all the good fortune that had come to the Rev. McPhule as a result of engaging in the Lord's work, he was still dissatisfied. He never passed a Baptist, Methodist or Holy Roller church without jealousy and ambition surging up within him. He wanted everybody in the county in his flock. He wanted to do God's work so effectually that the other churches would be put out of business. He could only do this, he knew, with the aid of a message straight from Heaven. That alone would impress them.

He began to talk in his meetings about a sign coming down from Heaven to convince all doubters and infidels like Methodists and Baptists. His flock was soon on the nervous edge of expectancy but the Lord failed, for some reason, to answer the prayer of his right-hand man.

Rev. McPhule began to wonder what he had done to offend the Almighty. He prayed long and fervently in the quiet of his bedchamber, except when he didn't have company, but no sign appeared. Possibly, thought the evangelist, some big demonstration might attract the attention of Jesus; something bigger than the revivals he had been staging. Then one day somebody brought him a copy of *The Warning* and upon reading it he got an idea. If the Lord would only send a nigger for his congregation to lynch! That would, indeed, be marked evidence of the power of Rev. Alex McPhule.

He prayed with increased fervency but no African put in an appearance. Two nights later as he sat before his altar, his "Bible" clutched in his hands, a bat flew in the window. It rapidly circled the room and flew out again. Rev. McPhule could feel the wind from its wings. He stood erect with a wild look in his watery blue eyes and screamed, "A sign! A sign! Oh, Glory be! The Lord has answered my prayer! Oh, thank you, God! A sign! A sign!" Then he grew dizzy, his eyes dimmed and he fell twitching across the altar, unconscious.

Next day he went around Happy Hill telling of his experience of the night before. An angel of the Lord, he told the gaping villagers, had flown through the window, alighted on his "Bible" and, kissing him on his forehead, had declared that the Lord would answer his prayer and send a sign. As proof of his tale, Rev. McPhule exhibited a red spot on his forehead which he had received when his head struck the marble altar top but which he claimed marked the place where the messenger of the Lord had kissed

The simple folk of Happy Hill were, with few exceptions, convinced that the Rev. McPhule stood in well with the celestial authorities. Nervous and expectant they talked of nothing but The Sign. They were on edge for the great revival scheduled for Election Day at which time they fervently hoped the Lord would make good.

At last the great day had arrived. From far and near came the good people of the countryside on horseback, in farm wagons and battered mud-caked flivvers. Many paused to cast their ballots for Givens and Snobbcraft, not having heard of the developments of the past twenty-four hours, but the bulk of the folk repaired immediately to the sacred grove where the preaching would take place.

Rev. Alex McPhule gloated inwardly at the many concentric circles of upturned faces. They were eager, he saw, to drink in his words of wisdom and be elevated. He noted with satisfaction that there were many strange people in the congregation. It showed that his power was growing. He glanced up apprehensively at the blue heavens. Would The Sign come? Would the Lord answer his prayers? He muttered another prayer and then proceeded to business.

He was an impressive figure today. He had draped himself in a long, white robe with a great red cross on the left breast and he looked not unlike one of the Prophets of old. He walked back and forth in the little circle surrounded by close-packed humanity, bending backward and forward, swinging his arms, shaking his head and rolling his eyes while he retold for the fiftieth time the story of the angel's visit. The man was a natural actor and his voice had that sepulchral tone universally associated with Men of God, court criers and Independence Day orators. In the first row squatted the Happy Hill True Faith Choir of eight young women with grizzled old man Yawbrew, the tub-thumper, among them. They groaned, amened and Yes-Lorded at irregular intervals.

Then, having concluded his story, the evangelist launched into song in a harsh, nasal voice:

> *I done come to Happy Hill to save you from Sin,*
> *Salvation's door is open and you'd better come in,*
> *Oh, Glory Hallelujah! you'd better come in.*
> *Jesus Christ has called me to save this white race,*
> *And with His Help I'll save you from awful disgrace.*
> *Oh, Glory Hallelujah! We must save this race.*

Old man Yawbrew beat on his tub while the sisters swayed and accompanied their pastor. The congregation joined in.

Suddenly Rev. McPhule stopped, glared at the rows of strained, upturned faces and extending his long arms to the sun, he shouted:

"It'll come I tell yuh. Yes Lord, the sign will come—ugh. I know that my Lord liveth and the sign will come—ugh. If—ugh —you just have faith—ugh. Oh, Jesus—ugh. Brothers and Sisters—ugh. Just have faith—ugh—and the Lord—ugh—will

answer your prayers . . . Oh, Christ—ugh. Oh, Little Jesus
—ugh . . . Oh, God—ugh—answer our prayers . . . Save
us—ugh. Send us the Sign . . ."

The congregation shouted after him "Send us the Sign!"
Then he again launched into a hymn composed on the spot:

> *He will send the Sign,*
> *Oh, He will send the Sign*
> *Loving Little Jesus Christ*
> *He will send the Sign.*

Over and over he sang the verse. The people joined him until
the volume of sound was tremendous. Then with a piercing
scream, Rev. McPhule fell on all fours and running among the
people hugged one after the other, crying "Christ is Love! . . .
He'll send the Sign! . . . Oh Jesus! send us The Sign!" The
cries of the others mingled with his and there was a general
kissing, embracing and rolling there in the green-walled grove
under the midday sun.

As the sun approached its zenith, Mr. Arthur Snobbcraft and
Dr. Samuel Buggerie, grotesque in their nondescript clothing
and their blackened skins, trudged along the dusty road in what
they hoped was the direction of a town. For three hours, now,
they had been on the way, skirting isolated farmhouses and
cabins, hoping to get to a place where they could catch a train.
They had fiddled aimlessly around the wrecked plane for two
or three hours before getting up courage enough to take to
the highroad. Suddenly they both thrilled with pleasure somewhat dampened by apprehension as they espied from a rise in
the road, a considerable collection of houses.

"There's a town," exclaimed Snobbcraft. "Now let's get this
damned stuff off our faces. There's probably a telegraph office
there."

"Oh, don't be crazy," Buggerie pleaded. "If we take off this
blacking we're lost. The whole country has heard the news
about us by this time, even in Mississippi. Let's go right in as
we are, pretending we're niggers, and I'll bet we'll be treated
all right. We won't have to stay long. With our pictures all over
the country, it would be suicidal to turn up here in one of
these hotbeds of bigotry and ignorance."

"Well, maybe you're right," Snobbcraft grudgingly admitted. He was eager to get the shoe polish off his skin. Both men had perspired freely during their hike and the sweat had mixed with the blacking much to their discomfort.

As they started toward the little settlement, they heard shouts and singing on their left.

"What's that?" cried Dr. Buggerie, stopping to listen.

"Sounds like a camp meeting," Snobbcraft replied. "Hope it is. We can be sure those folks will treat us right. One thing about these people down here they are real, sincere Christians."

"I don't think it will be wise to go where there's any crowds," warned the statistician. "You never can tell what a crowd will do."

"Oh, shut up, and come on!" Snobbcraft snapped. "I've listened to you long enough. If it hadn't been for you we would never have had all of this trouble. Statistics! Bah!"

They struck off over the fields toward the sound of the singing. Soon they reached the edge of the ravine and looked down on the assemblage. At about the same time, some of the people facing in that direction saw them and started yelling "The Sign! Look! Niggers! Praise God! The Sign! Lynch 'em!" Others joined in the cry. Rev. McPhule turned loose a buxom sister and stood wide-eyed and erect. His prayers had come true! "Lynch 'em!" he roared.

"We'd better get out of here," said Buggerie, quaking.

"Yes," agreed Snobbcraft, as the assemblage started to move toward them.

Over fences, through bushes, across ditches sped the two men, puffing and wheezing at the unaccustomed exertion, while in hot pursuit came Rev. McPhule followed by his enthusiastic flock.

Slowly the mob gained on the two Virginia aristocrats. Dr. Buggerie stumbled and sprawled on the ground. A dozen men and women fell upon him while he yelled to the speeding Snobbcraft for help. The angular Snobbcraft kept on but Rev. McPhule and several others soon overtook him.

The two men were marched protesting to Happy Hill. The enthused villagers pinched them, pulled them, playfully punched and kicked them during their triumphant march. No one paid the slightest attention to their pleas. Too long had Happy Hill waited for a Negro to lynch. Could the good people hesitate now that the Lord had answered their prayers?

Buggerie wept and Snobbcraft offered large sums of money for their freedom. The money was taken and distributed but the two men were not liberated. They insisted that they were not Negroes but they were only cudgeled for their pains.

At last the gay procession arrived at the long-unused iron post in front of the general store and post office in Happy Hill. As soon as Mr. Snobbcraft saw the post he guessed its significance. Something must be done quickly.

"We're not niggers," he yelled to the mob. "Take off our clothes and look at us. See for yourself. My God! don't lynch white men. We're white the same as you are."

"Yes, gentlemen," bleated Dr. Buggerie, "we're really white men. We just came from a masquerade ball over at Meridian and our plane wrecked. You can't do a thing like this. We're white men, I tell you."

The crowd paused. Even Rev. McPhule seemed convinced. Eager hands tore off the men's garments and revealed their pale white skins underneath. Immediately apology took the place of hatred. The two men were taken over to the general store and permitted to wash off the shoe polish while the crowd, a little disappointed, stood around wondering what to do. They felt cheated. Somebody must be to blame for depriving them of their fun. They began to eye Rev. McPhule. He glanced around nervously.

Suddenly, in the midst of this growing tenseness, an ancient Ford drove up to the outskirts of the crowd and a young man jumped out waving a newspaper.

"Looky here!" he yelled. "They've found out th' damned Demmycratic candidates is niggers. See here: Givens and Snobbcraft. Them's their pictures. They pulled out in airplanes last night or th' mobs wouldda lynched 'em." Men, women and children crowded around the newcomer while he read the account of the flight of the Democratic standard bearers. They gazed at each other bewildered and hurled imprecations upon the heads of the vanished candidates.

Washed and refreshed, Mr. Arthur Snobbcraft and Dr. Samuel Buggerie, each puffing a five-cent cigar (the most expensive sold in the store) appeared again on the porch of the general store. They felt greatly relieved after their narrow escape.

"I told you they wouldn't know who we were," said Snobbcraft disdainfully but softly.

"Who are you folks, anyway?" asked Rev. McPhule, suddenly at their elbow. He was holding the newspaper in his hand. The crowd was watching breathlessly.

"Why-why-y I'm-a-er-a that is . . ." spluttered Snobbcraft.

"Ain't that your pichure?" thundered the evangelist, pointing to the likeness on the front page of the newspaper.

"Why no," Snobbcraft lied, "but—but it looks like me, doesn't it?"

"You're mighty right it does!" said Rev. McPhule, sternly, "and it *is* you, too!"

"No, no, no, that's not me," cried the president of the Anglo-Saxon Association.

"Yes it is," roared McPhule, as the crowd closed in on the two hapless men. "It's you and you're a nigger, accordin' to this here paper, an' a newspaper wouldn't lie." Turning to his followers he commanded, "Take 'em. They're niggers just as I thought. The Lord's will be done. Idea of niggers runnin' on th' Demmycratic ticket!"

The crowd came closer. Buggerie protested that he was really white but it was of no avail. The crowd had sufficient excuse for doing what they had wanted to do at first. They shook their fists in the two men's faces, kicked them, tore off their nondescript garments, searched their pockets and found cards and papers proving their identity, and but for the calmness and presence of mind of the Rev. McPhule, the True Faith Christ Lovers would have torn the unfortunate men limb from limb. The evangelist restrained the more hot-headed individuals and insisted that the ceremonies proceed according to time-honored custom.

So the impetuous yielded to wiser counsel. The two men, vociferously protesting, were stripped naked, held down by husky and willing farm hands and their ears and genitals cut off with jack knives amid the fiendish cries of men and women. When this crude surgery was completed, some wag sewed their ears to their backs and they were released and told to run. Eagerly, in spite of their pain, both men tried to avail themselves of the opportunity. Anything was better than this. Staggering forward through an opening made in the crowd, they attempted to run down the dusty road, blood streaming down their bodies. They had only gone a few feet when, at a signal from the militant evangelist, a half-dozen revolvers cracked and the two Virginians pitched forward into the dust amid the uproarious laughter of the congregation.

The preliminaries ended, the two victims, not yet dead, were picked up, dragged to the stake and bound to it, back to back. Little boys and girls gaily gathered excelsior, scrap paper, twigs and small branches while their proud parents fetched logs, boxes, kerosene and the staves from a cider barrel. The fuel was piled up around the groaning men until only their heads were visible.

When all was in readiness, the people fell back and the Rev. McPhule, as master of ceremonies, ignited the pyre. As the flames shot upward, the dazed men, roused by the flames, strained vainly at the chains that held them. Buggerie found his voice and let out yelp after yelp as the flames licked at his fat flesh. The crowd whooped with glee and Rev. McPhule beamed with satisfaction. The flames rose higher and completely hid the victims from view. The fire crackled merrily and the intense heat drove the spectators back. The odor of cooking meat permeated the clear, country air and many a nostril was guiltily distended. The flames subsided to reveal a red-hot stake supporting two charred hulks.

There were in the assemblage two or three whitened Negroes, who, remembering what their race had suffered in the past, would fain have gone to the assistance of the two men but fear for their own lives restrained them. Even so they were looked at rather sharply by some of the Christ Lovers because they did not appear to be enjoying the spectacle as thoroughly as the rest. Noticing these questioning glances, the whitened Negroes began to yell and prod the burning bodies with sticks and cast stones at them. This exhibition restored them to favor and banished any suspicion that they might not be one-hundred-per-cent Americans.

When the roasting was over and the embers had cooled, the more adventurous members of Rev. McPhule's flock rushed to the stake and groped in the two bodies for skeletal souvenirs such as forefingers, toes and teeth. Proudly their pastor looked on. This was the crowning of a life's ambition. Tomorrow his name would be in every newspaper in the United States. God had indeed answered his prayers. He breathed again his thanks as he thrust his hand into his pocket and felt the soothing touch of the hundred-dollar bill he had extracted from Snobbcraft's pocket. He was supremely happy.

AND SO ON AND SO ON

In the last days of the Goosie administration, the Surgeon-General of the United States, Dr. Junius Crookman, published a monograph on the differences in skin pigmentation of the real whites and those he had made white by the Black-No-More process. In it he declared, to the consternation of many Americans, that in practically every instance the new Caucasians were from two to three shades lighter than the old Caucasians, and that approximately one-sixth of the population were in the first group. The old Caucasians had never been really white but rather were a pale pink shading down to a sand color and a red. Even when an old Caucasian contracted vitiligo, he pointed out, the skin became much lighter.

To a society that had been taught to venerate whiteness for over three hundred years, this announcement was rather staggering. What was the world coming to, if the blacks were whiter than the whites? Many people in the upper class began to look askance at their very pale complexions. If it were true that extreme whiteness was evidence of the possession of Negro blood, of having once been a member of a pariah class, then surely it were well not to be so white!

Dr. Crookman's amazing brochure started the entire country to examining shades of skin color again. Sunday magazine supplements carried long articles on the subject from the pens of hack writers who knew nothing whatever of pigmentation. Pale people who did not have blue eyes began to be whispered about. The comic weeklies devoted special numbers to the question that was on everyone's lips. Senator Bosh of Mississippi, about to run again for office, referred several times to it in the Congressional Record, his remarks interspersed with "Applauses." A popular song, "Whiter Than White" was being whistled by the entire nation. Among the working classes, in the next few months, there grew up a certain prejudice against all fellow workers who were exceedingly pale.

The new Caucasians began to grow self-conscious and resent the curious gazes bestowed upon their lily-white countenances in all public places. They wrote indignant letters to the newspapers about the insults and discriminations to which they were increasingly becoming subjected. They protested vehemently against the effort on the part of employers to pay them less and on the part of the management of public institutions to segregate them. A delegation that waited upon President Goosie firmly denounced the social trend and called upon the government to do something about it. The Down-With-White-Prejudice-League was founded by one Karl von Beerde, whom some accused of being the same Doctor Beard who had, as a Negro, once headed the National Social Equality League. Offices were established in the Times Square district of New York and the mails were soon laden with releases attempting to prove that those of exceedingly pale skin were just as good as anybody else and should not, therefore, be oppressed. A Dr. Cutten Prodd wrote a book proving that all enduring gifts to society came from those races whose skin color was not exceedingly pale, pointing out that the Norwegians and other Nordic peoples had been in savagery when Egypt and Crete were at the height of their development. Prof. Handen Moutthe, the eminent anthropologist (who was well known for his popular work on *The Sex Life of Left-Handed Morons among the Ainus*) announced that as a result of his long research among the palest citizens, he was convinced they were mentally inferior and that their children should be segregated from the others in school. Professor Moutthe's findings were considered authoritative because he had spent three entire weeks of hard work assembling his data. Four state legislatures immediately began to consider bills calling for separate schools for pale children.

Those of the upper class began to look around for ways to get darker. It became the fashion for them to spend hours at the seashore basking naked in the sunshine and then to dash back, heavily bronzed, to their homes, and, preening themselves in their dusky skins, lord it over their paler, and thus less fortunate, associates. Beauty shops began to sell face powders named *Poudre Nègre, Poudre le Egyptienne* and *L'Afrique*.

Mrs. Sari Blandine (formerly Mme. Sisseretta Blandish of Harlem), who had been working on a steam table in a Broadway Automat, saw her opportunity and began to study skin stains. She stayed away from work one week to read up on the subject at the Public Library and came back to find a recent arrival from Czecho-Slovakia holding down her job.

Mrs. Blandine, however, was not downhearted. She had the information and in three or four weeks time she had a skin stain that would impart a long-wearing light-brown tinge to the pigment. It worked successfully on her young daughter; so successfully, in fact, that the damsel received a proposal of marriage from a young millionaire within a month after applying it.

Free applications were given to all of the young women of the neighborhood. Mrs. Blandine's stain became most popular and her fame grew in her locality. She opened a shop in her front room and soon had it crowded from morning till night. The concoction was patented as Blandine's Egyptienne Stain.

By the time President-Elect Hornbill was inaugurated, her Egyptienne Stain Shoppes dotted the country and she had won three suits for infringement of patent. Everybody that was anybody had a stained skin. A girl without one was avoided by the young men; a young man without one was at a decided disadvantage, economically and socially. A white face became startlingly rare. America was definitely, enthusiastically mulatto-minded.

Imitations of Mrs. Blandine's invention sprang up like weeds in a cemetery. In two years there were fifteen companies manufacturing different kinds of stains and artificial tans. At last, even the Zulu Tan became the vogue among the smart set and it was a common thing to see a sweet young miss stop before a show window and dab her face with charcoal. Enterprising resort keepers in Florida and California, intent on attracting the *haute monde*, hired naturally black bathing girls from Africa until the white women protested against the practice on the ground that it was a menace to family life.

One Sunday morning Surgeon-General Crookman, in looking

over the rotogravure section of his favorite newspaper, saw a photograph of a happy crowd of Americans arrayed in the latest abbreviated bathing suits on the sands at Cannes. In the group he recognized Hank Johnson, Chuck Foster, Bunny Brown and his real Negro wife, former Imperial Grand Wizard and Mrs. Givens and Matthew and Helen Fisher. All of them, he noticed, were quite as dusky as little Matthew Crookman Fisher who played in a sandpile at their feet.

Dr. Crookman smiled wearily and passed the section to his wife.

THE CONJURE-MAN DIES

A MYSTERY TALE OF DARK HARLEM

Rudolph Fisher

Chapter One

Encountering the bright-lighted gaiety of Harlem's Seventh Avenue, the frigid midwinter night seemed to relent a little. She had given Battery Park a chill stare and she would undoubtedly freeze the Bronx. But here in this mid-realm of rhythm and laughter she seemed to grow warmer and friendlier, observing, perhaps, that those who dwelt here were mysteriously dark like herself.

Of this favor the Avenue promptly took advantage. Sidewalks barren throughout the cold white day now sprouted life like fields in spring. Along swung boys in camels' hair beside girls in bunny and muskrat; broad, flat heels clacked, high narrow ones clicked, reluctantly leaving the disgorging theaters or eagerly seeking the voracious dance halls. There was loud jest and louder laughter and the frequent uplifting of merry voices in the moment's most popular song:

> "*I'll be glad when you're dead, you rascal you,*
> *I'll be glad when you're dead, you rascal you.*
> *What is it that you've got*
> *Makes my wife think you so hot?*
> *Oh you dog—I'll be glad when you're gone!*"

But all of black Harlem was not thus gay and bright. Any number of dark, chill, silent side streets declined the relenting night's favor. 130th Street, for example, east of Lenox Avenue, was at this moment cold, still, and narrowly forbidding; one glanced down this block and was glad one's destination lay elsewhere. Its concentrated gloom was only intensified by an occasional spangle of electric light, splashed ineffectually against the blackness, or by the unearthly pallor of the sky, into which a wall of dwellings rose to hide the moon.

Among the houses in this looming row, one reared a little taller and gaunter than its fellows, so that the others appeared to shrink from it and huddle together in the shadow on either side. The basement of this house was quite black; its first floor, high above the sidewalk and approached by a long graystone stoop, was only dimly lighted; its second floor was lighted more dimly still, while the third, which was the top, was vacantly dark again like the basement. About the place hovered an oppressive silence, as if those who entered here were warned beforehand not to speak above a whisper. There was, like a footnote, in one of the two first-floor windows to the left of the entrance a black-on-white sign reading:

"Samuel Crouch, Undertaker."

On the narrow panel to the right of the doorway the silver letters of another sign obscurely glittered on an onyx background:

"N. Frimbo, Psychist."

Between the two signs receded the high, narrow vestibule, terminating in a pair of tall glass-paneled doors. Glass curtains, tightly stretched in vertical folds, dimmed the already too-subdued illumination beyond.

2

It was about an hour before midnight that one of the doors rattled and flew open, revealing the bareheaded, short, round figure of a young man who manifestly was profoundly agitated and in a great hurry. Without closing the door behind him, he rushed down the stairs, sped straight across the street, and in a moment was frantically pushing the bell of the dwelling directly opposite. A tall, slender, light-skinned man of obviously habitual composure answered the excited summons.

"Is—is you him?" stammered the agitated one, pointing to a shingle labeled "John Archer, M.D."

"Yes—I'm Dr. Archer."

"Well, arch on over here, will you, doc?" urged the caller. "Sump'm done happened to Frimbo."

"Frimbo? The fortune teller?"

"Step on it, will you, doc?"

Shortly, the physician, bag in hand, was hurrying up the graystone stoop behind his guide. They passed through the still

open door into a hallway and mounted a flight of thickly car-
peted stairs.

At the head of the staircase a tall, lank, angular figure awaited
them. To this person the short, round, black, and by now quite
breathless guide panted, "I got one, boy! This here's the doc
from 'cross the street. Come on, doc. Right in here."

Dr. Archer, in passing, had an impression of a young man as
long and lean as himself, of a similarly light complexion except
for a profusion of dark brown freckles, and of a curiously scowling countenance that glowered from either ill humor or apprehension. The doctor rounded the banister head and strode
behind his pilot toward the front of the house along the upper
hallway, midway of which, still following the excited short one,
he turned and swung into a room that opened into the hall at
that point. The tall fellow brought up the rear.

Within the room the physician stopped, looking about in
surprise. The chamber was almost entirely in darkness. The
walls appeared to be hung from ceiling to floor with black velvet drapes. Even the ceiling was covered, the heavy folds of
cloth converging from the four corners to gather at a central
point above, from which dropped a chain suspending the single
strange source of light, a device which hung low over a chair
behind a large desk-like table, yet left these things and indeed
most of the room unlighted. This was because, instead of
shedding its radiance downward and outward as would an ordinary shaded droplight, this mechanism focused a horizontal
beam upon a second chair on the opposite side of the table.
Clearly the person who used the chair beneath the odd spotlight could remain in relative darkness while the occupant of
the other chair was brightly illuminated.

"There he is—jes' like Jinx found him."

And now in the dark chair beneath the odd lamp the doctor
made out a huddled, shadowy form. Quickly he stepped forward.

"Is this the only light?"

"Only one I've seen."

Dr. Archer procured a flashlight from his bag and swept its
faint beam over the walls and ceiling. Finding no sign of another lighting fixture, he directed the instrument in his hand

toward the figure in the chair and saw a bare black head inclined limply sidewise, a flaccid countenance with open mouth
and fixed eyes staring from under drooping lids.

"Can't do much in here. Anybody up front?"

"Yes, suh. Two ladies."

"Have to get him outside. Let's see. I know. Downstairs.
Down in Crouch's. There's a sofa. You men take hold and get
him down there. This way."

There was some hesitancy. "Mean us, doc?"

"Of course. Hurry. He doesn't look so hot now."

"I ain't none too warm, myself," murmured the short one.
But he and his friend obeyed, carrying out their task with a
dispatch born of distaste. Down the stairs they followed Dr.
Archer, and into the undertaker's dimly lighted front room.

"Oh, Crouch!" called the doctor. "Mr. Crouch!"

"That 'mister' ought to get him."

But there was no answer. "Guess he's out. That's right—put
him on the sofa. Push that other switch by the door. Good."

Dr. Archer inspected the supine figure as he reached into his
bag. "Not so good," he commented. Beneath his black satin
robe the patient wore ordinary clothing—trousers, vest, shirt,
collar and tie. Deftly the physician bared the chest; with one
hand he palpated the heart area while with the other he adjusted the ear-pieces of his stethoscope. He bent over, placed
the bell of his instrument on the motionless dark chest, and listened a long time. He removed the instrument, disconnected
first one, then the other, rubber tube at their junction with the
bell, blew vigorously through them in turn, replaced them,
and repeated the operation of listening. At last he stood erect.

"Not a twitch," he said.

"Long gone, huh?"

"Not so long. Still warm. But gone."

The short young man looked at his scowling freckled companion.

"What'd I tell you?" he whispered. "Was I right or wasn't I?"

The tall one did not answer but watched the doctor. The
doctor put aside his stethoscope and inspected the patient's
head more closely, the parted lips and half-open eyes. He extended a hand and with his extremely long fingers gently
palpated the scalp. "Hello," he said. He turned the far side of

the head toward him and looked first at that side, then at his fingers.

"Wh-what?"

"Blood in his hair," announced the physician. He procured a gauze dressing from his bag, wiped his moist fingers, thoroughly sponged and reinspected the wound. Abruptly he turned to the two men, whom until now he had treated quite impersonally. Still imperturbably, but incisively, in the manner of lancing an abscess, he asked, "Who are you two gentlemen?"

"Why—uh—this here's Jinx Jenkins, doc. He's my buddy, see? Him and me——"

"And you—if I don't presume?"

"Me? I'm Bubber Brown——"

"Well, how did this happen, Mr. Brown?"

"'Deed I don' know, doc. What you mean—is somebody killed him?"

"You don't know?" Dr. Archer regarded the pair curiously a moment, then turned back to examine further. From an instrument case he took a probe and proceeded to explore the wound in the dead man's scalp. "Well—what do you know about it, then?" he asked, still probing. "Who found him?"

"Jinx," answered the one who called himself Bubber. "We jes' come here to get this Frimbo's advice 'bout a little business project we thought up. Jinx went in to see him. I waited in the waitin' room. Presently Jinx come bustin' out pop-eyed and beckoned to me. I went back with him—and there was Frimbo, jes' like you found him. We didn't even know he was over the river."

"Did he fall against anything and strike his head?"

"No, suh, doc." Jinx became articulate. "He didn't do nothin' the whole time I was in there. Nothin' but talk. He tol' me who I was and what I wanted befo' I could open my mouth. Well, I said that I knowed that much already and that I come to find out sump'm I didn't know. Then he went on talkin', tellin' me plenty. He knowed his stuff all right. But all of a sudden he stopped talkin' and mumbled sump'm 'bout not bein' able to see. Seem like he got scared, and he say, 'Frimbo, why don't you see?' Then he didn't say no more. He sound' so funny I got scared myself and jumped up and grabbed that light and turned it on him—and there he was."

"M-m."

Dr. Archer, pursuing his examination, now indulged in what appeared to be a characteristic habit: he began to talk as he worked, to talk rather absently and wordily on a matter which at first seemed inapropos.

"I," said he, "am an exceedingly curious fellow." Deftly, delicately, with half-closed eyes, he was manipulating his probe. "Questions are forever popping into my head. For example, which of you two gentlemen, if either, stands responsible for the expenses of medical attention in this unfortunate instance?"

"Mean who go'n' pay you?"

"That," smiled the doctor, "makes it rather a bald question."

Bubber grinned understandingly.

"Well here's one with hair on it, doc," he said. "Who got the medical attention?"

"M-m," murmured the doctor. "I was afraid of that. Not," he added, "that I am moved by mercenary motives. Oh, not at all. But if I am not to be paid in the usual way, in coin of the realm, then of course I must derive my compensation in some other form of satisfaction. Which, after all, is the end of all our getting and spending, is it not?"

"Oh, sho'," agreed Bubber.

"Now this case"—the doctor dropped the gauze dressing into his bag—"even robbed of its material promise, still bids well to feed my native curiosity—if not my cellular protoplasm. You follow me, of course?"

"With my tongue hangin' out," said Bubber.

But that part of his mind which was directing this discourse did not give rise to the puzzled expression on the physician's lean, light-skinned countenance as he absently moistened another dressing with alcohol, wiped off his fingers and his probe, and stood up again.

"We'd better notify the police," he said. "You men"—he looked at them again—"you men call up the precinct."

They promptly started for the door.

"No—you don't have to go out. The cops, you see"—he was almost confidential—"the cops will want to question all of us. Mr. Crouch has a phone back there. Use that."

They exchanged glances but obeyed.

"I'll be thinking over my findings."

Through the next room they scuffled and into the back of the long first-floor suite. There they abruptly came to a halt and again looked at each other, but now for an entirely different reason. Along one side of this room, hidden from view until their entrance, stretched a long narrow table draped with a white sheet that covered an unmistakably human form. There was not much light. The two young men stood quite still.

"Seem like it's—occupied," murmured Bubber.

"Another one," mumbled Jinx.

"Where's the phone?"

"Don't ask me. I got both eyes full."

"There 'tis—on that desk. Go on—use it."

"Use it yo' own black self," suggested Jinx. "I'm goin' back."

"No you ain't. Come on. We use it together."

"All right. But if that whosis says 'Howdy' tell it I said 'Goo'by.'"

"And where the hell you think I'll be if it says 'Howdy'?"

"What a place to have a telephone!"

"Step on it, slow motion."

"Hello!—Hello!" Bubber rattled the hook. "Hey operator! Operator!"

"My Gawd," said Jinx, "is the phone dead too?"

"Operator—gimme the station—quick. . . . Pennsylvania? No ma'am—New York—Harlem—listen, lady, not railroad. Police. *Please*, ma'am. . . . Hello—hey—send a flock o' cops around here—Frimbo's—the fortune teller's—yea—Thirteen West 130th—yea—somebody done put that thing on him! . . . Yea—O.K."

Hurriedly they returned to the front room where Dr. Archer was pacing back and forth, his hands thrust into his pockets, his brow pleated into troubled furrows.

"They say hold everything, doc. Be right over."

"Good." The doctor went on pacing.

Jinx and Bubber surveyed the recumbent form. Said Bubber, "If he could keep folks from dyin', how come he didn't keep hisself from it?"

"Reckon he didn't have time to put no spell on hisself," Jinx surmised.

"No," returned Bubber grimly. "But somebody else had time to put one on him. I knowed sump'm was comin'. I told you. First time I seen death on the moon since I been grown. And they's two mo' yet."

"How you reckon it happened?"

"You askin' me?" Bubber said. "You was closer to him than I was."

"It was plumb dark all around. Somebody could'a' snook up behind him and crowned him while he was talkin' to me. But I didn't hear a sound. Say—I better catch air. This thing's puttin' me on the well-known spot, ain't it?"

"All right, dumbo. Run away and prove you done it. Wouldn't that be a bright move?"

Dr. Archer said, "The wisest thing for you men to do is stay here and help solve this puzzle. You'd be called in anyway—you found the body, you see. Running away looks as if you were— well—running away."

"What'd I tell you?" said Bubber.

"All right," growled Jinx. "But I can't see how they could blame anybody for runnin' away from this place. Graveyard's a playground side o' this."

Chapter Two

O F THE ten Negro members of Harlem's police force to be promoted from the rank of patrolman to that of detective, Perry Dart was one of the first. As if the city administration had wished to leave no doubt in the public mind as to its intention in the matter, they had chosen, in him, a man who could not have been under any circumstances mistaken for aught but a Negro; or perhaps, as Dart's intimates insisted, they had chosen him because his generously pigmented skin rendered him invisible in the dark, a conceivably great advantage to a detective who did most of his work at night. In any case, the somber hue of his integument in no wise reflected the complexion of his brain, which was bright, alert, and practical within such territory as it embraced. He was a Manhattanite by birth, had come up through the public schools, distinguished himself in athletics at the high school he attended, and, having himself grown up with the black colony, knew Harlem from lowest dive to loftiest temple. He was rather small of stature, with unusually thin, fine features, which falsely accentuated the slightness of his slender but wiry body.

It was Perry Dart's turn for a case when Bubber Brown's call came in to the station, and to it Dart, with four uniformed men, was assigned.

Five minutes later he was in the entrance of Thirteen West 130th Street, greeting Dr. Archer, whom he knew. His men, one black, two brown, and one yellow, loomed in the hallway about him large and ominous, but there was no doubt as to who was in command.

"Hello, Dart," the physician responded to his greeting. "I'm glad you're on this one. It'll take a little active cerebration."

"Come on down, doc," the little detective grinned with a flash of white teeth. "You're talking to a cop now, not a college professor. What've you got?"

"A man that'll tell no tales." The physician motioned to the undertaker's front room. "He's in there."

Dart turned to his men. "Day, you cover the front of the place. Green, take the roof and cover the back yard. Johnson,

383

search the house and get everybody you find into one room. Leave a light everywhere you go if possible—I'll want to check up. Brady, you stay with me." Then he turned back and followed the doctor into the undertaker's parlor. They stepped over to the sofa, which was in a shallow alcove formed by the front bay windows of the room.

"How'd he get it, doc?" he asked.

"To tell you the truth, I haven't the slightest idea."

"Somebody crowned him," Bubber helpfully volunteered.

"Has anybody ast you anything?" Jinx inquired gruffly.

Dart bent over the victim.

The physician said:

"There is a scalp wound all right. See it?"

"Yea—now that you mentioned it."

"But that didn't kill him."

"No? How do you know it didn't, doc?"

"That wound is too slight. It's not in a spot that would upset any vital center. And there isn't any fracture under it."

"Couldn't a man be killed by a blow on the head that didn't fracture his skull?"

"Well—yes. If it fell just so that its force was concentrated on certain parts of the brain. I've never heard of such a case, but it's conceivable. But this blow didn't land in the right place for that. A blow at this point would cause death only by producing intracranial hemorrhage——"

"Couldn't you manage to say it in English, doc?"

"Sure. He'd have to bleed inside his head."

"That's more like it."

"The resulting accumulation of blood would raise the intra —the pressure inside his head to such a point that vital centers would be paralyzed. The power would be shut down. His heart and lungs would quit cold. See? Just like turning off a light."

"O.K. if you say so. But how do you know he didn't bleed inside his head?"

"Well, there aren't but two things that would cause him to."

"I'm learning, doc. Go on."

"Brittle arteries with no give in them—no elasticity. If he had them, he wouldn't even have to be hit—just excitement might shoot up the blood pressure and pop an artery. See what I mean?"

"That's apoplexy, isn't it?"

"Right. And the other thing would be a blow heavy enough to fracture the skull and so rupture the blood vessels beneath. Now this man is about your age or mine—somewhere in his middle thirties. His arteries are soft—feel his wrists. For a blow to kill this man outright, it would have had to fracture his skull."

"Hot damn!" whispered Bubber admiringly. "Listen to the doc do his stuff!"

"And his skull isn't fractured?" said Dart.

"Not if probing means anything."

"Don't tell me you've X-rayed him too?" grinned the detective.

"Any fracture that would kill this man outright wouldn't have to be X-rayed."

"Then you're sure the blow didn't kill him?"

"Not by itself, it didn't."

"Do you mean that maybe he was killed first and hit afterwards?"

"Why would anybody do that?" Dr. Archer asked.

"To make it seem like violence when it was really something else."

"I see. But no. If this man had been dead when the blow was struck, he wouldn't have bled at all. Circulation would already have stopped."

"That's right."

"But of one thing I'm sure: that wound is evidence of too slight a blow to kill."

"Specially," interpolated Bubber, "a hard-headed cullud man——"

"There you go ag'in," growled his lanky companion.

"He's right," the doctor said. "It takes a pretty hefty impact to bash in a skull. With a padded weapon," he went on, "a fatal blow would have had to be crushing to make even so slight a scalp wound as this. That's out. And a hard, unpadded weapon that would break the scalp just slightly like this, with only a little bleeding and without even cracking the skull, could at most have delivered only a stunning blow, not a fatal one. Do you see what I mean?"

"Sure. You mean this man was just stunned by the blow and actually died from something else."

"That's the way it looks to me."

"Well—anyhow he's dead and the circumstances indicate at least a possibility of death by violence. That justifies notifying us, all right. And it makes it a case for the medical examiner. But we really don't know that he's been killed, do we?"

"No. Not yet."

"All the more a case for the medical examiner, then. Is there a phone here, doc? Good. Brady, go back there and call the precinct. Tell 'em to get the medical examiner here double time and to send me four more men—doesn't matter who. Now tell me, doc. What time did this man go out of the picture?"

The physician smiled

"Call Meridian 7–1212."

"O.K., doc. But approximately?"

"Well, he was certainly alive an hour ago. Perhaps even half an hour ago. Hardly less."

"How long have you been here?"

"About fifteen minutes."

"Then he must have been killed—if he was killed—say anywhere from five to thirty-five minutes before you got here?"

"Yes."

Bubber, the insuppressible, commented to Jinx, "Damn! That's trimming it down to a gnat's heel, ain't it?" But Jinx only responded, "Fool, will you hush?"

"Who discovered him—do you know?"

"These two men."

"Both of you?" Dart asked the pair.

"No, suh," Bubber answered. "Jinx here discovered the man. I discovered the doctor."

Dart started to question them further, but just then Johnson, the officer who had been directed to search the house, reappeared.

"Been all over," he reported. "Only two people in the place. Women—both scared green."

"All right," the detective said. "Take these two men up to the same room. I'll be up presently."

Officer Brady returned. "Medical examiner's comin' right up."

The detective said, "Was he on this sofa when you got here, doc?"

"No. He was upstairs in his—his consultation room, I guess

you'd call it. Queer place. Dark as sin. Sitting slumped down in a chair. The light was impossible. You see, I thought I'd been called to a patient, not a corpse. So I had him brought where I knew I could examine him. Of course, if I had thought of murder——"

"Never mind. There's no law against your moving him or examining him, even if you had suspected murder—as long as you weren't trying to hide anything. People think there's some such law, but there isn't."

"The medical examiner'll probably be sore, though."

"Let him. We've got more than the medical examiner to worry about."

"Yes. You've got a few questions to ask."

"And answer. How, when, where, why, and who? Oh, I'm great at questions. But the answers——"

"Well, we've the 'when' narrowed down to a half-hour period." Dr. Archer glanced at his watch. "That would be between ten-thirty and eleven. And 'where' shouldn't be hard to verify—right here in his own chair, if those two fellows are telling it straight. 'Why' and 'who'—those'll be your little red wagon. 'How' right now is mine. I can't imagine——"

Again he turned to the supine figure, staring. Suddenly his lean countenance grew blanker than usual. Still staring, he took the detective by the arm. "Dart," he said reflectively, "we smart people are often amazingly—dumb."

"You're telling me?"

"We waste precious moments in useless speculation. We indulge ourselves in the extravagance of reason when a frugal bit of observation would suffice."

"Does prescription liquor affect you like that, doc?"

"Look at that face."

"Well—if you insist——"

"Just the general appearance of that face—the eyes—the open mouth. What does it look like?"

"Looks like he's gasping for breath."

"Exactly. Dart, this man might—might, you understand—have been choked."

"Ch——"

"Stunned by a blow over the ear——"

"To prevent a struggle!"

"—and choked to death. As simple as that."

"Choked! But just how?"

Eagerly, Dr. Archer once more bent over the lifeless countenance. "There are two ways," he dissertated in his roundabout fashion, "of interrupting respiration." He was peering into the mouth. "What we shall call, for simplicity, the external and the internal. In this case the external would be rather indeterminate, since we could hardly make out the usual bluish discolorations on a neck of this complexion." He procured two tongue depressors and, one in each hand, examined as far back into the throat as he could. He stopped talking as some discovery further elevated his already high interest. He discarded one depressor, reached for his flashlight with the hand thus freed, and, still holding the first depressor in place, directed his light into the mouth as if he were examining tonsils. With a little grunt of discovery, he now discarded the flashlight also, took a pair of long steel thumb-forceps from a flap in the side of his bag, and inserted the instrument into the victim's mouth alongside the guiding tongue-depressor. Dart and the uniformed officer watched silently as the doctor apparently tried to remove something from the throat of the corpse. Once, twice, the prongs snapped together, and he withdrew the instrument empty. But the next time the forceps caught hold of the physician's discovery and drew it forth.

It was a large, blue-bordered, white handkerchief.

Chapter Three

"**D**OC," said Dart, "you don't mind hanging around with us a while?"

"Try and shake me loose," grinned Dr. Archer. "This promises to be worth seeing."

"If you'd said no," Dart grinned back, "I'd have held you anyhow as a suspect. I'm going to need some of your brains. I'm not one of these bright ones that can do all the answers in my head. I'm just a poor boy trying to make a living, and this kind of a riddle hasn't been popped often enough in my life to be easy yet. I've seen some funny ones, but this is funnier. One thing I can see—that this guy wasn't put out by any beginner."

"The man that did this," agreed the physician, "thought about it first. I've seen autopsies that could have missed that handkerchief. It was pushed back almost out of sight."

"That makes you a smart boy."

"I admit it. Wonder whose handkerchief?"

"Stick it in your bag and hang on to it. And let's get going."

"Whither?"

"To get acquainted with this layout first. Whoever's here will keep a while. The bird that pulled the job is probably in Egypt by now."

"That wouldn't be my guess."

"You think he'd hang around?"

"He wouldn't do the expected thing—not if he was bright enough to think up a gag like this."

"Gag is good. Let's start with the roof. Brady, you come with me and the doc—and be ready for surprises. Where's Day?"

The doctor closed and picked up his bag. They passed into the hallway. Officer Day was on guard in the front vestibule according to his orders.

"There are four more men and the medical examiner coming,"

the detective told him. "The four will be right over. Put one on the rear of the house and send the others upstairs. Come on, doc."

The three men ascended two flights of stairs to the top floor. The slim Dart led, the tall doctor followed, the stalwart Brady brought up the rear. Along the uppermost hallway they made their way to the front of the third story of the house, moving with purposeful resoluteness, yet with a sharp-eyed caution that anticipated almost any eventuality. The physician and the detective carried their flashlights, the policeman his revolver.

At the front end of the hallway they found a closed door. It was unlocked. Dart flung it open, to find the ceiling light on, probably left by Officer Johnson in obedience to instructions.

This room was a large bedchamber, reaching, except for the width of the hallway, across the breadth of the house. It was luxuriously appointed. The bed was a massive four-poster of mahogany, intricately carved and set off by a counterpane of gold satin. It occupied the mid-portion of a large black-and-yellow Chinese rug which covered almost the entire floor. Two upholstered chairs, done also in gold satin, flanked the bed, and a settee of similar design guarded its foot. An elaborate smoking stand sat beside the head of the bed. A mahogany chest and bureau, each as substantial as the four-poster, completed the furniture.

"No question as to whose room this is," said Dart.

"A man's," diagnosed Archer. "A man of means and definite ideas, good or bad—but definite. Too bare to be a woman's room—look—the walls are stark naked. There aren't any frills" —he sniffed—"and there isn't any perfume."

"I guess you've been in enough women's rooms to know."

"Men's too. But this is odd. Notice anything conspicuous by its absence?"

"I'll bite."

"Photographs of women."

The detective's eyes swept the room in verification.

"Woman hater?"

"Maybe," said the doctor, "but——"

"Wait a minute," said the detective. There was a clothes closet to the left of the entrance. He turned, opened its door, and played his flashlight upon its contents. An array of masculine attire extended in orderly suspension—several suits of various patterns hanging from individual racks. On the back of the open door hung a suit of black pajamas. On the floor a half-dozen pairs of shoes were set in an orderly row. There was no suggestion of any feminine contact or influence; there was simply the atmosphere of an exceptionally well ordered, decided masculinity.

"What do you think?" asked Dr. Archer.

"Woman hater," repeated Dart conclusively.

"Or a Lothario of the deepest dye."

The detective looked at the doctor. "I get the deep dye—he was blacker'n me. But the Lothario——"

"Isn't it barely possible that this so very complete—er—repudiation of woman is too complete to be accidental? May it not be deliberate—a wary suppression of evidence—the recourse of a lover of great experience and wisdom, who lets not his right hand know whom his left embraceth?"

"Not good—just careful?"

"He couldn't be married—actively. His wife's influence would be—smelt. And if he isn't married, this over-absence of the feminine—well—it means something."

"I still think it could mean woman-hating. This other guesswork of yours sounds all bass-ackwards to me."

"Heaven forfend, good friend, that you should lose faith in my judgment. Woman-hater you call him and woman-hater he is. Carry on."

2

A narrow little room the width of the hallway occupied that extent of the front not taken up by the master bedroom. In this they found a single bed, a small table, and a chair, but nothing of apparent significance.

Along the hallway they now retraced their steps, trying each of three successive doors that led off from this passage. The first was an empty store-room, the second a white tiled bathroom, and the third a bare closet. These yielded no suggestion of the sort of character or circumstances with which they might be dealing. Nor did the smaller of the two rooms terminating the hallway at its back end, for this was merely a narrow kitchen, with a tiny range, a table, icebox, and cabinet. In these they found no inspiration.

But the larger of the two rear rooms was arresting enough. This was a study, fitted out in a fashion that would have warmed the heart and stirred the ambition of any student. There were two large brown-leather club chairs, each with its end table and reading lamp; a similarly upholstered divan in front of a fireplace that occupied the far wall, and over toward the windows at the rear, a flat-topped desk, upon which sat a bronze desk-lamp, and behind which sat a large swivel armchair. Those parts of the walls not taken up by the fireplace and windows were solid masses of books, being fitted from the floor to the level of a tall man's head with crowded shelves.

Dr. Archer was at once absorbed. "This man was no ordinary fakir," he observed. "Look." He pointed out several framed documents on the upper parts of the walls. "Here——" He approached the largest and peered long upon it. Dart came near, looked at it once, and grinned:

"Does it make sense, doc?"

"Bachelor's degree from Harvard. N'Gana Frimbo. N'Gana——"

"Not West Indian?"

"No. This sounds definitely African to me. Lots of them have that N'. The 'Frimbo' suggests it, too—mumbo—jumbo—sambo——"

"Limbo——"

"Wonder why he chose an American college? Most of the chiefs' sons'll go to Oxford or bust. I know—this fellow is probably from Liberia or thereabouts. American influence —see?"

"How'd he get into a racket like fortune telling?"

"Ask me another. Probably a better racket than medicine in this community. A really clever chap could do wonders."

The doctor was glancing along the rows of books. He noted such titles as Tankard's *Determinism and Fatalism, a Critical Contrast*, Bostwick's *The Concept of Inevitability*, Preem's *Cause and Effect*, Dessault's *The Science of History*, and Fairclough's *The Philosophical Basis of Destiny*. He took this last from its place, opened to a flyleaf, and read in script, "N'Gana

Frimbo" and a date. Riffling the pages, he saw in the same
script penciled marginal notes at frequent intervals. At the end
of the chapter entitled "Unit Stimulus and Reaction," the penciled notation read: "Fairclough too has missed the great
secret."

"This is queer."

"What?"

"A native African, a Harvard graduate, a student of philosophy—and a sorcerer. There's something wrong with that
picture."

"Does it throw any light on who killed him?"

"Anything that throws light on the man's character might
help."

"Well, let's get going. I want to go through the rest of the
house and get down to the real job. You worry about his character. I'll worry about the character of the suspects."

"Right-o. Your move, professor."

Chapter Four

MEANWHILE Jinx and Bubber, in Frimbo's waiting-room on the second floor, were indulging in one of their characteristic arguments. This one had started with Bubber's chivalrous endeavors to ease the disturbing situation for the two women, both of whom were bewildered and distraught and one of whom was young and pretty. Bubber had not only announced and described in detail just what he had seen, but, heedless of the fact that the younger woman had almost fainted, had proceeded to explain how he had known, long before it occurred, that he had been about to "see death." To dispel any remaining vestiges of tranquillity, he had added that the death of Frimbo was but one of three. Two more were at hand.

"Soon as Jinx here called me," he said, "I knowed somebody's time had come. I busted on in that room yonder with him—y'all seen me go—and sho' 'nough, there was the man, limp as a rag and stiff as a board. Y' see, the moon don't lie. 'Cose most signs ain't no 'count. As for me, you won't find nobody black as me that's less suprastitious."

"Jes' say we won't find nobody black as you and stop. That'll be the truth," growled Jinx.

"But a moonsign is different. Moonsign is the one sign you can take for sho'. Moonsign——"

"Moonshine is what you took for sho' tonight," Jinx said.

"Red moon mean bloodshed, new moon over your right shoulder mean good luck, new moon over your left shoulder mean bad luck, and so on. Well, they's one moonsign my grandmammy taught me befo' I was knee high and that's the worst sign of 'em all. And that's the sign I seen tonight. I was walkin' down the Avenue feelin' fine and breathin' the air——"

"What do you breathe when you don't feel so good?"

"—smokin' the gals over, watchin' the cars roll by—feelin' good, you know what I mean. And then all of a sudden I stopped. I store."

"You whiched?"

"Store. I stopped and I store."

"What language you talkin'?"

"I store at the sky. And as I stood there starin', sump'm didn't seem right. Then I seen what it was. Y' see, they was a full moon in the sky——"

"Funny place for a full moon, wasn't it?"

"—and as I store at it, they come up a cloud—wasn't but one cloud in the whole sky—and that cloud come up and crossed over the face o' the moon and blotted it out—jes' like that."

"You sho' 'twasn't yo' shadow?"

"Well there was the black cloud in front o' the moon and the white moonlight all around it and behind it. All of a sudden I seen what was wrong. That cloud had done took the shape of a human skull!"

"Sweet Jesus!" The older woman's whisper betokened the proper awe. She was an elongated, incredibly thin creature, ill-favored in countenance and apparel; her loose, limp, angular figure was grotesquely disposed over a stiff-backed arm-chair, and dark, nondescript clothing draped her too long limbs. Her squarish, fashionless hat was a little awry, her scrawny visage, already disquieted, was now inordinately startled, the eyes almost comically wide above the high cheek bones, the mouth closed tight over her teeth whose forward slant made the lips protrude as if they were puckering to whistle.

The younger woman, however, seemed not to hear. Those dark eyes surely could sparkle brightly, those small lips smile, that clear honey skin glow with animation; but just now the eyes stared unseeingly, the lips were a short, hard, straight line, the skin of her round pretty face almost colorless. She was obviously dazed by the suddenness of this unexpected tragedy. Unlike the other woman, however, she had not lost her poise, though it was costing her something to retain it. The trim, black, high-heeled shoes, the light sheer stockings, the black seal coat which fell open to reveal a white-bordered pimiento dress, even the small close-fitting black hat, all were quite as they should be. Only her isolating detachment betrayed the effect upon her of the presence of death and the law.

"A human skull!" repeated Bubber. "Yes, ma'am. Blottin' out the moon. You know what that is?"

"What?" said the older woman.

"That's death on the moon. It's a moonsign and it's never been known to fail."

"And it means death?"

"Worse 'n that, ma'am. It means three deaths. Whoever see death on the moon"—he paused, drew breath, and went on in an impressive lower tone—"gonna see death three times!"

"My soul and body!" said the lady.

But Jinx saw fit to summon logic. "Mean you go'n' see two more folks dead?"

"Gonna stare 'em in the face."

"Then somebody ought to poke yo' eyes out in self-defense."

Having with characteristic singleness of purpose discharged his duty as a gentleman and done all within his power to set the ladies' minds at rest, Bubber could now turn his attention to the due and proper quashing of his unappreciative commentator.

"Whyn't you try it?" he suggested.

"Try what?"

"Pokin' my eyes out."

"Huh. If I thought that was the onliest way to keep from dyin', you could get yo'self a tin cup and a cane tonight."

"Try it then."

" 'Tain't necessary. That moonshine you had'll take care o' everything. Jes' give it another hour to work and you'll be blind as a Baltimo' alley."

"Trouble with you," said Bubber, "is, you' ignorant. You' dumb. The inside o' yo' head is all black."

"Like the outside o' yourn."

"Is you by any chance alludin' to me?"

"I ain't alludin' to that policeman over yonder."

"Lucky for you he is over yonder, else you wouldn't be alludin' at all."

"Now you gettin' bad, ain't you? Jus' 'cause you know you got the advantage over me."

"What advantage?"

"How could I hit you when I can't even see you?"

"Well if I was ugly as you is, I wouldn't want nobody to see me."

"Don't worry, son. Nobody'll ever know how ugly you is. Yo' ugliness is shrouded in mystery."

"Well yo' dumbness ain't. It's right there for all the world to see. You ought to be back in Africa with the other dumb boogies."

"African boogies ain't dumb," explained Jinx. "They' jes' dark. You ain't been away from there long, is you?"

"My folks," returned Bubber crushingly, "left Africa ten generations ago."

"Yo' folks? Shuh. Ten generations ago, you-all wasn't folks. You-all hadn't qualified as apes."

Thus as always, their exchange of compliments flowed toward the level of family history, among other Harlemites a dangerous explosive which a single word might strike into instantaneous violence. It was only because the hostility of these two was actually an elaborate masquerade, whereunder they concealed the most genuine affection for each other, that they could come so close to blows that were never offered.

Yet to the observer this mock antagonism would have appeared alarmingly real. Bubber's squat figure sidled belligerently up to the long and lanky Jinx; solid as a fire-plug he stood, set to grapple; and he said with unusual distinctness:

"Yea? Well—yo' granddaddy was a hair on a baboon's tail. What does that make you?"

The policeman's grin of amusement faded. The older woman stifled a cry of apprehension.

The younger woman still sat motionless and staring, wholly unaware of what was going on.

Chapter Five

D ETECTIVE DART, Dr. Archer, and Officer Brady made a
rapid survey of the basement and cellar. The basement, a
few feet below sidewalk level, proved to be one long, low-
ceilinged room, fitted out, evidently by the undertaker, as a
simple meeting-room for those clients who required the use of
a chapel. There were many rows of folding wooden chairs facing a low platform at the far end of the room. In the middle of
this platform rose a pulpit stand, and on one side against the
wall stood a small reed organ. A heavy dark curtain across the
rear of the platform separated it and the meeting-place from a
brief unimproved space behind that led through a back door
into the back yard. The basement hallway, in the same relative
position as those above, ran alongside the meeting-room and
ended in this little hinder space. In one corner of this, which
must originally have been the kitchen, was the small door of a
dumbwaiter shaft which led to the floor above. The shaft contained no sign of a dumbwaiter now, as Dart's flashlight disclosed: above were the dangling gears and broken ropes of a
mechanism long since discarded, and below, an empty pit.

They discovered nearby the doorway to the cellar stairs,
which proved to be the usual precipitate series of narrow
planks. In the cellar, which was poorly lighted by a single central droplight, they found a large furnace, a coal bin, and, up
forward, a nondescript heap of shadowy junk such as cellars
everywhere seem to breed.

All this appeared for the time being unimportant, and so
they returned to the second floor, where the victim had originally been found. Dart had purposely left this floor till the last.
It was divided into three rooms, front, middle and back, and
these they methodically visited in order.

They entered the front room, Frimbo's reception room, just
as Bubber sidled belligerently up to Jinx. Apparently their
entrance discouraged further hostilities, for with one or two

upward, sidelong glares from Bubber, neutralized by an inarticulate growl or two from Jinx, the imminent combat faded
mysteriously away and the atmosphere cleared.

But now the younger woman's eyes lifted to recognize Dr.
John Archer. She jumped up and went to him.

"Hello, Martha," he said.

"What does it mean, John?"

"Don't let it upset you. Looks like the conjure-man had an
enemy, that's all."

"It's true—he really is——?"

"I'm afraid so. This is Detective Dart. Mrs. Crouch, Mr.
Dart."

"Good-evening," Mrs. Crouch said mechanically and turned
back to her chair.

"Dart's a friend of mine, Martha," said the physician. "He'll
take my word for your innocence, never fear."

The older woman, refusing to be ignored, said impatiently,
"How long you 'spect us to sit here? What we waitin' for? We
didn' kill him."

"Of course not," Dart smiled. "But you may be able to help
us find out who did. As soon as I've finished looking around
I'll want to ask you a few questions. That's all."

"Well," she grumbled, "you don't have to stand a seven-foot
cop over us to ask a few questions, do you?"

Ignoring this inquiry, the investigators continued with their
observations. This was a spacious room whose soft light came
altogether from three or four floor lamps; odd heavy silken
shades bore curious designs in profile, and the effect of the
obliquely downcast light was to reveal legs and bodies, while
countenances above were bedimmed by comparative shadow.
Beside the narrow hall door was a wide doorway hung with
portières of black velvet, occupying most of that wall. The lateral walls, which seemed to withdraw into the surrounding
dusk, were adorned with innumerable strange and awful shapes:
gruesome black masks with hollow orbits, some smooth and
bald, some horned and bearded; small misshapen statuettes of
near-human creatures, resembling embryos dried and blackened in the sun, with closed bulbous eyes and great protruding
lips; broad-bladed swords, slim arrows and jagged spear-heads
of forbidding designs. On the farther of the lateral walls was a

mantelpiece upon which lay additional African emblems. Dr. Archer pointed out a murderous-looking club, resting diagonally across one end of the mantel; it consisted of the lower half of a human femur, one extremity bulging into wicked-looking condyles, the other, where the original bone had been severed, covered with a silver knob representing a human skull.

"That would deliver a nasty crack."

"Wonder if it did?" said the detective.

2

They passed now through the velvet portières and a little isthmus-like antechamber into the middle room where the doctor had first seen the victim. Dr. Archer pointed out those peculiarities of this chamber which he had already noted: the odd droplight with its horizontally focused beam, which was the only means of illumination; the surrounding black velvet draping, its long folds extending vertically from the bottom of the walls to the top, then converging to the center of the ceiling above, giving the room somewhat the shape of an Arab tent; the one apparent opening in this drapery, at the side door leading to the hallway; the desk-like table in the middle of the room, the visitors' chair on one side of it, Frimbo's on the other, directly beneath the curious droplight.

"Let's examine the walls," said Dart. He and the doctor brought their flashlights into play. Like two offshoots of the parent beam, the smaller shafts of light traveled inquisitively over the long vertical folds of black velvet, which swayed this way and that as the two men pulled and palpated, seeking openings. The projected spots of illumination moved like two strange, twisting, luminous moths, constantly changing in size and shape, fluttering here and there from point to point, pausing, inquiring, abandoning. The detective and the physician began at the entrance from the reception room and circuited the black chamber in opposite directions. Presently they met at the far back wall, in whose midline the doctor located an opening. Pulling the hangings aside at this point, they discovered another door but found it locked.

"Leads into the back room, I guess. We'll get in from the hallway. What's this?"

"This" proved to be a switch-box on the wall beside the closed door. The physician read the lettering on its front. "Sixty amperes—two hundred and twenty volts. That's enough for an X-ray machine. What does he need special current for?"

"Search me. Come on. Brady, run downstairs and get that extension-light out of the back of my car. Then come back here and search the floor for whatever you can find. Specially around the table and chairs. We'll be right back."

3

They left the death chamber by its side door and approached the rearmost room from the hallway. Its hall door was unlocked, but blackness greeted them as they flung it open, a strangely sinister blackness in which eyes seemed to gleam. When they cast their flashlights into that blackness they saw whence the gleaming emanated, and Dart, stepping in, found a switch and produced a light.

"Damn!" said he as his eyes took in a wholly unexpected scene. Along the rear wall under the windows stretched a long flat chemical work-bench, topped with black slate. On its dull dark surface gleamed bright laboratory devices of glass or metal, flasks, beakers, retorts, graduates, pipettes, a copper water-bath, a shining instrument-sterilizer, and at one end, a gleaming black electric motor. The space beneath this bench was occupied by a long floor cabinet with a number of small oaken doors. On the wall at the nearer end was a glass-doored steel cabinet containing a few small surgical instruments, while the far wall, at the other end of the bench, supported a series of shelves, the lower ones bearing specimen-jars of various sizes, and the upper, bottles of different colors and shapes. Dart stooped and opened one of the cabinet doors and discovered more glassware, while Dr. Archer went over and investigated the shelves, removed one of the specimen-jars, and with a puzzled expression, peered at its contents, floating in some preserving fluid.

"What's that?" the detective asked, approaching.

"Can't be," muttered the physician.

"Can't be what?"

"What they look like."

"Namely?"

Ordinarily Dr. Archer would probably have indulged in a leisurely circumlocution and reached his decision by a flank attack. In the present instance he was too suddenly and wholly absorbed in what he saw to entertain even the slightest or most innocent pretense.

"Sex glands," he said.

"What?"

"Male sex glands, apparently."

"Are you serious?"

The physician inspected the rows of jars, none of which was labeled. There were other preserved biological specimens, but none of the same appearance as those in the jar which he still held in his hand.

"I'm serious enough," he said. "Does it stimulate your imagination?"

"Plenty," said Dart, his thin lips tightening. "Come on—let's ask some questions."

Chapter Six

THEY returned to the middle chamber. Officer Brady had plugged the extension into a hall socket and twisted its cord about the chain which suspended Frimbo's light. The strong white lamp's sharp radiance did not dispel the far shadows, but at least it brightened the room centrally.

Brady said, "There's three things I found—all on the floor by the chair."

"This chair?" Dart indicated the one in which the victim had been first seen by Dr. Archer.

"Yes."

The three objects were on the table, as dissimilar as three objects could be.

"What do you think of this, doc?" Dart picked up a small irregular shining metallic article and turned to show it to the physician. But the physician was already reaching for one of the other two discoveries.

"Hey—wait a minute!" protested the detective. "That's big enough to have finger prints on it."

"My error. What's that you have?"

"Teeth. Somebody's removable bridge."

He handed over the small shining object. The physician examined it. "First and second left upper bicuspids," he announced.

"You don't say?" grinned Dart.

"What do you mean, somebody's?"

"Well, if you know whose just by looking at it, speak up. Don't hold out on me."

"Frimbo's."

"Or the guy's that put him out."

"Hm—no. My money says Frimbo's. These things slip on and off easily enough."

"I see what you mean. In manipulating that handkerchief the murderer dislodged this thing."

403

"Yes. Too bad. If it was the murderer's it might help identify him."

"Why? There must be plenty of folks with those same teeth missing."

"True. But this bridge wouldn't fit—really fit—anybody but the person it was made for. The models have to be cast in plaster. Not two in ten thousand would be identical in every respect. This thing's practically as individual as a finger print."

"Yea? Well, we may be able to use it anyhow. I'll hang on to it. But wait. You looked down Frimbo's throat. Didn't you notice his teeth?"

"Not especially. I didn't care anything about his teeth then. I was looking for the cause of death. But we can easily check this when the medical examiner comes."

"O.K. Now—what's this?" He picked up what seemed to be a wad of black silk ribbon.

"That was his head cloth, I suppose. Very impressive with that flowing robe and all."

"Who could see it in the dark?"

"Oh, he might have occasion to come out into the light sometime."

The detective's attention was already on the third object.

"Say——!"

"I'm way ahead of you."

"That's the mate to the club on the mantel in the front room!"

"Right. That's made from a left femur, this from a right."

"That must be what crowned him. Boy, if that's got finger prints on it——"

"Ought to have. Look—it's not fully bleached out like the specimens ordinarily sold to students. Notice the surface—greasy-looking. It would take an excellent print."

"Did you touch it, Brady?"

"I picked it up by the big end. I didn't touch the rest of it."

"Good. Have the other guys shown up yet? All right. Wrap it—here"—he took a newspaper from his pocket, surrounded the thigh bone with it, stepped to the door and summoned one of the officers who had arrived meanwhile. "Take this over to the precinct, tell Mac to get it examined for finger prints pronto—anybody he can get hold of—wait for the result and bring it back here—wet. And bring back a set—if Tynie's around, let him bring it. Double time—it's a rush order."

"What's the use?" smiled the doctor. "You yourself said the offender's probably in Egypt by now."

"And you said different. Hey—look!"

He had been playing his flashlight over the carpet. Its rays passed obliquely under the table, revealing a grayish discoloration of the carpet. Closer inspection proved this to be due to a deposit of ash-colored powder. The doctor took a prescription blank and one of his professional cards and scraped up some of the powder onto the blank.

"Know what it is?" asked Dart.

"No."

"Save it. We'll have it examined."

"Meanwhile?"

"Meanwhile let's indulge in a few personalities. Let's see—I've got an idea."

"Shouldn't be at all surprised. What now?"

"This guy Frimbo was smart. He put his people in that spotlight and he stayed in the dark. All right—I'm going to do the same thing."

"You might win the same reward."

"I'll take precautions against that. Brady!"

Brady brought in the two officers who had not yet been assigned to a post. They were stationed now, one on either side of the black room toward its rear wall.

"Now," said Dart briskly. "Let's get started. Brady, call in that little short fat guy. You in the hall there—turn off this extension at that socket and be ready to turn it on again when I holler. I intend to sit pat as long as possible."

Thereupon he snapped off his flashlight and seated himself in Frimbo's chair behind the table, becoming now merely a deeper shadow in the surrounding dimness. The doctor put out his flashlight also and stood beside the chair. The bright shaft of light from the device overhead, directed away from them, shone full upon the back of the empty visitors' chair opposite, and on beyond toward the passageway traversed by those who entered from the reception room. They waited for Bubber Brown to come in.

2

Whatever he might have expected, Bubber Brown certainly was unprepared for this. With a hesitancy that was not in the least feigned, his figure came into view; first his extremely bowed legs, about which flapped the bottom of his imitation camels' hair overcoat, then the middle of his broad person, with his hat nervously fingered by both hands, then his chest and neck, jointly adorned by a bright green tie, and finally his round black face, blank as a door knob, loose-lipped, wide-eyed. Brady was prodding him from behind.

"Sit down, Mr. Brown," said a voice out of the dark.

The unaccustomed "Mr." did not dispel the unreality of the situation for Bubber, who had not been so addressed six times in his twenty-six years. Nor was he reassured to find that he could not make out the one who had spoken, so blinding was the beam of light in his eyes. What he did realize was that the voice issued from the place where he had a short while ago looked with a wild surmise upon a corpse. For a moment his eyes grew whiter; then, with decision, he spun about and started away from the sound of that voice.

He bumped full into Brady. "Sit down!" growled Brady.

Said Dart, "It's me, Brown—the detective. Take that chair and answer what I ask you."

"Yes, suh," said Bubber weakly, and turned back and slowly edged into the space between the table and the visitors' chair. Perspiration glistened on his too illuminated brow. By the least possible bending of his body he managed to achieve the mere rim of the seat, where, with both hands gripping the chair arms, he crouched as if poised on some gigantic spring which any sudden sound might release to send him soaring into the shadows above.

"Brady, you're in the light. Take notes. All right, Mr. Brown. What's your full name?"

"Bubber Brown," stuttered that young man uncomfortably.

"Address?"

"2100 Fifth Avenue."

"Age?"

"Twenty-six."

"Occupation?"

"Suh?"

"Occupation?"

"Oh. Detective."

"De—what!"

"Detective. Yes, suh."

"Let's see your shield."

"My which?"

"Your badge."

"Oh. Well—y'see I ain't the kind o' detective what has to have a badge. No, suh."

"What kind are you?"

"I'm a family detective."

Somewhat more composed by the questioning, Bubber quickly reached into his pocket and produced a business card. Dart took it and snapped his light on it, to read:

> BUBBER BROWN, INC., *Detective*
> (formerly with the City of
> New York)
> 2100 Fifth Avenue
> Evidence obtained in affairs of
> the heart, etc. Special attention
> to cheaters and backbiters.

Dart considered this a moment, then said:

"How long have you been breaking the law like this?"

"Breaking the law? Who, me? What old law, mistuh?"

"What about this 'Incorporated'? You're not incorporated."

"Oh, that? Oh, that's 'ink'—that means black."

"Don't play dumb. You know what it means, you know that you're not incorporated, and you know that you've never been a detective with the City. Now what's the idea? Who are you?"

Bubber had, as a matter of fact, proffered the card thoughtlessly in the strain of his discomfiture. Now he chose, wisely, to throw himself on Dart's good graces.

"Well, y'see times is been awful hard, everybody knows that. And I did have a job with the City—I was in the Distinguished Service Company——"

"The what?"

"The D. S. C.—Department of Street Cleaning—but we

never called it that, no, suh. Coupla weeks ago I lost that job and couldn't find me nothin' else. Then I said to myself, 'They's only one chance, boy—you got to use your head instead o' your hands.' Well, I figured out the situation like this: The only business what was flourishin' was monkey-business——"

"What are you talking about?"

"Monkey-business. Cheatin'—backbitin', and all like that. Don't matter how bad business gets, lovin' still goes on; and long as lovin' is goin' on, cheatin' is goin' on too. Now folks'll pay to catch cheaters when they won't pay for other things, see? So I figure I can hire myself out to catch cheaters as well as anybody—all I got to do is bust in on 'em and tell the judge what I see. See? So I had me them cards printed and I'm r'arin' to go. But I didn't know 'twas against the law sho' 'nough."

"Well it is and I may have to arrest you for it."

Bubber's dismay was great.

"Couldn't you jes'—jes' tear up the card and let it go at that?"

"What was your business here tonight?"

"Me and Jinx come together. We was figurin' on askin' the man's advice about this detective business."

"You and who?"

"Jinx Jenkins—you know—the long boy look like a giraffe you seen downstairs."

"What time did you get here?"

" 'Bout half-past ten I guess."

"How do you know it was half-past ten?"

"I didn't say I knowed it, mistuh. I said I guess. But I know it wasn't no later'n that."

"How do you know?"

Thereupon, Bubber told how he knew.

3

At eight o'clock sharp, as indicated by his new dollar watch, purchased as a necessary tool of his new profession, he had been walking up and down in front of the Lafayette Theatre, apparently idling away his time, but actually taking this opportunity to hand out his new business cards to numerous theatergoers. It was his first attempt to get a case and he was not surprised to find that it promptly bore fruit in that happy-go-lucky, care-free, irresponsible atmosphere. A woman to whom he had handed one of his announcements returned to him for further information.

"I should 'a' known better," he admitted, "than to bother with her, because she was bad luck jes' to look at. She was cross-eyed. But I figure a cross-eyed dollar'll buy as much as a straight-eyed one and she talked like she meant business. She told me if I would get some good first-class low-down on her big boy, I wouldn't have no trouble collectin' my ten dollars. I say 'O.K., sister. Show me two bucks in front and his Cleo from behind, and I'll track 'em down like a bloodhound.' She reached down in her stockin', I held out my hand and the deal was on. I took her name an' address an' she showed me the Cleo and left. That is, I thought she left.

"The Cleo was the gal in the ticket-box. Oh, mistuh, what a Sheba! Keepin' my eyes on her was the easiest work I ever did in my life. I asked the flunky out front what this honey's name was and he tole me Jessie James. That was all I wanted to know. When I looked at her I felt like givin' the cross-eyed woman back her two bucks.

"A little before ten o'clock Miss Jessie James turned the ticket-box over to the flunky and disappeared inside. It was too late for me to spend money to go in then, and knowin' I prob'ly couldn't follow her everywhere she was goin' anyhow, I figured I might as well wait for her outside one door as another. So I waited out front, and in three or four minutes out she come. I followed her up the Avenue a piece and round a corner to a private house on 134th Street. After she'd been in a couple o' minutes I rung the bell. A fat lady come to the door and I asked for Miss Jessie James.

"'Oh,' she say. 'Is you the gentleman she was expectin'?' I say, 'Yes ma'am. I'm one of 'em. They's another one comin'.' She say, 'Come right in. You can go up—her room is the top floor back. She jes' got here herself.' Boy, what a break. I didn' know for a minute whether this was business or pleasure.

"When I got to the head o' the stairs I walked easy. I snook up to the front-room door and found it cracked open 'bout half an inch. Naturally I looked in—that was business. But, friend, what I saw was nobody's business. Miss Jessie wasn't

gettin' ready for no ordinary caller. She look like she was gettin' ready to try on a bathin' suit and meant to have a perfect
fit. Nearly had a fit myself tryin' to get my breath back. Then I
had to grab a armful o' hall closet, 'cause she reached for a kimono and started for the door. She passed by and I see I've
got another break. So I seized opportunity by the horns and
slipped into her room. Over across one corner was——"

"Wait a minute," interrupted Dart. "I didn't ask for your life
history. I only asked——"

"You ast how I knowed it wasn't after half-past ten o'clock."

"Exactly."

"I'm tellin' you, mistuh. Listen. Over across one corner was
a trunk—a wardrobe trunk, standin' up on end and wide open.
I got behind it and squatted down. I looked at my watch. It
was ten minutes past ten. No sooner'n I got the trunk straight
'cross the corner again I heard her laughin' out in the hall and
I heard a man laughin', too. I say to myself, 'here 'tis. The
bathin'-suit salesman done arrived.'

"And from behind that trunk, y'see, I couldn't use nothin'
but my ears—couldn't see a thing. That corner had me pretty
crowded. Well, instead o' goin' on and talkin', they suddenly
got very quiet, and natchelly I got very curious. It was my
business to know what was goin' on.

"So instead o' scronchin' down behind the trunk like I'd
been doin', I begun to inch up little at a time till I could see
over the top. Lord—what did I do that for? Don' know jes'
how it happened, but next thing I do know is 'wham!'—the
trunk had left me. There it was flat on the floor, face down,
like a Hindu sayin' his prayers, and there was me in the corner,
lookin' dumb and sayin' mine, with the biggest boogy in
Harlem 'tween me and the door.

"Fact is, I forgot I was a detective. Only thing I wanted to
detect was the quickest way out. Was that guy evil-lookin'?
One thing saved me—the man didn't know whether to blame
me or her. Before he could make up his mind, I shot out o'
that corner past him like a cannon-ball. The gal yelled, 'Stop
thief!' And the guy started after me. But, shuh!—he never had
a chance—even in them runnin'-pants o' his. I flowed down
the stairs and popped out the front door, and who was waitin'
on the sidewalk but the cross-eyed lady. She'd done followed

me same as I followed the Sheba. Musta hid when her man
went by on the way in. But when he come by chasin' me on
the way out, she jumped in between us and ast him where was
his pants.

"Me, I didn't stop to hear the answer. I knew it. I made
Lenox Avenue in nothin' and no fifths. That wasn't no more
than quarter past ten. I slowed up and turned down Lenox
Avenue. Hadn' gone a block before I met Jinx Jenkins. I told
him 'bout it and ast him what he thought I better do next.
Well, somebody'd jes' been tellin' him 'bout what a wonderful
guy this Frimbo was for folks in need o' advice. We agreed to
come see him and walked on round here. Now, I know it didn't
take me no fifteen minutes to get from that gal's house here.
So I must 'a' been here before half-past ten, y'see?"

4

Further questioning elicited that when Jinx and Bubber arrived they had made their way, none too eagerly, up the stairs
in obedience to a sign in the lower hallway and had encountered no one until they reached the reception-room in front.
Here there had been three men, waiting to see Frimbo. One,
Bubber had recognized as Spider Webb, a number-runner who
worked for Harlem's well-known policy-king, Si Brandon.
Another, who had pestered Jinx with unwelcome conversation, was a notorious little drug-addict called Doty Hicks. The
third was a genial stranger who had talked pleasantly to everybody, revealing himself to be one Easley Jones, a railroad man.

After a short wait, Frimbo's flunky appeared from the hallway and ushered the railroad man, who had been the first to
arrive, out of the room through the wide velvet-curtained passage. While Jones was, presumably, with Frimbo, the two ladies
had come in—the young one first. Then Doty Hicks had gone
in to Frimbo, then Spider Webb, and finally Jinx. The usher
had not himself gone through the wide doorway at any time—
he had only bowed the visitors through, turned aside, and disappeared down the hallway.

"This usher—what was he like?"

"Tall, skinny, black, stoop-shouldered, and cockeyed. Wore

a long black silk robe like Frimbo's, but he had a bright yellow sash and a bright yellow thing on his head—you know—what d'y' call 'em? Look like bandages——"

"Turban?"

"That's it. Turban."

"Where is he now?"

"Don't ask me, mistuh. I ain't seen him since he showed Jinx in."

"Hm."

"Say!" Bubber had an idea.

"What?"

"I bet he done it!"

"Did what?"

"Scrambled the man's eggs!"

"You mean you think the assistant killed Frimbo?"

"Sho'!"

"How do you know Frimbo was killed?"

"Didn't—didn't you and the doc say he was when I was downstairs lookin' at you?"

"On the contrary, we said quite definitely that we didn't know that he was killed, and that even if he was, that blow didn't kill him."

"But—in the front room jes' now, didn't the doc tell that lady——"

"All the doctor said was that it looked like Frimbo had an enemy. Now you say Frimbo was killed and you accuse somebody of doing it."

"All I meant——"

"You were in this house when he died, weren't you? By your own time."

"I was here when the doc says he died, but——"

"Why would you accuse anybody of a crime if you didn't know that a crime had been committed?"

"Listen, mistuh, please. All I meant was, *if* the man *was* killed, the flunky *might* 'a' done it and hauled hips. He could be in Egypt by now."

Dart's identical remark came back to him. He said less sharply:

"Yes. But on the other hand you might be calling attention to that fact to avert suspicion from yourself."

"Who—me?" Bubber's eyes went incredibly large. "Good Lord, man, I didn't leave that room yonder—that waitin'-room —till Jinx called me in to see the man—and he was dead then. 'Deed that's the truth—I come straight up the stairs with Jinx —we went straight in the front room—and I didn't come out till Jinx called me—ask the others—ask them two women."

"I will. But they can only testify for your presence in that room. Who says you came up the stairs and went straight into that room? How can you prove you did that? How do I know you didn't stop in here by way of that side hall-door there, and attack Frimbo as he sat here in this chair?"

The utter unexpectedness of his own incrimination, and the detective's startling insistence upon it, almost robbed Bubber of speech, a function which he rarely relinquished. For a moment he could only gape. But he managed to sputter: "Judas Priest, mistuh, can't you take a man's word for nothin'?"

"I certainly can't," said the detective.

"Well, then," said Bubber, inspired, "ask Jinx. He seen me. He come in with me."

"I see. You alibi him and he alibis you. Is that it?"

"Damn!" exploded Bubber. "You is the most suspicious man I ever met!"

"You're not exactly free of suspicion yourself," Dart returned dryly.

"Listen, mistuh. If you bumped a man off, would you run get a doctor and hang around to get pinched? Would you?"

"If I thought that would make me look innocent I might —yes."

"Then you're dumber'n I am. If I'd done it, I'd been long gone by now."

"Still," Dart said, "you have only the word of your friend Jinx to prove you went straight into the waiting-room. That's insufficient testimony. Got a handkerchief on you?"

"Sho'." Bubber reached into his breast pocket and produced a large and flagrant affair apparently designed for appearance rather than for service; a veritable flag, crossed in one direction by a bright orange band and in another, at right angles to the first, by a virulent green one. "My special kind," he said; "always buy these. Man has to have a little color in his clothes, y'see?"

"Yes, I see. Got any others?"

"'Nother one like this—but it's dirty." He produced the mate, crumpled and matted, out of another pocket.

"O.K. Put 'em away. See anybody here tonight with a colored handkerchief of any kind?"

"No suh—not that I remember."

"All right. Now tell me this. Did you notice the decorations on the walls in the front room when you first arrived?"

"Couldn't help noticin' them things—'nough to scare anybody dizzy."

"What did you see?"

"You mean them false-faces and knives and swords and things?"

"Yes. Did you notice anything in particular on the mantelpiece?"

"Yea. I went over and looked at it soon as I come in. What I remember most was a pair o' clubs. One was on one end o' the mantelpiece, and the other was on the other. Look like they was made out o' bones."

"You are sure there were two of them?"

"Sho' they was two. One on——"

"Did you touch them?"

"No *suh*—couldn't pay me to touch none o' them things— might 'a' been conjured."

"Did you see anyone touch them?"

"No, suh."

"You saw no one remove one of them?"

"No, suh."

"So far as you know they are still there?"

"Yes, suh."

"Who was in that room, besides yourself, when you first saw the two clubs?"

"Everybody. That was befo' the flunky'd come in to get the railroad man."

"I see. Now these two women—how soon after you got there did they come in?"

"'Bout ten minutes or so."

"Did either of them leave the room while you were there?"

"No, suh."

"And the first man—Easley Jones, the railroad porter—he had come into this room before the women arrived?"

"Yes, suh. He was the first one here, I guess."

"After he went in to Frimbo, did he come back into the waiting-room?"

"No, suh. Reckon he left by this side door here into the hall."

"Did either of the other two return to the waiting-room?"

"No, suh. Guess they all left the same way. Only one that came back was Jinx, when he called me."

"And at that time, you and the women were the only people left in the waiting-room?"

"Yes, suh."

"Very good. Could you identify those three men?"

"'Deed I could. I could even find 'em if you said so."

"Perhaps I will. For the present you go back to the front room. Don't try anything funny—the house is lousy with policemen."

"Lousy is right," muttered Bubber.

"What's that?"

"I ain't opened my mouth, mistuh. But listen, you don't think I done it sho' 'nough do you?"

"That will depend entirely on whether the women corroborate your statement."

"Well, whatever that is, I sho' hope they do it."

Chapter Seven

"BRADY, ask the lady who arrived first to come in," said Dart, adding in a low aside to the physician, "if her story checks with Brown's on the point of his staying in that room, I think I can use him for something. He couldn't have taken that club out without leaving the room."

"He tells a straight story," agreed Dr. Archer. "Too scared to lie. But isn't it too soon to let anybody out?"

"I don't mean to let him go. But I can send him with a couple o' cops to identify the other men who were here and bring them back, without being afraid he'll start anything."

"Why not go with him and question them where you find 'em?"

"It's easier to have 'em all in one place if possible—saves everybody's time. Can't always do it of course. Here comes the lady—your friend."

"Be nice to her—she's the real thing. I've known her for years."

"O. K."

Uncertainly, the young woman entered, the beam of light revealing clearly her unusually attractive appearance. With undisguised bewilderment on her pretty face, but with no sign of fear, she took the visitors' chair.

"Don't be afraid, Mrs. Crouch. I want you to answer, as accurately as you can, a few questions which may help determine who killed Frimbo."

"I'll be glad to," she said in a low, matter-of-fact tone.

"What time did you arrive here tonight?"

"Shortly after ten-thirty."

"You're sure of the time?"

"I was at the Lenox. The feature picture goes on for the last time at ten-thirty. I had seen it already, and when it came on again I left. It is no more than four or five minutes' walk from there here."

"Good. You came directly to Frimbo's waiting-room?"

"No. I stopped downstairs to see if my husband was there."

"Your husband? Oh—Mr. Crouch, the undertaker, is your husband?"

"Yes. But he was out."

"Does he usually go out and leave his place open?"

"Late in the evening, yes. Up until then there is a clerk. Afterwards if he is called out he just leaves a sign saying when he will return. He never," she smiled faintly, "has to fear robbers, you see."

"But might not calls come in while he is out?"

"Yes. But they are handled by a telephone exchange. If he doesn't answer, the exchange takes the call and gives it to him later."

"I see. How long did stopping downstairs delay you?"

"Only a minute. Then I came right up to the waiting-room."

"Who was there when you got there?"

"Four men."

"Did you know any of them?"

"No, but I'd know them if I saw them again."

"Describe them."

"Well there was a little thin nervous man who looked like he was sick—in fact he was sick, because when he got up to follow the assistant he had a dizzy spell and fell, and all the men jumped to him and had to help him up."

"He was the first to go in to Frimbo after you arrived?"

"Yes. Then there was a heavy-set, rather flashily-dressed man in gray. He went in next. And there were two others who seemed to be together—the two who were in there a few minutes ago when you and Dr. Archer came in."

"A tall fellow and a short one?"

"Yes."

"About those two—did either of them leave the room while you were there?"

"The tall one did, when his turn came to see Frimbo."

"And the short one?"

"Well—when the tall one had been out for about five or six minutes, he came back—through the same way that he had gone. It was rather startling because nobody else had come back at all except Frimbo's man, and he always appeared in the hall doorway, not the other, and always left by the hall doorway also. And, too, this tall fellow looked terribly excited. He beckoned to the short one and they went back together through the passage—into this room."

"That was the first and only time the short man left that room while you were there?"

"Yes."

"And you yourself did not leave the room meanwhile?"

"No. Not until now."

"Did anyone else come in?"

"The other woman, who is in there now."

"Very good. Now, pardon me if I seem personal, but it's my business not to mind my business—to meddle with other people's. You understand?"

"Perfectly. Don't apologize—just ask."

"Thank you. Did you know anything about this man Frimbo —his habits, friends, enemies?"

"No. He had many followers, I know, and a great reputation for being able to cast spells and that sort of thing. His only companion, so far as I know, was his servant. Otherwise he seemed to lead a very secluded life. I imagine he must have been pretty well off financially. He'd been here almost two years. He was always our best tenant."

"Tell me why you came to see Frimbo tonight, please."

"Certainly. Mr. Crouch owns this house, among others, and Frimbo is our tenant. My job is collecting rents, and tonight I came to collect Frimbo's."

"I see. But do you find it more convenient to see tenants at night?"

"Not so much for me as for them. Most of them are working during the day. And Frimbo simply can't be seen in the daytime—he won't see anyone either professionally or on business until after dark. It's one of his peculiarities, I suppose."

"So that by coming during his office hours you are sure of finding him available?"

"Exactly."

"All right, Mrs. Crouch. That's all for the present. Will you return to the front room? I'd let you go at once, but you may be able to help me further if you will."

"I'll be glad to."

"Thank you. Brady, call in Bubber Brown and one of those extra men."

When Bubber reappeared, Dart said:

"You told me you could locate and identify the three men who preceded Jenkins?"

"Yes, suh. I sho' can."

"How?"

"Well, I been seein' that little Doty Hicks plenty. He hangs out 'round his brother's night club. 'Cose ev'ybody knows Spider Webb's a runner and I can find him from now till mornin' at Patmore's Pool Room. And that other one, the railroad man, he and I had quite a conversation before he come in to see Frimbo, and I found out where he rooms when he's in town. Jes' a half a block up the street here, in a private house."

"Good." The detective turned to the officer whom Brady had summoned:

"Hello, Hanks. Listen Hanks, you take Mr. Brown there around by the precinct, pick up another man, and then go with Mr. Brown and bring the men he identifies here. There'll be three of 'em. Take my car and make it snappy."

2

Jinx, behind a mask of scowling ill-humor, which was always his readiest defense under strain, sat now in the uncomfortably illuminated chair and growled his answers into the darkness whence issued Dart's voice. This apparently crusty attitude, which long use had made habitual, served only to antagonize his questioner, so that even the simplest of his answers were taken as unsatisfactory. Even in the perfectly routine but obviously important item of establishing his identity, he made a bad beginning.

"Have you anything with you to prove your identity?"

"Nothin' but my tongue."

"What do you mean?"

"I mean I say I'm who I is. Who'd know better?"

"No one, of course. But it's possible that you might say who you were not."

"Who I ain't? Sho' I can say who I ain't. I ain't Marcus Garvey,

I ain't Al Capone, I ain't Cal Coolidge—I ain't nobody but me—Jinx Jenkins, myself."

"Very well, Mr. Jenkins. Where do you live? What sort of work do you do?"

"Any sort I can get. Ain't doin' nothin' right now."

"M-m. What time did you get here tonight?"

On this and other similar points, Jinx's answers, for all their gruffness, checked with those of Bubber and Martha Crouch. He had come with Bubber a little before ten-thirty. They had gone straight to the waiting-room and found three men. The women had come in later. Then the detective asked him to describe in detail what had transpired when he left the others and went in to see Frimbo. And though Jinx's vocabulary was wholly inadequate, so deeply had that period registered itself upon his mind that he omitted not a single essential item. His imperfections of speech became negligible and were quite ignored; indeed, the more tutored minds of his listeners filled in or substituted automatically, and both the detective and the physician, the latter perhaps more completely, were able to observe the reconstructed scene as if it were even now being played before their eyes.

3

The black servitor with the yellow headdress and the cast in one eye ushered Jinx to the broad black curtains, saying in a low voice as he bowed him through, "Please go in, sit down, say nothing till Frimbo speaks." Thereupon the curtains fell to behind him and he was in a small dark passage, whose purpose was obviously to separate the waiting-room from the mystic chamber beyond and thus prevent Frimbo's voice from reaching the circle of waiting callers. Jinx shuffled forward toward the single bright light that at once attracted and blinded. He sidled in between the chair and table and sat down facing the figure beneath the hanging light. He was unable, because of the blinding glare, to descry any characteristic feature of the man he had come to see; he could only make out a dark shadow with a head that seemed to be enormous, cocked somewhat sidewise as if in a steady contemplation of the visitor.

For a time the shadow made no sound or movement, and Jinx squirmed about impatiently in his seat, trying to obey directions and restrain the impulse to say something. At one moment the figure seemed to fade away altogether and blend with the enveloping blackness beyond. This was the very limit of Jinx's endurance—but at this moment Frimbo spoke.

"Please do not shield your eyes. I must study your face."

The voice changed the atmosphere from one of discomfiture to one of assurance. It was a deep, rich, calm voice, so matter of fact and real, even in that atmosphere, as to dispel doubt and inspire confidence.

"You see, I must analyze your mind by observing your countenance. Only thus can I learn how to help you."

Here was a man that knew something. Didn't talk like an African native certainly. Didn't talk like any black man Jinx had ever heard. Not a trace of Negro accent, not a suggestion of dialect. He spoke like a white-haired judge on the bench, easily, smoothly, quietly.

"There are those who claim the power to read men's lives in crystal spheres. That is utter nonsense. I claim the power to read men's lives in their faces. That is completely reasonable. Every experience, every thought, leaves its mark. Past and present are written there clearly. He who knows completely the past and the present can deduce the inevitable future, which past and present determine. My crystal sphere, therefore, is your face. By reading correctly what is there I know what is scheduled to follow, and so can predict and guard you against your future."

"Yes, suh," said Jinx.

"I notice that you are at present out of work. It is this you wish to consult me about."

Jinx's eyes dilated. "Yes, suh, that's right."

"You have been without a job several weeks."

"Month come Tuesday."

"Yes. And now you have reached the point where you must seek the financial aid of your friends. Being of a proud and independent nature, you find this difficult. Yet even the fee which you will pay for the advice I give you is borrowed money."

There was no tone of question, no implied request for confirmation. The words were a simple statement of fact, presented as a comprehensive résumé of a situation, expressed merely as a basis for more important deductions to follow.

"So far, you see, my friend, I have done nothing at all mysterious. All this is the process of reason, based on observation. And now, though you may think it a strange power, let me add that there is nothing mysterious either in my being able to tell you that your name is Jenkins, that your friends call you Jinx, that you are twenty-seven years old, and that you are unmarried. All these matters have passed through your mind as you sat there listening to me. This is merely an acuteness of mental receptivity which anyone can learn; it is usually called telepathy. At this point, Mr. Jenkins, others whom you might have consulted stop. But at this point—Frimbo begins."

There was a moment's silence. The voice resumed with added depth and solemnity:

"For, in addition to the things that can be learned by anyone, Frimbo inherits the bequest of a hundred centuries, handed from son to son through four hundred unbroken generations of Buwongo kings. It is a profound and dangerous secret, my friend, a secret my fathers knew when the kings of the Nile still thought human flesh a delicacy."

The voice sank to a lower pitch still, inescapably impressive.

"Frimbo can change the future." He paused, then continued, "In the midst of a world of determined, inevitable events, of results rigidly fashioned by the past, Frimbo alone is free. Frimbo not only sees. Frimbo and Frimbo alone can step in at will and change the course of a life. Listen!"

The voice now became intimate, confidential, shading off from low vibrant tones into softly sibilant whispers:

"Your immediate needs will be taken care of but you will not be content. It is a strange thing that I see. For though food and shelter in abundance are to be your lot sooner than you think, still you will be more unhappy than you are now; and you will rejoice only when this physical security has been withdrawn. You will be overjoyed to return to the uncertain fortunes over which you now despair. I do not see the circumstances, at the moment, that will bring on these situations, because they are outside the present content of your mind which I am contemplating. But these things even now impatiently await you—adequate physical necessaries, but great mental distress.

"Now then, when you have passed through that paradoxical period, what will you do? Let me see. It is but a short way—a few days ahead—but——" Into that until now completely self-assured tone crept a quality of puzzlement. It was so unexpected and incongruous a change that Jinx, up to this point completely fascinated, was startled like one rudely awakened from deep sleep. "It is very dark——" There was a long pause. The same voice resumed, "What is this, Frimbo?" Again a pause; then: "Strange how suddenly it grows dark. Frimbo——" Bewilderment dilated into dismay. "Frimbo! Frimbo! *Why do you not see?*"

The voice of a man struck suddenly blind could not have been imbued with greater horror. So swift and definite was the transition that the alarmed Jinx could only grip the arms of his chair and stare hard. And despite the glaring beam, he saw a change in the figure beyond the table. That part of the shadow that had corresponded to the head seemed now to be but half its original size.

In a sudden frenzy of terror, Jinx jumped up and reached for the hanging light. Quickly he swung it around and tilted it so that the luminous shaft fell on the seated figure. What he saw was a bare black head, inclined limply sidewise, the mouth open, the eyes fixed, staring from under drooping lids.

He released the light, wheeled, and fled back to summon Bubber.

4

All this Jinx rehearsed in detail, making clear by implication or paraphrase those ideas whose original wording he was otherwise unable to describe or pronounce. The doctor emitted a low whistle of amazement; the detective, incredulous, said:

"Wait a minute. Let me get this straight. You mean to say that Frimbo actually talked to you, as you have related?"

"'Deed he did."

"You're sure that it was Frimbo talking to you?"

"Jest as sure as I am that you're talkin' to me now. He was right where you is."

"And when he tried to prophesy what would happen to you a few days hence, he couldn't?"

"Look like sump'm come over him all of a sudden—claim he couldn't see. And when he seen he couldn't see, he got scared-like and hollered out jes' like I said: 'Frimbo—why don't you see?'"

"Then you say *you* tried to see *him*, and it looked as though his head had shrunken?"

"Yes, suh."

"Evidently his head-piece had fallen off."

"His which?"

"Did you hear any sound just before this—like a blow?"

"Nope. Didn't hear nothin' but his voice. And it didn't stop like it would if he'd been hit. It jes' stopped like it would if he'd been tellin' 'bout sump'm he'd been lookin' at and then couldn't see no more. Only it scared him sump'm terrible not to be able to see it. Maybe he scared himself to death."

"Hm. Yea, maybe he even scared up that wound on his head."

"Well, maybe me and Bubber did that."

"How?"

"Carryin' him downstairs. We was in an awful hurry. His head might 'a' hit sump'm on the way down."

"But," said Dart, and Jinx couldn't know this was baiting, "if he was dead, that wound wouldn't have bled, even as little as it did."

"Maybe," Jinx insisted, "it stopped because he died jes' about that time—on the way down."

"You seem very anxious to account for his death, Jenkins."

"Humph," Jinx grunted. "You act kind o' anxious yourself, seems like to me."

"Yes. But there is this difference. By your own word, you were present and the only person present when Frimbo died. I was half a mile away."

"So what?"

"So that, while I'm as anxious as you are to account for this man's death, I am anxious for perhaps quite a different reason. For instance, I could not possibly be trying to prove my own innocence by insisting he died a natural death."

Jinx's memory was better than Bubber's.

"I ain't heard nobody say for sho' he was killed yet," said he.

"No? Well then, listen. We know that this man was murdered. We know that he was killed deliberately by somebody who meant to do a good job—and succeeded."

"And you reckon I done it?" There was no surprise in Jinx's voice, for he had long had the possibility in mind.

"I reckon nothing. I simply try to get the facts. When enough facts are gathered, they'll do all the reckoning necessary. One way of getting the facts is from the testimony of people who know the facts. The trouble with that is that anybody who knows the facts might have reasons for lying. I have to weed out the lies. I'm telling you this to show you that if you are innocent, you can best defend yourself by telling the truth, no matter how bad it looks."

"What you think I *been* doin'?"

"You've been telling a queer story, part of which we know to be absolutely impossible—unless——" The detective entertained a new consideration. "Listen. What time did you come into this room—as nearly as you can judge?"

"Musta been 'bout—'bout five minutes to eleven."

"How long did Frimbo talk to you?"

"'Bout five or six minutes I guess."

"That would be eleven o'clock. Then you got Bubber. Dr. Archer, what time were you called?"

"Three minutes past eleven—according to the clock on my radio."

"Not a lot of time—three minutes—Bubber took three minutes to get you and get back. During those three minutes Jenkins was alone with the dead man."

"Not me," denied Jinx. "I was out there in the hall right at the head o' the stairs where the doc found me—wonderin' what the hell was keepin' 'em so long." This was so convincingly ingenuous that the physician agreed with a smile. "He was certainly there when I got here."

"During those few minutes, Jenkins, when you were here alone, did you see or hear anything peculiar?"

"No, 'ndeed. The silence liked to drown me."

"And when you came back in this room with the doctor, was everything just as you left it?"

"Far as I could see."

"M-m. Listen, doc. Did you leave the body at all from the time you first saw it until I got here?"

"No. Not even to phone the precinct—I had the two men do it."

"Funny," Dart muttered. "Damn funny." For a moment he meditated the irreconcilable points in Jinx's story—the immobility of Frimbo's figure, from which nevertheless the turban had fallen, the absence of any sound of an attack, yet a sudden change in Frimbo's speech and manner just before he was discovered dead; the remoteness of any opportunity—except for Jinx himself—to reach the prostrate victim, cram that handkerchief in place, and depart during the three minutes when Jinx claimed to be in the hall, without noticeably disturbing the body; and the utter impossibility of any man's talking, dead or alive, when his throat was plugged with that rag which the detective's own eyes had seen removed. Clearly Jenkins was either mistaken in some of the statements he made so positively or else he was lying. If he was lying he was doing so to protect himself, directly or indirectly. In other words, if he was lying, either he knew who committed the crime or he had committed it himself. Only further evidence could indicate the true and the false in this curious chronicle.

And so Dart said, rather casually, as if he were asking a favor, "Have you a handkerchief about you, Mr. Jenkins?"

" 'Tain't what you'd call strictly clean," Jinx obligingly reached into his right-hand coat pocket, "but——" He stopped. His left hand went into his left coat pocket. Both hands came out and delved into their respective trousers pockets. "Guess I must 'a' dropped it," he said. "I had one."

"You're sure you had one?"

"M'hm. Had it when I come here."

"When you came into this room?"

"No. When I first went in the front room. I was a little nervous-like. I wiped my face with it. I think I put it——"

"Is that the last time you recall having it—when you first went into the front room?"

"Uh-huh."

"Can you describe it?"

Perhaps this odd insistence on anything so unimportant as a handkerchief put Jinx on his guard. At any rate he dodged.

"What difference it make?"

"Can you describe it?"

"No."

"No? Why can't you?"

"Nothin' to describe. Jes' a plain big white handkerchief with a——" He stopped.

"With a what?"

"With a hem," said Jinx.

"Hm."

"Yea—hem."

"A white hem?"

"It wasn' no black one," said Jinx, in typical Harlemese.

The detective fell silent a moment, then said:

"All right, Jenkins. That's all for the present. You go back to the front room."

Officer Brady escorted Jinx out, and returned.

"Brady, tell Green, who is up front, to take note of everything he overhears those people in there say. You come back here."

Obediently, Officer Brady turned away.

"Light!" called Dart, and the bluecoat in the hall pressed the switch that turned on the extension light.

Chapter Eight

"WHAT do you think of Jenkins' story?" Dr. Archer asked.
"Well, even before he balked on the handkerchief," answered Dart, "I couldn't believe him. Then when he balked on describing the blue border, it messed up the whole thing."

"He certainly was convincing about that interview, though. He couldn't have just conjured up that story—it's too definite."

"Yes. But I'm giving him a little time to cool off. Maybe the details won't be so exact next time."

"As I figure it, he could be right—at least concerning the time the fatal attack occurred. It would be right at the end of the one-half hour period in which I first estimated death to have taken place. And in the state of mind he was in when Frimbo seemed to be performing miracles of clairvoyance, he might easily have failed to hear the attack. Certainly he could have failed to see it—he didn't see me standing here beside you."

"You're thinking of the crack on the head. You surely don't suppose Jenkins could have failed to see anyone trying to push that handkerchief in place?"

"No. But that could have been done in the minute when he ran up front to get Bubber. It would have to be fast work, of course."

"Damn right it would. I really don't believe in considering the remote possibilities first. In this game you've got to be practical. Fit conclusions to the facts, not facts to conclusions. Personally I don't feel one way or the other about Jenkins—except that he is unnecessarily antagonistic. That won't help him at all. But I'm certainly satisfied, from testimony, that he is not the guilty party. His attitude, his impossible story, his balking on the blue-bordered handkerchief——"

"You think it's his handkerchief?"

"I think he could have described it—from the way he balked.

If he could have described it, why didn't he? Because it belonged either to him or to somebody he wanted to cover."

"He was balking all right."

"Of course, that wouldn't make him guilty. But it wouldn't exactly clear him either."

"Not exactly. On the other hand, the Frimbo part of his story—what Frimbo said to him—is stuff that a man like Jenkins couldn't possibly have thought up. It was Frimbo talking—that I'm sure of."

"Through a neckful of cotton cloth?"

"No. When he was talking to Jenkins, his throat was unobstructed."

"Well—that means that, the way it looks now, there are two possibilities: somebody did it either when Jenkins went up front to get Bubber or when Bubber went to get you. Let's get the other woman in. All right, Brady, bring in the other lady. Douse the glim, outside there."

Out went the extension light; the original bright horizontal shaft shot forth like an accusing finger pointing toward the front room, while the rest of the death chamber went black.

2

Awkwardly, not unlike an eccentric dancer, the tall thin woman took the spotlight, stood glaring a wide-eyed hostile moment, then disposed herself in a bristlingly erect attitude on the edge of the visitor's chair. Every angle of her meagre, poorly clad form, every feature of her bony countenance, exhibited resentment.

"What is your name, madam?"

"Who's that?" The voice was high, harsh, and querulous.

"Detective Dart. I'm sitting in a chair opposite you."

"Is you the one was in yonder a while ago?"

"Yes. Now——"

"What kind o' detective is you?"

"A police detective, madam, of the City of New York. And please let me ask the questions, while you confine yourself to the answers."

"Police detective? 'Tain't so. They don't have no black detectives."

"Your informant was either ignorant or color-blind, madam.
—Now would you care to give your answers here or around at
the police station?"

The woman fell silent. Accepting this as a change of heart,
the detective repeated:

"What is your name?"

"Aramintha Snead."

"Mrs. or Miss?"

"Mrs." The tone indicated that a detective should be able to
tell.

"Your address?"

"19 West 134th Street."

"You're an American, of course?"

"I is now. But I originally come from Savannah, Georgia."

"Occupation?"

"Occupation? You mean what kind o' work I do?"

"Yes, madam."

"I don't do no work at all—not for wages. I'm a church-
worker though."

"A church-worker? You spend a good deal of time in church
then?"

"Can't nobody spend too much time in church. Though I
declare I been wonderin' lately if there ain't some things the
devil can 'tend to better'n the Lord."

"What brought you here tonight?"

"My two feet."

Dart sighed patiently and pursued:

"How does it happen that a devoted church-worker like you,
Mrs. Snead, comes to seek the advice of a man like Frimbo, a
master of the powers of darkness? I should think you would
have sought the help of your pastor instead."

"I did, but it never done no good. Every time I go to the
Rev'n the Rev'n say, 'Daughter take it to the Lord in prayer.'
Well, I done like he said. I took it and took it. Tonight I got
tired takin' it."

"Tonight? Why tonight?"

"Tonight was prayer-meetin' night. I ain' missed a prayer-
meetin' in two years. And for two years, week after week—every
night for that matter, but specially at Friday night prayer-
meetin'—I been prayin' to the Lord to stop my husband from

drinkin'. Not that I object to the drinkin' itself, y'understand. The Lord made water into wine. But when Jake come home night after night jes' drunk enough to take pleasure in beatin' the breath out o' me—that's another thing altogether."

"I quite agree with you," encouraged Dart.

In the contemplation of her troubles, Mrs. Snead relinquished some of her indignation, or, more exactly, transferred it from the present to the past.

"Well, lo and behold, tonight I ain't no sooner got through prayin' for him at the meetin' and took myself on home than he greets me at the door with a cuff side o' the head. Jes' by way of interduction, he say, so next time I'd be there when he come in. And why in who-who ain't his supper ready? So I jes' turn around and walk off. And I thought to myself as I walked, 'If one medicine don' help, maybe another will.' So I made up my mind. Everybody know 'bout this man Frimbo—say he can conjure on down. And I figger I been takin' it to the Lord in prayer long enough. Now I'm goin' take it to the devil."

"So you came here?"

"Yes."

"How did you happen to choose Frimbo out of all the conjuremen in Harlem?"

"He was the only one I knowed anything about."

"What did you know about him?"

"Knowed what he done for Sister Susan Gassoway's boy, Lem. She was tellin' me 'bout it jes' a couple o' weeks ago— two weeks ago tonight. We was at prayer-meetin'. Old man Hezekiah Mosby was prayin' and when he gets to prayin' they ain't no stoppin' him. So Sister Gassoway and me, we was talkin' and she told me what this man Frimbo'd done for her boy, Lem. Lem got in a little trouble—wild boy he is, anyhow—and put the blame on somebody else. This other boy swore he'd kill Lem, and Lem believed him. So he come to this Frimbo and Frimbo put a charm on him—told him he'd come through it all right. Well you 'member that case what was in the *Amsterdam News* 'bout a boy havin' a knife stuck clean through his head and broke off and the hole closed over and he thought he was jes' cut and didn't know the knife was in there?"

"Yes. Went to Harlem Hospital, was X-rayed, and had the knife removed."

"And lived! That was Lem Gassoway. Nothin' like it ever heard of before. Anybody else'd 'a' been killed on the spot. But not Lem. Lem was under Frimbo's spell. That's what saved him."

"And that's why you chose Frimbo?"

" 'Deed so. Wouldn't you?"

"No doubt. At just what time did you get here, Mrs. Snead?"

"Little after half-past ten."

"Did anyone let you in?"

"No. I did like the sign say—open and walk in."

"You came straight upstairs and into the waiting-room?"

"Yes."

"Did you see anybody?"

"Nobody but that other girl and them two fellers that was 'bout to fight jes' now and a couple o' other men in the room. Oh, yes—the—the butler or whatever he was. Evilest-lookin' somebody y'ever see—liked to scared me to death."

"Did you notice anything of interest while you were waiting your turn?"

"Huh? Oh—yes. When one o' them other two men got up to go see the conjure-man, he couldn't hold his feet—must 'a' been drunker'n my Jake. 'Deed so, 'cause down he fell right in the middle o' the floor, and I guess he'd been there yet if them other men hadn't helped him up."

"Who helped him?"

"All of 'em."

"Did you notice the mantelpiece?"

"With all them conjures on it? I didn't miss."

"Did you see those two clubs with the silver tips?"

"Two? Uh–uh—I don't remember no two. I 'member one though. But I wasn't payin' much attention—might 'a' been a dozen of 'em for all I know. There was so many devilish-lookin' things 'round."

"Did you see anyone with a blue-bordered white handker-chief—a man's handkerchief?"

"No, suh."

"You are sure you did not see any such handkerchief—in one of the men's pockets, perhaps?"

"What men is got in they pockets ain't none my business."

3

There were, at this point, sounds of a new arrival in the hall. The officer at the hall door was speaking to a man who had just appeared. This man was saying:

"My name is Crouch. Yes, I have the funeral parlor downstairs. I'd like to see the officer in charge."

"Ask Mr. Crouch in, Brady," called Dart. "Mrs. Snead, you may return to the front room, if you will."

"To the front room!" expostulated the woman. "How long do you expect me to stay in this place?"

"Not very long, I hope. Brady, take the young lady up front. Come right in, Mr. Crouch. Take that chair, will you please? I'm glad you came by."

"Whew! It's dark as midnight in here," said the newcomer, vainly trying to make out who was present. He went promptly, however, to the illuminated chair, and sat down. His manner was pleasantly bewildered, and it was clear that he was as anxious to learn what had occurred as were the police. He grasped at once the value of the lighting arrangement of which Dart had taken advantage and grinned. "Judas, what a bright light! Clever though. Can't see a thing. Who are you, if I may ask?"

Dart told him.

"Glad to know you—though so far you're just a voice. Understand I've lost a tenant. Came back expecting to put the finishing touches on a little job down stairs, and found the place full of officers. Fellow in the door took my breath away—says Frimbo's been killed. How'd it happen?"

Dart's sharp black eyes were studying the undertaker closely. He observed a youngish man of medium build with skin the color of an English walnut, smooth, unblemished, and well cared for. The round face was clean shaven, the features blunt but not coarse, the eyes an indeterminate brown like most Negroes'. His hair was his most noteworthy possession, for it was as black and as straight as an Indian's and it shone with a bright gloss in the light that fell full upon it. His attire was quiet and his air was that of a matter-of-fact, yet genial business man on whom it would be difficult to play tricks. His manner, more than his inquiry, indicated that while there was no need of getting excited over something that couldn't be restored, still it was his right, as neighbor and landlord, to know just what had come about and how.

"Perhaps, Mr. Crouch," replied Dart, "you can answer your own question for us."

If the detective anticipated catching any twitch of feature that might have betrayed masquerading on the undertaker's part he was disappointed. Crouch's expression manifested only a curiosity which now became meditative.

"Well," he said reflectively, "let me see now. You know that he was killed, of course?"

"More than that. We know how he was killed. We know when. We even have evidence of the assailant's identity."

"Assailant? Oh, he was assaulted then? One of his customers, probably. Why, say, if you know that much, you shouldn't have much trouble. It would be narrowed down to whoever was here at the time who wanted to kill him. But that's just your difficulty. Who'd want to kill him?"

"Exactly. That's where you may be able to help us. You knew Frimbo, of course?"

"Only as a landlord knows a tenant." Crouch smiled. "Even that isn't quite true," he amended. "Landlords and tenants are usually enemies. Frimbo, on the contrary, was the best tenant I've ever had. Paid a good rent, always paid it on time, and never asked for a thing. A rare bird in that respect. I'll hardly get another one like him."

"How long was he your tenant here?"

"Nearly two years now. Built himself up quite a following here in Harlem—at least he always had plenty of people in here at night."

"You've had your place of business here how long?"

"Five years this winter."

"And in spite of the fact that you and he have been neighbors for two years, you knew nothing about him personally?"

"Well," again Crouch smiled, "we weren't exactly what you'd call associated. The proximity was purely—geographical, would you call it? You know, of course, that this isn't my residence."

"Yes."

"To be frank, Frimbo always seemed—and I don't mean this geographically—a little above me. Pretty distant, unapproachable sort of chap. Part of his professional pose, I guess. Solemn as an undertaker—I honestly envied him his manner. Could have used it myself. Occasionally we'd meet and pass the time of day. But otherwise I never knew he was here."

"Your relations were purely of a business nature, then?"

"Quite."

"In that case you really had to see him only once a month—to collect his rent."

"At first, yes. But during the last few months I didn't even have to do that. My wife collects all the rents now."

"Isn't that rather a dangerous occupation for a woman? Carrying money about?"

"I suppose so. We hadn't thought about that angle of it. You know how women are—if they haven't anything much to do they get restless and dissatisfied. We haven't any kids and she has a girl to do the housework. When she asked me to let her collect the rents it struck me as quite sensible—something to occupy her time and give me a little more freedom. I'm on call at all hours, you see, so I appreciated a little relief."

"I see. That is probably why she was here tonight."

"Was she? That's good."

"Good? Why?"

"Why—I guess it sounds a little hard—but—of course I'm sorry for Frimbo and all—but death is such a common experience to me that I suppose I take it as a matter of course. What I meant was that at least he didn't die in our debt."

So bald a statement rendered even the illusionless Dart silent a moment, while Dr. Archer audibly gasped. Then the detective said:

"Well—evidently you didn't know Frimbo as well as I had hoped. You knew no one who would want him out of the way?"

"No. And whoever it was certainly didn't do me any favor."

"You were here earlier this evening, weren't you, Mr. Crouch?"

"Yes. I left about nine o'clock. From then until a few minutes ago I was at the Forty Club around the corner playing cards." He smiled. "You can easily verify that by one of the attendants—or by my friend, Si Brandon, whom I plucked quite clean."

"Tell me—could any one get into this room and out without being seen by people in the hall or in the waiting-room?"

"Indeed I don't know. This is the first time since Frimbo came that I've been in here."

"Is that so?"

"Yes."

"Even when you collected rents yourself, you never had to come in here?"

"No. I used to wait in the hall there. Frimbo's man would tell him I was here for the rent and he would send it out. I'd hand the receipt over to the man and that was all."

"I see."

"And there are no concealed passages in this house by which some one could get about undetected?"

"Not unless Frimbo put 'em in himself. I never bothered him or nosed around to see what he was up to. His lease required him to leave things at the end as he found them at the beginning and I let it go at that. But in a room like this I should think a lot of undetected movement would be easy for anyone who put his mind to it. The darkness and those wall drapes and all——"

"Of course. How long did the lease still have to run?"

"Three more years—and at a rate considerably higher than I'll be able to get from anyone now in this depression."

"Was there anything peculiar about your lease agreement— special features and such?"

"No. Nothing. Except perhaps the agreement about heating. I paid for the coal and he paid for the labor. That is, he had his man keep the fires. There's only one boiler, of course."

"His man would have to pass through your part of the house quite often then to tend the fire, put out ashes, and so on?"

"Yes—he did."

"Well, Mr. Crouch, I suppose that's all then for the present. Except that an apology is due you for making use of your parlor downstairs without permission. Dr. Archer here moved the victim down there to examine him better—before he knew he was dead."

"Oh, is that you there, doc? Look like anybody else in the dark, don't you? Don't mention it—glad to have been able to help out. Perhaps if you'd tell me the circumstances, officer, I might run across something of value. Unless, of course, you have reasons for not disclosing what is known so far."

"Don't mind telling you at all," decided Dart. "The victim was stunned by a blow with a hard object—a sort of club—then stifled by a handkerchief pushed down his throat."

"Judas Priest!"

"We have the handkerchief. The club is being examined for finger prints. It was last seen—prior to Frimbo's death I mean —shortly after ten-thirty, resting in its apparently usual place on the mantelpiece in the front room. No one admits seeing it after that time until we found it here on the floor beside this chair, in which Frimbo's body was discovered. Testimony indicates that Frimbo was alive and talking as late as five minutes to eleven. The club was removed therefore by someone who was in the front room after ten-thirty and used by someone who was out of the front room by five minutes to eleven. Presumably the person who removed it was the person who used it. This person, of course, could have hidden until five minutes to eleven in the darkness or behind the drapes of the walls. But certainly he was one of the people who passed from that room into this room during that twenty-five-minute period."

"Say—that's a swell method. Beats a maxim silencer, doesn't it?"

"Well—I don't know. Leaves more evidence, apparently."

"Yes, but the more the evidence the more the possibility of confusion."

"True. But if the two clues we are studying—the ownership of the handkerchief and the identification of the finger prints—coincide, somebody'll be due for a toasting. On a specially designed toaster."

"I don't think you'll find any finger prints on your club though."

"Why not?"

"I'll bet the chap handled the club with the handkerchief."

"Hm—that's a good suggestion. But we'll have to wait for the results of the examination of the club to check that."

"Well," Crouch rose, "if I can think of anything or find anything that might help, I'll be glad to do so. I'm easy to get hold of if you need me again."

"Thank you, Mr. Crouch. I won't detain you." Dart called to the bluecoat at the hall door: "Pass Mr. Crouch out. Or did you say you had something to do downstairs, Mr. Crouch?"

"Well, I did, but it can wait till morning. I might be in your way now—searching around and all. Tomorrow'll be time enough—last few touches you know. Easier to handle a dead face than a live one—I've found that out."

"Interesting," commented Dart. "I never thought of an undertaker as a beautician."

"You'd be surprised. We can make the dark ones bright and the bright ones lighter—that seems to be the ambition in this community. We can fatten thin ones and reduce fat ones. I venture to say that, by the simplest imaginable changes, I could make Doc Archer there quite unrecognizable."

"The need," murmured the doctor, "may be present, but I trust the occasion does not soon arise."

"Well, good luck, officer. Good-night, doc. See you again sometime when things are brighter."

"Good-night."

"Good-night, Crouch."

4

"Why," asked Dr. Archer, "didn't you let him know his wife was still here?"

"She was here when the thing happened. I may need her. If I'd told him she was still here he'd have wanted to see her and she'd have wanted to leave with him."

"You could keep him too, then."

"Had no reason to keep him. His story checked perfectly with his wife's in spite of my efforts to trick him. And I can easily check his previous whereabouts, just as he said—he wouldn't have been so definite about 'em if they couldn't have been verified."

"He could pay liars."

"But he actually wasn't here. Brown, Jenkins, Mrs. Snead, or his wife—surely one of them would have mentioned him."

"That's so."

"And Frimbo was a goose that laid golden eggs for him."

"If it was anybody else besides Martha, I might be suspicious of——"

"Of what?"

"What she might have laid for Frimbo."

"Doctor—spare my blushes!" Then seriously, "But you're sure that she's an irreproachable character. And I'm just as sure Frimbo was not interested in women. That all argues against any outraged husband theory. There's absolutely no basis for it and even if there was, there's nothing that could possibly incriminate Crouch."

"You're right. But don't forget to check up." The doctor fell to ruminating in his wordy and roundabout way. "And keep your pupils dilated for more evidence. I have an impression— just an impression—that bright plumage oft adorns a bird of prey. Curious fellow, Crouch. Bright exterior, genial, cheerful even, despite his doleful occupation; but underneath, hard as a pawnbroker, with an extraordinarily keen awareness of his own possessions. Imagine a man congratulating himself on acquiring an extra month's rent before his tenant came to grief."

"Well, I don't know. Suppose a patient of yours died during an operation for which you had already collected the fee. Would you give back the fee—or would you be glad you had got it first?"

"I would desire with all my heart," murmured the doctor, "to reimburse the bereaved relatives. But since that would resemble an admission that my operation was at fault and would hence endanger my professional reputation, no course would remain except to rush speedily to the bank and deposit the amount to my credit."

"Self-preservation," grinned Dart. "Well, we can't blame Crouch for the same thing. He spoke bluntly, but maybe the man's just honest."

"Maybe everybody is," said Dr. Archer with a sigh.

Chapter Nine

M EANWHILE Bubber Brown, riding beside Officer Hanks in Detective Dart's touring car was evincing a decided appreciation of his new importance. Over his countenance spread a broad grin of satisfaction, and as the machine swung up the Avenue, he reared back in his seat and surveyed his less favored fellow men with a superior air. The car swung into 135th Street, pulled up at the curb in front of the station-house, and acquired presently a new passenger in the person of an enormous black giant named Small, who managed to crowd himself into the tonneau. As it drew away, Bubber could contain himself no longer.

"Hot damn!" he exclaimed. "In power at last!" As the little five-passenger car started off again— "Y'all s'posed to follow my directions now, ain't you?"

"Yep," said Hanks. "Where to now?"

"Henry Patmore's Pool Room—Fifth Avenue and 131st Street. And do me jes' one kind favor, will you Mr. Hanks?"

"What?"

"See that red traffic light yonder?"

"Yep."

"Run on past it, will you please?"

Shortly they reached their objective, got out, and, with Bubber expansively leading the way, entered Patmore's well-known meeting-place.

Patmore's boasted two separate entrances, one leading into the poolroom proper, the other into the barroom by its side. These two long, low rooms communicated within by means of a wide doorway in the middle of the intervening wall, and also by means of a small back gaming-room into which one might pass from either the speakeasy or the billiard parlor. It was into the poolroom that Bubber led the way. He and his uniformed escort paused just within the entrance to survey the scene.

Two long rows of green-topped tables extended the length of the bare wooden floor. Players in shirt sleeves moved about, hats on the backs of their heads, cigarettes drooping from their lips; leaned far over the felt to make impossible shots, whooped at their successes, cursed their failures, thrust cue-points aloft to mark off scores, or thumped cue-butts upon the floor to signal an attendant.

One of these gentlemen, seeing the entrance of Bubber's familiar rotund figure flanked by two officers of the law, called sympathetically:

"Tough titty, short-order. What they got you for this time?"

"They ain't got me," responded Mr. Brown glowing with his new importance. "I got them. And you get fly, I'll get you, too. Now what you think o' that?"

"I think you jes' a pop-eyed liar," said the other, dismissing the matter to sight on a new shot.

Bubber asked the manager, standing nearby, "Say, boy, you seen Spider Webb?"

The one addressed looked at him and looked at the policemen. Then he inquired blandly, "Who'n hell is Spider Webb?"

"Damn!" Bubber murmured, pushing back his hat and scratching his head. "You boogies sho' get dumb in the presence of the law. Listen, this ain' nothin' on him—jes' want to get some dope from him, that's all. Y'see, I'm doin' a little detective work now"—he produced one of the cards he had shown Detective Perry Dart—"and I want Spider's slant on a little case."

"So I *got* to know him?" bridled the other.

"You did know him."

"Well, I done forgot him, then."

"Thanks, liar."

"You welcome—stool."

Ordinarily Bubber would have resented the epithet, which was much worse than the one he himself had used; but he was now in such lofty spirits that the opinion of a mere poolroom manager could not touch him.

"You all wait here," he suggested to the officers. "The Spider might try a fast one if he feels guilty."

But before this expedition had started, Hanks had caught a

sign from Detective Dart that Mr. Bubber Brown must be brought back as well as those whom Mr. Brown identified; and so now Hanks offered an amendment:

"We'll leave Small at the door," he said, "and I'll come along with you."

So it was agreed, and Bubber with Hanks at his heels made his way to the back room of the establishment. As they approached it, Bubber saw the door open and Spider Webb start out. Looking up, Webb recognized Bubber at a distance, stopped, noted the policeman, stepped back and quickly shut the door. Bubber reached the door and flung it open a few seconds later, but his rapid survey revealed a total and astonishing absence of Spider Webb.

"Where'd that boogy go?" inquired Bubber blankly.

"Who?" said the house-man, sitting on a stool at the mid-point of one side of the table, running the game.

"Spider Webb."

The house-man looked about. "Any o' you all seen Spider Webb?" he asked the surrounding atmosphere. The players were so intent on the game that they did not even seem to hear. Upon receiving no response, the house-man appeared to dismiss the matter and also became absorbed again in the fall of cards. Bubber and his policeman were decidedly outside the world of their consideration.

But the newly appointed champion of the law now caught sight of the door at the other end of the room leading into the bar which paralleled the poolroom. With more speed than consideration for those he swept past, he bustled along to the far end of the chamber, opened that door and burst forth into the long narrow barroom. Hanks was but a moment behind him, for Hanks was as concerned with keeping close to Bubber as Bubber was with overtaking Webb. The barroom, however, was as innocent of Spider Webb as had been the blackjack chamber, and Bubber was still expressing his bewilderment in a vigorous scratching of the back of his head when the gentleman pursued appeared. He came through the wide doorway by which the barroom communicated directly with the poolroom. He came, in other words, out of the poolroom. The mystery of how he managed to appear from a place where he certainly had not been—for had not Bubber and Hanks just traversed the poolroom?—was submerged in the more important fact that he was proceeding now very rapidly toward the street door.

"Spider! Hey, Spider!" called Bubber.

Mr. Webb halted and turned in apparent surprise. Bubber and the policeman overtook him.

"What's on your mind?" inquired the Spider quite calmly and casually, quite, indeed, as though he had not been in any hurry whatever and had no other interest in the world than the answer to his question.

"How did you get in yonder?" Bubber wanted to know.

"How," inquired Webb, "did you and your boy friend get in here?"

Bubber abandoned the lesser mystery to pursue his interest in the original one. "Listen. Somebody put that thing on Frimbo tonight. We all got to get together over there and find out who done it. Everybody what was there."

"Put what thing on him?"

"Cut him loose, man. Put him on the well-known spot."

"Frimbo——"

"Hisself."

"Killed him?"

"If you want to put it that way."

"Good-night!" Spider Webb's astonishment yielded to a sense of his own implication. "So what?" he inquired rather harshly.

"So you, bein' among those present, you got to return to the scene of the tragedy. That's all."

"Yea? And who knew I was on the scene of the tragedy?"

"Everybody knew it."

"Reckon the police knew it, huh? All they had to do was walk in, and they knew I'd been there, huh? The peculiar perfume I use or somethin'?" There was somber menace in Spider's tone.

"Well," admitted Bubber, "you know I been doin' a little private detective work o' my own, see? So I'm helpin' the police out on this case. Naturally, knowin' you was there, I knew you'd want to give all the information you could, see? Anything else would look like runnin' away, y'understand?"

"I see. You're the one I got to thank for this little consideration."

"I'm givin' you a chance to protect yo'self," said Bubber.

"Thanks," Webb responded darkly. "I'll do the same by you sometime. Be watchin' out for it."

"Let's go," suggested Officer Hanks.

They went into the poolroom and with Small, returned to the car at the curb.

2

"Know how to drive?" Hanks asked Bubber.

"Who me? Sho'. I can drive anything but a bargain."

"Take the wheel—and plenty o' time."

Bubber obeyed. Shortly the expedition arrived at its next port of call, the Hip-Toe Club on Lenox Avenue. Leaving Small and the ominously silent Spider Webb in the car, Officer Hanks and Bubber left to seek Doty Hicks.

"How you know he's here?" Hanks said.

"His brother runs the place. Spats Oliver, they call him. Real name's Oliver Hicks. Everybody knows him, and everybody knows Doty. Doty's been up for dope-peddlin' coupla times— finally the dope got him—now it's all he can do to get enough for himself. This is his hang-out."

"It would be," observed Hanks. They had passed under a dingy canopy and into a narrow entrance, had negotiated a precipitate and angular staircase, and so with windings and twistings had descended eventually into a reclaimed cellar. The ceiling was oppressively low, the walls splotched with black sil-houetted grotesqueries, and the atmosphere thick with smoke. Two rows of little round white-topped tables hugged the two lateral walls, leaving between them a long narrow strip of bare wooden floor for dancing or entertainment. This strip termi-nated at a low platform at the far end of the room, whereon were mounted a pianist, a drummer, a banjo-player and a trumpeter, all properly equipped with their respective instru-ments and at the moment all performing their respective rites without restraint.

In the narrow strip of interspace, a tall brown girl was doing a song and dance to the absorbed delight of the patrons seated nearest her. Her flame chiffon dress, normally long and flowing, had been caught up bit by bit in her palms, which rested nonchalantly on her hips, until now it was not so much a dress as a sash, gathered about her waist. The long shapely smooth brown limbs below were bare from trim slippers to sash, and only a bit of silken underthing stood between her modesty and surrounding admiration.

With extraordinary ease and grace, this young lady was proving beyond question the error of reserving legs for mere locomotion, and no one who believed that the chief function of the hips was to support the torso could long have maintained so ridiculous a notion against the argument of her eloquent gestures.

Bubber caught sight of this vision and halted in his tracks. His abetting of justice, his stern immediate duty as a deputy of the law, faded.

"Boy!" he said softly. "What a pair of eyes!"

Sang the girl, with an irrelevance which no one seemed to mind:

> *I'll be standin' on the corner high*
> *When they drag your body by—*
> *I'll be glad when you're dead, you rascal you.*

"Where," said the unimpressionable Hanks, "is this bozo named Doty Hicks?"

"If he ain't here," returned Bubber, still captivated by the vision, "we'll jes' have to sit down and wait for him."

"I'll stand here. You look."

"I'm lookin'."

"For Hicks, if it ain't askin' too much."

Reluctantly obedient, Bubber moved slowly along the aisle, scanning the patrons at this table and that, acutely aware that his march was bringing him momentarily nearer the dancing girl. No one had he yet seen who faintly resembled Doty Hicks. The girl's number ended just as Bubber was on the point of passing her. As she terminated her dance with a flourish, she swung merrily about and chucked the newcomer under his plump chin.

"You're short and broad, but sweet, oh Gawd!"

Bubber, who was as much a child of the city as she, was by no means embarrassed. He grinned, did a little buck and wing step of his own, ended with a slap of his foot, and responded:

"You're long and tall and you've got it all!"

"O.K., big boy," laughed the girl and would have turned away, but he stopped her. Offering her one of his detective-cards, he said:

"Sis, if you ever need a friend, look me up."

She took the card, glanced at it, laughed again.

"Here on business, mister?"

"Business, no lie," he said ruefully. "Seen my friend Doty Hicks?"

"Oh—that kind o' business. Well who's that over in the corner by the orchestra?"

He looked, and there indeed was Doty Hicks, a little wizened black fellow, bent despondently over the table at which he sat alone, his elbows resting on the white porcelain surface, which he contemplated in deep meditation, his chin in his hands.

"Thanks, sister. I'll do better when I can see more of you. Right now at present, duty calls." And lamenting the hardships of working for law and order, Bubber approached the disconsolate figure at the corner table.

Remembering how he had been received by Spider Webb, Bubber approached the present responsibility differently:

"Hello, Doty," he said pleasantly and familiarly.

Doty Hicks looked up, the protrusiveness of his eyes accentuated by the thinness of his face. He stared somewhat like a man coming out of anesthesia.

"Don't know you," he said in a voice that was tremulous but none the less positive. And he resumed his contemplation of the table top.

"Sure you know me. You and me was at Frimbo's tonight —remember?"

"Couldn't see Frimbo," said Doty. "Too dark." Whether he referred to the darkness of Frimbo's room or of Frimbo's complexion was not clear. Bubber went on:

"Frimbo's got somethin' for you."

"Yea—talk. Thass all. Lot o' talk."

"He ain't expected to live—and he wants to see you befo' he dies."

For a moment the little man made no sound, his great round eyes staring blankly at Bubber Brown. Then, in a hoarse, unsteady whisper he repeated:

"Ain't expected to live?"

"Not long." Bubber was pursuing the vague notion that by hiding the actuality of the death he would achieve easier coöperation and less enmity. "It took him sort o' sudden."

"Mean—mean Frimbo's dyin'?"

"Don't mean maybe."

Doty Hicks, unsteadily, jerkily, more like a mechanism than like a man, got to his feet, pushed back his chair, stood teetering a dizzy moment, then rubbed the back of his hand across his nose, shook his head, became steadier, and fixed Bubber with an unwavering stare, a look in which there was a hint of triumph and more than a hint of madness.

"It worked!" he said softly. "It worked!" A grin, vacant, distant, unpleasant to see, came over his wasted features. "It worked! What you know 'bout that?" said he.

Bubber did not care for this at all. "I don't know nothin' 'bout it, but if you comin', come on, let's go."

"If I'm comin'? You couldn't keep me 'way. Where is he?"

Bubber had to hold him by the arm on the way out, partly to support him, partly to restrain the trembling eagerness with which he sought to reach Frimbo ere the latter should die.

3

"Where," inquired Bubber of Officer Hanks as they wedged the diminutive Doty Hicks into the already well-occupied rear seat and resumed their journey, "are we go'n' put Brother Easley Jones—if any?"

"We'll have to drop these men off and come back for him."

"Won't need no car for him—told me he lived right there in the same block, a few houses from Frimbo."

"You know everybody, don't you?"

"Well, I recognized these two in the waitin'-room there

tonight. Anybody that travels the sidewalks o' Harlem much as I do knows them by sight anyhow. This Easley Jones I struck up a conversation with on purpose. He was a jolly sort of a feller, easy to talk to, y' see, and when I found out he was a railroad man, I knew right off I might have a customer. Railroad men is the most back-bitten bozos in the world. They what you might call legitimate prey. That's, of co'se, if they married. Y' see, they come by it natural—they so crooked themselves. Any guy what lays over forty-eight hours one time in New York, where his wife is, and forty-eight hours another in Chicago, where she ain't, is gonna curve around a little in Chicago jes' to keep in practice for New York. Y' see what I mean?"

"Is that what this Easley Jones was doin'?"

"He didn't say. But he give me the number o' the house he rooms at in New York—*his* wife is in Chicago—and asked me to drop in and advise him some time."

"Some time'll be tonight."

"Right."

The two material witnesses were escorted back to Frimbo's and were left on the way upstairs in Officer Small's care. Hanks and Bubber walked the short distance back along the block to the address Easley Jones had given. Bubber mounted the stoop and rang the bell of a dwelling much like that in which the African mystic had lived and died.

After a moment the dark hall lighted up, the door opened, and a large, yellow woman wearing horn-rimmed spectacles gazed inquisitively upon them.

"Mr. Jones in?" asked Bubber.

"Mr. who?"

"Mr. Jones. Mr. Easley Jones."

The lady glanced at the uniformed officer and said resolutely, "Don' nobody stay here by that name. You-all must have the wrong address."

"We don't want to arrest him, lady. We want him to help us find somebody, that's all. He's a friend o' mine—else how'd I know he lived here?"

The woman considered this. "What'd you say his name was?"

"Jones. Easley Jones. Light brown-skin feller with freckles all over his face and kinks all over his head. He's a railroad man

—runs from here to Chicago—him and me used to work to-gether. Yes ma'am. Sho' did."

The horn-rimmed lenses were like the windows of a fortress. "Sorry—y'all done made a mistake somewhere. No sech person lives in this house. Know a Sam Jones," she added helpfully, "that lives in Jamaica, Long Island. He's a butler—don' run on no road, but he commutes to New York mos' ev'y night."

"Too bad, lady, but we can't take no substitutes. If it ain't genuwine Easley, we can't use it. Thanks jes' the same. But if you do run across a Easley Jones, tell him Frimbo wants to see him again tonight—right away—please."

"Hmph!" responded the gracious lady and shut the door abruptly.

"That's funny, ain't it?" reflected Bubber as the two turned back toward the house of tragedy.

"It's all funny to me," confessed Officer Hanks. "It's all jes' a mess, what I mean. Everybody I've seen acts guilty."

"You ain't been lookin' at me, is you, brother?"

"You? You're mighty anxious to put it on somebody else—I see that."

Bubber sighed at the hopelessness of ever weaning a cop from indiscriminate suspicion.

Chapter Ten

THE officer who had taken the club to be examined for finger prints returned and reported that the examination was
under way, that photographic reproductions would be sent
over as soon as they were ready, and that a finger-print man
would come with them to take additional data, make compari-
sons, and establish or eliminate such possible identities as Detective Dart might be seeking.

This officer was returned to his post as Doty Hicks and
Spider Webb were ushered up the stairs by the gigantic Officer
Small. Sensing their arrival, Dart had the extension light again
turned off.

"If those are the men we're waiting for send them up
front."

Accordingly, Small came in alone to report. "We got two of
'em. Little dopey guy and Spider Webb, the number-runner."

"Where are the others—Brown and Jones?"

"Brown's gone with Hanks to get Jones—right down the
street here."

"Good. You wait outside, Small. Brady, bring Hicks—the
little one—in first."

Doty Hicks, though of none too steady a gait, was by no
means reluctant to come in. With his protruding eyes popping
and mouth half open, he entered the shaft of light and stood
peering into the well-nigh impenetrable blackness that ob-
scured the seated detective and the doctor standing beside him.

Dart waited. After a long moment of fruitless staring, Doty
Hicks whispered, "Is you dead yet?"

"No," said the detective softly.

"But you dyin', ain't you?" The little fellow was trembling.
"They tol' me you was dyin'."

Dart followed the obvious lead, though he could only guess
its origin.

"So you tried to kill me?"

A puzzled look came over Doty Hick's thin black face.

"You don't sound right. Yo' voice don't sound——"

"Sit down," said Dart.

Still bewildered, Hicks mechanically obeyed.

"Why did you try to kill me?"

Hicks stared dumbly, groping for something. Suddenly his features changed to an aspect of unwilling comprehension, then of furious disappointment. He leaned forward in his chair, catching hold of the edge of the table. "You ain't him!" he cried. "You ain't him! You tryin' to fool me! Where's he at—I got to see him die. I got to——"

"Why?"

"Else it ain't no use—I got to see him! Where's he at?"

"Take it easy, Hicks. Maybe we'll let you see him. But you'll have to tell us all about it. Now, what's the idea?"

A plaintive almost sobbing tone came into Doty's high, quavering voice.

"Who is you, mister? What you want to fool me for?"

"I don't want to fool you, Hicks. I want to help you. You can tell me all about it—you can trust me. Tell me the whole thing, and if it's straight, I'll let you see Frimbo."

"Lemme see him first, will you, mistuh? He may die before I get to him."

"If he isn't dead yet he won't die till you get to him. You'll have to tell your story first, so you better tell it quickly. Why did you come here tonight at ten-thirty? Why did you try to kill Frimbo, and why must you see him before he dies?"

Doty sank back in his chair. "All right," he said, dully. Then, quickened by the realization of the urgency, he leaned forward again. "All right—I'll tell you, I'll tell you. Listen." He paused.

"I'm listening."

Drawing a deep breath, Doty Hicks proceeded:

"Frimbo's a conjure-man. You know that."

"Yes."

"I come here tonight because Frimbo was killin' my brother." He hesitated. "Killin' my brother," he repeated. Then, "You know my brother—everybody knows my brother—Spats Oliver Hicks—runs the Hip-Toe Club on Lenox Avenue. Good guy, my brother. Always looked out for me. Even when I went dopey and got down and out like I is now, he never turned me down. Always looked out for me. Good guy. If it'd been me Frimbo was killin', 'twouldn' matter. I'm jes' a dope—nobody'd miss me. But he was killin' my brother, see? Y'see, Frimbo's a conjure-man. He can put spells on folks. One kind o' spell to keep 'em from dyin' like that boy what got the knife stuck in his head. Another kind to set 'em to dyin'—like he was doin' my brother. Slow dyin'—misery all in through here, coughin' spells, night sweats, chills and fever, and wastin' away. That's what he was doin' to Spats."

"But why?" Dart couldn't help asking.

" 'Count o' my brother's wife. He's doin' it 'count o' my brother's wife. Spats married a show-gal, see? And hadn't been married a month befo' she met up with some guy with more sugar. So she quit my brother for the sugar-papa, see? And natchelly, bein' a regular man and not no good-for-nothin' dope like me, my brother went after her, see? He grabbed this sugar-daddy and pulled him inside out, like a glove. And one day he met the gal and asked her to come back and she called him somethin' and he smacked her cross-eyed. Well, 'cose, that give her a fever, and she come straight here to Frimbo. She could get plenty o' what it took from the new daddy, and she brought it with her. Frimbo told her what to do. She made believe she was goin' back to live with my brother, and he like a fool took her in. She stayed jes' long enough to do what Frimbo'd told her to do, whatever it was. Day she left, my brother had a fit—jes' like a cat in a alley—a fit. And ever since, he's been goin' from bad to worse. Doctor don' help, nothin' don' help. Y'see, it's Frimbo's spell."

"And that's why you tried to kill him?"

"Yea—that's why."

"How did you go about it?"

Doty Hicks looked around him into the enshrouding darkness. He shook his head. "Can't tell you that. Can't tell nobody how—that'd break the spell. All I can tell you is that they's only one way to kill a conjure-man—you got to out-conjure him. You got to put a back-conjure on him, and it's got to be stronger 'n the one he put on the other feller. 'Cose you can't do it alone. Got to have help."

"Help? What kind of help?"

"Somebody has to help you."

"Who helped you with this?"

"Can't tell you that neither—that'd break the spell. Can I see him now?"

"Why do you have to see him before he dies?"

"That's part of it. I have to see him and tell him how come he's dyin', else it don't do no good. But if I see him and tell him how come he's dyin', then, soon as he die, my brother gets well. See? Jes' like that—gets well soon as Frimbo die."

"Did you pay the person to help you?"

"Pay him? Sho'—had to pay him."

"And do you realize that you are making a confession of deliberate murder—for which you may be sentenced to die?"

"Hmph! What I care 'bout that? I been tired livin' a long time, mistuh. But you couldn't prove nothin' on me. I did a stretch once and I know. You got to have evidence. I got it fixed so they ain't no evidence—not against me."

"Against somebody else, maybe?" Doty Hicks did not answer.

"Frimbo was a pretty wise bird. He must have known you wanted to conjure him—the way he could read people's minds. What did he say when you came in?"

"Didn't say nothin' for a while. I asked him to lay off my brother—begged him, if he had to conjure somebody, to conjure me—but he jes' set there in the dark like he was thinkin' it over, and then he begins talkin'. Say: 'So you want to die in place of your brother? It is impossible. Your brother is incurably ill.' Then he kep' quiet a minute and he say, 'You have been misinformed, my friend. You are under the impression that I have put an evil spell upon your brother. That is superstitious nonsense. I am no caster of spells. I am a psychist—a kind of psychologist. I have done nothing to your brother. He simply has pulmonary tuberculosis—in the third stage. He had had it for at least three months when your sister-in-law came to me for advice. I could not possibly be responsible for that, since until then I did not know of his existence.' 'Course I didn' believe that, 'cause my brother hadn' been sick a day till after his wife came here, so I kep' on askin' him to take off the spell, so he finally says that everything'll be all right in a few days and don' worry. Well, I figure he's jes' gettin' rid o' me, and I gets up like I'm on my way out and come through that side door there, but 'stead o' goin' on downstairs, I slips back in again and—and——"

"Put your counter-spell on him?"

"I ain' sayin'," said Doty Hicks, "I'm jes' tellin' you enough so I can see him. I ain' sayin' enough to break the spell."

"And you refuse to say who helped you?"

"Not till I see Frimbo die; then I'll tell maybe. 'Twon' make no difference, then—the spell'll be broke. Now lemme see him, like you said."

"There's no hurry. You can wait up front a few minutes."

"You said if I tol' you——" Doty Hicks was changing from abjection and pleading to suspicion and anger. "What you want to say so for if you wasn't go'n'——"

"I said you must tell your story first. You've only told part of it. I also said that if Frimbo wasn't dead when you came in, he wouldn't be when you finished. That was true. He was already dead when you came in."

The face of the tremulous little man in the illumined chair was ordinarily ugly in a pitiful, dissolute, and rather harmless way. But as the meaning of Dart's statement now slowly sank into his consciousness that usual ugliness became an exceptionally evil and murderous ugliness. Doty Hicks leaned forward still further where he sat, his white eyes more protruding than ever, his breath coming in sharp gasps. And suddenly, as if a high tension current shot through him, he lurched to his feet and lunged forward toward Dart's voice.

"Gimme sump'm!" he screamed, his hands groping the table top in the dark. "Gimme sump'm in my hand! I'll bust yo' head open—you cheat! I'll——"

By that time Brady had him.

"Take him up front," instructed Detective Dart. "Have somebody keep a special eye on him. He's worth holding on to."

Struggling, cursing, and sobbing, Doty Hicks was dragged from the room.

2

"He wanted something with which to 'bust your head open,'" reflected Dr. Archer.

"So I noticed," said Detective Dart.

"Frimbo's head was—ever so slightly—'busted' open."

"Yes."

"Memory-suggestion?"

"Or coincidence? Anybody in a rage might want to get his hands on a weapon."

"With which to 'bust open' an offending cranium. No doubt. Rather over-effective way to 'put a spell' on a fellow though."

"Exactly. Wouldn't have to put a spell on him if you were going to brain him with a club."

"No. Yet—if you weren't going to brain him—if you just wanted him to keep still while the spell was being put on——"

"Yes—but a handkerchief is a pretty substantial thing, also, to use as a spell. And it wasn't put on. It was put in."

"In other words, whoever helped Doty Hicks, wasn't taking any chances."

"Something like that."

"Turn on the light a minute. I want to look at that—spell."

Dart gave the order. The extension lamp went on, throwing its sharp radiance into the darkness and giving an unnatural effect which disclosed well enough the men, the two chairs, the table, the black-hung walls, but somehow did not in any way relieve the oppressive somberness of the place—a light that cut through the shadow without actually dispelling it.

The physician stooped and, using his forceps, took the blue-bordered handkerchief out of his bag. He dropped it on the table, and with the instrument poked it about till it lay flat.

"What sort of a person," he meditated in a low tone, "would even think of using a device like that?"

3

Whatever Dart might have answered was cut off by the unceremonious and rather breathless entrance of Bubber Brown. Hanks, like a faithful guardian, was at his heels.

"We got two of 'em—see 'em?" Bubber breathed. "Doty Hicks was no trouble—too anxious to get here. But that Spider Webb—we had to chase that nigger all over Pat's."

"Yes, thanks. But where's Easley Jones?"

"We went to where he said he lived, couple o' doors up the street. But the landlady claim she didn' know him. I think she got leery when she saw my boy's brass buttons here and jes' shut up on general principles. But we left word for him to come by."

"That's not so good. Guess we'll have to put out feelers for him."

"How come 'tain' so good?"

"Nobody's anxious to get mixed up in a murder case."

"How he know it's a murder case?" Bubber said, using the same logic Dart had used on him earlier. "All I said was Frimbo wanted to see him right away. If he don't know it's a murder case, he'll figure Frimbo's got some more advice for him or sump'm and come a-runnin'. If he do know it's a murder case, he's long gone anyhow, so leavin' the message can't do no more harm than's done already."

Dart looked at Bubber with new interest.

"That's good reasoning—as far as it goes," he remarked. "But the woman—the landlady—may have been telling the truth. Maybe Easley Jones doesn't live there."

"Well then," Bubber concluded promptly, "if he lied 'bout his address in the first place, he was up to sump'm crooked all along. He didn't *have* to invite me to come advise him 'bout his trouble, jes' 'cause he saw my card. I can see why his landlady would lie—to protect him—but there wasn't no reason for him to lie to me."

"Then what is your opinion, Brown?"

"My 'pinion's like this: I believe he gimme the right address. She'll tell him—if he's still there to tell. If he had anything to do with this he'll stay 'way. If he didn't have nothin' to do with it, and don't know it's happened, curiosity to see what else Frimbo wants will bring him back."

"In other words, if Easley Jones does come back, he isn't the man we're after. Is that it?"

"Yes, suh. That's it. And if he don't come back, whether it's 'cause he lied 'bout the address or 'cause he got the message and is scared to come—y'all better find him. He knows sump'm. Any man that runs away, well, all I say is, is been up to sump'm."

"The attendant seems to have run away," Dart reminded him.

"It's between the two of 'em then—less'n they show up."

"What about Doty Hicks? He's confessed."

"No!"

"Sure—while you were out."

"He did? Well, I don't pay that no mind. That nigger's crazy. Smokes too many reefers."

"There may be a good deal in what you say, Brown. Anyhow, thanks for your help. Just go up front and keep your eyes and ears open, will you?"

"Sho' will," Bubber promised, proud of his commendation. But as he was on the point of turning away, his eye fell on the table where the blue-bordered handkerchief lay.

"Jinx been in here, ain't he?" said he.

"Jenkins? Yes, why?"

"I see he left his handkerchief. Want me to give it to him?"

Dart and the physician exchanged glances.

"Is that his?" the detective asked, feigning mild surprise.

"Sho' 'tis. I was kiddin' him 'bout it tonight. Great big old ugly boogy like Jinx havin' a handkerchief with a baby blue border on it. Can y' imagine? A baby blue border!"

"But," Dart said softly, "I asked you before if you'd seen anybody here with a colored handkerchief, and you said no."

"Yea—but I thought you meant really colored—like mine. That's white, all 'cep'n the hem. And anyhow, when you ast me if I'd seen any o' these people here with a colored handkerchief, I wasn't thinkin' 'bout Jinx. He ain't people. He never even crossed my mind. I was thinkin' 'bout them three men."

"Brady, ask Jenkins to come in again."

When Jinx returned, the unsuspecting Bubber, whose importance had by now grown large in his own eyes, did not wait for Dart to act. He picked up the handkerchief and thrust it toward Jinx saying:

"Here, boy, take your belongin's with you—don't leave 'em layin' 'round all over the place. You ain't home."

The tall, freckled, scowling Jinx was caught off guard. He looked doubtfully from the handkerchief to Bubber and from Bubber to the detective.

The detective was smiling quite guilelessly at him. "Take it if it's yours, Jenkins. We found it." Not even in his tone was there the slightest implication of any earlier mention of a hand-kerchief.

"Ole baby blue," mocked Bubber. "Take it boy, take it. You know it's yours—though it's no wonder you 'shamed to own it. Baby blue!"

But the redoubtable Jinx had by now grown normally wary.

"'Tain' none o' mine," he growled. "Never seen it before. This here's the boy that goes in for colors."

"Well," grinned Bubber, unaware that he was driving nails in his friend's coffin, "it may not be yours, but you sho' was wipin' yo' face with it when you come in here tonight."

Dart was still smiling. "Never mind," he remarked casually, "if it isn't Jenkins' he doesn't have to take it. That's all for the present. Just step up front again, will you please?"

A moment later, the doctor was saying, "Looks bad for Jenkins. If he'd accepted it right off, it would've been better for him."

"Right."

"But refusing to acknowledge it when it's now so clearly his—that's like being caught with the goods and saying 'I didn't take it.'"

"Jenkins is lying to cover up. That's a cinch."

"He may, of course—in ignorance—be just denying every-thing on general principles, without knowing specifically why himself."

"Yea," said Dart ironically. "He may. Brady, did you get that last down exactly?"

"Sho' did," said Brady.

"It wouldn't take much more," mused Dart, "to justify ar-resting our lanky friend, Jenkins."

"He hasn't admitted ownership of it."

"No. But knowing it's his, we can probably—er—persuade him to admit it, if necessary."

"But you've already got to hold that Hicks—on his own confession."

"His confession—if that's what it was—mentioned a sort of accomplice, as I remember it."

"So it did," reflected Dr. Archer.

"Jenkins might be that accomplice."

"Well—there's one strong argument against that."

"Name it."

"Jenkins' character. He just isn't the coöperating kind."

Detective Dart grinned.

"Doc, did you ever hear," he said, "of the so-called filthy lucre?"

Dr. Archer's serious face relaxed a little.

"I even saw some once," he murmured reminiscently.

Chapter Eleven

I

FROM the hall came the sound of an unsubdued and frankly astonished masculine voice, high-pitched in tone, firm, smooth in timbre, decidedly southern in accent, exclaiming:

"Great day in the mornin'! What all you polices doin' in this place? Policeman outside d' front door, policeman in d' hall, policeman on d' stairs, and hyer's another one. 'Deed I mus' be in d' wrong house! Is this Frimbo the conjure-man's house, or is it the jail?"

"Who you want to see?"

"There 'tis again. Policeman downstairs tole me come up hyer. Now you ask me same thing he did. Frimbo jes' sent for me, and I come to find out what he want."

"Wait a minute."

The officer thus addressed came in to Dart.

"Let him in," Dart said. But the order was unnecessary for the newcomer was already in.

"Bless mah soul!" he ejaculated. "I never see so many polices in all my life. Look like a lost parade." He came up to the physician and the detective. "Which a one o' y'all is Mr. Frimbo?" he inquired. "When I was hyer befo' it was so dark I couldn' see, though 'cose I heard every word what was said. Fact, if one o' y'all is him, jes' speak and I'll know it. Never fergit that voice as long as I got holes in my ears."

"You're Easley Jones?"

"At yo' service, brother."

"Mr. Frimbo is gone, Jones. Gone on a long journey."

"Is that a fact? Well, I'm a travelin' man myself. I run on the road—y' know—New York to Chicago. But say—how could he send me word to come back here if he's done gone away?"

"You received the message?"

"Sho' I did. Ha! That landlady o' mine's all right. Y' know, she figured I been up to sump'm, so she made out like she didn' know me when that cop come by jes' now. But I knowed

I ain' done nothin' wrong, and I figured best thing to do was breeze on back and see what's up. Where's he gone, mistuh?"

"Frimbo's dead. He was killed while you were here to-night."

For the first time, the appearance of Easley Jones became definite, as if this statement had suddenly turned a floodlight full upon him. He was of medium height, dressed in dark clothing, and he carried a soft gray felt hat in his hand. The hat dropped to the floor, the man stood motionless, his brown eyes went widely incredulous and his light brown face, which was spattered with black freckles, grew pale so that the freckles stood out even blacker still. Loose-mouthed, he gazed upon the detective a long moment. Then he drew a deep breath, slowly bent his kinky head and recovered his hat, stood erect again, and sighed:

"Well I be dog-goned!"

"I'm a police officer. It was I who sent for you, not Frimbo. It speaks in your favor that you have come. If you will be kind enough to sit down there in that chair, I'd like to ask you a few questions."

"Ask *me* questions? 'Deed, brother, I don' know what good askin' me anythin's go'n' do you. Look like to me I ought to be askin' you the questions. How long he been daid?"

"Sit down, please."

There was no evading the quiet voice, the steadfast bright black eyes of the little detective. Easley Jones sat down. At a word from Dart, the extension light went out. Thereupon, Easley Jones promptly got up. He made no effort to conceal the fact that the absence of surrounding illumination rendered the situation decidedly uncomfortable for him.

"Why—this is jes' like it was befo'—befo'. Listen, brother, if you 'specks to get a straight tale out o' me, you better gimme plenty o' light. Dark as 'tis in hyer now, I can't make out what I'm sayin'."

"Nothing's going to hurt you. Just sit down and answer truthfully what I ask you."

"Aw right, mistuh. But tellin' a man somebody been killed, and then turnin' out all the lights and talkin' right from wha' he was—dat ain't no way to get the truth. I ain' 'sponsible for nothin' I say, I tell you that much, now. And jes' lemme hear one funny little noise and you'll find yo'self starin' at a empty chair."

"You won't get far, my friend."

"Who? I tol' you I was a travelin' man. If anything funny happen, I'm go'n' prove it."

"You run on the railroad?"

"Yas, suh. Dat is, I rides on it."

"Company?"

"Never has no company. No suh. Always go alone."

"What railroad company?"

"Oh. Pullman—natchelly."

"Porter, of course?"

"Now what else do the Pullman Company put niggers on trains for?"

"How long've you been with them?"

"Ten years and five months yestiddy. Yestiddy was the first o' February, wasn't it?"

"What run?"

"You mean now?"

"Yes."

"New York to Chicago over the Central."

"Twentieth Century?"

"Yas indeedy—bes' train in the East."

"What's its schedule?"

"Two forty-five out o' New York, nine forty-five nex' morning in Chicago."

"Same hours on the return trip?"

"Yas, suh. 'Cep'n' week-ends. I lay over Saturday night and all day Sunday—one week in Chicago, nex' week in New York. Tonight's my Saturday in New York, y'see?"

"That's how you happened to choose tonight to see Frimbo?"

"Uh-huh. Yea."

"What time did you get here tonight?"

"Ten-twenty on the minute."

"How can you say that so positively?"

"Well, I tole you I'm a railroad man. I does ev'ything by the clock. When I arrive someplace I jes' natchelly look at my watch —fo'ce o' habit, y'see."

"You went straight into the waiting-room?"

"Yea—they was a flunky standin' in the hall; he showed me in."

"Describe him."

"Tall, black, and cock-eyed."

"Which eye had the cast in it?"

"Right eye—no—lemme see—left—tell you the truth I don' know. I never could tell, when it come to folks like that, which eye is lookin' at me and which ain't. But it was one of 'em—I knows that."

"Who was present when you arrived?"

"Nobody. I was first."

"What did you do?"

"I sat down and waited. Nothin' else for me to, was they?"

"What happened?"

"Nothin'. Too much nothin'. I sat there waitin' a while, 'bout eight or ten minutes I guess, and then a little feller come in that looked—well, he looked kind o' dopey to me. Nex', right behind him, come a sporty lookin' gent in gray—kind o' heavy-set he was, and tight-lookin', like he don' want no foolishness. Then two other men come in together, a long thin one and a short thick one. We all set around a minute or so, and then this short one begin to walk around and look at them decorations and charms in yonder, and the tall one with him. He started talkin' to the tall one 'bout them little freakish-lookin' figures on the wall, and them knives and spears. He say, 'Boy, you know what them is?' His boy say, 'No, what?' He say, 'Them's the folks this Frimbo's done chopped loose, and these implements hyer is what he chopped 'em loose with.' So the other say, 'What of it?' And the little one say, 'Know how come he kilt 'em?' 'No,' the long boy says. So the little one say, ' 'Cause they was so ugly. That make it look bad for you, son.' Long boy say, 'Why?' Shorty say, ' 'Cause they was all better lookin' than you is!' I figgered he might know sump'm 'bout them things sho' 'nough, so I went over where he was and struck up a conversation with him. Turned out he was a sort o' home detective, and I figgered he might be of some use to me, so I invited him to come by and see me some time when I was in town. Said he would. Say—I guess that's how y'all knowed where to find me at, huh? He must 'a' tol' you."

"What particular decorations or charms did you and he discuss?"

"None of 'em. Started—but right off he handed me his card and we got to talkin' 'bout other matters and fust thing I know, there was the flunky ready to show me in to Frimbo. So I went back to my chair, picked up my hat, and follered the flunky. Thought I might see this li'l detective ag'in, but 'stead o' goin' out the way I come in, Frimbo tole me to go out by this side hall-door hyer."

"Did you see two clubs on opposite ends of the mantel-piece?"

"Clubs? Uh-uh. Not far as I 'member now. Them funny-faces and things on the wall—I 'member them. Wait a min-ute—you mean two bones?"

"Yes."

"B'lieve I did. One 'cross one end of the mantelpiece, and one 'cross the other. Yea—sho' I did."

"What did you wish to see Frimbo about, Mr. Jones?"

"Now right there, brother, is where you gettin' personal. But I reckon I kin tell you—though I don' want to see it in no papers."

"There are no reporters here."

"Well, then, y'see it's like this. I got a wife in Chicago. I fig-ger she gets kind o' lonesome seein' me only every other week-end—that is, for any length o' time. Three four hours in the middle o' the day is jes' enough to say howdy and goo'by. So with all them evenin's full o' nothin' special to do, I got kind o' worried—y' understand? And one o' the New York boys on the train was tellin' me this Frimbo could tell the low-down on doings like that, so I figgered I'd come up and see him. So up I come."

"Did he give you the information you were looking for?"

" 'Deed he did, brother. He set my mind at rest."

"Just what was said when you came in to see him?"

"Well, I say I was hyer to ask 'bout my wife—was she true *to* me or f'ru *with* me. But he didn' say nothin' till he got good and ready, and then he didn' say much. Tole me I didn' have nothin' to worry 'bout—that he seen I had murder in my heart for somebody, but there wasn' no other mule in my stall sho' 'nough and to go on forgit it. 'Course them wasn' his 'zack words, but dass what he meant. So I went on—'cep'n' as I was 'bout to go down the stairs, the flunky 'peared in the hall there and collected my two bucks. Then I lef'."

Detective Dart turned his flashlight on the table where the blue-bordered handkerchief still lay.

"Ever see that before?"

The railroad porter leaned forward to inspect the object. "Seen one jes' like it," he admitted.

"When and where?"

"Tonight. In the front room yonder. That tall feller was wipin' his face with it when he fust come in. Couldn't miss it. 'Cose I can't say it's the self-same one——"

"That's all for the present, Jones. Thank you. Wait up front a few minutes, please."

"Yas, *suh*. And if they's anything I kin do, jes' lemme know. Who you reckon done it, chief?"

"When do you count up your tips, Jones?"

"Suh?"

"In the middle of the trip—or at the end?"

"Oh." Jones grinned widely, his round freckled face brightening. "I see what you mean. Yas, suh. I count 'em after the train's pulled in."

"Right. This train isn't in yet. But we know where it's headed and we know who's on board."

"O.K., brother engineer. But bring her in on time, please suh. I got me a little serious wringin' and twistin' to do later on tonight."

2

"I'm getting interested in the servant with the evil eye," murmured Dr. Archer. "Terribly careless of him to disappear like this."

"We'll find him, if it boils down that far."

"Are you by any manner of chance beginning to draw conclusions?"

"Not by chance, no. Getting tired?"

"The neurons of my pallium are confused but extraordinarily active. The soles of my feet, however, being, so to speak, at the other extreme as to both structure and function——"

"Brady, bring in Spider Webb and bring along a chair for Dr. Archer."

"Thoughtful of you," said Dr. Archer.

"Excuse me, doc. I forgot you were standing all this time."

"I only remember it in the intervals myself. And this is possibly the last. However, better tardy than when parallel lines meet—what's this?"

"Wait a minute, Brady. Lights, Joe," the detective called. "Who's there now? Oh, hello there, Tynes. This is our local finger-print hound, doc. What'd you find, Tynie?"

"They had some trouble," the Spaniard-like newcomer in civilian dress said, "gettin' a man up from downtown, and long as I was hangin' around——"

"Glad you were. Maybe we'll make a killing for our own office. Be nice to carry this through by ourselves. So what've you got?"

"I've got one isolated print. Smudgy, but definite. Didn't even have to bring it out—just photographed it like it was."

He reached into a small black Boston bag he was carrying. "Got the other stuff here, too." He brought forth a flat rectangular slab with a smooth metal surface a foot long and three inches wide, and placed it on the table, then a small roller with a handle, which he laid beside the slab. Next he withdrew a bundle wrapped in a silk cloth and handed it to Dart. "There's your bone or club or whatever it is. Next time wrap it in something soft like a silk handkerchief."

"Had a handkerchief all right," Dart said, "but it wasn't silk."

"Anything beats a newspaper—damn near scratched the thing useless."

"Don't hold us up for an argument, Tynie. Bring on your print."

"Well, there's probably lots of old finger marks on that bone—it's gooey as hell. But this one is new. It's a little spread, but there'd be no mistaking it."

He withdrew now a metal cigarette-case. "Best thing in the world to carry a moist print in—see?" He opened it, revealing, beneath either transverse guard, a single photograph of a thumb print. "The slight bulge accommodates the curl of the wet paper and the guards hold it in place without touching anything but the edges."

"Smart boy," said Dart.

"Smarter than that," said the physician, "if you can read those smudges."

"Now listen, young expert," said Dart, "hold that here a minute. After I see this next bird, I want you to print everybody here and see if you find a print identical with that one. If you do, there's a few free nights in jail for somebody."

"O.K., Perry."

"I hope so anyway—it'll save sending out an alarm for the tall dark gentleman with the cock-eye."

"External strabismus is the term," said the doctor gravely.

"The hell it is," said Dart. "Douse that light. All right Brady, let's have the Spider."

Chapter Twelve

SPIDER WEBB, an alert mouse-faced gentleman, perhaps thirty-five years old, was of dusky yellow complexion, rather sharp yet negroid features, and self-assured bearing. He was decidedly annoyed at the circumstances which had thus involved him, and his deep-set green-gray eyes glowed with a malicious impatience as he sat facing the well-nigh invisible detective.

His curt answers to Dart's incisive questioning revealed nothing to contradict the essential points already established. But the eliciting of his reasons for coming tonight to see Frimbo opened an entirely new realm of possibility.

At first he surlily refused to discuss the interview between himself and the African. It had been strictly personal he said.

"No more personal," the detective suggested, "than being held for murder on suspicion, was it?"

Spider was silent.

"Or being arrested for number-running? You know we can get you there on several counts, don't you?"

"Can't help that. Whatever you know, you also know I can't talk. That's suicide."

"So's silence. Telling the truth, Spider, will get you out of this—if you're not guilty—out of this and several other counts I could hold you on. You've enjoyed a lot of freedom, but this is a matter of life and death. A man has been killed. You're suspected. You can't keep quiet but so long. You know that?"

Webb said nothing.

"Now if it really was a personal matter you came here on tonight, telling me about it won't affect your—er—professional standing. If it wasn't, it had something to do with your number game. I know about that already—you won't be telling me anything new. The only thing talking now will do is clear you if you're innocent. Silence is equal to a confession."

Spider's receding chin quivered a bit; he started to speak, but didn't.

"You can get plenty, you know, for withholding evidence, too."

"I'd rather go to jail," Spider growled, "than take lead."

"Oh. So you're afraid of getting shot? Then you do know something. You'd better spill it, Spider, now that you've gone that far. Who sent you here to get Frimbo?"

A little of Webb's assurance dropped away.

"Nobody. On the level. Nobody."

"The man behind you is Brandon. Did he send you?"

"I said nobody."

"Let's see now. Brandon has only one real competitor as a policy-king here in Harlem. That's Spencer. Spider, your silence means one of two things. Either Brandon or Spencer had it in for Frimbo. If it was Spencer, you won't talk because you did it. If it was Brandon, you're afraid to squeal because he might find out."

In the bright illumination of the horizontal beam of light, Spider's face twitched and changed just enough to convince Dart that he was on the right track. He took a long chance:

"Spencer has been hit hard several times in the past month, hasn't he?"

"How—how'd you know?" came from the startled Spider.

"We watch such things, Spider. It helps us solve lots of crimes. Your chief, Brandon, however, has shown no signs of loss. He's going strong."

Again Spider Webb's expression betrayed a touch for the detective.

"Of course, if you let me do all the talking, Spider, I won't be able to give you any of the credit. I'll have to put you in jail just the same—on all the outstanding counts. Understand, the only reason you're not in jail now is that you might be of value in just such a case as this."

Uneasily, Spider stirred in his chair.

"You tried to escape coming here tonight, too, didn't you, Spider? In Pat's—when you saw a policeman with a man you had seen here earlier tonight. You tried to duck. I guess you're our man all right. Brady, put the bracelets on——"

"Wait a minute," said Spider. "Is this going to be on the level—no leaks?"

"Give you my word. Wait, Brady. Go ahead, Spider."

"O. K."

"Good. You're only protecting yourself," said Dart.

"This Frimbo was a smart guy—much too smart," Spider Webb began.

"Yes?"

"Yea. He had a system of playing the game that couldn't lose. I don't know how he did it—whether he worked out somethin' mathematical or was just a good guesser or what. But he could hit regular once a week without fail. And he played ten dollars a day, and I collected it."

"Go on."

"When he hit the third week in succession, the boss set up a howl. You know the percentage—six hundred to one. Hit for a dollar, you get six hundred minus the ten percent that goes to the runner. Hit for ten bucks, you're due six thousand minus the six hundred—five thousand four hundred dollars. Well, even a big banker like Brandon can't stand that—he only collects four grand a week."

"Only," murmured Dart.

"And when it happened the third week, it looked bad for me—I was gettin' six hundred out of each time this guy hit. I been with Brandon a long time, but he began to look at me awful doubtful. But he paid off—he always does—that's why he's successful at it. Also he told me, no more bets from this Frimbo. But then he begun to figure, and what he figured was this—that maybe he could use some o' this Frimbo's smartness for himself. Smart guy, Brandon. Here's what he did.

"First he accused me of playin' crooked. Runners try that once in a while, y' know. We have a list o' names on a slip, with the number and amount of money being played by each person beside the name. Well, the slips are s'posed to be turned in at nine forty-five every A.M., but it takes some time to get 'em in. Ten o'clock, the clearing-house number on which the winner is based is announced downtown. There's ways of holdin' the slip just a few seconds after ten, having a buddy telephone the winning number up, say, to the house next door, or downstairs someplace, where another buddy signals what it is by tapping on the wall or a radiator or something. Then the runner adds the winning number to his list beside a fake name, collects the money later, and splits with his buddies. Brandon, of course, knows all them tricks, and accused me of 'em. I showed him I wasn't dumb enough to try it three weeks in succession. So he had to admit this Frimbo must be just smart.

"So he figured he could trust me and he told me what to do. I was to keep on takin' Frimbo's ten bucks a day, and the numbers he played. Brandon had some of his boys play the same numbers with Spencer—but for twenty bucks. Result—when the numbers hit, Brandon lost six grand to Frimbo and won twelve from Spencer. The rest of his income stood like it was before. Spencer couldn't stand more than two or three twelve-grand hits—he'd have to quit. That would clear the field for Brandon. Then he could just stop taking Frimbo's bets and be sitting pretty."

"So what?" inquired Detective Dart.

"So that's why I was here tonight, that's all. To get Frimbo's number."

"Did he give you the number?"

"Sure he did—right from where you're sitting now."

"And the ten bucks?"

"Nope. He never handles money himself. The flunky collects all the people's fees as they go out of that door there. So I always got the ten bucks from the flunky. He'd either be waiting there or he'd come out in a moment."

"Come out? Out of where?"

"Out of the back room there."

"The back room? Oh. Could Spencer have learned of this and put Frimbo out of the way?"

"If he was smart enough. He'd be bound to get suspicious, no matter how Brandon played his twenty—it wouldn't look right. And he'd investigate. He'd check the bets each night before, find twenty bucks of the same number, and trace those players. But he'd have to pay 'em, once he'd taken the money. And he couldn't tell who not to take beforehand, either, because they could change their names, or if he did find a leak and got the lowdown, there'd be only one way out for him. He'd have to paralyze Frimbo or be ruined himself. Pure self-defense."

Perry Dart sat silent a moment, then said, "You know, doc, there's one thing that keeps worrying me. All these people agree up to now that Frimbo talked to them—talked to them personally about personal matters. How could a murdered man conduct an intelligent conversation *after* his death? That's why I haven't taken Jenkins already. The victim couldn't have been sitting here dead in the chair all the time, talking—through a stuffed neck."

"True," said the physician, "but the visitors preceding Jenkins might have found the man dead just as Jenkins did and slipped out without saying anything, to avoid incriminating themselves. Or the assistant might have been doing the talking through some trick or device, without knowing his master was dead. Everyone agrees the servant didn't come in here. So don't bank on the end of the conversation as the moment of death. Death could have occurred a half an hour or more earlier, without changing the testimony at all."

Another silence, then Dart said:

"Put on that light."

As the sharp radiance cut the shadow, Spider Webb exclaimed:

"Judas Priest! If I'd known you had all them listeners——"

"Don't worry—we'll see it doesn't cost you anything. Brady, bring everybody in here. All ready, Tynie?"

"All ready, Perry," said Tynes.

Chapter Thirteen

I N THE crystalline underlighting from the glaring extension, a thin brightness through which shot the horizontal beam from Frimbo's curious illumination, a semicircle of people stood facing the table. Behind it now stood the detective and the physician. The latter was busy with his handkerchief, wiping from his fingers a dark film which had stuck to them while he had been sitting in the chair which Brady had brought. It was a small, erect wooden chair with short arms on one of which he had rested a hand during Spider Webb's testimony. At the moment he paid the stuff no further attention, considering it merely a sort of furniture polish which had been too heavily applied, and had become gummy on standing.

The detective was addressing the people facing him. "I'm going to ask the coöperation of all of you folks. Before doing so, I want you to know just what I have in view." He paused a moment, considered, decided. "Among the facts brought out by what we have found and by your testimony are these: Frimbo, a man of close habits and no definitely known special friends or enemies, was killed here in this chair tonight between ten-thirty and eleven o'clock. He was stunned by a blow, presumably from this club, and then choked to death by this handkerchief, which was removed from his throat in my presence by Dr. Archer."

He paused again to observe the effect of this announcement. Outstanding were two reactions, quite opposite: Mrs. Crouch's horrified expression, and Bubber Brown's astonished comment:

"Doggone! They's some excuse for chokin' on a fish-bone— but a handkerchief!"

"There are several possible motives that have come to light. But before following these motives any further, we must establish or complete such evidence as we already have in hand. We have reliable testimony on the ownership of this handkerchief.

We must now determine who handled this club. You all know the meaning of finger prints. On this club, we have found a fresh print which will have to be compared with certain of your finger prints. But first I want to give you a chance now to admit having hold of this weapon tonight—if you did. Is anyone here ready to admit that he—even accidentally—touched this club tonight?"

Everyone looked at everyone else. No one spoke but the irrepressible Bubber. "Not tonight," murmured he, "nor las' night, either."

"Very well, then. I shall have to ask you all to submit to what you may consider an indignity, but it's quite necessary. And any who objects will have to be arrested on suspicion and for withholding of evidence, and will then have to submit anyhow. You will please come forward to this table in turn, one by one, beginning with Mrs. Crouch on that end, and allow Officer Tynes to take your prints. These prints will not be held as police records unless you are arrested in connection with this case."

"Wait a minute." It was Dr. Archer who spoke. "Better take mine first, hadn't you? I'm a suspect, too."

Dart agreed. "Right you are, doc. Go ahead."

Tynes had prepared his flat slab meanwhile by touching to it a dab of thick special ink from a flexible tube, then rolling this to a thin smooth even film which covered the rectangular surface. Dr. Archer submitted his hand. Tynes grasped the physician's right thumb, laid its outer edge upon the inky surface, rolled it skillfully over with a light even pressure till its inner edge rested as had its outer, lifted it, and repeated the maneuver within a labeled space on a prepared paper blank. The result was a perfectly rolled thumb print.

"I'm pretty sure it's a thumb on the club," Tynes said, "but I'll take the others, too, for safety."

"By all means," said the tall physician gravely. And in a few minutes Tynes had filled all ten of the spaces on the blank. Then he produced a small bottle of gasoline and a bit of cheese cloth. "That'll take it off," he said. He looked at the prints. "Your left thumb's blurred. Must have been dirty."

"Yes. It was, now that you mention it. Gummy furniture polish or something on the arm of that chair I was sitting in."

"Never mind, it'll do. Next."

"Mrs. Crouch—if you don't mind," said Dart.

Martha Crouch stepped forward without hesitation. The others followed in turn. The dexterous Tynes required only a minute for each person: Mrs. Snead, highly disgruntled, but silent save for an occasional disgusted grunt, Spider Webb, sullen, Easley Jones, grinning, Doty Hicks, trembling, and Jinx Jenkins scowling. Bubber's turn came last. Jinx's paper with his name across the head lay in plain view among those scattered out to dry on the table. Bubber cocked his head sidewise and peered at it as he submitted his digits to Tynes.

"Listen, brother—ain't you made a mistake?" he asked.

"How?" said Tynes, working on.

"Honest now, them ain't Jinx's *finger* prints, is they?"

"Sure, they are."

"Go on, man. You done took the boy's foot prints. Ain' no fingers made look like that."

"They're his, though."

"Tell me, mistuh, does apes have finger prints?"

"I suppose so."

"Well, listen. When you get time, see if them there don't belong to a gorilla or sump'm. I've had my doubts about Jinx Jenkins for quite a long time."

2

Tynes gathered the papers indiscriminately, so that they were not in any known order, faced them up in a neat pile, and procured a large hand-glass from his bag. He was the center of attention—even the officers in the corners of the room drew unconsciously a bit nearer. The doctor insisted on his sitting in one of the two chairs, he and the detective both being now on their feet. Tynes complied, sitting at the end of the table toward the hall with his back to the door. The physician stood so that he could direct his flashlight from the side upon the objects of Tynes' observations.

The latter now removed from the cigarette case one of the two photographs of the print which he had found on the club. This he kept in his left hand, the hand-glass in his right, and holding the original so that it was beside each labeled space in turn, methodically began to compare under the glass, the freshly made prints with the photograph.

Intently, silently, almost breathlessly, the onlookers stood watching the bent shoulders, the sleek black head, the expressionless tan face of Tynes. The whole room seemed to shift a little each time he passed from one comparison to the next, to hang suspended a moment, then shift with him again. So complete was the silence that the sound of a fire-siren on the Avenue a quarter-mile away came clearly into the room, and so absorbed was everyone in this important procedure that occasional odd sounds below were completely ignored.

It appeared that Tynes was making two separate piles, one of which, presumably, contained cases dismissed as out of the question, the other of which contained cases to be further studied and narrowed down. The long moments hung unrelaxed; the observers stared with the same fascinated expectancy that might have characterized their watching of a burning fuse, whose spark too slowly, too surely, approached some fatal explosive.

Yet Tynes' work was proceeding very rapidly, facilitated by the fortunate accident that the original print belonged to one of the simpler categories. In an apparent eternity which was actually but a few minutes, he had reduced the final number to two papers. One of these he laid decisively aside after a short reinspection. The other he examined at one point long and carefully. He nodded his head affirmatively once or twice, drew a deep breath, put down his hand-glass, and straightened up. He handed the paper to Detective Perry Dart, standing behind the table.

"This is it, Perry. Right thumb. Exactly like the photograph."

Dart took the paper, held it up, looked at it, lowered it again. His bright black eyes swept the waiting circle, halted.

"Jenkins," he said quietly, "you're under arrest."

Chapter Fourteen

"Y OU, Hicks," Dart continued, "will be held also on your own testimony, as a possible accessory. The rest of you be ready to be called at any time as witnesses. For the present, however——"

At this moment a newcomer pressed into the room, a large, bluff, red-faced man carrying a physician's bag, and puffing with the exertion of having climbed the stairs.

"Hello, Dart. Got you working, hey?"

"Hello, Dr. Winkler. How long've you been here?"

"Long enough to examine your case."

"Really? I heard some noises downstairs, but I didn't realize it was you. Shake hands with Dr. Archer here. He was called in, pronounced the case, and notified us. And he's a better detective than I am—missed his calling, I think."

"Howdy, doctor," said the florid medical examiner pleasantly. "This case puzzles me somewhat."

"I should think it would," said Dr. Archer. "We have the advantage over you."

"Can't figure out," went on Dr. Winkler, "just what evidence of violence there was to make you call in the police. Couldn't find any myself—looked pretty carefully, too."

"You mean you didn't see a scalp wound over the right ear?"

"Scalp wound? I should say I couldn't. There isn't any."

"No?" Dr. Archer turned to Dart. "Did you see that, Dart, or was it an optical illusion?"

"I saw it," admitted Dart.

"And unless I'm having hallucinations," the local physician went on, "it contained a fresh blood clot which I removed with a gauze dressing that now rests in my bag." He stooped deliberately, procured and displayed the soiled dressing, while the medical examiner looked first at him, then at Dart, as if he was not sure whether to doubt their sanity or his own. Dr.

Archer dropped the dressing back into his bag. "Then I probed it for a fracture," he concluded.

"Well," said Winkler, "I don't see how I could've missed anything like that. I went over her from head to foot, and if she wasn't a cardiorenal I never saw one——"

"You went—where?"

"I went over her from head to foot—every inch——"

"Her?" burst from Dart.

"Yes—her. She's been dead for hours——"

"Wait a minute. Doctor Winkler," said Dr. Archer, "we aren't discussing the same subject. I'm talking about the victim of this crime, a man known as Frimbo."

"A man! Well, if that corpse downstairs is a man, somebody played an awful dirty trick on him."

"Stand fast, everybody!" ordered Dart. "Tynes, take charge here till I get back. Come on, you medicos. Let's get this thing straight."

Out of the room and down the stairs they hurried, Archer, Dart, and Winkler. The door of Crouch's front room was open, but the couch on which the dead man had been placed was in a position that could not be seen from the hall. So far did Dr. Archer out-distance the others that by the time they got inside the room, he was already standing in the middle of the floor, staring dumbfoundedly at an unquestionably unoccupied couch.

"The elusive corpse," he murmured, as the other two came up. "First a man, then a woman, then—a memory."

"He was on that couch!" Dart said. "Where's Day? The cop covering the front? Day! Come here!"

Officer Day, large, cheese-colored, and bovine, loomed in the doorway. "Yas, suh."

"Day, where's the body that was on this couch?"

"Body? On that couch?" Day's face was blank as an egg.

"Are you on duty down here—or are you in a trance?"

" 'Deed, I ain' seen no body on that couch, chief. The only body down here is back yonder in the room where the telephone is. On a table under a sheet."

"He's right there," said Winkler.

"Day, don't repeat this question, please: When did you first come into this room?"

"When the medical examiner come. I took him in and showed him back yonder, but I didn' stay to look—I come right back here to my post."

"When you first came here tonight, didn't you see the corpse on this couch?"

"No 'ndeed. I was the last one in. You and the doc went in there and left the rest of us here in the hall. I couldn't see 'round the door. And when you come out, yo' orders to me was 'cover the front.' And I been coverin' it." Officer Day was a little resentful of Detective Dart's implied censure. "When the medical examiner got here I took him in. And they sho' wasn't no corpse on no couch then. Only corpse in here was back yonder, under the sheet. Natchelly I figured that was it."

"You would. Doc——"

But Dr. Archer was already returning from a quick trip to the rear room. "It's a woman all right," he said. "Frimbo is apparently A.W.O.L. Inconsiderate of him, isn't it?"

"Listen, Day," Dart said, refraining with difficulty from explosive language. "Has anyone come through this door since you came down here?"

"No 'ndeed. Nobody but him." He pointed to Dr. Winkler. "The undertaker started in, but when I told him what had happened he asked where y'all was, and I told him upstairs yonder, so he went straight up. Then, when he come down again, he went on out. Asked me to turn out the lights and slam this door when we was through, that's all."

"All right, Day. That's all. You keep on covering the front. Don't let it get away from you. Doc, you and the M. E. wait here and keep your eyes open. I'll tear this shack loose if necessary—nobody's going to get away with a stunt like that."

"Wait a second," said Dr. Archer. "How long has it been since we were down here?"

"Damn!" exploded Dart, looking at his watch. "Over an hour."

"Well," the local physician said, "whoever removed that stiff has had plenty of time to get it off the premises long before now. Just a hasty harum-scarum search won't dig up a thing, do you think?"

"I can't help it," Dart replied impatiently. "I've got to look, haven't I?" And out of the door he sped and bounded up the stairs.

2

The tall, pale, bespectacled Dr. Archer summarized the situation for the medical examiner's benefit while they waited. He described how they had found the strange instrument of death and later the club, devised of a human femur, which must have delivered the blow. He gave the evidence in support of his estimate of the period during which death had occurred, the medical examiner readily approving its probability.

"Testimony indicated," the local physician went on, "and Dart checked each witness against the others, that the two women and one of the six men present were very unlikely as suspects. Any one of the other five men, four of them visitors and one the assistant or servant, could have committed the crime. One of them, an obvious drug addict, even admitted having a hand in it—rather convincingly, too; although the person who voluntarily comes forward with an admission is usually ignored——"

"Some day," the medical examiner grinned, "that sort of suspect is going to be ignored once too often—he'll turn out guilty in spite of his admission."

"Well, there's more to this chap's admission than just an admission. He had a good motive—believed that Frimbo was slowly killing his brother by some mystic spell, which only Frimbo's own death could break. And he indicated, too, that he had a paid accomplice. That, plus his obvious belief in the superstition, was what really lent a little credibility to his admission. But there was another motive brought out by Dart: One of the other men was a policy-runner. He said Frimbo had a winning system that was being used to break his boss's rival, and that the rival might have found it out and eliminated Frimbo in self-defense. Even so, of course, the actual murderer would have to be one of those five men present. Because one of them had to take that club from the front room back to the middle room where we found it—it couldn't move by itself, even if it was a thigh-bone once. Of course, the same thing applies to the handkerchief. There was the servant too, who managed to disappear completely just before the murder was discovered. He'd hardly kill the goose that laid his golden eggs, though."

"But he did disappear?"

"To the naked eye."

"What about the undertaker who came in and went out?"

"He didn't enter the front room at any time. You see, both the handkerchief and the club were unquestionably in the front room before Frimbo was killed with them. The undertaker, or anybody else, would have had to be in that room at some time—and so be seen by the others—to have got possession of those two objects.— And the undertaker had every apparent reason to want Frimbo to stay alive. Frimbo paid him outrageously high rent—and always on time."

"So who did it?"

"Well, I'll give you a list—if I don't forget somebody—in the order of their probable guilt. First is Jenkins, against whom both the clues point. It's his handkerchief, as two others testify. What makes it look worse for him is that he denies it's his. It may be just apprehension or perversity that makes him deny it—he's a hard-boiled, grouchy sort of person; but it looks on the face of it, more like he's covering up. But worse still, his right thumb print was identified on the club—which, again, he'd denied touching."

"Dart's holding him then?"

"Has to. And that's evidence that even a smart lawyer—which Jenkins probably can't afford—couldn't easily explain away. Then next, I should say, is Doty Hicks, the drug-addict, about whom I just told you. Possibly the accomplice he admits paying is Jenkins. Then—let's see—then would come Spencer—the number-king mentioned by the runner, Spider Webb. Not Spencer himself, of course, but some one of those present, paid by Spencer. That again suggests Jenkins, who might be in Spencer's employ. Or the railroad porter, Jones—Easley Jones. He might be Spencer's agent, though he tells a simple, straightforward story which can easily be checked; and there isn't a scrap of evidence against him. In fact he went in to see Frimbo first and Frimbo talked to him, as well as to three others following him. Obviously even an African mystic couldn't tell fortunes through a throat plugged up as tightly as Frimbo's was."

"Not unless he used sign language," commented the medical examiner.

"Which he couldn't in the dark," answered Dr. Archer. "Well next—the servant, against whom the only charge is his disappearance. He could figure as somebody's agent too, I suppose. But it wasn't his thumb print on the club, nor his handkerchief. Then there was Brown, a likable sort of Harlem roustabout, who, however, did not leave the front room till after the attack on Frimbo. And finally the two women, who didn't even know the man had been killed till we told them, some time after examining him."

"Well, you know how the books tell it. It's always the least likely person."

"In that case, evidence or no evidence, the guilty party is Mrs. Aramintha Snead, devout church-member and long-suffering housewife."

"Oh, no. You've very adroitly neglected to mention the really most unlikely person. I'm thinking of the physician on the case. Dr. Archer is the name, I believe?"

"Quite possible," Dr. Archer returned gravely. "Motive—professional jealousy."

"If that theory applied here," the medical examiner laughed, "I'd have to clear out myself. I'm obviously the murderer: I was ten miles away when it happened."

"Of course. You put Jenkins' thumb print on that club by telephoto, and the handkerchief——"

"I blew the handkerchief out of Jenkins' pocket and down Frimbo's throat by means of a special electric fan!"

"Some day I'm going to write a murder mystery," mused Dr. Archer, "that will baffle and astound the world. The murderer will turn out to be the most likely suspect."

"You'd never write another," said the medical examiner.

3

For half an hour, Perry Dart and three of the more experienced bluecoats searched the house. They prowled from roof to cellar in vain. At one moment, Dart thought he had discovered an adequate hiding-place beneath the laboratory bench, which stretched across the posterior wall of the rear on the second floor; for the doors to the cabinets under the bench were locked. But he soon saw that this was an impossible lead: the two doors were not adjacent; an easily opened compartment was between them filled with mechanical bric-a-brac; and the size of this and all the other unlocked compartments indicated that the locked ones were far too small to accommodate a full sized cadaver.

Again a possibility appeared in the old dumbwaiter shaft, which extended from the basement to the first floor. But inspection of this, both from above and below, disclosed that it did not contain even the dumbwaiter which must originally have occupied it. A few old ropes and a set of pulleys dangled from its roof, at the level of the first floor ceiling; between these, flashlights revealed nothing but musty space.

Eventually, the detective returned alone to the two physicians. He was still grim and angry, but thoroughly composed again. "Somebody," he said, "is going to get in trouble."

The medical examiner grinned.

"What do you make of it?"

"Only one thing to make of it—you can't prove a murder without a corpse. It's an old trick, but it's the last thing I'd expect up here."

"Somebody's smart," commented Dr. Archer.

"Exactly. And the somebody isn't working alone. Everybody who could possibly have done the job is upstairs in that room now; not a single suspect has been down here since we left the body. Every one of them has been under some policeman's eye."

"The undertaker was down here."

"In the hall, but not in this room. Day might not be as bright as his name would indicate, but surely he could see whether Crouch came in here. Day says positively that he didn't; he went straight up, and came down and went straight out. He couldn't get back in here any other way without being seen, either. The back yard and back door are covered. The roof is covered. Every possible entrance and exit have been covered from almost the moment we left this room with Frimbo on that couch."

"Then," Dr. Archer said, "the fact of the matter must be that the gentleman is still in our midst. Maybe you're dealing with secret passages and mysterious compartments."

"Wouldn't be surprised," said the medical examiner amusedly. "He was a man of mystery, wasn't he? He ought to have a few hidden chambers and such."

"We can take care of them," Dart said. "I'll have a departmental expert here early tomorrow morning—even if it is Sunday. This morning, as a matter of fact. We'll go over the house with a pair of micrometer calipers. There never was a secret chamber that didn't take up space. And one thing is sure: Jenkins knows who did this. Whoever paid him, paid for the removal of the corpse also. It's the final stroke—protects everybody, you see. No corpse, no killing. Damn!"

"Somehow," Dr. Archer reflected, "I've a very uncomfortable feeling that something is wrong."

"Not really?"

"I mean something in the way we've been reasoning. It's so easy to ignore the obvious. What obvious circumstance can we have been ignoring?" He deliberated without benefit of the others' aid. Rather suddenly he drew a breath. "No," he contradicted his own inspiration, "that's a little too obvious. And yet——"

"What the dickens are you mumbling about?" Dart asked, with pardonable impatience.

"Let's divide all the suspects," said Dr. Archer, "whom we have considered here tonight into two groups. The first will be a group about whom we can definitely say they couldn't have made off with this body. The second will be a group about whom we can't say that."

"Go ahead."

"All right. Everybody that's been here will fall into the first group—except one."

"Who?"

"The servant."

"Mmm."

"Nobody knows that servant's whereabouts since he bowed Jenkins into Frimbo's room. And if it's a matter of knowing the layout, he ought to be more qualified than anybody else to bring off this last bit of sleight-of-hand."

"How'll we prove it?"

"Find him. He has all the additional information you need. He's your key."

"If he didn't leave before we got here."

"In that case he couldn't have got back to recover the remains—not if all avenues were covered. So that he may still be—with his gruesome companion. Keep your avenues guarded until you can go over the place with—calipers, did you say? And even if he isn't here, he's got to be found. I suspect his remarks on this whole matter would save us considerable energy, even if he didn't remove the body."

"All right, doc, I accept your suggestion. But Jenkins is a bird in the hand, and I think we can persuade him to talk. Hicks, too, may have something more to say under the right circumstances. And I've a mind to hold the other two also until the body is found. A few pertinent suggestions might improve their knowledge of the case. But it may be better to let 'em go, and have 'em trailed. Find out more that way. Yep—I'm going to have everybody I let out of here tonight trailed. I won't even tell 'em about this. That's the idea——"

"Well," the medical examiner sighed, gathering himself for departure, "I can't examine what isn't here. When you guys get a body let me know. But don't find it till I've had a few hours' sleep. And no more false alarms, please."

"O.K., Dr. Winkler. It won't be a false alarm next time."

"Good-night, doctor."

Before the outside door slammed behind the departing medical examiner, Dart had reached the telephone in the rear room. He got headquarters, made a brief preliminary report of the case, and instituted a sharp lookout, through police radio broadcast and all the other devices under headquarters' control, for a Negro of the servant's description, and any clues leading to possible recovery of the dead body.

Then he and the doctor returned to the death chamber above.

Chapter Fifteen

"GREAT day in the mornin'!" exclaimed Mrs. Aramintha Snead. "What under the sun is it now?"

"Sit tight, everybody," advised Tynes. "They'll be right back."

"'Twouldn' be so bad," commented Easley Jones good-humoredly, "if we was sittin'—tight or loose. But my dawgs is 'bout to let me down."

As for the customary volubility of Bubber, that had for the moment fled. The actuality of his friend's arrest had shocked him even more than it had Jinx, for Jinx had half-anticipated it, while Bubber hadn't given the possibility a thought. He stood near his long, lanky, uncomely friend, looking rather helplessly into his face. Jinx was scowling glumly into the distance. Finally Bubber spoke:

"Did you hear what the man said?"

"Hmph!" grunted Jinx.

"Is you got any idea what it means?"

"Hmph!" Jinx grunted again.

"Hmph hell-ie!" returned Bubber, sufficiently absorbed in his ally's predicament to be oblivious of the heretofore hampering presence of ladies. "Here you is headed straight for the fryin'-pan, and all you can do is grunt. What in the world is you tol' the man to make him think you done it?"

"Tol' him little as I could," muttered Jinx.

"Well, brother, you better get to talkin'. This here's serious."

"You tellin' me?"

"Somebody got to tell you. You don' seem to have sense enough to see it for yo'self. Look here—did you have a hand in this thing sho' 'nough?"

"Hmph!" said Jinx.

"Well, you could 'a'. Man might 'a' said sump'm 'bout yo' ancestors, and you might 'a' forgot yo'self and busted him one. It's possible."

486

"I tol' 'em what the man said—word for word—near as I could. This is what I get for that."

"Guess you jes' born for evil, boy. Good luck come yo' way, take one look at you, and turn 'round and run. You sho' you ain't done it?"

"Hmph," issued a fourth time from the tall boy's nose.

"Listen, Jinx. 'Hmph' don' mean nothin' in no language. You better learn to say 'no' and say it loud and frequent. You didn't fall asleep while the man was talkin' to you? Did y'?"

"How'm I go'n' sleep with all that light in my eyes?"

"Shuh, man, I've seen you sleep with the sun in yo' eyes."

"Hadn' been for you," Jinx grumbled, "I wouldn' be in this mess."

"Hadn' been for me? Listen to the fool! What'd I have to do with it?"

"You tol' the man that was my han'kerchief, didn' y'?"

"'Cose I did. It was yo' han'kerchief. But I sho' didn' tell 'im that was yo' finger print on that club yonder."

"'Tain' no finger print o' mine. I ain' touched no club."

"Now wait a minute, big boy. Don' give the man no argument 'bout no finger print. You in trouble enough now. This ain't the first time yo' fingers got away from you."

"And 'tain't the first time yo' tongue's got away from you. You talk too doggone much."

"Maybe. But everything I've said tonight is a whisper side o' what that finger print says. That thing shouts out loud."

2

Mrs. Aramintha Snead came up to them. "Young man," she addressed Jinx, "your time has come. I'm gonna pray for you."

At this, everyone exchanged uncomfortable, apprehensive glances, and Bubber, gathering the full significance of the church lady's intention, looked at Jinx as if the latter's time had indeed come.

"Stand one side, son," ordered the lady, elbowing Bubber well out of the way.

"Yas'm," said Bubber helplessly, his face a picture of distress.

"Young man, does you know the Ten Commandments?"

Jinx could only look at her.

"Does you know the *six'* commandment? Don't know even a single one of the commandments, does y'? Well, you's a hopeless sinner. You know that, don't y'? Hopeless—doomed—on yo' way," her voice trembled and rose, "to burn in hell, where the fire is not quenched and the worm dieth not."

"Lady, he ain't no worm," protested Bubber.

"Hush yo' mouf!" she rebuked; then resumed her more holy tone. "If you'd 'a' obeyed the commandments, you wouldn't 'a' been a sinner and you wouldn't 'a' sinned. But how could you obey 'em when you didn' even know 'em?"

The silence accompanying her pause proved that this was an unanswerable point.

"If you'd obeyed the six' commandment," her voice was low and impressive, "you wouldn't 'a' killed this conjure-man here tonight. 'Cause the six' commandment say, *'Thou shalt not kill!'* And now you done broke it. Done broke it—done kilt one o' yo' fellow men. Don' matter whether he was good or bad—you done kilt him—laid 'im out cold in the flesh. The Good Book say 'A eye for a eye and a toof for a toof.' And inasmuch as you did it unto him, it shall likewise be done unto you. And you got to go befo' that great tribunal on high and 'splain why—'splain why you done it. They's only one thing, you can do now—repent. Repent, sinner, befo' it is too late!"

"Can I do it for 'im, lady?" Bubber offered helpfully.

"Let us pray," said Mrs. Snead serenely. "Let us pray."

She stood erect, she folded her arms, she closed her prominent eyes. That helped. But the benefit to Jinx of what followed was extremely doubtful.

"Lawd, here he is. His earthly form returns to the dust frum whence it came, and befo' his undyin' soul goes to eternal judgment, we want to pray for 'im. We know he's got to go. We know that soon his mortal shell will be molderin' in the ground. It ain't for that we prayin'—it ain't for that——"

"The hell it ain't," devoutly mumbled Bubber.

"Hit's for his soul we prayin'—his soul so deep-dyed, so steeped, so black in sin. Wash him, Lawd. Wash him and he shall be whiter than snow. Take from him every stain of trans-

gression, and bleach him out like a clean garment in the sunlight of righteousness."

For an unconscionable length of time she went on lamenting the hopeless sinner's iniquitous past, that had culminated
in so shameful a present, and picturing the special torments reserved in hell for the impenitent dead.

"We know he's a hopeless sinner. But, oh, make him to see
his sins—make him know it was wrong to steal, wrong to gamble, wrong to drink, wrong to swear, wrong to lie, and wrong
to kill—and make him fall on his knees and confess unto salvation befo' it is too late. Make him realize that though he can't
save his body, they's still time to save his soul. So that when
that las' day comes, and he reaches Jordan's chilly shore, and
Death puts forth his cold icy hand and lays it on his shoulder
and whispers, 'Come,' he can rise up with a smile and say, 'I'm
ready—done made my peace callin', and election sho', done
cast off this old no'count flesh and took on the spirit.'"

Then she opened her eyes and looked at the young man for
whose soul she had so long pleaded. "There now," she said,
"Don't you feel better?"

"No, ma'am," said Jinx.

"Lawd have mercy!" breathed the lady, and shaking her
head sadly from side to side, she abandoned him to the fate of
the unrepentant, returning to her place with the air of one
who at least has done his duty.

3

When the second search was over and the detective and the
physician returned to the room where the others waited, they
found a restless and bewildered company.

"What was it, doc?" Bubber promptly wanted to know, "a
boy or a girl?"

"Neither," said the physician.

"Mph!" grunted Bubber. "Was Frimbo like that too? It's
gettin' so you don' know who to trust, ain't it?"

"Brown," said Detective Dart, "you heard what I told Jenkins
before I went out?"

"Sho' did."

"He's a good friend of yours, isn't he?"

"Who—Jenkins? Friend o' mine? No 'ndeed."

"What do you mean?"

"I mean I barely know the nigger. Up till night befo' las' we was perfect strangers."

"You were pretty chummy with him tonight. You and he came here together."

"Purely accidental, mistuh. Jes' happen' to meet him on the street; he was on his way here; I come along too, thinkin' the man might gimme some high lowdown. Chummy? Shuh! Didn' you and the doc burst in on us in the front room there where we was almost 'bout to fight? Friend o' mine! 'Deed you wrong there, brother. I don' have nothin' to do with gangsters, gunmen, killers, or no folks like that. I lives above reproach. Ask anybody."

Jinx's jaw sagged, his scowl faded into a stare of amazement. It was perhaps the first time in his life when he had failed to greet the unexpected obdurately. Not even the announcement of his arrest for murder had jolted him as did this. He had never been excessively articulate, but his silence now was the silence of one struck dumb.

"All right, Brown," Dart said. "I'm glad to hear that."

"Yes, *suh*," vowed Bubber, but he did not look at Jinx.

"Now listen, you people," went on Dart. "I'm letting you go, with the exception of Jenkins and Hicks, but you're not to leave town until further word from me. Jones, that means you too. I'm sorry to have you lose any time from your job, but you may have to. Can you manage it?"

"Yas, indeed," smiled Easley Jones. "I'm layin' over till Monday anyhow, y'see, and another day or two won' matter. I can fix it up with the boss-man—no trouble 'tall."

"Good. Then you and the others are free to go."

The word "go" was scarcely out of his mouth before the whole place went suddenly black.

"Hey—what the hell!"

Even the hall lights were gone. In the sudden dark, Mrs. Snead screamed aloud, "Sweet Jesus have mercy!" There was a quick soft rustle and bustle. Dart remembered that Jinx was nearest to the hall-door. "Look out for Jenkins!" he yelled. "Block that door—he's pullin' a fast one!"

He reached into his pocket for the flashlight he had dropped there, and at the same time Dr. Archer remembered his. The two fine beams of white light shot forth together, toward the spot where Jinx had been standing; he was not there. The lights swept toward the door, to reveal Officer Green, who had automatically obstructed the exit, earnestly embracing Jinx's long form, and experiencing no small difficulty in holding the young man back. At the same time Jinx looked back over his shoulder and saw the two spots of light. To him they must have appeared to be the malevolent eyes of some gigantic monster; for with a supreme effort he wriggled out of Green's uncertain hold, and might have fled down the stairs and out into the night, had he not tripped and fallen in the hall. Green, following him blindly, tripped over him, landed upon him, and so remained until Dart's pursuing flashlight revealed the tableau.

"Smart boy," muttered the detective grimly, for it did not seem to him that Jinx's behavior might have been occasioned by momentary panic. "Who's workin' with you? Who switched off those lights? Where's the switch?"

Under Green's weight, it was all Jinx could do to answer, "Dam' 'f I know!"

"Oh, no? Got bracelets, Green? Use 'em. Where the——"

A deep strong voice in the middle of the death room struck silence to all the rising babel.

"Wait!"

Profound, abrupt quiet.

"You will find a switch in this room beside the rear door."

Somebody drew a single sharp startled breath. Dr. Archer, who had not moved from where he had been standing, swung his light around toward the sound. It fell on the head and shoulders of a stranger, seated in Frimbo's chair.

Through the subsequent silence came Martha Crouch's voice, uttering one lone, incredulous word:

"*Frimbo!*"

From the hall Dart called: "Find that switch!" One of the patrolmen stationed inside the room obeyed. The horizontal beam, and the bright sharp extension light came on together as suddenly as they had gone out. Dart came rushing back into the room. He halted, staring like everyone else with utterly unbelieving eyes at the figure that sat in the chair from which the dead body had been removed: a black man wearing a black robe and a black silk head-band; a man with fine, almost delicate features, gleaming, deep-set black eyes, and an expression of supreme intelligence and tranquillity.

Quickly, ere Dart could speak, Martha Crouch stepped forward in wide-eyed wonder.

"Frimbo—you're—alive . . . ?"

"Yes, I am alive," said the deep clear voice of the man in the chair. Something just less than a smile touched the handsome dark face.

"But they said—they said you were dead——"

"They were correct," affirmed Frimbo, without emotion.

Chapter Sixteen

Everyone in the room perceptibly shrank. So terrible a thing, so calmly said, at once impelled them to flight and held them captive.

"My Gawd!" breathed Aramintha Snead. "The man done come back!" And she with the others drew away staring and terrified. For a moment it seemed they would have fled, had the air not been turned to jelly, holding them fast. "He done done a Lazarus!" Bubber Brown whispered.

But Perry Dart's amazement gave way to exasperation. He stepped forward. "Say, what is all this, anyway? Who the devil are you?"

There was something extraordinarily disconcerting in the unwavering deep-set black eyes of the man in the chair. Even the redoubtable Dart must have felt the penetrating, yet impenetrable calmness and vitality of that undisturbed gaze as it switched to meet his own.

"I am Frimbo. You heard this lady?"

"Oh, yea? Then who was killed?"

"I was."

"You were, were you? I suppose you've risen from the dead?"

"It is not the first time I have outwitted death, my friend."

"Do you mean to sit there and tell me that you are the man I saw lying dead on that couch downstairs?"

"I am the man. And if you will be patient, I will try to explain the matter to your satisfaction."

"But how did you—what did you do? Where did you go? What's the idea dousing the lights? What do you think we are, anyway?"

"I think you are a man of intelligence, who will appreciate that coöperation achieves more than antagonism. I trust I am correct?"

"Go ahead—talk," said Dart gruffly.

"Thank you. I hope you will understand. The facts are these:

At the time I was attacked—I am uncertain myself of the precise moment, for time is of little importance to me personally —I was in a state of what you would probably call suspended animation. More exactly, I was wholly immune to activities of the immediate present, for I had projected my mind into the future—that gentleman's future—Mr. Jenkins'. During that period I was assaulted—murderously. Physically, I *was* murdered. Mentally I could not be, because mentally I was elsewhere. Do you see?"

"I never heard of such thing," said Dart, but he spoke uncertainly, for nothing could have been more impressive than this cool, deliberate deep voice, stating a mystic paradox in terms of level reason.

"Your profession, Mr. Dart," returned Frimbo, "should embrace an understanding of such matters. They do occur, I assure you, but at the moment I must not take the time to convince you personally. I can, if necessary. Now, since my apparently lifeless body, which you and Dr. Archer abandoned downstairs, was not seriously damaged in any vital particular, the return of consciousness, which is to say, the return of present mental activity, was naturally accompanied by a return of physical activity also. In short, I came to. I realized what must have happened. Naturally, I decided to assist your further efforts.

"But I have certain aversions, Mr. Dart. One is to be impeded physically, particularly by such worthy but annoying persons as gigantic minions of the law. I therefore desired to return to this room, where you were, without being obstructed by your deputies. It was not difficult to reach my laboratory without being detected, but the hallway there could not be so easily negotiated. And so I adopted the simple, if theatrical, device of completing my journey under cover of darkness. It was much simpler and pleasanter for me, you see."

For the first time tonight Dart was uncertain of procedure. Nothing in his training, thorough as it had been, covered this situation where, with a murder on the verge of solution and the definitely incriminated assailant in handcuffs, the victim walked in, sat down, and pronounced himself thoroughly alive. It swept the very foundation out from under the structure which his careful reasoning had erected and rendered it all utterly and absurdly useless. So, for the present at least, it seemed.

But Frimbo continued with a statement altogether startling in its implications:

"The fact remains, of course, that a murder was committed. I live, but someone killed me. Someone is guilty." The voice took on a new hardness. "Someone must pay the penalty."

Something in that suggestion brought method back into Dart's mind. "Where were you when we were searching the house just now?" said he.

"Obviously, we simply were not in the same place at the same time. That is nothing extraordinary."

"How do I know it was you who was killed?"

"You saw me, did you not? My identity is easy to establish. Mrs. Crouch knows me, as she has indicated, by sight. The other visitors may not have been able to see me well, but they will perhaps recognize my voice."

"Sho' is the same voice," vowed Jinx, unaware that he was testifying against himself.

"Are you sure of that?" Dart asked.

"Sho' is," repeated Jinx, and the others murmured assent.

"Well," Dart turned to the doctor, "at least it wasn't the servant doing the talking."

But Dr. Archer now spoke. "I beg your pardon, Dart, but may I point out that it is of no consequence whether this gentleman is Frimbo or not. The only question of importance is whether he is the man whom we saw downstairs."

Thereupon Frimbo said, "Dr. Archer, who pronounced me dead, will naturally be most reluctant to identify me with the corpse, since the implication would be that he had been mistaken in his original pronouncement. Thereupon I must insist that he examine me now."

The physician was slightly surprised. "I should think you would prefer someone less prejudiced," he said.

"On the contrary. If you identify me with the man you yourself pronounced dead, there can be no further question. You are the only person who would be reluctant to do so. You will allow only the most reliable evidence to overcome that reluctance."

Dr. Archer stared for a moment from behind his spectacles

into the serene dark face of this astonishing fellow, sensing for the first time perhaps how his own irrepressible curiosity was to lead him shortly into an investigation of the most extraordinary personality he had ever confronted.

Then he went over to the seated figure. "Will you please remove your head-band? The wound would hardy be healed so soon."

"You will find the wound unhealed," said Frimbo, complying. The silken headdress removed, there appeared a small white dressing affixed by adhesive, over the right temple. "Look beneath the dressing," suggested the African.

Dr. Archer appreciated the ever so faintly malicious little irony, for he answered gravely:

"I shall look even further than that."

He detached the dressing, removed it, and examined a short scalp wound thus disclosed, a wound apparently identical with the one he had probed over an hour ago.

"I delayed a moment to dress it, of course," said Frimbo.

The physician inspected carefully every peculiarity of feature that might answer the question. To the lay eye, certainly there was nothing in this strikingly vivid countenance to recall that other death-distorted visage. But violent death—or even near death—often performs strange transfigurations. Dr. Archer eventually stood erect.

"As nearly as I can determine," he said, "this is the same man. I should request him to submit to a further test, however, before I commit myself finally—a test which will require some little time."

"Whatever the doctor wishes," agreed Frimbo.

"I have in my bag a small amount of blood on a dressing with which I swabbed the wound before probing it. There are one or two tests which can be used as convincing evidence, provided I may have a sample of your blood now for comparison."

"An excellent idea, doctor. Here"—Frimbo drew back the wide sleeve of his black satin robe, baring a well-formed forearm—"help yourself."

The physician promptly secured a tourniquet just above the elbow, moistened a sponge with alcohol, swabbed a small area, where large superficial veins stood out prominently, carefully removed a needle from its sterile tube container, deftly inserted it into a vein, caught a few drops of blood in the tube, loosed the tourniquet, withdrew the needle, and pressed firmly a moment with his swab on the point of puncture.

"Thank you," he said, the operation over.

"How long will this take you, doc?" Dart asked.

"At least an hour. Perhaps two. I'll have to go back to my office to do it."

"You will do the usual agglutination tests, of course?" Frimbo inquired.

"Yes," said Dr. Archer, unable to veil his astonishment that this apparent charlatan should even know there were such tests. "You are familiar with them?"

"Perfectly. I am somewhat of a biologist, you see. Psychology is really a branch of biology."

"You subscribe to the Spencerian classification?" Dr. Archer said.

It was Frimbo's turn to express surprise, which appeared in the slight lift of his lids.

"In that particular, yes."

"I should like to discuss the subject with you."

"I should be very glad indeed. I have met no one competent to do so for years. Today is Sunday. Why not later today?"

"At what hour?"

"Seven this evening?"

"Splendid."

"I shall look forward to seeing you."

2

At this point, a surreptitious remark from Bubber, who had been unwontedly silent, drew attention back to the matter in hand.

"He sho' can talk—for a dead man, can't he?"

"Listen, Frimbo," said Dart. "You say you were killed. All right. Who killed you?"

"I don't know, I'm sure."

"Why don't you?"

"I have tried to explain, Mr. Dart, that I was in a mental state equivalent to being absent. My entire mind was elsewhere—contemplating that gentleman's future. I can no more answer your question than if I had been sound asleep."

"Oh, I see. Would it be asking too much of this strange power of yours if I suggested that you use it to determine the identity of your assailant?"

"I'm glad you suggested it, even ironically. I was reluctant to interfere with your methods. You already have what you believe to be damning evidence against Jenkins. You may be right. But you still have to make sure of the items of motive and possible complicity. Is that not true?"

"Yes."

"Since I am the victim and thus the most personally interested party, I suggest that you allow me to solve this matter for you."

"How?"

"By the use of what you sarcastically call my strange power. If you will have all the suspects here on Monday night at eleven, I will provide you with the complete story of what took place here tonight and why."

"What are you going to do—reconstruct the crime?"

"In a sense, yes."

"Why can't you do that now? All the suspects are here. Here's Jenkins. His finger print on the club that inflicted that wound can't mean but one thing—he handled that club. Why don't you just read his mind and find out what made him do it?"

"It's not so simple as that, my friend. Such a thing requires preparation. Tonight there is not time. And I am tired. But see, I am not suggesting that you neglect doing any single thing that you would have done anyway. Proceed as if I had not returned—I insist that my being alive does not alter the fundamental criminal aspect of this case—proceed, hold whom you will, determine such facts as you can by every means at your disposal, establish your case—then accept my suggestion, if you care to, simply as a corroboration of what you have concluded. Consider what I shall show you on Monday night as just a check on what you already know."

Dart was impressed by the turn of the suggestion. "I

suppose," he mused, "I could change the charge to felonious assault——"

Frimbo said, "You are working on a common fallacy, my friend. You are making the common assumption that any creature who is alive cannot have been dead. This is pure assumption. If a body which has presented all the aspects of death, resumes the functions of life, we explain the whole thing away merely by saying, 'He was not dead.' We thus repudiate all our own criteria of death, you see. I cannot think in this self-contradictory fashion. Physically, I was dead by all the standards accepted throughout the years as evidence of death. I was so pronounced by this physician, who has already shown himself to be unusually competent. Had I been anyone else on earth, I should still be dead. But because I have developed special abilities and can separate my mental from my physical activities, the circumstances were such that I could resume the aspects of life. Why must you, on that account, assume that the death was any less actual than the life? Why must you change the charge from murder, which it unquestionably was, to assault, which is only part of the story? Must I pay a premium for special abilities? Must I continually reexpose myself to a criminal who has already carried out his purpose? He has killed—let him die also. If he is able, as I was, to resume life afterwards, I am sure I shall have no objection."

Dart shook his head. "No living person could convince a judge or a jury, that he'd been really murdered. Even if I believed your argument, which I don't, I couldn't arrest this man for murder. A conviction of murder requires the production of a corpse—or tangible evidence of a corpse. I can't present you as a corpse. I'd be the joke of the force."

"Perhaps you are right," Frimbo conceded. "I had not considered the—force."

"Still," Dr. Archer injected, "Mr. Frimbo's suggestion can do no harm. All he says is proceed as if he had not returned. That's what you'd have done anyway. Then, if you like, he will produce additional evidence—Monday night. Personally, I'd like to see it."

"So would I," Dart admitted. "Don't misunderstand me. My only point is that if this is the same man, it's no longer murder."

"There's still plenty to be answered, though," the doctor reminded him. "Jenkins' stout denial in the face of the strongest evidence, the probability of complicity, the motive——"

"And," popped unexpectedly from Bubber, "where that flunky disappeared to, all of a sudden."

Frimbo apparently rarely smiled, but now his awesome dark face relaxed a little. "That need not worry you. My assistant has been with me a long time. He is like a brother. He lives here. He could not possibly be guilty of this crime."

"Then," inquired Bubber, "how come he hauled hips so fast?"

"He is free to leave at eleven every night. It is our understanding and our custom. At that hour tonight, he no doubt took his departure as usual."

"Departure for where—if he lives here?" asked Dart.

"Even servants are entitled to their hour or two of relaxation. He takes his at that time. You need have no doubts about him. Even if I found him guilty, I should not press charges. And I assure you he will be present Monday night."

Later, Detective Dart conveyed to Dr. Archer the considerations which had influenced his decision. First, it had been his experience that in Harlem the most effective method of crime detection was to give your man enough rope with which to hang himself. If Jenkins' denial was true, in whole or part, careful observation of the behavior of the other suspects would reveal something incriminating. Believing himself free and unwatched, the actual criminal—or accomplice—would soon betray himself. The forty-eight hour interval would reveal much about all the suspects. Secondly, if any suspect demurred on the matter of returning or actually failed to return on Monday night, that fact, together with whatever was discovered meanwhile by trailers, would carry its own weight. In short, it was Dart's persuasion that in Harlem one learned most by seeking least—to force an issue was to seal it in silence forever.

And therefore, he now complied with the suggestion that the company be reassembled here on Monday night.

"Very well. I agree. Jenkins and Hicks will be returned under guard. Do any of you other ladies and gentlemen feel that you will be unable to be present?"

No one demurred.

"It is understood, then, that you will be present here at eleven P.M. on Monday. That is all. You are free to go."

The visitors departed, each in his own manner: Jinx, shackled to Officer Green, glowered unforgivingly at Bubber, who for once did not indulge in an opportunity to mock. Doty Hicks glared helplessly at the superbly calm figure of the man whose death he had admittedly sought and failed to effect. Martha Crouch seemed about to stop and speak to Frimbo, but simply smiled and said, "Good-night." Easley Jones and Aramintha Snead made their way out almost stumblingly, so unable were they to remove their fascinated stares from the man who had died and now lived.

3

The detective and the doctor took leave of each other in the street below.

"I will start this test tonight and finish it in the morning," promised the latter. "You'll get the result as soon as I am reasonably certain of it."

"Could he really be the same guy, doc? Is that suspended animation stuff on the level?"

"Cases have been reported. This is the first in my experience."

"You sound skeptical."

"I am more than skeptical in this case, my suspicious friend. I am positively repudiative. Somehow, I stubbornly cling to the belief that the man I examined was dead, completely and permanently."

"What? Well, why didn't——"

"And I too am of the common persuasion which Mr. Frimbo so logically exposed, that one who comes to life was never dead. Logic to the contrary notwithstanding, I still believe the dead stay dead. And, while the corpse may be hard to produce, I still believe you have a murder on your hands."

"But you practically admitted he was the same man. Why?"

"I found no evidence to the contrary—nothing decisive. He looked enough like the dead man, and he had an identically similar wound."

"Explainable how?"

"Self-inflicted, perhaps."

"Not unless he had seen the original."

"If he removed the corpse, he did see the original."

"Then why didn't you spring that removable bridge on him? I saw you look at his teeth."

"Because his teeth were perfect."

"What! Why, that would have shown he wasn't the same man right there!"

"Wait a minute now. When the bridge was first found, we considered the possibilities: It might be the corpse's, it might be his assailant's——"

"And decided it must be his—the corpse's."

"But we didn't check that up by going back to the corpse at once. We said we'd do so when the medical examiner arrived. But when the medical examiner arrived the corpse was gone."

"But you just said Frimbo's teeth were perfect. So the bridge can't possibly be his."

"That doesn't prove it belonged to the corpse. It might or might not—we never did establish the point."

"That's right—we didn't," Dart admitted.

"Which allows for a third possibility which we haven't even considered—that the bridge may belong to neither the victim nor the assailant. It could conceivably belong to anybody."

"You've got me there. Anybody who'd ever been in that room could have dropped it."

"Yes—out of a pocket with a hole in it—after having found the thing on the street."

"All Frimbo would have to do would be know nothing about it."

"Exactly. The identification of the ownership of that bridge is to find the person it was made for. And it must fit that person. So you see I had only a conviction—no tangible support whatever. It would have been worse than useless to show our cards then and there. But now, if these two blood specimens reposing in my bag present certain differences which I anticipate, I shall advise you to proceed with the total demolition of yonder dwelling—a vandalism which you have already contemplated, I believe?"

"Gosh, doc, it would be so much easier in French. Say it in French."

"And if you shouldn't find the elusive corpse there—a possibility with which I have already annoyed you tonight—you may proceed to demolish the house next to the right, then the next to the left, and so on until all Harlem lies in ruins. An excellent suggestion, I must say. You, after all, would only be doing your duty, while ever so many people would be infinitely better off if all Harlem did lie in ruins."

"And if we do find a corpse, Frimbo becomes a suspect himself!"

"With things to explain."

Dart whistled. "What a mess that would be!"

"Testicles," mused the other.

"All right, doc. It's irregular, of course, but I believe it's the best way. And I'd rather work with you than—some others. I'm dependin' on you."

"You have the house covered?"

"Sewed up back and front. And we'll keep it sewed up from now till we're satisfied."

"Satisfied—hm—have you reflected on the futility of satisfaction, Dart?"

"Never at one o'clock in the morning, doc. So long. Thanks a lot. See you in Macy's window."

"Shouldn't be at all surprised," murmured Dr. John Archer.

Chapter Seventeen

I

WITH an unquestionable sense of humor, the sun grinned down upon the proud pageantry of Seventh Avenue's Sunday noontime, beaming just a little more brightly and warmly than was strictly necessary for a day in February. Accordingly, the brisk air was tempered a little, and the flocks that flowed out from the innumerable churches could amble along at a more leisurely pace than winter usually permitted. This gave his celestial majesty time to observe with greater relish the colorful variety of this weekly promenade: the women with complexions from cream to black coffee and with costumes, individually and collectively, running the range of the rainbow; the men with derbies, canes, high collars, spats, and a dignity peculiar to doormen, chauffeurs, and headwaiters.

Bubber Brown had his place in the sun, too, and he swaggered proudly along with the others, for although Bubber was molded on the general plan of a sphere, his imitation camel's hair overcoat was designed to produce an illusion of slenderness and height, with broad shoulders, a narrowly belted waist and skirts long enough to conceal the extraordinary bowing of his legs. Although he boasted no derby, no cane, and no spats, still with his collar turned swankily up, the brim of his felt hat snapped nattily down, and his hands thrust nonchalantly into his coat pockets, even the rotund Bubber achieved fair semblance of a swagger.

This he maintained as he moved in the stream of church people by humming low yet lustily the anything but Christian song of the moment:

"I'll be glad when you're dead, you rascal you. . . ."

On he strolled past churches, drugstores, ice-cream parlors, cigar stores, restaurants, and speakeasies. Acquaintances standing in entrances or passing him by offered the genial insults which were characteristic Harlem greetings:

"What you say, blacker'n me?"

"How you doin', short-order?"

"Ole Eight-Ball! Where you rollin', boy?"

In each instance, Bubber returned some equivalent reply, grinned, waved, and passed on. He breathed deeply of the keen sweet air, appraised casually the trim, dark-eyed girls, admired the swift humming motors that flashed down the Avenue.

But at frequent intervals a frown ruffled his customarily bland countenance, and now and then he foreswore his humming and bowed his head in meditation, shaking it vainly from side to side.

When he reached the corner of 135th Street, he stopped. The stream flowed on past him. He looked westward toward the precinct station-house. Heaving a tremendous sigh, he turned and headed in that direction.

But when he reached the station-house, instead of stopping, he strode on past it as rapidly as if no destination had been further from his mind. At Eighth Avenue he turned south and walked three blocks, then east toward Seventh again. A moment later he halted, aware of a commotion just across the street.

This was a quiet side street, but people were stopping to look. Others, appearing from nowhere, began to run toward the point of agitation, and soon dozens were converging upon the scene like refuse toward a drain. Bubber approached the rim of the clutter of onlookers and craned his neck with normal curiosity.

The scene was the front stoop of an apartment house. Two men and a girl were engaged in loud and earnest disagreement.

"He did!" the girl accused hotly. "He come up to me on that corner——"

"If you was jes' man enough to admit it," menaced her champion.

"Aw, boogy, go diddle," the accused said contemptuously. "I never even seen your——"

Clearly, whatever his epithet might have signified at other times, at this moment it meant action; for hardly had Bubber time to comment, "Uh-oh—that's trouble——" before the girl's protector had smacked the offender quite off the stoop and into the crowd.

The latter, somewhat like a ball on an elastic, came instantaneously and miraculously back at the other. As he flew forward, the girl was heard to yell, "Look out, Jim! He's got a knife!" Jim somehow flung off the attack for the moment and reached for his hip. Apparently every onlooker saw that sinister gesture at the same instant, for the crowd, with one accord, dispersed as quickly and positively as a moment ago it had converged upon this spot—as though indeed, some sudden obstruction had caused the drain to belch back. Two quick loud pistol reports punctuated that divergent scattering. Inquisitive dark heads thrust out of surrounding windows vanished. The victim lay huddled with wide staring eyes at the foot of the stoop, and the man with the gun and his girl sped back into the foyer, appropriated the empty elevator, banged the gate shut, and vanished upward.

2

Bubber did not slacken his rapid pace till he was back at the corner of Eighth Avenue and 135th Street, a few feet from the precinct station. Then he removed his hat and with his bright-colored handkerchief mopped his beaded brow and swore.

"Damn! What a place! What is this—a epidemic?" The thought recalled his superstition. He opened his mouth and gazed awestruck into space. "Jordan River! That's number two! One las' night and another one today. Wonder whose turn it'll be nex'?"

Inadvertently, pondering the horror of the mysterious, he allowed his feet to wander whither they listed. They conveyed him slowly back toward the station-house, the abrupt presence of which struck so suddenly upon his consciousness as almost to startle him into further flight. But his feet were in no mood for further flight; they clung there to the pavement while Bubber's original purpose returned and made itself felt.

For a moment he stood hesitant before the imposing new structure, peering uncertainly in. There was no visible activity. He moved closer to the entrance, gazed into the spacious, not uninviting foyer, looked up and down the street and into the foyer again.

"They's an excuse," he mumbled, "for gettin' dragged into jail, but jes' walkin' in of yo' own free will—ain' no sense in that. . . ."

Nevertheless, with an air of final resolution, he mounted the steps, tried and opened the door. "Hope it works jes' as easy from the other side," he said, and entered.

He approached the desk sergeant.

"Y'all got a boy in here name Jinx Jenkins?"

"When was he brought in?"

"Las' night."

"Charge?"

"Suh?"

"What charge?"

"Couldn' been no charge, broke as he was."

"What was he brought in for—drunk, fightin', or what?"

"Oh. He didn' do nothin'. He jes' got in the wrong house."

"Whose house?"

"Frimbo's. You know—the conjure-man."

"Oh—that case. Sure he's here. Why?"

"Can I see him?"

"What for?"

"Well, y'see, he figgers sump'm I said put him in a bad light. I jes' wanted to let him know how come I said it, that's all."

"Oh, that's all, huh? Well that ain't enough."

But the lieutenant on duty happened to be crossing the foyer at the time and heard part of the conversation. He knew the circumstances of the case, and had planned to be present at the questioning for which, in part, Jinx was being held. With the quick grasp of every opportunity for information that marks the team-work of a well-trained investigative organization, he nodded significantly to the sergeant and promptly departed to arrange a complete recording of all that should transpire between Jinx and his visitor.

"You a friend o' his?" the sergeant asked.

"No—we ain' no special friends," said Bubber. "But I don't aim we should be no special enemies neither."

"I see. Well, in that case, I guess I could let you see him a few minutes. But no monkey-business, y'understand?"

"Monkey-business in a jail-house, mistuh? Do I look dumb, sho' 'nough?"

"O.K."

3

In due time and through proper channels, it came to pass that Bubber confronted his tall lean friend, who stood gloomily behind a fine steel grille.

"Hello, Judas," was Jinx's dark greeting.

"Boy," Bubber said, "it's everybody's privilege to be dumb, but they ain' no sense in abusin' it the way you do."

"Is that what you come here to say?"

"I done nearly had what I come here to say scared out o' me. I done seen number two."

"Number two?"

"Yea, man."

"Number two—that's what the little boy said to his mammy. You big and black enough to——"

"Death on the moon, boy. First one las' night, second one today—not ten minutes ago—'round on 132nd Street. Two boogies got in a li'l argument over a gal, and first thing you know—bong—bong! There was one of 'em stretched out dead on the ground and me lookin' at him."

"No."

"Yea, man. This Harlem is jes' too bad. But I tol' you I'm go'n' stare three corpses in the face. They's one mo' yet."

"Hmph. And you call me dumb."

"What you mean?"

"That wasn' no corpse you stared in the face las' night. Las' I remember, he was sittin' up in that chair talkin' pretty lively, like a natchel man."

"Yea, but he ain' no natchel man—he's a conjure-man. He was sho' 'nough dead, jes' like he said. He 'jes knows sump'm, that's all."

"He knows sump'm, I don't doubt that. Tol' me plenty. But any time a man knows enough to come to life after he's dead, he knows too much."

"Reckon that's how come he got kilt, 'cause he knows too much. Sho' was the same man though, wasn't he?"

"Far as I could see. But 'course that don' mean much—all coons look alike to me."

There was a moment's silence, whereupon Jinx added, with meaning, "And no matter how well you know 'em, you can't trust 'em."

"Listen, boy, you all wrong. 'Course I know you can't help it, 'cause what few brains you had is done dried up and been sneezed out long ago. But even you ought to be able to see my point."

"'Cose I see yo' point. Yo' point was, you was savin' yo' own black hide. If you admit you a friend o' mine, maybe you inhale some jail-air too. Jes' like all boogies—jes' let the man say 'Boo!' and yo' shirt tail roll up yo' back like a window shade."

"All right—all right. But see if this can penetrate yo' hard, kinky head. What good am I——"

"None whatsoever."

"Wait a minute, will you please? What good am I to you if I'm right here in jail alongside o' you?"

"What good is you to me anywhere?"

"Well, if I'm out, at least I got a chance to find out who done it, ain't I?"

Jinx relented a little, reluctantly comprehending.

"Yea, you got a chance," he muttered. "But you go'n' need mo'n a chance to find out who done that. Right under my nose, too, with me sittin' there—and if I seen anybody, you did."

"Well cheer up, long boy. You ain' got nothin' to worry 'bout. The man's alive and you heard what the detective said—all they can hold you for is assault."

"No," reflected Jinx sardonically. "I ain' got nothin' to worry 'bout. They tell me the most I can get for assault is twenty years."

"Twenty—whiches?"

"Years. Them things growin' out the side o' yo' head. And all twenty of 'em jes' that color. It sho' is a dark outlook."

"Mph!"

"Who's gruntin' now?"

"Both of us. But shuh, man, they can't do that to you."

"I know they can't. You know they can't. But do they know they can't?"

"Don't worry, boy. Leave everything to me. I'll find out who done this if it takes me the whole twenty years."

"Hmph! Well, it's time you done sump'm right. When you could 'a' kep' yo' mouth shut, you was talkin'. 'Sho' that's Jinx's handkerchief.' And when you could 'a' talked, you kep' yo' mouth shut. 'Friend o' mine? No 'ndeed!'—All right. Whatever you go'n' do, get to doin' it, 'cause these accommodations don't suit me. Twenty years! Twenty years from now Harlem'll be full o' Chinamen."

"Don't blame me for all of it. I never would 'a' been in the conjure-man's place if you hadn't said 'come on let's go.'"

"What you go'n' do?"

"I'm go'n' do some detectin', that's what. What's use o' bein' a private detective if I can't help out a friend? I'm workin' on a theory already, boy."

"First work you done since you quit haulin' ashes for the city."

"That was good trainin' for a detective. I used to figure out jes' what happened the night befo' by what I found in the ash can nex' mornin'. If I see a torn nightgown and a empty whiskey bottle——"

"I've heard all 'bout that. What's yo' theory?"

"The flunky, boy. He done it, sho's you born. I'm go'n' find him and trick him into a confession."

"What makes you think he done it?"

" 'Cause he run away, first thing."

"But didn't you hear the man say he was s'posed to leave by eleven o'clock?"

"That would make it all the easier for him, wouldn't it? If he s'posed to be gone th'ain't nothin' suspicious 'bout him *bein'* gone, don't you see?"

"M-m."

"He figured on that."

"How'n hell'd he get my handkerchief?"

"He took it out yo' pocket. 'Member when Doty Hicks fell down in a faint and we all scrambled 'round and helped him up?"

"Yea——"

"That's when he took it."

"He could 'a'. But what would he want to kill his boss for?"

"Boy, ain't you ever had a boss? They's times when you feel like killin' the best boss in the world, if you could get away with it."

"Well, whoever you hang it on, it's all right with me."

"If worse comes to worse," Bubber's voice sank to a whisper, "I can swear I seen him take yo' handkerchief out yo' pocket."

"No," Jinx demurred, "ain' no need o' you goin' to hell jes' 'cause I go to jail."

"I'm go'n' get you out o' this."

"When you startin'?"

"Tonight."

"Don' hurry. Nex' week'll be plenty o' time."

"Tonight. By tomorrer I'll have the dope on that flunky. You watch."

"I'm watchin'," said Jinx. "And all I got to say is, Sherlock, do yo' stuff."

Chapter Eighteen

B Y ELEVEN-THIRTY the same Sunday morning, Dr. Archer had completed his morning calls—both of them. He returned to his office, where he found three gentlemen awaiting him. Two were patients, the third was Detective Perry Dart.

"Urgent?" he asked Dart.

"Nope. Take the others."

The others were soon disposed of; the first pleaded a bad cold and got his liquor prescription, the second pleaded hard times and borrowed three dollars.

"Come in here," the physician then summoned Dart, and led the way through his treatment room with its adjustable table, porcelain stands, glass-doored steel cabinets shining with bright—and mostly virgin—instruments, into a smaller side room which had done duty as a butler's pantry in the days before Harlem changed color.

"Something like Frimbo's," commented the detective, looking admiringly around.

"In part, yes. That is, Frimbo has some clinical stuff, but that's only a fraction of his, while it's all of mine. He has chemistry apparatus that a physician's lab would never need except for research, and few practicing physicians have time for that kind of research. More than that, he has some electrical stuff there that only a physicist or mechanic would have, and I'm sure I saw something like a television receptor on one end of the bench—remember that affair like a big lens set in a square box? Those specimens sort of stole the show and we didn't take time to examine around carefully. But all I've got is what's necessary for routine clinical tests—some glassware, a few standard reagents, a centrifuge, a microscope, and that's about all."

"I guess all labs look alike to me."

"Well, there's enough here to investigate certain properties of our friend's blood, any day. If the two specimens present no differences that we can determine, we're stumped—so far as murder goes. But if they do——"

"Is this something new, doc?"

"New? No, why?"

"Well, of course I knew they could tell whether it was human blood. I know of plenty of cases where blood was found on a weapon, and the suspect claimed it was chicken's blood or sheep's blood, but the doctors came along and showed it was human. I should think that would be hard enough."

"Not so hard. A chap—Gay, I believe—sensitized some lab animals—guinea pigs or rabbits or whatever happened to be around—to various serums. You see, if you do it right, you can inject a little serum into an animal and he'll develop what they call antibodies for that serum. Antibody's a substance which the blood manufactures to combat certain things that get into it but haven't any business there. But the point is that each antibody is specific—hostile to just one certain thing. From the viewpoint of the health of the human family, that's too bad. Be swell if you could just inject a little of anything and get a general immunity to everything. But from the viewpoint of criminology it's useful, because if you're smart enough, you can tell whether your suspect is lying or not about the blood on his weapon. You just dissolve your blood off the weapon, and test it against the sensitized blood from each of your known animals. When you get a reaction you know, your unknown is the same as the one which reacted to it. See?"

Dart shook his head.

"I'll take you guys' word for that stuff. But if it's that hard to tell human blood from other kinds, I should think it would be still harder to tell one human's blood from another human's blood." Dart looked around. "And I don't see the first guinea pig."

"So it would seem. But there are many ways in which one man's blood differs from another's. Take the Wasserman reaction. Mine may be negative and yours positive——"

"Hold on, doc, don't get personal."

"Or we may both be positive, but different in degree."

"That's better."

"And there are plenty of other germs, which, like the germ of syphilis, bring about definite changes in the blood. In many cases these changes can be determined, so that you can say that this blood came from a fellow who had so-and-so, while that blood came from a fellow who didn't have so-and-so."

"Go ahead. How about Frimbo's?"

"Or take blood transfusions. You know everybody can't give his blood to everybody—in many cases it would be fatal—was fatal before blood types were known about. Now it's known a man might be eager to give his blood to save his sweetheart, and yet that might be the quickest way of killing her."

Dart's black eyes were alive with interest.

"That's right. I remember——"

"That's because one blood may contain something that doesn't harmonize with something in another blood."

"Like what, doc?"

"It's mainly a matter of serum and red corpuscles. Some serum will destroy some corpuscles——"

"Oh, I see," said Dart.

"So to make sure this doesn't happen, every transfusion now has to be preceded by a certain blood examination known as typing. Couple of bright gentlemen named Janski and Moss looked into the matter not so many years ago and found that all human blood falls into four general types. Since then a flock of sub-types have been established, but the four basic ones still suffice for ordinary procedures. Everybody falls into one of the four groups—and stays there."

Dart was eagerly curious.

"And Frimbo's blood isn't in the same group with the other?"

"I don't know. Haven't tested it out yet—just got ready and had to go deliver twins. That allowed you to get here just in time for the performance. But for intrahuman differences, you'd hardly find any two people with every degree of every blood reaction precisely identical."

"Do your stuff, doc. I'm getting nervous."

"All right. Now look. See this?" He held up a test tube in the bottom of which was a small amount of pinkish fluid. "This is the unknown serum, extracted from the dressing with which I sponged the wound in the dead man's scalp. It's diluted, of course, and discolored because of haemolysis of the red cells——"

"Don't mind me, doc. Go right ahead."

"—but that doesn't matter much. And this tube is Frimbo's serum, and this is a suspension of Frimbo's red cells, which I made last night. By the way, Dart, would you give up some of your blood to find this thing out?"

"How much, doc?"

"He hesitates in the pursuit of his duty," murmured the doctor. "Well, never mind—I may not need it. I may not even need my own."

"You mean you were figuring on bleeding yourself, too?"

"I happen to know I'm under Type II. You remember I mentioned that all tests are checks against a known specimen."

"And you've got to have a known specimen?"

"Unless we're very lucky. We may be able to prove these two specimens different without actually having to type them. Well, now look. We'll take this capillary pipette and remove a drop of this unknown serum and place it thus on a microscopic slide. Then we'll take a nichrome loop so, and remove a loopful of Professor Frimbo's best red cells, and stir them gently into the drop of serum, thus, spreading same smoothly into a small circular area in this manner. Watch carefully. The hand is quicker than the eye. Now then, a cover glass, and under the microscope it goes. We adjust the low power with a few deft turns and gaze into the mysteries of the beyond. Dart, we seldom reflect upon what goes on at the other end of the barrel of a microscope: challenge, conquest, combat, victory, defeat, life, death, reproduction—every possible relationship of living beings—the very birth of the world there in a droplet of moisture." With both eyes open he was manipulating the fine adjustment. "Do you know what a fellow said to me once? I came up behind him and asked him what he was staring down his mike so steadily for—what did he hope to find? He said one word without looking up. He said, 'God.'" He focused the instrument satisfactorily, peered a moment, then stood aside, "You and I are more practical, aren't we? All we hope to find is a murderer. Come on—try your luck."

"Me?"

"Of course. Look, look, and keep looking. If you see anything happen, don't keep it a secret."

Dart, squinting one eye shut, gazed with the other down the barrel. "A lot of little reddish dots," he announced.

"What are they doing?"

"Nothing." Dart grinned. "Must be Negro blood."

"Jest not, my friend. It is Sunday. All blood reposes. But keep looking."

"Well, maybe they are moving a little. Hey—sure! They *are* moving—so slow you can hardly see it, though."

"In what direction?"

"Every direction. Boy, this is good. They can't make up their minds."

"That sounds as though——"

"Hey—Judas Priest—what's this? Look, doc!"

"You look and tell me about it. I might let my imagination run away with me."

"These things are going into a huddle. No—into a flock of huddles. No kidding—they're slowly collecting in little bunches."

"Are you sure?"

"Am I sure? What does it mean, doc? Here, take a look."

Dr. Archer complied. "Hm—I think I can safely say your observations are correct—though 'agglutination' is a far more elegant term than 'huddle.'"

"But what's the answer?"

"The answer is that nobody's red cells could conceivably behave like that in their own serum. Not even a magician's."

"You mean that's the destruction you were talking about?"

"Yes, sir. The first step in it. That's as far as we need to go in vitro. In vivo, the process goes on to dissolution, disintegration, haemolysis—oh, there's lots of nice words you can call it. But whatever you call it, this serum gives those corpuscles —hell."

Dart's eyes glowed.

"Then Frimbo and the corpse were two different people?"

"And still are. And you and I are two lucky people, because we don't have to play school any longer—not with these, anyway."

"The son of a bedbug! I'm going to put him *under* the jail—trying to kid somebody like that. Where's my hat?"

"What's your hurry, mister? He isn't going anywhere."

"How do I know he isn't?"

"Can he get out without being seen by your men?"

"That's right. But why wait?"

"If you grab him now—if you even let him suspect what we know, he'll close up like a vault. My humble opinion is that he's got a lot of information you need—if he gets lockjaw, you'll never convict him."

"Then what's your idea?"

"Indulge me, my friend. I'm smart. I want to keep that appointment with him this evening——"

"He may be back in Bunghola, or wherever he hails from, by then."

"Not the slightest chance. Frimbo is staging a party tomorrow night for just one reason—he's going to fasten the blame for that murder, as he still calls it, and rightly, on somebody—somebody else. Your best bet is to have all the counter-evidence ready to confront him with at the same time. Don't worry, he'll be there."

"Well this certainly is enough to make him a suspect."

"You've got suspects enough already. What you want now is a murderer. It's true that Frimbo was not the corpse. This proves that. It is also true that he must have managed to make away with the corpse; then, to cover that, masqueraded as the corpse—even inflicted a wound on his head resembling that of the corpse." Dr. Archer could talk very plainly and directly on occasion. "But there are lots of things between that conclusion and proof of his being the murderer. All that we know is that Frimbo lied. We do not know why he lied. And he isn't the only liar in this case—Jenkins lied, probably Hicks lied, for all I know Webb lied——"

"Say that reminds me! That Webb was on the right track. He was telling the truth, at least in part. I meant to tell you, but I got so interested in this other thing. There was a knock-down and drag-out shooting this morning on 132nd Street. Apparently an argument over a girl, but who do you suppose the victim was? One of Brandon's best-known runners. Yes, sir. Well, it took the boys exactly forty-five minutes to nab the guy that did it. And who do you s'pose *he* was? Spencer's first lieutenant, boy named Eagle Watson. Of course he'll get out of it—good lawyers and all—girl'll swear the victim attacked her and turned on him when he came to her rescue—plenty o' bona fide witnesses—self-defense—easy. But we know what's behind it—and Webb told the truth about it. There actually is

a Spencer-Brandon policy feud on; Spencer's getting the worst
of it, and he's declared war on the whole Brandon outfit. The
reason why he's getting the worst of it can only be because he's
losing a lot of money and losing it fast, and the reason he de-
clares war on the rival outfit is because he figures they are responsible. If he figures that, he may have got wind of this
Frimbo's having a hand in it and tried to pull a fast one last
night. Only that doesn't hitch up with this blood business at
all, does it?"

"There was once a man—nice fellow, too, even though he
was a policeman—who delivered some remarks on premature
conclusions. His idea was to fit conclusions to facts, as I recall,
not facts to conclusions. And he admitted—nay, insisted—that,
by such a system, it would only be necessary to accumulate
enough facts and they'd sort of draw their own conclusions.
You will observe that this fellow was a lineal descendant of
Francis Bacon—despite their difference of complexion—in
that he inherited the tendency to reason inductively rather
than deductively. But such is the frailty of human-kind that
even this fortunate chap occasionally fell into the error of
letting his imagination, instead of his observation, draw the
conclusions; whereupon he would suddenly look about in bewilderment and say that something didn't hitch up with something."

"O.K., doc. The point of all that being it's still too soon to
speculate?"

"The point being that where more facts can be gathered, it
is always too soon to speculate."

"Well—I guess he'll keep. But if you let him get away from
me——"

"My dear fellow, permit me to remind you that in that case
the situation would be no different from what it was before I
suggested the blood comparison."

"Beg your pardon, doc. But what about the corpse? We've
got to have a corpse—you know that. If it's still somewhere in
that house, Frimbo's going to have plenty of time to destroy it."

"Have you—if I'm not too personal—ever tried to destroy a
corpse, Dart?"

"Almost impossible to destroy it completely by ordinary

methods. But there are acids. As much stuff as he's got there——"

"You searched the house pretty well."

"Yes, but we've got experts that do nothing else, doc. They could find places that I wouldn't dream of looking for. They measure and calculate and reconstruct to scale, and when they get through, there isn't a place left big enough to hide a bedbug in."

"They take time, though, and their presence would arouse Frimbo's suspicions and hostility. Believe me, Dart—Frimbo himself is the only answer to this riddle. Jump him too soon and you'll destroy the only chance. I'm sure of that. I'm as curious about this thing as you are. I'm funny that way. And I'd like to see you and the local boys get the credit for this whole thing—not a lot of Philistines from downtown. You said you were depending on me. All right. Do that. And let me depend on you."

"Gee, doc, I didn't realize you were as interested as all that. It sure would mean a lot to me personally to get credit for this. We don't grab off a funny one like this often. If that's really how you feel about it——"

"Fine. Now all you've got to do is make no report of this last finding and hold off Frimbo till I'm through with him. Before tomorrow night I hope to have a pretty good idea of what makes him go 'round. After all, a gentleman who turns out to be one of the suspects in his own murder case deserves a little personal consideration."

"A suspect in his own murder—say, that's right! That's a brand-new one on me! But he's smart all right. Wonder why he didn't object to the blood test? He must have known it might prove incriminating."

"Of course he knew it. But what could he do? To refuse would have put him in a bad light too. All he could gracefully do was acquiesce and take a chance on the two bloods being so much alike that the small amount of the unknown would be exhausted before we could distinguish it from his own. That failing, he would simply have to depend on his wits. Did you hear him ask me whether I would use the ordinary agglutination tests? He's ready with an alibi for this lie right now, I'll bet you. That's another reason for not rushing in yet. We've got to get something he can't anticipate."

Dart looked at the physician with genuine admiration. "Doc, you're all right, no lie. You ought to've been a detective."

"I am a detective," the other returned. "All my training and all my activities are those of a detective. The criminal I chase is as prime a rascal as you'll ever find—assailant, thief, murderer —disease. In each case I get, it's my job to track disease down, identify it, and arrest it. What else is diagnosis and treatment?"

"I never thought of it that way."

"In this Frimbo case, I'm your consultant—by your personal invitation. I'm going to make as extensive an examination as I can before I draw my conclusions. Your allowing me to do so is proper professional courtesy—a rare thing for which I thank you deeply." He bowed solemnly to the grinning Dart. "And meanwhile you will be finding out every move of every visitor to that place last night?"

"Right. They're all being tailed this minute. And I've already checked everybody's story, even the undertaker's. They're all O.K. Brown came around to the precinct this morning to see Jenkins—they eavesdropped on him but didn't get anything except that Jenkins is still denying guilt. And his friend is willing to perjure himself to save him."

"I still find it hard to believe that Jenkins, even for the dirty lucre you so cogently brought forward, actually did this. Jenkins is a hard one all right, but it's all external. He's probably got the heart of a baby, and has to masquerade as a tough customer to protect himself."

"As you like. But that very masquerade could lead him into something from which he couldn't turn back."

"But not murder."

"Well, explain how he masqueraded his finger print onto that club and you'll do him a great favor."

"He may be lying about not touching the club the same as he is about the handkerchief."

"He's lying all right if he says he didn't touch that club. There's no other way the print could have got there."

"Isn't there?" the physician said, but the detective missed the skepticism in the tone and went on with his enumeration.

"Doty Hick's brother really is sick with T.B. and refuses to go to a hospital. I told you this morning about the killing that harmonizes with Webb's story. And Easley Jones has been employed by the Pullman Company for ten years—the man spoke very highly of him. I went by the Forty Club last night after leaving you. Three different members told me Crouch the undertaker had been there as he said."

"What about the women?"

"Well, you yourself vouched for Mrs. Crouch. And I'm almost willing to vouch for that other one. If she's got anything to do with this, I have."

"I was wondering about that. Have you?"

"Sure, doc," Dart's bright smile flashed. "I'm the detective on the case, didn't you know?"

"Do you know who committed the crime?"

"Not for certain."

"I see. Then you couldn't have done it yourself. Because if you had, you'd know who did it and it would be a simple matter for you to track yourself down and arrest yourself. Of course you might have done it in your sleep."

"So might you."

"I have a perfect alibi, my friend. Doctors never sleep. If it isn't poker it's childbirth—a pair of aces or a pair of pickaninnies."

"Seriously, doc, there's one objection to your trying to get something on Frimbo tonight."

"What?"

"Why do you suppose that guy was so quick to invite you back alone? Because you're his chief worry. You may be the cause of putting him on the frying-pan. He's evil. He must know your purpose. And if you get too warm, he'll try to rub you out."

"He'll find me quite indelible, I'm sure," Dr. Archer said.

Chapter Nineteen

I

JOHN ARCHER opened a desk drawer and picked up a revolver which lay there. He gazed thoughtfully upon it a moment, then gently replaced it. He shut the drawer, turned and
made his way out of the house. His front door closed behind him,
and he stood contemplating the high narrow edifice across the
dark street. It was two minutes to seven; the air was sharp and
ill-disposed and snapped at him in passing. Absently he hunched
his ulster higher about his shoulders, thrust his hands, free of
the customary bag, deep into his pockets and studied Frimbo's
shadowy dwelling. Rearing a little above its fellows, it was like
a tall man peering over the heads of a crowd. "Wonder if I'm
expected?" the physician mused. As if in answer, two second-
story windows suddenly lighted up, like eyes abruptly opened.

"I am expected." Slowly he crossed the dim street, halted
again at the foot of the stoop to resume his meditative stare,
then resolutely mounted to the door and, finding it unlocked,
entered.

His host was awaiting him at the head of the stairs. Frimbo's
tall figure was clad tonight in a dressing-gown of figured maroon silk; this, with a soft shirt open at the throat, and the
absence of any native headdress, gave him a matter-of-fact appearance quite different from that of the night before. Tonight
he might have been any well-favored Harlemite taking his ease
on a Sunday evening in leisure which he could afford and intended to enjoy.

But the deep-set eyes still held their peculiar glow, and the
low resonant voice was the same.

"Let us go up to the library," he said. "It will be more
comfortable."

He reached into the front room as they passed and snapped
a wall switch, leaving the room dark. "I turned those on for
your benefit, doctor. We must not be disturbed by other visitors. I have been looking forward to seeing you."

He led the way to that rear third-floor chamber which the physician had visited the night before.

"Choose your own chair—you will find most of them comfortable." The man's attitude was entirely disarming, but Dr. Archer took a chair that was disposed diagonally in a corner with bookshelves to either side.

Frimbo smiled.

"I have some fair sherry and some execrable Scotch," he offered.

"Thank you. You evidently prefer the sherry—I'll follow your example."

Shortly the wine had been procured from the adjacent kitchen; glasses were filled—from the same container, the physician noted; cigarettes were lighted; Frimbo seated himself on the divan before the fireplace, in which artificial logs glowed realistically.

"You were speaking," he said, as if almost a whole day had not intervened, "of Herbert Spencer's classification of the sciences."

"Yes," the physician said. "Psychology considered as the physiology of the nervous system."

Easily and quickly they began to talk with that quick intellectual recognition which characterizes similarly reflective minds. Dr. Archer's apprehensions faded away and shortly he and his host were eagerly embarked on discussions that at once made them old friends: the hopelessness of applying physico-chemical methods to psychological problems; the nature of matter and mind and the possible relations between them; the current researches of physics, in which matter apparently vanished into energy, and Frimbo's own hypothesis that probably mind did likewise. Time sped. At the end of an hour Frimbo was saying:

"But as long as this mental energy remains mental, it cannot be demonstrated. It is like potential energy—to be appreciated it must be transformed into heat, light, motion—some form that can be grasped and measured. Still, by assuming its existence, just as we do that of potential energy, we harmonize psychology with mechanistic science."

"You astonish me," said the doctor. "I thought you were a mystic, not a mechanist."

"This," returned Frimbo, "*is* mysticism—an undemonstrable

belief. Pure faith in anything is mysticism. Our very faith in reason is a kind of mysticism."

"You certainly have the gift of harmonizing apparently opposite concepts. You should be a king—there'd be no conflicting parties under your régime."

"I am a king."

For a moment the physician looked at the serene dark countenance much as if he were seeing his first case of some unusual but clear-cut disease. Frimbo, however, tranquilly took a sip of sherry, gently replaced the fragile glass on a low table at his elbow, and allowed the phantom of a smile to soften his countenance.

"You forget," he said, lighting a fresh cigarette, "that I am an African native." There was a pride in the statement that was almost an affront. "I am of Buwongo, an independent territory to the northeast of Liberia, with a population of approximately a million people. My younger brother rules there in my stead." A reminiscent air descended momentarily upon him. "Often I long to go back, but it would be dull. I am too fond of adventure."

"Dull!" Archer exclaimed. "Why—most people would consider that an extraordinarily exciting life."

"Most people who know nothing of it. Excitement lies in the challenge of strange surroundings. To encounter life in the African brush would exhilarate you, certainly. But for the same reasons, life in a metropolis exhilarates me. The bush would be a challenge to all your resources. The city is a similar challenge to mine."

"But you can't be so unaccustomed to this now. You have finished an American college, you have mastered the ways of our thinking enough to have original contributions of your own to make—surely all that is behind you once and for all."

"No," said Frimbo softly. "There are things one never forgets."

"You make me very curious."

The kindled black eyes regarded him intently a long moment. Then Frimbo said, "Perhaps I should satisfy that curiosity somewhat . . . if you care to listen. . . ."

And the dark philosopher who called himself king, with a faraway look in his eyes and a rise and fall in his deep low voice, painted a picture twenty years past and five thousand miles away.

2

"In some countries night settles gently like a bird fluttering down into foliage; in Buwongo it drops precipitately like a bird that has been shot. It is as if the descending sun backed unaware upon the rim of a distant mountain, tripped on the peak, and tumbled headlong out of sight into the valley beyond. The bright day has been mysterious enough—the blank, blue sky, the level rice fields, the arrogant palms, the steaming jungle. But it is obvious, bold mystery—it must reveal itself before it can strike. Night clothes it in invisibility, renders it subtle, indeterminate, ominous. Brings it close.

"All day we have traveled southward—my father, a hundred fighting men, and I. I am only twelve, but that is enough. I must now begin to take part in the feasts of our tributary villages. We are on the way to Kimalu, a town of a thousand people. I am very tired—but I am the eldest son of a chief. I stride proudly beside my tireless father. Some day I shall be like him, tall, straight, strong; I shall wear the scarlet loin cloth and the white headdress of superior rank. I must not falter. We have not stopped for food or drink—for shall we not feast lavishly tonight? We have ignored the beckoning paths that lead off our main trail—paths to other villages, to cool green tributaries of the Niger, to who knows what animal's hideout. And in the flattening rays of the sinking sun we at last see the rice fields outside our destination and presently the far off thatched roofs of Kimalu's dwellings. We are on a slight rise of ground. Yet before we can reach Kimalu, night overtakes us and devours us.

"But already there is the glow of village fires, a hundred spots of wavering yellow light; and shortly we enter Kimalu, my father leading, with me by his side, the men in double file behind us. All fatigue drops away as the shouts of greeting and welcome deluge our company like a refreshing shower.

"The ceremonies are scheduled to begin three hours hence, at the height of the moon. Meanwhile preparations go on. Our company is welcomed respectfully by the elderly headman, who receives with effusive thanks our two bullocks, each suspended by its feet on a horizontal pole and carried on the shoulders of eight of our carriers. These will augment the feast that follows the ceremony and help provide for our party on the morrow. We are conducted to the central square before the dwelling of the headman, a large house, thatch-roofed, walled with palm and bamboo, and surrounded by a high rampart of tall interlaced *timwe* trunks, the sharpened top of each one treated with a poison that is death to touch. Even the most venomous snake could not crawl over that rampart and live. The square is large enough to accommodate all the people of the village, for here they must assemble at regular intervals to hear the issuing of edicts relative to their governing laws and their local and national taxes. Here too, the headman sits in judgment every other day and pronounces upon both moral and civil offenders sentences ranging from temporary banishment to castration—the latter a more dreaded penalty than beheading.

"Around the enormous square, as we enter it, we see many fires, over which stews are simmering in kettles, and barbecues of boar, bullock, or antelope are roasting on poles. Savory odors quicken our nostrils, cause our mouths to water. But we may not yet satisfy our appetites. First we must wash and rest. And so we go down to the edge of the river beside which the village lies; there is a broad clearing and a shallow bit of beach upon which more fires burn for illumination and protection. Here we wash. Then we return to the rim of the square and stretch out to doze and rest till the feast begins.

"It is the Malindo—the feast of procreation—and of all the rites of all our forty-eight tribes, none is more completely symbolic. An extremely wide circle—one hundred and fifty feet in diameter—of firewood has been laid in the center of the square. Outside this at intervals are piles of more firewood, short dry branches of fragrant trees.

"At the height of the moon, the headman gives the signal for the ceremony to begin. The band of drummers, stationed to one side of the rampart gate, is ready. The drums are hollow logs; one end is open; over the other is stretched a tympanum of boarskin; they lie horizontally side by side; vary in length from two to twenty feet, but are so placed that the closed ends are in alignment facing the circle of firewood; they vary in diameter also, but even the smallest is a foot high. Each drummer sits astride his instrument above its closed end, upon which he plays with his bare hands and fingers.

"At the chief's signal, the player of the largest drum stretches his arms high over his head and brings the heels of both hands down hard on the face of his instrument. There is a deep, resounding boom, a sound such as no other instrument has ever produced; as low and resonant as the deepest organ note, as startlingly sudden as an explosion. A prowling cat five miles away will halt and cringe at that sound. The stillness that follows trembles in the memory of it; as that tremor dwindles the drummer strikes again—the cadence is established. Again, again. Slowly, steadily the great drum booms, a measure so large, so stately, so majestic, that all that follows is subordinated to it and partakes of its dignity.

"The people of the village have already gathered around the margin of the square; some sit on the ground, some stand, all are raptly intent. My father is seated on a platform directly in front of the rampart gate; I am on his left, the headman on his right, our hundred men seated on the ground further along. There is no movement anywhere save the flicker of low fires, and no sound save the steady tremendous boom of the great drum.

"But now something is happening, for a new note creeps subtly into the slow period of the drumbeat—another smaller drum, then another, then another, sounding a submeasure of lesser beats, quicker pulsations that originate in the parent sound and lift away from it like dwindling echoes. From the far side of the clearing a procession of shadowy figures emerges, and in their midst appear six men bearing on their shoulders a large square chest. The figures move slowly, in time with the fundamental measure, till they are on this side of the circle of firewood; then the six bearers turn toward the circle, and the others, in front of them and behind them, turn toward us. The bearers, still in time, move forward toward the circle, step over the wood with their burden, and deposit it in the center of the ring, while the others, also keeping to the measure, approach our position, about face, and seat themselves on the ground to either side of our platform.

"Still another motif now enters the rhythmic cadence—all the remaining drums, at first softly, almost imperceptibly, then more definitely, take up this new, lighter, quicker variation, which weaves itself into the major pattern like brocaded figures into damask—the whole a rich fabric of strength, delicacy, and incredible complexity of design. And now a file of torches appears far across the clearing, comes closer—they seem numberless, but are forty-eight, I know—one for each of our tribes. And we see that they are borne aloft, each in the hand of a slim naked girl whose dancing movements are in accord with the new lighter measure of the drums. The file passes before us, each member gracefully maintaining the rhythmic motif, till, equally spaced, they face the circle, each the stem of a bright flower in a swaying garland of flame.

"For a few minutes they dance thus, keeping their relative positions around the circle, but advancing periodically a few feet toward the center then withdrawing; and they do this so perfectly in unison that, while their feet and bodily gestures obey the lighter, quicker rhythm, their advances and retreats are tuned to the original, fundamental pulse, and the flares in their hands become jewels of flame, set in a magic ring which contracts . . . dilates . . . contracts . . . dilates . . . like a living heart, pumping blood. Then, with a sudden swell and dwindling of the lesser drums, there is a terminal, maximal contracture—the girls have advanced quite to the circle of firewood, dropped their torches upon it each at her respective point; have then, without seeming to lose a rhythmic movement, executed a final retreat—faded back from the circle like so many shadows, and fallen on the ground perfectly straight, each in a radial line, each as motionless as if she were bound to a spoke of some gigantic wheel.

"The great circle of wood soon kindles into an unbroken ring of fire, symbol of eternal passion; and as the flames mount, the drumming grows louder and more turbulent, as if the fire were bringing it to a boil. A warrior, whose oiled skin gleams in the light, leaps through the flames into the inside of the circle, reaches the large square chest in the center, unfastens and turns back the lid, and vanishes through the far rim of the fire.

"Every eye is focused on the chest beyond the flames. There is a slight shift of the rhythm—so slight as entirely to escape an unaccustomed ear. But the dancing girls catch it, and instantly are on their feet again in another figure of their ceremonial gesture—a languorous, lithe, sinuous twist with which they again advance toward the fiery circle. They incorporate into this figure of their dance movements whereby they take branches from the extra piles and toss them into the fire. The blaze mounts steadily. No one is noticing the girls now, however; no one is aware of the pervasive incense from the fragrant burning wood. For something is rising from the chest—the head of a gigantic black python, that rears four—five—six feet above the rim and swings about bewildered by the encircling fire.

"Now the warrior reappears, holding aloft in his two hands an infant of the tribe. Swiftly, with the infant so held as to be out of reach of the licking flames, again he bounds through the fire into the circle. At the same time the most beautiful maiden of the tribe, her bare body oiled like the warrior's, appears within the ring from the opposite side. The python, still bewildered, swings back and forth. The warrior and the maiden dance three times in opposite directions around the serpent. And now, though none has seen it happen, the girl has the infant in her arms; the python, sensing danger in the entrapping flames and the tumult of the drums, withdraws into his chest. The warrior closes and fastens the lid and vanishes through the far wall of fire. The drums have gone mad. The girl, holding the baby aloft in both hands, faces us, dashes forward with a cry that transcends the crescendo of drumming, a shriek like that of a woman in the last spasm of labor, leaps high through the blaze, runs toward our platform, and gently lays the unharmed infant at our feet. . . ."

3

There was a long silence. Frimbo sat looking into the flickering mock-embers on his artificial hearth, seeing those faraway genuine ones of woods that burned with a fragrance like incense. John Archer was silent and still, absorbed in the other man's fine dark face. Perhaps he was wondering, "Could this man have committed a murder? Whom would he want to kill? Why?

What is he—charlatan or prophet? What is his part in this puzzle—what indeed is not possible to this mind that in a moment steps out of cold abstract reason into the warm symbolic beauty of a barbaric rite?"

But what the physician actually said was, "Rather a dangerous ceremony, isn't it?"

Frimbo gathered himself back into the present, smiled, and answered, "Are conception and birth without danger?"

After a moment the doctor said, "My own youth was so utterly different."

"Yet perhaps as interesting to me as mine would have been to you."

"The age of twelve," laughed the other, "recalls nothing more exciting than a strawberry festival in the vestry of my father's church."

"Your father was a minister?"

"Yes. He died shortly after I finished college. I wanted to study medicine. One of my profs had a wealthy friend. He saw me through. I've been practicing nearly ten years—and haven't finished paying him back yet. That's my biography. Hardly dramatic, is it?"

"You have omitted the drama, my friend. Your father's struggle to educate you, his clinging on to life just to see you complete a college training—which had been denied him; your desperate helplessness, facing the probability of not being able to go on into medicine; the impending alternative of teaching school in some Negro academy; the thrill of discovering help; the rigid economy, to keep the final amount of your debt as low as possible—the summers of menial work as a bell boy or waiter or porter somewhere, constantly taking orders from your inferiors, both white and black; the license to practice— and nothing to start on; more menial work—months of it—to accumulate enough for a down payment on your equipment; the first case that paid you and the next dozen that didn't; the prolonged struggle against your initial material handicaps—the resentment you feel at this moment against your inability to do what you are mentally equipped to do. If drama is struggle, my friend, your life is a perfect play."

Dr. Archer stared.

"I swear! You actually are something of a seer, aren't you?"

"Not at all. You told me all that in the few words you spoke. I filled in the gaps, that is all. I have done more with less. It is my livelihood."

"But—how? The accuracy of detail——"

"Even if it were as curious as you suggest, it should occasion no great wonder. It would be a simple matter of transforming energy, nothing more. So-called mental telepathy, even, is no mystery, so considered. Surely the human organism cannot create anything more than itself; but it has created the radio-broadcasting set and receiving set. Must there not be within the organism, then, some counterpart of these? I assure you, doctor, that this complex mechanism which we call the living body contains its broadcasting set and its receiving set, and signals sent out in the form of invisible, inaudible, radiant energy may be picked up and converted into sight and sound by a human receiving set properly tuned in."

He paused while the doctor sat speechless. Then he continued:

"But this is much simpler than that. Is it at all mystifying that you should walk into a sick room, make certain examinations, and say, 'This patient has so-and-so. He got it in such-and-such a way approximately so long ago; he has these-and-these changes in such-and-such organs; he will die in such-and-such a fashion in approximately so long'? No. I have merely practiced observation to the degree of great proficiency; that, together with complete faith in a certain philosophy enables me to do what seems mystifying. I can study a person's face and tell his past, present, and future."

The physician smiled. "Even his name?"

"That is never necessary," smiled Frimbo in the same spirit. "He always manages to tell me that without knowing it. There are tricks in all trades, of course. But fundamentally I deceive no one."

"I can understand your ability to tell the present—even the past, in a general way. But the future——"

"The future is as inevitably the outcome of the present as the present is of the past. That is the philosophy I mentioned."

"Determinism?"

"If you like. But a determinism so complete as to include everything—physical and mental. An applied determinism."

"I don't see how there can be any such thing as an applied determinism."

"Because——?"

"Because to apply it is to deny it. Assuming the ability to 'apply' anything is free will, pure and simple."

"You are correct," agreed Frimbo, "as far as you go."

"Why," the doctor continued warmly, "anyone who achieved a true freedom of will—a will that had no reference to its past —was not molded in every decision by its own history—a power that could step out of things and act as a cause without being itself an effect—good heavens!—such a creature would be a god!"

"Not quite a god, perhaps," said the other softly.

"What do you mean?"

"I mean that such a creature would be a god only to those bound by a deterministic order like ours. But you forget that ours is not—cannot be—the only order in the universe. There must be others—orders more complex perhaps than our simple cause-and-effect. Imagine, for instance, an order in which a cause followed its effect instead of preceding it—someone has already brought forward evidence of such a possibility. A creature of such an order could act upon our order in ways that would be utterly inconceivable to us. So far as our system is concerned, he would have complete freedom of will, for he would be subject only to his order, not to ours."

"That's too much metaphysics for me," confessed the physician. "Come on back to this little earth."

"Even on this little earth," said Frimbo, "minds occasionally arise that belong to another order. We call them prophets."

"And have you ever known a prophet?"

"I know," said the other in an almost inaudible voice, "that it is possible to escape this order and assume another."

"How do you know?"

"Because I can do it."

Had he shouted instead of whispering, John Archer could not have exhibited greater amazement.

"You can—what?"

"Do not ask me how. That is my secret. But we have talked together enough now for you to know I do not say anything lightly. And I tell you in all seriousness that here, in a world of rigidly determined causes and effects, Frimbo is free—as free as a being of another order."

The doctor simply could not speak.

"It is thus I am able to be of service to those who come to me. I act upon their lives. I do not have to upset their order. I simply change the velocity of what is going on. I am a catalyst. I accelerate or retard a reaction without entering into it. This changes the cross currents, so that the coincidences are different from what they would otherwise be. A husband reaches home twenty minutes too soon. A traveler misses his train—and escapes death in a wreck. Simple, is it not?"

"You've certainly retarded my reactions," said Dr. Archer. "You've paralyzed me."

4

It was ten o'clock when finally the physician rose to go. They had talked on diverse and curious topics, but no topic had been so diverse and curious as the extraordinary mind of Frimbo himself. He seemed to grasp the essentials of every discussion and whatever arose brought forth from him some peculiar and startling view that the physician had never hitherto considered. Dr. Archer had come to observe and found himself the object of the observation. To be sure, Frimbo had told how, as an adventurous lad, he had been sent to a mission school in Liberia; how at twenty he had assumed the leadership of his nation, his father having been fatally injured in a hunting expedition; but after a year, had turned it over to his brother, who was ten months younger than he, and had departed for America to acquire knowledge of western civilization—America because of his American mission school beginning. He had studied under private tutors for three years in preparation for college; had been irregularly allowed to take entrance examinations and had passed brilliantly; but had acquired a bitter prejudice against the dominant race that had seemed to be opposing his purpose. Many episodes had fostered this bitterness, making it the more acute in one accustomed to absolute authority and domination. But all this, even as it was being told, had somehow increased the physician's sense of failure in this first meeting. It was too much under Frimbo's direction. And so he suggested another call on the morrow, to which Frimbo agreed promptly.

"I have a little experiment in which you would be interested," he said.

"I had really intended to discuss the mystery of this assault," the doctor declared. "Perhaps we can do that tomorrow?"

Frimbo smiled.

"Mystery? That is no mystery. It is a problem in logic, and perfectly calculable. I have one or two short-cuts which I shall apply tomorrow night, of course, merely to save time. But genuine mystery is incalculable. It is all around us—we look upon it every day and do not wonder at it at all. We are fools, my friend. We grow excited over a ripple, but exhibit no curiosity over the depth of the stream. The profoundest mysteries are those things which we blandly accept without question. See. You are almost white. I am almost black. Find out why, and you will have solved a mystery."

"You don't think the causes of a mere death a worthy problem?"

"The causes of *a* death? No. The causes of death, yes. The causes of life and death and variation, yes. But what on earth does it really matter who killed Frimbo—except to Frimbo?"

They stood a moment in silence. Presently Frimbo added in an almost bitter murmur:

"The rest of the world would do better to concern itself with why Frimbo was black."

Dr. Archer shook hands and departed. He went out into the night in somewhat the state of mind of one waking from odd dreams in a dark room. A little later he was mounting his own stoop. Before opening his door he stopped for a moment, looking back at the house across the street. With a hand on the knob, he shook his head and, contrary to his custom, indulged in a popular phrase:

"What a man!" he said softly.

Chapter Twenty

EVENING had fallen and still Bubber Brown, Inc., had not been able to decide on a proper course of action. He had wandered about Harlem's streets unaware of its Sunday-best liveliness and color. Sly, come-hither eyes that fell upon him had kindled no sheikish response, trim silken calves had not even momentarily captured his dull, drifting stare, bright laughter of strolling dark crowds had not warmed his weary heart. Even his swagger had forsaken him. He had rolled along, a frankly bow-legged man, and the mind behind his blank features had rolled likewise, a rudderless bark on a troubled sea of indecision.

A mystery movie in which the villainous murderer turned out to be a sweet young girl of eighteen had not at all quickened Bubber's imagination. Leaving the theater, he had stopped in Nappy Shank's Café for supper; but the pigtails and hoppin'-john, which he meditatively consumed there from a platter on a white porcelain counter, likewise yielded no inspiration.

Eventually, in the early evening, his wandering brought him to Henry Patmore's Pool Room, and after standing about for a few minutes watching the ivory balls click, he made his way to the rear room where blackjack was the attraction.

An impish fate so contrived matters that the first player he saw was Spider Webb, whose detention he had brought about the night before. Spider at first glared at him, then grinned a trifle too pleasantly.

"Detective Brown, as I live!" he greeted. "Do you guys know the detective? Who you squealin' on tonight, detective?"

Bubber had forgotten until now Spider's threat last night. The abrupt reminder further upset his already unsteady poise. It was clear now that Spider really meant to square the account. To conceal his discomfiture, Bubber calmly seated himself at the table and bought two dollars' worth of chips.

"Deal me in," said he casually, ignoring Spider Webb.

"Sure—deal him in. He's a good guy."

Had the situation been normal it is likely that Bubber would promptly have lost his two dollars, got up, and departed. But inasmuch as his mind was now on anything but the cards, his customarily disastrous judgment was quite eliminated, and the laws of chance had an opportunity to operate to his advantage. In the course of an hour he had acquired twenty dollars' worth of his fellow players' chips and had become too fascinated at the miraculous, steady growth of his pile to leave the game. And of course, no one, not even an ordinarily poor gambler like Bubber, could run away from luck, not only because of what he might miss thereby but also because the losers expected a sporting chance to win back their money and could become remarkably disagreeable if it should be denied them.

But Bubber continued to win, the only disturbing part of this being that most of his gain was Spider Webb's loss. He did not know that Spider was gambling with money collected from policy-players, money that must be turned in early tomorrow morning; but he knew that Spider was taking risks that one rarely took with one's own hard-earned cash. And he soon saw whither this was directed. For whenever Bubber won a deal by holding a blackjack, Spider grimly undertook to break him by "stopping the bank"—that is by wagering at every opportunity an amount equal to whatever Bubber possessed, hoping thus to pluck him clean on the turn of a single hand.

With luck running in Bubber's direction, however, this plunging soon proved disastrous to Spider. By the time Bubber's twenty dollars had swelled to forty, Spider, certain that the moment was at hand when the tide must turn, "stopped" the forty dollars with all he had. Chance chose that moment to give Bubber another blackjack. Spider's curses were gems.

The heavy loser had now no recourse save to leave the game, and he did so with ill grace. A few minutes later, one Red Williams, a hanger-on at Pat's who was everybody's friend or enemy as profitable opportunity might direct, came into the card room from the pool parlor and called Bubber aside.

"Is you won money from Spider Webb?" he inquired in a

low tone that clearly indicated the importance of what hung on the answer.

"Sho'," admitted Bubber. "Does it pain you too?"

"Listen. I heard Spider talkin' to Tiger Shade jes' now. Seem like Spider had it in for you anyhow. I don't know what you done to him befo', but whatever 'twas he could 'a' scrambled you with pleasure. But when you ups and wins his money too, that jes' 'bout set 'im on fire. Fu'thermo', that wasn't his money he los'—that was players' money. If he don' turn in nothin' in the mornin', his boss Spencer knows he's been stealin' and that's his hips. If any o' his players git lucky and hit and don't git paid, that's his hips too. Either way it's his hips. So from what I heard him whisperin' to his boy, Tiger, he's plannin' to substitute yo' hips fo' his'n."

"Talk sense, man. What you mean?"

"Mean Tiger is done agreed to lay for you and remove both yo' winnin's and yo' school gal complexion. Tonight."

"You sho'?"

"I heard 'em. You better slip on out befo' they git wise you onto 'em."

"O. K. Thanks."

"Thanks? Is that all it's worth to you—much as you done won?"

"Wait a minute." Bubber made extravagant excuses to the house and cashed his chips. He returned to the waiting informer and handed him a dollar. "Here—git yo'self a pint o' gut-bucket. See y' later."

Sourly, Red Williams gazed upon the bill in his hand. "Hmph!" grumbled he. "Is this all that nigger thinks his life is worth?" Then he grinned. "But it won't be worth this much when Tiger Shade git hold of 'im. No, s*uh!*"

2

Bubber sought to elude those who conspired against him by making a hasty exit through the barroom instead of through the poolroom, where apparently the plot had been hatched. This would have been wholly successful had not Tiger Shade already taken his stand on the sidewalk outside, between the poolroom and barroom entrances.

"Hello, there, Bubber, ol' boy," he greeted as Bubber came out and started to walk rapidly away.

It was perhaps the most unwelcome greeting Bubber had ever heard. He returned it hurriedly and would have kept going, but the Tiger called pleasantly, "Hey, wait a minute—I'm goin' your way. What's y' hurry?"

"Got a heavy date and I'm way late," came over Bubber's shoulder.

But in what seemed like three strides, the Tiger had overtaken and was beside him. For Tiger Shade was by a fair margin the tallest, widest, and thickest man in Harlem. He was bigger than the gigantic Officer Small, one of Bubber's companions of last night—and one for whose presence Bubber would have been most grateful now. And the Tiger was as bad as he was big. His was no simulated malice like Jinx's, no feigned ill-humor arising as a sort of defense mechanism; no, the Tiger simply enjoyed a congenital absence of sympathy. This had been too extreme even for those occupations where it might have been considered an advantage. He might have been a great boxer, but he simply could not remember to take the rules seriously. When he got interested in putting an opponent out, he saw no sound objection to doing so by hitting him below the belt or by snapping his head back with one hand and smiting him on the Adam's apple with the other. And when the opponent thus disposed of lay writhing or gasping as the case might be, Tiger always thought the hisses of the crowd were meant for the fallen weakling.

Hence he didn't rise high in the pugilistic firmament; but nobody crossed his path in that lowly part of Harlem where he moved. His reputation was known, and his history of destruction was the more terrible because it was so impersonal. He proceeded in combat as methodically as a machine; was quite as effective when acting for someone else as when acting for himself, and in neither case did he ever exhibit any profound emotion. True, he had a light sense of humor. For example, he had once held an adversary's head in the crook of his elbow and with his free hand torn one of the unfortunate fellow's ears off. He was given to such little drolleries; they amused him much as it amuses a small boy to pull off the wings of a fly; but it was quite as impersonally innocent.

It is hardly accurate to say that Tiger walked along beside Bubber. He walked along above Bubber, looming ominously like a prodigious shadow, and fully as tenacious. He did so without effort, smoothly, taking approximately one step to Bubber's three; he glided. Bubber bounced along hurriedly, explaining how he had allowed the time to get away from him and must rush but did not want to inconvenience his unexpected companion by so swift a pace. Tiger assured him that the pace was anything but exhausting.

It was about the hour at which his moonsign had appeared to him on the night before. "Wonder do you see yo'self when you dead?" he asked himself. "Maybe the third one is me!"

"Huh?" inquired Tiger.

"Nothin'. Jes' thinkin' out loud."

It was a mistake that he did not make again. But what he thought further, as the two progressed southward along Harlem's Fifth Avenue, was evident from what he presently did.

"I ain't got but one chance to shake this boogy loose. That's 'cause he don't know that I know what he's aimin' to do. He didn't see Red come in the card-room and tell me the bad news. So the thing to do is surprise him; got to stay here on the Avenue till I get a chance to duck around a corner and run like hell up a side street. By the time he realize' what I've done, not expectin' me to know nothin', I'll have a start on him. When he look he won't see nothin' but the soles o' my feet. I'll be runnin' so fas' he'll think I'm layin' down.—But what's the use runnin' if I ain' got no place to run to? Lemme see. Hot damn—I got it! The doctor—right in the next street. I was goin' to see him anyhow, see if he could tell me how to help Jinx. Now I *got* to see him. Feet, get ready. And fo' Gawd's sake keep out o' each other's way!"

They crossed 130th Street. As they mounted the far curb and would have passed the building line, suddenly Bubber pointed in astonishment. "Good-night! Look a yonder! Done been a accident!" And as Tiger Shade innocently peered ahead, the trickster did a right turn, snatched off his hat, and flew.

He had estimated Tiger's reaction correctly. Tiger even walked on past the building line before he realized that he was alone, and Bubber was at the physician's stoop before Tiger's pursuit got under way.

The front door was at that moment opening to let out a patient who had come to see the doctor and found him out. The patient was in a bad humor. He needed treatment for certain scratches, abrasions, and bruises which his physiognomy had sustained before he had been able to subdue a violent wife. The wife had taken it upon herself to follow a certain private detective to a certain private residence the night before, and had come thus to discover her husband in an unexplainably trouserless state. The misunderstanding which had arisen then had waxed into an energetic physical encounter this morning; and though the lady had been duly subdued, she had, so to speak, made her mark first. Further the patient's present ill humor had been increased by the difficulty of getting a physician on a Sunday evening. Dr. Archer had been his fifth unsuccessful attempt, and he emerged from the hallway, where a housekeeper had told him the doctor was out for the evening, in a state of repressed, scowling rage which was the more rancorous because it was facially painful to scowl. Indeed he was at the moment praying to high heaven that the blippety-blipped so-and-so that got him in the jam in the first place be delivered into his hands just for sixty seconds.

It was therefore not coincidence but the efficacy of honest prayer which brought Bubber bounding up the stoop just as the large, disappointed gentleman turned to descend. There was just enough light before the door closed for each to recognize the other. And it might have inspired a new philosophy of the organism had some competent observer been there to see how so utterly different emotions in so utterly dissimilar men produced so completely identical reactions: malicious glee on the gentleman's part, consternation on Bubber's, but abrupt and total immobility in both cases. Before action could relieve that mutual paralysis, Tiger Shade was at hand.

At such moments, imbecility becomes genius. Bubber, accordingly, became a superman. "Come on, boy!" he shouted to the leaping Tiger. "Here he is—this the guy I was chasin'! He grabbed my money at the corner and run! Come on, let's get 'im!" Whereupon he lunged upward and tackled the dumbfounded husband about the knees. Tiger, whose real interest lay in recovering the money, of which he was to receive part, hesitated now but a moment; swept up the stairs and lay hold of the accused, whom Bubber promptly released below. When Doctor Archer's housekeeper opened the door again to see what the sudden rumpus was about, her astonished eyes beheld two heavyweights engaged in a wrestling match. It ended as she watched.

"Hand it over," she heard the victor, sitting astride the other, advise.

"I ain't been near no corner!" panted the uncomfortable underling. "I'm after that tubby runt, too! Where'd he go? Lemme up! Which a way'd he go?"

"Get off my stoop, you hoodlums," cried the outraged housekeeper, "else I'll call the police. Go on now! Get off o' my stoop!"

Her admonitions were unnecessary. Bubber's absence was sufficient evidence of his stratagem. Tiger desisted, whipping about just in time to see the elusive Bubber enter the house directly opposite across the street and carefully close the door behind him.

"There he goes!" exclaimed he. "Come on—let's get him!"

3

Across the street they sped, scuffled up the brownstone stoop and burst through the door. Tiger, who was first, glanced up the stairs, which the fugitive could not possibly yet have traversed.

"He's down here some place—on this floor. Let's look. Come on."

His new ally hesitated.

"Say—you know what this is?"

"What?"

"This place is a undertaker's parlor!"

"I don't care if it's a undertaker's bathroom, I'm goin' in here and look for that boogy. He can't pull no fast one on me like that."

They found Undertaker Crouch's rooms invitingly accessible and apparently quite empty. They went into the parlor and stopped. There was a faint funeral fragrance in the air, and a strange, unnatural quiet over all that immediately subdued their movements to cautious tiptoeing and their voices to low muttering.

"I ain' crazy 'bout lookin' for nobody in here," announced the husband.

"Aw, what you scared o'?" the Tiger reassured him. "Dead folks ain' no trouble."

"They ain' no trouble to me—I don't get that close to 'em."

"Well—you don't see none do you?"

"I ain' looked. First one I see, I bids you both good-evenin'."

"I thought you wanted some o' this guy?"

"Some of him? In a place like this, I couldn't use two of him. My mind wouldn't be on what I was doin'."

"Well, I'm go'n' get 'im tonight. He's got eighty bucks o' my buddy's dough. If he gives me the slip tonight, them bucks is long gone."

"And if I hear any funny noises, I'm long gone."

"Come on. Let's look back yonder."

"Go ahead—I'll wait for you."

"He's tricky—it'll take both of us to find 'im."

"O.K. I'm behind you. But I ain't lettin' nothin' get 'tween me and the door."

"Did you leave it open?"

"I sho' did."

But the words were no sooner out of his mouth than the door was heard to swing gently shut.

"The wind," explained Tiger Shade.

"Oh, yea?"

"What else could it be?"

"The Spirit of St. Louis for all I know."

"Come on."

"What you waitin' for?"

"Come on."

"O.K. Start out. If you turn round and don't see me you'll know I jes' lost my enthusiasm."

None too eagerly, Tiger started out, followed by his reluctant ally. Several tubbed palms stood supercilious and motionless along the walls, and these the two searchers eyed distrustfully as they passed. They reached the wide doorway of the rear room without noting any evidence of their quarry. The rear room was dark save for what shadowy illumination reached it from the dim light of the parlor. Close together, the husband peering around the more venturesome Tiger, their wide eyes trying vainly to discern the contents of the room, they halted on the threshold.

It occurred to both of them to feel for a switch-button on the wall beside the door, and still eyeing the shadows they simultaneously felt. Contact with an open live wire could have given either no greater shock than he got at this unexpected contact with a hand. For one palsied moment their fingers stuck together as if to an electrified object which, once grasped, could not be released. Then the husband snatched his hand away, wheeled and took the first stride in flight. Only the first. The Tiger, having wheeled also, was so close behind him as to be able to grab him from behind, and his comrade, not knowing what held him, gave a hoarse moan, slipped on the polished hardwood floor, and sprawled.

"Hey you dumbbell," muttered Tiger, recovered and master of himself again, but still noticeably dyspnœic. "That was only me. Come on—snap out of this monkey-business."

"I felt a human hand!" the other whispered getting up sheepishly.

"Well, don't I look human?"

"Was it you? Huh—well—yea, you look human all right. But if you grab hold o' me the next time I start to run, you won't look human no mo'. You'll look like you been ridin' a wild steer."

"Come on. That guy is hidin' in there."

"Somehow I done los' interest in that guy."

At this moment a curious sound rose to their ears.

"What's *that*?"

It was startlingly close—a distinct chorus of voices singing. Even the words of the song were easily distinguishable:

> "*Am I born to die?*
> *Oh, am I born to die?*
> *Lord, am I born to die—*
> *To lay this body down?*"

"What kind o' house is this?"

Tiger's wealth of reassurance was rapidly being exhausted. "Can't you think o' none o' the answers? That's somebody's radio."

> "*One of these mornings bright and fair,*
>   *Lay this body down—*
> *Going to take my wings and try the air,*
>   *Lay this body down—*
> *Lord am I born to die?*"

"No radio never sounded like that. Them's sho' 'nough voices and they's in this house."

> "*Oh, am I born to die*
>   *To lay this body down?*"

"Not me!"

"Listen," said Tiger. "That's only a radio. Let's give this place one mo' look. He got to be in there. If he can go in there, so can we."

"All right. But no holdin' in the clinches."

Again, in the closest possible formation and in utter silence, they advanced to the rear room door.

"Whyn't you feel for the light ag'in?"

"Wait. I'll strike a match." The Tiger did so with none too steady fingers. By its fluttering, feeble, yellow flare two pairs of dilated eyes surveyed what could be seen of the room—a large desk on the right in the far corner, two windows in the back wall, a chair or two, and—

"Lawd have mercy—look a yonder!"

But the Tiger had needed no such admonition—he was looking with one hundred percent of his eyesight. Along the left wall stretched a long table, upon which, covered with a sheet, lay an unmistakably human form.

The match went out.

The pair stood momentarily cataleptic, their eyes fixed on the body which, once seen, remained now vaguely but positively visible even in the shadows. Before their shock passed a mysterious thing, an awful thing, began to happen, holding them fast in a horrified moment of fascination: slowly the white form moved in the shadow, seemed to change shape, to lift and widen like vapor. At the moment when their very eyeballs seemed about to burst, singing voices came again with that disturbing query:

"Am I born to die?"

Their spastic paralysis broke into convulsions of activity.

"Not here!" gasped the husband. And this time Tiger Shade did not overtake him till they both hit the sidewalk at the base of the front stoop and headed in opposite directions for more light.

Bubber, sitting fully erect now on the side of the table, cast the sheet aside and stood up with a sigh of relief. "Frimbo ain't got a thing on me," said he. "If that ain't risin' from the dead, what is it?"

But the chorus of the singing was disturbing him as much as it had his pursuers. While allowing the latter time to retreat to a safe distance he decided to investigate the former. "Might as well find out all I can 'bout this morgue. Which a way——?"

He listened. He moved toward the door which led from the room directly into the back of the first-floor balcony. At the head of the stairs leading down to the basement he saw light below, and realized that the sound was coming from that direction. The singing had stopped. Just over his head, in the flight above, soft footsteps were distinctly audible. He waited, listening. Presently the front door clicked shut.

"Wonder if that was that flunky goin' out?"

It was too late to attempt to follow, however, and so he pursued his present investigation. The singing had stopped. Bubber went on down the stairs as noiselessly as he could. In the hall below, which corresponded to its fellows above, he paused and listened again. The light he had seen came from a door which was only partly open; the prowler could not see around it without going too close. But he heard significant sounds:

"Is they anybody heah," a deep evangelic voice was saying, "what don't expect to shake my hand up in glory?"

"No!" shouted a number of voices.

"The spirit of the Lord has been in this place tonight!"

"Yes!" avowed the chorus.

"Did you feel it?"

"Yes!"

"Did it stir yo' soul?"

"Yes, Jesus!"

"Move you to do good deeds?"

"Yes, indeed. Amen, brother!"

"Aw right then. Now let's take up the collection."

Silence, abrupt and unanimous.

Bubber grinned in the hall outside. "Church meetin'—and 'bout to break up."

He was right. Some of the members of the little group that evidently used Crouch's meeting-room Sundays were already shamelessly heading for the hall door, en route to the freer manifestations of divine presence out of doors. Bubber retreated to the rear of the hall so as to attract no attention, and found himself at the head of the cellar stairs. It occurred to him that his tour of inspection might as well include the cellar, especially since that would allow the occupants of the meeting-room time to take up their collection and depart. Then he could return and investigate the basement floor.

4

He had procured at a drugstore during his wanderings today, an inexpensive pocket flashlight in imitation of the physician and detective who had found such devices so useful last night. This he now produced and by its light started down the cellar stairs. He had to proceed cautiously for this staircase was not so firmly constructed as those above; but he was soon in the furnace-room below the sidewalk level, and his small pencil of light traced the objects which his predecessors had observed the night before: the furnace, the coal bin, the nondescript junk about the floor, the pile of trunks, boxes, and barrels up front. He saw the central droplight but could not turn it on, since its switch was at the head of the stairs he had already passed.

And so he moved inquisitively forward toward the pile of objects up front. A few minutes of nosing about revealed nothing exciting, and he became conscious that the sounds of shuffling feet overhead had stopped.

He was about to abandon the cellar, whose chilly dampness was beginning to penetrate, when, without sound or warning, the center droplight went on. Feeble as it was, its effect was startling in the extreme, and Bubber felt for the moment trapped and helpless. He recovered his wits enough to crouch down among the shadows of the objects around him, and slowly came to realize that no one else was in the place. He awaited a footfall on the staircase. None came. At the moment when curiosity would have overcome better judgment, he heard a sound which came from beyond the stairs, toward the distant back wall. Cautiously looking around the corner of a packing case, he saw a figure emerge from the dimness. The figure approached the foot of the stairs, and Bubber saw that it was Frimbo, bareheaded, clad in a black dressing-gown. Frimbo carefully and silently went up the stairs; there was the sound of a bolt sliding; then Frimbo came down again.

Fortunately Bubber's protection was now nothing so unstable as an outspread wardrobe trunk, for he was quite unmindful of anything but the strange man's movements. And curious enough they were. Frimbo grew dim again in the shadow, then reëmerged with a paper bundle in his arms. He laid this down several feet from, and in front of the furnace, which was against the left wall and facing toward the center. The bundle thus rested almost directly beneath the droplight, and Bubber could see that its paper wrapping had a greasy appearance, as if its contents had been dripping with oil. Frimbo went to the furnace door and flung it wide. The red of the bright coals touched his awesome face to a glow, contrasting oddly with the yellow light behind him. He seized a long-handled shovel standing beside the furnace and returning, lifted the bundle upon it, reapproached the open door and thrust the thing in. The ignition of the package was instantaneous, the flames from it belching out of the aperture before Frimbo closed it. Now he replaced the shovel, went up the stairs again, unbolted the door at the top, came down, and disappeared in the darkness at the rear. There was a soft sound like the one that had heralded Frimbo's appearance, and a moment later the center light went out.

Among all the bewildering questions which must have presented themselves to Bubber now, the greatest was surely, "What's he burnin'?" For a long time, perhaps half an hour, the spy remained where he was, afraid to move. Eventually, the compelling impulse to look into the furnace and trust to providence

for escape, if necessary, moved him out of his refuge and toward the fire.

Every foot or two he stopped to make sure there was no
sound. It was clear that Frimbo had some means of traveling
about the house other than the stairs, and it was probable that
he would not return to the cellar without switching on the
light from whatever distant connection he had contrived. But
Bubber had to reassure himself somewhat as to the mysterious
avenue of approach before satisfying his major curiosity. He invaded the territory through which Frimbo had departed, and
could discover no ordinary exit. There was no cellar door leading up to the back yard; the walls were solid cement. All that
he could find was the base of the dumbwaiter shaft, and his little
beam of light, directed up the channel, was sufficient to disclose, some feet above, the dangling gears and broken ropes
which attested the uselessness of the device.

In a state of mind which the shifting shadows about him did
nothing to relieve, he quickly returned to the furnace and
flung open the door. Whatever Frimbo had used to accelerate
combustion had already reduced his bundle to a fragile-looking
char; its more susceptible parts had already stopped blazing,
and the remainder lay crumbling like the embers of a frame
house that has burned down. Pocketing his light and working
by the illumination from the coals, Bubber took the shovel and,
with as little noise as possible, gently retrieved a part of what had
been consigned to the flames. He laid it, shovel and all, on the
floor, shut the furnace, and examined it with his flash. So intent
was he now that it would have been easy to approach and catch
him unawares. But the contents of the shovel, from which the
glow had already faded, presented nothing susceptible to
Bubber's knowledge; his puzzled stare disclosed to him only
that he must get the find out of this place and subject it to
more expert inspection.

It did not take him long to find a wooden box into which he
could deposit what he had retrieved. Having done so, he replaced the shovel beside the furnace, and with the box under
one arm, quietly mounted the stairs. The basement floor was
dark. He did not stop to investigate that now, however, but,
succeeding in making his exit by way of the basement front
door, without a moment's delay he ran across the street to Dr.

Archer's house and, no less excitedly than twenty-four hours before, rang the front-door bell.

Again the doctor himself answered the summons.

"Hello, Brown! What's up?"

"I done 'scovered sump'm!"

"In that box? What?"

"You'll have to answer that, doc. Damn 'f I know."

"Come in."

5

In the warmth and brightness of the physician's consulting-room, Bubber related what he had seen and done. Meanwhile the doctor was examining the contents of the box on his desk, poking about in it with a long paper knife. He stopped poking suddenly, then, very gently resumed. Much of what he touched crumbled dryly apart. At last he looked up.

"I should say you have discovered something."

"What is it, doc?"

"How long did you say this burned?"

"'Bout half an hour. Took me that long to make up my mind to get it out."

"Are you sure it didn't burn longer?"

"With me snoopin' 'round 'spectin' to be bumped off any second? No, s*uh!* If it was half an hour that was half an hour too long."

"Did it blaze when he first put it in the furnace?"

"'Deed it did. Looked like it was 'bout to explode."

"Let me see now. How could he have treated human flesh so as to make it so quickly destructible by fire?" The doctor mused, apparently forgetting Bubber's presence. "Alcohol would dehydrate it, if he could infiltrate the tissues pretty well. He could do that by injecting through the jugulars and carotids. But the alcohol would evaporate—that would explain the rapid oxidation. Greasy? Oh, I have it! He's simply reinjected with an inflammable oil—kerosene, probably. Of course. Hm—what a man!"

"Doc, would you mind tellin' me what you talkin' 'bout?"

"Have you any idea what this stuff is?"

"No, suh."

"It's what's left of a human head, neck and shoulder, a trifle over-cooked."

"Great day in the mornin'!"

"Quite so. The extent of destruction has been sped up by treating the dead tissues with substances which quickly reduced the water content and heightened the inflammability. Maybe alcohol and kerosene—maybe chemicals even more efficient—it doesn't matter."

He stopped his poking and gently lifted from the box an irregular, stiff, fragile cinder. He placed it very carefully on a piece of white paper on his desk.

"This is exhibit A. Notice anything? No, don't handle it—it's too crumbly and we can't afford to lose it. What do you——"

"Ain't them teeth?" Bubber pointed to three little lumps in the char.

"Yes. And apparently the only ones that haven't fallen loose. I believe we may be able to use them. Further, this cinder represents parts of two bones, the maxillary, in which the upper teeth are set, and the sphenoid which joins it at about this point."

"You don't mean to tell me?" gaped Bubber.

"I do. I do indeed. And I mean to tell you this also: that the presence of the sphenoid, or most of it, in a relatively free state like this is proof that its owner has left this world. On this bone, in life, rests a considerable part of the brain."

"S'posin' a guy's brainless, like Jinx?"

"Even Jinx couldn't make it without his sphenoid. So you see that in that fragile bit of the fruit of the crematory, we have an extraordinary bit of evidence. We have proof of a death. You see that?"

"Oh, sho' I see that."

"And we may have a means of identifying the corpse. You see that?"

"Well, that ain't quite so clear."

"Never mind. It will be. And finally we have your testimony to the effect that Frimbo was destroying this material."

"Huh. Don't look so good for Mr. Frimbo, do it?"

"Thanks to your discovery, it doesn't."

"Will that help Jinx out?"

"Possibly. Even probably. But the case against Frimbo is not quite complete, you see, even with this."

" 'Tain't? What mo' you need?"

"It might be important to know who was killed, don't you think?"

"Tha's right. Who?"

"I'm sure I don't know. Maybe nobody. These may be the remains of an old stiff he was dissecting—who knows? That we must find out. And there is one more thing to learn—Frimbo's motive. Not only whom did he kill—if anybody—but why?"

"Why you reckon?"

"That may be a hard point to convey to you, Mr. Brown, so late in the evening. But this much I will tell you. You see, while you have been ruminating in the depths of Frimbo's cellar, I have been ruminating in the depths of my mind."

"I hope 'tain't as full of trash as that cellar was."

"It has its share of rubbish, I'm not ashamed to say. But what it holds just now is the growing conviction that Frimbo is a paranoiac."

"A—which?"

"A paranoiac."

"The dirty son of a gun. Ought to be ashamed o' hisself, huh?"

"And so, my worthy collaborator, if you don't mind leaving this precious clue in my hands, I'll spend a little time and energy now freshening my mind on homicidal tendencies in paranoia —a most frequent symptom, if I recall correctly."

"Jes' what I was thinkin'," agreed Bubber. "Well, I'll come 'round again tomorrow, doc. I was on my way here tonight, but I got sorta side-tracked. I thought you might be able to tell me how to help Jinx out."

"If this is any indication," smiled the doctor, pointing to the evidence, "the best thing you can do for Jinx is to get side-tracked again."

Bubber thought over the day's episodes, grinned and shook his head.

"Uh—uh," he demurred resolutely. "He ain't wuth it, doc."

Chapter Twenty-one

I

"In this respect," Dr. Archer confessed to Detective Dart, who sat facing him across his desk the next morning, "Frimbo would call me a mystic. I have implicit faith in something I really can't prove."

"Is it a secret?"

"Yes, but I'll share it with you. I believe that the body, of which these humble remnants are ample evidence, is the same as the one I pronounced dead on Saturday night."

"Shouldn't think there'd be any doubt about that."

"There isn't. That's the mysticism of it. There isn't any doubt about it in my mind. But I haven't proved it. I have only yielded to a strong suspicion: somebody is killed, the body disappears. Frimbo steps up claiming to be the body. He is lying as our little blood test proved, and later he is seen destroying vital parts of a body. This might be another body, but I am too confirmed a mystic to believe so. I am satisfied to assume it is the same."

"You know damn well it's the same," said the practical Dart.

"We won't argue the point," smiled Dr. Archer. "Assuming it is the same—there will be reasons why Frimbo destroys a murdered man."

"Protecting himself."

"An omnipresent possibility. The victim was sped into the beyond either by Frimbo himself or by someone in league with Frimbo, whom Frimbo is trying to protect. Yes. But do you recall that we drew the same conclusions about Jinx Jenkins?"

"Well—bad as this looks for the conjure-man, it doesn't remove the evidence against Jenkins. That handkerchief could be explained, but that club—and the way he tried to scram when the lights went out——"

"Very well. Nor does it eliminate the actuality of a feud between the two policy kings, Spencer and Brandon, in which that runner was an unfortunate sacrifice yesterday. Personally, I pay no more attention to that than I do to the ravings of Doty Hicks."

"Me, personally," responded Dart, "I pay attention to both of 'em. I suspect 'em all till facts let 'em out. And I still think that the simplest thing may be so. Why make it hard? Hicks or Brandon, the one out of superstition, the other out of greed, either one may have hired Jenkins to do the job. Jenkins somehow didn't get Frimbo but got—say! I know—he got Frimbo's flunky! That's your dead body! The flunky!"

The physician demurred.

"Inspiration has its defects. Remember. The flunky ushered Jenkins to the entrance of the room. Jenkins went in. The victim was already in the chair waiting. Would the flunky have obligingly hurried around through the hall and got in place just so that Mr. Jenkins could dispose of him? That would be simple indeed—too simple."

"Well, maybe I'm prejudiced. But——"

"You are. Because that isn't all you ignore. Why would Frimbo claim to be the victim if what you suggest were true? Why would he destroy the body of his servant? One would rather expect him to want to find and punish the murderer."

"All right, doc. You can out-talk me. You give us the answer."

"I'm only part way through the problem. But I had an interesting interview with the gentleman last night. And I'm reasonably sure he's a full-fledged paranoiac."

"Too bad. If he was a Mason, now, or an Odd Fellow——"

"A paranoiac is a very special kind of a nut."

"Well, now, that's more like it. What's so special about this kind of a nut?"

"First, he has an extremely bright mind. Even flashes of brilliance."

"This bird is bright, all right."

"You don't know the half of it. You should hear him tie you up in mental knots the way he did me. Next thing, he has some trouble—some unfortunate experience, some maladjustment, or something—that starts him to believing the world is against him. He develops a delusion of persecution. Frimbo concealed his pretty well, but it cropped out once or twice. He came to America to study and had some trouble getting into college. He took it personally, and attributed it to his color."

"Where's the delusion in that?"

"The delusion in that is that plenty of students the same color, but with more satisfactory formal preparation, have no such difficulty. Also that plenty the same color with unsatisfactory preparation don't draw the same conclusion. And also that plenty *without* his generous inheritance of pigment and with unsatisfactory preparation have the same difficulty and don't draw the same conclusion."

"Call it a delusion if you want to——"

"Thanks. Now your paranoiac couldn't live if something didn't offset that plaguing conviction. So he develops another delusion to balance it. He says, 'Well, since I'm so persecuted, I must be a great guy.' He gets a delusion of grandeur."

"I know flocks of paranoiacs."

"Me too. But you don't know any with the kind of delusion of grandeur that Frimbo has. It's the most curious thing—and yet perfectly in case. You see, his first reaction to the persecution idea was flight into study. He got steeped in deterministic philosophy."

"What the hell is that?"

"The doctrine that everything, physical and mental, is inevitably a result of some previous cause. Well, Frimbo evidently accepted the logic of that philosophy, and that molded his particular delusion of grandeur. He said, 'Yes, everything is determined—nature, the will of man, his decisions, his choices—all are the products of their antecedents. This is the order of our existence. *But I—Frimbo—I am a creature of another order.* I can step out of the order of this existence and become, with respect to it, a free agent, independent of it, yet able to act upon it, reading past and present and modifying the future. Persecution cannot touch me—I am above it.' Do you see, Dart? Does it mean anything to you?"

"Not a damn thing. But it doesn't have to. Go on from there."

"Well, there you are—still paranoia. But when it gets as bad as in Frimbo's case, they get dangerous. They get homicidal. Either the first delusion moves them to eliminate their supposed persecutors, or the second generates such a contempt for their inferiors that they will remove them for any reason they choose."

"Gee! Nice people to ride in the subway with. Are you sure about this guy?"

"Reasonably. I'm going back for more evidence today."

"So he can remove you?"

"Not likely. I think he's taken a fancy to me. That's another symptom—they make quick decisions—accept certain people into their confidence as promptly as they repudiate others. I seem to be such a confidant. Something I said or did Saturday night appealed to him. That's why he accepted me so quickly—invited me back—took me in—exchanged confidences with me. No normal mind under similar circumstances would have done so."

"Well—be careful. I don't mind nuts when they're nuts. But when they're as fancy as that they may be poison."

"Don't worry. I know antidotes."

After a pause, Dart said:

"But who the hell did he kill?"

"You mean who's dead? We only surmise that Frimbo——"

"I mean who was the bird on the couch?"

"Have you that removable bridge in your pocket?"

"Sure. Here it is. What of it?"

"I don't dare hope anything. But let's see." He took the small device. Its two teeth were set in a dental compound tinted to resemble gums and its tiny gold clamps reached out from either end to grasp the teeth nearest the gap it bridged.

"Look." The doctor pointed to the three teeth in the bony char which still lay on the piece of white paper. "Upper left bicuspid, a two-space gap, and two molars. That means first bicuspid and second and third molars. Now this bridge. Second bicuspid and first molar. See?"

"Don't you ever talk English?"

"The gap, Dart, old swoop, corresponds to the bridge."

"Yea—but you yourself said that doesn't prove anything. It's got to fit. Fit perfect."

"Oh, thou of little faith. Well, here goes. Pray we don't break up the evidence trying to get a perfect fit." With deft and gentle fingers, the physician brought the bridge clamps in contact with the abutments of the cinder and ever so cautiously edged them in place, a millimeter at a time. He heaved a sigh.

"There you are, skeptic. The gums are gone of course. But

the distance between the teeth has been maintained, thanks to the high fusion point of calcium salts. Am I plain?"

"You are—but appearances are deceiving."

"Here's one you can depend on. Find out who belongs to this bridge and you'll know who, to put it quite literally, got it in the neck on Saturday night."

Dart reached for the bridge.

"Gently, kind friend," warned the doctor. "That's your case —maybe. And leave it in place."

"There's probably," observed the detective, "three thousand and three of these things made every day in this hamlet. All you want me to find out is whose this was."

"That's all. It'll be easy. See your dentist——"

"I know—twice a year. What time'll you be back here?"

"Four o'clock. And bring that club with you."

"Right. I'll see you—if Frimbo lets you out whole."

2

With the clue resting like a jewel upon soft cotton in a small wooden box, Detective Dart sought out one Dr. Chisholm Dell, known to his friends, including Perry Dart, as Chizzy. Chizzy was a young man of swarthy complexion, stocky build, and unfailing good humor, whose Seventh Avenue office had become a meeting-place for most of the time-killing youth of Harlem—ex-students, confidence boys, insurance agents, promoters, and other self-confessed "hustlers." The occasional presence of a pretty dancing girl from Connie's or the Cotton Club, presumably as a patient awaiting her turn, kept the boys lingering hopefully about Chizzy's reception room.

Detective Dart was not deceived, however, and rose promptly when Chizzy, in white tunic, came out of his operating-room.

"Can you give the law a hot minute?"

"I couldn't give anybody anything right now," grinned Chizzy. "But I'll lend you one. Come on in."

Dart obeyed. He produced his exhibit.

"Take a look."

"What the devil's that?" Chizzy exclaimed after glancing at it.

Dart explained, adding, "As I get it, this bridge is a pretty accurate means of identification. Is that right?"

"I've been practicing ten years," said Chizzy, "and I haven't seen two exactly alike yet."

"Good. Now is there any way to tell who this belonged to?"

"Sure. Whose bone is it?"

"Don't be funny. Would I ask for help if I knew that?"

Chizzy considered. "Well—it can be narrowed down, certainly. I can tell you one thing."

"No?"

"Sure. That bridge is less than two months old."

"Yea?"

"See this part here that looks like gums?"

"Is that what it's supposed to look like?"

"Yea. That's a new dental compound called deckalite. Deckalite has been on the market only two months. I haven't made a case yet."

"Know anybody in Harlem that might have?"

"When you limit it to Harlem, that makes it easy. Do you know it was made in Harlem?"

"No. But it was made for a Harlemite. The likelihood is that he went to a local dentist."

"I doubt it. I haven't seen a patient for so long I believe all the Harlemites must be going to Brooklyn for their teeth. But if he did go to a Harlem dentist, it's easy."

"Hurry up."

"Well, you see there are only two dental mechanics up here that can handle deckalite. As it's a recent product it requires a special technique. Not one of the regular dentists knows it, I'm sure. Whoever your unknown friend went to would just take the impression and send it to one of those two men to be made up. All you've got to do is to go to each of the two mechanics, find out what dentist he's made deckalite uppers for, go back to the referring dentist and trace down your particular bridge."

"Beautiful," said Dart. "Two names and addresses, please."

Chizzy complied. "You'll find 'em in now, sitting down with their chins in their hands, wishing for something to do."

"Thanks, Chizzy. If you weren't so damned funny-lookin', I'd kiss you."

"Is that all that prevents you?" Chizzy called—but Dart was already banging the outside door behind him.

3

"Come into my laboratory, doctor," Frimbo invited Dr. Archer. "I'm glad you could return, because, if you remember, I promised to demonstrate to you a little experiment. Let's see, this time you have your bag, haven't you? Good. Have you a gauze dressing?"

Dr. Archer produced the requested article and handed it over. Frimbo removed it from the small, sealed tissue paper envelope which kept it dry and sterile, and dropped it into a sealed glass beaker. Then he rolled up the left sleeve of his robe, the one he had worn the night before.

"Please, doctor, remove a few cubic centimeters of blood. Put a little in that test tube there, which contains a crystal of sodium citrate to prevent clotting, and the rest in the empty tube beside it. You will be interested in this, I'm sure."

The physician applied a tourniquet, procured a syringe, touched a distended vein of Frimbo's forearm with alcohol, and obeyed the latter's directions. Frimbo, the tourniquet removed, pressed the swabbing sponge on the point of puncture a moment, then discarded it and dropped his sleeve.

"Now, doctor, there are my red cells, are they not?" He indicated the first tube. "And in a moment we shall have a little of my serum in this other tube, as soon as the blood clots and squeezes the serum out." They awaited this process in silence.

"Good. Now I take your sterile dressing and pour onto it some of my serum. In a general way, now, this dressing might have wiped a bloody wound on some part of my body—except that it has upon it only serum instead of whole blood. A mere short cut to my little demonstration. I return the dressing to the beaker and add a few cubic centimeters of distilled water from this bottle. Then I remove the dressing, thus, leaving, you see, a dilute sample of my serum in the beaker."

"Yes," Dr. Archer said thoughtfully.

"Now on this slide, with this loop, I place a drop of my diluted serum"—he stressed "my" whenever he used it—"and mix with it a loopful of my red cells, so. Now. Will you observe with the microscope there, what takes place?"

The doctor put the slide on the stage of the microscope, adjusted the low power, and looked long and intently. Eventually he looked up. He was obviously astonished.

"Apparently your serum agglutinates its own cells. But that's impossible. One part of your blood couldn't destroy another—and you remain alive."

"Perhaps I am dead," murmured Frimbo. "But there is a much simpler explanation: Your dressings are evidently treated with some material which is hostile to red cells. In such a procedure as this, where the serum has to be soaked out of the dressing, this hostile material is soaked out also. It is this material that is responsible for the phenomenon which we usually attribute to hostile serum. Let us prove this."

Thereupon he repeated the experiment, discarding the dressing, and using a dilution of his serum made directly in another test tube. This time the microscope disclosed no clumping of red cells.

"You see?" the African said.

The doctor looked at him. "Why did you show me this?" he asked.

"Because I did not wish you to interpret falsely any observations you might have made in your investigation of night before last."

"Thank you," Dr. Archer said. "And may I say that you are the most remarkable person I have ever met in my life."

"Being remarkable also in my lack of modesty," smiled the other, "I quite agree with you. Tell me. How do you like my little laboratory?"

"It certainly reveals an unusual combination of interests. Biology, chemistry, electricity——"

"The electricity is, with me, but a convenience. The biochemistry is vital to my existence."

"Isn't that a television receiver over there?"

"Yes. I made it."

"Small, isn't it?"

"Therein lies its only originality."

"I hope you'll pardon my curiosity; you have taken me somewhat into your confidence, and if I presume you must pardon me. But you seem so absorbed in more or less serious pursuits—have you no lighter moments? I should think you would have to relax—at least occasionally—to offset your habitual concentration."

"I assure you I have—lighter moments," smiled the other.

"You are a bachelor?"

"Yes."

"And bachelors—you may look upon this as a confession if you like—are notoriously prone to seek relaxation in feminine company."

"I assure you," Frimbo returned easily, "that I am not abnormal in that respect. I admit I have denied myself little. I have even been, on occasion, indiscreet in my affairs of the heart—perhaps still am. But," he promptly grew serious, "this," he waved his hand at the surrounding apparatus, "this is my real pleasure. The other is necessary to comfort, like blowing one's nose. This I choose—I seek—because I like it. Or," he added after a pause, "because a part of it lifts me out of the common order of things."

"What do you mean?" The voice of Dr. Archer was not too eager.

"I mean that here in this room I perform the rite, which has been a secret of my family for many generations, whereby I am able to escape the set pattern of cause and effect. I wish I might share that secret with you, because you are the only person I have ever met who has the intelligence to comprehend it and the balance not to abuse it. And also because"—his voice dropped—"I am aware of the possibility that I may never use it again."

The doctor drew breath sharply. But he said quietly:

"It is always the greatest tragedy that a profound discovery should remain unshared."

"Yes. Yet it must be so. It is the oath of my dynasty. I can only name it for you." He paused. Then, "We call it the rite of the gonad."

"The rite of the gonad." With the greatest difficulty the physician withheld his glance from the direction of the shelf whereon he had observed a specimen jar containing sex glands.

"Yes," Frimbo said, a distant look creeping into his deep-set eyes. "The germplasm, of which the gonad is the only existing sample, is the unbroken heritage of the past. It is protoplasm which has been continuously maintained throughout thousands of generations. It's the only vital matter which goes back in a continuous line to the remotest origins of the organism. It is therefore the only matter which brings into the present every influence which the past has imprinted upon life. It is the epitome of the past. He who can learn its use can be master of his past. And he who can master his past—that man is free."

For a time there was complete silence. Presently Dr. Archer said, "You have been very kind. I must go now. I shall see you tonight."

"Yes. Tonight." A trace of irony entered the low voice. "Tonight we shall solve a mystery. An important mystery."

"Your death," said the doctor.

"My death—or my life. I am not sure."

"You—are not sure?"

"The life of this flesh, my friend."

"I do not follow you."

"Do not be surprised. Released of this flesh, I should be freer than ever."

"You mean—you think you may be—released?"

"I do not know. It is not important now. But Saturday night, an odd thing happened to me. I was talking to the man, Jenkins. I had projected my mind into his life. I could foresee his immediate future—up till tonight. Then everything went blank. There was nothing. I was as if struck blind. I could see no further. You see what that means?"

"A sort of premonition?"

"So it would be called. To me it is more than that. It meant the end. Whether of Jenkins' body or mine, I can not say at the moment. I was with him, of him, so to speak. But you see—the abrupt termination which cut off my vision could be either his—or—mine."

The doctor could say nothing. He turned, went out, and slowly descended the stairs.

Chapter Twenty-two

I

A GAIN Bubber Brown called on his friend Jinx Jenkins and again was permitted to see him. Jinx had never been of cheerful mien; but today he had sunk below the nadir of despondency as his glum countenance attested. But Bubber wore a halo of hope and his face was a garland of grins.

"Boy, I told you I'd get you out o' this!"

"Where," asked the sardonic prisoner, "is the key to the jail?"

"Far as you concerned, it's on Doc Archer's desk."

"That's a long way from this here lock."

"I been goin' after mo' evidence, boy. And I got it. I give it to the doc and, what I mean, yo' release is jes' a matter of time."

"So is twenty years."

"You' good as out, stringbean."

"Not so long as I'm in. Look." He laid hold of the grille between them and shook it. "That's real, man; that's sump'm I can believe, even the holes. But what you're sayin' don't widen nothin' but yo' mouth."

"Listen. You know what I found?"

And he related, how, at great personal risk, which he ignored because of his friend's predicament, he had voluntarily entered the stronghold of mystery and death, ignored the undertaker's several corpses—four or five of them lying around like chickens on a counter—descended past the company of voodoo worshipers who would have killed him on sight for spying on their secrets, and so into the pit of horror, where the furnace was merely a blind for the crematory habits of the conjure-man.

"He come straight out o' the wall," he related, "and me there hidin' lookin' at him. Come through the wall like a ghost."

"Ghos'es," Jinx demurred, "is white. Everybody know that."

"And so was I," avowed Bubber.

"Well," Jinx conceded, "you might 'a' turned white at that —when you seen Frimbo come out o' that wall."

Bubber went on with his story. "And," he eventually con-cluded, "when Doc Archer seen what I'd found, he said that settled it."

"Settled what?"

"That proved somebody's been killed sho' 'nough. See?"

Jinx gazed a long time upon his short, round friend. Finally he said, "Wait a minute. I know I didn't hear this thing straight. You say that what you found proves it was murder?"

"Sho' it do."

"Boy, I don't know how to thank you."

"Oh that's all right. You'd 'a' done the same for me."

"First you get me pulled in on a charge of assault. But you ain' satisfied with that. Tha's only twenty years. You got to go snoopin' around till you get the charge changed to murder. My pal."

"But—but——"

"But my ash can. You talkin' 'bout dumbness and ignorance. Well, you sho' ought to know—you invented 'em. All right; now what you go'n' do? You got me sittin' right in the electric fryin'-pan. Somebody got to throw the switch. You done ar-ranged that too?"

"Listen, boy. All I'm doin' is tryin' to find enough facts to clear you. You ain't guilty sho' 'nough, is you?"

"I didn't think so. But you got me b'lievin' I must be. If you keep on bein' helpful, I reckon I'll jes' have to break down and confess."

"Well, what would you 'a' done?"

"What would I 'a' done? First place, I wouldn' 'a' been there. Second place, if the man wanted to burn up sump'm in his own furnace, he could 'a' burned it. He could 'a' got in the furnace and burned hisself up for all I'd 'a' cared. But you—you got to run up and stop the thing from burnin'—you rather see me burn."

"Aw man, quit talkin' lamb-yap. If Frimbo's tryin' to get rid o' remains, who's responsible for 'em bein' remains? Frimbo, of course. Frimbo put his flunky up to killin' somebody; then he got the flunky away and tried to get rid o' the remains."

"Yea? Well, I don' see Frimbo in this jail house. I'm here. I'm holdin' the well-known bag. And all you doin' is fillin' it."

"I wish I could fill yo' head with some sense. Maybe when

you get yo' big flat feet out on the street again you'll appreciate what I'm doin' for you."

"Oh, I appreciate it now. But I never expect to get a chance
to show you how much. That'll be my only dyin' regret."

Bubber gave up. "All right. But you needn' never fear dyin'
in nobody's electric chair."

"No?"

"No. Not if they have to put that electric cap on yo' head to
kill you. Yo' head is a perfect non-conductor."

With this crushing remark Bubber terminated his call and
gloomily departed.

2

"You're ahead of time," said Dr. Archer.

"This won't wait," returned Perry Dart. "It took me less than
an hour to get the dope. Here's your club." He laid a package
on the desk. "And here," he put the box containing Bubber's
discovery down beside the other package, "is your removable
deckalite bridge. And I'll bet a week's wages you can't guess
who that bridge belonged to."

"I can't risk wages. Who?"

"A tall, slender, dark gentleman by the name of N. Frimbo."

The physician sat forward in his chair behind the desk. The
gray eyes behind his spectacles searched Dart's countenance
for some symptom of jest. Finding none, they fell to the box,
where they rested intently.

"And his address," the detective added, "is the house across
the street."

"Unless I've been seeing things," said Dr. Archer, "Frimbo's
teeth are very nearly perfect. Those two teeth are certainly
present."

"This patient differed from our friend in only one respect."

"How?"

"The dentist who treated him insists that he was cock-eyed."

"I'm beginning to wonder aren't we all?"

"Frimbo's servant was cock-eyed."

"And otherwise much like his master—tall, dark, slender."

"With the same name?"

The physician regarded the detective a solemn moment. "What's in a name?" he said.

3

Before the detective could answer, Dr. Archer's door bell rang again. The caller proved to be Bubber Brown; and a more disconsolate Bubber Brown had never appeared before these two observers.

"Sit down," said the doctor. "Found anything else?"

"Gee, doc," Bubber said, "my boy Jinx is got me worried. He brought up a point I hadn't thought about before."

"What point?"

"Well, if that clue I brought you last night changes the charge to murder, Jinx'll have to do life at least. 'Cose life in jail with nothin' to worry 'bout, like meals and room rent, has its advantages. But the accommodations is terrible they tell me, and I don't like the idea that I messed my boy up."

"Is that what he thinks?" asked Dart.

" 'Deed he do, mistuh, and it don't sweeten his temper. He's eviler than he would be if he really had killed the man."

"There is evidence that he did kill the man," Dart reminded him.

"Must be sump'm wrong with that evidence. Jinx wouldn't kill nobody."

"I thought you didn't know him so well?"

Bubber was too much concerned for his friend to attempt further subterfuge. "I know that much about him," he said. "That Negro ain't bad sho' 'nough. He's jes' bad-lookin'."

"You yourself identified his handkerchief. It had been stuffed down the victim's throat, you'll remember."

"Well—I knowed he didn't do it befo'. But, far as I see, that proved he didn't do it."

"How?"

"Listen, mistuh. Jinx might 'a' hit somebody with that club jes' sorter thoughtless like. But stuffin' a handkerchief down his throat—that wouldn't even occur to him. He's too dumb to think up a smart trick like that."

"An opinion," Dr. Archer said, "in which I wholly concur.

Nothing in Jenkins' character connects him with this offense, either as author or agent. Someone in that room simply made him the dupe."

"Possibly you can explain, then, how his thumb print got on that club," Dart said.

"Possibly I can. In fact I had just that in mind when I asked you to bring it along."

He reached for the first package which Dart had put on the desk, and unwrapped it carefully.

"Remember, we don't know," he observed meanwhile, "that this club or bone actually delivered the blow. There was no blood on it for the simple reason that it had bounced back from the point of impact before hemorrhage, which was moderate, got under way. But it is permissible to assume that it was used."

He lifted the club by its two ends, using the tips of his fingers, and slowly rotated it about its own axis. His glance shuttled back and forth over the ivory-colored surface. "This is the incriminating print?" he asked, indicating a dark smudge.

"Yes. That's what Tynie photographed."

"He didn't dust the bone with powder first, did he?"

"No. How'd you know?"

"Because there's no powder on it elsewhere. This surface has a thick viscous film over it as though it had been oiled or waxed. It isn't oil or wax. It's a film which oozes from the pores of the incompletely prepared specimens, due to the presence of undestroyed marrow inside. If Tynie had dusted this bone there'd be particles of powder stuck all over it. Fortunately, he looked first and found preparation unnecessary—his print had been prepared for him. Now let's have a look.

"I've a magnifying glass hereabouts somewhere—here it is." He studied the smudge a moment. Then he put the bone down, looked up at Dart and smiled. "Easiest thing in the world," he said.

"What is?"

"Transferring a finger print."

"Are you kidding me, doc?"

"Not at all. Simple statement of fact. The discovery of a finger print is not necessarily any better evidence of its owner's presence than the discovery of any other object belonging to

him. Don't misunderstand me. I know that as a means of identification, its value is established. But as proof that the owner's
fingers put it where it was found—that's another matter. That
is a belief based on an assumption. And the fact that the assumption is usually correct does not make it any the less an
assumption."

"But just what is the assumption?"

"That there is but one way to put finger prints on an object,
namely, direct contact between the fingers and the object. That
is the unconscious assumption that is always made the moment
a finger print is discovered. We say 'A-ha, finger print.' We
identify it as John Doe's finger print. Then we say, 'A-ha, John
Doe was here.'"

"Of course," said Dart. "What else would anyone think?"

"Apparently nothing else. But I assure you that as a matter
of demonstrable fact, John Doe may never have been near the
place. He may have been ten miles away when his finger print
was put on the object."

"You'll have to produce plenty evidence to convince me of
that, doc."

"Look. You were perfectly willing to believe that Jinx
Jenkins' handkerchief might have been taken by somebody
else and put where we found it, weren't you? So willing that
you did not arrest him on that evidence alone. But when his
thumb print was found on the club—that settled it: Jinx must
have had a hand in it. Now, I believe I can show you that, aside
from a lot of minor assumptions there, your major assumption
could have been wrong. Jinx Jenkins didn't have to be anywhere near this club. His finger print could have been deliberately put on it to incriminate him, just as his handkerchief
could have been used as it was for the same purpose."

"I'm looking, doc. Go ahead."

"All right. Let us suppose that I want to rob that safe in the
corner. I'd be an awful ass, because I wouldn't get a dime's
worth of anything. But I don't know that. I want to rob it and
I want the circumstances to incriminate you. I decide that since
people think as they do, it would incriminate you if right after
the robbery your finger prints—even a lone thumb print—
could be demonstrated on that safe door.

"Here is a box of fine grade talcum powder. It's a professional sample, otherwise it wouldn't be so fine. I'll put a little on the arm of your chair—smooth, polished wooden surface. Now grasp the arms of your chair with your hands, as you might if you didn't think I was putting something over on you. Good. Incidentally, look at your thumb—has a fair film of powder, hasn't it? All right. Change seats with me. . . . Now again grasp the arms of your chair naturally. Take your hands away. Look at the right arm of your chair. See anything?"

"Sure. A perfect thumb print in white powder! But——"

"Too early for buts. Get up now and stand behind the chair. You are now ten miles away. All right. Here is a rubber glove, such as I rarely nowadays have the opportunity to use. I put it on my hand thus. The rubber is of course perfectly smooth, and if I wish I can increase the coefficient of adhesion——"

"Wait a minute, doc."

"My error. I can make it just a very little bit sticky by rubbing into the palm of it thus, a bit of vaseline, cold cream or what have you. This is not strictly necessary, but tends to improve the clearness of the transfer. Now, with proper stealth, I approach the talcum-powder thumb print which you have so obligingly left on the arm of your chair. I lean over the chair thus and carefully, as if it were a curved blotter, I roll the heel of my hand once, only once, over our powder print. And you see, I have the powder tracing on my glove.

"Of course this is not your thumb print. It is the negative of your thumb print, or rather, the mirror-image of it. If now I go to the safe and smear a tiny bit of vaseline on the safe door thus, it is a simple matter to roll your thumb print off my glove onto the black surface of the door. And there it is. Doesn't even have to be dusted. Photograph it, bring it up on the high contrast paper, and you, my friend, are under arrest for robbing my safe. Yet you have never been near my safe and you were ten miles away when the crime was committed."

Perry Dart silently went over to the safe and gazed upon the smudge of powder. He came back to the desk, picked up the doctor's hand glass, returned to the safe door and studied the transferred print. It was not the crisp image of the original, but the fine granules of powder, primarily arranged in a definite pattern by the tiny grooves of his own skin, had not been sufficiently disarranged by the transposition to obliterate that pattern.

"If you wish," said Dr. Archer, "I can improve on that beautifully by using the same technique with printer's ink. It comes up astonishingly when dusted with finger-print powder afterwards. But this is sufficient to indicate the possibilities."

"You're going to get yourself in trouble thinking up things like that," muttered the detective.

"I didn't think it up," was the answer. "Our unknown murderer —if any—thought it up and used it. Only, since he had a light-colored and fairly gummy object to work toward, he used a black substance instead of a white. I remember getting some of it on my hand from that chair Brady brought me; possibly the same chair Jenkins used—or maybe several chair-arms had been so treated. Lamp-black would do nicely, plain or in a paste like shoe polish. If you examine that print on the bone as you did the one on the safe, you will note a general similarity. Both look as though they might have been put on by a somewhat dirty finger, that's all. Both, however, were actually put on by a smooth-surfaced applicator, which spread the lines just a little, but not too much."

"You know, I thought it was funny Tynes' saying he didn't even have to prepare the thing."

"Still," the physician said, "this only indicates that Jenkins didn't have to touch the club or deliver the blow. It doesn't indicate that he did not actually do so. But something else does."

"What?"

"The position of the print. Even if the transferability of a finger print couldn't be demonstrated, still this print would not prove that Jenkins delivered a blow with this club. On the contrary, it proves that he could not have delivered an effective blow with his thumb in that spot. Look. To deliver an effective blow he would grasp the club in his hand like this—no danger, I'm using my gloved hand and I've wiped off the remains of your thumb print—like this, near the smaller end, so that the condyles—those big bumps which help form the knee part of the bone—would land on the victim's head. Grasping it so, his fingers would surround the shaft thus, completely, and his thumb, you see, would rest on the outside of his fingers; it couldn't possibly produce a print on the surface of the bone because it wouldn't even touch the surface of the bone. But beyond that, the position of the print is near the big end—the clubbing-end here. Notice that the print is close to this condyle and directed obliquely toward it. If your hand grasped this bone so that your thumb fell in that position, your fingers would have to be around the club end like this, and the shaft of the bone, you see, would then fall along your forearm, so that you could not possibly deliver a blow. Any attempt to do so would only endanger your own fingers."

"Gee, doc, you ought to be a lawyer."

"I am. I'm Jenkins' lawyer right now. And I contend, your honor, that if the handkerchief was insufficient basis for indictment, so is the thumb print. Only more so."

"Hot damn!" came an unexpected cry from the admiring Bubber. "Go to it, doc! You're the best!"

4

Bubber's ensuing expressions of appreciation literally carried him away. He backed and sidled out through the doctor's several doors on a transporting flood of gratitude, much like a large rubber ball twisting this way and that on the surface of a flowing stream.

The physician turned again to the detective and smiled. "What does your honor say about Jenkins?"

"Sort of lost my enthusiasm for Jenkins," grinned Dart.

"Well, then, since we're beginning to eliminate, let's attempt a diagnosis."

"O.K. doc. Take 'em one by one. That'll bring up some things I've found out that I haven't told you. I was too interested in Frimbo's servant when I came in."

"Jinx Jenkins."

"Hardly, after your defense."

"Thanks. Doty Hicks."

"Oh, yes. Well, here's the dope on Hicks. Remember, he said that to break Frimbo's spell on his brother it was necessary to put a counter-spell equally fatal on Frimbo. But he had to have somebody's help. The immediate possibility was, of course, that Jenkins was that somebody. But your argument practically eliminates Jenkins on the one hand; and on the other we've found out by further questioning just who he meant. He was talking about a hoodoo artist named Bolus in 132nd Street, who gave him some kind of goofer dust to sprinkle on Frimbo's floor. That's the gray powder we found under the table."

"You found this Bolus?"

"Had no trouble getting a check-up out of him. I told him he was under suspicion for murder, having deliberately conjured and killed a professional competitor. Well, sir, he nearly died himself trying to convince me that his goofer dust was just ordinary coal ashes. Of course, I knew that already. Got the report last night. So then I promised to come back and take him for fraud."

"Doty Hicks, then, is no longer a suspect?"

"Hardly."

"Ironic business all around, Dart. Hicks, in all good faith, put his goofer dust at the feet of a man who may even then have been dead. And he and Jenkins, the only two you could reasonably have held, are probably the least likely suspects of the lot. Well—the two women."

"They're out. We know from checked testimony that they didn't enter the death room till after the thing was done."

"All right by me. Nice girl, Martha Crouch. Easley Jones, the railroad man?"

"Excellent record on his job. Long, faithful service. Hasn't been out of his rooming-house but twice since Saturday night, both times for food."

"Also decidedly untutored—same sort of man that Aramintha Snead is of woman. By no means the character of mind who would think up this particular scheme to incriminate someone else."

"Who's next?"

"Spider Webb."

"Yes, Webb. Well, Webb told a straight story. And Frimbo tried to dispose of the servant's remains. The only way to connect Webb with the crime now is to assume that he and Frimbo were conspiring. But why they'd be conspiring to kill Frimbo's servant—that's beyond me."

"You're sure Webb told a straight story?"

"About the feud, yes. We've gone into it thoroughly. That killing yesterday morning means all I told you it meant. Further, Brandon, Spencer's rival policy king, has disappeared. He always does when somebody has to take the rap."

"That leaves us Frimbo himself."

"Nobody else but."

"Hm—the house is open for suggestions."

"You know, I'm beginning to see daylight in this thing." An idea was growing on Dart. "By Judas! I do see daylight!"

"Show me, O master."

"Look. Suppose Brandon did find out that Frimbo was the cause of his downfall. It's not hard to believe you know. Dumber people than Frimbo are remarkably clever at this number-playing game. They hit on some system and it works. They get so good that bankers actually turn down their bets. Well, Frimbo could have doped out such a system. Suppose he did, and suppose that through it, Spencer was playing heavily with Brandon and winning. Brandon couldn't wipe out Spencer —that would be open confession. But nothing in the world would stop him from trying to wipe out Frimbo. Nothing except that Frimbo isn't easy to get at alone, except at night in a private interview. To take Frimbo, therefore, Brandon's got to finesse. You see?"

"So far."

"So what does he do? He finds somebody who is close to Frimbo, who has access to him, and who is not likely to be suspected. In short, he finds the servant. The servant, who no doubt is already envious of his master's success—the way black servants are with black masters—is offered a big handful of change to put his boss out—any way he can. All right. He agrees. But he's not going to jam himself by doing it during the day when he is known to be in the place alone with Frimbo! He's going to wait till night when the office is full. And he's going to bring the whole thing off in a way that will incriminate somebody else who happens to be present. Wouldn't you? Wait a minute—I know what you're going to say. The answer is that the servant was on the point of carrying the scheme through. He had snatched Jenkins' handkerchief in the scramble there when Doty Hicks fainted. He had already by some scheme such as you just demonstrated got Jenkins' finger print on the club. But Frimbo's smart. Frimbo reads his mind or gets a hunch or anything you want to call it. Frimbo discovers what's up just in time to turn the tables—frustrates the attack and gives the servant his own medicine, club, handkerchief, and all!"

Dart paused to emphasize this twist of interpretation; then went on:

"But Frimbo hasn't got time to dispose of the body then and there. So he exchanges the servant's yellow turban and sash for his own, props the body up in his own chair, hides in the dark and goes on telling visitors their fates, intending to get them all out without arousing any suspicions. But our crusty friend Jenkins discovers the fact that the man talking to him is a corpse—and that changes his plans. See?"

The physician meditated upon this. "You have lapsed into brilliance, Dart," he commented finally. "Brilliance is likely to be blinding. . . . Wasn't it the servant who ushered each visitor to Frimbo's door?"

"Hell, no. That was Frimbo, himself. He took each one to the door, then, while they were going in, blinded by that light, he'd run around, enter the hall door, hide behind the corpse, and talk to 'em."

"All coons look alike, to be sure. But I've seen no sign of external strabismus in either of Frimbo's eyes."

"What?"

"The servant in general resembled Frimbo. But he was cock-eyed. Frimbo isn't. The people who testified all saw the servant and all agreed that he was cock-eyed. Somehow, Dart, I dislike that term—extremely misleading isn't it? But strabismus, now —there's a word! External strabismus—internal strabismus— see how they roll off your tongue."

"I'm particular what rolls off my tongue."

"Nevertheless, external strabismus is not an easily assumed disguise. I have never heard of anyone who could render himself cock-eyed at will."

"You haven't?" grinned Dart. "Ever try cooked whiskey?"

"The phenomenon you have in mind is an illusion—an optical illusion, if you like. The victim enjoys diplopia—the impression of seeing the world double, an impression which he believes cock-eyed people must have at all times. Thus the illusion is twofold: cock-eyed people really don't see double; and the happy inebriate actually has no external strabismus, he has only a transitory internal strabismus. I insist therefore, that, remarkable as Frimbo is, voluntary external strabismus is an accomplishment which we must not grant him lightly. But all this is not the prime objection to your startling vision. The prime objection is that Frimbo would surely not leave thwarted his own plan. Would he?"

"He didn't. Jenkins——"

"He did. Jenkins would have gone on being mystified by Frimbo's revelations, had it not been for Frimbo's own startled words. The thing that made Jenkins jump up and turn the light on the corpse was Frimbo's sudden exclamation, 'Frimbo, why don't you see?' Frimbo would not have said that if he had been planning to get Jenkins and the others out as quickly and unsuspectingly as possible. Something happened to Frimbo about that moment."

"But Jenkins' word is all we have for that remark."

"Jenkins' word, now that he is pretty well exonerated, should be worth something. But even if by itself it isn't, I have Frimbo's word in support."

"You what?"

"Frimbo himself said to me today that he went blind, so to speak, while talking to Jenkins. He saw so far ahead—then everything went blank."

"Hooey."

"All right. Maybe this is hooey too: You say that Frimbo hid behind the corpse near enough to make his voice seem to come from the corpse."

"Yes."

"Then, when Jenkins suddenly jumped up and without warning swung the light around why didn't he see Frimbo hiding?"

"I don't know—maybe Frimbo ducked under the table or some place."

"Hooey. Hooey. An eloquent word, isn't it?"

"Well, the details may not be exact, but that isn't far from what happened. It's the only thing I can think of that even nearly fits the facts."

"Nearly won't do."

"All right, professor. You guess."

"There's something malicious in the way you say that. However, innocent and unsuspecting as I am, I will guess. And I guess, first off, I'll leave out the number racket. That'll make it easier for me, you see."

"But the number racket can't be ignored——"

"Who's doing this guessing?"

"O.K. doc. Guess away."

"I guess the same thing that you guess, that Frimbo killed his servant. But not because of the number racket, or any attack upon him growing out of the number racket."

"But because he's a nut."

"Please—not so bluntly. It sounds crude—robbed of its nuances and subtleties. You transform a portrait into a cartoon. Say, rather, that under the influence of certain compulsions, associated with a rather intricate psychosis, he was impelled to dispose of his servant for definite reasons."

"All right. Say it anyhow you like. But to me it's still because he was a nut."

" 'Nut' in no wise suggests the complexity of our friend's psychology. You recall my description of his condition; its origin in his type of mind, its actual onset in an experience, its primary and secondary delusions."

"Yes. I recall all that."

"Well, here's an item you don't recall because it hasn't been mentioned; Frimbo like other paranoiacs, has a specific act as a part of his compensatory mechanism. This act becomes a necessary routine which must be performed, and naturally takes its form from some earlier aspect of his life. In his case it derives from his native days in Buwongo, his African principality. He calls it the rite of the gonad. And though he declines to describe it, I can imagine what it amounts to. It is nothing more or less than his extracting, in that laboratory of his, a kind of testicular extract with which he periodically treats himself. By so doing, he believes that he partakes of matter actually carrying the impress of all the ages past, and so becomes master of that past."

"Deep stuff. Anything in it?"

"Well, I don't know anything about endocrines. But I should think such a practice would produce some kind of hyper-sexuality. Sex gland deficiency can be helped by such treat-ment, so perhaps a normal person would become, in some respects, oversexed."

"But sex has played no part in this picture."

"I was only answering your question. To return to my guess. Frimbo has to have sex glands—not those of lower animals such as biological houses use to make their commercial ex-tracts, but human sex glands, carrying, to his mind, the effects of human experience from time immemorial. With the com-pulsion strong upon him to secure human tissues for his rite, he could easily become as ruthless as a drug addict deprived of his drug. But he would be far more cunning. He would choose a victim who would not be missed, and he would arrange cir-cumstances to incriminate someone else. And the insanely bril-liant feature is that he would arrange to have himself appear to be the victim. I do not believe that the unusual devices used to commit this crime and divert suspicion indicate the workings of an ordinary mind or knowledge such as a servant would have. They indicate a sort of crazy ingenuity which would not be conceived and carried out by a normal person. Frimbo is the only one in the crowd whose mind fits the details of this crime."

"Well, you're disagreeing with me only on motive. I say self-defense. You say insanity. But both of us say Frimbo did it. From that point on I should think our difficulties would be alike: the cock-eyed business, the blind spot or whatever it was, and the—what was the other thing?"

"His sudden invisibility if he hid behind the dead servant."

"Yea—that."

"The cock-eyed business, yes. But the other business, no. I did not say that he hid behind the servant. I think he had some device or instrument—I'm not sure just what, but we'll find it —that placed his voice so that it seemed to come from the ser-vant. And I do not say that he acted under the urgency of a sudden encounter. I say that he planned the whole thing ahead, deliberately. Even foresaw the possibility of discovery and ar-ranged to rise from the dead, just for effect, as he did. That would be wholly in character. He even had an alibi ready for my blood test. He showed me this afternoon how I might easily have made an error in the little experiment I showed you. He did not know, of course, that Bubber Brown's discovery was on hand as a perfect check.

"He demonstrated how something in my gauze dressing might throw the test off—it would have been very disturbing indeed if I had not known what he was up to. What he did was to substitute for my gauze a piece which he had previously treated with the dead man's serum. He foresaw every possibility. Far from thwarting his own plans, even that sudden loss of prophetic vision, that premonition, did not change his main course of action. That exclamation, 'Frimbo, why don't you see?' startled Jenkins into action, to be sure, and resulted in our rushing on the scene. But even then he would have removed the body anyway from under our very noses—he could have done so simply by shutting off the lights.

"And there's another difference in our theories: If, as you say, it was just self-defense, he is not shown to be dangerous. He can be held for disposing of the remains, but not for murder; self-defense is manslaughter and is likely to go unpunished. But if, as I say, it is insanity, then he's liable to do the same thing again to some other unfortunate fellow; he must be put away in a cool dry place where he's no longer a menace. Don't you see?"

"That's so. You know, doc, just out of sportsmanship you might let me win an argument once in a while."

"We're not arguing. We're guessing. And I have a curious feeling that smart as we think we are, we're both guessing wrong."

"You're good, doc. Anyway it goes now, you're right."

"At least I know one thing."

"What?"

"I know I saw a new specimen jar on one of Frimbo's shelves today. It was next to the one that we noted before. And it contained two more sex glands."

"Judas H. Priest!" said Perry Dart softly.

Chapter Twenty-three

I

FOR the first time since the incarceration of his friend Jinx, Bubber Brown enjoyed a meal. The probability of Jinx's release later tonight, a happy eventuality which Bubber himself had helped bring about, more than restored Bubber's appetite to normal and he indulged in gleeful anticipation of what he would say to his grouchy comrade upon the latter's return to freedom. Mumbled mockery pushed its way through prodigious mouthfuls of food.

"Uh—huh," emerged stifled but determined through roast beef and mashed potatoes. "Here you is. Yo' flat feet is now out in the free air they probably need plenty of. Now get to thankin' me." A succulent forkful of kale crowded its way in with the roast and potatoes, and all this was stuffed securely back with a large folded layer of soft white bread. Even through this there somehow escaped sounds.

"Boy, you was due to go. Go where? Where do folks go what murder folks? I mean it was upon you. If it hadn' been for me and the doc, you'd be on your way to Swing Swing now. Your can was scheduled to rest on a 'lectric lounging chair—they even had the date set. I ain' kiddin' you, boy. You was jes' like that coffee they advertise on the radio—your can was dated."

The next few phrases were overwhelmed with hot coffee. Bubber grinned and substituted a dish of juicy apple cobbler for his denuded dinner plate. "From now on," he told it, "you listen and I talk, 'cause your head is a total loss to you—jes' extra weight you carryin' around for no purpose." The apple cobbler began miraculously to vanish. "You see, you don't appreciate my brains. I got brains enough for both of us. I don't even have to use all my brains—I got brains in the back o' my head I ain't never used. Some time when you admit how dumb you is, I'll lend you some for a few days, jes' to show you how it feels to have a thought once in a while."

The dessert became a sweet memory, vestiges of which were dislodged with a handy toothpick.

"Now, let's see. Got to be at the place at 'leven o'clock. Guess I'll drop in and see that picture at the Roosevelt Theatre —*Murder Between Drinks*. Wonder 'f I'm go'n' see that third one tonight? Maybe the one in the picture'll be number three. Now there's brains again. Jes' by goin' to see this picture I may save somebody's life. Doggone!—ain't I smart?"

2

Promptly at eleven, Bubber Brown mounted the stoop and entered the house. He started up the stairs toward Frimbo's floor, looking above. He stopped, his eyes popping. He brushed his hand across his lids, and stared again toward the head of the stairs. What he saw persisted. It might have been Saturday night again; for there motionless above him stood the tall, black-robed figure of Frimbo's servant, bright yellow turban and sash gleaming in the dim light, exactly as he had been before, even—yes, there it was—even to the definite cast in one solemn eye.

Bubber blinked twice, wheeled about, and would have vanished through the front door as magically as this corpse had reappeared. But at that particular moment the door opened and Perry Dart with half a dozen policemen obstructed the avenue of escape. Bubber came to in Jinx Jenkins' arms, pointed, and gasped:

"Look! is I dreamin'—or is I dreamin'?"

"What's the matter, Brown?" Dart asked.

"Didn't you say the flunky was the one got cooked?"

"Yes."

"Well, look up yonder! He's there—I seen him!"

"Yeah?" Dart stepped forward, looked up the stairs. He smiled. "So he is, Brown. We must have made a mistake. Come on, let's go—can't let a little error like that worry us."

"So," muttered Jinx, "you is wrong again. What a brain!"

"You can go if you want to, brother," demurred Bubber. "Me—I've never felt the need of fresh air the way I do now. People in this house don't suit me. They jes' don't pay death no mind."

"Come on, Brown," insisted Dart. "I'll need your help. Don't let me down now."

"All right. I'll follow. But don't count on me for no help. I'm go'n' stay 'live long as I can. I ain't learnt this Lazarus trick yet."

In the hallway above, Dart gave due orders in stationing his men, so that all natural exits were covered. The servant ushered them then to the reception room, where every one was present but Dr. Archer. The detective noted each person in turn: Mrs. Aramintha Snead, Mrs. Martha Crouch, Easley Jones, Doty Hicks, Spider Webb, and Jinx Jenkins, whom he had brought with him.

The physician arrived a moment later. "I summon Frimbo," said the servant who had escorted him in also. The servant bowed. The doctor looked after his retreating form quizzically, then turned to Detective Dart and smiled. Dart grinned back. Bubber observed the exchange and murmured, "You all could see jokes in tombstones, couldn't you?"

Perry Dart said to the physician, "Now what?"

"Wait," answered Dr. Archer. "It's his show."

They waited. Shortly the gold turban and sash returned. "This way, please," said the servitor, and gestured toward the wide entrance to the consulting-room.

"Everybody?"

"Please."

Again the servant retreated by way of the hall. The others, directed by the detective and led by the physician, entered the black chamber from the front room and stood in an expectant semicircle facing the table in the center. Over the far chair, which still sat behind the table just as it had when the body had been found in it, hung the device which projected a horizontal beam of light toward the entrance. Most of the visitors fell to the one or the other side of this beam, but at the distance of the semicircle, its rays diverged enough to include two figures directly in its path, those of Martha Crouch and Spider Webb. Mrs. Crouch's dark eyes were level and clear, her lips slightly compressed, her expression anticipative but not apprehensive. Spider Webb also betrayed interest without profound concern, his countenance manifesting only a sort of furtive malignancy. The rest were mere densities in the penumbra.

3

As they stood watching, the darkness beyond the table condensed into a black figure, much as mist might condense into a cloud. This figure silently came to occupy the chair beneath the light. Then from it issued the low rich voice of Frimbo.

"A return into the past," it said, "observes events in their reverse order. May I therefore ask Mr. Jenkins, who was the last to occupy that chair on Saturday evening, to be the first to do so tonight?"

Nobody moved.

Bubber's sharp whisper came forth.

"Go on, fool. Get yo'self freed."

With obvious and profound reluctance, Jinx's figure moved forward into the light. Those toward one side could see tiny beads of sweat glistening on his freckled countenance. He sidled into the chair on this side of the table, facing the voice and the shadow. His face was brightly illuminated and starkly troubled.

"Mr. Jenkins," Frimbo's voice went on smoothly, "it is again Saturday night. You have come to consult me. All that reached your consciousness is again before you. You will conceal nothing from the eyes of Frimbo. The light shall lay open your mind to me, book-wise. I shall read you. Be silent, please."

There was scant danger of Jinx's being anything else. Even his usual murderous scowl had been erased, and Frimbo's intent contemplation of his face could be sensed by every onlooker. They too were steadily staring upon him from behind or from the side, according to their position, much as if they expected him at any moment to leap to his feet and confess the crime.

Then a change of color came over Jinx's face. Those who were in position to see observed that the light freckled skin over the eminences of his bony countenance was growing darker. Alarmingly the change progressed, like an attack of some grave cyanotic disease. Jinx was actually turning blue. But it at once became apparent that his color was due to a change in the light which illumined him. Slowly that light changed again.

"Each hue," said Frimbo's voice, "makes its particular disclosure."

Jinx became yellow.

"Got to do mo'n that to make a Chinaman out o' him," came Bubber's whisper.

Diabolically red flushed the subject's lean visage, and finally a ghastly green. Throughout it all Frimbo's intense inspection created an atmosphere of vibrant expectancy. One felt that the lines of vision between his eyes and Jinx's face were almost tangible—could be plucked and made to sing like the strings of an instrument.

Eventually Frimbo said, "No," and the spell was broken. "This is not the man." The light came white again. "That is all, Mr. Jenkins."

There was a general sigh of relief. Jinx returned to the circle, where Bubber greeted him with an inevitable comment:

"The red light turned you red, boy, and that green light turned you green. But that white light couldn't do a thing for you. It was jes' wasted."

Frimbo said, "Now, Mr. Webb, please."

But Perry Dart interrupted. "Just a minute, Frimbo." He stepped forward to the side of the table. "Before we go any further, don't you think it fair to have your servant present?"

Frimbo's voice became grave. "I regret that I have already permitted my servant to leave."

"Why did you do that?"

"It is his custom to leave at eleven, may I remind you?"

"And may I remind you that we are investigating a serious crime; also that you promised to have him present?"

"I kept my promise. He was here. You all saw him. I did not promise that he would remain after his hours."

"Very well. You say he is gone?"

"Yes."

"He has left the house?"

"Yes."

"Then perhaps you will tell me just how he got out. Every exit is covered by an officer, with orders to bring to me anyone who tries to leave this house."

There was a pause; but Frimbo said easily, "That I cannot tell you. I can tell you, however, that by interrupting this procedure you are defeating your own investigation, with which I am endeavoring to help you."

Dart achieved a trace of Frimbo's own irony. "Your consideration for my interest touches me, Frimbo. I am overwhelmed with gratitude. But your servant is a necessary witness. I must insist on his being here—with you."

"That is impossible."

"Well, now you are at least telling the truth. Or perhaps you can do for him what you did for yourself?"

"You are obscure."

"Look harder, Frimbo. It's the bad lighting. I mean that perhaps you can make him rise from the dead, as you did."

Bubber could not suppress a mumbled, "Come on, Lazarus. Do yo' stuff."

"You believe then," Frimbo said, "that my servant is dead?"

"I know that your servant is dead. I have in my hand positive evidence of his death."

"Of what nature?"

"Evidence that was retrieved from your furnace downstairs by one of my men——"

"Hot damn!" breathed Bubber. "Tell 'em 'bout me!"

"—when you were trying to destroy it. I have a piece of the bone upon which his brain rested during life. I have a removable bridge which is known to be his, and which fits that bone—or rather the teeth in the bone joined to it. Frimbo, this is a farce. You killed your servant, who also went by the name of Frimbo. You slipped around through this house somehow on Saturday night while I was investigating this case, and moved his body to some hiding-place on these premises. You treated that body to make it burn quickly and to make what bone was left crumble easily. You dismembered it and tried to dispose of it by way of your furnace. You were seen doing this by Bubber Brown, who was in your cellar last night and who recovered a part of the bone before it crumbled. To avert suspicion, you masqueraded as your servant by a trick of your eyes. I see no point in continuing this nonsense. You're the guilty party and you're under arrest. Am I still obscure?"

4

For a long moment no other word was spoken. At last Frimbo said quietly:

"Since I am already under arrest, it would be useless, perhaps, to point out certain errors in your charges. . . . However, if you would care to know the truth——"

"You are at liberty to make any statement you please. But don't try anything funny. We've anticipated some of your tricks."

"Tricks," Frimbo said softly, "is an unkind word. The fact is, however, that I have killed no one. It is true that I have disposed of my servant's remains. If that box contains what you say it does, and if Brown was in the cellar when you say he was, he undoubtedly saw me in the course of performing what was nothing more or less than a tribal duty."

"Tribal duty?"

"The servant was a fellow tribesman of mine whom I took in and protected when his venture into this civilization proved to be less fortunate than mine. He was of my clan and entitled to use the name, Frimbo. His distinguishing name, however—what you would call his Christian name, had he not been a heathen and a savage—was N'Ogo. It is our tradition that the spirit of one of our number who meets death at the hands of an—an outsider, can be purged of that disgrace and freed from its flesh only by fire. The body must be burned before sunset of the third day. Since the circumstances made this impossible, I assumed the risk of removing and properly destroying my tribesman's flesh. For that and for whatever penalty attaches to it, I have no regret. My only regret, Mr. Dart, is that you have interrupted, and perhaps for the time defeated, my effort to complete the duty which this death has imposed upon me."

Dart was impressed. The man's total lack of embarrassment, his dignity, his utter composure, could not fail to produce effect.

"Complete the duty——?"

"It is a part of my duty, as the king of my people, to find the killer and bring him to the just punishment which he has earned. In my own land I should take that part of the matter into my own hands. Here in yours it was my intention to find the killer and turn him over to you. But as for killing N'Ogo myself—you would have to be one of us, my friend, to appreciate how horribly absurd that is. I would sooner kill myself than one of my clan. And he—he could not under the most extraordinary circumstances imaginable bring himself to do a thing against his king. He simply could not have committed an offense against me that would have caused me to decree or execute his death. Against one of his own or lower rank, perhaps, but not against me."

The detective, ordinarily prompt in decision, was for the moment bewildered. But habit was strong. "Look here," he said, "how can you prove that what you say is true—that you didn't kill this man?"

"It is not of the slightest importance to me, Mr. Dart, whether you or the authorities you represent believe me or not. My concern is not for my own protection but for the discharge of my obligation as king. If I can not complete my duty to this member of my clan, I do not deserve to have been his king. The greatest humiliation I could suffer would be death at the hands of a strange people. That is no more than he has suffered."

This was an attitude which Dart had never encountered. The complete and convincing unimportance to Frimbo of what was paramount to the detective left the latter for the moment without resource. He was silent, considering. Finally he asked:

"But why did you have to do so much play-acting? Accepting what you say as true, why did you have to pull all that hokum about rising from the dead?"

"Do you not see that it was necessary to my plans? I had to have time in which to dispose of N'Ogo's body. I had to account for its disappearance. It is easy for me to pass undiscovered from almost any part of this house to any other part. I have a lift, electrically operated and practically undiscoverable, in the old dumbwaiter shaft. It travels from this floor to the cellar. What appears on examination to be the roof of the old shaft, with rusty gears and frazzled rope hanging down, is really not the roof but the bottom of the floor of the lift. N'Ogo's remains reposed on that lift, securely hidden, during the latter part of your search. So did I until the proper moment for my entrance. What better way can you think of to account for the disappearance of a body than to claim to be that body? I even wounded myself as N'Ogo had been wounded, in anticipation of the good doctor's examination. I took every possible precaution—even inviting the doctor alone here to determine the extent of his investigations and divert him from the truth if possible."

"What about those sex glands?"

"They too are a part of the tradition. They alone, of all his flesh, must be preserved as a necessary item in the performance of one of our tribal rites, one which I went so far as to mention to Dr. Archer today. That I can not speak further of, but I think the doctor's excellent mind will comprehend what it can not fully know."

"But this is unheard of. You haven't told the whole story yet. You say you don't know who killed this servant or tribesman of yours. Do you know when he was killed?"

"Not even that. I know only that one of the people who came here to see me killed him, thinking he was I."

"How could anybody make that mistake?"

"Easily. You see, it has always been our custom, as is true of many peoples, that the chief, in whom resides the most important secrets of the nation, should not be unnecessarily exposed to physical danger. Just as a lesser warrior in medieval days donned the white plume of his commander to deceive the enemy and prevent the possibility of their concentrating upon the leader, killing him early, and demoralizing the troops by eliminating competent direction, so with us for many hundreds of years a similar practice has been in effect. The king is prohibited by tribal law from unnecessarily endangering the tribal secrets residing in his person. My servant knew of certain dangers to which I was exposed here. I had devised a mathematical formula whereby I was able to predict a certain probability in the popular policy game of this community. My part in the dwindling fortunes of one of the so-called bankers was discovered through the disloyalty of a disgruntled underling in the rival camp which my information was aiding. The loser intended to eliminate me. Whether this actual killing was his doing or not I am not sure—that was one possibility. There was another.

"At any rate, N'Ogo and I exchanged rôles. It had been so

for several days. I am able through a divertissement learned in youth to diverge my eyes as easily as most people converge theirs, and so, to the casual observer, could easily pass for my own servant.

"My servant had only to sit here in this chair in the darkness. I myself, dressed in his costume, would usher the visitor to the entrance there, turn aside, and come down the hall to my laboratory at the rear. There a device of mine enabled me to convince the visitor, now seated in that chair opposite, that it was really I who sat there. This light over my head is far more than a light. It is also a mechanism whereby I can see the illuminated face of whoever occupies that chair, and whereby also I can transmit my voice to this point. It comprises nothing mechanically original or unusual, except, perhaps, its compactness. By means of it, I was able to carry on my observation of a visitor and talk to him quite as if I were really in this chair, except that I could see only his face. Thus, you see, by the use of two rather simple mechanisms, my lift and my light, I enjoyed remarkable freedom of movement and considerable personal security in case of necessity.

"But on Saturday night, I had no need, any more than on any other night, for entering this room. Visitors were always accustomed to paying their fees to the assistant in the hall as they departed. So negative was my assistant's part in this masquerade that I did not—and do not—know just when he was attacked. But the strange experience—what you will call a premonition—that momentarily startled me during Mr. Jenkins' interview made me exclaim in a way that startled him also, so that he jumped up to investigate. The crime had been done before that moment. It was done between the time when some prior visitor rose to go—disappearing from view in my mechanism—and the time when I collected the same visitor's fee in the hall. Or perhaps between the time when I bowed him into this room and reached my laboratory.

"From that point on you know what happened. I could do only what I did do. Tonight I had every reason to believe, before your interruption, that I should determine the identity of the murderer. Perhaps I may do so yet—I have arranged certain traps. In case of the unexpected, Mr. Dart, be careful what you touch——"

A wholly strange voice suddenly shot out from the deep shadow behind Frimbo.

"So it's really you this time, Frimbo? Why weren't you careful what you touched?"

At the last word a pistol banged twice.

In that frozen instant, before any of the dumbfounded bystanders could move, Frimbo's light was abruptly blotted out and the room went utterly black. At the same moment a shriek of unmistakable pain and terror broke through the dark from the direction of the two shots.

"Brady—that light—quick!" came Dart's sharp voice. The powerful extension light flashed brilliantly on.

There was no need for haste, however. Against the wall at the rear of the black-draped chamber, whence the distressed cry had come, everyone saw a figure slumped limply down, as if it would fall but could not. It moaned and twitched as if in a convulsion, and one arm was extended upward as if held by something on the wall.

Dr. Archer reached the figure before the detective, started to lift it, looked up at the point where the hand was clinging, and changed his intention.

"Wait—be careful!" he warned the detective. The man's hand was grasping the handle of the switch-box which occupied that point on the wall. "That handle's live in that position. Here—push it up by lifting him by his clothing—that's it—a little more—I'll push up his elbow—there!" The hand fell free.

Supporting his limp figure between them, they got the man to his feet. They swung him, more unnerved than hurt, around into the light and drew him forward.

It was the railroad porter, Easley Jones.

5

Dr. Archer first did what he could for Frimbo, who, still sitting in the chair, had fallen face-down on the table; lifted his shoulders so that he resumed an erect posture, and began to loosen his clothing in order to examine his wounds. Frimbo, rapidly weakening, yet was able to lift one hand in protest. He smiled ever so faintly and managed a low whisper:

"Thank you, my friend, but it is of no use. This is what I foresaw."

Martha Crouch had come forward like one walking in a daze. Now she was beside Frimbo. Her face was a portrait of bewilderment and dread. Frimbo's head sank forward on his chest.

"The Buwongo secret," he murmured, "dies. . . ."

The young woman put her arm about his sagging shoulders. Her horror-struck face turned to Dr. Archer, mutely questioning. He shook his head a little sadly.

"How about the car downstairs, doc?" Dart was asking. "Shoot right over to Harlem Hospital if you say so."

Dr. Archer stood beside Frimbo a moment longer without answering. Then he sighed and turned away. "It's too late," he said. "Have him taken up to his room."

He approached Easley Jones, who stood between two policemen, looking down at the palm of his left hand, where the live switch handle had burned him. The doctor picked up the railroad porter's hand, inspected it, dropped it.

"Just what under the sun," he said, looking the man up and down, "could you have had against Frimbo?"

Easley Jones said nothing. His head remained sullenly lowered, the bushy kinks standing out like a black wool wig, the dark freckles sharply defined against pale brown skin.

"Have you anything to say?" Dart asked him.

Still he was silent.

"You sneaked around in the dark until you were near that switch Frimbo mentioned Saturday night. Then you shot Frimbo from behind, intending to throw off the switch and get back to your place during the excitement. We were looking for something like that, otherwise this extension would have been useless. We plugged it in downstairs on another circuit."

"But it was Frimbo," Dr. Archer said, "who caught him. Frimbo had wired that switch box so that the handle would go live when it was pulled down. Frimbo anticipated all this—he said so. Deliberately exposed himself to another attack in order to catch the killer. He even knew he was going to die."

"What this guy's grudge was I can't imagine. But he's saved us a lot of trouble by trying again. I suppose he would have tried it before if he hadn't known he was being trailed. How'd you know we were trailing you, Jones?"

No answer.

"Incredible," Dr. Archer was muttering. "Nothing about him to suggest the ingenuity——"

"Frimbo!"

The physician swung around, stepped back to Martha Crouch, who had uttered the name as one might cry out in torture. Never on any face had he seen such intense grief.

"Why, Martha—what in the world? Does this mean all that to you?"

Her eyes, wide and dry, stared impotently about in a suppressed frenzy of despair. Clearly, she would have screamed, but could not.

"You mean"—the physician could not bring himself to accept the obvious—"that you and Frimbo——?"

It was as if that name coupled with her own was more than she could endure. She wheeled away from him, and from the sudden tense immobility of her figure he knew that in a moment all that she was now curbing by long self-discipline would explode in one relieving outburst.

Suddenly she about-faced again. This time her eyes, fixed on a point behind John Archer, had in them the madness of hysteria. The doctor manifested an impulse to restrain her as she passed him. He hesitated a trifle too long. Before anyone knew her intention, she had swept like a Fury upon the man whose arms were in the grasp of the two officers. Low words came from between her clenched teeth as her hands tore at his face.

"You—killed—the only man——"

They managed after a moment to pull her away. What shocked her, however, out of that moment of mania into a sudden stupor of immobility was not the firm grasp of friendly hands but the realization that in her tightly closed fingers was a wig of kinky black hair, and that the sleek, black scalp of the man before her, despite the freckles which so well disguised his complexion, was that of her husband, the undertaker, Samuel Crouch.

Chapter Twenty-four

JINX JENKINS, released, and his ally, Bubber Brown, walked together down Seventh Avenue. It was shortly after midnight and the Avenue at this point was alive. The Lafayette Theatre was letting out somewhat later than usual, flooding the sidewalk with noisy crowds. Cabs were jostling one another to reach the curb. Brightly dressed downtowners were streaming into Connie's Inn next door. Habitués of the curb stood about in commenting groups, swapping jibes. The two friends ambled through the animated turbulence, unaware of the gaiety swirling around them, still awed by the experience through which they had passed.

"Death on the moon, boy," Bubber said. "What'd I tell you?"

"You tol' me," Jinx unkindly reminded him, "it was the flunky done it."

"The flunky done plenty," returned Bubber. "Got hisself killed, didn't he?"

"Yea—he done that, all right."

"His name was N'Ogo," Bubber said, "but he went."

They emerged from the bedlam of that carnival block.

"Smart guy that Frimbo," observed Bubber. "Y' know, I wouldn't mind bein' kind o' crazy if it made me that smart."

"That Crouch wasn't no dumbbell."

"Dart say Crouch must 'a' known all about a railroad porter named Easley Jones, and made out he was him."

"Hmph. Guess now he wishes he was him sho' 'nough."

"Sho' was different from his own self—act different, talk different."

"He wasn't so different. He was still actin' and talkin' cullud, only more so."

Bubber's hand was on the roll of bills in his pocket which he had won at blackjack, but his mind was still in Frimbo's death chamber.

"Them artificial freckles—that man must 'a' been kind o' crazy too—jealous crazy—to sit down and think up a thing like that. Freckles sump'm like yourn, only his comes off."

"Mine liked to come off too when I seen who he was. How you reckon he got my finger print on that thing?"

Bubber described with enthusiasm the physician's demonstration.

"Say, that's right," Jinx recalled. "My chair arm was kind o' messy on one side, but I thought it was jes' furniture polish and sorter blotted it off on a clean place."

"Then we got up and went over to the mantelpiece and was talkin' 'bout all them false-faces and things."

"Yea."

"That's when this guy come up and joined the conversation. But he had dropped his hat in your chair. While he was standin' there talkin' so much, he got your han'kerchief and that club. Then it come his turn to go in to Frimbo. On the way he leaned over your chair to pick up his hat. That's when he got your thumb print—off the clean place. Didn't take him a second."

"The grave-digger," Jinx muttered. "He sho' meant to dig me in, didn't he?"

"If it hadn't been you, 'twould 'a' been somebody else. He jes' didn't mean to lose his wife and his life both. Couldn't blame him for that. Jes' ordinary common sense."

A gay young man on the edge of the pavement burst into song for the benefit of some acquaintance passing by with a girl:

> "*I'll be glad when you're dead, you rascal you—*
> *I'll be glad when you're dead, you rascal you—*
> *Since you won't stop messin' 'round,*
> *I'm go'n' turn yo' damper down—*
> *Oh, you dog—I'll be glad when you're gone!*"

"Boy," murmured Bubber, if he only knew what he was singin'."

And deep in meditation the two wandered on side by side down Seventh Avenue.

BLACK THUNDER

Arna Bontemps

TO
ALBERTA

CONTENTS

Book One   JACOBINS 597

Book Two   HAND ME DOWN MY SILVER TRUMPET 671

Book Three   MAD DOGS 709

Book Four   A BREATHING OF THE COMMON WIND 747

Book Five   PALE EVENING. . . . A TALL SLIM TREE 785

BOOK ONE

JACOBINS

One

VIRGINIA COURT records for September 15, 1800, mention a certain Mr. Moseley Sheppard who came quietly to the witness stand in Richmond and produced testimony that caused half the States to shudder. The disclosures, disturbing as they were, preceded rumors that would positively let no Virginian sleep. A troop of United States cavalry was urgently dispatched, and Governor James Monroe, himself an old soldier, paced the halls of Ash Lawn with quaking knees and appointed for his estate three special aides-de-camp.

It is safe to say, however, that on the night this history begins, early in June of the same year, Mr. Moseley Sheppard slept well. That night the planter's great house was as dark as death. The rooms, cavernous and deep, were without sound, except when a gray squirrel scampered over the roof or when Ben, the old slave, rattled a plate in the pantry. A tall clock, ticking hoarsely on a landing, changed its tone occasionally and suggested the croaking of a bullfrog. Mr. Moseley Sheppard breathed heavily behind his mosquito netting, turned now and again on his high-piled mattresses, but slept well.

Old Ben twisted a scrap of paper, got a fragment of flame over the pantry lamp and went into the kitchen. There were candles on a table in the corner. He lit one and threw the punk that was burning his fingers into a kettle of ashes.

Following the taper, the old servant's face glowed like a drunken moon behind a star. He was smiling. There was gray wool on the sides of his face as well as on his head. Ben wore satin breeches and shoes with white paste buckles; his savage hair was long and tied with a black string at the back of his neck.

On the landing he opened the clock and began winding it with a brass key. He had placed the candle above his head, and it threw on his shoulders a dull blue radiance weaker than the light a ghost carries. Ben's thin hands kept turning the key, winding the tall clock. He was still turning, still winding, when young Robin Sheppard let himself in by a side door and came quietly through the unlighted great room. He reached the staircase and paused. Ben closed the clock, took his candle and came down. The boy's embroidered cuffs covered his pale hands. There was glossy braid on his knee-length coat.

"Listen, Ben," he said. "You're not supposed to see things, and you're not supposed to hear."

"No, suh, young Marse Robin. I don't hear and I don't see."

"You don't know what time I came in—understand?"

"I don't know nothing," Ben said, "nothing."

"That's it. Have you got anything handy in the pantry, Ben?"

The boy followed him out to the larder, took a stool beneath the pantry lamp and waited while Ben trimmed the breast of a cold roasted duck, opened an earthen jar of preserves and poured wine from a reed-covered jug. Home from the College of William and Mary, Robin seemed strangely unfamiliar to Ben, not at all like the youngster he had seen grow up in that same house; but he was showing his Sheppard blood all right, keeping such hours before he was twenty-one and drinking like a congressman. Ben knew what to expect of the quality.

"You know where I've been, Ben?"

"I don't know nothing, young Marse Robin. Not a thing."

"You know, but you're not supposed to say. I want you to know, Ben. I might need you some time. You see, she's yellow."

"Yes, suh. I know and *don't* know."

"The horse is tied to a tree on the drive."

"I'll put him up myself," Ben said. "No need to call Pharoah."

"Thanks, Ben. You're a good boy."

The old gray-haired Negro smiled. He went through the kitchen and out on the gravel way. His heart fluttered with pleasure; he was a good boy.

Mr. Moseley Sheppard was still asleep behind his mosquito netting, his toes peeping out of the cover, but cocks were crowing. The handsome great house was dark as death inside, but in the fields thousands of gleaming birds were crowing up the sun. Old Ben, a shadow among shadows, wavered on the path that led beneath the walnut trees. He was smoking a corncob pipe, and in his hand there was an empty bowl covered with a napkin. He let himself into the kitchen.

Later, when Drucilla came with her grown daughter and started cooking breakfast, Ben returned to the back steps, bringing the silverware in a plush bag, and commenced polishing the pieces one by one on a bench. It was a big job, one that would take most of the morning, and he was glad to get an early start.

He worked steadily. By and by the sky flushed. There was a blue mist on the world. Ben always felt mellow at that hour. Somewhere, in some hedge or thicket a thrasher called; a thrasher called him somewhere. A few moments passed. The mist stretched and broke like a cobweb, and through it crept Bundy, an extremely thin Negro carrying a fat earthen jug.

" 'Mawnin', Ben."

They were near the same age, but Bundy was not gray, had no hair to be gray, in fact, and had no frizzly whiskers on his face.

"What's on yo' mind?" Ben said.

Bundy turned his jug bottom up.

"Look: dry's a bone," he said. "Can't you give me another little taste of that old pizen rum, Ben?"

"You drinks worser'n a gentaman, Bundy. But I reckon maybe Marse Sheppard can spare you one mo' jugful. I'll just fill it anyhow and ask him about it some other time. He sleep now."

"That's the ticket, Ben. You oughta be a mason."

"A mason?"

"Sure. I'm one. You oughta come j'ine."

Ben came out of the cellar a few moments later hammering with his palm on the cork of Bundy's jug.

"There you be."

"Much obliged, Ben. But sure 'nough, you oughta come on j'ine the masons."

"I ain't got time for no such chillun's foolishness as that, Bundy."

"If you come find out what it is, you might change that song."

"Nah, not me, boy."

"Listen. I'm going to come get you next week just the same."

"Don't bother, Bundy. I'm too busy."

"I just want you to talk to Gabriel; I ain't asking you to j'ine no mo'."

"I'm too busy," Ben said. "That's all chillun's foolishness."

"You just wait'll Gabriel 'splains it. I'm going to come get you next week."

"Aw, Bundy——"

"Don't say a word. Just you wait'll you talks to Gabriel. Much obliged, Ben."

"Don't mention it, Bundy. It wa'n't nothing."

Bundy left with his jug. The mist had broken into scraps. Ben could feel the softness of the young day. It amused him to see Bundy making his way across the fields on such unsteady legs with such a fat jug. Join the masons! Lordy, what a notion! Where was it the thrasher called him, to what green clump? Mr. Moseley Sheppard was probably still sleeping, his toes looking out from under the sheet, but bacon was frying in the kitchen and Ben thought he had better go up and wake him now.

Two

M R. THOMAS PROSSER was waiting beside a water oak in the low field when the sky flushed that morning. His lips were soiled with snuff; his pippin cheeks were bright. He had on a wig, a three-cornered hat and a pair of riding breeches, but he had neglected his shirt, and he stood expanding a hairy chest in the dewy air and smiting his boot with the firm head of a riding whip. His horse whinnied and pawed the earth.

Some Negroes were already in the field hoeing. Old Bundy came over a knoll, crossed a meadow and climbed a fence. Still toiling with the fat jug, he got in a corn row and followed it. His legs seemed less and less secure.

Mr. Thomas Prosser flung himself into the saddle, drove his horse up to the end of the corn. The lines around his mouth and eyes tightened. A worthless old scavenger, that Bundy. Too old for hard work, too trifling and unreliable for lighter responsibilities. Not worth his keep. No better'n a lame mule. And here coming home from God knows where with a jug of rum as big as himself.

Old Bundy saw something coming and veered away, his arm thrown up to protect his head. He saw it again and started side-stepping. He dropped the jug, threw the other hand up and felt the butt end of a riding whip on his elbow. His arms became suddenly paralyzed. Again he veered anxiously. This time he went down on his knees in a clump of rank polk and began crying like a child.

The jug rolled into the corn row without loosing its cork. The Negroes, hoeing in another field, raised their heads, their faces wrenched with agony. Somewhere the thrashers called. The Negroes cupped their hands, whispered through the tall corn.

Something struck Bundy's head. Was it the horse or the man? Both were above him now; both showed him clinched teeth. Bundy regained his feet and made a leap for the bridle. He grasped something, something. . . . But there was darkness now.

Old Bundy's eyes were open, but he didn't see. His mouth was open, and his face had a tortured look, but he said nothing.

Mr. Thomas Prosser was obliged to use his foot to break the critter's grip on the stirrup. Was Bundy trying to resist? The old sway-backed mule. The lick-spittle scavenger. Well, take that. And here is some more. This. And this.

Yes, suh, Marse Prosser, I'm taking it all. I can't prance and gallop no mo'; I'm 'bliged to take it. Yo' old sway-backed mule —that's me. Can't nobody lay it on like you, Marse Prosser, and don't nobody know it better'n me. Me and my jug has a hard time with you, a hard time. That jug done got to be bad luck for a fact. Every time I puts it under my arm I meets trouble. Lordy, me. Ain't that 'nough, Marse Prosser? Ain't you done laid on 'nough for this one time? You see me crumpled up here in the bushes. Howcome you keeps on hitting? Howcome you keeps on hitting me around the head, Marse Prosser? I won't be no mo' good to you directly. Lordy, what was that? Felt like a horse's foot. Lordy. . . .

Three

THE colt called Araby kicked up his heels in the deep clover. He swept his lowered head over the sweet green surf that broke and foamed about his knees and struck across the field in a joyous race with his shadow. He was as glossy and black as anthracite; his legs, still a trifle long for his body, twinkled in the sunlight. After the fetid stable, the stale straw for a bed and the damp planks underfoot, after the dark indoor prison and the days and weeks of longing at a tiny window, the meadow seemed too good to be true. He bounded again, inscribed a huge circle in the fine gritty turf and came back to the whitewashed gate, the water trough and the cake of salt under the chestnut tree.

The young coachman in varnished hat, high boots and tailed coat turned toward the barn, the halter in his hand. Then he paused, put his foot on the gate again. That jet colt was happiness itself, pure joy let loose. The coachman shook his head. His own eyes were wretched; old Bundy was dying.

"That's all right for you, Araby," Gabriel said. "You ain't a horse yet, and you ain't a nigger neither. That's mighty fine for you, feeling yo' oats and trying to out-run the wind. You don't know nothing yet. Was you a white colt, I reckon I'd have to call you *mister* Araby."

He took a lump of sugar from a pocket in his coat tail and held it between the crosspieces of the gate. Araby's lips touched the immense boyish hand. Gabriel could have cried with melancholy pleasure at the sudden feeling of this confidence, but instead he smiled.

"Nothing like that," he said. "Get on back there in the clover, you and them monstrous flies. I'm got to drive Marse Prosser to town directly."

The horses were hitched, waiting in the door of the carriage room. Taking Araby to the meadow had been an afterthought. Gabriel was fond of the colt. Criddle, the stable boy, would never have thought of it; he was too busy pitching manure out the back window. His little stupid head was a bullet; his eyes were no more than the white spots on a domino.

All about the place Negroes were whispering. They stood in pairs behind the stable, under the low trees, in the tobacco rows, bowed till their corncob pipes nearly touched, cupped their hands and whispered.

High on the driver's seat Gabriel gave the lines a twitch. He was almost a giant for size, but his head was bowed. The tall shiny hat seemed ready to fall on his knees at any minute. One leg hanging loosely beside the footboard gave a suggestion of his extraordinary length. His features were as straight as a Roman's, but he was not a mulatto. He was just under twenty-four and the expression of hurt pride that he wore was in keeping with his years and station. He was too old for joy, as a slave's life went in Henrico County, Virginia, too young for despair as black men despaired in 1800. The gleaming golden horses were out from under the shed with a leap. The newly painted carriage flashed on the gravel path.

The tallest of three uncommonly tall brothers, Gabriel was also what they considered a man of destiny. His reputation was about a year old. It dated from an encounter with Ditcher, Negro "driver" on a near-by plantation.

Long before, Solomon and Ditcher had fought. Gabriel was fifteen then, but he remembered well the fierce struggle his oldest brother put up against the powerful barrel-chested black that ruled the Bowler slaves in the place of the usual white overseer. He remembered the shiver of powerful muscles and the blowing of powerful nostrils near the ground, and he remembered the thuds of blows in the darkness after night fell on the contest. Finally, too, he remembered how they brought Solomon home unconscious.

Three years later Martin, the second brother, met Ditcher in the clump of trees behind the barn. He and Ditcher were nearer the same age, but Martin didn't last as long as did Solomon against the roaring beast. Two or three years passed, and it was Gabriel's turn, the third of the Prosser giants.

Ditcher, naked to the waist, came to the little grove in the twilight. He carried a whip that had been in his hand all day; and when Gabriel approached him in the clearing, straight and unflinching, he tossed it on the ground and slapped his great chest with a proud air. They locked mighty grips. Again there was that wanton display of strength. Again the muscles tightening till they shivered and the two giants tumbling on the ground.

A score of round-eyed blacks encircled the two. For them the earth rocked. The stars shook like lamps swinging in a storm. They thought: Them three big Prosser boys is *some* pun'kins, and this here Gabriel is just too fine to talk about, but that there Ditcher ain't no man: he's a demon. Yet and still, Gabriel ain't scairt of devils or nothing else, he ain't. Look a-yonder. God bless me, he's giving Ditcher the time of his life.

Suddenly Gabriel shook himself free and sprang to his feet. Ditcher rose slowly. The tide had turned. Gabriel leaped to the attack with a bitter grin on his boyish face. He showered blows on the demon that had whipped his two older brothers. It couldn't last. Ditcher curled up on the ground, and the Bowler crowd carried him home, snickering and giggling as they crossed the fields. One of the youngsters took the whip for a plaything.

"That there Gabriel can whup anything on two feet," an old man said. "He ain't biggity neither."

Gabriel didn't like to think about it any more, because he and Ditcher were friends now. Ditcher wasn't really mean; he simply had a loud ugly way of talking and doing things. He had been somewhat spoiled by the feeling of authority. But Ditcher could be depended on to stand by a friend. Of course Ditcher knew right well who was the biggest and the baddest nigger in Henrico County, but Gabriel didn't see any reason to talk about it or rub it in.

The horses stopped in the drive near the front steps. Gabriel's varnished hat inclined a little forward as he waited. His eyes were sad. Being massive and strong didn't make one happy. Being a great slave made Marse Prosser richer, perhaps, but it didn't put any pennies in Gabriel's pocket. Of course there was some compensation in the fine clothes of a coachman, and it was a pleasure to drive to town occasionally and to sport around in a tall hat instead of working in the fields or the shop. These were compensations, but they were brief, very brief.

Beyond the tall columns the door swung open. A lackey

with white stockings stepped out first and stood bowing till the master followed. The pippin-cheeked man with three-cornered hat, knee breeches, a white wig and a cane under his arm came down the path fingering a small sheaf of papers.

"I'm going to the notary first, Gabriel."

"Yes, suh."

"Walk the horses. I have some things to read over."

"H'm."

Having only recently inherited the plantation on the outskirts of Richmond, Mr. Thomas Prosser seemed endlessly occupied with legal papers and long conversations at the notary's office. And it may have been, Gabriel imagined, that these concerns were responsible for his curt manners and quick flashes of indignation. At any rate, he was a hard man to serve.

The morning sun mounted. There were grouse dusting in the road and bluejays annoying squirrels in the low branches of trees. A swarm of sparrows covered a green coppice like flies on a carcass. The horses were eager to be gone; at first Gabriel had to hold them in check. Marse Prosser was still fingering his papers, still belching periodically and periodically snapping the top of his snuffbox.

The road went over a hill and down along the edge of a creek. Later it found another rise and beyond that some green slopes and low fields. At best it gave a jolting ride; but it did not stop the flutter of Mr. Thomas Prosser's papers; it failed even to topple the coachman's varnished hat. In time Gabriel was so deeply absorbed by his daydream that his chin fell against his shirt front, the reins fell slack in his hands and he awakened to hear Marse Prosser shouting in his ears.

"Are you asleep there, billy goat? Or are you trying to turn the carriage over?"

"Nah, suh," Gabriel murmured in a deep voice. "I ain't going to turn you over, Marse Prosser."

"Well, if you can't keep those horses in the road, I have a cane here that I can bloody well teach you with."

"Yes, suh."

Gabriel got his wheels out of the ditch promptly. He drew himself more erect in the seat.

"You can let them take a trot from here in."

"H'm."

*

The streets had a quiet air in the forenoon. Richmond's six or seven thousand people were so scattered the town seemed even smaller than it was for population. Shops were doing a slow business here and there; carriages and saddle horses were tied at hitching bars, and little groups of free blacks and poor whites lolled at the public watering troughs and under the oak trees. There were slaves too, trusted family servants going through the town on errands, the males trotting in the dusty streets, carrying little mashed-up hats in their hands, the women balancing huge baskets on their heads, slapping their bare feet in the footpaths.

There was always the hum of fiddles at the dancing school and the flutter of clean, crisp-looking children in crinolins with pompous black attendants. The dancing master was a Frenchman, as was also his friend the printer, whose shop attracted Gabriel while he waited for Marse Prosser to complete his conversations with the notary.

M. Creuzot had a visitor, and the two were talking very rapidly and in deep earnestness. The rather young visitor wore thick-lensed glasses; he was short and dark and his hair was thick. M. Creuzot was tall and fair and his hair was thin. The printer had also a hoarseness in his throat and a perpetual cough on his chest. He shook a long nervous finger before his face as he talked.

Gabriel walked over to the window where M. Creuzot's red-haired shop boy was setting type so fast it was scarcely possible to follow his fingers. The boy had moved a case and his copy near the window in order to enjoy the better light and the suggestion of a breeze outside. He did not seem interested in the conversation of M. Creuzot and his Philadelphia visitor. But Gabriel, his eyes on the plump red-haired fellow, was innocent of letters and interested only in the words of the other men.

Presently M. Creuzot grew tired, his voice weak.

"Here in Richmond," he said with an accent, "I am an outsider. I am not trusted too far."

"I know," the younger man said. "I know."

"They have catalogued me with the radicals for some reason. I don't know why. I never talk."

"They have heard of Sonthonaz and the *Amis des Noirs*."

"It is an inconvenience," M. Creuzot said.

They paused. There were blue shadows outside the back window. Through the front, yellow sunlight slanted in shafts. After a while Alexander Biddenhurst said vigorously, "The equality of man—there's the pill. You had the filthy nobles in France. Here we have the planter aristocrats. We have the merchants, the poor whites, the free blacks, the slaves—classes, classes, classes. . . . I tell you, M. Creuzot, the whole world must know that these are not natural distinctions but artificial ones. Liberty, equality and fraternity will have to be won for the poor and the weak everywhere if your own revolution is to be permanent. It is for us to awaken the masses."

"Perhaps," said M. Creuzot weakly. "Perhaps. I do not say. It baffles me. I have read Mr. Jefferson's *Notes on Virginia*, and I understand that Judge Tucker, here at William and Mary College, makes a strong proposal for gradual abolition in his *Dissertation on Slavery*, but it all seems hopeless in this country."

"Never say hopeless, M. Creuzot. Even now the blacks are whispering."

"Perhaps not hopeless entirely. But the blacks are *always* whispering. It baffles me."

"The trouble is that those statesmen you named do not go far enough in the direction they indicate."

They were all just words, but they put gooseflesh on Gabriel's arms and shoulders. He felt curiously tremulous. Standing at the window he felt one chill after another run along his spine. He knew that he was delaying longer than he should, but his feet were planted. He was as helpless as a man of wood. He stood facing the funny little typesetter but seeing nothing; he was bewitched. Here were words for things that had been in his mind, things that he didn't know had names. Liberty, equality, frater—it was a strange music, a strange music. And was it true that in another country white men fought for these things, died for them? Gabriel reeled a trifle, but his feet were hopelessly fastened. So they had noticed the blacks whispering, had they?

The men talked on. After a while the young man from Philadelphia came out, slapped the immense Negro on the shoulder and pointed to the typesetter.

"Would you like to learn things like that?"

Gabriel came out of his trance. He managed to get turned around so that he faced the carelessly dressed visitor.

"I reckon I would, suh. I reckon so."

"Are you a free man?"

Gabriel's shoulders rounded, his arms hung a bit in front of his body, the tall hat tilted forward on his head.

"No." His head went lower. "I ain't free."

Young Mr. Biddenhurst looked at him a long time in silence, looked up at the great stature, the powerful shoulders, looked at the sober melancholy face.

"That's a pity. Listen. Peep in the wine shop by the river bridge some time. I do my reading there. I'll buy you a drink, maybe."

When he had turned away, Gabriel felt the hand on his shoulder again. He was so embarrassed by the white man's attention he could not speak. He was now thinking about Marse Prosser and the danger of keeping him waiting, but that was a small thing as compared to Mr. Biddenhurst's astonishing words.

M. Creuzot went back to the form he was making up on the flat stone in the corner. The red-haired boy threw a glance or two out of the window, but he had not interrupted his work. Across the street and down a few paces the fiddles were still humming. They were upstairs over a tailoring establishment, and there were young girls, dancing pupils, at the windows with fans. Downstairs two black crones sat on a stone smoking corncob pipes. Others, like them, were leaning against carriage wheels, giggling with the glossy males who held the horses. Alexander Biddenhurst carried a book under his arm, but he wore no hat. His long natural hair looked odd and wild, and he walked with a sharp step. Gabriel went the other way, staggering.

Marse Prosser was walking back and forth beside his carriage, the sheaf of papers in one hand, his cane in the other. Gabriel came up like a drunken man.

"You left the horses, fool."

"They wa'n't fidgety. I just walked a little piece."

"But you kept me *waiting*. I'll teach you to gad around when I'm on business. There. Let that be a lesson to you. And that."

Twice the cane whistled. Once it fell on Gabriel's arm, the

second time across the side of his face. He raised his head slowly. Something tightened in his shoulders.

"Yes, suh. Yes, suh, Marse Prosser."

Mr. Thomas Prosser took a pinch of snuff and climbed to his seat. His pippin cheeks were no redder than they had been, but his three-cornered hat and the wig under it were sitting a bit off kilter. Gabriel took his place and gave the driving lines a jerk. For some reason he felt less wretched than he had felt earlier. Marse Prosser's licks didn't actually hurt him much; even though they left a long welt on his arm and another on his face, they were really nothing.

Four

M. CREUZOT's shop apron suggested a huge penwiper. It
was inked so thoroughly he must have long ago despaired of making a new smear on a fresh spot. Had the cloth
been black from the beginning, the effect might have been less
like a stipple job now, but the garment could hardly have been
more completely darkened. He stood at the window rubbing
his fingers on it sadly and looking out at the shaded street—
stood and rubbed as if his sadness were occasioned by his failure
to make another impression on the hopeless apron.

Once, apparently, he had chosen to wipe his hands on his
cheek, and there he had been more successful. A vivid three-
fingered smudge ran downward, reached his chin. But this did
not reassure M. Creuzot's despondent eyes. They were as melancholy as if the whole world were blackened and all smears
made.

Not that M. Creuzot pined to besmear the earth actually—
possibly the picture suggests too much. M. Creuzot longed to
see justice prevail. He had come to the new world before the
storm broke in his former home, but he had been deeply
stirred by the triumph of the third estate, and he often cried in
his heart for another sight of the little singing village he had left
too soon. In this city where he was not trusted, where the poor
man was as wretched as a feudal serf, he stood at his window,
hearing violins that seemed to be playing in the branches of
the trees across the street, seeing poverty-stricken youngsters
flee before the approach of proud horses on the cobblestones,
and felt sick for another breath of Norman air, for another
night in a little stone house he remembered and another stroll
in a field of tiny haycocks.

Yet he did not think, as did the young man with the bushy
hair, the thick-lensed spectacles and the copy of the *Diction-
naire Philosophique* under his arm, that there was hope for the
masses in Virginia, that white and black workers, given a torch,
could be united in a quest. He could not feel hopeful or buoyant as did Alexander Biddenhurst. His own head was usually

low. Perhaps, he thought, it was because of his lungs, that confounded barking cough, that persistent rattle in his chest. There were many who said that a man's thoughts could make him ill; perhaps it was also true that a man's illness could corrupt his thoughts. M. Creuzot turned to the pudgy red-haired boy who was no longer standing before the case of type.

"Have you finished that galley, Laurent?"

"Yes, sir. This is the last."

Even as he spoke he was removing the type from his stick, balancing the orderly pile between his fingers.

"Good. Perhaps I can read the proof before the children bring my lunch."

"I'll take it directly."

The boy inked the type with a small hand roller, took an impression and brought it to the pale man. M. Creuzot moved a stool to the window.

"This is very clear. You might make another one, though, so that we can compare our corrections."

"Yes, sir."

They read a few moments in silence, M. Creuzot on his stool, Laurent standing with his elbows on the sill. Suddenly the older man looked up astonished.

"Something's wrong. This doesn't make sense."

"Where's that?"

"Between the third and forth paragraphs. He is giving here instances in which great fish have been known to swallow men, in support of the Jonah legend, and then in the next sentence he is speaking of the various ranks of angels."

"I followed copy."

"Yes? Where is that copy?"

The fat, round-faced boy gathered all the scattered pages, assembled them and handed them to M. Creuzot.

"It was all hard to follow."

"Yes, these pamphlet-writing preachers are generally as incoherent as they are dull. They write like schoolboys."

"I thought perhaps the fault was mine."

"Just partly, Laurent. Your wits are normal, but it may be true that some spiritual things elude you for *other* reasons."

The boy became intensely red. He dropped his eyes as he tried to smile.

"I hadn't thought I was so wicked as all that."

M. Creuzot looked up with a twinkle.

"Perhaps not. Perhaps I misjudged you. But, seriously, if pamphlet-writing clergymen are no credit to letters, they *are* a boon to printers. Here—just what I thought—there *is* a page missing."

"I didn't discover it."

"The pages were unnumbered when we got them. I suppose you had better run over there and ask the Rev. Youngblood if he can supply the other sheet."

Laurent looked out at the sun. It stood almost directly above the street.

"Shall I eat my lunch first?"

"I'd rather not. I can work while you eat if you go now."

The boy put an absurd little round cap on his head and went out, walking reluctantly. The stockings he wore with his knee breeches had been white. They were dust-colored now, and there were holes in them, and they had a tendency to wrinkle on his legs.

On his stool at the window M. Creuzot smiled without mirth and gave his thought once more to the pages in his hand.

The youngsters André and Jean were as dark and rugged as Tartars and nothing at all like M. Creuzot; nothing, that is, except that André was inclined to be a trifle tall for his years and that Jean's eyes were bluish. The little heavy fellow carried the lunch in a basket, and André brought a warm dish with a cover and the bottle of wine, and each had a hoop that he was not able to roll because his hands were too full.

"Papa, there's something here that will surprise you. May I have a little taste of it?"

"Now, what is that? What have you brought that you want to eat from me, little pig?"

"He had one already," André said. "They're tarts."

"Mine was awfully small," Jean protested. "May I have just a taste of yours? You have two big ones."

M. Creuzot uncovered the small basket and divided one of his tarts between his sons. Then he spread the lunch on the stone make-up table in the corner and sat down and blessed himself. The boys went past the window slapping their hoops with one hand, clasping the fragments of their dainty in the other. M. Creuzot coughed behind his napkin, munched his bread sullenly and at intervals drank from the bottle.

For some reason Laurent delayed. He was gone longer than it would ordinarily require for a boy to go and return twice. And when M. Creuzot's bottle was nearly empty, he began throwing anxious glances at the door. He finished the mutton stew and raked the crumbs of bread from the table into the bowl. The table cleared, he folded his napkin, put the bowl in the basket and went back to the stool at the window with his bottle and tart.

A fastidious young man with fancy riding gloves and frills on his shirt-front went by on a white horse. A poor farmer walked beside his ox cart, and a barefoot boy was sleeping on a sack of meal thrown across a scrawny mare's back. There were people walking too, more of them than there had been an hour or two earlier, but Laurent was not among them. His round, moth-eaten cap was nowhere in sight; his round, pock-marked face was nowhere. M. Creauzot took another bite of his tart, another swallow from his bottle.

When the boy did finally return, his cap was in his hand; he had been running, and he was breathless. His red hair had fallen on his forehead in a shaggy bang.

"You had to run?"

"Yes, sir. Here's the other page of copy."

"But you could have gone and returned three times at the gait of an ox."

"I was detained," Laurent said with embarrassment.

"Not by the Rev. Youngblood?"

"Some town boys."

"The same ones as usual?"

"Some were the same, but there were others. They were hiding behind a fence. When I passed, they leaped over and gave me a broadside of green apples."

"Were you hurt?"

"Just a little. I ran for it. I was at the Rev. Youngblood's in a wink, but I couldn't stop. They stayed at my heels till I reached the edge of town, and I had to wait there till they went away."

"You should have led them into our own neighborhood and there returned their fire."

"There wasn't time to think."

"Did they call you a Jacobin?"

"Yes, that's always the first thing. Then something about my red hair. Some of the big fellows were really men."

"They are dogs, not men. That's their amusement as mine is my fiddle and a game of chess."

"It's a mean sport," Laurent said.

"Perhaps when they learn that we do not wish to impose our views on them, they may be more willing to tolerate us, Laurent. Even now *some* conditions are improving a trifle."

"You wouldn't have thought so had you been in my shoes a few minutes ago."

M. Creuzot smiled, took a few steps toward the back of the shop.

"I suppose that *was* a hypothetical remark. You'd better eat your lunch now. I'll set that."

Five

THE impartial sun kept its course. The first pearl-gray flush gave the great Prosser house a silver glow, and the same flush filled the chink holes in Gabriel's cabin with a duller silver. There was still the reek of fried greens, ham hocks and coffee grounds in the hut. Gabriel turned fretfully on his bed of rags. Something like a powerful cobweb constricted his arms, bore down upon his chest. He was neither asleep nor awake; he felt paralyzed, yet he continued to struggle. The same thoughts ran through his mind over and over again and he couldn't stop them. They were like snakes crawling. Suddenly the cobweb tightened, tightened till he thought the breath would go out of him, and he wakened in the arms of Juba, the tempestuous brown wench.

"Go on back to sleep, big sugar," she said. "You ain't slept enough to do a scarecrow."

"I know, gal. I know I ain't slept much."

"Put yo' head on my breast, boy. Sleep some mo'. There, like that. Go on back to sleep now."

"H'm."

A pause.

"Soft?" she asked.

"Soft as goose feathers."

"Well, howcome you can't sleep no mo'? Howcome that?"

"I can't sleep, and I don't know howcome, gal."

Her arms half-around him, she patted his shoulders and looked frightened. Her eyes were bright in the dark corner, her mouth round. She raised her head and saw the dull silver in the chink holes. There was a bitter sweetness in her voice.

"Big sugar?"

"Little bit."

"Maybe it's a yellow woman on yo' mind?"

"No womens but you, gal, no womens."

"That yellow white man's woman that they calls Melody, maybe?"

618

"No woman they calls Melody; just you."

"Ain't the place where you's laying sweet no mo'? Ain't it sweet and soft no mo', boy?"

"Too sweet, gal, too sweet. Yo' breast, soft. Yo' lips, sweet, sweet as ripe persimmons."

"Sweet, hunh?"

She patted his shoulders with both her hands, rocking a little as she patted.

"Too sweet. Yet and still—I can't sleep no mo'."

He yawned and stretched the length of a giant. The muscles quavered and ran under his skin. He saw the silver welding in the chink holes and wondered why the bell hadn't rung. There was a pig outside, rooting against the bottom log.

"Is you—" She stopped short.

"What you go to say, gal?"

"Ne' mind."

"Go on, say it."

"Is you thinking, boy?" she whispered. "Is that howcome you can't sleep no mo'?"

He looked ashamed.

"I reckon so. I reckon that's it, gal."

"That's bad."

"I know. I can't help it, though."

"What you thinking about, big sugar?"

"Thinking about I don't know my mind and I ain't satisfied no mo'."

"Ain't satisfied?"

"No mo'n a wriggletail."

She clasped him tighter, rocking, patting his shoulders again.

"Stop it, boy; stop thinking like that. It ain't good."

"You say stop, but you don't say how."

"Yo' head on my breast; there. . . . Yo' arms; there. . . . Stop thinking."

"Soft. Sweet too, but I can't stop thinking."

"Thinking about *what*?"

"Thinking about how I'd like to be free—how I'd feel."

Juba cried. Real tears came in her eyes.

"You thinking it too, hunh? You fixing to leave me soon."

"No, I ain't fixing to run away, and I ain't going to leave you soon. But I wants to be free. I wonder how it'd feel."

"The police'll get you for just thinking like that, boy. It's bad, bad."

"I reckon so, but I can't help it."

The bell rang. Criddle, the short black stable boy with the bullet head and the eyes like white spots on a domino, was already in the barn. The mules were geared. Presently there were little puffs of smoke above each cabin. The sleepy slave folks, as crochety as things scissored from black paper, crept out half-naked. Each had his corncob pipe, his tuft of rebellious wool. Here and there one cupped his hand, threw a glance over his shoulder and whispered to a round-eyed neighbor.

Gabriel and Juba came up from the creek dripping. They lit their pipes at an outdoor fire, and the girl, who wasn't yet eighteen, ran back to the hut. Gabriel walked down toward the shops.

Six

Old Bundy was dying when Ben got the word. It was night again, and the old great house was still and dark, but Ben was not alone. While Mr. Moseley Sheppard and his son slept in the large bedrooms at the top of the stairs, the frizzly whiskered major-domo and the female house servants buzzed quietly in the kitchen.

Drucilla was preparing her next day's vegetables by the flicker of a candle, and Mousie, the grown daughter that did the scrubbing, had stayed to help her. Mousie was picking and cleaning greens while her old black mother shelled peas. Ben stood at the lamp table blowing his breath on a smoked chimney and polishing it with a soft cloth. There was an octagonal ring on his finger. It was about the thickness of a woman's wedding band, and it kept clicking against the glass as Ben turned his hand inside the chimney.

Presently there was a little scraping noise at the back door, a sound like the pawing of a dog. Ben opened it and looked out. Criddle was there, terrified and panting, the two little domino spots showing plain on his bullet head.

"Bundy——"

"Hush that loud talk, boy. The white folks is sleep," Ben said.

"Well, I help you to say hush," Drucilla whispered.

"What about Bundy?"

"He's dying, I reckon."

"Dying!"

"H'm."

"Dying from what?"

"From day before yestiddy; from what happened in the field."

They all became silent and looked one at the other. The candle on the table gasped as if catching its breath. Ben put the lamp chimney down, knotted his brow and looked at the boy.

"I ain't heard nothing about day before yestiddy."

"Marse Prosser whupped Bundy about coming here," Criddle said. "He whupped him all up about the head and stepped on him with his horse."

621

Mousie turned her head petulantly.

"That's one mo' mean white man, that Marse Prosser."

"H'm," Criddle murmured. "That's what Gabriel and the rest of them is saying now. They say it ain't no cause to beat a nigger up about the head and step on him in the bushes with a horse."

"Po' old Bundy," Ben said. "He was worried about making me a mason."

"That's howcome he sent me," Criddle said. "He say don't you stay away on account of him. He want you to talk to Gabriel about j'ining up."

"I wasn't aiming to go," Ben said. "I ain't strong on that chillun's foolishness, but you needn't mention it to Bundy if he's all that bad off."

"I reckon he dying all right."

"Bundy used to talk a heap about freedom," Drucilla said. "Used to swear he's going to die free."

"He ain't apt to do that now."

"Nah," Criddle said; "leastwise, not less'n the good Lord sets him free."

"Po' old Bundy," Ben said. "He kept drinking up all that rum because he couldn't get up enough nerve to make his getaway."

"Must I tell him you said yes, Uncle Ben?"

"Tell him I said I reckon. That mason business is chillun's foolishness."

Criddle slipped away, dissolved in the shadows. Ben took a candle and went through the dark house trying the doors, adjusting the windows and hangings. His hand trembled on the brass knobs. Old Bundy was dying. A squirrel sprang from a bough, ran across the roof. Poor old Bundy. It seemed like just the other day since he was a young buck standing cross-legged against a tree and telling the world he was going to die free. He had grown old and given up the notion, it seemed, but Ben could well imagine his feelings. A slave's life was bad enough when he belonged to quality white folks; it must have been torment on that Prosser plantation.

They were praying for old Bundy's life when Criddle returned. Moonlight made shadows of uplifted arms on the wall above his heap of rags. There was a chorus of moaning voices. There were faces bowing to the earth and bodies swaying like barley.

Oh, Lord, Lord-Lord. . . . Knee-bent and body-bound, thy unworthy chilluns is crying in Egypt land. . . . Laaawd, Lord. . . . Wilt thou please, Oh, Massa Jesus, to look upon him what's lowly bowed and raise him up if it is thy holy and righteous will. Oh, La-aawd. La-aaaawd-Lord! . . .

"Amen," old Bundy said feebly. *"Amen!"*

They were praying for old Bundy's life, but there was one who didn't pray. He stood naked to the waist in the hot cabin, stood above the others with hands on his hips and head bowed sorrowfully. His shadow, among the waving hands on the wall, was like a giant in a field of grain.

Old Bundy's eyes opened; he looked at the big fellow.

"That there head of yo's is mighty low, long boy, mighty low."

"Yeah, old Bundy, I reckon it is. I reckon it is," Gabriel said.

"And it don't pleasure me a bit to see it like that neither."

"I'm sorry, old man; I'm sorry as all-out-doors. I'd lift it up for a penny, and I'd pleasure you if I could."

"It's that yellow woman, I 'spect, that white men's Melody waving her hand out the window."

"No woman, old Bundy, no woman."

"That brown gal Juba then—her with her petticoats on fire?"

"She belongs to me, that Juba, but she ain't got my head hung down."

"Not her? Well, you's thinking again, boy."

"Thinking again. It's all like we been talking. You know."

"H'm. I was aiming to die free, me. I heard tell how in San Domingo——"

"Listen, old man. You ain't gone yet."

"I don't mind dying, but I hates to die not free. I wanted to see y'-all do something like Toussaint done. I always wanted to be free powerful bad."

"That you did, and we going to do something too. You know how we talked it, you and me. And you know right well how I feel when my head's bowed low."

"Feel bad—I know. I feel bad too, plenty times."

One of the moaners on the ground raised a fervent voice, cried in a wretched sing-song.

"When Marse Prosser beat you with a stick, how you feel, old man?"

"Feel like I wants to be free, chile."

Gabriel gave the others his back, strolled to the door, rested one hand on the sill overhead. The chant went on.

"When the jug get low and you can't go to town, how you feel?"

"Bound to be free, chillun, bound to be free."

Gabriel left the others, walked outdoors.

"When the preacher preach about Moses and the chillun, about David and the Philistines, how you feel, old man?"

"Amen, boy. Bound to be free. You hear me? Bound to be free."

Gabriel did not turn. Even when the moaning and chanting stopped, he continued to walk.

Seven

THEN the days hastened. M. Creuzot and his friend the dancing master were at a game of chess when sharp heels clicked on the doorstep. Both of them paused, looked up and waited for the knocker. When it sounded, M. Creuzot rose slowly. Hugo Baptiste took the board. The two men had been holding it on their knees, but now M. Baptiste placed it on the edge of a table. The eager, hopeful voice of Alexander Biddenhurst came from the vestibule. Laurent, the red-haired boy, was with him.

"We had a bottle of wine at the *Dirty Spoon*," Biddenhurst said. "All the blacks have the jumps. Something's up."

"It's nothing. The Negroes are always jumpy, always whispering."

"I think they're waking up. I really do."

"More's the pity," M. Creuzot said. "They are far better off asleep."

M. Baptiste stroked his fine chin whiskers with a wan hand.

"Better to sleep," he echoed.

"But I disagree," said Biddenhurst. "Think of the white peasantry, our own poor."

"Yes, do," said M. Creuzot, "but it is better to sit while thinking of them. Laurent, go in the kitchen and ask my wife to put one of her aprons on you. You know your job."

M. Creuzot pushed open the tall shutters of his living room. There was a light flutter of hangings before a frame of stars. M. Baptiste reclined in a straw-stuffed seat; Biddenhurst took a straight-backed chair, tilted it on its hind legs. In the kitchen Angelique and her small sons were laughing boisterously at Laurent.

"This may interest you," Biddenhurst said, taking a handbill from his pocket.

The dancing master read it aloud.

"Slavery and the Rights of Man."

"More of that stuff intended to incite the proletariat," the printer said, bowing over the other's shoulder. "Trouble is the proletariat is innocent of letters. They know of only one use for clean sheets of paper like this."

"A boon to the outhouses—that's what they are. Especially at a time when cornshucks are not plentiful."

Biddenhurst laughed with them.

"But there is a striking thing about this one," he said seriously.

"The subject is trite."

"That's true. But the gossips in town have it that this one was written by Callender."

"Callender?"

"Yes, sir, Thomas Callender, Jefferson's friend, right here in the Richmond prison where he's serving time for sedition. They are saying everywhere that he's the anonymous author."

"What a mad thing to distribute at a time like this," M. Baptiste said. "Where did you get this copy?"

"Two French Negroes, boys from Martinique, were distributing them among the free colored folks and the slaves—who probably took them for wedding certificates or something of the sort. The boys were assisted by a United Irishman. All there were strangers. The boys were from the French boat that was docked here yesterday. They have just sailed."

"Do you suppose they knew what they were scattering?"

"Of course not, but they knew to whom they should give them. I had the devil's own time wrangling them out of one."

Laurent came in with bottles and tall greenish glasses. He looked grotesque in the white apron Mme. Creuzot had pinned around him. Beyond the dining room the faces of Jean and André could be seen in the candlelight, giggling in the kitchen door. They felt sure they had made a clown of Laurent, but the men did not notice the apron or the way the boy's red hair had been ruffled. M. Baptiste continued to read, M. Creuzot looking over his shoulder and both holding full glasses.

"I doubt that Callender would be guilty of an attempt to incite the Negroes," M. Creuzot said.

"Possibly not," said Biddenhurst, "but it gives you an idea what they're whispering about. *Some*body published it."

"It mentions the San Domingo uprisings, I see."

"Yes, the Negroes talk about that too. It's one of the things that make me suspect they're awakening."

M. Creuzot emptied his glass and held it out for the boy to refill.

Then something occurred to him. A twinkle came into his eye.

"It would be too bad for poor Laurent should we live to see any real discontent among the masses here. They call him a Jacobin on the streets now, and sometimes they pelt him when he passes."

Laurent blushed a deeper red.

"That's partly because of his red hair," said M. Baptiste laughing. "But it is true that all Virginians have a tendency to associate the slogans of the *States-Général* with every show of discontent among slaves. They blame those principles for the San Domingo uprisings, and they resent the resumption of commercial relations with that country. Such things as that possibly come into their minds when they see poor Laurent with his round face and run-down stockings. He is just the type. He could scarcely suit them better if he had a shaggy beard. A Jacobin, they fancy, is an abandoned, villianous person with a foreign accent and a soiled shirt."

"I hadn't thought of that," Laurent lamented. "I'll have to spruce up."

"Don't grieve, Laurent," Biddenhurst said lightly. "The worm can turn. You may well pelt them some day."

"Let us hope that M. Baptiste and I, poor souls like us with our less combative spirits, have moved on by then. There'll be bitter days ahead when Laurent pelts the town boys in Richmond. It will be an omen."

They all laughed. Laurent went into the kitchen and returned with a tray of cheese, cold meat and bread. The men laughed again. Young Biddenhurst threw out his feet with hearty pleasure.

"Will John Adams be re-elected this fall, Mr. Biddenhurst?"

"No, I think not. Mr. Jefferson's popularity is increasing. This sliced turkey—it *is* good, M. Creuzot. Where do you shoot these days?"

"There's a bottom out of town, a place where the creek broadens and the thicket is dense. The Brook Swamp."

"Well, now, that's a fortune."

"One can't amuse himself with the fiddle *all* the time, and M. Baptiste is occasionally unavailable for chess."

"By the by," M. Baptiste said, "you were in Paris last year?"

"Yes."

"Ah——"

"One gets homesick some time, I daresay?"

"Homesick? *Mon Dieu!* Who is seen at the old Procope nowadays, Mr. Biddenhurst?"

"A very interesting crowd. Poets, musicians, artists, and a great many others who'd like to be poets or musicians or artists. They were mostly young. Perhaps they're a new crowd, a younger generation than you knew."

"Yes, yes. Of course, they are. What memories that café holds! I can remember seeing Voltaire there when I was a student in the Latin Quarter. Murat and Danton and Robespierre came too. Time flies, Mr. Biddenhurst. You do not know yet. Wait till you pass fifty-five."

"I shall not mind passing fifty-five at all if I am as nimble as M. Hugo Baptiste, the dancing master, is at that age."

They all laughed. Laurent stumbled going into the kitchen with his empty tray, but he did not fall. The small boys came to the kitchen door again, laughing hard. Laurent had stepped on his apron.

Eight

MELODY, the apricot-colored mulattress, swept her rooms with a sage-straw broom, dusted the chairs and table with a spray of turkey feathers. The windows were open, the curtains knotted high and the shutters thrown out as she cleaned, and through the house there went an early morning breeze from the river. Her skirt was folded up and caught at the back, and her leaf-green petticoat kept turning at the bottom, turning up the frill of a yellow one underneath. Melody's headcloth was a faded red, but beneath it there was enameled black hair and barbarous hoops in her ears.

The broom, a handful of straw bound to the stick with a cord, was in her hand when she stood at the window looking down at the quiet street. She nipped a twig with her fingernails and chewed it a moment. Then she dipped the frayed tip into a snuff-box on the table and put it in her mouth against the gums.

A few minutes passed. Melody twirled the broom. She thought: He's a funny one with them thick specks of his'n and that book underneath of his arm all the time. Favors a Jew more'n he does a Englishman. I reckon he reads too much. One thing's mighty sure, though: Him and his equality of mens, his planter aristocrats, as he calls them, and all like of that is going to get his Philadelphia pants hung wrong-side-out on a sour apple tree if he don't mind out. And it's worse'n a shame, too, because he talks like he mean what he say, and I thinks he likes poor folks a heap.

Another thing too: My name'll be mud if folks start saying he come up here to get drunk on peach brandy and to big-talk about how all the money in the country ought to be divided up equal amongst everybody. The rich white folks in this here town, leastwise the menfolks, ain't going to put up with no such running on. Next time he knock on the door, I'm going to have company, full house. If I don't, I'm going to come across myself leaving town one these fine mornings.

The old slave called General John Scott was cutting weeds in the back yard with a scythe. He had no teeth, strictly speaking, only a half-dozen crooked brown fangs in front, and it was a miracle how he managed a chew of tobacco. Yet there was always that lump in his cheek, that busy gnawing of his lower jaw and that periodic dark spout. His whiskers were gray and frizzled, and his butternut pants, suspended from his shoulder by a single strap, were perhaps the most thoroughly patched homespuns in Virginia. His old arched body was as scrawny and shriveled as a dead oak leaf. He paused once, fished into a pocket that dropped below his knee and brought out a whetstone with which he touched up his blade. In a moment, the edge restored, his lower jaw was busy again, his sharp blade was whispering to the grass roots.

"How you come along, Gen'l John?" Melody called from the back window.

"Tolerably, Miss Melody," he said. "Just tolerably."

"Well, did you hear all that commotion down by the river just now?"

He straightened up as best he could, let the blade touch the ground.

"I ain't heard a thing," he said. "Did it sound like something to you?"

"Indeed it did, Gen'l. Some of them was hollering loud enough for it to of been a boat coming up."

"Well, bless me, I ain't heard a thing. There was a Norfolk boat just the other day."

"I know," she said. "There it is again. Hear them, Gen'l? Hear that hollering?"

"I'm got both ears pricked."

"Run down to the river road and see what it is."

"I'm gone already, Miss Melody. I'll tell you about it directly."

Melody's rooms were upstairs over an abandoned shop; weeds were high on either side, and there were no other houses near. The place had once been a grove, and still many trees were standing, but people passed on a carriage path now, and only a stone's throw away was the big road that ran by the river.

General Scott snatched the tiny crown of a hat off his head

and shambled around to the front. Melody was there looking out of her little plush parlor when he got on the path. A lock of the enameled black hair had fallen down on her neck; one end of the red headcloth was hanging. Her smile, compounded not only of excitement and pure pleasure, was no less comely. She leaned over the row of tiny plants in earthen pots and watched the ragged old slave scuffling the dust on the foot-path.

Partly, General John Scott came to cut weeds in Melody's back yard because he was too old to do a real day's work in the field where the other slaves were cutting tobacco, and partly he came because his tipsy middle-aged master wanted to do something handsome for a rosy buff-colored girl. It made no difference at all to General John. He didn't have to work any harder than he was pleased to work; Melody usually put a shilling in his hand when he finished, and just a short way down the river road was the rum shop beloved of the black folks. Melody had a habit of sending him there before the day's work was done.

The old fellow couldn't run, his time for that sort of kicking up had passed, but he swung his arms gingerly as he went and threw enough dust with his excited heels to well represent a running man. A boat! Children dancing along the river. Black folks opening their eyes in the warm sunlight, rousing from sleep on the stacked boxes at the landing, coming out of the *Dirty Spoon*, whistling, waving their hands. . . . It was mighty fine. The old man's heart fluttered.

Yes, sir, that was it; a boat was coming up the river just as Melody suspected. General John crossed the road and went on to the crest of a slope. There he stood, hat in hand, mouth open and eyes fixed. The patches in his pants were as bright as stars. He had lost his chew of tobacco, perhaps swallowed it, but that didn't matter now. He was busy thinking.

Yonder she come. And a pretty one she is, I thank you. Them white sails and that rigging. They ain't giving her much canvas now, just enough to bring her upstream easy and slow-like. Them flags—well, what kind of flags *is* them? Aw, sail it, Cap'n Bud, sail it.

A finger touched General's elbow, touched it a second time, then a third. He felt it. It was just a little push, nothing to hurt a body. He didn't mind it; he was looking at the boat. There were children scampering around, and the air was full of voices. He didn't mind them either; he was looking at the boat, thinking.

There's some black boys on her too, hauling at them ropes. Well, bust my breeches, what kind of nigger is that one? Red pants fastened at the ankles like a woman's bloomers, bare feet, no shirt and a pair of earrings in his ears. And will you look at that head? Just like a briar patch. He oughta cut some of that mess off if he don't aim to keep it combed and plaited. But he sure looks sassy in that pretty boat. She's fixing to land, too.

That finger on his elbow pushed again, pushed so hard General John dropped his hat and turned to see what touched him. He smiled when he saw the huge young fellow standing beside him in a two-foot hat.

"Quit yo' foolishness, boy," he grinned.

"Was you visioning, Gen'l John?"

"Sure I's visioning. I visions all the time."

Gabriel laughed.

"That's the boat from San Domingo," he said. "Indigo, coffee, cocoa and all like of that."

"Howcome it ain't stopped at Norfolk?"

"I reckon it did stop there. What you doing here?"

"Melody wanted me to find out what all the noise was about. How you come?"

"Taking a walk," Gabriel said. "Just strolling-like."

"Where'bouts yo' Marse Prosser?"

Gabriel shrugged insolently.

"I'm bigger'n him, ain't I?"

"Yes, you's bigger, but you might ain't so loud."

"They're pulling her up at the landing."

"H'm."

"How much money we got in the treasury now, Gen'l?"

"Well, sir, I ain't spent nothing this week, and I laid hands on ten dollar more."

"That's good."

The two started down toward the landing and toward the *Dirty Spoon* that wasn't far away. There was a good crowd in the road, all hurrying. They quickly rushed past old General John and Gabriel. But after them came one who did not rush.

She carried a leaf-green parasol, and she had changed to a plum-colored dress. And when the two men stopped by the lamp post to talk, she went past them, walking with a languid and insolent twitch, and entered the wine shop called the *Dirty Spoon*.

"Money ain't nothing to us," Gabriel said. "We going to have plenty to eat from the crops and cattle and hogs and all. But you and Ben'll need a little for expenses. Pharoah, too."

"Pharoah?"

"Yes. I made up my mind to send Pharoah up to Caroline County with Ben."

"Howcome?"

"I don't trust that pun'kin-colored nigger."

"I thought he was hankering to lead a line."

"He was. I don't trust him, though."

"Well, maybe you did right. Get him far way as you can if his eye ain't right."

The ragged old man looked at Gabriel long and earnestly. His own eyes rounded, then sharpened. Now, take Gabriel here —there was an eye you could bank on. He'd stand up to the last, that Gabriel; he was a nachal-born general, him. General John's mouth dropped open, but he did not speak.

Some noisy sailors came up from the boat, went into the *Dirty Spoon*.

Nine

MINGO knew how to read. He held the Book on his knee and fluttered the crimped leaves with a damp forefinger. A freedman and a saddle-maker, Mingo was also a friend to the slaves. They came to his house on Sundays because he welcomed them and because they liked to hear him read. The room was hot and small, and Gabriel stood in the midst of the tattered circle that surrounded the reader's chair with his coachman's hat pushed back, his coachman's coat flung open.

"There, there," he said abruptly. "Hold on a minute, Mingo. Read that once mo'."

Mingo looked over his square spectacles. A cataracted left eye blinked. He smiled, turned the page back and repeated.

"He that stealeth a man and selleth him, or if he be found in his hand, he shall surely be put to death. . . ."

"That's the Scripture," Gabriel said. "That's the *good* Book what Mingo's reading out of."

The Negroes murmured audibly, but they made no words. Mingo fluttered a few more pages.

"Thou shalt neither vex a stranger nor oppress him; for ye were strangers in the land of Egypt. . . . Thou shalt not oppress a stranger, for ye know the heart of a stranger. . . .

"Therefore thus saith the Lord: Ye have not harkened unto me, in proclaiming liberty, every one to his brother, and every one to his neighbor: behold, I proclaim a liberty for you, saith the Lord, to the sword——"

"Listen!" Gabriel said.

"——to the pestilence, and to the famine; and I will make you to be removed into all the kingdoms of the earth. And I will give the men that have transgressed my covenant, which have not performed the words of the covenant which they had made before me, when they cut the calf in twain, and passed between the parts thereof, the princes of Judah, and the princes of Jerusalem, the eunuchs, and the priests, and all the people of the land, which passed between the parts of the calf; I will even give them into the hand of their enemies, and into the hand of them that seek their life; and their dead bodies shall be for meat unto the fowls of the heaven, and to the beasts of the earth. . . ."

Mingo thumbed the crimped pages awkwardly.

"Don't stop, Mingo. Read some mo'," Gabriel said. "That's the Scripture, ain't it?"

"Scripture," Mingo said. "Scripture——

"Is not this the fast that I have chosen to loose the bands of wickedness, to undo the heavy burdens, to let the oppressed go free, and that ye break every yoke?"

"Read some mo', Mingo. Keep on reading some mo'."

"He sent a man before them, even Joseph,

"Who was sold for a servant;

"Whose feet they hurt with fetters:

"He was laid in iron——"

"Lord help; Lord help."

"Mm-mm. Do, Jesus. Do help."

"—Until the time that his word came,

"The word of the Lord tried him.

"The king sent and loosed him——

"Even the ruler of the people, and let him go free."

"Yes, Jesus, let him go free. Let him go free."

Mingo cleared his throat. The black folks in chairs, on boxes, kneeling with folded arms, sitting on the floor, rocked reverently as they murmured. Gabriel flipped his coat a little self-consciously and went to the window, giving the others his back.

"One is your master, even Christ; and all ye are brethren . . .

"Rob not the poor because he is poor; neither oppress the afflicted in the gate: for the Lord will plead their cause, and spoil the soul of those that spoil them. . . .

"The people of the land have used oppression, and exercised robbery, and have vexed the poor and needy; yea they have oppressed the stranger wrongfully. And I sought for a man among them that should make up the hedge, and stand in the gap before me in the land, that I should not destroy it: but I found none. Therefore have I poured out mine indignation upon them. . . .

"Woe unto him that buildeth his house by unrighteousness,

and his chambers by wrong; that useth his neighbor's service without wages, and giveth him not for his work. . . .

"Behold the hire of the labourers who have reaped down your fields, which is of you kept back by fraud, crieth; and the cries of them which have reaped are entered into the ears of the Lord of Saboath. . . .

"And I will come near you to judgment; and I will be a swift witness against the sorcerers, and against the adulterers, and against false swearers and against those that oppress the hireling in his wages. . . ."

Gabriel swung around, one hand at his side, the other still on his hip.

"God's hard on them, Mingo. He don't like ugly, do he?"

Mingo shook his head.

"God's hard on them, and he don't like ugly," he said.

"It say so in the book, and it's plain as day," Gabriel said. "And, let push come to shove, He going to fight them down like a flock of pant'ers, He is. Y'-all heard what he read. God's aiming to give them in the hands of they enemies and all like of that. He say he just need a man to make up the hedge and stand in the gap. He's going to cut them down his own self. See?"

The Negroes stopped rocking and looked up. There was a glint of something bright in Gabriel's eye. Their mouths dropped open; they gazed without speaking.

Ten

M R. MOSELEY SHEPPARD, slim, silvered, a man with a military air, waited at the foot of the stairs for his candle. Ben brought it to him in a saucer with a handle like a teacup. The old Negro bowed gravely in the shadows.

"All the black folks are terribly nervous, Ben. What's the trouble?"

Ben shook his head slowly.

"I don't get round a heap, Marse Sheppard. I don't hear much talk."

"There must be *some*thing. Why, you see little groups of them whispering under every tree. When you start toward them, they bow their heads and break up."

Ben thought for a long moment. Then he looked up.

"Old Bundy's dead," he said. "You reckon it's that?"

"Who's Bundy?"

"Marse Thomas Prosser's old Bundy. He died from a whupping he got for slipping away, and they's aiming to bury him tomorrow."

"Oh, him."

"Yes, suh, him."

"Well, I suspect that's it. I reckon the niggers are learning that Mr. Prosser doesn't take the foolishness from his slaves that some of us take."

"H'm. They's learning that, Marse Sheppard."

"Good-night, Ben."

"Good-night, suh."

Ben stood at the foot of the stairs till the frail, slim man closed a door overhead. Then he went into the front room and started trying the doors and windows. He remembered that young Marse Robin wasn't in yet, so he left the bolt unfastened on the side door.

Drucilla and Mousie were still slipping about softly in the kitchen and pantry. Ben heard the click of plates they touched, heard the chair legs drag when they moved. He was standing at a tall window, looking out through a lacework of shadows on the lawn.

Marse Sheppard must be the most lonesomest old man in the country, he thought. He must of been that for a fact, what with no mo' womens in the house and him going to bed early like he did because he didn't have nobody to sit around and drink and talk with. And it was just like him to worry hisself about a lot of niggers that didn't even belong to him and that wasn't no ways as lonesome as him.

Ben's heart melted.

And there was young Marse Robin that wasn't a heap of comfort to the old man neither. That college boy had his daddy's quality and manners all right, but he went in stronger for merry times. His heart was a leaf. There he was this very evening out getting hisself drunk with a yellow woman with enameled black hair and hoops in her ears. He wasn't a heap of comfort to his daddy—leastwise, not when the old man felt his lonesomeness coming down.

A small wind fluttered the curtain. Ben closed the window and went through the large dining hall to the kitchen. Mousie was pealing peaches, fishing them out of a bucket of water. Drucilla was getting ready to set her light rolls before leaving for the night. Her hands were full of dough. Ben went into the pantry and came out with a plate of food he had left here half-eaten. He placed it on the kitchen table across from Mousie and went back for his coffee.

"Maybe I can get through eating now," he said.

"I reckon so," Drucilla smiled. "Here, let me set yo' coffee on the back of the stove. I bound you it's stone cold now."

"You's right about that. Thanks."

There was a pone of bread on the plate in a puddle of pot liquor. A small ham hock, partly demolished, stood at the side like a mountain. There had been a half-dozen pots from which to choose, but Ben knew his own mind and he knew his own palate. Let others tear at the tenderloin steaks; let them mop up the gravy and devour the garnishings; let them lick the artichoke's succulent petals if they chose; he would bear them no malice and no envy. He crushed his pone quietly in the puddle of pot liquor and smiled somewhere amid his frizzly whiskers.

"Old Bundy's dead," Mousie muttered over her peaches. "Lord, it don't seem real."

"The last thing I heard him say was something another about rum," Drucilla said.

Ben's mouth was full, but not too full to for him to talk.

"He was worrying me to be one of them colored masons, and I reckon he died with it on his mind."

"H'm," Drucilla answered. "And he'll come back to you with it, if you don't mind out."

"He didn't 'zactly ask me to j'ine up," Ben said. "He ended with asking me to see Gabriel and listen to him talk. He didn't say j'ine, not 'zactly."

"Was I you, Ben, I'd do just about like Gabriel say do about that when you see him. That is, I'd do it if I didn't want to be pestered by no dead mens. It won't cost nothing to oblige him that little bit on account of his last request."

"I reckon it won't cost nothing, but it's a peck of trouble. Yet and still, I ain't after having trouble with no devilish hants and the like of that."

Mousie looked up sharply, her eyes round.

"Lordy, what was that noise I heard?"

"Nothing," Ben said. "Just a squirrel jumped on the roof, I reckon."

They all waited a moment without speaking or moving. Then there was something again.

"Squirrel nothing," Drucilla said. "It's upstairs, Ben."

"Upstairs, hunh?"

"Sound like Marse Sheppard stumbling."

Ben got his feet from under the table as quickly as he could, snatched one of the candles and started through the dining room. When he reached the stairs, he heard the old man opening the bedroom door. Ben rushed up.

Marse Sheppard came into the hall supporting himself by keeping one hand on the door frame. He was pale and his candle trembled in his hand. He looked like an old woman in his nightcap and his long sleeping shirt, but Ben saw only the distressed face.

"My God," he said, "my knees gave away, Ben."

"Yes, suh, Marse Sheppard. Here, lean on me. You oughta

be laying down. There, now, suh. Easy. Lean on me, Marse Sheppard, you be all right."

"Get me the salts, Ben."

"Yes, suh. Lay down there; I'll get them directly. There . . . now."

Ben darted around the room while the old silvered man lay in his nightcap. He held the smelling salts to Marse Sheppard's nose, then poured a peg of whiskey into a small glass. The old man tossed it off and leaned back on his pillow. Ben lit two long rows of candles in the room and picked up a coat his master had dropped on the floor.

"Funny, these confounded spells. I'm not as old as you, am I, Ben?"

"No, suh, Marse Sheppard, but you got so much mo' to think about. That's howcome I don't have no spells like you. I got *you* looking out after me, but who's you got?"

The old man smiled a little.

"You're a good boy, Ben, but you're an awful liar about some things."

"Nah, suh, that ain't no tale."

"You'd make me feel good if you could, Ben."

Ben was glad to hear that; glad, too, that Marse Sheppard had called him a good boy.

Drucilla and her grown daughter were in the door now, gawking foolishly, waiting for a word from Ben. But he didn't need them, and after a few moments they went back downstairs. Ben took a seat near the bed and prepared to sit up with the sick man. Half an hour later young Marse Robin crept upstairs on unsteady legs, went directly to his own room. Ben did not call him. That tipsy boy wouldn't be able to help any, he thought; besides, Robin was too young for troubles like sickness in the family, too young, too merry.

Eleven

THEY were burying old Bundy in the low field by the swamp. They were throwing themselves on the ground and wailing savagely. (The Negroes remembered Africa in 1800.) But there was one that did not wail, and there were some that did not wail for grief. Some were too mean to cry; some were too angry. They had made a box for him, and black men stood with ropes on either side the hole.

Down, down, down: old Bundy's long gone now. Put a jug of rum at his feet. Old Bundy with his legs like knotty canes. Roast a hog and put it on his grave. Down, down. How them victuals suit you, Bundy? How you like what we brung you? Anybody knows that dying ain't nothing. You got one eye shut and one eye open, old man. We going to miss you just the same, though, we going to miss you bad, but we'll meet you on t'other side, Bundy. We'll do that sure's you born. One eye shut and one eye open: down, down, down. Lord, Lord. Mm-mm-mm-mm. Don't let them black boys cover you up in that hole, brother.

They had raised a song without words. They were kneeling with their faces to the sun. Their hands were in the air, the fingers apart, and they bowed and rose together as they sang. Up came the song like a wave, and down went their faces in the dirt.

Easy down, black boys, easy down. I heard tell of niggers dropping a coffin one time. They didn't have no more rest the balance of their borned days. The dead man's spirit never would excuse a carelessness like that. Easy down, black boys. Keep one eye open, Bundy. Don't let them sprinkle none of that dirt on you. Dying ain't nothing. You know how wood burns up to ashes and smoke? Well, it's just the same way when you's dying. The spirit and the skin been together like the smoke and the ashes in the wood; when you dies, they separates. Dying ain't nothing. The smoke goes free. Can't nobody hurt smoke. A smoke man—that's you now, brother. A *real* smoke man. Smoke what gets in yo' eyes and makes you blink. Smoke what gets in yo' throat and chokes you. Don't let them cover you up in that hole, Bundy. Mm-mm-mm-mm.

Ben crossed a field and came to the place. The sun was far in the west; it was slipping behind the hills fast. But there were small suns now in every window on the countryside, numberless small suns. A blue and gold twilight sifted into the low field. The black folks, some of them naked to the waist, kept bowing to the sun, bowing and rising as they sang. Their arms quivered above their heads.

That's all right about you, Bundy, and it's all right about us. Marse Prosser thunk it was cheaper to kill a old wo'-out mule than to feed him. But they's plenty things Marse Prosser don't know. He don't even know a tree got a soul same as a man, and he don't know you ain't in that there hole, Bundy. We know, though. We can see you squatting there beside that pile of dirt, squatting like a old grinning bullfrog on a bank. Marse Prosser act like he done forgot smoke get in his eyes and make him blink. You'll be in his eyes and in his throat too, won't you, Bundy?

Ben knelt down and joined the song, moaning with the others at the place where the two worlds meet. He watched the young black fellows cover the hole, and he kept thinking about the old crochety slave who loved a jug of rum. Bundy wanted Ben to talk with Gabriel, and Ben knew now he would have to do it. There was something about a dead man's wish that commanded respect. The twilight thickened in the low field. Two or three stray whites who had been standing near by walked away.

Dead and gone, old Bundy. Something—something no denser than smoke—squatting by the hole, grinning pleasantly with one eye on the jug of rum.

The Negroes became still; and Martin, the smaller of Gabriel's two brothers, stood up to speak.

"Is there anybody what ain't swore?"

Ben wrinked his forehead, scratched his frizzly salt-and-pepper whiskers.

"Swore about what?" he murmured.

"I reckon you don't know," Martin said. "Here's the Book, and here's the pot of blood, and here's the black-cat bone. Swear."

"Swear what?"

"You won't tell none of what you's apt to hear in this meeting. You'll take a curse and die slow death if you tells. On'erstand?"

Ben felt terrified. All eyes were on him. All the others seemed to know. Something like a swarm of butterflies was suddenly let loose in his mind. After a dreadful pause his thought became clear again. Well, he wouldn't be swearing to do anything he didn't want to do; he would just be swearing that he'd keep his mouth closed. It was no more than he'd have done had he not come to the burying. And by now, anyhow, so great was his curiosity, he couldn't possibly resist the desire to hear. Gossip was sweet at his age.

"I won't tell nobody, Martin," he said. "I swears."

There were a few others to be sworn. This done, Martin knelt quietly, and Gabriel took his place in the center of the circle. Near him on the ground was Ditcher, powerful and beast-like. General John Scott knelt in his rags. Criddle looked up, his mouth hanging open, the domino spots bright in his bullet head. Juba, the thin-waisted brown girl with hair bushed on her head, curled both feet under her body and leaned back insolently, her hands behind her on the ground. Solomon, Gabriel's oldest brother, sat with his chin in his palm like a thinker. His head was bald in front, and his forehead glistened. Something imaginary, perhaps the smoke of old Bundy, squatted beside the hole that the black boys had covered, squatted and grinned humorously, one eye on the jug of rum. Gabriel called for a prayer.

Oh, battle-fighting God, listen to yo' little chilluns; listen to yo' lambs. Remember how you brung deliverance to the Israelites in Egypt land; remember how you fit for Joshua. Remember Jericho. Remember Goliath, Lord. Listen to yo' lambs. Oh, battle-fighting God. . . .

"That's enough," Gabriel said. "Hush moaning and listen to me now. God don't like ugly. Some of y'-all heard Mingo read it."

He gave a quick summary of the Scriptures Mingo had read. Then he paused a long time. His eye flashed in the growing dusk. He looked at those near him in the circle, one by one, and one by one they broke their gaze and dropped their heads.

Another sweeping gaze. Then he spoke abruptly.

"We's got enough to take the town already. This going to be the sign: When you see somebody riding that black colt Araby,

galloping him for all he's worth in the big road, wearing a pair
of Marse Prosser's shiny riding boots, you can know that the
time's come. You going to know yo' captains, and that's going
to be the sign to report. You on'erstand me?"

Ben caught his breath with difficulty. Lordy. The young
speaker was deeply in earnest, but Ben couldn't make himself
believe that Gabriel meant what his words seemed to mean. It
sounded like a dream. Two or three phrases, a few words, fluttered in his mind like rags on a clothes wire. Take the town.
Captains. . . . Ben shuddered violently. Somebody wearing
Marse Prosser's riding boots, galloping Araby in the big road.
Where would Marse Prosser be when they took his shiny boots
off him? Did they mean that they were going to murder?

And so this was what old Bundy wanted him to hear from
Gabriel, was it? Did he think Ben would get mixed up in any
such crazy doings? Ben's lips twitched. His thought broke off
abruptly. Something squatting beside the covered hole turned
a quizzical eye toward the frizzly whiskered house servant. Ben
wrung his hands; he bowed his head, and heavy jolting sobs
wrenched his body. He wasn't in for no such cutting up as all
that. The devil must of got in Bundy before he died. What
could he do now with that eye on him? Ben bowed lower.

"Oh, Lord Jesus," he said, crying.

A powerful elbow punched his ribs, and Ben raised his head
without opening his eyes.

"What's the matter, nigger, don't you want to be free?"

Ben stopped sobbing, thought a long moment.

"I don't know," he said.

Gabriel was talking again by now.

"This the way how you line up: Ditcher's the head man of
all y'-all from across the branch. Gen'l John is going to—" He
stopped talking for a moment. A little later he whispered,
"Who that coming across that field?"

"Marse Prosser."

"It is, hunh? Well, strike up a song, Martin."

They began moaning softly. The voices rose bit by bit, a full
wave. Again there was the same swaying of bodies, the same
shouts punctuating the song. Gabriel faced the west, his hands
locked behind him, his varnished coachman's hat tilted forward. Ben fell on his face crying. It became quite dark.

Twelve

MELODY watered the pot plants between the green shutters of her upstairs window. A lock of the enameled black hair fell against her cheek and the large earrings jangled beneath the rose-colored headcloth. General John came around from the back, passed beneath the window and walked toward the river road. There was no bounce in his stride, but he stepped briskly and walked with an air of great importance despite his hopeless rags. He was the busiest man in Richmond.

Three languid blacks lolled in front of the *Dirty Spoon*, one on a chair tilted against the brick wall, one on the doorstep and one standing with legs crossed and hands thrust into the pockets of tattered jeans. There was only the ghost of a breeze in the bright, quiet morning, but the old lamp post swayed in its place a few steps from the door of the wine shop. A tall three-master, its canvas all in, rocked against the river wharf.

General John purchased the wine for which he had been sent and hurried back to Melody's upstairs rooms. She poured him a drink in a tumbler. He stood at the head of the back steps, his mashed-up hat in his hand, and tossed it off.

"Well, if you ain't got nothing else for me to do, I reckon I'll trot along, Miss Melody."

"No need to hurry, Gen'l John. You can sit on the bench under my fig tree and rest yourself some."

He looked at her earnestly.

"Can't rest," he said. "Leastwise, not yet nohow."

She had a slow eye, that yellow woman called Melody. She had finished her sweeping and dusting, and she stood against the door in her billowing furbelows.

"It's mighty funny about you and Gabriel getting so busy all of a sudden."

"It ain't nothing, Miss Melody. Just I'm got to see a friend of mine about something another this morning."

"I ain't seen that Gabriel standing still since I-don't-know-when."

"A brown gal named Juba—that's all."

"His head been mighty low for a nigger what's got the gal he wants. You better tell me right, Gen'l John. You and Gabriel got something up yo' sleeve."

"Just thinking, maybe," he said. "Just thinking how it would feel to be free, I reckon."

"See there. You been talking to that Philadelphia lawyer, ain't you?"

General John shook his head.

"I ain't talked to no white man about nothing," he said. "But you couldn't on'erstand like us. Things ain't the same with you. You's free."

"I got a good mind how you feels," she said. Then after a pause, "That ain't telling me howcome you always keeps so busy, though."

General John just grinned a wide crooked-toothed grin.

"I'm got to trot along."

He hurried down the stairs and around the house to the street.

Suddenly Melody thought of something. She ran through her rooms to the front window and called down to General John.

"Wait a minute," she said.

She went quickly to a table and dipped a quill into an ink pot. Then she began writing hastily on a sheet of notepaper. When she had finished and sealed the brief missive, she returned to the window and tossed it down to General John.

"Mail it?" he asked.

"No, leave it with M. Creuzot at his printing shop. Ask him if he will deliver it, please."

"H'm."

She remained at the window, watching the old black man out of sight.

Thirteen

THE days were not long enough now. Gabriel and a young fellow called Blue went to get Ben at night. They left a group whispering on the floor of a hut, crept silently down a corn row, climbed a fence and went over a low hill. Then, finding a wagon path beneath a line of poplars, they walked another half-mile.

Ben was not in his cabin yet, so they started up toward the big house and met him on the path.

"Did Criddle give you the word?" Gabriel said.

Ben quaked.

"Yes, he been here."

"Well, ain't you coming?"

"I reckon so. But I ain't fit for a lot of cutting up now. I ain't young like y'-all."

"Don't you want to be free, fool," Blue said.

"I reckon I does."

"You *reckon*?"

"Listen," Gabriel said, "you ain't got to fight none. We got something else for you to do. Come along."

Ben walked between the other two.

Solomon, General John and Ditcher lay on their bellies in the hut. They were whispering with their faces near the dirt floor. Gabriel and Blue came in with Ben. No greetings, no useless words passed. The three got down and made a circle. An eery blue light pierced a crack in the wall, separated the dull silhouettes. No preliminary words, no Biblical extenuations preceded the essential plans this time. Ben knelt beside Gabriel and saw the huge young coachman touch the earth with his extended index finger.

"Listen. All the black folks'll j'ine us when we get our power. This here thing'll spread like fire. That's howcome we's sending Gen'l John down to Petersburg. He's aiming to get up a crowd there and start kicking up dust directly after we done made

647

our attack. We want Ben to go to Caroline County. Him and Gen'l John can get off and travel 'thout nobody thinking nothing. They's old and trusted-like. Nothing much they going to have to do: just be there to tell folks what's what when the time come.

"But the main plan is right here. We going to meet at the Brook Swamp where the creek go through the grove. On'erstand? There ought to be about eleven hundred of us by then. Mingo's got the names. We going to divide in three lines. One'll go on each side the town; one'll take the old penitentiary what they's using for a arsenal (they ain't but a handful of guards there), and the left wing'll hit at the powder house. The third band is the one that carries the guns and the best of the pikes and blades. Them's the ones that's got to hit the town in the middle and mop up. They ain't going to spare nothing what raises its hand—nothing. By daybreak, and maybe befo', every one of us'll have a musket and all the bullets and powder we can shoot. The arsenal is busting open with ammunition.

"The middle column is going to break in two so it can come in town from both ends at the same time. They's been some talk about not hurting the French folks. We'll find out about that later on. But we's aiming to make one of the biggest fires these here white folks is ever seen. Ditcher and Blue is captains of them two lines, and we can let them carry all the guns we got, all the scythe-swords, all the pikes, everything like that. I'm leading the wing what goes after the arsenal. That's a touchy spot. Everything hangs on that. But we can take it with sticks about as well as we could with guns. We got to move on cat feet there and take the guards by surprise. We got to be all around them like shadows, snatching the guns out of they hands and bashing they skulls with sticks. Solomon will take the powder house the same way."

Ben tried hard to keep his lips moist, but they kept drying up like paper. His breath made so much noise he felt ashamed. He imagined the others were listening to it and judging him harshly. Suddenly there were tears in his eyes and a moment later he cried audibly, his face in his hands.

"I can't do it," he said. "Lordy, it's killing and murder and burning down houses. I can't do it."

Gabriel turned sternly, paused and then spoke.

"It's the onliest way. Besides, I reckon that wa'n't murder when Marse Prosser kilt old Bundy."

Ben sniffled and became silent again. The picture of that scrawny old good-humored ghost squatting near his fat jug came into his mind again and his flesh quaked, but he made no other sound. Then there was another man in his thoughts, too, a man whose feet they hurt with fetters, according to the Book, who was laid in irons—*until the time that his word came.*

Curiously, at the same instant Gabriel said, "This here is the time. There ain't no backing up now. Is you going to Caroline County or must we get somebody else?"

"I reckon I'm going," Ben said faintly.

"Well, that's settled. Gen'l John is carrying the money. He'll give you some for expense. We got a peck of bullets and about a dozen scythe-swords now. Solomon's fixing these in the black-smith shop and I'm making the handles. They'll do the work."

"We need mo' weapons," Blue said.

"We can have them too," Gabriel answered. "But we don't need many's you reckon. They ain't mo'n twenty-three muskets in the town, and we ain't going to give them time to put they hands on them what they's got. What's mo' God's going to fight them because they oppresses the poor. Mingo read it in the Book and you heard it same as me."

"H'm."

They all murmured. Their assent, so near the ground, seemed to rise from the earth itself. H'm. There was something warm and musical in the sound, a deep tremor. It was the earth that spoke, the fallen star.

Ben's eyes burned for sleep. He went from window to window raising blinds and throwing open shutters, but there was no sun and the handsome high-ceilinged rooms remained dull and cheerless. Ben was tortured with a vision of filthy black slaves coming suddenly through those windows with pikes and cut-lasses in their hands, their eyes burning with murderous pas-sion and their feet dripping mud from the swamp. He saw the lovely hangings crash, the furniture reel and topple, piece by piece, and he saw the increasing black host storm the stairway.

In another moment there were the quick, choked cries of the dying, followed by wild jungle laughter. Then it occurred to Ben which side he was on, and he covered his eyes with his hand. It was going to be an impossible thing for him to do, a desecrating, sinful thing.

Fourteen

M. CREUZOT stopped in the open door of Mingo's saddle-shop. Outside a horse hitched to a small buck wagon was tied to the crossbar. The printer rested his musket and held a wild turkey up for the free Negro to inspect.

"He one mo' beauty," Mingo said, passing his hand over the enameled feathers. "Where'bouts you shoot him, Mistah Creuzot?"

"Out on the creek. I prefer duck, but you don't see many of them this early."

"I reckon not. They start coming this way about October."

"Yes, or possibly later. I want to hang the bird behind your shop here, Mingo. When Laurent comes, I'll have him carry it home."

"Yes, suh. Help yo'self," Mingo said.

"Thanks."

M. Creuzot went out into the small yard behind. Weeds were tall, and there was a rubbish pile that had grown remarkably. He tied the feet of his turkey to a hook as high as he could reach on the wall. Mingo was busy with an awl when he returned.

"How about leaving that there musket here a few days too?" the Negro suggested.

"Well, I don't mind. You want to try your luck?"

"H'm. I might."

"You'll have to get some small shot."

When he was gone, something that Alexander Biddenhurst had said occurred to M. Creuzot. The blacks are whispering; something's up. Suddenly, and for the first time, the Frenchman seriously wondered if there were reason for the observation. Actually, *could* it be? Could these tamed things imagine liberty, equality? Of course, he knew about San Domingo, many stories had filtered through, but whether or not the blacks themselves were capable of that divine discontent that turns the mill of destiny was not answered. There had been, or so he had been told, strong forces at work in France; there had possibly been paid and experienced agitators supported by groups of people who sometimes had political as well as humanitarian aims. Young mulattos had been to Paris to school and had met certain of the *Amis des Noirs.* . . . M. Creuzot found the long thread tiresome. The blacks were not discontented: they couldn't be. They were without the necessary faculties.

He let himself into his printing shop, picked up two small jobs that had been slipped under the door with written instructions and went to the back windows to let in light and air. The morning was fine, and a shaft of yellow sun fell across the room. M. Creuzot tied on his ink-spattered apron and began clearing the composing stone.

Laurent looked drowsy when he came in a little later. His hair had not been combed and the queer little cap seemed ready to fall at any moment.

"Shame," said M. Creuzot. "You look as if you could hardly drag your feet. And such a fine morning it is. Why, I've been out to the grove and shot a turkey already."

"I didn't sleep well," Laurent said weakly.

"Too much rum?"

"No, I only took a trifle."

"That was too much. Did you see Biddenhurst last night?"

"Yes, it was he that bought the drink."

"Well, I hope you reminded him that we have a note for him here."

"He said he'd be by this morning. Where's the turkey?"

"Hanging behind Mingo's saddle-shop. I want you to carry it home for me when you deliver that job to the greengrocer on our corner."

A little later M. Creuzot looked up from the job he was locking in the form. Laurent had taken his place on a stool in front of his case and his fingers were darting rapidly.

"I keep remembering what Biddenhurst said about the Africans."

"They do whisper a lot," Laurent said. "Has some one else mentioned the same thing?"

"No, I don't know what put it in my mind."

They became silent again, but after a short time M. Creuzot did conclude what suggested the thought to him. It must have been Mingo. He had thought about it first when leaving the saddle-shop. Mingo had mentioned or inferred nothing suspicious, of course; it must have been his asking to use the musket. That *was* it. M. Creuzot rejoiced to trace his thought successfully to its source.

It would surely be a grave thing for Alexander Biddenhurst, following his bold quotations from Voltaire and other makers of the French Revolution, should discontent be manifest among the proletariat and particularly among the blacks. They bore so many insults that might call forth horrible retaliation. It would be miserable for Laurent, whom the town boys already, quite absurdly, called a Jacobin. The ground might even get hot under the feet of M. Creuzot and his friend the dancing master, what with the Presidential election approaching and with the Federalist press accusing the party of Thomas Jefferson of getting its philosophy from the *States-Général* and inclining very radically toward the left. No Federalist paper, wishing to win votes, missed an opportunity to hurl the anathema of that dreaded word *Jacobin* into the air. They didn't bother to analyze or define carefully. They were glad to have the public catch the misleading implications they had succeeded in putting into the term: redistribution of wealth, snatching of private property, elevation of the blacks, equality, immediate and compulsory miscegenation. The masses were pitifully abused and frightened, M. Creuzot thought. But the fact that he had a more temperate burden for their rise than had Alexander Biddenhurst would help him little in a moment of general passion. The same mark was on him. He was sorry that he had let Mingo have his gun; it gave him unpleasant thoughts, made him nervous. He would get it back as soon as possible.

The writing on the envelope was an illiterate scrawl. Alexander Biddenhurst read the misspelled name, smiled and dropped it into his pocket.

"It is just for laughter, M. Creuzot. Nothing important."

The sunlight was so fine in the back of the shop that Biddenhurst removed his coat, took a chair beneath the window and opened his book. A customer came in and engaged M. Creuzot in the front doorway. Biddenhurst read from his book with quiet absorption.

Man is a stranger to his own research;
He knows not whence he comes, nor whither goes.
Tormented atoms in a bed of mud,
Devoured by death, a mockery of fate;
But thinking atoms, whose far-seeing eyes,
Guided by thoughts, have measured the faint stars.
Our being mingles with the infinite;
Ourselves we never see, nor come to know.
This world, this theatre of pride and wrong,
Swarms with sick fools who talk of happiness . . .
Seeking a light amid the deepening gloom. . . .

Fifteen

The brown girl curled on the floor in front of the circle of men. Mingo sat on a stool; the others had drawn up benches, work tables and boxes. They were meeting in the saddle-shop because Mingo had said, "Never twice in the same place—on'erstand? Here this time and somewheres else the next."

"That's enough reading this time," Gabriel said. "We going to have all the help we needs once we get our hands in. It's most nigh time to strike, and we got to make haste."

Gabriel, silent and dreamy usually, spoke with a quick excitement these days. There was an urgency in his manner that got under the skin at once. He didn't talk in a loud voice; in fact, he didn't talk at all. He simply whispered. Yet Ditcher's mouth dropped open as he listened; he leaned forward and the muscles tightened on his shoulders. His huge hands, dangling at his sides, closed gradually and gradually opened again. He was ready to strike. Blue, hearing every word, pulled the heavy lips over his large protruding teeth, hunched himself somberly on his box. General John Scott, as scrawny and ragged as a scarecrow, rubbed his brown bark-like hands together, blinked nervously. Ben, wearing gloves, stood with a new Sunday hat in his hand, his head bowed. Some of the group trembled. They were all ready.

They had come into the shop through the back way. They had selected this place for their Sunday gathering because the shops on either side were closed and they were able to feel safely secluded.

"What's going to be the day?" Ditcher said.

"The first day in September," Gabriel told him.

"That falls on a Sad-dy," a pumpkin-colored fellow said quietly.

General John showed his brown fangs without malevolence.

"Sad-dy, hunh?"

"Yes, the first day of September come next Sad-dy," Ben said.

"I's just thinking," the yellow Negro muttered. "I's just thinking it might be better to strike on a Sunday."

"Howcome that?" Gabriel asked.

"Well, it's just like today. The country folks can leave home and travel mo' better on a Sunday. Nobody's going to ask where they's going or if they's got a note. That's what I's thinking. Sunday's a mo' better day for the back-country folks to get together."

"We don't need none of them what lives that far in the country—not right now nohow. We done set Sad-dy for the day and Sad-dy it's going to be—hear? We got all the mens we need to hit the first lick right round here close."

"Well, I reckon maybe that's right too. That other was just something what come in my head."

"This what *you* got to remember, Pharoah: You's leaving for Caroline County with Ben next Sad-dy evening. You can send word up by the boys going that a-way so everything'll be in shape. We going to write up something like that what Mingo read from Toussaint, soon's we get our power, and you ain't got to do nothing up there but spread the news. Them's all our brothers. I bound you they'll come when they hears the proclamation."

"H'm. They'll come," General John said. "They'll come soon's they hears what we's done."

Ben turned the new Sunday hat round and round in his hands. He was nervous and tremulous again. He turned General John's words in his mind: They'll come. Anything wants to be free. Well, Ben reckoned so; yet and still, it seemed like some folks was a heap mo' anxious about it than others. It was true that they were brothers—not so much because they were black as because they were the outcasts and the unwanted of the land—and for that reason he followed against his will. Then, too, there was old Bundy buried in the low field and that something else that squatted by the hole where he lay.

"They'll come," Ben echoed weakly. "Anything wants to be free—I reckon."

"You mighty right," Gabriel whispered. "Some of y'-all can commence leaving now. Remember just two by two, and don't go till the ones in front of you is had time to get round the square. That's right, Criddle, you and George. You two go first. Ben and Pharoah—you next. Keep moving and don't make no fuss."

Now they were getting away slowly. They were slipping down the ally by twos and the saddle-shop was emptying gradually. Gabriel stood above the thin-waisted brown girl, his foot on the edge of the bench, one elbow on his knee.

"It's a man's doings, Juba. You ain't obliged to keep following along."

"I hears what you say."

"The time ain't long, and it's apt to get worse and worser."

"H'm."

"And it's going to be fighting and killing till you can't rest, befo' it's done."

"I know," she said.

"And you still wants to follow on?"

"Yes."

"Well, it ain't for me to tell you no, gal."

"I'm in it. Long's you's in it, I'm in it too."

"And it's win all or lose all—on'erstand?"

"I'm in it. Win all or lose all."

Mingo stood by listening. His spectacles had slipped down on his nose. He had a thin face for a black and a high receding forehead. He listened to Gabriel's words and Juba's short answers and tried to tear himself away. Somehow he couldn't move. It was win all or lose all. He became pale with that peculiar lavender paleness that comes to terrified black men. There was death in the offing, death or freedom, but until now Mingo had thought only in terms of the latter. The other was an ugly specter to meet.

He looked at Gabriel's face, noted the powerful resolution

in his expression. Sometimes, he thought, the unlearned lead the learned and teach them courage, teach them to die with a handsome toss of the head. He looked at Juba and saw that she was bewitched. She would indeed follow to the end. He was a free Negro and these were slaves, but somehow he envied them. Suddenly a strange exaltation came to his mind.

"Yes," he said, breaking into their conversation. "It's win all or lose all. It's a game, but it's worth trying and I got a good notion we can win. I'm free now, but it ain't no good being free when all yo' people's slaves, yo' wife and chilluns and all."

"A wild bird what's in a cage will die anyhow, sooner or later," Gabriel said. "He'll pine hisself to death. He just is well to break his neck trying to get out."

Sixteen

THE pumpkin-colored mulatto was outside, standing beneath a willow tree near the back doorstep. Ben could see him from the kitchen window, and at first he was puzzled, but in a moment he recognized that it was Pharoah. He was a field-hand, that Pharoah, and his jeans were encrusted with earth. He was obsequious beyond reason, and he had a wide, open-mouth smile and little obscure eyes like the eyes of a swine. He belonged to Marse Sheppard, but Ben saw him rarely.

Standing over the lamp table, cleaning chimneys with a silk cloth, Ben could watch him from the window without even rising on his tiptoes. Pharoah waited patiently in the dusk, his back against the willow, his hands in his pockets. And Ben could have gone out promptly, but he delayed. He felt certain that Pharoah had come on some mission connected with the bloody business just ahead, and for that reason Ben was in no hurry.

Drucilla was at the stove, her head tied in a cloth, bowing over a pot of something she was stirring with a long wooden spoon. Presently she went into the pantry for a pinch of salt, and Ben put down his lamp chimney and slipped out of doors. Pharoah began to grin and bow almost as if he had forgotten that it was not a white person who was approaching him.

"S-sorry, Uncle Ben," he said. "I didn't go to disturb you."

"You ain't disturbing me. What's on yo' mind?"

"Well, I been thinking a heap, Uncle Ben."

"Too late to be thinking now, ain't it?"

"I don't know if it is or if it ain't. I been thinking just the same. Is you going to let them send you up to Caroline County, Uncle Ben?"

Ben averted his face. Pharoah came a step nearer, his shoulders hunched, his mouth open.

"You heard the plan well as me. There ain't nothing else left for me *but* go."

"Gabriel's getting biggity," Pharoah said. "You ain't obliged to do *everything* he says, is you?"

"It'll be better going there than staying here. It'll be murder and killing here. Up there it'll just be——"

"I don't know," Pharoah said. "I can't help thinking sometimes, though. Here. Gabriel sent this here."

"Three shillings, hunh?"

"Yes. It's the money for our expense in Caroline County."

"Kind of skimpy change."

"That's what I been thinking. Gen'l John had a roll of bills in his old raggety pockets fit to choke a crocodile. They could of give us a little mo'n this."

Ben kept looking at Pharoah and trying to make out what he meant by talking that way. But he learned nothing. Pharoah just naturally seemed dissatisfied and peeved and possibly sorry that he was involved in the plot at all.

"I reckon we can make out," Ben said absently. "When do we go?"

"Sad-dy evening, I reckon. That's the last thing Gabriel said at the meeting. We is supposed to get up a good crowd that'll rise up like a flock of sparrows in a wheat field soon's they get the news that Richmond's in Gabriel's hands."

"If we don't get no news, they don't rise up?"

"I reckon they don't." Then after a pause, "I wanted to lead a line into Richmond, me. Gabriel's so biggity he won't listen to nobody. He say I got to go with you."

"You can lead the Caroline County crowd," Ben said.

Suddenly twilight came to the trees behind the great house. The fat, pumpkin-colored Negro crossed the yard and followed the gravel carriage path out to the big road. Ben returned to the kitchen.

Ben placed the candles on the supper table and touched a small brass gong on the sideboard. He had an eye for niceties, that Ben, and he refrained from drawing the blinds against the blue dusk till Marse Sheppard and young Marse Robin were seated at the table. When grace had been said, he served the soup. This done, he hung his cloth neatly across his left wrist and made the rounds of the windows. Ben knew that that was as it should have been. He could even feel the warmth and security that came to Mr. Moseley Sheppard's supper table. Ben stood in a corner of the room, the white cloth on his wrist, his back against an old-rose hanging. There, without warning, the devil spoke to his mind.

What cause you got feeling sorry for a rich old white man that God don't even love? You ought to know them kind by now. They oppress the stranger, and they oppresses the poor. They kills the old horse when he gets wind-broke. Wa'n't it Marse Prosser that said it's cheaper to kill a wo'-out nigger than to feed him? Leastwise, he must of thought it if he didn't say it. He kilt old Bundy with his riding whip, stepped on him with his horse. Old rum-drinking Bundy with his spindle legs and his laughing and his cutting up. Lord, it was a shame; it was a shame befo' Jesus.

Robin waited for his father to finish his soup, and Ben promptly carried the two bowls into the kitchen. The food was ready; Drucilla was waiting, slightly provoked at the lazy tempo of things. Ben took the steaming platters out to the table. It was a routine that called for little thought. Yet in doing it he did reflect upon the trustfulness of masters who eat food prepared by servants they have despitefully used. Of course they had no reason to fear; he had heard of attempts by slaves to poison their masters, but he had never witnessed an instance. Well, it was good that folks couldn't read one another's minds. Yes, suh, and that wa'n't no lie. Ben returned to the kitchen when he had placed the food on the table. Once he came back with warm rolls and again with warm gravy, but he tried to be inconspicuous while the father and son talked across the platters and candles.

In the kitchen Drucilla's glossy round face became increasingly serious. Her forehead wrinkled.

"Marse Sheppard didn't clean his soup dish."

"No, he left some," Ben said.

"That ain't his way. He ain't supposed to turn away from no oyster soup."

"He ain't got the appetite he used to had. He ain't as young, I reckon."

"Maybe he ain't as well, neither. Them spells——"

A little later Ben went in with the sweet dish. Marse Sheppard looked at his and shook his head. Then while young Robin was at his, the old man pushed his chair back and started to rise. But something stopped him, a sudden weakness and a constriction near the base of his ribs on the left side. Robin didn't see it, didn't even raise his eyes, but Ben was by the old planter's side in a wink, saying nothing, but lending his arm and leading Marse Sheppard toward the staircase. They climbed the steps slowly, and Ben blinked with sorrow in his eyes.

He was playing out, Marse Sheppard was, like some old plush-covered music box running down. Yes, suh, his days was few and they was numbered. Ben was getting old too, but somehow he seemed to be lasting a little bit better, thanks the Lord. Nobody couldn't tell, though. He might kick the bucket hisself befo' long. Time didn't stand still. Funny too: it didn't seem long. Yet he had been a full-grown man when Marse Sheppard bought him from old Sol Woodfolk, and that was yonder about fifty year ago. Marse Sheppard had out-lived two young wives since then, but he wouldn't out-live nara another two. No, nor one either.

It was right sad to think about it all. And it was going to be hard to go away to Caroline County and leave him like this. But it would be a heap better'n staying home and seeing the crowd of mad savages coming through the windows with scythe-swords and pikes. Lordy!

They reached the top of the stairs.

"I'm going to be all right," Marse Sheppard said. "Fix the candles."

"Yes, suh."

But Ben knew that when Marse Sheppard became so anxious about light in his room it was because he feared he *wasn't* going to be all right.

Seventeen

ALEXANDER BIDDENHURST hastily took the coach to Fredericksburg. Something was in the air. There was no longer room for doubt. It was leaving time. The Negroes were whispering, and some had whispered a bit too loudly. Nothing was certain, of course, but the prudent act for a stranger who had quoted Rousseau quite freely on the equality of man was to secure passage on the first public conveyance going north.

Laurent was outside, standing on the cobblestones when the horses pulled away. The stagecoach was filled, and there were other people at the junction for saying farewells. They bustled noisily in the street, waving handkerchiefs and, in one case at least, throwing kisses. There were two women with small bright parasols; they wore furbelows and little dainty hats that didn't cover the back of the head. There was a young man with white stockings and a three-cornered hat. And there were others, like Laurent, whose clothes were plain and whose appearance left no remarkable impression.

Laurent followed the footpath beneath the trees along the street. The dust was deep. It had powdered the trees, and Laurent recalled that there had been no drop of rain in more than seven weeks. The earth thirsted. Some small birds rested beneath a shrub, their wings hanging, their tiny throats quavering.

In the shop door he confronted the tall, gentle printer.

"Biddenhurst just took the stage to Fredericksburg."

"So? Is he returning directly?"

"Hardly. He said it was becoming unhealthy for him here."

M. Creuzot looked at his ruddy apprentice with a long puzzled gaze. Then his mouth dropped open. Laurent heard the breath wheezing between the older man's teeth.

"So there *is* something up?"

"He didn't say so to me, not as pointedly as that, anyway."

"He'd have no other reason to flee. He's gotten himself involved in mischief all right. Are you in it too, Laurent?"

"There is nothing that I know, nothing more than I've talked with you."

Again that look on M. Creuzot's face, that serious, intent gaze. But when he spoke finally, his voice was tired and he seemed that he would presently cry.

"Anything may happen, Laurent. They think we're Jacobins and revolutionaries. If the mob spirit is aroused, we'll just have to be ready for the worst."

The two went to the front window and looked out on the parched leaves and the dusty street. Heavy green flies boomed above a puddle of filth beside the nearest hitching bar. There were fiddles overhead, sounding through the trees that shaded M. Baptiste's dancing school.

"We're innocent, though," Laurent murmured. "We've done nothing to injure anyone."

"It's all the same. If they say we're Jacobins, that's quite enough to put them on us."

Alexander Biddenhurst re-read Melody's letter as the stage-coach lumbered over the difficult road. The dust and heat made a vile journey of it, and the large woman and her handsome daughter, who shared the coach with the young lawyer and an older gentleman, kept their handkerchiefs before their faces most of the time. The traveling bags jostled in their carrier overhead. Disregarding the faces around him, Alexander Biddenhurst read:

> I think you're right about what you said the other night. Something *is* up among the slaves. And if you been talking round town like you talked here when you was drinking I think you best to lay low till it quiets down. If anything was to happen somebody might be apt to blame you beingst you're a stranger and all and throw up to you all that book-reading about the natural-born equality of men and all like of that I never did hear no such talking as that amongst the rich white men down here and I reckon as to how they'd hate it a plenty so don't come here again whilst all this whispering is going around and if you are bound and determined to stay in town and see it through it might be healthy to lay mighty low something is up amongst the colored folks and that's a fact as sure's you born. I never before seen them carrying on like now and I'm scared a little myself so don't come here again till it all blows over. Somebody is apt to start looking at me funny too. . . .

Biddenhurst folded his arms tightly when he settled back into his seat. If the town boys pelted Laurent with green apples and called him Jacobin just because he was a Frenchman with red hair, the men were likely to have little mercy on a stranger whom they suspected of inciting slaves to rise against their masters. It was definitely leaving time. Yet the signs were hopeful, in one way of thinking, Biddenhurst thought; there was a definite foment among the masses in this state. The revolution of the American proletariat would soon be something more than an idle dream. Soon the poor, the despised of the earth, would join hands around the globe; there would be no more serfs, no more planters, no more classes, no more slaves, only men.

The stagecoach lurched; dust poured through the open windows.

Eighteen

NOBODY questioned Criddle's presence in the stable after dark. Even Marse Prosser, slapping his boots with a riding whip, went by without raising his head. But the domino spots in the boy's black face were like silver dollars now. Criddle set the lantern against a stanchion wall and crept into the next room. There he went to a loose floorboard that he knew by sound, removed it and, falling on his belly, ran his arm far back underneath and brought out a monstrous hand-made cutlass with a well-turned handle. Criddle got his hands on a whetstone, and in the dark alone he worked on the edge of his blade.

"Everything what's equal to a groundhog want to be free," he thought.

Ditcher spat on the ground in the door of his cabin. A round orange moon confronted him on a low hill. He was without a shirt, and his jeans were frayed away at the knees. But he carried a driver's whip and wore leather bands on his wrists.

"Pretty night, woman," he said, addressing the moon.

A voice in the black hut said, "Yes, I reckon so."

A pause, the earth whispering, the thrashers speaking in the thickets.

"Tomorrow's our night, woman."

"Yes, I knows. You better be getting yo'self together, too."

"H'm. *You* better be having that there baby, you."

"Soon be daylight, son."

The dreamy mulatto boy was fishing in the creek. A few paces away sat his old black mammy. The moon was gone now.

"Yes, mammy."

"I'm going to cook you a breakfast what'll make yo' mouth water, dreamy boy."

"You always cooks good, mammy."

Silence, the earth whispering, the water lapping the bank with a black tongue. . . .

"What you thinking about, son?"

"A heap of things, mammy."

"You ain't fixing to go with Gabriel tomorrow night, is you?"

"I's just thinking, that's all. Didn't you ever want to be free, mammy? Didn't you ever wonder how you'd feel?"

"Hush, boy. Hush that kind of talk."

"Yes, mammy."

Mingo, the freed Negro, locked the door of his shop and said farewell to the stimulating odors of new saddles and leather trimmings. The whole adventure was going to be a plunge into the dark, he reasoned, but at least one thing was certain—nothing would be the same thereafter. The saddle-shop, if he returned to it again, would hold a new experience. His slave wife and children out on Marse Prosser's place—well, they could count on something different. It looked like win all or lose all to Mingo, but he was ready for the throw. Anything would be better than the sight of his own woman stripped and bleeding at a whipping post. Lordy, anything. He raised a hand to cover his eyes from the punishing recollection, but he failed to put by the memory of the woman's cries.

"Pray, massa; pray, massa—I'll do better next time. Oh, pray, massa."

Mingo locked his shop with a three-ounce key, turned away from the familiar door and hurried down the tree-shaded street. Nothing was going to be the same in the future, but anything would be better than Julie stripped and bleeding at a whipping post and the two little girls with white dresses and little wiry braids growing up to the same thing. Lord Jesus, anything would be better than that, anything.

"Well, here's where us parts company, boy," Blue said. He unhooked the mule's collar and slapped the critter's flank. "Kick up yo' heels if you's a-mind to. Sun's going down directly and it might not rise no mo'. Right here me and you parts company for keeps."

He tossed the harness on the barn floor and hurried down the path to the cabins. Fast moving clouds streaked the mauve sky. The other field Negroes were knocking off too; they followed the line of mules up the narrow path. Blue tried to imagine how it would feel to be free. He could see himself, in his mind's eye, shooting ducks in the marsh when he should have been following a plow, riding in a public stagecoach with a cigar in his mouth, his clothes well-ordered, his queue neatly tied, drinking rum in a waterfront tavern, his legs crossed, one foot swinging proudly, but he couldn't imagine how it would feel.

"About time to stir now," he said aloud.

Old Catfish Primus was busy all day.

"Here, boy, tie this round yo' neck likea that—on'erstand? It'll do the work. Leastwise, it'll do the work if somebody else ain't already put a bad hand on you."

"Thanks a heap, Old Primus. What I really needs is a black cat bone, but it's too late to get one now."

"Ne'mind, this'll do the work. This a fighting 'hand.' You heard tell about a money hand, a gambling hand, a woman hand and all like of that to help a man out? Well, this fighting hand is just the thing now. I don't reckon nobody else is done put a bad hand on none of y'-all."

"Thanks a heap."

"You other boys—you want the same kind?"

"Same kind, Catfish."

"Well, wait outside then."

"Us ain't got long to wait."

"I knows. Look kinda like rain, don't it?"

"H'm. Mind out what you's doing there, Old Primus. Don't get yo' conjur mixed up, hear?"

"Hush, boy."

"Well, I just don't want no hand to make the womens love me when I needs to be fighting. That's all."

The streaks moved faster and faster across the sky. Then suddenly there were flashes playing on the rushing clouds. Araby whimpered, his lovely head at the open window of his stall. He was bridled and ready. The stables were peopled with shadows slipping from place to place. Outside a few dry leaves were gathered up in a quick swirl. They danced for a moment like tiny wretched ghosts on the barn roof, then fled.

There was a girl's hand on the colt's bridle.

She wore a shiny pair of men's riding boots and a cut-off skirt that failed to reach her knees.

"Not yet," she said, seeking the colt's forelock. "Not yet, boy."

A taller shadow bowed its head and entered the door.

"You, Juba?"

"H'm."

"I's just seeing was everything ready."

"Everything ready," she said.

"Good. I'll be back directly, then."

Gabriel hurried out. The lightning crackled around him like the sound of a young pine fire. The clouds were growing darker.

Nineteen

"A LITTLE rain won't hurt none," Gabriel kept saying. "Let it rain, if that's what it's up to. A little rain won't hurt and it might can help some."

Presently it was full night, full night with heavy clouds scudding up the sky.

Rain or no rain, wet or dry, it was all the same to Juba. That brown gal wasn't worried. She sat astride Araby's bare back, her fragmentary skirt curled about her waist, her naked thighs flashing above the riding boots, leaned forward till her face was almost touching the wild mane and felt the warm body of the colt straining between her clinched knees.

Out from behind the stable, across a field, down a shaded lane, over a low fence and across another field and she came to the big road. The gangling young horse, warming to the gait, beat a smooth rhythm with his small porcelain feet. Juba heard the footfalls now, heard the sweet, muffled clatter on the hardened earth and her breathing became quick and excited. It occurred to her benumbed mind that she was giving the sign.

Those were not shadows running down to the roadside, pausing briefly and then darting back into the thickets. Those were not shadows, merely. Juba knew better. She understood.

Y'-all sees me, every lasting one of you. And you knows what this here means. Gabriel said it plain. Dust around now, you old big-foot boys. Get a move on. Remember how Gabriel say it: you got to go on cat feet. You got to get around like the wind. Quick. On'erstand? Always big-talking about what booming bed-men you is. Always trying to turn the gals' heads like that. Well, let's see what you is good for sure 'nough. Let's see if you knows how to go free; let's see if you knows how to die, you big-footses, you.

There it was now—thunder. Yes, and rain too. There it was, a sudden spray in her face, a few big broken drops.

Araby tossed his head, nickered, caught his second wind and bounded forward like a creature drunk with pleasure. His heart was a leaf.

670

BOOK TWO

HAND ME DOWN
MY SILVER TRUMPET

One

THEY were going against Richmond with eleven hundred men and one woman. They were gathering like shadows at the Brook Swamp. Through the relentless downpour there went the motley rattle of their scythe-swords and the thump of bludgeons hanging from their belts. The ghostly insurrection-naires raked wet leaves overhead with pikes that stood against their shoulders. They splashed water ankle-deep in the honey-locust grove.

"A little rain won't hurt none," Gabriel said, his back against a sapling.

"No, I reckon it won't," Martin whispered. "Yet and still, it might be a sign, mightn't it?"

"Sign of what?"

"I don't know. Bad hand or something like that, maybe."

"Humph! Whoever heard tell about rain being a sign of a bad hand against you?"

Martin's voice faded into the slosh of water, the swish and thrum in the tree-tops and the rattle of home-made side arms. Bare feet churned the mud. One of the Negroes with an ex-tremely heavy voice had a barking cough on his chest. All of them were restless; they kept plop-plopping like cattle in a bog. Now and again a flash brightened their drenched bodies.

Near Gabriel, beneath the next tree, the thin-waisted girl sat like a statue on the black colt. Her wet hair had tightened into a savage bush. She still wore Marse Prosser's high riding boots, but above her knees her thighs were wet and gleaming. She sat rapt, only the things she had fastened to her ears moving.

"How many's here?" Gabriel asked.

"Near about fo'-hundred."

"Some of them's slow coming."

"The rain's holding them back, I reckon."

"They needs to get a move on. Time ain't waiting and the rain ain't fixing to let up. Leastwise, it don't seem like it is."

"It's getting worser. We going to have a time crossing the branches between here and town if we don't start soon."

"You better go on back with the other womens, gal; you's apt to catch yo' death out in all this water."

"Anybody what's studying about freedom is apt to catch his death, one way or another, ain't he?"

"But it's a men-folks' job just the same. It ain't a fitten way for womens to die."

Thunder broke and a fresh shower began before the old one had diminished. Presently another followed and again another, like waves succeeding waves on a tortured reef. The invisible Negroes milled more and more restlessly in the sloppy grove.

"I don't aim to go back, though."

Gabriel knew how to answer that. He decided to forget the matter.

"Ditcher and his crowd ain't here yet," he said.

"It's the rain, I reckon."

"We got to get started just the same. It ain't good to wait. Some of them'll start talking about signs and one thing and another. We got to keep on the move now we's here. Martin. You Martin!"

The older brother wasn't far away. He came near enough to whisper.

"You 'spect it's too much water tonight, Gabriel?"

"Too much water for what?"

"I's just thinking maybe Ditcher and the country crowd's hemmed in. Them creeks out that a-way might be too deep and swift to cross after all this."

"Well we's here. There's near about fo'-hundred of us, and we'll go without the others if they don't come soon. You and Solomon and Blue line them up. Find Criddle and send him here. We got to get a move on. There's creeks for us 'tween here and town, and I bound you there's high water in them too. Hush all the talking and make everyone stand still for orders. Hurry. Get Criddle first."

Martin was gone, splashing a lot of water.

"What line you want me in?" Juba said.

"You can take Ditcher's place till he come. Araby'll be something for the line to follow. That you, Criddle?"

"Yes, this here me."

"You know your first job?"

"H'm. That little old house this side of town."

"That's it. Just stay in the yard till the line pass by. There's a old po' white man there that's apt to jump on his horse and start waking up the town folks do he hear us passing. You stay in the yard till the line get by—on'erstand?"

"H'm. I on'erstands."

"Well, light out then. You's going to wait there for us. If anything happen, you's got yo' blade and you oughta know by now what you got it for. Blue——"

"I'm right here."

"Get my crowd in line. We got to lead the way—hear?"

"They's ready."

"Well and good then. That you, Martin?"

"Yes, this me."

"Why in the nation don't you hurry and get yo' crowd in line?"

"Some of them's thinking maybe all this here thunder and lightning and rain's a sure 'nough bad sign."

"Listen. Listen, all y'-all." Gabriel raised his voice, turning around in excitement. "They ain't a lasting man nowheres ever heard tell of rain being a sign of a bad hand or nothing else. If any one of you's getting afeared, he can tuck his tail and go on back. I'm going to give the word directly, and them what's coming can come, and them what ain't can talk about signs. Thunder and lightning ain't nothing neither. If it is, I invites it to try me a barrel." He put out a massive chest, struck it a resounding smack. "Touch me if you's so bad, Big Man." A huge roar filled the sky. The lightning snapped bitterly. Gabriel roared with laughter, slapping his chest again and again. "Sign, hunh! Is y'-all ready to come with me?"

"We's ready," Blue said.

There was a strong murmur of assent. Then a pause, waiting for the orders. The colt whinneyed and the thin rider pulled him around so that his face was away from the force of the rain.

"Remember, we's falling on them like eagles. We's hushing up everything what opens its mouth—all but the French folks. And we ain't aiming to miss, neither, but if anything *do* go wrong, there won't be no turning back. The mountains is the only place for us then." No one spoke. After a pause he turned to the girl. "Juba, I reckon you could hurry back and see for sure is Ditcher and his crowd coming. Tell them we's starting down the creek and they can meet us at the first crossing place."

Araby wheeled, sloshing water noisily, hastened away. Lightning played on the girl's wet garment. Solomon's voice came out of a pocket of darkness.

"We's waiting for the word," he said.

"Stay ready," Gabriel told him. "I'm going to give it directly."

Two

NOTHING like it had happened before in Virginia. The downpour came first in swirls; then followed diagonal blasts that bore down with withering strength. The thirsting earth sucked up as much water as it could but presently spewed little slobbery streams into the wrinkles of the ground. Small gullies took their fill with open mouths and let the rest run out. Rivulets wriggled in the wheel paths, cascaded over small embankments. The creeks grew fat. Water rose in the swamps and in the low fields, and gradually Henrico County became a sea with islands and bays, reefs and currents and atolls.

Cattle, knee-deep in their stalls, set up a vast lamentation. An old sow, nursing her young in a puddle of slime, let out a sudden prolonged wail and scampered into a hay mow with her eleven pigs. Down by a barn fence a lean and sullen mule stood with lowered head, his hinder parts lashed tender by the storm. A flock of speckled chickens went down screaming when the wind whipped off a peach bough.

General John Scott stood in a barn door with a lantern in his hand. He wore a frayed overcoat with sleeves that covered his hands and a wet, fallen-down hat with a brim that covered his eyes. His light hollowed out an orange hole in the blackness, and into it rain poured.

"Here I'm is," the old slave muttered, "'tween the earth and the sea and the sky, and how I'm going to get the rest of the way to Richmond to catch the stagecoach is mo'n a nachal man can tell."

The door flew open and a gust like a bucket of water slopped into his face.

Well, suh, if this here storm ain't the beatingest thing yet. Just when everybody was all fixed and fitten to go, here comes a plague of rain to put the whole countryside under water. Now how in the nation is folks going to get together? Lordy, Lordy. Listen, Lordy. You remember about the chillun of Israel, don't you? Well, this here is the very same thing perzactly. . . .

The Lord was on their side, sure as you're born, but some of his ways was mysterious plus.

Another bucket of water splashed in the General's face.

"Confound this tarnation door," he said aloud. "It keep on blowing open. This here rain don't let up directly, I'm going to light out walking again anyhow."

In a thicket on the edge of town wind raked the shingles of a small log house. The undersized cabin, hidden in a tangle of wild plum, columbine and honeysuckle, squatted like a hurt thing under a bush. A light burned inside one of the tiny rooms.

Grisselda stood at the window in an outing night dress that covered her feet. She held a lamp so that it would throw a small beam into the yard. Presently the withered voice of her old father came out of the little dark chamber beyond the kitchen.

"You ain't scairt of the wind, air ye, Grisselda?"

"Oh, no. I don't mind the wind, papa."

"Well, why don't you blow the lamp out then?"

"I was just going to blow it out, papa."

She returned to the high bed. In a moment she was again conscious of the old man's snoring. She lay very still, hearing beams groan after the gusts and squalls. Her face must have been flushed; it felt very warm. Suddenly she heard the thing again and the sound brought her bolt upright in the bed. It was a noise the rain could not make, a tearing of twigs that was unlike wind, and Grisselda knew that if it were not a living creature, it was the very beast of ill weather. She waited and heard it rubbing against the house, something heavier than a cat, something with softer feet than a yearling, a more elastic body than a dog. And the girl would have sprung from the bed and rushed into the kitchen screaming, but at that moment the breath was out of her and she could not move.

For many moments she was sitting there imagining the kind of things that might seek a tangled thicket off the big road on a night like this. A panther? A thug? Was the creature hiding or prowling? What would he seek in the cabin of a widowed old man and his young daughter, destitude white folks who were poorer than black slaves?

Grisselda remembered that she was sixteen now; she knew why a young farmer had noticed the color of her hair and why the middle-aged storekeeper had recently pinched her cheek. A lewd word dropped into her thought like a pebble falling into a well. She curled her feet uneasily, but in the next moment she was cold with fear again. The thing seemed to be setting its weight against the door. Grisselda sprang from the bed and ran into the kitchen.

"Papa!"

"Still prowling, air ye?"

"Didn't you hear nothing at all, papa?"

"God bless me, who could help hearing a storm like this, gal?"

"Not that—something in the yard, something against the door?"

"Against the door, hunh?"

She put a hand on the table and felt her own quaking for the first time. The old man murmured something. They waited.

Three

I T WAS going to be like hog-killing day. Criddle had a picture in his mind; he remembered the feel of warm blood. He knew how it gushed out after the cut. He remembered the stricken eyes. Then more blood, thicker and deeper in color. Criddle knew.

The only difference was that hogs were killed on a wintry day nearer the end of the year. Hog-killing required weather that was cold enough to chill the meat but not cold enough to freeze it. On such a morning three stakes were driven into the earth and bound at the top to form a tripod. From the apex a fat, corn-fed swine was suspended by his hind feet. After a very few moments, exhausted by struggle, the blood forced down into his head, he was ready for the blade.

Criddle knew how to hush their squeals: for a long time that had been his job. It was right funny too, the way Marse Prosser always called on him to use the knife. But it wasn't hard; you just stuck the knife in where that big vein comes down the throat; you gave the blade a turn and it was all over. Hog-killing wasn't a bad preparation for tonight's business.

"I'm going to start in right here, me."

He had lost the path, so it was necessary to tear a way through the undergrowth. Later there appeared a lighted window in the house and that helped. In his bare feet and naked chest Criddle felt as drenched and slick as a frog. When he reached the yellow patch of light, he squatted silently beneath a bush and paused to make up his mind about several small details. It was then that he noticed the face beside the lamp.

He passed a thumb meditatively down the edge of his scythe-sword and derived an unaccountable pleasure from the thought of thrusting it through the pale young female that stood looking into the darkness with such a disturbed face. Yet she looked flower-like and beautiful to him there, and Criddle, though he didn't know his own mind, was sure he meant the girl no harm. She reminded him of a certain indentured white girl in town, a girl who made free with the black slaves of the same master and woke up one morning with a chocolate baby. That wasn't the kind of cutting he was up against tonight, though. Yet and still, there *were* similarities. The domino spots brightened.

Listen here, church, y'-all white folks better stay in yo' seats and look nice. They ain't going to be no wringing and twisting this night. Anything what's equal to a gray squirrel want to be free. That's what kind of business this here is. Us ain't sparing nothing, nothing what raises its hand. The good and the bad goes together this night, the pretty and the ugly. We's going to be as hard as God hisself. That's right, gal; you just as well to blow out that lamp. It'll help you get used to the dark. That's about the very best thing for you now.

The rain was almost taking his breath there under the bush. Could he really hurt that girl? Could he make his hands do it? Well, they had nobody to blame but themselves. Had no business buying and selling humans like hogs and mules. That rain! Criddle darted over to the house, crept along the rough, mud-plastered walls and came around to the door. There was a tiny ledge overhead; it offered a partial shelter. He wondered how long he would have to wait for the columns with Gabriel leading. The road passed near the house. There was a rise just above the clump through which he had wormed his way, and over it the road passed. But there were other ways to town, and the old farmer, detecting the black rabble, could easily beat the lines into town by leaping on a horse. He would be sure to hear them on the road. Somebody would be sure to talk too loud. But the lucky thing about it all was that these possibilities had been provided for. Criddle could visualize a small, ineffectual old man squirming on the end of his sword. He leaned against the door, laughing. Then abruptly he became silent.

What was that sound? Voices inside?

The black stable boy stepped back a stride, faced the door coldly and waited. Don't you come out here, Mistah Man. If you does, you ain't going nowheres. On'erstand? You ain't carrying no news to town this night.

He held his sword arm tense; the scythe blade rose, stiffened, stiffened and remained erect.

"I'm going to start in right here, me."

Four

M R. MOSELEY SHEPPARD enjoyed a good rainstorm as much as anybody, but his enjoyment of this one was tempered by the thought that possibly it would prove more costly than he could afford. Then there was this cursed wind. Though the windows were closed, he noticed that Ben found it difficult to keep a flame on his wicks.

"Is it still in your head to make that trip you spoke to me about, Ben?"

"Yes, suh—please you, Marse Sheppard."

The old planter moved a window drape aside. Two fingers of the other hand went into the pocket of his satin waistcoat. Ben was laying kindling for a small fire. The night hadn't turned cold, but with such sloppy weather outside the house seemed damp and uncomfortable.

"You shouldn't do it, though. It's not a fit night for ducks, much less people."

"Niggers ain't people, Marse Sheppard."

"I won't argue that with you. They cost a lot of money just the same. If I did right, I wouldn't let you expose yourself like that."

"That's a fact for true," Ben agreed. "Yet and still, them grown gal young-uns of mine ain't seen me in I don't-know-how-long. I done sent the word and they going to be hanging they head out the window, looking. Since you sold them——"

"If they hang their heads out in this rain, they won't have any heads left when you come, not if it's storming there like it is here."

"You know how a nigger feel about his own chillun what he don't see much. Since you sold them gals——"

"I'm not stopping you, remember," Marse Sheppard said quickly.

Ben grinned. Now and again he could hear Drucilla and Mousie moving about in the kitchen. Young Marse Robin was in his room early for once, perhaps writing a careful letter to a

pretty cousin who lived in Roanoke. Ben's hand trembled with
the splinters and small wood. The fire was catching on and the
pink warmth of the great living room reminded him that colossal things were supposed to happen tonight, colossal things
in which he was supposed to have a part. Ben knew that by
now the Negroes were gathering in the grove by the creek, the
place called the Brook Swamp, that when they had gone against
Richmond, God willing, they would turn on the planters and
their rich harvests, their country homes. Oh, it was hard to
love freedom. Of course, it was the self-respecting thing to do.
Everything that was equal to a groundhog wanted to be free.
But it was so expensive, this love; it was such a disagreeable
compulsion, such a bondage.

Ben grieved with his thoughts. Here he was getting fixed to
call on his gal young-uns. Bless God, he'd never told Marse
Sheppard such a bare-faced lie in all his days. And God might
take it on hisself to let a certain lying colored man meet the
devil the best way he could, since the fellow was so careless
with the truth. Come to think about it, all this big rain just at
this time was a caution in itself. How in God's name was all
them eleven hundred folks going to cross the streams going
into Richmond? There wasn't a sign of a bridge across most of
them.

But dying wasn't the only hold-back. Everybody had to die
some time. Another thing was leaving this house. Then there
was the old frail man standing at the window. It had been so
long, their association. They understood each other so well.
They were both so well satisfied with their present status. It
was a pretty thing to think about and a right sad one too. Ben
began to wilt. Then suddenly another thought shouted in his
head.

Licking his spit because he done fed you, hunh? Fine nigger
you is. Good old Marse Sheppard, hunh? Is he ever said anything about setting you free? He wasn't too good to sell them
two gal young-uns down the river soon's they's old enough to
know the sight of a cotton-chopping hoe. How'd he treat yo'
old woman befo' she died? And you love it, hunh? Anything
what's equal——

"Get the toddy bowl, Ben."

"Yes, suh."

Rain poured against the tall windows, rattled the overfilled gutters. Ben went into the kitchen and found Drucilla and Mousie trying to shoo a frightened bird out of the house. Pharoah was standing near the stove, his coat and hat drying on a chair. The bird had evidently come in when he opened the door. It was a bad luck sign and had to be driven out at once. Drucilla and her daughter were shaking towels at it and giving the poor creature no rest. They were still swiping at it when Ben went into the living room with his bowl of toddy.

Marse Sheppard had taken a chair.

"This is good. Did you taste it, Ben?"

Ben, smiling, set the bowl at his master's elbow.

"No, suh," he said.

Then, rather nervously, he busied himself by needlessly touching the window hangings and adjusting chairs. Mr. Moseley Sheppard drank meditatively, his gaze on the small red fire. With the second glass he put out his feet and relaxed.

"What's going on in the kitchen, Ben?"

"They's shooing a bird."

"Shooing what kind of a bird?"

"Just a little old something or other like a field lark or a swift. It come in when Pharoah opened the do', I reckon."

"Pharoah?"

"H'm."

"What's Pharoah doing here?"

"Drying his coat."

"Oh. Well, maybe you'd better tell those gals to keep the door closed from now on."

"I done told them that, Marse Sheppard."

"And tell Pharoah that's a new wrinkle, him coming in the kitchen here to dry his coat by the stove."

"Yes, suh, I'm going to tell him too."

"If you change your mind about that trip, Ben, you can keep the lights burning till the rain lets up."

"Yes, suh."

"If you go, tell Drucilla to keep them."

The two black women stood wilted and panting in the middle of the floor when Ben returned to the kitchen. Fat, pumpkin-colored Pharoah was behind the stove, his back to the fire. The kitchen was in disorder, and a chair had been upset.

"The bird gone yet?" Ben said.

"Yes, thanks the Lord. Us got to start scrubbing now. All that there water slopped in whilst George was holding the door open for us to shoo it out."

Mousie got buckets and rags from a small closet. She tied her skirt above her knees and got down to dry the floor. Drucilla followed.

"If anything give me the all-overs, it's to see a devilish bird get in the house," Mousie said.

"I ain't never seen it to fail," Drucilla said. "It's a sign, sure's you born."

"Sign of what?" Pharoah shot a glance over his right shoulder.

"Sign of death, that's what. Somebody's going to die."

"Peoples is dying all the time," Ben said.

"Well, this just mean one mo' gone," Drucilla told him. "And it's most apt to be somebody close by."

"Hush, gal."

She turned her head languidly, looked up at him from the floor with a strangely quizzical face.

"You don't believe it, hunh?"

"I ain't said I does and I ain't said I doesn't. I said hush up."

"Oh."

"Pharoah, you best throw something round you and get on out somewheres. Marse Sheppard's asking me howcome you in here drying yo' coat like as if you lived here."

"You reckon we can make it in all this rain, Ben?"

Ben went into the pantry without answering. When he returned, he said, "Maybe the rain'll let up soon."

"Better say you *reckon* it'll let up. There ain't no signs of good weather out there now."

"I said maybe."

"But what good it going to do us even do it stop raining after the water get chin-deep over everything?"

Ben put on a hat and a long cape that had been hanging on a nail behind the pantry door. He offered Pharoah a blanket.

"Marse Sheppard say keep the lights burning long's the storm keep up," he told Drucilla.

The two men stood in the doorway a few moments. They looked as solemn as ghosts. A gust of wind flickered the lights as the door opened. The tumult and agony of great trees filled the night. Ben uttered a small, audible groan. Pharoah walked behind him with fearful steps and a wrenched face.

Five

THE crackle of lightning ceased in the fields, but the sky still gave a pulsating blue light. Pharoah stood beneath a live oak holding the jack's bridle while Ben climbed into the buck wagon.

"It's a fool's doing," Ben admitted. "The Lord don't like it."

Pharoah lowered his head, his forehead touching the animal's hard face.

"Gabriel won't listen to sense. It ain't a fit night to break free."

"For a penny I'd stay home."

"Me too."

Pharoah made no move to follow Ben into the wagon. He stroked the jack a few times, and suddenly a palsied frenzy shook him. A moment later, when he heard Ben speaking again, he recovered partially, but his strength was gone so that he needed support to keep him on his feet.

"We can't get to no Caroline County tonight," Ben said. "That's all there is to it."

"H'm. That's what I been——"

"We couldn't make it way up there tonight in all this was we birds with wings. I didn't know it was this bad."

"Reckon we ought to tell Gabriel?"

"I bound you they's left already."

"It ain't late," Pharoah said. "They's most like to be at the Brook Swamp yet."

"We's going to be obliged to get this here jackass and wagon of Mingo's back to town anyhow. They ain't no place to keep it out here. Leastwise, we better get it back if we don't want to answer too many questions."

"That's a fact."

They reached the big road, jogging miserably in the slush. There was still the noisy lamentation of the trees and the downpour slopping against them by the bucketful. Pharoah held the driving lines sullenly.

"Hold on a minute," Ben said abruptly.

"Whop! Hold on for what?"

"Ain't that somebody yonder?"

They waited and presently a half-naked black boy slipped from the roadside shadows. He seemed, in the pitch darkness, as if he gave a strange light from his body, an unearthly luster such as the sky offered. Quickly, without waiting for him to speak, a curious animal-like sense of recognition passed between him and the Negroes on the wagon.

"Daniel?" Pharoah said.

"Yes, this me."

"What done happen—you lost?" Ben said.

"No. Me and Ditcher was going down to the Swamp to meet Gabriel."

"Well, howcome you going back?"

"We met Juba."

"Talk sense, boy. What's the trouble?"

Ben's voice showed excitement now. Daniel fumbled for words.

"The country crowd is hemmed in. They can't make it over here, and they is scairt stiff. Me and Ditcher swimmed and paddled and pulled till we got across, and we went to tell Gabriel. But we met Juba."

"Well, howcome you going back?"

"Juba and Ditcher say tell them to come what's coming and them to stay what's staying. They's going free tonight, them. They's hitting Richmond tonight, do they have to hit it by their lonesomes."

"The others wa'n't fixing to come, hunh?"

"No. They wants to put it off two-three days."

There was a pause. Ben struggled to keep his thoughts in order. He could hear his own heartbeats screaming in his ears.

"Where'bouts you seen Juba?"

"Up the road. She was coming on the colt to see what done happen to us—us taking so long to get there and all."

Ben turned his head. At his side he saw Pharoah faintly, a shadow ready to jump off the seat.

The wagon got started again, the wheels churning mud almost axle-deep, the jack behaving like the wild thing he was. Daniel splashed away very excited. The tiny storm-ridden earth rocked like a great eye in a vast socket. There had been nothing to equal it among all the cloudbursts and tempests in Ben's long memory.

Six

"ROMANCE won't mend the roof of your house," Midwick observed cautiously.

"No, but it's useless to fight against a thing like that when it's in your blood—don't you think so too?"

Fat and red and round of face, Ovid, who had just discovered that the seat of his pants was scorching, wheeled around, rubbing the spot briskly, and gave the other guard his face across the fire.

"Well, if you fail to grow out of it normally at the proper age, perhaps, God willing, it might be a hopeless fight."

There was a plenty of wood, the fire burned well, and the stable was a luxury on such a night. Midwick still relished a dark neglected hole where he could smell earth. That was the thing in his blood; it reminded him of Bunker Hill, Valley Forge and White Plains. The most vivid part of these campaigns, as he remembered them, was the smell of the earth. A thing could get in your blood all right. Midwick was pulling on his shoes. They were not thoroughly dry, but it was about time to go out again and take a stroll around the arsenal. The blasted muskets of the sovereign state might start popping off if a man in uniform failed to go around and try the doors every half-hour. And if an unimportant official should get drunk and run into the place by mistake, he'd end his natural life when he failed to see a guard immediately, even in such weather as this. Ovid looked at the bats clinging overhead, his hands locked behind him.

"You don't really understand me, Midwick. It's a very adult sentiment—the thing I mentioned. I feel sort of like a caged thing that needs the open."

"Open country?"

"No, no. That's figurative. My blood requires adventure—delightful women, that sort of thing."

"Oh, God willing, it's a hankering after harlots. The town's got its share. And Norfolk——"

"Not ill-famed women. Lovely women. You know—young

and dimpled. Can't you get the picture? One is standing on a white beach in threatening weather. Her hair is loose, her feet bare; white birds circle above her head."

"Yes, God bless me, I know. I know the kind that goes traipsing around barefoot when rain's coming up and she ought to be to home, but I can't see why a family man like you would worry his head about that kind."

"You don't understand." Ovid looked sorrowful. "Maybe you've wanted to put out with a good ship some time?"

"Not much. It was always soldiering for me when I was a lad, and now it's staying at home."

"I should have soldiered. It might have cured me," Ovid said. "Now, it's my luck to cry over what I've missed. But I'm still a good man. There might be a fling for me yet. Maybe a ship. A year in the Caribbees, taverns, orange trees, Spanish galleons anchored a mile or two out, pirate's daughters left at home."

"You should have soldiered. But here, give me the blanket. I'll make a turn around the place."

He went outside. A short while later Ovid heard him talking to someone in the rain, so he buttoned his own coat, snatched his musket and followed him around to the street side of the old penitentiary building. There were other men there, but he could not see them. They were talking to Midwick.

"Stand there," Ovid said boyishly.

"The night watch of Richmond, Ovid," Midwick answered.

"Oh. A nasty night, I'd say."

"Not even fit for ducks and geese. Good-night."

When they returned to the stable again, Midwick promptly removed his shoes once more.

"They won't turn water," he said.

Ovid sat on a heap of litter within reach of a jug. A little later he threw out his feet, leaned back and tilted the thing above his head.

Seven

THAT same blue brightness flickered over the line of stumbling shadows. Gabriel could hear a boisterous plop-plopping behind him, and he could see, when he turned his head, a parade of blurred silhouettes in the rain. Juba was back now, moving at his side on the fretful colt.

"We's got a crowd what can do the work. On'erstand?"

"I reckon so. They'll do the work if you's leading. But the country folks was many again as this. We's obliged to get along without them, and that's a care for sure."

"Too many is a trouble some time. A nigger ain't equal to a grasshopper when he scairt, and a scairt crowd is worser'n a scairt one."

The leader's immense shoulders slouched. He tramped in the heavy mud with a melodious swing of loose limbs. He had shed his coachman's frock-tailed coat, but the coachman's tall hat was still on his head; the front of his drenched shirt was open.

"Whoa, suh. Easy now, Araby," the girl said, pulling up the bridle and slapping the colt's face. "Easy, suh."

The rain was whipping him badly, but Araby decided to behave.

"We can do as good 'thout the others. Ditcher's here. It's bad to turn back."

"They's feeling mighty low-down now, I bound you—beingst they's left out."

"I reckon—maybe. The rain's bad and all, but I don't just know."

"You don't know what?"

"I don't know was it the deep water or was it something else that's holding them up."

"You talk funny. What you mean something else?"

Gabriel threw a glance over his shoulder. The line was coming down a rise. Here and there, in the blur and the downpour, a stray glint caught the point of a tall pike. Gabriel led them beneath a clump of willows and discovered an immense bough torn from one of the trees and hurled across the way. He went around it, churning mud up to his knees. Araby had a brief struggle before regaining firm ground.

"You ain't seen nothing, gal? You ain't noticed nothing funny?"

"I don't know what you means, boy."

Again Gabriel refrained from answering promptly. He walked a short way, swinging arms meditatively, then paused to wipe the water from his face with an open hand.

"The line's getting slimmer and slimmer," he said.

Juba took a sudden quick breath through her open mouth. "No!"

"It's the God's truth. I can tell by they feet. They ain't as many back there now."

"Hush, boy. I ain't seen none leave."

"Some's left, though. But that ain't nothing. They'll all come back tomorrow, the country crowd too. There won't be nothing else for them to do after we gets in our lick. Nobody's going to want a black face around they place tomorrow. You mind what I say, it's going to be who shall and who sha'n't, do we get in a good lick tonight. Do we fall down, the niggers what's left'll be looking for us too. They going to find out that the safest place is with yo' own crowd, sticking together."

"What make you so sure they's leaving, though? What you think make them go way like that?"

"Afeared," Gabriel said.

"Afeared to fight?"

"No, not afeared to fight. Scairt of the signs. Scairt of the stars, as you call it. You heard them talking. 'The stars is against us,' they says. They says, 'All this here rain and storm ain't a nachal thing.'"

There was a light in a tiny house beyond the thicket to the left. The line didn't pause, however. Gabriel swung along beside the colt, his elbow now and again touching the naked thigh of the girl astride. He glanced at the light, but he knew that no stone had been left unturned. The thing for the present was to keep going. The rain was no lighter; the wind was not letting up, and somewhere ahead a branch could be heard roaring like a river.

A little later Gabriel whispered, "I'm tired of being a devilish slave."

"Me, too. I'm tired too, boy."

"There ain't nothing but hard times waiting when a man get to studying about freedom."

"H'm. Like a gal what love a no-'count man."

"He just as well to take the air right away. He can't get well."

"No, not lessen he got a pair of wings. They ain't no peace for him lessen he can fly."

"H'm. No peace."

"Didn't you used to loved a yellow woman, boy? A yellow woman hanging her head out the window?"

"Hush, gal. I'm a bird in the air, but it's freedom I been dreaming about. Not no womens."

"You got good wings, I reckon."

"Good wings, gal. Us both two got good wings."

There was still the line of stumbling shadows behind. Suddenly they halted. They were at the crossing of the stream that lay between the plantations and the town. The colt whinnied and shivered, his front feet in the fast water.

"Wide," Juba said. "Deep, too."

Gabriel stood with his feet in it. Rain whipped his back. There was grief in the treetops, a tall wind bearing down. Gabriel could see the flash and sparkle of water through the blackness. He bowed his head, heavy with thoughts, and waited a long moment without speaking.

Meanwhile the storm boomed. The small branch, swollen beyond reason, twisted and curled in its channel, hurled its length like a serpent, spewed water into the air and splashed with its tail.

Eight

MEANWHILE, too, each in his place, the quaint confederates fought the storm, kept their posts or carried on as occasion demanded.

General John, his strength failing, crept into an abandoned pig sty and gave up the journey. He bent above his lantern, muttering aloud and trying to shield it from the wind.

'Twa'n't no use, nohow. Nothing outdoors this night but wind and water, God helping. Lord a-mercy, what I'm going to do with my old raw-boned self? Here I is halfway 'twixt town and home and as near played out as ever I been. They ain't no call to turn back, though. After Gabriel and Ditcher and them gets done mopping up, it ain't going to be no place for we-all but right with the crowd. Gabriel said it and he said right. Do they get whupped, us going to have to hit for the mountains anyhow, so there ain't no cause to study about turning back. Yet and still, Richmond ain't for this here black man tonight, much less Petersburg. No, suh, not this night.

He squatted, his hands locked around his knees, and gave himself to meditation. Now and again a humorless grin altered his face, exposed the sparse brown fangs. The general's mood became first sluggish then mellow.

His head fell on his knees. A little later, his lantern gone out, he tumbled over on a heap of damp litter and slept.

The buck wagon came to a standstill midway the creek. The jack fretted and presently got himself at right angles with the cart.

"It's way yonder too deep for driving across," Ben said.

"Well, what I'm going to do now?" Pharoah asked.

"Turn round or stay here—one thing or t'other."

Pharoah moaned softly, sawing the reins back and forth while the animal danced in the fast current.

"These is bad doings," he said passionately. "I ain't never seen no sense in running a thing in the ground."

"Listen," Ben told him curtly. "Come to think about it, you

was the nigger kneeling down side of me at old Bundy's bury-ing."

"Maybe I was. What that got to do with all this here fool-headed mess?"

"Nothing. Only I remembers as to how you jugged yo' elbow in my belly that day and says, 'Don't you want to be free, fool?' Seem to me you was a big one on the rising then."

"Anybody gets mad some time. Freedom's all right, I reckon."

"But if you'd kept yo' elbow out of my belly, I'd of like as not been in my bed this very minute."

"You can't put it on me, Ben."

"No. Not trying to. Just getting you told. You making mo' fuss than me."

The jack whimpered and danced. Suddenly Pharoah rose to his feet in the cart, braced himself and put all his strength on the lines. The terrified, half-wild animal threw up his heels, bounded forward with a violent effort that jerked the shafts from the cart and sent the fat, pumpkin-colored Negro hur-tling forward into the creek. The jack leaped again, and Pharoah felt the hot lines tear through his hands, heard the broken thills pounding the ground and the terrified animal galloping against the rain, fury against fury.

Ben climbed over the wheel and waded waist deep to the sloppy bank. He heard Pharoah slushing the mud on his hands and knees, heard him calling God feverishly.

"Lord Jesus, help. Lord a-mercy, do."

Ben felt a quick chill. He noticed that his good clothes were near ruined; and as he stood there trembling, he closed his eyes and tried to imagine himself tucked in a dry feather bed at home. But it was no good. He was wet to the bone, and that was a fact.

It was like hog-killing day to Criddle. He knew the feel of warm blood, and he knew his own mind. He knew, as well, that his scythe-sword was ready to drink. He could feel the thing getting stiffer and stiffer in his hand. Well, anyhow, he hadn't told anyone to snatch that door open and come legging it outside without looking where he was going.

Criddle had heard the columns in the road. They were not
noisy, but there was something different in the sound they
made. It was something like the rumble of the creek, nothing
like the swish and whisper of poplars. He heard them go by,
and he felt as if he were free already. He could just as well run
and catch up with them now. Why not? But for some reason
there wasn't much run left in his legs. They were, for the moment, scarcely strong enough to hold him up.

Cheap old white man, poorer'n a nigger. That's you, and it's
just like you, hopping around like a devilish frog. You won't
hop no mo' soon. Plague take yo' time, I didn't tell you to be
so fidgety. You could of stayed in yonder and woke up in the
morning. This here ain't no kind of night to be busting outdoors like something crazy.

And that there gal in the long nightgown and the lamp in
her hand. Humph! She don't know nothing. Squeeling and
a-hollering round here like something another on fire. She
need a big buck nigger to—no, not that. Gabriel done say too
many times don't touch no womens. This here is all business
this night. What that they calls it? Freedom? Yes, that's the
ticket, and I reckon it feel mighty good too.

Where the nation that gal go to? Don't reckon I ought to
leave her running round here in that there nightgown like a
three-year filly. Where she go?

Criddle knew what blood was like. He remembered hog-
killing day.

Nine

GABRIEL heard the murmur that passed down the line as he stood in the water. He turned slowly, put out his hand and touched the nearest shadow.

"You, Blue?"

"Yes, this me."

"Where'bouts Martin and Solomon?"

"Back in the line, I reckon."

"Call them here."

He was gone with the word, and the confused and frightened Negroes began circling like cattle in the soft mud. Now and again one groaned at the point of hysteria. Gabriel didn't doubt that the groaners presently vanished and that the others lapsed directly into their former animal-like desperation. Juba was on the ground now, twitching her wet skirt lasciviously and clinging to the colt's bridle.

"Tired, boy?"

He shook his head.

"Tired ain't the word," he said. "Low."

"Niggers won't do."

"They's still leaving, slipping away—scairt white. How we's going to get them across this high-water branch is mo'n I know."

"We could of been gone from here, was it just me and you. Biggest part of these others ain't got the first notion about freedom."

"Maybe. That wouldn't do me, though. I reckon it's a birthmark. Running away won't do me no good long's the others stays. The littlest I can think about is a thousand at a time when it come to freedom. I reckon it's a conjure or something like that on me. I'm got to do it the big way, do I do it at all. And something been telling me this the night, the onliest night for us."

"It won't be the night if they keeps slipping away, though."

"I reckon it won't, gal. It won't be the night if we can't get them across this high-water branch."

"H'm. It's wasting time staying here if we can't cross. Just as well to be home pleasuring yo'self in a good sleeping place, dry, warm maybe, two together maybe."

"H'm."

They gathered quickly, Martin, Solomon, Blue and Ditcher with Gabriel and Juba. The others kept mulling in a sloppy low thicket beneath boughs that drooped under the relentless punishment.

"The branch is deep," Gabriel said. "And they's two mo' to cross like it further on. Y'-all reckon we can get this crowd in town tonight?"

Blue lost his breath.

"Quit the game now?"

"The weather's bad," Gabriel said. "It ain't too bad, but the niggers is leaving fast. They's scairt white, and they ain't more'n two hundred left, I reckon. We might could get them together again in two-three days."

"They's leaving for true," Ditcher said. "I heard some talk and I seen some go. They's afeared of the water and they's scairt to fight 'thout the whole eleven hundred. But they's most scairt of the signs. It look like bad luck, all this flood."

"It's bad to turn round and go back," Gabriel said. "Something keep telling me this here's the night, but you can't fight with mens what's scairt. What you say, Solomon?"

"You done said it all, Bubber. They ain't no mo'."

Gabriel turned first to one, then to the other, the question still open.

"You said it all," Blue echoed.

"They ain't no mo'," Juba murmured. "No mo' to say, boy."

"Well, then, it's pass the word along. Pass it fast and tell them all to get home soon's they can. On'erstand? If they don't mind out somebody'll catch up with them going back. Send somebody to tell Criddle ne'mind now and somebody to town to head off Ben and Gen'l John and tell Mingo and them that's with him. Somebody got to wade out to tell the country folks, too. We's got to turn round fast. It's bad to quit and go back. It's more dangerouser than going frontwise. These fools don't know it."

In a few moments the crowd left the low thicket, scurrying across fields by twos and threes. Gabriel walked in the slushy path, his shoulders slouched wistfully, his hand hooked in Araby's bridle. Rain blew in Juba's face. She sat erect, feeling the pure warmth of the colt's fine muscles gnawing back and forth between her naked thighs. There was something sadly pleasant about retreat under these circumstances. Hope was not gone.

"We's got tomorrow," she said.

"Not yet," Gabriel answered. "The sun ain't *obliged* to rise, you know."

"I hope it do."

"H'm."

The storm boomed weakly, flapping the shreds of a torn banner.

Ten

THE cabins on the Prosser place were running a foot of water. Negroes sleeping in the haymow opened their eyes stupidly and tottered over to the loft window. A village of corn shocks in the low field was completely inundated. A scrawny red rooster, looking very tall and awkward on a small raft, drifted steadily downstream. He had not lost his strut, but his feathers were wet and he seemed, in his predicament, as dismayed as an old beau. The rain was over; there was a vague promise of sunshine in a sky that was lead-colored.

Mingo's frightened jack was still running, an arm of the broken thills dangling from his harness, sliding over the ground with a bump-bump-bump. Something had snapped in his head. He imagined the devil would pounce on him if he lost a single bound. He was running in circles sometimes and sometimes straightening out for a mile at a stretch. Leaping streams, plowing up flower beds, tearing through thickets and underbrush, it did not occur to him that the storm was over.

Ben and Pharoah stood in mud by the roadside, their heads together. They were still dripping wet and their clothes were mud-spattered from heel to crown. The wagon in the creek near by had been thrown on its side by the current; its wheels were lodged on the underside.

"It was a pure fool's doings, Ben."

"No need to stand here saying that all day. We best get gone."

"I reckon."

"That's all what's left to do. Come on."

Pharoah cried shamelessly.

Ben whispered beneath his breath.

Criddle was bewildered when he met the other two on the road.

"What done come of everybody?"

"Gone home. Ain't you heard?"

"I ain't heard nothing. Gone home for what?"

"Tell him, Pharoah."

The pumpkin-faced Negro tried to explain.

"They couldn't make it on account of the water and all. They's telling everybody to lay low two-three days and wait till the weather clear up. They didn't get across the first branch. Somebody was looking for you directly after the lines broke up."

"They broke up, hunh?"

"They *been* broke up. They been gone since before midnight, I reckon."

Criddle's domino spots got smaller and smaller. Finally they disappeared altogether.

"You ain't fixing to cry about it, is you?" Ben said. "It just going to be two-three mo' days."

"I ain't crying, but I don't see how they going to wait no two-three days with that white gal running lose in her nightgown. She'll let it out befo' you can spit."

"How she know?"

"Gabriel told me what to do, and I done it, me. I don't know what come of the gal?"

"I help you to say she going to tell it."

Ben thought of nothing but the broken wagon in the creek and Mingo's half-wild jack running furiously. He began to pray under his breath again, crying in his mind like a child. Pharoah stood like a wooden man, his mouth hanging open, his swine-like eyes extremely bright. Suddenly he quaked violently. Then he covered his face and cried, cried absurdly loud and long for a grown man. When he recovered again and looked up, his eyes were quite empty. Some strange, inarticulate decision of his blood made a new man of him. It was evident on his face.

The three of them started walking. Ben led the dazed Pharoah by the hand a little way. Criddle followed, his shoulders rounded, his long arms hanging a bit in front of his short body as he walked. It was sloppy weather for a Sunday.

Eleven

M R. MOSELEY SHEPPARD was early to his counting room that Monday. A shaft of fine sunlight stood against the window. The silvered old man sat at a desk profuse with papers. He was carefully dressed; the small pink flower in his buttonhole was responsible for an appearance of almost springtime cheerfulness.

The planter was feeling fit again, and his spirits rose accordingly. His cares seemed small that morning. The fact that young Robin was strong for a yellow wench was nothing. That crops had undoubtedly suffered by the storm (such of them as remained in the fields) was only an incident. That he was growing old and lonesome in a great house, that his friends were few (those he could really count on)—these were no more than moods that good health dispelled.

Leaning far back in his chair, Mr. Moseley Sheppard took an inconsiderable pinch of snuff and looked out on a clean, fresh world tinted with pastel shades. And so pleased was he with the view he did not hear the door open. He was not astonished, however, when he saw a Negro standing timidly before him. The old fellow had been careful to close the door, but now, confronting his master, he was nervous and mute. He was neatly dressed, his face covered with salt-and-pepper whiskers, and he waited with bowed head. Plainly, there was something of moment that he wanted to say, but he was in no hurry whatever to say it.

"Well——"

The Negro's head went lower. His shoulders tightened and the flesh of his arms was suddenly pricked by innumerable needles. His fingernails hurt the palms of his hands.

"Marse Sheppard——"

"Yes." Then after a pause, "Go ahead, Ben."

Suddenly the aged Negro dropped to one knee, his hands resting on the arm of the planter's chair, and began weeping aloud.

Twelve

"HUSH," Gabriel said. "Don't talk. A nigger done kilt a old white trash. That ain't telling nothing about the rising. That ain't so much as telling who done the killing. That ain't a thing to stop us. On'erstand?"

He was polishing the carriage with an oily cloth. Martin and Criddle and Juba were under the shed, Martin keeping watch in the doorway, Criddle leaning on a manure shovel, and Juba, sitting in the carriage like a great lady, twitching her foot and pulling on a corncob pipe.

"The Book said the stars in they courses fit against Sistra," Martin said.

"H'm. I reckon that Sistra must of been a rich old white man then," Gabriel said. "Them's the ones Jesus don't like. You mind my word. God's against them like a gold eagle is against a chipmunk. You heard Mingo read it."

None of them had rested well. Their faces were drawn and tired; Criddle's mouth snapped open with a tremendous yawn. He failed to follow the others in their allusions to Sistra or to the possible effect of the white man's death on the whole scheme.

"I could do with about two-three days' sleep, me."

"Us both two," Martin said. "All I can do to drag."

"Y'-all had yestiddy to sleep," Gabriel said.

"I laid down, Bubber, but sleep ain't been here yet."

"Tonight's another day," Gabriel told them. "The rain done played out. We's got to beat the drum and beat it hard this evening."

Juba got a sensuous pleasure out of the excitement. A little familiar shiver ran over her flesh. She could hardly wait to put on Marse Prosser's stolen riding boots again. She could still feel Araby twitching and fretting between her clinched knees. Lordy, that colt. He was pure joy itself. Almost as much fun as a man, that half-wild Araby.

Then very soon, as the day waxed and the puddles gradually diminished in the road, a half-crazed yellow Negro was streaking toward Richmond, his hat in his hand, his queue in the air. Before sundown he would reach the town if his wind lasted. In half-an-hour they would all know. Drums would beat. Bells would ring. Insurrection. Insurrection. Insurrection. The blacks were rising against their masters. The dogs had gone mad. They were in arms and organized to the number of eleven hundred. Richmond was threatened with fire and butchery. Other near-by cities were not safe. . . . His face wrenched, his eyes empty, the heavy Negro ran as if spurs were digging into his ribs.

Later Ditcher and General John came to the shed, and after them Mingo. Blue and Solomon joined the circle, and they lay on their bellies in a dying coppice as dusk came to the trees behind the stables.

"Ben and Pharoah ought to done been here," Gabriel said. "Us got to be turning round mighty fast two-three hours from now."

"Four-five hour," Martin said.

"Ne' mind. Some's going to be dusting befo' that even —hear?"

"H'm."

"Well, I'm telling you so. Listen. We wants them all to meet like how we planned it befo'. Onliest thing different is we's going down the line this time, and I don't mean I *reckon* so. On'erstand?"

Ditcher felt the flames in Gabriel's angry eyes. Blue ground his teeth.

"Hush a minute. What's that yonder?" General John said, straining his old cataracted eyes.

The others rose on their elbows or knees. A running fury inscribed an arc in the low field half-mile away. The thing was only a trifle more substantial than the twilight itself, but it gave the Negroes a breathless moment.

"Yo' jack, Mingo," Gabriel said. "He still running. Ne' mind that, though. Do we take Richmond, you going to have mo' horses and things than you can shake a stick at. Do we get whupped, us going to have to run so fast a lazy old jack like that couldn't keep up. Let me tell you the whole plan one mo' time."

"Everybody know the plan," Ditcher said. "Tell us what time."

Gabriel waited a moment, apparently irritated.

"Make sure you does then. Midnight is the time. We's meeting in the grove and marching double quick. And do anything go wrong, we ain't coming back here no mo'. Them hills off yonder was made special for niggers what's obliged to use they wings."

"It sound good," General John said. "It sound mighty good, Gabriel, and I like it a heap, I *tell* you. I been had my mind set on freedom a long time."

"H'm, but it ain't no good 'thout all the rest goes free too," Mingo said. "You ain't free for true till all yo' kin peoples is free with you. You ain't sure 'nough free till you gets treated like any other mens."

"That's good to talk about. We's got to start turning around now. Get yo' bellies off of these here leaves and start doing something now. Come on, all y'-all."

Six miles never did seem so long before. But he'd get there if his wind lasted. By night there would be a troop in front of the courthouse. The local guard would be in the streets with long, out-of-date muskets. There would be drums. There would be bells. Pharoah tore through the dry hedges, splashed through muddy water. He had to tell it now. He was sure he would burst if he didn't tell it right away. Bloody insurrection. Bloody, bloody . . .

Little splinters of moonlight showered the dark hut. They fell in gusts as faint and fine as the spray of imaginary sparklers on an imaginary holiday. The tall Negro tossed his limbs boyishly on the floor. Beside him the thin-waisted girl tossed.

"It was right pretty how Toussaint writ that note. I'm going to get Mingo to write me some just like it. We can send them to all the black folks in all the States. Let me see now. How it going to read. 'My name is Gabriel—*Gen'l* Gabriel, I reckon—you's heard tell about me by now.' Ha-ha! How that sound, gal?"

"Right pretty, boy."

"Well, that's how it going to begin."

He couldn't lie still with the hour so near. He twitched his head, flipped an arm and threw one leg out. Juba stretched and drew up to a sitting position, her skirt in a tangle around her waist. Broken splinters of light still came through the chink holes overhead. Presently there were a few Negroes outside, moving on cat feet, whispering.

"Some of them's ready, gal."

"Yes, I hears."

A pause—Gabriel's hands locked under his head, the girl's shoulders gleaming in the darkness.

"That was right pretty how Toussaint writ that note all right."

"What else he say?"

"Come and unite with us, brothers, and combat with us for the same cause." He slapped his flank. "Sing it, church! Ain't that pretty?"

"Pretty 'nough, boy."

"I have undertaken to avenge your wrongs. You hear it, don't you?"

"H'm."

"It is my desire that liberty and equality shall reign in—well, when Mingo write mine, I'll have him say *shall reign in Virginia.—I am striving to this end. Come and unite with us, brothers."*

"It do sound good a-plenty."

"Them folks is getting noisy outdoors."

"Maybe scairt."

"Sound like a big crowd now."

"They's mo' now than they was a few minutes ago."

"And they's scuffling round a *heap* mo'."

Gabriel lay on his elbow a moment, his brow furrowed. Then he sprang to his feet and rushed outside. Presently a thought halted him, the memory of a single word he had dictated into his imaginary letter to the black folks of the States. *Gen'l* Gabriel. He turned abruptly, went back into the hut and put on his shiny boots, his frock-tailed coat and his varnished coachman's hat. It was all very important when you really thought it over.

Scrawny black figures milled up and down the cabin row. They seemed unnecessarily jumpy. At first Gabriel got the impression they were running in circles. There was a great deal of whispering, all very rapid, very breathless. All the crochety old silhouettes had their corncob pipes in their hands. Humorous little tufts stood on their heads or stuck out behind for those who had enough hair to make queues. They were all gesturing with their pipes, throwing out excited arms.

Gabriel started toward a small group by a woodpile. A pale fragmentary moon was pushing up. There was no mistaking the alarm that had spread among the blacks. Their agitation was too plain. Solomon slipped from a shadow and met Gabriel on the path.

"It's something what'll burn yo' ears like fire to hear, Bubber."

"Tell me. Tell me!"

Gabriel forgot to whisper. His voice was a roar.

"The game's up, Bubber."

"What you mean? Tell me, I say!"

Solomon, fluttering like a bird, put his hand on his taller brother and tried to speak. Gradually the thought took shape. Pharoah had betrayed them. Volunteers were already being armed in Richmond to meet the attack. There was another tempest in the offing.

Every bell in the town was ringing. For nearly an hour drums had gone up and down the streets. Men and boys gathered in groups under the trees. They were being assigned to their leaders; they were listening prick-eared to the hasty instructions. Consternation, terror, confusion increased with every bell toll, with every drum beat. All the available horses were being herded into an enclosure behind the courthouse.

And on a near-by street corner, empty-eyed, exhausted, alone, stood Pharoah, the pumpkin-colored mulatto. He was breathing hard. Now he could start home, he thought. Nobody would know who gave the alarm. The white folks would thank him. They wouldn't tell. They would protect him. Now he could start home in the heavy shadows.

"If Gabriel had of listened to me, he'd of fared a heap better. He wasn't fixing to do no good nohow, the way how he was going about it. I wanted to lead a line, me."

BOOK THREE

MAD DOGS

One

GET down, Criddle. Get down underneath of them sassafras switches, down amongst the dead leaves and all. Moon bright as day out yonder—get down low. You knows right well they ain't far away. They done nipped you once already. They nipped you like a man nips a grouse on the wing.

Killing a nachal man ain't nothing like hog-killing, boy. On'erstand?

You's got yo' chance now, maybe. You's free, I reckon. You's got a chance equal to the chance a gray squirrel's got—a gray squirrel what's been nipped. A gray squirrel bleeding with a chunk of lead in his belly. You's got a equal chance, Criddle. Get down; hush.

Marse Jesus, I knows you is a-listening. You's got yo' hand behind yo' ear. You is listening to hear me pray. But I don't know nothing about no praying, me. I's low-down as I-don't-know-what, but I ain't no moaning man, Jesus. I been working for Marse Prosser all the time. I ain't seen nothing but the hind parts of horses, me. I been shoveling up manure in the stable; I ain't had time for no praying. You know yo'self I ain't, Marse Jesus. Howcome you looking at me with yo' hand behind yo' ear? I don't know nothing about no praying. I been pitching manure all the time, me.

Get down, boy. You don't hear them horses yonder? Can't bend, hunh? Look across the hill. Ah, Gabriel is the one to entertain them biggity white mens. They better be studying about him, too—do they know what's good.

Them's them all right: soldiers. Scratch down underneath of the leaves and switches and things. No? Hurt too bad, hunh?

"Well, ne' mind. That there chunk of lead was mo'n a nip maybe. Feel bigger'n a watermellon now. Manure pitching in Marse Prosser's stable wasn't bad, was it? And the smell of the horses and the smell of the harness was right good, come to think about it. What you say, Criddle? What you say now? No mo' hog-killings, I reckon. No mo' Decembers, maybe. No mo' manure. Hush; get down, boy, low.

Two

MEANWHILE the young nation gasped and caught its breath, trembled with excitement. Fanned by newspaper tales and swift rumors, its amazement flared.

"For the week past," wrote the Virginia correspondent to the Philadelphia *United-States Gazette*, "we have been under momentary expectation of a rising among the Negroes, who have assembled to the number of nine hundred or a thousand, and threatened to massacre all the whites. They are armed with desperate weapons and now secrete themselves in the woods. God only knows our fate: we have strong guards every night under arms. . . ."

Another reported: "Their arms consist of muskets, bludgeons, pikes, knives and the frightful scythe-swords. These cutlasses are made of scythes cut in two and fitted with well-turned handles. I have never seen arms so murderous. One shudders with horror at the sight of these instruments of death."

A gentle letter writer remarked to a distant friend that "Last night twenty-five hundred of our citizens were under arms to guard our property and lives. But it is a subject *not to be mentioned*; and unless you hear of it elsewhere, say nothing about it."

A score of Federalist editorials, quick to make a political use of the plot by applying it to the campaign between Thomas Jefferson and John Quincy Adams, hurled Mr. Jefferson's own words disrespectfully into his face with profuse capital letters, "The Spirit of the Master is abating, that of the Slave rising from the dust, his condition mollifying."

Elsewhere the disturbed country sawed at its morning bacon and read the story with bulging eyes—

"It is evident that the French principles of liberty and equality have been infused into the minds of the Negroes and that the incautious and intemperate use of the words by some whites among us have inspired them with confidence. . . .

"While the fiery Hotspurs of the State vociferate their *French babble* of the natural equality of man, the insulted Negro will be constantly stimulated to cast away his cords and to sharpen his pike. . . .

"It is, moreover, believed, though not yet confirmed, that a great many of our profligate and abandoned whites (who are disguised by the burlesque appellation of *Democrats*) are implicated with the blacks. . . . Never was terror more strongly depicted in the countenances of men. . . ."

And as the nation read, it had the assurance that a strong detachment of United States cavalry was moving on to Richmond, the arrogant horses striking a brisk jog, splashing now and again in the little lingering puddles. . . .

A mellow golden morning arched the road. There was a pleasant rattle of side arms, a delicious squeak of new saddle leather, an immoderate splendor of buttons and chevrons. Captain Orian Des Mukes, straight, aristocratic, cavalier, gave his young orderly a profile on which was written a type of languid, moonlight bravery. He was talkative this morning, but for some reason he had insisted on such an immense chew of tobacco that he was obliged, periodically, to suspend a phrase long enough to avert his face and spit with a solemn gurgle.

"Well (splut), this, I bound you, is no exception. Men fight for just three things. The rest (hep) is all (splut) sham. There is no such thing as equality."

At Ash Lawn, Governor James Monroe slumped into a stuffed settee, festooning his arms on the high back. Beyond his window he could see gawdy autumn trees so heavy with color they seemed unreal. The tireless bluejays were still annoying the gray squirrels. On the gravel drive an inexpensive cariole waited at a respectful distance, a small Negro holding the bridle. The nearer bustle of surreys and coaches he could not see from his window, but their presence was disturbingly manifest. There was increasing excitement in the outer rooms. And presently, the Governor knew, the throng would be upon him. His attendants could delay but not withhold them.

A slender man at the writing desk tapped the inkpot with his quill.

"There's a strong impression that it comes of a too hasty re-sumption of commercial relations with the revolutionary gov-ernment in San Domingo," he said.

"I don't know. I don't know. But there is no need to deny the obvious. The blacks are in an uprising. Frustrated for the moment by betrayal, they have fled to the swamps and hills. Minimizing their powers will not help us quell the disturbance. By all means, let us have a price offered for the arrest of the chiefs. The cavalry has been dispatched. Let us have added guards here for our own safety and suggest that the night pa-trols be at least doubled in Petersburg, Norfolk, Roanoke and the other cities."

"But these evidences of serious concern on our part may hearten the blacks. They may imagine that they have a chance if they see us showing them attention."

"By the very nature of things in our state, the very number of blacks and the personal trust that is imposed in so many of them, we are left exceedingly vulnerable to this sort of hostil-ity. I would like to feel that it could be disregarded. There is the political angle that I also regret, but who is going to tell us the extent of our *actual* danger? Who knows exactly how far-reaching this thing is? What Negro can you point to and say definitely he is not involved?"

The younger man curled his feet beneath his chair. The fine yellow sunlight, mocking former tempests, seemed to fairly burst upon them as the morning waxed. Outside on the lawn a uniformed guard strode across the view, a tall musket on his shoulder. The Governor let his arms fall, rose from the settee and paced the room with a far-away smile while the secretary busied himself with his pen.

Three

A BLUE light sifted through the small barred window overhead. In his Richmond cell a man with agitated eyes paced the floor, folding and unfolding his hands with a transparent, remote air. He was a Scotsman, his queue tied with a black ribbon, his face furrowed beyond his years. Now and again his eye caught the flicker of a bright leaf falling past his window like a flake of gold, his ear caught the tiny golden clang as it touched the ground.

But the melancholy of Thomas Callender was compounded of more than autumn leaves and a blue window. Certainly there were brighter leaves than these in his memory, bluer skies. In his youth there had been well-heads clothed with growing vines and singing peasants with pitchers in their arms. But the shattering came so early, the broken wheel, the neglected watering place, the leaves falling sorrowfully, one by one—so early.

Perhaps, he thought, this was the end of his gawdy talents, the reward of his brilliance. Fate always chose the strangest turnings in his case. Once he had written poetry, and it had seemed then that a fire burned in his breast, a fire that would consume his life if he failed to put verses upon it. But the verses were second-rate and later the fire demanded prose. So prose it had been, pages and pages of it, the biting, acid prose of a man sick with the need of liberty.

It had seemed almost certain, a few years ago, that the bright fulfillment was at hand; but now, after all the blood, after the writhing, after the breathless flights, the dream was still a faraway thing. He had found it necessary to flee England to escape punishment for political writings. Then came Philadelphia and the job on the *Gazette*, that lasted till 1796 and again his own need proved his undoing. Hoping to escape again, perhaps for good and all this time, he became a teacher. But it was laughable, this notion that he could live without writing, and almost at once he was publishing the *American Annual Register* with the support of Thomas Jefferson and others. This brought no immediate disaster, so presently he was off to Richmond, at Jefferson's suggestion, to become a writer for the *Examiner*. But even then the gods were conspiring. The rest was too disgusting to recall. That foul medievalism, the *Sedition Act*. A sharply barbed pamphlet entitled *The Prospect Before Us*. And then the gaol.

Good men had come to grief before, Callender reflected wistfully, but the thought failed to cure his own melancholy. In fact, it was more agreeable to consider the slow golden rain of autumn leaves outside his high blue window. He was sick to his belly from the offal stench of political wrangling. Far better the red leaves. Far better. But now there were voices at the door. A guard was turning a key in the lock.

A tired young man followed the uniformed attendant into the cell. There was urgency on his face but he seemed almost too worn to speak.

"They are saying you caused it, sir."

"I don't know what you're talking about."

"The insurrection of the blacks. One hears no name so often as Callender."

"Cant. Federalist cant. The nincompoops of John Quincy Adams are braying again. Where is the insurrection?"

The young man told him briefly what had happened.

"Everyone knows that Mr. Jefferson has been your friend. It hasn't taken them a day to make a campaign use of the disturbance."

Callender slumped into a chair, folding and unfolding his hands. His gaze strayed upward to the small indigo window.

"An asinine lie. No Democrat would have been fool enough to encourage a thing that could only help the opposition."

"What do you suggest?"

"I'll write a piece to the *Epitome*."

"Thanks. That may help."

Four

A LL that afternoon they gathered in rum shops and taverns and in the public square. Excited and nervous, the men of the town wanted eagerly to be doing something but couldn't make up their minds where to start. There were so many things to be considered. At dusk somebody lit a flambeau in an apple grove and a crowd of gangling boys began to mill under the small trees.

"They'll thank us for doing it," a thick-chested boy said.

"Sure—Jacobins. That's what they are. They're Jacobins," whispered a boy with a harelip.

"Lots of times I've heard the old man say they're dangerous." The third speaker was lank; his face was small, lorn and doll-like.

The thick-chested boy twitched impatiently.

"Fits, yes. Let's get together. They're next things to—to— why they're almost heathen when it comes to being low."

They were all of a class accustomed to running the streets after dark, when they could elude the watch, and there were among them boys with holes in their stockings and some who were emphatically unwashed. But they were all intoxicated by the bold light of their flambeau and by the delicious whisper of loose leaves underfoot. There was also a holiday feeling of license based on the general bewilderment of their elders and the continuous parade of soldiers and volunteers through the streets.

"They're against religion, too," the whisperer said with an effort. "Infidels. The cursed Africans practice devil-worship and nakedness, but these are next thing to them."

There were bugles in another part of town and occasionally the sound of drums. The streets were far from empty, and it was hard to imagine that night had come. The boys with their little minute-man hats, their loose hair falling on their shoulders, clustered nearer the leaders shouting their readiness to undertake anything, relevant or absurd, so long as it was immediate.

Above all things they wanted to move. Waiting was the one torture they couldn't endure.

The lean, doll-faced boy deposited a slingshot in his pocket. "Why, I've even heard the old man say——"

"Never mind," the heavy fellow said. "Let's start. Everybody'll need two big stones. We can get a crowbar behind the blacksmith shop."

They followed the torch and rallied like any other troopers under its glow, but the light was unnecessary. A moon rose and brightened the footpath so that they could even see the color of the trees. Heaven, perhaps, the lorn, small-faced boy imagined, had spilled its paint pots on the leaves too soon. Autumn was early this year, bright and early.

There were farmers in the streets, delaying their ox carts after dark, still exchanging impressions in high-pitched voices and trembling at the prospect of long journeys into the infested country. Their cheeks were bulged, but the incredible spouts they sent splashing into the road were now invisible. Yet the farmers kept drawing the backs of their hands across their mouths and talking very rapidly.

"I've heard the old man say some pretty hard things about some of them foreign radicals."

"Never mind, we'll show them something."

The crowd delayed noisily while two or three of the larger boys plundered the blacksmith's back yard for irons that would serve as crowbars. They returned promptly and again the crowd moved. Presently they came to a final halt. That portion of town was as dark and tree-shaded as any and as quiet, but overhead across the street there were lights and fiddles sawing on little childish gavots. Apparently there were no pupils in the dancing school.

"Save your stones, boys."

"Stand back a minute. Let Hamlin and Willowby at the door. There; get the bar under the lock. Both together. Now push. Good, she's coming."

A terrified black child went by on a mule. Shadows were darting under the trees now and again, shadows deeply preoccupied with their own errands. Presently a wild beast shout went up from the crowd, a shout at once joyful, fiendish, playful and victorious, and the young animals swept into the print shop. M. Baptiste hastened to his window and tried futilely to see through the leaves.

Then the real storm broke. Cases went over with a clash and boom. Some boys began at once to tug on the presses with their wild, intoxicated strength, having the debauch of their young lives. The composing table was upturned, smashed to splinters. The stools instantly got the same medicine. Then followed a hideous dismemberment of the small pieces; one by one, the last clinging joints were separated.

Meanwhile, by some miracle of happy exuberance, the presses were drawn outside. There, by dint of stones and crowbars, they were wantonly leveled. Then the boys remembered the windows and let their remaining stones fly.

M. Baptiste started across the street but retreated promptly when a stone careered near his feet. Others ran out into the darkness and started turning round and round in a hopeless bewilderment. What, in God's name, was happening?

"Dash the light," the harelipped youngster whispered. "Run for it."

Inside somebody stumbled over the wreckage, scrambled to his feet and came thundering out with the horde.

"Cut across the fields. Over that fence and back to the grove from behind. Scatter when you get out there. You can't tell——"

Five

M. CREUZOT's first thought ran to his musket; he was now quite certain that his mind had warned him against lending it to Mingo. It was a tall weapon of a French make and easily recognizable. No need to weep now, though, now with the town full of drums, militiamen and men and boys who had volunteered. The situation, where M. Creuzot and his family were concerned, was beyond tears. The wan printer blessed himself at the draped window of his front room and tried to extricate himself, mentally, from the desperate snare. Would he bow down and face the music, or would he attempt flight with a stout wife and two small boys? And Laurent. He would have to be considered one of them now; their problem was the same.

A few moments later, eating supper around a rude kitchen table, M. Creuzot looked at his meat and wine without desire. André and Jean were ravenous as usual. Their mother stood over the stove like one unaccustomed to a table and moistened a morsel of bread in the gravy left in a pot.

"They're everywhere," André said. "Listen, I hear drums over by the river."

"Can't we go out tonight, papa?" Jean said. "We've been in the house all day."

"Maybe. If your mama wants to walk with you."

"You come too," André said.

"Not tonight."

"Are you sick, papa?"

"No, not sick."

"Well, why don't you eat?"

"Why, oh, yes, I'm going to begin now, son."

His wife rattled a kettle self-consciously. Her heavy black hair seemed almost sinister without a direct view of her large smiling face, but when she turned there was reassurance enough.

"Never mind your papa. Eat, Jean. Don't sit staring," she said.

"It's an awful confusion," M. Creuzot said. "Maybe we'll be going away from Richmond soon."

"Why?" Jean said.

"Well, lots of things. All this noise—these soldiers."

"Will they hurt us?"

"No. Business is not so good here, you know. Mr. Biddenhurst says Philadelphia is a finer place."

The boys still looked bewildered. M. Creuzot drank his wine, nibbled at his meat and pretended to disregard their rigid attention. Soon someone was at the front door and M. Creuzot sprang up with a suddenness that frightened the others. Taking one of the candles, he went through the door and into the adjoining room. M. Baptiste materialized from the empty blackness of the doorway. His face, apart from his pointed whiskers, was chalk-white, and there was a ghostly distress on his features.

"Mon Dieu," the printer said, looking at him.

"Have you heard it?"

"We haven't heard anything. But your face——"

"Hell's loose, my friend."

"I know that, but what's happened?"

"Vandals. They've broken in your shop."

"*Broken* in?"

"They've annihilated everything. 'Jacobin' is the word they used. We're all involved somehow in the uprising of the blacks."

"The blacks? What are the blacks doing?"

"Who knows?"

They went into the next room and stood facing each other over a round table. Mme. Creuzot came in, wiping her hands on her apron, and the youngsters followed as far as the door. There they stood, gazing in wonder. The white-paste buckles of the dancing master twinkled nervously. M. Creuzot's face suddenly went haggard.

"Mingo borrowed my musket," he whispered. "Is he among the blacks who have made trouble?"

"A leader of some sort, I daresay."

"The musket *could* be offered as evidence against me, but I am innocent. What can one do?"

"The stages are running. Had you thought of that?"

"I'd like to find Laurent."

"I'll send him. I'll go by his room from here."

"Thanks. Tell him to hurry."

"I've been thinking about Charleston for myself. I have friends there."

There were a few more words, a few more details and M. Baptiste was outside again, facing the candle with that same woe-begone countenance. Then he turned and was gone, and the door closed. Mme. Creuzot was back at the kitchen door, entreating the youngsters to finish their supper, while her husband kept blessing himself in the shadows of the front door.

Six

"AND you acknowledge complicity?"

"Don't know as I does *that*, yo' honor."

"But you were one of them? You plotted with the others to massacre the people of Richmond?"

"No, suh. Befo' God, I ain't done that."

The court of *Oyer and Terminer*, composed of Henrico County justices, had no occasion to nod. Crowded into a clerk's small office, the wigged justices wearing hats and street clothes had taken seats on tables, stools and desks. Three or four newspaper reporters had wormed in with guards and spectators; they had promptly appropriated the writing places. The wheels of customary court justice were too sluggish for a crisis such as this one. The fastidious old slave, the salt-and-pepper whiskers quivering on his face, stood before the circle of men twisting a pair of faun-colored driving gloves in his hands. Presently, for no apparent reason, the tone of inquisition changed. The questioner paused abstractedly. When he opened his mouth again, his voice took a new note.

"You Ben Woodfolk?"

"Yes, suh."

"You the property of Mr. Moseley Sheppard?"

"I is, suh."

"How long?"

"Fifty year, I reckon. Near about that long, leastwise."

"Well, how did you become associated with the plot?"

The Negro's eyes roved. There was a bough sweeping against the blue window at his shoulder. Ben became aware of perspiration on his face and of the new Sunday hat crushed under his arm. He recalled an ugly grinning thing squatted beside a burying hole in Marse Prosser's low field. Suddenly the experiences of the past weeks seemed far away.

Ben moistened his lips and began telling the impromptu court how it had been that old Bundy's invitation to become a "mason" had led to his reluctant interview with Gabriel and

Blue and how the long net, against his will, had seemed to involve him without actually taking him in.

The newspaper men began writing rapidly.

"Who were the leaders?"

"Too many to talk about, suh. Gabriel's the head man. Him and Ditcher."

"Ditcher?"

"Yes, suh. He is named Jack Bowler. They calls him Ditcher."

"Oh. And who else that you know?"

"Gabriel's two brothers, Solomon and Martin. Marse Prosser's Blue. Gen'l John Scott——"

"Who is he?"

"Gen'l John belong to Marse Greenhow. He work for Marse McCrea some time."

"Well, what was his part in the plan?"

"Gen'l John? He carried the biggest end of the money, him. He was going to lead a rising in Petersburg, too."

"Yes, yes. Possibly he is the one somebody saw take ten dollars from his ragged jeans recently."

"H'm. I reckon so."

"Were there any free Negroes? Any white people?"

"Well, suh, Mingo was one. He kept the names. I don't know was there any white folks, yo' honor."

"But how were they going about it, Ben? What weapons do they have, and how did they hope to take the city?"

"They's got plenty scythe-swords and pikes and like of that."

"Any muskets?"

"About a dozen flintlocks, I reckon."

"Um hunh. How many bullets?"

"A peck," Ben said soberly.

"That's pretty slim ammunition, isn't it?"

"I don't know. They figured how they wasn't many guards at the arsenal or the powder house. I reckon they figured on starting in there."

At this disclosure the justices all became sober and ceased to smile.

Mr. Moseley Sheppard twitched fretfully in his seat. He had noted the scarlet bough outside the tall window, but his eyes were now on the perplexed old Negro trembling before the circle of inquisitors. The justices sat with their hats on, and some of them rested gloved hands on the knobs of canes that stood between their feet. Now and again a quick sniffle came from the dour circle, a short catch of the breath attending the intake of snuff. Mr. Moseley Sheppard could almost have wept for Ben's distress. In fact, his eyes were watery when the presiding justice abruptly turned to him with a question.

"Mr. Sheppard——"

"Yes."

"Is that substantially the same confession that the defendant made to you?"

"Yes, sir. Quite the same."

"How long ago was it made?"

"Monday morning last."

"And you'd be disposed to vouch for the credibility of the testimony?"

"Quite."

"Well, now, a few more questions to the defendant——"

The voices continued, purged of emotion, repressed, cold, unmoved, yet quavering faintly with a guarded, hidden excitement that amounted to terror. The sky darkened, and a great shadowy leaf fell from the bough.

Thus it befell that Mr. Moseley Sheppard produced his astonishing testimony in a Richmond court. How could any Virginian sleep? How could he be sure from now on that the black slave who trimmed his lamps was not waiting to put a knife in his heart while he slept? How could he know his cook was not brewing belladonna with his tea? This sickness called the desire for liberty, equality, was plainly among the pack. Where would the madness end?

Seven

A BLANKET had been thrown over the seat to protect the cariole's upholstery from early dew. Ben threw it aside nervously, climbed to his place and twitched the driving lines. The old Negro felt like a child new-born. His heart was a leaf.

He say I's clear, that's what he say. He say, You's a good boy, Ben. Don't you let none of these evil niggers tangle you up in nara another such mess, though. Hear? He sure was scairt a heap, I know that. Him and the rest of them white mens was scairt *plenty*. I reckon they won't feel right good again long's Gabriel and Ditcher and the others is on the wing neither.

Ben's heart quickened at the thought of the big crowd at large on the countryside and perhaps in the hills. For some reason it *did* tickle him to see a mighty powerful black fellow acting right sassy, scampering and cutting up like a devilish pant'er or a lion. It did him more good than a pint of rum. But it was bad doings and dangerous this time. Ben wasn't ready to die. He was past that reckless age. He wasn't even studying about freedom any more. At first, of course, he had been drawn along, but he was glad to be out of it now—now that he was clear and didn't have Gabriel's eyes to face. It was a burden lifted; yes, it was like a new day for Ben.

New-borned, Lordy. New-borned, new-borned, thanks Jesus. I heard tell about a woman come walking up out of the ocean, a brand-new woman come up dripping clean out of that there green water and them white waves and all. I heard tell about such a woman plenty times, but I just now knows how she felt. The man say I's clear's the day I's borned. Marse Sheppard he say——

Suddenly in the midst of his rejoicing a kind of nausea commenced rising from Ben's stomach. Nothing from his head, mind you, nothing in his thought telling him he was a no-'count swine and lower than any dog, just something from his stomach making him so sick he wanted to vomit. He pictured his ruffled shirt-front soiled by his sickness, smeared loathsomely, and with a shiver of revulsion, he found his hand across his breast.

Lordy, Jesus, I ain't being no dog. I ain't being lowdown. I's just being like you made me, Marse Jesus. This here freedom and all ain't nothing to me. There's blood in it, Lordy, and the sight of blood make me sick as I-don't-know-what.

The little mare had a pleasant gait. For a while the cariole rattled over cobblestones, then came the gritty dirt path with tiny lanes for the wheels. There was a flambeau burning in front of the *Dirty Spoon*; the river, with a burnished metallic brightness, gave an indigo flash. There were shadows creeping along the waterfront, and in the light of the rum shop a ragged Negro sleeping face downward on the ground. Ben heard only the whir of wheels, a small legendary whir resounding against the dim wall of sound that was the river.

On it rolled, the night darkening steadily, the feet of the small alert animal showing like upturned teacups on the black road. In less than an hour Ben observed that the mare had turned without his direction and that the little hooves were twinkling on Marse Sheppard's own gravel drive.

"Well, suh, bless me if you don't know the way home, little Miss. Was I blind I wouldn't need no better guiding. You is all eyes and footses once you get yo' head turned this way."

For once there was no lantern hanging in the carriage shed. Ben drew up the reins and stepped to the ground. The broken, fragmentary moon sprang up beyond the stable. The place was frightfully quiet. But Ben knew better than to expect a stable boy now with half the black men on the wing and the other half quaking in their huts. He began unhitching the little mare. Presently a heavy figure tumbled out of the haymow and crept down beside the cariole.

"Listen——"

"That you, Pharoah?"

"Yes, this me. You heard anything?"

"Anything like what?"

"Somebody say Criddle is long gone."

"Long gone, hunh?"

"H'm. He dead out yonder 'neath of a palma Christe tree."

"Bullets?"

"Yes, I reckon. Soldiers. That ain't the beginning neither."

"It ain't?"

"No."

Ben carried an armful of harness into the stable. He was inside several minutes, feeling his way along the wall and putting things on the proper hooks. When he returned he did not speak at once but began passing a dry cloth over the neck and flanks of the horse. Pharoah stood with a petrified stare, hunched at the shoulders and breathing audibly. His arms hung loose.

"Well, what in the nation was you doing in that there devilish haymow?"

"I tell you things is a-popping round here."

"I reckon," Ben said. "They is a-popping in town too. But you—*you* ain't obliged to hide from nobody, is you?"

Pharoah chose to ignore the question. He put his hands together and began twisting an old hat. His queue was untied and his hair had risen on his head like a porcupine's bristles.

"They went by just now with two-three of Marse Bowler's slaves."

"Which ones?"

"Don't know which ones. Mousie say they pulled them out a pigsty. Them pudden-head boys crawled in there in such a big hurry they left they feet sticking out."

"Nobody's hunting *you*, is they?"

"The niggers is saying I'm the one what told——"

Pharoah lost his voice. His eyes kept darting across the yard.

"Saying you's the one what told, hunh?"

"Somebody was hiding in the bushes, and when I passed, they throwed this here out at me."

He held a knife in his hand.

"You should of stayed in town."

"Did somebody tell you it was me that told?"

Ben became uncommonly grave. He walked the little mare around to the barnyard. When he returned, he was shivering. He backed the cariole into the shed by hand and raised the thills.

"Everybody know you told."

"I ain't named no names."

"Naming names ain't nothing. You just as well to named

names. You told plenty. White folks can look and see for they-
selves who's gone. Naming names ain't a thing."

"Where you been? Ain't *you* told nothing?"

"Me told?"

Ben coughed. Then he became silent for a space.

"I been in court. They was trying me."

"Is you clear?"

"H'm."

"Well, ain't you had to tell nothing?"

"Nothing much. Nothing amounting to nothing."

"I wish I's locked up in jail."

Pharoah disappeared beneath some fruit trees, and Ben
started up the path to the great house. There were candles in
the kitchen and in the front a porch lamp flickered in its sconce.
Ben's feet seemed heavy on the gravel path. Somewhere, in
some dying thicket, a brown thrasher called. Shadows of leaves
made a charcoal lacework on the ground. A nervous little
cough escaped Ben and he raised a thin palsied hand to muffle
it. At the same instant something whistled through the shrub-
bery; something as damp and cold as an icicle brushed his coat
sleeve and slipped through his hand. The old slave swayed back
on his heels, tottered a moment and then went down on his
knees.

It was as Ben imagined. There was at once a scuffling and
scampering on the dead leaves beneath the hedge, followed by
running feet on the slope beyond. Ben waited to reassure himself, then rose, his hand sopped by unaccountable mud, and
started toward the house again. In the light before the window
he saw the cut in his palm and was about to go back and look
for the knife when a sudden panic took him. The first thing, he
decided, was to staunch the blood. Furthermore, daylight
would be safer time for prowling in the leaves. He cupped his
wounded hand to hold the blood and let himself into the
kitchen.

Eight

A LEXANDER BIDDENHURST got the story from newspapers and the accounts he read, like those read by the country at large, were marked by hinted implications more serious than were indicated in the testimony of Ben and the report of Pharoah. It is true that the Salem *Gazette*, with other papers, resented this campaign of reticence and suggestion, but the same veiled reports continued. "The minutiæ of the conspiracy have not been detailed to the public," this journal remarked, "and perhaps, through a mistaken notion of prudence and policy, will not be detailed in the Richmond papers." New York's *Commercial Advertiser* had been informed that a conditional amnesty was to be sought, since the plot, it was felt, involved immense numbers and would demand that nearly all the Africans in that part of the country be apprehended and punished. Later that paper expected the whole procedure to wait on a special secret session of the Virginia legislature, scheduled to meet as soon as the men could be gathered.

Yet reports came through and, straight or warped, the newspapers printed and reprinted them. They told of Gabriel's sober, thoughtful face, his obsession for the same romantic dream that was the lasting creed of the poor, the unwanted, the world over. An immense fellow, amazingly young to exercise such influence, was conjured into the imaginations of thousands; he was a black of vast abilities and life-long preparations. Since the age of twenty-one (he was twenty-four now) he had traveled about, with apparent innocence, recruiting confederates and accumulating stores of arms. He was now at large with hundreds of followers, and his shadowy figure standing on the summit of a twilight hill recalled the savage uprisings in San Domingo that put the slaves in the masters' saddles. The possibility of such a wide conspiracy, when one considered the desperate and fatalistic temper of the serfs, was hard to overestimate.

Mr. Alexander Biddenhurst polished the thick lenses of his spectacles with a silk handkerchief. In his upstairs rooms at the corner of Coats Alley and Budd Street he had drawn away from the writing desk and reclined in a low chair surrounded by frayed Ottomans, shabby cushions and books turned face downward on the floor. His lamp was spitting feebly, and it occurred to him that there was no more oil in the house. He decided to dash the flame and conserve his little remaining fuel for a possible need during the night. One never knew, when he tucked his coverlet over his shoulders, who would knock on his door before morning. That, at least, had been Mr. Biddenhurst's experience in Philadelphia, at the corner of Coats and Budd. He went into the bedroom, feeling the way by hand, and began undressing.

He awakened to a crisp morning and a shaft of golden light against his window. Mr. Chubbs had already let herself into the small apartment and was busy with the coffee pot. Mr. Biddenhurst pulled on his shirt and tied his curly black hair indifferently. A moment later, one arm in his coat, he was flying to the door in answer to urgent raps.

Alexander Biddenhurst felt singularly exuberant this morning, and the noise of his own heels gave him an immense pleasure.

"Hail, goddess," he shouted to the fat housekeeper as he whisked past the door without giving her a chance to reply. But an instant later, his hand on the knob, the sound of voices downstairs gave him pause. They were nervous, covered voices, and Mr. Biddenhurst's speculation ran at once to the fugitive blacks who were stopping at his door more and more frequently these recent days, seeking brief succor and guidance to the next imaginary post on their shadowy flight to the town of St. Catherine, across the Canadian border. Why it would come to be a business soon—these runaways would develop a regular transit line if they continued this system, he reflected. And always it was like this too: just after daybreak, following a night of travel, they would call on him and he would give them directions to one of the addresses on his list. At the homes of freed Negroes or gracious whites they would find pallets in attic or cellar and warm porridge for their bones sometimes. An unimportant young lawyer, a foreign-born citizen of a great city that knew him hardly at all, Mr. Biddenhurst felt that this small contribution to the cause of freedom and equality in

the large, cheerfully rendered, justified in some part a life that
otherwise meant but little to anyone now. And there was melancholy in the thought, too, though indeed it gave him no hurt
at this exuberant hour of the morning. The door swung open.

Gasps and shrieks of astonishment.

The roly-poly red-haired fellow stood with arms dangling,
his face rent with an embarrased smile, his ill-fitting hat clinging to his head by a strand, but Mr. Biddenhurst threw his own
arms into the air, embraced the boy and began presently to
slap him on the back.

"Laurent!"

"It's me. I'm sorry to take you like this, so sudden-like."

"But I don't believe it. That's *not* you."

"Did you ever see a Frenchman you could mistake for me?"

Mr. Biddenhurst laughed heartily and made a motion to
close the door behind the excited boy.

"Hardly," he said. "But you could be an apparition. Let me
touch the wounds."

"Fortunately I have none, no serious ones at any rate. But
you have another surprise in store."

"Let me get near the sofa. Now. You can tell me now."

"There are others downstairs," Laurent said. "Shall I call
them?"

"Of course. I heard the voices but seeing you made me forget. Who is it?"

"I'll go down. I had the feeling you were spying me through
the keyhole—your hand was on the knob so long."

"The incurable dreamer, you know. Who's down there?"

"I'll get them."

In a moment the little group was on the stair, their hesitant,
disciplined steps scarcely audible in the rooms above. Mr. Biddenhurst stood in the door and recognized with a jolt the top
of M. Creuzot's hat. The printer was followed by his wife and
small sons, and behind them all came Laurent, a heavy traveling bag in each hand this time. There were warm embraces all
around.

"But I'm speechless, M. Creuzot."

"It's the season of blowing leaves," the printer said mirth-
lessly. "You know how leaves behave."

"Sudden, delightful swirls—I know, but still——"

"There's a tempest in Richmond," the other murmured. "A crowd of boys, shouting 'Jacobin' at the top of their lungs, demolished my shop."

"And you suspected they'd demolish you?"

"That's one way of saying it."

Mr. Biddenhurst managed to be silent for a spell. His eyes ran to the small boys peeping into the kitchen, to their mother busy with the folds of her shawl and to the lugubrious red-haired Laurent holding a drape aside as he peered out on the street.

"We cannot escape it," he said at length. "There is a struggle that takes us in. It takes us in against our wills. There is no escape for men of conscience."

"It is unjust."

"Of course, just as poverty is unjust. Just as slavery and class distinctions are unjust. The consequences of these evils fall back on us indirectly. We're marked."

André and Jean had inched their way into the kitchen. They were making friends with Mrs. Chubbs. Suddenly they were laughing. Mr. Biddenhurst, hearing them, threw out his feet and laughed too. M. Creuzot's blue eyes were still downcast.

"We'll want to get settled somewhere today," he said.

"Let's think about coffee now. That other will follow in its time."

Meanwhile the sun went higher. A beam fell across the shelves of inexpensive books, and Laurent turned and began scanning the titles along the wall, his eye obviously running to typographical features rather than subject matter. Mme. Creuzot, wearied of fussing with folds, finally decided to remove her shawl completely. A fresh burst of laughter came from the kitchen, and Mr. Biddenhurst threw out his feet again.

Nine

STILL the blurred rattle of kettle drums was unbroken, and swarms of uniformed guardsmen gave the streets of Richmond no rest. A hysterical woman wearing a night shift ran out of her house in the early dawn with screams and declarations that she had heard voices in her cellar. A crochety old man leading a cow by a tether carried an immense stone in his right hand. He was followed by a linty old hag who walked with a gnarled corkscrew cane. In the public square a jittery morning crowd was slowly dispersing. Half a dozen obscure blacks had just been hanged following a summary hearing before the wigged justices who composed the *Oyer and Terminer* tribunal for the emergency. This stern show of retribution, as had been expected, was proving itself a useful sedative, but the city was still mad, still frothing at the mouth; and now that the real slave chiefs were known, it was not likely to be long pacified by the blood of a nameless rabble. An immense dog, imprisoned in an outhouse, scratched at the wall and howled bitterly. A fine, silvery mist stretched over the city, over the trees and lawns and finally broke like a cobweb.

A pippin-cheeked man wearing a brown suit and brown shoes with buckles came out of a notary's office and tacked a full-page leaflet on the announcement board. A moment later, leaving a circle of gawking peasants around the bulletin, he spat gingerly into the gutter and walked away. Carriages were on the streets early, rumbling on the cobblestones. And just the night before, the man reflected, there had been such a crowd of them wedged and jammed at the square, it had seemed they would never be disentangled; yet here they were again coming back as eagerly as they had gone. And so much the better, too; why, here was an announcement from Governor Monroe that would raise their hair. The brown-clad man selected a lamp post near the waiting rooms of the stagecoach line and again put up a copy of his bulletin. There was still a small sheaf of the papers in his hand, so he slipped away again as a new crowd began to gawk over his shoulders.

In the courtyard stood the yellow woman with the black enameled hair. She was swinging a scarlet parasol with a vacuous air. There were two horses at the hitching bar and a swarm of pigeons near the water trough and on the ground. Melody's heavy bracelets jangled softly but her furbelows were still. She was watching a troop of guards haul a cowed Negro through the streets. They were flogging him freely and making a scene that drew a medley of spectators.

She began walking again, the lacey parasol twirling, and passed through the crowd with quiet self-conscious hauteur. Suddenly she saw the face of Mingo the freed Negro flickering between the other heads like a drowned moon in a bog. He had lost his hat, and his queue was untied so that he had momentarily the look of a savage. Melody thought: It's ugly doings for true. This here town is going to the dogs, and the peoples is getting meaner'n apes. I wonder how Philadelphia is.

A moment later she turned her face on the sight and began walking once more. Down the empty blue street she passed half a dozen squares. Shops were opening to the soft morning, and there was a string of carts beneath the cottonwoods on a noisy side street. Farmers in filthy homespuns were holding up yams, cabbages, rutabagas and ears of corn and vying noisily for the small indifferent trade. Melody passed them and turned into a neatly arranged shop where she was known.

"He was putting up a fight, that Mingo."

"I wasn't looking. A dozen bananas, please. Some grapes."

"Grapes, bananas—yes. He was the third this morning."

"Third?"

"Yes, the others I didn't know."

"These quinces——"

"A penny for two. We've got the Democrats to thank—plague take them."

"I reckon we has. Four, please."

A little later she stopped before the announcement board outside the notary's office. Two farmers in leather jackets had put their heads together and were reading the small type laboriously. Melody, glancing over their shoulders, between their heads, paused long enough to spell out in part the bold headline of the governor's offer. REWARDS FOR CAPTURE.

. . . SLAVE CHIEFS. . . . PLOT TO MASSACRE. . . .
GABRIEL PROSSER $300.00. . . . Jack Bowler. . . . The
lines were broken up and confused by the two heads that
bobbed and shifted before her line of vision; and presently
such letters as she saw clearly, wrinkled and curled and danced
in her excited eyes. Suddenly she became aware of coarse remarks coming from a crowd of men withdrawn to the edge of
the road. Melody gave them a slow, bitter, sidewise glance and
started walking again. She twirled her parasol lightly, but there
was perspiration in the palm of her hand and she was not gay.

Ten

THOMAS CALLENDER put down his heels hopelessly. Even now, though a prisoner by reason of the Sedition Act, he seemed as actively involved as ever in the political snares of his day. It didn't seem right. He was a sensitive writing man, a poet at heart. Those conscienceless men who were trying to bring about the re-election of John Quincy Adams would halt at no lying inference, no false interpretation to befuddle the voters. Everyone knew, for example, where he (Callender) stood on the question of slavery and on the question of wealth and private property and the equality of men; everyone knew where Thomas Jefferson stood. Yet these Federalist swine now sought to identify both of them with hated atheistic propaganda and with the French *Amis des Noirs* and their encouragement to the slaves to free themselves by armed insurrection. It was fairly obvious guile, Callender thought. He curled his feet beneath the writing table and put another paragraph on his paper.

> . . . An insurrection at this critical moment by the Negroes of the Southern States would have thrown everything into confusion, and consequently it was to have prevented the choice of electors in the whole or the greater part of the states south of the Potomac. Such a disaster must have tended directly to injure the interests of Mr. Jefferson, and to promote the slender possibility of a second election of Mr. Adams.

Such a statement should not be necessary, he told himself, but dishonesty was so rife in the opposing party one had to say something to spare the innocents. Callender leaned back, festooning his writing arm on the back of his chair, and waited for the approach of a guard whose heels were at the moment clicking in the aisle outside.

"A young man wants to know if the letter to the Norfolk *Epitome of the Times* is ready."

"Tell him to wait. He can take it presently."

"Could you say how long?"

"Half an hour, possibly."

Callender dipped his pen in the inkpot and set to work again, more hastily this time.

The sun was pushing up rapidly. An overgrown boy with large feet and a slow wit dashed out of a house and came plop-plopping through the yard carrying an antique matchlock. He shot wild glances in both directions then fled down the street to an open shop at the corner.

"Will this do?" he asked the shoemaker, handing the musket across the counter.

"It's powerfully old."

"Grampa shot turkeys with it, turkeys and Indians."

"I reckon it'll need some tending to."

"There ain't time to fiddle around, is there?" He failed to get an answer from the tiny wizened man with the pipe in his mouth, so he went on talking. "With a lot of wild Africans fixing to scalp us, somebody's got to do something, they're a lot of mad dogs let loose, them niggers. It's true—I heard it from one of the volunteers."

"This won't do. Too much rust. You might scare them with it, though. If somebody seen this looking out of your window, he might change his mind about coming inside."

The boy's eyes rounded; his mouth became a circle. For a moment he could not utter a word. Then his voice returned in a whisper, a whisper that grew with each word.

"Yes, yes. That's topping. I know how: poke it out at them. Like this. Sure, that's it. I know. Thanks. This is it. See? Like this."

He was pointing the thing venomously, driving the unseen savage into a corner. The shoemaker took his pipe in his hand, nodded agreement. The boy bounded out of the store so blindly he ran into a squad of militiamen. But he was up like a cat, hastening to the small inconspicuous house down the road.

The men with Captain Orian Des Mukes were in and out of town at intervals of less than an hour. By turn they followed every road into the country; returning periodically, they offered the townsfolk the pleasant reassurance of squeaky new saddles, burnished sabers and the tock-tock of metal horse-shoes on the cobblestones.

This had continued nearly a week now, but still there had been no clash with insurgents, and the impression was going out that maybe there would be none, that perhaps the blacks were scattered and would have to be ferreted from their holes by searching detachments.

"This parading," Captain Des Mukes said. "It's a cursed tomfoolery, Sergeant."

"I reckon it is for a fact, Cap'n. What's your idea?"

"We'd just as well be hunting rabbits with this outfit. Some-body's got to get out and comb the hills and thickets. Nothing against stationing the cavalry in town, understand. They could be ready for an eventuality."

"That's sense, suh."

"But them ringleaders are like as not out of the state by now. Mark my word, when them black sons hit the bush, they went down on all fours like they been wanting to do for years. They dusted, that's what they did, every blasted one of them. This is nonsense, drilling around here like we were waiting for an attack by an artillery division."

"You're talking sense, Cap'n."

At nightfall Mingo lay face downward on a wooden floor. The room might have been a cave or a den, so far as he could tell; nothing was distinguishable in the blackness. Yet they had taken pains to bind his wrists to the flooring so that he lay on his belly with arms flung out. He wriggled helplessly, his nose pressed against the boards.

No mo' little buck wagon, Mistah Mingo, no mo' saddle shop, no mo' nothing now. Reading's bad for a nigger. You just reads and you reads and pretty soon you sees where it say, Brothers, come and unite with us and let us combat for a com-mon good; then you is plum done for. You ain't no mo' count for bowing and scraping and licking boots. Oh, it's bad when niggers get to holding out they arms, touching hands, saying Brother this and Brother that, they is about to meet the whirl-wind then.

The stars in they courses fought against Sistra, and that's a fact for true. That's howcome all the rain and wind that night. We was fixed to wear them out that night; dog it, we was *ready*. Black folks was as sure to go free here Sad-dy night week ago as God is sure to judge the wicked. We was ready to fall on this here town so fast they wouldn't had time to whistle. The stars was against us, though.

Mingo knew that night had come to the streets and that the night watch had been doubled; he knew too how many times the hangman's trap had been sprung since morning. The sounds came to him distinctly. But he couldn't tell exactly where he was, and he failed at first to understand the strategy that delayed his hanging while others were being rushed to the gallows so breathlessly. Now at last a possible reason was dawning. He had just heard a strange voice talking outside.

"Keep that one," it had said. "There were hands in this plot that haven't been suspected yet. Why, Lord, man, the thing could hardly have failed of success. A surprise blow like this— you mark my word, such audacity and diabolical invention came from a trained mind, possibly a professional revolutionary. Search carefully for papers that might point to Callender, Duane, United Irishmen or to France by way of San Domingo. And by all means hold this Mingo; *he knows how to read*. He was free and in open communication with radical elements. He carried the lists."

Mingo groaned and fretted and twitched till he rubbed the skin off the tip of his nose. His nerves blunted by the torturous anxiety of the past days, he felt that he would sooner take his punishment at once and have it over with than to writhe longer on the floor clutching at a hope too slender for any comfort at all.

Now among the townspeople, however, the first paralyzing consternation was past. The attack, depending entirely upon surprise and audacity for success, had been delayed by the most severe tempest in the memory of any living Virginian. The band of drenched savages, with their chiefs, were scattered. It was not likely that they would reunite, their numbers having dwindled greatly and their design having been betrayed. Many of the rebelling slaves were back at their places, protesting their innocence and laying all blame on the leaders who inveigled them; more than a score had been punished publicly.

Now the town was gathering its wits, but the ringleaders were still at large. That wizened and sinister old sack of rags they called General John Scott—what had become of him and his grinning brown fangs? That giant stud called Ditcher, the one with the immense shock of hair, where was he? And the incredible Gabriel, twenty-four, massive, dour-visaged and un-disputed leader of them all, had he given up the game?

There was a woman too, they said, a thin-waisted brown gal with a penchant for wearing her master's riding boots, twisting her skirt around her hips and galloping a fiery black colt in the big road. There were lots of stories about her. Not much was known definitely.

Richmond was armed to the teeth now, and men could sleep. Ovid, night guard at the arsenal, stood long at his picket gate as night darkened. The sky was too heavy with stars. Leaves were falling like shadows on the gabled roof of his small house, and through the door he could see the numerous faces of his children in the circle of light around a lamp. Ovid filled his pipe leisurely.

"No more cause to fret yourself, Birdie." He stroked a small hand.

The woman's voice came out of the shadows.

"Not fretting, Ovid, thanking God. Think how it might have been with you and Mr. Midwick there alone."

He could toss his head about it now.

"I don't know. There's always something in a brave man that rises to the occasion. My taste for adventure and danger——"

"Oh, it's fine to think about it like that."

"I must trot now, Birdie."

Eleven

A LEXANDER BIDDENHURST read Governor Monroe's proclamation in the newspapers, and the thing that struck him was the smallness of the price placed on the rebel heads as compared with the gravity and earnestness of the governor's statement and the obvious concern of the state manifest in their calling of the United States cavalry and the doubling of patrols and guards in every city of consequence. Possibly, he concluded, the very gravity of the situation made a larger money offer unnecessary.

He was standing beneath a tree, his elbows resting on a cobblestone fence. Before him and beyond this wall crisp fields tumbled away into knolls and broken declivities. Small bright pumpkins were scattered across dun acres of reaped cornstalks. Mr. Biddenhurst folded his paper, shoved it into a coat pocket and resumed his morning walk.

Would the frustration of this bold plot delay or hasten the great emancipation of all serfs and bondmen? Surely it was becoming increasingly plain that liberty and equality for any poor class could not prevail so long as the system of chattel slavery continued to mock them. But this thwarted attempt by Gabriel, this colossal advertisement of wild discontent and desperate hope, would it not put the planter class on its guard, give them a chance to fortify their inequitable position?

Certainly no one could be blamed, especially since it was everywhere conceded that, barring the storm, the blacks could hardly have failed to duplicate the recent success (within certain bounds) of their brothers in San Domingo. But life was like that: beauty beats a frail wing and the scales of fate are shaken by a bubble. Now the hope of freeing the slaves was more remote than ever in the United States and would have to wait for the slow drip of spring to cut a way through stone. And eventually the stone *would* fail; there could be no doubt of that. Only now, at this moment, Alexander Biddenhurst felt his own efforts so futile and unnecessary.

The only thing left for him was to continue his same endeavors. There were many tender old people (with time and money to burn) who longed to see justice triumph, though it reduce their own fortunes. More and more these would be willing to support the small, semi-secret groups working for the deliverance of bondsmen here and there, singly, as the occasion arose. Romantically excited, they would continue to aid those who were trying to establish a secret highway to the Canadian city of St. Catherine. And young men like Alexander Biddenhurst, lawyers, scholars, poets, would receive their support in the discharge of this work while neglecting the saner courses of business. They would keep the spark alive by agitating, agitating, agitating. They would work into the schools, winning the youngsters and the teachers; they would go among the blacks, flaunt the old taboos, slap the hands of the wretches, tell them there was deliverance ahead and to be ready for the revolution at any hour. Comforted by the philosophers and writers, they would carry on their near-hopeless mission; they would be the drip of spring on the determined rock.

An ox cart trudged slovenly in the fine sunlight. A handsome young fellow wearing a red jacket and shiny boots came jauntily out of town with a falcon on his wrist.

On Budd Street, before he reached his own doorstep, Mr. Biddenhurst met the Creuzots coming in from a narrow lane. The tall printer was swinging a cane, but his wife's hands were twisted into the folds of her shawl, her covered head bowed slightly. The boys trotted ahead.

"I think we've found the house we want," Mme Creuzot said with her usual calm cheerfulness. "But Philadelphia's not as pretty as Richmond."

"No, not as pretty. But you'll grow to like it better. There's something about the place that takes hold on you after a time."

"People are straight-laced down there," M. Creuzot said.

"It's something like that—the real difference is. It's a matter of temperament, viewpoint. There's a false, crêpe-paper grandeur down there, a hollowness. How near is the house you're looking at?"

"Only a few squares. Look—I don't know the streets yet—two houses around the second turn there, just beyond the lamp post."

The plump woman, smiling eagerly now, did her best to point.

"People walk faster here," M. Creuzot observed. "We'll have to get adjusted. I don't imagine there'll be time for much chess. Or music."

The younger man laughed.

"You'll manage to squeeze them in."

They were walking again, nearing the doorway where Jean and André waited. Mrs. Chubbs, looking very linty and fluffed in her bonnet and shawl, came down the steps with a basket on her arm. She hurried up the street as if she feared the green grocer would presently close shop; in a moment or two she turned a corner. Mr. Biddenhurst led his guests upstairs and stood against the door while they entered.

"If you're not going to be reading your newspaper right away——"

"Of course not, it's yours, M. Creuzot."

"Thanks."

"Not at all. You know, it offends me just a trifle to see you all so jubilant about leaving my humble——"

"Listen to him," Mme Creuzot laughed. "He's just a boy. As if we could stay here always."

"Why not?"

"He loves to play, that boy. Laurent is still out."

"He's inspecting the town, no doubt."

Jean's eyes were round.

"Are you really a boy, Mr. Biddenhurst?"

"Well, not quite yet, but I soon shall be. You see I used to be an old bent man—like this. I walked with a crooked stick and my back wouldn't straighten up, but now I'm getting younger and younger, and I've just begun getting *smaller*, too. Soon I shall be a little boy, then perhaps a baby."

"Aw, mama, that isn't true, is it?"

"Well—" She threw off her shawl and ran to the window. "Look down there—a man with a monkey."

"But is it true, mama. Is Mr. Biddenhurst——"

She had to face him.

"Well, we'll have to wait and see."

They all laughed, but the smaller boy's eyes were still round.

Twelve

BEN slept fretfully on chairs behind the great cookstove. Then after daybreak, when he had let Drucilla and Mousie into the kitchen, he went out to the stable and hitched the cariole. There was no hurry, of course; Marse Sheppard was still asleep behind his mosquito nets, and Drucilla's griddle couldn't be heated in a minute. Ben drove the little mare around the gravel path and fastened her reins to a hitching post.

The old Negro had rested poorly, his bones had an aching stiffness, but he was not drowsy. He delayed on the piazza, adjusting a cluster of wooden outdoor chairs around a small table, then walked around to the back and took two wooden water buckets from a stand on the back porch. These were not empty, but Ben poured their remaining contents on the ground and carried them out to the well shed. A moment later he was busy with the sweep, amused by the delightful splash and spatter of water down under the earth.

The two buckets were considerably more than a load for Ben at his age, but there was something about carrying only one at a time that made him unhappy—he had carried two for so many years—and he was more willing to strain his back than to make a second trip. Drucilla opened the door.

"Here you come again, trying to out-do yo'self like some half-grown boy. You ain't fooling nobody but yo'self."

"I ain't old as you might reckon, Miss."

"You done spilt half that water on yo' feet just the same. Now look a-there."

Ben went upstairs and began arranging the old planter's washstand. The great bed on which Marse Sheppard lay looked as feathery and fluffed as a sitting hen. Under one wing and only partly revealed was the white bedroom crock, a shell of a hatched egg. After a while Mousie brought fresh water for the pitcher, and the silvered old man rolled over on the side of the bed so that Ben could untie his nightcap.

Ben sipped a second saucer of coffee behind the stove; and when Marse Sheppard was nearly finished with his meal, he hurried around to the cariole and stood holding the mare's bridle. Marse Sheppard came down the wide white steps, the ruffles of his shirt-front falling like a cascade on his bosom, and took the place beside Ben in the small carriage. A moment later they were in the big road headed for town.

"I reckon they haven't seen hide or hair of them yet? Nothing of Gabriel or of Bowler's big stud either?"

"No, suh, nothing."

"At any rate, nobody that could bring them in has seen them yet."

"I reckon they ain't."

"There was that General John, as they call him, too. How about him?"

"They ain't found him neither."

"Those boys must have meant business."

"H'm. Must of did."

There was a crowd at the courthouse when they reached town. In the midst of them stood Ditcher, surrounded by officers and soldiers. He seemed incredibly large as he stood there. Ben pulled up the little mare. One of the officers had just spoken to the giant Negro. Then a hush fell on the entire group.

"*Nobody* ain't brung me in, suh. I walked down that street yonder on my own two feets. On'erstand?"

"Well, you're under arrest *now*, by——"

"H'm. That's howcome I'm here. I heard tell that the Governor wanted me, and it look like nobody wasn't ever coming to get me."

The swarm of men and boys buzzed around him like hornets. In a moment he walked meekly through a double door, following an officer, followed by dozens of others.

"Well, that accounts for one of them," Marse Sheppard said.

"Gabriel's apt to give them mo' trouble than that," Ben said.

BOOK FOUR

A BREATHING OF
THE COMMON WIND

One

THEY slipped out of one thicket, ran across a lane and plunged into another. Darkness came down hurriedly like a curtain. Gabriel stroked the girl's long wiry fingers.

"This here's the fork of the road, gal, and yonder's the way back."

"Yonder's the way back, but I ain't a-mind to go, boy. On'erstand?"

The coachman's boots that had suited him so well as a general were far from comfortable now. They squeaked and pinched his toes. The purple coat, the coachman's varnished hat and the ruffles on his shirt bosom were all a care to Gabriel now that the ranks of his crowd were broken, now that every man had his own skin to save.

"Which way Blue go?"

"Through the swamps, I reckon. Trying to catch up with Solomon and Martin."

"He should of gone with them what crossed the river."

"Which way you going, boy?"

His eyes darted, but his face did not alter, and he waited long enough to let her know that some of his thoughts were his own.

"I ain't got a heap of rabbit blood in me," he said. "I ain't got no mind to go scratching through the woods. You better start back now. They ain't studying much about womens in this rising. Maybe Marse Prosser don't know you's in it even."

"Maybe he don't. Maybe he do. I ain't studying Marse Prosser."

"What you studying about, gal?"

"About not leaving you."

He pressed the tenuous fingers again and felt a quick suggestion of their real strength.

"Ne' mind that. No need to hold back. What's going to be is bound to be. On'erstand?"

She shook her head.

"I ain't got no mind for nothing like that. All I knows is I feel bad as all-out-doors and I'd heap sooner take a pure killing 'n go the other way."

"I knows. H'm. Some birds is like that too," he said. "That ain't the thing now, though. You might can help me some time if you go back. See? You might could draw me a drink at the well some morning befo' day. You might could help me out some time when I'm near 'bout give out. You could bring me a jug or a chunk of meat some night, maybe. Down in the low field I might be squatting side of a corn shock some night."

There was nothing she could say to that. Nothing she *would* say, at any rate. They began walking, threading a way through the switches of undergrowth. Presently the carcass of a dead animal was under their feet. Buzzards and possums had already cleaned the bones, but shreds of harness were still on the skeleton and the arm of a broken thill lay under the heap. They looked at it briefly, and Gabriel thought of Mingo and of Pharoah and of Ben. He had a fleeting impression that now Juba would surely speak. But there was nothing she could say.

"See, gal, it's going to be me and them from now till the rope snaps. On'erstand? I ain't fixing to go way and hide in the Dismal Swamp. I ain't got no head to fly across the line or nothing like that. I'm after getting up a crowd of don't-care niggers and punishing them white folks till they hollers calf-rope, me. I'm out to plague them like a hornet. God's against them what oppresses the po'. I ain't fixing to quit now."

"They is all scattered now—Ditcher and Solomon and Mingo and all. You going to be one man by yo' lonesome, boy."

"One man. That's a fact and a caution; but just the same I ain't running away nowheres. I'm laying low but I'm staying here, gal. It ain't the same with me like it is with them. I been the gen'l, I reckon."

"Listen there——"

"Nothing but cottontails."

"You reckon so?"

"You better go back now. Keep one eye on the edge of them trees yonder and the other'n on that little dumpy hill—you know how."

She wasn't paying attention.

"It ain't no trouble to keep the way."

"Well——"

"Well what?"

"Howcome you don't get going?"

"I ain't going now," she said. Then after a pause, "You's right nigh played out, boy. Lay down and rest yo'self."

"Who played out?"

"Stop puffing out yo' chest. You going to pop open one these times. You's tired a plenty."

"Not me, gal. I ain't tired."

"Lay down anyhow. Here, side of me."

"When you going then?"

"Just befo' day, maybe. I want you to sleep some first."

She twisted and turned like an animal on the switches and leaves. Finally, working down to a place of comfort, she stretched tremulously then curled beside the big solemn-faced male. Gabriel threw out his feet but did not lie down at once. He sat with hands behind him on the ground, his face upraised, his varnished hat gleaming bright black in a clump of dull shadows.

Two

WHOEVER piled light wood against this here fence must of knowed what he was doing, but I'd lay a pretty he didn't know about this here hole he was leaving underneath of the bottom. I bound you he didn't know it was just my size neither. Onliest thing about it is I can't straighten out good and I can't sit up none. Good place to sleep, though. Martin or some of them other lazy niggers is the ones what ought to found this. Yes, suh, sweet as you please for somebody what's studying sleep. I should of put my feet in first. Better crawl out and do that *now*. I'm got to put a knot front of that hole too. Back on out, gen'l; let's go and come again, suh.

Heap better this a-way. I'll be so I can see out some, soon's day come. Whos'n'ever's woodpile this is sure ain't been bothering it much. Weeds about to cover the devilish thing from top to bottom. Don't look like nobody's touched it in a year or mo'. Humph! Just laying out here begging for somebody to crawl under it. . . .

Nothing for a general to crow about, though. Crawling down underneath of a woodpile on his belly. Lordy. I counted on a heap of things, but I sure ain't never counted on this. I heard tell about generals getting kilt and hanged and one thing and another, but I is got my first time to hear tell about one scratching around like a dog under a woodpile. It don't suit a general, this here hole; and it don't suit me a *little* bit. Laying on this sword don't feel good neither. Swords belong to hang down. This here hole ain't going to do me—I see that sticking way out. A general, do he lay down at all, supposes to hang up his sword. Lordy, this ain't me, this sure ain't Gabriel down under here. Gabriel ain't scairt of the living devil; and do he lay down at all for a nachal man, he lay down dead. That's Gen'l Gabriel, Lord, not this here crawling thing.

Yet and still, a good general might would get down low to win; he might would eat some dirt, when his time ain't come, waiting till he can get in his licks good. But that don't look like me. I don't look good to myself eating dirt no kind of way. I'm going to get out of here and hang up my sword, me. Yes, suh, I invites whoever can to come and take the general. 'Member this, though: you takes him standing up, do you take him at all. On'erstand?

The low morning sky was streaked like marble. The peak of a roof here, the silhouette of a grove there, the shape of a hill beyond, each gradually, one by one, took its form from the blackness and assumed its place on the horizon. Cows came to life on a dim slope and a broken-down rail fence suddenly appeared.

The immense Negro, distraught and sleepless, crawled from beneath the light wood and staggered along the fence. The cumbersome sword whipped his left leg. There was a noticeable dent in the top of his two-foot hat. His shirt-front was as smeared and colorless as a gunny sack. He wavered weakly a few steps then leaned against the fence, crossing his legs proudly and festooning his arms on the shoulder-high boards. There, without smiling, he faced the east and soberly invited the sun to rise.

Humble—yes—*humble*—I reckon—*humble yo'self, the bell done rung*. Yes, suh, I hears what you say, and I knows what you means. I heard you say see God, too; *see God 'n see God 'n see God*. That's well and good; *see* God then. You say *He'll come riding down the line of time*. Talk about it if you's a-mind to; I reckon He *will* come riding down the line of time; I reckon you's right. You ain't said nothing to the general, though. On'erstand? I know right well you don't mean Gabriel. Humble —humph!

Ring all the bells you please, peoples. The general ain't scratching down underneath of no mo' light-wood pile. This here general is crossing his legs, spitting through his two fingers and calling the turns. Come on up, Mr. Sun. Let's have some daylight. This here is my own neck and I'll keep it if I can, but I ain't wallering in no dirt to keep it. This here country is mo' fulled up with soldiers and mens with guns than it is fulled up with groundhogs. And that's mighty well and good too. I'm going to run them till they tongues hang out, run them till they start going round and round in one place. But I ain't crawling in no hole, peoples. They takes the general standing up, do they take him at all. They takes him with his sword in the air, do he have one then. On'erstand?

Three

THE village of shocks in the field of slain hay was, at that hour, peopled by sparrows. Along the boundary of the acres someone had been building a new stone fence. A drag, neglected in the field, had a dozen egg-shaped boulders still on it, and there was a mortar trough and a sand heap near the spot where work had last ceased. A pair of stolid plow oxen grazed beyond a narrow draw. A lantern blossomed like a yellow flower in the stable door, but already the sky was pale and streaks of light stood ready to show the day.

Gabriel, more the general than ever, followed an obscure lane between hedges of dying spiræa; then, strolling easily with a hand on his steel, he swung into the open, crossed a knoll and came down into a poplar clump.

When they tongues is hanging out and they's running round and round in the same place, that's the time to hit back fast. Me and Ditcher could mash up near about a hundred of them by our lonesomes. But plenty mo' niggers'll come; they'll drop out of the sky when they hears sticks a-cracking together and drums a-beating. They'll came shouting like jackals and hyenas. Something'll happen. Something'll happen for good. Can't say as to how. Maybe all of them get kilt. Good'll come, though. I bound you that, peoples.

It's hitting fast what counts, hitting fast at the right time. Them soldiers and all is feeling mighty spry now, killing off niggers by the dozen—I know about them. Ain't nothing to dying. Humph; you's got to die to find out things, I reckon. You's got to die to find out what you don't know. I ain't moaning about them what dies. Good'll come. I'm worried about getting in hard licks when my time come.

His hand was still on his steel when he came to the stubble field and passed between the tall well-made haycocks. A dewy sweetness rose from the field, and Gabriel was suddenly constrained to loiter. Now and again the muscles tightened on his shoulders,

755

quivered and ran. Then without warning something ripped the air; a musket reported near at hand, and Gabriel, off with the crack, plunged forward with raised hands, his hat tumbling before him. Only one knee touched the ground, however, and his stride was scarcely broken by the business of snatching the jittery headgear from between his feet. Running low, cutting arcs and curlicues between the stacks, dashing, changing pace, the big Negro faded like a mist in the hay field. There was a sort of superiority in his flight, an air not mingled with fear or distress or urgency. It was easy, calculated, catch-me-if-you-can running, and Gabriel pulled up proudly where the haystacks ended. He examined his hat and found that nearly a score of buckshot holes dotted its high crown.

"H'm. Close," he said.

Then, a little self-consciously and with a lordly lassitude, he turned, feet apart, and watched the excitement five hundred yards away. The farmer who had fired the shot was still in the field fiddling with his flintlock. Another armed man had materialized from the blue slope behind the barns and was skirting the field by way of the stone fence. There was a vague commotion around the houses too, doors banging and a blur of voices audible half a mile on the unruffled morning.

Gabriel considered the question of striking out again. Should he wait until they were within musket range and then outdistance them once more, or should he go at once, allowing himself the sweet luxury of walking insolently into the thicket while they tore the dust? A horse and rider left the barn, galloped down toward the big road. Gabriel fancied the spread of alarm on the countryside, perhaps the coming of a squad to comb the woods behind him. He decided to walk nevertheless. So the pursuers, if they saw him at all before he vanished into the thicket, saw him with hat cocked, a hand resting easily on his steel, his shoulders rocking arrogantly.

Safely out of view, he hastened again. Switches whipped his legs. He went through puddles of crisp airy leaves and felt them foam up around his knees and settle down again with a tiny golden splash. Somewhere, incredibly sweet, there was the voice of a brown thrasher. Gabriel recalled a marsh of shallow water, a marsh dense with trees and vines. And now, without his taking thought, something was drawing him toward it.

Four

JUBA moped. She stood outside the circle of savage gossiping hags and settled her weight on one leg. She had given
them her left shoulder and an arm set akimbo on her hip, and
now, running nervous fingers through her wild shock of hair,
she cut her eyes at them spitefully.

At intervals the others leaned forward confidentially, their
heads coming together near the ground, their blunt posteriors
rising and broadening simultaneously. At the center of the circle, beside the outdoor fire, squatted a woman with a baby.
She was moistening a rag in a cup of gruel and offering it to
the infant. Her teeth jutted between sagging lips; lean wrinkled
breasts hung against her belly.

"The way that gal is putting on you'd think he's the last man
in the state what's got a seed to give."

An older woman, wrinkled and witch-like, clasping a clay
pipe in her mouth, picked at the toenails of a scaly foot.

"Gabriel's all right. He a mighty fine boy, even if he is got a
face longer'n a mule's. But all this Jesus talk I hears ain't helping him none."

The sleeves were torn from Juba's garment, and the rag
that remained of the upper half was drawn tight around her
breasts. It had parted from the skirt, too, and there was a
streak of nakedness at her waist. Now that she knew what
they were getting at, she gave her hips a twitch and moved a
few steps.

"You ain't never heard Gabriel moaning and praying. What
you talking about?"

The others looked a little surprised, but they were far from
displeased with their success in piquing her interest and finally
drawing words from her. She had ignored them so long they
had begun to imagine that she failed to hear them, even when
they talked in her presence. The woman with the baby leaned
forward and spat into the fire.

"No sense of you trying to get yo'self hanged, though. You's
a fool; that's what you is."

"Ne' mind about that. If I don't care do I get hanged, that's me. If I's a plum fool, that's me too. On'erstand?"

The shadows gathered quickly, almost hastily, and now, in no time at all, it was night at the cooking place. Juba walked completely around the circle of slave women. Somewhere among the folds of her butternut garment she found a pipe and a moment later she was kneeling at the fire. But she was not one of the crowd on the ground; even when she brushed against them while holding her pipe to the flame, she was as haughty and aloof as a harlot. The old woman scraping at her crusted toenails did not look up.

"A man, do he 'spect to win, is obliged to fight the way he know. That's what's ailing Gabriel and all them. He is obliged to go at it with something he can manage."

Juba looked perplexed, but she did not speak till she was on her feet again.

"What you mean, woman?"

"They talks about Toussaint over yonder in San Domingo. They done forget something."

Her face grew more hideous in the firelight. A frayed stick that she had been chewing hung on her lip.

"Go on. What Gabriel forget?"

"I don't know about all that reading in the Book. All that what say God is going to fight against them what oppresses the po'. That might be well and good—I don't know. Toussaint and them kilt a hog in the woods. Drank the blood."

"He did, hunh?"

"H'm. Gabriel done forget to take something to protect hisself. The stars wasn't right. See? All that rain. Too much listening to Mingo read a white man's book. They ain't paid attention to the signs."

"Gabriel don't know a heap of conjure and signs and charms. He ain't never had no head for nothing like that."

The old female drew up the other foot. Suddenly she seemed far-away and cruelly unconcerned.

"Nah, I reckon he ain't," she said.

"Well, he ain't done for yet. He going to be a peck of trouble to them yet, I bound you."

"Maybe. I tell you there's a heap of them what *is* done for, though. Criddle, Ditcher, Mingo and I don't know how many mo'. Then they's a lot mo' what nobody's seen hide or hair of and what's just as apt to be dead as they is apt to be live."

Juba shrugged.

"Plenty niggers died with Toussaint too, didn't they?"

"It didn't work out the same. You'll see. Toussaint kilt a hog. There's plenty things Gabriel could of done."

"Listen, woman. Maybe some time I might see Gabriel *now* —some night maybe. Has you got a good hand I can give him to put in his pocket?"

The infant, not satisfied with its rag, whimpered and presently set up a faint, croaking lamentation. The four or five women who were not smoking had snuff-smeared mouths; periodically they leaned forward and spat into the fire. Juba squatted down beside the old creature who was still preoccupied with her scaly black feet and waited for an answer.

"Maybe."

"Listen, woman," Juba said. "I don't know nothing about *maybe*. Is you going to make me a hand for Gabriel, one what'll keep him safe whilst he's running?"

"He ought to come hisself. That's the most surest way. I could make you one for him that might help *some*, though."

"Come on." Juba pulled at the other's rags. "Come on now. Some time I might can bring him to you, some night late, but that ain't now. Come on, woman."

"Take yo' hands off'n me, gal. See there, you done pulled it off. I can't be sitting out here buck naked, old as I'm getting."

Juba put the garment under her arm. The old female gave up her toes reluctantly, struggled to her feet.

"Come on now," Juba said. "Here's yo' rag."

"Gabriel should of come hisself. Matter of fact, he should of come long time ago, did he have any sense."

Night had come with emphasis, but bats were still leaving the peaked gable of the barn. They wavered upward, shadowy and fabulous, like legendary birds. When Juba and the old crone reached the door, a foul stench came out of the hut and assailed them like a plague. Juba halted and heard the women they had left cackling around the fire. Then, puffing fast to keep the smoke in her nostrils, she followed the older woman into the hovel.

Five

THE town of Richmond breathed a bitter murderous resentment, but much of the original excitement had now abated. Militiamen still mulled the streets, however, periodically dragging anonymous Negroes before the justices. For the most part, the first-fruits of this messy harvest were inconspicuous nobodies, but the leaders were marked now and grimly promised to the noose.

Meanwhile the trap was not idle. A crowd swarmed in the open yard. Among them was the dazed, vacuous girl whose parent got himself impaled on Criddle's scythe-sword. All were restless and touchy during the intervals, but the arrival of a fresh victim gave them a moment of pause that permitted the trap to fall during a hush. Then, blinking hard after the jolt, one by one they regained their wits and sought to show a casual air. But the girl, waiting hungrily for each new kill, neither blinked nor recovered. She stared, leaning a little forward, tearing her homespuns absently. There seemed to be an impression among those who had ceased to regard her presence that she was entitled to whatever compensation she could wring from the sights, but she got little attention now.

Somewhere near by, bound face downward to the floor, Mingo caught a change in the voices he heard, discerned the pause and waited for the trap. He could feel gooseflesh rising, and he kicked the floor wildly, imagining that he could not bear the gruesome horror another time. But there it was, a bungling clap-clap, and he wilted again, cold and tremulous and with tears in his eyes. What was it Touissaint said? *Brothers, come and unite with me.* Suddenly Mingo awakened to a meaning he had not previously seen in the words. Toussaint was in jail now, maybe dead. *Brothers, come and unite with me.* Mingo felt momentarily stronger. Do the dead combat for a common cause? Well, he thought, it was possible that they did, quite possible.

Near by old Ben, clean and well-favored, wearing new driving gloves and a hat in neat trim, stood at the curbstone, his arm hooked in the horse's bridle. His satin breeches were fresh and glossy, but they were also a bit too loose around his scrawny old knees. He scarcely filled his coat. A mournful dignity bowed his head, though his shoulders stood back fairly strong; and as he waited, his lips parted now and again and his tongue slipped between them, but they were never moistened. They remained as white as if they had been painted. Hearing the blurred bustle in the yard and finally the rattle of the sprung trap, he put a hand over his eyes and groaned aloud.

At the same moment two men came out of a shop door.

"They're at it again."

"H'm. Lot of live stock they're wasting, too."

"Can't be helped. They've gone mad, the black dogs. Some kind of disease, I reckon. It's got to be stamped out."

Ben opened his eyes and saw their backs against the clear afternoon sky. A barefoot rustic, standing on his horse to see above the crowd, got down and kicked the animal's ribs.

Gabriel heard nothing that he could distinguish, but he saw a crowd breaking at the head of the alley and he could imagine the rest. Presently he threw himself over a back fence and slipped into an abandoned stable. Frayed and perplexed and desperate for food, he could at the moment see no special danger in his position. Matter of fact, the woods had become unsafe; they were not seeking him in town. Lordy, where was old Ditcher? What had befell Solomon and Martin? How about Blue—had he caught up with the others? And General John— where, where? A good many had swung. Were any of these among the number? They could swing as many as they were a-mind to, plague take their time, but the nigger they really wanted was Gabriel, the general. And it just happened that there was a plenty fight left in that individual, if they only knew it. Of course, he couldn't whip a whole squad single-handed, but he could well-nigh worry them to death if his luck held out, if he managed to keep his hide free of buckshots.

His hat was battered beyond recognition, and the purple coat had begun to show its hard use. His shirt was gone. A strip of bright black nakedness flashed between his buttons. Gabriel rested his hand on an overhead beam and leaned forward, his long insidious gaze fixed rigidly on nothing. A little later he sat on a heap of filthy straw, rested his back against the wall; presently his chin fell against his chest, his eyes closed. His exhaustion was so profound he did not awaken when he finally toppled over on his side.

Then the hours were lost until at length he sprang up fiercely and began hacking at the shadows that crowded the stable. In the midst of this vastly satisfying set-to he awakened, his nerves tingling pleasantly, his feet no heavier than feathers, and replaced his blade. Sleep was gone now. He went out, threw himself over the fence and started up the alleyway. His mind became splendidly active.

Well, now, ain't this a pretty. We-all could of been doing a heap better'n we is doing. Somebody need to be going round and round this town at night; every now and then he need to stop and beat a drum and holler like the devil. Folks would think there was near about a million man-eating Africans in the woods; they wouldn't get no sleep, and that's how we could wear them out. Me and Ditcher and Blue and Solomon and Martin and a few mo' could do that. I'm got to find them. If we can't make no drums, we can sure pop up underneath of a bush every now and then and holler like devils. The others'll hear us, too; they'll come. I'm got to find my crowd, me.

"Stop." The word had been on the surprised man's lips and it leaped out involuntarily and without meaning, for Gabriel was facing him like a beast and in the same instant he sprang at the soldier's face. "Bloody swine—my musket—get your hands off—I'll kill you. Damn black—help, help! No, don't shoot— Oh, God please, no, no. Don't, don't, don'——"

"Here, take yo' musket, suh. Generals don't use 'em. Anyhow a sword'll do the work mo' quiet-like. Got to leave you now. Wa'n't no cause for you to make all that fuss, hollering for help. You wasted yo' breath, Mistah. You could of breathed two-three mo' times, did you keep yo' mouth shut."

There were running feet on the walk. Somebody opened an upstairs window and held a candle out. Presently a horse clattered on the cobblestones. Gabriel charted his directions deliberately. Then, pulling himself together, he slipped between two buildings, leaped a fence, ran a few paces in a lane, scaled another fence and presently faded in a clump of fruit trees.

Six

NORFOLK was unruffled. News filtered through from Richmond, of course, and the papers had much to say about the disclosed plot, but there was less to worry about here. It was true, if one accepted the rumors, that Norfolk had been included by the blacks in their dream of empire, and there had been reports of unexplained slave gatherings outside the town, but nothing had come of these thus far, and, aside from doubling the night patrol, nothing thus far had been done.

The waterfront was the same. Sailing boats tugged at the wharf, rocked sleeplessly as the seas came in. Barefoot deck Negroes shambled along the landing, twisting little useless hats in their hands and kicking up dust along the landing. Without the hats to occupy their hands, they let their arms fly back and forth with an air of important hustle. The fact that it was all mockery and that they were usually bent on a sleeping nook struck them as being apparent, yet their faces disclosed nothing but innocence and industry.

The streets in that part of town were forever cluttered with ox carts, carriages, wains and saddle horses. The air had a flavor. Heaping cargoes of indigo, tobacco and hides waited on the landings. Incoming boats brought sugar, tea, coffee, dates, cinnamon, bananas, cocoanuts, rum and fragrant woods. Some of the argosies were unloaded by black rousters in loin cloths, some by brown men in turbans, emissaries of legendary worlds. A medley of languages was heard.

General John was intoxicated by the aroma of things. He stood behind a crude shed and watched the labor of tiny fishing craft out near the rim of the sky. His long oversized coat was in strings, but he had caught it together at the throat in an effort to cover his naked belly. The coat was a blessing, too. It had pockets, which his jeans had not, and just now pockets were powerfully useful to General John; he had something to put in them.

These here Norfolk people ain't studying me. They ain't paying me no mo' mind than if I wasn't here. Dog take my time,
though, they is apt to think something do they see me slipping
round here behind this old shed. Yes, suh, bless Jesus, I'm
going to walk out yonder big as life, I'm is; I'm going to go
over there to the stagecoach station like as if I owned the devilish place. Peoples ain't paying me no mind. This here diving
and ducking'll make them think something's rotten. Here go
me, peoples.

There now, see? Didn't know me from Adam. Nice down
here, all the spice and things, the barrels of rum and the sweet-
smelling wood and all, mighty nice. I'd catch me a boat, too,
was there one fixing to sail directly. But I can't be waiting
around now. Even if they ain't studying me, I can't wait all
week. That there stagecoach is the thing. Looka there—see
that? This tarnation town is busting wide open with niggers,
and every lasting one of them look just alike to the white folks.
These peoples don't know me no better'n I knows them, and
that suits both two of us mighty fine. Looka there—see?

Go on there, brother, don't *you* start turning round and looking me up and down now. You neither, Mistah Man. Go on
about yo' business—on'erstand? H'm. Now, that's a little mo'
better. Y'-all don't know me from bullfrog, and if you did, it
wouldn't do you a speck of good. The Governor ain't said he's
going to pay you for catching anybody excepty Gabriel and
Ditcher. Go catch them if you's big enough. Next town I hits,
leastwise the first one across the line, I'm going to buy me
some clothes to wear. These rags ain't fitten for a hog. Look
a-them shoes: nothing but tops. And my pants, Lord a'mighty,
they don't even hide my privates. This old coat is a caution to
look at, but it sure do do a heap of good. They wouldn't let a
nigger walk through town with pants like this, showing all
his— Lordy, no they sure wouldn't.

Well, now, I'm here, ain't I? Soon's that there stage-driving
man get his horses out in the yard I'm going to get in and set
down too. I sure is tired a plenty; peoples, that ain't no tale,
neither. For a fact, I believes I could sleep two-three days
'thout waking up or turning over. Well, suh, what in the name
of lands is them folks doing? Oh, buying tickets, hunh? That's
something I can do whilst I'm waiting, I reckon.

"Howdy, Mistah Man. Yes, suh, I'm aiming to travel some, I sure am."

The stranger was promptly joined by another, and it occurred to General John that the two looked very little like stagecoach officials. Their eyes were uncommonly stern. And their interest in the wizened old Negro was, to say the least, not a casual curiosity.

"Your papers," General John heard one of them say in the course of a long period, the remainder of which escaped him.

"Papers, hunh? Papers for what, suh?"

Out of a tiny waiting room, curiously, came a uniformed guard. He was armed. Suddenly the three men dropped the veil.

"Where the hell you come from, old nigger? Who you belong to anyhow?"

General John became tense; his old withered lips went white. He shot quick glances at first one man and then another. His head fell forward, but under his rags his shoulders tightened and the quaking old fellow rose on the balls of his feet. His anguished smile revealed the horrid dark fangs that were his teeth, but there was now a shadow of cunning in his eyes that suggested an ancient fox.

"I's a free nigger, suh. I ain't *no*body's, me."

He bowed lower, thinking fast, still poised on his toes, as ready and elastic as a cat. Then his mind fastened on something. One way was hopeless, to be sure, but there were other things he needed to consider. He snatched a paper from his pockets. It was too large; it should have been only half the size. Yet in a flash he crammed more than half of it into his mouth and began swallowing hard as the guards laid hands on him. They snatched a crimped fragment from between his lips, boxed his head severely and bent him double in a frantic attempt to make him cough up what he had swallowed.

"Just what I thought. Search his pockets, rip the insides out of that old coat. Money, too. H'm, I thought so. Calm yourself there, you old dog's vomit, or I'll run you through now. He's one of them. By God, he looked *too* harmless; I thought something was rotten. Here, look——"

General John's courage began to melt. His thought, racing like a squirrel in a cage, slowed down to a walk. The men's hands were on him, clasping viciously. His face smarted from the blows, his head ached. He grinned at them weakly. He was a weird sight.

On the portion of the note that he had saved, the guard read: *Alexander Biddenhurst, corner Coats Alley and Budd Street, Philad—* The writing was a clear, though illiterate, scrawl. The man's eyes danced. Suddenly, harking back to General John's last remark, he added, "You're not going anywhere, old dog." The armed guard had to almost chop a way through the circle of spectators.

Seven

A<small>ND</small> in Richmond, bound to the floor of his cell, Mingo could still hear the hangman's trap falling periodically. Obscure Negroes were dragged before the justices in the morning and hanged the same day. The known leaders, as they were taken, were not punished immediately, however. There was still that question of Jacobin hands turning the spoon in the kettle: Fries, Gallatin, Duane, Callender and certain United Irishmen had not yet been cleared of suspicion, either. Their French babble about the natural equality of man had taken root like dragons' teeth. The black chiefs would have to be held for questioning. So Mingo, who knew how to read, who kept the lists, lay with his face to the floor. Ditcher, chained like a bear, sat on a stool in a dungeon. Rats romped about his bare feet.

Meanwhile Ben brought the cariole into town alone. The afternoon was fine, and the autumn trees were growing brighter and brighter. God's upturned paint pots had indeed spattered them all with red. At the edge of town he saw a familiar young man standing beneath a balcony, his arm hooked in a horse's bridle, his hat off, his wig exceedingly white, but Ben had to look twice before he fully recognized young Marse Robin. Leaves were falling. The face above had a taunting way of vanishing and reappearing every moment or two. It was wonderful, Ben thought, how oblivious young folks could be to death and woe. Maybe it was being white that enabled them to be unconcerned. What did a few niggers more or less mean to them? God bless them, they weren't studying any evil; they were just thinking about their own problems. And right now, seeing that young Robin was just getting himself cured of a honey-colored woman with hoops in her ears, he must have had his hands full. Ben twitched his lines, and the little mare's porcelain-clean feet twinkled again.

You're a good boy, Ben.

Yes, suh, young Marse Robin; thank you, suh. It do pleasure me a heap to hear you talk that a-way. I's aiming to be good, befo' God I is. You and yo' pappy is two mo' sure 'nough quality white mens. God bless me, I was about ready to turn my back on y'-alls once, but I bound you I won't do it nara 'nother time. That old dead Bundy—him squatting side of that hole in the low field. Jesus! He the one what was cause of it— him and Gabriel. But God beingst my helper, I'm standing by you from here on, suh. I ain't strong for no such cutting up as Gabriel and them was talking. I been a good nigger, suh, and I's too old to change now.

Pharoah, the pumpkin-colored one, came out of a shop carrying a full basket. Seeing Ben, he threw up his hand pleasantly and stepped down on the street.

"Well, now, what time you make it, old man?"

Ben looked at the sky.

"Two-three hours befo' dark, I reckon. Where you's bound?"

"Home."

"Well, howcome you can't wait and ride piece-ways back with me?"

"I ain't aiming for dark to catch me on the road, Ben."

"Scairt?"

"Nah, just careful-like, I reckon." He shuddered a moment. "The niggers is just nachal-born tired of seeing me live."

Ben didn't answer.

"Listen, Ben, ain't you told it, too?"

"Seem like somebody think I has. Tried to hit me with a knife."

"No?"

"Yes, they did. Leastwise, they throwed it at me. Look at this hand. I ain't saying whether they was trying to kill me or whether they wasn't. It sure look like somebody don't love me much, though."

"Lordy, I can't stand it, Ben. Seem like I'm all the time about half-sleep and half-wake. You reckon they's poisoned me?"

"Conjure poisoning? Well, ain't you carrying nothing?"

"String round my neck. That's all."

"I don't know, Pharoah. Some time I feels mighty funny myself."

"Got to hurry along now. Don't want night to catch me on the road."

"You can just as well ride piece-ways with me."

"Ne' mind, Ben. I can't wait."

Ben clucked to the mare.

An hour later he was back at the same spot, driving out of town. He had tucked the lap rug around his knees and now sat gravely erect in the small carriage. A North African sailor passed him in the road, a turbaned Negro, bright black, barefoot and without a shirt. He looked up, giving his pendants a toss, then promptly averted his face. Suddenly a host of swifts flecked the sky above an old chimney. They kept rising, gushing up like blown-out cinders. Ben set his eyes on the road again. Between the small ears of the small horse he discovered a distant spot near the bend of the road where the bushes were troubled.

Ben took a quick breath, stiffened in his seat and tried to prepare himself for danger. The bushes rustled again, then became still. There was the steady tock-tock of little porcelain feet on the firm road, and the eager animal never slackened pace a moment. In another moment they were at the bend. Ben pulled up the reins and at the same instant the bushes parted. Pharoah sprang out and ran down to the cariole.

"Let me ride some, Ben."

"You ain't home yet?"

"Somebody's after me. Let me ride piece-ways."

"Nobody ain't studying you—not here in the broad daylight, nohow. That's 'magination."

"'Magination nothing. Let me ride some now. Marse Sheppard won't care none."

"I tried to get you to wait in the first place."

"It's getting dark heap quicker'n I reckoned. Somebody done spied me, too. I heard them amongst the trees. You know I done already had one knife throwed at me."

"Climb on up."

"Much obliged, Ben."

"Maybe you shouldn't of been so burning up to run tell everything you knows. Leastwise, not if you's aiming to live a long time. Get up, Miss."

"It wasn't me what give them the names and all. Ain't you told nothing, Ben?"

"Ne' mind me. It ain't helped *you* none to talk yo'self near about crazy."

"You said they picked you up once, then let you go?"

"Now if you hadn't gone busting to town like you did——"

"Somebody say the white folks let you go cause you told, cause you told them plenty."

"I told them about me. They come and got me. They was aiming to hang me with the rest, I reckon."

The blood left Ben's lips. Pharoah shivered. Again there was a brisk tock-tock on the firm road.

"Some's catching the rope what ain't done nothing, Ben. Howcome they let you go—seeingst you told them about yo'self?"

Ben turned his face.

Eight

THE small chest-like trunk had been dragged into the middle of the floor, and the young mulattress stood above it
in a billowing leaf-green dress. The window hangings were
down now, and the room was flooded with yellow light. Melody passed a bright velvet garment through her hands, inspected it lovingly from top to bottom, then knelt to pack the
garment away as neatly as possible. There were other articles,
too: petticoats hanging on the backs of chairs, capes thrown
across the table, pieces of china worth saving, a silver vase, a
decanter, a medley of footgear strewn around the gilded box.

Melody felt a certain sadness, but she knew her own mind
and she had made her decision. Richmond had suddenly become too small for her. She had a *feeling*. Something told her
that she couldn't stay there, enjoying so many conflicting confidences, without becoming entangled. Her imagination was at
work, too. Why, for example, was young Marse Robin losing
interest? Not that she cared, but might it not have a meaning,
coming as it did at this turbulent time? Oh, there were so many
angles, so many things involved. Was it suspicion that she saw
on his face these last few times?

Well, let it be; she was leaving town. Philadelphia, according
to Alexander Biddenhurst, would be a more wholesome place
for a young freed woman, particularly an alert and handsome
one, despite, in this case, her obvious inclination toward easy
virtue. Why, it was a hateful thing, he thought, to sell one's
graces to the sons of aristocratic planters. Being the favorite of
such men would never help her to serve the cause of liberty
and equality. She was selling out her own class, the masses of
black folks, the poor, the enslaved. Of course, her sympathies
were all right, but of what good was sympathy for the unwanted coming from the darling of their oppressors? No, it
was leaving time now. Good-by, peoples. Good-by, church.
These zebra-striped stockings—well, toss them into the trunk
too. They wouldn't take up much space.

There were, in fact, very definite and substantial things that could bring her trouble if she delayed her departure. There was the flight of General John with the address she had given him in his pockets. Lordy, what had come of him? How was he getting along—him and his raggety self? Do tell, Lordy—po' old General John. Yes, and there were heaps of people who remembered that Biddenhurst himself had—maybe it was infatuation and maybe it was something very different—at least, he had known her. And it was funny about him, very funny. Not very ardent, to be sure, not warm or sensuous, but a curiously exciting person. All on fire. Liberty, equality, book learning. . . . He was a case, that Philadelphia man. Looked as if he might have been part Jew, but he hobnobbed with the French.

Presently shadows streaked the bright room, and Melody, rising from her knees, saw clouds in the sky. The storm was less than a month past, but here was a promise of rain again. No matter about that, though; old Benbow Bowler understood that he was to come for her trunk before day in the morning and deposit it on the schooner *Mary*, scheduled to leave Richmond at dawn. Melody untied her headcloth, went into the front room and swung the shutters out. She couldn't let folks see her through the front windows with her hair tied, but by now she was bored with packing and curious to see who might be passing.

The street was empty. A mist was gathering down toward the river. In the other direction two oxen were tied to a tree in a field where they had been pulled off the road with their cart. The clouds mounted. Melody leaned across the sill on her elbows, her feet off the floor and swinging childishly. After a while she closed the shutters and lit a candle. It was time to prepare supper.

Her mind told her to dash the light. If anyone knocked at the door, she would lie still and make no sound till the person was gone. Her house was upset from front to back. She wanted no visitors, and she wanted no one to carry out the news that she was leaving town. She wanted to answer no questions. Melody lay across the bed in a rumpled dress and listened to the drip of water in the roof drains. The shower itself was so fine and veil-like it made no sound. Three times she heard the rattle of broughams on the road. Not one stopped. Melody drew the coverlet above her shoulders and slept.

She awakened to a violent banging downstairs at her back door. And when she snatched on her cape and ran to the window that overlooked the yard, she saw a magical glow over the wet earth. Sheet lightning played like a blue fairy light, seemed to emanate from the very earth. In it she could see a burnished black figure, naked above the waist, wearing a badly battered hat, tottering like a man in a daze: an uncommonly large Negro, sorrowful yet dignified, undismayed, unafraid, turning a slow insidious eye up to her. And suddenly, with a burst of recognition, she put her hand on the sill and felt her own quaking.

"You, Gabriel."

"H'm. Me."

"Lord, boy, howcome you knock at my door this time of night?"

"Ain't nobody here but you," he told her.

"You right sure about that?"

"Right sure, yellow woman."

"Well—" She went to a shelf for the key. He hadn't moved when she returned. "—here then."

It struck the ground at his feet. She went into the next room and waited for him to let himself in. No, better not make a light. She drew the remaining curtains, pushed back the shutters. That was a help. One wouldn't have to stumble over the table with this blue brightness playing on things. Presently Gabriel came through the kitchen, handed her the key.

"Thank you, gal."

"What's that rag in yo' hand?"

"My coat. It's sopping wet."

"Here—let me have it. There's still some coals in the grate."

"I ain't got long."

"I know. Just as well to hang it here, though."

"Thanks a heap." He raised his head. "Mm-mm. Lordy!"

"Lordy what?"

"The perfume and sweetness and all. It's fit to kill and cripple in here."

He was luminous like the earth, giving the same blue light

in the murky darkness. The muscles quivered and ran on his arms and back. When Melody came out of the next room, there was a blanket in her arms.

"Put this round you, boy. Take that old broken-up hat off yo' head, too. Sit down. Rest yo'self some, beingst you's here."

He obeyed. His sword fell against the floor with a clank. If he had only been dry, he would have felt like some*body*. But a general can't feel like somebody as long as he's wearing a pair of sopping wet pants, as long as he can hear water slushing in his shoes. Gabriel's chin fell against his chest. After a long while he looked up slowly.

"Is you seen anybody, gal? Is you heard any talk?"

"Some, I reckon. Why don't you fly, though. Howcome you keep hanging round town, beingst everything's like it is?"

"I don't feel like running. I just feels like fighting, me."

She stared at him for a moment and decided to let that point rest.

"Has you et a plenty?"

"Little bit. Don't feel much like eating here of late."

"No, I reckon you don't. Just the same you need to keep something in yo' stomach if you aims to keep moving."

"Some time I picks up a apple, some time a ear of dry corn, some time nuts or berries or eggs. I ain't plum empty."

"You could do with mo', though; I bound you that."

"Maybe so. What is you heard? Who is you seen?"

"Wait. Let me see what's left in my kettle."

"Tell me now. Has you set eyes on Ditcher or Mingo or Blue? Has you heard tell of Gen'l John or my brothers?"

She reached the door.

"Some of them," she said. "Wait."

Nine

GABRIEL, warmed by the food, relaxing in his chair, threw out one foot majestically, leaned back, his elbows on the arms of the chair, his chin in the palm of his right hand. There, almost lost in shadows, his dark insidious gaze ran from an uncertain point on the floor to the woman on the couch. She had a lazy, indolent air, that Melody, but her presence was so soft and delicate, so charged with fragrant odors, that Gabriel began to feel himself dirtier even than he was, a befouled thing and sorely out of place. His flesh tingled, but there was a drowsiness on his eyes. He could have slept. His head began to rock.

"There, rest yo'self if you's a-mind to, boy. Sleep some. Want to lay down?"

Gabriel remembered his wet pants, his grimy, unclean person. It embarrassed him.

"No," he said, "ne' mind that. Just got to nodding here. What was that about Ditcher?"

"Ditcher give himself up directly after the Governor put up the reward for you and him."

Only Gabriel's eyes showed surprise. His voice came back deep, troubled, but unastonished.

"He in the lock-up, hunh?"

"Been there two-three weeks."

"Not two-three weeks."

"Well, maybe one-two."

"Where'bouts Gen'l John?"

"Philadelphia—if they ain't headed him off."

Gabriel spent several moments with his thoughts. Then suddenly he twitched his feet, stirred in his chair.

"Well, here's one what ain't going to give hisself up. Here's one that ain't aiming to fly away neither."

Melody rose on her elbow, tossing one foot indifferently.

"Was you right *smart*, you'd fly, though."

"I reckon I ain't smart. Not smart 'nough to run."

"Whose house you going to knock at tomorrow night?"

"I don't know. Howcome you say that?"

"See that thing yonder?"

"That there box? Yes."

"That's my trunk. It's all packed up and locked. Benbow be here for it any time now. I'm leaving befo' day on the *Mary*, boy."

"You?"

"Nobody else. It's leaving time, if you ask me."

"Somebody got to stay and fight. It's well and good for you, kicking up yo' heels; you's free. You don't know how it feels."

" 'Pears to me, you's free too. Who been telling *you* where to go and what to do these here last two-three weeks?"

"Well, now, I reckon so, me. But a plenty mo' niggers ain't free."

"You can help them mo' better if you's live than if you's dead."

"I might could get up another crowd here."

"You might couldn't, too. Who you think's going to fight now, after seeing all them black mens get kilt—hanged? You can't do a heap by yo'self."

"There ain't nothing else for me, though. I just as well to get kilt. Maybe I can get in two-three mo' good licks befo' my time come. That might would help some others what ain't free."

"It ain't sense. You's big and strong and mighty fine, boy. Was you away somewhere, way away and live, well then, maybe——"

Gabriel pulled himself together in the chair. His hands gripped the arm-rests, and he let the blanket slip down from one shoulder.

"Listen——"

"I hear. A wagon or cart or something."

"It done stop now."

"Benbow, maybe."

She ran to the front window and looked down. The shadowy cart had halted, but no one was apparently getting to the ground. It was a cart, too, a crude two-wheeled affair and not a carriage or brougham or cariole. If it was Benbow, why didn't he come in? He knew where she lived; he knew all the details. Surely he didn't expect to see a light in the window. . . . Come on up, Benbow, stupid nigger; you can't be wasting time. The *Mary* ain't fixing to wait on nobody.

Not getting down, hunh? Moving along. Well, maybe it wasn't Benbow. Funny, though, stopping out yonder like that. Funny as the devil. What's that, now? Sound like something scuffling up leaves across in the field. Something scuffling underneath of them trees all right. Somebody's hogs or something.

"H'm," Gabriel said.

He could not see her across the room, but a shadow was shaking its head.

"Gone now," she said. "Whoever it was. Nobody didn't even get down from the thing."

She waited at the window. Down at the river landing things had begun to stir. There were flares. Now and again a voice identified itself. There was no doubt that they were making ready the *Mary*.

Gabriel rested his chin in his palm again, and his eyes promptly closed. They did not open till Melody returned from the window some time later.

"That's him for sure now. He's coming round to the back," she said, excited.

Gabriel sprang up, confused.

"Coming, hunh?"

"Benbow. Coming to take my trunk."

"Oh. I was about to go to sleep. I couldn't make out who you meant was coming."

"*About* sleep?"

"Maybe I *was* sleep—just that one minute."

"You need to rest, I bound you, but it's near about leaving time now." She ran from window to window, drawing the shutters and pulling together such hangings as were still up. Then she ran into the kitchen and made a small light. "Come on up, Benbow, That's you, ain't it?"

"H'm. This me, Miss Melody."

He came in directly and stood in the door: a short pudgy black with masses of woolly hair pulled together ruthlessly and tied in a queue. Gabriel rose, dropped the blanket, slapped on his hat and stood looking down, his hands on his hips. His air, unintentionally lofty, seemed to disturb the smaller fellow. Benbow's lips went white with surprise.

"Didn't you pass by few minutes ago?" Melody said.

"Mm—yes. Seem like I seed somebody, though; seem like they was police or something—so I kept on moving. Maybe, though, they was looking for Gabriel. Maybe they know he's here."

"No cause for them to stand down there," Gabriel said indifferently. "They got they guns."

Benbow trembled a little.

"You' trunk ready now?"

"That's it there. You better hurry, too, Benbow. Look like they's getting things ready down there at the landing."

"Here," Gabriel said. He raised the small, solidly packed box and waited for Benbow to get under it. "Take it that a-way. See? No trouble to it. Did you see the boys working on the *Mary*, Benbow?"

"Two or three of them was a-stirring."

"That's a good-size schooner, Gabriel. You just as well to be down in it when she pull away. These police and all here waiting to see you come out the front door——"

"Well, maybe I ain't going out the front door."

Benbow was creeping down the steps. Then he was on the path, going around to the front.

"I got to dress in a hurry," Melody said. "Believe I'll ride on the cart with Benbow. It's powerfully dark out yonder."

Gabriel got his coat from the kitchen chair, tossed it across his arm.

"What time you say the *Mary*'s aiming to pull out?"

"Just about day. You better get on it if you can."

"There's a heap of things to think about when you's a general. Right now I don't know my mind. But I'm leaving here, though."

"You better forget some of them things on yo' mind—hot as they is on yo' track. Thing you need to do is see how fast a good general can run when push come to shove." Gabriel was walking away absently, hardly hearing what she said. "Here, wait a minute," she said. She wrote something on a sheet of paper. "Here's somewheres you can go in Philadelphia, do you get away."

Gabriel took it, started down the rear stairs. At the bottom he tore the note up, tossed the pieces on the ground.

Ten

H<small>E SAID</small> he might be squatting side of a corn shock some night. Down in the low field, maybe. That's how I heard him say it, and I sure do wish he'd come right now. He allowed how I might could help him some. A jug of water, maybe, when he's near played out, some meat or bread or like of that. It's all here, boy. Howcome you don't come get it? Everything I can tote, tall boy, everything you talk about I got. It all come out of the big-house kitchen, too, right off of Marse Prosser's table. See here—yams, meat, corn bread, collards, a jug of rum, everything. Me, too; I'm here, boy. What else mo' you want?

Yes, and I got this here charm, too. I know you ain't got no mind for such doings, but it's what you needs. On'erstand? That big rain and all—that was the stars against you, boy. Toussaint and them, they kilt a live hog, drunk the nachal blood underneath of a tree. It made a big difference. You never did hear tell of nobody hunting him like a dog. Martin and all his Jesus; Mingo reading out the Book—nothing to that. Come on back, boy, and get this charm. Come lay down, rest. Nobody's studying you down here this time of night, nobody in the low field but me. Come pleasure yo'self with a blue-gummed gal, boy. Might change yo' luck.

He said he might be squatting side of some corn shock. I heard him say it like that, and I been here time and time again since he said it. But, peoples, it's a heart-sickening thing to keep on waiting when he don't show up.

Nasty night this evening. This little slow misty-like rain. Fit to give a body his death of dampness. Mighty dark, too. Funny how you can see things though. Everything look like it got its own light. Everything got a purple-like shine. Me, too, my hands and legs, this old rag, all shining. I reckon it's the sheet lightning on things.

He'd be shining too, did he come. He'd be something tall, something with a purple shine slipping through the high bushes, wriggling, coming this way. Lordy! He'd slip down side of me.

I know how. I know how. I'll see him easy, do he come. He'll be shining.

Better be stirring now. Freeze yo' round yonder, sitting on this damp ground all night. Need to stir about some.

There were cattle splashing in the bog. Now and again a coon barked in a black clump of trees. The thin-waisted brown girl wriggled out of her rags and stood for a moment rejoicing beside the creek. Lightning played around her. She stood with feet apart, arms thrust overhead. Then, splash! And she was slipping through the water like a moonbeam, a slim, transparent thing that disturbed the stream hardly at all.

Why didn't he come some time? When he was nearly played out, thirsty, hungry, lonesome, why didn't he look for her in the low field? She might be able to help him. It was just like he said. But she couldn't help him if he stayed away. Here was this charm, for one thing. It would be a protection to him. It was a thing he had neglected, an important thing. Was he right safe? Could he possibly be unable to come, or afraid? Had he changed his mind and made a dash for safer ground?

She pulled herself out of the creek, shook the water from her matted hair. The air was cold. Lordy, it was colder than she could endure. She snatched up her rags and ran to the row of huts.

"There's plenty to eat and drink out there, do he come now," she told herself. "But the charm is here in my hand. He wouldn't know what to do with that 'less'n I told him, nohow. Maybe he'll come tomorrow when it ain't so rainy and wet."

Eleven

I T WAS a rat, sure as you're born, back behind the rum kegs,
down in the hold of the schooner *Mary*. The devilish thing
was as big as a cottontail, as full of fight as a porcupine.

Down on his hands and knees, eyes starting from his head
and nostrils dilating, Gabriel saw the thing vaguely like a
shadow. A moment later, when a scrap of light broke through,
he drew his steel and held out a challenge. The rat, desperate
in his corner, quickly showed a set of willing teeth. Gabriel
came a trifle nearer, put the sword-point practically in the varmint's face.

Bad, hunh? Wants something to set yo' teeth into, do you?
Try this here blade one time. See how this taste in yo' mouth,
suh. Back on up if you's a-mind to. You can't go nowhere but
in that corner. You's got to fight now. Showing me them teeth
so big—you got to use them now. There: bite that. There, suh.
Just as well to die fighting. I'm got you where I can say what's
what now. Oop-oo-oop! No, you don't neither. You ain't getting by me that slick. There now, see what you done? Kilt
yo'self. Jumped right straddle across my blade. Well, suh, that's
you all right. Look just as nachal as can be. Got on yo' last
clean shirt, too.

The schooner was moving along pleasantly. Now and again
the kegs jostled. Cries of the men on deck rent the air at intervals. A peculiar lassitude settled on Gabriel. His eyes kept closing involuntarily. None of the usual feelings of sleepiness
accompanied it, but periodically his eyes closed and things
went black for a few moments.

Just as well be sleep as wake here now. No way to break and
run, back behind here with the rats. Just as well to sleep from
here to Norfolk. Yes, suh, just as well—ho-hum, just as well to
stretch out—just as well—ho-hum.

His body was still asleep when his mind went to work again.
He couldn't follow a train of thought, but he was aware of a

781

parched throat. He was thirsty, near perishing for a drink. Water, rum, anything. Lordy——

His eyes opened. He raised himself on an elbow. Were they in Norfolk yet? How long had they been there? Now if he could only get Mott's ear. Lucky for Gabriel, he had seen that young cousin of his as he came on. Otherwise he might not have been so neatly stored. He might not have enjoyed such a long sleep. It was plainly dark outside. Things were quiet aboard. If he could only get Mott's ear about now. He went down on his belly and slept again. Later Mott came and Gabriel put two coins in his hand.

"Norfolk, hunh? Well, I'm staying down here a spell anyhow. I ain't getting off yet a while. That yellow woman——"

"Gone."

"H'm. Well, you can fill me a jug somewheres, if you's a-mind to."

"Stay long is you wants. The *Mary* going to be here a mont', I reckon. Maybe mo'."

"Where it going then?"

"To some them islands."

"Well, I feels like sailing awhile. I ain't getting off just yet."

"I'll bring you the jug directly."

Eleven days had passed. Gabriel had sent Mott to have the jug refilled. Then as he lay on his elbow, he heard stern voices on the deck. He caught a few words. Men were questioning Mott.

"You don't know? We'll take *you* then. Maybe you'll find out before it's too late."

They were fixing to arrest Mott, hunh? Well, suh, nothing like that. They was suspicioning Mott because he kept going and coming with that jug, with bread and meat in a basket, was they? They was aiming to lock him up, hunh? Nothing like that. Mott was powerfully afeard, and that was plain.

"No, suh, I ain't been in no Richmond, me. Leastwise, suh, I ain't been off'n the boat there. No, suh. No, suh, not me."

Gabriel slipped between the stacks of cargo. Then he remembered a bludgeon that had lain beside him and returned for it. Now he was doubly armed. Sunlight was like transparent gold on the deck. He came up, staggered in the intense light and started toward the four policemen who were at the moment haranguing the frightened Mott. The boy clung to his jug, but his knees were smiting.

Gabriel, towering like a giant, reeling noticeably, his clothes in outlandish shape, his eyes vacuous, was upon the group when they first noticed him.

"No, suh," Mott was protesting. "Not me—I ain't seen——"

"I'm the one," Gabriel said in a trance.

They all wheeled in confusion and excitement. For an instant a shadow of fear hung over the entire circle. The men stuttered. He was so obviously the wanted chief, that even Gabriel could see that they were parrying when the first one got a few words out.

"You? You Gabriel?"

They had been too astonished to draw their muskets. Gabriel had been too absorbed in his own daydream to take advantage of their delay. Now they all stepped back, leveled nervously. Gabriel dropped his club.

"I'm Gabriel. You oughta could see that boy ain't——"

"You—you giving up?"

"I ain't running. I wants a drink of water. I'm perishing for something to drink."

They got his blade. Suddenly a thought struck one of the policemen.

"Papers. Letters. Search him."

In a few seconds his clothes were ribbons. He looked at them with calm, detached eyes. His gaze, commonly dark and insidious, became indifferent, far-away.

"Is y'-all through?"

"Funny. Nothing but his money. No letters at all. Mighty funny——"

"You think he could have conceived it all himself?"

"Hard to tell."

"Through now?" Gabriel said.

Mott was slouched against the rain barrel, moaning audibly.

"He does have the look of one that——"

"I ain't got much rabbit in me," Gabriel said. "I ain't much hand at running. I was in for fighting, me."

He was very tired.

BOOK FIVE

PALE EVENING. . . .
A TALL SLIM TREE

One

Now for the second time Virginia was paralyzed with excitement. Benjamin Lundy, living in Richmond, but wisely contemplating a move to Tennessee, wrote letters.

"So well had they matured their plot, and so completely had they organized their system of operation, that nothing but a miraculous intervention of the arm of Providence was supposed to have been capable of saving the city from pillage and flames, and the inhabitants thereof from butchery."

So dreadful was the alarm and so great the consternation, that Congressman John Randolph of Roanoke, speaking with hand on heart, exclaimed, "The night bell is nevermore heard to toll in the city of Richmond, but the anxious mother presses her infant more closely to her bosom."

In Norfolk, meanwhile, crowds surged around the old jail. Bayonets bristled before the gates. In the mulling rabble were dozens of incurably curious blacks. Someone had reported that the dusky chief was about to be moved to Richmond. They had all come to catch a glimpse.

Yes, apparently something was going to happen. Police officers kept going and coming, passing the guards at will, exercising to the limit their prideful prerogative. Each time a lock turned, each time the gate cracked to admit an officer, a ripple of anticipation swept the crowd. Everyone went up on tiptoes, bobbed his head.

Where? Where? Is he coming now?

A sullen black sailor from a San Domingo boat stood with the others. He did not rise on his toes as the rest did; he did not bob his head. He had seen Dessalines ride a horse. He knew the sight of Christophe. He understood now that words like *freedom* and *liberty* drip blood—always, everywhere, there is blood on such words. Still he'd like to see this Gabriel. Was he as tall as Christophe, as broad as Dessalines? Was he as stern-faced as Toussaint, the tiger? They were saying now that the stars were against this Gabriel, that he had neglected the signs.

Yes, something *was* going to happen. They were about ready. Curse those long-necked white people. Couldn't they keep still a single minute? The officers were clearing a way. Evidently they were going to return the prisoner by river boat. There was the coach. Plague take those skinny white people; there they went crowding like swine.

Gabriel stood a moment, seen of all, then walked to the waiting coach. Mounted guards swirled around the conveyance. The crowd broke. The miserable young sailor stood alone, his thick lips hanging wretchedly.

It was an unsatisfactory glimpse. In twenty-four days the legend had become too great; the crowd wanted to know more. They were obliged to get it from the newspapers. In Norfolk they read the *Epitome* story.

"When he was apprehended, he manifested the greatest marks of firmness and confidence, showing not the least disposition to equivocate or screen himself from justice—but making no confession that would implicate any one else. . . . The behavior of Gabriel under his misfortunes was such as might be expected from a mind capable of forming the daring project which he had conceived."

Excitement spread like a fire catching up barn after barn. Wherever there was a black population, slave or free, there was consternation. The Negro became suddenly a dangerous man. In Philadelphia fear was rife. It was proposed there that the use of sky-rockets be forbidden, because in San Domingo they had been employed by the blacks as signals. And Alexander Biddenhurst, hearing the argument, went home and made a note in his journel.

"I can well understand how men's startled consciences make cowards of them. They recognize in the Negro a dangerous man, because they recognize in him an injured one. Injured men like injured beasts are always dangerous. By the same token extremely poor men are dangerous."

Then, pleased with his own words, he went out again, walked beneath the maples and filled his lungs with fresh air.

The *Daily Advertiser* pointed out that "even in Boston fears are expressed and measures of prevention adopted." This reference, of course, was to the advertisement then appearing in Boston newspapers. The police, it seemed, were taking this occasion to enforce an old ordinance for suppressing rogues, vagabonds and the like, an Act which forbade all persons of African descent, with stated exceptions, from remaining more than two months within the Commonwealth. Above a list of about three hundred names the advertisement read:

NOTICE TO BLACKS

The officers of the police having made returns to the subscriber of the names of the following persons who are Africans or Negroes, not subjects of the Emperor of Morocco nor citizens of any of the United States, the same are hereby warned and directed to depart out of this Commonwealth before the tenth day of October next, as they would avoid the pains and penalties of the law in that case provided, which was passed by the Legislature March 26, 1788.

CHARLES BULFINCH, *Superintendent.*
By order and direction of the Selectmen.

Virginians, for their part, could look forward with hope to the next meeting of the state legislature. With gossips estimating a larger and larger number of Negroes involved, with the reporter for the *Epitome* discovering a meeting of one hundred and fifty blacks near Whitlock's Mills in Suffolk County and getting the assurance that some of these were from Norfolk, with the story of a similar gathering appearing in Petersburg newspapers, with a real insurrection being suppressed near Edinton, N. C., and with all these things being linked more and more closely to the one large design of Gabriel, the opinions of legislators became increasingly necessary. People couldn't sleep as things stood.

Two

WELL, suh, I done sung my song, I reckon. It wasn't much, though. Nothing like Toussaint. The rain was against us. That Pharoah and his mouth wa'n't no mo'n I looked for. Something told me we was done when we turned back the first time. It was a bad night for such doings as we was counting on. A nachal man can't beat the weather, though. Nothing to do but take the medicine now.

The blacks boys there, working the boat and all—faces longer'n a mule's, every lasting one of them. They'd a-come with us once we got our hand in. They been powerfully polite to me. They know. They know I'm the gen'l. The weather turned out bad, that's all. There's a heap of things what could of been by now. Heap of black mens could of been free in this state, only that big rain come up. Befo' God, it looked to me like the sky was emptying plum bottomside up. Excusing that, niggers would of gone free as rabbits. These black boys know. They know I been a gen'l, me. They been polite, too.

Trees and all, all along the river there, little old houses in the thickets, red leaves a-blowing—mighty pretty. H'm. Didn't see none of this when I was going down two weeks ago. Lordy, me and that old rat was too busy having it out back behind them kegs and things. Yes, suh, worth seeing, too. I shouldn't of come, though. My mind ain't never told me to fly away. There ain't nothing good for Gabriel nowhere but right here where I was borned. Right here with my kinfolks and all. If I can't be free here, I don't want to be free nowheres else, me.

Bless me if I ain't had my time last three-four weeks, though. Ain't seen old Marse Prosser's face since I-don't-know-when. I been free. And, Lordy, I's free from now on, too. Plenty things they might can do to me now, but there ain't but one I'm looking for. Look at them here, lined up round me like the petals round a sunflower. All of them with they guns and everything—they knows what's what. They all know right good and well that they's riding with the gen'l. They know I'm a free man, me.

*

They kept going downstairs. Then, when he could see nothing at all, they opened a door and led him inside.

"Down there—understand?"

He bowed on his knees.

"Flat on yo' belly, nigger. There's points on these muskets if you need a little help."

He put his face on the floor.

"Stretch your arms out. Wide. There now."

They locked the heavy bands around his wrists. Then for the first time he seemed to perceive, without seeing, that there was some one else in the cell, bound to the floor beside him. He couldn't imagine who it was. He wasn't even concerned.

Some of the guards went out. Two remained, and some other men came a moment later. Someone walked over and slapped Gabriel's back with a sword.

"Say, who were some of the foreigners that put it in your head?"

No answer. Then a prick of the pointed blade.

"You—where'd you get the sweet notion to butcher the people of Richmond?"

Gabriel heard the other prisoner squirm. Neither spoke.

"You had money. White men gave it to you, didn't they?"

There was an end of patience. A boot thudded—not against Gabriel's ribs but against the ribs of his companion.

"Talk, dog. You had the lists and the records. Who gave you those pamphlets?"

Then, with a jolt of surprise, Gabriel heard Mingo's voice.

"We didn't read no pamphlets. Them pamphlets didn't have nothing to do with us. We was started long before——"

"How many names did you have listed? Why did you plan to spare the French residents? Why were *you* so active in the thing? You were free."

"We was——"

Gabriel raised his head abruptly.

"Die like a free man, Mingo."

His voice, as he said it, had a savage quaver that suggested a lion. Mingo felt the air suddenly chilled. Trembling, he put his face against the rough boards again. Presendy the other men left the two with their guards.

Three

THE wrinkled black crones made a half-circle before the cabin door. Near by, within easy eyeshot, a host of naked youngsters scampered like little midnight trolls. The old bird-like women sat with scaly bare feet curled beneath them, heads tied in rags, and smoked their pipes in a dreamy haze. Now and again a heavy lip curled, disclosed the want of teeth.

"Ain't that gal young-un of yo's getting heavy, Tisha?"

"Lordy, she *been* getting heavy, chile."

"I thought so all the time. Well, that's good. Two-three days rest from the field'll do her good."

"Yes, she do need a rest. Beulah works so hard. Having a baby'll give her two-three days to kind of catch her breath."

"H'm."

"Hagar, what's that you was saying a little while ago?"

"Oh, about when I was a gal on Marse Bowler's place?"

"Yes, what about it?"

"Well, it look for a long time like I wasn't going to have no chilluns. Marse Bowler, the old one what's dead now, commenced to get worried-like and started talking about selling me down the river whilst I's young. One day I heard him tell some strange white man he didn't believe I could make a baby. That stranger he just turned down the corners of his mouth and say, Bullfrogs! I'm got a stud nigger on my place that'll——"

"Hush that foolishment, Hagar."

"It's truth, gal. And, well-suh, when me and that roaring bull——"

"Hush, gal. You's fixing to say that right away you commenced to spitting out all them ten-twelve babies of yo's. You need to get religion and hush lying. Ain't that Juba coming yonder?"

"She need to be in the field working, do she know what's good for her roundyonder."

"That Juba don't care nothing about her skin."

"She would, did she know what I knows."

"What you doing round here, gal?"

Juba came nearer, her hands on her hips.

"What it look like I'm doing?"

"Snappy, hunh?"

"No, not snappy. Just telling what you ask me."

"You ain't sound to me like you was telling. Sound to me like you was asking me something back."

"Well, I'm doing just what it look like I'm doing. On'er-stand?"

"Oh. Give him that charm yet?"

"I ain't seen him."

"Well, I heard somebody say it's too late now."

Juba put her nose in the air, gave her shoulders a toss.

"I heard that."

"It's true, hunh?"

"I reckon so. Mott say they brung him back this morning."

"Well, now, that's howcome you put down yo' hoe and come back here?"

Juba shrugged. A moment later she slid down beside the others, took a pipe out of her bosom.

It was evening when Marse Prosser called her from her hut.

"You, Juba."

"Yes, suh, Marse Prosser."

She came out into the twilight, her eyes wild, bloodshot. His scowl seized her at once, but she avoided the burning pin-points of his stare. For some reason she had a feeling of being undressed. It was nothing, of course. She waited sullenly.

"How much tobacco you cut this afternoon, gal?"

She rolled her eyes, her gaze rising to meet his attention, then straying off into the darkness. It was an insolent maneuver, but she refrained from speaking.

"I'll teach you, sow."

"You talking to me, Marse Prosser?"

A deep purple red flushed his cheeks.

"You—you varmint. Get on down to the stake. Trot along —trot, I tell you." He prodded her with the butt of his lash. She halted, planted her feet, every time he poked her, and eventually he was obliged to use the lash end on her bare legs.

At the stake she snarled and tossed her hips as she took the place indicated beneath the yard lantern. A crowd of frightened blacks materialized in the dusk, followed at a safe distance, the whites of their eyes, the palms of their hands, their rounded white mouths distinct in the shadows. Later they set up a soft dove-like lamentation.

"Pray, massa, pray. Oh, pray, massa."

"H'ist them clothes."

She understood and obeyed, snatching the old tattered skirt up over her naked buttocks.

The white palms, uplifted, fluttered in the darkness. The mouths, as round as O's, grew large, then small again.

"Lord a-mercy."

"Here's something else to toss up your petticoats for, ma'm. Here's something worth fluttering your hips *about*. Understand?"

She didn't speak, didn't even flinch. Presently her thighs were raw like cut beef and bloody. Once or twice she turned her head and threw a swift, hateful glance at the powerful man pouring the hot melted lead on her flesh, but she didn't cry out or shrink away. The end of the lash became wet and began making words like *sa-lack, sa-lack, sa-lack* as it twined around her thin hips. *Sa-lack, sa-lack, sa-lack.*

"Oh, pray, massa; pray."

Something shook the lantern overhead, and the near shadows began to tremble and bounce back and forth like dervishes. When would Marse Prosser get tired? Maybe he was waiting for that Juba to break down. Maybe he was aiming to take the starch out of her hide. Well, he was certainly a powerful hand at laying it on, anyhow. The voices increased in the thicket, the quaking hands multiplied.

"Another such caper from you, and I'll fix you so you *can't* cut tobacco—then sell you down the river for good measure— sell you down to one of them Georgia cotton raisers—where you'll eat hog slop and sleep in a stable with mules."

She said nothing. She wouldn't even let herself cry. Lordy, she was just so full of meanness, she could almost taste it. Cry? Humph!

Sa-lack, sa-lack—

"Pray, massa. Oh, pray, massa."

Four

THE plight of Mrs. Cassandra Rainwater was that she was now too old to accomplish the things she dreamed. In her taffeta and lace she was even too wan and fragile to get around Philadelphia in her own carriage as she wished, and more and more she was obliged to leave with young Biddenhurst errands and contacts that might well have profited by her own attention. This in no wise inferred that the young man's talents were at all short of remarkable or his understanding, his sympathies, less than splendid; but her years, her feminine discernment, her lightness of touch must have offered advantages. Yet her plight was a common one; the sword was outwearing its sheath.

And indeed, over and over again, she had reason to be thankful that she had discovered Alexander Biddenhurst, discovered in him a romantic love of liberty like her own and a rather special burden for abused minority groups. At first there had been their mutual resentment against those who stole the Indians' hunting grounds. And now they were together convinced that liberty, equality and fraternity should prevail in the American States as well as in France. Each had read Rousseau and Voltaire with conviction, and each had been intrigued by the *Amis des Noirs*. Each hoped that somehow slavery would end promptly, even if the end had to come with blood as in San Domingo. The spirit of the master was abating, that of the slave rising from the dust. Jefferson was right; though, of course, he failed to go far enough. They themselves were not afraid to say (to each other, at least) that they approved the Jacobin ideal of utter equality for all men, everywhere. They enjoyed working for it as best they could. But Mrs. Rainwater, widowed and old, could do little of herself now, very little.

Yet she could still contribute her vision—her vision, her insight and, of course, her money. Fortunately she had a plenty of that, and scarcely any dependents. She rested the needlework that had occupied her fingers and adjusted her cushions. The young man rose to go, the afternoon sunlight making grotesque blurs behind his thick-lensed spectacles.

"I don't think you told me you were in a hurry, Alec."

"It's only the stagecoach that I was expecting to meet."

"Oh, yes. You did say—but about your moving. You didn't finish."

"I thought it would be well if they found my lodgings at Coats Alley and Budd Street empty. Of course, it proves nothing that that slave had my name and address when he was captured, but moving will save me the necessity of talking. They may want to make something of my being in Richmond at the beginning of the summer."

"Oh, that. Possibly."

"I couldn't have gone at a more suspicious time, had I actually been inciting the slaves to insurrection."

"You think those with axes to grind would be slow to believe that I sent you merely to look around, to study sentiment and get a cross-section view?"

"They'd never be satisfied with the facts. Being unsuspecting, I *did* say a good many strong things. Mostly I said them to draw out their thoughts, but you see how it's all coming to appear to an outsider."

"Possibly you're right, but they'll find you if they want you badly enough. Be sure to leave your new number anyhow. And come to think about it, why don't you use my carriage to meet the stage?"

"Well, if you say——"

"Of course. Didn't you say she's a young woman?"

"Yes. You and I are becoming a sort of bureau for the aid of fugitives—if nothing more."

"That's something. I hope we're getting at something far deeper, however. Whenever we succor a fleeing creature, I hope we make a soldier for liberty."

"No doubt we do."

"How about the Creuzots and Laurent?"

"Doing well. Their home is simpler than the one they left, but I have no doubt they'll become the kind of influences we want."

"I must have a talk with M. Creuzot. Is he coughing more than usual?"

"Not more."

"That's good. I'm especially eager to get some Negroes, some escaped slaves. They'll bring such an emotional fervor to the work."

"If I may go now——"

"Yes, of course, Alec. Take the carriage."

"Thank you."

Twilight had fallen. There was a cheerful confusion and bustle beneath the elms where the stagecoach unloaded. Mrs. Rainwater's amber coachman held his horses in a soft rain of leaves, while Alexander Biddenhurst ran across the road to meet the veiled woman traveling alone.

A little later, as the horses jogged along indolently, Biddenhurst realized that the carriage was too heavily scented. A dreamy lassitude had settled upon the tired, excited woman. Ah, he thought, it's a strange free-masonry, this love of freedom, a strange free-masonry. Of course, any man might be drawn to a fragrant, faintly tinted creature like this one, but that he should be a partner with her, sharing a secret, working for other ends, was strange. Yet all that did not forestall the joy of living, the pride of the eye.

"Melody—that's the name for you all right."

"You think so, Mist' Alec?"

"Listen. I'm not a rich planter's son, and you're not in Virginia now. *Mist' Alec!*"

She smiled in a drowsy haze. She was very tired.

Five

"... and are you the one they call the General?"

"I'm name Gabriel."

"I've heard slaves refer to a General something or other."

"Gen'l John, maybe."

"Didn't they call you General?"

"Some time—not so much."

"Then old John there was the leader, not you?"

"No. I been the leader, *me*. I'm the one. Gen'l John is just named that. I'm the one."

"You *are* the General?"

"I reckon so. Leastwise, I'm the leader. I ain't never turned my back to a nachal man. I don't know if I'm a sure 'nough general or if I ain't."

Gabriel, still in the frayed coachman's clothes, sank back into a lordly slouch. Now, suh, curse they ugly hides, they could make up they own minds about the gen'l part. Is I, or ain't I? One hand clasped the arm of the witness chair; the other hung idly across his knee. His eye kept its penetrating gaze, but now there was a vague sadness on his face. It was as if shadows passed before him now and again. It may have been woe or remorse rising in him, but the look was more like the dark, uncertain torment one sees in the countenance of a crushed beast whose spirit remains unbroken.

Only that morning there had been another execution, a small herd of anonymous field Negroes. The townsfolk were hardened to the spectacle now. Even the customary eyewitnesses were missing. The word had gotten about that these were not the ringleaders, and the mere sight of slaughter for its own sake was no longer attractive or stimulating. So many little groups like this had come to the scaffold since mid-September—five, ten, fifteen at a time—so many. It was a routine. These blacks had contracted a malady, a sort of hydrophobia; they were mad. It was necessary to check the spread of the thing. It was a common-sense matter. Only this morning there had been a difference.

At first no one had seen or heard the wiry old man with the turn-down mouth. He had seen the first of the executions, and he had raised his voice then.

"You idiots. You're putting them through too fast, I tell you. No sense in killing off a man's live stock in herds like that unless you know for sure what you're doing."

He scrambled in the crowd and tried to fight his way through. But they thought he was talking about the blacks being idiots. A chorus of approval rose around him. No one saw him as an individual, only as a part of a snarling crowd.

Today, with things much quieter, they had heard, for he succeeded in delaying the hangings half-an-hour.

"See that long yellow boy there. Well, that's John Thomas. That boy's been to Norfolk for me. He just got back last week. And, by God, if you hang him without proof, you'll pay me his worth. Bloody apes, what's wrong with you? Have you gone stone crazy for life?"

John Thomas did not swing. There was a rumor that several other planters had also been to the justices since morning. And already a statement had been issued—some "mistakes" had been made, admittedly. But Gabriel, lying on his face beside Mingo, knew only what the swinging trap indicated. Yet it occurred to him that all this pause, this unhurried questioning, could not possibly have been in keeping with the trials that had preceded his. He concluded at length that the "General" was simply receiving his due recognition, this in spite of the prosecutor's whining, sarcastic voice.

"Here, now, you mean to say you were the one that thought up the whole idea?"

"I was the one. Me."

"Yes, but not all alone, surely——"

"Maybe not all alone."

"Well, then, who were your accomplices? Who helped you think it up?"

Gabriel shrugged.

"You got Ditcher and Mingo and Gen'l John. You done hanged a plenty mo'. I talked to some of them. I told them to come on."

"It's plain that you do not intend to implicate anyone not already in custody. You're not telling all you know."

Gabriel looked at the man long and directly.

"I ain't got cause to talk a heap, suh."

"You haven't?"

"H'm."

Then the prosecutor spun quickly on his heel, barked.

"What do you mean by that, you——"

Gabriel's eyes strayed indolently to the window, to the golden leaves of an oak bough. The court was oppressively rigid, the justices in their wigs and robes, the spectators gaping, straining their necks.

"A man what's booked to hang anyhow—" he mused.

"Oh. So you think—" Then a diplomatic change of tone. "You know, Gabriel, it is not impossible to alter the complexion of things even yet. A—I mean, you have a fine chance to let the court know if you have been made the tool of foreign agitators. If there were white men who talked to you, encouraged——"

That sounded foolish to Gabriel.

"White mens?"

"Yes, men talking about equality, setting the poor against the rich, the blacks against their masters, things like that."

Gabriel was now convinced that the man was resorting to some sort of guile. He fixed his eyes earnestly.

"I tell you. I been studying about freedom a heap, me. I heard a plenty folks talk and I listened a heap. And everything I heard made me feel like I wanted to be free. It was on my mind hard, and it's right there the same way yet. On'erstand? That's all. Something keep telling me that anything what's equal to a gray squirrel wants to be free. That's how it all come about."

"Well, was it necessary to plot such a savage butchery? Couldn't you have contrived an easier way?"

Gabriel shook his head slowly. After a long pause he spoke.

"I ain't got no head for flying away. A man is got a right to have his freedom in the place where he's born. He is got cause to want all his kinfolks free like hisself."

"Oh, why don't you come clean? Don't you realize you're on the verge of hanging? The court wants to know who planted the damnable seeds, what Jacobins worked on you. Were you not treated well by your master?"

Gabriel ignored most of what he said.

"Might just as well to hang."

"That's bravado. You want to live. And the best way for you——"

"A lion what's tasted man's blood is a caution to keep around after that."

"Don't strut, nigger."

"No, suh, no strutting. But I been free this last four-five weeks. On'erstand? I been a gen'l, and I been ready to die since first time I hooked on a sword. The others too—they been ready. We all knowed it was one thing or the other. The stars was against us, though; that's all."

It was astonishing how the thing dragged on, astonishing how they worried and cajoled, threatened and flattered the captive. "Mistakes" *had* been made, due to haste and excitement, but there was no possibility of a mistake here. Gabriel seemed, if anything, anxious to have them get the thing straight, to have them place responsibility where responsibility belonged.

In another room, under heavy guard and awaiting their call, the last of the accused Negroes sulked. Ditcher's massive head was bowed, his wiry queue curled like a pig's tail. It had never been more apparent that he was a giant. His legs suggested tree stumps. The depth of his chest, the spread of his shoulders seemed unreal. His skin was amber. Now, delaying in the guarded room, he was perfectly relaxed. Indeed, he might have nodded had it not been for the jittery, nervous activity of the armed men around him. They annoyed him.

"We could had them on they knees long ago," he was saying in his mind. "Only that devilish big rain. That's what stopped us. We could all been free as squirrels by now. It wasn't the time to hit. We should had a sign."

Mingo's clothes were better, but his hair had been torn from its braid. He had lost his spectacles. His eyes had an uncertain, watery stare. He was not merely downcast; he looked definitely disappointed. Words were going through his mind too, but they made a briefer strain.

"Toussaint's crowd was luckier. Toussaint's crowd was luckier."

There were others, a dozen or more, unimportant fellows. Then near the door the withered old dead-leaf clad in a rag that had once been an overcoat. He kept licking his white, shriveled lips, kept showing the brown fangs. He was trembling now.

"Somebody's obliged to foot the bill," his mind was saying. "Ne' mind, though. Near about everybody dies *one* time. And there ain't many niggers what gets to cross the river free—not many."

Any one of them would have sped the business along had it been his to do it. No cause for a heap of aggravating questions. Them white mens ought to could see that Gabriel didn't care nothing about them; he was going to tell them just what it was good for them to know, and precious little more. But there was nothing they could do, nothing but wait.

". . . and how did you imagine you'd be able to take the city?"

"We was ready to hit fast. We had three lines, and the one in the middle was going to split in two. They was coming in town from both ends at once. They wasn't going to spare nothing what helt up its hand against us."

"How about the other two?"

"Them's the ones what was ready to take the arsenal and the powder house."

"Which line were you to lead?"

"The one what went against the arsenal."

"What arms had you?"

"We didn't need no guns—us what went against the arsenal there. All we needed was to slip by in the dark with good stout sticks. We could manage them few guards."

"Mad dogs—that's what you are. The audacity! It's inconceivable that well-treated servants like——"

"We was tired being slaves. We never heard tell about no other way."

"You'd take the arsenal and powder house by surprise; then with ample arms, with the city in ashes, with the countryside and crops for your food, you thought you'd be able to stand your ground?"

"H'm."

"How many bullets had you to start with?"

"About a peck."

"And powder?"

" 'Nough for that many bullets."

"Any other arms?"

"Pikes, scythe-swords, knives, clubs, all like of that—'nough to do the work."

"How'd you know it would do the work?"

"There wa'n't but twenty-three muskets in town outside the arsenal."

"You knew that!"

Gabriel felt that it was unnecessary to answer.

There was a hush; a shiver passed over the courtroom.

"It was a diabolical thing. Gentlemen——"

He talked for a time with his back to Gabriel. Later he turned to the prisoner again, but this time he spoke like a changed man, an awakened man who had had an evil dream.

"Did you imagine other well-fed, well-kept slaves would join you?"

"Wouldn't you j'ine us, was you a slave, suh?"

"Don't be impudent. You're still a black——"

"I been a free man—and a gen'l, I reckon."

"And stop saying general, too. Ringleader of mad dogs. That's what you've been. I call on this court of justice——"

Gabriel felt the scene withdrawing. It was almost like a dream, almost mystic. Further and further away it receded. Again there was that insulting mockery of words he could not understand, that babble of legal language and political innuendo. It was all moving away from him, leaving him clinging to an arm of his chair, slouched on one elbow. A lordly insolence rose in him. Suddenly he was vaguely aware of that whiney voice again.

"The only question yet raised, sir, was whether or not the wretch was capable of conceiving such a masterpiece of deviltry, such a demon-inspired——"

It was far away. Gabriel's eyes strayed again. The window—blue. The crisp oak leaves—like gold. Demons. Freedom. Deviltry. Justice. Funny words. All of them sounded like conjure now.

"Maybe we should paid attention to the signs. Maybe we should done that," Gabriel thought.

Six

BEN stood in the kitchen door and watched the fellow sitting on a chopping block beside the woodpile. Early-morning sunlight flooded the yard, and the pumpkin-colored slave sat beneath a bright arch of transparent gold. His elbows rested on his sprawled knees, his brown ham-like hands dangled between. Trouble had dogged old Pharoah since the day he carried the news to Richmond, and now his thoughts were in a whirl.

Lordy, me, I couldn't help telling. I just couldn't live and know all them peoples was fixing to meet they master 'thout knowing it. Seemed like I'd go hog-crazy if I didn't tell it. I *had* to; I didn't mean Gabriel and them no hurt. Just the same, they wants my meat. They wants a piece of my skin, Lord.

Ben watched him and saw the daydream play on his face, saw his lips curl, his eyes flicker. He saw, too, a crisp golden shower of oak leaves on the sorrowful mulatto and on the woodpile. Ben turned to Drucilla who was stirring something in a kettle, her immobile, mask-like face glowing in the heat.

"They's wearing Pharoah down all right, following him around like they do, throwing knives at him every chance they gets."

"What else he 'spect?"

"I don't know."

"H'm. I reckon you don't."

"But it's a powerful bad thing to sit around waiting for yo' medicine when you know you's sure to get it."

"*You* ought to know."

"What you mean, gal?"

"Nothing—just you ought know."

"Howcome *I* ought know mo'n anybody else?"

"I didn't say you ought to know mo'n anybody else."

"It sounded like you meant that."

"Did it?"

He leaned against the doorpost again. She shifted a few pots, stirred a while longer. Ben kept watching Pharoah's bowed head.

A few moments later, when he had decided to say nothing more to Drucilla, he heard her speaking to his back.

"Just like that yellow varmint. Least thing he could do, was he equal to a hound dog, was keep his mouth shut. But, no, he wanted to lead one line; and when they wouldn't let him, nothing would do but he must go tell everything. You and him——"

"Me and him what?"

"Nothing."

"What you keep on hinting at me, gal?"

"Nothing. Call him and see do he want a cup of coffee to ease his mind. You can put a drop of Marse Sheppard's rum in it."

Such fall weather. . . . Lordy! Ben preferred not to raise his voice. He strolled down the gravel walk, went over to the woodpile. He spoke to Pharoah; but the latter, shaking his head woefully, showed no immediate interest in Ben's suggestion. Later, however, he rose reluctantly and followed the other to the kitchen door.

"No need mopping yo'self sick, though."

"I ain't so scairt. That ain't it."

"Howcome you do it, then?"

"I'm sick, Ben. Sure's you borned, I been poisoned."

"Hush. Ain't nothing wrong with you."

"Don't tell me. I been finding frogs' toes and like of that in my pipe. They keeps my bed sprinkled with conjure dust. I been doing everything I know how to fight it, but it don't amount to nothing. I'm got slow poisoning sure's I'm a foot tall."

"Hush. A cup of coffee'll do you good. Then walk around till work time. You can make *yo'self* sick just studying like that."

Drucilla had placed a cup on the stove and poured an inch of rum in it. When they reached the door, she poured the boiling coffee.

"Wait there," she ordered Pharoah.

"H'm."

"Here, now. This'll ease yo' mind."

"You reckon?"

He stood cooling it a few moments, then raised the cup and poured the contents down his throat. His eyes were wide, startled, as if he had seen a spirit. Suddenly he began trembling violently. A moment later he was crying, his hand over his eyes. Ben and Drucilla stood before him paralyzed. Then, abruptly, his shoulders rounded, he gave a little hiccough and the coffee came out of his mouth in an ugly geyser that spouted on the floor of the porch. And when he removed his hand from his eyes and saw it there, he began crying louder.

"Lordy, Ben, look at it. See there. There it is. I told you so. They fixed me. I done puked up a varmint. What is it—a snake or a lizard? Lordy! They done fixed me. Look at it there, Ben."

His crying became louder and louder. Then, without warning, he left Ben and Drucilla in the doorway, bounded across the yard, raising his voice higher and higher, wailing insanely, and raced toward the clump beyond the stables.

Negroes began leaving the outhouses and cabins, coming into the early sun with amazed faces. One by one they started after Pharoah, pursuing him hesitantly, partly curious, partly concerned, but unable to resist following. Ben and Drucilla remained like statues in the doorway.

It was five minutes later when Drucilla went outside and recovered the cup and saucer the crazed fellow had tossed there as he left. She saw some of the black men returning from the tree clump, walking slowly.

"Catch him, George?" Ben called.

"It wasn't no use, Uncle Ben."

"Lord help."

"Done climbed a tree already. Up there barking like a dog."

"Barking, hunh?"

They went on. Drucilla went back into the kitchen. Ben stood wringing his hands. So Drucilla thought it was no more than Pharoah should expect for telling a thing like that? Telling a thing like that! Lordy, what could anybody expect. Anybody.

Ben's hands felt scaly and cold to himself. They were so thin and brittle he imagined they were like the hands of a skeleton. Still he could not restrain the impulse to pass one in and out of the other. He could not move his feet from the place where he stood on the path, either.

Seven

A<small>N AIR</small> of mystery invaded the Virginia State Legislature. Assembled in secret session with drawn blinds and guards at every door, the men sat with bowed heads in a haze of tobacco smoke and flickering lamplight. A warm proud voice engulfed them. Subdued yet distinct in the small chamber, it laid before the group a possible solution for the baffling problem.

"*Resolved*, that the Senators of this state in the Congress of the United States be instructed, and the Representatives be requested, to use their best efforts for the obtaining from the General Government a competent portion of territory in the State of Louisiana, to be appropriated to the residence of such people of color as have been or shall be emancipated, or hereafter may become dangerous to the public safety. . . ."

At length the reading was finished and discussion was allowed. The black-clad men, intensely sober, deeply concerned, shook their heads and murmured. Somewhere in the rear a tired voice was heard saying, "Sir, not yet. The time is not ripe. Our present situation only delays the possibility of such action. There are so many angles. Perhaps slavery itself——"

Yes, the Governor told himself at Oak Lawn, it all led back to the same colossal bugbear. Why such a widespread fret about slavery? Hadn't there always been slaves? But with liberty the fad of the hour, it might well be expected. Some fanatic would always be absent-minded enough to apply his cant to the black man's condition in the American States. Whenever there was a nonsensical thing to be said, nature would provide a fool to say it. So it always went. At any rate, he was still the Governor of Virginia; his personal responsibilities had not ceased. He could at least write the President a letter looking forward to such action by the United States Congress as his own legislature was hesitant to suggest at the moment.

He walked to the window, withdrew the hangings. A frame

of stars. A moment later he returned to his writing table. In the pale orchid light he took a quill and began writing.

"Honorable Sir——"

Now it was different with Gabriel in his cell. He had not been returned to the hole where he had lain chained to the floor beside Mingo. Here there were chains, but now he sat upright on a stool when he wished, rolled on the floor when he felt inclined. There was a barred window, too, a frame of indigo sky with little near stars.

Them white folks is sure a sight. Now they's aiming to make Mingo talk some mo'. They is sure got great heads for figuring out something what ain't. They sure loves to wring and twist about nothing. Nothing going to do them now but to make somebody say white mens was telling us to rise up. Never heard tell of nobody being so set on a thing before.

When the night watch passed, Ovid walked around the corner and whistled for Midwick. Later, plowing his feet through the loose leaves, the older guard came to a pool of light near the main gate.

"Well, doesn't anyone know why she left, Midwick?"

"Don't seem to. Not unless some politician caused it—him or somebody mixed up with this insurrection business."

"Now that's a thing to blind you. I always thought that young Robin Sheppard was great on her."

"Just getting his education, I reckon." He snickered. "They say he's sparking somebody he can marry now."

"The other one was really something to look at, though. Kind of a—I suppose you call it exotic. Apricot-colored, enameled-like hair—most any man could enjoy a little recklessness with——"

"Steady, Ovid. Remember you're a——"

"Dash it all, Midwick. I'm sick of being steady. I want to do incredible things."

"Incredible?"

"Yes, outlandish, glamorous——"

"Well, now, if we go to war again——"

"Oh, you don't understand me, Midwick."

Eight

A WEEK passed. The gallows-day came, and Gabriel awakened to the clatter of heels and the rattle of side arms outside his cell.

This the day all right. They is sure here early a plenty. Trying to be good as they word, I reckon. Beating the sun up so I won't get to thinking they's gone back on me. Never got up this soon in the morning to feed me, not as I can recollect, nohow.

H'm. Yes, suh, it's still night.

He curled his legs and sat upright, his hands resting on the floor to spare them the weight of the iron wristbands and chains. His naked shoulders gave a faint glow in the darkness. There was a brightness on his cheekbones, on his forehead.

Suddenly there was silence outside. A brief hush blanketed the men with the flambeaus and sabers.

Them is the mens with the milk-white horses, I reckon. I ain't seen nara one of them, but I know right well how they looks. H'm. I got a good mind how they come. I know about *them* all right, all right. . . . Galloping down a heap of clouds piled up like mountains. I know them milk-white horses, me.

His eyes, large, the whites prominent, turned listlessly. He was still sitting on his feet, his hands resting on the floor. Again the sabers rattled, heels clattered and a medley of gross voices rose in confusion.

Put yo' key in the lock, Mistah Man. Give the sign and come in, please you, suh. I heard a nigger say Death is his mammy. His old black mammy is name Death, he say. Well and good, onliest thing about it is Death is a man.

Come on in, suh, if you's a-mind to. I'm ready and waiting, me. I ain't been afeared of a nachal man, and I don't know's I mind the old Massa hisself. I ain't been afeared of thunder and lightning, and I don't reckon I'll mind the hurricane. I don't know's I'll mind when the trees bend down and the tombstones commence to bust. Don't reckon I'll mind, suh. Come on in.

The sky flushed as they put him in the cart, and suddenly Gabriel thought of the others, the ones who were to follow him, the ones who waited in their cells because of his leadership, these and others, others, and still others, a world of others who were to follow.

There was a long over-sized box on the cart, and Gabriel knew its use. It had to be long, over-sized, for a body of his dimensions. He sat on the thing, threw out his feet. A flood of color burst in the east, rose and orchid and pale gold. The cart jogged. A clatter of feet went before, and a clatter of feet came after. Sabers rattled from the belts of shadowy, uniformed men. Above their heads a score of muskets pointed toward heaven, pointed like the stiff fingers of black workers rising from their prayers.

The trumpet sounds within-a my soul.

Ditcher, even then was standing at his small window with bloodshot, sleepless eyes. His face was marked by numerous small scars. He had been a fighter. Not that he was petulant or touchy, but the nature of his work frequently got him embroiled. The nature of his reputation, before Gabriel deflated it, obliged him to meet all comers. But fighting had never been a pleasure to Ditcher; this morning, his massive hands clasping the window bars, he lamented all wars. Presently, he thought, so far as he was concerned, the trumpets would blow their last blast. The sky would flush, redden like a sea of blood, and the sun would go down on all conflict. . . . Presently. Presently. Outside the cart lumbered. The pale torches blossomed like white flowers.

Good-by, Gabriel. Don't nobody need tell *you* how to die, I reckon. You's the gen'l, you.

Distraught, fluttery, Mingo chewed his lips and dug his fingernails into the palms of his hands. The Book said some powerfully hopeful things about the stranger, the servant, the outcast. The Book was all for abused folks like Negroes. Other books too, in fact. Mostly them men what writ books was a little better kind than them what made speeches at the town meetings.

Wagon, hunh? Bright and early, too. Gabriel be the first, I

reckon. Yes, the first, all right. Toussaint was first across yonder; Gabriel's first here. The first robin going north. It was too
soon for Gabriel, though. It wasn't summer. The cold caught
us here, the rain and all. Toussaint drunk blood. Gabriel never
had no head for such doings as that. They was the first, them
two.

Ne' mind, boy.

General John was as scrawny as a hawk now. The days of
waiting had drawn his face so tight and hard it suggested a
bird's face. Inside his torn garment, his shaggy feathers, he
twitched a rattling skeleton-like body.

Was I a singing man, I'd sing me a song now, he thought.
I'd sing me a song about lonesome, about a song-singing man
long gone. No need crying about a nigger what's about to die
free. I'd sing me a song, me.

The horizon was pearl-gray now, but overhead a star or two
lingered. A man gave the word, and Gabriel climbed the steps
to the platform. For an instant he was still, his hands idle.
Across some roof-tops a limp flag rose, ever so lightly, fluttered
a little.

They had chosen to bring him without shirt or coat. He
stood, naked above the waist, excellent in strength, the first for
freedom of the blacks, savage and baffled, perplexed but unafraid, waiting for the dignity of death.

"Have you anything to——"

Then an interruption, another voice.

"Would you ask that of a—of a black?"

"Well, seeing he's getting a hanging like this, I thought
maybe——"

"As you wish."

Then a stuttering followed by bluster.

"You want to talk now, you a—a—scoundrel?"

No answer.

"Want to talk now, I say?"

"Let the rope talk, suh."

"No statement?"

"The rope, please you, suh—let it talk."

The vein grew big in the executioner's forehead. His face
became livid. The narrow scar that was his mouth tightened,

tightened, tightened. Another man, standing beside the one with the ax, stepped forward, stood on tiptoes and placed the cowl on the tall Negro's head.

Somewhere down below feet tramped. The escort jostled, wheeled and withdrew a few paces.

Like night, Gabriel thought, like night with this thing on your head.

A command to the soldiers broke the absolute stillness. A wagon moved. A horse nickered. Then, here and there, the sudden, surprised intake of breath filled the air with a tiny whispering. The sheriff's ax inscribed a vivid arc. The trap banged, and the rope hummed like a violin string. And still there was that arc, inscribed by the ax, lingering there against the sky like a wreath of smoke.

Seated in a cariole a hundred yards away, a blanket tucked about his knees, Ben saw it and gasped. Near him a small crowd of Negroes bowed their heads, covered their faces with their hands. Even when Ben closed his eyes, he could see that arc, hear that violin string.

Nine

BEN did not wait to see them remove the body. There were errands for him in town. Later he was expected to meet Marse Sheppard and drive him home.

So the morning was spent. Then it occurred to Ben that the sky was no longer clear, clouds were gathering. But now there was no further need for haste. Marse Sheppard was not ready. The old Negro drove his carriage down a street he knew well and remained in the seat, watching something in a corral beyond a low fence. A crowd of white men were mulling in a yard. Saddle horses were strung along all the near hitching bars; and wherever there was space, driving rigs were hitched.

Ben could see the slave block from his seat, could hear the auctioneer's voice, but he had been watching a long while before he realized that the brown girl up for bids was Gabriel's Juba, the tempestuous wench with the slim hips and the savage mop of hair. Her feet were bare. Her clothes were scant. And there was something about her figure, something about the bold rise of her exposed breasts, that put gooseflesh on a man. But her look was downcast, bitter, almost threatening.

Yet the bidding continued lively. Ben decided abruptly that he did not wish to see it through. He pulled on his lines and began threading a way through the thronged carriages of the planters. It was definitely going to rain.

Ben was waiting at a curb for Marse Sheppard when the first flurry came. Then the silvered old man, wrapped to the eyes in his cape, came out, and they started home in the downpour. When they were in the heart of town, lightning flashed, and Ben saw an array of bright red and yellow and green and purple parasols suddenly raised. Men dashed across the wet street, seeking shelter in shops. Carriages jostled. Voices called in the rain and received something better than their own echoes for answer. The clouds bore down. The air had a melancholy sweetness. But Ben could not forget Gabriel's shining naked body or the arc inscribed by the executioner's ax. He could not feel reassured about the knives that waited for him with the sweet brown thrashers in every hedge and clump. For him the rain-swept streets had a carnival sadness.

The little mare's feet played a soothing tune on the cobble-stones.

CHRONOLOGY

BIOGRAPHICAL NOTES

NOTE ON THE TEXTS

NOTES

Chronology

1919   February 17: Returning veterans of the Fifteenth Regiment of New York's National Guard march triumphally through Harlem. February 19–21: While the Paris Peace Conference is taking place, W.E.B. Du Bois organizes Pan-African Conference in Paris, attended by fifty-seven delegates from the United States, the West Indies, Europe, and Africa; conference calls for acknowledgment and protection of the rights of Africans under colonial rule. March: Release of *The Homesteader*, directed and produced by self-published novelist and entrepreneur Oscar Micheaux, first feature-length film by an African American. May: Hair-care entrepreneur Madam C. J. Walker dies at her estate in Irvington, New York; her daughter A'Lelia Walker assumes control of the Madam C.J. Walker Manufacturing Company. May–October: In what becomes known as "the Red Summer," racial conflicts boil over in the wake of the return of African American veterans; incidents of racial violence erupt across the United States, including outbreaks in Charleston, South Carolina; Longview, Texas; Omaha; Washington, D.C.; Chicago; Knoxville; and Elaine, Arkansas. June: Marcus Garvey establishes his Black Star Line (the shipping concern will operate until 1922). July: Claude McKay's poem "If We Must Die," written in response to the summer of violence, appears in Max Eastman's magazine *The Liberator*. September: Jessie Redmon Fauset joins staff of *The Crisis*, the literary magazine of the NAACP founded in 1910, as literary editor.

1920   January: *The Brownie's Book*, a magazine for African American children, founded by W.E.B. Du Bois with Jessie Redmon Fauset and Augustus Dill, begins its run of twenty-four issues. Oscar Micheaux releases the anti-lynching film, *Within Our Gates*, an answer both to D. W. Griffith's inflammatory *The Birth of a Nation* (1915) and the Red Summer of 1919. April: In an article in *The Crisis*, W.E.B. Du Bois writes: "A renaissance of American Negro literature is due." August: The Universal Negro Improvement Association (UNIA), founded by Jamaican immigrant and Pan-Africanist Marcus Garvey, holds its first convention at Madison Square Garden in New York City, attended by some 25,000 delegates. November: James Weldon Johnson becomes executive secretary (and first black officer) of the NAACP. Mamie Smith's "Crazy Blues" is released by Okeh Records. Eugene O'Neill's *The Emperor Jones*, starring Charles Gilpin, opens at the Provincetown Playhouse in Greenwich Village.

Books

W.E.B. Du Bois: *Darkwater: Voices from Within the Veil* (Harcourt, Brace & Howe)

Claude McKay: *Spring in New Hampshire and Other Poems* (Grant Richards)

1921   February: Max Eastman invites Claude McKay, just returned from England, to become associate editor of *The Liberator*. March: Harry Pace forms Black Swan Phonograph Company, one of the first black-owned record companies in Harlem; its most successful recording artist is Ethel Waters. May: *Shuffle Along*, a pioneering all–African American production, with book by Flournoy Miller and Aubrey Lyles and music and lyrics by Eubie Blake and Noble Sissle, opens on Broadway and becomes a hit. It showcases such stars as Florence Mills and Josephine Baker. June: Langston Hughes publishes his poem "The Negro Speaks of Rivers" in *The Crisis*. August–September: Exhibit of African American art at the 135th Street branch of the New York Public Library, including work by Henry Ossawa Tanner, Meta Fuller, and Laura Wheeler Waring. December: René Maran, a native of Martinique, becomes the first black recipient of the Prix Goncourt, for his novel *Batouala*; soon translated into English, it will be widely discussed in the African American press.

1922   January: The Dyer Anti-Lynching Bill is passed by the House of Representatives; it is subsequently blocked in the Senate. Spring: *Birthright*, novel of African American life by the white novelist T. S. Stribling, is published by Century Publications. (Oscar Micheaux will make two films based on the book, in 1924 and 1938.) White real estate magnate William E. Harmon establishes the Harmon Foundation to advance African American achievements.

Books

Georgia Douglas Johnson: *Bronze* (B. J. Brimmer)

James Weldon Johnson, editor: *The Book of American Negro Poetry* (Harcourt, Brace)

Claude McKay: *Harlem Shadows* (Harcourt, Brace; expanded version of *Spring in New Hampshire*)

T. S. Stribling: *Birthright* (Century)

1923   January: *Opportunity: A Journal of Negro Life*, published by the National Urban League and edited by sociologist Charles S. Johnson, is founded. Claude McKay addresses the Fourth Congress of the Third International in Moscow. February: Bessie Smith's "Downhearted Blues" (written and originally recorded by Alberta Hunter) is released by Columbia Records and sells nearly a million copies within six months. May: Willis Richardson's *The Chip Woman*, produced by the National Ethiopian Art Players, becomes the first serious play by an African American playwright to open on Broadway. June: Marcus Garvey receives a five-year sentence for mail fraud. December: Tenor Roland Hayes, having won acclaim in London as a singer of classical music, gives a concert of lieder and spirituals at Town Hall in New York. *The Messenger*, founded in 1917 by Asa Philip Randolph and Chandler Owen as a black trade unionist magazine with socialist sympathies, begins publishing more literary material under editorial guidance of George S. Schuyler and Theophilus Lewis.

Books
Marcus Garvey: *Philosophy and Opinion of Marcus Garvey* (Universal Publishing House)

Jean Toomer: *Cane* (Boni & Liveright)

1924   March: The Civic Club dinner, held in honor of Jessie Redmon Fauset on publishing her first novel *There Is Confusion*, is sponsored by *Opportunity* and Charles S. Johnson. Those in attendance include Alain Locke, W.E.B. Du Bois, Countee Cullen, Eric Walrond, Gwendolyn Bennett, and such representatives of the New York publishing world as Alfred A. Knopf and Horace Liveright. (In retrospect the occasion is often taken to mark the beginning of the Harlem Renaissance.) May: W.E.B. Du Bois attacks Marcus Garvey in *The Crisis* article "A Lunatic or a Traitor." Eugene O'Neill's play *All God's Chillun Got Wings*, starring Paul Robeson and controversial for its theme of miscegenation, opens. Autumn: Countee Cullen is the first recipient of Witter Bynner Poetry Competition. September: René Maran publishes poems by Countee Cullen, Langston Hughes, Claude McKay, and Jean Toomer in his Paris newspaper, *Les Continents*. Louis Armstrong comes to New York from Chicago to join Fletcher Henderson's band at the Roseland Ballroom.

Books

W.E.B. Du Bois: *The Gift of Black Folk: The Negroes in the Making of America* (Stratford)

Jessie Redmon Fauset: *There Is Confusion* (Boni & Liveright)

Walter White: *The Fire in the Flint* (Knopf)

1925   February: After his appeals are denied, Marcus Garvey begins serving his sentence for mail fraud at Atlanta Federal Penitentiary. March: Howard Philosophy Professor Alain Locke edits a special issue of *The Survey Graphic* titled "Harlem: Mecca of the New Negro"; in November *The New Negro*, an expanded book version, is published by Albert and Charles Boni. The volume features six pages of painter Aaron Douglas's African-inspired illustrations, and includes writing by Jean Toomer, Rudolph Fisher, Zora Neale Hurston, Eric Walrond, Countee Cullen, James Weldon Johnson, Langston Hughes, Georgia Douglas Johnson, Richard Bruce Nugent, Anne Spencer, Claude McKay, Jessie Redmon Fauset, Arthur Schomburg, Charles S. Johnson, W.E.B. Du Bois, and E. Franklin Frazier. May: *Opportunity* holds its first awards dinner, recognizing, among others, Langston Hughes ("The Weary Blues," first prize), Countee Cullen, Zora Neale Hurston, Eric Walrond, and Sterling Brown. Paul Robeson appears at Greenwich Village Theatre in a concert entirely devoted to spirituals, accompanied by Lawrence Brown. August: A. Phillip Randolph organizes the Brotherhood of Sleeping Car Porters. October: The American Negro Labor Congress is founded in Chicago. November: First prize of *The Crisis* awards goes to poet Countee Cullen. Paul Robeson stars in Oscar Micheaux's film *Body and Soul*. December: Marita Bonner publishes essay "On Being Young—A Woman—And Colored" in *The Crisis*, about the predicament and possibilities of the educated black woman.

Books

Countee Cullen: *Color* (Harper)

James Weldon Johnson and J. Rosamond Johnson, editors: *The Book of American Negro Spirituals* (Viking Press)

Alain Locke, editor: *The New Negro: An Interpretation* (Albert and Charles Boni)

1926   January: The Harmon Foundation announces its first awards for artistic achievement by African Americans. Palmer Hayden, a World War I veteran and menial laborer, wins the gold medal for painting. February: Jessie Redmon Fauset steps down as editor of *The Crisis*. The play *Lulu Belle*, starring Lenore Ulric in blackface as well as the African American actress Edna Thomas, opens to great success on Broadway; it helps create a vogue of whites frequenting Harlem nightspots. March: The Savoy Ballroom opens on Lenox Avenue between 140th and 141st Streets. June: Successive issues of *The Nation* feature Langston Hughes's "The Negro Artist and the Racial Mountain" and George S. Schuyler's "The Negro-Art Hokum." July: W.E.B. Du Bois founds Krigwa Players, Harlem theater group devoted to plays depicting African American life. August: Carl Van Vechten, white novelist and close friend to many Negro Renaissance figures, publishes his roman à clef, *Nigger Heaven*, with Knopf. Although many of his friends—including James Weldon Johnson, Nella Larsen, and Langston Hughes—are supportive, the book is widely disliked by African American readers, and notably condemned by W.E.B. Du Bois. October: Arthur Schomburg's collection of thousands of books, manuscripts, and artworks is purchased for the New York Public Library by the Carnegie Corporation; it will form the basis of what will become the Schomburg Center for Research in Black Culture. November: *Fire!!*, a journal edited by Wallace Thurman, makes its sole appearance. Contributors include Langston Hughes, Zora Neale Hurston, and Gwendolyn Bennett, among others. "Smoke, Lilies and Jade," a short story by Richard Bruce Nugent published in *Fire!!*, shocks many by its delineation of a homosexual liaison as well as by Nugent's suggestive line drawings. Most copies are accidentally destroyed in a fire. December: Countee Cullen begins contributing a column, "The Dark Tower," to *Opportunity*. (It will run until September 1928.)

Books
W. C. Handy, editor: *Blues: An Anthology* (Boni & Boni)
Langston Hughes: *The Weary Blues* (Knopf)
Alain Locke, editor: *Four Negro Poets* (Simon & Schuster)

Carl Van Vechten: *Nigger Heaven* (Knopf)

Eric Walrond: *Tropic Death* (Boni & Liveright; story collection)

Walter White: *Flight* (Knopf)

1927   July: Ethel Waters stars on Broadway in the revue *Africana*. August: Rudolph Fisher's essay "The Caucasian Storms Harlem" is published in *The American Mercury*. September: James Weldon Johnson's *The Autobiography of an Ex-Colored Man*, first published anonymously in 1912, is republished by Knopf. October: A'Lelia Walker, cosmetics heiress and Harlem socialite, opens The Dark Tower, a tearoom intended as a cultural gathering place, at her home on West 130th Street: "We dedicate this tower to the aesthetes. That cultural group of young Negro writers, sculptors, painters, music artists, composers, and their friends." The Theatre Guild production of DuBose Heyward's play *Porgy*, with an African American cast, opens to great success. December: Marcus Garvey, pardoned by Calvin Coolidge after serving more than half of five-year sentence for mail fraud, is deported. Duke Ellington and his orchestra begin what will prove a years-long engagement at the Cotton Club of Harlem.

Books

Countee Cullen: *Copper Sun* (Harper)

Countee Cullen, editor: *Caroling Dusk: An Anthology of Verse by Negro Poets* (Harper)

Langston Hughes: *Fine Clothes to the Jew* (Knopf)

Charles S. Johnson, editor: *Ebony and Topaz* (Journal of Negro Life/National Urban League)

James Weldon Johnson: *God's Trombones: Seven Negro Sermons in Verse* (Knopf)

Alain Locke and Montgomery Gregory, editors: *Plays of Negro Life* (Harper)

1928   January: The first Harmon Foundation art exhibition opens at New York's International House. April 9: Countee Cullen marries Nina Yolande, daughter of W.E.B. Du Bois; the wedding is a major social event, attended by thousands of people. (The marriage breaks up several months later.) May: Bill "Bojangles" Robinson appears on Broadway in the revue *Blackbirds of 1928*. June: *The Messenger* ceases publication when the Brotherhood of Sleeping Car Porters can no longer financially support the journal. November:

Wallace Thurman publishes the first and only issue of the magazine *Harlem: A Forum of Negro Life*.

Books

W.E.B. Du Bois: *Dark Princess: A Romance* (Harcourt, Brace)

Jessie Redmon Fauset: *Plum Bun* (Frederick Stokes)

Rudolph Fisher: *The Walls of Jericho* (Knopf)

Georgia Douglas Johnson: *An Autumn Love Cycle* (Harold Vinal)

Nella Larsen: *Quicksand* (Knopf)

Claude McKay: *Home to Harlem* (Harper)

1929   February: *Harlem*, co-authored by Wallace Thurman and William Rapp, opens on Broadway to mixed reviews. Archibald Motley, Jr. wins gold medal for painting from the Harmon Foundation. October 29: The New York stock market plunges, eliminating much of the funding powering "New Negro" literature and arts.

Books

Countee Cullen: *The Black Christ and Other Poems* (Harper)

Nella Larsen: *Passing* (Knopf)

Claude McKay: *Banjo: A Story Without a Plot* (Harper)

Wallace Thurman: *The Blacker the Berry* (Macaulay)

Walter White: *Rope and Faggot: A Biography of Judge Lynch* (Knopf)

1930   February: *The Green Pastures*, a play by Marc Connelly, based on Roark Bradford's *Ol' Man Adam an' His Chillun* (1928), opens on Broadway with an all-black cast; it will be one of the most successful plays of its era. July: The Nation of Islam, colloquially known as the Black Muslims, founded by W. D. Fard in Detroit at the Islam Temple. Dancer and anthropology student Katharine Dunham founds Ballet Nègre in Chicago. James Weldon Johnson publishes a limited edition of "Saint Peter Relates an Incident of the Resurrection Day," a poem protesting the insulting treatment accorded to African American Gold Star Mothers visiting American cemeteries in Europe.

Books

Langston Hughes: *Not Without Laughter* (Macmillan)

Charles S. Johnson: *The Negro in American Civilization: A Study of Negro Life and Race Relations* (Henry Holt)

James Weldon Johnson: *Black Manhattan* (Knopf)

James Weldon Johnson: *Saint Peter Relates an Incident of the Resurrection Day* (Viking Press)

1931   April–July: The "Scottsboro Boys," a group of young African American men accused of raping two white women, are tried and convicted; a massive, lengthy, and only partly successful campaign to free them begins. Sculptor Augusta Savage, whose real-life rebuff by the white art establishment becomes part of the back story for *Plum Bun*, establishes the Savage Studio of Arts and Crafts in Harlem.

Books

Arna Bontemps: *God Sends Sunday* (Harcourt, Brace)
Sterling Brown: *Outline for the Study of Poetry of American Negroes* (Harcourt, Brace)
Countee Cullen: *One Way to Heaven* (Harper)
Jessie Redmon Fauset: *The Chinaberry Tree* (Frederick Stokes)
Langston Hughes: *Dear Lovely Death* (Troutbeck Press)
George S. Schuyler: *Black No More* (Macaulay)
Jean Toomer: *Essentials: Definitions and Aphorisms* (Lakeside Press)

1932   June: Langston Hughes, Dorothy West, Louise Thompson, and more than a dozen other African Americans travel to the Soviet Union to film *Black and White*, a movie about American racism. (Due to shifting Soviet policies, the movie will never be made.)

Books

Sterling Brown: *Southern Road* (Harcourt, Brace)
Rudolph Fisher: *The Conjure-Man Dies* (Covici-Friede)
Langston Hughes: *The Dream Keeper* (Knopf)
Claude McKay: *Gingertown* (Harper; story collection)
George S. Schuyler: *Slaves Today* (Brewer, Warren, and Putnam)
Wallace Thurman: *Infants of the Spring* (Macaulay)
Wallace Thurman and Abraham Furman: *Interne* (Macaulay)

1933   **Books**

Jessie Redmon Fauset: *Comedy: American Style* (Frederick A. Stokes)
James Weldon Johnson: *Along This Way* (Knopf)

Alain Locke: *The Negro in America* (American Library Association)

Claude McKay: *Banana Bottom* (Harper)

1934 January: The Apollo Theater opens. February: *Negro*, an anthology of work by and about African Americans, edited by Nancy Cunard, is published by Wishart in London. March: Dorothy West founds the magazine *Challenge*. May: W.E.B. Du Bois resigns from the NAACP; he is replaced as editor of *The Crisis* by Roy Wilkins. November: Aaron Douglas completes *Aspects of Negro Life*, four murals commissioned by the New York Public Library. December: Wallace Thurman and Rudolph Fisher die within days of one another. Richard Wright writes the initial draft of his first novel, *Lawd Today*, published posthumously in 1963. M. B. Tolson completes sequence of poems *A Gallery of Harlem Portraits*, published posthumously in 1979.

Books

Langston Hughes: *The Ways of White Folks* (Knopf; story collection)

Zora Neale Hurston: *Jonah's Gourd Vine* (Lippincott)

James Weldon Johnson: *Negro Americans, What Now?* (Viking Press)

1935 March 19: A riot sparked by rumors of white violence against a Puerto Rican youth results in three African American deaths and millions of dollars in damage to white-owned properties. April: In "Harlem Runs Wild," published in *The Nation*, Claude McKay asserts that the riot is "the gesture of despair of a bewildered, baffled, and disillusioned people." The Works Progress Administration (WPA) established by U.S. President Franklin Delano Roosevelt; writers and artists who will eventually find employment under its aegis include Richard Wright, Ralph Ellison, Dorothy West, Margaret Walker, Augusta Savage, Romare Bearden, and Jacob Lawrence. October: Langston Hughes's play *Mulatto* and George Gershwin's opera *Porgy and Bess* open on Broadway.

Books

Countee Cullen: *The Medea and Some Poems* (Harper)

Frank Marshall Davis: *Black Man's Verse* (Black Cat Press)

W.E.B. Du Bois: *Black Reconstruction in America, 1860–1880* (Harcourt, Brace)

Zora Neale Hurston: *Mules and Men* (Lippincott)
James Weldon Johnson: *Saint Peter Relates an Incident:
Selected Poems* (Viking Press)

1936   February: The National Negro Congress, representing
some 600 organizations, holds its first meeting in Chicago.
June: Mary McLeod Bethune is appointed Director of the
Division of Negro Affairs of the National Youth Administration, becoming the highest-ranking African American
official of the Roosevelt administration.

Books
Arna Bontemps: *Black Thunder* (Macmillan)
Alain Locke: *Negro Art—Past and Present* (Associates in
Negro Folk Education)
Alain Locke: *The Negro and His Music* (Associates in Ne-
gro Folk Education)

Biographical Notes

Langston Hughes   Born James Langston Hughes in Joplin, Missouri, on February 1, 1902, son of James Nathaniel Hughes, a stenographer for a mining company, and Carrie Mercer Langston Hughes, an aspiring writer and actress. (In later years, Hughes used the form James Langston Mercer Hughes as his full name.) Hughes's father left the family shortly after his son's birth, relocating to Mexico. In the absence of his father, and with his mother also frequently away, Hughes was raised mostly by his grandmother, Mary Langston, in Lawrence, Kansas. (Mary Langston's first husband, Lewis Leary, was an associate of John Brown who was killed in the Harpers Ferry raid in 1859; her second husband was also an abolitionist.) After briefly reuniting with his mother in Topeka, Kansas, in 1907, Hughes returned to Lawrence to live with his grandmother until her death in 1915. Subsequently he lived with his mother and her second husband in Lincoln, Illinois, and Cleveland, Ohio. He began to publish poems and stories in school publications. After graduating high school he spent a year with his father in Mexico; relations between the two were stormy, as Hughes's literary ambitions were strongly opposed by his father. He published the poem "The Negro Speaks of Rivers" in *The Crisis* in June 1921, and that autumn began attending Columbia University with support from his father (and majoring in engineering at his father's request); he left Columbia after a year following a break with his father. In Harlem he formed friendships with Jessie Redmon Fauset, Countee Cullen, and other writers. A series of odd jobs was followed in 1923 by a job on a steamship which visited ports in West Africa; the following year he worked his way to Europe but jumped ship and remained in Paris, working at a jazz club in Montmartre. He returned to the United States in 1925, living with his mother in Washington, D.C. for a year before settling in Harlem. He continued to befriend many writers, including Alain Locke, Arna Bontemps, Wallace Thurman, and Carl Van Vechten. In 1926 he published his first collection of poems, *The Weary Blues*, as well as the essay "The Negro Artist and the Racial Mountain"; a second poetry collection, *Fine Clothes to the Jew*, appeared the next year. From 1926 to 1929 he attended Lincoln University in Pennsylvania. A wealthy white woman, Charlotte Mason (whom at her request he referred to as "Godmother"), supported him for three years, underwriting trips to Cuba (1930) and Haiti (1931) and encouraging his first novel, *Not Without*

Laughter, published in 1930; the relationship with Mason ended abruptly the same year when she broke with him for reasons not clear to him. Around the same time his friendship with Zora Neale Hurston ended as the result of a quarrel over the authorship of a play, *Mulebone*, on which they had collaborated. Hughes continued to work prolifically in a range of genres, collaborating with Arna Bontemps on the children's book *Popo and Fifina* (1932), and publishing the poetry collections *Dear Lovely Death* (1931) and *The Negro Mother* (1931) and the story collection *The Ways of White Folks* (1934). With Louise Thompson and a contingent of African American writers and intellectuals he traveled to the Soviet Union in 1932 for the purpose of making a film, never realized, about American race relations. He remained in the Soviet Union, traveling widely in Soviet Asia and going in 1933 to China and Japan; he was expelled from Japan for leftist activities and arrived in San Francisco in August 1933. After residences in Carmel, California, and Mexico (where he lived for a time with the photographer Henri Cartier-Bresson), Hughes returned to New York, where his play *Mulatto* opened in 1935 despite Hughes's protests against changes made by the producers. He traveled to Europe and addressed the Paris Writers' Congress in July 1937, meeting Bertolt Brecht, W. H. Auden, and many others; in Spain, where he reported on the civil war for the Baltimore *Afro-American*, he stayed for three months in Madrid while it was under siege; the following year he returned to Paris with Theodore Dreiser to address a conference of the International Association of Writers. A collection of radical poems, *A New Song*, was published in 1938 by the International Workers Order, and the memoir *The Big Sea*, focusing on his travels in the 1920s, appeared in 1940. In the following year Hughes lived briefly in Los Angeles (where he wrote a film script) and Chicago before settling again in Harlem in 1941. Knopf published the poetry collection *Shakespeare in Harlem* in 1942. His newspaper column "Here to Yonder," which began appearing in the Chicago *Defender* in November 1942, introduced in 1943 the character Jesse B. Semple ("Simple"); these columns were ultimately collected in a popular series of books, beginning with *Simple Speaks His Mind* (1950). Hughes's involvement in many left-wing and anti-fascist organizations came under steady right-wing attack during the 1940s and was denounced repeatedly in testimony before the House Un-American Activities Committee. Beginning in 1944 he organized national reading tours which helped provide him with financial support. In 1953 he was subpoenaed to testify before Senator Joseph McCarthy's anti-subversive subcommittee, and gave testimony disavowing communism but not implicating any individuals. In addition to the Simple books, Hughes in the postwar period published the poetry collections *Fields of Wonder* (1947), *Montage of a Dream Deferred* (1951), *Selected Poems* (1959), and *Ask Your Mama: 12 Moods for Jazz* (1961); the memoir *I Wonder As I Wander* (1954); the story collection *Laughing to Keep From Crying* (1952); the novella *Tambourines to Glory* (1958, based on Hughes's 1956 musical play); and a series of books for children. He continued to be involved in a range of musical and theatrical projects, collaborating with Kurt Weill on *Street Scene* (1947) and William Grant Still on *Troubled Island* (1949). He gave readings of his poetry accompanied by bassist Charles Mingus, published translations of Gabriela Mistral and Federico Garcia Lorca, collaborated with photographer Roy DeCarava on *The Sweet Flypaper of Life* (1955), and with Arna Bontemps edited the anthology *The Poetry of the Negro, 1746–1949* (1949). He was elected in 1961 to membership in the National Institute of Arts and Letters. During the 1960s Hughes traveled widely, making repeated visits to Africa and Europe, and participating in a State Department–sponsored tour of Senegal, Nigeria, Ethiopia, and Tanzania in 1966. A private man, Hughes never married and is not known to have had a longtime companion. He died of complications following prostate surgery on May 22, 1967. The poetry collection *The Panther and the Lash: Poems of Our Times* was published posthumously the same year.

George S. Schuyler   Born George Samuel Schuyler on February 25, 1895; his birthplace was Providence, Rhode Island, according to Schuyler's account, although little direct evidence supports this. His parents were George Frances, a chef, and Eliza Jane Fischer Schuyler, a cook; it has been speculated that he may have been adopted. After his father died when he was three, he was raised in Syracuse, New York, by his mother, who remarried in 1900, and his grandmother Helen Fischer. At seventeen he dropped out of high school and enlisted in the Armed Services, joining the 25th Infantry and serving in Seattle and Hawaii; eventually he became a drill instructor and rose to the rank of first lieutenant at Fort Des Moines, Iowa. While based in Hawaii he began to contribute writing to the *Honolulu Commercial Advertiser* and other local publications. With a racist incident in 1918 as catalyst, Schuyler deserted; after turning himself in, he was sentenced to five years on Governor's Island in New York, a term finally reduced to nine months. (Until the end of his life Schuyler never acknowledged this episode.) He worked as an army clerk during and after his imprisonment; discharged at the end of the war, he held a succession of low-paying jobs (porter, factory worker, dishwasher) and returned briefly to live in Syracuse, where he worked in construction. He joined the Socialist Party in 1921 and served as the party's educational director in Syracuse. Returning to New York, he took a room in Harlem and immersed himself in literary and political currents, attending Garveyite meetings at Liberty Hall and taking classes at the Rand School, where his teachers included Thorstein Veblen. Out of work, he lived briefly with a group of hobos in a church basement on the Lower East Side before being hired in 1923 as office messenger and staff writer for *The Messenger*, edited by A. Phillip Randolph and Chandler Owen. He remained at the magazine until it closed in 1928, contributing a column, "Shafts and Darts: A Page of Calumny and Satire," along with much other writing, including stories, essays, and reviews. In 1925 he was invited by the *Pittsburgh Courier* to contribute a weekly column, which after several name changes became "Views and Reviews" and which he continued to write until 1966. Schuyler wrote for many other print outlets as well, including *The Nation*, *The Crisis*, and *The American Mercury*, whose editor H. L. Mencken was an enthusiastic supporter of Schuyler's work. For the *Courier* Schuyler undertook a lengthy investigative tour of the South (1925–26), resulting in the series "Aframerica Today." In January 1928 he married Josephine Codgell, the daughter of a wealthy Texas banker and cattle rancher; their daughter Philippa was born in 1931. The interracial marriage—which Schuyler discussed in "Racial Intermarriage in the United States" (1928)—along with Philippa's recognition as a child prodigy on the piano (as well as her exceptionally high scores on intelligence tests) brought much media attention to the Schuylers. His satirical novel *Black No More* was published by the Macaulay Company in 1931. A second novel, *Slaves Today: A Story of Liberia* (1932), grew out of Schuyler's 1931 trip to Liberia to investigate allegations of domestic slavery as well as the use of forced labor by the Firestone Rubber Company. (In articles and in his novel, Schuyler affirmed the practice of slavery but exonerated Firestone.) Schuyler also published in the *Courier*, under pseudonyms, a series of novellas with African settings, including "Devil Town" (1933), "Golden Gods" (1933–34), "Strange Valley" (1934), "The Ethiopian Murder Mystery" (1935–36), "The Black Internationale" (1936–37), "Black Empire" (1937–38), and "Revolt in Ethiopia" (1938–39). Schuyler vigorously protested the Italian invasion of Ethiopia and the U.S. internment of Japanese Americans during World War II. In other respects, his political views moved steadily to the right. He published *The Communist Conspiracy Against the Negroes* in 1947, and supported the anticommunist campaign of Senator Joseph McCarthy. A virulent attack on Dr. Martin Luther King, Jr. in 1964 attracted much attention, and the *Courier* dismissed him two years later. Subsequently Schuyler published *Black and Conservative: The Autobiography of George S. Schuyler* (1966) and contributed to the conservative New Hampshire newspaper *Manchester Union Leader*, which had published the attack on King; he had joined the

John Birch Society in 1965 and began to write for its publications. Philippa Schuyler became a journalist in the 1960s, and while on a humanitarian mission in Vietnam was killed in a U.S. Army helicopter crash in 1967. Schuyler's wife, who had been in declining health, committed suicide in 1969. Schuyler died on August 31, 1977, at New York Hospital.

Rudolph Fisher   Born Rudolph John Chauncey Fisher on May 9, 1897, in Washington, D.C., one of three children of Reverend John Wesley Fisher and Glendora Williamson Fisher. As a small child, Fisher moved with the family to Providence, Rhode Island, where he attended public schools, graduating with honors from Classical High School. In 1919 he graduated from Brown University with a BA in English and biology, and a year later received an MA from Brown. In addition, he won prizes in German and public speaking, and was elected to Phi Beta Kappa. While at Brown he formed a friendship with Paul Robeson (a fellow Phi Beta Kappa attending Rutgers), whom he would sometimes accompany on piano. He received a medical degree from Howard University in 1924. Following graduation he took up a residency at the Freedman's Hospital in Washington, D.C., and a postdoctoral fellowship at Columbia University Hospital, working in bacteriology. His work on viruses and ultraviolet rays led to the publication of two scientific articles, one in the *Journal of Infectious Diseases*. He married Jane Ryder, an elementary school teacher, in 1924; their son Hugh was born two years later. He had begun writing while in college, and his story "The City of Refuge" was published in *The Atlantic Monthly* in 1925, and reprinted the same year in Alain Locke's anthology *The New Negro* (1925) along with "Vestiges: Harlem Sketches." He worked at Bronx and Mount Sinai hospitals in New York before opening a private practice and X-ray laboratory in Harlem in the late 1920s; he was head of the roentgenology department at International Hospital in Manhattan, 1930–32. During the same period he moved to Jamaica, Queens, where he relocated his private practice. Fisher (known to his friends as "Bud") socialized widely in Harlem, and was described by Langston Hughes (in his memoir *The Big Sea*) as "the wittiest of these New Negroes of Harlem . . . who always frightened me a little, because he could think of the most incisively clever things to say—and I could never think of anything to answer." Fisher contributed an article on Harlem nightlife, "The Caucasian Storms Harlem," to H. L. Mencken's *American Mercury* in 1927. In a 1933 radio interview he remarked: "If I should be fortunate enough to become known as Harlem's interpreter, I should be very happy." Other short stories appeared in *The Atlantic Monthly, McClure's Magazine, The Crisis, Opportunity,* and *Story Magazine,* and he published reviews of

books by George S. Schuyler, Jessie Redmon Fauset, Wallace Thurman, Countee Cullen, and Claude McKay in the *New York Herald
Tribune*. His first novel, *The Walls of Jericho*, was published in 1928 by
Knopf. *The Conjure-Man Dies*, often described as the first detective
novel written by an African American, was published in 1932 by Covici-
Friede. Fisher underwent a series of stomach operations during 1934,
and died on December 26, 1934, at Edgecombe Sanitarium in Harlem
(Wallace Thurman had died four days earlier). As an officer with the
reserve medical corps of the New York National Guard's 369th Infantry, Fisher was buried with an honor guard from his unit in attendance.
A dramatization of *The Conjure-Man Dies* was produced in Harlem
by the Federal Theater Project in 1936. (Fisher's stories were collected
posthumously in 1991 in *The City of Refuge: The Collected Stories of
Rudolph Fisher*, edited by John McCluskey, Jr.)

Arna Bontemps   Born Arnaud Wendell Bontemps on October
13, 1902, in Alexandria, Louisiana, to Paul Bismark Bontemps, a brick
and stone mason also sometimes employed as a jazz trombonist, and
his wife Maria Caroline, a public school teacher. In 1906 Bontemps
moved with his parents and his mother's parents to California, where
they were eventually joined by other members of the extended family,
settling in the "Furlough Track," a rural area north of Watts in Los
Angeles. During the first year in California, his parents left the Catholic church and converted to Seventh Day Adventism, his father becoming a lay minister. Bontemps's mother died in 1914. He attended
predominantly white Adventist schools in Los Angeles, graduating
from Pacific Union College in 1923. He spent much time reading in-
dependently at the Los Angeles Public Library, and early on developed
an interest in African American history. Following graduation he went
to work in the post office; after he had a poem accepted by *The Crisis*
he decided (apparently on the advice of his friend Wallace Thurman)
to move to New York. Of his first year in the city he would write: "In
some places the autumn of 1924 may have been an unremarkable season. In Harlem it was like a foretaste of paradise." Supporting himself
by teaching at the Adventist high school Harlem Academy, he continued to publish poems, winning several prizes; worked on a novel
which remained unfinished; and immersed himself in the social and
cultural life of Harlem. Countee Cullen introduced Bontemps to Langston Hughes, with whom he formed a lifelong friendship. In 1926 he
married Alberta Johnson; they had six children, born between 1927
and 1945. His novel *God Sends Sunday*, inspired by the wandering life
of his great-uncle Joseph Ward ("Uncle Buddy"), was published in
1931 by Harcourt, Brace; the book received some good reviews but
was condemned by W.E.B. Du Bois for its "low-life" subject matter.

After Harlem Academy closed, Bontemps relocated to Huntsville, Alabama where he taught at the Adventist-affiliated Oakwood College, 1931–34. He was unhappy at Oakwood and came under criticism from the school's conservative and theologically rigid directors, but continued to keep in touch with Cullen and Hughes; with Cullen he collaborated on a dramatization of *God Sends Sunday*, which was produced in Cleveland in 1934, and with Hughes he wrote a children's book, *Popo and Fifina: Children of Haiti*, published by Macmillan in 1932. After resigning his position at Oakwood he returned to his father's home in Watts, where he completed his second novel, *Black Thunder*, based on the Gabriel Prosser slave revolt of 1800, published by Macmillan in 1936. He moved to Chicago, serving as principal of another Adventist school, Shiloh Academy, 1936–38, until conflicts with the school's administration led to his withdrawal from the Adventist church. He found employment with the Illinois Writers Project while pursuing graduate studies at the University of Chicago. Another historical novel, *Drums at Dusk*, about the Haitian revolution, appeared in 1939. He completed a degree in library science in 1943 and was hired as head librarian at Fisk University, where he remained on staff until 1966 and achieved preeminence as a pioneering archivist and historian in the field of African American studies. In 1946 *St. Louis Woman*, the musical dramatization of *God Sends Sunday* on which he and Countee Cullen had continued to work for years, opened successfully on Broadway. After retiring from Fisk in the 1960s, Bontemps taught at the University of Illinois and Yale University as a visiting professor. In addition to numerous volumes of fiction and nonfiction, much of it aimed at young adult readers, he edited a number of anthologies, including *The Poetry of the Negro, 1746–1949* (with Langston Hughes, 1949), *The Book of Negro Folklore* (also with Hughes, 1958), and *American Negro Poetry* (1963). He died on June 4, 1973 of heart failure.

Note on the Texts

This volume collects four novels—*Not Without Laughter* (1930), by Langston Hughes; *Black No More* (1931), by George S. Schuyler; *The Conjure-Man Dies* (1932), by Rudolph Fisher; and *Black Thunder* (1936), by Arna Bontemps—associated with what has come to be known as the Harlem Renaissance, a period of great creativity and change in African American cultural life, with its epicenter in New York's Harlem neighborhood. A companion volume in the Library of America series, *Harlem Renaissance: Five Novels of the 1920s*, vol. 1, presents five earlier novels: Jean Toomer's *Cane* (1923), Claude McKay's *Home to Harlem* (1928), Nella Larsen's *Quicksand* (1928), Jessie Redmon Fauset's *Plum Bun* (1928), and Wallace Thurman's *The Blacker the Berry* (1929). The texts of all of these novels have been taken from the first printings of the first editions.

Not Without Laughter. Though Langston Hughes had written short stories and two books of poetry—*The Weary Blues* (1926) and *Fine Clothes to the Jew* (1927)—he was reluctant, at first, to tackle the longer form of the novel. He was encouraged to do so by a new patron, Charlotte Mason, who suggested the goal in August 1927 and then in November added a proposal of financial assistance: she would provide Hughes a regular stipend for a year (or longer, if their arrangement proved successful), freeing him of the need to support himself. Hughes would retain the rights to his work, but in return Mason expected to be regularly apprised of his progress. Accepting Mason's terms, Hughes finished his junior year at Lincoln University and then began "The Novel" (as his first draft was called) in June 1928. He finished the draft within about six weeks, in mid-August. "At first I did a chapter or two a day," he later recalled in his autobiography *The Big Sea* (1940), "and revised them the next day. But they seemed bad; in fact, so bad I finally decided to write the whole story straight through to the end before re-reading anything." Hughes made further revisions to the initial draft during the fall (his hand-corrected typescript bears the date December 19, 1928), but he did not return to full-time work on the book until the summer of 1929, after his graduation. In May 1929, Mason sent Hughes a twenty-four-page letter offering detailed comments on his initial draft, enthusiastically praising some sections, recommending "literary welding together" for the whole, and at points registering her objections: "the quality of the writing . . . becomes

834

self-conscious, and has the air of the author's propaganda." (She also dissuaded him from using the titles *So Moves This Swift World* and *Roots of Dawn*; the former, she explained, was "not characteristic enough of you and your writing, which is always original and arresting.")

One scholar has argued that this "literary censorship" on Mason's part "forced Hughes to suppress his increasingly strong left-wing political notions in the novel" (see John P. Shields, "'Never Cross the Divide': Reconstructing Langston Hughes's *Not Without Laughter*," *African American Review* 28.4 [1994]: 601–13). Hughes's manuscripts of successive drafts of the novel (all of which he donated, after publication, to the Negro Collection of the 135th Street Branch Library, now the Schomburg Center for Research in Black Culture) suggest that he did make changes to his work in response to Mason's suggestions, in the midst of his own thoroughgoing process of revision. Mason herself was happy with Hughes's second draft, finished on August 15. Hughes—returning from a trip to Canada—insisted it needed more work. ("I couldn't bear to have the people I had grown to love," he remembered in *The Big Sea*, "locked up in long pages of uncomfortable words, awkward sentences, and drawn-out passages.")

With the help of Louise Thompson, a stenographer Mason had hired to facilitate Hughes's progress on the novel, he finished a third draft during the fall. Alfred A. Knopf—who had been asked by Carl Van Vechten to extend "every tenderness and consideration" to Hughes's work—agreed to publish the book. Alain Locke, enlisted by Knopf as a reader, sought further changes after it was accepted (asking for more detail about the protagonist's "inner emotional conflict" in its later sections), and Mason again noted that "propaganda utterances" had re-emerged in the revised manuscript. Hughes addressed Locke and Mason's suggestions and gave his finished manuscript to Blanche Knopf on February 17, 1930. Hughes read galleys and page proofs with great care, reversing many small changes in spelling and the handling of dialect that had been introduced by Knopf's copy editor and making a few further revisions. *Not Without Laughter* was published in July 1930. Knopf reprinted the novel at least nine times during Hughes's lifetime, without Hughes's involvement. The present volume prints the text of the 1930 Knopf first printing.

Black No More. In his 1966 autobiography *Black and Conservative*, George S. Schuyler credits V. F. Calverton—the pen name under which George Goetz edited *Modern Quarterly*—for the suggestion that he begin *Black No More*. Schuyler said that Calverton, who had previously published essays by him, "encouraged me to write my first book . . . a satire on the American race question," and was "instrumental in getting the Macaulay Company to publish it." Another impetus for the novel was the widely publicized claim by Japanese biologist Yusaburo Noguchi that he had "developed a technique for changing racial characteristics, even to the pigment colorings" (*The New York Times*, October 24, 1929). Writing in the *Pittsburgh Courier* on November 2, Schuyler commented: "I have been prophesying it for some years, and have even written something built around such a discovery." Schuyler worked on this initial "something" for "about six or seven months," he recalled in a 1975 interview with Michael W. Peplow; he had completed a draft of *Black No More* by July 1930. In late August, he solicited a preface from H. L. Mencken, in whose *American Mercury* he had been publishing since 1927. Mencken declined in mid-September, explaining that he did not wish to seem to patronize. ("I think you are quite right about the requested preface, as you are about most things," Schuyler replied. "One thing I am very anxious to avoid is patronizing. There has, I believe, been altogether too much of it, especially in connection with work done by the dark brethren.") By September 4, 1930, Schuyler had returned a corrected set of proofs to his publisher. Later that month, he made a number of small changes in "expression" and "characterization" after receiving belated suggestions from the novelist and NAACP national secretary Walter White, to whom he had written about the novel in July. White went on to suggest further changes, but on October 3, Schuyler informed him that he had returned his final page proofs "about ten days ago." The Macaulay Company published *Black No More* in January 1931. It was reprinted, much later in Schuyler's career, by Negro Universities Press in 1969 and Collier Books in 1971, without any authorial revision. This volume prints the text of the 1931 first edition.

The Conjure-Man Dies. Little evidence is known to have appeared in print about the composition and textual history of *The Conjure-Man Dies*, Rudolph Fisher's second novel. It was published in New York by Covici-Friede in late July 1932 and was reprinted once, without revision, before Fisher's death in December 1934. No manuscripts or other prepublication versions of the novel are known to be extant, and the main repository of Fisher's papers, Brown University Library, does not hold any correspondence about it. (Other archival sources, such as the unpublished correspondence of Carl Van Vechten or Walter White, may contain further information.) Asked about his recently published book by a reporter from the *Pittsburgh Courier* at an August 18, 1932, Harlem gala for African American authors, Fisher explained that he chose to write a mystery novel "against the wishes of his friends," because "there is more money in it, he gets more fun out of this kind of writing, and it isn't necessary after all, to cater to one's friends in writing." He returned to *The Conjure-Man*'s main characters, John Archer and Perry Dart, in a novelette, "John Archer's Nose," published posthumously (*Metropolitan*, January 1935). The present volume prints the text of the 1932 Covici-Friede first printing.

Black Thunder. Arna Bontemps described the genesis of his second novel, *Black Thunder*, in an introduction he wrote for a new edition in 1968. After "three horrifying years of preparation in a throbbing region of the deep South," he moved with his family into his father's home in Watts, Los Angeles, in the summer of 1934, where he drafted the novel "on the top of a folded-down sewing machine." He had had the book in mind for at least a couple of years. In an undated letter to Langston Hughes, written around March 1932, he reported "working a bit on a draft of a new adult novel," probably *Black Thunder*. He had ultimately been inspired, during an earlier visit to Fisk University in Nashville, Tennessee, by the Fisk Library's collection of slave narratives, and in particular by accounts of the Gabriel Prosser conspiracy of 1800. *Black Thunder*, which is closely based on these accounts, was completed by the spring of 1935. Harper & Brothers in New York expressed interest in publishing the book but requested extensive changes. "Gabriel's Attempt"—an unfinished typescript of 105 pages now in the Arna Bontemps Papers at Syracuse University Library—represents Bontemps's effort to revise the novel in response to the firm's suggestions. He abandoned this effort when he learned that Macmillan, with whom he and Langston Hughes had published a children's book, *Popo and Fifina*, in 1932, was willing to accept his original manuscript without alteration: it was published as *Black Thunder* on January 28, 1936. The novel was reprinted without Bontemps's involvement in 1964, by Seven Seas Press in Berlin. In 1968, Beacon Press in Boston published a new edition for which Bontemps contributed a new introduction (reprinted in the Notes to this volume) but which he did not otherwise alter. The text in the present volume has been taken from the first edition.

This volume presents the texts of the editions chosen for inclusion here but does not attempt to reproduce every feature of their typographic design. The texts are reprinted without change, except for the correction of typographical errors. Spelling, punctuation, and capitalization are often expressive features, and they are not altered, even when inconsistent or irregular. The following is a list of typographical errors corrected, cited by page and line number: 14.5, 'Get; 21.23, outside!; 22.19, 'Does; 22.20, right!; 77.35, passengers,; 131.25, dear;'; 165.36, Old-timy; 185.3, Tempy's; 251.6, frauliens; 266.37–38, Givens viewed; 301.7, gaunt,; 323.34, he had; 334.18, its a; 340.24, Quite; 340.28, Snobbcraft).; 350.7, chubby, ball; 358.3, passengers, managed; 358.23, fact They; 405.3, doctor." You; 550.7, imflammability; 559.31, as unusual; 566.17, glanced; 651.31, imaagine, liberty; 653.25, Creauzot; 669.1, boats; 673.6–7, insurrectionaires; 761.13, helped:.; 807.14, or small.

Notes

In the notes below, the reference numbers denote page and line of the present volume; the line count includes titles and headings but not blank lines. Notes are not generally made for material found in standard desk-reference works. For additional information and references to other studies, see: Jeffrey B. Ferguson, *The Sage of Sugar Hill: George S. Schuyler and the Harlem Renaissance* (New Haven: Yale University Press, 2005); Nathan Irvin Huggins, *Harlem Renaissance* (New York: Oxford University Press, 1971); Kirkland C. Jones, *Renaissance Man from Louisiana: A Biography of Arna Wendell Bontemps* (Westport, Connecticut: Greenwood Press, 1992); David Levering Lewis, *When Harlem Was in Vogue* (New York: Alfred A. Knopf, 1980); John McCluskey Jr., ed., *The City of Refuge: The Collected Stories of Rudolph Fisher* (Columbia: University of Missouri Press, 2008); Charles H. Nichols, ed., *Arna Bontemps–Langston Hughes Letters, 1925–1967* (New York: Dodd, Mead, 1980); Michael W. Peplow, *George S. Schuyler* (Boston: Twayne, 1980); Arnold Rampersad, *The Life of Langston Hughes*, 2 vols. (New York: Oxford University Press, 1986–88); Steven Watson, *The Harlem Renaissance: Hub of African-American Culture, 1920–1930* (New York: Pantheon, 1995); Oscar R. Williams, *George S. Schuyler: Portrait of a Black Conservative* (Knoxville: University of Tennessee Press, 2007).

NOT WITHOUT LAUGHTER

2.2   *J. E. and Amy Spingarn.*] Joel Elias Spingarn (1875–1939) and his wife Amy Einstein Spingarn (1883–1980) were among Hughes's patrons; he had attended Lincoln University with their financial help. Joel, a former Columbia professor of comparative literature, was elected president of the NAACP in 1930. Amy, an heiress and artist, published a limited edition of Hughes poems, *Dear Lovely Death*, at her Troutbeck Press in 1931.

32.21   dicty] African American slang: snobbish, high-class.

36.3–8   THROW yo' arms . . . done!] Hughes's adaptation of contemporary blues lyrics. A variant of the opening couplet, credited to Gus Cannon (c. 1883–1979), was recorded by the Memphis Jug Band in 1928 in "Stealin' Stealin'"; see also the "Western Bound Blues" by Tampa Red (1904–1981), first recorded in 1932.

37.29   Ada Walker's] Ada ("Aïda") Overton Walker (1880–1914), vaudeville dancer and choreographer.

38.10–11   I wonder where . . . watch in pawn.] See "I Wonder Where My Easy Rider's Gone," a 1913 blues song by Shelton Brooks (1886–1975).

39.6   *parse me la*] A dance step, also spelled *pasmala*, *possumala*, or *pas ma la*, possibly from the French *pas mêlé*, or mixed step. Ernest Hogan (1859–1909), a minstrel performer, published the song "La Pas Ma La" in 1895 and is credited with popularizing the dance.

40.35   *Casey Jones*] Folk ballad about railroad engineer Casey Jones (1863–1900), written by Wallace Saunders and first published in 1909.

41.7   W. C. Handy] Alabama-born musician and composer (1873–1958), sometimes referred to as "father of the blues."

64.28   Sen Sens] Licorice-flavored candies used as a breath freshener.

68.34–35   *St. Louis Blues*] 1914 twelve-bar blues song by W. C. Handy.

69.21   *Memphis . . . Yellow Dog*] Blues songs by W. C. Handy, first published in 1912 and 1915, respectively.

72.21   P. I.] Pimp.

118.24   *Dear Old Southland*] Popular song (1921) with words by Harry Creamer (1879–1930) and music by Turner Layton (1894–1978).

126.9   "Layovers to catch meddlers."] A widely varying traditional phrase, persistent especially in the South, used to evade impertinently curious questions.

159.33   balling-the-jack.] From "Ballin' the Jack," a 1913 dance instruction song with words by James Henry (Jim) Burris (1874–1923) and music by Chris Smith (1879–1949).

167.38–39   Dark was the night . . . ground] African American spiritual based on a 1792 hymn by Thomas Haweis (1734–1820); a version by Blind Willie Johnson (1897–1945) was recorded in 1927.

174.16–17   Senator Bruce . . . Frederick Douglass.] Blanche Kelso Bruce (1841–1898), senator from Mississippi, 1875–81; John Mercer Langston (1829–1897), congressman from Virginia, 1890–91 (and Langston Hughes's great uncle); Pinckney Benton Stewart Pinchback (1837–1921), Louisiana governor, 1872–73 (and maternal grandfather of Jean Toomer); and abolitionist Frederick Douglass (c. 1818–1895).

175.16–18   some modern novels . . . Gene Stratton Porter] Tempy's novels and favored novelists were all bestsellers: *The Rosary* (1909), by English romantic writer Florence L. Barclay (1862–1921); *The Little Shepherd of Kingdom Come* (1903), by Kentucky-born John Fox Jr. (1862–1919); Harold Bell Wright (1872–1944), prolific popular novelist, and Gene Stratton-Porter (1863–1924), Indiana novelist most often remembered for *A Girl of the Limberlost* (1909).

183.12–13   all beat up like Jim Jeffries . . . Jack Johnson]   On July 4, 1910, in what came to be known as the "fight of the century," former heavyweight boxing champion James J. Jeffries (1875–1953) was defeated by the African American current champion Jack Johnson (1878–1946). Jeffries was billed as the "Great White Hope"; widespread rioting followed Johnson's victory.

183.14   sweet-papa Stingaree's]   See "Stingaree Blues" (1920), by Clinton A. Kemp (b. 1895).

187.15–16   The Doors of Life]   See The Doors of Life; or, Little Studies in Self-Healing (1909), by Walter DeVoe.

192.24–25   Love, O love . . . wine!]   From the traditional song "Careless Love"; a popular blues version was recorded in 1925 by Bessie Smith (1894–1937).

BLACK NO MORE

222.7–8   Mr. V. F. Calverton]   Victor Francis Calverton, pen name of George Goetz (1900–1940), editor of the radical magazine The Modern Quarterly; Calverton had encouraged Schuyler to write Black No More.

229.31   "Numbers" banker]   Operator of an illegal betting scheme, supplied with customers' bets by a "runner."

234.38   Lafayette Theater]   A celebrated Harlem theater located at 132nd Street and Seventh Avenue, reputed to have been the first in New York City to offer desegregated seating to its audiences.

242.37   "Beale Street"]   A street in Memphis, Tennessee associated with the development of the blues.

243.21   Volstead Law]   The Volstead Act of 1919 regulated the manufacture and sale of alcohol during Prohibition.

248.39   dicty]   See note 32.21.

276.10   Shakespeare Agamemnon Beard]   Commentators on Black No More have noted that many characters appear to be thinly veiled satiric portraits of public figures. Beard in some respects resembles W.E.B. Du Bois (1868–1963); Napoleon Wellington Jackson, James Weldon Johnson (1871–1938); Mortimer Roberts, Robert Russa Moton (1867–1940), of the Tuskegee Institute; Walter Williams, Walter White (1893–1955) of the NAACP; Santop Licorice, Marcus Garvey (1887–1940); Mme Blandish, Mme. C. J. Walker (1867–1919) or her daughter A'Lelia (1885–1931).

296.36   Tudor City.]   A large, luxurious residential development on the East Side of Manhattan, begun in 1927.

311.26   "white mule"]   Colorless moonshine or grain alcohol.

320.28   Mann Act]   Officially known as the White-Slave Traffic Act, a 1910 anti-prostitution law; the boxer Jack Johnson was the first to be convicted under the law, in 1912, for transporting a white sex worker across state lines.

330.15–17   to quote Abraham Lincoln . . . earth.'] See Lincoln's Gettysburg Address (1863).

350.40–351.1   Sherlock Holmes . . . Pinkertons] Holmes and Carter were fictional detectives, the former the creation of Sir Arthur Conan Doyle (1859–1930) and the latter a character in dime novels and magazine stories by many authors, beginning with *The Old Detective's Pupil; or, The Mysterious Crime of Madison Square* in 1886. The Pinkertons were agents of the Pinkerton National Detective Agency, founded in 1850.

THE CONJURE-MAN DIES

375.18–22   *"I'll be glad . . . you're gone!"*] From "I'll Be Glad When You're Dead, You Rascal You" (1929), written by "Lovin'" Sam Theard (1904–1982) and popularized by Louis Armstrong (1901–1971) and others.

445.20–22   *I'll be standin' . . . rascal you.*] See note above.

497.16   the Spencerian classification] See "The Classification of the Sciences," an 1864 essay by English philosopher and sociologist Herbert Spencer (1820–1903).

543.35–38   *"Am I born . . . body down?"*] Hymn (1763) by Charles Wesley (1707–1788).

578.20   Swing Swing] Sing Sing, a prison in Ossining, New York ("up the river" from New York City).

BLACK THUNDER

593.1   Bontemps added an introduction to the novel in 1968 when Beacon Press published it in a new edition:

Time is not a river. Time is a pendulum. The thought occurred to me first in Watts in 1934. After three horrifying years of preparation in a throbbing region of the deep south, I had settled there to write my second novel, away from it all.

At the age of thirty, or thereabouts, I had lived long enough to become aware of intricate patterns of recurrence, in my own experience and in the history I had been exploring with almost frightening attention. I suspect I was preoccupied with those patterns when, early in *Black Thunder*, I tried to make something of the old major-domo's mounting the dark steps of the Sheppard mansion near Richmond to wind the clock.

The element of time was crucial to Gabriel's attempt, in historical fact as in *Black Thunder*, and the hero of that action knew well the absolute necessity of a favorable conjunction. When this did not occur, he realized that the outcome was no longer in his own hands. Perhaps it was in the stars, he reasoned.

If time is the pendulum I imagined, the snuffing of Martin Luther King, Jr.'s career may yet appear as a kind of repetition of Gabriel's shattered dream during the election year of 1800. At least the occurrence of the former as this is written serves to recall for me the tumult in my own thoughts when I began to read extensively about slave insurrections and to see in them a possible metaphor of turbulence to come.

Not having space for my typewriter, I wrote the book in longhand on the top of a folded-down sewing machine in the extra bedroom of my parents' house at 10310 Wiegand Avenue where my wife and I and our children (three at that time) were temporarily and uncomfortably quartered. A Japanese truck farmer's asparagus field was just outside our back door. From a window on the front, above the sewing machine, I could look across 103rd Street at the buildings and grounds of Jordan High School, a name I did not hear again until I came across it in some of the news accounts reporting the holocaust that swept Watts a quarter of a century later. In the vacant lot across from us on Wiegand a friendly Mexican neighbor grazed his milk goat. We could smell eucalyptus trees when my writing window was open and when we walked outside, and nearly always the air was like transparent gold in those days. I could have loved the place under different circumstances, but as matters stood there was no way to disguise the fact that our luck had run out.

My father and stepmother were bearing up reasonably well, perhaps, under the strain our presence imposed on them, but only a miracle could have healed one's own hurt pride, one's sense of shame and failure at an early age. Meanwhile, it takes time to write a novel, even one that has been painstakingly researched, and I do not blame my father for his occasional impatience. I had flagellated myself so thoroughly, I was numb to such criticism, when he spoke in my presence, and not very tactfully, about young people with bright prospects who make shipwreck of their lives.

What he had in mind, mainly, I am sure, were events which had brought me home at such an awkward time and with such uncertain plans, but somehow I suspected more. At the age at which I made my commitment to writing, he had been blowing a trombone in a Louisiana marching band under the direction of Claiborne Williams. But he had come to regard such a career as a deadend occupation unworthy of a young family man, married to a schoolteacher, and he renounced it for something more solid: bricklaying. Years later when the building trades themselves began to fade as far as black workers were concerned, under pressure of the new labor unions, he had made another hard decision and ended his working years in the ministry.

He was reproaching me for being less resourceful, by his lights, and I was too involved in my novel to even reply. The work I had undertaken, the new country into which I had ventured when I began to explore Negro history had rendered me immune for the moment, even to implied insults.

Had the frustrations dormant in Watts at that date suddenly exploded in flame and anger, as they were eventually to do, I don't think they would have shaken my concentration; but I have a feeling that more readers might then have been in a mood to hear a tale of volcanic rumblings among angry blacks—and the end of patience. At the time, however, I began to suspect that it was fruitless for a Negro in the United States to address serious writing to my generation, and I began to consider the alternative of trying to reach young readers not yet hardened or grown insensitive to man's inhumanity to man, as it is called.

For this, as for so much else that has by turn intrigued or troubled me in subsequent years, my three-year sojourn in northern Alabama had been a kind of crude conditioning. Within weeks after the publication of my first book, as it happened, I had been caught up in a quaint and poignant disorder that failed to attract wide attention. It was one of the side effects of the crash that bought on the Depression, and it brought instant havoc to the Harlem Renaissance of the twenties. I was one of the hopeful young people displaced, so to speak. The jobs we had counted on to keep us alive and writing in New York vanished, as some observed, quicker than a cat could wink. Not knowing where else to turn, I wandered into northern Alabama, on the promise of employment as a teacher, and hopefully to wait out the bad times, but at least to get my bearings. I did not stay long enough to see any improvement in the times, but a few matters, which now seem important, did tend to become clearer as I waited.

Northern Alabama had a primitive beauty when I saw it first. I remember writing something in which I called the countryside a green Eden, but I awakened to find it dangerously infested. Two stories dominated the news as well as the daydreams of the people I met. One had to do with the demonstrations by Mahatma Gandhi and his followers in India; the other, the trials of the Scottsboro boys then in progress in Decatur, Alabama, about thirty miles from where we were living. Both seemed to foreshadow frightening consequences, and everywhere I turned someone demanded my opinions, since I was recently arrived and expected to be knowledgeable. Eventually their questions upset me as much as the news stories. We had fled here to escape our fears in the city, but the terrors we encountered here were even more upsetting than the ones we had left behind.

I was, frankly, running scared when an opportunity came for me to visit Fisk University in Nashville, Tennessee, about a hundred miles away, get a brief release from tension, perhaps, and call on three old friends from the untroubled years of the Harlem Renaissance: James Weldon Johnson, Charles S. Johnson, and Arthur Schomburg. All, in a sense, could have been considered as refugees living in exile, and the three, privately could have been dreaming of planting an oasis at Fisk where, surrounded by bleak hostility in the area, the region, and the nation, if not indeed the world, they might not only stay alive but, conceivably, keep alive a flicker of the impulse they had detected and helped to encourage in the black awakening in Renaissance Harlem.

Each of them could and did recite by heart Countée Cullen's lines dedicated to Charles S. Johnson in an earlier year:

> We shall not always plant while others reap
> The golden increment of bursting fruit,
> Not always countenance, abject and mute,
> That lesser men should hold their brothers cheap;
> Not everlastingly while others sleep
> Shall we beguile their limbs with mellow flute,
> Not always bend to some more subtle brute,
> We were not made eternally to weep.
>
> The night whose sable breast relieves the stark,
> White stars is no less lovely being dark,
> And there are buds that cannot bloom at all
> In light, but crumple, piteous, and fall;
> So in the dark we hide the heart that bleeds,
> And wait, and tend our agonizing seeds.

Separately and with others we made my visit a time for declaring and reasserting sentiments we had stored in our memories for safekeeping against the blast that had already dispersed their young protégés and my friends and the disasters looming ahead.

Discovering in the Fisk Library a larger collection of slave narratives than I knew existed, I began to read almost frantically. In the gloom of the darkening Depression settling all around us, I began to ponder the stricken slave's will to freedom. Three historic efforts at self-emancipation caught my attention and promptly shattered peace of mind. I knew instantly that one of them would be the subject of my next novel. First, however, I would have to make a choice, and this involved research. Each had elements the others did not have, or at least not to the same degree, and except for the desperate need of freedom they had in common, each was attempted under different conditions and led by unlike personalities.

Denmark Vesey's effort I dismissed first. It was too elaborately planned for its own good. His plot was betrayed, his conspiracy crushed too soon, but it would be a mistake to say nothing came of it in Vesey's own time. The shudder it put into the hearts and minds of slaveholders was never quieted. *Nat Turner's Confession*, which I read in the Fisk Library at a table across from Schomburg's desk, bothered me on two counts. I felt uneasy about the amanuensis to whom his account was related and the conditions under which he confessed. Then there was the business of Nat's "visions" and "dreams."

Gabriel's attempt seemed to reflect more accurately for me what I felt then and feel now might have motivated slaves capable of such boldness and inspired daring. The longer I pondered, the more convinced I became. Gabriel had not opened his mind too fully and hence had not been betrayed as had Vesey. He had by his own dignity and by the esteem in which he was held inspired and maintained loyalty. He had not depended on trance-like mumbo jumbo. Freedom was a less complicated affair in his case. It was, it seemed to me, a more unmistakable equivalent of the yearning I felt and which I imagined to be general. Finally, there was the plan itself, a strategy which some contemporaries, prospective victims, felt could scarcely have failed had not the weather miraculously intervened in their behalf. Gabriel attributed his reversal, ultimately, to the stars in their courses, the only factor that had been omitted in his calculations. He had not been possessed, not even overly optimistic.

Back in Alabama, I began to sense quaint hostilities. Borrowing library books by mail, as I sometimes did, was unusual enough to attract attention. Wasn't there a whole room of books in the school where I worked—perhaps as many as a thousand? How many books could a man read in one lifetime anyway? We laughed together at the questions, but I realized they were not satisfied with my joking answers. How could I tell them about Gabriel's adventure in such an atmosphere?

Friends from Harlem years learned from our mutual friends at Fisk that we were in the vicinity and began dropping in to say howdy en route to Decatur or Montgomery or Birmingham. There was an excitement in the state similar to that which recurred twenty-five years later when black folk began confronting hardened oppression by offering to put their bodies in escrow, if that was required. In 1931, however, the effort was centered around forlorn attempts to save the lives of nine black boys who had been convicted, in a travesty of justice, of ravishing two white girls in the empty boxcars in which all were hoboing.

The boyish poet Langston Hughes was one of those who came to protest, to interview the teen-age victims in their prison cells, and to write prose and poetry aimed at calling the world's attention to the enormity about to be perpetrated. It was natural that he should stop by to visit us. He and I had recently collaborated, mainly by mail, on the writing of a children's story, *Popo and Fifina: Children of Haiti*. He had the story and I had the children, so my publisher thought it might work. Perhaps it would not be too much to say they were justified. The story lasted a long time and was translated into a number of languages. The friendship between the two authors also lasted and yielded other collaborations over the next thirty-five years. But the association was anathema to the institution which had, with some admitted reluctance, given me employment.

As my year ended, I was given an ultimatum. I would have to make a clean break with the unrest in the world as represented by Gandhi's efforts abroad and the Scottsboro protests here at home. Since I had no connection or involvement with either, other than the fact that I had known some of the people who were shouting their outrage, I was not sure how a break could be made. The head of the school had a plan, however. I could do it, he demanded publicly, by burning most of the books in my small library, a number of which were trash in his estimation anyway, the rest, race-conscious and provocative. *Harlem Shadows*, *The Blacker the Berry*, *My Bondage and Freedom*, *Black Majesty*, *The Souls of Black Folk*, and *The Autobiography of an Ex-Coloured Man* were a few of those indicated.

I was too horrified to speak, but I swallowed my indignation. My wife was expecting another child, and the options before us had been reduced to none. At the end of the following term we drove to California, sold our car, and settled down in the small room in Watts in the hope that what we had received for the car would buy food till I could write my book. By the next spring *Black Thunder* was finished, and the advance against royalties was enough to pay our way to Chicago.

Black Thunder, when published later that year, earned no more than its advance. As discouraging as this was, I was not permitted to think of it as a total loss. The reviews were more than kind. John T. Frederick, director of the Illinois Writers Project, read the book and decided to add me to his staff. He also commended it warmly in his anthology, *Out of the Midwest*, and in his CBS broadcasts. Robert Morss Lovett mentioned it in his class at the University of Chicago. But the theme of self-assertion by black men whose endurance was strained to the breaking point was not one that readers of fiction were prepared to contemplate at the time. Now that *Black Thunder* is published again, after more than thirty years, I cannot help wondering if its story will be better understood by Americans, both black and white. I am, however, convinced that time is not a river.

Chicago
April 1968

594.2 ALBERTA] Alberta Bontemps (1906–2004), née Johnson, Bontemps' wife.

599.2 VIRGINIA COURT records] For information about the historicity of *Black Thunder* and Bontemps's sources, see Mary Kemp Davis, "Arna Bontemps' *Black Thunder*: The Creation of an Authoritative Text of 'Gabriel's Defeat'," *Black American Literature Forum* 23.1 (Spring 1989): 17–36, and Davis, "The Historical Slave Revolt and the Literary Imagination" (PhD diss., University of North Carolina, Chapel Hill, 1984).

610.1 Sonthonaz . . . *des Noirs*."] Léger-Félicité Sonthonax (1763–1813), a member of the French abolitionist group Société des amis des Noirs (1788–93), served as civil commissioner of Saint-Domingue (now Haiti) from 1792–95, during the Haitian Revolution. Sent to keep the colony under

French control, he upheld the citizenship rights of "free men of color," which had been granted by France in 1792, and emancipated Haitian slaves in 1793, while also seeking their return to plantation life.

610.16–18   Judge Tucker . . . *on Slavery*]   St. George Tucker (1752–1827) published his *Dissertation on Slavery* in 1796.

626.9   Callender]   James Thomson Callender (1758–1803), Scottish-born political writer who emigrated to Philadelphia around 1793, where he attained notoriety as an anti-Federalist pamphleteer. Beginning in June 1800 he served a six-month prison sentence for sedition.

626.19   United Irishman.]   A member of the Society of United Irishmen, an Irish nationalist organization inspired by the American and French revolutions and founded in 1791.

628.7   the old Procope]   Reputedly the world's oldest coffeehouse, founded in 1686 and a center of Parisian literary and political life in the eighteenth and nineteenth centuries.

654.1–11   *Man is a stranger . . . deepening gloom*]   See Voltaire's 1755 "Poem on the Lisbon Disaster," as translated in 1911 by Joseph McCabe.

740.20   Duane]   William John Duane (1780–1865), editor of the anti-Federalist Philadelphia *Aurora*; he later served as Postmaster General (1776–82) and Secretary of the Treasury (1833).

767.8   Fries, Gallatin]   John Fries (1750–1818), convicted of treason for his role in Fries's Rebellion, an armed anti-taxation protest among the Pennsylvania Dutch (1799–1800), and pardoned by John Adams in 1800; Albert Gallatin (1761–1849), an advocate for western Pennsylvanians opposed to new taxes on whiskey during the Whiskey Rebellion of the early 1790s and later Secretary of the Treasury (1801–14).

810.15   *The trumpet . . . my soul.*]   From "Steal Away," an African American spiritual first performed by the Fisk Jubilee Singers in 1871 and attributed to Choctaw freedman Wallace Willis (fl. 1840s–1850s).

THE LIBRARY OF AMERICA SERIES

The Library of America fosters appreciation and pride in America's literary heritage by publishing, and keeping permanently in print, authoritative editions of America's best and most significant writing. An independent nonprofit organization, it was founded in 1979 with seed funding from the National Endowment for the Humanities and the Ford Foundation.

1. Herman Melville: *Typee, Omoo, Mardi*
2. Nathaniel Hawthorne: *Tales and Sketches*
3. Walt Whitman: *Poetry and Prose*
4. Harriet Beecher Stowe: *Three Novels*
5. Mark Twain: *Mississippi Writings*
6. Jack London: *Novels and Stories*
7. Jack London: *Novels and Social Writings*
8. William Dean Howells: *Novels 1875–1886*
9. Herman Melville: *Redburn, White-Jacket, Moby-Dick*
10. Nathaniel Hawthorne: *Collected Novels*
11. Francis Parkman: *France and England in North America*, vol. I
12. Francis Parkman: *France and England in North America*, vol. II
13. Henry James: *Novels 1871–1880*
14. Henry Adams: *Novels, Mont Saint Michel, The Education*
15. Ralph Waldo Emerson: *Essays and Lectures*
16. Washington Irving: *History, Tales and Sketches*
17. Thomas Jefferson: *Writings*
18. Stephen Crane: *Prose and Poetry*
19. Edgar Allan Poe: *Poetry and Tales*
20. Edgar Allan Poe: *Essays and Reviews*
21. Mark Twain: *The Innocents Abroad, Roughing It*
22. Henry James: *Literary Criticism: Essays, American & English Writers*
23. Henry James: *Literary Criticism: European Writers & The Prefaces*
24. Herman Melville: *Pierre, Israel Potter, The Confidence-Man, Tales & Billy Budd*
25. William Faulkner: *Novels 1930–1935*
26. James Fenimore Cooper: *The Leatherstocking Tales*, vol. I
27. James Fenimore Cooper: *The Leatherstocking Tales*, vol. II
28. Henry David Thoreau: *A Week, Walden, The Maine Woods, Cape Cod*
29. Henry James: *Novels 1881–1886*
30. Edith Wharton: *Novels*
31. Henry Adams: *History of the U.S. during the Administrations of Jefferson*
32. Henry Adams: *History of the U.S. during the Administrations of Madison*
33. Frank Norris: *Novels and Essays*
34. W.E.B. Du Bois: *Writings*
35. Willa Cather: *Early Novels and Stories*
36. Theodore Dreiser: *Sister Carrie, Jennie Gerhardt, Twelve Men*
37a. Benjamin Franklin: *Silence Dogood, The Busy-Body, & Early Writings*
37b. Benjamin Franklin: *Autobiography, Poor Richard, & Later Writings*
38. William James: *Writings 1902–1910*
39. Flannery O'Connor: *Collected Works*
40. Eugene O'Neill: *Complete Plays 1913–1920*
41. Eugene O'Neill: *Complete Plays 1920–1931*
42. Eugene O'Neill: *Complete Plays 1932–1943*
43. Henry James: *Novels 1886–1890*
44. William Dean Howells: *Novels 1886–1888*
45. Abraham Lincoln: *Speeches and Writings 1832–1858*
46. Abraham Lincoln: *Speeches and Writings 1859–1865*
47. Edith Wharton: *Novellas and Other Writings*
48. William Faulkner: *Novels 1936–1940*
49. Willa Cather: *Later Novels*
50. Ulysses S. Grant: *Memoirs and Selected Letters*
51. William Tecumseh Sherman: *Memoirs*
52. Washington Irving: *Bracebridge Hall, Tales of a Traveller, The Alhambra*
53. Francis Parkman: *The Oregon Trail, The Conspiracy of Pontiac*
54. James Fenimore Cooper: *Sea Tales: The Pilot, The Red Rover*
55. Richard Wright: *Early Works*
56. Richard Wright: *Later Works*
57. Willa Cather: *Stories, Poems, and Other Writings*
58. William James: *Writings 1878–1899*
59. Sinclair Lewis: *Main Street & Babbitt*
60. Mark Twain: *Collected Tales, Sketches, Speeches, & Essays 1852–1890*
61. Mark Twain: *Collected Tales, Sketches, Speeches, & Essays 1891–1910*
62. *The Debate on the Constitution: Part One*
63. *The Debate on the Constitution: Part Two*
64. Henry James: *Collected Travel Writings: Great Britain & America*
65. Henry James: *Collected Travel Writings: The Continent*

66. *American Poetry: The Nineteenth Century*, Vol. 1

67. *American Poetry: The Nineteenth Century*, Vol. 2

68. Frederick Douglass: *Autobiographies*

69. Sarah Orne Jewett: *Novels and Stories*

70. Ralph Waldo Emerson: *Collected Poems and Translations*

71. Mark Twain: *Historical Romances*

72. John Steinbeck: *Novels and Stories 1932–1937*

73. William Faulkner: *Novels 1942–1954*

74. Zora Neale Hurston: *Novels and Stories*

75. Zora Neale Hurston: *Folklore, Memoirs, and Other Writings*

76. Thomas Paine: *Collected Writings*

77. *Reporting World War II: American Journalism 1938–1944*

78. *Reporting World War II: American Journalism 1944–1946*

79. Raymond Chandler: *Stories and Early Novels*

80. Raymond Chandler: *Later Novels and Other Writings*

81. Robert Frost: *Collected Poems, Prose, & Plays*

82. Henry James: *Complete Stories 1892–1898*

83. Henry James: *Complete Stories 1898–1910*

84. William Bartram: *Travels and Other Writings*

85. John Dos Passos: *U.S.A.*

86. John Steinbeck: *The Grapes of Wrath and Other Writings 1936–1941*

87. Vladimir Nabokov: *Novels and Memoirs 1941–1951*

88. Vladimir Nabokov: *Novels 1955–1962*

89. Vladimir Nabokov: *Novels 1969–1974*

90. James Thurber: *Writings and Drawings*

91. George Washington: *Writings*

92. John Muir: *Nature Writings*

93. Nathanael West: *Novels and Other Writings*

94. *Crime Novels: American Noir of the 1930s and 40s*

95. *Crime Novels: American Noir of the 1950s*

96. Wallace Stevens: *Collected Poetry and Prose*

97. James Baldwin: *Early Novels and Stories*

98. James Baldwin: *Collected Essays*

99. Gertrude Stein: *Writings 1903–1932*

100. Gertrude Stein: *Writings 1932–1946*

101. Eudora Welty: *Complete Novels*

102. Eudora Welty: *Stories, Essays, & Memoir*

103. Charles Brockden Brown: *Three Gothic Novels*

104. *Reporting Vietnam: American Journalism 1959–1969*

105. *Reporting Vietnam: American Journalism 1969–1975*

106. Henry James: *Complete Stories 1874–1884*

107. Henry James: *Complete Stories 1884–1891*

108. *American Sermons: The Pilgrims to Martin Luther King Jr.*

109. James Madison: *Writings*

110. Dashiell Hammett: *Complete Novels*

111. Henry James: *Complete Stories 1864–1874*

112. William Faulkner: *Novels 1957–1962*

113. John James Audubon: *Writings & Drawings*

114. *Slave Narratives*

115. *American Poetry: The Twentieth Century*, Vol. 1

116. *American Poetry: The Twentieth Century*, Vol. 2

117. F. Scott Fitzgerald: *Novels and Stories 1920–1922*

118. Henry Wadsworth Longfellow: *Poems and Other Writings*

119. Tennessee Williams: *Plays 1937–1955*

120. Tennessee Williams: *Plays 1957–1980*

121. Edith Wharton: *Collected Stories 1891–1910*

122. Edith Wharton: *Collected Stories 1911–1937*

123. *The American Revolution: Writings from the War of Independence*

124. Henry David Thoreau: *Collected Essays and Poems*

125. Dashiell Hammett: *Crime Stories and Other Writings*

126. Dawn Powell: *Novels 1930–1942*

127. Dawn Powell: *Novels 1944–1962*

128. Carson McCullers: *Complete Novels*

129. Alexander Hamilton: *Writings*

130. Mark Twain: *The Gilded Age and Later Novels*

131. Charles W. Chesnutt: *Stories, Novels, and Essays*

132. John Steinbeck: *Novels 1942–1952*

133. Sinclair Lewis: *Arrowsmith, Elmer Gantry, Dodsworth*

134. Paul Bowles: *The Sheltering Sky, Let It Come Down, The Spider's House*

135. Paul Bowles: *Collected Stories & Later Writings*

136. Kate Chopin: *Complete Novels & Stories*

137. *Reporting Civil Rights: American Journalism 1941–1963*

138. *Reporting Civil Rights: American Journalism 1963–1973*

139. Henry James: *Novels 1896–1899*

140. Theodore Dreiser: *An American Tragedy*

141. Saul Bellow: *Novels 1944–1953*

142. John Dos Passos: *Novels 1920–1925*

143. John Dos Passos: *Travel Books and Other Writings*

144. Ezra Pound: *Poems and Translations*
145. James Weldon Johnson: *Writings*
146. Washington Irving: *Three Western Narratives*
147. Alexis de Tocqueville: *Democracy in America*
148. James T. Farrell: *Studs Lonigan: A Trilogy*
149. Isaac Bashevis Singer: *Collected Stories I*
150. Isaac Bashevis Singer: *Collected Stories II*
151. Isaac Bashevis Singer: *Collected Stories III*
152. Kaufman & Co.: *Broadway Comedies*
153. Theodore Roosevelt: *The Rough Riders, An Autobiography*
154. Theodore Roosevelt: *Letters and Speeches*
155. H. P. Lovecraft: *Tales*
156. Louisa May Alcott: *Little Women, Little Men, Jo's Boys*
157. Philip Roth: *Novels & Stories 1959–1962*
158. Philip Roth: *Novels 1967–1972*
159. James Agee: *Let Us Now Praise Famous Men, A Death in the Family*
160. James Agee: *Film Writing & Selected Journalism*
161. Richard Henry Dana, Jr.: *Two Years Before the Mast & Other Voyages*
162. Henry James: *Novels 1901–1902*
163. Arthur Miller: *Collected Plays 1944–1961*
164. William Faulkner: *Novels 1926–1929*
165. Philip Roth: *Novels 1973–1977*
166. *American Speeches: Part One*
167. *American Speeches: Part Two*
168. Hart Crane: *Complete Poems & Selected Letters*
169. Saul Bellow: *Novels 1956–1964*
170. John Steinbeck: *Travels with Charley and Later Novels*
171. Capt. John Smith: *Writings with Other Narratives*
172. Thornton Wilder: *Collected Plays & Writings on Theater*
173. Philip K. Dick: *Four Novels of the 1960s*
174. Jack Kerouac: *Road Novels 1957–1960*
175. Philip Roth: *Zuckerman Bound*
176. Edmund Wilson: *Literary Essays & Reviews of the 1920s* & 30s
177. Edmund Wilson: *Literary Essays & Reviews of the 1930s* & 40s
178. *American Poetry: The 17th & 18th Centuries*
179. William Maxwell: *Early Novels & Stories*
180. Elizabeth Bishop: *Poems, Prose, & Letters*
181. A. J. Liebling: *World War II Writings*
182s. *American Earth: Environmental Writing Since Thoreau*
183. Philip K. Dick: *Five Novels of the 1960s & 70s*
184. William Maxwell: *Later Novels & Stories*
185. Philip Roth: *Novels & Other Narratives 1986–1991*
186. Katherine Anne Porter: *Collected Stories & Other Writings*
187. John Ashbery: *Collected Poems 1956–1987*
188. John Cheever: *Collected Stories & Other Writings*
189. John Cheever: *Complete Novels*
190. Lafcadio Hearn: *American Writings*
191. A. J. Liebling: *The Sweet Science & Other Writngs*
192s. *The Lincoln Anthology: Great Writers on His Life and Legacy from 1860 to Now*
193. Philip K. Dick: *VALIS & Later Novels*
194. Thornton Wilder: *The Bridge of San Luis Rey and Other Novels 1926–1948*
195. Raymond Carver: *Collected Stories*
196. *American Fantastic Tales: Terror and the Uncanny from Poe to the Pulps*
197. *American Fantastic Tales: Terror and the Uncanny from the 1940s to Now*
198. John Marshall: *Writings*
199s. *The Mark Twain Anthology: Great Writers on His Life and Works*
200. Mark Twain: *A Tramp Abroad, Following the Equator, Other Travels*
201. Ralph Waldo Emerson: *Selected Journals 1820–1842*
202. Ralph Waldo Emerson: *Selected Journals 1841–1877*
203. *The American Stage: Writing on Theater from Washington Irving to Tony Kushner*
204. Shirley Jackson: *Novels & Stories*
205. Philip Roth: *Novels 1993–1995*
206. H. L. Mencken: *Prejudices: First, Second, and Third Series*
207. H. L. Mencken: *Prejudices: Fourth, Fifth, and Sixth Series*
208. John Kenneth Galbraith: *The Affluent Society and Other Writings 1952–1967*
209. Saul Bellow: *Novels 1970–1982*
210. Lynd Ward: *Gods' Man, Madman's Drum, Wild Pilgrimage*
211. Lynd Ward: *Prelude to a Million Years, Song Without Words, Vertigo*
212. The Civil War: *The First Year Told by Those Who Lived It*
213. John Adams: *Revolutionary Writings 1755–1775*
214. John Adams: *Revolutionary Writings 1775–1783*
215. Henry James: *Novels 1903–1911*
216. Kurt Vonnegut: *Novels & Stories 1963–1973*
217. *Harlem Renaissance: Five Novels of the 1920s*

218. *Harlem Renaissance: Four Novels of the 1930s*
219. Ambrose Bierce: *The Devil's Dictionary, Tales, & Memoirs*
220. Philip Roth: *The American Trilogy 1997–2000*

To subscribe to the series or to order individual copies, please visit www.loa.org or call (800) 964.5778.

This book is set in 10 point Linotron Galliard,
a face designed for photocomposition by Matthew Carter
and based on the sixteenth-century face Granjon. The paper
is acid-free lightweight opaque and meets the requirements
for permanence of the American National Standards Institute.
The binding material is Brillianta, a woven rayon cloth made
by Van Heek-Scholco Textielfabrieken, Holland. Compo-
sition by Dedicated Book Services. Printing by
Malloy Incorporated. Binding by Dekker Book-
binding. Designed by Bruce Campbell.

Harlem Renaissance

Five Novels of the 1920s

HARLEM RENAISSANCE

FIVE NOVELS OF THE 1920s

Cane • Jean Toomer
Home to Harlem • Claude McKay
Quicksand • Nella Larsen
Plum Bun • Jessie Redmon Fauset
The Blacker the Berry • Wallace Thurman

Rafia Zafar, *editor*

THE LIBRARY OF AMERICA

Home to Harlem reprinted courtesy of the Literary Representative
for the Works of Claude McKay, Schomburg Center for Research
in Black Culture, The New York Public Library, Astor, Lenox
and Tilden Foundations. *Plum Bun* reprinted
by arrangement with Beacon Press.

The paper used in this publication meets the
minimum requirements of the American National Standard for
Information Sciences–Permanence of Paper for Printed
Library Materials, ANSI Z39.48–1984.

Distributed to the trade in the United States
by Penguin Group (USA) Inc.
and in Canada by Penguin Books Canada Ltd.

Library of Congress Control Number: 2010942023
ISBN 978-1-59853-099-5

———

First Printing
The Library of America—217

Harlem Renaissance: Five Novels of the 1920s
is published with support from

THE SHELLEY & DONALD RUBIN FOUNDATION

Contents

CANE by Jean Toomer. 1

HOME TO HARLEM by Claude McKay. 135

QUICKSAND by Nella Larsen 297

PLUM BUN by Jessie Redmon Fauset 433

THE BLACKER THE BERRY by Wallace Thurman 687

Chronology 835

Biographical Notes 845

Note on the Texts 853

Notes 859

CANE

Jean Toomer

Oracular.
Redolent of fermenting syrup,
Purple of the dusk,
Deep-rooted cane.

To my grandmother . . .

Contents

Karintha 5
Reapers 8
November Cotton Flower 9
Becky 10
Face 13
Cotton Song 14
Carma 15
Song of the Son 18
Georgia Dusk 19
Fern 20
Nullo 25
Evening Song 26
Esther 27
Conversion 34
Portrait in Georgia 35
Blood-Burning Moon 36

Seventh Street 47
Rhobert 48
Avey 50
Beehive 56
Storm Ending 57
Theater 58
Her Lips Are Copper Wire 63
Calling Jesus 64
Box Seat 65
Prayer 78
Harvest Song 79
Bona and Paul 81

Kabnis 93

Karintha

Her skin is like dusk on the eastern horizon,
O cant you see it, O cant you see it,
Her skin is like dusk on the eastern horizon
. . . When the sun goes down.

Men had always wanted her, this Karintha, even as a child, Karintha carrying beauty, perfect as dusk when the sun goes down. Old men rode her hobby-horse upon their knees. Young men danced with her at frolics when they should have been dancing with their grown-up girls. God grant us youth, secretly prayed the old men. The young fellows counted the time to pass before she would be old enough to mate with them. This interest of the male, who wishes to ripen a growing thing too soon, could mean no good to her.

Karintha, at twelve, was a wild flash that told the other folks just what it was to live. At sunset, when there was no wind, and the pine-smoke from over by the sawmill hugged the earth, and you couldnt see more than a few feet in front, her sudden darting past you was a bit of vivid color, like a black bird that flashes in light. With the other children one could hear, some distance off, their feet flopping in the two-inch dust. Karintha's running was a whir. It had the sound of the red dust that sometimes makes a spiral in the road. At dusk, during the hush just after the sawmill had closed down, and before any of the women had started their supper-getting-ready songs, her voice, high-pitched, shrill, would put one's ears to itching. But no one ever thought to make her stop because of it. She stoned the cows, and beat her dog, and fought the other children. . . Even the preacher, who caught her at mischief, told himself that she was as innocently lovely as a November cotton flower. Already, rumors were out about her. Homes in Georgia are most often built on the two-room plan. In one, you cook and eat, in the other you sleep, and there love goes on. Karintha had seen or heard, perhaps she had felt her parents loving. One could but imitate one's parents, for to follow them was the way of God. She played "home" with a small boy who was not afraid to do her bidding. That started the whole thing. Old men could no longer ride her hobby-horse upon their knees. But young men counted faster.

> Her skin is like dusk,
> O cant you see it,
> Her skin is like dusk,
> When the sun goes down.

Karintha is a woman. She who carries beauty, perfect as dusk when the sun goes down. She has been married many times. Old men remind her that a few years back they rode her hobby-horse upon their knees. Karintha smiles, and indulges them when she is in the mood for it. She has contempt for them. Karintha is a woman. Young men run stills to make her money. Young men go to the big cities and run on the road. Young men go away to college. They all want to bring her money. These are the young men who thought that all they had to do was to count time. But Karintha is a woman, and she has had a child. A child fell out of her womb onto a bed of pine-needles in the forest. Pine-needles are smooth and sweet. They are elastic to the feet of rabbits. . . A sawmill was nearby. Its pyramidal sawdust pile smouldered. It is a year before one completely burns. Meanwhile, the smoke curls up and hangs in odd wraiths about the trees, curls up, and spreads itself out over the valley. . . Weeks after Karintha returned home the smoke was so heavy you tasted it in water. Some one made a song:

> Smoke is on the hills. Rise up.
> Smoke is on the hills, O rise
> And take my soul to Jesus.

Karintha is a woman. Men do not know that the soul of her was a growing thing ripened too soon. They will bring their money; they will die not having found it out. . . Karintha at twenty, carrying beauty, perfect as dusk when the sun goes down. Karintha. . .

Her skin is like dusk on the eastern horizon,
O cant you see it, O cant you see it,
Her skin is like dusk on the eastern horizon
. . . When the sun goes down.

Goes down. . .

REAPERS

Black reapers with the sound of steel on stones
Are sharpening scythes. I see them place the hones
In their hip-pockets as a thing that's done,
And start their silent swinging, one by one.
Black horses drive a mower through the weeds,
And there, a field rat, startled, squealing bleeds,
His belly close to ground. I see the blade,
Blood-stained, continue cutting weeds and shade.

NOVEMBER COTTON FLOWER

Boll-weevil's coming, and the winter's cold,
Made cotton-stalks look rusty, seasons old,
And cotton, scarce as any southern snow,
Was vanishing; the branch, so pinched and slow,
Failed in its function as the autumn rake;
Drouth fighting soil had caused the soil to take
All water from the streams; dead birds were found
In wells a hundred feet below the ground—
Such was the season when the flower bloomed.
Old folks were startled, and it soon assumed
Significance. Superstition saw
Something it had never seen before:
Brown eyes that loved without a trace of fear,
Beauty so sudden for that time of year.

Becky

Becky was the white woman who had two Negro sons. She's dead; they've gone away. The pines whisper to Jesus. The Bible flaps its leaves with an aimless rustle on her mound.

BECKY had one Negro son. Who gave it to her? Damn buck nigger, said the white folks' mouths. She wouldnt tell. Common, God-forsaken, insane white shameless wench, said the white folks' mouths. Her eyes were sunken, her neck stringy, her breasts fallen, till then. Taking their words, they filled her, like a bubble rising—then she broke. Mouth setting in a twist that held her eyes, harsh, vacant, staring. . . Who gave black folks' mouths. She wouldnt tell. Poor Catholic poor-white crazy woman, said the black folks' mouths. White folks and black folks built her cabin, fed her and her growing baby, prayed secretly to God who'd put His cross upon her and cast her out.

When the first was born, the white folks said they'd have no more to do with her. And black folks, they too joined hands to cast her out. . . The pines whispered to Jesus. . The railroad boss said not to say he said it, but she could live, if she wanted to, on the narrow strip of land between the railroad and the road. John Stone, who owned the lumber and the bricks, would have shot the man who told he gave the stuff to Lonnie Deacon, who stole out there at night and built the cabin. A single room held down to earth. . . O fly away to Jesus . . . by a leaning chimney. . .

Six trains each day rumbled past and shook the ground under her cabin. Fords, and horse- and mule-drawn buggies went back and forth along the road. No one ever saw her. Train-men, and passengers who'd heard about her, threw out papers and food. Threw out little crumpled slips of paper scribbled with prayers, as they passed her eye-shaped piece of sandy ground. Ground islandized between the road and railroad track. Pushed up where a blue-sheen God with listless eyes could look at it.

Folks from the town took turns, unknown, of course, to each other, in bringing corn and meat and sweet potatoes. Even sometimes snuff. . . O thank y Jesus. . . Old David Georgia, grinding cane and boiling syrup, never went her way without some sugar sap. No one ever saw her. The boy grew up and ran around. When he was five years old as folks reckoned it, Hugh Jourdon saw him carrying a baby. "Becky has another son," was what the whole town knew. But nothing was said, for the part of man that says things to the likes of that had told itself that if there was a Becky, that Becky now was dead.

The two boys grew. Sullen and cunning. . . O pines, whisper to Jesus; tell Him to come and press sweet Jesus-lips against their lips and eyes. . . It seemed as though with those two big fellows there, there could be no room for Becky. The part that prayed wondered if perhaps she'd really died, and they had buried her. No one dared ask. They'd beat and cut a man who meant nothing at all in mentioning that they lived along the road. White or colored? No one knew, and least of all themselves. They drifted around from job to job. We, who had cast out their mother because of them, could we take them in? They answered black and white folks by shooting up two men and leaving town. "Godam the white folks; godam the niggers," they shouted as they left town. Becky? Smoke curled up from her chimney; she must be there. Trains passing shook the ground. The ground shook the leaning chimney. Nobody noticed it. A creepy feeling came over all who saw that thin wraith of smoke and felt the trembling of the ground. Folks began to take her food again. They quit it soon because they had a fear. Becky if dead might be a hant, and if alive—it took some nerve even to mention it. . . O pines, whisper to Jesus. . .

It was Sunday. Our congregation had been visiting at Pulverton, and were coming home. There was no wind. The autumn sun, the bell from Ebenezer Church, listless and heavy. Even the pines were stale, sticky, like the smell of food that makes you sick. Before we turned the bend of the road that would show us the Becky cabin, the horses stopped stock-still, pushed back their ears, and nervously whinnied. We urged, then whipped them on. Quarter of a mile away thin smoke curled up from the leaning chimney. . . O pines, whisper to Jesus. . . Goose-flesh came on my skin though there still was neither chill nor wind. Eyes left their sockets for the cabin. Ears burned and throbbed. Uncanny eclipse! fear closed my mind. We were just about to pass. . . Pines shout to Jesus! . . the ground trembled as a ghost train rumbled by. The chimney fell into the cabin. Its thud was like a hollow re-port, ages having passed since it went off. Barlo and I were pulled out of our seats. Dragged to the door that had swung open. Through the dust we saw the bricks in a mound upon the floor. Becky, if she was there, lay under them. I thought I heard a groan. Barlo, mumbling something, threw his Bible on the pile. (No one has ever touched it.) Somehow we got away. My buggy was still on the road. The last thing that I remember was whipping old Dan like fury; I remember nothing after that—that is, until I reached town and folks crowded round to get the true word of it.

Becky was the white woman who had two Negro sons. She's dead; they've gone away. The pines whisper to Jesus. The Bible flaps its leaves with an aimless rustle on her mound.

FACE

Hair—
silver-gray,
like streams of stars,
Brows—
recurved canoes
quivered by the ripples blown by pain,
Her eyes—
mist of tears
condensing on the flesh below
And her channeled muscles
are cluster grapes of sorrow
purple in the evening sun
nearly ripe for worms.

COTTON SONG

Come, brother, come. Lets lift it;
Come now, hewit! roll away!
Shackles fall upon the Judgment Day
But lets not wait for it.

God's body's got a soul,
Bodies like to roll the soul,
Cant blame God if we dont roll,
Come, brother, roll, roll!

Cotton bales are the fleecy way
Weary sinner's bare feet trod,
Softly, softly to the throne of God,
"We aint agwine t wait until th Judgment Day!

Nassur; nassur,
Hump.
Eoho, eoho, roll away!
We aint agwine t wait until th Judgment Day!"

God's body's got a soul,
Bodies like to roll the soul,
Cant blame God if we dont roll,
Come, brother, roll, roll!

Carma

Wind is in the cane. Come along.
Cane leaves swaying, rusty with talk,
Scratching choruses above the guinea's squawk,
Wind is in the cane. Come along.

CARMA, in overalls, and strong as any man, stands behind the old brown mule, driving the wagon home. It bumps, and groans, and shakes as it crosses the railroad track. She, riding it easy. I leave the men around the stove to follow her with my eyes down the red dust road. Nigger woman driving a Georgia chariot down an old dust road. Dixie Pike is what they call it. Maybe she feels my gaze, perhaps she expects it. Anyway, she turns. The sun, which has been slanting over her shoulder, shoots primitive rockets into her mangrove-gloomed, yellow flower face. Hi! Yip! God has left the Moses-people for the nigger. "Gedap." Using reins to slap the mule, she disappears in a cloudy rumble at some indefinite point along the road.

(The sun is hammered to a band of gold. Pine-needles, like mazda, are brilliantly aglow. No rain has come to take the rustle from the falling sweet-gum leaves. Over in the forest, across the swamp, a sawmill blows its closing whistle. Smoke curls up. Marvelous web spun by the spider sawdust pile. Curls up and spreads itself pine-high above the branch, a single silver band along the eastern valley. A black boy . . . you are the most sleepiest man I ever seed, Sleeping Beauty . . . cradled on a gray mule, guided by the hollow sound of cowbells, heads for them through a rusty cotton field. From down the railroad track, the chug-chug of a gas engine announces that the repair gang is coming home. A girl in the yard of a whitewashed shack not much larger than the stack of worn ties piled before it, sings. Her voice is loud. Echoes, like rain, sweep the valley. Dusk takes the polish from the rails. Lights twinkle in scattered houses. From far away, a sad strong song. Pungent and composite, the smell of farmyards is the fragrance of the woman. She does not sing; her body is a song. She is in the forest, dancing.

Torches flare . . juju men, greegree, witch-doctors . . torches
go out. . . The Dixie Pike has grown from a goat path in
Africa.

Night.

Foxie, the bitch, slicks back her ears and barks at the rising
moon.)

> Wind is in the corn. Come along.
> Corn leaves swaying, rusty with talk,
> Scratching choruses above the guinea's squawk,
> Wind is in the corn. Come along.

Carma's tale is the crudest melodrama. Her husband's in the
gang. And its her fault he got there. Working with a contrac-
tor, he was away most of the time. She had others. No one
blames her for that. He returned one day and hung around the
town where he picked up week-old boasts and rumors. . . Bane
accused her. She denied. He couldnt see that she was becoming hysterical. He would have liked to take his fists and beat
her. Who was strong as a man. Stronger. Words, like cork-
screws, wormed to her strength. It fizzled out. Grabbing a gun
she rushed from the house and plunged across the road into a
cane-brake. . There, in quarter heaven shone the crescent
moon. . . Bane was afraid to follow till he heard the gun go
off. Then he wasted half an hour gathering the neighbor men.
They met in the road where lamp-light showed tracks dissolv-
ing in the loose earth about the cane. The search began. Moths
flickered the lamps. They put them out. Really, because she
still might be live enough to shoot. Time and space have no
meaning in a canefield. No more than the interminable
stalks. . . Some one stumbled over her. A cry went up. From
the road, one would have thought that they were cornering a
rabbit or a skunk. . . It is difficult carrying dead weight
through cane. They placed her on the sofa. A curious, nosey
somebody looked for the wound. This fussing with her clothes
aroused her. Her eyes were weak and pitiable for so strong a
woman. Slowly, then like a flash, Bane came to know that
the shot she fired, with averted head, was aimed to whistle like
a dying hornet through the cane. Twice deceived, and one

deception proved the other. His head went off. Slashed one of
the men who'd helped, the man who'd stumbled over her.
Now he's in the gang. Who was her husband. Should she not
take others, this Carma, strong as a man, whose tale as I have
told it is the crudest melodrama?

> Wind is in the cane. Come along.
> Cane leaves swaying, rusty with talk,
> Scratching choruses above the guinea's squawk,
> Wind is in the time. Come along.

SONG OF THE SON

Pour O pour that parting soul in song,
O pour it in the sawdust glow of night,
Into the velvet pine-smoke air to-night,
And let the valley carry it along.
And let the valley carry it along.

O land and soil, red soil and sweet-gum tree,
So scant of grass, so profligate of pines,
Now just before an epoch's sun declines
Thy son, in time, I have returned to thee,
Thy son, I have in time returned to thee.

In time, for though the sun is setting on
A song-lit race of slaves, it has not set;
Though late, O soil, it is not too late yet
To catch thy plaintive soul, leaving, soon gone,
Leaving, to catch thy plaintive soul soon gone.

O Negro slaves, dark purple ripened plums,
Squeezed, and bursting in the pine-wood air,
Passing, before they stripped the old tree bare
One plum was saved for me, one seed becomes

An everlasting song, a singing tree,
Caroling softly souls of slavery,
What they were, and what they are to me,
Caroling softly souls of slavery.

GEORGIA DUSK

The sky, lazily disdaining to pursue
  The setting sun, too indolent to hold
  A lengthened tournament for flashing gold,
Passively darkens for night's barbecue,

A feast of moon and men and barking hounds,
  An orgy for some genius of the South
  With blood-hot eyes and cane-lipped scented mouth,
Surprised in making folk-songs from soul sounds.

The sawmill blows its whistle, buzz-saws stop,
  And silence breaks the bud of knoll and hill,
  Soft settling pollen where plowed lands fulfill
Their early promise of a bumper crop.

Smoke from the pyramidal sawdust pile
  Curls up, blue ghosts of trees, tarrying low
  Where only chips and stumps are left to show
The solid proof of former domicile.

Meanwhile, the men, with vestiges of pomp,
  Race memories of king and caravan,
  High-priests, an ostrich, and a juju-man,
Go singing through the footpaths of the swamp

Their voices rise . . the pine trees are guitars,
  Strumming, pine-needles fall like sheets of rain . .
  Their voices rise . . the chorus of the cane
Is caroling a vesper to the stars. .

O singers, resinous and soft your songs
  Above the sacred whisper of the pines,
  Give virgin lips to cornfield concubines,
Bring dreams of Christ to dusky cane-lipped throngs.

Fern

FACE flowed into her eyes. Flowed in soft cream foam and plaintive ripples, in such a way that wherever your glance may momentarily have rested, it immediately thereafter wavered in the direction of her eyes. The soft suggestion of down slightly darkened, like the shadow of a bird's wing might, the creamy brown color of her upper lip. Why, after noticing it, you sought her eyes, I cannot tell you. Her nose was aquiline, Semitic. If you have heard a Jewish cantor sing, if he has touched you and made your own sorrow seem trivial when compared with his, you will know my feeling when I follow the curves of her profile, like mobile rivers, to their common delta. They were strange eyes. In this, that they sought nothing—that is, nothing that was obvious and tangible and that one could see, and they gave the impression that nothing was to be denied. When a woman seeks, you will have observed, her eyes deny. Fern's eyes desired nothing that you could give her; there was no reason why they should withhold. Men saw her eyes and fooled themselves. Fern's eyes said to them that she was easy. When she was young, a few men took her, but got no joy from it. And then, once done, they felt bound to her (quite unlike their hit and run with other girls), felt as though it would take them a lifetime to fulfill an obligation which they could find no name for. They became attached to her, and hungered after finding the barest trace of what she might desire. As she grew up, new men who came to town felt as almost everyone did who ever saw her: that they would not be denied. Men were everlastingly bringing her their bodies. Something inside of her got tired of them, I guess, for I am certain that for the life of her she could not tell why or how she began to turn them off. A man in fever is no trifling thing to send away. They began to leave her, baffled and ashamed, yet vowing to themselves that some day they would do some fine thing for her: send her candy every week and not let her know whom it came from, watch out for her wedding-day and give her a magnificent something with no name on it, buy a house and deed it to her, rescue her from some unworthy fellow who had tricked her into marrying him. As you know, men are apt to idolize or fear that which they cannot understand, especially if it be a woman. She did not deny them, yet the fact was that they were denied. A sort of superstition crept into their consciousness of her being somehow above them. Being above them meant that she was not to be approached by anyone. She became a virgin. Now a virgin in a small southern town is by no means the usual thing, if you will believe me. That the sexes were made to mate is the practice of the South. Particularly, black folks were made to mate. And it is black folks whom I have been talking about thus far. What white men thought of Fern I can arrive at only by analogy. They let her alone.

Anyone, of course, could see her, could see her eyes. If you walked up the Dixie Pike most any time of day, you'd be most like to see her resting listless-like on the railing of her porch, back propped against a post, head tilted a little forward because there was a nail in the porch post just where her head came which for some reason or other she never took the trouble to pull out. Her eyes, if it were sunset, rested idly where the sun, molten and glorious, was pouring down between the fringe of pines. Or maybe they gazed at the gray cabin on the knoll from which an evening folk-song was coming. Perhaps they followed a cow that had been turned loose to roam and feed on cotton-stalks and corn leaves. Like as not they'd settle on some vague spot above the horizon, though hardly a trace of wistfulness would come to them. If it were dusk, then they'd wait for the search-light of the evening train which you could see miles up the track before it flared across the Dixie Pike, close to her home. Wherever they looked, you'd follow them and then waver back. Like her face, the whole countryside seemed to flow into her eyes. Flowed into them with the soft listless cadence of Georgia's South. A young Negro, once, was looking at her, spellbound, from the road. A white man passing in a buggy had to flick him with his whip if he was to get by without running him over. I first saw her on her porch. I was passing with a fellow whose crusty numbness (I was from the North and suspected of being prejudiced and stuck-up) was melting as he found me warm. I asked him who she was. "That's Fern," was all that I could get from him. Some folks already thought that I was given to nosing around; I let it go at that, so far as questions were concerned. But at first sight of her I felt as if I heard a Jewish cantor sing. As if his singing rose above the unheard chorus of a folk-song. And I felt bound to her. I too had my dreams: something I would do for her. I have knocked about from town to town too much not to know the futility of mere change of place. Besides, picture if you can, this cream-colored solitary girl sitting at a tenement window looking down on the indifferent throngs of Harlem. Better that she listen to folk-songs at dusk in Georgia, you would say, and so would I. Or, suppose she came up North and married. Even a doctor or a lawyer, say, one who would be sure to get along—that is, make money. You and I know, who have had experience in such things, that love is not a thing like prejudice which can be bettered by changes of town. Could men in Washington, Chicago, or New York, more than the men of Georgia, bring her something left vacant by the bestowal of their bodies? You and I who know men in these cities will have to say, they could not. See her out and out a prostitute along State Street in Chicago. See her move into a southern town where white men are more aggressive. See her become a white man's concubine. . . Something I must do for her. There was myself. What could I do for her? Talk, of course. Push back the fringe of pines upon new horizons. To what purpose? and what for? Her? Myself? Men in her case seem to lose their selfishness. I lost mine before I touched her. I ask you, friend (it makes no difference if you sit in the Pullman or the Jim Crow as the train crosses her road), what thoughts would come to you—that is, after you'd finished with the thoughts that leap into men's minds at the sight of a pretty woman who will not deny them; what thoughts would come to you, had you seen her in a quick flash, keen and intuitively, as she sat there on her porch when your train thundered by? Would you have got off at the next station and come back for her to take her where? Would you have completely forgotten her as soon as you reached Macon, Atlanta, Augusta, Pasadena, Madison, Chicago, Boston, or New Orleans? Would you tell your wife or sweetheart about a girl you saw? Your thoughts can help me, and I would like to know. Something I would do for her. . .

One evening I walked up the Pike on purpose, and stopped to say hello. Some of her family were about, but they moved away to make room for me. Damn if I knew how to begin. Would you? Mr. and Miss So-and-So, people, the weather, the crops, the new preacher, the frolic, the church benefit, rabbit and possum hunting, the new soft drink they had at old Pap's store, the schedule of the trains, what kind of town Macon was, Negro's migration north, boll-weevils, syrup, the Bible— to all these things she gave a yassur or nassur, without further comment. I began to wonder if perhaps my own emotional sensibility had played one of its tricks on me. "Lets take a walk," I at last ventured. The suggestion, coming after so long an isolation, was novel enough, I guess, to surprise. But it wasnt that. Something told me that men before me had said just that as a prelude to the offering of their bodies. I tried to tell her with my eyes. I think she understood. The thing from her that made my throat catch, vanished. Its passing left her visible in a way I'd thought, but never seen. We walked down the Pike with people on all the porches gaping at us. "Doesnt it make you mad?" She meant the row of petty gossiping people. She meant the world. Through a canebrake that was ripe for cutting, the branch was reached. Under a sweet-gum tree, and where reddish leaves had dammed the creek a little, we sat down. Dusk, suggesting the almost imperceptible procession of giant trees, settled with a purple haze about the cane. I felt strange, as I always do in Georgia, particularly at dusk. I felt that things unseen to men were tangibly immediate. It would not have surprised me had I had vision. People have them in Georgia more often than you would suppose. A black woman once saw the mother of Christ and drew her in charcoal on the courthouse wall. . . When one is on the soil of one's ancestors, most anything can come to one. . . From force of habit, I suppose, I held Fern in my arms—that is, without at first noticing it. Then my mind came back to her. Her eyes, unusually weird and open, held me. Held God. He flowed in as I've seen the countryside flow in. Seen men. I must have done something—what, I dont know, in the confusion of my emotion. She sprang up. Rushed some distance from me. Fell to her knees, and began swaying, swaying. Her body was tortured with something it could not let out. Like boiling sap it flooded arms and fingers till she shook them as if they burned her. It found her throat, and spattered inarticulately in plaintive, convulsive sounds, mingled with calls to Christ Jesus. And then she sang, brokenly. A Jewish cantor singing with a broken voice. A child's voice, uncertain, or an old man's. Dusk hid her; I could hear only her song. It seemed to me as though she were pounding her head in anguish upon the ground. I rushed to her. She fainted in my arms.

There was talk about her fainting with me in the canefield. And I got one or two ugly looks from town men who'd set themselves up to protect her. In fact, there was talk of making me leave town. But they never did. They kept a watch-out for me, though. Shortly after, I came back North. From the train window I saw her as I crossed her road. Saw her on her porch, head tilted a little forward where the nail was, eyes vaguely focused on the sunset. Saw her face flow into them, the countryside and something that I call God, flowing into them. . . Nothing ever really happened. Nothing ever came to Fern, not even I. Something I would do for her. Some fine unnamed thing. . . And, friend, you? She is still living, I have reason to know. Her name, against the chance that you might happen down that way, is Fernie May Rosen.

NULLO

A spray of pine-needles,
Dipped in western horizon gold,
Fell onto a path.
Dry moulds of cow-hoofs.
In the forest.
Rabbits knew not of their falling,
Nor did the forest catch aflame.

EVENING SONG

Full moon rising on the waters of my heart,
Lakes and moon and fires,
Cloine tires,
Holding her lips apart.

Promises of slumber leaving shore to charm the moon,
Miracle made vesper-keeps,
Cloine sleeps,
And I'll be sleeping soon.

Cloine, curled like the sleepy waters where the moon-waves
    start,
Radiant, resplendently she gleams,
Cloine dreams,
Lips pressed against my heart.

Esther

I

Nine.

ESTHER'S hair falls in soft curls about her high-cheek-boned
chalk-white face. Esther's hair would be beautiful if there
were more gloss to it. And if her face were not prematurely
serious, one would call it pretty. Her cheeks are too flat and
dead for a girl of nine. Esther looks like a little white child,
starched, frilled, as she walks slowly from her home towards
her father's grocery store. She is about to turn in Broad from
Maple Street. White and black men loafing on the corner hold
no interest for her. Then a strange thing happens. A clean-
muscled, magnificent, black-skinned Negro, whom she had
heard her father mention as King Barlo, suddenly drops to his
knees on a spot called the Spittoon. White men, unaware of
him, continue squirting tobacco juice in his direction. The saf-
fron fluid splashes on his face. His smooth black face begins to
glisten and to shine. Soon, people notice him, and gather
round. His eyes are rapturous upon the heavens. Lips and nostrils quiver. Barlo is in a religious trance. Town folks know it.
They are not startled. They are not afraid. They gather round.
Some beg boxes from the grocery stores. From old McGregor's
notion shop. A coffin-case is pressed into use. Folks line the
curb-stones. Business men close shop. And Banker Warply parks
his car close by. Silently, all await the prophet's voice. The sheriff, a great florid fellow whose leggings never meet around his
bulging calves, swears in three deputies. "Wall, y cant never tell
what a nigger like King Barlo might be up t." Soda bottles, five
fingers full of shine, are passed to those who want them. A
couple of stray dogs start a fight. Old Goodlow's cow comes
flopping up the street. Barlo, still as an Indian fakir, has not
moved. The town bell strikes six. The sun slips in behind a
heavy mass of horizon cloud. The crowd is hushed and expectant. Barlo's under jaw relaxes, and his lips begin to move.

"Jesus has been awhisperin strange words deep down, O way down deep, deep in my ears."

Hums of awe and of excitement.

"He called me to His side an said, 'Git down on your knees beside me, son, Ise gwine t whisper in your ears.'"

An old sister cries, "Ah, Lord."

"'Ise agwine t whisper in your ears,' he said, an I replied, 'Thy will be done on earth as it is in heaven.'"

"Ah, Lord. Amen. Amen."

"An Lord Jesus whispered strange good words deep down, O way down deep, deep in my ears. An He said, 'Tell em till you feel your throat on fire.' I saw a vision. I saw a man arise, an he was big an black an powerful—"

Some one yells, "Preach it, preacher, preach it!"

"—but his head was caught up in th clouds. An while he was agazin at th heavens, heart filled up with th Lord, some little white-ant biddies came an tied his feet to chains. They led him t th coast, they led him t th sea, they led him across th ocean an they didnt set him free. The old coast didnt miss him, an th new coast wasnt free, he left the old-coast brothers, t give birth t you an me. O Lord, great God Almighty, t give birth t you an me."

Barlo pauses. Old gray mothers are in tears. Fragments of melodies are being hummed. White folks are touched and curiously awed. Off to themselves, white and black preachers confer as to how best to rid themselves of the vagrant, usurping fellow. Barlo looks as though he is struggling to continue. People are hushed. One can hear weevils work. Dusk is falling rapidly, and the customary store lights fail to throw their feeble glow across the gray dust and flagging of the Georgia town. Barlo rises to his full height. He is immense. To the people he assumes the outlines of his visioned African. In a mighty voice he bellows:

"Brothers an sisters, turn your faces t th sweet face of the Lord, an fill your hearts with glory. Open your eyes an see th dawnin of th mornin light. Open your ears—"

Years afterwards Esther was told that at that very moment a great, heavy, rumbling voice actually was heard. That hosts of angels and of demons paraded up and down the streets all night. That King Barlo rode out of town astride a pitch-black bull that had a glowing gold ring in its nose. And that old

Limp Underwood, who hated niggers, woke up next morning
to find that he held a black man in his arms. This much is certain: an inspired Negress, of wide reputation for being sanctified, drew a portrait of a black madonna on the court-house
wall. And King Barlo left town. He left his image indelibly
upon the mind of Esther. He became the starting point of the
only living patterns that her mind was to know.

2

Sixteen.

Esther begins to dream. The low evening sun sets the windows of McGregor's notion shop aflame. Esther makes believe
that they really are aflame. The town fire department rushes
madly down the road. It ruthlessly shoves black and white idlers
to one side. It whoops. It clangs. It rescues from the second-
story window a dimpled infant which she claims for her own.
How had she come by it? She thinks of it immaculately. It is a
sin to think of it immaculately. She must dream no more. She
must repent her sin. Another dream comes. There is no fire
department. There are no heroic men. The fire starts. The
loafers on the corner form a circle, chew their tobacco faster,
and squirt juice just as fast as they can chew. Gallons on top of
gallons they squirt upon the flames. The air reeks with the
stench of scorched tobacco juice. Women, fat chunky Negro
women, lean scrawny white women, pull their skirts up above
their heads and display the most ludicrous underclothes. The
women scoot in all directions from the danger zone. She alone
is left to take the baby in her arms. But what a baby! Black,
singed, woolly, tobacco-juice baby—ugly as sin. Once held to
her breast, miraculous thing: its breath is sweet and its lips can
nibble. She loves it frantically. Her joy in it changes the town
folks' jeers to harmless jealousy, and she is left alone.

Twenty-two.

Esther's schooling is over. She works behind the counter of her
father's grocery store. "To keep the money in the family," so

he said. She is learning to make distinctions between the business and the social worlds. "Good business comes from remembering that the white folks dont divide the niggers, Esther. Be just as black as any man who has a silver dollar." Esther listlessly forgets that she is near white, and that her father is the richest colored man in town. Black folk who drift in to buy lard and snuff and flour of her, call her a sweet-natured, accommodating girl. She learns their names. She forgets them. She thinks about men. "I dont appeal to them. I wonder why." She recalls an affair she had with a little fair boy while still in school. It had ended in her shame when he as much as told her that for sweetness he preferred a lollipop. She remembers the salesman from the North who wanted to take her to the movies that first night he was in town. She refused, of course. And he never came back, having found out who she was. She thinks of Barlo. Barlo's image gives her a slightly stale thrill. She spices it by telling herself his glories. Black. Magnetically so. Best cotton picker in the county, in the state, in the whole world for that matter. Best man with his fists, best man with dice, with a razor. Promoter of church benefits. Of colored fairs. Vagrant preacher. Lover of all the women for miles and miles around. Esther decides that she loves him. And with a vague sense of life slipping by, she resolves that she will tell him so, whatever people say, the next time he comes to town. After the making of this resolution which becomes a sort of wedding cake for her to tuck beneath her pillow and go to sleep upon, she sees nothing of Barlo for five years. Her hair thins. It looks like the dull silk on puny corn ears. Her face pales until it is the color of the gray dust that dances with dead cotton leaves. .

3

Esther is twenty-seven.

Esther sells lard and snuff and flour to vague black faces that drift in her store to ask for them. Her eyes hardly see the people to whom she gives change. Her body is lean and beaten. She rests listlessly against the counter, too weary to sit down. From the street some one shouts, "King Barlo has come back to town." He passes her window, driving a large new car. Cut-out open. He veers to the curb, and steps out. Barlo has made money on cotton during the war. He is as rich as anyone. Esther suddenly is animate. She goes to her door. She sees him at a distance, the center of a group of credulous men. She hears the deep-bass rumble of his talk. The sun swings low. McGregor's windows are aflame again. Pale flame. A sharply dressed white girl passes by. For a moment Esther wishes that she might be like her. Not white; she has no need for being that. But sharp, sporty, with get-up about her. Barlo is connected with that wish. She mustnt wish. Wishes only make you restless. Emptiness is a thing that grows by being moved. "I'll not think. Not wish. Just set my mind against it." Then the thought comes to her that those purposeless, easy-going men will possess him, if she doesnt. Purpose is not dead in her, now that she comes to think of it. That loose women will have their arms around him at Nat Bowle's place to-night. As if her veins are full of fired sun-bleached southern shanties, a swift heat sweeps them. Dead dreams, and a forgotten resolution are carried upward by the flames. Pale flames. "They shant have him. Oh, they shall not. Not if it kills me they shant have him." Jerky, aflutter, she closes the store and starts home. Folks lazing on store window-sills wonder what on earth can be the matter with Jim Crane's gal, as she passes them. "Come to remember, she always was a little off, a little crazy, I reckon." Esther seeks her own room, and locks the door. Her mind is a pink mesh-bag filled with baby toes.

Using the noise of the town clock striking twelve to cover the creaks of her departure, Esther slips into the quiet road. The town, her parents, most everyone is sound asleep. This fact is a stable thing that comforts her. After sundown a chill wind came up from the west. It is still blowing, but to her it is a steady, settled thing like the cold. She wants her mind to be like that. Solid, contained, and blank as a sheet of darkened ice. She will not permit herself to notice the peculiar phosphorescent glitter of the sweet-gum leaves. Their movement would excite her. Exciting too, the recession of the dull familiar homes she knows so well. She doesnt know them at all. She closes her eyes, and holds them tightly. Wont do. Her being aware that they are closed recalls her purpose. She does not want to think of it. She opens them. She turns now into the deserted business street. The corrugated iron canopies and mule- and horse-gnawed hitching posts bring her a strange composure. Ghosts of the commonplaces of her daily life take stride with her and become her companions. And the echoes of her heels upon the flagging are rhythmically monotonous and soothing. Crossing the street at the corner of McGregor's notion shop, she thinks that the windows are a dull flame. Only a fancy. She walks faster. Then runs. A turn into a side street brings her abruptly to Nat Bowle's place. The house is squat and dark. It is always dark. Barlo is within. Quietly she opens the outside door and steps in. She passes through a small room. Pauses before a flight of stairs down which people's voices, muffled, come. The air is heavy with fresh tobacco smoke. It makes her sick. She wants to turn back. She goes up the steps. As if she were mounting to some great height, her head spins She is violently dizzy. Blackness rushes to her eyes. And then she finds that she is in a large room. Barlo is before her.

"Well, I'm sholy damned—skuse me, but what, what brought you here, lil milk-white gal?"

"You." Her voice sounds like a frightened child's that calls homeward from some point miles away.

"Me?"

"Yes, you Barlo."

"This aint th place fer y. This aint th place fer y."

"I know. I know. But I've come for you."

"For me for what?"

She manages to look deep and straight into his eyes. He is slow at understanding. Guffaws and giggles break out from all around the room. A coarse woman's voice remarks, "So thats how th dictie niggers does it." Laughs. "Mus give em credit fo their gall."

Esther doesnt hear. Barlo does. His faculties are jogged. She sees a smile, ugly and repulsive to her, working upward through thick licker fumes. Barlo seems hideous. The thought comes suddenly, that conception with a drunken man must be a mighty sin. She draws away, frozen. Like a somnambulist she wheels around and walks stiffly to the stairs. Down them. Jeers and hoots pelter bluntly upon her back. She steps out. There is no air, no street, and the town has completely disappeared.

CONVERSION

African Guardian of Souls,
Drunk with rum,
Feasting on a strange cassava,
Yielding to new words and a weak palabra
Of a white-faced sardonic god—
Grins, cries
Amen,
Shouts hosanna.

PORTRAIT IN GEORGIA

Hair—braided chestnut,
    coiled like a lyncher's rope,
Eyes—fagots,
Lips—old scars, or the first red blisters,
Breath—the last sweet scent of cane,
And her slim body, white as the ash
    of black flesh after flame.

Blood-Burning Moon

I

Up from the skeleton stone walls, up from the rotting floor boards and the solid hand-hewn beams of oak of the pre-war cotton factory, dusk came. Up from the dusk the full moon came. Glowing like a fired pine-knot, it illumined the great door and soft showered the Negro shanties aligned along the single street of factory town. The full moon in the great door was an omen. Negro women improvised songs against its spell.

Louisa sang as she came over the crest of the hill from the white folks' kitchen. Her skin was the color of oak leaves on young trees in fall. Her breasts, firm and up-pointed like ripe acorns. And her singing had the low murmur of winds in fig trees. Bob Stone, younger son of the people she worked for, loved her. By the way the world reckons things, he had won her. By measure of that warm glow which came into her mind at the thought of him, he had won her. Tom Burwell, whom the whole town called Big Boy, also loved her. But working in the fields all day, and far away from her, gave him no chance to show it. Though often enough of evenings he had tried to. Somehow, he never got along. Strong as he was with hands upon the ax or plow, he found it difficult to hold her. Or so he thought. But the fact was that he held her to factory town more firmly than he thought for. His black balanced, and pulled against, the white of Stone, when she thought of them. And her mind was vaguely upon them as she came over the crest of the hill, coming from the white folks' kitchen. As she sang softly at the evil face of the full moon.

A strange stir was in her. Indolently, she tried to fix upon Bob or Tom as the cause of it. To meet Bob in the canebrake, as she was going to do an hour or so later, was nothing new. And Tom's proposal which she felt on its way to her could be indefinitely put off. Separately, there was no unusual significance to either one. But for some reason, they jumbled when her eyes gazed vacantly at the rising moon. And from the jumble came the stir that was strangely within her. Her lips trembled. The slow rhythm of her song grew agitant and restless. Rusty black and tan spotted hounds, lying in the dark corners of porches or prowling around back yards, put their noses in the air and caught its tremor. They began plaintively to yelp and howl. Chickens woke up and cackled. Intermittently, all over the countryside dogs barked and roosters crowed as if heralding a weird dawn or some ungodly awakening. The women sang lustily. Their songs were cotton-wads to stop their ears. Louisa came down into factory town and sank wearily upon the step before her home. The moon was rising towards a thick cloud-bank which soon would hide it.

> Red nigger moon. Sinner!
> Blood-burning moon. Sinner!
> Come out that fact'ry door.

2

Up from the deep dusk of a cleared spot on the edge of the forest a mellow glow arose and spread fan-wise into the low-hanging heavens. And all around the air was heavy with the scent of boiling cane. A large pile of cane-stalks lay like ribboned shadows upon the ground. A mule, harnessed to a pole, trudged lazily round and round the pivot of the grinder. Beneath a swaying oil lamp, a Negro alternately whipped out at the mule, and fed cane-stalks to the grinder. A fat boy waddled pails of fresh ground juice between the grinder and the boiling stove. Steam came from the copper boiling pan. The scent of cane came from the copper pan and drenched the forest and the hill that sloped to factory town, beneath its fragrance. It drenched the men in circle seated around the stove. Some of them chewed at the white pulp of stalks, but there was no need for them to, if all they wanted was to taste the cane. One tasted it in factory town. And from factory town one could see the soft haze thrown by the glowing stove upon the low-hanging heavens.

Old David Georgia stirred the thickening syrup with a long

ladle, and ever so often drew it off. Old David Georgia tended
his stove and told tales about the white folks, about moon-
shining and cotton picking, and about sweet nigger gals, to
the men who sat there about his stove to listen to him. Tom
Burwell chewed cane-stalk and laughed with the others till
someone mentioned Louisa. Till some one said something
about Louisa and Bob Stone, about the silk stockings she
must have gotten from him. Blood ran up Tom's neck hotter
than the glow that flooded from the stove. He sprang up.
Glared at the men and said, "She's my gal." Will Manning
laughed. Tom strode over to him. Yanked him up and knocked
him to the ground. Several of Manning's friends got up to
fight for him. Tom whipped out a long knife and would have
cut them to shreds if they hadnt ducked into the woods. Tom
had had enough. He nodded to Old David Georgia and
swung down the path to factory town. Just then, the dogs
started barking and the roosters began to crow. Tom felt
funny. Away from the fight, away from the stove, chill got to
him. He shivered. He shuddered when he saw the full moon
rising towards the cloud-bank. He who didnt give a godam
for the fears of old women. He forced his mind to fasten on
Louisa. Bob Stone. Better not be. He turned into the street
and saw Louisa sitting before her home. He went towards her,
ambling, touched the brim of a marvelously shaped, spotted,
felt hat, said he wanted to say something to her, and then
found that he didnt know what he had to say, or if he did, that
he couldnt say it. He shoved his big fists in his overalls,
grinned, and started to move off.

"Youall want me, Tom?"

"Thats what us wants, sho, Louisa."

"Well, here I am—"

"An here I is, but that aint ahelpin none, all th same."

"You wanted to say something? . ."

"I did that, sho. But words is like th spots on dice: no matter
how y fumbles em, there's times when they jes wont come. I
dunno why. Seems like th love I feels fo yo done stole m
tongue. I got it now. Whee! Louisa, honey, I oughtnt tell y, I
feel I oughtnt cause yo is young an goes t church an I has had
other gals, but Louisa I sho do love y. Lil gal, Ise watched y
from them first days when youall sat right here befo yo door

befo th well an sang sometimes in a way that like t broke m
heart. Ise carried y with me into the fields, day after day, an
after that, an I sho can plow when yo is there, an I can pick
cotton. Yassur! Come near beatin Barlo yesterday. I sho did.
Yassur! An next year if ole Stone'll trust me, I'll have a farm.
My own. My bales will buy yo what y gets from white folks
now. Silk stockings an purple dresses—course I dont believe
what some folks been whisperin as t how y gets them things
now. White folks always did do for niggers what they likes. An
they jes cant help alikin yo, Louisa. Bob Stone likes y. Course
he does. But not th way folks is awhisperin. Does he, hon?"

"I dont know what you mean, Tom."

"Course y dont. Ise already cut two niggers. Had t hon, t
tell em so. Niggers always tryin t make somethin out a nothin.
An then besides, white folks aint up t them tricks so much
nowadays. Godam better not be. Leastawise not with yo.
Cause I wouldnt stand f it. Nassur."

"What would you do, Tom?"

"Cut him jes like I cut a nigger."

"No, Tom—"

"I said I would an there aint no mo to it. But that aint th
talk f now. Sing, honey Louisa, an while I'm listenin t y I'll be
makin love."

Tom took her hand in his. Against the tough thickness of his
own, hers felt soft and small. His huge body slipped down to
the step beside her. The full moon sank upward into the deep
purple of the cloud-bank. An old woman brought a lighted
lamp and hung it on the common well whose bulky shadow
squatted in the middle of the road, opposite Tom and Louisa.
The old woman lifted the well-lid, took hold the chain, and
began drawing up the heavy bucket. As she did so, she sang.
Figures shifted, restless-like, between lamp and window in the
front rooms of the shanties. Shadows of the figures fought
each other on the gray dust of the road. Figures raised the windows and joined the old woman in song. Louisa and Tom, the
whole street, singing:

> Red nigger moon. Sinner!
> Blood-burning moon. Sinner!
> Come out that fact'ry door.

3

Bob Stone sauntered from his veranda out into the gloom of fir trees and magnolias. The clear white of his skin paled, and the flush of his cheeks turned purple. As if to balance this outer change, his mind became consciously a white man's. He passed the house with its huge open hearth which, in the days of slavery, was the plantation cookery. He saw Louisa bent over that hearth. He went in as a master should and took her. Direct, honest, bold. None of this sneaking that he had to go through now. The contrast was repulsive to him. His family had lost ground. Hell no, his family still owned the niggers, practically. Damned if they did, or he wouldnt have to duck around so. What would they think if they knew? His mother? His sister? He shouldnt mention them, shouldnt think of them in this connection. There in the dusk he blushed at doing so. Fellows about town were all right, but how about his friends up North? He could see them incredible, repulsed. They didnt know. The thought first made him laugh. Then, with their eyes still upon him, he began to feel embarrassed. He felt the need of explaining things to them. Explain hell. They wouldnt understand, and moreover, who ever heard of a Southerner getting on his knees to any Yankee, or anyone. No sir. He was going to see Louisa to-night, and love her. She was lovely—in her way. Nigger way. What way was that? Damned if he knew. Must know. He'd known her long enough to know. Was there something about niggers that you couldnt know? Listening to them at church didnt tell you anything. Looking at them didnt tell you anything. Talking to them didnt tell you anything—unless it was gossip, unless they wanted to talk. Of course, about farming, and licker, and craps—but those werent nigger. Nigger was something more. How much more? Something to be afraid of, more? Hell no. Who ever heard of being afraid of a nigger? Tom Burwell. Cartwell had told him that Tom went with Louisa after she reached home. No sir. No nigger had ever been with his girl. He'd like to see one try. Some position for him to be in. Him, Bob Stone, of the old Stone family, in a scrap with a nigger over a nigger girl. In the good old

days. . . Ha! Those were the days. His family had lost ground.
Not so much, though. Enough for him to have to cut through
old Lemon's canefield by way of the woods, that he might
meet her. She was worth it. Beautiful nigger gal. Why nigger?
Why not, just gal? No, it was because she was nigger that he
went to her. Sweet. . . The scent of boiling cane came to him.
Then he saw the rich glow of the stove. He heard the voices of
the men circled around it. He was about to skirt the clearing
when he heard his own name mentioned. He stopped.
Quivering. Leaning against a tree, he listened.

"Bad nigger. Yassur, he sho is one bad nigger when he gets
started."

"Tom Burwell's been on th gang three times fo cuttin
men."

"What y think he's agwine t do t Bob Stone?"

"Dunno yet. He aint found out. When he does— Baby!"

"Aint no tellin."

"Young Stone aint no quitter an I ken tell y that. Blood of
th old uns in his veins."

"Thats right. He'll scrap, sho."

"Be gettin too hot f niggers round this away."

"Shut up, nigger. Y dont know what y talkin bout."

Bob Stone's ears burned as though he had been holding
them over the stove. Sizzling heat welled up within him. His
feet felt as if they rested on red-hot coals. They stung him to
quick movement. He circled the fringe of the glowing. Not a
twig cracked beneath his feet. He reached the path that led to
factory town. Plunged furiously down it. Halfway along, a
blindness within veered aside. He crashed into the bordering
canebrake. Cane leaves cut his face and lips. He tasted blood.
He threw himself down and dug his fingers in the ground. The
earth was cool. Cane-roots took the fever from his hands. After
a long while, or so it seemed to him, the thought came to him
that it must be time to see Louisa. He got to his feet and
walked calmly to their meeting place. No Louisa. Tom Burwell
had her. Veins in his forehead bulged and distended. Saliva
moistened the dried blood on his lips. He bit down on his lips.
He tasted blood. Not his own blood; Tom Burwell's blood.
Bob drove through the cane and out again upon the road. A
hound swung down the path before him towards factory town.

Bob couldnt see it. The dog loped aside to let him pass. Bob's blind rushing made him stumble over it. He fell with a thud that dazed him. The hound yelped. Answering yelps came from all over the countryside. Chickens cackled. Roosters crowed, heralding the bloodshot eyes of southern awakening. Singers in the town were silenced. They shut their windows down. Palpitant between the rooster crows, a chill hush settled upon the huddled forms of Tom and Louisa. A figure rushed from the shadow and stood before them. Tom popped to his feet.

"Whats y want?"

"I'm Bob Stone."

"Yassur—an I'm Tom Burwell. Whats y want?"

Bob lunged at him. Tom side-stepped, caught him by the shoulder, and flung him to the ground. Straddled him.

"Let me up."

"Yassur—but watch yo doins, Bob Stone."

A few dark figures, drawn by the sound of scuffle, stood about them. Bob sprang to his feet.

"Fight like a man, Tom Burwell, an I'll lick y."

Again he lunged. Tom side-stepped and flung him to the ground. Straddled him.

"Get off me, you godam nigger you."

"Yo sho has started somethin now. Get up."

Tom yanked him up and began hammering at him. Each blow sounded as if it smashed into a precious, irreplaceable soft something. Beneath them, Bob staggered back. He reached in his pocket and whipped out a knife.

"Thats my game, sho."

Blue flash, a steel blade slashed across Bob Stone's throat. He had a sweetish sick feeling. Blood began to flow. Then he felt a sharp twitch of pain. He let his knife drop. He slapped one hand against his neck. He pressed the other on top of his head as if to hold it down. He groaned. He turned, and staggered towards the crest of the hill in the direction of white town. Negroes who had seen the fight slunk into their homes and blew the lamps out. Louisa, dazed, hysterical, refused to go indoors. She slipped, crumbled, her body loosely propped against the woodwork of the well. Tom Burwell leaned against it. He seemed rooted there.

Bob reached Broad Street. White men rushed up to him. He collapsed in their arms.

"Tom Burwell. . ."

White men like ants upon a forage rushed about. Except for the taut hum of their moving, all was silent. Shotguns, revolvers, rope, kerosene, torches. Two high-powered cars with glaring search-lights. They came together. The taut hum rose to a low roar. Then nothing could be heard but the flop of their feet in the thick dust of the road. The moving body of their silence preceded them over the crest of the hill into factory town. It flattened the Negroes beneath it. It rolled to the wall of the factory, where it stopped. Tom knew that they were coming. He couldnt move. And then he saw the search-lights of the two cars glaring down on him. A quick shock went through him. He stiffened. He started to run. A yell went up from the mob. Tom wheeled about and faced them. They poured down on him. They swarmed. A large man with dead-white face and flabby cheeks came to him and almost jabbed a gun-barrel through his guts.

"Hands behind y, nigger."

Tom's wrist were bound. The big man shoved him to the well. Burn him over it, and when the woodwork caved in, his body would drop to the bottom. Two deaths for a godam nigger. Louisa was driven back. The mob pushed in. Its pressure, its momentum was too great. Drag him to the factory. Wood and stakes already there. Tom moved in the direction indicated. But they had to drag him. They reached the great door. Too many to get in there. The mob divided and flowed around the walls to either side. The big man shoved him through the door. The mob pressed in from the sides. Taut humming. No words. A stake was sunk into the ground. Rotting floor boards piled around it. Kerosene poured on the rotting floor boards. Tom bound to the stake. His breast was bare. Nails scratches let little lines of blood trickle down and mat into the hair. His face, his eyes were set and stony. Except for irregular breathing, one would have thought him already dead. Torches were flung onto the pile. A great flare muffled in black smoke shot upward. The mob yelled. The mob was silent. Now Tom could be seen within the flames. Only his head, erect, lean, like a blackened stone. Stench of burning flesh soaked the air. Tom's eyes popped. His head settled downward. The mob yelled. Its yell echoed against the skeleton stone walls and sounded like a hundred yells. Like a hundred mobs yelling. Its yell thudded against the thick front wall and fell back. Ghost of a yell slipped through the flames and out the great door of the factory. It fluttered like a dying thing down the single street of factory town. Louisa, upon the step before her home, did not hear it, but her eyes opened slowly. They saw the full moon glowing in the great door. The full moon, an evil thing, an omen, soft showering the homes of folks she knew. Where were they, these people? She'd sing, and perhaps they'd come out and join her. Perhaps Tom Burwell would come. At any rate, the full moon in the great door was an omen which she must sing to:

> Red nigger moon. Sinner!
> Blood-burning moon. Sinner!
> Come out that fact'ry door.

Seventh Street

Money burns the pocket, pocket hurts,
Bootleggers in silken shirts,
Ballooned, zooming Cadillacs,
Whizzing, whizzing down the street-car tracks.

SEVENTH STREET is a bastard of Prohibition and the War. A crude-boned, soft-skinned wedge of nigger life breathing its loafer air, jazz songs and love, thrusting unconscious rhythms, black reddish blood into the white and whitewashed wood of Washington. Stale soggy wood of Washington. Wedges rust in soggy wood. . . Split it! In two! Again! Shred it! . . the sun. Wedges are brilliant in the sun; ribbons of wet wood dry and blow away. Black reddish blood. Pouring for crude-boned soft-skinned life, who set you flowing? Blood suckers of the War would spin in a frenzy of dizziness if they drank your blood. Prohibition would put a stop to it. Who set you flowing? White and whitewash disappear in blood. Who set you flowing? Flowing down the smooth asphalt of Seventh Street, in shanties, brick office buildings, theaters, drug stores, restaurants, and cabarets? Eddying on the corners? Swirling like a blood-red smoke up where the buzzards fly in heaven? God would not dare to suck black red blood. A Nigger God! He would duck his head in shame and call for the Judgment Day. Who set you flowing?

Money burns the pocket, pocket hurts,
Bootleggers in silken shirts,
Ballooned, zooming Cadillacs,
Whizzing, whizzing down the street-car tracks.

Rhobert

RHOBERT wears a house, like a monstrous diver's helmet, on his head. His legs are banty-bowed and shaky because as a child he had rickets. He is way down. Rods of the house like antennæ of a dead thing, stuffed, prop up in the air. He is way down. He is sinking. His house is a dead thing that weights him down. He is sinking as a diver would sink in mud should the water be drawn off. Life is a murky, wiggling, microscopic water that compresses him. Compresses his helmet and would crush it the minute that he pulled his head out. He has to keep it in. Life is water that is being drawn off.

> Brother, life is water that is being drawn off.
> Brother, life is water that is being drawn off.

The dead house is stuffed. The stuffing is alive. It is sinful to draw one's head out of live stuffing in a dead house. The propped-up antennæ would cave in and the stuffing be strewn . . shredded life-pulp . . in the water. It is sinful to have one's own head crushed. Rhobert is an upright man whose legs are banty-bowed and shaky because as a child he had rickets. The earth is round. Heaven is a sphere that surrounds it. Sink where you will. God is a Red Cross man with a dredge and a respiration-pump who's waiting for you at the opposite periphery. God built the house. He blew His breath into its stuffing. It is good to to die obeying Him who can do these things.

A futile something like the dead house wraps the live stuffing of the question: how long before the water will be drawn off? Rhobert does not care. Like most men who wear monstrous helmets, the pressure it exerts is enough to convince him of its practical infinity. And he cares not two straws as to whether or not he will ever see his wife and children again. Many a time he's seen them drown in his dreams and has kicked about joyously in the mud for days after. One thing about him goes straight to the heart. He has an Adam's-apple which strains sometimes as if he were painfully gulping great globules of air . . air floating shredded life-pulp. It is a sad thing to see a banty-bowed, shaky, ricket-legged man straining the raw insides of his throat against smooth air. Holding furtive thoughts about the glory of pulp-heads strewn in water. . He is way down. Down. Mud, coming to his banty knees, almost hides them. Soon people will be looking at him and calling him a strong man. No doubt he is for one who has had rickets. Lets give it to him. Lets call him great when the water shall have been all drawn off. Lets build a monument and set it in the ooze where he goes down. A monument of hewn oak, carved in nigger-heads. Lets open our throats, brother, and sing "Deep River" when he goes down.

> Brother, Rhobert is sinking.
> Lets open our throats, brother,
> Lets sing Deep River when he goes down.

Avey

FOR a long while she was nothing more to me than one of those skirted beings whom boys at a certain age disdain to play with. Just how I came to love her, timidly, and with secret blushes, I do not know. But that I did was brought home to me one night, the first night that Ned wore his long pants. Us fellers were seated on the curb before an apartment house where she had gone in. The young trees had not outgrown their boxes then. V Street was lined with them. When our legs grew cramped and stiff from the cold of the stone, we'd stand around a box and whittle it. I like to think now that there was a hidden purpose in the way we hacked them with our knives. I like to feel that something deep in me responded to the trees, the young trees that whinnied like colts impatient to be let free. . . On the particular night I have in mind, we were waiting for the top-floor light to go out. We wanted to see Avey leave the flat. This night she stayed longer than usual and gave us a chance to complete the plans of how we were going to stone and beat that feller on the top floor out of town. Ned especially had it in for him. He was about to throw a brick up at the window when at last the room went dark. Some minutes passed. Then Avey, as unconcerned as if she had been paying an old-maid aunt a visit, came out. I don't remember what she had on, and all that sort of thing. But I do know that I turned hot as bare pavements in the summertime at Ned's boast: "Hell, bet I could get her too if you little niggers weren't always spying and crabbing everything." I didnt say a word to him. It wasnt my way then. I just stood there like the others, and something like a fuse burned up inside of me. She never noticed us, but swung along lazy and easy as anything. We sauntered to the corner and watched her till her door banged to. Ned repeated what he'd said. I didnt seem to care. Sitting around old Mush-Head's bread box, the discussion began. "Hang if I can see how she gets away with it," Doc started. Ned knew, of course. There was nothing he didnt know when it came to women. He dilated on the emotional needs of girls. Said they werent much different from men in that respect. And concluded with the solemn avowal: "It does em good." None of us liked Ned much. We all talked dirt; but it was the way he said it. And then too, a couple of the fellers had sisters and had caught Ned playing with them. But there was no disputing the superiority of his smutty wisdom. Bubs Sanborn, whose mother was friendly with Avey's, had overheard the old ladies talking. "Avey's mother's ont her," he said. We thought that only natural and began to guess at what would happen. Some one said she'd marry that feller on the top floor. Ned called that a lie because Avey was going to marry nobody but him. We had our doubts about that, but we did agree that she'd soon leave school and marry some one. The gang broke up, and I went home, picturing myself as married.

Nothing I did seemed able to change Avey's indifference to me. I played basket-ball, and when I'd make a long clean shot she'd clap with the others, louder than they, I thought. I'd meet her on the street, and there'd be no difference in the way she said hello. She never took the trouble to call me by my name. On the days for drill, I'd let my voice down a tone and call for a complicated maneuver when I saw her coming. She'd smile appreciation, but it was an impersonal smile, never for me. It was on a summer excursion down to Riverview that she first seemed to take me into account. The day had been spent riding merry-go-rounds, scenic-railways, and shoot-the-chutes. We had been in swimming and we had danced. I was a crack swimmer then. She didnt know how. I held her up and showed her how to kick her legs and draw her arms. Of course she didnt learn in one day, but she thanked me for bothering with her. I was also somewhat of a dancer. And I had already noticed that love can start on a dance floor. We danced. But though I held her tightly in my arms, she was way away. That college feller who lived on the top floor was somewhere making money for the next year. I imagined that she was thinking, wishing for him. Ned was along. He treated her until his money gave out. She went with another feller. Ned got sore. One by one the boys' money gave out. She left them. And they got sore. Every one of them but me got sore. This is the reason, I guess, why I had her to myself on the top deck of the *Jane Mosely* that night as we puffed up the Potomac, coming home. The moon was brilliant. The air was sweet like clover. And every now and then, a salt tang, a stale drift of sea-weed. It was not my mind's fault if it went romancing. I should have taken her in my arms the minute we were stowed in that old lifeboat. I dallied, dreaming. She took me in hers. And I could feel by the touch of it that it wasnt a man-to-woman love. It made me restless. I felt chagrined. I didnt know what it was, but I did know that I couldnt handle it. She ran her fingers through my hair and kissed my forehead. I itched to break through her tenderness to passion. I wanted her to take me in her arms as I knew she had that college feller. I wanted her to love me passionately as she did him. I gave her one burning kiss. Then she laid me in her lap as if I were a child. Helpless. I got sore when she started to hum a lullaby. She wouldnt let me go. I talked. I knew damned well that I could beat her at that. Her eyes were soft and misty, the curves of her lips were wistful, and her smile seemed indulgent of the irrelevance of my remarks. I gave up last and let her love me, silently, in her own way. The moon was brilliant. The air was sweet like clover, and every now and then, a salt tang, a stale drift of sea-weed. . .

The next time I came close to her was the following summer at Harpers Ferry. We were sitting on a flat projecting rock they give the name of Lover's Leap. Some one is supposed to have jumped off it. The river is about six hundred feet beneath. A railroad track runs up the valley and curves out of sight where part of the mountain rock had to be blasted away to make room for it. The engines of this valley have a whistle, the echoes of which sound like iterated gasps and sobs. I always think of them as crude music from the soul of Avey. We sat there holding hands. Our palms were soft and warm against each other. Our fingers were not tight. She would not let them be. She would not let me twist them. I wanted to talk. To explain what I meant to her. Avey was as silent as those great trees whose tops we looked down upon. She has always been like that. At least, to me. I had the notion that if I really wanted to, I could do with her just what I pleased. Like one can strip a tree. I did kiss her. I even let my hands cup her breasts. When I was through, she'd seek my hand and hold it till my pulse cooled down. Evening after evening we sat there. I tried to get her to talk about that college feller. She never would. There was no set time to go home. None of my family had come down. And as for hers, she didnt give a hang about them. The general gossips could hardly say more than they had. The boarding-house porch was always deserted when we returned. No one saw us enter, so the time was set conveniently for scandal. This worried me a little, for I thought it might keep Avey from getting an appointment in the schools. She didnt care. She had finished normal school. They could give her a job if they wanted to. As time went on, her indifference to things began to pique me; I was ambitious. I left the Ferry earlier than she did. I was going off to college. The more I thought of it, the more I resented, yes, hell, thats what it was, her downright laziness. Sloppy indolence. There was no excuse for a healthy girl taking life so easy. Hell! she was no better than a cow. I was certain that she was a cow when I felt an udder in a Wisconsin stock-judging class. Among those energetic Swedes, or whatever they are, I decided to forget her. For two years I thought I did. When I'd come home for the summer she'd be away. And before she returned, I'd be gone. We never wrote; she was too damned lazy for that. But what a bluff I put up about forgetting her. The girls up that way, at least the ones I knew, havent got the stuff: they dont know how to love. Giving themselves completely was tame beside just the holding of Avey's hand. One day I received a note from her. The writing, I decided, was slovenly. She wrote on a torn bit of note-book paper. The envelope had a faint perfume that I remembered. A single line told me she had lost her school and was going away. I comforted myself with the reflection that shame held no pain for one so indolent as she. Nevertheless, I left Wisconsin that year for good. Washington had seemingly forgotten her. I hunted Ned. Between curses, I caught his opinion of her. She was no better than a whore. I saw her mother on the street. The same old pinch-beck, jerky-gaited creature that I'd always known.

Perhaps five years passed. The business of hunting a job or something or other had bruised my vanity so that I could recognize it. I felt old. Avey and my real relation to her, I thought I came to know. I wanted to see her. I had been told that she was in New York. As I had no money, I hiked and bummed my way there. I got work in a ship-yard and walked the streets at night, hoping to meet her. Failing in this, I saved enough to pay my fare back home. One evening in early June, just at the time when dusk is most lovely on the eastern horizon, I saw Avey, indolent as ever, leaning on the arm of a man, strolling under the recently lit arc-lights of U Street. She had almost passed before she recognized me. She showed no surprise. The puff over her eyes had grown heavier. The eyes themselves were still sleepy-large, and beautiful. I had almost concluded— indifferent. "You look older," was what she said. I wanted to convince her that I was, so I asked her to walk with me. The man whom she was with, and whom she never took the trouble to introduce, at a nod from her, hailed a taxi, and drove away. That gave me a notion of what she had been used to. Her dress was of some fine, costly stuff. I suggested the park, and then added that the grass might stain her skirt. Let it get stained, she said, for where it came from there are others.

I have a spot in Soldier's Home to which I always go when I want the simple beauty of another's soul. Robins spring about the lawn all day. They leave their footprints in the grass. I imagine that the grass at night smells sweet and fresh because of them. The ground is high. Washington lies below. Its light spreads like a blush against the darkened sky. Against the soft dusk sky of Washington. And when the wind is from the South, soil of my homeland falls like a fertile shower upon the lean streets of the city. Upon my hill in Soldier's Home. I know the policeman who watches the place of nights. When I go there alone, I talk to him. I tell him I come there to find the truth that people bury in their hearts. I tell him that I do not come there with a girl to do the thing he's paid to watch out for. I look deep in his eyes when I say these things, and he believes me. He comes over to see who it is on the grass. I say hello to him. He greets me in the same way and goes off searching for other black splotches upon the lawn. Avey and I went there. A band in one of the buildings a fair distance off was playing a march. I wished they would stop. Their playing was like a tin spoon in one's mouth. I wanted the Howard Glee Club to sing "Deep River," from the road. To sing "Deep River, Deep

River," from the road. . . Other than the first comments, Avey had been silent. I started to hum a folk-tune. She slipped her hand in mine. Pillowed her head as best she could upon my arm. Kissed the hand that she was holding and listened, or so I thought, to what I had to say. I traced my development from the early days up to the present time, the phase in which I could understand her. I described her own nature and temperament. Told how they needed a larger life for their expression. How incapable Washington was of understanding that need. How it could not meet it. I pointed out that in lieu of proper channels, her emotions had overflowed into paths that dissipated them. I talked, beautifully I thought, about an art that would be born, an art that would open the way for women the likes of her. I asked her to hope, and build up an inner life against the coming of that day. I recited some of my own things to her. I sang, with a strange quiver in my voice, a promise-song. And then I began to wonder why her hand had not once returned a single pressure. My old-time feeling about her laziness came back. I spoke sharply. My policeman friend passed by. I said hello to him. As he went away, I began to visualize certain possibilities. An immediate and urgent passion swept over me. Then I looked at Avey. Her heavy eyes were closed. Her breathing was as faint and regular as a child's in slumber. My passion died. I was afraid to move lest I disturb her. Hours and hours, I guess it was, she lay there. My body grew numb. I shivered. I coughed. I wanted to get up and whittle at the boxes of young trees. I withdrew my hand. I raised her head to waken her. She did not stir. I got up and walked around. I found my policeman friend and talked to him. We both came up, and bent over her. He said it would be all right for her to stay there just so long as she got away before the workmen came at dawn. A blanket was borrowed from a neighbor house. I sat beside her through the night. I saw the dawn steal over Washington. The Capitol dome looked like a gray ghost ship drifting in from sea. Avey's face was pale, and her eyes were heavy. She did not have the gray crimson-splashed beauty of the dawn. I hated to wake her. Orphan-woman. . .

BEEHIVE

Within this black hive to-night
There swarm a million bees;
Bees passing in and out the moon,
Bees escaping out the moon,
Bees returning through the moon,
Silver bees intently buzzing,
Silver honey dripping from the swarm of bees
Earth is a waxen cell of the world comb,
And I, a drone,
Lying on my back,
Lipping honey,
Getting drunk with silver honey,
Wish that I might fly out past the moon
And curl forever in some far-off farmyard flower.

STORM ENDING

Thunder blossoms gorgeously above our heads,
Great, hollow, bell-like flowers,
Rumbling in the wind,
Stretching clappers to strike our ears . .
Full-lipped flowers
Bitten by the sun
Bleeding rain
Dripping rain like golden honey—
And the sweet earth flying from the thunder.

Theater

L IFE of nigger alleys, of pool rooms and restaurants and near-beer saloons soaks into the walls of Howard Theater and sets them throbbing jazz songs. Black-skinned, they dance and shout above the tick and trill of white-walled buildings. At night, they open doors to people who come in to stamp their feet and shout. At night, road-shows volley songs into the mass-heart of black people. Songs soak the walls and seep out to the nigger life of alleys and near-beer saloons, of the Poodle Dog and Black Bear cabarets. Afternoons, the house is dark, and the walls are sleeping singers until rehearsal begins. Or until John comes within them. Then they start throbbing to a subtle syncopation. And the space-dark air grows softly luminous.

John is the manager's brother. He is seated at the center of the theater, just before rehearsal. Light streaks down upon him from a window high above. One half his face is orange in it. One half his face is in shadow. The soft glow of the house rushes to, and compacts about, the shaft of light. John's mind coincides with the shaft of light. Thoughts rush to, and compact about it. Life of the house and of the slowly awakening stage swirls to the body of John, and thrills it. John's body is separate from the thoughts that pack his mind.

Stage-lights, soft, as if they shine through clear pink fingers. Beneath them, hid by the shadow of a set, Dorris. Other chorus girls drift in. John feels them in the mass. And as if his own body were the mass-heart of a black audience listening to them singing, he wants to stamp his feet and shout. His mind, contained above desires of his body, singles the girls out, and tries to trace origins and plot destinies.

A pianist slips into the pit and improvises jazz. The walls awake. Arms of the girls, and their limbs, which . . jazz, jazz . . by lifting up their tight street skirts they set free, jab the air and clog the floor in rhythm to the music. (Lift your skirts, Baby, and talk t papa!) Crude, individualized, and yet . . monotonous. . .

John: Soon the director will herd you, my full-lipped,

distant beauties, and tame you, and blunt your sharp thrusts in loosely suggestive movements, appropriate to Broadway. (O dance!) Soon the audience will paint your dusk faces white, and call you beautiful. (O dance!) Soon I. . . (O dance!) I'd like. . .

Girls laugh and shout. Sing discordant snatches of other jazz songs. Whirl with loose passion into the arms of passing show-men.

John: Too thick. Too easy. Too monotonous. Her whom I'd love I'd leave before she knew that I was with her. Her? Which? (O dance!) I'd like to. . .

Girls dance and sing. Men clap. The walls sing and press inward. They press the men and girls, they press John towards a center of physical ecstasy. Go to it, Baby! Fan yourself, and feed your papa! Put . . nobody lied . . and take . . when they said I cried over you. No lie! The glitter and color of stacked scenes, the gilt and brass and crimson of the house, converge towards a center of physical ecstasy. John's feet and torso and his blood press in. He wills thought to rid his mind of passion.

"All right, girls. Alaska. Miss Reynolds, please."

The director wants to get the rehearsal through with.

The girls line up. John sees the front row: dancing ponies. The rest are in shadow. The leading lady fits loosely in the front. Lack-life, monotonous. "One, two, three—" Music starts. The song is somewhere where it will not strain the leading lady's throat. The dance is somewhere where it will not strain the girls. Above the staleness, one dancer throws herself into it. Dorris. John sees her. Her hair, crisp-curled, is bobbed. Bushy, black hair bobbing about her lemon-colored face. Her lips are curiously full, and very red. Her limbs in silk purple stockings are lovely. John feels them. Desires her. Holds off.

John: Stage-door johnny; chorus-girl. No, that would be all right. Dictie, educated, stuck-up; show-girl. Yep. Her suspicion would be stronger than her passion. It wouldnt work. Keep her loveliness. Let her go.

Dorris sees John and knows that he is looking at her. Her own glowing is too rich a thing to let her feel the slimness of his diluted passion.

"Who's that?" she asks her dancing partner.

"Th manager's brother. Dictie. Nothin doin, hon."

Dorris tosses her head and dances for him until she feels she has him. Then, withdrawing disdainfully, she flirts with the director.

Dorris: Nothin doin? How come? Aint I as good as him? Couldnt I have got an education if I'd wanted one? Dont I know respectable folks, lots of em, in Philadelphia and New York and Chicago? Aint I had men as good as him? Better. Doctors an lawyers. Whats a manager's brother, anyhow?

Two steps back, and two steps front.

"Say, Mame, where do you get that stuff?"

"Whatshmean, Dorris?"

"If you two girls cant listen to what I'm telling you, I know where I can get some who can. Now listen."

Mame: Go to hell, you black bastard.

Dorris: Whats eatin at him, anyway?

"Now follow me in this, you girls. Its three counts to the right, three counts to the left, and then you shimmy—"

John: —and then you shimmy. I'll bet she can. Some good cabaret, with rooms upstairs. And what in hell do you think you'd get from it? Youre going wrong. Here's right: get her to herself—(Christ, but how she'd bore you after the first five minutes)—not if you get her right she wouldnt. Touch her, I mean. To herself—in some room perhaps. Some cheap, dingy bedroom. Hell no. Cant be done. But the point is, brother John, it can be done. Get her to herself somewhere, anywhere. Go down in yourself—and she'd be calling you all sorts of asses while you were in the process of going down. Hold em, bud. Cant be done. Let her go. (Dance and I'll love you!) And keep her loveliness.

"All right now, Chicken Chaser. Dorris and girls. Where's Dorris? I told you to stay on the stage, didnt I? Well? Now thats enough. All right. All right there, Professor? All right. One, two, three—"

Dorris swings to the front. The line of girls, four deep, blurs within the shadow of suspended scenes. Dorris wants to dance. The director feels that and steps to one side. He smiles, and picks her for a leading lady, one of these days. Odd ends of stage-men emerge from the wings, and stare and clap. A crap game in the alley suddenly ends. Black faces crowd the rear stage doors. The girls, catching joy from Dorris, whip up within the footlights' glow. They forget set steps; they find their own. The director forgets to bawl them out. Dorris dances.

John: Her head bobs to Broadway. Dance from yourself. Dance! O just a little more.

Dorris' eyes burn across the space of seats to him.

Dorris: I bet he can love. Hell, he cant love. He's too skinny. His lips are too skinny. He wouldnt love me anyway, only for that. But I'd get a pair of silk stockings out of it. Red silk. I got purple. Cut it, kid. You cant win him to respect you that away. He wouldnt anyway. Maybe he would. Maybe he'd love. I've heard em say that men who look like him (what does he look like?) will marry if they love. O will you love me? And give me kids, and a home, and everything? (I'd like to make your nest, and honest, hon, I wouldnt run out on you.) You will if I make you. Just watch me.

Dorris dances. She forgets her tricks. She dances.

Glorious songs are the muscles of her limbs.

And her singing is of canebrake loves and mangrove feastings

The walls press in, singing. Flesh of a throbbing body, they press close to John and Dorris. They close them in. John's heart beats tensely against her dancing body. Walls press his mind within his heart. And then, the shaft of light goes out the window high above him. John's mind sweeps up to follow it. Mind pulls him upward into dream. Dorris dances. . . John dreams:

Dorris is dressed in a loose black gown splashed with lemon ribbons. Her feet taper long and slim from trim ankles. She waits for him just inside the stage door. John, collar and tie colorful and flaring, walks towards the stage door. There are no trees in the alley. But his feet feel as though they step on autumn leaves whose rustle has been pressed out of them by the passing of a million satin slippers. The air is sweet with roasting chestnuts, sweet with bonfires of old leaves. John's melancholy is a deep thing that seals all senses but his eyes, and makes him whole.

Dorris knows that he is coming. Just at the right moment she steps from the door, as if there were no door. Her face is tinted like the autumn alley. Of old flowers, or of a southern canefield, her perfume.

"Glorious Dorris." So his eyes speak. And their sadness is too deep for sweet untruth. She barely touches his arm. They glide off with footfalls softened on the leaves, the old leaves powdered by a million satin slippers.

They are in a room. John knows nothing of it. Only, that the flesh and blood of Dorris are its walls. Singing walls. Lights, soft, as if they shine through clear pink fingers. Soft lights, and warm.

John reaches for a manuscript of his, and reads. Dorris, who has no eyes, has eyes to understand him. He comes to a dancing scene. The scene is Dorris. She dances. Dorris dances. Glorious Dorris. Dorris whirls, whirls, dances. . .

Dorris dances.

The pianist crashes a bumper chord. The whole stage claps. Dorris, flushed, looks quick at John. His whole face is in shadow. She seeks for her dance in it. She finds it a dead thing in the shadow which is his dream. She rushes from the stage. Falls down the steps into her dressing-room. Pulls her hair. Her eyes, over a floor of tears, stare at the whitewashed ceiling. (Smell of dry paste, and paint, and soiled clothing.) Her pal comes in. Dorris flings herself into the old safe arms, and cries bitterly.

"I told you nothin doin," is what Mame says to comfort her.

HER LIPS ARE COPPER WIRE

whisper of yellow globes
gleaming on lamp-posts that sway
like bootleg licker drinkers in the fog

and let your breath be moist against me
like bright beads on yellow globes

telephone the power-house
that the main wires are insulate

(her words play softly up and down
dewy corridors of billboards)

then with your tongue remove the tape
and press your lips to mine
till they are incandescent

Calling Jesus

HER soul is like a little thrust-tailed dog that follows her, whimpering. She is large enough, I know, to find a warm spot for it. But each night when she comes home and closes the big outside storm door, the little dog is left in the vestibule, filled with chills till morning. Some one . . . eoho Jesus . . . soft as a cotton boll brushed against the milk-pod cheek of Christ, will steal in and cover it that it need not shiver, and carry it to her where she sleeps upon clean hay cut in her dreams.

When you meet her in the daytime on the streets, the little dog keeps coming. Nothing happens at first, and then, when she has forgotten the streets and alleys, and the large house where she goes to bed of nights, a soft thing like fur begins to rub your limbs, and you hear a low, scared voice, lonely, calling, and you know that a cool something nozzles moisture in your palms. Sensitive things like nostrils, quiver. Her breath comes sweet as honeysuckle whose pistils bear the life of coming song. And her eyes carry to where builders find no need for vestibules, for swinging on iron hinges, storm doors.

Her soul is like a little thrust-tailed dog, that follows her, whimpering. I've seen it tagging on behind her, up streets where chestnut trees flowered, where dusty asphalt had been freshly sprinkled with clean water. Up alleys where niggers sat on low door-steps before tumbled shanties and sang and loved. At night, when she comes home, the little dog is left in the vestibule, nosing the crack beneath the big storm door, filled with chills till morning. Some one . . . eoho Jesus . . . soft as the bare feet of Christ moving across bales of southern cotton, will steal in and cover it that it need not shiver, and carry it to her where she sleeps: cradled in dream-fluted cane.

Box Seat

I

HOUSES are shy girls whose eyes shine reticently upon the dusk body of the street. Upon the gleaming limbs and asphalt torso of a dreaming nigger. Shake your curled wool-blossoms, nigger. Open your liver lips to the lean, white spring. Stir the root-life of a withered people. Call them from their houses, and teach them to dream.

Dark swaying forms of Negroes are street songs that woo virginal houses.

Dan Moore walks southward on Thirteenth Street. The low limbs of budding chestnut trees recede above his head. Chest-nut buds and blossoms are wool he walks upon. The eyes of houses faintly touch as he passes them. Soft girl-eyes, they set him singing. Girl-eyes within him widen upward to promised faces. Floating away, they dally wistfully over the dusk body of the street. Come on, Dan Moore, come on. Dan sings. His voice is a little hoarse. It cracks. He strains to produce tones in keeping with the houses' loveliness. Cant be done. He whistles. His notes are shrill. They hurt him. Negroes open gates, and go indoors, perfectly. Dan thinks of the house he's going to. Of the girl. Lips, flesh-notes of a forgotten song, plead with him. . .

Dan turns into a side-street, opens an iron gate, bangs it to. Mounts the steps, and searches for the bell. Funny, he cant find it. He fumbles around. The thought comes to him that some one passing by might see him and not understand. Might think that he is trying to sneak, to break in.

Dan: Break in. Get an ax and smash in. Smash in their faces. I'll show em. Break into an engine-house, steal a thousand horse-power fire truck. Smash in with the truck. I'll show em. Grab an ax and brain em. Cut em up. Jack the Ripper. Baboon from the zoo. And then the cops come. "No, I aint a baboon. I aint Jack the Ripper. I'm a poor man out of work. Take your hands off me, you bull-necked bears. Look into my eyes. I am

65

Dan Moore. I was born in a canefield. The hands of Jesus touched me. I am come to a sick world to heal it. Only the other day, a dope fiend brushed against me— Dont laugh, you mighty, juicy, meat-hook men. Give me your fingers and I will peel them as if they were ripe bananas."

Some one might think he is trying to break in. He'd better knock. His knuckles are raw bone against the thick glass door. He waits. No one comes. Perhaps they havent heard him. He raps again. This time, harder. He waits. No one comes. Some one is surely in. He fancies that he sees their shadows on the glass. Shadows of gorillas. Perhaps they saw him coming and dont want to let him in. He knocks. The tension of his arms makes the glass rattle. Hurried steps come towards him. The door opens.

"Please, you might break the glass—the bell—oh, Mr. Moore! I thought it must be some stranger. How do you do? Come in, wont you? Muriel? Yes. I'll call her. Take your things off, wont you? And have a seat in the parlor. Muriel will be right down. Muriel! Oh Muriel! Mr. Moore to see you. She'll be right down. You'll pardon me, wont you? So glad to see you."

Her eyes are weak. They are bluish and watery from reading newspapers. The blue is steel. It gimlets Dan while her mouth flaps amiably to him.

Dan: Nothing for you to see, old mussel-head. Dare I show you? If I did, delirium would furnish you headlines for a month. Now look here. Thats enough. Go long, woman. Say some nasty thing and I'll kill you. Huh. Better damned sight not. Ta-ta, Mrs. Pribby.

Mrs. Pribby retreats to the rear of the house. She takes up a newspaper. There is a sharp click as she fits into her chair and draws it to the table. The click is metallic like the sound of a bolt being shot into place. Dan's eyes sting. Sinking into a soft couch, he closes them. The house contracts about him. It is a sharp-edged, massed, metallic house. Bolted. About Mrs. Pribby. Bolted to the endless rows of metal houses. Mrs. Pribby's house. The rows of houses belong to other Mrs. Pribbys. No wonder he couldn't sing to them.

Dan: What's Muriel doing here? God, what a place for her. Whats she doing? Putting her stockings on? In the bathroom.

Come out of there, Dan Moore. People must have their privacy. Peeping-toms. I'll never peep. I'll listen. I like to listen.

Dan goes to the wall and places his ear against it. A passing street car and something vibrant from the earth sends a rumble to him. That rumble comes from the earth's deep core. It is the mutter of powerful underground races. Dan has a picture of all the people rushing to put their ears against walls, to listen to it. The next world-savior is coming up that way. Coming up. A continent sinks down. The new-world Christ will need consummate skill to walk upon the waters where huge bubbles burst. . . Thuds of Muriel coming down. Dan turns to the piano and glances through a stack of jazz music sheets. Ji-ji-bo, JI-JI-BO!" . .

"Hello, Dan, stranger, what brought you here?"

Muriel comes in, shakes hands, and then clicks into a high-armed seat under the orange glow of a floor-lamp. Her face is fleshy. It would tend to coarseness but for the fresh fragrant something which is the life of it. Her hair like an Indian's. But more curly and bushed and vagrant. Her nostrils flare. The flushed ginger of her cheeks is touched orange by the shower of color from the lamp.

"Well, you havent told me, you havent answered my question, stranger. What brought you here?"

Dan feels the pressure of the house, of the rear room, of the rows of houses, shift to Muriel. He is light. He loves her. He is doubly heavy.

"Dont know, Muriel—wanted to see you—wanted to talk to you—to see you and tell you that I know what you've been through—what pain the last few months must have been—"

"Lets dont mention that."

"But why not, Muriel? I—"

"Please."

"But Muriel, life is full of things like that. One grows strong and beautiful in facing them. What else is life?"

"I dont know, Dan. And I dont believe I care. Whats the use? Lets talk about something else. I hear there's a good show at the Lincoln this week."

"Yes, so Harry was telling me. Going?"

"To-night."

Dan starts to rise.

"I didnt know. I dont want to keep you."

"Its all right. You dont have to go till Bernice comes. And she wont be here till eight. I'm all dressed. I'll let you know."

"Thanks."

Silence. The rustle of a newspaper being turned comes from the rear room.

Muriel: Shame about Dan. Something awfully good and fine about him. But he don't fit in. In where? Me? Dan, I could love you if I tried. I dont have to try. I do. O Dan, dont you know I do? Timid lover, brave talker that you are. Whats the good of all you know if you dont know that? I wont let myself. I? Mrs. Pribby who reads newspapers all night wont. What has she got to do with me? She *is* me, somehow. No she's not. Yes she is. She is the town, and the town wont let me love you, Dan. Dont you know? You could make it let me if you would. Why wont you? Youre selfish. I'm not strong enough to buck it. Youre too selfish to buck it, for me. I wish you'd go. You irritate me. Dan, please go.

"What are you doing now, Dan?"

"Same old thing, Muriel. Nothing, as the world would have it. Living, as I look at things. Living as much as I can without—"

"But you cant live without money, Dan. Why dont you get a good job and settle down?"

Dan: Same old line. Shoot it at me, sister. Hell of a note, this loving business. For ten minutes of it youve got to stand the torture of an intolerable heaviness and a hundred platitudes. Well, damit, shoot on.

"To what? my dear. Rustling newspapers?"

"You mustnt say that, Dan. It isnt right. Mrs. Pribby has been awfully good to me."

"Dare say she has. Whats that got to do with it?"

"Oh, Dan, youre so unconsiderate and selfish. All you think of is yourself."

"I think of you."

"Too much—I mean, you ought to work more and think less. Thats the best way to get along."

"Mussel-heads get along, Muriel. There is more to you than that—"

"Sometimes I think there is, Dan. But I dont know. I've tried. I've tried to do something with myself. Something real and beautiful, I mean. But whats the good of trying? I've tried to make people, every one I come in contact with, happy—"

Dan looks at her, directly. Her animalism, still unconquered by zoo-restrictions and keeper-taboos, stirs him. Passion tilts upward, bringing with it the elements of an old desire. Muriel's lips become the flesh-notes of a futile, plaintive longing. Dan's impulse to direct her is its fresh life.

"Happy, Muriel? No, not happy. Your aim is wrong. There is no such thing as happiness. Life bends joy and pain, beauty and ugliness, in such a way that no one may isolate them. No one should want to. Perfect joy, or perfect pain, with no contrasting element to define them, would mean a monotony of consciousness, would mean death. Not happy, Muriel. Say that you have tried to make them create. Say that you have used your own capacity for life to cradle them. To start them upward-flowing. Or if you cant say that you have, then say that you will. My talking to you will make you aware of your power to do so. Say that you will love, that you will give yourself in love—"

"To you, Dan?"

Dan's consciousness crudely swerves into his passions. They flare up in his eyes. They set up quivers in his abdomen. He is suddenly over-tense and nervous.

"Muriel—"

The newspaper rustles in the rear room.

"Muriel—"

Dan rises. His arms stretch towards her. His fingers and his palms, pink in the lamplight, are glowing irons. Muriel's chair is close and stiff about her. The house, the rows of houses locked about her chair. Dan's fingers and arms are fire to melt and bars to wrench and force and pry. Her arms hang loose. Her hands are hot and moist. Dan takes them. He slips to his knees before her.

"Dan, you mustnt."

"Muriel—"

"Dan, really you mustnt. No, Dan. No."

"Oh, come, Muriel. Must I—"

"Shhh. Dan, please get up. Please. Mrs. Pribby is right in the next room. She'll hear you. She may come in. Dont, Dan. She'll see you—"

"Well then, lets go out."

"I cant. Let go, Dan. Oh, wont you please let go."

Muriel tries to pull her hands away. Dan tightens his grip. He feels the strength of his fingers. His muscles are tight and strong. He stands up. Thrusts out his chest. Muriel shrinks from him. Dan becomes aware of his crude absurdity. His lips curl. His passion chills. He has an obstinate desire to possess her.

"Muriel, I love you. I want you, whatever the world of Pribby says. Damn your Pribby. Who is she to dictate my love? I've stood enough of her. Enough of you. Come here."

Muriel's mouth works in and out. Her eyes flash and waggle. She wrenches her hands loose and forces them against his breast to keep him off. Dan grabs her wrists. Wedges in between her arms. Her face is close to him. It is hot and blue and moist. Ugly.

"Come here now."

"Dont, Dan. Oh, dont. What are you killing?"

"Whats weak in both of us and a whole litter of Pribbys. For once in your life youre going to face whats real, by God—"

A sharp rap on the newspaper in the rear room cuts between them. The rap is like cool thick glass between them. Dan is hot on one side. Muriel, hot on the other. They straighten. Gaze fearfully at one another. Neither moves. A clock in the rear room, in the rear room, the rear room, strikes eight. Eight slow, cool sounds. Bernice. Muriel fastens on her image. She smooths her dress. She adjusts her skirt. She becomes prim and cool. Rising, she skirts Dan as if to keep the glass between them. Dan, gyrating nervously above the easy swing of his limbs, follows her to the parlor door. Muriel retreats before him till she reaches the landing of the steps that lead upstairs. She smiles at him. Dan sees his face in the hall mirror. He runs his fingers through his hair. Reaches for his hat and coat and puts them on. He moves towards Muriel. Muriel steps backward up one step. Dan's jaw shoots out. Muriel jerks her arm in warning of Mrs. Pribby. She gasps and turns and starts to run. Noise of a chair scraping as Mrs. Pribby rises from it, ratchets down the hall. Dan stops. He makes a wry face, wheels round, goes out, and slams the door.

2

People come in slowly . . . mutter, laughs, flutter, whish-adwash, "I've changed my work-clothes—" . . . and fill vacant seats of Lincoln Theater. Muriel, leading Bernice who is a cross between a washerwoman and a blue-blood lady, a washer-blue, a washer-lady, wanders down the right aisle to the lower front box. Muriel has on an orange dress. Its color would clash with the crimson box-draperies, its color would contradict the sweet rose smile her face is bathed in, should she take her coat off. She'll keep it on. Pale purple shadows rest on the planes of her cheeks. Deep purple comes from her thick-shocked hair. Orange of the dress goes well with these. Muriel presses her coat down from around her shoulders. Teachers are not supposed to have bobbed hair. She'll keep her hat on. She takes the first chair, and indicates that Bernice is to take the one directly behind her. Seated thus, her eyes are level with, and near to, the face of an imaginary man upon the stage. To speak to Berny she must turn. When she does, the audience is square upon her.

People come in slowly . . . "—for my Sunday-go-to-meeting dress. O glory God! O shout Amen!" . . . and fill vacant seats of Lincoln Theater. Each one is a bolt that shoots into a slot, and is locked there. Suppose the Lord should ask, where was Moses when the light went out? Suppose Gabriel should blow his trumpet! The seats are slots. The seats are bolted houses. The mass grows denser. Its weight at first is impalpable upon the box. Then Muriel begins to feel it. She props her arm against the brass box-rail, to ward it off. Silly. These people are friends of hers: a parent of a child she teaches, an old school friend. She smiles at them. They return her courtesy, and she is free to chat with Berny. Berny's tongue, started, runs on, and on. O washer-blue! O washer-lady!

Muriel: Never see Dan again. He makes me feel queer. Starts things he doesnt finish. Upsets me. I am not upset. I am perfectly calm. I am going to enjoy the show. Good show. I've

had some show! This damn tame thing. O Dan. Wont see Dan
again. Not alone. Have Mrs. Pribby come in. She *was* in. Keep
Dan out. If I love him, can I keep him out? Well then, I dont
love him. Now he's out. Who is that coming in? Blind as a bat.
Ding-bat. Looks like Dan. He mustnt see me. Silly. He cant
reach me. He wont dare come in here. He'd put his head down
like a goring bull and charge me. He'd trample them. He'd
gore. He'd rape! Berny! He won't dare come in here.

"Berny, who was that who just came in? I havent my
glasses."

"A friend of yours, a *good* friend so I hear. Mr. Daniel Moore,
Lord."

"Oh. He's no friend of mine."

"No? I hear he is."

"Well, he isnt."

Dan is ushered down the aisle. He has to squeeze past the
knees of seated people to reach his own seat. He treads on a
man's corns. The man grumbles, and shoves him off. He shriv-
els close beside a portly Negress whose huge rolls of flesh meet
about the bones of seat-arms. A soil-soaked fragrance comes
from her. Through the cement floor her strong roots sink
down. They spread under the asphalt streets. Dreaming, the
streets roll over on their bellies, and suck their glossy health
from them. Her strong roots sink down and spread under the
river and disappear in blood-lines that waver south. Her roots
shoot down. Dan's hands follow them. Roots throb. Dan's
heart beats violently. He places his palms upon the earth to
cool them. Earth throbs. Dan's heart beats violently. He sees
all the people in the house rush to the walls to listen to the
rumble. A new-world Christ is coming up. Dan comes up. He
is startled. The eyes of the woman dont belong to her. They
look at him unpleasantly. From either aisle, bolted masses press
in. He doesnt fit. The mass grows agitant. For an instant, Dan's
and Muriel's eyes meet. His weight there slides the weight on
her. She braces an arm against the brass rail, and turns her head
away.

Muriel: Damn fool; dear Dan, what did you want to follow
me here for? Oh cant you ever do anything right? Must you always pain me, and make me hate you? I do hate you. I wish
some one would come in with a horse-whip and lash you out.

I wish some one would drag you up a back alley and brain you with the whip-butt.

Muriel glances at her wrist-watch.

"Quarter of nine. Berny, what time have you?"

"Eight-forty. Time to begin. Oh, look Muriel, that woman with the plume; doesnt she look good! They say she's going with, oh, whats his name. You know. Too much powder. I can see it from here. Here's the orchestra now. O fine! Jim Clem at the piano!"

The men fill the pit. Instruments run the scale and tune. The saxophone moans and throws a fit. Jim Clem, poised over the piano, is ready to begin. His head nods forward. Opening crash. The house snaps dark. The curtain recedes upward from the blush of the footlights. Jazz overture is over. The first act is on.

Dan: Old stuff. Muriel—bored. Must be. But she'll smile and she'll clap. Do what youre bid, you she-slave. Look at her. Sweet, tame woman in a brass box seat. Clap, smile, fawn, clap. Do what youre bid. Drag me in with you. Dirty me. Prop me in your brass box seat. I'm there, am I not? because of you. He-slave. Slave of a woman who is a slave. I'm a damned sight worse than you are. I sing your praises, Beauty! I exalt thee, O Muriel! A slave, thou art greater than all Freedom because I love thee.

Dan fidgets, and disturbs his neighbors. His neighbors glare at him. He glares back without seeing them. The man whose corns have been trod upon speaks to him.

"Keep quiet, cant you, mister. Other people have paid their money besides yourself to see the show."

The man's face is a blur about two sullen liquid things that are his eyes. The eyes dissolve in the surrounding vagueness. Dan suddenly feels that the man is an enemy whom he has long been looking for.

Dan bristles. Glares furiously at the man.

"All right. All right then. Look at the show. I'm not stopping you."

"Shhh," from some one in the rear.

Dan turns around.

"Its that man there who started everything. I didnt say a thing to him until he tried to start something. What have I got to do with whether he has paid his money or not? Thats the manager's business. Do I look like the manager?"

"Shhhh. Youre right. Shhhh."

"Dont tell me to shhh. Tell him. That man there. He started everything. If what he wanted was to start a fight, why didnt he say so?"

The man leans forward.

"Better be quiet, sonny. I aint said a thing about fight, yet."

"Its a good thing you havent."

"Shhhh."

Dan grips himself. Another act is on. Dwarfs, dressed like prize-fighters, foreheads bulging like boxing gloves, are led upon the stage. They are going to fight for the heavyweight championship. Gruesome. Dan glances at Muriel. He imagines that she shudders. His mind curves back into himself, and picks up tail-ends of experiences. His eyes are open, mechanically. The dwarfs pound and bruise and bleed each other, on his eyeballs.

Dan: Ah, but she was some baby! And not vulgar either. Funny how some women can do those things. Muriel dancing like that! Hell. She rolled and wabbled. Her buttocks rocked. She pulled up her dress and showed her pink drawers. Baby! And then she caught my eyes. Dont know what my eyes had in them. Yes I do. God, dont I though! Sometimes I think, Dan Moore, that your eyes could burn clean . . . burn clean . . . BURN CLEAN! . .

The gong rings. The dwarfs set to. They spar grotesquely, playfully, until one lands a stiff blow. This makes the other sore. He commences slugging. A real scrap is on. Time! The dwarfs go to their corners and are sponged and fanned off. Gloves bulge from their wrists. Their wrists are necks for the tight-faced gloves. The fellow to the right lets his eyes roam over the audience. He sights Muriel. He grins.

Dan: Those silly women arguing feminism. Here's what I should have said to them. "It should be clear to you women, that the proposition must be stated thus:

> Me, horizontally above her.
> Action: perfect strokes downward oblique.
> Hence, man dominates because of limitation.
> Or, so it shall be until women learn their stuff.

So framed, the proposition is a mental-filler, Dentist, I want gold teeth. It should become cherished of the technical intellect. I hereby offer it to posterity as one of the important machine-age designs. P. S. It should be noted, that because it *is* an achievement of this age, its growth and hence its causes, up to the point of maturity, antedate machinery. Ery . . ."

The gong rings. No fooling this time. The dwarfs set to. They clinch. The referee parts them. One swings a cruel uppercut and knocks the other down. A huge head hits the floor. Pop! The house roars. The fighter, groggy, scrambles up. The referee whispers to the contenders not to fight so hard. They ignore him. They charge. Their heads jab like boxing-gloves. They kick and spit and bite. They pound each other furiously. Muriel pounds. The house pounds. Cut lips. Bloody noses. The referee asks for the gong. Time! The house roars. The dwarfs bow, are made to bow. The house wants more. The dwarfs are led from the stage.

Dan: Strange I never really noticed him before. Been sitting there for years. Born a slave. Slavery not so long ago. He'll die in his chair. Swing low, sweet chariot. Jesus will come and roll him down the river Jordan. Oh, come along, Moses, you'll get lost;, stretch out your rod and come across. LET MY PEOPLE GO! Old man. Knows everyone who passes the corners. Saw the first horse-cars. The first Oldsmobile. And he was born in slavery. I did see his eyes. Never miss eyes. But they were bloodshot and watery. It hurt to look at them. It hurts to look in most people's eyes. He saw Grant and Lincoln. He saw Walt—old man, did you see Walt Whitman? Did you see Walt Whitman! Strange force that drew me to him. And I went up to see. The woman thought I saw crazy. I told him to look into the heavens. He did, and smiled. I asked him if he knew what that rumbling is that comes up from the ground. Christ, what a stroke that was. And the jabberin idiots crowding around. And the crossing-cop leaving his job to come over and wheel him away . . .

The house applauds. The house wants more. The dwarfs are led back. But no encore. Must give the house something. The attendant comes out and announces that Mr. Barry, the champion, will sing one of his own songs, "for your approval." Mr. Barry grins at Muriel as he wabbles from the wing. He holds a fresh white rose, and a small mirror. He wipes blood from his nose. He signals Jim Clem. The orchestra starts. A sentimental love song, Mr. Barry sings, first to one girl, and then another in the audience. He holds the mirror in such a way that it flashes in the face of each one he sings to. The light swings around.

Dan: I am going to reach up and grab the girders of this building and pull them down. The crash will be a signal. Hid by the smoke and dust Dan Moore will arise. In his right hand will be a dynamo. In his left, a god's face that will flash white light from ebony. I'll grab a girder and swing it like a walking-stick. Lightning will flash. I'll grab its black knob and swing it like a crippled cane. Lightning . . . Some one's flashing . . . some one's flashing . . . Who in hell is flashing that mirror? Take it off me, godam you.

Dan's eyes are half blinded. He moves his head. The light follows. He hears the audience laugh. He hears the orchestra. A man with a high-pitched, sentimental voice is singing. Dan sees the dwarf. Along the mirror flash the song comes. Dan ducks his head. The audience roars. The light swings around to Muriel. Dan looks. Muriel is too close. Mr. Barry covers his mirror. He sings to her. She shrinks away. Nausea. She clutches the brass box-rail. She moves to face away. The audience is square upon her. Its eyes smile. Its hands itch to clap. Muriel turns to the dwarf and forces a smile at him. With a showy blare of orchestration, the song comes to its close. Mr. Barry bows. He offers Muriel the rose, first having kissed it. Blood of his battered lips is a vivid stain upon its petals. Mr. Barry offers Muriel the rose. The house applauds. Muriel flinches back. The dwarf steps forward, diffident; threatening. Hate pops from his eyes and crackles like a brittle heat about the box. The thick hide of his face is drawn in tortured wrinkles. Above his eyes, the bulging, tight-skinned brow. Dan looks at it. It grows calm and massive. It grows profound. It is a thing of wisdom and tenderness, of suffering and beauty. Dan looks down. The eyes are calm and luminous. Words come from them . . . Arms of the audience reach out, grab Muriel, and hold her there. Claps are steel fingers that manacle her wrists and move them forward to acceptance. Berny leans forward and whispers:

"Its all right. Go on—take it."

Words form in the eyes of the dwarf:

> Do not shrink. Do not be afraid of me.
> *Jesus*
> See how my eyes look at you.
> *the Son of God*
> I too was made in His image.
> *was once—*
> I give you the rose.

Muriel, tight in her revulsion, sees black, and daintily reaches for the offering. As her hand touches it, Dan springs up in his seat and shouts:

"JESUS WAS ONCE A LEPER!"

Dan steps down.

He is as cool as a green stem that has just shed its flower.

Rows of gaping faces strain towards him. They are distant, beneath him, impalpable. Squeezing out, Dan again treads upon the corn-foot man. The man shoves him.

"Watch where youre going, mister. Crazy or no, you aint going to walk over me. Watch where youre going there."

Dan turns, and serenely tweaks the fellow's nose. The man jumps up. Dan is jammed against a seat-back. A slight swift anger flicks him. His fist hooks the other's jaw.

"Now you have started something. Aint no man living can hit me and get away with it. Come on on the outside."

The house, tumultuously stirring, grabs its wraps and follows the men.

The man leads Dan up a black alley. The alley-air is thick and moist with smells of garbage and wet trash. In the morning, singing niggers will drive by and ring their gongs. . . Heavy with the scent of rancid flowers and with the scent of fight. The crowd, pressing forward, is a hollow roar. Eyes of houses, soft girl-eyes, glow reticently upon the hubbub and blink out. The man stops. Takes off his hat and coat. Dan, having forgotten him, keeps going on.

PRAYER

My body is opaque to the soul.
Driven of the spirit, long have I sought to temper it unto the
     spirit's longing,
But my mind, too, is opaque to the soul.
A closed lid is my soul's flesh-eye.
O Spirits of whom my soul is but a little finger,
Direct it to the lid of its flesh-eye.
I am weak with much giving.
I am weak with the desire to give more.
(How strong a thing is the little finger!)
So weak that I have confused the body with the soul,
And the body with its little finger.
(How frail is the little finger.)
My voice could not carry to you did you dwell in stars,
O Spirits of whom my soul is but a little finger . .

HARVEST SONG

I am a reaper whose muscles set at sundown. All my oats are
  cradled.
But I am too chilled, and too fatigued to bind them. And I
  hunger.

I crack a grain between my teeth. I do not taste it.
I have been in the fields all day. My throat is dry. I hunger.

My eyes are caked with dust of oatfields at harvest-time.
I am a blind man who stares across the hills, seeking stack'd
  fields of other harvesters.

It would be good to see them . . crook'd, split, and iron-
  ring'd handles of the scythes. It would be good to see
  them, dust-caked and blind. I hunger.

(Dusk is a strange fear'd sheath their blades are dull'd in.)
My throat is dry. And should I call, a cracked grain like the
  oats . . . eoho—

I fear to call. What should they hear me, and offer me their
  grain, oats, or wheat, or corn? I have been in the fields
  all day. I fear I could not taste it. I fear knowledge of my
  hunger.

My ears are caked with dust of oatfields at harvest-time.
I am a deaf man who strains to hear the calls of other harvesters whose throats are also dry.

It would be good to hear their songs . . reapers of the sweet-
  stalk'd cane, cutters of the corn . . even though their
  throats cracked and the strangeness of their voices deafened me.

I hunger. My throat is dry. Now that the sun has set and I am
  chilled, I fear to call. (Eoho, my brothers!)

I am a reaper. (Eoho!) All my oats are cradled. But I am too
  fatigued to bind them. And I hunger. I crack a grain. It
  has no taste to it. My throat is dry. . .

O my brothers, I beat my palms, still soft, against the stubble of my harvesting. (You beat your soft palms, too.) My pain is sweet. Sweeter than the oats or wheat or corn. It will not bring me knowledge of my hunger.

Bona and Paul

I

ON the school gymnasium floor, young men and women are drilling. They are going to be teachers, and go out into the world . . thud, thud . . and give precision to the movements of sick people who all their lives have been drilling. One man is out of step. In step. The teacher glares at him. A girl in bloomers, seated on a mat in the corner because she has told the director that she is sick, sees that the footfalls of the men are rhythmical and syncopated. The dance of his blue-trousered limbs thrills her.

Bona: He is a candle that dances in a grove swung with pale balloons.

Columns of the drillers thud towards her. He is in the front row. He is in no row at all. Bona can look close at him. His red-brown face—

Bona: He is a harvest moon. He is an autumn leaf. He is a nigger. Bona! But dont all the dorm girls say so? And dont you, when you are sane, say so? Thats why I love— Oh, nonsense. You have never loved a man who didnt first love you. Besides—

Columns thud away from her. Come to a halt in line formation. Rigid. The period bell rings, and the teacher dismisses them.

A group collects around Paul. They are choosing sides for basket-ball. Girls against boys. Paul has his. He is limbering up beneath the basket. Bona runs to the girl captain and asks to be chosen. The girls fuss. The director comes to quiet them. He hears what Bona wants.

"But, Miss Hale, you were excused—"

"So I was, Mr. Boynton, but—

"—you can play basket-ball, but you are too sick to drill."

"If you wish to put it that way."

She swings away from him to the girl captain.

"Helen, I want to play, and you must let me. This is the first time I've asked and I dont see why—"

"Thats just it, Bona. We have our team."

"Well, team or no team, I want to play and thats all there is to it."

She snatches the ball from Helen's hands, and charges down the floor.

Helen shrugs. One of the weaker girls says that she'll drop out. Helen accepts this. The team is formed. The whistle blows. The game starts. Bona, in center, is jumping against Paul. He plays with her. Out-jumps her, makes a quick pass, gets a quick return, and shoots a goal from the middle of the floor. Bona burns crimson. She fights, and tries to guard him. One of her team-mates advises her not to play so hard. Paul shoots his second goal.

Bona begins to feel a little dizzy and all in. She drives on. Almost hugs Paul to guard him. Near the basket, he attempts to shoot, and Bona lunges into his body and tries to beat his arms. His elbow, going up, gives her a sharp crack on the jaw. She whirls. He catches her. Her body stiffens. Then becomes strangely vibrant, and bursts to a swift life within her anger. He is about to give way before her hatred when a new passion flares at him and makes his stomach fall. Bona squeezes him. He suddenly feels stifled, and wonders why in hell the ring of silly gaping faces that's caked about him doesnt make way and give him air. He has a swift illusion that it is himself who has been struck. He looks at Bona. Whir. Whir. They seem to be human distortions spinning tensely in a fog. Spinning . . dizzy . . spinning. . . Bona jerks herself free, flushes a startling crimson, breaks through the bewildered teams, and rushes from the hall.

2

Paul is in his room of two windows.

Outside, the South-Side L track cuts them in two.

Bona is one window. One window, Paul.

Hurtling Loop-jammed L trains throw them in swift shadow.

Paul goes to his. Gray slanting roofs of houses are tinted

lavender in the setting sun. Paul follows the sun, over the stock-yards where a fresh stench is just arising, across wheat lands that are still waving above their stubble, into the sun. Paul follows the sun to a pine-matted hillock in Georgia. He sees the slanting roofs of gray unpainted cabins tinted lavender. A Negress chants a lullaby beneath the mate-eyes of a southern planter. Her breasts are ample for the suckling of a song. She weans it, and sends it, curiously weaving, among lush melodies of cane and corn. Paul follows the sun into himself in Chicago.

He is at Bona's window.

With his own glow he looks through a dark pane.

Paul's room-mate comes in.

"Say, Paul, I've got a date for you. Come on. Shake a leg, will you?"

His blonde hair is combed slick. His vest is snug about him.

He is like the electric light which he snaps on.

"Whatdoysay, Paul? Get a wiggle on. Come on. We havent got much time by the time we eat and dress and everything."

His bustling concentrates on the brushing of his hair.

Art: What in hell's getting into Paul of late, anyway? Christ, but he's getting moony. Its his blood. Dark blood: moony. Doesnt get anywhere unless you boost it. You've got to keep it going—

"Say, Paul!"

—or it'll go to sleep on you. Dark blood; nigger? Thats what those jealous she-hens say. Not Bona though, or she . . from the South . . wouldnt want me to fix a date for him and her. Hell of a thing, that Paul's dark: you've got to always be answering questions

"Say, Paul, for Christ's sake leave that window, cant you?"

"Whats it, Art?"

"Hell, I've told you about fifty times. Got a date for you. Come on."

"With who?"

Art: He didnt use to ask; now he does. Getting up in the air. Getting funny.

"Heres your hat. Want a smoke? Paul! Here. I've got a match. Now come on and I'll tell you all about it on the way to supper."

Paul: He's going to Life this time. No doubt of that. Quit your kidding. Some day, dear Art, I'm going to kick the living slats out of you, and you wont know what I've done it for. And your slats will bring forth Life . . beautiful woman. . .

Pure Food Restaurant.

"Bring me some soup with a lot of crackers, understand? And then a roast-beef dinner. Same for you, eh, Paul? Now as I was saying, you've got a swell chance with her. And she's game. Best proof: she dont give a damn what the dorm girls say about you and her in the gym, or about the funny looks that Boynton gives her, or about what they say about, well, hell, you know, Paul. And say, Paul, she's a sweetheart. Tall, not puffy and pretty, more serious and deep—the kind you like these days. And they say she's got a car. And say, she's on fire. But you know all about that. She got Helen to fix it up with me. The four of us—remember the last party? Crimson Gardens! Boy!"

Paul's eyes take on a light that Art can settle in.

3

Art has on his patent-leather pumps and fancy vest. A loose fall coat is swung across his arm. His face has been massaged, and over a close shave, powdered. It is a healthy pink the blue of evening tints a purple pallor. Art is happy and confident in the good looks that his mirror gave him. Bubbling over with a joy he must spend now if the night is to contain it all. His bubbles, too, are curiously tinted purple as Paul watches them. Paul, contrary to what he had thought he would be like, is cool like the dusk, and like the dusk, detached. His dark face is a floating shade in evening's shadow. He sees Art, curiously. Art is a purple fluid, carbon-charged, that effervesces besides him. He loves Art. But is it not queer, this pale purple facsimile of a red-blooded Norwegian friend of his? Perhaps for some reason, white skins are not supposed to live at night. Surely, enough nights would transform them fantastically, or kill them. And their red passion? Night paled that too, and made it moony. Moony. Thats what Art thought of him. Bona didnt, even in the daytime. Bona, would she be pale? Impossible. Not that red glow. But the conviction did not set his emotion flowing.

"Come right in, wont you? The young ladies will be right down. Oh, Mr. Carlstrom, do play something for us while you are waiting. We just love to listen to your music. You play so well."

Houses, and dorm sitting-rooms are places where white faces seclude themselves at night. There is a reason. . .

Art sat on the piano and simply tore it down. Jazz. The picture of Our Poets hung perilously.

Paul: I've got to get the kid to play that stuff for me in the daytime. Might be different. More himself. More nigger. Different? There is. Curious, though.

The girls come in. Art stops playing, and almost immediately takes up a petty quarrel, where he had last left it, with Helen.

Bona, black-hair curled staccato, sharply contrasting with Helen's puffy yellow, holds Paul's hand. She squeezes it. Her own emotion supplements the return pressure. And then, for no tangible reason, her spirits drop. Without them, she is nervous, and slightly afraid. She resents this. Paul's eyes are critical. She resents Paul. She flares at him. She flares to poise and security.

"Shall we be on our way?"

"Yes, Bona, certainly."

The Boulevard is sleek in asphalt, and, with arc-lights and limousines, aglow. Dry leaves scamper behind the whir of cars. The scent of exploded gasoline that mingles with them is faintly sweet. Mellow stone mansions overshadow clapboard homes which now resemble Negro shanties in some southern alley. Bona and Paul, and Art and Helen, move along an island-like, far-stretching strip of leaf-soft ground. Above them, worlds of shadow-planes and solids, silently moving. As if on one of these, Paul looks down on Bona. No doubt of it: her face is pale. She is talking. Her words have no feel to them.

One sees them. They are pink petals that fall upon velvet cloth. Bona is soft, and pale, and beautiful.

"Paul, tell me something about yourself—or would you rather wait?"

"I'll tell you anything you'd like to know."

"Not what I want to know, Paul; what you want to tell me."

"You have the beauty of a gem fathoms under sea."

"I feel that, but I dont want to be. I want to be near you. Perhaps I will be if I tell you something. Paul, I love you."

The sea casts up its jewel into his hands, and burns them furiously. To tuck her arm under his and hold her hand will ease the burn.

"What can I say to you, brave dear woman—I cant talk love. Love is a dry grain in my mouth unless it is wet with kisses."

"You would dare? right here on the Boulevard? before Arthur and Helen?"

"Before myself? I dare."

"Here then."

Bona, in the slim shadow of a tree trunk, pulls Paul to her. Suddenly she stiffens. Stops.

"But you have not said you love me."

"I cant—yet—Bona."

"Ach, you never will. Youre cold. Cold."

Bona: Colored; cold. Wrong somewhere. She hurries and catches up with Art and Helen.

4

Crimson Gardens. Hurrah! So one feels. People . . . University of Chicago students, members of the stock exchange, a large Negro in crimson uniform who guards the door . . had watched them enter. Had leaned towards each other over ash-smeared tablecloths and highballs and whispered: What is he, a Spaniard, an Indian, an Italian, a Mexican, a Hindu, or a Japanese? Art had at first fidgeted under their stares . . what are *you* looking at, you godam pack of owl-eyed hyenas? . . but soon settled into his fuss with Helen, and forgot them. A strange thing happened to Paul. Suddenly he knew that he was apart from the people around him. Apart from the pain which they had unconsciously caused. Suddenly he knew that people saw, not attractiveness in his dark skin, but difference. Their stares, giving him to himself, filled something long empty within him, and were like green blades sprouting in his consciousness. There was fullness, and strength and peace about it all. He saw himself, cloudy, but real. He saw the faces of the people at the tables round him. White lights, or as now, the pink lights of the Crimson Gardens gave a glow and immediacy to white faces. The pleasure of it, equal to that of love or dream, of seeing this. Art and Bona and Helen? He'd look. They were wonderfully flushed and beautiful. Not for himself; because they were. Distantly. Who were they, anyway? God, if he knew them. He'd come in with them. Of that he was sure. Come where? Into life? Yes. No. Into the Crimson Gardens. A part of life. A carbon bubble. Would it look purple if he went out into the night and looked at it? His sudden starting to rise almost upset the table.

"What in hell—pardon—whats the matter, Paul?"

"I forgot my cigarettes—"

"Youre smoking one."

"So I am. Pardon me."

The waiter straightens them out. Takes their order.

Art: What in hell's eating Paul? Moony aint the word for it. From bad to worse. And those godam people staring so. Paul's a queer fish. Doesnt seem to mind. . . He's my pal, let me tell you, you horn-rimmed owl-eyed hyena at that table, and a lot better than you whoever you are. . . Queer about him. I could stick up for if he'd only come out, one way or the other, and tell a feller. Besides, a room-mate has a right to know. Thinks I wont understand. Said so. He's got a swell head when it comes to brains, all right. God, he's a good straight feller, though. Only, moony. Nut. Nuttish. Nuttery. Nutmeg. . . "What'd you say, Helen?"

"I was talking to Bona, thank you."

"Well, its nothing to get spiffy about."

"What? Oh, of course not. Please lets dont start some silly argument all over again."

"Well."

"Well."

"Now thats enough. Say, waiter, whats the matter with our order? Make it snappy, will you?"

Crimson Gardens. Hurrah! So one feels. The drinks come. Four highballs. Art passes cigarettes. A girl dressed like a bare-back rider in flaming pink, makes her way through tables to the dance floor. All lights are dimmed till they seem a lush afterglow of crimson. Spotlights the girl. She sings. "Liza, Little Liza Jane."

Paul is rosy before his window.

He moves, slightly, towards Bona.

With his own glow, he seeks to penetrate a dark pane.

Paul: From the South. What does that mean, precisely, except that you'll love or hate a nigger? Thats a lot. What does it mean except that in Chicago you'll have the courage to neither love or hate. A priori. But it would seem that you have. Queer words, arent these, for a man who wears blue pants on a gym floor in the daytime. Well, never matter. You matter. I'd like to know you whom I look at. Know, not love. Not that knowing is a greater pleasure; but that I have just found the joy of it. You came just a month too late. Even this afternoon I dreamed. To-night, along the Boulevard, you found me cold. Paul Johnson, cold! Thats a good one, eh, Art, you fine old stupid fellow, you! But I feel good! The color and the music and the song. . . A Negress chants a lullaby beneath the mate-eyes of a southern planter. O song! . . And those flushed faces. Eager brilliant eyes. Hard to imagine them as awakened. Your own. Oh, they're awake all right. "And you know it too, dont you Bona?"

"What, Paul?"

"The truth of what I was thinking."

"I'd like to know I know—something of you."

"You will—before the evening's over. I promise it."

Crimson Gardens. Hurrah! So one feels. The bare-back rider balances agilely on the applause which is the tail of her song. Orchestral instruments warm up for jazz. The flute is a cat that ripples its fur against the deep-purring saxophone. The drum throws sticks. The cat jumps on the piano keyboard. Hi diddle, hi diddle, the cat and the fiddle. Crimson Gardens . . hurrah! . . jumps over the moon. Crimson Gardens! Helen . . O

Eliza . . rabbit-eyes sparkling, plays up to, and tries to placate what she considers to be Paul's contempt. She always does that . . Little Liza Jane. . . Once home, she burns with the thought of what she's done. She says all manner of snidy things about him, and swears that she'll never go out again when he is along. She tries to get Art to break with him, saying, that if Paul, whom the whole dormitory calls a nigger, is more to him than she is, well, she's through. She does not break with Art. She goes out as often as she can with Art and Paul. She explains this to herself by a piece of information which a friend of hers had given her: men like him (Paul) can fascinate. One is not responsible for fascination. Not one girl had really loved Paul; he fascinated them. Bona didnt; only thought she did. Time would tell. And of course, *she* didnt. Liza. . . She plays up to, and tries to placate, Paul.

"Paul is so deep these days, and I'm so glad he's found some one to interest him."

"I dont believe I do."

The thought escapes from Bona just a moment before her anger at having said it.

Bona: You little puffy cat, I do. I do!

Dont I, Paul? her eyes ask.

Her answer is a crash of jazz from the palm-hidden orchestra. Crimson Gardens is a body whose blood flows to a clot upon the dance floor. Art and Helen clot. Soon, Bona and Paul. Paul finds her a little stiff, and his mind, wandering to Helen (silly little kid who wants every highball spoon her hands touch, for a souvenir), supple, perfect little dancer, wishes for the next dance when he and Art will exchange.

Bona knows that she must win him to herself.

"Since when have men like you grown cold?"

"The first philosopher."

"I thought you were a poet—or a gym director."

"Hence, your failure to make love."

Bona's eyes flare. Water. Grow red about the rims. She would like to tear away from him and dash across the clotted floor.

"What do you mean?"

"Mental concepts rule you. If they were flush with mine—good. I dont believe they are."

"How do you know, Mr. Philosopher?"

"Mostly a priori."

"You talk well for a gym director."

"And you—"

"I hate you. Ou!"

She presses away. Paul, conscious of the convention in it, pulls her to him. Her body close. Her head still strains away. He nearly crushes her. She tries to pinch him. Then sees people staring, and lets her arms fall. Their eyes meet. Both, contemptuous. The dance takes blood from their minds and packs it, tingling, in the torsos of their swaying bodies. Passionate blood leaps back into their eyes. They are a dizzy blood clot on a gyrating floor. They know that the pink-faced people have no part in what they feel. Their instinct leads them away from Art and Helen, and towards the big uniformed black man who opens and closes the gilded exit door. The cloak-room girl is tolerant of their impatience over such trivial things as wraps. And slightly superior. As the black man swings the door for them, his eyes are knowing. Too many couples have passed out, flushed and fidgety, for him not to know. The chill air is a shock to Paul. A strange thing happens. He sees the Gardens purple, as if he were way off. And a spot is in the purple. The spot comes furiously towards him. Face of the black man. It leers. It smiles sweetly like a child's. Paul leaves Bona and darts back so quickly that he doesnt give the door-man a chance to open. He swings in. Stops. Before the huge bulk of the Negro.

"Youre wrong."

"Yassur."

"Brother, youre wrong.

"I came back to tell you, to shake your hand, and tell you that you are wrong. That something beautiful is going to happen. That the Gardens are purple like a bed of roses would be at dusk. That I came into the Gardens, into life in the Gardens with one whom I did not know. That I danced with her, and did not know her. That I felt passion, contempt and passion for her whom I did not know. That I thought of her. That my thoughts were matches thrown into a dark window. And all the while the Gardens were purple like a bed of roses would be at dusk. I came back to tell you, brother, that white faces are petals of roses. That dark faces are petals of dusk. That I am going out and gather petals. That I am going out and know her whom I brought here with me to these Gardens which are purple like a bed of roses would be at dusk."

Paul and the black man shook hands.

When he reached the spot where they had been standing, Bona was gone.

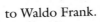

to Waldo Frank.

Kabnis

RALPH KABNIS, propped in his bed, tries to read. To read himself to sleep. An oil lamp on a chair near his elbow burns unsteadily. The cabin room is spaced fantastically about it. Whitewashed hearth and chimney, black with sooty sawteeth. Ceiling, patterned by the fringed globe of the lamp. The walls, unpainted, are seasoned a rosin yellow. And cracks between the boards are black. These cracks are the lips the night winds use for whispering. Night winds in Georgia are vagrant poets, whispering. Kabnis, against his will, lets his book slip down, and listens to them. The warm whiteness of his bed, the lamp-light, do not protect him from the weird chill of their song:

> White-man's land.
> Niggers, sing.
> Burn, bear black children
> Till poor rivers bring
> Rest, and sweet glory
> In Camp Ground.

Kabnis' thin hair is streaked on the pillow. His hand strokes the slim silk of his mustache. His thumb, pressed under his chin, seems to be trying to give squareness and projection to it. Brown eyes stare from a lemon face. Moisture gathers beneath his arm-pits. He slides down beneath the cover, seeking release.

Kabnis: Near me. Now. Whoever you are, my warm glowing sweetheart, do not think that the face that rests beside you is the real Kabnis. Ralph Kabnis is a dream. And dreams are faces with large eyes and weak chins and broad brows that get smashed by the fists of square faces. The body of the world is bull-necked. A dream is a soft face that fits uncertainly upon it. . . God, if I could develop that in words. Give what I know a bull-neck and a heaving body, all would go well with me, wouldnt it, sweetheart? If I could feel that I came to the South to face it. If I, the dream (not what is weak and afraid in me) could become the face of the South. How my lips would sing for it, my songs being the lips of its soul. Soul. Soul hell. There aint no such thing. What in hell was that?

A rat had run across the thin boards of the ceiling. Kabnis thrusts his head out from the covers. Through the cracks, a powdery faded red dust sprays down on him. Dust of slave-fields, dried, scattered. . . No use to read. Christ, if he only could drink himself to sleep. Something as sure as fate was going to happen. He couldnt stand this thing much longer. A hen, perched on a shelf in the adjoining room begins to tread. Her nails scrape the soft wood. Her feathers ruffle.

"Get out of that, you egg-laying bitch."

Kabnis hurls a slipper against the wall. The hen flies from her perch and cackles as if a skunk were after her.

"Now cut out that racket or I'll wring your neck for you."

Answering cackles arise in the chicken yard.

"Why in Christ's hell cant you leave me alone? Damn it, I wish your cackle would choke you. Choke every mother's son of them in this God-forsaken hole. Go away. By God I'll wring your neck for you if you dont. Hell of a mess I've got in: even the poultry is hostile. Go way. Go way. By God, I'll . . ."

Kabnis jumps from his bed. His eyes are wild. He makes for the door. Bursts through it. The hen, driving blindly at the windowpane, screams. Then flies and flops around trying to elude him. Kabnis catches her.

"Got you now, you she-bitch."

With his fingers about her neck, he thrusts open the outside door and steps out into the serene loveliness of Georgian autumn moonlight. Some distance off, down in the valley, a band of pine-smoke, silvered gauze, drifts steadily. The half-moon is a white child that sleeps upon the tree-tops of the forest. White winds croon its sleep-song:

rock a-by baby . .
Black mother sways, holding a white child on her bosom.
when the bough bends . .
Her breath hums through pine-cones.
cradle will fall . .

Teat moon-children at your breasts,
down will come baby . .
Black mother.

Kabnis whirls the chicken by its neck, and throws the head
away. Picks up the hopping body, warm, sticky, and hides it in
a clump of bushes. He wipes blood from his hands onto the
coarse scant grass.

Kabnis: Thats done. Old Chromo in the big house there
will wonder whats become of her pet hen. Well, it'll teach her
a lesson: not to make a hen-coop of my quarters. Quarters.
Hell of a fine quarters, I've got. Five years ago; look at me
now. Earth's child. The earth my mother. God is a profligate
red-nosed man about town. Bastardy; me. A bastard son has
got a right to curse his maker. God. . .

Kabnis is about to shake his fists heavenward. He looks up,
and the night's beauty strikes him dumb. He falls to his knees.
Sharp stones cut through his thin pajamas. The shock sends a
shiver over him. He quivers. Tears mist his eyes. He writhes.

"God Almighty, dear God, dear Jesus, do not torture me
with beauty. Take it away. Give me an ugly world. Ha, ugly.
Stinking like unwashed niggers. Dear Jesus, do not chain me
to myself and set these hills and valleys, heaving with folk-
songs, so close to me that I cannot reach them. There is a radiant beauty in the night that touches and . . . tortures me. Ugh.
Hell. Get up, you damn fool. Look around. Whats beautiful
there? Hog pens and chicken yards. Dirty red mud. Stinking
outhouse. Whats beauty anyway but ugliness if it hurts you?
God, he doesnt exist, but nevertheless He is ugly. Hence, what
comes from Him is ugly. Lynchers and business men, and that
cockroach Hanby, especially. How come that he gets to be
principal of a school? Of the school I'm driven to teach in?
God's handiwork, doubtless. God and Hanby, they belong together. Two godam moral-spouters. Oh, no, I wont let that
emotion come up in me. Stay down. Stay down, I tell you. O
Jesus, Thou art beautiful. . . Come, Ralph, pull yourself together. Curses and adoration dont come from what is sane.
This loneliness, dumbness, awful, intangible oppression is
enough to drive a man insane. Miles from nowhere. A speck
on a Georgia hillside. Jesus, can you imagine it—an atom of

dust in agony on a hillside? Thats a spectacle for you. Come, Ralph, old man, pull yourself together."

Kabnis has stiffened. He is conscious now of the night wind, and of how it chills him. He rises. He totters as a man would who for the first time uses artificial limbs. As a completely artificial man would. The large frame house, squatting on brick pillars, where the principal of the school, his wife, and the boarding girls sleep, seems a curious shadow of his mind. He tries, but cannot convince himself of its reality. His gaze drifts down into the vale, across the swamp, up over the solid dusk bank of pines, and rests, bewildered-like, on the court-house tower. It is dull silver in the moonlight. White child that sleeps upon the top of pines. Kabnis' mind clears. He sees himself yanked beneath that tower. He sees white minds, with indolent assumption, juggle justice and a nigger. . . Somewhere, far off in the straight line of his sight, is Augusta. Christ, how cut off from everything he is. And hours, hours north, why not say a lifetime north? Washington sleeps. Its still, peaceful streets, how desirable they are. Its people whom he had always halfway despised. New York? Impossible. It was a fiction. He had dreamed it. An impotent nostalgia grips him. It becomes intolerable. He forces himself to narrow to a cabin silhouetted on a knoll about a mile away. Peace. Negroes within it are content. They farm. They sing. They love. They sleep. Kabnis wonders if perhaps they can feel him. If perhaps he gives them bad dreams. Things are so immediate in Georgia.

Thinking that now he can go to sleep, he reenters his room. He builds a fire in the open hearth. The room dances to the tongues of flames, and sings to the crackling and spurting of the logs. Wind comes up between the floor boards, through the black cracks of the walls.

Kabnis: Cant sleep. Light a cigarette. If that old bastard comes over here and smells smoke, I'm done for. Hell of a note, cant even smoke. The stillness of it: where they burn and hang men, you cant smoke. Cant take a swig of licker. What do they think this is, anyway, some sort of temperance school? How did I ever land in such a hole? Ugh. One might just as well be in his grave. Still as a grave. Jesus, how still everything is. Does the world know how still it is? People make noise.

They are afraid of silence. Of what lives, and God, of what dies in silence. There must be many dead things moving in silence. They come here to touch me. I swear I feel their fingers. . . Come, Ralph, pull yourself together. What in hell was that? Only the rustle of leaves, I guess. You know, Ralph, old man, it wouldnt surprise me at all to see a ghost. People dont think there are such things. They rationalize their fear, and call their cowardice science. Fine bunch, they are. Damit, that was a noise. And not the wind either. A chicken maybe. Hell, chickens dont wander around this time of night. What in hell is it?

A scraping sound, like a piece of wood dragging over the ground, is coming near.

"Ha, ha. The ghosts down this way havent got any chains to rattle, so they drag trees along with them. Thats a good one. But no joke, something is outside this house, as sure as hell. Whatever it is, it can get a good look at me and I cant see it. Jesus Christ!"

Kabnis pours water on the flames and blows his lamp out. He picks up a poker and stealthily approaches the outside door. Swings it open, and lurches into the night. A calf, carrying a yoke of wood, bolts away from him and scampers down the road.

"Well, I'm damned. This godam place is sure getting the best of me. Come, Ralph, old man, pull yourself together. Nights cant last forever. Thank God for that. Its Sunday already. First time in my life I've ever wanted Sunday to come. Hell of a day. And down here there's no such thing as ducking church. Well, I'll see Halsey and Layman, and get a good square meal. Thats something. And Halsey's a damn good feller. Cant talk to him though. Who in Christ's world can I talk to? A hen. God. Myself. . . I'm going bats, no doubt of that. Come now, Ralph, go in and make yourself go to sleep. Come now . . in the door . . thats right. Put the poker down. There. All right. Slip under the sheets. Close your eyes. Think nothing . . a long time . . nothing, nothing. Dont even think nothing. Blank. Not even blank. Count. No, mustnt count. Nothing . . blank . . nothing . . blank . . space without stars in it. No, nothing . . nothing . .

Kabnis sleeps. The winds, like soft-voiced vagrant poets sing:

White-man's land.
Niggers, sing.
Burn, bear black children
Till poor rivers bring
Rest, and sweet glory
In Camp Ground.

2

The parlor of Fred Halsey's home. There is a seediness about
it. It seems as though the fittings have given a frugal service to
at least seven generations of middle-class shop-owners. An
open grate burns cheerily in contrast to the gray cold changed
autumn weather. An old-fashioned mantelpiece supports a
family clock (not running), a figure or two in imitation bronze,
and two small group pictures. Directly above it, in a heavy oak
frame, the portrait of a bearded man. Black hair, thick and
curly, intensifies the pallor of the high forehead. The eyes are
daring. The nose, sharp and regular. The poise suggests a tendency to adventure checked by the necessities of absolute
command. The portrait is that of an English gentleman who
has retained much of his culture, in that money has enabled
him to escape being drawn through a land-grubbing pioneer
life. His nature and features, modified by marriage and circumstances, have been transmitted to his great-grandson, Fred. To
the left of this picture, spaced on the wall, is a smaller portrait
of the great-grandmother. That here there is a Negro strain,
no one would doubt. But it is difficult to say in precisely what
feature it lies. On close inspection, her mouth is seen to be
wistfully twisted. The expression of her face seems to shift
before one's gaze—now ugly, repulsive; now sad, and somehow
beautiful in its pain. A tin wood-box rests on the floor below.
To the right of the great-grandfather's portrait hangs a family
group: the father, mother, two brothers, and one sister of Fred.
It includes himself some thirty years ago when his face was an
olive white, and his hair luxuriant and dark and wavy. The father is a rich brown. The mother, practically white. Of the children, the girl, quite young, is like Fred; the two brothers,

darker. The walls of the room are plastered and painted green. An old upright piano is tucked into the corner near the window. The window looks out on a forlorn, box-like, whitewashed frame church. Negroes are gathering, on foot, driving questionable gray and brown mules, and in an occasional Ford, for afternoon service. Beyond, Georgia hills roll off into the distance, their dreary aspect heightened by the gray spots of unpainted one- and two-room shanties. Clumps of pine trees here and there are the dark points the whole landscape is approaching. The church bell tolls. Above its squat tower, a great spiral of buzzards reaches far into the heavens. An ironic comment upon the path that leads into the Christian land. . . Three rocking chairs are grouped around the grate. Sunday papers scattered on the floor indicate a recent usage. Halsey, a well-built, stocky fellow, hair cropped close, enters the room. His Sunday clothes smell of wood and glue, for it is his habit to potter around his wagon-shop even on the Lord's day. He is followed by Professor Layman, tall, heavy, loose-jointed Georgia Negro, by turns teacher and preacher, who has traveled in almost every nook and corner of the state and hence knows more than would be good for anyone other than a silent man. Kabnis, trying to force through a gathering heaviness, trails in behind them. They slip into chairs before the fire.

Layman: Sholy fine, Mr. Halsey, sholy fine. This town's right good at feedin folks, better'n most towns in th state, even for preachers, but I ken say this beats um all. Yassur. Now aint that right, Professor Kabnis?

Kabnis: Yes sir, this beats them all, all right—best I've had, and thats a fact, though my comparison doesnt carry far, y'know.

Layman: Hows that, Professor?

Kabnis: Well, this is my first time out—

Layman: For a fact. Aint seed you round so much. Whats th trouble? Dont like our folks down this away?

Halsey: Aint that, Layman. He aint like most northern niggers that way. Aint a thing stuck up about him. He likes us, you an me, maybe all—its that red mud over yonder—gets stuck in it an cant get out. (Laughs.) An then he loves th fire so, warm as its been. Coldest Yankee I've ever seen. But I'm goin t get him out now it a jiffy, eh, Kabnis?

Kabnis: Sure, I should say so, sure. Dont think its because I dont like folks down this way. Just the opposite, in fact. Theres more hospitality and everything. Its diff—that is, theres lots of northern exaggeration about the South. Its not half the terror they picture it. Things are not half bad, as one could easily figure out for himself without ever crossing the Mason and Dixie line: all these people wouldnt stay down here, especially the rich, the ones that could easily leave, if conditions were so mighty bad. And then too, sometime back, my family were southerners y'know. From Georgia, in fact—

Layman: Nothin t feel proud about, Professor. Neither your folks nor mine.

Halsey (in a mock religious tone):   Amen t that, brother Layman. Amen (turning to Kabnis, half playful, yet somehow dead in earnest). An Mr. Kabnis, kindly remember youre in th land of cotton—hell of a land. Th white folks get th boll; th niggers get th stalk. An dont you dare touch th boll, or even look at it. They'll swing y sho. (Laughs.)

Kabnis: But they wouldnt touch a gentleman—fellows, men like us three here—

Layman: Nigger's a nigger down this away, Professor. An only two dividins: good an bad. An even they aint permanent categories. They sometimes mixes um up when it comes t lynchin. I've seen um do it.

Halsey: Dont let th fear int y, though, Kabnis. This county's a good un. Aint been a stringin up I can remember. (Laughs.)

Layman: This is a good town an a good county. But theres some that makes up fer it.

Kabnis: Things are better now though since that stir about those peonage cases, arent they?

Layman: Ever hear tell of a single shot killin moren one rabbit, Professor?

Kabnis: No, of course not, that is, but then—

Halsey: Now I know you werent born yesterday, sprung up so rapid like you aint heard of th brick thrown in th hornets' nest. (Laughs.)

Kabnis: Hardly, hardly, I know—

Halsey: Course y do. (To Layman) See, northern niggers aint as dumb as they make out t be.

Kabnis (overlooking the remark): Just stirs them up to sting.

Halsey: T perfection. An put just like a professor should put it.

Kabnis: Thats what actually did happen?

Layman: Well, if it aint sos only because th stingers already movin jes as fast as they ken go. An been goin ever since I ken remember, an then some mo. Though I dont usually make mention of it.

Halsey: Damn sight better not. Say, Layman, you come from where theyre always swarmin, dont y?

Layman: Yassur. I do that, sho. Dont want t mention it, but its a fact. I've seed th time when there werent no use t even stretch out flat upon th ground. Seen um shoot an cut a man t pieces who had died th night befo. Yassur. An they didnt stop when they found out he was dead—jes went on ahackin at him anyway.

Kabnis: What did you do? What did you say to them, Professor?

Layman: Thems th things you neither does a thing or talks about if y want t stay around this away, Professor.

Halsey: Listen t what he's tellin y, Kabnis. May come in handy some day.

Kabnis: Cant something be done? But of course not. This preacher-ridden race. Pray and shout. Theyre in the preacher's hands. Thats what it is. And the preacher's hands are in the white man's pockets.

Halsey: Present company always excepted.

Kabnis: The Professor knows I wasnt referring to him.

Layman: Preacher's a preacher anywheres you turn. No use exceptin.

Kabnis: Well, of course, if you look at it that way. I didnt mean— But cant something be done?

Layman: Sho. Yassur. An done first rate an well. Jes like Sam Raymon done it.

Kabnis: Hows that? What did he do?

Layman: Th white folks (reckon I oughtnt tell it) had jes knocked two others like you kill a cow—brained um with an ax, when they caught Sam Raymon by a stream. They was about t do fer him when he up an says, "White folks, I gotter die, I knows that. But wont y let me die in my own way?" Some was fer gettin after him, but th boss held um back an says, "Jes so longs th nigger dies—" An Sam fell down ont his knees an prayed, "O Lord, Ise comin to y," an he up an jumps int th stream.

Singing from the church becomes audible. Above it, rising and falling in a plaintive moan, a woman's voice swells to shouting. Kabnis hears it. His face gives way to an expression of mingled fear, contempt, and pity. Layman takes no notice of it. Halsey grins at Kabnis. He feels like having a little sport with him.

Halsey: Lets go t church, eh, Kabnis?

Kabnis (seeking control):   All right—no sir, not by a damn sight. Once a days enough for me. Christ, but that stuff gets to me. Meaning no reflection on you, Professor.

Halsey: Course not. Say, Kabnis, noticed y this morning. What'd y get up for an go out?

Kabnis: Couldnt stand the shouting, and thats a fact. We dont have that sort of thing up North. We do, but, that is, some one should see to it that they are stopped or put out when they get so bad the preacher has to stop his sermon for them.

Halsey: Is that th way youall sit on sisters up North?

Kabnis: In the church I used to go to no one ever shouted—

Halsey: Lungs weak?

Kabnis: Hardly, that is—

Halsey: Yankees are right up t th minute in tellin folk how t turn a trick. They always were good at talkin.

Kabnis: Well, anyway, they should be stopped.

Layman: Thats right. Thats true. An its th worst ones in th community that comes int th church t shout. I've sort a made a study of it. You take a man what drinks, th biggest licker-head around will come int th church an yell th loudest. An th sister whats done wrong, an is always doin wrong, will sit down in th Amen corner an swing her arms an shout her head off. Seems as if they cant control themselves out in th world; they cant control themselves in church. Now dont that sound logical, Professor?

Halsey: Reckon its as good as any. But I heard that queer

cuss over yonder—y know him, dont y, Kabnis? Well, y ought
t. He had a run-in with your boss th other day—same as you'll
have if you dont walk th chalk-line. An th quicker th better. I
hate that Hanby. Ornery bastard. I'll mash his mouth in one of
these days. Well, as I was sayin, that feller, Lewis's name, I
heard him sayin somethin about a stream whats dammed has
got t cut loose somewheres. An that sounds good. I know th
feelin myself. He strikes me as knowin a bucketful bout most
things, that feller does. Seems like he doesnt want t talk, an
does, sometimes, like Layman here. Damn queer feller, him.

Layman: Cant make heads or tails of him an I've seen lots
o queer possums in my day. Everybody's wonderin about him.
White folks too. He'll have t leave here soon, thats sho. Always
askin questions. An I aint seed his lips move once. Pokin round
an notin somethin. Noted what I said th other day, an that
werent fer notin down.

Kabnis: What was that?

Layman: Oh, a lynchin that took place bout a year ago. Th
worst I know of round these parts.

Halsey: Bill Burnam?

Layman: Na. Mame Lamkins

Halsey grunts, but says nothing.

The preacher's voice rolls from the church in an insistent
chanting monotone. At regular intervals it rises to a crescendo
note. The sister begins to shout. Her voice, high-pitched and
hysterical, is almost perfectly attuned to the nervous key of
Kabnis. Halsey notices his distress, and is amused by it.
Layman's face is expressionless. Kabnis wants to hear the story
of Mame Lamkins. He does not want to hear it. It can be no
worse than the shouting.

Kabnis (his chair rocking faster):   What about Mame
Lamkins?

Halsey: Tell him, Layman.

The preacher momentarily stops. The choir, together with
the entire congregation, sings an old spiritual. The music seems
to quiet the shouter. Her heavy breathing has the sound of
evening winds that blow through pinecones. Layman's voice is
uniformly low and soothing. A canebrake, murmuring the tale
to its neighbor-road would be more passionate.

Layman: White folks know that niggers talk, an they dont

mind jes so long as nothing comes of it, so here goes. She was in th family-way, Mame Lamkills was. They killed her in th street, an some white man seein th risin in her stomach as she lay there soppy in her blood like any cow, took an ripped her belly open, an th kid fell out. It was living; but a nigger baby aint supposed t live. So he jabbed his knife in it an stuck it t a tree. An then they all went away.

Kabnis: Christ no! What had she done?

Layman: Tried t hide her husband when they was after him.

A shriek pierces the room. The bronze pieces on the mantel hum. The sister cries frantically: "Jesus, Jesus, I've found Jesus. O Lord, glory t God, one mo sinner is acomin home." At the height of this, a stone, wrapped round with paper, crashes through the window. Kabnis springs to his feet, terror-stricken. Layman is worried. Halsey picks up the stone. Takes off the wrapper, smooths it out, and reads: "You northern nigger, its time fer y t leave. Git along now." Kabnis knows that the command is meant for him. Fear squeezes him. Caves him in. As a violent external pressure would. Fear flows inside him. It fills him up. He bloats. He saves himself from bursting by dashing wildly from the room. Halsey and Layman stare stupidly at each other. The stone, the crumpled paper are things, huge things that weight them. Their thoughts are vaguely concerned with the texture of the stone, with the color of the paper. Then they remember the words, and begin to shift them about in sentences. Layman even construes them grammatically. Suddenly the sense of them comes back to Halsey. He grips Layman by the arm and they both follow after Kabnis.

A false dusk has come early. The countryside is ashen, chill. Cabins and roads and canebrakes whisper. The church choir, dipping into a long silence, sings:

> My Lord, what a mourning,
> My Lord, what a mourning,
> My Lord, what a mourning,
> When the stars begin to fall.

Softly luminous over the hills and valleys, the faint spray of a scattered star. . .

3

A splotchy figure drives forward along the cane- and corn-stalk hemmed-in road. A scarecrow replica of Kabnis, awkwardly animate. Fantastically plastered with red Georgia mud. It skirts the big house whose windows shine like mellow lanterns in the dusk. Its shoulder jogs against a sweet-gum tree. The figure caroms off against the cabin door, and lunges in. It slams the door as if to prevent some one entering after it.

"God Almighty, theyre here. After me. On me. All along the road I saw their eyes flaring from the cane. Hounds. Shouts. What in God's name did I run here for? A mud-hole trap. I stumbled on a rope. O God, a rope. Their clammy hands were like the love of death playing up and down my spine. Trying to trip my legs. To trip my spine. Up and down my spine. My spine. . . My legs. . . why in hell didn't they catch me?"

Kabnis wheels around, half defiant, half numbed with a more immediate fear.

"Wanted to trap me here. Get out o there. I see you."

He grabs a broom from beside the chimney and violently pokes it under the bed. The broom strikes a tin wash-tub. The noise bewilders. He recovers.

"Not there. In the closet."

He throws the broom aside and grips the poker. Starts towards the closet door, towards somewhere in the perfect blackness behind the chimney.

"I'll brain you."

He stops short. The barks of hounds, evidently in pursuit, reach him. A voice, liquid in distance, yells, "Hi! Hi!"

"O God, theyre after me. Holy Father, Mother of Christ—hell, this aint no time for prayer—"

Voices, just outside the door:

"Reckon he's here."

"Dont see no light though."

The door is flung open.

Kabnis: Get back or I'll kill you.

He braces himself, brandishing the poker.

Halsey (coming in):   Aint as bad as all that. Put that thing down.

Layman: Its only us, Professor. Nobody else after y.

Kabnis: Halsey. Layman. Close that door. Dont light that light. For godsake get away from there.

Halsey: Nobody's after y, Kabnis, I'm tellin y. Put that thing down an get yourself together.

Kabnis: I tell you they are. I saw them. I heard the hounds.

Halsey: These aint th days of hounds an Uncle Tom's Cabin, feller. White folks aint in fer all them theatrics these days. Theys more direct than that. If what they wanted was t get y, theyd have just marched right in an took y where y sat. Somebodys down by th branch chasin rabbits an atreein possums.

A shot is heard.

Halsey: Got him, I reckon. Saw Tom goin out with his gun. Tom's pretty lucky most times.

He goes to the bureau and lights the lamp. The circular fringe is patterned on the ceiling. The moving shadows of the men are huge against the bare wall boards. Halsey walks up to Kabnis, takes the poker from his grip, and without more ado pushes him into a chair before the dark hearth.

Halsey: Youre a mess. Here, Layman. Get some trash an start a fire.

Layman fumbles around, finds some newspapers and old bags, puts them in the hearth, arranges the wood, and kindles the fire. Halsey sets a black iron kettle where it soon will be boiling. Then takes from his hip-pocket a bottle of corn licker which he passes to Kabnis.

Halsey: Here. This'll straighten y out a bit.

Kabnis nervously draws the cork and gulps the licker down.

Kabnis: Ha. Good stuff. Thanks. Thank y, Halsey.

Halsey: Good stuff! Youre damn right. Hanby there dont think so. Wonder he doesnt come over t find out whos burnin his oil. Miserly bastard, him. Th boys what made this stuff—are y listenin t me, Kabnis? th boys what made this stuff have got th art down like I heard you say youd like t be with words. Eh? Have some, Layman?

Layman: Dont think I care for none, thank y jes th same, Mr. Halsey.

Halsey: Care hell. Course y care. Everybody cares around these parts. Preachers an school teachers an everybody. Here. Here, take it. Dont try that line on me.

Layman limbers up a little, but he cannot quite forget that he is on school ground.

Layman: Thats right. Thats true, sho. Shinin is th only business what pays in these hard times.

He takes a nip, and passes the bottle to Kabnis. Kabnis is in the middle of a long swig when a rap sounds on the door. He almost spills the bottle, but manages to pass it to Halsey just as the door swings open and Hanby enters. He is a well-dressed, smooth, rich, black-skinned Negro who thinks there is no one quite so suave and polished as himself. To members of his own race, he affects the manners of a wealthy white planter. Or, when he is up North, he lets it be known that his ideas are those of the best New England tradition. To white men he bows, without ever completely humbling himself. Tradesmen in the town tolerate him because he spends his money with them. He delivers his words with a full consciousness of his moral superiority.

Hanby: Hum. Erer, Professor Kabnis, to come straight to the point: the progress of the Negro race is jeopardized whenever the personal habits and examples set by its guides and mentors fall below the acknowledged and hard-won standard of its average member. This institution, of which I am the humble president, was founded, and has been maintained at a cost of great labor and untold sacrifice. Its purpose is to teach our youth to live better, cleaner, more noble lives. To prove to the world that the Negro race can be just like any other race. It hopes to attain this aim partly by the salutary examples set by its instructors. I cannot hinder the progress of a race simply to indulge a single member. I have thought the matter out beforehand, I can assure you. Therefore, if I find your resignation on my desk by to-morrow morning, Mr. Kabnis, I shall not feel obliged to call in the sheriff. Otherwise. . .

Kabnis: A fellow can take a drink in his own room if he wants to, in the privacy of his own room.

Hanby: His room, but not the institution's room, Mr. Kabnis.

Kabnis: This is my room while I'm in it.

Hanby: Mr. Clayborn (the sheriff) can inform you as to that.

Kabnis: Oh, well, what do I care—glad to get out of this mud-hole.

Hanby: I should think so from your looks.

Kabnis: You neednt get sarcastic about it.

Hanby: No, that is true. And I neednt wait for your resignation either, Mr. Kabnis.

Kabnis: Oh, you'll get that all right. Dont worry.

Hanby: And I should like to have the room thoroughly aired and cleaned and ready for your successor by to-morrow noon, Professor.

Kabnis (trying to rise):   You can have your godam room right away. I dont want it.

Hanby: But I wont have your cursing.

Halsey pushes Kabnis back into his chair.

Halsey: Sit down, Kabnis, till I wash y.

Hanby (to Halsey):   I would rather not have drinking men on the premises, Mr. Halsey. You will oblige me—

Halsey: I'll oblige you by stayin right on this spot, this spot, get me? till I get damned ready t leave.

He approaches Hanby. Hanby retreats, but manages to hold his dignity.

Halsey: Let me get you told right now, Mr. Samuel Hanby. Now listen t me. I aint no slick an span slave youve hired, an dont y think it for a minute. Youve bullied enough about this town. An besides, wheres that bill youve been owin me? Listen t me. If I dont get it paid in by tmorrer noon, Mr. Hanby (he mockingly assumes Hanby's tone and manner), I shall feel obliged t call th sheriff. An that sheriff'll be myself who'll catch y in th road an pull y out your buggy an rightly attend t y. You heard me. Now leave him alone. I'm takin him home with me. I got it fixed. Before you came in. He's goin t work with me. Shapin shafts and buildin wagons'll make a man of him what nobody, y get me? what nobody can take advantage of. Thats all. . .

Halsey burrs off into vague and incoherent comment.

Pause. Disagreeable.

Layman's eyes are glazed on the spurting fire.

Kabnis wants to rise and put both Halsey and Hanby in their places. He vaguely knows that he must do this, else the power of direction will completely slip from him to those outside. The conviction is just strong enough to torture him. To bring a feverish, quick-passing flare into his eyes. To mutter words soggy in hot saliva. To jerk his arms upward in futile protest. Halsey, noticing his gestures, thinks it is water that he desires. He brings a glass to him. Kabnis slings it to the floor. Heat of the conviction dies. His arms crumple. His upper lip, his mustache, quiver. Rap! rap, on the door. The sounds slap Kabnis. They bring a hectic color to his cheeks. Like huge cold finger tips they touch his skin and goose-flesh it. Hanby strikes a commanding pose. He moves toward Layman. Layman's face is innocently immobile.

Halsey: Whos there?

Voice: Lewis.

Halsey: Come in, Lewis. Come on in.

Lewis enters. He is the queer fellow who has been referred to. A tall wiry copper-colored man, thirty perhaps. His mouth and eyes suggest purpose guided by an adequate intelligence. He is what a stronger Kabnis might have been, and in an odd faint way resembles him. As he steps towards the others, he seems to be issuing sharply from a vivid dream. Lewis shakes hands with Halsey. Nods perfunctorily to Hanby, who has stiffened to meet him. Smiles rapidly at Layman, and settles with real interest on Kabnis.

Lewis: Kabnis passed me on the road. Had a piece of business of my own, and couldnt get here any sooner. Thought I might be able to help in some way or other.

Halsey: A good baths bout all he needs now. An somethin t put his mind t rest.

Lewis: I think I can give that. That note was meant for me. Some Negroes have grown uncomfortable at my being here—

Kabnis: You mean, Mr. Lewis, some colored folks threw it? Christ Almighty!

Halsey: Thats what he means. An just as I told y. White folks more direct than that.

Kabnis: What are they after you for?

Lewis: Its a long story, Kabnis. Too long for now. And it might involve present company. (He laughs pleasantly and gestures vaguely in the direction of Hanby.) Tell you about it later on perhaps.

Kabnis: Youre not going?

Lewis: Not till my month's up.

Halsey: Hows that?

Lewis: I'm on a sort of contract with myself. (Is about to leave.) Well, glad its nothing serious—

Halsey: Come round t th shop sometime why dont y, Lewis? I've asked y enough. I'd like t have a talk with y. I aint as dumb as I look. Kabnis an me'll be in most any time. Not much work these days. Wish t hell there was. This burg gets to me when there aint. (In answer to Lewis' question.) He's goin t work with me. Ya. Night air this side th branch aint good fer him. (Looks at Hanby. Laughs.)

Lewis: I see. . .

His eyes turn to Kabnis. In the instant of their shifting, a vision of the life they are to meet. Kabnis, a promise of a soil-soaked beauty; uprooted, thinning out. Suspended a few feet above the soil whose touch would resurrect him. Arm's length removed from him whose will to help. . . There is a swift intuitive interchange of consciousness. Kabnis has a sudden need to rush into the arms of this man. His eyes call, "Brother." And then a savage, cynical twist-about within him mocks his impulse and strengthens him to repulse Lewis. His lips curl cruelly. His eyes laugh. They are glittering needles, stitching. With a throbbing ache they draw Lewis to. Lewis brusquely wheels on Hanby.

Lewis: I'd like to see you, sir, a moment, if you dont mind.

Hanby's tight collar and vest effectively preserve him.

Hanby: Yes, erer, Mr. Lewis. Right away.

Lewis: See you later, Halsey.

Halsey: So long—thanks—sho hope so, Lewis.

As he opens the door and Hanby passes out, a woman, miles down the valley, begins to sing. Her song is a spark that travels swiftly to the near-by cabins. Like purple tallow flames, songs jet up. They spread a ruddy haze over the heavens. The haze swings low. Now the whole countryside is a soft chorus. Lord. O Lord. . . Lewis closes the door behind him. A flame jets out. . .

The kettle is boiling. Halsey notices it. He pulls the wash-tub from beneath the bed. He arranges for the bath before the fire.

Halsey: Told y them theatrics didnt fit a white man. Th niggers, just like I told y. An after him. Aint surprisin though. He aint bowed t none of them. Nassur. T nairy a one of them nairy an inch nairy a time. An only mixed when he was good an ready—

Kabnis: That song, Halsey, do you hear it?

Halsey: Thats a man. Hear me, Kabnis? A man—

Kabnis: Jesus, do you hear it.

Halsey: Hear it? Hear what? Course I hear it. Listen t what I'm tellin y. A man, get me? They'll get him yet if he dont watch out.

Kabnis is jolted into his fear.

Kabnis: Get him? What do you mean? How? Not lynch him?

Halsey: Na. Take a shotgun an shoot his eyes clear out. Well, anyway, it wasnt fer you, just like I told y. You'll stay over at th house an work with me, eh, boy? Good t get away from his nobs, eh? Damn big stiff though, him. An youre not th first an I can tell y. (Laughs.)

He bustles and fusses about Kabnis as if he were a child. Kabnis submits, wearily. He has no will to resist him.

Layman (his voice is like a deep hollow echo): Thats right. Thats true, sho. Everybody's been expectin that th bust up was comin. Surprised um all y held on as long as y did. Teachin in th South aint th thing fer y. Nassur. You ought t be way back up North where sometimes I wish I was. But I've hung on down this away so long—

Halsey: An there'll never be no leavin so fer y.

4

A month has passed.

Halsey's workshop. It is an old building just off the main street of Sempter. The walls to within a few feet of the ground are of an age-worn cement mixture. On the outside they are considerably crumbled and peppered with what looks like musket-shot. Inside, the plaster has fallen away in great chunks, leaving the laths, grayed and cobwebbed, exposed. A sort of loft above the shop proper serves as a break-water for the rain and sunshine which otherwise would have free entry to the main floor. The shop is filled with old wheels and parts of wheels, broken shafts, and wooden litter. A double door, midway the street wall. To the left of this, a work-bench that holds a vise and a variety of wood-work tools. A window with as many panes broken as whole, throws light on the bench. Opposite, in the rear wall, a second window looks out upon the back yard. In the left wall, a rickety smoke-blackened chimney, and hearth with fire blazing. Smooth-worn chairs grouped about the hearth suggest the village meeting-place. Several large wooden blocks, chipped and cut and sawed on their upper surfaces are in the middle of the floor. They are the supports used in almost any sort of wagon-work. Their idleness means that Halsey has no worth-while job on foot. To the right of the central door is a junk heap, and directly behind this, stairs that lead down into the cellar. The cellar is known as "The Hole." Besides being the home of a very old man, it is used by Halsey on those occasions when he spices up the life of the small town.

Halsey, wonderfully himself in his work overalls, stands in the doorway and gazes up the street, expectantly. Then his eyes grow listless. He slouches against the smooth-rubbed frame. He lights a cigarette. Shifts his position. Braces an arm against the door. Kabnis passes the window and stoops to get in under Halsey's arm. He is awkward and ludicrous, like a schoolboy in his big brother's new overalls. He skirts the large blocks on the floor, and drops into a chair before the fire. Halsey saunters towards him.

Kabnis: Time f lunch.

Halsey: Ya.

He stands by the hearth, rocking backward and forward. He stretches his hands out to the fire. He washes them in the warm glow of the flames. They never get cold, but he warms them.

Kabnis: Saw Lewis up th street. Said he'd be down.

Halsey's eyes brighten. He looks at Kabnis. Turns away. Says nothing. Kabnis fidgets. Twists his thin blue cloth-covered limbs. Pulls closer to the fire till the heat stings his shins. Pushes back.

Pokes the burned logs. Puts on several fresh ones. Fidgets. The town bell strikes twelve.

Kabnis: Fix it up f tnight?

Halsey: Leave it t me.

Kabnis: Get Lewis in?

Halsey: Tryin t.

The air is heavy with the smell of pine and resin. Green logs spurt and sizzle. Sap trickles from an old pine-knot into the flames. Layman enters. He carries a lunch-pail. Kabnis, for the moment, thinks that he is a day laborer.

Layman: Evenin, gen'lemun.

Both: Whats say, Layman.

Layman squares a chair to the fire and droops into it. Several town fellows, silent unfathomable men for the most part, saunter in. Overalls. Thick tan shoes. Felt hats marvelously shaped and twisted. One asks Halsey for a cigarette. He gets it. The blacksmith, a tremendous black man, comes in from the forge. Not even a nod from him. He picks up an axle and goes out. Lewis enters. The town men look curiously at him. Suspicion and an open liking contest for possession of their faces. They are uncomfortable. One by one they drift into the street.

Layman: Heard y was leavin, Mr. Lewis.

Kabnis: Months up, eh? Hell of a month I've got.

Halsey: Sorry y goin, Lewis. Just getting acquainted like.

Lewis: Sorry myself, Halsey, in a way—

Layman: Gettin t like our town, Mr. Lewis?

Lewis: I'm afraid its on a different basis, Professor.

Halsey: An I've yet t hear about that basis. Been waitin long enough, God knows. Seems t me like youd take pity on a feller if nothin more.

Kabnis: Somethin that old black cockroach over yonder doesnt like, whatever it is.

Layman: Thats right. Thats right, sho.

Halsey: A feller dropped in here tother day an said he knew what you was about. Said you had queer opinions. Well, I could have told him you was a queer one, myself. But not th way he was driftin. Didnt mean anything by it, but just let drop he thought you was a little wrong up here—crazy, y'know. (Laughs.)

Kabnis: Y mean old Blodson? Hell, he's bats himself.

Lewis: I remember him. We had a talk. But what he found queer, I think, was not my opinions, but my lack of them. In half an hour he had settled everything: boll weevils, God, the World War. Weevils and wars are the pests that God sends against the sinful. People are too weak to correct themselves: the Redeemer is coming back. Get ready, ye sinners, for the advent of Our Lord. Interesting, eh, Kabnis? but not exactly what we want.

Halsey: Y could have come t me. I've sho been after y enough. Most every time I've seen y.

Kabnis (sarcastically):   Hows it y never came t us professors?

Lewis: I did—to one.

Kabnis: Y mean t say y got somethin from that celluloid-collar-eraser-cleaned old codger over in th mud hole?

Halsey: Rough on th old boy, aint he? (Laughs.)

Lewis: Something, yes. Layman here could have given me quite a deal, but the incentive to his keeping quiet is so much greater than anything I could have offered to open up, that I crossed him off my mind. And you—

Kabnis: What about me?

Halsey: Tell him, Lewis, for godsake tell him. I've told him. But its somethin else he wants so bad I've heard him downstairs mumblin with th old man.

Lewis: The old man?

Kabnis: What about me? Come on now, you know so much.

Halsey: Tell him, Lewis. Tell it t him.

Lewis: Life has already told him more than he is capable of knowing. It has given him in excess of what he can receive. I have been offered. Stuff in his stomach curdled, and he vomited me.

Kabnis' face twitches. His body writhes.

Kabnis: You know a lot, you do. How about Halsey?

Lewis: Yes. . . Halsey? Fits here. Belongs here. An artist in your way, arent you, Halsey?

Halsey: Reckon I am, Lewis. Give me th work and fair pay an I aint askin nothin better. Went over-seas an saw France; an I come back. Been up North; an I come back. Went t school;

but there aint no books whats got th feel t them of them there tools. Nassur. An I'm atellin y.

A shriveled, bony white man passes the window and enters the shop. He carries a broken hatchet-handle and the severed head. He speaks with a flat, drawn voice to Halsey, who comes forward to meet him.

Mr. Ramsay: Can y fix this fer me, Halsey?

Halsey (looking it over):   Reckon so, Mr. Ramsay. Here, Kabnis. A little practice fer y.

Halsey directs Kabnis, showing him how to place the handle in the vise, and cut it down. The knife hangs. Kabnis thinks that it must be dull. He jerks it hard. The tool goes deep and shaves too much off. Mr. Ramsay smiles brokenly at him.

Mr. Ramsay (to Halsey):   Still breakin in the new hand, eh, Halsey? Seems like a likely enough faller once he gets th hang of it.

He gives a tight laugh at his own good humor. Kabnis burns red. The back of his neck stings beneath his collar. He feels stifled. Through Ramsay, the whole white South weighs down upon him. The pressure is terrific. He sweats under the arms. Chill beads run down his body. His brows concentrate upon the handle as though his own life was staked upon the perfect shaving of it. He begins to out and out botch the job. Halsey smiles.

Halsey: He'll make a good un some of these days, Mr. Ramsay.

Mr. Ramsay: Y ought t know. Yer daddy was a good un before y. Runs in th family, seems like t me.

Halsey: Thats right, Mr. Ramsay.

Kabnis is hopeless. Halsey takes the handle from him. With a few deft strokes he shaves it. Fits it. Gives it to Ramsay.

Mr. Ramsay: How much on this?

Halsey: No charge, Mr. Ramsay.

Mr. Ramsay (going out):   All right, Halsey. Come down an take it out in trade. Shoe-strings or something.

Halsey: Yassur, Mr. Ramsay.

Halsey rejoins Lewis and Layman. Kabnis, hangdog-fashion, follows him.

Halsey: They like y if y work fer them.

Layman: Thats right, Mr. Halsey. Thats right, sho.

The group is about to resume its talk when Hanby enters. He is all energy, bustle, and business. He goes direct to Kabnis.

Hanby: An axle is out in the buggy which I would like to have shaped into a crow-bar. You will see that it is fixed for me.

Without waiting for an answer, and knowing that Kabnis will follow, he passes out. Kabnis, scowling, silent, trudges after him.

Hanby (from the outside):   Have that ready for me by three o'clock, young man. I shall call for it.

Kabnis (under his breath as he comes in):   Th hell you say, you old black swamp-gut.

He slings the axle on the floor.

Halsey: Wheeee!

Layman, lunch finished long ago, rises, heavily. He shakes hands with Lewis.

Layman: Might not see y again befo y leave, Mr. Lewis. I enjoys t hear y talk. Y might have been a preacher. Maybe a bishop some day. Sho do hope t see y back this away again sometime, Mr. Lewis.

Lewis: Thanks, Professor. Hope I'll see you.

Layman waves a long arm loosely to the others, and leaves. Kabnis goes to the door. His eyes, sullen, gaze up the street.

Kabnis: Carrie K.'s comin with th lunch. Bout time.

She passes the window. Her red girl's-cap, catching the sun, flashes vividly. With a stiff, awkward little movement she crosses the doorsill and gives Kabnis one of the two baskets which she is carrying. There is a slight stoop to her shoulders. The curves of her body blend with this to a soft rounded charm. Her gestures are stiffly variant. Black bangs curl over the forehead of her oval-olive face. Her expression is dazed, but on provocation it can melt into a wistful smile. Adolescent. She is easily the sister of Fred Halsey.

Carrie K.:   Mother says excuse her, brother Fred an Ralph, fer bein late.

Kabnis: Everythings all right an O.K., Carrie Kate. O.K. an all right.

The two men settle on their lunch. Carrie, with hardly a glance in the direction of the hearth, as is her habit, is about to take the second basket down to the old man, when Lewis rises. In doing so he draws her unwitting attention. Their meeting is a swift sun-burst. Lewis impulsively moves towards her. His mind flashes images of her life in the southern town. He sees the nascent woman, her flesh already stiffening to cartilage, drying to bone. Her spirit-bloom, even now touched sullen, bitter. Her rich beauty fading. . . He wants to— He stretches forth his hands to hers. He takes them. They feel like warm cheeks against his palms. The sun-burst from her eyes floods up and haloes him. Christ-eyes, his eyes look to her. Fearlessly she loves into them. And then something happens. Her face blanches. Awkwardly she draws away. The sin-bogies of respectable southern colored folks clamor at her: "Look out! Be a *good* girl. A *good* girl. Look out!" She gropes for her basket that has fallen to the floor. Finds it, and marches with a rigid gravity to her task of feeding the old man. Like the glowing white ash of burned paper, Lewis' eyelids, wavering, settle down. He stirs in the direction of rear window. From the back yard, mules tethered to odd trees and posts blink dumbly at him. They too seem burdened with an impotent pain. Kabnis and Halsey are still busy with their lunch. They havent noticed him. After a while he turns to them.

Lewis: Your sister, Halsey, whats to become of her? What are you going to do for her?

Halsey: Who? What? What am I goin t do? . .

Lewis: What I mean is, what does she do down there?

Halsey: Oh. Feeds th old man. Had lunch, Lewis?

Lewis: Thanks, yes. You have never felt her, have you, Halsey? Well, no, I guess not. I dont suppose you can. Nor can she. . . Old man? Halsey, some one lives down there? I've never heard of him. Tell me—

Kabnis takes time from his meal to answer with some emphasis:

Kabnis: Theres lots of things you aint heard of.

Lewis: Dare say. I'd like to see him.

Kabnis: You'll get all th chance you want tnight.

Halsey: Fixin a little somethin up fer tnight, Lewis. Th three of us an some girls. Come round bout ten-thirty.

Lewis: Glad to. But what under the sun does he do down there?

Halsey: Ask Kabnis. He blows off t him every chance he gets.

Kabnis gives a grunting laugh. His mouth twists. Carrie returns from the cellar. Avoiding Lewis, she speaks to her brother.

Carrie K.:   Brother Fred, father hasnt eaten now goin on th second week, but mumbles an talks funny, or tries t talk when I put his hands ont th food. He frightens me, an I dunno what t do. An oh, I came near fergettin, brother, but Mr. Marmon—he was eatin lunch when I saw him—told me t tell y that th lumber wagon busted down an he wanted y t fix it fer him. Said he reckoned he could get it t y after he ate.

Halsey chucks a half-eaten sandwich in the fire. Gets up. Arranges his blocks. Goes to the door and looks anxiously up the street. The wind whirls a small spiral in the gray dust road.

Halsey: Why didnt y tell me sooner, little sister?

Carrie K.:   I fergot t, an just remembered it now, brother.

Her soft rolled words are fresh pain to Lewis. He wants to take her North with him What for? He wonders what Kabnis could do for her. What she could do for him. Mother him. Carrie gathers the lunch things, silently, and in her pinched manner, curtsies, and departs. Kabnis lights his after-lunch cigarette. Lewis, who has sensed a change, becomes aware that he is not included in it. He starts to ask again about the old man. Decides not to. Rises to go.

Lewis: Think I'll run along, Halsey.

Halsey: Sure. Glad t see y any time.

Kabnis: Dont forget tnight.

Lewis: Dont worry. I wont. So long.

Kabnis: So long. We'll be expectin y.

Lewis passes Halsey at the door. Halsey's cheeks form a vacant smile. His eyes are wide awake, watching for the wagon to turn from Broad Street into his road.

Halsey: So long.

His words reach Lewis halfway to the corner.

5

Night, soft belly of a pregnant Negress, throbs evenly against the torso of the South. Night throbs a womb-song to the South. Cane- and cotton-fields, pine forests, cypress swamps, sawmills, and factories are fecund at her touch. Night's womb-song sets them singing. Night winds are the breathing of the unborn child whose calm throbbing in the belly of a Negress sets them somnolently singing. Hear their song.

> White-man's land.
> Niggers, sing.
> Burn, bear black children
> Till poor rivers bring
> Rest, and sweet glory
> In Camp Ground.

Sempter's streets are vacant and still. White paint on the wealthier houses has the chill blue glitter of distant stars. Negro cabins are a purple blur. Broad Street is deserted. Winds stir beneath the corrugated iron canopies and dangle odd bits of rope tied to horse- and mule-gnawed hitching-posts. One store window has a light in it. Chesterfield cigarette and Chero-Cola cardboard advertisements are stacked in it. From a side door two men come out. Pause, for a last word and then say good night. Soon they melt in shadows thicker than they. Way off down the street four figures sway beneath iron awnings which form a sort of corridor that imperfectly echoes and jumbles what they say. A fifth form joins them. They turn into the road that leads to Halsey's workshop. The old building is phosphorescent above deep shade. The figures pass through the double door. Night winds whisper in the eaves. Sing weirdly in the ceiling cracks. Stir curls of shavings on the floor. Halsey lights a candle. A good-sized lumber wagon, wheels off, rests upon the blocks. Kabnis makes a face at it. An unearthly hush is upon the place. No one seems to want to talk. To move, lest the scraping of their feet . .

Halsey: Come on down this way, folks.

He leads the way. Stella follows. And close after her, Cora,

Lewis, and Kabnis. They descend into the Hole. It seems huge, limitless in the candle light. The walls are of stone, wonderfully fitted. They have no openings save a small iron-barred window toward the top of each. They are dry and warm. The ground slopes away to the rear of the building and thus leaves the south wall exposed to the sun. The blacksmith's shop is plumb against the right wall. The floor is clay. Shavings have at odd times been matted into it. In the right-hand corner, under the stairs, two good-sized pine mattresses, resting on cardboard, are on either side of a wooden table. On this are several half-burned candles and an oil lamp. Behind the table, an irregular piece of mirror hangs on the wall. A loose something that looks to be a gaudy ball costume dangles from a near-by hook. To the front, a second table holds a lamp and several whiskey glasses. Six rickety chairs are near this table. Two old wagon wheels rest on the floor. To the left, sitting in a high-backed chair which stands upon a low platform, the old man. He is like a bust in black walnut. Gray-bearded. Gray-haired. Prophetic. Immobile. Lewis' eyes are sunk in him. The others, unconcerned, are about to pass on to the front table when Lewis grips Halsey and so turns him that the candle flame shines obliquely on the old man's features.

Lewis: And he rules over—

Kabnis: Th smoke an fire of th forge.

Lewis: Black Vulcan? I wouldnt say so. That forehead. Great woolly beard. Those eyes. A mute John the Baptist of a new religion—or a tongue-tied shadow of an old.

Kabnis: His tongue is tied all right, an I can vouch f that.

Lewis: Has he never talked to you?

Halsey: Kabnis wont give him a chance. He laughs. The girls laugh. Kabnis winces.

Lewis: What do you call him?

Halsey: Father.

Lewis: Good. Father what?

Kabnis: Father of hell.

Halsey: Father's th only name we have fer him. Come on. Lets sit down an get t th pleasure of the evenin.

Lewis: Father John it is from now on. . .

Slave boy whom some Christian mistress taught to read the

Bible. Black man who saw Jesus in the ricefields, and began preaching to his people. Moses- and Christ-words used for songs. Dead blind father of a muted folk who feel their way upward to a life that crushes or absorbs them. (Speak, Father!) Suppose your eyes could see, old man. (The years hold hands. O Sing!) Suppose your lips. . .

Halsey, does he never talk?

Halsey: Na. But sometimes. Only seldom. Mumbles. Sis says he talks—

Kabnis: I've heard him talk.

Halsey: First I've ever heard of it. You dont give him a chance. Sis says she's made out several words, mostly one—an like as not cause it was "sin."

Kabnis: All those old fogies stutter about sin.

Cora laughs in a loose sort of way. She is a tall, thin, mulatto woman. Her eyes are deep-set behind a pointed nose. Her hair is coarse and bushy. Seeing that Stella also is restless, she takes her arm and the two women move towards the table. They slip into chairs. Halsey follows and lights the lamp. He lays out a pack of cards. Stella sorts them as if telling fortunes. She is a beautifully proportioned, large-eyed, brown-skin girl. Except for the twisted line of her mouth when she smiles or laughs, there is about her no suggestion of the life she's been through. Kabnis, with great mock-solemnity, goes to the corner, takes down the robe, and dons it. He is a curious spectacle, acting a part, yet very real. He joins the others at the table. They are used to him. Lewis is surprised. He laughs. Kabnis shrinks and then glares at him with a furtive hatred. Halsey, bringing out a bottle of corn licker, pours drinks.

Halsey: Come on, Lewis. Come on, you fellers. Heres lookin at y.

Then, as if suddenly recalling something, he jerks away from the table and starts towards the steps.

Kabnis: Where y goin, Halsey?

Halsey: Where? Where y think? That oak beam in th wagon—

Kabnis: Come ere. Come ere. Sit down. What in hell's wrong with you fellers? You with your wagon. Lewis with his Father John. This aint th time fer foolin with wagons. Daytime's bad enough f that. Ere, sit down. Ere, Lewis, you too sit down. Have a drink. Thats right. Drink corn licker, love th girls, an listen t th old man mumblin sin.

There seems to be no good-time spirit to the party. Something in the air is too tense and deep for that. Lewis, seated now so that his eyes rest upon the old man, merges with his source and lets the pain and beauty of the South meet there. White faces, pain-pollen, settle downward through a cane-sweet mist and touch the ovaries of yellow flowers. Cotton-bolls bloom, droop. Black roots twist in a parched red soil beneath a blazing sky. Magnolias, fragrant, a trifle futile, lovely, far off. . . His eyelids close. A force begins to heave and rise. . . Stella is serious, reminiscent.

Stella: Usall is brought up t hate sin worse than death—

Kabnis: An then before you have y eyes half open, youre made t love it if y want t live.

Stella: Us never—

Kabnis: Oh, I know your story: that old prim bastard over yonder, an then old Calvert's office—

Stella: It wasnt them—

Kabnis: I know. They put y out of church, an then I guess th preacher came around an asked f some. But thats your body. Now me—

Halsey (passing the bottle):   All right, kid, we believe y. Here, take another. Wheres Clover, Stel?

Stella: You know how Jim is when he's just out th swamp. Done up in shine an wouldnt let her come. Said he'd bust her head open if she went out.

Kabnis: Dont see why he doesnt stay over with Laura, where he belongs.

Stella: Ask him, an I reckon he'll tell y. More than you want.

Halsey: Th nigger hates th sight of a black woman worse than death. Sorry t mix y up this way, Lewis. But y see how tis.

Lewis' skin is tight and glowing over the fine bones of his face. His lips tremble. His nostrils quiver. The others notice this and smile knowingly at each other. Drinks and smokes are passed around. They pay no neverminds to him. A real party is being worked up. Then Lewis opens his eyes and looks at them. Their smiles disperse in hot-cold tremors. Kabnis chokes his laugh. It sputters, gurgles. His eyes flicker and turn away. He tries to pass the thing off by taking a long drink which he makes considerable fuss over. He is drawn back to Lewis. Seeing Lewis' gaze still upon him, he scowls.

Kabnis: Whatsha lookin at me for? Y want t know who I am? Well, I'm Ralph Kabnis—lot of good its goin t do y. Well? Whatsha keep lookin for? I'm Ralph Kabnis. Aint that enough f y? Want th whole family history? Its none of your godam business, anyway. Keep off me. Do y hear? Keep off me. Look at Cora. Aint she pretty enough t look at? Look at Halsey, or Stella. Clover ought t be here an you could look at her. An love her. Thats what you need. I know—

Lewis: Ralph Kabnis gets satisfied that way?

Kabnis: Satisfied? Say, quit your kiddin. Here, look at that old man there. See him? He's satisfied. Do I look like him? When I'm dead I dont expect t be satisfied. Is that enough f y, with your godam nosin, or do you want more? Well, y wont get it, understand?

Lewis: The old man as symbol, flesh, and spirit of the past, what do you think he would say if he could see you? You look at him, Kabnis.

Kabnis: Just like any done-up preacher is what he looks t me. Jam some false teeth in his mouth and crank him, an youd have God Almighty spit in torrents all around th floor. Oh, hell, an he reminds me of that black cockroach over yonder. An besides, he aint my past. My ancestors were Southern blue-bloods—

Lewis: And black.

Kabnis: Aint much difference between blue an black.

Lewis: Enough to draw a denial from you. Cant hold them, can you? Master; slave. Soil; and the overarching heavens. Dusk; dawn. They fight and bastardize you. The sun tint of your cheeks, flame of the great season's multicolored leaves, tarnished, burned. Split, shredded: easily burned. No use . . .

His gaze shifts to Stella. Stella's face draws back, her breasts come towards him.

Stella: I aint got nothin f y, mister. Taint no use t look at me.

Halsey: Youre a queer feller, Lewis, I swear y are. Told y
so, didnt I, girls? Just take him easy though, an he'll be ridin
just th same as any Georgia mule, eh, Lewis? (Laughs.)

Stella: I'm goin t tell y somethin, mister. It aint t you, t th
Mister Lewis what noses about. Its t somethin different, I
dunno what. That old man there—maybe its him—is like m father used t look. He used t sing. An when he could sing no
mo, they'd allus come f him an carry him t church an there
he'd sit, befo th pulpit, aswayin an aleadin every song. A white
man took m mother an it broke th old man's heart. He died;
an then I didnt care what become of me, an I dont now. I dont
care now. Dont get it in y head I'm some sentimental Susie
askin for yo sop. Nassur. But theres somethin t yo th others
aint got. Boars an kids an fools—thats all I've known. Boars
when their fever's up. When their fever's up they come t me.
Halsey asks me over when he's off th job. Kabnis—it ud be a
sin t play with him. He takes it out in talk.

Halsey knows that he has trifled with her. At odd things he
has been inwardly penitent before her tasking him. But now he
wants to hurt her. He turns to Lewis.

Halsey: Lewis, I got a little licker in me, an thats true.
True's what I said. True. But th stuff just seems t wake me up
an make my mind a man of me. Listen. You know a lot, queer
as hell as y are, an I want t ask y some questions. Theyre too
high fer them, Stella an Cora an Kabnis, so we'll just excuse
em. A chat between ourselves. (Turns to the others.) You-all
cant listen in on this. Twont interest y. So just leave th table t
this gen'lemun an myself. Go long now.

Kabnis gets up, pompous in his robe, grotesquely so, and
makes as if to go through a grand march with Stella. She shoves
him off, roughly, and in a mood swings her body to the steps.
Kabnis grabs Cora and parades around, passing the old man,
to whom he bows in mock-curtsy. He sweeps by the table,
snatches the licker bottle, and then he and Cora sprawl on the
mattresses. She meets his weak approaches after the manner
she thinks Stella would use.

Halsey contemptuously watches them until he is sure that
they are settled.

Halsey: This aint th sort o thing f me, Lewis, when I got
work upstairs. Nassur. You an me has got things t do. Wastin

time on common low-down women—say, Lewis, look at her now—Stella—aint she a picture? Common wench—na she aint, Lewis. You know she aint. I'm only tryin t fool y. I used t love that girl. Yassur. An sometimes when th moon is thick an I hear dogs up th valley barkin an some old woman fetches out her song, an th winds seem like th Lord made them fer t fetch an carry th smell o pine an cane, an there aint no big job on foot, I sometimes get t thinkin that I still do. But I want t talk t y, Lewis, queer as y are. Y know, Lewis, I went t school once. Ya. In Augusta. But it wasnt a regular school. Na. It was a pussy Sunday-school masqueradin under a regular name. Some goody-goody teachers from th North had come down t teach th niggers. If you was nearly white, they liked y. If you was black, they didnt. But it wasnt that—I was all right, y see. I couldnt stand em messin an pawin over m business like I was a child. So I cussed em out an left. Kabnis there ought t have cussed out th old duck over yonder an left. He'd a been a better man tday. But as I was sayin, I couldnt stand their ways. So I left an came here an worked with my father. An been here ever since. He died. I set in f myself. An its always been; give me a good job an sure pay an I aint far from being satisfied, so far as satisfaction goes. Prejudice is everywheres about this country. An a nigger aint in much standin anywheres. But when it comes t pottin round an doin nothing, with nothin bigger'n an ax-handle t hold a feller down, like it was a while back befo I got this job—that beam ought t be—but tmorrow mornin early's time enough f that. As I was sayin, I gets t thinkin. Play dumb naturally t white folks. I gets t thinkin. I used to subscribe t th *Literary Digest* an that helped along a bit. But there werent nothing I could sink m teeth int. Theres lots I want t ask y, Lewis. Been askin y t come around. Couldnt get y. Cant get in much tnight. (He glances at the others. His mind fastens on Kabnis.) Say, tell me this, whats on your mind t say on that feller there? Kabnis' name. One queer bird ought t know another, seems like t me.

Licker has released conflicts in Kabnis and set them flowing. He pricks his ears, intuitively feels that the talk is about him, leaves Cora, and approaches the table. His eyes are watery, heavy with passion. He stoops. He is a ridiculous pathetic figure in his showy robe.

Kabnis: Talkin bout me. I know. I'm th topic of conversation everywhere theres talk about this town. Girls an fellers. White folks as well. An if its me youre talkin bout, guess I got a right t listen in. Whats sayin? Whats sayin bout his royal guts, the Duke? Whats sayin, eh?

Halsey (to Lewis):   We'll take it up another time.

Kabnis: No nother time bout it. Now. I'm here now an talkin's just begun. I was born an bred in a family of orators, thats what I was.

Halsey: Preachers.

Kabnis: Na. Preachers hell. I didnt say wind-busters. Y misapprehended me. Y understand what that means, dont y? All right then, y misapprehended me. I didnt say preachers. I said orators. ORATORS. Born one an I'll die one. You understand me, Lewis. (He turns to Halsey and begins shaking his finger in his face.) An as f you, youre all right f choppin things from blocks of wood. I was good at that th day I ducked th cradle. An since then, I've been shapin words after a design that branded here. Know whats here? M soul. Ever heard o that? Th hell y have. Been shapin words t fit m soul. Never told y that before, did I? Thought I couldnt talk. I'll tell y. I've been shapin words; ah, but sometimes theyre beautiful an golden an have a taste that makes them fine t roll over with y tongue. Your tongue aint fit f nothin but t roll an lick hog-meat.

Stella and Cora come up to the table.

Halsey: Give him a shove there, will y, Stel?

Stella jams Kabnis in a chair. Kabnis springs up.

Kabnis: Cant keep a good man down. Those words I was tellin y about, they wont fit int th mold thats branded on m soul. Rhyme, y see? Poet, too. Bad rhyme. Bad poet. Somethin else youve learned tnight. Lewis dont know it all, an I'm atellin y. Ugh. Th form thats burned int my soul is some twisted awful thing that crept in from a dream, a godam nightmare, an wont stay still unless I feed it. An it lives on words. Not beautiful words. God Almighty no. Misshapen, split-gut, tortured, twisted words. Layman was feedin it back there that day you thought I ran out fearin things. White folks feed it cause their looks are words. Niggers, black niggers feed it cause theyre evil an their looks are words. Yallar niggers feed it. This whole damn bloated purple country feeds it cause its goin down t hell in a holy avalanche of words. I want t feed th soul—I know what that is; th preachers dont—but I've got t feed it. I wish t God some lynchin white man ud stick his knife through it an pin it to a tree. An pin it to a tree. You hear me? Thats a wish f y, you little snot-nosed pups who've been makin fun of me, an fakin that I'm weak. Me, Ralph Kabnis weak. Ha.

Halsey: Thats right, old man. There, there. Here, so much exertion merits a fittin reward. Help him t be seated, Cora.

Halsey gives him a swig of shine. Cora glides up, seats him, and then plumps herself down on his lap, squeezing his head into her breasts. Kabnis mutters. Tries to break loose. Curses. Cora almost stifles him. He goes limp and gives up. Cora toys with him. Ruffles his hair. Braids it. Parts it in the middle. Stella smiles contemptuously. And then a sudden anger sweeps her. She would like to lash Cora from the place. She'd like to take Kabnis to some distant pine grove and nurse and mother him. Her eyes flash. A quick tensioning throws her breasts and neck into a poised strain. She starts towards them. Halsey grabs her arms and pulls her to him. She struggles. Halsey pins her arms and kisses her. She settles, spurting like a pine-knot afire.

Lewis finds himself completely cut out. The glowing within him subsides. It is followed by a dead chill. Kabnis, Carrie, Stella, Halsey, Cora, the old man, the cellar, and the work-shop, the southern town descend upon him. Their pain is too intense. He cannot stand it. He bolts from the table. Leaps up the stairs. Plunges through the work-shop and out into the night.

6

The cellar swims in a pale phosphorescence. The table, the chairs, the figure of the old man are amœba-like shadows which move about and float in it. In the corner under the steps, close to the floor, a solid blackness. A sound comes from it. A forcible yawn. Part of the blackness detaches itself so that it may be seen against the grayness of the wall. It moves forward and then seems to be clothing itself in odd dangling bits of shadow. The voice of Halsey, vibrant and deepened, calls.

Halsey: Kabnis. Cora. Stella.

He gets no response. He wants to get them up, to get on the job. He is intolerant of their sleepiness.

Halsey: Kabnis! Stella! Cora!

Gutturals, jerky and impeded, tell that he is shaking them.

Halsey: Come now, up with you.

Kabnis (sleepily and still more or less intoxicated):   Whats th big idea? What in hell—

Halsey: Work. But never you mind about that. Up with you.

Cora: Oooooo! Look here, mister, I aint used t bein thrown int th street befo day.

Stella: Any bunk whats worked is worth in wages moren this. But come on. Taint no use t arger.

Kabnis: I'll arger. Its preposterous—

The girls interrupt him with none too pleasant laughs.

Kabnis: Thats what I said. Know what it means, dont y? All right, then. I said its preposterous t root an artist out o bed at this ungodly hour, when there aint no use t it. You can start your damned old work. Nobody's stoppin y. But what we got t get up for? Fraid somebody'll see th girls leavin? Some sport, you are. I hand it t y.

Halsey: Up you get, all th same.

Kabnis: Oh, th hell you say.

Halsey: Well, son, seeing that I'm th kind-hearted father, I'll give y chance t open your eyes. But up y get when I come down.

He mounts the steps to the work-shop and starts a fire in the hearth. In the yard he finds some chunks of coal which he brings in and throws on the fire. He puts a kettle on to boil. The wagon draws him. He lifts an oak-beam, fingers it, and becomes abstracted. Then comes to himself and places the beam upon the work-bench. He looks over some newly cut wooden spokes. He goes to the fire and pokes it. The coals are red-hot. With a pair of long prongs he picks them up and places them in a thick iron bucket. This he carries downstairs. Outside, darkness has given way to the impalpable grayness of dawn. This early morning light, seeping through the four barred cellar windows, is the color of the stony walls. It seems to be an emanation from them. Halsey's coals throw out a rich warm glow. He sets them on the floor, a safe distance from the beds.

Halsey: No foolin now. Come. Up with you.

Other than a soft rustling, there is no sound as the girls slip into their clothes. Kabnis still lies in bed.

Stella (to Halsey):   Reckon y could spare us a light?

Halsey strikes a match, lights a cigarette, and then bends over and touches flame to the two candles on the table between the beds. Kabnis asks for a cigarette. Halsey hands him his and takes a fresh one for himself. The girls, before the mirror, are doing up their hair. It is bushy hair that has gone through some straightening process. Character, however, has not all been ironed out. As they kneel there, heavy-eyed and dusky, and throwing grotesque moving shadows on the wall, they are two princesses in Africa going through the early-morning ablutions of their pagan prayers. Finished, they come forward to stretch their hands and warm them over the glowing coals. Red dusk of a Georgia sunset, their heavy, coal-lit faces. . . Kabnis suddenly recalls something.

Kabnis: Th old man talked last night.

Stella: An so did you.

Halsey: In your dreams.

Kabnis: I tell y, he did. I know what I'm talkin about. I'll tell y what he said. Wait now, lemme see.

Halsey: Look out, brother, th old man'll be getting int you by way o dreams. Come, Stel, ready? Cora? Coffee an eggs f both of you.

Halsey goes upstairs.

Stella: Gettin generous, aint he?

She blows the candles out. Says nothing to Kabnis. Then she and Cora follow after Halsey. Kabnis, left to himself, tries to rise. He has slept in his robe. His robe trips him. Finally, he manages to stand up. He starts across the floor. Half-way to the old man, he falls and lies quite still. Perhaps an hour passes. Light of a new sun is about to filter through the windows. Kabnis slowly rises to support upon his elbows. He looks hard, and internally gathers himself together. The side face of Father John is in the direct line of his eyes. He scowls at him. No one is around. Words gush from Kabnis.

Kabnis: You sit there like a black hound spiked to an ivory pedestal. An all night long I heard you murmurin that devilish word. They thought I didnt hear y, but I did. Mumblin, feedin that ornery thing thats livin on my insides. Father John. Father of Satan, more likely. What does it mean t you? Youre dead already. Death. What does it mean t you? To you who died way back there in th 'sixties. What are y throwin it in my throat for? Whats it goin t get y? A good smashin in th mouth, thats what. My fist'll sink int y black mush face clear t y guts—if y got any. Dont believe y have. Never seen signs of none. Death. Death. Sin an Death. All night long y mumbled death. (He forgets the old man as his mind begins to play with the word and its associations.) Death . . . these clammy floors . . . just like th place they used t stow away th worn-out, no-count niggers in th days of slavery . . . that was long ago; not so long ago . . . no windows (he rises higher on his elbows to verify this assertion. He looks around, and, seeing no one but the old man, calls.) Halsey! Halsey! Gone an left me. Just like a nigger. I thought he was a nigger all th time. Now I know it. Ditch y when it comes right down t it. Damn anyway. Godam him. (He looks and re-sees the old man.) Eh, you? T hell with you too. What do I care whether you can see or hear? You know what hell is cause youve been there. Its a feelin an its ragin in my soul in a way that'll pop out of me an run you through, an scorch y, an burn an rip your soul. Your soul. Ha. Nigger soul. A gin soul that gets drunk on a preacher's words. An screams. An shouts. God Almighty, how I hate that shoutin. Where's th beauty in that? Gives a buzzard a windpipe an I'll bet a dollar t a dime th buzzard ud beat y to it. Aint surprisin th white folks hate y so. When you had eyes, did you ever see th beauty of th world? Tell me that. Th hell y did. Now dont tell me. I know y didnt. You couldnt have. Oh, I'm drunk an just as good as dead, but no eyes that have seen beauty ever lose their sight. You aint got no sight. If you had, drunk as I am, I hope Christ will kill me if I couldnt see it. Your eyes are dull and watery, like fish eyes. Fish eyes are dead eyes. Youre an old man, a dead fish man, an black at that. Theyve put y here t die, damn fool y are not t know it. Do y know how many feet youre under ground? I'll tell y. Twenty. An do y think you'll ever see th light of day again, even if you wasnt blind? Do y think youre out of slavery? Huh? Youre where they used t throw th worked-out, no-count slaves. On a damp clammy floor of a dark scum-hole. An they called that an infimary. Th sons-a . . . . Why I can already see you toppled off that stool an stretched out on th floor beside me—not beside me, damn you, by yourself, with th flies buzzin an lickin God knows what they'd find on a dirty, black, foul-breathed mouth like yours . . .

Some one is coming down the stairs. Carrie, bringing food for the old man. She is lovely in her fresh energy of the morning, in the calm untested confidence and nascent maternity which rise from the purpose of her present mission. She walks to within a few paces of Kabnis.

Carrie K.:   Brother says come up now, brother Ralph.

Kabnis: Brother doesnt know what he's talkin bout.

Carrie K.:   Yes he does, Ralph. He needs you on th wagon.

Kabnis: He wants me on th wagon, eh? Does he think some wooden thing can lift me up? Ask him that.

Carrie K.:   He told me t help y.

Kabnis: An how would you help me, child, dear sweet little sister?

She moves forward as if to aid him.

Carrie K.:   I'm not a child, as I've more than once told you, brother Ralph, an as I'll show you now.

Kabnis: Wait, Carrie. No, thats right. Youre not a child. But twont do t lift me bodily. You dont understand. But its th soul of me that needs th risin.

Carrie K: Youre a bad brother an just wont listen t me when I'm tellin y t go t church.

Kabnis doesnt hear her. He breaks down and talks to himself.

Kabnis: Great God Almighty, a soul like mine cant pin itself onto a wagon wheel an satisfy itself in spinnin round. Iron prongs an hickory sticks, an God knows what all . . all right for Halsey . . . use him. Me? I get my life down in this scum-hole. Th old man an me—

Carrie K.:   Has he been talkin?

Kabnis: Huh? Who? Him? No. Dont need to. I talk. An when I really talk, it pays th best of them t listen. Th old man is a good listener. He's deaf; but he's a good listener. An I can talk t him. Tell him anything.

Carrie K.:   He's deaf an blind, but I reckon he hears, an sees too, from th things I've heard.

Kabnis: No. Cant. Cant I tell you. How's he do it?

Carrie K.:   Dunno, except I've heard that th souls of old folks have a way of seein things.

Kabnis: An I've heard them call that superstition.

The old man begins to shake his head slowly. Carrie and Kabnis watch him, anxiously. He mumbles. With a grave motion his head nods up and down. And then, on one of the down-swings—

Father John (remarkably clear and with great conviction): Sin.

He repeats this word several times, always on the downward nodding. Surprised, indignant, Kabnis forgets that Carrie is with him.

Kabnis: Sin! Shut up. What do you know about sin, you old black bastard. Shut up, an stop that swayin an noddin your head.

Father John: Sin.

Kabnis tries to get up.

Kabnis: Didnt I tell y t shut up?

Carrie steps forward to help him. Kabnis is violently shocked at her touch. He springs back.

Kabnis: Carrie! What . . how . . Baby, you shouldnt be down here. Ralph says things. Doesnt mean to. But Carrie, he doesnt know what he's talkin about. Couldnt know. It was only a preacher's sin they knew in those old days, an that wasnt sin at all. Mind me, th only sin is whats done against th soul. Th whole world is a conspiracy t sin, especially in America, an against me. I'm th victim of their sin. I'm what sin is. Does he look like me? Have you ever heard him say th things youve heard me say? He couldn't if he had th Holy Ghost t help him. Dont look shocked, little sweetheart, you hurt me.

Father John: Sin.

Kabnis: Aw, shut up, old man.

Carrie K.:   Leave him be. He wants t say somethin. (She turns to the old man.) What is it, Father?

Kabnis: Whatsha talkin t that old deaf man for? Come away from him.

Carrie K.:   What is it, Father?

The old man's lips begin to work. Words are formed incoherently. Finally, he manages to articulate—

Father John: Th sin whats fixed . . . (Hesitates.)

Carrie K. (restraining a comment from Kabnis):   Go on, Father.

Father John: . . . upon th white folks—

Kabnis: Suppose youre talkin about that bastard race thats roamin round th country. It looks like sin, if thats what y mean. Give us somethin new an up t date.

Father John: —f tellin Jesus—lies. O th sin th white folks 'mitted when they made th Bible lie.

Boom. Boom. BOOM! Thuds on the floor above. The old man sinks back into his stony silence. Carrie is wet-eyed. Kabnis, contemptuous.

Kabnis: So thats your sin. All these years t tell us that th white folks made th Bible lie. Well, I'll be damned. Lewis ought t have been here. You old black fakir—

Carrie K.:   Brother Ralph, is that your best Amen?

She turns him to her and takes his hot cheeks in her firm cool hands. Her palms draw the fever out. With its passing, Kabnis crumples. He sinks to his knees before her, ashamed, exhausted. His eyes squeeze tight. Carrie presses his face tenderly against her. The suffocation of her fresh starched dress feels good to him. Carrie is about to lift her hands in prayer, when Halsey, at the head of the stairs, calls down.

Halsey: Well, well. Whats up? Aint you ever comin? Come on. Whats up down there? Take you all mornin t sleep off a pint? Youre weakenin, man, youre weakenin. Th axle an th beam's all ready waitin f y. Come on.

Kabnis rises and is going doggedly towards the steps. Carrie notices his robe. She catches up to him, points to it, and helps him take it off. He hangs it, with an exaggerated ceremony, on its nail in the corner. He looks down on the tousled beds. His lips curl bitterly. Turning, he stumbles over the bucket of dead coals. He savagely jerks it from the floor. And then, seeing Carrie's eyes upon him, he swings the pail carelessly and with eyes downcast and swollen, trudges upstairs to the work-shop. Carrie's gaze follows him till he is gone. Then she goes to the old man and slips to her knees before him. Her lips murmur, "Jesus, come."

Light streaks through the iron-barred cellar window. Within its soft circle, the figures of Carrie and Father John.

Outside, the sun arises from its cradle in the tree-tops of the forest. Shadows of pines are dreams the sun shakes from its eyes. The sun arises. Gold-glowing child, it steps into the sky and sends a birth-song slanting down gray dust streets and sleepy windows of the southern town.

HOME TO HARLEM

Claude McKay

To My Friend
Louise Bryant

CONTENTS

FIRST PART

I	GOING BACK HOME	139
II	ARRIVAL	143
III	ZEDDY	146
IV	CONGO ROSE	151
V	ON THE JOB AGAIN	158
VI	MYRTLE AVENUE	165
VII	ZEDDY'S RISE AND FALL	174
VIII	THE RAID OF THE BALTIMORE	187
IX	JAKE MAKES A MOVE	192

SECOND PART

X	THE RAILROAD	196
XI	SNOWSTORM IN PITTSBURGH	204
XII	THE TREEING OF THE CHEF	213
XIII	ONE NIGHT IN PHILLY	226
XIV	INTERLUDE	234
XV	RELAPSE	241
XVI	A PRACTICAL PRANK	246
XVII	HE ALSO LOVED	253
XVIII	A FAREWELL FEED	261

THIRD PART

XIX	SPRING IN HARLEM	267
XX	FELICE	277
XXI	THE GIFT THAT BILLY GAVE	284

I
Going Back Home

A LL that Jake knew about the freighter on which he stoked was that it stank between sea and sky. He was working with a dirty Arab crew. The captain signed him on at Cardiff because one of the Arabs had quit the ship. Jake was used to all sorts of rough jobs, but he had never before worked in such a filthy dinghy.

The white sailors who washed the ship would not wash the stokers' water-closet, because they despised the Arabs. And the Arabs themselves made no effort to keep the place clean, although it adjoined their sleeping berth.

The cooks hated the Arabs because they did not eat pork. Whenever there was pork for dinner, something else had to be prepared for the Arabs. The cooks put the stokers' meat, cut in unappetizing chunks, in a broad pan, and the two kinds of vegetables in two other pans. The stoker who carried the food back to the bunks always put one pan inside of the other, and sometimes the bottoms were dirty and bits of potato peelings or egg shells were mixed in with the meat and the vegetables.

The Arabs took up a chunk of meat with their coal-powdered fingers, bit or tore off a piece, and tossed the chunk back into the pan. It was strange to Jake that these Arabs washed themselves after eating and not before. They ate with their clothes stiff-starched to their bodies with coal and sweat. And when they were finished, they stripped and washed and went to sleep in the stinking-dirty bunks. Jake was used to the lowest and hardest sort of life, but even his leather-lined stomach could not endure the Arabs' way of eating. Jake also began to despise the Arabs. He complained to the cooks about the food. He gave the chef a ten-shilling note, and the chef gave him his eats separately.

One of the sailors flattered Jake. "You're the same like us chaps. You ain't like them dirty jabbering coolies."

But Jake smiled and shook his head in a non-committal way.

He knew that if he was just like the white sailors, he might
have signed on as a deckhand and not as a stoker. He didn't
care about the dirty old boat, anyhow. It was taking him back
home—that was all he cared about. He made his shift all right,
stoking four hours and resting eight. He didn't sleep well. The
stokers' bunks were lousy, and fetid with the mingled smell of
stale food and water-closet. Jake had attempted to keep the
place clean, but to do that was impossible. Apparently the
Arabs thought that a sleeping quarters could also serve as a
garbage can.

"Nip me all you wanta, Mister Louse," said Jake. "Roll on,
Mister Ship, and stinks all the way as you rolls. Jest take me
'long to Harlem is all I pray. I'm crazy to see again the brown-
skin chippies 'long Lenox Avenue. Oh boy!"

Jake was tall, brawny, and black. When America declared
war upon Germany in 1917 he was a longshoreman. He was
working on a Brooklyn pier, with a score of men under him.
He was a little boss and a very good friend of his big boss, who
was Irish. Jake thought he would like to have a crack at the
Germans. . . . And he enlisted.

In the winter he sailed for Brest with a happy chocolate
company. Jake had his own daydreams of going over the top.
But his company was held at Brest. Jake toted lumber—boards,
planks, posts, rafters—for the hundreds of huts that were built
around the walls of Brest and along the coast between Brest
and Saint-Pierre, to house the United States soldiers.

Jake was disappointed. He had enlisted to fight. For what
else had he been sticking a bayonet into the guts of a stuffed
man and aiming bullets straight into a bull's-eye? Toting planks
and getting into rows with his white comrades at the Bal
Musette were not adventure.

Jake obtained leave. He put on civilian clothes and lit out
for Havre. He liquored himself up and hung round a low-down
café in Havre for a week.

One day an English sailor from a Channel sloop made up to
Jake. "Darky," he said, "you 'arvin' a good time 'round 'ere."

Jake thought how strange it was to hear the Englishman say
"darky" without being offended. Back home he would have
been spoiling for a fight. There he would rather hear "nigger"
than "darky," for he knew that when a Yankee said "nigger" he

meant hatred for Negroes, whereas when he said "darky" he meant friendly contempt. He preferred white folks' hatred to their friendly contempt. To feel their hatred made him strong and aggressive, while their friendly contempt made him ridiculously angry, even against his own will.

"Sure Ise having a good time, all right," said Jake. He was making a cigarette and growling cusses at French tobacco. "But Ise got to get a move on 'fore very long."

"Where to?" his new companion asked.

"Any place, Buddy. I'm always ready for something new," announced Jake.

"Been in Havre a long time?"

"Week or two," said Jake. "I tooks care of some mules over heah. Twenty, God damn them, days across the pond. And then the boat plows round and run off and leaves me behind. Kain you beat that, Buddy?"

"It wasn't the best o' luck," replied the other. "Ever been to London?"

"Nope, Buddy," said Jake. "France is the only country I've struck yet this side the water."

The Englishman told Jake that there was a sailor wanted on his tug.

"We never 'ave a full crew—since the war," he said.

Jake crossed over to London. He found plenty of work there as a docker. He liked the West India Docks. He liked Limehouse. In the pubs men gave him their friendly paws and called him "darky." He liked how they called him "darky." He made friends. He found a woman. He was happy in the East End.

The Armistice found him there. On New-Year's Eve, 1919, Jake went to a monster dance with his woman, and his docker friends and their women, in the Mile End Road.

The Armistice had brought many more black men to the East End of London. Hundreds of them. Some of them found work. Some did not. Many were getting a little pension from the government. The price of sex went up in the East End, and the dignity of it also. And that summer Jake saw a big battle staged between the colored and white men of London's East End. Fisticuffs, razor and knife and gun play. For three days his woman would not let him out-of-doors. And when it was all over he was seized with the awful fever of lonesomeness. He felt all alone in the world. He wanted to run away from the kind-heartedness of his lady of the East End.

"Why did I ever enlist and come over here?" he asked himself. "Why did I want to mix mahself up in a white folks' war? It ain't ever was any of black folks' affair. Niggers am evah always such fools, anyhow. Always thinking they've got something to do with white folks' business."

Jake's woman could do nothing to please him now. She tried hard to get down into his thoughts and share them with him. But for Jake this woman was now only a creature of another race—of another world. He brooded day and night.

It was two years since he had left Harlem. Fifth Avenue, Lenox Avenue, and One Hundred and Thirty-fifth Street, with their chocolate-brown and walnut-brown girls, were calling him.

"Oh, them legs!" Jake thought. "Them tantalizing brown legs! . . . Barron's Cabaret! . . . Leroy's Cabaret! . . . Oh, boy!"

Brown girls rouged and painted like dark pansies. Brown flesh draped in soft colorful clothes. Brown lips full and pouted for sweet kissing. Brown breasts throbbing with love.

"Harlem for mine!" cried Jake. "I was crazy thinkin' I was happy over heah. I wasn't mahself. I was like a man charged up with dope every day. That's what it was. Oh, boy! Harlem for mine!

"Take me home to Harlem, Mister Ship! Take me home to the brown gals waiting for the brown boys that done show their mettle over there. Take me home, Mister Ship. Put your beak right into that water and jest move along." . . .

II
Arrival

JAKE was paid off. He changed a pound note he had brought with him. He had fifty-nine dollars. From South Ferry he took an express subway train for Harlem.

Jake drank three Martini cocktails with cherries in them. The price, he noticed, had gone up from ten to twenty-five cents. He went to Bank's and had a Maryland fried-chicken feed—a big one with candied sweet potatoes.

He left his suitcase behind the counter of a saloon on Lenox Avenue. He went for a promenade on Seventh Avenue between One Hundred and Thirty-fifth and One Hundred and Fortieth Streets. He thrilled to Harlem. His blood was hot. His eyes were alert as he sniffed the street like a hound. Seventh Avenue was nice, a little too nice that night.

Jake turned off on Lenox Avenue. He stopped before an ice-cream parlor to admire girls sipping ice-cream soda through straws. He went into a cabaret. . . .

A little brown girl aimed the arrow of her eye at him as he entered. Jake was wearing a steel-gray English suit. It fitted him loosely and well, perfectly suited his presence. She knew at once that Jake must have just landed. She rested her chin on the back of her hands and smiled at him. There was something in his attitude, in his hungry wolf's eyes, that went warmly to her. She was brown, but she had tinted her leaf-like face to a ravishing chestnut. She had on an orange scarf over a green frock, which was way above her knees, giving an adequate view of legs lovely in fine champagne-colored stockings. . . .

Her shaft hit home. . . . Jake crossed over to her table. He ordered Scotch and soda.

"Scotch is better with soda or even water," he said. "English folks don't take whisky straight, as we do."

But she preferred ginger ale in place of soda. The cabaret singer, seeing that they were making up to each other, came expressly over to their table and sang. Jake gave the singer fifty cents. . . .

143

Her left hand was on the table. Jake covered it with his right.

"Is it clear sailing between us, sweetie?" he asked.

"Sure thing. . . . You just landed from over there?"

"Just today!"

"But there wasn't no boat in with soldiers today, daddy."

"I made it in a special one."

"Why, you lucky baby! . . . I'd like to go to another place, though. What about you?"

"Anything you say, I'm game," responded Jake.

They walked along Lenox Avenue. He held her arm. His flesh tingled. He felt as if his whole body was a flaming wave. She was intoxicated, blinded under the overwhelming force.

But nevertheless she did not forget her business.

"How much is it going to be, daddy?" she demanded.

"How much? *How* much? Five?"

"Aw no, daddy. . . ."

"Ten?"

She shook her head.

"Twenty, sweetie!" he said, gallantly.

"Daddy," she answered, "I wants fifty."

"Good," he agreed. He was satisfied. She was responsive. She was beautiful. He loved the curious color on her cheek.

They went to a buffet flat on One Hundred and Thirty-seventh Street. The proprietress opened the door without removing the chain and peeked out. She was a matronly mulatto woman. She recognized the girl, who had put herself in front of Jake, and she slid back the chain and said, "Come right in."

The windows were heavily and carefully shaded. There was beer and wine, and there was plenty of hard liquor. Black and brown men sat at two tables in one room, playing poker. In the other room a phonograph was grinding out a "blues," and some couples were dancing, thick as maggots in a vat of sweet liquor, and as wriggling.

Jake danced with the girl. They shuffled warmly, gloriously about the room. He encircled her waist with both hands, and she put both of hers up to his shoulders and laid her head against his breast. And they shuffled around.

"Harlem! Harlem!" thought Jake. "Where else could I have

all this life but Harlem? Good old Harlem! Chocolate Harlem! Sweet Harlem! Harlem, I've got you' number down. Lenox Avenue, you're a bear, I know it. And, baby honey, sure enough youse a pippin for your pappy. Oh, boy!" . . .

After Jake had paid for his drinks, that fifty-dollar note was all he had left in the world. He gave it to the girl. . . .

"Is we going now, honey?" he asked her.

"Sure, daddy. Let's beat it." . . .

Oh, to be in Harlem again after two years away. The deep-dyed color, the thickness, the closeness of it. The noises of Harlem. The sugared laughter. The honey-talk on its streets. And all night long, ragtime and "blues" playing somewhere, . . . singing somewhere, dancing somewhere! Oh, the contagious fever of Harlem. Burning everywhere in dark-eyed Harlem. . . . Burning now in Jake's sweet blood. . . .

He woke up in the morning in a state of perfect peace. She brought him hot coffee and cream and doughnuts. He yawned. He sighed. He was satisfied. He breakfasted. He washed. He dressed. The sun was shining. He sniffed the fine dry air. Happy, familiar Harlem.

"I ain't got a cent to my name," mused Jake, "but ahm as happy as a prince, all the same. Yes, I is."

He loitered down Lenox Avenue. He shoved his hand in his pocket—pulled out the fifty-dollar note. A piece of paper was pinned to it on which was scrawled in pencil:

"Just a little gift from a baby girl to a honey boy!"

III
Zeddy

"GREAT balls of fire! Looka here! See mah luck!" Jake stopped in his tracks . . . went on . . . stopped again . . . retraced his steps . . . checked himself. "Guess I won't go back right now. Never let a woman think you're too crazy about her. But she's a particularly sweet piece a business. . . . Me and her again tonight. . . . Handful o' luck shot straight outa heaven. Oh, boy! Harlem is mine!"

Jake went rolling along Fifth Avenue. He crossed over to Lenox Avenue and went into Uncle Doc's saloon, where he had left his bag. Called for a glass of Scotch. "Gimme the siphon, Doc. I'm off the straight stuff."

"Iszh you? Counta what?"

"Hits the belly better this way. I l'arned it over the other side."

A slap on the shoulder brought him sharply round. "Zeddy Plummer! What grave is you arisen from?" he cried.

"Buddy, you looks so good to me, I could kish you," Zeddy said.

"Where?"

"Everywhere. . . . French style."

"One on one cheek and one on the other."

"Savee-vous?"

"Parlee-vous?"

Uncle Doc set another glass on the counter and poured out pure Bourbon. Zeddy reached a little above Jake's shoulders. He was stocky, thick-shouldered, flat-footed, and walked like a bear. Some more customers came in and the buddies eased round to the short side of the bar.

"What part of the earth done belch you out?" demanded Zeddy. "Nevah heared no God's tidings a you sence we missed you from Brest."

"And how about you?" Jake countered. "Didn't them Germans git you scrambling over the top?"

"Nevah see'd them, buddy. None a them showed the goose-

146

step around Brest. Have a shot on me. . . . Well, dawg bite
me, but—say, Jake, we've got some more stuff to booze over."

Zeddy slapped Jake on his breast and looked him over again.
"Tha's some stuff you're strutting in, boh. 'Tain't 'Merican and
it ain't French." . . .

"English." Jake showed his clean white teeth.

"Mah granny an' me! You been in that theah white folks'
country, too?"

"And don't I look as if Ise been? Where else could a fellow
git such good and cheap man clothes to cover his skin?"

"Buddy, I know it's the trute. What you doing today?"

"No, when you make me think ovit, particular thing. And
you?"

"I'm alongshore but—I ain't agwine to work thisaday."

"I guess I've got to be heaving along right back to it, too, in
pretty short time. I got to get me a room but——"

Uncle Doc reminded Jake that his suit-case was there.

"I ain't nevah fohgitting all mah worldly goods," responded
Jake.

Zeddy took Jake to a pool-room where they played. Jake
was the better man. From the pool-room they went to Aunt
Hattie's chitterling joint in One Hundred and Thirty-second
Street, where they fed. Fricassee chicken and rice. Green peas.
Stewed corn.

Aunt Hattie's was renowned among the lowly of Harlem's
Black Belt. It was a little basement joint, smoke-colored. And
Aunt Hattie was weather-beaten dark-brown, cheery-faced,
with two rusty-red front teeth sticking together conspicuously
out of her twisted, spread-away mouth. She cooked delicious
food—home-cooked food they called it. None of the boys
loafing round that section of Fifth Avenue would dream of going to any other place for their "poke chops."

Aunt Hattie admired her new customer from the kitchen
door and he quite filled her sight. And when she went with the
dish rag to wipe the oil-cloth before setting down the cocoanut
pie, she rubbed her breast against Jake's shoulder and a sensual
light gleamed in her aged smoke-red eyes.

The buddies talked about the days of Brest. Zeddy recalled the everlasting unloading and unloading of ships and the
toting of lumber. The house of the Young Men's Christian

Association, overlooking the harbor, where colored soldiers were not wanted. . . . The central Rue de Siam and the point near the Prefecture of Marine, from which you could look down on the red lights of the Quartier Réservé. The fatal fights between black men and white in the *maisons closes*. The encounters between apaches and white Americans. The French sailors that couldn't get the Yankee idea of amour and men. And the cemetery, just beyond the old mediæval gate of the town, where he left his second-best buddy.

"Poor boh. Was always belly-aching for a chance over the top. Nevah got it nor nothing. Not even a baid in the hospital. Strong like a bull, yet just knocked off in the dark through raw cracker cussedness. . . . Some life it was, buddy, in them days. We was always on the defensive as if the boches, as the froggies called them, was right down on us."

"Yet you stuck t'rough it toting lumber. Got back to Harlem all right, though."

"You bet I did, boh. You kain trust Zeddy Plummer to look out for his own black hide. . . . But you, buddy. How come you just vanished thataway like a spook? How did you take your tail out ovit?"

Jake told Zeddy how he walked out of it straight to the station in Brest. Le Havre. London. The West India Docks. And back home to Harlem.

"But you must keep it dark, buddy," Zeddy cautioned. "Don't go shooting off your mouth too free. Gov'mant still smoking out deserters and draft dodgers."

"I ain't told no nigger but you, boh. Nor ofay, neither. Ahm in your confidence, chappie."

"That's all right, buddy." Zeddy put his hand on Jake's knee. "It's better to keep your business close all the time. But I'll tell you this for your perticular information. Niggers am awful close-mouthed in some things. There is fellows here in Harlem that just telled the draft to mount upstairs. Pohlice and soldiers were hunting ev'where foh them. And they was right here in Harlem. Fifty dollars apiece foh them. All their friends knowed it and not a one gived them in. I tell you, niggers am amazing sometimes. Yet other times, without any natural reason, they will just go vomiting out their guts to the ofays about one another."

"God; but it's good to get back home again!" said Jake.

"I should think you was hungry foh a li'l' brown honey. I tell you trute, buddy. I made mine ovah there, spitin' ov ev'thing. I l'arned her a little z'inglise and she l'arned me beaucoup plus the French stuff. . . . The real stuff, buddy. But I was tearin' mad and glad to get back all the same. Take it from me, buddy, there ain't no honey lak to that theah comes out of our own belonging-to-us honeycomb."

"Man, what you telling me?" cried Jake. "Don't I knows it? What else you think made me leave over the other side? And dog mah doggone ef I didn't find it just as I landed."

"K-hhhhhhh! K-hhhhhhhh!" Zeddy laughed. "Dog mah cats! You done tasted the real life a'ready?"

"Last night was the end of the world, buddy, and tonight ahm going back there," chanted Jake as he rose and began kicking up his heels round the joint.

Zeddy also got up and put on his gray cap. They went back to the pool-room. Jake met two more fellows that he knew and got into a ring of Zeddy's pals. . . . Most of them were longshoremen. There was plenty of work, Jake learned. Before he left the pool-room he and Zeddy agreed to meet the next evening at Uncle Doc's.

"Got to work tomorrow, boh," Zeddy informed Jake.

"Good old New York! The same old wench of a city. Elevated racketing over you' head. Subway bellowing under you' feet. Me foh wrastling round them piers again. Scratching down to the bottom of them ships and scrambling out. All alongshore for me now. No more fooling with the sea. Same old New York. Everybody dashing round like crazy. . . . Same old New York. But the ofay faces am different from those ovah across the pond. Sure they is. Stiffer. Tighter. Yes, they is that. . . . But the sun does better here than over there. And the sky's so high and dry and blue. And the air it—O Gawd it works in you' flesh and blood like Scotch. O Lawdy, Lawdy! I wants to live to a hundred and finish mah days in New York."

Jake threw himself up as if to catch the air pouring down from the blue sky. . . .

"Harlem! Harlem! Little thicker, little darker and noisier and smellier, but Harlem just the same. The niggers done plowed

through Hundred and Thirtieth Street. Heading straight foh
One Hundred and Twenty-fifth. Spades beyond Eighth Avenue. Going, going, going Harlem! Going up! Nevah befoh I
seed so many dickty shines in sich swell motor-cars. Plenty moh
nigger shops. Seventh Avenue done gone high-brown. O Lawdy!
Harlem bigger, Harlem better . . . and sweeter."

"Street and streets! One Hundred and Thirty-second, Thirty-
third, Thirty-fourth. It wasn't One Hundred and Thirty-fifth
and it wasn't beyond theah. . . . O Lawd! how did I fohgit to
remember the street and number. I reeled outa there like a
drunken man. I been so happy. . . .

   "Thirty-fourth, Thirty-second, Thirty-third. . . . Only difference in the name. All the streets am just the same and all the
houses 'like as peas. I could try this one heah or that one there
but—— Rabbit foot! I didn't even git her name. Oh, Jakie,
Jake! What a big Ah-Ah you is.

   "I was a fool not to go back right then when I feeled like it.
What did I want to tighten up mahself and crow and strut like
a crazy cat for? A grand Ah-Ah I is. Feet in mah hands! Take
me back to the Baltimore tonight. I ain't gwine to know no
peace till I lay these here hands on mah tantalizing brown
again."

IV
Congo Rose

A LL the old cabarets were going still. Connor's was losing ground. The bed of red roses that used to glow in the ceiling was almost dim now. The big handsome black girl that always sang in a red frock was no longer there. What a place Connor's was from 1914 to 1916 when that girl was singing and kicking and showing her bright green panties there! And the little ebony drummer, beloved of every cabaret lover in Harlem, was a fiend for rattling the drum!

Barron's was still Barron's, depending on its downtown white trade. Leroy's, the big common rendezvous shop for everybody. Edmond's still in the running. A fine new place that was opened in Brooklyn was freezing to death. Brooklyn never could support anything.

Goldgraben's on Lenox Avenue was leading all the Negro cabarets in a cruel dance. The big-spirited Jew had brought his cabaret up from the basement and established it in a hall blazing with lights, overlooking Lenox Avenue. He made a popular Harlem Negro manager. There the joy-loving ladies and gentlemen of the Belt collected to show their striking clothes and beautiful skin. Oh, it was some wonderful sight to watch them from the pavement! No wonder the lights of Connor's were dim. And Barron's had plunged deeper for the ofay trade. Goldgraben was grabbing all the golden-browns that had any spendable dough.

But the Congo remained in spite of formidable opposition and foreign exploitation. The Congo was a real throbbing little Africa in New York. It was an amusement place entirely for the unwashed of the Black Belt. Or, if they were washed, smells lingered telling the nature of their occupation. Pot-wrestlers, third cooks, W.C. attendants, scrub maids, dish-washers, stevedores.

Girls coming from the South to try their future in New York always reached the Congo first. The Congo was African in spirit and color. No white persons were admitted there. The proprietor knew his market. He did not cater to the fast trade. "High yallers" were scarce there. Except for such sweetmen that lived off the low-down dark trade.

When you were fed up with the veneer of Seventh Avenue, and Goldgraben's Afro-Oriental garishness, you would go to the Congo and turn rioting loose in all the tenacious odors of service and the warm indigenous smells of Harlem, fooping or jig-jagging the night away. You would if you were a black kid hunting for joy in New York.

Jake went down to the Baltimore. No sign of his honey girl anywhere. He drank Scotch after Scotch. His disappointment mounted to anger against himself—turned to anger against his honey girl. His eyes roved round the room, but saw nobody.

"Oh what a big Ah-Ah I was!"

All round the den, luxuriating under the little colored lights, the dark dandies were loving up their pansies. Feet tickling feet under tables, tantalizing liquor-rich giggling, hands busy above.

"Honey gal! Honey gal! What other sweet boy is loving you now? Don't you know your last night's daddy am waiting for you?"

The cabaret singer, a shiny coffee-colored girl in a green frock and Indian-waved hair, went singing from table to table in a man's bass voice.

> "You wanta know how I do it,
>   How I look so good, how I am so happy,
>   All night on the blessed job—
>   How I slide along making things go snappy?
>   It is easy to tell,
>   I ain't got no plan—
>   But I'm crazy, plumb crazy
>   About a man, mah man.
>
> "It ain't no secret as you think,
>   The glad heart is a state o' mind—
>   Throw a stone in the river and it will sink;
>   But a feather goes whirling on the wind.
>   It is easy to tell. . . ."

She stopped more than usual at Jake's table. He gave her a half dollar. She danced a jagging jig before him that made the giggles rise like a wave in the room. The pansies stared and tightened their grip on their dandies. The dandies tightened their hold on themselves. They looked the favored Jake up and down. All those perfection struts for him. Yet he didn't seem aroused at all.

"I'm crazy, plumb crazy
    About a man, mah man. . . ."

The girl went humming back to her seat. She had poured every drop of her feeling into the song.

"Crazy, plumb crazy about a man, mah man. . . ."

Dandies and pansies, chocolate, chestnut, coffee, ebony, cream, yellow, everybody was teased up to the high point of excitement. . . .

"Crazy, plumb crazy about a man, mah man. . . ."

The saxophone was moaning it. And feet and hands and mouths were acting it. Dancing. Some jigged, some shuffled, some walked, and some were glued together swaying on the dance floor.

Jake was going crazy. A hot fever was burning him up. . . . Where was the singing gal that had danced to him? That dancing was for him all right. . . .

A crash cut through the music. A table went jazzing into the drum. The cabaret singer lay sprawling on the floor. A raging putty-skinned mulattress stamped on her ribs and spat in her face! "That'll teach you to leave mah man be every time." A black waiter rushed the mulattress. "Git off'n her. 'Causen she's down."

A potato-yellow man and a dull-black were locked. The proprietor, a heavy brown man, worked his elbow like a hatchet between them.

The antagonists glowered at each other.

"What you want to knock the gal down like that for, I acks you?"

"Better acks her why she done spits on mah woman."

"*Woman!* White man's wench, you mean. You low-down tripe. . . ."

The black man heaved toward the yellow, but the waiters

hooked and hustled him off. . . . Sitting at a table, the cabaret singer was soothing her eye.

"Git out on the sidewalk, all you trouble-makers," cried the proprietor. "And you, Bess," he cried to the cabaret singer, "nevah you show your face in mah place again."

The cabaret was closed for the rest of the night. Like dogs flicked apart by a whipcord, the jazzers stood and talked resentfully in the street.

"Hi, Jake"—Zeddy, rocking into the group with a nosy air, spotted his buddy—"was you in on the li'l' fun?"

"Yes, buddy, but I wasn't mixed up in it. Sometimes they turn mah stomach, the womens. The same in France, the same in England, the same in Harlem. White against white and black against white and yellow against black and brown. We's all just crazy-dog mad. Ain't no peace on earth with the womens and there ain't no life anywhere without them."

"You said it, boh. It's a be-be itching life"—Zeddy scratched his flank—"and we're all sons of it. . . . But what is you hitting round this joint? I thought you would be feeding off milk and honey tonight?"

"Hard luck, buddy. Done lose out counta mah own indiligence. I fohgit the street and the house. Thought I'd find her heah but. . . ."

"What you thinking 'bout, boh?"

"That gal got beat up in the Baltimore. She done sings me into a tantalizing mood. Ahm feeling like."

"Let's take a look in on the Congo, boh. It's the best pick-me-up place in Harlem."

"I'm with you, buddy."

"Always packed with the best pickings. When the chippies come up from down home, tha's where they hangs out first. You kain always find something that New York ain't done made a fool of yet. Theah's a high-yaller entertainer there that I'se got a crush on, but she ain't nevah gived me a encouraging eye."

"I ain't much for the high-yallers after having been so much fed-up on the ofays," said Jake. "They's so doggone much alike."

"Ah no, boh. A sweet-lovin' high-yaller queen's got something different. K-hhhhhhh, K-hhhhhhh. Something nigger."

The Congo was thick, dark-colorful, and fascinating. Drum and saxophone were fighting out the wonderful drag "blues" that was the favorite of all the low-down dance halls. In all the better places it was banned. Rumor said it was a police ban. It was an old tune, so far as popular tunes go. But at the Congo it lived fresh and green as grass. Everybody there was giggling and wriggling to it.

And it is ashes to ashes and dust to dust,
Can you show me a woman that a man can trust?

Oh, baby, how are you?
Oh, baby, what are you?
Oh, can I have you now,
Or have I got to wait?
Oh, let me have a date,
Why do you hesitate?

And there is two things in Harlem I don't understan'
It is a bulldycking woman and a faggotty man.

Oh, baby how are you?
Oh, baby, what are you? . . .

Jake and Zeddy picked two girls from a green bench and waded into the hot soup. The saxophone and drum fought over the punctuated notes. The cymbals clashed. The excitement mounted. Couples breasted each other in rhythmical abandon, grinned back at their friends and chanted:

"Oh, baby, how are you?
Oh, baby, what are you? . . ."

Clash! The cymbal snuffed out saxophone and drum, the dancers fell apart,—reeled, strutted, drifted back to their green places. . . .

Zeddy tossed down the third glass of Gordon gin and became aware of Rose, the Congo entertainer, singing at the table. Happy for the moment, he gave her fifty cents. She sang some more, but Zeddy saw that it was all for Jake. Finished, she sat down, uninvited, at their table.

How many nights, hungry nights, Zeddy had wished that Rose would sit down voluntarily at his table. He had asked her

sometimes. She would sit, take a drink and leave. Nothing doing. If he was a "big nigger," perhaps—but she was too high-
priced for him. Now she was falling for Jake. Perhaps it was
Jake's nifty suit. . . .

"Gin for mine," Rose said. Jake ordered two gins and a
Scotch. "Scotch! That's an ofay drink," Rose remarked. "And
I've seen the monkey-chasers order it when they want to put
on style."

"It's good," Jake said. "Taste it."

She shook her head. "I have befoh. I don't like the taste.
Gimme gin every time or good old red Kentucky."

"I got used to it over the other side," Jake said.

"Oh! You're an over-yonder baby! Sure enough!" She fondled his suit in admiration.

Zeddy, like a good understanding buddy, had slipped away.
Another Scotch and Gordon Dry. The glasses kissed. Like a
lean lazy leopard the mulattress reclined against Jake.

The milk cans were sounding on the pavements and a few pale
stars were still visible in the sky when Rose left the Congo with
both hands entwined in Jake's arm.

"You gwina stay with me, mah brown?"

"I ain't got me a room yet," he said.

"Come stay with me always. Got any stuff to bring along?"

"Mah suitcase at Uncle Doc's."

They went to her room in One Hundred and Thirty-third
street. Locking the door, she said: "You remember the song
they used to sing before you all went over there, mah brown?"

Softly she chanted:

"If I had some one like you at home
  I wouldn't wanta go out, I wouldn't wanta go out. . . .
  If I had some one like you at home,
  I'd put a padlock on the door. . . ."

She hugged him to her.

"I love you. I ain't got no man."

"Gwan, tell that to the marines," he panted.

"Honest to God. Lemme kiss you nice."

It was now eating-time in Harlem. They were hungry. They washed and dressed.

"If you'll be mah man always, you won't have to work," she said.

"Me?" responded Jake. "I've never been a sweetman yet. Never lived off no womens and never will. I always works."

"I don't care what you do whilst you is mah man. But hard work's no good for a sweet-loving papa."

V
On the Job Again

JAKE stayed on in Rose's room. He could not feel about her as he did for his little lost maroon-brown of the Baltimore. He went frequently to the Baltimore, but he never saw her again. Then he grew to hate that cabaret and stopped going there.

The mulattress was charged with tireless activity and Jake was her big, good slave. But her spirit lacked the charm and verve, the infectious joy, of his little lost brown. He sometimes felt that she had no spirit at all—that strange, elusive something that he felt in himself, sometimes here, sometimes there, roaming away from him, going back to London, to Brest, Le Havre, wandering to some unknown new port, caught a moment by some romantic rhythm, color, face, passing through cabarets, saloons, speakeasies, and returning to him. . . . The little brown had something of that in her, too. That night he had felt a reaching out and marriage of spirits. . . . But the mulattress was all a wonderful tissue of throbbing flesh. He had never once felt in her any tenderness or timidity or aloofness. . . .

Jake was working longshore. Hooking barrels and boxes, wrestling with chains and cranes. He didn't have a little-boss job this time. But that didn't worry him. He was one blackamoor that nourished a perfect contempt for place. There were times when he divided his days between Rose and Uncle Doc's saloon and Dixie Red's pool-room.

He never took money from her. If he gambled away his own and was short, he borrowed from Nije Gridley, the longshoreman broker. Nije Gridley was a tall, thin, shiny black man. His long eyelashes gave his sharp eyes a sleepy appearance, but he was always wide awake. Before Jake was shipped to France, Nije had a rooming-house in Harlem's Fifth Avenue, worked a little at longshoring himself, and lent money on the checks of the hard-gambling boys. Now he had three rooming-houses, one of which, free of mortgage, he owned. His lean belly bore a heavy gold chain and he strutted Fifth and Lenox in a minis-terial crow-black suit. With the war boom of wages, the boys had gambled heavily and borrowed recklessly.

Ordinarily, Nije lent money at the rate of a dollar on four and two on eight per week. He complained bitterly of losses. Twenty-five dollars loaned on a check which, presented, brought only a day's pay. There were tough fellows that played him that game sometimes. They went and never returned to borrow again. But Nije's interest covered up such gaps. And sometimes he gave ten dollars on a forty-dollar check, drew the wages, and never saw his customer again, who had vanished entirely out of that phase of Harlem life.

One week when they were not working, Zeddy came to Jake with wonderful news. Men were wanted at a certain pier to unload pineapples at eight dollars a day. Eight dollars was ex-ceptional wages, but the fruit was spoiling.

Jake went with Zeddy and worked the first day with a group of Negroes and a few white men. The white men were not reg-ular dock workers. The only thing that seemed strange to Jake was that all the men ate inside and were not allowed outside the gates for lunch. But, on the second day, his primitive pas-sion for going against regulation urged him to go out in the street after lunch.

Heaving casually along West Street, he was hailed by a white man. "Hello, fellow-worker!"

"Hello, there! What's up?" Jake asked.

"You working in there?"

"Sure I is. Since yestidday."

The man told Jake that there was a strike on and he was scabbing. Jake asked him why there were no pickets if there was a strike. The man replied that there were no pickets be-cause the union leaders were against the strike, and had con-nived with the police to beat up and jail the pickets.

"Well, pardner," Jake said, "I've done worked through a tur'ble assortments o' jobs in mah lifetime, but I ain't nevah yet scabbed it on any man. I done work in this heah country, and I works good and hard over there in France. I works in London and I nevah was a blackleg, although I been the only black man in mah gang."

"Fine, fellow-worker; that's a real man's talk," said the white

man. He took a little red book out of his pocket and asked
Jake to let him sign him up in his union.

"It's the only one in the country for a red-blooded worker,
no matter what race or nation he belongs to."

"Nope, I won't scab, but I ain't a joiner kind of a fellah,"
said Jake. "I ain't no white folks' nigger and I ain't no poah
white's fool. When I longshored in Philly I was a good union
man. But when I made New York I done finds out that they
gived the colored mens the worser piers and holds the bes'n a'
them foh the Irishmen. No, pardner, keep you' card. I take the
best I k'n get as I goes mah way. But I tells you, things ain't
none at all lovely between white and black in this heah Gawd's
own country."

"We take all men in our union regardless——" But Jake was
haunching along out of hearing down West Street. . . .
Suddenly he heard sharp, deep, distressful grunts, and saw behind some barrels a black man down and being kicked perilously in the rear end by two white men. Jake drew his hook
from his belt and, waving it in the air, he rushed them. The
white men shot like rats to cover. The down man scrambled to
his feet. One of Zeddy's pals, Jake recognized him.

"What's the matter, buddy, the peckawoods them was doing
you in?"

"Becaz they said there was a strike in theah. And I said I
didn't give a doughnut, I was going to work foh mah money
all the same. I got one o' them bif! in the eye, though. . . ."

"Don't go back, buddy. Let the boss-men stick them jobs
up. They are a bunch of rotten aigs. Just using us to do their
dirty work. Come on, let's haul bottom away from here to
Harlem."

At Dixie Red's pool-room that evening there were some fellows with bandaged arms and heads. One iron-heavy, blue-
black lad (he was called Liver-lip behind his back, because of
the plankiness of his lips) carried his arm in a sling, and told
Jake how he happened to be like that.

"They done jumped on me soon as I turned mah black
moon on that li'l saloon tha's catering to us niggers. Heabenly
God! But if the stars them didn't twinkle way down in mah
eyes. But easy, easy, old man, I got out mah shaving steel and
draws it down the goosey flesh o' one o' them, and, buddy,

you shoulda heah him squeal. . . . The pohlice?" His massive mouth molded the words to its own form. "They tooks me, yes, but tunned me loose by'n'by. They's with us this time, boh, but, Lawdy! if they hadn't did entervention I woulda gutted gizzard and kidney outa that white tripe."

Jake was angry with Zeddy and asked him, when he came in, why he had not told him at first that the job was a scab job.

"I won't scab on nobody, not even the orneriest crackers," he said.

"Bull Durham!" cried Zeddy. "What was I going to let on about anything for? The boss-man done paid me to git him mens, and I got them. Ain't I working there mahself? I'll take any job in this heah Gawd's country that the white boss make it worf mah while to work at."

"But it ain't decent to scab," said Jake.

"Decent mah black moon!" shouted Zeddy. "I'll scab through hell to make mah living. Scab job or open shop or union am all the same jobs to me. White mens don't want niggers in them unions, nohow. Ain't you a good carpenter? And ain't I a good blacksmith? But kain we get a look-in on our trade heah in this white man's city? Ain't white mens done scabbed niggers outa all the jobs they useter hold down heah in this city? Waiter, bootblack, and barber shop?"

"With all a that scabbing is a low-down deal," Jake maintained.

"Me eye! Seems lak youse gittin' religion, boh. Youse talking death, tha's what you sure is. One thing I know is niggers am made foh life. And I want to live, boh, and feel plenty o' the juice o' life in mah blood. I wanta live and I wanta love. And niggers am got to work hard foh that. Buddy, I'll tell you this and I'll tell it to the wo'l'—all the crackers, all them poah white trash, all the nigger-hitting and nigger-breaking white folks—I loves life and I got to live and I'll scab through hell to live."

Jake did not work again that week. By Saturday morning he didn't have a nickel, so he went to Nije Gridley to borrow money. Nije asked him if he was going that evening to Billy Biasse's railroad flat, the longshoremen gaming rendezvous. Jake said no, he was going with Zeddy to a buffet flat in One Hundred and Fortieth Street. The buffet flat was the rendez-vous of a group of railroad porters and club waiters who

gambled for big stakes. Jake did not go there often because he
had to dress up as if he were going to a cabaret. Also, he was
not a big-stake gambler. . . . He preferred Billy Biasse's,
where he could go whenever he liked with hook and overalls.

"Oh, that's whar Zeddy's hanging out now," Nije commented, casually.

For some time before Jake's return from Europe Zeddy had
stopped going to Billy Biasse's. He told Jake he was fed up
with it. Jake did not know that Zeddy owed Nije money and
that he did not go to Billy Biasse's because Nije often went
there. . . .

Later in the evening Nije went to Billy Biasse's and found a
longshoreman who was known at the buffet flat, to take him
there.

Gambling was a bigger game than sex at this buffet flat. The
copper-hued lady who owned it was herself a very good poker-
player. There were only two cocoa-brown girls there. Not
young or attractive. They made a show of doing something,
serving drinks and trying hard to make jokes. In dining- and
sitting-room, five tables were occupied by card-players. Railroad porters, longshoremen, waiters; tight-faced, anxious-eyed.
Zeddy sat at the same table with the lady of the flat. He had
just eliminated two cards and asked for two when Nije and his
escort were let into the flat. Zeddy smelled his man and knew
it was Nije without looking up.

Nije swaggered past Zeddy and joined a group at another
table. The gaming went on with intermittent calls for drinks.
Nije sat where he could watch Zeddy's face. Zeddy also, although apparently intent on the cards, kept a wary eye on Nije.
Sometimes their eyes met. No one was aware of the challenge
that was developing between the two men.

There was a little slackening in the games, a general call for
drinks, and a shifting of chairs. Nije got nearer to Zeddy. . . .
Half-smiling and careless-like, he planted his bootheel upon
Zeddy's toes.

"Git off mah feets," Zeddy barked. The answer was a hard
blow in the face. Zeddy tasted blood in his mouth. He threw
his muscular gorilla body upon the tall Nije and hugged him
down to the floor.

"You blasted black Jew, say you' prayers!" cried Zeddy.

"Ain't scared o' none o' you barefaced robber niggers." Nije was breathing hard under Zeddy and trying to get the better of him by the help of the wall.

"Black man," growled Zeddy, "I'se gwineta cut your throat just so sure as God is white."

With his knee upon Nije's chest and his left hand on his windpipe, Zeddy flashed the deadly-gleaming blade out of his back pocket. The proprietress let loose a blood-curdling scream, but before Zeddy's hand could achieve its purpose, Jake aimed a swift kick at his elbow. The razor flew spinning upward and fell chopping through a glass of gin on the pianola.

The proprietress fell upon Zeddy and clawed at him. "Wha's the matter all you bums trying to ruin mah place?" she cried. "Ain't I been a good spoht with you all, making everything here nice and respectable?"

Jake took charge of Zeddy. Two men hustled Nije off away out of the flat.

"Who was it put the krimp on me?" asked Zeddy.

"You ought to praise the Lawd you was saved from Sing Sing and don't ask no questions," the woman replied.

Everybody was talking.

"How did that long, tall, blood-suckin' nigger get in heah?"

"Soon as this heah kind a business stahts, the dicks will sartain sure git on to us."

"It ain't no moh than last week they done raided Madame Jerkin's, the niftiest buffet flat in Harlem. O Lawdy!"

"That ole black cock," growled Zeddy, "he wouldn'a' crowed round Harlem no moh after I'd done made that theah fine blade talk in his throat."

"Shut up you," the proprietress said, "or I'll throw you out." And Zeddy, the ape, who was scared of no man in the place, became humble before the woman. She began setting the room to order, helped by the two cocoa-brown girls. A man shuffling a pack of cards called to Zeddy and Jake.

But the woman held up her hand. "No more card-playing tonight. I feel too nervous."

"Let's dance, then," suggested the smaller cocoa-brown girl.

A "blues" came trotting out of the pianola. The proprietress bounced into Jake's arms. The men sprang at the two girls. The unlucky ones paired off with each other.

Oh, "blues," "blues," "blues." Black-framed white grinning. Finger-snapping. Undertone singing. The three men with women teasing the stags. Zeddy's gorilla feet dancing down the dark death lurking in his heart. Zeddy dancing with a pal. "Blues," "blues," "blues." Red moods, black moods, golden moods. Curious, syncopated slipping-over into one mood, back-sliding back to the first mood. Humming in harmony, barbaric harmony, joy-drunk, chasing out the shadow of the moment before.

VI
Myrtle Avenue

ZEDDY was excited over Jake's success in love. He thought how often he had tried to make up to Rose, without succeeding. He was crazy about finding a woman to love him for himself.

He had been married when he was quite a lad to a crust-yellow girl in Petersburg. Zeddy's wife, after deceiving him with white men, had run away from him to live an easier life. That was before Zeddy came North. Since then he had had many other alliances. But none had been successful.

It was true that no Black Belt beauty would ever call Zeddy "mah han'some brown." But there were sweetmen of the Belt more repulsive than he, that women would fight and murder each other for. Zeddy did not seem to possess any of that magic that charms and holds women for a long time. All his attempts at home-making had failed. The women left him when he could not furnish the cash to meet the bills. They never saw his wages. For it was gobbled up by his voracious passion for poker and crap games. Zeddy gambled in Harlem. He gambled with white men down by the piers. And he was always losing.

"If only I could get those kinda gals that falls foh Jake," Zeddy mused. "And Jake is such a fool spade. Don't know how to handle the womens."

Zeddy's chance came at last. One Saturday a yellow-skinned youth, whose days and nights were wholly spent between pool-rooms and Negro speakeasies, invited Zeddy to a sociable at a grass-widow's who lived in Brooklyn and worked as a cook downtown in New York. She was called Gin-head Susy. She had a little apartment in Myrtle Avenue near Prince Street.

Susy was wonderfully created. She was of the complexion known among Negroes as spade or chocolate-to-the-bone. Her eyes shone like big white stars. Her chest was majestic and the general effect like a mountain. And that mountain was overgrand because Susy never wore any other but extremely

French-heeled shoes. Even over the range she always stood poised in them and blazing in bright-hued clothes.

The burning passion of Susy's life was the yellow youth of her race. Susy came from South Carolina. A yellow youngster married her when she was fifteen and left her before she was eighteen. Since then she had lived with a yellow complex at the core of her heart.

Civilization had brought strikingly exotic types into Susy's race. And like many, many Negroes, she was a victim to that. . . . Ancient black life rooted upon its base with all its fascinating new layers of brown, low-brown, high-brown, nut-brown, lemon, maroon, olive, mauve, gold. Yellow balancing between black and white. Black reaching out beyond yellow. Almost-white on the brink of a change. Sucked back down into the current of black by the terribly sweet rhythm of black blood. . . .

Susy's life of yellow complexity was surcharged with gin. There were whisky and beer also at her sociable evenings, but gin was the drink of drinks. Except for herself, her parties were all-male. Like so many of her sex, she had a congenital contempt for women. All-male were her parties and as yellow as she could make them. A lemon-colored or paper-brown poolroom youngster from Harlem's Fifth Avenue or from Prince Street. A bellboy or railroad waiter or porter. Sometimes a chocolate who was a quick, nondiscriminating lover and not remote of attitude like the pampered high-browns. But chocolates were always a rarity among Susy's front-roomful of gin-lovers.

Yet for all of her wages drowned in gin, Susy carried a hive of discontents in her majestic breast. She desired a lover, something like her undutiful husband, but she desired in vain. Her guests consumed her gin and listened to the phonograph, exchanged rakish stories, and when they felt fruit-ripe to dropping, left her place in pursuit of pleasures elsewhere.

Sometimes Susy managed to lay hold of a yellow one for some time. Something all a piece of dirty rags and stench picked up in the street. Cleansed, clothed, and booted it. But so soon as he got his curly hair straightened by the process of Harlem's Ambrozine Palace of Beauty, and started in strutting the pavement of Lenox Avenue, feeling smart as a moving-picture dandy, he would leave Susy.

Apart from Susy's repellent person, no youthful sweetman attempting to love her could hold out under the ridicule of his pals. Over their games of pool and craps the boys had their cracks at Susy.

"What about Gin-head Susy tonight?"

"Sure, let's go and look the crazy old broad over."

"I'll go anywheres foh swilling of good booze."

"She's sho one ugly spade, but she's right there with her Gordon Dry."

"She ain't got 'em from creeps to crown and her trotters is B flat, but her gin is regal."

But now, after all the years of gin sociables and unsatisfactory lemons, Susy was changing just a little. She was changing under the influence of her newly-acquired friend, Lavinia Curdy, the only woman whom she tolerated at her parties. That was not so difficult, as Miss Curdy was less attractive than Susy. Miss Curdy was a putty-skinned mulattress with purple streaks on her face. Two of her upper front teeth had been knocked out and her lower lip slanted pathetically leftward. She was skinny and when she laughed she resembled an old braying jenny.

When Susy came to know Miss Curdy, she unloaded a quantity of the stuff of her breast upon her. Her drab childhood in a South Carolina town. Her early marriage. No girlhood. Her husband leaving her. And all the yellow men that had beaten her, stolen from her, and pawned her things.

Miss Curdy had been very emphatic to Susy about "yaller men." "I know them from long experience. They never want to work. They're a lazy and shiftless lot. Want to be kept like women. I found that out a long, long time ago. And that's why when I wanted a man foh keeps I took me a black plug-ugly one, mah dear."

It wouldn't have supported the plausibility of Miss Curdy's advice if she had mentioned that more than one black plug-ugly had ruthlessly cut loose from her. As the black woman had had her entanglements in yellow, so had the mulattress hers of black. But, perhaps, Miss Curdy did not realize that she could not help desiring black. In her salad days as a business girl her purse was controlled by many a black man. Now, however, her old problems did not arise in exactly the same way, —her purse was old and worn and flat and attracted no attention.

"A black man is as good to me as a yaller when I finds a real one." Susy lied a little to Miss Curdy from a feeling that she ought to show some pride in her own complexion.

"But all these sociables—and you spend so much coin on gin," Miss Curdy had said.

"Well, that's the trute, but we all of us drinks it. And I loves to have company in mah house, plenty of company."

But when Susy came home from work one evening and found that her latest "yaller" sweetie had stolen her suitcase and best dresses and pawned even her gas range, she resolved never to keep another of his kind as a "steady." At least she made that resolve to Miss Curdy. But the sociables went on and the same types came to drink the Saturday evenings away, leaving the two women at the finish to their empty bottles and glasses. Once Susy did make a show of a black lover. He was the house man at the boarding-house where she cooked. But the arrangement did not hold any time, for Susy demanded of the chocolate extremely more than she ever got from her yellows.

"Well, boh, we's Brooklyn bound tonight," said Zeddy to Jake.

"You got to show me that Brooklyn's got any life to it," replied Jake.

"Theah's life anywheres theah's booze and jazz, and theah's cases o' gin and a gramophone whar we's going."

"Has we got to pay foh it, buddy?"

"No, boh, eve'ything is f.o.c. ef the lady likes you."

"Blimey!" A cockney phrase stole Jake's tongue. "Don't bull me."

"I ain't. Honest-to-Gawd Gordon Dry, and moh—ef you're the goods, all f.o.c."

"Well, I'll be browned!" exclaimed Jake.

Zeddy also took along Strawberry Lips, a new pal, burnt-cork black, who was thus nicknamed from the peculiar stage-red color of his mouth. Strawberry Lips was typically the stage Negro. He was proof that a generalization has some foundation in truth. . . . You might live your life in many black belts and arrive at the conclusion that there is no such thing as a typical Negro—no minstrel coon off the stage, no Thomas Nelson Page's nigger, no Octavus Roy Cohen's porter, no lineal descendant of Uncle Tom. Then one day your theory may be upset through meeting with a type by far more perfect than any created counterpart.

"Myrtle Avenue used to be a be-be itching of a place," said Strawberry Lips, "when Doc Giles had his gambling house on there and Elijah Bowers was running his cabaret. H'm. But Bowers was some big guy. He knew swell white folks in politics, and had a grand automobile and a high-yaller wife that hadn't no need of painting to pass. His cabaret was running neck and neck with Marshall's in Fifty-third Street. Then one night he killed a man in his cabaret, and that finished him. The lawyers got him off. But they cleaned him out dry. Done broke him, that case did. And today he's plumb down and out."

Jake, Zeddy, and Strawberry Lips had left the subway train at Borough Hall and were walking down Myrtle Avenue.

"Bowers' cabaret was some place for the teasing-brown pick-me-up then, brother—and the snow. The stuff was cheap then. You sniff, boh?" Strawberry Lips asked Jake and Zeddy.

"I wouldn't know befoh I sees it," Jake laughed.

"I ain't no habitual prisoner," said Zeddy, "but I does any little thing for a change. Keep going and active with anything, says I."

The phonograph was discharging its brassy jazz notes when they entered the apartment. Susy was jerking herself from one side to the other with a potato-skinned boy. Miss Curdy was half-hopping up and down with the only chocolate that was there. Five lads, ranging from brown to yellow in complexion, sat drinking with jaded sneering expressions on their faces. The one that had invited Zeddy was among them. He waved to him to come over with his friends.

"Sit down and try some gin," he said. . . .

Zeddy dipped his hand in his pocket and sent two bones rolling on the table.

"Ise with you, chappie," his yellow friend said. The others

crowded around. The gramophone stopped and Susy, hugging a bottle, came jerking on her French heels over to the group. She filled the glasses and everybody guzzled gin.

Miss Curdy looked the newcomers over, paying particular attention to Jake. A sure-enough eye-filling chocolate, she thought. I would like to make a steady thing of him.

Over by the door two light-brown lads began arguing about an actress of the leading theater of the Black Belt.

"I tell you I knows Gertie Kendall. I know her more'n I know you."

"Know her mah granny. You knows her just like I do, from the balcony of the Lafayette. Don't hand me none o' that fairy stuff, for I ain't gwine to swallow it."

"Youse an aching pain. I knows her, I tell you. I even danced with her at Madame Mulberry's apartment. You thinks I only hangs out with low-down trash becassin Ise in a place like this, eh? I done met mos'n all our big niggers: Jack Johnson, James Reese Europe, Adah Walker, Buddy, who used to play that theah drum for them Castle Walkers, and Madame Walker."

"Yaller, it 'pears to me that youse jest a nacherally-born story-teller. You really spec's me to believe youse been associating with the mucty-mucks of the race? Gwan with you. You'll be telling me next you done speaks with Charlie Chaplin and John D. Rockefeller——"

Miss Curdy had tuned her ears to the conversation and broke in: "Why, what is that to make so much fuss about? Sure he can dance with Gertie Kendall and know the dickty niggers. In my sporting days I knew Bert Williams and Walker and Adah Overton and Editor Tukslack and all that upstage race gang that wouldn't touch Jack Johnson with a ten-foot pole. I lived in Washington and had Congressmen for my friends— foop! Why you can get in with the top-crust crowd at any swell ball in Harlem. All you need is clothes and the coin. I know them all, yet I don't feel a bit haughty mixing here with Susy and you all."

"I guess you don't now," somebody said.

Gin went round . . . and round . . . and round. . . . Desultory dancing. . . . Dice. . . . Blackjack. . . . Poker. . . . The room became a close, live, intense place. Tight-faced, the men seemed interested only in drinking and gaming, while Susy and Miss Curdy, guzzling hard, grew uglier. A jungle atmosphere pervaded the room, and, like shameless wild animals hungry for raw meat, the females savagely searched the eyes of the males. Susy's eyes always came back to settle upon the lad that had invited Zeddy. He was her real object. And Miss Curdy was ginned up with high hopes of Jake.

Jake threw up the dice and Miss Curdy seized her chance to get him alone for a little while.

"The cards do get so tiresome," she said. "I wonder how you men can go on and on all night long poking around with poker."

"Better than worser things," retorted Jake. Disgusted by the purple streaks, he averted his eyes from the face of the mulattress.

"I don't know about that," Miss Curdy bridled. "There's many nice ways of spending a sociable evening between ladies and gentlemen."

"Got to show me," said Jake, simply because the popular phrase intrigued his tongue.

"And that I can."

Irritated, Jake turned to move away.

"Where you going? Scared of a lady?"

Jake recoiled from the challenge, and shuffled away from the hideous mulattress. From experience in seaport towns in America, in France, in England, he had concluded that a woman could always go farther than a man in coarseness, depravity, and sheer cupidity. Men were ugly and brutal. But beside women they were merely vicious children. Ignorant about the aim and meaning and fulfillment of life; uncertain and indeterminate; weak. Rude children who loved excelling in spectacular acts to win the applause of women.

But women were so realistic and straight-going. *They* were the real controlling force of life. Jake remembered the bal-musette fights between colored and white soldiers in France. Blacks, browns, yellows, whites. . . . He remembered the interracial sex skirmishes in England. Men fought, hurt, wounded, killed each other. Women, like blazing torches, egged them on or denounced them. Victims of sex, the men seemed foolish, apelike blunderers in their pools of blood. Didn't know what they were fighting for, except it was to gratify some vague feeling about women. . . .

Jake's thoughts went roaming after his little lost brown of the Baltimore. The difference! She, in one night, had revealed a fine different world to him. Mystery again. A little stray girl. Finer than the finest!

Some of the fellows were going. In a vexed spirit, Susy had turned away from her unresponsive mulatto toward Zeddy. Relieved, the mulatto yawned, threw his hands backwards and said: "I guess mah broad is home from Broadway by now. Got to final on home to her. Harlem, lemme see you."

Miss Curdy was sitting against the mantelpiece, charming Strawberry Lips. Marvellous lips. Salmon-pink and planky. She had hoisted herself upon his knees, her arm around his thick neck.

Jake went over to the mantelpiece to pour a large chaser of beer and Miss Curdy leered at him. She disgusted him. His life was a free coarse thing, but he detested nastiness and ugliness. Guess I'll haul bottom to Harlem, he thought. Congo Rose was a rearing wild animal, all right, but these women, these boys. . . . Skunks, tame skunks, all of them!

He was just going out when a chocolate lad pointed at a light-brown and said: "The pot calls foh four bits, chappie. Come across or stay out."

"Lemme a quarter!"

"Ain't got it. Staying out?"

Biff! Square on the mouth. The chocolate leaped up like a tiger-cat at his assailant, carrying over card table, little pile of money, and half-filled gin glasses with a crash. Like an enraged ram goat, he held and butted the light-brown boy twice, straight on the forehead. The victim crumpled with a thud to the floor. Susy jerked over to the felled boy and hauled him, his body leaving a liquid trail, to the door. She flung him out in the corridor and slammed the door.

"Sarves him right, pulling off that crap in mah place. And you, Mis'er Jack Johnson," she said to the chocolate youth, "lemme miss you quick."

"He done hits me first," the chocolate said.

"I knows it, but I ain't gwina stand foh no rough-house in

mah place. Ise got a dawg heah wif me all ready foh bawking."

"K-hhhhh, K-hhhhh," laughed Strawberry Lips. "Oh, boh,
I know it's the trute, but——"

The chocolate lad slunk out of the flat.

"Lavinia," said Susy to Miss Curdy, "put on that theah
'Tickling Blues' on the victroly."

The phonograph began its scraping and Miss Curdy started
jig-jagging with Strawberry Lips. Jake gloomed with disgust
against the door.

"Getting outa this, buddy?" he asked Zeddy.

"Nobody's chasing *us*, boh." Zeddy commenced stepping
with Susy to the "Tickling Blues."

Outside, Jake found the light-brown boy still half-stunned
against the wall.

"Ain't you gwine at home?" Jake asked him.

"I can't find a nickel foh car fare," said the boy.

Jake took him into a saloon and bought him a lemon squash.
"Drink that to clear you' haid," he said. "And heah's car fare."
He gave the boy a dollar. "Whar you living at?"

"San Juan Hill."

"Come on, le's git the subway, then."

The Myrtle Avenue Elevated train passed with a high raucous rumble over their heads.

"Myrtle Avenue," murmured Jake. "Pretty name, all right,
but it stinks like a sewer. Legs and feets! Come take me outa it
back home to Harlem."

VII
Zeddy's Rise and Fall

Z EDDY was scarce in Harlem. And Strawberry Lips was also scarce. It was fully a week after the Myrtle Avenue gin-fest before Jake saw Zeddy again. They met on the pavement in front of Uncle Doc's saloon.

"Why, where in the sweet name of niggers in Harlem, buddy, you been keeping you'self?"

"Whar you think?"

"Think? I been very much thinking that Nije Gridley done git you."

"How come you git thataway, boh? Nije Gridley him ain't got a chawnst on the carve or the draw ag'inst Zeddy Plummer so long as Ise got me a black moon."

"Well, what's it done git you, then?"

"Myrtle Avenue."

"Come outa that; you ain't talking. . . ."

"The trute as I knows it, buddy."

"Crazy dog bite mah laig!" cried Jake. "You ain't telling me that you done gone. . . ."

"Transfer mah suitcase and all mah pohsitions to Susy."

"Gin-head Susy!"

"Egsactly; that crechur is mah ma-ma now. I done express mahself ovah theah on that very mahv'lously hang-ovah after-noon of that ginnity mawnin' that you left me theah. And Ise been right theah evah since."

"Well, Ise got to wish you good luck, buddy, although youse been keeping it so dark."

"It's the darkness of new loving, boh. But the honeymoon is good and well ovah, and I'll be li'l moh in Harlem as usual, looking the chippies and chappies ovah. I ain't none at all stuck on Brooklyn."

"It's a swah hole all right," said Jake.

"But theah's sweet stuff in it." Zeddy tongue-wiped his fleshy lips with a salacious laugh.

"It's all right, believe me, boh," he informed Jake. "Susy

ain't nothing to look at like you' fair-brown queen, but she's tur'bly sweet loving. You know when a ma-ma ain't the goods in looks and figure, she's got to make up foh it some. And that Susy does. And she treats me right. Gimme all I wants to drink and brings home the goodest poke chops and fried chicken foh me to put away under mah shirt. . . . Youse got to come and feed with us all one o' these heah evenings."

It was a party of five when Jake went again to Myrtle Avenue for the magnificent free-love feast that Susy had prepared. It was Susy's free Sunday. Miss Curdy and Strawberry Lips were also celebrating. Susy had concocted a pitcherful of knock-out gin cocktails. And such food! Susy could cook. Perhaps it was her splendid style that made her sink all her wages in gin and sweet-men. For she belonged to the ancient aristocracy of black cooks, and knew that she was always sure of a good place, so long as the palates of rich Southerners retained their discriminating taste.

Cream tomato soup. Ragout of chicken giblets. Southern fried chicken. Candied sweet potatoes. Stewed corn. Rum-flavored fruit salad waiting in the ice-box. . . . The stars rolling in Susy's shining face showed how pleased she was with her art.

She may be fat and ugly as a turkey, thought Jake, but her eats am sure beautiful.

"Heah! Pass me you' plate," Susy gave Jake a leg. Zeddy held out his plate again and got a wing. Strawberry Lips received a bit of breast. . . .

"No more chicken for me, Susy," Miss Curdy mumbled, "but I *will* have another helping of that there stewed corn. I don't know what ingredients yo-all puts in it, but, Lawdy! I never tasted anything near so good."

Susy beamed and dipped up three spoonfuls of corn. "Plenty, thank you," Miss Curdy stopped her from filling up her saucer. . . . Susy drank off a tumbler of cocktail at a draught, and wiped her lips with the white serviette that was stuck into the low neck of her vermillion crepe-de-chine blouse. . . .

When Jake was ready to leave, Zeddy announced that he would take a little jaunt with him to Harlem.

"You ain'ta gwine to do no sich thing as that," Susy said.

"Yes I is," responded Zeddy. "Wha' there is to stop me?"

"I is," said Susy.

"And what foh?"

" 'Causen I don't wanchu to go to Harlem. What makes you niggers love Harlem so much? Because it's a bloody ungodly place where niggers nevah go to bed. All night running around speakeasies and cabarets, where bad, hell-bent nigger womens am giving up themselves to open sin."

Susy stood broad and aggressive against the window overlooking Myrtle Avenue.

"Harlem is all right," said Zeddy. "I ain't knocking round no cabarets and speakeasies. Ahm just gwine ovah wif Jake to see somathem boys."

"Can that boy business!" cried Susy. "I've had anuff hell scrapping wif the women ovah mah mens. I ain't agwine to have no Harlem boys seducin' mah man away fwom me. The boy business is a fine excuse indeedy foh sich womens as ain't wise. I always heah the boss say to the missus, 'I gwine out foh a little time wif the boys, dearie,' when him wants an excuse foh a night off. I ain't born yestiday, honey. If you wants the boys foh a li'l' game o' poky, you bring 'em ovah heah. I ain't got the teeeniest bit of objection, and Ise got plenty o' good Gordon Dry foh eve'body."

"Ise got to go scares them up to bring them heah," said Zeddy.

"But not tonight or no night," declared Susy. "You kain do that in the daytime, foh you ain't got nothing to do."

Zeddy moved toward the mantelpiece to get his cap, but Susy blocked his way and held the cap behind her.

Zeddy looked savagely in her eyes and growled: "Come outa that, sistah, and gimme mah cap. It ain't no use stahting trouble."

Susy looked steadily in his eyes and chucked the cap at him. "Theah's you cap, but ef you stahts leaving me nights you . . ."

"What will you do?" asked Zeddy.

"I'll put you' block in the street."

Zeddy's countenance fell flat from its high aggressiveness.

"Well s'long, eve'body," said Jake.

Zeddy put on his cap and rocked out of the apartment after him. In the street he asked Jake, "Think I ought to take a crack at Harlem with you tonight, boh?"

"Not ef you loves you' new home, buddy," Jake replied.

"Bull! That plug-ugly black women is ornery like hell. I ain't gwineta let her bridle and ride me. . . . You ain't in no pickle like that with Rose, is you?"

"Lawd, no! I do as I wanta. But I'm one independent cuss, buddy. We ain't sitchuate the same. I works."

"Black womens when theyse ugly am all sistahs of Satan," declared Zeddy.

"It ain't the black ones only," said Jake.

"I wish I could hit things off like you, boh," said Zeddy. . . . "Well, I'll see you all some night at Billy Biasse's joint. . . . S'long. Don't pick up no bad change."

From that evening Zeddy began to discover that it wasn't all fine and lovely to live sweet. Formerly he had always been envious when any of his pals pointed out an extravagantly-dressed dark dandy and remarked, "He was living sweet." There was something so romantic about the sweet life. To be the adored of a Negro lady of means, or of a pseudo grass-widow whose husband worked on the railroad, or of a hard-working laundress or cook. It was much more respectable and enviable to be sweet—to belong to the exotic aristocracy of sweetmen than to be just a common tout.

But there were strings to Susy's largesse. The enjoyment of Harlem's low night life was prohibited to Zeddy. Susy was jealous of him in the proprietary sense. She believed in free love all right, but not for the man she possessed and supported. She warned him against the ornery hussies of her race.

"Nigger hussies nevah wanta git next to a man 'cep'n' when he's a-looking good to another woman," Susy declared. "I done gived you fair warning to jest keep away from the buffet-flat widdahs and thim Harlem street floaters; foh ef I ketch you making a fool woman of me, I'll throw you' pants in the street."

"Hi, but youse talking sistah. Why don't you wait till you see something before you staht in chewing the rag?"

"I done give you the straight stuff in time so you kain watch you'self when I kain't watch you. I ain't bohding and lodging no black man foh'm to be any other nigger woman's daddy."

So, in a few pointed phrases, Susy let Zeddy understand precisely what she would stand for. Zeddy was well kept like a prince of his type. He could not complain about food . . . and bed. Susy was splendid in her matriarchal way, rolling her eyes with love or disapproval at him, according to the exigencies of the moment.

The Saturday-night gin parties went on as usual. The brown and high-brown boys came and swilled. Miss Curdy was a constant visitor, frequently toting Strawberry Lips along. About her general way of handling things Susy brooked no criticism from Zeddy. She had bargained with him in the interest of necessity and of rivalry and she paid and paid fully, but grimly. She was proud to have a man to boss about in an intimate, casual way.

"Git out another bottle of gin, Zeddy. . . ."

"Bring along that packet o' saltines. . . ."

"Put on that theah 'Tickling Blues' that we's all just crazy about."

To have an aggressive type like Zeddy at her beck and call considerably increased Susy's prestige and clucking pride. She noticed, with carefully-concealed delight, that the interest of the yellow gin-swillers was piqued. She became flirtatious and coy by turns. And she was rewarded by fresh attentions. Even Miss Curdy was now meeting with new adventures, and she was prompted to expatiate upon men and love to Susy.

"Men's got a whole lot of women in their nature, I tell you. Just as women never really see a man until he's looking good to another woman and the hussies want to steal him, it's the same thing with men, mah dear. So soon as a woman is all sugar and candy for another man, you find a lot of them heartbreakers all trying to get next to her. Like a set of strutting game cocks all priming themselves to crow over a li'l' piece o' nothing."

"That's the gospel trute indeed," agreed Susy. "I done have a mess of knowledge 'bout men tucked away heah." Susy tapped her head of tight-rolled kinks knotted with scraps of ribbon of different colors. "I pays foh what I know and I've nevah been sorry, either. Yes, mam, I done larned about mah own self fust. Had no allusions about mahself. I knowed that I was black and ugly and no-class and unejucated. And I knowed that I was bohn foh love. . . . Mah mammy did useter warn me about love. All what the white folks call white slavery these-adays. I dunno ef theah's another name foh the nigger-an'-white side ovit down home in Dixie. Well, I soon found out it wasn't womens alone in the business, sposing thimselves like vigitables foh sale in the market. No, mam! I done soon l'arned that the mens was most buyable thimselves. Mah heart-breaking high-yaller done left me sence—how miny wintahs I been counting this heah Nothan snow? All thim and some moh—dawggone ef I remimber. But evah since I been paying sistah, paying good and hard foh mah loving feelings."

"Life ain't no country picnic with sweet flute and fiddle," Miss Curdy sighed.

"Indeed not," Susy was emphatic. "It ain't got nothing to do with the rubbish we l'arn at Sunday school and the sweet snooziness I used to lap up in thim blue-cover story books. My God! the things I've seen! Working with white folks, so dickty and high-and-mighty, you think theyse nevah oncet naked and thim feets nevah touch ground. Yet all the silks and furs and shining diamonds can't hide the misery a them lives. . . . Servants and heartbreakers from outside stealing the husband's stuff. And all the men them that can't find no sweet-loving life at home. Lavinia, I done seen life."

"Me, too, I have seen the real life, mixing as I used to in *real* society," said Miss Curdy.

"I know society, too, honey, even though I only knows it watching from the servant window. And I know it ain't no different from *us*. It's the same life even ef they drink champagne and we drink gin."

"You said it and said it right," responded Miss Curdy.

Zeddy discovered that in his own circles in Harlem he had become something of a joke. It was known that he was living sweet. But his buddies talked about his lady riding him with a cruel bit.

"He was kept, all right," they said, "kept under 'Gin-head' Susy's skirt."

He had had to fight a fellow in Dixie Red's pool-room, for calling him a "skirt-man."

He was even teased by Billy Biasse or Billy, the Wolf, as he was nicknamed. Billy boasted frankly that he had no time for women. Black women, or the whole diversified world of the sex were all the same to him.

"So Harlem, after the sun done set, has no fun at all foh you, eh, boh?" Billy asked Zeddy.

Zeddy growled something indistinct.

"Sweet with the bit in you' mouf. Black woman riding her nigger. Great life, boh, ef you don't weaken."

"Bull! Wha's the matter with you niggers, anyhow?" Zeddy said in a sort of general way. "Ain't it better than being a wolf?"

"Ise a wolf, all right, but I ain't a lone one," Billy grinned. "I guess Ise the happiest, well-feddest wolf in Harlem. Oh, boy!"

Zeddy spent that evening in Harlem drinking with Jake and two more longshoremen at Uncle Doc's saloon. Late in the night they went to the Congo. Zeddy returned to Myrtle Avenue, an hour before it was time for Susy to rise, fully ginned up.

To Susy's "Whar you been?" he answered, "Shut up or I'll choke you," staggered, swayed, and swept from the dresser a vase of chrysanthemums that broke on the floor.

"Goddam fool flowers," he growled. "Why in hell didn't you put them out of the way, hey, you Suze?"

"Oh, keep quiet and come along to bed," said Susy.

A week later he repeated the performance, coming home with alarming symptoms of gin hiccough. Susy said nothing. After that Zeddy began to prance, as much as a short, heavy-made human could, with the bit out of his mouth. . . .

One Saturday night Susy's gin party was a sad failure. Nobody came beside Miss Curdy with Strawberry Lips. (Zeddy had left for Harlem in the afternoon.) They drank to themselves and played coon-can. Near midnight, when Miss Curdy was going, she said offhandedly, "I wouldn't mind sampling one of those Harlem cabarets now." Susy at once seized upon the idea.

"Sure. Let's go to Harlem for a change."

They caught the subway train for Harlem. Arrived there they gravitated to the Congo.

Before Susy left Myrtle Avenue, Zeddy was already at the Congo with a sweet, timid, satin-faced brown just from down home, that he had found at Aunt Hattie's and induced to go with him to the cabaret. Jake sat at Zeddy's table. Zeddy was determined to go the limit of independence, to show the boys that he was a cocky sweetman and no skirt-man. Plenty of money. He was treating. He wore an elegant nigger-brown sports suit and patent-leather shoes with cream-light spats such as all the sweet swells love to strut in. If Zeddy had only been taller, trimmer, and well-arched he would have been one of Harlem's dandiest sports.

His new-found brown had a glass of Virginia Dare before her; he was drinking gin. Jake, Scotch-and-soda; and Rose, who sat with them when she was not entertaining, had ordered White Rock. The night before, or rather the early morning after her job was done, she had gone on a champagne party and now she was sobering up.

Billy Biasse was there at a neighboring table with a long-shoreman and a straw-colored boy who was a striking advertisement of the Ambrozine Palace of Beauty. The boy was made up with high-brown powder, his eyebrows were elongated and blackened up, his lips streaked with the dark rouge so popular in Harlem, and his carefully-straightened hair lay plastered and glossy under Madame Walker's absinthe-colored salve "for milady of fashion and color."

"Who's the doll baby at the Wolf's table?" Zeddy asked.

"Tha's mah dancing pardner," Rose answered.

"Another entertainer? The Congo is gwine along fast enough."

"You bet you," said Jake. "And the ofays will soon be nosing it out. Then we'll have to take a back seat."

"Who's the Wolf?" Timidly Zeddy's girl asked.

Zeddy pointed out Billy.

"But why Wolf?"

"Khhhhhhh—Khhhhhhhh . . ." Zeddy laughed. " 'Causen he eats his own kind."

It was time for Rose to dance. Her partner had preceded her to the open space and was standing, arm akimbo against the piano, talking to the pianist. The pianist was a slight-built, long-headed fellow. His face shone like anthracite, his eyes were arresting, intense, deep-yellow slits. He seemed in a continual state of swaying excitement, whether or not he was playing.

They were ready, Rose and the dancer-boy. The pianist began, his eyes toward the ceiling in a sort of savage ecstatic dream. Fiddler, saxophonist, drummer, and cymbalist seemed to catch their inspiration from him. . . .

> When Luty dances, everything
>> Is dancing in the cabaret.
> The second fiddle asks the first:
>> What makes you sound that funny way?
> The drum talks in so sweet a voice,
>> The cymbal answers in surprise,
> The lights put on a brighter glow
>> To match the shine of Luty's eyes.
>
> For he's a foot-manipulating fool
>> When he hears that crazy moan
>> Come rolling, rolling outa that saxophone. . . .
> Watch that strut; there's no keeping him cool
>> When he's a-rearing with that saxophone. . . .
>> Oh, the tearing, tantalizing tone!
>> Of that moaning saxophone. . . .
>>> That saxophone. . . .
>>> That saxophone. . . .

They danced, Rose and the boy. Oh, they danced! An exercise of rhythmical exactness for two. There was no motion she made that he did not imitate. They reared and pranced together, smacking palm against palm, working knee between knee, grinning with real joy. They shimmied, breast to breast, bent themselves far back and shimmied again. Lifting high her short skirt and showing her green bloomers, Rose kicked. And in his tight nigger-brown suit, the boy kicked even with her. They were right there together, neither going beyond the other. . . .

And the pianist! At intervals his yellow eyes, almost bloodshot, swept the cabaret with a triumphant glow, gave the dancers a caressing look, and returned to the ceiling. Lean, smart fingers beating barbaric beauty out of a white frame. Brown bodies, caught up in the wild rhythm, wiggling and swaying in their seats.

For he's a foot-manipulating fool
When he hears that crazy moan
Come rolling, rolling outa that saxophone. . . .
  That saxophone. . . .
  That saxophone. . . .

Rose was sipping her White Rock. Her partner, at Billy's table, sucked his iced creme-de-menthe through a straw. The high wave of joyful excitement had subsided and the customers sat casually drinking and gossiping as if they had not been soaring a minute before in a realm of pure joy.

From his place, giving a good view of the staircase, Zeddy saw two apparently familiar long legs swinging down the steps. Sure enough, he knew those big, thick-soled red boots.

"Them feets look jest laka Strawberry Lips' own," he said to Jake. Jake looked and saw first Strawberry Lips enter the cabaret, with Susy behind balancing upon her French heels, and Miss Curdy. Susy was gorgeous in a fur coat of rich shiny black, like her complexion. Opened, it showed a cérise blouse and a yellow-and-mauve check skirt. Her head of thoroughly-straightened hair flaunted a green hat with a decoration of red ostrich plumes.

"Great balls of fire! Here's you doom, buddy," said Jake.

"Doom, mah granny," retorted Zeddy. "Ef that theah black ole cow come fooling near me tonight, I'll show her who's wearing the pants."

Susy did not see Zeddy until her party was seated. It was Miss Curdy who saw him first. She dug into Susy's side with her elbow and cried:

"For the love of Gawd, looka there!"

Susy's star eyes followed Miss Curdy's. She glared at Zeddy and fixed her eyes on the girl with him for a moment. Then she looked away and grunted: "He thinks he's acting smart, eh? Him and I will wrastle that out to a salution, but I ain't agwine to raise no stink in heah."

"He's got some more nerve pulling off that low-down stuff, and on your money, too," said Miss Curdy.

"Who that?" asked Strawberry Lips.

"Ain't you seen your best friends over there?" retorted Miss Curdy.

Strawberry Lips waved at Zeddy and Jake, but they were deliberately keeping their eyes away from Susy's table. He got up to go to them.

"Where you going?" Miss Curdy asked.

"To chin wif——"

A yell startled the cabaret. A girl had slapped another's face and replied to her victim's cry of pain with, "If you no like it you can lump it!"

"You low an' dutty bobbin-bitch!"

"Bitch is bobbin in you' sistah's coffin."

They were West Indian girls.

"I'll mek mah breddah beat you' bottom foh you."

"Gash it and stop you' jawing."

They were interrupted by another West Indian girl, who wore a pink-flowered muslin frock and a wide jippi-jappa hat from which charmingly hung two long ends of broad pea-green ribbon.

"It's a shame. Can't you act like decent English people?" she said. Gently she began pushing away the assaulted girl, who burst into tears.

"She come boxing me up ovah a dutty-black 'Merican coon."

"Mek a quick move or I'll box you bumbole ovah de moon," her assailant cried after her. . . .

"The monkey-chasers am scrapping," Zeddy commented.

"In a language all their own," said Jake.

"They are wild womens, buddy, and it's a wild language they're using, too," remarked a young West Indian behind Jake.

"Hmm! but theyse got the excitement fever," a lemon-colored girl at a near table made her contribution and rocked and twisted herself coquettishly at Jake. . . .

Susy had already reached the pavement with Miss Curdy and Strawberry Lips. Susy breathed heavily.

"Lesh git furthest away from this low-down vice hole," she said. "Leave that plug-ugly nigger theah. I ain't got no more use foh him nohow."

"I never did have any time for Harlem," said Miss Curdy. "When I was high up in society all respectable colored people lived in Washington. There was no Harlem full a niggers then. I declare——"

"I should think the nigger heaven of a theater downtown is better than anything in this heah Harlem," said Susy. "When we feels like going out, it's better we enjoy ourse'f in the li'l' corner the white folks 'low us, and then shuffle along back home. It's good and quiet ovah in Brooklyn."

"And we can have all the inside fun we need," said Miss Curdy.

"Brooklyn ain't no better than Harlem," said Strawberry Lips, running the words rolling off his tongue. "Theah's as much shooting-up and cut-up in Prince Street and——"

"There ain't no compahrison atall," stoutly maintained Susy. "This here Harlem is a stinking sink of iniquity. Nigger hell! That's what it is. Looka that theah ugly black nigger loving up a scrimpy brown gal right befoh mah eyes. Jest daring me to turn raw and loose lak them monkey-chasing womens thisanight. But that I wouldn't do. I ain't a woman abandoned to sich publicity stunts. Not even though mah craw was full to bursting. Lemme see'm tonight. . . . Yessam, this heah Harlem is sure nigger hell. Take me way away from it."

When Zeddy at last said good night to his new-found brown, he went straight to an all-night barrel-house and bought a half a pint of whisky. He guzzled the liquor and smashed the flask on the pavement. Drew up his pants, tightened his belt and growled, "Now I'm ready for Susy."

He caught the subway train for Brooklyn. Only local trains were running and it was quite an hour and a half before he got home. He staggered down Myrtle Avenue well primed with the powerful stimulation of gin-and-whisky.

At the door of Susy's apartment he was met by his suitcase. He recoiled as from a blow struck at his face. Immediately he became sober. His eyes caught a little white tag attached to the handle. Examining it by the faint gaslight he read, in Susy's handwriting: "Kip owt that meen you."

Susy had put all Zeddy's belongings into the suitcase, keeping back what she had given him: two fancy-colored silk shirts, silk handkerchiefs, a mauve dressing-gown, and a box of silk socks.

"What he's got on that black back of his'n he can have," she had said while throwing the things in the bag.

Zeddy beat on the door with his fists.

"Wha moh you want?" Susy's voice bawled from within. "Ain'tchu got all you stuff theah? Gwan back where youse coming from."

"Lemme in and quit you joking," cried Zeddy.

"You ugly flat-footed zigaboo," shouted Susy, "may I ketch the 'lectric chair without conversion ef I 'low you dirty black pusson in mah place again. And you better git quick foh I staht mah dawg bawking at you."

Zeddy picked up his suitcase. "Come on, Mistah Bag. Le's tail along back to Harlem. Leave black woman 'lone wif her gin and ugly mug. Black woman is hard luck."

VIII
The Raid of the Baltimore

THE blazing lights of the Baltimore were put out and the entrance was padlocked. Fifth Avenue and Lenox talked about nothing else. Buddy meeting buddy and chippie greeting chippie, asked: "Did you hear the news?" . . . "Well, what do you know about that?"

Yet nothing sensational had happened in the Baltimore. The police had not, on a certain night, swept into it and closed it up because of indecent doings. No. It was an indirect raid. Oh, and that made the gossip toothier! For the Baltimore was not just an ordinary cabaret. It had mortgages and policies in the best of the speakeasy places of the Belt. And the mass of Harlem held the Baltimore in high respect because (it was rumored and believed) it was protected by Tammany Hall.

Jake, since he had given up hoping about his lost brown, had stopped haunting the Baltimore, yet he had happened to be very much in on the affair that cost the Baltimore its license. Jake's living with Rose had, in spite of himself, projected him into a more elegant atmosphere of worldliness. Through Rose and her associates he had gained access to buffet flats and private rendezvous apartments that were called "nifty."

And Jake was a high favorite wherever he went. There was something so naturally beautiful about his presence that everybody liked and desired him. Buddies, on the slightest provocation, were ready to fight for him, and the girls liked to make an argument around him.

Jake had gained admission to Madame Adeline Suarez's buffet flat, which was indeed a great feat. He was the first longshoreman, colored or white, to tread that magnificent red carpet. Madame Suarez catered to sporty colored persons of consequence only and certain groups of downtown whites that used to frequent Harlem in the good old pre-prohibition days.

"Ain't got no time for cheap- no-'count niggers," Madame Suarez often said. "Gimme their room to their company any time, even if they've got money to spend." Madame Suarez

came from Florida and she claimed Cuban descent through
her father. By her claim to that exotic blood she moved like a
queen among the blue-veins of the colored sporting world.

But Jake's rough charm could conquer anything.

"Ofay's mixing in!" he exclaimed to himself the first night
he penetrated into Madame Suarez's. "But ofay or ofay not,
this here is the real stuff," he reflected. And so many nights he
absented himself from the Congo (he had no interest in Rose's
art of flirting money out of hypnotized newcomers) to luxuri-
ate with charmingly painted pansies among the colored cushions and under the soft, shaded lights of Madame Suarez's
speakeasy. It was a new world for Jake and he took it easily.
That was his natural way, wherever he went, whatever new
people he met. It had helped him over many a bad crossing at
Brest at Havre and in London. . . . Take it easy . . . take
life easy. Sometimes he was disgusted with life, but he was
never frightened of it.

Jake had never seen colored women so carefully elegant as
these rich-browns and yellow-creams at Madame Suarez's.
They were fascinating in soft bright draperies and pretty pumps
and they drank liquor with a fetching graceful abandon. Gin
and whisky seemed to lose their barbaric punch in that atmosphere and take on a romantic color. The women's coiffure was
arranged in different striking styles and their arms and necks
and breasts tinted to emphasize the peculiar richness of each
skin. One girl, who was the favorite of Madame Suarez, and
the darkest in the group, looked like a breathing statue of burnished bronze. With their arresting poses and gestures, their
deep shining painted eyes, they resembled the wonderfully
beautiful pictures of women of ancient Egypt.

Here Jake brushed against big men of the colored sporting
world and their white friends. That strange un-American world
where colored meets and mingles freely and naturally with
white in amusement basements, buffet flats, poker establish-
ments. Sometimes there were two or three white women, who
attracted attention because they were white and strange to
Harlem, but they appeared like faded carnations among those
burning orchids of a tropical race.

One night Jake noticed three young white men, clean-
shaven, flashily-dressed, who paid for champagne for everybody

in the flat. They were introduced by a perfectly groomed dark-brown man, a close friend of the boss of the Baltimore. Money seemed worthless to them except as a means of getting fun out of it. Madame Suarez made special efforts to please them. Showed them all of the buffet flat, even her own bedroom. One of them, very freckled and red-haired, sat down to the piano and jazzed out popular songs. The trio radiated friendliness all around them. Danced with the colored beauties and made lively conversation with the men. They were gay and recklessly spendthrift. . . .

They returned on a Saturday night, between midnight and morning, when the atmosphere of Madame Suarez's was fairly bacchic and jazz music was snake-wriggling in and out and around everything and forcing everybody into amatory states and attitudes. The three young white men had two others with them. At the piano a girl curiously made up in mauve was rendering the greatest ragtime song of the day. Broadway was wild about it and Harlem was crazy. All America jazzed to it, and it was already world-famous. Already being jazzed perhaps in Paris and Cairo, Shanghai, Honolulu, and Java. It was a song about cocktails and cherries. Like this in some ways:

Take a juicy cocktail cherry,
    Take a dainty little bite,
And we'll all be very merry
    On a cherry drunk tonight.

We'll all be merry when you have a cherry,
    And we'll twine and twine like a fruitful vine,
Grape vine, red wine, babe mine, bite a berry,
    You taste a cherry and twine, rose vine, sweet wine.
        Cherry-ee-ee-ee-ee, cherry-ee-ee-ee-ee-ee, ee-ee-ee
        Cherry-ee-ee-ee-ee, cherry-ee-ee-ee-ee-ee, ee-ee-ee
        Grape vine, rose vine, sweet wine. . . .

Love is like a cocktail cherry,
    Just a fruity little bit,
And you've never yet been merry,
    If you've not been drunk on it.

We'll all be merry when you have. . . .

The women, carried away by the sheer rhythm of delight, had risen above their commercial instincts (a common trait of Negroes in emotional states) and abandoned themselves to pure voluptuous jazzing. They were gorgeous animals swaying there through the dance, punctuating it with marks of warm physical excitement. The atmosphere was charged with intensity and over-charged with currents of personal reaction. . . .

Then the five young white men unmasked as the Vice Squad and killed the thing.

Dicks! They had wooed and lured and solicited for their trade. For two weeks they had spilled money like water at the Baltimore. Sometimes they were accompanied by white girls who swilled enormous quantities of champagne and outshrieked the little ginned-up Negresses and mulattresses of the cabaret. They had posed as good fellows, regular guys, looking for a good time only in the Black Belt. They were wearied of the pleasures of the big white world, wanted something new—the primitive joy of Harlem.

So at last, with their spendthrift and charming ways, they had convinced the wary boss of the Baltimore that they were fine fellows. The boss was a fine fellow himself, who loved life and various forms of fun and had no morals about them. And so one night when the trio had left their hired white ladies behind, he was persuaded to give his youthful white guests an introduction to Madame Adeline Suarez's buffet flat. . . .

The uniformed police were summoned. Madame Suarez and her clients were ordered to get ready to go down to the Night Court. The women asked permission to veil themselves. Many windows were raked up in the block and heads craned forth to watch the prisoners bundled into waiting taxicabs. The women were afraid. Some of them were false grass-widows whose husbands were working somewhere. Some of them were church members. Perhaps one could claim a place in local society!

They were all fined. But Madame Suarez, besides being fined, was sent to Blackwell's Island for six months.

To the two white girls that were also taken in the raid the judge remarked that it was a pity he had no power to order them whipped. For whipping was the only punishment he considered suitable for white women who dishonored their race by associating with colored persons.

The high point of the case was the indictment of the boss of the Baltimore as accessory to the speakeasy crime. The boss was not convicted, but the Baltimore was ordered to be padlocked. That decision was appealed. But the cabaret remained padlocked. A black member of Tammany had no chances against the Moral Arm of the city.

The Belt's cabaret sets licked their lips over the sensation for weeks. For a long time Negro proprietors would not admit white customers into their cabarets and near-white members of the black race, whose features were unfamiliar in Harlem, had a difficult time proving their identity.

IX
Jake Makes a Move

COMING home from work one afternoon, Jake remarked a taxicab just driving away from his house. He was quite a block off, but he thought it was his number. When he entered Rose's room he immediately detected an unfamiliar smell. He had an uncanny sharp nose for strange smells. Rose always had visitors, of course. Girls, and fellows, too, of her circle. But Jake had a feeling that his nose had scented something foreign to Harlem. The room was close with tobacco smoke; there were many Melachrino butts in a tray, and a half-used box of the same cigarettes on a little table drawn up against the scarlet-covered couch. Also, there was a half-filled bottle of Jake's Scotch whisky on the table and glasses for two. Rose was standing before the dresser, arranging her hair.

"Been having company?" Jake asked, carelessly.

"Yep. It was only Gertie Blake."

Jake knew that Rose was lying. Her visitor had not been Gertie Blake. It had been a man, a strange man, doubtless a white man. Yet he hadn't the slightest feeling of jealousy or anger, whatever the visitor was. Rose had her friends of both sexes and was quite free in her ways. At the Congo she sat and drank and flirted with many fellows. That was a part of her business. She got more tips that way, and the extra personal bargains that gave her the means to maintain her style of living. All her lovers had always accepted her living entirely free. For that made it possible for her to keep them living carefree and sweet.

Rose was disappointed in Jake. She had wanted him to live in the usual sweet way, to be brutal and beat her up a little, and take away her money from her. Once she had a rough leather-brown man who used to beat her up regularly. Sometimes she was beaten so badly she had to stay indoors for days, and to her visiting girl pals she exhibited her bruises and blackened eyes with pride.

As Jake was not brutally domineering, she cooled off from

him perceptibly. But she could not make him change. She confided to her friends that he was "good loving but" (making use
of a contraction that common people employ) "a big Ah-Ah
all the same." She felt no thrill about the business when her
lover was not interested in her earnings.

Jake did not care. He did not love her, had never felt any
deep desire for her. He had gone to live with her simply because she had asked him when he was in a fever mood for a
steady mate. There was nothing about Rose that touched and
roused him as his vivid recollection of his charming little
brown-skin of the Baltimore. Rose's room to him was like any
ordinary lodging in Harlem. While the room of his little lost
brown lived in his mind a highly magnified affair: a bed of
gold, fresh, white linen, a magic carpet, all bathed in the rarest
perfume. . . . Rose's perfume made his nose itch. It was
rank.

He came home another afternoon and found her with a bright
batik kimono carelessly wrapped around her and stretched
full-length on the couch. There were Melachrino stubs lying
about and his bottle of Scotch was on the mantelpiece.
Evidently the strange visitor of the week before had been there
again.

"Hello!" She yawned and flicked off her cigarette ash and
continued smoking. A chic veneer over a hard, restless, insensitive body. Fascinating, nevertheless. . . . For the moment,
just as she was, she was desirable and provoked responses in
him. He shuffled up to the couch and caressed her.

"Leave me alone, I'm tired," she snarled.

The rebuff hurt Jake. "You slut!" he cried. He went over to
the mantelpiece and added, "Youse just everybody's teaser."

"You got a nearve talking to me that way," said Rose. "Since
when you staht riding the high horse?"

"It don't take no nearve foh me to tell you what you is. Fact
is I'm right now sure tiahd to death of living with you."

"You poor black stiff!" Rose cried. And she leaped over at
Jake and scratched at his face.

Jake gave her two savage slaps full in her face and she
dropped moaning at his feet.

"There! You done begged foh it," he said. He stepped over
her and went out.

Walking down the street, he looked at his palms. "Ahm shame o' you, hands," he murmured. "Mah mother useter tell me, 'Nevah hit no woman,' but that hussy jest made me do it . . . jest *made* me. . . . Well, I'd better pull outa that there mud-hole. . . . It wasn't what I come back to Gawd's own country foh. No, sirree! You bet it wasn't. . . ."

When he returned to the house he heard laughter in the room. Gertie Blake was there and Rose was telling a happy tale. He stood by the closed door and listened for a while.

"Have another drink, Gertie. Don't ever get a wee bit delicate when youse with me. . . . My, mah dear, but he did slap the daylights outa me. When I comed to I wanted to kiss his feet, but he was gone."

"Rose! You're the limit. But didn't it hurt awful?"

"Didn't hurt enough. Honey, it's the first time I ever felt his real strength. A hefty-looking one like him, always acting so nice and proper. I almost thought he was getting sissy. But he's a *ma-an* all right. . . ."

A nasty smile stole into Jake's features. He could not face those women. He left the house again. He strolled down to Dixie Red's pool-room and played awhile. From there he went with Zeddy to Uncle Doc's saloon.

He went home again and found Rose stunning in a new cloth-of-gold frock shining with brilliants. She was refixing a large artificial yellow rose to the side of a pearl-beaded green turban. Jake, without saying a word, went to the closet and took down his suitcase. Then he began tossing shirts, underwear, collars, and ties on to the couch.

"What the devil you're doing?" Rose wheeled round and stared at him in amazement, both hands gripping the dresser behind her.

"Kain't you see?" Jake replied.

She moved down on him like a panther, swinging her hips in a wonderful, rhythmical motion. She sprang upon his neck and brought him down.

"Oh, honey, you ain't mad at me 'counta the little fuss tonight?"

"I don't like hitting no womens," returned Jake's hard-breathing muffled voice.

"Daddy! I love you the more for that."

"You'll spile you' new clothes," Jake said, desperately.

"Hell with them! I love mah daddy moh'n anything. And mah daddy loves me, don't he? Daddy!"

Rose switched on the light and looked at her watch.

"My stars, daddy! We been honey-dreaming some! I am two hours late."

She jumped up and jig-stepped. "I should worry if the Congo . . . I should worry mumbo-jumbo."

She smoothed out her frock, arranged her hair, and put the turban on. "Come along to the Congo a little later," she said to Jake. "Let's celebrate on champagne."

The door closed on him. . . .

"O Lawdy!" he yawned, stretched himself, and got up. He took the rest of his clothes out of the closet, picked up the crumpled things from the couch, packed, and walked out with his suitcase.

SECOND PART

X
The Railroad

O VER the heart of the vast gray Pennsylvania country the huge black animal snorted and roared, with sounding rods and couplings, pulling a long chain of dull-brown boxes packed with people and things, trailing on the blue-cold air its white masses of breath.

Hell was playing in the hot square hole of a pantry and the coffin-shaped kitchen of the dining-car. The short, stout, hard-and-horny chef was terrible as a rhinoceros. Against the second, third, and fourth cooks he bellied his way up to the little serving door and glared at the waiters. His tough, aproned front was a challenge to them. In his oily, shining face his big white eyes danced with meanness. All the waiters had squeezed into the pantry at once, excitedly snatching, dropping and breaking things.

"Hey, you there! You mule!"* The chef shouted at the fourth waiter. "Who told you to snitch that theah lamb chops outa the hole?"

"I done think they was the one I ordered——"

"Done think some hell, you down-home black fool. Ain't no thinking to be done on here——"

"Chef, ain't them chops ready yet?" a waiter asked.

"Don't rush me, nigger," the chef bellowed back. "Wha' yu'all trying to do? Run me up a tree? Kain't run this here chef up no tree. Jump off ef you kain't ride him." His eyes gleamed with grim humor. "Jump off or lay down. This heah white man's train service ain't no nigger picnic."

The second cook passed up a platter of chops. The chef rushed it through the hole and licked his fingers.

"There you is, yaller. Take it away. Why ain't you gone yet? Show me some service, yaller, show me some service." He

*The fourth waiter on the railroad is nick-named "mule" because he works under the orders of the pantry-man.

rocked his thick, tough body sideways in a sort of dance, licked the sweat from his brow with his forefinger and grunted with aggressive self-satisfaction. Then he bellied his way back to the range and sent the third cook up to the serving window.

"Tha's the stuff to hand them niggers," he told the third cook. "Keep 'em up a tree all the time, but don't let 'em get you up there."

Jake, for he was the third cook, took his place by the window and handed out the orders. It was his first job on the railroad, but from the first day he managed his part perfectly. He rubbed smoothly along with the waiters by remaining himself and not trying to imitate the chef nor taking his malicious advice.

Jake had taken the job on the railroad just to break the hold that Harlem had upon him. When he quitted Rose he felt that he ought to get right out of the atmosphere of Harlem. If I don't git away from it for a while, it'll sure git me, he mused. But not ship-and-port-town life again. I done had enough a that here and ovah there. . . . So he had picked the railroad. One or two nights a week in Harlem. And all the days on the road. He would go on like that until he grew tired of that rhythm. . . .

The rush was over. Everything was quiet. The corridors of the dining-car were emptied of their jam of hungry, impatient guests. The "mule" had scrubbed the slats of the pantry and set them up to dry. The other waiters had put away silver and glasses and soiled linen. The steward at his end of the car was going over the checks. Even the kitchen work was finished and the four cooks had left their coffin for the good air of the dining-room. They sat apart from the dining-room boys. The two grades, cooks and waiters, never chummed together, except for gambling. Some of the waiters were very haughty. There were certain light-skinned ones who went walking with pals of their complexion only in the stopover cities. Others, among the older men, were always dignified. They were fathers of families, their wives moved in some sphere of Harlem society, and their movements were sometimes chronicled in the local Negro newspapers.

Sitting at one of the large tables, four of the waiters were playing poker. Jake wanted to join them, but he had no money. One waiter sat alone at a small table. He was reading. He was of average size, slim, a smooth pure ebony with straight features and a suggestion of whiskers. Jake shuffled up to him and asked him for the loan of two dollars. He got it and went to play. . . .

Jake finished playing with five dollars. He repaid the waiter and said: "Youse a good sport. I'll always look out for you in that theah hole."

The waiter smiled. He was very friendly. Jake half-sprawled over the table. "Wha's this here stuff you reading? Looks lak Greek to me." He spelled the title, "S-A-P-H-O, Sapho."

"What's it all about?" Jake demanded, flattening down the book on the table with his friendly paw. The waiter was reading the scene between Fanny and Jean when the lover discovers the letters of his mistress's former woman friend and exclaims: "Ah *Oui . . . Sapho . . . toute la lyre. . . .*"

"It's a story," he told Jake, "by a French writer named Alphonse Daudet. It's about a sporting woman who was beautiful like a rose and had the soul of a wandering cat. Her lovers called her Sapho. I like the story, but I hate the use of Sapho for its title."

"Why does you?" Jake asked.

"Because Sappho was a real person. A wonderful woman, a great Greek poet——"

"So theah *is* some Greek in the book!" said Jake.

The waiter smiled. "In a sense, yes."

And he told Jake the story of Sappho, of her poetry, of her loves and her passion for the beautiful boy, Phaon. And of her leaping into the sea from the Leucadian cliff because of her love for him.

"Her story gave two lovely words to modern language," said the waiter.

"Which one them?" asked Jake.

"Sapphic and Lesbian . . . beautiful words."

"What is that there Leshbian?"

". . . Lovely word, eh?"

"Tha's what we calls bulldyker in Harlem," drawled Jake. "Them's all ugly womens."

"Not *all.* And that's a damned ugly name," the waiter said.

"Harlem is too savage about some things. *Bulldyker*," the waiter stressed with a sneer.

Jake grinned. "But tha's what they is, ain't it?"

He began humming:

"And there is two things in Harlem I don't understan'
It is a bulldyking woman and a faggoty man. . . ."

Charmingly, like a child that does not know its letters, Jake turned the pages of the novel. . . .

"Bumbole! This heah language is most different from how they talk it."

"Bumbole" was now a popular expletive for Jake, replacing such expressions as "Bull," "bawls," "walnuts," and "blimey." Ever since the night at the Congo when he heard the fighting West Indian girl cry, "I'll slap you bumbole," he had always used the word. When his friends asked him what it meant, he grinned and said, "Ask the monks."

"You know French?" the waiter asked.

"*Parlee-vous? Mademoiselle, un baiser, s'il vous plait. Voilà!* I larned that much offn the froggies."

"So you were over there?"

"*Au oui, camarade,*" Jake beamed. "I was way, way ovah there after Democracy and them boches, and when I couldn't find one or the other, I jest turned mah black moon from the A.E.F. . . . But you! How come you jest plowing through this here stuff lak that? I could nevah see no light at all in them print, chappie. *Eh bien. Mais vous compris beaucoup.*"

"*C'est ma langue maternelle.*"

"Hm!" Jake made a face and scratched his head. "*Comprendre pas*, chappie. Tell me in straight United States."

"French is my native language. I——"

"Don't crap me," Jake interrupted. "Ain'tchu—ain'tchu one of us, too?"

"Of course I'm Negro," the waiter said, "but I was born in Hayti and the language down there is French."

"Hayti . . . Hayti," repeated Jake. "Tha's where now? Tha's——"

"An island in the Caribbean—near the Panama Canal."

Jake sat like a big eager boy and learned many facts about

Hayti before the train reached Pittsburgh. He learned that the
universal spirit of the French Revolution had reached and lifted
up the slaves far away in that remote island; that Black Hayti's
independence was more dramatic and picturesque than the
United States' independence and that it was a strange, almost
unimaginable eruption of the beautiful ideas of the "Liberté,
Egalité, Fraternité" of Mankind, that shook the foundations of
that romantic era.

For the first time he heard the name Toussaint L'Ouverture,
the black slave and leader of the Haytian slaves. Heard how he
fought and conquered the slave-owners and then protected
them; decreed laws for Hayti that held more of human wisdom
and nobility than the Code Napoleon; defended his baby revolution against the Spanish and the English vultures; defeated
Napoleon's punitive expedition; and how tragically he was captured by a civilized trick, taken to France, and sent by Napoleon
to die broken-hearted in a cold dungeon.

"A black man! A black man! Oh, I wish I'd been a soldier
under sich a man!" Jake said, simply.

He plied his instructor with questions. Heard of Dessalines,
who carried on the fight begun by Toussaint L'Ouverture and
kept Hayti independent. But it was incredible to Jake that a little island of freed slaves had withstood the three leading
European powers. The waiter told him that Europe was in a
complex state of transition then, and that that wonderful age
had been electrified with universal ideas—ideas so big that they
had lifted up ignorant people, even black, to the stature of gods.

"The world doesn't know," he continued, "how great
Toussaint L'Ouverture really was. He was not merely great.
He was lofty. He was good. The history of Hayti today might
have been different if he had been allowed to finish his work.
He was honored by a great enigmatic poet of that period. And
I honor both Toussaint and the poet by keeping in my memory
the wonderful, passionate lines."

He quoted Wordsworth's sonnet.

> "Toussaint, the most unhappy Man of Men!
>   Whether the whistling Rustic tend his plough
>   Within thy hearing, or thy head be now
> Pillowed in some deep dungeon's earless den;—

Oh miserable Chieftain! Where and when
  Wilt thou find patience? Yet die not; do thou
  Wear rather in thy bonds a cheerful brow:
Though fallen Thyself never to rise again,
Live, and take comfort. Thou hast left behind
  Powers that will work for thee, air, earth, and skies;
There's not a breathing of the common wind
  That will forget thee; thou hast great allies;
  Thy friends are exultations, agonies,
And love, and Man's unconquerable Mind."

Jake felt like one passing through a dream, vivid in rich, var-ied colors. It was revelation beautiful in his mind. That brief account of an island of savage black people, who fought for collective liberty and were struggling to create a culture of their own. A romance of his race, just down there by Panama. How strange!

Jake was very American in spirit and shared a little of that comfortable Yankee contempt for poor foreigners. And as an American Negro he looked askew at foreign niggers. Africa was jungle, and Africans bush niggers, cannibals. And West Indians were monkey-chasers. But now he felt like a boy who stands with the map of the world in colors before him, and feels the wonder of the world.

The waiter told him that Africa was not jungle as he dreamed of it, nor slavery the peculiar rôle of black folk. The Jews were the slaves of the Egyptians, the Greeks made slaves of their conquered, the Gauls and Saxons were slaves of the Romans. He told Jake of the old destroyed cultures of West Africa and of their vestiges, of black kings who struggled stoutly for the independence of their kingdoms: Prempreh of Ashanti, Tofa of Dahomey, Gbehanzin of Benin, Cetawayo of Zulu-Land, Menelik of Abyssinia. . . .

Had Jake ever heard of the little Republic of Liberia, founded by American Negroes? And Abyssinia, deep-set in the shoulder of Africa, besieged by the hungry wolves of Europe? The only nation that has existed free and independent from the earliest records of history until today! Abyssinia, oldest unconquered nation, ancient-strange as Egypt, persistent as Palestine, leg-endary as Greece, magical as Persia.

There was the lovely legend of her queen who visited the court of the Royal Rake of Jerusalem, and how he fell in love with her. And her beautiful black body made the Sage so lyrical, he immortalized her in those wonderful pagan verses that are sacred to the hearts of all lovers—even the heart of the Church. . . . The catty ladies of the court of Jerusalem were jealous of her. And Sheba reminded them that she was black but beautiful. . . . And after a happy period she left Jerusalem and returned to her country with the son that came of the royal affair. And that son subsequently became King of Abyssinia. And to this day the rulers of Abyssinia carry the title, Lion of Judah, and trace their descent direct from the liaison of the Queen of Sheba with King Solomon.

First of Christian nations also is the claim of this little kingdom! Christian since the time when Philip, the disciple of Jesus, met and baptized the minister of the Queen of Abyssinia and he returned to his country and converted the court and people to Christianity.

Jake listened, rapt, without a word of interruption.

"All the ancient countries have been yielding up the buried secrets of their civilizations," the waiter said. "I wonder what Abyssinia will yield in her time? Next to the romance of Hayti, because it is my native country, I should love to write the romance of Abyssinia . . . Ethiopia."

"Is that theah country the same Ethiopia that we done l'arned about in the Bible?" asked Jake.

"The same. The Latin peoples still call it Ethiopia."

"Is you a professor?"

"No, I'm a student."

"Whereat? Where did you l'arn English?"

"Well, I learned English home in Port-au-Prince. And I was at Howard. You know the Negro university at Washington. Haven't even finished there yet."

"Then what in the name of mah holy rabbit foot youse doing on this heah white man's chuh-chuh? It ain't no place foh no student. It seems to me you' place down there sounds a whole lot better."

"Uncle Sam put me here."

"Whadye mean Uncle Sam?" cried Jake. "Don't hand me that bull."

"Let me tell you about it," the waiter said. "Maybe you don't know that during the World War Uncle Sam grabbed Hayti. My father was an official down there. He didn't want Uncle Sam in Hayti and he said so and said it loud. They told him to shut up and he wouldn't, so they shut him up in jail. My brother also made a noise and American marines killed him in the street. I had nobody to pay for me at the university, so I had to get out and work. *Voilà!*"

"And you ain't gwine to study no moh?"

"Never going to stop. I study now all the same when I get a little time. Every free day I have in New York I spend at the library downtown. I read there and I write."

Jake shook his head. "This heah work is all right for me, but for a chappie like you. . . . Do you like waiting on them ofays? 'Sall right working longshore or in a kitchen as I does it, but to be rubbing up against them and bowing so nice and all a that. . . ."

"It isn't so bad," the waiter said. "Most of them are pretty nice. Last trip I waited on a big Southern Senator. He was perfectly gentlemanly and tipped me half a dollar. When I have the blues I read Dr. Frank Crane."

Jake didn't understand, but he spat and said a stinking word. The chef called him to do something in the kitchen.

"Leave that theah professor and his nonsense," the chef said. . . .

The great black animal whistled sharply and puff-puffed slowly into the station of Pittsburgh.

XI
Snowstorm in Pittsburgh

I N the middle of the little bridge built over the railroad crossing he was suddenly enveloped in a thick mass of smoke
spouted out by an in-rushing train. That was Jake's first impression of Pittsburgh. He stepped off the bridge into a saloon. From there along a dull-gray street of grocery and fruit
shops and piddling South-European children. Then he was on
Wiley Avenue, the long, gray, uphill street.

Brawny bronze men in coal-blackened and oil-spotted blue
overalls shadowed the doorways of saloons, pool-rooms, and
little basement restaurants. The street was animated with dark
figures going up, going down. Houses and men, women, and
squinting cats and slinking dogs, everything seemed touched
with soot and steel dust.

"So this heah is the niggers' run," said Jake. "I don't like its
'pearance, nohow." He walked down the street and remarked a
bouncing little chestnut-brown standing smartly in the entrance of a basement eating-joint. She wore a knee-length
yellow-patterned muslin frock and a white-dotted blue apron.
The apron was a little longer than the frock. Her sleeves were
rolled up. Her arms were beautiful, like smooth burnished bars
of copper.

Jake stopped and said, "Howdy!"

"Howdy again!" the girl flashed a row of perfect teeth at
him.

"Got a bite of anything good?"

"I should say so, Mister Ma-an."

She rolled her eyes and worked her hips into delightful free-
and-easy motions. Jake went in. He was not hungry for food.
He looked at a large dish half filled with tapioca pudding. He
turned to the pie-case on the counter.

"The peach pie is the best," said the girl, her bare elbow on
the counter; "it's fresh." She looked straight in his eyes. "All
right, I'll try peach," he said, and, magnetically, his long, shining fingers touched her hand. . . .

*

In the evening he found the Haytian waiter at the big Wiley Avenue pool-room. Quite different from the pool-rooms in Harlem, it was a sort of social center for the railroad men and the more intelligent black workmen of the quarter. Tobacco, stationery, and odds and ends were sold in the front part of the store. There was a table where customers sat and wrote letters. And there were pretty chocolate dolls and pictures of Negroid types on sale. Curious, pathetic pictures; black Madonna and child; a kinky-haired mulatto angel with African lips and Nordic nose, soaring on a white cloud up to heaven; Jesus blessing a black child and a white one; a black shepherd carrying a white lamb—all queerly reminiscent of the crude prints of the great Christian paintings that are so common in poor religious homes.

"Here he is!" Jake greeted the waiter. "What's the new?"

"Nothing new in Soot-hill; always the same."

The railroad men hated the Pittsburgh run. They hated the town, they hated Wiley Avenue and their wretched free quarters that were in it. . . .

"What're you going to do?"

"Ahm gwine to the colored show with a li'l' brown piece," said Jake.

"You find something already? My me! You're a fast-working one."

"Always the same whenever I hits a new town. Always in cock-tail luck, chappie."

"Which one? Manhattan or Bronx?"

"It's Harlem-Pittsburgh thisanight," Jake grinned. "Wachyu gwine make?"

"Don't know. There's nothing ever in Pittsburgh for me. I'm in no mood for the leg-show tonight, and the colored show is bum. Guess I'll go sleep if I can."

"Awright, I'll see you li'l' later, chappie." Jake gripped his hand. "Say—whyn't you tell a fellow you' name? Youse sure more'n second waiter as Ise more'n third cook. Ev'body calls me Jake. And you?"

"Raymond, but everybody calls me Ray."

Jake heaved off. Ray bought some weekly Negro newspapers: *The Pittsburgh Courier, The Baltimore American, The Negro*

World, The Chicago Defender. Here he found a big assortment
of all the Negro publications that he never could find in
Harlem. In a next-door saloon he drank a glass of sherry and
started off for the waiters' and cooks' quarters.

It was long after midnight when Jake returned to quarters.
He had to pass through the Western men's section to get to
the Eastern crews. Nobody was asleep in the Western men's
section. No early-morning train was chalked up on their board.
The men were grouped off in poker and dice games. Jake
hesitated a little by one group, fascinated by a wiry little long-
headed finger-snapping black, who with strenuous h'h, h'h,
h'h, h'h, was zestfully throwing the bones. Jake almost joined
the game but he admonished himself: "You winned five dollars
thisaday and you made a nice li'l' brown piece. Wha'more you
want?" . . .

He found the beds assigned to the members of his crew.
They were double beds, like Pullman berths. Three of the
waiters had not come in yet. The second and the fourth cooks
were snoring, each a deep frothy bass and a high tenor, and
scratching themselves in their sleep. The chef sprawled like
the carcass of a rhinoceros, half-naked, mouth wide open.
Tormented by bedbugs, he had scratched and tossed in his
sleep and hoofed the covers off the bed. Ray was sitting on a
lower berth on his Negro newspapers spread out to form a
sheet. He had thrown the sheets on the floor, they were so
filthy from other men's sleeping. By the thin flame of gaslight
he was killing bugs.

"Where is I gwine to sleep?" asked Jake.

"Over me, if you can. I saved the bunk for you," said Ray.

"Some music the niggers am making," remarked Jake, nodding in the direction of the snoring cooks. "But whasmat,
chappie, you ain't sleeping?"

"Can't you see?"

"Bugs. Bumbole! This is a hell of a dump for a man to
sleep in."

"The place is rocking crazy with them," said Ray. "I hauled
the cot away from the wall, but the mattress is just swarming."

Hungry and bold, the bugs crept out of their chinks and
hunted for food. They stopped dead-still when disturbed

by the slightest shadow, and flattened their bellies against the wall.

"Le's get outa this stinking dump and chase a drink, chappie."

Ray jumped out of his berth, shoved himself into his clothes and went with Jake. The saloon near by the pool-room was still open. They went there. Ray asked for sherry.

"You had better sample some hard liquor if youse gwine back to wrastle with them bugs tonight," Jake suggested.

Ray took his advice. A light-yellow fellow chummed up with the boys and invited them to drink with him. He was as tall as Jake and very thin. There was a vacant, wandering look in his kindly-weak eyes. He was a waiter on another dining-car of the New York–Pittsburg run. Ray mentioned that he had to quit his bed because he couldn't sleep.

"This here town is the rottenest lay-over in the whole railroad field," declared the light-yellow. "I don't never sleep in the quarters here."

"Where do you sleep, then?" asked Ray.

"Oh, I got a sweet baby way up yonder the other side of the hill."

"Oh, ma-ma!" Jake licked his lips. "So youse all fixed up in this heah town?"

"Not going there tonight, though," the light-yellow said in a careless, almost bored tone. "Too far for mine."

He asked Jake and Ray if they would like to go to a little open-all-night place. They were glad to hear of that.

"Any old thing, boh," Jake said, "to get away from that theah Pennsy bug house."

The little place was something of a barrel-house speak-easy, crowded with black steel-workers in overalls and railroad men, and foggy with smoke. They were all drinking hard liquor and playing cards. The boss was a stocky, genial brown man. He knew the light-yellow waiter and shook hands with him and his friends. He moved away some boxes in a corner and squeezed a little table in it, specially for them. They sat down, jammed into the corner, and drank whisky.

"Better here than the Pennsy pigpen," said the light-yellow.

He was slapped on the back by a short, compact young black.

"Hello, you! What you think youse doing theah?"

"Ain't figuring," retorted the light-yellow, "is you?"

"On the red moon gwine around mah haid, yes. How about a li'l' good snow?"

"Now you got mah number down, Happy."

The black lad vanished again through a mysterious back door.

The light-yellow said: "He's the biggest hophead I ever seen. Nobody can sniff like him. Yet he's always the same happy nigger, stout and strong like a bull."

He took another whisky and went like a lean hound after Happy. Jake looked mischievously at the little brown door, remarking: "It's a great life ef youse in on it." . . .

The light-yellow came back with a cold gleam in his eyes, like arsenic shining in the dark. His features were accentuated by a rigid, disturbing tone and he resembled a smiling wax figure.

"Have a li'l' stuff with the bunch?" he asked Jake.

"I ain't got the habit, boh, but I'll try anything once again."

"And you?" The light-yellow turned to Ray.

"No, chief, thank you, but I don't want to."

The waiter went out again with Jake on his heels. Beyond the door, five fellows, kneeling in the sawdust, were rolling the square bones. Others sat together around two tables with a bottle of red liquor and thimble-like glasses before them.

"Oh, boy!" one said. "When I get home tonight it will be some more royal stuff. I ain'ta gwine to work none 'tall tomorrow."

"Shucks!" Another spread away his big mouth. "This heah ain't nothing foh a fellow to turn royal loose on. I remimber when I was gwine with a money gang that hed no use foh nothing but the pipe. That theah time was life, buddy."

"Wha' sorta pipe was that there?" asked Jake.

"The Chinese stuff, old boy."

Instead of deliberately fisting his, like the others, Jake took it up carelessly between his thumb and forefinger and inhaled.

"Say what you wanta about Chinee or any other stuff," said Happy, "but theah ain't nothing can work wicked like snow and whisky. It'll flip you up from hell into heaven befoh you knows it."

Ray looked into the room.

"Who's you li'l' mascot?" Happy asked the light-yellow.

"Tha's mah best pal," Jake answered. "He's got some moh stuff up here," Jake tapped his head.

"Better let's go on back to quarters," said Ray.

"To them bugs?" demanded Jake.

"Yes, I think we'd better."

"Awright, anything you say, chappie. I kain sleep through worser things." Jake took a few of the little white packets from Happy and gave him some money. "Guess I might need them some day. You never know."

Jake fell asleep as soon as his head touched the dirty pillow. Below him, Ray lay in his bunk, tormented by bugs and the snoring cooks. The low-burning gaslight flickered and flared upon the shadows. The young man lay under the untellable horror of a dead-tired man who wills to sleep and cannot.

In other sections of the big barn building the faint chink of coins touched his ears. Those men gambling the hopeless Pittsburg night away did not disturb him. They were so quiet. It would have been better, perhaps, if they were noisy. He closed his eyes and tried to hypnotize himself to sleep. Sleep . . . sleep . . . sleep . . . sleep . . . sleep. . . . He began counting slowly. His vigil might break and vanish somnolently upon some magic number. He counted a million. Perhaps love would appease this unwavering angel of wakefulness. Oh, but he could not pick up love easily on the street as Jake. . . .

He flung himself, across void and water, back home. Home thoughts, if you can make them soft and sweet and misty-beautiful enough, can sometimes snare sleep. There was the quiet, chalky-dusty street and, jutting out over it, the front of the house that he had lived in. The high staircase built on the outside, and pots of begonias and ferns on the landing. . . .

All the flowering things he loved, red and white and pink hibiscus, mimosas, rhododendrons, a thousand glowing creepers, climbing and spilling their vivid petals everywhere, and bright-buzzing humming-birds and butterflies. All the tropic-warm lilies and roses. Giddy-high erect thatch palms, slender, tall,

fur-fronded ferns, majestic cotton trees, stately bamboos creating a green grandeur in the heart of space. . . .

Sleep remained cold and distant. Intermittently the cooks
broke their snoring with masticating noises of their fat lips, like
animals eating. Ray fixed his eyes on the offensive bug-bitten
bulk of the chef. These men claimed kinship with him. They
were black like him. Man and nature had put them in the same
race. He ought to love them and feel them (if they felt anything). He ought to if he had a shred of social morality in him.
They were all chain-ganged together and he was counted as
one link. Yet he loathed every soul in that great barrack-room,
except Jake. Race. . . . Why should he have and love a race?

Races and nations were things like skunks, whose smells
poisoned the air of life. Yet civilized mankind reposed its faith
and future in their ancient, silted channels. Great races and big
nations! There must be something mighty inspiriting in being
the citizen of a great strong nation. To be the white citizen of
a nation that can say bold, challenging things like a strong
man. Something very different from the keen ecstatic joy a man
feels in the romance of being black. Something the black man
could never feel nor quite understand.

Ray felt that as he was conscious of being black and impotent, so, correspondingly, each marine down in Hayti must be
conscious of being white and powerful. What a unique feeling
of confidence about life the typical white youth of his age must
have! Knowing that his skin-color was a passport to glory,
making him one with ten thousands like himself. All perfect
Occidentals and investors in that grand business called civilization. That grand business in whose pits sweated and snored,
like the cooks, all the black and brown hybrids and mongrels,
simple earth-loving animals, without aspirations toward
national unity and racial arrogance.

He remembered when little Hayti was floundering uncontrolled, how proud he was to be the son of a free nation. He
used to feel condescendingly sorry for those poor African natives; superior to ten millions of suppressed Yankee "coons."
Now he was just one of them and he hated them for being one
of them. . . .

But he was not entirely of them, he reflected. He possessed
another language and literature that they knew not of. And

some day Uncle Sam might let go of his island and he would escape from the clutches of that magnificent monster of civilization and retire behind the natural defenses of his island, where the steam-roller of progress could not reach him. Escape he would. He had faith. He had hope. But, oh, what would become of that great mass of black swine, hunted and cornered by slavering white canaille! Sleep! oh, sleep! Down Thought!

But all his senses were burning wide awake. Thought was not a beautiful and reassuring angel, a thing of soothing music and light laughter and winged images glowing with the rare colors of life. No. It was suffering, horribly real. It seized and worried him from every angle. Pushed him toward the sheer precipice of imagination. It was awful. He was afraid. For thought was a terrible tiger clawing at his small portion of gray substance, throttling, tearing, and tormenting him with pitiless ferocity. Oh, a thousand ideas of life were shrieking at him in a wild orgy of mockery! . . .

He was in the middle of a world suspended in space. A familiar line lit up, like a flame, the vast, crowded, immensity of his vision.

Et l'âme du monde est dans l'air.

A moment's respite. . . .

A loud snore from the half-naked chef brought him back to the filthy fact of the quarters that the richest railroad in the world had provided for its black servitors. Ray looked up at Jake, stretched at full length on his side, his cheek in his right hand, sleeping peacefully, like a tired boy after hard playing, so happy and sweet and handsome. He remembered the neatly-folded white papers in Jake's pocket. Maybe that was the cause of his sleeping so soundly. He reached his hand up to the coat hanging on the nail above his head. It was such an innocent little thing—like a headache powder the paper of which you wipe with your tongue, so that none should be wasted. Apparently the first one had no effect and Ray took the rest.

Sleep capitulated.

Immediately he was back home again. His father's house was a vast forest full of blooming hibiscus and mimosas and giant evergreen trees. And he was a gay humming-bird, fluttering and darting his long needle beak into the heart of a bell-flower. Suddenly he changed into an owl flying by day. . . . Howard University was a prison with white warders. . . . Now he was a young shining chief in a marble palace; slim, naked negresses dancing for his pleasure; courtiers reclining on cushions soft like passionate kisses; gleaming-skinned black boys bearing goblets of wine and obedient eunuchs waiting in the offing. . . .

And the world was a blue paradise. Everything was in gorgeous blue of heaven. Woods and streams were blue, and men and women and animals, and beautiful to see and love. And he was a blue bird in flight and a blue lizard in love. And life was all blue happiness. Taboos and terrors and penalties were transformed into new pagan delights, orgies of Orient-blue carnival, of rare flowers and red fruits, cherubs and seraphs and fetishes and phalli and all the most-high gods. . . .

A thousand pins were pricking Ray's flesh and he was shouting for Jake, but his voice was so faint he could not hear himself. Jake had him in his arms and tried to stand him upon his feet. He crumpled up against the bunk. All his muscles were loose, his cells were cold, and the rhythm of being arrested.

It was high morning and time to go to the train. Jake had picked up the empty little folds of paper from the floor and restored them to his pocket. He knew what had happened to them, and guessed why. He went and called the first and fourth waiters.

The chef bulked big in the room, dressed and ready to go to the railroad yards. He gave a contemptuous glance at Jake looking after Ray and said: "Better leave that theah nigger professor alone and come on 'long to the dining-car with us. That theah nigger is dopey from them books o' hisn. I done told befoh them books would git him yet."

The chef went off with the second and fourth cooks. Jake stayed with Ray. They got his shoes and coat on. The first waiter telephoned the steward, and Ray was taken to the hospital.

"We may all be niggers aw'right, but we ain't nonetall all the same," Jake said as he hurried along to the dining-car, thinking of Ray.

XII
The Treeing of the Chef

PERHAPS the chef of Jake's dining-car was the most hated chef in the service. He was repulsive in every aspect. From the elevated bulk of his gross person to the matted burrs of his head and the fat cigar, the constant companion of his sloppy mouth, that he chewed and smoked at the same time. The chef deliberately increased his repulsiveness of form by the meannesses of his spirit.

"I know Ise a mean black nigger," he often said, "and I'll let you all know it on this heah white man's car, too."

The chef was a great black bundle of consciously suppressed desires. That was doubtless why he was so ornery. He was one of the model chefs of the service. His kitchen was well-ordered. The checking up of his provisions always showed a praiseworthy balance. He always had his food ready on time, feeding the heaviest rush of customers as rapidly as the lightest. He fed the steward excellently. He fed the crew well. In a word, he did his duty as only a martinet can.

A chef who is "right-there" at every call is the first asset of importance on an *à la carte* restaurant-car. The chef lived rigidly up to that fact and above it. He was also painfully honest. He had a mulatto wife and a brown boy-child in New York and he never slipped away any of the company's goods to them. Other dining-car men had devised a system of getting by the company's detectives with choice brands of the company's foodstuffs. The chef kept away from that. It was long since the yard detectives had stopped searching any parcel that *he* carried off with him.

"I don't want none o' the white-boss stuff foh mine," he declared. "Ise making enough o' mah own to suppoht mah wife and kid."

And more, the chef had a violent distaste for all the stock things that "coons" are supposed to like to the point of stealing them. He would not eat watermelon, because white people called it "the niggers' ice-cream." Pork chops he fancied not.

Nor corn pone. And the idea of eating chicken gave him a spasm. Of the odds and ends of chicken gizzard, feet, head, rump, heart, wing points, and liver—the chef would make the most delicious stew for the crew, which he never touched himself. The Irish steward never missed his share of it. But for his meal the chef would grill a steak or mutton chop or fry a fish. Oh, chef was big and haughty about not being "no regular darky"! And although he came from the Alabama country, he pretended not to know a coon tail from a rabbit foot.

"All this heah talk about chicken-loving niggers," he growled chuckingly to the second cook. "The way them white passengers clean up on mah fried chicken I wouldn't trust one o' them anywheres near mah hen-coop."

Broiling tender corn-fed chicken without biting a leg. Thus, grimly, the chef existed. Humored and tolerated by the steward and hated by the waiters and undercooks. Jake found himself on the side of the waiters. He did not hate the chef (Jake could not hate anybody). But he could not be obscenely sycophantic to him as the second cook, who was just waiting for the chance to get the chef's job. Jake stood his corner in the coffin, doing his bit in diplomatic silence. Let the chef bawl the waiters out. He would not, like the second cook, join him in that game.

Ray, perhaps, was the chief cause of Jake's silent indignation. Jake had said to him: "I don't know how all you fellows can stand that theah God-damn black bull. I feels like falling down mahself." But Ray had begged Jake to stay on, telling him that he was the only decent man in the kitchen. Jake stayed because he liked Ray. A big friendship had sprung up between them and Jake hated to hear the chef abusing his friend along with the other waiters. The other cooks and waiters called Ray "Professor." Jake had never called him that. Nor did he call him "buddy," as he did Zeddy and his longshoremen friends. He called him "chappie" in a genial, semi-paternal way.

Jake's life had never before touched any of the educated of the ten dark millions. He had, however, a vague idea of who they were. He knew that the "big niggers" that were gossiped about in the saloons and the types he had met at Madame Adelina Suarez's were not *the* educated ones. The educated "dick-tees," in Jake's circles were often subjects for raw and

funny sallies. He had once heard Miss Curdy putting them in
their place while Susy's star eyes gleamed warm approval.

"Honey, I lived in Washington and I knowed inside and naked out the stuck-up bush-whackers of the race. They all talks
and act as if loving was a sin, but I tell you straight, I wouldn't
trust any of them after dark with a preacher. . . . Don't ask
me, honey. I seen and I knows them all."

"I guess you does, sistah," Susy had agreed. "Nobody kaint
hand *me* no fairy tales about niggers. Wese all much of a much-
ness when you git down to the real stuff."

Difficulties on the dining-car were worsened by a feud between the pantry and the kitchen. The first waiter, who was
pantryman by regulation, had a grievance against the chef and
was just waiting to "get" him. But, the chef being such a paragon, the "getting" was not easy.

Nothing can be worse on a dining-car than trouble between
the pantry and the kitchen, for one is as necessary to the other
as oil is to salad. But the war was covertly on and the chef was
prepared to throw his whole rhinoceros weight against the
pantry. The first waiter had to fight cautiously. He was quite
aware that a first-class chef was of greater value than a first-class
pantryman.

The trouble had begun through the "mule." The fourth
man—a coffee-skinned Georgia village boy, timid like a country girl just come to town—hated the nickname, but the chef
would call him nothing else.

"Call him 'Rhinoceros' when he calls you 'Mule,'" Ray told
the fourth waiter, but he was too timid to do it. . . .

The dining-car was resting on the tracks in the Altoona
yards, waiting for a Western train. The first, third, and fifth
waiters were playing poker. Ray was reading Dostoievski's
Crime and Punishment. The fourth waiter was working in the
pantry. Suddenly the restaurant-car was shocked by a terrible
roar.

"Gwan I say! Take that theah ice and beat it, you black
sissy." . . .

"This ice ain't good for the pantry. You ought to gimme the
cleaner one," the timid fourth man stood his ground.

The cigar of the chef stood up like a tusk. Fury was dancing in his enraged face and he would have stamped the guts out of the poor, timid boy if he was not restrained by the fear of losing his job. For on the dining-car, he who strikes the first blow catches the punishment.

"Quit jawing with me, nigger waiter, or I'll jab this heah ice-pick in you' mouf."

"Come and do it," the fourth waiter said, quietly.

"God dam' you' soul!" the chef bellowed. "Ef you don't quit chewing the rag—ef you git fresh with me, I'll throw you off this bloody car. S'elp mah Gawd, I will. You disnificant down-home mule."

The fourth waiter glanced behind him down the corridor and saw Ray, book in hand, and the other waiters, who had left their cards to see the cause of the tumult. Ray winked at the fourth waiter. He screwed up his courage and said to the chef: "I ain't no mule, and youse a dirty rhinoceros."

The chef seemed paralyzed with surprise. "Wha's that name you done call me? Wha's rhinasras?"

All the waiters laughed. The chef looked ridiculous and Ray said: "Why, chef, don't you know? That's the ugliest animal in all Africa."

The chef looked apoplectic. . . . "I don't care a dime foh all you nigger waiters and I ain't joking wif any of you. Cause you manicuring you' finger nails and rubbing up you' stinking black hide against white folks in that theah diner, you all think youse something. But lemme tell you straight, you ain't nothing atall."

"But, chef," cried the pantryman, "why don't you stop riding the fourth man? Youse always riding him."

"Riding who? I nevah rode a man in all mah life. I jest tell that black skunk what to do and him stahts jawing with me. I don't care about any of you niggers, nohow."

"Wese all tiahd of you cussin' and bawking," said the pantry-man. "Why didn't you give the boy a clean piece of ice and finish? You know we need it for the water."

"Yaller nigger, you'd better gwan away from here."

"Don't call me no yaller nigger, you black and ugly cotton-field coon."

"Who dat? You bastard-begotten dime-snatcher, you'd

better gwan back to you' dining-room or I'll throw this heah garbage in you' crap-yaller face. . . . I'd better git long far away from you all 'foh I lose mah haid." The chef bounced into the kitchen and slammed the door.

That "bastard-begotten dime-snatcher" grew a cancer in the heart of the pantryman. It rooted deep because he *was* an "illegitimate" and he bitterly hated the whites he served ("crackers," he called them all) and the tips he picked up. He knew that his father was some red-necked white man who had despised his mother's race and had done nothing for him.

The sight of the chef grew more and more unbearable each day to the pantryman. He thought of knifing or plugging him with a gun some night. He had nursed his resentment to the point of madness and was capable of any act. But getting the chef in the dark would not have been revenge enough. The pantryman wanted the paragon to live, so that he might invent a way of bringing him down humiliatingly from his perch.

But the chef was hard to "get." He had made and kept his place by being a perfect brutal machine, with that advantage that all mechanical creatures have over sensitive human beings. One day the pantryman thought he almost had his man. The chef had fed the steward, but kept the boys waiting for their luncheon. The waiters thought that he had one of his ornery spells on and was intentionally punishing them. They were all standing in the pantry, except Ray.

The fifth said to the first: "Ask him why he don't put the grub in the hole, partner. I'm horse-ways hungry."

"Ask him you'self. I ain't got nothing to do with that black hog moh'n giving him what b'longs to him in this heah pantry."

"Mah belly's making a most beautiful commotion. Jest lak a bleating lamb," drawled the third.

The fifth waiter pushed up the little glass door and stuck his head in the kitchen: "Chef, when are we gwine to go away from here?"

"Keep you' shirt on, nigger," flashed back from the kitchen. "Youall'll soon be stuffing you'self full o' the white man's poke chops. Better than you evah smell in Harlem."

"Wese werking foh't same like you is," the fifth man retorted.

"I don't eat no poke chops, nigger. I cooks the stuff, but I don't eat it, nevah."

"P'raps youse chewing a worser kind o' meat."

"Don't gimme no back talk, nigger waiter. Looka heah ——"

The steward came into the pantry and said: "Chef, it's time to feed the boys. They're hungry. We had a hard day, today."

The chef's cigar drooped upon his slavering lip and almost fell. He turned to the steward with an injured air. "Ain't I doing mah best? Ain't I been working most hard mahself? I done get yourn lunch ready and am getting the crew's own and fixing foh dinner at the same time. I ain't tuk a mouful mahse'f——"

The steward had turned his heels on the pantry. The chef was enraged that he had intervened on behalf of the waiters.

"Ef you dime-chasing niggers keep fooling with me on this car," he said, "I'll make you eat mah spittle. I done do it a'ready and I'll do it again. I'll spit in you' eats——"

"Wha's that? The boss sure gwine to settle this." The pantryman dashed out of the pantry and called the steward. . . . "Ain't any of us waiters gwine to stay on heah Mis'r Farrel, with a chef like this."

"What's that, now?" The steward was in the pantry again. "What's this fine story, chef?"

"Nothing at all, Sah Farrel. I done pull a good bull on them fellars, tha's all. Cause theyse all trying to get mah goat. L'em quit fooling with the kitchen, Sah Farrel. I does mah wuk and I don't want no fooling fwom them nigger waiters, nohow."

"I guess you spit in it as you said, all right," cried the pantryman. . . . "Yes, you! You'd wallow in a pigpen and eat the filth, youse so doggone low-down."

"Now cut all o' that out," said the steward. "How could he do anything like that, when he eats the food, and I do meself?"

"In the hole!" shouted Jake.

The third and fifth waiters hurried into the pantry and brought out the waiters' food. . . . First a great platter of fish and tomatoes, then pork chops and mashed potatoes, steaming Java and best Borden's cream. The chef had made home-made bread baked in the form of little round caps. Nice and hot,

they quickly melted the butter that the boys sandwiched between them. He was a splendid cook, an artist in creating
palatable stuff. He came out of the kitchen himself, to eat in
the dining-room and, diplomatically, he helped himself from
the waiters' platter of fish. . . . Delicious food. The waiters
fell to it with keen relish. Obliterated from their memory the
sewer-incident of the moment before. . . . Feeding, feeding,
feeding.

But Ray remembered and visualized, and his stomach
turned. He left the food and went outside, where he found
Jake taking the air. He told Jake how he felt.

"Oh, the food is all right," said Jake. "I watch him close
anough in that there kitchen, and he knows I ain't standing in
with him in no low-down stuff."

"But do you think he would ever do such a thing?" asked
Ray.

Jake laughed. "What won't a bad nigger do when he's good
and mean way down in his heart? I ain't 'lowing mahself careless with none o' that kind, chappie."

Two Pullman porters came into the dining-car in the middle
of the waiters' meal.

"Here is the chambermaids," grinned the second cook.

"H'm, but how you all loves to call people names, though,"
commented the fourth waiter.

The waiters invited the porters to eat with them. The pantryman went to get them coffee and cream. The chef offered
to scramble some eggs. He went back to the kitchen and, after
a few minutes, the fourth cook brought out a platter of scrambled eggs for the two porters. The chef came rocking importantly behind the fourth cook. A clean white cap was poised on
his head and fondly he chewed his cigar. A perfect menial of
the great railroad company. He felt a wave of goodness sweeping over him, as if he had been patted on the head by the
Angel Gabriel for his good works. He asked the porters if they
had enough to eat and they thanked him and said they had
more than enough and that the food was wonderful. The chef
smiled broadly. He beamed upon steward, waiters, and porters,
and his eyes said: See what a really fine fellow I am in spite of
all the worries that go with the duties of a chef?

*

One day Ray saw the chef and the pantryman jesting while the pantryman was lighting his cigarette from the chef's stump of cigar. When Ray found the pantryman alone, he laughingly asked him if he and the chef had smoked the tobacco of peace.

"Fat chance!" retorted the first waiter. "I gotta talk to him, for we get the stores together and check up together with the steward, and I gotta hand him the stuff tha's coming to him outa the pantry, but I ain't settle mah debt with him yet. I ain't got no time for no nigger that done calls me 'bastard-begotten' and means it."

"Oh, forget it!" said Ray. "Christ was one, too, and we all worship him."

"Wha' you mean?" the pantryman demanded.

"What I said," Ray replied. . . .

"Oh! . . . Ain't you got no religion in you none 'tall?"

"My parents were Catholic, but I ain't nothing. God is white and has no more time for niggers than you've got for the chef."

"Well, I'll be browned but once!" cried the pantryman. "Is that theah what youse l'arning in them books? Don't you believe in getting religion?"

Ray laughed.

"You kain laugh, all right, but watch you' step Gawd don't get you yet. Youse sure trifling."

The coldness between the kitchen and the pantry continued, unpleasantly nasty, like the wearing of wet clothes, after the fall of a heavy shower, when the sun is shining again. The chef was uncomfortable. A waiter had never yet opposed open hostility to his personality like that. He was accustomed to the crew's surrendering to his ways with even a little sycophancy. It was always his policy to be amicable with the pantryman, playing him against the other waiters, for it was very disagreeable to keep up a feud when the kitchen and the pantry had so many unavoidable close contacts.

So the chef made overtures to the pantryman with special toothsome tidbits, such as he always prepared for the only steward and himself. But the pantryman refused to have any specially-prepared-for-his-Irishness-the-Steward's stuff that the other waiters could not share. Thereupon the chef gave up trying to placate him and started in hating back with profound African hate. African hate is deep down and hard to stir up, but there is no hate more realistic when it is stirred up.

One morning in Washington the iceman forgot to supply ice to the dining-car. One of the men had brought a little brass top on the diner and the waiters were excited over an easy new game called "put-and-take." The pantryman forgot his business. The chef went to another dining-car and obtained ice for the kitchen. The pantryman did not remember anything about ice until the train was well on its way to New York. He remembered it because the ice-cream was turning soft. He put his head through the hole and asked Jake for a piece of ice. The chef said no, he had enough for the kitchen only.

With a terrible contented expression the chef looked with malicious hate into the pantryman's yellow face. The pantryman glared back at the villainous black face and jerked his head in rage. The ice-cream turned softer. . . .

Luncheon was over, all the work was done, everything in order, and the entire crew was ready to go home when the train reached New York. The steward wanted to go directly home. But he had to wait and go over to the yards with the keys, so that the pantryman could ice up. And the pantryman was severely reprimanded for his laxity in Washington. . . .

The pantryman bided his time, waiting on the chef. He was cordial. He even laughed at the jokes the chef made at the other waiters' expense. The chef swelled bigger in his hide, feeling that everything had bent to his will. The pantryman waited, ignoring little moments for the big moment. It came.

One morning both the second and the fourth cook "fell down on the job," neither of them reporting for duty. The steward placed an order with the commissary superintendent for two cooks. Jake stayed in the kitchen, working, while the chef and the pantryman went to the store for the stock. . . .

The chef and the pantryman returned together with the large baskets of provisions for the trip. The eggs were carried by the chef himself in a neat box. Remembering that he had forgotten coffee, he sent Jake back to the store for it. Then he began putting away the kitchen stuff. The pantryman was putting away the pantry stuff. . . .

A yellow girl passed by and waved a smile at the chef. He grinned, his teeth champing his cigar. The chef hated yellow men with "cracker" hatred, but he loved yellow women with "cracker" love. His other love was gin. But he never carried a liquor flask on the diner, because it was against regulations. And he never drank with any of the crew. He drank alone. And he did other things alone. In Philadelphia or Washington he never went to a buffet flat with any of the men.

The girls working in the yards were always flirting with him. He fascinated them, perhaps because he was so Congo mask-like in aspect and so duty-strict. They could often wheedle something nice out of other chefs, but nothing out of *the* chef. He would rather give them his money than a piece of the company's raw meat. The chef was generous in his way; Richmond Pete, who owned the saloon near the yards in Queensborough, could attest to that. He had often gossiped about the chef. How he "blowed them gals that he had a crush on in the family room and danced an elephant jig while the gals were pulling his leg."

The yellow girl that waved at the chef through the window was pretty. Her gesture transformed his face into a foolish broad-smiling thing. He stepped outside the kitchen for a moment to have a tickling word with her.

In that moment the pantryman made a lightning-bolt move; and shut down the little glass door between the pantry and the kitchen. . . .

The train was speeding its way west. The first call for dinner had been made and the dining-room was already full. Over half a dozen calls for eggs of different kinds had been bawled out before the chef discovered that the basket of eggs was missing. The chef asked the pantryman to call the steward. The pantryman, curiously preoccupied, forgot. Pandemonium was loose in the pantry and kitchen when the steward, radish-red, stuck his head in.

The chef's lower lip had flopped low down, dripping, and the cigar had fallen somewhere. "Cut them aiggs off o' the bill, Sah Farrel. O Lawd!" he moaned, "Ise sartain sure I brought them aiggs on the car mahself, and now I don't know where they is."

"What kind o' blah is that?" cried the steward. "The eggs must be there in the kitchen. I saw them with the stock meself."

"And I brought them here hugging them, Boss, ef I ain't been made fool of by something." The rhinoceros had changed into a meek black lamb. "O Lawd! and I ain't been outa the kitchen sence. Ain't no mortal hand could tuk them. Some evil hand. O Lawd!——"

"Hell!" The steward dashed out of the pantry to cut all the egg dishes off the bill. The passengers were getting clamorous. The waiters were asking those who had ordered eggs to change to something else. . . .

The steward suggested searching the pantry. The pantry was ransacked. "Them ain't there, cep'n' they had feets to walk. O Lawd of Heaben!" the chef groaned. "It's something deep and evil, I knows, for I ain't been outa this heah kitchen." His little flirtation with the yellow girl was completely wiped off his memory.

Only Jake was keeping his head in the kitchen. He was acting second cook, for the steward had not succeeded in getting one. The fourth cook he had gotten was new to the service and he was standing, conspicuously long-headed, with gaping mouth.

"Why'n the debbil's name don't you do some'n, nigger?" bellowed the chef, frothy at the corners of his mouth.

"The chef is up a tree, all right," said Ray to the pantryman.

"And he'll break his black hide getting down," the pantryman replied, bitterly.

"Chef!" The yellow pantryman's face carried a royal African grin. "What's the matter with you and them aiggs?"

"I done gived them to you mammy."

"And fohget you wife, ole timer? Ef you ain't a chicken-roost nigger, as you boast, you surely loves the nest."

Gash! The chef, at last losing control of himself, shied a huge ham bone at the pantryman. The pantryman sprang back as the ham bone flew through the aperture and smashed a bottle of milk in the pantry.

"What's all this bloody business today?" cried the steward,

who was just entering the pantry. . . . "What nonsense is this, chef? You've made a mess of things already and now you start fighting with the waiters. You can't do like that. You losing your head?"

"Lookahere, Sah Farrel, I jes' want ev'body to leave me 'lone."

"But we must all team together on the dining-car. That's the only way. You can't start fighting the waiters because you've lost the eggs."

"Sah Farrel, leave me alone, I say," half roared, half moaned the chef, "or I'll jump off right now and let you run you' kitchen you'self."

"What's that?" The steward started.

"I say I'll jump off, and I mean it as Gawd's mah maker."

The steward slipped out of the pantry without another word.

The steward obtained a supply of eggs in Harrisburg the next morning. The rest of the trip was made with the most dignified formalities between him and the chef. Between the pantry and the chef the atmosphere was tenser, but there were no more explosions.

The dining-car went out on its next trip with a new chef. And the old chef, after standing a little of the superintendent's notoriously sharp tongue, was sent to another car as second cook.

"Hit those fellahs in the pocket-book is the only way," the pantryman overheard the steward talking to one of his colleagues. "Imagine an old experienced chef threatening to jump off when I was short of a second cook."

They were getting the stock for the next trip in the commissary. Jake turned to the pantryman: "But it was sure peculiar, though, how them aiggs just fly outa that kitchen lak that way."

"Maybe they all hatched and growed wings when ole black bull was playing with that sweet yaller piece," the pantryman laughed.

"Honest, though, how do you think it happened?" persisted Jake. "Did you hoodoo them aiggs, or what did you do?"

"I wouldn't know atall. Better ask them rats in the yards ef they sucked the shells dry. What you' right hand does don't tell it to the left, says I."

"You done said a mou'ful, but how did you get away with it so quiet?"

"I ain't said nothing discrimination and I ain't nevah."

"Don't figure against me. Ise with you, buddy," said Jake, "and now that wese good and rid of him, I hope all we niggers will pull together like civilization folks."

"Sure we will. There ain't another down-home nigger like him in this white man's service. He was riding too high and fly, brother. I knew he would tumble and bust something nasty. But I ain't said I knowed a thing about it, all the same."

XIII
One Night in Philly

O NE night in Philadelphia Jake breezed into the waiters' quarters in Market Street, looking for Ray. It was late. Ray was in bed. Jake pulled him up.

"Come on outa that, you slacker. Let's go over to North Philly."

"What for?"

"A li'l' fun. I knows a swell outfit I wanta show you."

"Anything new?"

"Don't know about anything *new*, chappie, but I know there's something *good* right there in Fifteenth Street."

"Oh, I know all about that. I don't want to go."

"Come on. Don't be so particular about you' person. You gotta go with me."

"I have a girl in New York."

"Tha's awright. This is Philly."

"I tell you, Jake, there's no fun in those kinds for me. They'll bore me just like that night in Baltimore."

"Oh, these here am different chippies, I tell you. Come on, le's spend the night away from this damn dump. Wese laying ovah all day tomorrow."

"And some of them will say such rotten things. Pretty enough, all right, but their mouths are loaded with filth, and that's what gets me."

"Them's different ovah there, chappie. I'll kiss the Bible on it. Come on, now. It's no fun me going alone."

They went to a house in Fifteenth Street. As they entered Jake was greeted by a mulatto woman in the full vigor of middle life.

"Why, *you* heart-breaker! It's ages and ages since I saw you. You and me sure going to have a bust-up tonight."

Jake grinned, prancing a little, as if he were going to do the old cake-walk.

"Here, Laura, this is mah friend," he introduced Ray casually.

"Bring him over here and sit down," Madame Laura commanded.

She was a big-boned woman, but very agile. A long, irregular, rich-brown face, roving black eyes, deep-set, and shiny black hair heaped upon her head. She wore black velvet, a square-cut blouse low down on her breasts, and a string of large coral beads. The young girls of that house envied her finely-preserved form and her carriage and wondered if they would be anything like that when they reached her age.

The interior of this house gave Ray a shock. It looked so much like a comfortable boarding-house where everybody was cheerful and nice coquettish girls in colorful frocks were doing the waiting. . . . There were a few flirting couples, two groups of men playing cards, and girls hovering around. An attractive black woman was serving sandwiches, gin and bottled beer. At the piano, a slim yellow youth was playing a "blues." . . . A pleasant house party, similar to any other among colored people of that class in Baltimore, New Orleans, Charleston, Richmond, or even Washington, D.C. Different, naturally, from New York, which molds all peoples into a hectic rhythm of its own. Yet even New York, passing its strange thousands through its great metropolitan mill, cannot rob Negroes of their native color and laughter.

"Mah friend's just keeping me company," Jake said to the woman. "He ain't regular—you get me? And I want him treated right."

"He'll be treated better here than he would in church." She laughed and touched Ray's calf with the point of her slipper.

"What kind o' bust-up youse gwine to have with me?" demanded Jake.

"I'll show you just what I'm going to do with you for forgetting me so long."

She got up and went into an adjoining room. When she returned an attractively made-up brown girl followed her carrying a tray with glasses and a bottle of champagne. . . . The cork hit the ceiling, bang! And deftly the woman herself poured the foaming liquor without a wasted drop.

"There! That's our bust-up," she said. "Me and you and
your friend. Even if he's a virgin he's all right. I know you ain't
never going around with no sap-head."

"Give me some, too," a boy of dull-gold complexion materialized by the side of Madame Laura and demanded a drink. He
was about eleven years old.

Affectionately she put her arm around him and poured out a
small glass of champagne. The frailness of the boy was pathetic;
his eyes were sleepy-sad. He resembled a reed fading in a
morass.

"Who is he?" Ray asked.

"He's my son," responded Madame Laura. "Clever kid, too.
He loves books."

"Ray will like him, then," said Jake. "Books is his middle
name."

Ray suddenly felt a violent dislike for the atmosphere. At
first he had liked the general friendliness and warmth and natu-
ralness of it. All so different from what he had expected. But
something about the presence of the little boy there and his
being the woman's son disgusted him. He could not analyse
his aversion. It was just an instinctive, intolerant feeling that
the boy did not belong to that environment and should not be
there.

He went from Madame Laura and Jake over to the piano
and conversed with the pianist. When he glanced again at the
table he had left, Madame Laura had her arm around Jake's
neck and his eyes were strangely shining.

Madame Laura had set the pace. There were four other couples making love. At one table a big-built, very black man was
amusing himself with two attractive girls, one brown-skinned
and the other yellow. The girls' complexion was heightened by
High-Brown Talc powder and rouge. A bottle of Muscatel
stood on the table. The man was well dressed in nigger-brown
and he wore an expensive diamond ring on his little finger.

The stags were still playing cards, with girls hovering over
them. The happy-faced black woman was doing the managing,
as Madame Laura was otherwise engaged. The pianist began
banging another blues.

Ray felt alone and a little sorry for himself. Now that he was there, he would like to be touched by the spirit of that atmosphere and, like Jake, fall naturally into its rhythm. He also envied Jake. Just for this night only he would like to be like him. . . .

They were dancing. The little yellow girl, her legs kicked out at oblique angles, appeared as if she were going to fall through the big-built black man.

> We'll all be merry when you taste a cherry,
> And we'll twine and twine like a fruitful vine.

In the middle of the floor, a young railroad porter had his hand flattened straight down the slim, cérise-chiffoned back of a brown girl. Her head was thrown back and her eyes held his gleaming eyes. Her lips were parted with pleasure and they stood and rocked in an ecstasy. Their feet were not moving. Only their bodies rocked, rocked to the "blues." . . .

Ray remarked that Jake was not in the room, nor was Madame Laura in evidence. A girl came to him. "Why is you so all by you'self, baby? Don't you wanta dance some? That there is some more temptation 'blues.'"

Tickling, enticing syncopation. Ray felt that he ought to dance to it. But some strange thing seemed to hold him back from taking the girl in his arms.

"Will you drink something, instead?" he found a way out.

"Awwww-right," disappointed, she drawled.

She beckoned to the happy-faced woman.

"Virginia Dare."

"I'll have some, too," Ray said.

Another brown girl joined them.

"Buy mah pal a drink, too?" the first girl asked.

"Why, certainly," he answered.

The woman brought two glasses of Virginia Dare and Ray ordered a third.

Such a striking exotic appearance the rouge gave these brown girls. Rouge that is so cheap in its general use had here an uncommon quality. Rare as the red flower of the hibiscus would be in a florist's window on Fifth Avenue. Rouge on brown, a warm, insidious chestnut color. But so much more

subtle than chestnut. The round face of the first girl, the carnal
sympathy of her full, tinted mouth, touched Ray. But something was between them. . . .

The piano-player had wandered off into some dim, far-away,
ancestral source of music. Far, far away from music-hall syncopation and jazz, he was lost in some sensual dream of his own.
No tortures, banal shrieks and agonies. Tum-tum . . . tum-
tum . . . tum-tum . . . tum-tum. . . . The notes were
naked acute alert. Like black youth burning naked in the bush.
Love in the deep heart of the jungle. . . . The sharp spring of
a leopard from a leafy limb, the snarl of a jackal, green lizards
in amorous play, the flight of a plumed bird, and the sudden
laughter of mischievous monkeys in their green homes. Tum-
tum . . . tum-tum . . . tum-tum . . . tum-tum. . . .
Simple-clear and quivering. Like a primitive dance of war or of
love . . . the marshaling of spears or the sacred frenzy of a
phallic celebration.

Black lovers of life caught up in their own free native rhythm,
threaded to a remote scarce-remembered past, celebrating the
midnight hours in themselves, for themselves, of themselves,
in a house in Fifteenth Street, Philadelphia. . . .

"Raided!" A voice screamed. Standing in the rear door, a
policeman, white, in full uniform, smilingly contemplated the
spectacle. There was a wild scramble for hats and wraps. The
old-timers giggled, shrugged, and kept their seats. Madame
Laura pushed aside the policeman.

"Keep you' pants on, all of you and carry on with you' fun.
What's matter? Scared of a uniform? Pat"—she turned to the
policeman—"what you want to throw a scare in the company
for? Come on here with you."

The policeman, twirling his baton, marched to a table and
sat down with Madame Laura.

"Geewizard!" Jake sat down, too. "Tell 'em next time not to
ring the fire alarm so loud."

"You said it, honey-stick. There are no cops in Philly going
to mess with this girl. Ain't it the truth, Pat?" Madame Laura
twisted the policeman's ear and bridled.

"I know it's the Bible trute," the happy-faced black lady
chanted in a sugary voice, setting a bottle of champagne and

glasses upon the table and seating herself familiarly beside the policeman.

The champagne foamed in the four glasses.

"Whar's mah li'l' chappie?" Jake asked.

"Gone, maybe. Don't worry," said Madame Laura. "Drink!"

Four brown hands and one white. Chink!

"Here's to you, Pat," cried Madame Laura. "There's Irish in me from the male line." She toasted:

> "Flixy, flaxy, fleasy,
>   Make it good and easy,
>   Flix for start and flax for snappy,
>   Niggers and Irish will always be happy."

The policeman swallowed his champagne at a gulp and got up. "Gotta go now. Time for duty."

"You treat him nice. Is it for love or protection?" asked Jake.

"He's loving *her*"—Madame Laura indicated the now coy lady who helped her manage—"but he's protecting *me*. It's a long time since I ain't got no loving inclination for any skin but chocolate. Get me?"

When Jake returned to the quarters he found Ray sleeping quietly. He did not disturb him. The next morning they walked together to the yards.

"Did the policeman scare you, too, last night?" asked Jake.

"What policeman?"

"Oh, didn't you see him? There was a policeman theah and somebody hollered 'Raid!' scaring everybody. I thought you'd done tuk you'self away from there in quick time becasn a that."

"No, I left before that, I guess. Didn't even smell one walking all the way to the quarters in Market Street."

"Why'd you beat it? One o' the li'l' chippies had a crush on you. Oh, boy! and she was some piece to look at."

"I know it. She was kind of nice. But she had some nasty perfume on her that turned mah stomach."

"Youse awful queer, chappie," Jake commented.

"Why, don't you ever feel those sensations that just turn you back in on yourself and make you isolated and helpless?"

"Wha'd y'u mean?"

"I mean if sometimes you don't feel as I felt last night?"

"Lawdy no. Young and pretty is all I feel."

They stopped in a saloon. Jake had a small whisky and Ray an egg-nogg.

"But Madame Laura isn't young," resumed Ray.

"Ain't she?" Jake showed his teeth. "I'd back her against some of the youngest. She's a wonder, chappie. Her blood's like good liquor. She gave me a present, too. Looka here." Jake took from his pocket a lovely slate-colored necktie sprinkled with red dots. Ray felt the fineness of it.

"Ef I had the sweetman disinclination I wouldn't have to work, chappie," Jake rocked proudly in his walk. "But tha's the life of a pee-wee cutter, says I. Kain't see it for mine."

"She was certainly nice to you last night. And the girls were nice, too. It was just like a jolly parlor social."

"Oh, sure! Them gals not all in the straight business, you know. Some o' them works and just go there for a good time, a li'l' extra stuff. . . . It ain't like that nonetall ovah in Europe, chappie. They wouldn't 'a' treated you so nice. Them places I sampled ovah there was all straight raw business and no camoflage."

"Did you prefer them?"

"Hell, no! I prefer the niggers' way every time. They does it better. . . ."

"Wish I could feel the difference as you do, Jakie. I lump all those ladies together, without difference of race."

"Youse crazy, chappie. You ain't got no experience about it. There's all kinds a difference in that theah life. Sometimes it's the people make the difference and sometimes it's the place. And as foh them sweet marchants, there's as much difference between them as you find in any other class a people. There is them slap-up private-apartmant ones, and there is them of the dickty buffet flats; then the low-down speakeasy customers; the cabaret babies, the family-entrance clients, and the street fliers."

They stopped on a board-walk. The dining-car stood before them, resting on one of the hundred tracks of the great Philadelphia yards.

"I got a free permit to a nifty apartmant in New York, chappie, and the next Saturday night we lay over together in the big city Ise gwine to show you some real queens. It's like everything else in life. Depends on you' luck."

"And you are one lucky dog," Ray laughed.

Jake grinned: "I'd tell you about a li'l' piece o' sweetness I picked up in a cabaret the first day I landed from ovah the other side. But it's too late now. We gotta start work."

"Next time, then," said Ray.

Jake swung himself up by the rear platform and entered the kitchen. Ray passed round by the other side into the dining-room.

XIV
Interlude

Dusk gathered in blue patches over the Black Belt. Lenox Avenue was vivid. The saloons were bright, crowded with drinking men jammed tight around the bars, treating one another and telling the incidents of the day. Longshoremen in overalls with hooks, Pullman porters holding their bags, waiters, elevator boys. Liquor-rich laughter, banana-ripe laughter. . . .

The pavement was a dim warm bustle. Women hurrying home from day's work to get dinner ready for husbands who worked at night. On their arms brown bags and black containing a bit of meat, a head of lettuce, butter. Young men who were stagging through life, passing along with brown-paper packages, containing a small steak, a pork chop, to do their own frying.

From out of saloons came the savory smell of corned beef and cabbage, spare-ribs, Hamburger steaks. Out of little cook-joints wedged in side streets, tripe, pigs' feet, hogs' ears and snouts. Out of apartments, steak smothered with onions, liver and bacon, fried chicken.

The composite smell of cooked stuff assaulted Jake's nostrils. He was hungry. His landlady was late bringing his food. Maybe she was out on Lenox Avenue chewing the rag with some other Ebenezer soul, thought Jake.

Jake was ill. The doctor told him that he would get well very quickly if he remained quietly in bed for a few days.

"And you mustn't drink till you are better. It's bad for you," the doctor warned him.

But Jake had his landlady bring him from two to four pails of beer every day. "I must drink some'n," he reasoned, "and beer can't make me no harm. It's light."

When Ray went to see him, Jake laughed at his serious mien.

"Tha's life, chappie. I goes way ovah yonder and wander and fools around and I hed no mind about nothing. Then I come back to mah own home town and, oh, you snakebite! When I was in the army, chappie, they useter give us all sorts o' lechers about canshankerous nights and prophet-lactic days, but I nevah pay them no mind. Them things foh edjucated guys like you who lives in you' head."

"They are for you, too," Ray said. "This is a new age with new methods of living. You can't just go on like a crazy ram goat as if you were living in the Middle Ages."

"Middle Ages! I ain't seen them yet and don't nevah wanta. All them things you talk about am kill-joy things, chappie. The trute is they make me feel shame."

Ray laughed until tears trickled down his cheeks. . . . He visualized Jake being ashamed and laughed again.

"Sure," said Jake. "I'd feel ashame' ef a chippie—No, chappie, them stuff is foh you book fellahs. I runs around all right, but Ise lak a sailor that don't know nothing about using a compass, but him always hits a safe port."

"You didn't this time, though, Jakie. Those devices that you despise are really for you rather than for me or people like me, who don't live your kind of free life. If you, and the whole strong race of workingman who live freely like you, don't pay some attention to them, then you'll all wither away and rot like weeds."

"Let us pray!" said Jake.

"*That* I don't believe in."

"Awright, then, chappie."

On the next trip, the dining-car was shifted off its scheduled run and returned to New York on the second day, late at night. It was ordered out again early the next day. Ray could not get round to see Jake, so he telephoned his girl and asked her to go.

Agatha had heard much of Ray's best friend, but she had never met him. Men working on a train have something of the spirit of men working on a ship. They are, perforce, bound together in comradeship of a sort in that close atmosphere. In the stopover cities they go about in pairs or groups. But the camaraderie breaks up on the platform in New York as soon as the dining-car returns there. Every man goes his own way unknown to his comrades. Wife or sweetheart or some other magnet of the great magic city draws each off separately.

Agatha was a rich-brown girl, with soft amorous eyes. She worked as assistant in a beauty parlor of the Belt. She was a Baltimore girl and had been living in New York for two years. Ray had met her the year before at a basket-ball match and dance.

She went to see Jake in the afternoon. He was sitting in a Morris chair, reading the Negro newspaper, *The Amsterdam News*, with a pail of beer beside him, when Agatha rapped on the door.

Jake thought it was the landlady. He was thrown off his balance by the straight, beautiful girl who entered the room and quietly closed the door behind her.

"Oh, keep your seat, please," she begged him. "I'll sit there," she indicated a brown chair by the cherrywood chiffonier.

"Ray asked me to come. He was doubled out this morning and couldn't get around to see you. I brought these for you."

She put a paper bag of oranges on the table. "Where shall I put these?" She showed him a charming little bouquet of violets. Jake's drinking-glass was on the floor, half full, beside the pail of beer.

"It's all right, here!" On the chipped, mildew-white washstand there was another glass with a tooth-brush. She took the tooth-brush out, poured some water in the glass, put the violets in, and set it on the chiffonier.

"There!" she said.

Jake thanked her. He was diffident. She was so different a girl from the many he had known. She was certainly one of those that Miss Curdy would have sneered at. She was so full of simple self-assurance and charm. Mah little sister down home in Petersburg, he thought, might have turned out something lak this ef she'd 'a' had a chance to talk English like in books and wear class-top clothes. Nine years sence I quite home. She must be quite a li'l' woman now herself.

Jake loved women's pretty clothes. The plain nigger-brown coat Agatha wore, unbuttoned, showed a fresh peach-colored frock. He asked after Ray.

"I didn't see him myself this trip," she said. "He telephoned me about you."

Jake praised Ray as his best pal.

"He's a good boy," she agreed. She asked Jake about the

railroad. "It must be lots of fun to ride from one town to the other like that. I'd love it, for I love to travel. But Ray hates it."

"It ain't so much fun when youse working," replied Jake.

"I guess you're right. But there's something marvelous about meeting people for a little while and serving them and never seeing them again. It's romantic. You don't have that awful personal everyday contact that domestic workers have to get along with. If I was a man and had to be in service, I wouldn't want better than the railroad."

"Some'n to that, yes," agreed Jake. . . . "But it ain't all peaches, neither, when all them passengers rush you like a herd of hungry swine."

Agatha stayed twenty minutes.

"I wish you better soon," she said, bidding Jake good-by. "It was nice to know you. Ray will surely come to see you when he gets back this time."

Jake drank a glass of beer and eased his back, full length on the little bed.

"She is sure some wonderful brown," he mused. "Now I sure does understand why Ray is so scornful of them easy ones." He gazed at the gray door. It seemed a shining panel of gold through which a radiant vision had passed.

"She sure does like that theah Ray an unconscionable lot. I could see the love stuff shining in them mahvelous eyes of hers when I talked about him. I s'pose it's killing sweet to have some'n loving you up thataway. Some'n real fond o' you for you own self lak, lak—jest lak how mah mammy useter love pa and do everything foh him bafore he done took and died off without giving no notice. . . ."

His thoughts wandered away back to his mysterious little brown of the Baltimore. She was not elegant and educated, but she was nice. Maybe if he found her again—it would be better than just running wild around like that! Thinking honestly about it, after all, he was never satisfied, flopping here and sleeping there. It gave him a little cocky pleasure to brag of his conquests to the fellows around the bar. But after all the swilling and boasting, it would be a thousand times nicer to have a little brown woman of his own to whom he could go home and be his simple self with. Lay his curly head between her brown breasts and be fondled and be the spoiled child that every man loves sometimes to be when he is all alone with a woman. *That* he could never be with the Madame Lauras. They expected him always to be the prancing he-man. Maybe it was the lack of a steady girl that kept him running crazy around. Boozing and poking and rooting around, jolly enough all right, but not altogether contented.

The landlady did not appear with Jake's dinner.

"Guess she is somewhere rocking soft with gin," he thought. "Ise feeling all right enough to go out, anyhow. Guess I'll drop in at Uncle Doc's and have a good feed of spare-ribs. Hm! but the stuff coming out of these heah Harlem kitchens is enough to knock me down. They smell so good."

He dressed and went out. "Oh, Lenox Avenue, but you look good to me, now. Lawdy! though, how the brown-skin babies am humping it along! Strutting the joy-stuff! Invitation for a shimmy. O Lawdy! Pills and pisen, you gotta turn me loose, quick."

Billy Biasse was drinking at the bar of Uncle Doc's when Jake entered.

"Come on, you, and have a drink," Billy cried. "Which hole in Harlem youse been burying you'self in all this time?"

"Which you figure? There is holes outside of Harlem too, boh." Jake ordered a beer.

"Beer!" exclaimed Billy. "Quit you fooling and take some real liquor, nigger. Ise paying foh it. Order that theah ovah-water liquor you useter be so dippy about. That theah Scotch."

"I ain't quite all right, Billy. Gotta go slow on the booze."

"Whasmat? . . . Oh, foh Gawd's sake! Don't let the li'l' beauty break you' heart. Fix her up with gin."

"Might as well, and then a royal feed o' spare-ribs," agreed Jake.

He asked for Zeddy.

"Missing sence all the new moon done bless mah luck that you is, too. Last news I heard 'bout him, the gen'man was Yonkers anchored."

"And Strawberry Lips?"

"That nigger's back home in Harlem where he belongs. He done long ago quit that ugly yaller razor-back. And you, boh.

Who's providing foh you' wants sence you done turn Congo Rose down?"

"Been running wild in the paddock of the Pennsy."

"Oh, boh, you sure did breaks the sweet-loving haht of Congo Rose. One night she stahted to sing 'You broke mah haht and went away' and she jest bust out crying theah in the cabaret and couldn't sing no moh. She hauled harself whimpering out there, and she laid off o' the Congo foh moh than a week. That li'l' goosey boy had to do the strutting all by himse'f."

"She was hot stuff all right." Jake laughed richly. "But I had to quit her or she would have made me either a no-'count or a bad nigger."

Warmed up by meeting an old pal and hearing all the intimate news of the dives, Jake tossed off he knew not how many gins. He told Billy Biasse of the places he had nosed out in Baltimore and Philadelphia. The gossip was good. Jake changed to Scotch and asked for the siphon.

He had finished the first Scotch and asked for another, when a pain gripped his belly with a wrench that almost tore him apart. Jake groaned and doubled over, staggered into a corner, and crumpled up on the floor. Perspiration stood in beads on his forehead, trickled down his rigid, chiseled features. He heard the word "ambulance" repeated several times. He thought first of his mother. His sister. The little frame house in Petersburg. The backyard of bleached clothes on the line, the large lilac tree and the little forked lot that yielded red tomatoes and green peas in spring.

"No hospital foh me," he muttered. "Mah room is jest next doh. Take me theah."

Uncle Doc told his bar man to help Billy Biasse lift Jake.

"Kain you move you' laigs any at all, boh?" Billy asked.

Jake groaned: "I kain try."

The men took him home. . . .

Jake's landlady had been invited to a fried-chicken feed in the basement lodging of an Ebenezer sister and friend on Fifth Avenue. The sister friend had rented the basement of the old-fashioned house and appropriated the large backyard for her laundry work. She went out and collected soiled linen every Monday. Her wealthiest patrons sent their chauffeurs round with their linen. And the laundress was very proud of white chauffeurs standing their automobiles in front of her humble basement. She noticed with heaving chest that the female residents of the block rubber-necked. Her vocation was very profitable. And it was her pleasure sometimes to invite a sister of her church to dinner. . . .

The fried chicken, with sweet potatoes, was excellent. Over it the sisters chinned and ginned, recounting all the contemporary scandals of the Negro churches. . . .

At last Jake's landlady remembered him and staggered home to prepare his beef broth. But when she took it up to him she found that Jake was out. Returning to the kitchen, she stumbled and broke the white bowl, made a sign with her rabbit foot, and murmured, foggily: "Theah's sure a cross coming to thisa house. I wonder it's foh who?"

The bell rang and rang again and again in spite of the notice: Ring once. And when the landlady opened the door and saw Jake supported between two men, she knew that the broken white bowl was for him and that his time was come.

XV
Relapse

BILLY BIASSE telephoned to the doctor, a young chocolate-complexioned man. He was graduate of a Negro medical college in Tennessee and of Columbia University. He was struggling to overcome the prejudices of the black populace against Negro doctors and wedge himself in among the Jewish doctors that prescribed for the Harlem clientele. A clever man, he was trying, through Democratic influence, to get an appointment in one of the New York hospitals. Such an achievement would put him all over the Negro press and get him all the practice and more than he could handle in the Belt.

Ray had sent Jake to him. . . .

The landlady brought Jake a rum punch. He shook his head. With a premonition of tragedy, she waited for the doctor, standing against the chiffonier, a blue cloth carelessly knotted round her head. . . .

In the corridor she questioned Billy Biasse about Jake's seizure.

"All you younger generation in Harlem don't know no God," she accused Billy and indicted Young Harlem. "All you know is cabarets and movies and the young gals them exposing them legs a theirs in them jumper frocks."

"I wouldn't know 'bout that," said Billy.

"You all ought to know, though, and think of God Almighty before the trumpet sound and it's too late foh black sinners. I nevah seen so many trifling and ungodly niggers as there is in this heah Harlem." She thought of the broken white bowl. "And I done had a warning from heaben."

The doctor arrived. Ordered a hot-water bottle for Jake's belly and a hot lemon drink. There was no other remedy to help him but what he had been taking.

"You've been drinking," the doctor said.

"Jest a li'l' beer," Jake murmured.

"O Lawdy! though, listen at him!" cried the landlady.

"Mister, if he done had a glass, he had a barrel a day. Ain't I been getting it foh him?"

"Beer is the worst form of alcohol you could ever take in your state," said the doctor. "Couldn't be anything worse. Better you had taken wine."

Jake growled that he didn't like wine.

"It's up to you to get well," said the doctor. "You have been ill like that before. It's a simple affair if you will be careful and quiet for a little while. But it's very dangerous if you are foolish. I know you chaps take those things lightly. But you shouldn't, for the consequences are very dangerous."

Two days later Ray's diner returned to New York. It was early afternoon and the crew went over to the yards to get the stock for the next trip. And after stocking up Ray went directly to see Jake.

Jake was getting along all right again. But Ray was alarmed when he heard of his relapse. Indeed, Ray was too easily moved for the world he lived in. The delicate-fibered mechanism of his being responded to sensations that were entirely beyond Jake's comprehension.

"The doctor done hand me his. The landlady stahted warning me against sin with her mouth stinking with gin. And now mah chappie's gwina join the gang." Jake laughed heartily.

"But you must be careful, Jake. You're too sensible not to know good advice from bad."

"Oh, sure, chappie, I'll take care. I don't wanta be crippled up as the doctor says I might. Mah laigs got many moh miles to run yet, chasing after the sweet stuff o' life, chappie."

"Good oh Jake! I know you love life too much to make a fool of yourself like so many of those other fellows. I've never knew that this thing was so common until I started working on the railroad. You know the fourth had to lay off this trip."

"You don't say!"

"Yes, he's got a mean one. And the second cook on Bowman's diner he's been in a chronic way for about three months."

"But how does he get by the doctor? All them crews is examined every week."

"Hm! . . ." Ray glanced carelessly through *The Amsterdam*

News. "I saw Madame Laura in Fairmount Park and I told her you were sick. I gave her your address, too."

"Bumbole! What for?"

"Because she asked me for it. She was sympathetic."

"I never give mah address to them womens, chappie. Bad system that."

"Why?"

"Because you nevah know when they might bust in on you and staht a rough-house. Them's all right, them womens . . . in their own parlors."

"I guess you ought to know. I don't," said Ray. "Say, why don't you move out of this dump up to the Forties? There's a room in the same house I stay in. Cheap. Two flights up, right on the court. Steam heat and everything."

"I guess I could stand a new place to lay mah carcass in, all right," Jake drawled. "Steam heats you say? I'm sure sick o' this here praying-ma-ma hot air. And the trute is it ain't nevah much hotter than mah breath."

"All right. When do you want me to speak to the landlady about the room?"

"This heah very beautiful night, chappie. Mah rent is up to-morrow and I moves. But you got to do me a li'l' favor. Go by Billy Biasse this night and tell him to come and git his ole buddy's suitcase and see him into his new home tomorrow morning."

Jake was as happy as a kid. He would be frisking if he could. But Ray was not happy. The sudden upset of affairs in his home country had landed him into the quivering heart of a naked world whose reality was hitherto unimaginable. It was what they called in print and polite conversation "the underworld." The compound word baffled him, as some English words did sometimes. Why *under*-world he could never understand. It was very much upon the surface as were the others divisions of human life. Having its heights and middle and depths and se-cret places even as they. And the people of this world, waiters, cooks, chauffeurs, sailors, porters, guides, ushers, hod-carriers, factory hands—all touched in a thousand ways the people of the other divisions. They worked over there and slept over here, divided by a street.

Ray had always dreamed of writing words some day. Weaving words to make romance, ah! There were the great books that dominated the bright dreaming and dark brooding days when he was a boy. *Les Misérables, Nana, Uncle Tom's Cabin, David Copperfield, Nicholas Nickleby, Oliver Twist.*

From them, by way of free-thought pamphlets, it was only a stride to the great scintillating satirists of the age—Bernard Shaw, Ibsen, Anatole France, and the popular problemist, H. G. Wells. He had lived on that brilliant manna that fell like a flame-fall from those burning stars. Then came the great mass carnage in Europe and the great mass revolution in Russia.

Ray was not prophetic-minded enough to define the total evil that the one had wrought nor the ultimate splendor of the other. But, in spite of the general tumults and threats, the perfectly-organized national rages, the ineffectual patching of broken, and hectic rebuilding of shattered, things, he had perception enough to realize that he had lived over the end of an era.

And also he realized that his spiritual masters had not crossed with him into the new. He felt alone, hurt, neglected, cheated, almost naked. But he was a savage, even though he was a sensitive one, and did not mind nakedness. What had happened? Had they refused to come or had he left them behind? Something had happened. But it was not desertion nor young insurgency. It was death. Even as the last scion of a famous line prances out this day and dies and is set aside with his ancestors in their cold whited sepulcher, so had his masters marched with flags and banners flying all their wonderful, trenchant, critical, satirical, mind-sharpening, pity-evoking, constructive ideas of ultimate social righteousness, into the vast international cemetery of this century.

Dreams of patterns of words achieving form. What would he ever do with the words he had acquired? Were they adequate to tell the thoughts he felt, describe the impressions that reached him vividly? What were men making of words now? During the war he had been startled by James Joyce in *The Little Review*. Sherwood Anderson had reached him with *Winesburg, Ohio*. He had read, fascinated, all that D. H. Lawrence published. And wondered if there was not a great Lawrence reservoir of words too terrible and too terrifying for nice printing. Henri Barbusse's *Le Feu* burnt like a flame in his memory. Ray loved the book because it was such a grand anti-romantic presentation of mind and behavior in that hell-pit of life. And literature, story-telling, had little interest for him now if thought and feeling did not wrestle and sprawl with appetite and dark desire all over the pages.

Dreams of making something with words. What could he make . . . and fashion? Could he ever create Art? Art, around which vague, incomprehensible words and phrases stormed? What was art, anyway? Was it more than a clear-cut presentation of a vivid impression of life? Only the Russians of the late era seemed to stand up like giants in the new. Gogol, Dostoievski, Tolstoy, Chekhov, Turgeniev. When he read them now he thought: Here were elements that the grand carnage swept over and touched not. The soil of life saved their roots from the fire. They were so saturated, so deep-down rooted in it.

Thank God and Uncle Sam that the old dreams were shattered. Nevertheless, he still felt more than ever the utter blinding nakedness and violent coloring of life. But what of it? Could he create out of the fertile reality around him? Of Jake nosing through life, a handsome hound, quick to snap up any tempting morsel of poisoned meat thrown carelessly on the pavement? Of a work pal he had visited in the venereal ward of Bellevue, where youths lolled sadly about? And the misery that overwhelmed him there, until life appeared like one big disease and the world a vast hospital?

XVI
A Practical Prank

MY DEAR HONEY-STICK

"I was riding in Fairmount Park one afternoon, just taking the air as usual, when I saw your proper-speaking friend with a mess of books. He told me you were sick and I was so mortified for I am giving a big evening soon and was all set on fixing it on a night when you would certain sure be laying over in Philadelphia. Because you are such good company I may as well say how much you are appreciated here. I guess I'll put it off till you are okay again, for as I am putting my hand in my own pocket to give all of my friends and wellwishers a dandy time it won't be no fun for *me* if I leave out the *principal* one. Guess who!

"I am expecting to come to New York soon on a shopping bent. You know all us weak women who can afford it have got the Fifth Avenue fever, my dear. If I come I'll sure look you up, you can bank on it.

"Bye, bye, honeystick and be good and quiet and better yourself soon. Philadelphia is lonesome without you.

"Lovingly, LAURA."

Billy Biasse, calling by Jake's former lodging, found this letter for him, lying there among a pile of others, on the little black round table in the hall. . . .

"Here you is, boh. Whether youse well or sick, them's after you."

"Is they? Lemme see. Hm . . . Philly." . . .

"Who is you' pen-pusher?" asked Billy.

"A queen in Philly. Says she might pay me a visit here. I ain't send out no invitation foh no womens yet."

"Is she the goods?"

"She's a wang, boh. Queen o' Philly, I tell you. And foh me, everything with her is f.o.c. But I don't want that yaller piece o' business come nosing after me here in Harlem."

"She ain't got to find you, boh. Jest throws her a bad lead."

"Tha's the stuff to give 'm. Ain't you a buddy with a haid on, though?"

" 'Deed I is. And all you niggers knows it who done frequent mah place."

And so Jake, in a prankish mood, replied to Madame Laura on a picture post-card saying he would be well and up soon and be back on the road and on the job again, and he gave Congo Rose's address.

Madame Laura made her expected trip to New York, traveling "Chair," as was her custom when she traveled. She wore a mauve dress, vermilion-shot at the throat, and short enough to show the curved plumpness of her legs encased in fine un-rumpled rose-tinted stockings. Her modish overcoat was lilac-gray lined with green and a large marine-blue rosette was bunched at the side of her neat gray hat.

In the Fifth Avenue shops she was waited upon as if she were a dark foreign lady of title visiting New York. In the afternoon she took a taxi-cab to Harlem.

Now all the fashionable people who called at Rose's house were generally her friends. And so Rose always went herself to let them in. She could look out from her window, one flight up, and ho-ho down to them.

When Madame Laura rang the bell, Rose popped her head out. Nobody I know, she thought, but the attractive woman in expensive clothes piqued her curiosity. Hastily she dabbed her face with a powder pad, patted her hair into shape, and descended.

"Is Mr. Jacob Brown living here?" Madame Laura asked.

"Well, he was—I mean——" This luxurious woman demanding Jake tantalized Rose. She still referred to him as her man since his disappearance. No reports of his living with another woman having come to her, she had told her friends that Jake's mother had come between them.

"He always had a little some'n' of a mamma's boy about him, you know."

Poor Jake. Since he left home, his mother had become for him a loving memory only. When you saw him, talked to him, he stood forth as one of those unique types of humanity who

lived alone and were never lonely. You would hardly wonder
who were his father and mother and what they were like. He,
in his frame and atmosphere, was the Alpha and Omega himself.

"I mean—— Can you tell me what you want?" asked Rose.

"Must I? I didn't know he—— Why, he wrote to me. Said
he was ill. And sent his friend to tell me he was ill. Can't I see
him?"

"Did he write to you from this here address?"

"Why, certainly. I have his card here." Madame Laura was
fumbling in her handbag.

A triumphant smile stole into Rose's face. Jake had no real
home and had to use her address.

"Is you his sister or what?"

"I'm a friend," Madame Laura said, sharply.

"Well, he's got a nearve." Rose jerked herself angrily. "He's
mah man."

"I didn't come all the way here to hear that," said Madame
Laura. "I thought he was sick and wanting attention."

"Ain't I good enough to give him all the attention required
without another woman come chasing after him?"

"Disgusting!" cried Madame Laura. "I would think this was
a spohting house."

"Gwan with you before I spit in you' eye," cried Rose. "You
look like some'n just outa one you'self."

"You're no lady," retorted Madame Laura, and she hurried
down the steps.

Rose amplified the story exceedingly in telling it to her
friends. "I slapped her face for insulting me," she said.

Billy Biasse heard of it from the boy dancer of the Congo.
When Billy went again to see Jake, one of the patrons of his
gaming joint went with him. It was that yellow youth, the
same one that had first invited Zeddy over to Gin-head Susy's
place. He was a prince of all the day joints and night holes of
the Belt. All the shark players of Dixie Red's pool-room were
proud of losing a game to him, and at the Congo the waiters
danced around to catch his orders. For Yaller Prince, so they
affectionately called him, was living easy and sweet. Three girls,
they said, were engaged in the business of keeping him princely
—one chocolate-to-the-bone, one teasing-brown, and one

yellow. He was always well dressed in a fine nigger-brown or bottle-green suit, excessively creased, and spats. Also he was happy-going and very generous. But there was something slimy about him.

Yaller Prince had always admired Jake, in the way a common-bred admires a thoroughbred, and hearing from Billy that he was ill, he had brought him fruit, cake, and ice cream and six packets of Camels. Yaller Prince was more intimate with Jake's world than Billy, who swerved off at a different angle and was always absorbed in the games and winnings of men.

Jake and Yaller had many loose threads to pick up again and follow for a while. Were the gin parties going on still at Susy's? What had become of Miss Curdy? Yaller didn't know. He had dropped Myrtle Avenue before Zeddy did.

"Susy was free with the gin all right, but, gee whizzard! She was sure black and ugly, buddy," remarked Yaller.

"You said it, boh," agreed Jake. "They was some pair all right, them two womens. Black and ugly is exactly Susy, and that there other Curdy creachur all streaky yaller and ugly. I couldn't love them theah kind."

Yaller uttered a little goat laugh. "I kain't stand them ugly grannies, either. But sometimes they does pay high, buddy, and when the paying is good, I can always transfer mah mind."

"I couldn't foh no price, boh," said Jake. "Gimme a nice sweet-skin brown. I ain't got no time foh none o' you' ugly hard-hided dames."

Jake asked for Strawberry Lips. He was living in Harlem again and working longshore. Up in Yonkers Zeddy was endeavoring to overcome his passion for gambling and start housekeeping with a steady home-loving woman. He was beginning to realize that he was not big enough to carry two strong passions, each pulling him in opposite directions. Some day a grandson of his born in Harlem might easily cope with both passions, might even come to sacrifice woman to gambling. But Zeddy himself was too close to the savage swell of life.

Ray entered with a friend whom he introduced as James Grant. He was also a student working his way through college. But lacking funds to continue, he had left college to find a job. He was fourth waiter on Ray's diner, succeeding the timid boy from Georgia. As both chairs were in use, Grant sat on the edge of the bed and Ray tipped up Jake's suitcase. . . .

Conversation veered off to the railroad.

"I am getting sick of it," Ray said. "It's a crazy, clattering, nerve-shattering life. I think I'll fall down for good."

"Why, ef you quit, chappie, I'll nevah go back on that there white man's sweet chariot," said Jake.

"Whasmat?" asked Billy Biasse. "Kain't you git along on theah without him?"

"It's a whole lot the matter you can't understand, Billy. The white folks' railroad ain't like Lenox Avenue. You can tell on theah when a pal's a real pal."

"I got a pal, I got a gal," chanted Billy, "heah in mah pocket-book." He patted his breast pocket.

"Go long from here with you' lonesome haht, you wolf," cried Jake.

"Wolf is mah middle name, but . . . I ain't bad as I hear, and ain't you mah buddy, too?" Billy said to Jake. "Git you'self going quick and come on down to mah place, son. The bones am lonesome foh you."

Billy and Yaller Prince left.

"Who is the swell strutter?" Ray's friend asked.

"Hm! . . . I knowed him long time in Harlem," said Jake. "He's a good guy. Just brought me all them eats and ciga-rettes."

"What does he work at?" asked Ray.

"Nothing menial. He's a p-i." . . .

"Low-down yaller swine," said Ray's friend. "Harlem is stinking with them."

"Oh, Yaller is all right, though," said Jake. "A real good-hearted scout."

"Good-hearted!" Grant sneered. "A man's heart is cold dead when he has women doing that for him. How can a man live that way and strut in public, instead of hiding himself under-ground like a worm?" He turned indignantly to Ray.

"Search me!" Ray laughed a little. "You might as well ask why all mulattoes have unpleasant voices."

Grant was slightly embarrassed. He was yellow-skinned and his voice was hard and grainy. Jake he-hawed.

"Not all, chappie, I know some with sweet voice."

"Mulat*tress, mon ami.*" Ray lifted a finger. "That's an exception. And now, James, let us forget Jake's kind friend."

"Oh, I don't mind him talking," said Jake. "I don't approve of Yaller's trade mahself, but ef he can do it, well— It's because you don't know how many womens am running after the fellahs jest begging them to do that. They been after me moh time I can remember. There's lots o' folks living easy and living sweet, but . . ."

"There are as many forms of parasitism as there are ways of earning a living," said Ray.

"But to live the life of carrion," sneered Grant, "fatten on rotting human flesh. It's the last ditch, where dogs go to die. When you drop down in that you cease being human."

"You done said it straight out, brother," said Jake. "It's a stinking life and I don't like stinks."

"Your feeling against that sort of thing is fine, James," said Ray. "But that's the most I could say for it. It's all right to start out with nice theories from an advantageous point in life. But when you get a chance to learn life for yourself, it's quite another thing. The things you call fine human traits don't belong to any special class or nation or race of people. Nobody can pull that kind of talk now and get away with it, least of all a Negro."

"Why not?" asked Grant. "Can't a Negro have fine feelings about life?"

"Yes, but not the old false-fine feelings that used to be monopolized by educated and cultivated people. You should educate yourself away from that sort of thing."

"But education is something to make you fine!"

"No, modern education is planned to make you a sharp, snouty, rooting hog. A Negro getting it is an anachronism. We ought to get something new, we Negroes. But we get our education like—like our houses. When the whites move out, we move in and take possession of the old dead stuff. Dead stuff that this age has no use for."

"How's that?"

"Can you ask? You and I were born in the midst of the illness of this age and have lived through its agony. . . . Keep your fine feelings, indeed, but don't try to make a virtue of them. You'll lose them, then. They'll become all hollow inside, false and dry as civilization itself. And civilization is rotten. We are all rotten who are touched by it."

"I am not rotten," retorted Grant, "and I couldn't bring myself and my ideas down to the level of such filthy parasites."

"All men have the disease of pimps in their hearts," said Ray. "We can't be civilized and not. I have seen your high and mighty civilized people do things that some pimps would be ashamed of——"

"You said it, then, and most truly," cried Jake, who, lying on the bed, was intently following the dialogue.

"Do it in the name of civilization," continued Ray. "And I have been forced down to the level of pimps and found some of them more than human. One of them was so strange. . . . I never thought he could feel anything. Never thought he could do what he did. Something so strange and wonderful and awful, it just lifted me up out of my little straight thoughts into a big whirl where all of life seemed hopelessly tangled and colored without point or purpose."

"Tell us about it," said Grant.

"All right," said Ray. "I'll tell it."

XVII
He Also Loved

IT was in the winter of 1916 when I first came to New York to hunt for a job. I was broke. I was afraid I would have to pawn my clothes, and it was dreadfully cold. I didn't even know the right way to go about looking for a job. I was always timid about that. For five weeks I had not paid my rent. I was worried, and Ma Lawton, my landlady, was also worried. She had her bills to meet. She was a good-hearted old woman from South Carolina. Her face was all wrinkled and sensitive like finely-carved mahogany.

Every bed-space in the flat was rented. I was living in the small hall bedroom. Ma Lawton asked me to give it up. There were four men sleeping in the front room; two in an old, chipped-enameled brass bed, one on a davenport, and the other in a folding chair. The old lady put a little canvas cot in that same room, gave me a pillow and a heavy quilt, and said I should try and make myself comfortable there until I got work.

The cot was all right for me. Although I hate to share a room with another person and the fellows snoring disturbed my rest. Ma Lawton moved into the little room that I had had, and rented out hers—it was next to the front room—to a man and a woman.

The woman was above ordinary height, chocolate-colored. Her skin was smooth, too smooth, as if it had been pressed and fashioned out for ready sale like chocolate candy. Her hair was straightened out into an Indian Straight after the present style among Negro ladies. She had a mongoose sort of a mouth, with two top front teeth showing. She wore a long mink coat.

The man was darker than the woman. His face was longish, with the right cheek somewhat caved in. It was an interesting face, an attractive, salacious mouth, with the lower lip protruding. He wore a bottle-green peg-top suit, baggy at the hips. His coat hung loose from his shoulders and it was much longer than the prevailing style. He wore also a Mexican hat, and in his breast pocket he carried an Ingersoll watch attached to a heavy gold chain. His name was Jericho Jones, and they called him Jerco for short. And she was Miss Whicher—Rosalind Whicher.

Ma Lawton introduced me to them and said I was broke, and they were both awfully nice to me. They took me to a big feed of corned beef and cabbage at Burrell's on Fifth Avenue. They gave me a good appetizing drink of gin to commence with. And we had beer with the eats; not ordinary beer, either, but real Budweiser, right off the ice.

And as good luck sometimes comes pouring down like a shower, the next day Ma Lawton got me a job in the little free-lunch saloon right under her flat. It wasn't a paying job as far as money goes in New York, but I was glad to have it. I had charge of the free-lunch counter. You know the little dry crackers that go so well with beer, and the cheese and fish and the potato salad. And I served, besides, spare-ribs and whole boiled potatoes and corned beef and cabbage for those customers who could afford to pay for a lunch. I got no wages at all, but I got my eats twice a day. And I made a few tips, also. For there were about six big black men with plenty of money who used to eat lunch with us, specially for our spare-ribs and sweet potatoes. Each one of them gave me a quarter. I made enough to pay Ma Lawton for my canvas cot.

Strange enough, too, Jerco and Rosalind took a liking to me. And sometimes they came and ate lunch perched up there at the counter, with Rosalind the only woman there, all made up and rubbing her mink coat against the men. And when they got through eating, Jerco would toss a dollar bill at me.

We got very friendly, we three. Rosalind would bring up squabs and canned stuff from the German delicatessen in One Hundred and Twenty-fifth Street, and sometimes they asked me to dinner in their room and gave me good liquor.

I thought I was pretty well fixed for such a hard winter. All I had to do as extra work was keeping the saloon clean. . . .

One afternoon Jerco came into the saloon with a man who looked pretty near white. Of course, you never can tell for sure about a person's race in Harlem, nowadays, when there are so many high-yallers floating round—colored folks that would make Italian and Spanish people look like Negroes beside them. But I figured out from his way of talking and acting that the man with Jerco belonged to the white race. They went in through the family entrance into the back room, which was unusual, for the family room of a saloon, as you know, is only for women in the business and the men they bring in there with them. Real men don't sit in a saloon here as they do at home. I suppose it would be sissified. There's a bar for them to lean on and drink and joke as long as they feel like.

The boss of the saloon was a little fidgety about Jerco and his friend sitting there in the back. The boss was a short pumpkin-bellied brown man, a little bald off the forehead. Twice he found something to attend to in the back room, although there was nothing at all there that wanted attending to. . . . I felt better, and the boss, too, I guess, when Rosalind came along and gave the family room its respectable American character. I served Rosalind a Martini cocktail extra dry, and afterward all three of them, Rosalind, Jerco, and their friend, went up to Ma Lawton's.

The two fellows that slept together were elevator operators in a department store, so they had their Sundays free. On the afternoon of the Sunday of the same week that the white-looking man had been in the saloon with Jerco, I went upstairs to change my old shoes—they'd got soaking wet behind the counter—and I found Ma Lawton talking to the two elevator fellows.

The boys had given Ma Lawton notice to quit. They said they couldn't sleep there comfortably together on account of the goings-on in Rosalind's room. The fellows were members of the Colored Y.M.C.A. and were queerly quiet and pious. One of them was studying to be a preacher. They were the sort of fellows that thought going to cabarets a sin, and that parlor socials were leading Harlem straight down to hell. They only went to church affairs themselves. They had been rooming with Ma Lawton for over a year. She called them her gentlemen lodgers.

Ma Lawton said to me: "Have you heard anything phony outa the next room, dear?"

"Why, no, Ma," I said, "nothing more unusual than you can hear all over Harlem. Besides, I work so late, I am dead tired when I turn in to bed, so I sleep heavy."

"Well, it's the truth I do like that there Jerco an' Rosaline," said Ma Lawton. "They did seem quiet as lambs, although they was always havin' company. But Ise got to speak to them, 'cause I doana wanta lose ma young mens. . . . But theyse a real nice-acting couple. Jerco him treats me like him was mah son. It's true that they doan work like all poah niggers, but they pays that rent down good and prompt ehvery week."

Jerco was always bringing in ice-cream and cake or something for Ma Lawton. He had a way about him, and everybody liked him. He was a sympathetic type. He helped Ma Lawton move beds and commodes and he fixed her clothes lines. I had heard somebody talking about Jerco in the saloon, however, saying that he could swing a mean fist when he got his dander up, and that he had been mixed up in more than one razor cut-up. He did have a nasty long razor scar on the back of his right hand.

The elevator fellows had never liked Rosalind and Jerco. The one who was studying to preach Jesus said he felt pretty sure that they were an ungodly-living couple. He said that late one night he had pointed out their room to a woman that looked white. He said the woman looked suspicious. She was perfumed and all powdered up and it appeared as if she didn't belong among colored people.

"There's no sure telling white from high-yaller these days," I said. "There are so many swell-looking quadroons and octoroons of the race."

But the other elevator fellow said that one day in the tenderloin section he had run up against Rosalind and Jerco together with a petty officer of marines. And that just put the lid on anything favorable that could be said about them.

But Ma Lawton said: "Well, Ise got to run mah flat right an' try mah utmost to please youall, but I ain't wanta dip mah nose too deep in a lodger's affairs."

Late that night, toward one o'clock, Jerco dropped in at the saloon and told me that Rosalind was feeling badly. She hadn't eaten a bite all day and he had come to get a pail of beer, because she had asked specially for draught beer. Jerco was worried, too.

"I hopes she don't get bad," he said. "For we ain't got a cent o' money. Wese just in on a streak o' bad luck."

"I guess she'll soon be all right," I said.

The next day after lunch I stole a little time and went up to see Rosalind. Ma Lawton was just going to attend to her when I let myself in, and she said to me: "Now the poor woman is sick, poor chile, ahm so glad mah conscience is free and that I hadn't a said nothing evil t' her."

Rosalind was pretty sick. Ma Lawton said it was the grippe. She gave Rosalind hot whisky drinks and hot milk, and she kept her feet warm with a hot-water bottle. Rosalind's legs were lead-heavy. She had a pain that pinched her side like a pair of pincers. And she cried out for thirst and begged for draught beer.

Ma Lawton said Rosalind ought to have a doctor. "You'd better go an' scares up a white one," she said to Jerco. "Ise nevah had no faith in these heah nigger doctors."

"I don't know how we'll make out without money," Jerco whined. He was sitting in the old Morris chair with his head heavy on his left hand.

"You kain pawn my coat," said Rosalind. "Old man Greenbaum will give you two hundred down without looking at it."

"I won't put a handk'chief o' yourn in the hock shop," said Jerco. "You'll need you' stuff soon as you get better. Specially you' coat. You kain't go anywheres without it."

"S'posin' I don't get up again," Rosalind smiled. But her countenance changed suddenly as she held her side and moaned. Ma Lawton bent over and adjusted the pillows.

Jerco pawned his watch chain and his own overcoat, and called in a Jewish doctor from the upper Eighth Avenue fringe of the Belt. But Rosalind did not improve under medical treatment. She lay there with a sad, tired look, as if she didn't really care what happened to her. Her lower limbs were apparently paralyzed. Jerco told the doctor that she had been sick unto death like that before. The doctor shot a lot of stuff into her system. But Rosalind lay there heavy and fading like a felled tree.

The elevator operators looked in on her. The student one gave her a Bible with a little red ribbon marking the chapter in St. John's Gospel about the woman taken in adultery. He also wanted to pray for her recovery. Jerco wanted the prayer, but Rosalind said no. Her refusal shocked Ma Lawton, who believed in God's word.

The doctor stopped Rosalind from drinking beer. But Jerco slipped it in to her when Ma Lawton was not around. He said he couldn't refuse it to her when beer was the only thing she cared for. He had an expensive sweater. He pawned it. He also pawned their large suitcase. It was real leather and worth a bit of money.

One afternoon Jerco sat alone in the back room of the saloon and began to cry.

"I'd do anything. There ain't anything too low I wouldn't do to raise a little money," he said.

"Why don't you hock Rosalind's fur coat?" I suggested. "That'll give you enough money for a while."

"Gawd, no! I wouldn't touch none o' Rosalind's clothes. I jest kain't," he said. "She'll need them as soon as she's better."

"Well, you might try and find some sort of a job, then," I said.

"Me find a job? What kain I do? I ain't no good foh no job. I kain't work. I don't know how to ask for no job. I wouldn't know how. I wish I was a woman."

"Good God! Jerco," I said, "I don't see any way out for you but some sort of a job."

"What kain I do? What kain I do?" he whined. "I kain't do nothing. That's why I don't wanta hock Rosalind's fur coat. She'll need it soon as she's better. Rosalind's so wise about picking up good money. Just like that!" He snapped his fingers.

I left Jerco sitting there and went into the saloon to serve a customer a plate of corned beef and cabbage.

After lunch I thought I'd go up to see how Rosalind was making out. The door was slightly open, so I slipped in without knocking. I saw Jerco kneeling down by the open wardrobe and kissing the toe of one of her brown shoes. He started as he saw me, and looked queer kneeling there. It was a high old-fashioned wardrobe that Ma Lawton must have picked up at some sale. Rosalind's coat was hanging there, and it gave me a spooky feeling, for it looked so much more like the real Rosalind than the woman that was dozing there on the bed.

Her other clothes were hanging there, too. There were three gowns—a black silk, a glossy green satin, and a flimsy chiffon-like yellow thing. In a corner of the lowest shelf was a bundle of soiled champagne-colored silk stockings and in the other four pairs of shoes—one black velvet, one white kid, and another gold-finished. Jerco regarded the lot with dog-like affection.

"I wouldn't touch not one of her things until she's better," he said. "I'd sooner hock the shirt off mah back."

Which he was preparing to do. He had three expensive striped silk shirts, presents from Rosalind. He had just taken two out of the wardrobe and the other off his back, and made a parcel of them for old Greenbaum. . . . Rosalind woke up and murmured that she wanted some beer. . . .

A little later Jerco came to the saloon with the pail. He was shivering. His coat collar was turned up and fastened with a safety pin, for he only had an undershirt on.

"I don't know what I'd do if anything happens to Rosalind," he said. "I kain't live without her."

"Oh yes, you can," I said in a not very sympathetic tone. Jerco gave me such a reproachful pathetic look that I was sorry I said it.

The tall big fellow had turned into a scared, trembling baby. "You ought to buck up and hold yourself together," I told him. "Why, you ought to be game if you like Rosalind, and don't let her know you're down in the dumps."

"I'll try," he said. "She don't know how miserable I am. When I hooks up with a woman I treat her right, but I never let her know everything about me. Rosalind is an awful good woman. The straightest woman I ever had, honest."

I gave him a big glass of strong whisky.

Ma Lawton came in the saloon about nine o'clock that evening and said that Rosalind was dead. "I told Jerco we'd have to sell that theah coat to give the poah woman a decent fun'ral, an' he jest brokes down crying like a baby."

That night Ma Lawton slept in the kitchen and put Jerco in

her little hall bedroom. He was all broken up. I took him up a pint of whisky.

"I'll nevah find another one like Rosalind," he said, "nevah!" He sat on an old black-framed chair in which a new yellow-varnished bottom had just been put. I put my hand on his shoulder and tried to cheer him up: "Buck up, old man. Never mind, you'll find somebody else." He shook his head. "Perhaps you didn't like the way me and Rosalind was living. But she was one naturally good woman, all good inside her."

I felt foolish and uncomfortable. "I always liked Rosalind, Jerco," I said, "and you, too. You were both awfully good scouts to me. I have nothing against her. I am nothing myself."

Jerco held my hand and whimpered: "Thank you, old top. Youse all right. Youse always been a regular fellar."

It was late, after two a. m. I went to bed. And, as usual, I slept soundly.

Ma Lawton was an early riser. She made excellent coffee and she gave the two elevator runners and another lodger, a porter who worked on Ellis Island, coffee and hot homemade biscuits every morning. The next morning she shook me abruptly out of my sleep.

"Ahm scared to death. Thar's moah tur'ble trouble. I kain't git in the barfroom and the hallway's all messy."

I jumped up, hauled on my pants, and went to the bath-room. A sickening purplish liquid coming from under the door had trickled down the hall toward the kitchen. I took Ma Lawton's rolling-pin and broke through the door.

Jerco had cut his throat and was lying against the bowl of the water-closet. Some empty coke papers were on the floor. And he sprawled there like a great black boar in a mess of blood.

XVIII
A Farewell Feed

R AY and Grant had found jobs on a freighter that was going down across the Pacific to Australia and from there to Europe. Ray had reached the point where going any further on the railroad was impossible. He had had enough to vomit up of Philadelphia and Baltimore, Pittsburgh and Washington. More than enough of the bar-to-bar camaraderie of railroad life.

And Agatha was acting wistfully. He knew what would be the inevitable outcome of meeting that subtle wistful yearning halfway. Soon he would become one of the contented hogs in the pigpen of Harlem, getting ready to litter little black piggies. If he could have felt about things as Jake, how different his life might have been! Just to hitch up for a short while and be irresponsible! But he and Agatha were slaves of the civilized tradition. . . . Harlem nigger strutting his stuff. . . . Harlem niggers! How often he had listened to those phrases, like jets of saliva, spewing from the lips of his work pals. They pursued, scared, and haunted him. He was afraid that some day the urge of the flesh and the mind's hankering after the pattern of respectable comfort might chase his high dreams out of him and deflate him to the contented animal that was a Harlem nigger strutting his stuff. "No happy-nigger strut for me," he would mutter, when the feeling for Agatha worked like a fever in his flesh. He saw destiny working in her large, dream-sad eyes, filling them with the passive softness of resignation to life, and seeking to encompass and yoke him down as just one of the thousand niggers of Harlem. And he hated Agatha and, for escape, wrapped himself darkly in self-love.

Oh, he was scared of that long red steel cage whose rumbling rollers were eternally heavy-lipped upon shining, continent-circling rods. If he forced himself to stay longer he would bang right off his head. Once upon a time he used to wonder at that great body of people who worked in nice cages: bank clerks in steel-wire cages, others in wooden cages, salespeople behind counters, neat, dutiful, respectful, all of them. God! how could they carry it on from day to day and remain quietly obliging and sane? If the railroad had not been cacophonous and riotous enough to balance the dynamo roaring within him, he would have jumped it long ago.

Life burned in Ray perhaps more intensely than in Jake. Ray felt more and his range was wider and he could not be satisfied with the easy, simple things that sufficed for Jake. Sometimes he felt like a tree with roots in the soil and sap flowing out and whispering leaves drinking in the air. But he drank in more of life than he could distill into active animal living. Maybe that was why he felt he had to write.

He was a reservoir of that intense emotional energy so peculiar to his race. Life touched him emotionally in a thousand vivid ways. Maybe his own being was something of a touch-stone of the general emotions of his race. Any upset—a terror-breathing, Negro-baiting headline in a metropolitan newspaper or the news of a human bonfire in Dixie—could make him miserable and despairingly despondent like an injured child. While any flash of beauty or wonder might lift him happier than a god. It was the simple, lovely touch of life that charmed and stirred him most. . . . The warm, rich-brown face of a Harlem girl seeking romance . . . a late wet night on Lenox Avenue, when all forms are soft-shadowy and the street gleams softly like a still, dim stream under the misted yellow lights. He remembered once the melancholy-comic notes of a "Blues" rising out of a Harlem basement before dawn. He was going to catch an early train and all that trip he was sweetly, deliciously happy humming the refrain and imagining what the interior of the little dark den he heard it in was like. "Blues" . . . melancholy-comic. That was the key to himself and to his race. That strange, child-like capacity for wistfulness-and-laughter. . . .

No wonder the whites, after five centuries of contact, could not understand his race. How could they when the instinct of comprehension had been cultivated out of them? No wonder they hated them, when out of their melancholy environment the blacks could create mad, contagious music and high laughter. . . .

Going away from Harlem. . . . Harlem! How terribly Ray

could hate it sometimes. Its brutality, gang rowdyism, promis-
cuous thickness. Its hot desires. But, oh, the rich blood-red
color of it! The warm accent of its composite voice, the fruiti-
ness of its laughter, the trailing rhythm of its "blues" and the
improvised surprises of its jazz. He had known happiness, too,
in Harlem, joy that glowed gloriously upon him like the high-
noon sunlight of his tropic island home.

How long would he be able to endure the life of a cabin boy
or mess boy on a freighter? Jake had tried to dissuade him. "A
seaman's life is no good, chappie, and it's easier to jump off a
train in the field than offn a ship gwine across the pond."

"Maybe it's not so bad in the mess," suggested Ray.

" 'Deed it's worse foh mine, chappie. Stoking and A.B.S. is
cleaner work than messing with raw meat and garbage. I never
was in love with no kitchen job. And tha's why I ain't none
crazy about the white man's chu-chuing buggy."

Going away from Harlem. . . .

Jake invited Ray and Grant to a farewell feed, for which Billy
Biasse was paying. Billy was a better pal for Jake than Zeddy.
Jake was the only patron of his gambling house that Billy really
chummed with. They made a good team. Their intimate interests never clashed. And it never once entered Jake's head that
there was anything ugly about Billy's way of earning a living.
Tales often came roundabout to Billy of patrons grumbling
that "he was swindling poah hardworking niggers outa their
wages." But he had never heard of Jake backbiting.

"The niggers am swindling themselves," Billy always retorted. "I runs a gambling place foh the gang and they pays
becas they love to gamble. I plays even with them mahself. I
ain't no miser hog like Nije Gridley."

Billy liked Jake because Jake played for the fun of the game
and then quit. Gambling did not have a strangle hold upon
him any more than dope or desire did. Jake took what he
wanted of whatever he fancied and . . . kept going.

The feed was spread at Aunt Hattie's cook-shop. Jake maintained that Aunt Hattie's was the best place for good eats in
Harlem. A bottle of Scotch whisky was on the table and a bottle
of gin.

While the boys sampled the fine cream tomato soup, Aunt
Hattie bustled in and out of the kitchen, with a senile-fond

look for Jake and an affectionate phrase, accompanied by a salacious lick of her tongue.

"Why, it's good and long sence you ain't been in reg'lar to
see me, chile. Whar's you been keeping you'self?"

"Ain't been no reg'lar chile of Harlem sence I done jump on
the white man's chu-chu," said Jake.

"And is you still on that theah business?" Aunt Hattie
asked.

"I don't know ef I is and I don't know ef I ain't. Ise been laid
off sick."

"Sick! Poah chile, and I nevah knowed so I could come
off'ring you a li'l' chicken broth. You jest come heah and eats
any time you wanta, whether youse got money or not."

Aunt Hattie shuffled back to the kitchen to pick the nicest
piece of fried chicken for Jake.

"Always in luck, Jakey," said Billy. "It's no wonder you nevah
see niggers in the bread line. And you'll nevah so long as
theah's good black womens like Aunt Hattie in Harlem."

Jake poured Scotch for three.

"Gimme gin," said Billy.

Jake called to Aunt Hattie to bring her glass. "What you
gwine to have, Auntie?"

"Same thing youse having, chile," replied Aunt Hattie.

"This heah stuff is from across the pond."

"Lemme taste it, then. Ef youse always so eye-filling drinking it, it might ginger up mah bones some."

"Well, here's to us, fellahs," cried Billy. "Let's hope that hard
luck nevah turn our glasses down or shet the door of a saloon
in our face."

Glasses clinked and Aunt Hattie touched Jake's twice and
closed her eyes as with trembling hand she guzzled.

"You had better said, 'Le's hope that this heah Gawd's own
don't shut the pub in our face'," replied Jake. "Prohibition is
right under our tail."

Everybody laughed. . . . Ray bit into the tender leg of his
fried chicken. The candied sweet potatoes were sweeter than
honey to his palate.

"Drink up, fellahs," said Billy.

"Got to leave you, Harlem," Ray sang lightly. "Got to turn
our backs on you."

"And our black moon on the Pennsy," added Jake.

"Tomorrow the big blue beautiful ocean," said Ray.

"You'll puke in it," Jake grinned devilishly. "Why not can the idea, chappie? The sea is hell and when you hits shore it's the same life all ovah."

"I guess you are right," replied Ray. "Goethe said the same thing in *Werther*."

"Who is that?" Jake asked.

"A German——"

"A boche?"

"Yes, a great one who made books instead of war. He was mighty and contented like a huge tame elephant. Genteel lovers of literature call that Olympian."

Jake gripped Ray's shoulder: "Chappie, I wish I was edjucated mahself."

"Christ! What for?" demanded Ray.

"Becaz I likes you." Like a black Pan out of the woods Jake looked into Ray's eyes with frank savage affection and Billy Biasse exclaimed:

"Lawdy in heaben! A li'l' foreign booze gwine turn you all soft?"

"Can't you like me just as well as you are?" asked Ray. "I can't feel any difference at all. If I was famous as Jack Johnson and rich as Madame Walker I'd prefer to have you as my friend than—President Wilson."

"Like bumbole you would!" retorted Jake. "Ef I was edjucated, I could understand things better and be proper-speaking like you is. . . . And I mighta helped mah li'l' sister to get edjucated, too (she must be a li'l' woman, now), and she would be nice-speaking like you' sweet brown, good enough foh you to hitch up with. Then we could all settle down and make money like edjucated people do, instead a you gwine off to throw you'self away on some lousy dinghy and me chasing around all the time lak a hungry dawg."

"Oh, you heart-breaking, slobbering nigger!" cried Billy Biasse. "That's the stuff youse got tuck away there under your tough black hide."

"Muzzle you' mouf," retorted Jake. "Sure Ise human. I ain't no lonesome wolf lak you is."

"A wolf is all right ef he knows the jungle."

"The fact is, Jake," Ray said, "I don't know what I'll do with my little education. I wonder sometimes if I could get rid of it and go and lose myself in some savage culture in the jungles of Africa. I am a misfit—as the doctors who dole out newspaper advice to the well-fit might say—a misfit with my little education and constant dreaming, when I should be getting the nightmare habit to hog in a whole lot of dough like everybody else in this country. Would you like to be educated to be like me?"

"If I had your edjucation I wouldn't be slinging no hash on the white man's chu-chu," Jake responded.

"Nobody knows, Jake. Anyway, you're happier than I as you are. The more I learn the less I understand and love life. All the learning in this world can't answer this little question, Why are we living?"

"Why, becaz Gawd wants us to, chappie," said Billy Biasse.

"Come on le's all go to Uncle Doc's," said Jake, "and finish the night with a li'l' sweet jazzing. This is you last night, chappie. Make the most of it, foh there ain't no jazzing like Harlem jazzing over the other side."

They went to Uncle Doc's, where they drank many ceremonious rounds. Later they went to Leroy's Cabaret. . . .

The next afternoon the freighter left with Ray signed on as a mess boy.

THIRD PART

XIX
Spring in Harlem

THE lovely trees of Seventh Avenue were a vivid flame-green. Children, lightly clad, skipped on the pavement. Light open coats prevailed and the smooth bare throats of brown girls were a token as charming as the first pussy-willows. Far and high over all, the sky was a grand blue benediction, and beneath it the wonderful air of New York tasted like fine dry champagne.

Jake loitered along Seventh Avenue. Crossing to Lenox, he lazied northward and over the One Hundred and Forty-ninth Street bridge into the near neighborhood of the Bronx. Here, just a step from compactly-built, teeming Harlem, were frame houses and open lots and people digging. A colored couple dawdled by, their arms fondly caressing each other's hips. A white man forking a bit of ground stopped and stared expressively after them.

Jake sat down upon a mound thick-covered with dandelions. They glittered in the sun away down to the rear of a rusty-gray shack. They filled all the green spaces. Oh, the common little things were glorious there under the sun in the tender spring grass. Oh, sweet to be alive in that sun beneath that sky! And to be in love—even for one hour of such rare hours! One day! One night! Somebody with spring charm, like a dandelion, seasonal and haunting like a lovely dream that never repeats itself. . . . There are hours, there are days, and nights whose sheer beauty overwhelm us with happiness, that we seek to make even more beautiful by comparing them with rare human contacts. . . . It was a day like this we romped in the grass . . . a night as soft and intimate as this on which we forgot the world and ourselves. . . . Hours of pagan abandon, celebrating ourselves. . . .

And Jake felt as all men who love love for love's sake can feel. He thought of the surging of desire in his boy's body and of his curious pure nectarine beginnings, without pain,

267

without disgust, down home in Virginia. Of his adolescent breaking-through when the fever-and-pain of passion gave him a wonderful strange-sweet taste of love that he had never known again. Of rude contacts and swift satisfactions in Norfolk, Baltimore, and other coast ports. . . . Havre. . . . The West India Dock districts of London. . . .

"Only that cute heart-breaking brown of the Baltimore," he mused. "A day like this sure feels like her. Didn't even get her name. O Lawdy! what a night that theah night was. Her and I could sure make a hallelujah picnic outa a day like this." . . .

Jake and Billy Biasse, leaving Dixie Red's pool-room together, shuffled into a big excited ring of people at the angle of Fifth Avenue and One Hundred and Thirty-third Street. In the ring three bad actors were staging a rough play—a yellow youth, a chocolate youth, and a brown girl.

The girl had worked herself up to the highest pitch of obscene frenzy and was sicking the dark strutter on to the yellow with all the filthiest phrases at her command. The two fellows pranced round, menacing each other with comic gestures.

"Why, ef it ain't Yaller Prince!" said Jake.

"Him sure enough," responded Billy Biasse. "Guess him done laid off from that black gal why she's shooting her stinking mouth off at him."

"Is she one of his producing goods?"

"She was. But I heard she done beat up anether gal of hisn—a fair-brown that useta hand over moh change than her and Yaller turn' her loose foh it." . . .

"You lowest-down face-artist!" the girl shrieked at Yaller Prince. "I'll bawl it out so all a Harlem kain know what you is." And ravished by the fact that she was humiliating her one-time lover, she gesticulated wildly.

"Hit him, Obadiah!" she yelled to the chocolate chap. "Hit him I tell you. Beat his mug up foh him, beat his mug and bleed his mouf." Over and over again she yelled: "Bleed his mouf!" As if that was the thing in Yaller Prince she had desired most. For it she had given herself up to the most unthinkable acts of degradation. Nothing had been impossible to do. And now she would cut and bruise and bleed that mouth that had once loved her so well so that he should not smile upon her rivals for many a day.

"Two-faced yaller nigger, you does ebery low-down thing, but you nevah done a lick of work in you lifetime. Show him, Obadiah. Beat his face and bleed his mouf."

"Yaller nigger," cried the extremely bandy-legged and grimfaced Obadiah, "Ise gwine kick you pants."

"I ain't scared a you, black buzzard," Yaller Prince replied in a thin, breathless voice, and down he went on his back, no one knowing whether he fell or was tripped up. Obadiah lifted a bottle and swung it down upon his opponent. Yaller Prince moaned and blood bubbled from his nose and his mouth.

"He's a sweet-back, all right, but he ain't a strong one," said some one in the crowd. The police had been conspicuously absent during the fracas, but now a baton tap-tapped upon the pavement and two of them hurried up. The crowd melted away.

Jake had pulled Yaller Prince against the wall and squatted to rest the bleeding head against his knee.

"What's matter here now? What's matter?" the first policeman, with revolver drawn, asked harshly.

"Nigger done beat this one up and gone away from heah, tha's whatsmat," said Billy Biasse.

They carried Yaller Prince into a drugstore for first aid, and the policeman telephoned for an ambulance. . . .

"We gotta look out foh him in hospital. He was a pretty good skate for a sweetman," Billy Biasse said.

"Poor Yaller!" Jake, shaking his head, commented; "it's a bad business."

"He's plumb crazy gwine around without a gun when he's a-playing that theah game," said Billy, "with all these cutthwoat niggers in Harlem ready to carve up one another foh a li'l' insisnificant humpy."

"It's the same ole life everywhere," responded Jake. "In white man's town or nigger town. Same bloody-sweet life across the pond. I done lived through the same blood-battling foh womens ovah theah in London. Between white and white and between white and black. Done see it in the froggies' country, too. A mess o' fat-headed white soldiers them was

knocked off by apaches. Don't tell *me* about cut-thwoat niggers in Harlem. The whole wul' is boody-crazy——"

"But Harlem is the craziest place foh that, I bet you, boh,"
Billy laughed richly. "The stuff it gives the niggers brain-fevah,
so far as I see, and this heah wolf has got a big-long horeezon.
Wese too thick together in Harlem. Wese all just lumped together without a chanst to choose and so we nacherally hate
one another. It's nothing to wonder that you' buddy Ray done
runned away from it. Why, jest the other night I witnessed a
nasty stroke. You know that spade prof that's always there on
the Avenue handing out the big stuff about niggers and their
rights and the wul' and bolschism. . . . He was passing by
the pool-room with a bunch o' books when a bad nigger jest
lunges out and socks him bif! in the jaw. The poah frightened
prof. started picking up his books without a word said, so I ups
and asks the boxer what was the meaning o' that pass. He
laughed and asked me ef I really wanted to know, and before
he could squint I landed him one in the eye and pulled mah
gun on him. I chased him off that corner all right. I tell you,
boh, Harlem is lousy with crazy-bad niggers, as tough as Hell's
Kitchen, and I always travel with mah gun ready."

"And ef all the niggers did as you does," said Jake, "theah'd
be a regular gun-toting army of us up here in the haht of the
white man's city. . . . Guess ef a man stahts gunning after you
and means to git you he will someways——"

"But you might git him fierst, too, boh, ef youse in luck."

"I mean ef you don't know he's gunning after you," said Jake.
"I don't carry no weapons nonetall, but mah two long hands."

"Youse a punk customer, then, I tell you," declared Billy
Biasse, "and no real buddy o' mine. Ise got a A number one
little barker I'll give it to you. You kain't lay you'self wide open
lak thataways in this heah burg. No boh!"

Jake went home alone in a mood different from the lyrical
feelings that had fevered his blood among the dandelions.
"Niggers fixing to slice one another's throats. Always fighting.
Got to fight if youse a man. It ain't because Yaller was a p-i.
. . . It coulda been me or anybody else. Wese too close and
thick in Harlem. Need some moh fresh air between us. . . .
Hitting out at a edjucated nigger minding his own business
and without a word said. . . . Guess Billy is right toting his

silent dawg around with him. He's gotta, though, when he's running a gambling joint. All the same, I gambles mahself and you nevah know when niggers am gwineta git crazy-mad. Guess I'll take the li'l' dawg offn Billy, all right. It ain't costing me nothing." . . .

In the late afternoon he lingered along Seventh Avenue in a new nigger-brown suit. The fine gray English suit was no longer serviceable for parade. The American suit did not fit him so well. Jake saw and felt it. . . . The only thing he liked better about the American suit was the pantaloons made to wear with a belt. And the two hip pockets. If you have the American habit of carrying your face-cloth on the hip instead of sticking it up in your breast pocket like a funny decoration, and if, like Billy Biasse, you're accustomed to toting some steely thing, what is handier than two hip pockets?

Except for that, Jake had learned to prefer the English cut of clothes. Such first-rate tweed stuff, and so cheap and durable compared with American clothes! Jake knew nothing of tariff laws and naïvely wondered why the English did not spread their fine cloth all over the American clothes market. . . . He worked up his shoulders in his nigger-brown coat. It didn't feel right, didn't hang so well. There was something a little too chic in American clothes. Not nearly as awful as French, though, Jake horse-laughed, vividly remembering the popular French styles. Broad-pleated, long-waisted, tight-bottomed pants and close-waisted coats whose breast pockets stick out their little comic signs of color. . . . Better color as a savage wears it, or none at all, instead of the Frenchman's peeking bit. The French must consider the average bantam male killing handsome, and so they make clothes to emphasize all the angular elevated rounded and pendulated parts of the anatomy. . . .

The broad pavements of Seventh Avenue were colorful with promenaders. Brown babies in white carriages pushed by little black brothers wearing nice sailor suits. All the various and varying pigmentation of the human race were assembled there: dim brown, clear brown, rich brown, chestnut, copper, yellow, near-white, mahogany, and gleaming anthracite. Charming brown matrons, proud yellow matrons, dark nursemaids pulled a zigzag course by their restive little charges. . . .

And the elegant strutters in faultless spats; West Indians, carrying canes and wearing trousers of a different pattern from their coats and vests, drawing sharp comments from their Afro-Yank rivals.

Jake mentally noted: "A dickty gang sure as Harlem is black, but———"

The girls passed by in bright batches of color, according to station and calling. High class, menial class, and the big trading class, flaunting a front of chiffon-soft colors framed in light coats, seizing the fashion of the day to stage a lovely leg show and spilling along the Avenue the perfume of Djer-kiss, Fougère, and Brown Skin.

"These heah New York gals kain most sartainly wear some moh clothes," thought Jake, "jest as nifty as them French gals." . . .

Twilight was enveloping the Belt, merging its life into a soft blue-black symphony. . . . The animation subsided into a moment's pause, a muffled, tremulous soul-stealing note . . . then electric lights flared everywhere, flooding the scene with dazzling gold.

Jake went to Aunt Hattie's to feed. Billy Biasse was there and a gang of longshoremen who had boozed and fed and were boozing again and, touched by the tender spring night, were swapping love stories and singing:

"Back home in Dixie is a brown gal there,
  Back home in Dixie is a brown gal there,
  Back home in Dixie is a brown gal there,
    Back home in Dixie I was bawn in.

"Back home in Dixie is a gal I know,
  Back home in Dixie is a gal I know,
  Back home in Dixie is a gal I know,
    And I wonder what nigger is saying to her a bootiful
      good mawnin'."

A red-brown West Indian among them volunteered to sing a Port-of-Spain song. It immortalized the drowning of a young black sailor. It was made up by the bawdy colored girls of the port, with whom the deceased had been a favorite, and became very popular among the stevedores and sailors of the island.

> "Ring the bell again,
> Ring the bell again,
> Ring the bell again,
> But the sharks won't puke him up.
> Oh, ring the bell again.
>
> "Empty is you' room,
> Empty is you' room,
> Empty is you' room,
> But you find one in the sea.
> Oh, empty is you' room.
>
> "Ring the bell again,
> Ring the bell again,
> Ring the bell again,
> But we know who feel the pain.
> Oh, ring the bell again."

The song was curious, like so many Negro songs of its kind, for the strange strengthening of its wistful melody by a happy rhythm that was suitable for dancing.

Aunt Hattie, sitting on a low chair, was swaying to the music and licking her lips, her wrinkled features wearing an expression of ecstatic delight. Billy Biasse offered to stand a bottle of gin. Jake said he would also sing a sailor song he had picked up in Limehouse. And so he sang the chanty of Bullocky Bill who went up to town to see a fair young maiden. But he could not remember most of the words, therefore Bullocky Bill cannot be presented here. But Jake was boisterously applauded for the scraps of it that he rendered.

The singing finished, Jake confided to Billy: "I sure don't feel lak spending a lonesome night this heah mahvelous night."

"Ain't nobody evah lonely in Harlem that don't wanta be," retorted Billy. "Even yours truly lone Wolf ain't nevah lonesome."

"But I want something as mahvelous as mah feelings."

Billy laughed and fingered his kinks: "Harlem has got the right stuff, boh, for all feelings."

"Youse right enough," Jake agreed, and fell into a reverie of full brown mouth and mischievous brown eyes all composing a perfect whole for his dark-brown delight.

"You wanta take a turn down the Congo?" asked Billy.

"Ah no."

"Rose ain't there no moh."

Rose had stepped up a little higher in her profession and had been engaged to tour the West in a Negro company.

"All the same, I don't feel like the Congo tonight," said Jake. "Le's go to Sheba Palace and jazz around a little."

Sheba Palace was an immense hall that was entirely monopolized for the amusements of the common workaday Negroes of the Belt. Longshoremen, kitchen-workers, laundresses, and W.C. tenders—all gravitated to the Sheba Palace, while the upper class of servitors—bell-boys, butlers, some railroad workers and waiters, waitresses and maids of all sorts—patronized the Casino and those dancings that were given under the auspices of the churches.

The walls of Sheba Palace were painted with garish gold, and tables and chairs were screaming green. There were green benches also lined round the vast dancing space. The music stopped with an abrupt clash just as Jake entered. Couples and groups were drinking at tables. Deftly, quickly the waiters slipped a way through the tables to serve and collect the money before the next dance. . . . Little white-filled glasses, little yellow-filled glasses, general guzzling of gin and whisky. Little saucy brown lips, rouged maroon, sucking up iced crème de menthe through straws, and many were sipping the golden Virginia Dare, in those days the favorite wine of the Belt. On the green benches couples lounged, sprawled, and, with the juicy love of spring and the liquid of Bacchus mingled in fascinating white eyes curious in their dark frames, apparently oblivious of everything outside of themselves, were loving in every way but . . .

The orchestra was tuning up. . . . The first notes fell out like a general clapping for merrymaking and chased the dancers running, sliding, shuffling, trotting to the floor. Little girls energetically chewing Spearmint and showing all their teeth dashed out on the floor and started shivering amorously, itching for their partners to come. Some lads were quickly on their feet, grinning gayly and improvising new steps with snapping of fingers while their girls were sucking up the last of their crème de menthe. The floor was large and smooth enough for anything.

They had a new song-and-dance at the Sheba and the black fellows were playing it with *éclat.*

> Brown gal crying on the corner,
>   Yaller gal done stole her candy,
> Buy him spats and feed him cream,
>   Keep him strutting fine and dandy.

> Tell me, pa-pa, Ise you' ma-ma,
>   Yaller gal can't make you fall,
> For Ise got some loving pa-pa
>   Yaller gal ain't got atall.

"Tell me, pa-pa, Ise you' ma-ma." The black players grinned and swayed and let the music go with all their might. The yellow in the music must have stood out in their imagination like a challenge, conveying a sense of that primitive, ancient, eternal, inexplicable antagonism in the color taboo of sex and society. The dark dancers picked up the refrain and jazzed and shouted with delirious joy, "Tell me, pa-pa, Ise you' ma-ma." The handful of yellow dancers in the crowd were even more abandoned to the spirit of the song. "White," "green," or "red" in place of "yaller" might have likewise touched the same deep-sounding, primitive chord. . . .

> Yaller gal sure wants mah pa-pa,
>   But mah chocolate turns her down,
> 'Cause he knows there ain't no loving
>   Sweeter than his loving brown.

> Tell me, pa-pa, Ise you' ma-ma,
>   Yaller gal can't make you fall,
> For Ise got some loving pa-pa
>   Yaller gal ain't got atall.

Jake was doing his dog with a tall, shapely quadroon girl when, glancing up at the balcony, he spied the little brown that he had entirely given over as lost. She was sitting at a table while "Tell me pa-pa" was tickling everybody to the uncontrollable point—she was sitting with her legs crossed and well exposed, and, with the aid of the mirror attached to her vanity case, was saucily and nonchalantly powdering her nose.

The quadroon girl nearly fell as Jake, without a word of explanation, dropped her in the midst of a long slide and, dashing across the floor, bounded up the stairs.

"Hello, sweetness! What youse doing here?"

The girl started and knocked over a glass of whisky on the floor: "O my Gawd! it's mah heartbreaking daddy! Where was you all this time?"

Jake drew a chair up beside her, but she jumped up: "Lawdy, no! Le's get outa here quick, 'cause Ise got somebody with me and now I don't want see him no moh."

"'Sawright, I kain take care of mahself," said Jake.

"Oh, honey, no! I don't want no trouble and he's a bad actor, that nigger. See, I done break his glass o' whisky and tha's bad luck. Him's just theah in the lav'try. Come quick. I don't want him to ketch us."

And the flustered little brown heart hustled Jake down the stairs and out of the Sheba Palace.

"Tell me, pa-pa, Ise you' ma-ma . . ."

The black shouting chorus pursued them outside.

"There ain't no yaller gal gwine get mah honey daddy thisanight." She took Jake's arm and cuddled up against his side.

"Aw no, sweetness. I was dogging it with one and jest drops her flat when I seen you."

"And there ain't no nigger in the wul' I wouldn't ditch foh you, daddy. O Lawdy! How Ise been crazy longing to meet you again."

XX
Felice

"WHAR's we gwine?" Jake asked.

They had walked down Madison Avenue, turned on One Hundred and Thirtieth Street, passing the solid gray-grim mass of the whites' Presbyterian church, and were under the timidly whispering trees of the decorously silent and distinguished Block Beautiful. . . . The whites had not evacuated that block yet. The black invasion was threatening it from One Hundred and Thirty-first Street, from Fifth Avenue, even from behind in One Hundred and Twenty-ninth Street. But desperate, frightened, blanch-faced, the ancient sepulchral Respectability held on. And giving them moral courage, the Presbyterian church frowned on the corner like a fortress against the invasion. The Block Beautiful was worth a struggle. With its charming green lawns and quaint white-fronted houses, it preserved the most Arcadian atmosphere in all New York. When there was a flat to let in that block, you would have to rubberneck terribly before you saw in the corner of a window-pane a neat little sign worded, Vacancy. But groups of loud-laughing-and-acting black swains and their sweethearts had started in using the block for their afternoon promenade. That was the limit: the desecrating of that atmosphere by black love in the very shadow of the gray, gaunt Protestant church! The Ancient Respectability was getting ready to flee. . . .

The beautiful block was fast asleep. Up in the branches the little elfin green things were barely whispering. The Protestant church was softened to a shadow. The atmosphere was perfect, the moment sweet for something sacred.

The burning little brownskin cuddled up against Jake's warm tall person: "Kiss me, daddy," she said. He folded her closely to him and caressed her. . . .

"But whar was you all this tur'bly long time?" demanded Jake.

Light-heartedly, she frisky like a kitten, they sauntered along

Seventh Avenue, far from the rough environment of Sheba Palace.

"Why, daddy, I waited foh you all that day after you went away and all that night! Oh, I had a heart-break on foh you, I was so tur'bly disappointed. I nev' been so crazy yet about no man. Why didn't you come back, honey?"

Jake felt foolish, remembering why. He said that shortly after leaving her he had discovered the money and the note. He had met some of his buddies of his company who had plenty of money, and they all went celebrating until that night, and by then he had forgotten the street.

"Mah poor daddy!"

"Even you' name, sweetness, I didn't know. Ise Jake Brown— Jake for ev'body. What is you', sweetness?"

"They calls me Felice."

"Felice. . . . But I didn't fohget the cabaret nonatall. And I was back theah hunting foh you that very night and many moh after, but I nevah finds you. Where was you?"

"Why, honey, I don't lives in cabarets all mah nights 'cause Ise got to work. Furthermore, I done went away that next week to Palm Beach———"

"Palm Beach! What foh?"

"Work of course. What you think? You done brokes mah heart in one mahvelous night and neveh returns foh moh. And I was jest right down sick and tiahd of Harlem. So I went away to work. I always work. . . . I know what youse thinking, honey, but I ain't in the reg'lar business. 'Cause Ise a funny gal. I kain't go with a fellah ef I don't like him some. And ef he kain make me like him enough I won't take nothing off him and ef he kain make me fall the real way, I guess I'd work like a wop for him."

"Youse the baby I been waiting foh all along," said Jake. "I knowed you was the goods."

"Where is we gwine, daddy?"

"Ise got a swell room, sweetness, up in 'Fortiet' Street whar all them dickty shines live."

"But kain you take me there?"

"Sure thing, baby. Ain't no nigger renting a room in Harlem whar he kain't have his li'l' company."

"Oh, goody, goody, honey-stick!"

Jake took Felice home to his room. She was delighted with it. It was neat and orderly.

"Your landlady must be one of them proper persons," she remarked. "How did you find such a nice place way up here?"

"A chappie named Ray got it foh me when I was sick——"

"O Lawdy! was it serious? Did they all take good care a you?"

"It wasn't nothing much and the fellahs was all awful good spohts, especially Ray."

"Who is this heah Ray?"

Jake told her. She smoothed out the counterpane on the bed, making a mental note that it was just right for two. She admired the geraniums in the window that looked on the large court.

"These heah new homes foh niggers am sure nice," she commented.

She looked behind the curtain where his clothes were hanging and remarked his old English suit. Then she regarded archly his new nigger-brown rig-out.

"You was moh illegant in that other, but I likes you in this all the same."

Jake laughed. "Everything's gotta wear out some day."

Felice hung round his neck, twiddling her pretty legs.

He held her as you might hold a child and she ruffled his thick mat of hair and buried her face in it. She wriggled down with a little scream:

"Oh, I gotta go get mah bag!"

"I'll come along with you," said Jake.

"No, lemme go alone. I kain manage better by mahself."

"But suppose that nigger is waiting theah foh you? You better lemme come along."

"No, honey, I done figure he's waiting still in Sheba Palace, or boozing. Him and some friends was all drinking befoh and he was kinder full. Ise sure he ain't gone home. Anyway, I kain manage by mahself all right, but ef you comes along and we runs into him— No, honey, you stays right here. I don't want messing up in no blood-baff. Theah's too much a that in Harlem."

They compromised, Felice agreeing that Jake should accompany her to the corner of Seventh Avenue and One Hundred

and Thirty-fifth Street and wait for her there. She had not the
faintest twinge of conscience herself. She had met the male
that she preferred and gone with him, leaving the one that she
was merely makeshifting with. It was a very simple and natural
thing to her. There was nothing mean about it. She was too
nice to be mean. However, she was aware that in her world
women scratched and bit into each other's flesh and men ra-
zored and gunned at each other over such things. . . .

Felice recalled one memorable afternoon when two West
Indian women went for each other in the back yard of a house
in One Hundred and Thirty-second Street. One was a laundress, a whopping brown woman who had come to New York
from Colon, and the other was a country girl, a buxom Negress
from Jamaica. They were quarreling over a vain black bantam,
one of the breed that delight in women's scratching over them.
The laundress had sent for him to come over from the Canal
Zone to New York. They had lived together there and she had
kept him, making money in all the ways that a gay and easy
woman can on the Canal Zone. But now the laundress be-
moaned the fact that "sence mah man come to New Yawk,
him jest gone back on me in the queerest way you can imagine."

Her man, in turn, blamed the situation upon her, said she
was too aggressive and mannish and had harried the energy
out of him. But the other girl seemed to endow him again
with virility. . . . After keeping him in Panama and bringing
him to New York, the laundress hesitated about turning her
male loose in Harlem, although he was apparently of no more
value to her. But his rejuvenating experience with the younger
girl had infuriated the laundress. A sister worker from Alabama,
to whom she had confided her secret tragedy, had hinted:
"Lawdy! sistah, that sure sounds phony-like. Mebbe you' man
is jest playing 'possum with you." And the laundress was crazy
with suspicion and jealousy and a feeling for revenge. She challenged her rival to fight the affair out. They were all living in
the same house. . . .

Felice also lived in that house. And one afternoon she was
startled by another girl from an adjoining room pounding on
her door and shrieking: "Open foh the love of Jesus! . . .
Theah's sweet hell playing in the back yard."

The girls rushed to the window and saw the two black women squaring off at each other down in the back yard. They were stark naked.

After the challenge, the women had decided to fight with their clothes off. An old custom, perhaps a survival of African tribalism, had been imported from some remote West Indian hillside into a New York back yard. Perhaps, the laundress had thought, that with her heavy and powerful limbs she could easily get her rival down and sit on her, mauling her properly. But the black girl was as nimble as a wild goat. She dodged away from the laundress who was trying to get ahold of her big bush of hair, and suddenly sailing fullfront into her, she seized the laundress, shoulder and neck, and butted her twice on the forehead as only a rough West Indian country girl can butt. The laundress staggered backward, groggy, into a bundle of old carpets. But she rallied and came back at the grinning Negress again. The laundress had never learned the brutal art of butting. The girl bounded up at her forehead with another well-aimed butt and sent her reeling flop on her back among the carpets. The girl planted her knees upon the laundress's high chest and wrung her hair.

"You don't know me, but I'll make you remember me for-eber. I'll beat you' mug ugly. There!" Bam! Bam! She slapped the laundress's face.

"Git off mah stomach, nigger gal, and leave me in peace," the laundress panted. The entire lodging-house was in a sweet fever over the event. Those lodgers whose windows gave on the street had crowded into their neighbors' rear rooms and some had descended into the basement for a close-up view. Apprised of the naked exhibition, the landlord hurried in from the corner saloon and threatened the combatants with the police. But there was nothing to do. The affair was settled and the women had already put their shifts on.

The women lodgers cackled gayly over the novel staging of the fight.

"It sure is better to disrobe like that, befoh battling," one declared. "It turn you' hands and laigs loose for action."

"And saves you' clothes being ripped into ribbons," said another.

A hen-fight was more fun than a cock-fight, thought Felice, as she hastily threw her things into her bag. The hens pluck feathers, but they never wring necks like the cocks.

And Jake. Standing on the corner, he waited, restive, nervous. But, unlike Felice, his thought was not touched by the faintest fear of a blood battle. His mind was a circle containing the girl and himself only, making a thousand plans of the joys they would create together. She was a prize to hold. Had slipped through his fingers once, but he wasn't ever going to lose her again. That little model of warm brown flesh. Each human body has its own peculiar rhythm, shallow or deep or profound. Transient rhythms that touch and pass you, unrememberable, and rhythms unforgetable. Imperial rhythms whose vivid splendor blinds your sight and destroys your taste for lesser ones.

Jake possessed a sure instinct for the right rhythm. He was connoisseur enough. But although he had tasted such a varied many, he was not raw animal enough to be undiscriminating, nor civilized enough to be cynical. . . .

Felice came hurrying as much as she could along One Hundred and Thirty-fifth Street, bumping a cumbersome portmanteau on the pavement and holding up one unruly lemon-bright silk stocking with her left hand. Jake took the bag from her. They went into a delicatessen store and bought a small cold chicken, ham, mustard, olives, and bread. They stopped in a sweet shop and bought a box of chocolate-and-vanilla ice-cream and cake. Felice also took a box of chocolate candy. Their last halt was at a United Cigar Store, where Jake stocked his pockets with a half a dozen packets of Camels. . . .

Felice had just slipped out of her charming strawberry frock when her hands flew down to her pretty brown leg. "O Gawd! I done fohget something!" she cried in a tone that intimated something very precious.

"What's it then?" demanded Jake.

"It's mah luck," she said. "It's the fierst thing that was gived to me when I was born. Mah gran'ma gived it and I wears it always foh good luck."

This lucky charm was an old plaited necklace, leathery in appearance, with a large, antique blue bead attached to it, that Felice's grandmother (who had superintended her coming into the world) had given to her immediately after that event. Her grandmother had dipped the necklace into the first water that Felice was washed in. Felice had religiously worn her charm around her neck all during her childhood. But since she was grown to ripe girlhood and low-cut frocks were the fashion and she loved them so much, she had transferred the unsightly necklace from her throat to her leg. But before going to the Sheba Palace she had unhooked the thing. And she had forgotten it there in the closet, hanging by a little nail against the wash-bowl.

"I gotta go get it," she said.

"Aw no, you won't bother," drawled Jake. And he drew the little agitated brown body to him and quieted it. "It was good luck you fohget it, sweetness, for it made us find one another."

"Something to that, daddy," Felice said, and her mouth touched his mouth.

They wove an atmosphere of dreams around them and were lost in it for a week. Felice asked the landlady to let her use the kitchen to cook their meals at home. They loitered over the wide field and lay in the sweet grass of Van Cortlandt Park. They went to the Negro Picture Theater and held each other's hand, gazing in raptures at the crude pictures. It was odd that all these cinematic pictures about the blacks were a broad burlesque of their home and love life. These colored screen actors were all dressed up in expensive evening clothes, with automobiles, and menials, to imitate white society people. They laughed at themselves in such rôles and the laughter was good on the screen. They pranced and grinned like good-nigger servants, who know that "mas'r" and "missus," intent on being amused, are watching their antics from an upper window. It was quite a little funny and the audience enjoyed it. Maybe that was the stuff the Black Belt wanted.

XXI
The Gift That Billy Gave

"WE gotta celebrate to-night," said Felice when Saturday came round again. Jake agreed to do anything she wanted. Monday they would have to think of working. He wanted to dine at Aunt Hattie's, but Felice preferred a "niftier" place. So they dined at the Nile Queen restaurant on Seventh Avenue. After dinner they subwayed down to Broadway. They bought tickets for the nigger heaven of a theater, whence they watched high-class people make luxurious love on the screen. They enjoyed the exhibition. There is no better angle from which one can look down on a motion picture than that of the nigger heaven.

They returned to Harlem after the show in a mood to celebrate until morning. Should they go to Sheba Palace where chance had been so good to them, or to a cabaret? Sentiment was in favor of Sheba Palace but her love of the chic and novel inclined Felice toward an attractive new Jewish-owned Negro cabaret. She had never been there and could not go under happier circumstances.

The cabaret was a challenge to any other in Harlem. There were one or two cabarets in the Belt that were distinguished for their impolite attitude toward the average Negro customer, who could not afford to swill expensive drinks. He was pushed off into a corner and neglected, while the best seats and service were reserved for notorious little gangs of white champagne-guzzlers from downtown.

The new cabaret specialized in winning the good will of the average blacks and the approval of the fashionable set of the Belt. The owner had obtained a college-bred Negro to be manager, and the cashier was a genteel mulatto girl. On the opening night the management had sent out special invitations to the high lights of the Negro theatrical world and free champagne had been served to them. The new cabaret was also drawing nightly a crowd of white pleasure-seekers from downtown. The war was just ended and people were hungry for any amusements that were different from the stale stock things.

Besides its spacious floor, ladies' room, gentlemen's room and coat-room, the new cabaret had a bar with stools, where men could get together away from their women for a quick drink and a little stag conversation. The bar was a paying innovation. The old-line cabarets were falling back before their formidable rival. . . .

The fashionable Belt was enjoying itself there on this night. The press, theatrical, and music world were represented. Madame Mulberry was there wearing peacock blue with patches of yellow. Madame Mulberry was a famous black beauty in the days when Fifty-third Street was the hub of fashionable Negro life. They called her then, Brown Glory. She was the wife of Dick Mulberry, a promoter of Negro shows. She had no talent for the stage herself, but she knew all the celebrated stage people of her race. She always gossiped reminiscently of Bert Williams, George Walker and Aida Overton Walker, Anita Patti Brown and Cole and Johnson.

With Madame Mulberry sat Maunie Whitewing with a dapper cocoa-brown youth by her side, who was very much pleased by his own person and the high circle to which it gained him admission. Maunie was married to a nationally-known Negro artist, who lived simply and quietly. But Maunie was notorious among the scandal sets of Brooklyn, New York, and Washington. She was always creating scandals wherever she went, gallivanting around with improper persons at improper places, such as this new cabaret. Maunie's beauty was Egyptian in its exoticism and she dared to do things in the manner of ancient courtesans. Dignified colored matrons frowned upon her ways, but they had to invite her to their homes, nevertheless, when they asked her husband. But Maunie seldom went.

The sports editor of *Colored Life* was also there, with a prominent Negro pianist. It was rumored that Bert Williams might drop in after midnight. Madame Mulberry was certain he would.

James Reese Europe, the famous master of jazz, was among a group of white admirers. He had just returned from France, full of honors, with his celebrated band. New York had acclaimed

him and America was ready to applaud. . . . That was his last
appearance in a Harlem cabaret before his heart was shot out
during a performance in Boston by a savage buck of his
race. . . .

Prohibition was on the threshold of the country and drinking was becoming a luxury, but all the joy-pacers of the Belt
who adore the novel and the fashionable and had a dollar to
burn had come together in a body to fill the new cabaret.

The owner of the cabaret knew that Negro people, like his
people, love the pageantry of life, the expensive, the fine, the
striking, the showy, the trumpet, the blare—sumptuous settings and luxurious surroundings. And so he had assembled his
guests under an enchanting-blue ceiling of brilliant chandeliers
and a dome of artificial roses bowered among green leaves.
Great mirrors reflected the variegated colors and poses. Shaded,
multi-colored sidelights glowed softly along the golden walls.

It was a scene of blazing color. Soft, barbaric, burning, savage, clashing, planless colors—all rioting together in wonderful
harmony. There is no human sight so rich as an assembly of
Negroes ranging from lacquer black through brown to cream,
decked out in their ceremonial finery. Negroes are like trees.
They wear all colors naturally. And Felice, rouged to a ravishing maroon, and wearing a close-fitting, chrome-orange frock
and cork-brown slippers, just melted into the scene.

They were dancing as Felice entered and she led Jake right
along into it.

"Tell me, pa-pa, Ise you ma-ma . . ."

Every cabaret and dancing-hall was playing it. It was the
tune for the season. It had carried over from winter into spring
and was still the favorite. Oh, ma-ma! Oh, pa-pa!

The dancing stopped. . . . A brief interval and a dwarfish,
shiny black man wearing a red-brown suit, with kinks straightened and severely plastered down in the Afro-American manner, walked into the center of the floor and began singing. He
had a massive mouth, which he opened wide, and a profoundly
big and quite good voice came out of it.

"I'm so doggone fed up, I don't know what to do.
 Can't find a pal that's constant, can't find a gal that's true.

But I ain't gwine to worry 'cause mah buddy was a ham;
Ain't gwine to cut mah throat 'cause mah gal ain't worf a
  damn.
Ise got the blues all ovah, the coal-black biting blues,
Like a prowling tom-cat that's got the low-down mews.

"I'm gwine to lay me in a good supply a gin,
Foh gunning is a crime, but drinking ain't no sin.
I won't do a crazy deed 'cause of a two-faced pal,
Ain't gwineta break mah heart ovah a no-'count gal
Ise got the blues all ovah, the coal-black biting blues,
Like a prowling tom-cat that's got the low-down mews."

There was something of the melancholy charm of Tschaikovsky in the melody. The black singer made much of the triumphant note of strength that reigned over the sad motif. When he sang, "I ain't gwine to cut mah throat," "Ain't gwine to break mah heart," his face became grim and full of will as a bulldog's.

He conquered his audience and at the finish he was greeted with warm applause and a shower of silver coins ringing on the tiled pavement. An enthusiastic white man waved a dollar note at the singer and, to show that Negroes could do just as good or better, Maunie Whitewing's sleek escort imitated the gesture with a two-dollar note. That started off the singer again.

"Ain't gwine to cut mah throat . . .
Ain't gwine to break mah heart . . ."

"That zigaboo is a singing fool," remarked Jake.

Billy Biasse entered resplendent in a new bottle-green suit, and joined Jake and Felice at their table.

"What you say, Billy?" Jake's greeting.

"I say Ise gwineta blow. Toss off that theah liquor, you two. Ise gwineta blow champagne as mah compliments, old top." . . .

"Heah's good luck t'you, boh, and plenty of joy-stuff and happiness," continued Billy, when the champagne was poured. "You sure been hugging it close this week."

Jake smiled and looked foolish. . . . The second cook, whom he had not seen since he quitted the railroad, entered

the cabaret with a mulatto girl on his arm and looked round
for seats. Jake stood up and beckoned him over to his table.

"It's awright, ain't it Billy?" he asked his friend.

"Sure. Any friend a yourn is awright."

The two girls began talking fashion around the most striking
dresses in the place. Jake asked about the demoted rhinoceros.
He was still on the railroad, the second cook said, taking orders
from another chef, "jest as savage and mean as ever, but not
so moufy. I hear you friend Ray done quit us for the ocean,
Jakey." . . .

There was still champagne to spare, nevertheless the second
cook invited the boys to go up to the bar for a stiff drink of real
liquor.

Negroes, like all good Americans, love a bar. I should have
said, Negroes under Anglo-Saxon civilization. A bar has a
charm all of its own that makes drinking there pleasanter. We
like to lean up against it, with a foot on the rail. We will leave
our women companions and choice wines at the table to snatch
a moment of exclusive sex solidarity over a thimble of gin at
the bar.

The boys left the girls to the fashions for a little while. Billy
Biasse, being a stag as always, had accepted the invitation with
alacrity. He loved to indulge in naked man-stuff talk, which
would be too raw even for Felice's ears. As they went out
Maunie Whitewing (she was a traveled woman of the world
and had been abroad several times with and without her husband) smiled upon Jake with a bold stare and remarked to
Madame Mulberry: "*Quel beau garçon! J'aimerais beaucoup
faire l'amour avec lui.*"

"Superb!" agreed Madame Mulberry, appreciating Jake
through her lorgnette.

Felice caught Maunie Whitewing's carnal stare at her man
and said to the mulatto girl: "Jest look at that high-class
hussy!"

And the dapper escort tried to be obviously unconcerned.

At the bar the three pals had finished one round and the bar-
man was in the act of pouring another when a loud scream
tore through music and conversation. Jake knew that voice
and dashed down the stairs. What he saw held him rooted at

the foot of the stairs for a moment. Zeddy had Felice's wrists in a hard grip and she was trying to wrench herself away.

"Leggo a me, I say," she bawled.

"I ain't gwineta do no sich thing. Youse mah woman."

"You lie! I ain't and you ain't mah man, black nigger."

"We'll see ef I ain't. Youse gwine home wif me right now."

Jake strode up to Zeddy. "Turn that girl loose."

"Whose gwineta make me?" growled Zeddy.

"I is. She's mah woman. I knowed her long before you. For Gawd's sake quit you' fooling and don't let's bust up the man's cabaret."

All the fashionable folk had already fled.

"She's *my* woman and I'll carve any damn-fool nigger for her." Lightning-quick Zeddy released the girl and moved upon Jake like a terrible bear with open razor.

"Don't let him kill him, foh Gawd's sake don't," a woman shrieked, and there was a general stampede for the exit.

But Zeddy had stopped like a cowed brute in his tracks, for leveled straight at his heart was the gift that Billy gave.

"Drop that razor and git you' hands up," Jake commanded, "and don't make a fool move or youse a dead nigger."

Zeddy obeyed. Jake searched him and found nothing. "I gotta good mind fixing you tonight, so you won't evah pull a razor on another man."

Zeddy looked Jake steadily in the face and said: "You kain kill me, nigger, ef you wanta. You come gunning at me, but you didn't go gunning after the Germans. Nosah! You was scared and runned away from the army."

Jake looked bewildered, sick. He was hurt now to his heart and he was dumb. The waiters and a few rough customers that the gun did not frighten away looked strangely at him.

"Yes, mah boy," continued Zeddy, "that's what life is everytime. When youse good to a buddy, he steals you woman and pulls a gun on you. Tha's what I get for prohceeding a slacker. A-llll right, boh, I was a good sucker, but—I ain't got no reason to worry sence youse down in the white folks' books." And he ambled away.

Jake shuffled off by himself. Billy Biasse tried to say a decent word, but he waved him away.

These miserable cock-fights, beastly, tigerish, bloody. They had always sickened, saddened, unmanned him. The wild, shrieking mad woman that is sex seemed jeering at him. Why should love create terror? Love should be joy lifting man out of the humdrum ways of life. He had always managed to delight in love and yet steer clear of the hate and violence that govern it in his world. His love nature was generous and warm without any vestige of the diabolical or sadistic.

Yet here he was caught in the thing that he despised so thoroughly. . . . Brest, London, and his America. Their vivid brutality tortured his imagination. Oh, he was infinitely disgusted with himself to think that he had just been moved by the same savage emotions as those vile, vicious, villainous white men who, like hyenas and rattlers, had fought, murdered, and clawed the entrails out of black men over the common, commercial flesh of women. . . .

He reached home and sat brooding in the shadow upon the stoop.

"Zeddy. My own friend in some ways. Naturally lied about me and the army, though. Playing martyr. How in hell did *he* get hooked up with her? Thought he was up in Yonkers. Would never guess one in a hundred it was he. What a crazy world! He must have passed us drinking at the bar. Wish I'd seen him. Would have had him drinking with us. And maybe we would have avoided that stinking row. Maybe and maybe not. Can't tell about Zeddy. He was always a bad-acting razor-flashing nigger."

A little hand timidly took his arm.

"Honey, you ain't mad at you sweetness, is you?"

"No. . . . I'm jest sick and tiah'd a everything."

"I nevah know you knowed one anether, honey. Oh, I was so scared. . . . But how could I know?"

"No, you couldn't. I ain't blaming nothing on you. I nevah would guess it was him mahself. I ain't blaming nobody at all."

Felice cuddled closer to Jake and fondled his face. "It was a good thing you had you' gun, though, honey, or—— O Lawd! what mighta happened!"

"Oh, I woulda been a dead nigger this time or a helpless one," Jake laughed and hugged her closer to him. "It was Billy gived me that gun and I didn't even wanta take it."

"Didn't you? Billy is a good friend, eh?"

"You bet he is. Nevah gets mixed up with—in scraps like that."

"Honest, honey, I nevah liked Zeddy, but———"

"Oh, you don't have to explain me nothing. I know it's jest connexidence. It coulda been anybody else. That don't worry mah skin."

"I really didn't like him, though, honey. Lemme tell you. I was kinder sorry for him. It was jest when I got back from Palm Beach I seen him one night at a buffet flat. And he was that nice to me. He paid drinks for the whole houseful a people and all because a me. I couldn't act mean, so I had to be nice mahself. And the next day he ups and buys me two pair a shoes and silk stockings and a box a chocolate candy. So I jest stayed on and gived him a li'l' loving, honey, but I nevah did tuk him to mah haht."

"It's awright, sweetness. What do I care so long as wese got one another again?"

She drew down his head and sought his mouth. . . .

"But what is we gwineta do, daddy? Sence they say that youse a slacker or deserter, I don't which is which———"

"He done lied about that, though," Jake said, angrily. "I didn't run away because I was scared a them Germans. But I beat it away from Brest because they wouldn't give us a chance at them, but kept us in that rainy, sloppy, Gawd-forsaken burg working like wops. They didn't seem to want us niggers foh no soldiers. We was jest a bunch a despised hod-carriers, and Zeddy know that."

Now it was Felice's turn. "You ain't telling me a thing, daddy. I'll be slack with you and desert with you. What right have niggers got to shoot down a whole lot a Germans for? Is they worse than Americans or any other nation a white people? You done do the right thing, honey, and Ise with you and I love you the more for that. . . . But all the same, we can't stay in Harlem no longer, for the bulls will sure get you."

"I been thinking a gitting away from the stinking mess and go on off to sea again."

"Ah no, daddy," Felice tightened her hold on his arm. "And what'll become a me? I kain't go 'board a ship with you and I needs you."

Jake said nothing.

"What you wanta go knocking around them foreign countries again for like swallow come and swallow go from year to
year and nevah settling down no place? This heah is you' country, daddy. What you gwine away from it for?"

"And what kain I do?"

"Do? Jest le's beat it away from Harlem, daddy. This heah
country is good and big enough for us to git lost in. You know
Chicago?"

"Haven't made that theah burg yet."

"Why, le's go to Chicago, then. I hear it's a mahvelous place
foh niggers. Chicago, honey."

"When?"

"This heah very night. Ise ready. Ain't nothing in Harlem
holding *me*, honey. Come on. Le's pack."

Zeddy rose like an apparition out of the shadow. Automatically Jake's hand went to his pocket.

"Don't shoot!" Zeddy threw up his hands. "I ain't here foh
no trouble. I jest wanta ast you' pahdon, Jake. Excuse me, boh.
I was crazy-mad and didn't know what I was saying. Ahm
bloody well ashamed a mahself. But you know how it is when
a gal done make a fool outa you. I done think it ovah and said
to mah inner man: Why, you fool fellah, whasmat with you? Ef
Zeddy slit his buddy's thwoat for a gal, that won't give back
the gal to Zeddy. . . . So I jest had to come and tell it to you
and ast you pahdon. You kain stay in Harlem as long as you
wanta. Zeddy ain'ta gwineta open his mouf against you. You was
always a good man-to-man buddy and nevah did wears you
face bahind you. Don't pay no mind to what I done said in that
theah cabaret. Them niggers hanging around was all drunk
and wouldn't shoot their mouf off about you nohow. You ain't
no moh slacker than me. What you done was all right, Jakey,
and I woulda did it mahself ef I'd a had the guts to."

"It's all right, Zeddy," said Jake. "It was jest a crazy mix-up
we all got into. I don't bear you no grudge."

"Will you take the paw on it?"

"Sure!" Jake gripped Zeddy's hand.

"So long, buddy, and fohgit it."

"So long, Zeddy, ole top." And Zeddy bear-walked off,
without a word or a look at Felice, out of Jake's life forever.
Felice was pleased, yet, naturally, just a little piqued. He might

have said good-by to *me*, too, she thought. I would even have kissed him for the last time. She took hold of Jake's hands and swung them meditatively: "It's all right daddy, but——"

"But what?"

"I think we had better let Harlem miss us foh a little while."

"Scared?"

"Yes, daddy, but for you only. Zeddy won't go back on you. I guess not. But news is like a traveling agent, honey, going from person to person. I wouldn't take no chances."

"I guess youse right, sweetness. Come on, le's get our stuff together."

The two leather cases were set together against the wall. Felice sat upon the bed dangling her feet and humming "Tell me, pa-pa, Ise you ma-ma." Jake, in white shirt-sleeves, was arranging in the mirror a pink-yellow-and-blue necktie.

"All set! What you say, sweetness?"

"I say, honey, le's go to the Baltimore and finish the night and ketch the first train in the morning."

"Why, the Baltimore is padlocked!" said Jake.

"It was, daddy, but it's open again and going strong. White folks can't padlock niggers outa joy forever. Let's go, daddy."

She jumped down from the bed and jazzed around.

"Oh, I nearly made a present of these heah things to the landlady!" She swept from the bed a pink coverlet edged with lace, and pillow-slips of the same fantasy (they were her own make), with which she had replaced the flat, rooming-house-white ones, and carefully folded them to fit in the bag that Jake had ready open for her. He slid into his coat, made certain of his pocket-book, and picked up the two bags.

The Baltimore was packed with happy, grinning wrigglers. Many pleasure-seekers who had left the new cabaret, on account of the Jake-Zeddy incident, had gone there. It was brighter than before the raid. The ceiling and walls were kalsomined in white and lilac and the lights glared stronger from new chandeliers.

The same jolly, compact manager was there, grinning a welcome to strange white visitors, who were pleased and never guessed what cautious reserve lurked under that grin.

Tell me, pa-pa, Ise you' ma-ma. . . .

Jake and Felice squeezed a way in among the jazzers. They were all drawn together in one united mass, wriggling around to the same primitive, voluptuous rhythm.

Tell me, pa-pa, Ise you' ma-ma. . . .

Haunting rhythm, mingling of naïve wistfulness and charming gayety, now sheering over into mad riotous joy, now, like a jungle mask, strange, unfamiliar, disturbing, now plunging headlong into the far, dim depths of profundity and rising out as suddenly with a simple, childish grin. And the white visitors laugh. They see the grin only. Here are none of the well-patterned, well-made emotions of the respectable world. A laugh might finish in a sob. A moan end in hilarity. That gorilla type wriggling there with his hands so strangely hugging his mate, may strangle her tonight. But he has no thought of that now. He loves the warm wriggle and is lost in it. Simple, raw emotions and real. They may frighten and repel refined souls, because they are too intensely real, just as a simple savage stands dismayed before nice emotions that he instantly perceives are false.

Tell me, pa-pa, Ise you' ma-ma. . . .

Jake was the only guest left in the Baltimore. The last wriggle was played. The waiters were picking up things and settling accounts.

"Whar's the little hussy?" irritated and perplexed, Jake wondered.

Felice was not in the cabaret nor outside on the pavement. Jake could not understand how she had vanished from his side.

"Maybe she was making a high sign when you was asleep," a waiter laughed.

"Sleep hell!" retorted Jake. He was in no joking mood.

"We gwineta lock up now, big boy," the manager said.

Jake picked up the bags and went out on the sidewalk again. "I kain't believe she'd ditch me like that at the last moment," he said aloud. "Anyhow, I'm bound foh Chicago. I done made up mah mind to go all becausing a her, and I ain'ta gwineta change it whether she throws me down or not. But sure she kain'ta run off and leaves her suitcase. What the hell is I gwine do with it?"

Felice came running up to him, panting, from Lenox Avenue.

"Where in hell you been all this while?" he growled.

"Oh, daddy, don't get mad!"

"Whar you been I say?"

"I done been to look for mah good-luck necklace. I couldn't go to Chicago without it."

Jake grinned. "Whyn't you tell me you was gwine? Weren't you scared a Zeddy?"

"I was and I wasn't. Ef I'd a told you, you woulda said it wasn't worth troubling about. So I jest made up mah mind to slip off and git it. The door wasn't locked and Zeddy wasn't home. It was hanging same place where I left it and I slipped it on mah leg and left the keys on the table. You know I had the keys. Ah, daddy, ef I'd a had mah luck with me, we nevah woulda gotten into a fight at that cabaret."

"You really think so, sweetness?"

They were walking to the subway station along Lenox Avenue.

"I ain't thinking, honey. I knows it. I'll nevah fohgit it again and it'll always give us good luck."

QUICKSAND

Nella Larsen

For E. S. I.

My old man died in a fine big house.
My ma died in a shack.
I wonder where I'm gonna die,
Being neither white nor black?

LANGSTON HUGHES

One

HELGA CRANE sat alone in her room, which at that hour, eight in the evening, was in soft gloom. Only a single reading lamp, dimmed by a great black and red shade, made a pool of light on the blue Chinese carpet, on the bright covers of the books which she had taken down from their long shelves, on the white pages of the opened one selected, on the shining brass bowl crowded with many-colored nasturtiums beside her on the low table, and on the oriental silk which covered the stool at her slim feet. It was a comfortable room, furnished with rare and intensely personal taste, flooded with Southern sun in the day, but shadowy just then with the drawn curtains and single shaded light. Large, too. So large that the spot where Helga sat was a small oasis in a desert of darkness. And eerily quiet. But that was what she liked after her taxing day's work, after the hard classes, in which she gave willingly and unsparingly of herself with no apparent return. She loved this tranquillity, this quiet, following the fret and strain of the long hours spent among fellow members of a carelessly unkind and gossiping faculty, following the strenuous rigidity of conduct required in this huge educational community of which she was an insignificant part. This was her rest, this intentional isolation for a short while in the evening, this little time in her own attractive room with her own books. To the rapping of other teachers, bearing fresh scandals, or seeking information, or other more concrete favors, or merely talk, at that hour Helga Crane never opened her door.

An observer would have thought her well fitted to that framing of light and shade. A slight girl of twenty-two years, with narrow, sloping shoulders and delicate, but well-turned, arms and legs, she had, none the less, an air of radiant, careless health. In vivid green and gold negligee and glistening brocaded mules, deep sunk in the big high-backed chair, against whose dark tapestry her sharply cut face, with skin like yellow satin, was distinctly outlined, she was—to use a hackneyed word—attractive. Black, very broad brows over soft, yet penetrating, dark eyes, and a pretty mouth, whose sensitive and

sensuous lips had a slight questioning petulance and a tiny dissatisfied droop, were the features on which the observer's attention would fasten; though her nose was good, her ears
delicately chiseled, and her curly blue-black hair plentiful and
always straying in a little wayward, delightful way. Just then it
was tumbled, falling unrestrained about her face and on to her
shoulders.

Helga Crane tried not to think of her work and the school as
she sat there. Ever since her arrival in Naxos she had striven to
keep these ends of the days from the intrusion of irritating
thoughts and worries. Usually she was successful. But not this
evening. Of the books which she had taken from their places
she had decided on Marmaduke Pickthall's *Saïd the Fisherman*.
She wanted forgetfulness, complete mental relaxation, rest
from thought of any kind. For the day had been more than
usually crowded with distasteful encounters and stupid perversities. The sultry hot Southern spring had left her strangely
tired and a little unnerved. And annoying beyond all other
happenings had been that affair of the noon period, now again
thrusting itself on her already irritated mind.

She had counted on a few spare minutes in which to indulge
in the sweet pleasure of a bath and a fresh, cool change of
clothing. And instead her luncheon time had been shortened,
as had that of everyone else, and immediately after the hurried
gulping down of heavy hot meal the hundreds of students and
teachers had been herded into the sun-baked chapel to listen
to the banal, the patronizing, and even the insulting remarks
of one of the renowned white preachers of the state.

Helga shuddered a little as she recalled some of the statements made by that holy white man of God to the black folk
sitting so respectfully before him.

This was, he had told them with obvious sectional pride, the
finest school for Negroes anywhere in the country, north or
south; in fact, it was better even than a great many schools for
white children. And he had dared any Northerner to come
south and after looking upon this great institution to say that
the Southerner mistreated the Negro. And he had said that if
all Negroes would only take a leaf out of the book of Naxos
and conduct themselves in the manner of the Naxos products,
there would be no race problem, because Naxos Negroes knew

what was expected of them. They had good sense and they had good taste. They knew enough to stay in their places, and that, said the preacher, showed good taste. He spoke of his great admiration for the Negro race, no other race in so short a time had made so much progress, but he had urgently besought them to know when and where to stop. He hoped, he sincerely hoped, that they wouldn't become avaricious and grasping, thinking only of adding to their earthly goods, for that would be a sin in the sight of Almighty God. And then he had spoken of contentment, embellishing his words with scriptural quotations and pointing out to them that it was their duty to be satisfied in the estate to which they had been called, hewers of wood and drawers of water. And then he had prayed.

Sitting there in her room, long hours after, Helga again felt a surge of hot anger and seething resentment. And again it subsided in amazement at the memory of the considerable applause which had greeted the speaker just before he had asked his God's blessing upon them.

The South. Naxos. Negro education. Suddenly she hated them all. Strange, too, for this was the thing which she had ardently desired to share in, to be a part of this monument to one man's genius and vision. She pinned a scrap of paper about the bulb under the lamp's shade, for, having discarded her book in the certainty that in such a mood even *Saïd* and his audacious villainy could not charm her, she wanted an even more soothing darkness. She wished it were vacation, so that she might get away for a time.

"No, forever!" she said aloud.

The minutes gathered into hours, but still she sat motionless, a disdainful smile or an angry frown passing now and then across her face. Somewhere in the room a little clock ticked time away. Somewhere outside, a whippoorwill wailed. Evening died. A sweet smell of early Southern flowers rushed in on a newly-risen breeze which suddenly parted the thin silk curtains at the opened windows. A slender, frail glass vase fell from the sill with tingling crash, but Helga Crane did not shift her position. And the night grew cooler, and older.

At last she stirred, uncertainly, but with an overpowering desire for action of some sort. A second she hesitated, then rose abruptly and pressed the electric switch with determined firmness, flooding suddenly the shadowy room with a white glare of light. Next she made a quick nervous tour to the end of the long room, paused a moment before the old bow-legged secretary that held with almost articulate protest her school-teacher paraphernalia of drab books and papers. Frantically Helga Crane clutched at the lot and then flung them violently, scornfully toward the wastebasket. It received a part, allowing the rest to spill untidily over the floor. The girl smiled ironically, seeing in the mess a simile of her own earnest endeavor to inculcate knowledge into her indifferent classes.

Yes, it was like that; a few of the ideas which she tried to put into the minds behind those baffling ebony, bronze, and gold faces reached their destination. The others were left scattered about. And, like the gay, indifferent wastebasket, it wasn't their fault. No, it wasn't the fault of those minds back of the diverse colored faces. It was, rather, the fault of the method, the general idea behind the system. Like her own hurried shot at the basket, the aim was bad, the material drab and badly prepared for its purpose.

This great community, she thought, was no longer a school. It had grown into a machine. It was now a show place in the black belt, exemplification of the white man's magnanimity, refutation of the black man's inefficiency. Life had died out of it. It was, Helga decided, now only a big knife with cruelly sharp edges ruthlessly cutting all to a pattern, the white man's pattern. Teachers as well as students were subjected to the paring process, for it tolerated no innovations, no individualisms. Ideas it rejected, and looked with open hostility on one and all who had the temerity to offer a suggestion or ever so mildly express a disapproval. Enthusiasm, spontaneity, if not actually suppressed, were at least openly regretted as unladylike or ungentlemanly qualities. The place was smug and fat with self-satisfaction.

A peculiar characteristic trait, cold, slowly accumulated unreason in which all values were distorted or else ceased to exist, had with surprising ferociousness shaken the bulwarks of that self-restraint which was also, curiously, a part of her nature. And now that it had waned as quickly as it had risen, she smiled again, and this time the smile held a faint amusement, which

wiped away the little hardness which had congealed her lovely
face. Nevertheless she was soothed by the impetuous discharge
of violence, and a sigh of relief came from her.

She said aloud, quietly, dispassionately: "Well, I'm through
with that," and, shutting off the hard, bright blaze of the overhead lights, went back to her chair and settled down with an
odd gesture of sudden soft collapse, like a person who had
been for months fighting the devil and then unexpectedly had
turned round and agreed to do his bidding.

Helga Crane had taught in Naxos for almost two years, at
first with the keen joy and zest of those immature people who
have dreamed dreams of doing good to their fellow men. But
gradually this zest was blotted out, giving place to a deep
hatred for the trivial hypocrisies and careless cruelties which
were, unintentionally perhaps, a part of the Naxos policy of
uplift. Yet she had continued to try not only to teach, but to
befriend those happy singing children, whose charm and dis-
tinctiveness the school was so surely ready to destroy. Instinctively Helga was aware that their smiling submissiveness
covered many poignant heartaches and perhaps much secret
contempt for their instructors. But she was powerless. In Naxos
between teacher and student, between condescending authority and smoldering resentment, the gulf was too great, and too
few had tried to cross it. It couldn't be spanned by one sympathetic teacher. It was useless to offer her atom of friendship,
which under the existing conditions was neither wanted nor
understood.

Nor was the general atmosphere of Naxos, its air of self-
rightness and intolerant dislike of difference, the best of medi-
ums for a pretty, solitary girl with no family connections. Helga's
essentially likable and charming personality was smudged out.
She had felt this for a long time. Now she faced with determination that other truth which she had refused to formulate in
her thoughts, the fact that she was utterly unfitted for teaching, even for mere existence, in Naxos. She was a failure here.
She had, she conceded now, been silly, obstinate, to persist for
so long. A failure. Therefore, no need, no use, to stay longer.
Suddenly she longed for immediate departure. How good, she
thought, to go now, tonight!—and frowned to remember how

impossible that would be. "The dignitaries," she said, "are not in their offices, and there will be yards and yards of red tape to unwind, gigantic, impressive spools of it."

And there was James Vayle to be told, and much-needed money to be got. James, she decided, had better be told at once. She looked at the clock racing indifferently on. No, too late. It would have to be tomorrow.

She hated to admit that money was the most serious difficulty. Knowing full well that it was important, she nevertheless rebelled at the unalterable truth that it could influence her actions, block her desires. A sordid necessity to be grappled with. With Helga it was almost a superstition that to concede to money its importance magnified its power. Still, in spite of her reluctance and distaste, her financial situation would have to be faced, and plans made, if she were to get away from Naxos with anything like the haste which she now so ardently desired.

Most of her earnings had gone into clothes, into books, into the furnishings of the room which held her. All her life Helga Crane had loved and longed for nice things. Indeed, it was this craving, this urge for beauty which had helped to bring her into disfavor in Naxos—"pride" and "vanity" her detractors called it.

The sum owing to her by the school would just a little more than buy her ticket back to Chicago. It was too near the end of the school term to hope to get teaching-work anywhere. If she couldn't find something else, she would have to ask Uncle Peter for a loan. Uncle Peter was, she knew, the one relative who thought kindly, or even calmly, of her. Her step-father, her step-brothers and sisters, and the numerous cousins, aunts, and other uncles could not be even remotely considered. She laughed a little, scornfully, reflecting that the antagonism was mutual, or, perhaps, just a trifle keener on her side than on theirs. They feared and hated her. She pitied and despised them. Uncle Peter was different. In his contemptuous way he was fond of her. Her beautiful, unhappy mother had been his favorite sister. Even so, Helga Crane knew that he would be more likely to help her because her need would strengthen his oft-repeated conviction that because of her Negro blood she would never amount to anything, than from motives of affection or loving memory. This knowledge, in its present aspect of truth, irritated her to an astonishing degree. She regarded Uncle Peter almost vindictively, although always he had been extraordinarily generous with her and she fully intended to ask his assistance. "A beggar," she thought ruefully, "cannot expect to choose."

Returning to James Vayle, her thoughts took on the frigidity of complete determination. Her resolution to end her stay in Naxos would of course inevitably end her engagement to James. She had been engaged to him since her first semester there, when both had been new workers, and both were lonely. Together they had discussed their work and problems in adjustment, and had drifted into a closer relationship. Bitterly she reflected that James had speedily and with entire ease fitted into his niche. He was now completely "naturalized," as they used laughingly to call it. Helga, on the other hand, had never quite achieved the unmistakable Naxos mold, would never achieve it, in spite of much trying. She could neither conform, nor be happy in her unconformity. This she saw clearly now, and with cold anger at all the past futile effort. What a waste! How pathetically she had struggled in those first months and with what small success. A lack somewhere. Always she had considered it a lack of understanding on the part of the community, but in her present new revolt she realized that the fault had been partly hers. A lack of acquiescence. She hadn't really wanted to be made over. This thought bred a sense of shame, a feeling of ironical disillusion. Evidently there were parts of her she couldn't be proud of. The revealing picture of her past striving was too humiliating. It was as if she had deliberately planned to steal an ugly thing, for which she had no desire, and had been found out.

Ironically she visualized the discomfort of James Vayle. How her maladjustment had bothered him! She had a faint notion that it was behind his ready assent to her suggestion anent a longer engagement than, originally, they had planned. He was liked and approved of in Naxos and loathed the idea that the girl he was to marry couldn't manage to win liking and approval also. Instinctively Helga had known that secretly he had placed the blame upon her. How right he had been! Certainly his attitude had gradually changed, though he still gave her his attentions. Naxos pleased him and he had become content with life as it was lived there. No longer lonely, he was now one of the community and so beyond the need or the desire to discuss its affairs and its failings with an outsider. She was, she knew, in a queer indefinite way, a disturbing factor. She knew too that a something held him, a something against which he was powerless. The idea that she was in but one nameless way necessary to him filled her with a sensation amounting almost to shame. And yet his mute helplessness against that ancient appeal by which she held him pleased her and fed her vanity— gave her a feeling of power. At the same time she shrank away from it, subtly aware of possibilities she herself couldn't predict.

Helga's own feelings defeated inquiry, but honestly confronted, all pretense brushed aside, the dominant one, she suspected, was relief. At least, she felt no regret that tomorrow would mark the end of any claim she had upon him. The surety that the meeting would be a clash annoyed her, for she had no talent for quarreling—when possible she preferred to flee. That was all.

The family of James Vayle, in near-by Atlanta, would be glad. They had never liked the engagement, had never liked Helga Crane. Her own lack of family disconcerted them. No family. That was the crux of the whole matter. For Helga, it accounted for everything, her failure here in Naxos, her former loneliness in Nashville. It even accounted for her engagement to James. Negro society, she had learned, was as complicated and as rigid in its ramifications as the highest strata of white society. If you couldn't prove your ancestry and connections, you were tolerated, but you didn't "belong." You could be queer, or even attractive, or bad, or brilliant, or even love beauty and such nonsense if you were a Rankin, or a Leslie, or a Scoville; in other words, if you had a family. But if you were just plain Helga Crane, of whom nobody had ever heard, it was presumptuous of you to be anything but inconspicuous and conformable.

To relinquish James Vayle would most certainly be social suicide, for the Vayles were people of consequence. The fact that they were a "first family" had been one of James's attractions for the obscure Helga. She had wanted social background, but—she had not imagined that it could be so stuffy.

She made a quick movement of impatience and stood up. As she did so, the room whirled about her in an impish, hateful way. Familiar objects seemed suddenly unhappily distant. Faintness closed about her like a vise. She swayed, her small, slender hands gripping the chair arms for support. In a moment the faintness receded, leaving in its wake a sharp resentment at the trick which her strained nerves had played upon her. And after a moment's rest she got hurriedly into bed, leaving her room disorderly for the first time.

Books and papers scattered about the floor, fragile stockings and underthings and the startling green and gold negligee dripping about on chairs and stool, met the encounter of the amazed eyes of the girl who came in the morning to awaken Helga Crane.

Two

SHE woke in the morning unrefreshed and with that feeling of half-terrified apprehension peculiar to Christmas and birthday mornings. A long moment she lay puzzling under the sun streaming in a golden flow through the yellow curtains. Then her mind returned to the night before. She had decided to leave Naxos. That was it.

Sharply she began to probe her decision. Reviewing the situation carefully, frankly, she felt no wish to change her resolution. Except—that it would be inconvenient. Much as she wanted to shake the dust of the place from her feet forever, she realized that there would be difficulties. Red tape. James Vayle. Money. Other work. Regretfully she was forced to acknowledge that it would be vastly better to wait until June, the close of the school year. Not so long, really. Half of March, April, May, some of June. Surely she could endure for that much longer conditions which she had borne for nearly two years. By an effort of will, her will, it could be done.

But this reflection, sensible, expedient, though it was, did not reconcile her. To remain seemed too hard. Could she do it? Was it possible in the present rebellious state of her feelings? The uneasy sense of being engaged with some formidable antagonist, nameless and un-understood, startled her. It wasn't, she was suddenly aware, merely the school and its ways and its decorous stupid people that oppressed her. There was something else, some other more ruthless force, a quality within herself, which was frustrating her, had always frustrated her, kept her from getting the things she had wanted. Still wanted.

But just what did she want? Barring a desire for material security, gracious ways of living, a profusion of lovely clothes, and a goodly share of envious admiration, Helga Crane didn't know, couldn't tell. But there was, she knew, something else. Happiness, she supposed. Whatever that might be. What, exactly, she wondered, was happiness. Very positively she wanted it. Yet her conception of it had no tangibility. She couldn't define it, isolate it, and contemplate it as she could some other abstract things. Hatred, for instance. Or kindness.

The strident ringing of a bell somewhere in the building brought back the fierce resentment of the night. It crystallized her wavering determination.

From long habit her biscuit-coloured feet had slipped mechanically out from under the covers at the bell's first unkind jangle. Leisurely she drew them back and her cold anger vanished as she decided that, now, it didn't at all matter if she failed to appear at the monotonous distasteful breakfast which was provided for her by the school as part of her wages.

In the corridor beyond her door was a medley of noises incident to the rising and preparing for the day at the same hour of many schoolgirls—foolish giggling, indistinguishable snatches of merry conversation, distant gurgle of running water, patter of slippered feet, low-pitched singing, good-natured admonitions to hurry, slamming of doors, clatter of various unnamable articles, and—suddenly—calamitous silence.

Helga ducked her head under the covers in the vain attempt to shut out what she knew would fill the pregnant silence—the sharp sarcastic voice of the dormitory matron. It came.

"Well! Even if every last one of you did come from homes where you weren't taught any manners, you might at least try to pretend that you're capable of learning some here, now that you have the opportunity. Who slammed the shower-baths door?"

Silence.

"Well, you needn't trouble to answer. It's rude, as all of you know. But it's just as well, because none of you can tell the truth. Now hurry up. Don't let me hear of a single one of you being late for breakfast. If I do there'll be extra work for everybody on Saturday. And *please* at least try to act like ladies and not like savages from the backwoods."

On her side of the door, Helga was wondering if it had ever occurred to the lean and desiccated Miss MacGooden that most of her charges had actually come from the backwoods. Quite recently too. Miss MacGooden, humorless, prim, ugly, with a face like dried leather, prided herself on being a "lady" from one of the best families—an uncle had been a congressman in the period of the Reconstruction. She was therefore, Helga Crane reflected, perhaps unable to perceive that the inducement to act like a lady, her own acrimonious example, was slight, if not altogether negative. And thinking on Miss Mac-Gooden's "ladyness," Helga grinned a little as she remembered that one's expressed reason for never having married, or intending to marry. There were, so she had been given to understand, things in the matrimonial state that were of necessity entirely too repulsive for a lady of delicate and sensitive nature to submit to.

Soon the forcibly shut-off noises began to be heard again, as the evidently vanishing image of Miss MacGooden evaporated from the short memories of the ladies-in-making. Preparations for the intake of the day's quota of learning went on again. Almost naturally.

"So much for that!" said Helga, getting herself out of bed.

She walked to the window and stood looking down into the great quadrangle below, at the multitude of students streaming from the six big dormitories which, two each, flanked three of its sides, and assembling into neat phalanxes preparatory to marching in military order to the sorry breakfast in Jones Hall on the fourth side. Here and there a male member of the faculty, important and resplendent in the regalia of an army officer, would pause in his prancing or strutting, to jerk a negligent or offending student into the proper attitude or place. The massed phalanxes increased in size and number, blotting out pavements, bare earth, and grass. And about it all was a depressing silence, a sullenness almost, until with a horrible abruptness the waiting band blared into "The Star Spangled Banner." The goose-step began. Left, right. Left, right. Forward! March! The automatons moved. The squares disintegrated into fours. Into twos. Disappeared into the gaping doors of Jones Hall. After the last pair of marchers had entered, the huge doors were closed. A few unlucky latecomers, apparently already discouraged, tugged half-heartedly at the knobs, and finding, as they had evidently expected, that they were indeed barred out, turned resignedly away.

Helga Crane turned away from the window, a shadow dimming the pale amber loveliness of her face. Seven o'clock it was now. At twelve those children who by some accident had been a little minute or two late would have their first meal after five hours of work and so-called education. Discipline, it was called.

There came a light knocking on her door.

"Come in," invited Helga unenthusiastically. The door opened to admit Margaret Creighton, another teacher in the English department and to Helga the most congenial member of the whole Naxos faculty. Margaret, she felt, appreciated her.

Seeing Helga still in night robe seated on the bedside in a mass of cushions, idly dangling a mule across bare toes like one with all the time in the world before her, she exclaimed in dismay: "Helga Crane, do you know what time it is? Why, it's long after half past seven. The students—"

"Yes, I know," said Helga defiantly, "the students are coming out from breakfast. Well, let them. I, for one, wish that there was some way that they could forever stay out from the poisonous stuff thrown at them, literally thrown at them, Margaret Creighton, for food. Poor things."

Margaret laughed. "That's just ridiculous sentiment, Helga, and you know it. But you haven't had any breakfast, yourself. Jim Vayle asked if you were sick. Of course nobody knew. You never tell anybody anything about yourself. I said I'd look in on you."

"Thanks awfully," Helga responded, indifferently. She was watching the sunlight dissolve from thick orange into pale yellow. Slowly it crept across the room, wiping out in its path the morning shadows. She wasn't interested in what the other was saying.

"If you don't hurry, you'll be late to your first class. Can I help you?" Margaret offered uncertainly. She was a little afraid of Helga. Nearly everyone was.

"No. Thanks all the same." Then quickly in another, warmer tone: "I do mean it. Thanks, a thousand times, Margaret. I'm really awfully grateful, but—you see, it's like this, I'm not going to be late to my class. I'm not going to be there at all."

The visiting girl, standing in relief, like old walnut against the buff-colored wall, darted a quick glance at Helga. Plainly she was curious. But she only said formally: "Oh, then you *are* sick." For something there was about Helga which discouraged questionings.

No, Helga wasn't sick. Not physically. She was merely disgusted. Fed up with Naxos. If that could be called sickness.

The truth was that she had made up her mind to leave. That very day. She could no longer abide being connected with a place of shame, lies, hypocrisy, cruelty, servility, and snobbishness. "It ought," she concluded, "to be shut down by law."

"But, Helga, you can't go now. Not in the middle of the term." The kindly Margaret was distressed.

"But I can. And I am. Today."

"They'll never let you," prophesied Margaret.

"*They* can't stop me. Trains leave here for civilization every day. All that's needed is money," Helga pointed out.

"Yes, of course. Everybody knows that. What I mean is that you'll only hurt yourself in your profession. They won't give you a reference if you jump up and leave like this now. At this time of the year. You'll be put on the black list. And you'll find it hard to get another teaching-job. Naxos has enormous influence in the South. Better wait till school closes."

"Heaven forbid," answered Helga fervently, "that I should ever again want work anywhere in the South! I hate it." And fell silent, wondering for the hundredth time just what form of vanity it was that had induced an intelligent girl like Margaret Creighton to turn what was probably nice live crinkly hair, perfectly suited to her smooth dark skin and agreeable round features, into a dead straight, greasy, ugly mass.

Looking up from her watch, Margaret said: "Well, I've really got to run, or I'll be late myself. And since I'm staying— Better think it over, Helga. There's no place like Naxos, you know. Pretty good salaries, decent rooms, plenty of men, and all that. Ta-ta." The door slid to behind her.

But in another moment it opened. She was back. "I do wish you'd stay. It's nice having you here, Helga. We all think so. Even the dead ones. We need a few decorations to brighten our sad lives." And again she was gone.

Helga was unmoved. She was no longer concerned with what anyone in Naxos might think of her, for she was now in love with the piquancy of leaving. Automatically her fingers adjusted the Chinese-looking pillows on the low couch that served for her bed. Her mind was busy with plans for departure. Packing, money, trains, and—could she get a berth?

Three

O N one side of the long, white, hot sand road that split the flat green, there was a little shade, for it was bordered with trees. Helga Crane walked there so that the sun could not so easily get at her. As she went slowly across the empty campus she was conscious of a vague tenderness for the scene spread out before her. It was so incredibly lovely, so appealing, and so facile. The trees in their spring beauty sent through her restive mind a sharp thrill of pleasure. Seductive, charming, and beckoning as cities were, they had not this easy unhuman loveliness. The trees, she thought, on city avenues and boulevards, in city parks and gardens, were tamed, held prisoners in a surrounding maze of human beings. Here they were free. It was human beings who were prisoners. It was too bad. In the midst of all this radiant life. They weren't, she knew, even conscious of its presence. Perhaps there was too much of it, and therefore it was less than nothing.

In response to her insistent demand she had been told that Dr. Anderson could give her twenty minutes at eleven o'clock. Well, she supposed that she could say all that she had to say in twenty minutes, though she resented being limited. Twenty minutes. In Naxos, she was as unimportant as that.

He was a new man, this principal, for whom Helga remembered feeling unaccountably sorry, when last September he had first been appointed to Naxos as its head. For some reason she had liked him, although she had seen little of him: he was so frequently away on publicity and money-raising tours. And as yet he had made but few and slight changes in the running of the school. Now she was a little irritated at finding herself wondering just how she was going to tell him of her decision. What did it matter to him? Why should she mind if it did? But there returned to her that indistinct sense of sympathy for the remote silent man with the tired gray eyes, and she wondered again by what fluke of fate such a man, apparently a humane and understanding person, had chanced into the command of this cruel educational machine. Suddenly, her own resolve loomed as an almost direct unkindness. This increased her annoyance and discomfort. A sense of defeat, of being cheated of justification, closed down on her. Absurd!

She arrived at the administration building in a mild rage, as unreasonable as it was futile, but once inside she had a sudden attack of nerves at the prospect of traversing that great outer room which was the workplace of some twenty-odd people. This was a disease from which Helga had suffered at intervals all her life, and it was a point of honor, almost, with her never to give way to it. So, instead of turning away, as she felt inclined, she walked on, outwardly indifferent. Half-way down the long aisle which divided the room, the principal's secretary, a huge black man, surged toward her.

"Good-morning, Miss Crane, Dr. Anderson will see you in a few moments. Sit down right here."

She felt the inquiry in the shuttered eyes. For some reason this dissipated her self-consciousness and restored her poise. Thanking him, she seated herself, really careless now of the glances of the stenographers, book-keepers, clerks. Their curiosity and slightly veiled hostility no longer touched her. Her coming departure had released her from the need for conciliation which had irked her for so long. It was pleasant to Helga Crane to be able to sit calmly looking out of the window on to the smooth lawn, where a few leaves quite prematurely fallen dotted the grass, for once uncaring whether the frock which she wore roused disapproval or envy.

Turning from the window, her gaze wandered contemptuously over the dull attire of the women workers. Drab colors, mostly navy blue, black, brown, unrelieved, save for a scrap of white or tan about the hands and necks. Fragments of a speech made by the dean of women floated through her thoughts— "Bright colors are vulgar"—"Black, gray, brown, and navy blue are the most becoming colors for colored people"— "Dark-complected people shouldn't wear yellow, or green or red."—The dean was a woman from one of the "first families" —a great "race" woman; she, Helga Crane, a despised mulatto, but something intuitive, some unanalyzed driving spirit of loyalty to the inherent racial need for gorgeousness told her that bright colours *were* fitting and that dark-complexioned people *should* wear yellow, green, and red. Black, brown, and gray were ruinous to them, actually destroyed the luminous tones lurking in their dusky skins. One of the loveliest sights Helga had ever seen had been a sooty black girl decked out in a flaming orange dress, which a horrified matron had next day consigned to the dyer. Why, she wondered, didn't someone write *A Plea for Color*?

These people yapped loudly of race, of race consciousness, of race pride, and yet suppressed its most delightful manifestations, love of color, joy of rhythmic motion, naïve, spontaneous laughter. Harmony, radiance, and simplicity, all the essentials of spiritual beauty in the race they had marked for destruction.

She came back to her own problems. Clothes had been one of her difficulties in Naxos. Helga Crane loved clothes, elaborate ones. Nevertheless, she had tried not to offend. But with small success, for, although she had affected the deceptively simple variety, the hawk eyes of dean and matrons had detected the subtle difference from their own irreproachably conventional garments. Too, they felt that the colors were queer; dark purples, royal blues, rich greens, deep reds, in soft, luxurious woolens, or heavy, clinging silks. And the trimmings—when Helga used them at all—seemed to them odd. Old laces, strange embroideries, dim brocades. Her faultless, slim shoes made them uncomfortable and her small plain hats seemed to them positively indecent. Helga smiled inwardly at the thought that whenever there was an evening affair for the faculty, the dear ladies probably held their breaths until she had made her appearance. They existed in constant fear that she might turn out in an evening dress. The proper evening wear in Naxos was afternoon attire. And one could, if one wished, garnish the hair with flowers.

Quick, muted footfalls sounded. The secretary had returned.

"Dr. Anderson will see you now, Miss Crane."

She rose, followed, and was ushered into the guarded sanctum, without having decided just what she was to say. For a moment she felt behind her the open doorway and then the gentle impact of its closing. Before her at a great desk her eyes picked out the figure of a man, at first blurred slightly in outline in that dimmer light. At his "Miss Crane?" her lips formed for speech, but no sound came. She was aware of inward confusion. For her the situation seemed charged, unaccountably, with strangeness and something very like hysteria. An almost overpowering desire to laugh seized her. Then, miraculously, a complete ease, such as she had never known in Naxos, possessed her. She smiled, nodded in answer to his questioning salutation, and with a gracious "Thank you" dropped into the chair which he indicated. She looked at him frankly now, this man still young, thirty-five perhaps, and found it easy to go on in the vein of a simple statement.

"Dr. Anderson, I'm sorry to have to confess that I've failed in my job here. I've made up my mind to leave. Today."

A short, almost imperceptible silence, then a deep voice of peculiarly pleasing resonance, asking gently: "You don't like Naxos, Miss Crane?"

She evaded. "Naxos, the place? Yes, I like it. Who wouldn't like it? It's so beautiful. But I—well—I don't seem to fit here."

The man smiled, just a little. "The school? You don't like the school?"

The words burst from her. "No, I don't like it. I hate it!"

"Why?" The question was detached, too detached.

In the girl blazed a desire to wound. There he sat, staring dreamily out of the window, blatantly unconcerned with her or her answer. Well, she'd tell him. She pronounced each word with deliberate slowness.

"Well, for one thing, I hate hypocrisy. I hate cruelty to students, and to teachers who can't fight back. I hate backbiting, and sneaking, and petty jealousy. Naxos? It's hardly a place at all. It's more like some loathsome, venomous disease. Ugh! Everybody spending his time in a malicious hunting for the weaknesses of others, spying, grudging, scratching."

"I see. And you don't think it might help to cure us, to have someone who doesn't approve of these things stay with us? Even just one person, Miss Crane?"

She wondered if this last was irony. She suspected it was humor and so ignored the half-pleading note in his voice.

"No, I don't! It doesn't do the disease any good. Only irritates it. And it makes me unhappy, dissatisfied. It isn't pleasant to be always made to appear in the wrong, even when I know I'm right."

His gaze was on her now, searching. "Queer," she thought,

"how some brown people have gray eyes. Gives them a strange, unexpected appearance. A little frightening."

The man said, kindly: "Ah, you're unhappy. And for the reasons you've stated?"

"Yes, partly. Then, too, the people here don't like me. They don't think I'm in the spirit of the work. And I'm not, not if it means suppression of individuality and beauty."

"And does it?"

"Well, it seems to work out that way."

"How old are you, Miss Crane?"

She resented this, but she told him, speaking with what curtness she could command only the bare figure: "Twenty-three."

"Twenty-three. I see. Some day you'll learn that lies, injustice, and hypocrisy are a part of every ordinary community. Most people achieve a sort of protective immunity, a kind of callousness, toward them. If they didn't, they couldn't endure. I think there's less of these evils here than in most places, but because we're trying to do such a big thing, to aim so high, the ugly things show more, they irk some of us more. Service is like clean white linen, even the tiniest speck shows." He went on, explaining, amplifying, pleading.

Helga Crane was silent, feeling a mystifying yearning which sang and throbbed in her. She felt again the urge for service, not now for her people, but for this man who was talking so earnestly of his work, his plans, his hopes. An insistent need to be a part of them sprang in her. With compunction tweaking at her heart for even having entertained the notion of deserting him, she resolved not only to remain until June, but to return next year. She was shamed, yet stirred. It was not sacrifice she felt now, but actual desire to stay, and to come back next year.

He came, at last, to the end of the long speech, only part of which she had heard. "You see, you understand?" he urged.

"Yes, oh yes, I do."

"What we need is more people like you, people with a sense of values, and proportion, an appreciation of the rarer things of life. You have something to give which we badly need here in Naxos. You mustn't desert us, Miss Crane."

She nodded, silent. He had won her. She knew that she

would stay. "It's an elusive something," he went on. "Perhaps I can best explain it by the use of that trite phrase, 'You're a lady.' You have dignity and breeding."

At these words turmoil rose again in Helga Crane. The intricate pattern of the rug which she had been studying escaped her. The shamed feeling which had been her penance evaporated. Only a lacerated pride remained. She took firm hold of the chair arms to still the trembling of her fingers.

"If you're speaking of family, Dr. Anderson, why, I haven't any. I was born in a Chicago slum."

The man chose his words, carefully he thought. "That doesn't at all matter, Miss Crane. Financial, economic circumstances can't destroy tendencies inherited from good stock. You yourself prove that!"

Concerned with her own angry thoughts, which scurried here and there like trapped rats, Helga missed the import of his words. Her own words, her answer, fell like drops of hail.

"The joke is on you, Dr. Anderson. My father was a gambler who deserted my mother, a white immigrant. It is even uncertain that they were married. As I said at first, I don't belong here. I shall be leaving at once. This afternoon. Good-morning."

Four

L ONG, soft white clouds, clouds like shreds of incredibly fine cotton, streaked the blue of the early evening sky. Over the flying landscape hung a very faint mist, disturbed now and then by a languid breeze. But no coolness invaded the heat of the train rushing north. The open windows of the stuffy day coach, where Helga Crane sat with others of her race, seemed only to intensify her discomfort. Her head ached with a steady pounding pain. This, added to her wounds of the spirit, made traveling something little short of a medieval torture. Desperately she was trying to right the confusion in her mind. The temper of the morning's interview rose before her like an ugly mutilated creature crawling horribly over the flying landscape of her thoughts. It was no use. The ugly thing pressed down on her, held her. Leaning back, she tried to doze as others were doing. The futility of her effort exasperated her.

Just what had happened to her there in that cool dim room under the quizzical gaze of those piercing gray eyes? Whatever it was had been so powerful, so compelling, that but for a few chance words she would still be in Naxos. And why had she permitted herself to be jolted into a rage so fierce, so illogical, so disastrous, that now after it was spent she sat despondent, sunk in shameful contrition? As she reviewed the manner of her departure from his presence, it seemed increasingly rude.

She didn't, she told herself, after all, like this Dr. Anderson. He was too controlled, too sure of himself and others. She detested cool, perfectly controlled people. Well, it didn't matter. He didn't matter. But she could not put him from her mind. She set it down to annoyance because of the cold discourtesy of her abrupt action. She disliked rudeness in anyone.

She had outraged her own pride, and she had terribly wronged her mother by her insidious implication. Why? Her thoughts lingered with her mother, long dead. A fair Scandinavian girl in love with life, with love, with passion, dreaming, and risking all in one blind surrender. A cruel sacrifice. In forgetting all but love she had forgotten, or had perhaps never known, that some things the world never forgives. But as Helga knew, she had remembered, or had learned in suffering and longing all the rest of her life. Her daughter hoped she had been happy, happy beyond most human creatures, in the little time it had lasted, the little time before that gay suave scoundrel, Helga's father, had left her. But Helga Crane doubted it. How could she have been? A girl gently bred, fresh from an older, more polished civilization, flung into poverty, sordidness, and dissipation. She visualized her now, sad, cold, and— yes, remote. The tragic cruelties of the years had left her a little pathetic, a little hard, and a little unapproachable.

That second marriage, to a man of her own race, but not of her own kind—so passionately, so instinctively resented by Helga even at the trivial age of six—she now understood as a grievous necessity. Even foolish, despised women must have food and clothing; even unloved little Negro girls must be somehow provided for. Memory, flown back to those years following the marriage, dealt her torturing stabs. Before her rose the pictures of her mother's careful management to avoid those ugly scarifying quarrels which even at this far-off time caused an uncontrollable shudder, her own childish self-effacement, the savage unkindness of her stepbrothers and sisters, and the jealous, malicious hatred of her mother's husband. Summers, winters, years, passing in one long, changeless stretch of aching misery of soul. Her mother's death, when Helga was fifteen. Her rescue by Uncle Peter, who had sent her to school, a school for Negroes, where for the first time she could breathe freely, where she discovered that because one was dark, one was not necessarily loathsome, and could, therefore, consider oneself without repulsion.

Six years. She had been happy there, as happy as a child unused to happiness dared be. There had been always a feeling of strangeness, of outsideness, and one of holding her breath for fear that it wouldn't last. It hadn't. It had dwindled gradually into eclipse of painful isolation. As she grew older, she became gradually aware of a difference between herself and the girls about her. They had mothers, fathers, brothers, and sisters of whom they spoke frequently, and who sometimes visited them. They went home for the vacations which Helga spent in the city where the school was located. They visited each other and knew many of the same people. Discontent for which there was no remedy crept upon her, and she was glad almost when these most peaceful years which she had yet known came to their end. She had been happier, but still horribly lonely.

She had looked forward with pleasant expectancy to working in Naxos when the chance came. And now this! What was it that stood in her way? Helga Crane couldn't explain it, put a name to it. She had tried in the early afternoon in her gentle but staccato talk with James Vayle. Even to herself her explanation had sounded inane and insufficient; no wonder James had been impatient and unbelieving. During their brief and unsatisfactory conversation she had had an odd feeling that he felt somehow cheated. And more than once she had been aware of a suggestion of suspicion in his attitude, a feeling that he was being duped, that he suspected her of some hidden purpose which he was attempting to discover.

Well, that was over. She would never be married to James Vayle now. It flashed upon her that, even had she remained in Naxos, she would never have been married to him. She couldn't have married him. Gradually, too, there stole into her thoughts of him a curious sensation of repugnance, for which she was at a loss to account. It was new, something unfelt before. Certainly she had never loved him overwhelmingly, not, for example, as her mother must have loved her father, but she *had* liked him, and she had expected to love him, after their marriage. People generally did love then, she imagined. No, she had not loved James, but she had wanted to. Acute nausea rose in her as she recalled the slight quivering of his lips sometimes when her hands had unexpectedly touched his; the throbbing vein in his forehead on a gay day when they had wandered off alone across the low hills and she had allowed him frequent kisses under the shelter of some low-hanging willows. Now she shivered a little, even in the hot train, as if she had suddenly come out from a warm scented place into cool, clear air. She must have been mad, she thought; but she couldn't tell why she thought so. This, too, bothered her.

Laughing conversation buzzed about her. Across the aisle a bronze baby, with bright staring eyes, began a fretful whining, which its young mother essayed to silence by a low droning croon. In the seat just beyond, a black and tan young pair were absorbed in the eating of a cold fried chicken, audibly crunching

the ends of the crisp, browned bones. A little distance away a
tired laborer slept noisily. Near him two children dropped the
peelings of oranges and bananas on the already soiled floor.
The smell of stale food and ancient tobacco irritated Helga like
a physical pain. A man, a white man, strode through the packed
car and spat twice, once in the exact centre of the dingy door
panel, and once into the receptacle which held the drinking-
water. Instantly Helga became aware of stinging thirst. Her
eyes sought the small watch at her wrist. Ten hours to Chicago.
Would she be lucky enough to prevail upon the conductor to
let her occupy a berth, or would she have to remain here all
night, without sleep, without food, without drink, and with
that disgusting door panel to which her purposely averted eyes
were constantly, involuntarily straying?

Her first effort was unsuccessful. An ill-natured "No, you
know you can't," was the answer to her inquiry. But farther on
along the road, there was a change of men. Her rebuff had
made her reluctant to try again, but the entry of a farmer carrying a basket containing live chickens, which he deposited on
the seat (the only vacant one) beside her, strengthened her
weakened courage. Timidly, she approached the new conductor,
an elderly gray-mustached man of pleasant appearance, who
subjected her to a keen, appraising look, and then promised to
see what could be done. She thanked him, gratefully, and went
back to her shared seat, to wait anxiously. After half an hour he
returned, saying he could "fix her up," there was a section she
could have, adding: "It'll cost you ten dollars." She murmured:
"All right. Thank you." It was twice the price and she needed
every penny, but she knew she was fortunate to get it even at
that, and so was very thankful, as she followed his tall, loping
figure out of that car and through seemingly endless others,
and at last into one where she could rest a little.

She undressed and lay down, her thoughts still busy with
the morning's encounter. Why hadn't she grasped his meaning? Why, if she had said so much, hadn't she said more about
herself and her mother? He would, she was sure, have understood, even sympathized. Why had she lost her temper and
given way to angry half-truths?— Angry half-truths— Angry
half—

Five

GRAY Chicago seethed, surged, and scurried about her. Helga shivered a little, drawing her light coat closer. She had forgotten how cold March could be under the pale skies of the North. But she liked it, this blustering wind. She would even have welcomed snow, for it would more clearly have marked the contrast between this freedom and the cage which Naxos had been to her. Not but what it was marked plainly enough by the noise, the dash, the crowds.

Helga Crane, who had been born in this dirty, mad, hurrying city, had no home here. She had not even any friends here. It would have to be, she decided, the Young Women's Christian Association. "Oh dear! The uplift. Poor, poor colored people. Well, no use stewing about it. I'll get a taxi to take me out, bag and baggage, then I'll have a hot bath and a really good meal, peep into the shops—mustn't buy anything—and then for Uncle Peter. Guess I won't phone. More effective if I surprise him."

It was late, very late, almost evening, when finally Helga turned her steps northward, in the direction of Uncle Peter's home. She had put it off as long as she could, for she detested her errand. The fact that that one day had shown her its acute necessity did not decrease her distaste. As she approached the North Side, the distaste grew. Arrived at last at the familiar door of the old stone house, her confidence in Uncle Peter's welcome deserted her. She gave the bell a timid push and then decided to turn away, to go back to her room and phone, or, better yet, to write. But before she could retreat, the door was opened by a strange red-faced maid, dressed primly in black and white. This increased Helga's mistrust. Where, she wondered, was the ancient Rose, who had, ever since she could remember, served her uncle.

The hostile "Well?" of this new servant forcibly recalled the reason for her presence there. She said firmly: "Mr. Nilssen, please."

"Mr. Nilssen's not in," was the pert retort. "Will you see Mrs. Nilssen?"

Helga was startled. "Mrs. Nilssen! I beg your pardon, did you say Mrs. Nilssen?"

"I did," answered the maid shortly, beginning to close the door.

"What is it, Ida?" A woman's soft voice sounded from within.

"Someone for Mr. Nilssen, m'am." The girl looked embarrassed.

In Helga's face the blood rose in a deep-red stain. She explained: "Helga Crane, his niece."

"She says she's his niece, m'am."

"Well, have her come in."

There was no escape. She stood in the large reception hall, and was annoyed to find herself actually trembling. A woman, tall, exquisitely gowned, with shining gray hair piled high, came forward murmuring in a puzzled voice: "His niece, did you say?"

"Yes, Helga Crane. My mother was his sister, Karen Nilssen. I've been away. I didn't know Uncle Peter had married." Sensitive to atmosphere, Helga had felt at once the latent antagonism in the woman's manner.

"Oh, yes! I remember about you now. I'd forgotten for a moment. *Well*, he isn't exactly your uncle, is he? Your mother wasn't married, was she? I mean, to your father?"

"I—I don't know," stammered the girl, feeling pushed down to the uttermost depths of ignominy.

"Of course she wasn't." The clear, low voice held a positive note. "Mr. Nilssen has been very kind to you, supported you, sent you to school. But you mustn't expect anything else. And you mustn't come here any more. It—well, frankly, it isn't convenient. I'm sure an intelligent girl like yourself can understand that."

"Of course," Helga agreed, coldly, freezingly, but her lips quivered. She wanted to get away as quickly as possible. She reached the door. There was a second of complete silence, then Mrs. Nilssen's voice, a little agitated: "And please remember that my husband is not your uncle. No indeed! Why, that, that would make me your aunt! He's not—"

But at last the knob had turned in Helga's fumbling hand. She gave a little unpremeditated laugh and slipped out. When she was in the street, she ran. Her only impulse was to get as far away from her uncle's house, and this woman, his wife, who so plainly wished to dissociate herself from the outrage of her very existence. She was torn with mad fright, an emotion against which she knew but two weapons: to kick and scream, or to flee.

The day had lengthened. It was evening and much colder, but Helga Crane was unconscious of any change, so shaken she was and burning. The wind cut her like a knife, but she did not feel it. She ceased her frantic running, aware at last of the curious glances of passers-by. At one spot, for a moment less frequented than others, she stopped to give heed to her disordered appearance. Here a man, well groomed and pleasant-spoken, accosted her. On such occasions she was wont to reply scathingly, but, tonight, his pale Caucasian face struck her breaking faculties as too droll. Laughing harshly, she threw at him the words: "You're not my uncle."

He retired in haste, probably thinking her drunk, or possibly a little mad.

Night fell, while Helga Crane in the rushing swiftness of a roaring elevated train sat numb. It was as if all the bogies and goblins that had beset her unloved, unloving, and unhappy childhood had come to life with tenfold power to hurt and frighten. For the wound was deeper in that her long freedom from their presence had rendered her the more vulnerable. Worst of all was the fact that under the stinging hurt she understood and sympathized with Mrs. Nilssen's point of view, as always she had been able to understand her mother's, her step-father's, and his children's points of view. She saw herself for an obscene sore in all their lives, at all costs to be hidden. She understood, even while she resented. It would have been easier if she had not.

Later in the bare silence of her tiny room she remembered the unaccomplished object of her visit. Money. Characteristically, while admitting its necessity, and even its undeniable desirability, she dismissed its importance. Its elusive quality she had as yet never known. She would find work of some kind. Perhaps the library. The idea clung. Yes, certainly the library. She knew books and loved them.

She stood intently looking down into the glimmering street,

far below, swarming with people, merging into little eddies
and disengaging themselves to pursue their own in individual
ways. A few minutes later she stood in the doorway, drawn by
an uncontrollable desire to mingle with the crowd. The purple
sky showed tremulous clouds piled up, drifting here and there
with a sort of endless lack of purpose. Very like the myriad human beings pressing hurriedly on. Looking at these, Helga
caught herself wondering who they were, what they did, and
of what they thought. What was passing behind those dark
molds of flesh. Did they really think at all? Yet, as she stepped
out into the moving multi-colored crowd, there came to her a
queer feeling of enthusiasm, as if she were tasting some agreeable, exotic food—sweetbreads, smothered with truffles and
mushrooms—perhaps. And, oddly enough, she felt, too, that
she had come home. She, Helga Crane, who had no home.

Six

HELGA woke to the sound of rain. The day was leaden gray, and misty black, and dullish white. She was not surprised, the night had promised it. She made a little frown, remembering that it was today that she was to search for work.

She dressed herself carefully, in the plainest garments she possessed, a suit of fine blue twill faultlessly tailored, from whose left pocket peeped a gay kerchief, an unadorned, heavy silk blouse, a small, smart, fawn-colored hat, and slim, brown oxfords, and chose a brown umbrella. In a near-by street she sought out an appealing little restaurant, which she had noted in her last night's ramble through the neighborhood, for the thick cups and the queer dark silver of the Young Women's Christian Association distressed her.

After a slight breakfast she made her way to the library, that ugly gray building, where was housed much knowledge and a little wisdom, on interminable shelves. The friendly person at the desk in the hall bestowed on her a kindly smile when Helga stated her business and asked for directions.

"The corridor to your left, then the second door to your right," she was told.

Outside the indicated door, for half a second she hesitated, then braced herself and went in. In less than a quarter of an hour she came out, in surprised disappointment. "Library training"—"civil service"—"library school"—"classification" —"cataloguing"—"training class"—"examination"—"probation period"—flitted through her mind.

"How erudite they must be!" she remarked sarcastically to herself, and ignored the smiling curiosity of the desk person as she went through the hall to the street. For a long moment she stood on the high stones steps above the avenue, then shrugged her shoulders and stepped down. It *was* a disappointment, but of course there were other things. She would find something else. But what? Teaching, even substitute teaching, was hopeless now, in March. She had no business training, and the shops didn't employ colored clerks or sales-people, not even the smaller ones. She couldn't sew, she couldn't cook. Well, she *could* do housework, or wait on table, for a short time at least. Until she got a little money together. With this thought she remembered that the Young Women's Christian Association maintained an employment agency.

"Of course, the very thing!" she exclaimed, aloud. "I'll go straight back."

But, though the day was still drear, rain had ceased to fall, and Helga, instead of returning, spent hours in aimless strolling about the hustling streets of the Loop district. When at last she did retrace her steps, the business day had ended, and the employment office was closed. This frightened her a little, this and the fact that she had spent money, too much money, for a book and a tapestry purse, things which she wanted, but did not need and certainly could not afford. Regretful and dismayed, she resolved to go without her dinner, as a self-inflicted penance, as well as an economy—and she would be at the employment office the first thing tomorrow morning.

But it was not until three days more had passed that Helga Crane sought the Association, or any other employment office. And then it was sheer necessity that drove her there, for her money had dwindled to a ridiculous sum. She had put off the hated moment, had assured herself that she was tired, needed a bit of vacation, was due one. It had been pleasant, the leisure, the walks, the lake, the shops and streets with their gay colors, their movement, after the great quiet of Naxos. Now she was panicky.

In the office a few nondescript women sat scattered about on the long rows of chairs. Some were plainly uninterested, others wore an air of acute expectancy, which disturbed Helga. Behind a desk two alert young women, both wearing a superior air, were busy writing upon and filing countless white cards. Now and then one stopped to answer the telephone.

"Y.W.C.A. employment. . . . Yes. . . . Spell it, please. . . . Sleep in or out? Thirty dollars? . . . Thank you, I'll send one right over."

Or, "I'm awfully sorry, we haven't anybody right now, but I'll send you the first one that comes in."

Their manners were obtrusively business-like, but they ignored the already embarrassed Helga. Diffidently she approached the desk. The darker of the two looked up and turned on a little smile.

"Yes?" she inquired.

"I wonder if you can help me? I want work," Helga stated simply.

"Maybe. What kind? Have you references?"

Helga explained. She was a teacher. A graduate of Devon. Had been teaching in Naxos.

The girl was not interested. "Our kind of work wouldn't do for you," she kept repeating at the end of each of Helga's statements. "Domestic mostly."

When Helga said that she was willing to accept work of any kind, a slight, almost imperceptible change crept into her manner and her perfunctory smile disappeared. She repeated her question about the references. On learning that Helga had none, she said sharply, finally: "I'm sorry, but we never send out help without references."

With a feeling that she had been slapped, Helga Crane hurried out. After some lunch she sought out an employment agency on State Street. An hour passed in patient sitting. Then came her turn to be interviewed. She said, simply, that she wanted work, work of any kind. A competent young woman, whose eyes stared frog-like from great tortoise-shell-rimmed glasses, regarded her with an appraising look and asked for her history, past and present, not forgetting the "references." Helga told her that she was a graduate of Devon, had taught in Naxos. But even before she arrived at the explanation of the lack of references, the other's interest in her had faded.

"I'm sorry, but we have nothing that you would be interested in," she said and motioned to the next seeker, who immediately came forward, proffering several much worn papers.

"References," thought Helga, resentfully, bitterly, as she went out the door into the crowded garish street in search of another agency, where her visit was equally vain.

Days of this sort of thing. Weeks of it. And of the futile scanning and answering of newspaper advertisements. She traversed acres of streets, but it seemed that in that whole energetic place nobody wanted her services. At least not the kind that she offered. A few men, both white and black, offered her money, but the price of the money was too dear. Helga Crane did not feel inclined to pay it.

She began to feel terrified and lost. And she was a little hungry too, for her small money was dwindling and she felt the need to economize somehow. Food was the easiest.

In the midst of her search for work she felt horribly lonely too. This sense of loneliness increased, it grew to appalling proportions, encompassing her, shutting her off from all of life around her. Devastated she was, and always on the verge of weeping. It made her feel small and insignificant that in all the climbing massed city no one cared one whit about her.

Helga Crane was not religious. She took nothing on trust. Nevertheless on Sundays she attended the very fashionable, very high services in the Negro Episcopal church on Michigan Avenue. She hoped that some good Christian would speak to her, invite her to return, or inquire kindly if she was a stranger in the city. None did, and she became bitter, distrusting religion more than ever. She was herself unconscious of that faint hint of offishness which hung about her and repelled advances, an arrogance that stirred in people a peculiar irritation. They noticed her, admired her clothes, but that was all, for the self-sufficient uninterested manner adopted instinctively as a protective measure for her acute sensitiveness, in her child days, still clung to her.

An agitated feeling of disaster closed in on her, tightened. Then, one afternoon, coming in from the discouraging round of agencies and the vain answering of newspaper wants to the stark neatness of her room, she found between door and sill a small folded note. Spreading it open, she read:

> *Miss Crane:*
> *Please come into the employment office*
> *as soon as you return.*
>
> *Ida Ross*

Helga spent some time in the contemplation of this note. She was afraid to hope. Its possibilities made her feel a little hysterical. Finally, after removing the dirt of the dusty streets, she went down, down to that room where she had first felt the smallness of her commercial value. Subsequent failures had augmented her feeling of incompetence, but she resented the fact that these clerks were evidently aware of her unsuccess. It required all the pride and indifferent hauteur she could summon to support her in their presence. Her additional arrogance passed unnoticed by those for whom it was assumed. They were interested only in the business for which they had summoned her, that of procuring a traveling-companion for a lecturing female on her way to a convention.

"She wants," Miss Ross told Helga, "someone intelligent, someone who can help her get her speeches in order on the train. We thought of you right away. Of course, it isn't permanent. She'll pay your expenses and there'll be twenty-five dollars besides. She leaves tomorrow. Here's her address. You're to go to see her at five o'clock. It's after four now. I'll phone that you're on your way."

The presumptuousness of their certainty that she would snatch at the opportunity galled Helga. She became aware of a desire to be disagreeable. The inclination to fling the address of the lecturing female in their face stirred in her, but she remembered the lone five-dollar bill in the rare old tapestry purse swinging from her arm. She couldn't afford anger. So she thanked them very politely and set out for the home of Mrs. Hayes-Rore on Grand Boulevard, knowing full well that she intended to take the job, if the lecturing one would take her. Twenty-five dollars was not to be looked at with nose in air when one was the owner of but five. And meals—meals for four days at least.

Mrs. Hayes-Rore proved to be a plump lemon-colored woman with badly straightened hair and dirty finger-nails. Her direct, penetrating gaze was somewhat formidable. Notebook in hand, she gave Helga the impression of having risen early for consultation with other harassed authorities on the race problem, and having been in conference on the subject all day. Evidently, she had had little time or thought for the careful donning of the five-years-behind-the-mode garments which covered her, and which even in their youth could hardly have fitted or suited her. She had a tart personality, and prying. She approved of Helga, after asking her endless questions about her education and her opinions on the race problem, none of which she was permitted to answer, for Mrs. Hayes-Rore either

went on to the next or answered the question herself by remarking: "Not that it matters, if you can only do what I want
done, and the girls at the 'Y' said that you could. I'm on the
Board of Managers, and I know they wouldn't send me anybody who wasn't all right." After this had been repeated twice
in a booming, oratorical voice, Helga felt that the Association
secretaries had taken an awful chance in sending a person about
whom they knew as little as they did about her.

"Yes, I'm sure you'll do. I don't really need ideas, I've plenty
of my own. It's just a matter of getting someone to help me
get my speeches in order, correct and condense them, you
know. I leave at eleven in the morning. Can you be ready by
then? . . . That's good. Better be here at nine. Now, don't
disappoint me. I'm depending on you."

As she stepped into the street and made her way skillfully
through the impassioned human traffic, Helga reviewed the
plan which she had formed, while in the lecturing one's presence, to remain in New York. There would be twenty-five
dollars, and perhaps the amount of her return ticket. Enough
for a start. Surely she could get work there. Everybody did.
Anyway, she would have a reference.

With her decision she felt reborn. She began happily to paint
the future in vivid colors. The world had changed to silver and
life ceased to be a struggle and became a gay adventure. Even
the advertisements in the shop windows seemed to shine with
radiance.

Curious about Mrs. Hayes-Rore, on her return to the "Y"
she went into the employment office, ostensibly to thank the
girls and to report that that important woman would take her.
Was there, she inquired, anything that she needed to know?
Mrs. Hayes-Rore had appeared to put such faith in their
recommendation of her that she felt almost obliged to give
satisfaction. And she added: "I didn't get much chance to ask
questions. She seemed so—er—busy."

Both the girls laughed. Helga laughed with them, surprised
that she hadn't perceived before how really likable they were.

"We'll be through here in ten minutes. If you're not busy,
come in and have your supper with us and we'll tell you about
her," promised Miss Ross.

Seven

HAVING finally turned her attention to Helga Crane, Fortune now seemed determined to smile, to make amends for her shameful neglect. One had, Helga decided, only to touch the right button, to press the right spring, in order to attract the jade's notice.

For Helga that spring had been Mrs. Hayes-Rore. Ever afterwards on recalling that day on which with wellnigh empty purse and apprehensive heart she had made her way from the Young Women's Christian Association to the Grand Boulevard home of Mrs. Hayes-Rore, always she wondered at her own lack of astuteness in not seeing in the woman someone who by a few words was to have a part in the shaping of her life.

The husband of Mrs. Hayes-Rore had at one time been a dark thread in the soiled fabric of Chicago's South Side politics, who, departing this life hurriedly and unexpectedly and a little mysteriously, and somewhat before the whole of his suddenly acquired wealth had had time to vanish, had left his widow comfortably established with money and some of that prestige which in Negro circles had been his. All this Helga had learned from the secretaries at the "Y." And from numerous remarks dropped by Mrs. Hayes-Rore herself she was able to fill in the details more or less adequately.

On the train that carried them to New York, Helga had made short work of correcting and condensing the speeches, which Mrs. Hayes-Rore as a prominent "race" woman and an authority on the problem was to deliver before several meetings of the annual convention of the Negro Women's League of Clubs, convening the next week in New York. These speeches proved to be merely patchworks of others' speeches and opinions. Helga had heard other lecturers say the same things in Devon and again in Naxos. Ideas, phrases, and even whole sentences and paragraphs were lifted bodily from previous orations and published works of Wendell Phillips, Frederick Douglass, Booker T. Washington, and other doctors of the race's ills. For variety Mrs. Hayes-Rore had seasoned hers with a peppery dash of Du Bois and a few vinegary statements of her own. Aside from these it was, Helga reflected, the same old thing.

But Mrs. Hayes-Rore was to her, after the first short, awkward period, interesting. Her dark eyes, bright and investigating, had, Helga noted, a humorous gleam, and something in the way she held her untidy head gave the impression of a cat watching its prey so that when she struck, if she so decided, the blow would be unerringly effective. Helga, looking up from a last reading of the speeches, was aware that she was being studied. Her employer sat leaning back, the tips of her fingers pressed together, her head a bit on one side, her small inquisitive eyes boring into the girl before her. And as the train hurled itself frantically toward smoke-infested Newark, she decided to strike.

"Now tell me," she commanded, "how is it that a nice girl like you can rush off on a wildgoose chase like this at a moment's notice. I should think your people'd object, or'd make inquiries, or something."

At that command Helga Crane could not help sliding down her eyes to hide the anger that had risen in them. Was she to be forever explaining her people—or lack of them? But she said courteously enough, even managing a hard little smile: "Well you see, Mrs. Hayes-Rore, I haven't any people. There's only me, so I can do as I please."

"Ha!" said Mrs. Hayes-Rore.

Terrific, thought Helga Crane, the power of that sound from the lips of this woman. How, she wondered, had she succeeded in investing it with so much incredulity.

"If you didn't have people, you wouldn't be living. Everybody has people, Miss Crane. Everybody."

"*I* haven't, Mrs. Hayes-Rore."

Mrs. Hayes-Rore screwed up her eyes. "Well, that's mighty mysterious, and I detest mysteries." She shrugged, and into those eyes there now came with alarming quickness, an accusing criticism.

"It isn't," Helga said defensively, "a mystery. It's a fact and a mighty unpleasant one. Inconvenient too," and she laughed a little, not wishing to cry.

Her tormentor, in sudden embarrassment, turned her sharp eyes to the window. She seemed intent on the miles of red clay sliding past. After a moment, however, she asked gently: "You wouldn't like to tell me about it, would you? It seems to bother you. And I'm interested in girls."

Annoyed, but still hanging, for the sake of the twenty-five dollars, to her self-control, Helga gave her head a little toss and flung out her hands in a helpless, beaten way. Then she shrugged. What did it matter? "Oh, well, if you really want to know. I assure you, it's nothing interesting. Or nasty," she added maliciously. "It's just plain horrid. For me." And she began mockingly to relate her story.

But as she went on, again she had that sore sensation of revolt, and again the torment which she had gone through loomed before her as something brutal and undeserved. Passionately, tearfully, incoherently, the final words tumbled from her quivering petulant lips.

The other woman still looked out of the window, apparently so interested in the outer aspect of the drab sections of the Jersey manufacturing city through which they were passing that, the better to see, she had now so turned her head that only an ear and a small portion of cheek were visible.

During the little pause that followed Helga's recital, the faces of the two women, which had been bare, seemed to harden. It was almost as if they had slipped on masks. The girl wished to hide her turbulent feelings and to appear indifferent to Mrs. Hayes-Rore's opinion of her story. The woman felt that the story, dealing as it did with race intermingling and possibly adultery, was beyond definite discussion. For among black people, as among white people, it is tacitly understood that these things are not mentioned—and therefore they do not exist.

Sliding adroitly out from under the precarious subject to a safer, more decent one, Mrs. Hayes-Rore asked Helga what she was thinking of doing when she got back to Chicago. Had she anything in mind?

Helga, it appeared, hadn't. The truth was she had been thinking of staying in New York. Maybe she could find something there. Everybody seemed to. At least she could make the attempt.

Mrs. Hayes-Rore sighed, for no obvious reason. "Um, maybe I can help you. I know people in New York. Do you?"

"No."

"New York's the lonesomest place in the world if you don't know anybody."

"It couldn't possibly be worse than Chicago," said Helga savagely, giving the table support a violent kick.

They were running into the shadow of the tunnel. Mrs. Hayes-Rore murmured thoughtfully: "You'd better come up-town and stay with me a few days. I may need you. Something may turn up."

It was one of those vicious mornings, windy and bright. There seemed to Helga, as they emerged from the depths of the vast station, to be a whirling malice in the sharp air of this shining city. Mrs. Hayes-Rore's words about its terrible loneliness shot through her mind. She felt its aggressive unfriendliness. Even the great buildings, the flying cabs, and the swirling crowds seemed manifestations of purposed malevolence. And for that first short minute she was awed and frightened and inclined to turn back to that other city, which, though not kind, was yet not strange. This New York seemed somehow more appalling, more scornful, in some inexplicable way even more terrible and uncaring than Chicago. Threatening almost. Ugly. Yes, perhaps she'd better turn back.

The feeling passed, escaped in the surprise of what Mrs. Hayes-Rore was saying. Her oratorical voice boomed above the city's roar. "I suppose I ought really to have phoned Anne from the station. About you, I mean. Well, it doesn't matter. She's got plenty of room. Lives alone in a big house, which is something Negroes in New York don't do. They fill 'em up with lodgers usually. But Anne's funny. Nice, though. You'll like her, and it will be good for you to know her if you're going to stay in New York. She's a widow, my husband's sister's son's wife. The war, you know."

"Oh," protested Helga Crane, with a feeling of acute misgiving, "but won't she be annoyed and inconvenienced by having me brought in on her like this? I supposed we were going to the 'Y' or a hotel or something like that. Oughtn't we really to stop and phone?"

The woman at her side in the swaying cab smiled, a peculiar invincible, self-reliant smile, but gave Helga Crane's suggestion no other attention. Plainly she was a person accustomed to having things her way. She merely went on talking of other plans. "I think maybe I can get you some work. With a new Negro insurance company. They're after me to put quite a tidy sum into it. Well, I'll just tell them that they may as well take you with the money," and she laughed.

"Thanks awfully," Helga said, "but will they like it? I mean being made to take me because of the money."

"They're not being made," contradicted Mrs. Hayes-Rore. "I intended to let them have the money anyway, and I'll tell Mr. Darling so—after he takes you. They ought to be glad to get you. Colored organizations always need more brains as well as more money. Don't worry. And don't thank me again. You haven't got the job yet, you know."

There was a little silence, during which Helga gave herself up to the distraction of watching the strange city and the strange crowds, trying hard to put out of her mind the vision of an easier future which her companion's words had conjured up; for, as had been pointed out, it was, as yet, only a possibility.

Turning out of the park into the broad thoroughfare of Lenox Avenue, Mr. Hayes-Rore said in a too carefully casual manner: "And, by the way, I wouldn't mention that my people are white, if I were you. Colored people won't understand it, and after all it's your own business. When you've lived as long as I have, you'll know that what others don't know can't hurt you. I'll just tell Anne that you're a friend of mine whose mother's dead. That'll place you well enough and it's all true. I never tell lies. She can fill in the gaps to suit herself and anyone else curious enough to ask."

"Thanks," Helga said again. And so great was her gratitude that she reached out and took her new friend's slightly soiled hand in one of her own fastidious ones, and retained it until their cab turned into a pleasant tree-lined street and came to a halt before one of the dignified houses in the center of the block. Here they got out.

In after years Helga Crane had only to close her eyes to see herself standing apprehensively in the small cream-colored hall, the floor of which was covered with deep silver-hued carpet; to see Mrs. Hayes-Rore pecking the cheek of the tall slim creature beautifully dressed in a cool green tailored frock; to hear herself being introduced to "my niece, Mrs. Grey" as "Miss Crane, a little friend of mine whose mother's died, and I think perhaps a while in New York will be good for her"; to feel her hand grasped in quick sympathy, and to hear Anne Grey's pleasant voice, with its faint note of wistfulness, saying: "I'm so sorry, and I'm glad Aunt Jeanette brought you here. Did you have a good trip? I'm sure you must be worn out. I'll have Lillie take you right up." And to feel like a criminal.

Eight

A YEAR thick with various adventures had sped by since that spring day on which Helga Crane had set out away from Chicago's indifferent unkindness for New York in the company of Mrs. Hayes-Rore. New York she had found not so unkind, not so unfriendly, not so indifferent. There she had been happy, and secured work, had made acquaintances and another friend. Again she had had that strange transforming experience, this time not so fleetingly, that magic sense of having come home. Harlem, teeming black Harlem, had welcomed her and lulled her into something that was, she was certain, peace and contentment.

The request and recommendation of Mrs. Hayes-Rore had been sufficient for her to obtain work with the insurance company in which that energetic woman was interested. And through Anne it had been possible for her to meet and to know people with tastes and ideas similar to her own. Their sophisticated cynical talk, their elaborate parties, the unobtrusive correctness of their clothes and homes, all appealed to her craving for smartness, for enjoyment. Soon she was able to reflect with a flicker of amusement on that constant feeling of humiliation and inferiority which had encompassed her in Naxos. Her New York friends looked with contempt and scorn on Naxos and all its works. This gave Helga a pleasant sense of avengement. Any shreds of self-consciousness or apprehension which at first she may have felt vanished quickly, escaped in the keenness of her joy at seeming at last to belong somewhere. For she considered that she had, as she put it, "found herself."

Between Anne Grey and Helga Crane there had sprung one of those immediate and peculiarly sympathetic friendships. Uneasy at first, Helga had been relieved that Anne had never returned to the uncomfortable subject of her mother's death so intentionally mentioned on their first meeting by Mrs. Hayes-Rore, beyond a tremulous brief: "You won't talk to me about it, will you? I can't bear the thought of death. Nobody ever talks to me about it. My husband, you know." This Helga discovered to be true. Later, when she knew Anne better, she suspected that it was a bit of a pose assumed for the purpose of doing away with the necessity of speaking regretfully of a husband who had been perhaps not too greatly loved.

After the first pleasant weeks, feeling that her obligation to Anne was already too great, Helga began to look about for a permanent place to live. It was, she found, difficult. She eschewed the "Y" as too bare, impersonal, and restrictive. Nor did furnished rooms or the idea of a solitary or a shared apartment appeal to her. So she rejoiced when one day Anne, looking up from her book, said lightly: "Helga, since you're going to be in New York, why don't you stay here with me? I don't usually take people. It's too disrupting. Still, it *is* sort of pleasant having somebody in the house and I don't seem to mind you. You don't bore me, or bother me. If you'd like to stay— Think it over."

Helga didn't, of course, require to think it over, because lodgment in Anne's home was in complete accord with what she designated as her "æsthetic sense." Even Helga Crane approved of Anne's house and the furnishings which so admirably graced the big cream-colored rooms. Beds with long, tapering posts to which tremendous age lent dignity and interest, bonneted old highboys, tables that might be by Duncan Phyfe, rare spindle-legged chairs, and others whose ladder backs gracefully climbed the delicate wall panels. These historic things mingled harmoniously and comfortably with brass-bound Chinese tea-chests, luxurious deep chairs and davenports, tiny tables of gay color, a lacquered jade-green settee with gleaming black satin cushions, lustrous Eastern rugs, ancient copper, Japanese prints, some fine etchings, a profusion of precious bric-a-brac, and endless shelves filled with books.

Anne Grey herself was, as Helga expressed it, "almost too good to be true." Thirty, maybe, brownly beautiful, she had the face of a golden Madonna, grave and calm and sweet, with shining black hair and eyes. She carried herself as queens are reputed to bear themselves, and probably do not. Her manners were as agreeably gentle as her own soft name. She possessed an impeccably fastidious taste in clothes, knowing what suited her and wearing it with an air of unconscious assurance. The unusual thing, a native New Yorker, she was also a person of distinction, financially independent, well connected and much sought after. And she was interesting, an odd confusion of wit and intense earnestness; a vivid and remarkable person. Yes, undoubtedly, Anne was almost too good to be true. She was almost perfect.

Thus established, secure, comfortable, Helga soon became thoroughly absorbed in the distracting interests of life in New York. Her secretarial work with the Negro insurance company filled her day. Books, the theater, parties, used up the nights. Gradually in the charm of this new and delightful pattern of her life she lost that tantalizing oppression of loneliness and isolation which always, it seemed, had been a part of her existence.

But, while the continuously gorgeous panorama of Harlem fascinated her, thrilled her, the sober mad rush of white New York failed entirely to stir her. Like thousands of other Harlem dwellers, she patronized its shops, its theaters, its art galleries, and its restaurants, and read its papers, without considering herself a part of the monster. And she was satisfied, unenvious. For her this Harlem was enough. Of that white world, so distant, so near, she asked only indifference. No, not at all did she crave, from those pale and powerful people, awareness. Sinister folk, she considered them, who had stolen her birthright. Their past contribution to her life, which had been but shame and grief, she had hidden away from brown folk in a locked closet, "never," she told herself, "to be reopened."

Some day she intended to marry one of those alluring brown or yellow men who danced attendance on her. Already financially successful, any one of them could give to her the things which she had now come to desire, a home like Anne's, cars of expensive makes such as lined the avenue, clothes and furs from Bendel's and Revillon Frères', servants, and leisure.

Always her forehead wrinkled in distaste whenever, involuntarily, which was somehow frequently, her mind turned on the speculative gray eyes and visionary uplifting plans of Dr. Anderson. That other, James Vayle, had slipped absolutely from her consciousness. Of him she never thought. Helga Crane meant, now, to have a home and perhaps laughing, appealing dark-eyed children in Harlem. Her existence was bounded by Central Park, Fifth Avenue, St. Nicholas Park, and One Hundred and Forty-fifth street. Not at all a narrow life, as

Negroes live it, as Helga Crane knew it. Everything was there, vice and goodness, sadness and gayety, ignorance and wisdom, ugliness and beauty, poverty and richness. And it seemed to her that somehow of goodness, gayety, wisdom, and beauty always there was a little more than of vice, sadness, ignorance, and ugliness. It was only riches that did not quite transcend poverty.

"But," said Helga Crane, "what of that? Money isn't everything. It isn't even the half of everything. And here we have so much else—and by ourselves. It's only outside of Harlem among those others that money really counts for everything."

In the actuality of the pleasant present and the delightful vision of an agreeable future she was contented, and happy. She did not analyze this contentment, this happiness, but vaguely, without putting it into words or even so tangible a thing as a thought, she knew it sprang from a sense of freedom, a release from the feeling of smallness which had hedged her in, first during her sorry, unchildlike childhood among hostile white folk in Chicago, and later during her uncomfortable sojourn among snobbish black folk in Naxos.

Nine

B UT it didn't last, this happiness of Helga Crane's.
Little by little the signs of spring appeared, but strangely the enchantment of the season, so enthusiastically, so lavishly greeted by the gay dwellers of Harlem, filled her only with restlessness. Somewhere, within her, in a deep recess, crouched discontent. She began to lose confidence, in the fullness of her life, the glow began to fade from her conception of it. As the days multiplied, her need of something, something vaguely familiar, but which she could not put a name to and hold for definite examination, became almost intolerable. She went through moments of overwhelming anguish. She felt shut in, trapped. "Perhaps I'm tired, need a tonic, or something," she reflected. So she consulted a physician, who, after a long, solemn examination, said that there was nothing wrong, nothing at all. "A change of scene, perhaps for a week or so, or a few days away from work," would put her straight most likely. Helga tried this, tried them both, but it was no good. All interest had gone out of living. Nothing seemed any good. She became a little frightened, and then shocked to discover that, for some unknown reason, it was of herself she was afraid.

Spring grew into summer, languidly at first, then flauntingly. Without awareness on her part, Helga Crane began to draw away from those contacts which had so delighted her. More and more she made lonely excursions to places outside of Harlem. A sensation of estrangement and isolation encompassed her. As the days became hotter and the streets more swarming, a kind of repulsion came upon her. She recoiled in aversion from the sight of the grinning faces and from the sound of the easy laughter of all these people who strolled, aimlessly now, it seemed, up and down the avenues. Not only did the crowds of nameless folk on the street annoy her, she began also actually to dislike her friends.

Even the gentle Anne distressed her. Perhaps because Anne was obsessed by the race problem and fed her obsession. She frequented all the meetings of protest, subscribed to all the complaining magazines, and read all the lurid newspapers spewed out by the Negro yellow press. She talked, wept, and ground her teeth dramatically about the wrongs and shames of her race. At times she lashed her fury to surprising heights for one by nature so placid and gentle. And, though she would not, even to herself, have admitted it, she reveled in this orgy of protest.

"Social equality," "Equal opportunity for all," were her slogans, often and emphatically repeated. Anne preached these things and honestly thought that she believed them, but she considered it an affront to the race, and to all the vari-colored peoples that made Lenox and Seventh Avenues the rich spectacles which they were, for any Negro to receive on terms of equality any white person.

"To me," asserted Anne Grey, "the most wretched Negro prostitute that walks One Hundred and Thirty-fifth Street is more than any president of these United States, not excepting Abraham Lincoln." But she turned up her finely carved nose at their lusty churches, their picturesque parades, their naïve clowning on the streets. She would not have desired or even have been willing to live in any section outside the black belt, and she would have refused scornfully, had they been tendered, any invitation from white folk. She hated white people with a deep and burning hatred, with the kind of hatred which, finding itself held in sufficiently numerous groups, was capable some day, on some great provocation, of bursting into dangerously malignant flames.

But she aped their clothes, their manners, and their gracious ways of living. While proclaiming loudly the undiluted good of all things Negro, she yet disliked the songs, the dances, and the softly blurred speech of the race. Toward these things she showed only a disdainful contempt, tinged sometimes with a faint amusement. Like the despised people of the white race, she preferred Pavlova to Florence Mills, John McCormack to Taylor Gordon, Walter Hampden to Paul Robeson. Theoretically, however, she stood for the immediate advancement of all things Negroid, and was in revolt against social inequality.

Helga had been entertained by this racial ardor in one so little affected by racial prejudice as Anne, and by her inconsistencies. But suddenly these things irked her with a great irksomeness and she wanted to be free of this constant prattling of the incongruities, the injustices, the stupidities, the viciousness of white people. It stirred memories, probed hidden wounds, whose poignant ache bred in her surprising oppression and corroded the fabric of her quietism. Sometimes it took all her self-control to keep from tossing sarcastically at Anne Ibsen's remark about there being assuredly something very wrong with the drains, but after all there were other parts of the edifice.

It was at this period of restiveness that Helga met again Dr. Anderson. She had gone, unwillingly, to a meeting, a health meeting, held in a large church—as were most of Harlem's uplift activities—as a substitute for her employer, Mr. Darling. Making her tardy arrival during a tedious discourse by a pompous saffron-hued physician, she was led by the irritated usher, whom she had roused from a nap in which he had been pleasantly freed from the intricacies of Negro health statistics, to a very front seat. Complete silence ensued while she subsided into her chair. The offended doctor looked at the ceiling, at the floor, and accusingly at Helga, and finally continued his lengthy discourse. When at last he had ended and Helga had dared to remove her eyes from his sweating face and look about, she saw with a sudden thrill that Robert Anderson was among her nearest neighbors. A peculiar, not wholly disagreeable, quiver ran down her spine. She felt an odd little faintness. The blood rushed to her face. She tried to jeer at herself for being so moved by the encounter.

He, meanwhile, she observed, watched her gravely. And having caught her attention, he smiled a little and nodded.

When all who so desired had spouted to their hearts' content —if to little purpose—and the meeting was finally over, Anderson detached himself from the circle of admiring friends and acquaintances that had gathered around him and caught up with Helga half-way down the long aisle leading out to fresher air.

"I wondered if you were really going to cut me. I see you were," he began, with that half-quizzical smile which she remembered so well.

She laughed. "Oh, I didn't think you'd remember me." Then she added: "Pleasantly, I mean."

The man laughed too. But they couldn't talk yet. People

kept breaking in on them. At last, however, they were at the door, and then he suggested that they share a taxi "for the sake of a little breeze." Helga assented.

Constraint fell upon them when they emerged into the hot street, made seemingly hotter by a low-hanging golden moon and the hundreds of blazing electric lights. For a moment, before hailing a taxi, they stood together looking at the slow moving mass of perspiring human beings. Neither spoke, but Helga was conscious of the man's steady gaze. The prominent gray eyes were fixed upon her, studying her, appraising her. Many times since turning her back on Naxos she had in fancy rehearsed this scene, this re-encounter. Now she found that rehearsal helped not at all. It was so absolutely different from anything that she had imagined.

In the open taxi they talked of impersonal things, books, places, the fascination of New York, of Harlem. But underneath the exchange of small talk lay another conversation of which Helga Crane was sharply aware. She was aware, too, of a strange ill-defined emotion, a vague yearning rising within her. And she experienced a sensation of consternation and keen regret when with a lurching jerk the cab pulled up before the house in One Hundred and Thirty-ninth Street. So soon, she thought.

But she held out her hand calmly, coolly. Cordially she asked him to call some time. "It is," she said, "a pleasure to renew our acquaintance." Was it, she was wondering, merely an acquaintance?

He responded seriously that he too thought it a pleasure, and added: "You haven't changed. You're still seeking for something, I think."

At his speech there dropped from her that vague feeling of yearning, that longing for sympathy and understanding which his presence evoked. She felt a sharp stinging sensation and a recurrence of that anger and defiant desire to hurt which had so seared her on that past morning in Naxos. She searched for a biting remark, but, finding none venomous enough, she merely laughed a little rude and scornful laugh and, throwing up her small head, bade him an impatient good-night and ran quickly up the steps.

Afterwards she lay for long hours without undressing, thinking angry self-accusing thoughts, recalling and reconstructing that other explosive contact. That memory filled her with a sort of aching delirium. A thousand indefinite longings beset her. Eagerly she desired to see him again to right herself in his thoughts. Far into the night she lay planning speeches for their next meeting, so that it was long before drowsiness advanced upon her.

When he did call, Sunday, three days later, she put him off on Anne and went out, pleading an engagement, which until then she had not meant to keep. Until the very moment of his entrance she had had no intention of running away, but something, some imp of contumacy, drove her from his presence, though she longed to stay. Again abruptly had come the uncontrollable wish to wound. Later, with a sense of helplessness and inevitability, she realized that the weapon which she had chosen had been a boomerang, for she herself had felt the keen disappointment of the denial. Better to have stayed and hurled polite sarcasms at him. She might then at least have had the joy of seeing him wince.

In this spirit she made her way to the corner and turned into Seventh Avenue. The warmth of the sun, though gentle on that afternoon, had nevertheless kissed the street into marvelous light and color. Now and then, greeting an acquaintance, or stopping to chat with a friend, Helga was all the time seeing its soft shining brightness on the buildings along its sides or on the gleaming bronze, gold, and copper faces of its promenaders. And another vision, too, came haunting Helga Crane; level gray eyes set down in a brown face which stared out at her, coolly, quizzically, disturbingly. And she was not happy.

The tea to which she had so suddenly made up her mind to go she found boring beyond endurance, insipid drinks, dull conversation, stupid men. The aimless talk glanced from John Wellinger's lawsuit for discrimination because of race against a downtown restaurant and the advantages of living in Europe, especially in France, to the significance, if any, of the Garvey movement. Then it sped to a favorite Negro dancer who had just then secured a foothold on the stage of a current white musical comedy, to other shows, to a new book touching on Negroes. Thence to costumes for a coming masquerade dance, to a new jazz song, to Yvette Dawson's engagement to a Boston lawyer who had seen her one night at a party and proposed to her the next day at noon. Then back again to racial discrimination.

Why, Helga wondered, with unreasoning exasperation, didn't they find something else to talk of? Why must the race problem always creep in? She refused to go on to another gathering. It would, she thought, be simply the same old thing.

On her arrival home she was more disappointed than she cared to admit to find the house in darkness and even Anne gone off somewhere. She would have liked that night to have talked with Anne. Get her opinion of Dr. Anderson.

Anne it was who the next day told her that he had given up his work in Naxos; or rather that Naxos had given him up. He had been too liberal, too lenient, for education as it was inflicted in Naxos. Now he was permanently in New York, employed as a welfare worker by some big manufacturing concern, which gave employment to hundreds of Negro men.

"Uplift," sniffed Helga contemptuously, and fled before the onslaught of Anne's harangue on the needs and ills of the race.

Ten

WITH the waning summer the acute sensitiveness of Helga Crane's frayed nerves grew keener. There were days when the mere sight of the serene tan and brown faces about her stung her like a personal insult. The care-free quality of their laughter roused in her the desire to scream at them: "Fools, fools! Stupid fools!" This passionate and unreasoning protest gained in intensity, swallowing up all else like some dense fog. Life became for her only a hateful place where one lived in intimacy with people one would not have chosen had one been given choice. It was, too, an excruciating agony. She was continually out of temper. Anne, thank the gods! was away, but her nearing return filled Helga with dismay.

Arriving at work one sultry day, hot and dispirited, she found waiting a letter, a letter from Uncle Peter. It had originally been sent to Naxos, and from there it had made the journey back to Chicago to the Young Women's Christian Association, and then to Mrs. Hayes-Rore. That busy woman had at last found time between conventions and lectures to readdress it and had sent it on to New York. Four months, at least, it had been on its travels. Helga felt no curiosity as to its contents, only annoyance at the long delay, as she ripped open the thin edge of the envelope, and for a space sat staring at the peculiar foreign script of her uncle.

> *715 Sheridan Road*
> *Chicago, Ill.*
>
> Dear Helga:
>
> It is now over a year since you made your unfortunate call here. It was unfortunate for us all, you, Mrs. Nilssen, and myself. But of course you couldn't know. I blame myself. I should have written you of my marriage.
>
> I have looked for a letter, or some word from you; evidently, with your usual penetration, you understood thoroughly that I must terminate my outward relation with you. You were always a keen one.
>
> Of course I am sorry, but it can't be helped. My

*wife must be considered, and she feels very strongly
about this.*

*You know, of course, that I wish you the best of
luck. But take an old man's advice and don't do as
your mother did. Why don't you run over and visit
your Aunt Katrina? She always wanted you. Maria
Kirkeplads, No. 2, will find her.*

*I enclose what I intended to leave you at my death.
It is better and more convenient that you get it now. I
wish it were more, but even this little may come in
handy for a rainy day.*

Best wishes for your luck.

                                        Peter Nilssen

Beside the brief, friendly, but none the less final, letter there
was a check for five thousand dollars. Helga Crane's first feeling
was one of unreality. This changed almost immediately into one
of relief, of liberation. It was stronger than the mere security
from present financial worry which the check promised. Money
as money was still not very important to Helga. But later, while
on an errand in the big general office of the society, her puzzled
bewilderment fled. Here the inscrutability of the dozen or more
brown faces, all cast from the same indefinite mold, and so like
her own, seemed pressing forward against her. Abruptly it
flashed upon her that the harrowing irritation of the past weeks
was a smoldering hatred. Then, she was overcome by another,
so actual, so sharp, so horribly painful, that forever afterwards
she preferred to forget it. It was as if she were shut up, boxed
up, with hundreds of her race, closed up with that something in
the racial character which had always been, to her, inexplicable,
alien. Why, she demanded in fierce rebellion, should she be
yoked to these despised black folk?

Back in the privacy of her own cubicle, self-loathing came
upon her. "They're my own people, my own people," she kept
repeating over and over to herself. It was no good. The feeling
would not be routed. "I can't go on like this," she said to herself. "I simply can't."

There were footsteps. Panic seized her. She'd have to get out.
She terribly needed to. Snatching hat and purse, she hurried to
the narrow door, saying in a forced, steady voice, as it opened

to reveal her employer: "Mr. Darling, I'm sorry, but I've got to go out. Please, may I be excused?"

At his courteous "Certainly, certainly. And don't hurry. It's much too hot," Helga Crane had the grace to feel ashamed, but there was no softening of her determination. The necessity for being alone was too urgent. She hated him and all the others too much.

Outside, rain had begun to fall. She walked bare-headed, bitter with self-reproach. But she rejoiced too. She didn't, in spite of her racial markings, belong to these dark segregated people. She was different. She felt it. It wasn't merely a matter of color. It was something broader, deeper, that made folk kin.

And now she was free. She would take Uncle Peter's money and advice and revisit her aunt in Copenhagen. Fleeting pleasant memories of her childhood visit there flew through her excited mind. She had been only eight, yet she had enjoyed the interest and the admiration which her unfamiliar color and dark curly hair, strange to those pink, white, and gold people, had evoked. Quite clearly now she recalled that her Aunt Katrina had begged for her to be allowed to remain. Why, she wondered, hadn't her mother consented? To Helga it seemed that it would have been the solution to all their problems, her mother's, her stepfather's, her own.

At home in the cool dimness of the big chintz-hung living-room, clad only in a fluttering thing of green chiffon, she gave herself up to day-dreams of a happy future in Copenhagen, where there were no Negroes, no problems, no prejudice, until she remembered with perturbation that this was the day of Anne's return from her vacation at the sea-shore. Worse. There was a dinner-party in her honor that very night. Helga sighed. She'd have to go. She couldn't possibly get out of a dinner-party for Anne, even though she felt that such an event on a hot night was little short of an outrage. Nothing but a sense of obligation to Anne kept her from pleading a splitting headache as an excuse for remaining quietly at home.

Her mind trailed off to the highly important matter of clothes. What should she wear? White? No, everybody would, because it was hot. Green? She shook her head, Anne would be sure to. The blue thing. Reluctantly she decided against it; she loved it, but she had worn it too often. There was that

cobwebby black net touched with orange, which she had
bought last spring in a fit of extravagance and never worn,
because on getting it home both she and Anne had considered
it too *décolleté*, and too *outré*. Anne's words: "There's not
enough of it, and what there is gives you the air of something
about to fly," came back to her, and she smiled as she decided
that she would certainly wear the black net. For her it would
be a symbol. She was about to fly.

She busied herself with some absurdly expensive roses which
she had ordered sent in, spending an interminable time in their
arrangement. At last she was satisfied with their appropriateness in some blue Chinese jars of great age. Anne *did* have
such lovely things, she thought, as she began conscientiously
to prepare for her return, although there was really little to do;
Lillie seemed to have done everything. But Helga dusted the
tops of the books, placed the magazines in ordered carelessness, redressed Anne's bed in fresh-smelling sheets of cool
linen, and laid out her best pale-yellow pajamas of *crêpe de
Chine*. Finally she set out two tall green glasses and made a
great pitcher of lemonade, leaving only the ginger-ale and
claret to be added on Anne's arrival. She was a little conscience-
stricken, so she wanted to be particularly nice to Anne, who
had been so kind to her when she first came to New York, a
forlorn friendless creature. Yes, she was grateful to Anne; but,
just the same, she meant to go. At once.

Her preparations over, she went back to the carved chair
from which the thought of Anne's home-coming had drawn
her. Characteristically she writhed at the idea of telling Anne of
her impending departure and shirked the problem of evolving
a plausible and inoffensive excuse for its suddenness. "That,"
she decided lazily, "will have to look out for itself; I can't be
bothered just now. It's too hot."

She began to make plans and to dream delightful dreams of
change, of life somewhere else. Some place where at last she
would be permanently satisfied. Her anticipatory thoughts
waltzed and eddied about to the sweet silent music of change.
With rapture almost, she let herself drop into the blissful sensation of visualizing herself in different, strange places, among
approving and admiring people, where she would be appreciated, and understood.

Eleven

IT was night. The dinner-party was over, but no one wanted to go home. Half-past eleven was, it seemed, much too early to tumble into bed on a Saturday night. It was a sulky, humid night, a thick furry night, through which the electric torches shone like silver fuzz—an atrocious night for cabareting, Helga insisted, but the others wanted to go, so she went with them, though half unwillingly. After much consultation and chatter they decided upon a place and climbed into two patiently waiting taxis, rattling things which jerked, wiggled, and groaned, and threatened every minute to collide with others of their kind, or with inattentive pedestrians. Soon they pulled up before a tawdry doorway in a narrow crosstown street and stepped out. The night was far from quiet, the streets far from empty. Clanging trolley bells, quarreling cats, cackling phonographs, raucous laughter, complaining motor-horns, low singing, mingled in the familiar medley that is Harlem. Black figures, white figures, little forms, big forms, small groups, large groups, sauntered, or hurried by. It was gay, grotesque, and a little weird. Helga Crane felt singularly apart from it all. Entering the waiting doorway, they descended through a furtive, narrow passage, into a vast subterranean room. Helga smiled, thinking that this was one of those places characterized by the righteous as a hell.

A glare of light struck her eyes, a blare of jazz split her ears. For a moment everything seemed to be spinning round; even she felt that she was circling aimlessly, as she followed with the others the black giant who led them to a small table, where, when they were seated, their knees and elbows touched. Helga wondered that the waiter, indefinitely carved out of ebony, did not smile as he wrote their order—"four bottles of White Rock, four bottles of ginger-ale." Bah! Anne giggled, the others smiled and openly exchanged knowing glances, and under the tables flat glass bottles were extracted from the women's evening scarfs and small silver flasks drawn from the men's hip pockets. In a little moment she grew accustomed to the smoke and din:

They danced, ambling lazily to a crooning melody, or violently twisting their bodies, like whirling leaves, to a sudden
streaming rhythm, or shaking themselves ecstatically to a
thumping of unseen tomtoms. For the while, Helga was
oblivious of the reek of flesh, smoke, and alcohol, oblivious of
the oblivion of other gyrating pairs, oblivious of the color, the
noise, and the grand distorted childishness of it all. She was
drugged, lifted, sustained, by the extraordinary music, blown
out, ripped out, beaten out, by the joyous, wild, murky orchestra. The essence of life seemed bodily motion. And when
suddenly the music died, she dragged herself back to the present with a conscious effort; and a shameful certainty that not
only had she been in the jungle, but that she had enjoyed it,
began to taunt her. She hardened her determination to get
away. She wasn't, she told herself, a jungle creature. She
cloaked herself in a faint disgust as she watched the entertainers throw themselves about to the bursts of syncopated jangle,
and when the time came again for the patrons to dance, she
declined. Her rejected partner excused himself and sought an
acqaintance a few tables removed. Helga sat looking curiously
about her as the buzz of conversation ceased, strangled by the
savage strains of music, and the crowd became a swirling mass.
For the hundredth time she marveled at the gradations within
this oppressed race of hers. A dozen shades slid by. There was
sooty black, shiny black, taupe, mahogany, bronze, copper,
gold, orange, yellow, peach, ivory, pinky white, pastry white.
There was yellow hair, brown hair, black hair; straight hair,
straightened hair, curly hair, crinkly hair, woolly hair. She saw
black eyes in white faces, brown eyes in yellow faces, gray eyes
in brown faces, blue eyes in tan faces. Africa, Europe, perhaps
with a pinch of Asia, in a fantastic motley of ugliness and
beauty, semi-barbaric, sophisticated, exotic, were here. But she
was blind to its charm, purposely aloof and a little contemptuous, and soon her interest in the moving mosaic waned.

She had discovered Dr. Anderson sitting at a table on the
far side of the room, with a girl in a shivering apricot frock.
Seriously he returned her tiny bow. She met his eyes gravely
smiling, then blushed, furiously, and averted her own. But they
went back immediately to the girl beside him, who sat indifferently sipping a colorless liquid from a high glass, or puffing a

precariously hanging cigarette. Across dozens of tables, littered with corks, with ashes, with shriveled sandwiches, through slits in the swaying mob, Helga Crane studied her.

She was pale, with a peculiar, almost deathlike pallor. The brilliantly red, softly curving mouth was somehow sorrowful. Her pitch-black eyes, a little aslant, were veiled by long, drooping lashes and surmounted by broad brows, which seemed like black smears. The short dark hair was brushed severely back from the wide forehead. The extreme *décolleté* of her simple apricot dress showed a skin of unusual color, a delicate, creamy hue, with golden tones. "Almost like an alabaster," thought Helga.

Bang! Again the music died. The moving mass broke, separated. The others returned. Anne had rage in her eyes. Her voice trembled as she took Helga aside to whisper: "There's your Dr. Anderson over there, with Audrey Denney."

"Yes, I saw him. She's lovely. Who is she?"

"She's Audrey Denney, as I said, and she lives downtown. West Twenty-second Street. Hasn't much use for Harlem any more. It's a wonder she hasn't some white man hanging about. The disgusting creature! I wonder how she inveigled Anderson? But that's Audrey! If there is any desirable man about, trust her to attach him. She ought to be ostracized."

"Why?" asked Helga curiously, noting at the same time that three of the men in their own party had deserted and were now congregated about the offending Miss Denney.

"Because she goes about with white people," came Anne's indignant answer, "and they know she's colored."

"I'm afraid I don't quite see, Anne. Would it be all right if they didn't know she was colored?"

"Now, don't be nasty, Helga. You know very well what I mean." Anne's voice was shaking. Helga didn't see, and she was greatly interested, but she decided to let it go. She didn't want to quarrel with Anne, not now, when she had that guilty feeling about leaving her. But Anne was off on her favorite subject, race. And it seemed, too, that Audrey Denney was to her particularly obnoxious.

"Why, she gives parties for white and colored people together. And she goes to white people's parties. It's worse than disgusting, it's positively obscene."

"Oh, come, Anne, you haven't been to any of the parties, I know, so how can you be so positive about the matter?"

"No, but I've heard about them. I know people who've been."

"Friends of yours, Anne?"

Anne admitted that they were, some of them.

"Well, then, they can't be so bad. I mean, if your friends sometimes go, can they? Just what goes on that's so terrible?"

"Why, they drink, for one thing. Quantities, they say."

"So do we, at the parties here in Harlem," Helga responded. An idiotic impulse seized her to leave the place, Anne's presence, then, forever. But of course she couldn't. It would be foolish, and so ugly.

"And the white men dance with the colored women. Now you know, Helga Crane, that can mean only one thing." Anne's voice was trembling with cold hatred. As she ended, she made a little clicking noise with her tongue, indicating an abhorrence too great for words.

"Don't the colored men dance with the white women, or do they sit about, impolitely, while the other men dance with their women?" inquired Helga very softly, and with a slowness approaching almost to insolence. Anne's insinuations were too revolting. She had a slightly sickish feeling, and a flash of anger touched her. She mastered it and ignored Anne's inadequate answer.

"It's the principle of the thing that I object to. You can't get round the fact that her behavior is outrageous, treacherous, in fact. That's what's the matter with the Negro race. They won't stick together. She certainly ought to be ostracized. I've nothing but contempt for her, as has every other self-respecting Negro."

The other women and the lone man left to them—Helga's own escort—all seemingly agreed with Anne. At any rate, they didn't protest. Helga gave it up. She felt that it would be useless to tell them that what she felt for the beautiful, calm, cool girl who had the assurance, the courage, so placidly to ignore racial barriers and give her attention to people, was not contempt, but envious admiration. So she remained silent, watching the girl.

At the next first sound of music Dr. Anderson rose. Languidly the girl followed his movement, a faint smile parting her sorrowful lips at some remark he made. Her long, slender body swayed with an eager pulsing motion. She danced with grace and abandon, gravely, yet with obvious pleasure, her legs, her hips, her back, all swaying gently, swung by that wild music from the heart of the jungle. Helga turned her glance to Dr. Anderson. Her disinterested curiosity passed. While she still felt for the girl envious admiration, that feeling was now augmented by another, a more primitive emotion. She forgot the garish crowded room. She forgot her friends. She saw only two figures, closely clinging. She felt her heart throbbing. She felt the room receding. She went out the door. She climbed endless stairs. At last, panting, confused, but thankful to have escaped, she found herself again out in the dark night alone, a small crumpled thing in a fragile, flying black and gold dress. A taxi drifted toward her, stopped. She stepped into it, feeling cold, unhappy, misunderstood, and forlorn.

Twelve

HELGA CRANE felt no regret as the cliff-like towers faded. The sight thrilled her as beauty, grandeur, of any kind always did, but that was all.

The liner drew out from churning slate-colored waters of the river into the open sea. The small seething ripples on the water's surface became little waves. It was evening. In the western sky was a pink and mauve light, which faded gradually into a soft gray-blue obscurity. Leaning against the railing, Helga stared into the approaching night, glad to be at last alone, free of that great superfluity of human beings, yellow, brown, and black, which, as the torrid summer burnt to its close, had so oppressed her. No, she hadn't belonged there. Of her attempt to emerge from that inherent aloneness which was part of her very being, only dullness had come, dullness and a great aversion.

Almost at once it was time for dinner. Somewhere a bell sounded. She turned and with buoyant steps went down. Already she had begun to feel happier. Just for a moment, outside the dining-salon, she hesitated, assailed with a tiny uneasiness which passed as quickly as it had come. She entered softly, unobtrusively. And, after all, she had had her little fear for nothing. The purser, a man grown old in the service of the Scandinavian-American Line, remembered her as the little dark girl who had crossed with her mother years ago, and so she must sit at his table. Helga liked that. It put her at her ease and made her feel important.

Everyone was kind in the delightful days which followed, and her first shyness under the politely curious glances of turquoise eyes of her fellow travelers soon slid from her. The old forgotten Danish of her childhood began to come, awkwardly at first, from her lips, under their agreeable tutelage. Evidently they were interested, curious, and perhaps a little amused about this Negro girl on her way to Denmark alone.

Helga was a good sailor, and mostly the weather was lovely with the serene calm of the lingering September summer, under whose sky the sea was smooth, like a length of watered silk, unruffled by the stir of any wind. But even the two rough days found her on deck, reveling like a released bird in her returned feeling of happiness and freedom, that blessed sense of belonging to herself alone and not to a race. Again, she had put the past behind her with an ease which astonished even herself. Only the figure of Dr. Anderson obtruded itself with surprising vividness to irk her because she could get no meaning from that keen sensation of covetous exasperation that had so surprisingly risen within her on the night of the cabaret party. This question Helga Crane recognized as not entirely new; it was but a revival of the puzzlement experienced when she had fled so abruptly from Naxos more than a year before. With the recollection of that previous flight and subsequent half-questioning a dim disturbing notion came to her. She wasn't, she couldn't be, in love with the man. It was a thought too humiliating, and so quickly dismissed. Nonsense! Sheer nonsense! When one is in love, one strives to please. Never, she decided, had she made an effort to be pleasing to Dr. Anderson. On the contrary, she had always tried, deliberately, to irritate him. She was, she told herself, a sentimental fool.

Nevertheless, the thought of love stayed with her, not prominent, definite; but shadowy, incoherent. And in a remote corner of her consciousness lurked the memory of Dr. Anderson's serious smile and gravely musical voice.

On the last morning Helga rose at dawn, a dawn outside old Copenhagen. She lay lazily in her long chair watching the feeble sun creeping over the ship's great green funnels with sickly light; watching the purply gray sky change to opal, to gold, to pale blue. A few other passengers, also early risen, excited by the prospect of renewing old attachments, of glad home-comings after long years, paced nervously back and forth. Now, at the last moment, they were impatient, but apprehensive fear, too, had its place in their rushing emotions. Impatient Helga Crane was not. But she *was* apprehensive. Gradually, as the ship drew into the lazier waters of the dock, she became prey to sinister fears and memories. A deep pang of misgiving nauseated her at the thought of her aunt's husband, acquired since Helga's childhood visit. Painfully, vividly, she remembered the frightened anger of Uncle Peter's new wife, and looking back at her precipitate departure from America, she was amazed at her own stupidity. She had not even considered the remote possibility that her aunt's husband might be like Mrs. Nilssen. For the first time in nine days she wished herself back in New York, in America.

The little gulf of water between the ship and the wharf lessened. The engines had long ago ceased their whirring, and now the buzz of conversation, too, died down. There was a sort of silence. Soon the welcoming crowd on the wharf stood under the shadow of the great sea-monster, their faces turned up to the anxious ones of the passengers who hung over the railing. Hats were taken off, handkerchiefs were shaken out and frantically waved. Chatter. Deafening shouts. A little quiet weeping. Sailors and laborers were yelling and rushing about. Cables were thrown. The gangplank was laid.

Silent, unmoving, Helga Crane stood looking intently down into the gesticulating crowd. Was anyone waving to her? She couldn't tell. She didn't in the least remember her aunt, save as a hazy pretty lady. She smiled a little at the thought that her aunt, or anyone waiting there in the crowd below, would have no difficulty in singling her out. But—had she been met? When she descended the gangplank she was still uncertain and was trying to decide on a plan of procedure in the event that she had not. A telegram before she went through the customs? Telephone? A taxi?

But, again, she had all her fears and questionings for nothing. A smart woman in olive-green came toward her at once. And, even in the fervent gladness of her relief, Helga took in the carelessly trailing purple scarf and correct black hat that completed the perfection of her aunt's costume, and had time to feel herself a little shabbily dressed. For it was her aunt; Helga saw that at once, the resemblance to her own mother was unmistakable. There was the same long nose, the same beaming blue eyes, the same straying pale-brown hair so like sparkling beer. And the tall man with the fierce mustache who followed carrying hat and stick must be Herr Dahl, Aunt Katrina's husband. How gracious he was in his welcome, and how anxious to air his faulty English, now that her aunt had finished kissing her and exclaimed in Danish: "Little Helga! Little Helga! Goodness! But how you have grown!"

Laughter from all three.

"Welcome to Denmark, to Copenhagen, to our home," said the new uncle in queer, proud, oratorical English. And to Helga's smiling, grateful "Thank you," he returned: "Your trunks? Your checks?" also in English, and then lapsed into Danish.

"Where in the world are the Fishers? We must hurry the customs."

Almost immediately they were joined by a breathless couple, a young gray-haired man and a fair, tiny, doll-like woman. It developed that they had lived in England for some years and so spoke English, real English, well. They were both breathless, all apologies and explanations.

"So early!" sputtered the man, Herr Fisher. "We inquired last night and they said nine. It was only by accident that we called again this morning to be sure. Well, you can imagine the rush we were in when they said eight! And of course we had trouble in finding a cab. One always does if one is late." All this in Danish. Then to Helga in English: "You see, I was especially asked to come because Fru Dahl didn't know if you remembered your Danish, and your uncle's English—well—"

More laughter.

At last, the customs having been hurried and a cab secured, they were off, with much chatter, through the toy-like streets, weaving perilously in a nd out among the swarms of bicycles.

It had begun, a new life for Helga Crane.

Thirteen

SHE liked it, this new life. For a time it blotted from her mind all else. She took to luxury as the proverbial duck to water. And she took to admiration and attention even more eagerly.

It was pleasant to wake on that first afternoon, after the insisted-upon nap, with that sensation of lavish contentment and well-being enjoyed only by impecunious sybarites waking in the houses of the rich. But there was something more than mere contentment and well-being. To Helga Crane it was the realization of a dream that she had dreamed persistently ever since she was old enough to remember such vague things as day-dreams and longings. Always she had wanted, not money, but the things which money could give, leisure, attention, beautiful surroundings. Things. Things. Things.

So it was more than pleasant, it was important, this awakening in the great high room which held the great high bed on which she lay, small but exalted. It was important because to Helga Crane it was the day, so she decided, to which all the sad forlorn past had led, and from which the whole future was to depend. This, then, was where she belonged. This was her proper setting. She felt consoled at last for the spiritual wounds of the past.

A discreet knocking on the tall paneled door sounded. In response to Helga's "Come in" a respectful rosy-faced maid entered and Helga lay for a long minute watching her adjust the shutters. She was conscious, too, of the girl's sly curious glances at her, although her general attitude was quite correct, willing and disinterestd. In New York, America, Helga would have resented this sly watching. Now, here, she was only amused. Marie, she reflected, had probably never seen a Negro outside the pictured pages of her geography book.

Another knocking. Aunt Katrina entered, smiling at Helga's quick, lithe spring from the bed. They were going out to tea, she informed Helga. What, the girl inquired, did one wear to tea in Copenhagen, meanwhile glancing at her aunt's dark purple dress and bringing forth a severely plain blue *crêpe* frock. But no! It seemed that that wouldn't at all do.

"Too sober," pronounced Fru Dahl. "Haven't you something lively, something bright?" And, noting Helga's puzzled glance at her own subdued costume, she explained laughingly: "Oh, I'm an old married lady, and a Dane. But you, you're young. And you're a foreigner, and different. You must have bright things to set off the color of your lovely brown skin. Striking things, exotic things. You must make an impression."

"I've only these," said Helga Crane, timidly displaying her wardrobe on couch and chairs. "Of course I intend to buy here. I didn't want to bring over too much that might be useless."

"And you were quite right too. Umm. Let's see. That black there, the one with the cerise and purple trimmings. Wear that."

Helga was shocked. "But for tea, Aunt! Isn't it too gay? Too—too—*outré*?"

"Oh dear, no. Not at all, not for you. Just right." Then after a little pause she added: "And we're having people in to dinner tonight, quite a lot. Perhaps we'd better decide on our frocks now." For she was, in spite of all her gentle kindness, a woman who left nothing to chance. In her own mind she had determined the role that Helga was to play in advancing the social fortunes of the Dahls of Copenhagen, and she meant to begin at once.

At last, after much trying on and scrutinizing, it was decided that Marie should cut a favorite emerald-green velvet dress a little lower in the back and add some gold and mauve flowers, "to liven it up a bit," as Fru Dahl put it.

"Now that," she said, pointing to the Chinese red dressing-gown in which Helga had wrapped herself when at last the fitting was over, "suits you. Tomorrow we'll shop. Maybe we can get something that color. That black and orange thing there is good too, but too high. What a prim American maiden you are, Helga, to hide such a fine back and shoulders. Your feet are nice too, but you ought to have higher heels—and buckles."

Left alone, Helga began to wonder. She was dubious, too,

and not a little resentful. Certainly she loved color with a passion that perhaps only Negroes and Gypsies know. But she had a deep faith in the perfection of her own taste, and no mind to be bedecked in flaunting flashy things. Still—she had to admit that Fru Dahl was right about the dressing-gown. It did suit her. Perhaps an evening dress. And she knew that she had lovely shoulders and her feet *were* nice.

When she was dressed in the shining black taffeta with its bizarre trimmings of purple and cerise, Fru Dahl approved her and so did Herr Dahl. Everything in her responded to his "She's beautiful; beautiful!" Helga Crane knew she wasn't that, but it pleased her that he could think so, and say so. Aunt Katrina smiled in her quiet, assured way, taking to herself her husband's compliment to her niece. But a little frown appeared over the fierce mustache, as he said, in his precise, faintly feminine voice: "She ought to have ear-rings, long ones. Is it too late for Garborg's? We could call up."

And call up they did. And Garborg, the jeweler, in Fredericksgaarde waited for them. Not only were ear-rings bought, long ones brightly enameled, but glittering shoe-buckles and two great bracelets. Helga's sleeves being long, she escaped the bracelets for the moment. They were wrapped to be worn that night. The ear-rings, however, and the buckles came into immediate use and Helga felt like a veritable savage as they made their leisurely way across the pavement from the shop to the waiting motor. This feeling was intensified by the many pedestrians who stopped to stare at the queer dark creature, strange to their city. Her cheeks reddened, but both Herr and Fru Dahl seemed oblivious of the stares or the audible whispers in which Helga made out the one frequently recurring word "*sorte*," which she recognized as the Danish word for "black."

Her Aunt Katrina merely remarked: "A high color becomes you, Helga. Perhaps tonight a little rouge—" To which her husband nodded in agreement and stroked his mustache meditatively. Helga Crane said nothing.

They were pleased with the success she was at the tea, or rather the coffee—for no tea was served—and later at dinner. Hegla herself felt like nothing so much as some new and strange species of pet dog being proudly exhibited. Everyone was very polite and very friendly, but she felt the massed curiosity and interest, so discreetly hidden under the polite greetings. The very atmosphere was tense with it. "As if I had horns, or three legs," she thought. She was really nervous and a little terrified, but managed to present an outward smiling composure. This was assisted by the fact that it was taken for granted that she knew nothing or very little of the language. So she had only to bow and look pleasant. Herr and Fru Dahl did the talking, answered the questions. She came away from the coffee feeling that she had acquitted herself well in the first skirmish. And, in spite of the mental strain, she had enjoyed her prominence.

If the afternoon had been a strain, the evening was something more. It was more exciting too. Marie had indeed "cut down" the prized green velvet, until, as Helga put it, it was "practically nothing but a skirt." She was thankful for the barbaric bracelets, for the dangling ear-rings, for the beads about her neck. She was even thankful for the rouge on her burning cheeks and for the very powder on her back. No other woman in the stately pale-blue room was so greatly exposed. But she liked the small murmur of wonder and admiration which rose when Uncle Poul brought her in. She liked the compliments in the men's eyes as they bent over her hand. She liked the subtle half-understood flattery of her dinner partners. The women too were kind, feeling no need for jealousy. To them this girl, this Helga Crane, this mysterious niece of the Dahls, was not to be reckoned seriously in their scheme of things. True, she was attractive, unusual, in an exotic, almost savage way, but she wasn't one of them. She didn't at all count.

Near the end of the evening, as Helga sat effectively posed on a red satin sofa, the center of an admiring group, replying to questions about America and her trip over, in halting, inadequate Danish, there came a shifting of the curious interest away from herself. Following the others' eyes, she saw that there had entered the room a tallish man with a flying mane of reddish blond hair. He was wearing a great black cape, which swung gracefully from his huge shoulders, and in his long, nervous hand he held a wide soft hat. An artist, Helga decided at once, taking in the broad streaming tie. But how affected! How theatrical!

With Fru Dahl he came forward and was presented. "Herr Olsen, Herr Axel Olsen." To Helga Crane that meant nothing.

The man, however, interested her. For an imperceptible second he bent over her hand. After that he looked intently at her for what seemed to her an incredibly rude length of time from under his heavy drooping lids. At last, removing his stare of startled satisfaction, he wagged his leonine head approvingly.

"Yes, you're right. She's amazing. Marvelous," he muttered.

Everyone else in the room was deliberately not staring. About Helga there sputtered a little staccato murmur of manufactured conversation. Meanwhile she could think of no proper word of greeting to the outrageous man before her. She wanted, very badly, to laugh. But the man was as unaware of her omission as of her desire. His words flowed on and on, rising and rising. She tried to follow, but his rapid Danish eluded her. She caught only words, phrases, here and there. "Superb eyes . . . color . . . neck column . . . yellow . . . hair . . . alive . . . wonderful. . . ." His speech was for Fru Dahl. For a bit longer he lingered before the silent girl, whose smile had become a fixed aching mask, still gazing appraisingly, but saying no word to her, and then moved away with Fru Dahl, talking rapidly and excitedly to her and her husband, who joined them for a moment at the far side of the room. Then he was gone as suddenly as he had come.

"Who is he?" Helga put the question timidly to a hovering young army officer, a very smart captain just back from Sweden. Plainly he was surprised.

"Herr Olsen, Herr Axel Olsen, the painter. Portraits, you know."

"Oh," said Helga, still mystified.

"I guess he's going to paint you. You're lucky. He's queer. Won't do everybody."

"Oh, no. I mean, I'm sure you're mistaken. He didn't ask, didn't say anything about it."

The young man laughed. "Ha ha! That's good! He'll arrange that with Herr Dahl. He evidently came just to see you, and it was plain that he was pleased." He smiled, approvingly.

"Oh," said Helga again. Then at last she laughed. It was too funny. The great man hadn't addressed a word to her. Here she was, a curiosity, a stunt, at which people came and gazed. And was she to be treated like a secluded young miss, a Danish *frøkken*, not to be consulted personally even on matters affecting her personally? She, Helga Crane, who almost all her life had looked after herself, was she now to be looked after by Aunt Katrina and her husband? It didn't seem real.

It was late, very late, when finally she climbed into the great bed after having received an auntly kiss. She lay long awake reviewing the events of the crowded day. She was happy again. Happiness covered her like the lovely quilts under which she rested. She was mystified too. Her aunt's words came back to her. "You're young and a foreigner and—and different." Just what did that mean, she wondered. Did it mean that the difference was to be stressed, accented? Helga wasn't so sure that she liked that. Hitherto all her efforts had been toward similarity to those about her.

"How odd," she thought sleepily, "and how different from America!"

Fourteen

THE young officer had been right in his surmise. Axel Olsen was going to paint Helga Crane. Not only was he going to paint her, but he was to accompany her and her aunt on their shopping expedition. Aunt Katrina was frankly elated. Uncle Poul was also visibly pleased. Evidently they were not above kotowing to a lion. Helga's own feelings were mixed; she was amused, grateful, and vexed. It had all been decided and arranged without her, and, also, she was a little afraid of Olsen. His stupendous arrogance awed her.

The day was an exciting, not easily to be forgotten one. Definitely, too, it conveyed to Helga her exact status in her new environment. A decoration. A curio. A peacock. Their progress through the shops was an event; an event for Copenhagen as well as for Helga Crane. Her dark, alien appearance was to most people an astonishment. Some stared surreptitiously, some openly, and some stopped dead in front of her in order more fully to profit by their stares. "*Den Sorte*" dropped freely, audibly, from many lips.

The time came when she grew used to the stares of the population. And the time came when the population of Copenhagen grew used to her outlandish presence and ceased to stare. But at the end of that first day it was with thankfulness that she returned to the sheltering walls of the house on Maria Kirkeplads.

They were followed by numerous packages, whose contents all had been selected or suggested by Olsen and paid for by Aunt Katrina. Helga had only to wear them. When they were opened and the things spread out upon the sedate furnishings of her chamber, they made a rather startling array. It was almost in a mood of rebellion that Helga faced the fantastic collection of garments incongruously laid out in the quaint, stiff, pale old room. There were batik dresses in which mingled indigo, orange, green, vermilion, and black; dresses of velvet and chiffon in screaming colors, blood-red, sulphur-yellow, sea-green; and one black and white thing in striking combination. There was a black Manila shawl strewn with great scarlet and lemon flowers, a leopard-skin coat, a glittering opera-cape. There were turban-like hats of metallic silks, feathers and furs, strange jewelry, enameled or set with odd semi-precious stones, a nauseous Eastern perfume, shoes with dangerously high heels. Gradually Helga's perturbation subsided in the unusual pleasure of having so many new and expensive clothes at one time. She began to feel a little excited, incited.

Incited. That was it, the guiding principle of her life in Copenhagen. She was incited to make an impression, a voluptuous impression. She was incited to inflame attention and admiration. She was dressed for it, subtly schooled for it. And after a little while she gave herself up wholly to the fascinating business of being seen, gaped at, desired. Against the solid background of Herr Dahl's wealth and generosity she submitted to her aunt's arrangement of her life to one end, the amusing one of being noticed and flattered. Intentionally she kept to the slow, faltering Danish. It was, she decided, more attractive than a nearer perfection. She grew used to the extravagant things with which Aunt Katrina chose to dress her. She managed, too, to retain that air of remoteness which had been in America so disastrous to her friendships. Here in Copenhagen it was merely a little mysterious and added another clinging wisp of charm.

Helga Crane's new existence was intensely pleasant to her; it gratified her augmented sense of self-importance. And it suited her. She had to admit that the Danes had the right idea. To each his own milieu. Enhance what was already in one's possession. In America Negroes sometimes talked loudly of this, but in their hearts they repudiated it. In their lives too. They didn't want to be like themselves. What they wanted, asked for, begged for, was to be like their white overlords. They were ashamed to be Negroes, but not ashamed to beg to be something else. Something inferior. Not quite genuine. Too bad!

Helga Crane didn't, however, think often of America, excepting in unfavorable contrast to Denmark. For she had resolved never to return to the existence of ignominy which the New World of opportunity and promise forced upon Negroes. How stupid she had been ever to have thought that she could marry and perhaps have children in a land where every dark child was handicapped at the start by the shroud of color! She saw,

suddenly, the giving birth to little, helpless, unprotesting
Negro children as a sin, an unforgivable outrage. More black
folk to suffer indignities. More dark bodies for mobs to lynch.
No, Helga Crane didn't think often of America. It was too
humiliating, too disturbing. And she wanted to be left to the
peace which had come to her. Her mental difficulties and questionings had become simplified. She now believed sincerely
that there was a law of compensation, and that sometimes it
worked. For all those early desolate years she now felt recom-
pensed. She recalled a line that had impressed her in her lonely
school-days, "The far-off interest of tears."

To her, Helga Crane, it had come at last, and she meant to
cling to it. So she turned her back on painful America, resolutely shutting out the griefs, the humiliations, the frustrations,
which she had endured there.

Her mind was occupied with other and nearer things.

The charm of the old city itself, with its odd architectural
mixture of medievalism and modernity, and the general air
of well-being which pervaded it, impressed her. Even in the
so-called poor sections there was none of that untidiness and
squalor which she remembered as the accompaniment of poverty in Chicago, New York, and the Southern cities of America.
Here the door-steps were always white from constant scrub-
bings, the women neat, and the children washed and provided
with whole clothing. Here were no tatters and rags, no beggars. But, then, begging, she learned, was an offense punishable
by law. Indeed, it was unnecessary in a country where everyone
considered it a duty somehow to support himself and his family by honest work; or, if misfortune and illness came upon
one, everyone else, including the State, felt bound to give assistance, a lift on the road to the regaining of independence.

After the initial shyness and consternation at the sensation
caused by her strange presence had worn off, Helga spent hours
driving or walking about the city, at first in the protecting
company of Uncle Poul or Aunt Katrina or both, or sometimes Axel Olsen. But later, when she had become a little familiar with the city, and its inhabitants a little used to her, and
when she had learned to cross the streets in safety, dodging
successfully the innumerable bicycles like a true Copenhagener,
she went often alone, loitering on the long bridge which

spanned the placid lakes, and watching the pageant of the blue-clad, sprucely tailored soldiers in the daily parade at Amalien-borg Palace, or in the historic vicinity of the long, low-lying Exchange, a picturesque structure in picturesque surround-ings, skirting as it did the great canal, which always was alive with many small boats, flying broad white sails and pressing close on the huge ruined pile of the Palace of Christiansborg. There was also the Gammelstrand, the congregating-place of the venders of fish, where daily was enacted a spirited and in-teresting scene between sellers and buyers, and where Helga's appearance always roused lively and audible, but friendly, inter-est, long after she became in other parts of the city an accepted curiosity. Here it was that one day an old countrywoman asked her to what manner of mankind she belonged and at Helga's replying: "I'm a Negro," had become indignant, retorting an-grily that, just because she was old and a countrywoman she could not be so easily fooled, for she knew as well as everyone else that Negroes were black and had woolly hair.

Against all this walking the Dahls had at first uttered mild protest. "But, Aunt dear, I have to walk, or I'll get fat," Helga asserted. "I've never, never in all my life, eaten so much." For the accepted style of entertainment in Copenhagen seemed to be a round of dinner-parties, at which it was customary for the hostess to tax the full capacity not only of her dining-room, but of her guests as well. Helga enjoyed these dinner-parties, as they were usually spirited affairs, the conversation brilliant and witty, often in several languages. And always she came in for a goodly measure of flattering attention and admiration.

There were, too, those popular afternoon gatherings for the express purpose of drinking coffee together, where between much talk, interesting talk, one sipped the strong and steaming beverage from exquisite cups fashioned of Royal Danish por-celain and partook of an infinite variety of rich cakes and *smørrebrød*. This *smørrebrød*, dainty sandwiches of an endless and tempting array, was distinctly a Danish institution. Often Helga wondered just how many of these delicious sandwiches she had consumed since setting foot on Denmark's soil. Always, wherever food was served, appeared the inevitable *smørrebrød*, in the home of the Dahls, in every other home that she visited, in hotels, in restaurants.

At first she had missed, a little, dancing, for, though excellent dancers, the Danes seemed not to care a great deal for that pastime, which so delightfully combines exercise and pleasure. But in the winter there was skating, solitary, or in gay groups. Helga liked this sport, though she was not very good at it. There were, however, always plenty of efficient and willing men to instruct and to guide her over the glittering ice. One could, too, wear such attractive skating-things.

But mostly it was with Axel Olsen that her thoughts were occupied. Brilliant, bored, elegant, urbane, cynical, worldly, he was a type entirely new to Helga Crane, familiar only, and that but little, with the restricted society of American Negroes. She was aware, too, that this amusing, if conceited, man was interested in her. They were, because he was painting her, much together. Helga spent long mornings in the eccentric studio opposite the Folkemuseum, and Olsen came often to the Dahl home, where, as Helga and the man himself knew, he was something more than welcome. But in spite of his expressed interest and even delight in her exotic appearance, in spite of his constant attendance upon her, he gave no sign of the more personal kind of concern which—encouraged by Aunt Katrina's mild insinuations and Uncle Poul's subtle questionings—she had tried to secure. Was it, she wondered, race that kept him silent, held him back. Helga Crane frowned on this thought, putting it furiously from her, because it disturbed her sense of security and permanence in her new life, pricked her self-assurance.

Nevertheless she was startled when on a pleasant afternoon while drinking coffee in the Hotel Vivili, Aunt Katrina mentioned, almost casually, the desirability of Helga's making a good marriage.

"Marriage, Aunt dear!"

"Marriage," firmly repeated her aunt, helping herself to another anchovy and olive sandwich. "You are," she pointed out, "twenty-five."

"Oh, Aunt, I couldn't! I mean, there's nobody here for me to marry." In spite of herself and her desire not to be, Helga was shocked.

"Nobody?" There was, Fru Dahl asserted, Captain Frederick Skaargaard—and very handsome he was too—and he would

have money. And there was Herr Hans Tietgen, not so handsome, of course, but clever and a good business man; he too
would be rich, very rich, some day. And there was Herr Karl
Pedersen, who had a good berth with the Landmands-bank
and considerable shares in a prosperous cement-factory at
Aalborg. There was, too, Christian Lende, the young owner of
the new Odin Theater. Any of these Helga might marry, was
Aunt Katrina's opinion. "And," she added, "others." Or maybe
Helga herself had some ideas.

Helga had. She didn't, she responded, believe in mixed marriages, "between races, you know." They brought only trouble
—to the children—as she herself knew but too well from bitter
experience.

Fru Dahl thoughtfully lit a cigarette. Eventually, after a satisfactory glow had manifested itself, she announced: "Because
your mother was a fool. Yes, she was! If she'd come home after
she married, or after you were born, or even after your father
—er—went off like that, it would have been different. If even
she'd left you when she was here. But why in the world she
should have married again and a person like that, I can't see. She
wanted to keep you, she insisted on it, even over his protest, I
think. She loved you so much, she said.—And so she made you
unhappy. Mothers, I suppose, are like that. Selfish. And Karen
was always stupid. If you've got any brains at all they came
from your father."

Into this Helga would not enter. Because of its obvious partial truths she felt the need for disguising caution. With a detachment that amazed herself she asked if Aunt Katrina didn't
think, really, that miscegenation was wrong, in fact as well as
principle.

"Don't," was her aunt's reply, "be a fool too, Helga. We
don't think of those things here. Not in connection with individuals, at least." And almost immediately she inquired: "Did
you give Herr Olsen my message about dinner tonight?"

"Yes, Aunt." Helga was cross, and trying not to show it.

"He's coming?"

"Yes, Aunt," with precise politeness.

"What about him?"

"I don't know. *What* about him?"

"He likes you?"

"I don't know. How can I tell that?" Helga asked with irritating reserve, her concentrated attention on the selection of a
sandwich. She had a feeling of nakedness. Outrage.

Now Fru Dahl was annoyed and showed it. "What nonsense!
Of course you know. Any girl does," and her satin-covered foot
tapped, a little impatiently, the old tiled floor.

"Really, I don't know, Aunt," Helga responded in a strange
voice, a strange manner, coldly formal, levelly courteous. Then
suddenly contrite, she added: "Honestly, I don't. I can't tell a
thing about him," and fell into a little silence. "Not a thing,"
she repeated. But the phrase, though audible, was addressed to
no one. To herself.

She looked out into the amazing orderliness of the street.
Instinctively she wanted to combat this searching into the one
thing which, here, surrounded by all other things which for so
long she had so positively wanted, made her a little afraid.
Started vague premonitions.

Fru Dahl regarded her intently. It would be, she remarked
with a return of her outward casualness, by far the best of all
possibilities. Particularly desirable. She touched Helga's hand
with her fingers in a little affectionate gesture. Very lightly.

Helga Crane didn't immediately reply. There was, she knew,
so much reason—from one viewpoint—in her aunt's statement. She could only acknowledge it. "I know that," she told
her finally. Inwardly she was admiring the cool, easy way in
which Aunt Katrina had brushed aside the momentary acid
note of the conversation and resumed her customary pitch. It
took, Helga thought, a great deal of security. Balance.

"Yes," she was saying, while leisurely lighting another of
those long, thin, brown cigarettes which Helga knew from dis-
tressing experience to be incredibly nasty tasting, "it would be
the ideal thing for you, Helga." She gazed penetratingly into the
masked face of her niece and nodded, as though satisfied with
what she saw there. "And you of course realize that you are a
very charming and beautiful girl. Intelligent too. If you put
your mind to it, there's no reason in the world why you
shouldn't—" Abruptly she stopped, leaving her implication at
once suspended and clear. Behind her there were footsteps. A
small gloved hand appeared on her shoulder. In the short

moment before turning to greet Fru Fischer she said quietly, meaningly: "Or else stop wasting your time, Helga."

Helga Crane said: "Ah, Fru Fischer. It's good to see you." She meant it. Her whole body was tense with suppressed indignation. Burning inside like the confined fire of a hot furnace. She was so harassed that she smiled in self-protection. And suddenly she was oddly cold. An intimation of things distant, but none the less disturbing, oppressed her with a faintly sick feeling. Like a heavy weight, a stone weight, just where, she knew, was her stomach.

Fru Fischer was late. As usual. She apologized profusely. Also as usual. And, yes, she would have some coffee. And some *smørrebrød*. Though she must say that the coffee here at the Vivili was atrocious. Simply atrocious. "I don't see how you stand it." And the place was getting so common, always so many Bolsheviks and Japs and things. And she didn't—"begging your pardon, Helga"—like that hideous American music they were forever playing, even if it was considered very smart. "Give me," she said, "the good old-fashioned Danish melodies of Gade and Heise. Which reminds me, Herr Olsen says that Nielsen's 'Helios' is being performed with great success just now in England. But I suppose you know all about it, Helga. He's already told you. What?" This last was accompanied with an arch and insinuating smile.

A shrug moved Helga Crane's shoulders. Strange she'd never before noticed what a positively disagreeable woman Fru Fischer was. Stupid, too.

Fifteen

WELL into Helga's second year in Denmark, came an indefinite discontent. Not clear, but vague, like a storm gathering far on the horizon. It was long before she would admit that she was less happy than she had been during her first year in Copenhagen, but she knew that it was so. And this subconscious knowledge added to her growing restlessness and little mental insecurity. She desired ardently to combat this wearing down of her satisfaction with her life, with herself. But she didn't know how.

Frankly the question came to this: what was the matter with her? Was there, without her knowing it, some peculiar lack in her? Absurd. But she began to have a feeling of discouragement and hopelessness. Why couldn't she be happy, content, somewhere? Other people managed, somehow, to be. To put it plainly, didn't she know how? Was she incapable of it?

And then on a warm spring day came Anne's letter telling of her coming marriage to Anderson, who retained still his shadowy place in Helga Crane's memory. It added, somehow, to her discontent, and to her growing dissatisfaction with her peacock's life. This, too, annoyed her.

What, she asked herself, was there about that man which had the power always to upset her? She began to think back to her first encounter with him. Perhaps if she hadn't come away— She laughed. Derisively. "Yes, if I hadn't come away, I'd be stuck in Harlem. Working every day of my life. Chattering about the race problem."

Anne, it seemed, wanted her to come back for the wedding. This, Helga had no intention of doing. True, she had liked and admired Anne better than anyone she had ever known, but even for her she wouldn't cross the ocean.

Go back to America, where they hated Negroes! To America, where Negroes were not people. To America, where Negroes were allowed to be beggars only, of life, of happiness, of security. To America, where everything had been taken from those dark ones, liberty, respect, even the labor of their hands. To America, where if one had Negro blood, one mustn't expect money, education, or, sometimes, even work whereby one might earn bread. Perhaps she was wrong to bother about it now that she was so far away. Helga couldn't, however, help it. Never could she recall the shames and often the absolute horrors of the black man's existence in America without the quickening of her heart's beating and a sensation of disturbing nausea. It was too awful. The sense of dread of it was almost a tangible thing in her throat.

And certainly she wouldn't go back for any such idiotic reason as Anne's getting married to that offensive Robert Anderson. Anne was really too amusing. Just why, she wondered, and how had it come about that he was being married to Anne. And why did Anne, who had so much more than so many others—more than enough—want Anderson too? Why couldn't she— "I think," she told herself, "I'd better stop. It's none of my business. I don't care in the least. Besides," she added irrelevantly, "I hate such nonsensical soul-searching."

One night not long after the arrival of Anne's letter with its curious news, Helga went with Olsen and some other young folk to the great Circus, a vaudeville house, in search of amusement on a rare off night. After sitting through several numbers they reluctantly arrived at the conclusion that the whole entertainment was dull, unutterably dull, and apparently without alleviation, and so not to be borne. They were reaching for their wraps when out upon the stage pranced two black men, American Negroes undoubtedly, for as they danced and cavorted, they sang in the English of America an old rag-time song that Helga remembered hearing as a child, "Everybody Gives Me Good Advice." At its conclusion the audience applauded with delight. Only Helga Crane was silent, motionless.

More songs, old, all of them old, but new and strange to that audience. And how the singers danced, pounding their thighs, slapping their hands together, twisting their legs, waving their abnormally long arms, throwing their bodies about with a loose ease! And how the enchanted spectators clapped and howled and shouted for more!

Helga Crane was not amused. Instead she was filled with a fierce hatred for the cavorting Negroes on the stage. She felt shamed, betrayed, as if these pale pink and white people among whom she lived had suddenly been invited to look

upon something in her which she had hidden away and wanted
to forget. And she was shocked at the avidity at which Olsen
beside her drank it in.

But later, when she was alone, it became quite clear to her
that all along they had divined its presence, had known that in
her was something, some characteristic, different from any that
they themselves possessed. Else why had they decked her out
as they had? Why subtly indicated that she was different? And
they hadn't despised it. No, they had admired it, rated it as a
precious thing, a thing to be enhanced, preserved. Why? She,
Helga Crane, didn't admire it. She suspected that no Negroes,
no Americans, did. Else why their constant slavish imitation of
traits not their own? Why their constant begging to be considered as exact copies of other people? Even the enlightened, the
intelligent ones demanded nothing more. They were all beggars like the motley crowd in the old nursery rhyme:

> *Hark! Hark!*
> *The dogs do bark.*
> *The beggars are coming to town.*
> *Some in rags,*
> *Some in tags,*
> *And some in velvet gowns.*

The incident left her profoundly disquieted. Her old unhappy questioning mood came again upon her, insidiously
stealing away more of the contentment from her transformed
existence.

But she returned again and again to the Circus, always alone,
gazing intently and solemnly at the gesticulating black figures,
an ironical and silently speculative spectator. For she knew that
into her plan for her life had thrust itself a suspensive conflict
in which were fused doubts, rebellion, expediency, and urgent
longings.

It was at this time that Axel Olsen asked her to marry him.
And now Helga Crane was surprised. It was a thing that at one
time she had much wanted, had tried to bring about, and had
at last relinquished as impossible of achievement. Not so much
because of its apparent hopelessness as because of a feeling, intangible almost, that, excited and pleased as he was with her,
her origin a little repelled him, and that, prompted by some

impulse of racial antagonism, he had retreated into the fastness of a protecting habit of self-ridicule. A mordantly personal pride and sensitiveness deterred Helga from further efforts at incitation.

True, he had made, one morning, while holding his brush poised for a last, a very last stroke on the portrait, one admirably draped suggestion, speaking seemingly to the pictured face. Had he insinuated marriage, or something less—and easier? Or had he paid her only a rather florid compliment, in somewhat dubious taste? Helga, who had not at the time been quite sure, had remained silent, striving to appear unhearing.

Later, having thought it over, she flayed herself for a fool. It wasn't, she should have known, in the manner of Axel Olsen to pay florid compliments in questionable taste. And had it been marriage that he had meant, he would, of course, have done the proper thing. He wouldn't have stopped—or, rather, have begun—by making his wishes known to her when there was Uncle Poul to be formally consulted. She had been, she told herself, insulted. And a goodly measure of contempt and wariness was added to her interest in the man. She was able, however, to feel a gratifying sense of elation in the remembrance that she had been silent, ostensibly unaware of his utterance, and therefore, as far as he knew, not affronted.

This simplified things. It did away with the quandary in which the confession to the Dahls of such a happening would have involved her, for she couldn't be sure that they, too, might not put it down to the difference of her ancestry. And she could still go attended by him, and envied by others, to openings in Kongens Nytorv, to showings at the Royal Academy or Charlottenborg's Palace. He could still call for her and Aunt Katrina of an afternoon or go with her to Magasin du Nord to select a scarf or a length of silk, of which Uncle Poul could say casually in the presence of interested acquaintants: "Um, pretty scarf"—or "frock"—"you're wearing, Helga. Is that the new one Olsen helped you with?"

Her outward manner toward him changed not at all, save that gradually she became, perhaps, a little more detached and indifferent. But definitely Helga Crane had ceased, even remotely, to consider him other than as someone amusing, desirable, and convenient to have about—if one was careful.

She intended, presently, to turn her attention to one of the others. The decorative Captain of the Hussars, perhaps. But in the ache of her growing nostalgia, which, try as she might, she could not curb, she no longer thought with any seriousness on either Olsen or Captain Skaargaard. She must, she felt, see America again first. When she returned—

Therefore, where before she would have been pleased and proud at Olsen's proposal, she was now truly surprised. Strangely, she was aware also of a curious feeling of repugnance, as her eyes slid over his face, as smiling, assured, with just the right note of fervor, he made his declaration and request. She was astonished. Was it possible? Was it really this man that she had thought, even wished, she could marry?

He was, it was plain, certain of being accepted, as he was always certain of acceptance, of adulation, in any and every place that he deigned to honor with his presence. Well, Helga was thinking, that wasn't as much his fault as her own, her aunt's, everyone's. He was spoiled, childish almost.

To his words, once she had caught their content and recovered from her surprise, Helga paid not much attention. They would, she knew, be absolutely appropriate ones, and they didn't at all matter. They meant nothing to her—now. She was too amazed to discover suddenly how intensely she disliked him, disliked the shape of his head, the mop of his hair, the line of his nose, the tones of his voice, the nervous grace of his long fingers; disliked even the very look of his irreproachable clothes. And for some inexplicable reason, she was a little frightened and embarrassed, so that when he had finished speaking, for a short space there was only stillness in the small room, into which Aunt Katrina had tactfully had him shown. Even Thor, the enormous Persian, curled on the window ledge in the feeble late afternoon sun, had rested for the moment from his incessant purring under Helga's idly stroking fingers.

Helga, her slight agitation vanished, told him that she was surprised. His offer was, she said, unexpected. Quite.

A little sardonically, Olsen interrupted her. He smiled too. "But of course I expected surprise. It is, is it not, the proper thing? And always you are proper, Frøkken Helga, always."

Helga, who had a stripped, naked feeling under his direct

glance, drew herself up stiffly. Herr Olsen needn't, she told him, be sarcastic. She *was* surprised. He must understand that she was being quite sincere, quite truthful about that. Really, she hadn't expected him to do her so great an honor.

He made a little impatient gesture. Why, then, had she refused, ignored, his other, earlier suggestion?

At that Helga Crane took a deep indignant breath and was again, this time for an almost imperceptible second, silent. She had, then, been correct in her deduction. Her sensuous, petulant mouth hardened. That he should so frankly—so insolently, it seemed to her—admit his outrageous meaning was too much. She said, coldly: "Because, Herr Olsen, in my country the men, of my race, at least, don't make such suggestions to decent girls. And thinking that you were a gentleman, introduced to me by my aunt, I chose to think myself mistaken, to give you the benefit of the doubt."

"Very commendable, my Helga—and wise. Now you have your reward. Now I offer you marriage."

"Thanks," she answered, "thanks, awfully."

"Yes," and he reached for her slim cream hand, now lying quiet on Thor's broad orange and black back. Helga let it lie in his large pink one, noting their contrast. "Yes, because I, poor artist that I am, cannot hold out against the deliberate lure of you. You disturb me. The longing for you does harm to my work. You creep into my brain and madden me," and he kissed the small ivory hand. Quite decorously, Helga thought, for one so maddened that he was driven, against his inclination, to offer her marriage. But immediately, in extenuation, her mind leapt to the admirable casualness of Aunt Katrina's expressed desire for this very thing, and recalled the unruffled calm of Uncle Poul under any and all circumstances. It was, as she had long ago decided, security. Balance.

"But," the man before her was saying, "for me it will be an experience. It may be that with you, Helga, for wife, I will become great. Immortal. Who knows? I didn't want to love you, but I had to. That is the truth. I make of myself a present to you. For love." His voice held a theatrical note. At the same time he moved forward putting out his arms. His hands touched air. For Helga had moved back. Instantly he dropped

his arms and took a step away, repelled by something suddenly
wild in her face and manner. Sitting down, he passed a hand
over his face with a quick, graceful gesture.

Tameness returned to Helga Crane. Her ironic gaze rested
on the face of Axel Olsen, his leonine head, his broad nose—
"broader than my own"—his bushy eyebrows, surmounting
thick, drooping lids, which hid, she knew, sullen blue eyes. He
stirred sharply, shaking off his momentary disconcertion.

In his assured, despotic way he went on: "You know, Helga,
you are a contradiction. You have been, I suspect, corrupted
by the good Fru Dahl, which is perhaps as well. Who knows?
You have the warm impulsive nature of the women of Africa,
but, my lovely, you have, I fear, the soul of a prostitute. You
sell yourself to the highest buyer. I should of course be happy
that it is I. And I am." He stopped, contemplating her, lost apparently, for the second, in pleasant thoughts of the future.

To Helga he seemed to be the most distant, the most unreal
figure in the world. She suppressed a ridiculous impulse to
laugh. The effort sobered her. Abruptly she was aware that in
the end, in some way, she would pay for this hour. A quick
brief fear ran through her, leaving in its wake a sense of impending calamity. She wondered if for this she would pay all
that she'd had.

And, suddenly, she didn't at all care. She said, lightly, but
firmly: "But you see, Herr Olsen, I'm not for sale. Not to you.
Not to any white man. I don't at all care to be owned. Even by
you."

The drooping lids lifted. The look in the blue eyes was,
Helga thought, like the surprised stare of a puzzled baby. He
hadn't at all grasped her meaning.

She proceeded, deliberately. "I think you don't understand
me. What I'm trying to say is this, I don't want you. I wouldn't
under any circumstances marry you," and since she was, as she
put it, being brutally frank, she added: " *Now.* "

He turned a little away from her, his face white but composed, and looked down into the gathering shadows in the little
park before the house. At last he spoke, in a queer frozen voice:
"You refuse me?"

"Yes," Helga repeated with intentional carelessness. "I refuse
you."

The man's full upper lip trembled. He wiped his forehead, where the gold hair was now lying flat and pale and lusterless. His eyes still avoided the girl in the high-backed chair before him. Helga felt a shiver of compunction. For an instant she regretted that she had not been a little kinder. But wasn't it after all the greatest kindness to be cruel? But more gently, less indifferently, she said: "You see, I couldn't marry a white man. I simply couldn't. It isn't just you, not just personal, you understand. It's deeper, broader than that. It's racial. Some day maybe you'll be glad. We can't tell, you know; if we were married, you might come to be ashamed of me, to hate me, to hate all dark people. My mother did that."

"I have offered you marriage, Helga Crane, and you answer me with some strange talk of race and shame. What nonsense is this?"

Helga let that pass because she couldn't, she felt, explain. It would be too difficult, too mortifying. She had no words which could adequately, and without laceration to her pride, convey to him the pitfalls into which very easily they might step. "I might," she said, "have considered it once—when I first came. But you, hoping for a more informal arrangement, waited too long. You missed the moment. I had time to think. Now I couldn't. Nothing is worth the risk. We might come to hate each other. I've been through it, or something like it. I know. I couldn't do it. And I'm glad."

Rising, she held out her hand, relieved that he was still silent. "Good afternoon," she said formally. "It has been a great honor—"

"A tragedy," he corrected, barely touching her hand with his moist finger-tips.

"Why?" Helga countered, and for an instant felt as if something sinister and internecine flew back and forth between them like poison.

"I mean," he said, and quite solemnly, "that though I don't entirely understand you, yet in a way I do too. And—" He hesitated. Went on. "I think that my picture of you is, after all, the true Helga Crane. Therefore—a tragedy. For someone. For me? Perhaps."

"Oh, the picture!" Helga lifted her shoulders in a little impatient motion.

Ceremoniously Axel Olsen bowed himself out, leaving her grateful for the urbanity which permitted them to part without too much awkwardness. No other man, she thought, of her acquaintance could have managed it so well—except, perhaps, Robert Anderson.

"I'm glad," she declared to herself in another moment, "that I refused him. And," she added honestly, "I'm glad that I had the chance. He took it awfully well, though—for a tragedy." And she made a tiny frown.

The picture—she had never quite, in spite of her deep interest in him, and her desire for his admiration and approval, forgiven Olsen for that portrait. It wasn't, she contended, herself at all, but some disgusting sensual creature with her features. Herr and Fru Dahl had not exactly liked it either, although collectors, artists, and critics had been unanimous in their praise and it had been hung on the line at an annual exhibition, where it had attracted much flattering attention and many tempting offers.

Now Helga went in and stood for a long time before it, with its creator's parting words in mind: ". . . a tragedy . . . my picture is, after all, the true Helga Crane." Vehemently she shook her head. "It isn't, it isn't at all," she said aloud. Bosh! Pure artistic bosh and conceit. Nothing else. Anyone with half an eye could see that it wasn't, at all, like her.

"Marie," she called to the maid passing in the hall, "do you think this is a good picture of me?"

Marie blushed. Hesitated. "Of course, Frøkken, I know Herr Olsen is a great artist, but no, I don't like that picture. It looks bad, wicked. Begging your pardon, Frøkken."

"Thanks, Marie, I don't like it either."

Yes, anyone with half an eye could see that it wasn't she.

Sixteen

GLAD though the Dahls may have been that their niece had had the chance of refusing the hand of Axel Olsen, they were anything but glad that she had taken that chance. Very plainly they said so, and quite firmly they pointed out to her the advisability of retrieving the opportunity, if, indeed, such a thing were possible. But it wasn't, even had Helga been so inclined, for, they were to learn from the columns of *Politikken*, Axel Olsen had gone off suddenly to some queer place in the Balkans. To rest, the newspapers said. To get Frøkken Crane out of his mind, the gossips said.

Life in the Dahl ménage went on, smoothly as before, but not so pleasantly. The combined disappointment and sense of guilt of the Dahls and Helga colored everything. Though she had resolved not to think that they felt that she had, as it were, "let them down," Helga knew that they did. They had not so much expected as hoped that she would bring down Olsen, and so secure the link between the merely fashionable set to which they belonged and the artistic one after which they hankered. It was of course true that there were others, plenty of them. But there was only one Olsen. And Helga, for some idiotic reason connected with race, had refused him. Certainly there was no use in thinking, even, of the others. If she had refused him, she would refuse any and all for the same reason. It was, it seemed, all-embracing.

"It isn't," Uncle Poul had tried to point out to her, "as if there were hundreds of mulattoes here. That, I can understand, might make it a little different. But there's only you. You're unique here, don't you see? Besides, Olsen has money and enviable position. Nobody'd dare to say, or even to think anything odd or unkind of you or him. Come now, Helga, it isn't this foolishness about race. Not here in Denmark. You've never spoken of it before. It can't be just that. You're too sensible. It must be something else. I wish you'd try to explain. You don't perhaps like Olsen?"

Helga had been silent, thinking what a severe wrench to Herr Dahl's ideas of decency was this conversation. For he had an almost fanatic regard for reticence, and a peculiar shrinking from what he looked upon as indecent exposure of the emotions.

"Just what is it, Helga?" he asked again, because the pause had grown awkward, for him.

"I can't explain any better than I have," she had begun tremulously, "it's just something—something deep down inside of me," and had turned away to hide a face convulsed by threatening tears.

But that, Uncle Poul had remarked with a reasonableness that was wasted on the miserable girl before him, was nonsense, pure nonsense.

With a shaking sigh and a frantic dab at her eyes, in which had come a despairing look, she had agreed that perhaps it was foolish, but she couldn't help it. "Can't you, won't you understand, Uncle Poul?" she begged, with a pleading look at the kindly worldly man who at that moment had been thinking that this strange exotic niece of his wife's was indeed charming. He didn't blame Olsen for taking it rather hard.

The thought passed. She was weeping. With no effort at restraint. Charming, yes. But insufficiently civilized. Impulsive. Imprudent. Selfish.

"Try, Helga, to control yourself," he had urged gently. He detested tears. "If it distresses you so, we won't talk of it again. You, of course, must do as you yourself wish. Both your aunt and I want only that you should be happy." He had wanted to make an end of this fruitless wet conversation.

Helga had made another little dab at her face with the scrap of lace and raised shining eyes to his face. She had said, with sincere regret: "You've been marvelous to me, you and Aunt Katrina. Angelic. I don't want to seem ungrateful. I'd do anything for you, anything in the world but this."

Herr Dahl had shrugged. A little sardonically he had smiled. He had refrained from pointing out that this was the only thing she could do for them, the only thing that they had asked of her. He had been too glad to be through with the uncomfortable discussion.

So life went on. Dinners, coffees, theaters, pictures, music, clothes. More dinners, coffees, theaters, clothes, music. And that nagging aching for America increased. Augmented by the uncomfortableness of Aunt Katrina's and Uncle Poul's disappointment with her, that tormenting nostalgia grew to an unbearable weight. As spring came on with many gracious tokens of following summer, she found her thoughts straying with increasing frequency to Anne's letter and to Harlem, its dirty streets, swollen now, in the warmer weather, with dark, gay humanity.

Until recently she had had no faintest wish ever to see America again. Now she began to welcome the thought of a return. Only a visit, of course. Just to see, to prove to herself that there was nothing there for her. To demonstrate the absurdity of even thinking that there could be. And to relieve the slight tension here. Maybe when she came back—

Her definite decision to go was arrived at with almost bewildering suddenness. It was after a concert at which Dvořák's "New World Symphony" had been wonderfully rendered. Those wailing undertones of "Swing Low, Sweet Chariot" were too poignantly familiar. They struck into her longing heart and cut away her weakening defenses. She knew at least what it was that had lurked formless and undesignated these many weeks in the back of her troubled mind. Incompleteness.

"I'm homesick, not for America, but for Negroes. That's the trouble."

For the first time Helga Crane felt sympathy rather than contempt and hatred for that father, who so often and so angrily she had blamed for his desertion of her mother. She understood, now, his rejection, his repudiation, of the formal calm her mother had represented. She understood his yearning, his intolerable need for the inexhaustible humor and the incessant hope of his own kind, his need for those things, not material, indigenous to all Negro environments. She understood and could sympathize with his facile surrender to the irresistible ties of race, now that they dragged at her own heart. And as she attended parties, the theater, the opera, and mingled with people on the streets, meeting only pale serious faces when she longed for brown laughing ones, she was able to forgive him. Also, it was as if in this understanding and forgiving she had come upon knowledge of almost sacred importance.

Without demur, opposition, or recrimination Herr and Fru Dahl accepted Helga's decision to go back to America. She had expected that they would be glad and relieved. It was agreeable to discover that she had done them less than justice. They were, in spite of their extreme worldliness, very fond of her, and would, as they declared, miss her greatly. And they did want her to come back to them, as they repeatedly insisted. Secretly they felt as she did, that perhaps when she returned— So it was agreed upon that it was only for a brief visit, "for your friend's wedding," and that she was to return in the early fall.

The last day came. The last good-byes were said. Helga began to regret that she was leaving. Why couldn't she have two lives, or why couldn't she be satisfied in one place? Now that she was actually off, she felt heavy at heart. Already she looked back with infinite regret at the two years in the country which had given her so much, of pride, of happiness, of wealth, and of beauty.

Bells rang. The gangplank was hoisted. The dark strip of water widened. The running figures of friends suddenly grown very dear grew smaller, blurred into a whole, and vanished. Tears rose in Helga Crane's eyes, fear in her heart.

Good-bye Denmark! Good-bye. Good-bye!

Seventeen

A SUMMER had ripened and fall begun. Anne and Dr. Anderson had returned from their short Canadian wedding journey. Helga Crane, lingering still in America, had tactfully removed herself from the house in One Hundred and Thirty-ninth Street to a hotel. It was, as she could point out to curious acquaintances, much better for the newly-married Andersons not to be bothered with a guest, not even with such a close friend as she, Helga, had been to Anne.

Actually, though she herself had truly wanted to get out of the house when they came back, she had been a little surprised and a great deal hurt that Anne had consented so readily to her going. She might at least, thought Helga indignantly, have acted a little bit as if she had wanted her to stay. After writing for her to come, too.

Pleasantly unaware was Helga that Anne, more silently wise than herself, more determined, more selfish, and less inclined to leave anything to chance, understood perfectly that in a large measure it was the voice of Robert Anderson's inexorable conscience that had been the chief factor in bringing about her second marriage—his ascetic protest against the sensuous, the physical. Anne had perceived that the decorous surface of her new husband's mind regarded Helga Crane with that intellectual and æsthetic appreciation which attractive and intelligent women would always draw from him, but that underneath that well-managed section, in a more lawless place where she herself never hoped or desired to enter, was another, a vagrant primitive groping toward something shocking and frightening to the cold asceticism of his reason. Anne knew also that though she herself was lovely—more beautiful than Helga—and interesting, with her he had not to struggle against that nameless and to him shameful impulse, that sheer delight, which ran through his nerves at mere proximity to Helga. And Anne intended that her marriage should be a success. She intended that her husband should be happy. She was sure that it could be managed by tact and a little cleverness on her own part. She was truly fond of Helga, but seeing how she had grown more

charming, more aware of her power, Anne wasn't so sure that
her sincere and urgent request to come over for her wedding
hadn't been a mistake. She was, however, certain of herself.
She could look out for her husband. She could carry out
what she considered her obligation to him, keep him undisturbed, unhumiliated. It was impossible that she could fail.
Unthinkable.

Helga, on her part, had been glad to get back to New York.
How glad, or why, she did not truly realize. And though she
sincerely meant to keep her promise to Aunt Katrina and Uncle
Poul and return to Copenhagen, summer, September, October,
slid by and she made no move to go. Her uttermost intention
had been a six or eight weeks' visit, but the feverish rush of
New York, the comic tragedy of Harlem, still held her. As time
went on, she became a little bored, a little restless, but she
stayed on. Something of that wild surge of gladness that had
swept her on the day when with Anne and Anderson she had
again found herself surrounded by hundreds, thousands, of
dark-eyed brown folk remained with her. *These* were her people.
Nothing, she had come to understand now, could ever change
that. Strange that she had never truly valued this kinship until
distance had shown her its worth. How absurd she had been
to think that another country, other people, could liberate her
from the ties which bound her forever to these mysterious,
these terrible, these fascinating, these lovable, dark hordes.
Ties that were of the spirit. Ties not only superficially entangled
with mere outline of features or color of skin. Deeper. Much
deeper than either of these.

Thankful for the appeasement of that loneliness which had
again tormented her like a fury, she gave herself up to the miraculous joyousness of Harlem. The easement which its heedless abandon brought to her was a real, a very definite thing.
She liked the sharp contrast to her pretentious stately life in
Copenhagen. It was as if she had passed from the heavy solemnity of a church service to a gorgeous care-free revel.

Not that she intended to remain. No. Helga Crane couldn't,
she told herself and others, live in America. In spite of its glamour, existence in America, even Harlem, was for Negroes too
cramped, too uncertain, too cruel; something not to be endured for a lifetime if one could escape; something demanding

a courage greater than was in her. No. She couldn't stay. Nor, she saw now, could she remain away. Leaving, she would have to come back.

This knowledge, this certainty of the division of her life into two parts in two lands, into physical freedom in Europe and spiritual freedom in America, was unfortunate, inconvenient, expensive. It was, too, as she was uncomfortably aware, even a trifle ridiculous, and mentally she caricatured herself moving shuttle-like from continent to continent. From the prejudiced restrictions of the New World to the easy formality of the Old, from the pale calm of Copenhagen to the colorful lure of Harlem.

Nevertheless she felt a slightly pitying superiority over those Negroes who were apparently so satisfied. And she had a fine contempt for the blatantly patriotic black Americans. Always when she encountered one of those picturesque parades in the Harlem streets, the Stars and Stripes streaming ironically, insolently, at the head of the procession tempered for her, a little, her amusement at the childish seriousness of the spectacle. It was too pathetic.

But when mental doors were deliberately shut on those skeletons that stalked lively and in full health through the consciousness of every person of Negro ancestry in America—conspicuous black, obvious brown, or indistinguishable white—life was intensely amusing, interesting, absorbing, and enjoyable; singularly lacking in that tone of anxiety which the insecurities of existence seemed to ferment in other peoples.

Yet Helga herself had an acute feeling of insecurity, for which she could not account. Sometimes it amounted to fright almost. "I must," she would say then, "get back to Copenhagen." But the resolution gave her not much pleasure. And for this she now blamed Axel Olsen. It was, she insisted, he who had driven her back, made her unhappy in Denmark. Though she knew well that it wasn't. Misgivings, too, rose in her. Why hadn't she married him? Anne was married—she would not say Anderson— Why not she? It would serve Anne right if she married a white man. But she knew in her soul that she wouldn't. "Because I'm a fool," she said bitterly.

Eighteen

ONE November evening, impregnated still with the kindly warmth of the dead Indian summer, Helga Crane was leisurely dressing in pleasant anticipation of the party to which she had been asked for that night. It was always amusing at the Tavernors'. Their house was large and comfortable, the food and music always of the best, and the type of entertainment always unexpected and brilliant. The drinks, too, were sure to be safe.

And Helga, since her return, was more than ever popular at parties. Her courageous clothes attracted attention, and her deliberate lure—as Olsen had called it—held it. Her life in Copenhagen had taught her to expect and accept admiration as her due. This attitude, she found, was as effective in New York as across the sea. It was, in fact, even more so. And it was more amusing too. Perhaps because it was somehow a bit more dangerous.

In the midst of curious speculation as to the possible identity of the other guests, with an indefinite sense of annoyance she wondered if Anne would be there. There was of late something about Anne that was to Helga distinctly disagreeable, a peculiar half-patronizing attitude, mixed faintly with distrust. Helga couldn't define it, couldn't account for it. She had tried. In the end she had decided to dismiss it, to ignore it.

"I suppose," she said aloud, "it's because she's married again. As if anybody couldn't get married. Anybody. That is, if mere marriage is all one wants."

Smoothing away the tiny frown between the broad black brows, she got herself into a little shining, rose-colored slip of a frock knotted with a silver cord. The gratifying result soothed her ruffled feelings. It didn't really matter, this new manner of Anne's. Nor did the fact that Helga knew that Anne disapproved of her. Without words Anne had managed to make that evident. In her opinion, Helga had lived too long among the enemy, the detestable pale faces. She understood them too well, was too tolerant of their ignorant stupidities. If they had been Latins, Anne might conceivably have forgiven the disloyalty.

394

But Nordics! Lynchers! It was too traitorous. Helga smiled a little, understanding Anne's bitterness and hate, and a little of its cause. It was of a piece with that of those she so virulently hated. Fear. And then she sighed a little, for she regretted the waning of Anne's friendship. But, in view of diverging courses of their lives, she felt that even its complete extinction would leave her undevastated. Not that she wasn't still grateful to Anne for many things. It was only that she had other things now. And there would, forever, be Robert Anderson between them. A nuisance. Shutting them off from their previous confident companionship and understanding. "And anyway," she said again, aloud, "he's nobody much to have married. Anybody could have married him. Anybody. If a person wanted only to be married— If it had been somebody like Olsen— That would be different—something to crow over, perhaps."

The party was even more interesting than Helga had expected. Helen, Mrs. Tavenor, had given vent to a malicious glee, and had invited representatives of several opposing Harlem political and social factions, including the West Indian, and abandoned them helplessly to each other. Helga's observing eyes picked out several great and near-great sulking or obviously trying hard not to sulk in widely separated places in the big rooms. There were present, also, a few white people, to the open disapproval or discomfort of Anne and several others. There too, poised, serene, certain, surrounded by masculine black and white, was Audrey Denney.

"Do you know, Helen," Helga confided, "I've never met Miss Denney. I wish you'd introduce me. Not this minute. Later, when you can manage it. Not so—er—apparently by request, you know."

Helen Tavenor laughed. "No, you wouldn't have met her, living as you did with Anne Grey. Anderson, I mean. She's Anne's particular pet aversion. The mere sight of Audrey is enough to send her into a frenzy for a week. It's too bad, too, because Audrey's an awfully interesting person and Anne's said some pretty awful things about her. *You'll* like her, Helga."

Helga nodded. "Yes, I expect to. And I know about Anne. One night—" She stopped, for across the room she saw, with a stab of surprise, James Vayle. "Where, Helen did you get him?"

"Oh, that? That's something the cat brought in. Don't ask which one. He came with somebody, I don't remember who. I think he's shocked to death. Isn't he lovely? The dear baby. I was going to introduce him to Audrey and tell her to do a good job of vamping on him as soon as I could remember the darling's name, or when it got noisy enough so he wouldn't hear what I called him. But you'll do just as well. Don't tell me you know him!" Helga made a little nod. "Well! And I suppose you met him at some shockingly wicked place in Europe. That's always the way with those innocent-looking men."

"Not quite. I met him ages ago in Naxos. We were engaged to be married. Nice, isn't he? His name's Vayle. James Vayle."

"Nice," said Helen throwing out her hands in a characteristic dramatic gesture—she had beautiful hands and arms—"is exactly the word. Mind if I run off? I've got somebody here who's going to sing. *Not* spirituals. And I haven't the faintest notion where he's got to. The cellar, I'll bet."

James Vayle hadn't, Helga decided, changed at all. Someone claimed her for a dance and it was some time before she caught his eyes, half questioning, upon her. When she did, she smiled in a friendly way over her partner's shoulder and was rewarded by a dignified little bow. Inwardly she grinned, flattered. He hadn't forgotten. He was still hurt. The dance over, she deserted her partner and deliberately made her way across the room to James Vayle. He was for the moment embarrassed and uncertain. Helga Crane, however, took care of that, thinking meanwhile that Helen was right. Here he did seem frightfully young and delightfully unsophisticated. He must be, though, every bit of thirty-two or more.

"They say," was her bantering greeting, "that if one stands on the corner of One Hundred and Thirty-fifth Street and Seventh Avenue long enough, one will eventually see all the people one has ever known or met. It's pretty true, I guess. Not literally of course." He was, she saw, getting himself together. "It's only another way of saying that everybody, almost, some time sooner or later comes to Harlem, even you."

He laughed. "Yes, I guess that is true enough. I didn't come to stay, though." And then he was grave, his earnest eyes searchingly upon her.

"Well, anyway, you're here now, so let's find a quiet corner if that's possible, where we can talk. I want to hear all about you."

For a moment he hung back and a glint of mischief shone in Helga's eyes. "I see," she said, "you're just the same. However, you needn't be anxious. This isn't Naxos, you know. Nobody's watching us, or if they are, they don't care a bit what we do."

At that he flushed a little, protested a little, and followed her. And when at last they had found seats in another room, not so crowded, he said: "I didn't expect to see you here. I thought you were still abroad."

"Oh, I've been back some time, ever since Dr. Anderson's marriage. Anne, you know, is a great friend of mine. I used to live with her. I came for the wedding. But, of course, I'm not staying. I didn't think I'd be here this long."

"You don't mean that you're going to live over there? Do you really like it so much better?"

"Yes and no, to both questions. I was awfully glad to get back, but I wouldn't live here always. I couldn't. I don't think that any of us who've lived abroad for any length of time would ever live here altogether again if they could help it."

"Lot of them do, though," James Vayle pointed out.

"Oh, I don't mean tourists who rush over to Europe and rush all over the continent and rush back to America thinking they know Europe. I mean people who've actually lived there, actually lived among the people."

"I still maintain that they nearly all come back here eventually to live."

"That's because they can't help it," Helga Crane said firmly. "Money, you know."

"Perhaps, I'm not so sure. I was in the war. Of course, that's not really living over there, but I saw the country and the difference in treatment. But, I can tell you, I was pretty darn glad to get back. All the fellows were." He shook his head solemnly. "I don't think anything, money or lack of money, keeps us here. If it was only that, if we really wanted to leave, we'd go all right. No, it's something else, something deeper than that."

"And just what do you think it is?"

"I'm afraid it's hard to explain, but I suppose it's just that we like to be together. I simply can't imagine living forever away from colored people."

A suspicion of a frown drew Helga's brows. She threw out rather tartly: "I'm a Negro too, you know."

"Well, Helga, you were always a little different, a little dissatisfied, though I don't pretend to understand you at all. I never did," he said a little wistfully.

And Helga, who was beginning to feel that the conversation had taken an impersonal and disappointing tone, was reassured and gave him her most sympathetic smile and said almost gently: "And now let's talk about you. You're still at Naxos?"

"Yes I'm still there. I'm assistant principal now."

Plainly it was a cause for enthusiastic congratulation, but Helga could only manage a tepid "How nice!" Naxos was to her too remote, too unimportant. She did not even hate it now.

How long, she asked, would James be in New York?

He couldn't say. Business, important business for the school, had brought him. It was, he said, another tone creeping into his voice, another look stealing over his face, awfully good to see her. She was looking tremendously well. He hoped he would have the opportunity of seeing her again.

But of course. He must come to see her. Any time, she was always in, or would be for him. And how did he like New York, Harlem?

He didn't, it seemed, like it. It was nice to visit, but not to live in. Oh, there were so many things he didn't like about it, the rush, the lack of home life, the crowds, the noisy meaninglessness of it all.

On Helga's face there had come that pityingly sneering look peculiar to imported New Yorkers when the city of their adoption is attacked by alien Americans. With polite contempt she inquired: "And is that all you don't like?"

At her tone the man's bronze face went purple. He answered coldly, slowly, with a faint gesture in the direction of Helen Tavenor, who stood conversing gayly with one of her white guests: "And I don't like that sort of thing. In fact I detest it."

"Why?" Helga was striving hard to be casual in her manner.

James Vayle, it was evident, was beginning to be angry. It was also evident that Helga Crane's question had embarrassed him. But he seized the bull by the horns and said: "You know as well as I do, Helga, that it's the colored girls these men come up here to see. They wouldn't think of bringing their wives." And he blushed furiously at his own implication. The blush restored Helga's good temper. James was really too funny.

"That," she said softly, "is Hugh Wentworth, the novelist, you know." And she indicated a tall olive-skinned girl being whirled about to the streaming music in the arms of a towering black man. "And that is his wife. She isn't colored, as you've probably been thinking. And now let's change the subject again."

"All right! And this time let's talk about you. You say you don't intend to live here. Don't you ever intend to marry, Helga?"

"Some day, perhaps. I don't know. Marriage—that means children, to me. And why add more suffering to the world? Why add any more unwanted, tortured Negroes to America? Why *do* Negroes have children? Surely it must be sinful. Think of the awfulness of being responsible for the giving of life to creatures doomed to endure such wounds to the flesh, such wounds to the spirit, as Negroes have to endure."

James was aghast. He forgot to be embarrassed. "But Helga! Good heavens! Don't you see that if we—I mean people like us—don't have children, the others will still have. That's one of the things that's the matter with us. The race is sterile at the top. Few, very few Negroes of the better class have children, and each generation has to wrestle again with the obstacles of the preceding ones, lack of money, education, and background. I feel very strongly about this. We're the ones who must have the children if the race is to get anywhere."

"Well, I for one don't intend to contribute any to the cause. But how serious we are! And I'm afraid that I've really got to leave you. I've already cut two dances for your sake. Do come to see me."

"Oh, I'll come to see you all right. I've got several things that I want to talk to you about and one thing especially."

"Don't," Helga mocked, "tell me you're going to ask me again to marry you."

"That," he said, "is just what I intend to do."

Helga Crane was suddenly deeply ashamed and very sorry for James Vayle, so she told him laughingly that it was shameful of him to joke with her like that, and before he could answer, she had gone tripping off with a handsome coffee-colored youth whom she had beckoned from across the room with a little smile.

Later she had to go upstairs to pin up a place in the hem of her dress which had caught on a sharp chair corner. She finished the temporary repair and stepped out into the hall, and somehow, she never quite knew exactly just how, into the arms of Robert Anderson. She drew back and looked up smiling to offer an apology.

And then it happened. He stooped and kissed her, a long kiss, holding her close. She fought against him with all her might. Then, strangely, all power seemed to ebb away, and a long-hidden, half-understood desire welled up in her with the suddenness of a dream. Helga Crane's own arms went up about the man's neck. When she drew away, consciously confused and embarrassed, everything seemed to have changed in a space of time which she knew to have been only seconds. Sudden anger seized her. She pushed him indignantly aside and with a little pat for her hair and dress went slowly down to the others.

Nineteen

THAT night riotous and colorful dreams invaded Helga Crane's prim hotel bed. She woke in the morning weary and a bit shocked at the uncontrolled fancies which had visited her. Catching up a filmy scarf, she paced back and forth across the narrow room and tried to think. She recalled her flirtations and her mild engagement with James Vayle. She was used to kisses. But none had been like that of last night. She lived over those brief seconds, thinking not so much of the man whose arms had held her as of the ecstasy which had flooded her. Even recollection brought a little onrush of emotion that made her sway a little. She pulled herself together and began to fasten on the solid fact of Anne and experienced a pleasant sense of shock in the realization that Anne was to her exactly what she had been before the incomprehensible experience of last night. She still liked her in the same degree and in the same manner. She still felt slightly annoyed with her. She still did not envy her marriage with Anderson. By some mysterious process the emotional upheaval which had racked her had left all the rocks of her existence unmoved. Outwardly nothing had changed.

Days, weeks, passed; outwardly serene; inwardly tumultuous. Helga met Dr. Anderson at the social affairs to which often they were both asked. Sometimes she danced with him, always in perfect silence. She couldn't, she absolutely couldn't, speak a word to him when they were thus alone together, for at such times lassitude encompassed her; the emotion which had gripped her retreated, leaving a strange tranquillity, troubled only by a soft stir of desire. And shamed by his silence, his apparent forgetting, always after these dances she tried desperately to persuade herself to believe what she wanted to believe: that it had not happened, that she had never had that irrepressible longing. It was of no use.

As the weeks multiplied, she became aware that she must get herself out of the mental quagmire into which that kiss had thrown her. And she should be getting herself back to Copenhagen, but she had now no desire to go.

Abruptly one Sunday in a crowded room, in the midst of teacups and chatter, she knew that she couldn't go, that she hadn't since that kiss intended to go without exploring to the end that unfamiliar path into which she had strayed. Well, it was of no use lagging behind or pulling back. It was of no use trying to persuade herself that she didn't want to go on. A species of fatalism fastened on her. She felt that, ever since that last day in Naxos long ago, somehow she had known that this thing would happen. With this conviction came an odd sense of elation. While making a pleasant assent to some remark of a fellow guest she put down her cup and walked without haste, smiling and nodding to friends and acquaintances on her way to that part of the room where he stood looking at some examples of African carving. Helga Crane faced him squarely. As he took the hand which she held out with elaborate casualness, she noted that his trembled slightly. She was secretly congratulating herself on her own calm when it failed her. Physical weariness descended on her. Her knees wobbled. Gratefully she slid into the chair which he hastily placed for her. Timidity came over her. She was silent. He talked. She did not listen. He came at last to the end of his long dissertation on African sculpture, and Helga Crane felt the intentness of his gaze upon her.

"Well?" she questioned.

"I want very much to see you, Helga. Alone."

She held herself tensely on the edge of her chair, and suggested: "Tomorrow?"

He hesitated a second and then said quickly: "Why, yes, that's all right."

"Eight o'clock?"

"Eight o'clock," he agreed.

Eight o'clock tomorrow came. Helga Crane never forgot it. She had carried away from yesterday's meeting a feeling of increasing elation. It had seemed to her that she hadn't been so happy, so exalted, in years, if ever. All night, all day, she had mentally prepared herself for the coming consummation; physically too, spending hours before the mirror.

Eight o'clock had come at last and with it Dr. Anderson. Only then had uneasiness come upon her and a feeling of fear for possible exposure. For Helga Crane wasn't, after all, a rebel from society, Negro society. It did mean something to her. She had no wish to stand alone. But these late fears were overwhelmed by the hardiness of insistent desire; and she had got herself down to the hotel's small reception room.

It was, he had said, awfully good of her to see him. She instantly protested. No, she had wanted to see him. He looked at her surprised. "You know, Helga," he had begun with an air of desperation, "I can't forgive myself for acting such a swine at the Travenors' party. I don't at all blame you for being angry and not speaking to me except when you had to."

But that, she exclaimed, was simply too ridiculous. "I wasn't angry a bit." And it had seemed to her that things were not exactly going forward as they should. It seemed that he had been very sincere, and very formal. Deliberately. She had looked down at her hands and inspected her bracelets, for she had felt that to look at him would be, under the circumstances, too exposing.

"I was afraid," he went on, "that you might have misunderstood; might have been unhappy about it. I could kick myself. It was, it must have been, Tavenor's rotten cocktails."

Helga Crane's sense of elation had abruptly left her. At the same time she had felt the need to answer carefully. No, she replied, she hadn't thought of it at all. It had meant nothing to her. She had been kissed before. It was really too silly of him to have been at all bothered about it. "For what," she had asked, "is one kiss more or less, these days, between friends?" She had even laughed a little.

Dr. Anderson was relieved. He had been, he told her, no end upset. Rising, he said: "I see you're going out. I won't keep you."

Helga Crane too had risen. Quickly. A sort of madness had swept over her. She felt that he had belittled and ridiculed her. And thinking this, she had suddenly savagely slapped Robert Anderson with all her might, in the face.

For a short moment they had both stood stunned, in the deep silence which had followed that resounding slap. Then, without a word of contrition or apology, Helga Crane had gone out of the room and upstairs.

She had, she told herself, been perfectly justified in slapping

Dr. Anderson, but she was not convinced. So she had tried hard to make herself very drunk in order that sleep might come to her, but had managed only to make herself very sick.

Not even the memory of how all living had left his face, which had gone a taupe gray hue, or the despairing way in which he had lifted his head and let it drop, or the trembling hands which he had pressed into his pockets, brought her any scrap of comfort. She had ruined everything. Ruined it because she had been so silly as to close her eyes to all indications that pointed to the fact that no matter what the intensity of his feelings or desires might be, he was not the sort of man who would for any reason give up one particle of his own good opinion of himself. Not even for her. Not even though he knew that she had wanted so terribly something special from him.

Something special. And now she had forfeited it forever. Forever. Helga had an instantaneous shocking perception of what forever meant. And then, like a flash, it was gone, leaving an endless stretch of dreary years before her appalled vision.

Twenty

THE day was a rainy one. Helga Crane, stretched out on her bed, felt herself so broken physically, mentally, that she had given up thinking. But back and forth in her staggered brain wavering, incoherent thoughts shot shuttle-like. Her pride would have shut out these humiliating thoughts and painful visions of herself. The effort was too great. She felt alone, isolated from all other human beings, separated even from her own anterior existence by the disaster of yesterday. Over and over, she repeated: "There's nothing left but to go now." Her anguish seemed unbearable.

For days, for weeks, voluptuous visions had haunted her. Desire had burned in her flesh with uncontrollable violence. The wish to give herself had been so intense that Dr. Anderson's surprising, trivial apology loomed as a direct refusal of the offering. Whatever outcome she had expected, it had been something else than this, this mortification, this feeling of ridicule and self-loathing, this knowledge that she had deluded herself. It was all, she told herself, as unpleasant as possible.

Almost she wished she could die. Not quite. It wasn't that she was afraid of death, which had, she thought, its picturesque aspects. It was rather that she knew she would not die. And death, after the debacle, would but intensify its absurdity. Also, it would reduce her, Helga Crane, to unimportance, to nothingness. Even in her unhappy present state, that did not appeal to her. Gradually, reluctantly, she began to know that the blow to her self-esteem, the certainty of having proved herself a silly fool, was perhaps the severest hurt which she had suffered. It was her self-assurance that had gone down in the crash. After all, what Dr. Anderson thought didn't matter. She could escape from the discomfort of his knowing gray eyes. But she couldn't escape from sure knowledge that she had made a fool of herself. This angered her further and she struck the wall with her hands and jumped up and began hastily to dress herself. She couldn't go on with the analysis. It was too hard. Why bother when she could add nothing to the obvious fact that she had been a fool?

"I can't stay in this room any longer. I must get out or I'll choke." Her self-knowledge had increased her anguish. Distracted, agitated, incapable of containing herself, she tore open drawers and closets trying desperately to take some interest in the selection of her apparel.

It was evening and still raining. In the streets, unusually deserted, the electric lights cast dull glows. Helga Crane, walking rapidly, aimlessly, could decide on no definite destination. She had not thought to take umbrella or even rubbers. Rain and wind whipped cruelly about her, drenching her garments and chilling her body. Soon the foolish little satin shoes which she wore were sopping wet. Unheeding these physical discomforts, she went on, but at the open corner of One Hundred and Thirty-eighth Street a sudden more ruthless gust of wind ripped the small hat from her head. In the next minute the black clouds opened wider and spilled their water with unusual fury. The streets became swirling rivers. Helga Crane, forgetting her mental torment, looked about anxiously for a sheltering taxi. A few taxis sped by, but inhabited, so she began desperately to struggle through wind and rain toward one of the buildings, where she could take shelter in a store or a doorway. But another whirl of wind lashed her and, scornful of her slight strength, tossed her into the swollen gutter.

Now she knew beyond all doubt that she had no desire to die, and certainly not there nor then. Not in such a messy wet manner. Death had lost all of its picturesque aspects to the girl lying soaked and soiled in the flooded gutter. So, though she was very tired and very weak, she dragged herself up and succeeded finally in making her way to the store whose blurred light she had marked for her destination.

She had opened the door and had entered before she was aware that, inside, people were singing a song which she was conscious of having heard years ago—hundreds of years it seemed. Repeated over and over, she made out the words:

> . . . *Showers of blessings,*
> *Showers of blessings* . . .

She was conscious too of a hundred pairs of eyes upon her as she stood there, drenched and disheveled, at the door of this improvised meeting-house.

. . . Showers of blessings . . .

The appropriateness of the song, with its constant reference to showers, the ridiculousness of herself in such surroundings, was too much for Helga Crane's frayed nerves. She sat down on the floor, a dripping heap, and laughed and laughed and laughed.

It was into a shocked silence that she laughed. For at the first hysterical peal the words of the song had died in the singers' throats, and the wheezy organ had lapsed into stillness. But in a moment there were hushed solicitous voices; she was assisted to her feet and led haltingly to a chair near the low platform at the far end of the room. On one side of her a tall angular black woman under a queer hat sat down, on the other a fattish yellow man with huge outstanding ears and long, nervous hands.

The singing began again, this time a low wailing thing:

> *Oh, the bitter shame and sorrow*
> *That a time could ever be,*
> *When I let the Savior's pity*
> *Plead in vain, and proudly answered:*
> *"All of self and none of Thee,*
> *All of self and none of Thee."*

> *Yet He found me, I beheld Him,*
> *Bleeding on the cursed tree;*
> *Heard Him pray: "Forgive them, Father."*
> *And my wistful heart said faintly,*
> *"Some of self and some of Thee,*
> *Some of self and some of Thee."*

There were, it appeared, endless moaning verses. Behind Helga a woman had begun to cry audibly, and soon, somewhere else, another. Outside, the wind still bellowed. The wailing singing went on:

> *. . . Less of self and more of Thee,*
> *Less of self and more of Thee.*

Helga too began to weep, at first silently, softly; then with great racking sobs. Her nerves were so torn, so aching, her body so wet, so cold! It was a relief to cry unrestrainedly, and she gave herself freely to soothing tears, not noticing that the groaning and sobbing of those about her had increased, unaware that the grotesque ebony figure at her side had begun gently to pat her arm to the rhythm of the singing and to croon softly: "Yes, chile, yes, chile." Nor did she notice the furtive glances that the man on her other side cast at her between his fervent shouts of "Amen!" and "Praise God for a sinner!"

She did notice, though, that the tempo, the atmosphere of the place, had changed, and gradually she ceased to weep and gave her attention to what was happening about her. Now they were singing:

> . . . *Jesus knows all about my troubles* . . .

Men and women were swaying and clapping their hands, shouting and stamping their feet to the frankly irreverent melody of the song. Without warning the woman at her side threw off her hat, leaped to her feet, waved her long arms, and shouted shrilly: "Glory! Hallelujah!" and then, in wild ecstatic fury jumped up and down before Helga clutching at the girl's soaked coat, and screamed: "Come to Jesus, you pore los' sinner!" Alarmed for the fraction of a second, involuntarily Helga had shrunk from her grasp, wriggling out of the wet coat when she could not loosen the crazed creature's hold. At the sight of the bare arms and neck growing out of the clinging red dress, a shudder shook the swaying man at her right. On the face of the dancing woman before her a disapproving frown gathered. She shrieked: "A scarlet 'oman. Come to Jesus, you pore los' Jezebel!"

At this the short brown man on the platform raised a placating hand and sanctimoniously delivered himself of the words: "Remembah de words of our Mastah: 'Let him that is without sin cast de first stone.' Let us pray for our errin' sistah."

Helga Crane was amused, angry, disdainful, as she sat there, listening to the preacher praying for her soul. But though she was contemptuous, she was being too well entertained to leave. And it was, at least, warm and dry. So she stayed, listening to the fervent exhortation to God to save her and to the zealous shoutings and groanings of the congregation. Particularly she was interested in the writhings and weepings of the feminine portion, which seemed to predominate. Little by little the performance took on an almost Bacchic vehemence. Behind her, before her, beside her, frenzied women gesticulated, screamed, wept, and tottered to the praying of the preacher, which had gradually become a cadenced chant. When at last he ended, another took up the plea in the same moaning chant, and then another. It went on and on without pause with the persistence of some unconquerable faith exalted beyond time and reality.

Fascinated, Helga Crane watched until there crept upon her an indistinct horror of an unknown world. She felt herself in the presence of a nameless people, observing rites of a remote obscure origin. The faces of the men and women took on the aspect of a dim vision. "This," she whispered to herself, "is terrible. I must get out of here." But the horror held her. She remained motionless, watching as if she lacked the strength to leave the place—foul, vile, and terrible, with its mixture of breaths, its contact of bodies, its concerted convulsions, all in wild appeal for a single soul. Her soul.

And as Helga watched and listened, gradually a curious influence penetrated her, she felt an echo of the weird orgy resound in her own heart; she felt herself possessed by the same madness; she too felt a brutal desire to shout and to sling herself about. Frightened at the strength of the obsession, she gathered herself for one last effort to escape, but vainly. In rising, weakness and nausea from last night's unsuccessful attempt to make herself drunk overcame her. She had eaten nothing since yesterday. She fell forward against the crude railing which enclosed the little platform. For a single moment she remained there in silent stillness, because she was afraid she was going to be sick. And in that moment she was lost—or saved. The yelling figures about her pressed forward, closing her in on all sides. Maddened, she grasped at the railing, and with no previous intention began to yell like one insane, drowning every other clamor, while torrents of tears streamed down her face. She was unconscious of the words she uttered, or their meaning: "Oh God, mercy, mercy. Have mercy on me!" but she repeated them over and over.

From those about her came a thunderclap of joy. Arms were stretched toward her with savage frenzy. The women dragged themselves upon their knees or crawled over the floor like reptiles, sobbing and pulling their hair and tearing off their clothing. Those who succeeded in getting near to her leaned forward to encourage the unfortunate sister, dropping hot tears and beads of sweat upon her bare arms and neck.

The thing became real. A miraculous calm came upon her. Life seemed to expand, and to become very easy. Helga Crane felt within her a supreme aspiration toward the regaining of simple happiness, a happiness unburdened by the complexities of the lives she had known. About her the tumult and the shouting continued, but in a lesser degree. Some of the more exuberant worshipers had fainted into inert masses, the voices of others were almost spent. Gradually the room grew quiet and almost solemn, and to the kneeling girl time seemed to sink back into the mysterious grandeur and holiness of far-off simpler centuries.

Twenty-One

O N leaving the mission Helga Crane had started straight back to her room at the hotel. With her had gone the fattish yellow man who had sat beside her. He had introduced himself as the Reverend Mr. Pleasant Green in proffering his escort for which Helga had been grateful because she had still felt a little dizzy and much exhausted. So great had been this physical weariness that as she had walked beside him, without attention to his verbose information about his own "field," as he called it, she had been seized with a hateful feeling of vertigo and obliged to lay firm hold on his arm to keep herself from falling. The weakness had passed as suddenly as it had come. Silently they had walked on. And gradually Helga had recalled that the man beside her had himself swayed slightly at their close encounter, and that frantically for a fleeting moment he had gripped at a protruding fence railing. That man! Was it possible? As easy as that?

Instantly across her still half-hypnotized consciousness little burning darts of fancy had shot themselves. No. She couldn't. It would be too awful. Just the same, what or who was there to hold her back? Nothing. Simply nothing. Nobody. Nobody at all.

Her searching mind had become in a moment quite clear. She cast at the man a speculative glance, aware that for a tiny space she had looked into his mind, a mind striving to be calm. A mind that was certain that it was secure because it was concerned only with things of the soul, spiritual things, which to him meant religious things. But actually a mind by habit at home amongst the mere material aspect of things, and at that moment consumed by some longing for the ecstasy that might lurk behind the gleam of her cheek, the flying wave of her hair, the pressure of her slim fingers on his heavy arm. An instant's flashing vision it had been and it was gone at once. Escaped in the aching of her own senses and the sudden disturbing fear that she herself had perhaps missed the supreme secret of life.

After all, there was nothing to hold her back. Nobody to

care. She stopped sharply, shocked at what she was on the verge of considering. Appalled at where it might lead her.

The man—what was his name?—thinking that she was almost about to fall again, had reached out his arms to her. Helga Crane had deliberately stopped thinking. She had only smiled, a faint provocative smile, and pressed her fingers deep into his arms until a wild look had come into his slightly bloodshot eyes.

The next morning she lay for a long while, scarcely breathing, while she reviewed the happenings of the night before. Curious. She couldn't be sure that it wasn't religion that had made her feel so utterly different from dreadful yesterday. And gradually she became a little sad, because she realized that with every hour she would get a little farther away from this soothing haziness, this rest from her long trouble of body and of spirit; back into the clear bareness of her own small life and being, from which happiness and serenity always faded just as they had shaped themselves. And slowly bitterness crept into her soul. Because, she thought, all I've ever had in life has been things—except just this one time. At that she closed her eyes, for even remembrance caused her to shiver a little.

Things, she realized, hadn't been, weren't, enough for her. She'd have to have something else besides. It all came back to that old question of happiness. Surely this was it. Just for a fleeting moment Helga Crane, her eyes watching the wind scattering the gray-white clouds and so clearing a speck of blue sky, questioned her ability to retain, to bear, this happiness at such cost as she must pay for it. There was, she knew, no getting round that. The man's agitation and sincere conviction of sin had been too evident, too illuminating. The question returned in a slightly new form. Was it worth the risk? Could she take it? Was she able? Though what did it matter—now?

And all the while she knew in one small corner of her mind that such thinking was useless. She had made her decision. Her resolution. It was a chance at stability, at permanent happiness, that she meant to take. She had let so many other things, other chances, escape her. And anyway there was God, He would perhaps make it come out all right. Still confused and not so sure that it wasn't the fact that she was "saved" that had contributed to this after feeling of well-being, she clutched the hope, the desire to believe that now at last she had found some One, some Power, who was interested in her. Would help her.

She meant, however, for once in her life to be practical. So she would make sure of both things, God and man.

Her glance caught the calendar over the little white desk. The tenth of November. The steamer *Oscar II* sailed today. Yesterday she had half thought of sailing with it. Yesterday. How far away!

With the thought of yesterday came the thought of Robert Anderson and a feeling of elation, revenge. She had put herself beyond the need of help from him. She had made it impossible for herself ever again to appeal to him. Instinctively she had the knowledge that he would be shocked. Grieved. Horribly hurt even. Well, let him!

The need to hurry suddenly obsessed her. She must. The morning was almost gone. And she meant, if she could manage it, to be married today. Rising, she was seized with a fear so acute that she had to lie down again. For the thought came to her that she might fail. Might not be able to confront the situation. That would be too dreadful. But she became calm again. How could he, a naïve creature like that, hold out against her? If she pretended to distress? To fear? To remorse? He couldn't. It would be useless for him even to try. She screwed up her face into a little grin, remembering that even if protestations were to fail, there were other ways.

And, too, there was God.

Twenty-Two

Aɴᴅ so in the confusion of seductive repentance Helga Crane was married to the grandiloquent Reverend Mr. Pleasant Green, that rattish yellow man, who had so kindly, so unctuously, proffered his escort to her hotel on the memorable night of her conversion. With him she willingly, even eagerly, left the sins and temptations of New York behind her to, as he put it, "labor in the vineyard of the Lord" in the tiny Alabama town where he was pastor to a scattered and primitive flock. And where, as the wife of the preacher, she was a person of relative importance. Only relative.

Helga did not hate him, the town, or the people. No. Not for a long time.

As always, at first the novelty of the thing, the change, fascinated her. There was a recurrence of the feeling that now, at last, she had found a place for herself, that she was really living. And she had her religion, which in her new status as a preacher's wife had of necessity become real to her. She believed in it. Because in its coming it had brought this other thing, this anæsthetic satisfaction for her senses. Hers was, she declared to herself, a truly spiritual union. This one time in her life, she was convinced, she had not clutched a shadow and missed the actuality. She felt compensated for all previous humiliations and disappointments and was glad. If she remembered that she had had something like this feeling before, she put the unwelcome memory from her with the thought: "This time I know I'm right. This time it will last."

Eagerly she accepted everything, even that bleak air of poverty which, in some curious way, regards itself as virtuous, for no other reason than that it is poor. And in her first hectic enthusiasm she intended and planned to do much good to her husband's parishioners. Her young joy and zest for the uplifting of her fellow men came back to her. She meant to subdue the cleanly scrubbed ugliness of her own surroundings to soft inoffensive beauty, and to help the other women to do likewise. Too, she would help them with their clothes, tactfully point out that sunbonnets, no matter how gay, and aprons, no matter how frilly, were not quite the proper things for Sunday church wear. There would be a sewing circle. She visualized herself instructing the children, who seemed most of the time to run wild, in ways of gentler deportment. She was anxious to be a true helpmate, for in her heart was a feeling of obligation, of humble gratitude.

In her ardor and sincerity Helga even made some small beginnings. True, she was not very successful in this matter of innovations. When she went about to try to interest the women in what she considered more appropriate clothing and in inexpensive ways of improving their homes according to her ideas of beauty, she was met, always, with smiling agreement and good-natured promises. "Yuh all is right, Mis' Green," and "Ah suttinly will, Mis' Green," fell courteously on her ear at each visit.

She was unaware that afterwards they would shake their heads sullenly over their wash-tubs and ironing-boards. And that among themselves they talked with amusement, or with anger, of "dat uppity, meddlin' No'the'nah," and "pore Reve'end," who in their opinion "would 'a done bettah to a ma'ied Clementine Richards." Knowing, as she did, nothing of this, Helga was unperturbed. But even had she known, she would not have been disheartened. The fact that it was difficult but increased her eagerness, and made the doing of it seem only the more worth while. Sometimes she would smile to think how changed she was.

And she was humble too. Even with Clementine Richards, a strapping black beauty of magnificent Amazon proportions and bold shining eyes of jet-like hardness. A person of awesome appearance. All chains, strings of beads, jingling bracelets, flying ribbons, feathery neck-pieces, and flowery hats. Clementine was inclined to treat Helga with an only partially concealed contemptuousness, considering her a poor thing without style, and without proper understanding of the worth and greatness of the man, Clementine's own adored pastor, whom Helga had somehow had the astounding good luck to marry. Clementine's admiration of the Reverend Mr. Pleasant Green was open. Helga was at first astonished. Until she learned that there was really no reason why it should be concealed. Everybody was aware of it. Besides, open adoration was the prerogative, the almost religious duty, of the female portion of the flock. If this unhidden and exaggerated approval contributed to his already oversized pomposity, so much the better. It was what they expected, liked, wanted. The greater his own sense of superiority became, the more flattered they were by his notice and small attentions, the more they cast at him killing glances, the more they hung enraptured on his words.

In the days before her conversion, with its subsequent blurring of her sense of humor, Helga might have amused herself by tracing the relation of this constant ogling and flattering on the proverbially large families of preachers; the often disastrous effect on their wives of this constant stirring of the senses by extraneous women. Now, however, she did not even think of it.

She was too busy. Every minute of the day was full. Necessarily. And to Helga this was a new experience. She was charmed by it. To be mistress in one's own house, to have a garden, and chickens, and a pig; to have a husband—and to be "right with God"—what pleasure did that other world which she had left contain that could surpass these? Here, she had found, she was sure, the intangible thing for which, indefinitely, always she had craved. It had received embodiment.

Everything contributed to her gladness in living. And so for a time she loved everything and everyone. Or thought she did. Even the weather. And it was truly lovely. By day a glittering gold sun was set in an unbelievably bright sky. In the evening silver buds sprouted in a Chinese blue sky, and the warm day was softly soothed by a slight, cool breeze. And night! Night, when a languid moon peeped through the wide-opened windows of her little house, a little mockingly, it may be. Always at night's approach Helga was bewildered by a disturbing medley of feelings. Challenge. Anticipation. And a small fear.

In the morning she was serene again. Peace had returned. And she could go happily, inexpertly, about the humble tasks of her household, cooking, dish-washing, sweeping, dusting, mending, and darning. And there was the garden. When she worked there, she felt that life was utterly filled with the glory and the marvel of God.

Helga did not reason about this feeling, as she did not at that time reason about anything. It was enough that it was there, coloring all her thoughts and acts. It endowed the four rooms of her ugly brown house with a kindly radiance, obliterating the stark bareness of its white plaster walls and the nakedness of its uncovered painted floors. It even softened the choppy lines of the shiny oak furniture and subdued the awesome horribleness of the religious pictures.

And all the other houses and cabins shared in this illumination. And the people. The dark undecorated women unceasingly concerned with the actual business of life, its rounds of births and christenings, of loves and marriages, of deaths and funerals, were to Helga miraculously beautiful. The smallest, dirtiest, brown child, barefooted in the fields or muddy roads, was to her an emblem of the wonder of life, of love, and of God's goodness.

For the preacher, her husband, she had a feeling of gratitude, amounting almost to sin. Beyond that, she thought of him not at all. But she was not conscious that she had shut him out from her mind. Besides, what need to think of him? He was there. She was at peace, and secure. Surely their two lives were one, and the companionship in the Lord's grace so perfect that to think about it would be tempting providence. She had done with soul-searching.

What did it matter that he consumed his food, even the softest varieties, audibly? What did it matter that, though he did no work with his hands, not even in the garden, his finger-nails were always rimmed with black? What did it matter that he failed to wash his fat body, or to shift his clothing, as often as Helga herself did? There were things that more than outweighed these. In the certainty of his goodness, his righteousness, his holiness, Helga somehow overcame her first disgust at the odor of sweat and stale garments. She was even able to be unaware of it. Herself, Helga had come to look upon as a finicky, showy thing of unnecessary prejudices and fripperies. And when she sat in the dreary structure, which had once been a stable belonging to the estate of a wealthy horse-racing man and about which the odor of manure still clung, now the church and social center of the Negroes of the town, and heard him expound with verbal extravagance the gospel of blood and love, of hell and heaven, of fire and gold streets, pounding with clenched fists the frail table before him or shaking those fists in the faces of the congregation like direct personal threats, or pacing wildly back and forth and even sometimes shedding great tears as he besought them to repent, she was, she told herself, proud and gratified that he belonged to her. In some strange way she was able to ignore the atmosphere of self-satisfaction which poured from him like gas from a leaking pipe.

And night came at the end of every day. Emotional, palpitating, amorous, all that was living in her sprang like rank weeds at the tingling thought of night, with a vitality so strong that it devoured all shoots of reason.

Twenty-Three

A FTER the first exciting months Helga was too driven, too
occupied, and too sick to carry out any of the things for
which she had made such enthusiastic plans, or even to care
that she had made only slight progress toward their accomplishment. For she, who had never thought of her body save as
something on which to hang lovely fabrics, had now constantly
to think of it. It had persistently to be pampered to secure
from it even a little service. Always she felt extraordinarily and
annoyingly ill, having forever to be sinking into chairs. Or, if
she was out, to be pausing by the roadside, clinging desperately to some convenient fence or tree, waiting for the horrible
nausea and hateful faintness to pass. The light, care-free days
of the past, when she had not felt heavy and reluctant or weak
and spent, receded more and more and with increasing vagueness, like a dream passing from a faulty memory.

The children used her up. There were already three of them,
all born within the short space of twenty months. Two great
healthy twin boys, whose lovely bodies were to Helga like rare
figures carved out of amber, and in whose sleepy and mysterious black eyes all that was puzzling, evasive, and aloof in life
seemed to find expression. No matter how often or how long
she looked at these two small sons of hers, never did she lose a
certain delicious feeling in which were mingled pride, tenderness, and exaltation. And there was a girl, sweet, delicate, and
flower-like. Not so healthy or so loved as the boys, but still miraculously her own proud and cherished possession.

So there was no time for the pursuit of beauty, or for the
uplifting of other harassed and teeming women, or for the instruction of their neglected children.

Her husband was still, as he had always been, deferentially
kind and incredulously proud of her—and verbally encouraging. Helga tried not to see that he had rather lost any personal
interest in her, except for the short spaces between the times
when she was preparing for or recovering from childbirth. She
shut her eyes to the fact that his encouragement had become a
little platitudinous, limited mostly to "The Lord will look out

419

for you," "We must accept what God sends," or "My mother
had nine children and was thankful for every one." If she was
inclined to wonder a little just how they were to manage with
another child on the way, he would point out to her that her
doubt and uncertainty were a stupendous ingratitude. Had
not the good God saved her soul from hell-fire and eternal
damnation? Had He not in His great kindness given her three
small lives to raise up for His glory? Had He not showered her
with numerous other mercies (evidently too numerous to be
named separately)?

"You must," the Reverend Mr. Pleasant Green would say
unctuously, "trust the Lord more fully, Helga."

This pabulum did not irritate her. Perhaps it was the fact
that the preacher was, now, not so much at home that even
lent to it a measure of real comfort. For the adoring women of
his flock, noting how with increasing frequency their pastor's
house went unswept and undusted, his children unwashed,
and his wife untidy, took pleasant pity on him and invited him
often to tasty orderly meals, specially prepared for him, in their
own clean houses.

Helga, looking about in helpless dismay and sick disgust at
the disorder around her, the permanent assembly of partly
emptied medicine bottles on the clock-shelf, the perpetual array of drying baby-clothes on the chair-backs, the constant debris of broken toys on the floor, the unceasing litter of half-dead
flowers on the table, dragged in by the toddling twins from the
forlorn garden, failed to blame him for the thoughtless selfishness of these absences. And, she was thankful, whenever possible, to be relieved from the ordeal of cooking. There were
times when, having had to retreat from the kitchen in lumbering haste with her sensitive nose gripped between tightly
squeezing fingers, she had been sure that the greatest kindness
that God could ever show to her would be to free her forever
from the sight and smell of food.

How, she wondered, did other women, other mothers,
manage? Could it be possible that, while presenting such smiling and contented faces, they were all always on the edge of
health? All always worn out and apprehensive? Or was it only
she, a poor weak city-bred thing, who felt that the strain of
what the Reverend Mr. Pleasant Green had so often gently and

patiently reminded her was a natural thing, an act of God, was almost unendurable?

One day on her round of visiting—a church duty, to be done no matter how miserable one was—she summoned up sufficient boldness to ask several women how they felt, how they managed. The answers were a resigned shrug, or an amused snort, or an upward rolling of eyeballs with a mention of "de Lawd" looking after us all.

"'Tain't nothin', nothin' at all, chile," said one, Sary Jones, who, as Helga knew, had had six children in about as many years. "Yuh all takes it too ha'd. Jes' remembah et's natu'al fo' a 'oman to hab chilluns an' don' fret so."

"But," protested Helga, "I'm always so tired and half sick. That can't be natural."

"Laws, chile, we's all ti'ed. An' Ah reckons we's all gwine a be ti'ed till kingdom come. Jes' make de bes' of et, honey. Jes' make de bes' yuh can."

Helga sighed, turning her nose away from the steaming coffee which her hostess had placed for her and against which her squeamish stomach was about to revolt. At the moment the compensations of immortality seemed very shadowy and very far away.

"Jes' remembah," Sary went on, staring sternly into Helga's thin face, "we all gits ouah res' by an' by. In de nex' worl' we's all recompense'. Jes' put yo' trus' in de Sabioah."

Looking at the confident face of the little bronze figure on the opposite side of the immaculately spread table, Helga had a sensation of shame that she should be less than content. Why couldn't she be as trusting and as certain that her troubles would not overwhelm her as Sary Jones was? Sary, who in all likelihood had toiled every day of her life since early childhood except on those days, totalling perhaps sixty, following the birth of her six children. And who by dint of superhuman saving had somehow succeeded in feeding and clothing them and sending them all to school. Before her Helga felt humbled and oppressed by the sense of her own unworthiness and lack of sufficient faith.

"Thanks, Sary," she said, rising in retreat from the coffee, "you've done me a world of good. I'm really going to try to be more patient."

So, though with growing yearning she longed for the great ordinary things of life, hunger, sleep, freedom from pain, she resigned herself to the doing without them. The possibility of alleviating her burdens by a greater faith became lodged in her mind. She gave herself up to it. It *did* help. And the beauty of leaning on the wisdom of God, of trusting, gave to her a queer sort of satisfaction. Faith was really quite easy. One had only to yield. To ask no questions. The more weary, the more weak she became, the easier it was. Her religion was to her a kind of protective coloring, shielding her from the cruel light of an unbearable reality.

This utter yielding in faith to what had been sent her found her favor, too, in the eyes of her neighbors. Her husband's flock began to approve and commend this submission and humility to a superior wisdom. The womenfolk spoke more kindly and more affectionately of the preacher's Northern wife. "Pore Mis' Green, wid all dem small chilluns at once. She suah do hab it ha'd. An' she don' nebah complains an' frets no mo'e. Jes' trus' in de Lawd lak de Good Book say. Mighty sweet lil' 'oman too."

Helga didn't bother much about the preparations for the coming child. Actually and metaphorically she bowed her head before God, trusting in Him to see her through. Secretly she was glad that she had not to worry about herself or anything. It was a relief to be able to put the entire responsibility on someone else.

Twenty-Four

IT began, this next child-bearing, during the morning services of a breathless hot Sunday while the fervent choir soloist was singing: "Ah am freed of mah sorrow," and lasted far into the small hours of Tuesday morning. It seemed, for some reason, not to go off just right. And when, after that long frightfulness, the fourth little dab of amber humanity which Helga had contributed to a despised race was held before her for maternal approval, she failed entirely to respond properly to this sob of consolation for the suffering and horror through which she had passed. There was from her no pleased, proud smile, no loving, possessive gesture, no manifestation of interest in the important matters of sex and weight. Instead she deliberately closed her eyes, mutely shutting out the sickly infant, its smiling father, the soiled midwife, the curious neighbors, and the tousled room.

A week she lay so. Silent and listless. Ignoring food, the clamoring children, the comings and goings of solicitous, kind-hearted women, her hovering husband, and all of life about her. The neighbors were puzzled. The Reverend Mr. Pleasant Green was worried. The midwife was frightened.

On the floor, in and out among the furniture and under her bed, the twins played. Eager to help, the church-women crowded in and, meeting there others on the same laudable errand, stayed to gossip and to wonder. Anxiously the preacher sat, Bible in hand, beside his wife's bed, or in a nervous half-guilty manner invited the congregated parishioners to join him in prayer for the healing of their sister. Then, kneeling, they would beseech God to stretch out His all-powerful hand on behalf of the afflicted one, softly at first, but with rising vehemence, accompanied by moans and tears, until it seemed that the God to whom they prayed must in mercy to the sufferer grant relief. If only so that she might rise up and escape from the tumult, the heat, and the smell.

Helga, however, was unconcerned, undisturbed by the commotion about her. It was all part of the general unreality. Nothing reached her. Nothing penetrated the kind darkness

into which her bruised spirit had retreated. Even that red-letter
event, the coming to see her of the old white physician from
downtown, who had for a long time stayed talking gravely to
her husband, drew from her no interest. Nor for days was she
aware that a stranger, a nurse from Mobile, had been added to
her household, a brusquely efficient woman who produced order out of chaos and quiet out of bedlam. Neither did the absence of the children, removed by good neighbors at Miss
Hartley's insistence, impress her. While she had gone down
into that appalling blackness of pain, the ballast of her brain
had got loose and she hovered for a long time somewhere in
that delightful borderland on the edge of unconsciousness,
an enchanted and blissful place where peace and incredible
quiet encompassed her.

After weeks she grew better, returned to earth, set her reluctant feet to the hard path of life again.

"Well, here you are!" announced Miss Hartley in her slightly
harsh voice one afternoon just before the fall of evening. She
had for some time been standing at the bedside gazing down
at Helga with an intent speculative look.

"Yes," Helga agreed in a thin little voice, "I'm back." The
truth was that she had been back for some hours. Purposely
she had lain silent and still, wanting to linger forever in that serene haven, that effortless calm where nothing was expected of
her. There she could watch the figures of the past drift by.
There was her mother, whom she had loved from a distance
and finally so scornfully blamed, who appeared as she had
always remembered her, unbelievably beautiful, young, and remote. Robert Anderson, questioning, purposely detached, affecting, as she realized now, her life in a remarkably cruel
degree; for at last she understood clearly how deeply, how passionately, she must have loved him. Anne, lovely, secure, wise,
selfish. Axel Olsen, conceited, worldly, spoiled. Audrey Denney,
placid, taking quietly and without fuss the things which she
wanted. James Vayle, snobbish, smug, servile. Mrs. Hayes-Rore,
important, kind, determined. The Dahls, rich, correct, climbing. Flashingly, fragmentarily, other long-forgotten figures,
women in gay fashionable frocks and men in formal black and
white glided by in bright rooms to distant, vaguely familiar
music.

It was refreshingly delicious, this immersion in the past. But it was finished now. It was over. The words of her husband, the Reverend Mr. Pleasant Green, who had been standing at the window looking mournfully out at the scorched melon-patch, ruined because Helga had been ill so long and unable to tend it, were confirmation of that.

"The Lord be praised," he said, and came forward. It was distinctly disagreeable. It was even more disagreeable to feel his moist hand on hers. A cold shiver brushed over her. She closed her eyes. Obstinately and with all her small strength she drew her hand away from him. Hid it far down under the bed-covering, and turned her face away to hide a grimace of unconquerable aversion. She cared nothing, at that moment, for his hurt surprise. She knew only that, in the hideous agony that for interminable hours—no, centuries—she had borne, the luster of religion had vanished; that revulsion had come upon her; that she hated this man. Between them the vastness of the universe had come.

Miss Hartley, all-seeing and instantly aware of a situation, as she had been quite aware that her patient had been conscious for some time before she herself had announced the fact, intervened, saying firmly: "I think it might be better if you didn't try to talk to her now. She's terribly sick and weak yet. She's still got some fever and we mustn't excite her or she's liable to slip back. And we don't want that, do we?"

No, the man, her husband, responded, they didn't want that. Reluctantly he went from the room with a last look at Helga, who was lying on her back with one frail, pale hand under her small head, her curly black hair scattered loose on the pillow. She regarded him from behind dropped lids. The day was hot, her breasts were covered only by a nightgown of filmy *crêpe*, a relic of prematrimonial days, which had slipped from one carved shoulder. He flinched. Helga's petulant lip curled, for she well knew that this fresh reminder of her desirability was like the flick of a whip.

Miss Hartley carefully closed the door after the retreating husband. "It's time," she said, "for your evening treatment, and then you've got to try to sleep for a while. No more visitors tonight."

Helga nodded and tried unsuccessfully to make a little smile.

She was glad of Miss Hartley's presence. It would, she felt, protect her from so much. She mustn't, she thought to herself, get well too fast. Since it seemed she was going to get well. In bed she could think, could have a certain amount of quiet. Of aloneness.

In that period of racking pain and calamitous fright Helga had learned what passion and credulity could do to one. In her was born angry bitterness and an enormous disgust. The cruel, unrelieved suffering had beaten down her protective wall of artificial faith in the infinite wisdom, in the mercy, of God. For had she not called in her agony on Him? And He had not heard. Why? Because, she knew now, He wasn't there. Didn't exist. Into that yawning gap of unspeakable brutality had gone, too, her belief in the miracle and wonder of life. Only scorn, resentment, and hate remained—and ridicule. Life wasn't a miracle, a wonder. It was, for Negroes at least, only a great disappointment. Something to be got through with as best one could. No one was interested in them or helped them. God! Bah! And they were only a nuisance to other people.

Everything in her mind was hot and cold, beating and swirling about. Within her emaciated body raged disillusion. Chaotic turmoil. With the obscuring curtain of religion rent, she was able to look about her and see with shocked eyes this thing that she had done to herself. She couldn't, she thought ironically, even blame God for it, now that she knew that He didn't exist. No. No more than she could pray to Him for the death of her husband, the Reverend Mr. Pleasant Green. The white man's God. And His great love for all people regardless of race! What idiotic nonsense she had allowed herself to believe. How could she, how could anyone, have been so deluded? How could ten million black folk credit it when daily before their eyes was enacted its contradiction? Not that she at all cared about the ten million. But herself. Her sons. Her daughter. These would grow to manhood, to womanhood, in this vicious, this hypocritical land. The dark eyes filled with tears.

"I wouldn't," the nurse advised, "do that. You've been dreadfully sick, you know. I can't have you worrying. Time enough for that when you're well. Now you must sleep all you possibly can."

Helga did sleep. She found it surprisingly easy to sleep. Aided by Miss Hartley's rather masterful discernment, she took advantage of the ease with which this blessed enchantment stole over her. From her husband's praisings, prayers, and caresses she sought refuge in sleep, and from the neighbors' gifts, advice, and sympathy.

There was that day on which they told her that the last sickly infant, born of such futile torture and lingering torment, had died after a short week of slight living. Just closed his eyes and died. No vitality. On hearing it Helga too had just closed her eyes. Not to die. She was convinced that before her there were years of living. Perhaps of happiness even. For a new idea had come to her. She had closed her eyes to shut in any telltale gleam of the relief which she felt. One less. And she had gone off into sleep.

And there was that Sunday morning on which the Reverend Mr. Pleasant Green had informed her that they were that day to hold a special thanksgiving service for her recovery. There would, he said, be prayers, special testimonies, and songs. Was there anything particular she would like to have said, to have prayed for, to have sung? Helga had smiled from sheer amusement as she replied that there was nothing. Nothing at all. She only hoped that they would enjoy themselves. And, closing her eyes that he might be discouraged from longer tarrying, she had gone off into sleep.

Waking later to the sound of joyous religious abandon floating in through the opened windows, she had asked a little diffidently that she be allowed to read. Miss Hartley's sketchy brows contracted into a dubious frown. After a judicious pause she had answered: "No, I don't think so." Then, seeing the rebellious tears which had sprung into her patient's eyes, she added kindly: "But I'll read to you a little if you like."

That, Helga replied, would be nice. In the next room on a high-up shelf was a book. She'd forgotten the name, but its author was Anatole France. There was a story, "The Procurator of Judea." Would Miss Hartley read that? "Thanks. Thanks awfully."

"'Lælius Lamia, born in Italy of illustrious parents,'" began the nurse in her slightly harsh voice.

Helga drank it in.

"'. . . For to this day the women bring down doves to the altar as their victims. . . .'"

Helga closed her eyes.

"'. . . Africa and Asia have already enriched us with a considerable number of gods. . . .'"

Miss Hartley looked up. Helga had slipped into slumber while the superbly ironic ending which she had so desired to hear was yet a long way off. A dull tale, was Miss Hartley's opinion, as she curiously turned the pages to see how it turned out.

"'Jesus? . . . Jesus—of Nazareth? I cannot call him to mind.'"

"Huh!" she muttered, puzzled. "Silly." And closed the book.

Twenty-Five

DURING the long process of getting well, between the dreamy intervals when she was beset by the insistent craving for sleep, Helga had had too much time to think. At first she had felt only an astonished anger at the quagmire in which she had engulfed herself. She had ruined her life. Made it impossible ever again to do the things that she wanted, have the things that she loved, mingle with the people she liked. She had, to put it as brutally as anyone could, been a fool. The damnedest kind of a fool. And she had paid for it. Enough. More than enough.

Her mind, swaying back to the protection that religion had afforded her, almost she wished that it had not failed her. An illusion. Yes. But better, far better, than this terrible reality. Religion had, after all, its uses. It blunted the perceptions. Robbed life of its crudest truths. Especially it had its uses for the poor—and the blacks.

For the blacks. The Negroes.

And this, Helga decided, was what ailed the whole Negro race in America, this fatuous belief in the white man's God, this childlike trust in full compensation for all woes and privations in "kingdom come." Sary Jones's absolute conviction, "In de nex' worl' we's all recompense'," came back to her. And ten million souls were as sure of it as was Sary. How the white man's God must laugh at the great joke he had played on them! Bound them to slavery, then to poverty and insult, and made them bear it unresistingly, uncomplainingly, almost, by sweet promises of mansions in the sky by and by.

"Pie in the sky," Helga said aloud derisively, forgetting for the moment Miss Hartley's brisk presence, and so was a little startled at hearing her voice from the adjoining room saying severely: "My goodness! No! I should say you can't have pie. It's too indigestible. Maybe when you're better—"

"That," assented Helga, "is what I said. Pie—by and by. That's the trouble."

The nurse looked concerned. Was this an approaching relapse? Coming to the bedside, she felt at her patient's pulse

429

while giving her a searching look. No. "You'd better," she admonished, a slight edge to her tone, "try to get a little nap. You haven't had any sleep today, and you can't get too much of it. You've got to get strong, you know."

With this Helga was in full agreement. It seemed hundreds of years since she had been strong. And she would need strength. For in some way she was determined to get herself out of this bog into which she had strayed. Or—she would have to die. She couldn't endure it. Her suffocation and shrinking loathing were too great. Not to be borne. Again. For she had to admit that it wasn't new, this feeling of dissatisfaction, of asphyxiation. Something like it she had experienced before. In Naxos. In New York. In Copenhagen. This differed only in degree. And it was of the present and therefore seemingly more reasonable. The other revulsions were of the past, and now less explainable.

The thought of her husband roused in her a deep and contemptuous hatred. At his every approach she had forcibly to subdue a furious inclination to scream out in protest. Shame, too, swept over her at every thought of her marriage. Marriage. This sacred thing of which parsons and other Christian folk ranted so sanctrimoniously, how immoral—according to their own standards—it could be! But Helga felt also a modicum of pity for him, as for one already abandoned. She meant to leave him. And it was, she had to concede, all of her own doing, this marriage. Nevertheless, she hated him.

The neighbors and churchfolk came in for their share of her all-embracing hatred. She hated their raucous laughter, their stupid acceptance of all things, and their unfailing trust in "de Lawd." And more than all the rest she hated the jangling Clementine Richards, with her provocative smirkings, because she had not succeeded in marrying the preacher and thus saving her, Helga, from that crowning idiocy.

Of the children Helga tried not to think. She wanted not to leave them—if that were possible. The recollection of her own childhood, lonely, unloved, rose too poignantly before her for her to consider calmly such a solution. Though she forced herself to believe that this was different. There was not the element of race, of white and black. They were all black together. And they would have their father. But to leave them would be a tearing agony, a rending of deepest fibers. She felt that through all the rest of her lifetime she would be hearing their cry of "Mummy, Mummy, Mummy," through sleepless nights. No. She couldn't desert them.

How, then, was she to escape from the oppression, the degradation, that her life had become? It was so difficult. It was terribly difficult. It was almost hopeless. So for a while—for the immediate present, she told herself—she put aside the making of any plan for her going. "I'm still," she reasoned, "too weak, too sick. By and by, when I'm really strong—"

It was so easy and so pleasant to think about freedom and cities, about clothes and books, about the sweet mingled smell of Houbigant and cigarettes in softly lighted rooms filled with inconsequential chatter and laughter and sophisticated tuneless music. It was so hard to think out a feasible way of retrieving all these agreeable, desired things. Just then. Later. When she got up. By and by. She must rest. Get strong. Sleep. Then, afterwards, she could work out some arrangement. So she dozed and dreamed in snatches of sleeping and waking, letting time run on. Away.

And hardly had she left her bed and become able to walk again without pain, hardly had the children returned from the homes of the neighbors, when she began to have her fifth child.

PLUM BUN
A NOVEL WITHOUT A MORAL

Jessie Redmon Fauset

"To Market, to Market
To buy a Plum Bun;
Home again, Home again,
Market is done."

CONTENTS

	PAGE
HOME	437
MARKET	487
PLUM BUN	546
HOME AGAIN	589
MARKET IS DONE	652

HOME

Chapter I

OPAL STREET, as streets go, is no jewel of the first water. It is merely an imitation, and none too good at that. Narrow, unsparkling, uninviting, it stretches meekly off from dull Jefferson Street to the dingy, drab market which forms the north side of Oxford Street. It has no mystery, no allure, either of exclusiveness or of downright depravity; its usages are plainly significant,—an unpretentious little street lined with unpretentious little houses, inhabited for the most part by unpretentious little people.

The dwellings are three stories high, and contain six boxes called by courtesy, rooms—a "parlour", a midget of a dining-room, a larger kitchen and, above, a front bedroom seemingly large only because it extends for the full width of the house, a mere shadow of a bathroom, and another back bedroom with windows whose possibilities are spoiled by their outlook on sad and diminutive back-yards. And above these two, still two others built in similar wise.

In one of these houses dwelt a father, a mother and two daughters. Here, as often happens in a home sheltering two generations, opposite, unevenly matched emotions faced each other. In the houses of the rich the satisfied ambition of the older generation is faced by the overwhelming ambition of the younger. Or the elders may find themselves brought in opposition to the blank indifference and ennui of youth engendered by the realization that there remain no more worlds to conquer; their fathers having already taken all. In houses on Opal Street these niceties of distinction are hardly to be found; there is a more direct and concrete contrast. The satisfied ambition of maturity is a foil for the restless despair of youth.

Affairs in the Murray household were advancing towards this stage; yet not a soul in that family of four could have foretold its coming. To Junius and Mattie Murray, who had known poverty and homelessness, the little house on Opal Street represented the *ne plus ultra* of ambition; to their daughter Angela it seemed the dingiest, drabbest chrysalis that had ever fettered the wings of a brilliant butterfly. The stories which Junius and Mattie told of difficulties overcome, of the arduous learning of trades, of the pitiful scraping together of infinitesimal savings; would have made a latter-day Iliad, but to Angela they were merely a description of a life which she at any cost would avoid living. Somewhere in the world were paths which lead to broad thoroughfares, large, bright houses, delicate niceties of existence. Those paths Angela meant to find and frequent. At a very early age she had observed that the good things of life are unevenly distributed; merit is not always rewarded; hard labour does not necessarily entail adequate recompense. Certain fortuitous endowments, great physical beauty, unusual strength, a certain unswerving singleness of mind,—gifts bestowed quite blindly and disproportionately by the forces which control life,—these were the qualities which contributed toward a glowing and pleasant existence.

Angela had no high purpose in life; unlike her sister Virginia, who meant some day to invent a marvellous method for teaching the pianoforte, Angela felt no impulse to discover, or to perfect. True she thought she might become eventually a distinguished painter, but that was because she felt within herself an ability to depict which as far as it went was correct and promising. Her eye for line and for expression was already good and she had a nice feeling for colour. Moreover she possessed the instinct for self-appraisal which taught her that she had much to learn. And she was sure that the knowledge once gained would flower in her case to perfection. But her gift was not for her the end of existence; rather it was an adjunct to a life which was to know light, pleasure, gaiety and freedom.

Freedom! That was the note which Angela heard oftenest in the melody of living which was to be hers. With a wildness that fell just short of unreasonableness she hated restraint. Her father's earlier days as coachman in a private family, his later successful, independent years as boss carpenter, her mother's youth spent as maid to a famous actress, all this was to Angela a manifestation of the sort of thing which happens to those enchained it might be by duty, by poverty, by weakness or by colour.

Colour or rather the lack of it seemed to the child the one

absolute prerequisite to the life of which she was always dreaming. One might break loose from a too hampering sense of duty; poverty could be overcome; physicians conquered weakness; but colour, the mere possession of a black or a white skin, that was clearly one of those fortuitous endowments of the gods. Gratitude was no strong ingredient in this girl's nature, yet very often early she began thanking Fate for the chance which in that household of four had bestowed on her the heritage of her mother's fair skin. She might so easily have been, like her father, black, or have received the melange which had resulted in Virginia's rosy bronzeness and her deeply waving black hair. But Angela had received not only her mother's creamy complexion and her soft cloudy, chestnut hair, but she had taken from Junius the aquiline nose, the gift of some remote Indian ancestor which gave to his face and his eldest daughter's that touch of chiselled immobility.

It was from her mother that Angela learned the possibilities for joy and freedom which seemed to her inherent in mere whiteness. No one would have been more amazed than that same mother if she could have guessed how her daughter interpreted her actions. Certainly Mrs. Murray did not attribute what she considered her happy, busy, sheltered life on tiny Opal Street to the accident of her colour; she attributed it to her black husband whom she had been glad and proud to marry. It is equally certain that that white skin of hers had not saved her from occasional contumely and insult. The famous actress for whom she had worked was aware of Mattie's mixed blood and, boasting temperament rather than refinement, had often dubbed her "white nigger".

Angela's mother employed her colour very much as she practised certain winning usages of smile and voice to obtain indulgences which meant much to her and which took nothing from anyone else. Then, too, she was possessed of a keener sense of humour than her daughter; it amused her when by herself to take lunch at an exclusive restaurant whose patrons would have been panic-stricken if they had divined the presence of a "coloured" woman no matter how little her appearance differed from theirs. It was with no idea of disclaiming her own that she sat in orchestra seats which Philadelphia denied to coloured patrons. But when Junius or indeed any other dark friend accompanied her she was the first to announce that she liked to sit in the balcony or gallery, as indeed she did; her infrequent occupation of orchestra seats was due merely to a mischievous determination to flout a silly and unjust law.

Her years with the actress had left their mark, a perfectly harmless and rather charming one. At least so it seemed to Junius, whose weakness was for the qualities known as "essentially feminine". Mrs. Murray loved pretty clothes, she liked shops devoted to the service of women; she enjoyed being even on the fringe of a fashionable gathering. A satisfaction that was almost ecstatic seized her when she drank tea in the midst of modishly gowned women in a stylish tea-room. It pleased her to stand in the foyer of a great hotel or of the Academy of Music and to be part of the whirling, humming, palpitating gaiety. She had no desire to be of these people, but she liked to look on; it amused and thrilled and kept alive some unquenchable instinct for life which thrived within her. To walk through Wanamaker's on Saturday, to stroll from Fifteenth to Ninth Street on Chestnut, to have her tea in the Bellevue Stratford, to stand in the lobby of the St. James' fitting on immaculate gloves; all innocent, childish pleasures pursued without malice or envy contrived to cast a glamour over Monday's washing and Tuesday's ironing, the scrubbing of kitchen and bathroom and the fashioning of children's clothes. She was endowed with a humorous and pungent method of presentation; Junius, who had had the wit not to interfere with these little excursions and the sympathy to take them at their face value, preferred one of his wife's sparkling accounts of a Saturday's adventure in "passing" to all the tall stories told by cronies at his lodge.

Much of this pleasure, harmless and charming though it was, would have been impossible with a dark skin.

In these first years of marriage, Mattie, busied with the house and the two babies had given up those excursions. Later, when the children had grown and Junius had reached the stage where he could afford to give himself a half-holiday on Saturdays, the two parents inaugurated a plan of action which eventually became a fixed programme. Each took a child, and Junius went off to a beloved but long since suspended pastime of exploring old Philadelphia, whereas Mattie embarked once more on her

social adventures. It is true that Mattie accompanied by brown
Virginia could not move quite as freely as when with Angela.
But her maternal instincts were sound; her children, their feel-
ings and their faith in her meant much more than the pleasure
which she would have been first to call unnecessary and silly.
As it happened the children themselves quite unconsciously
solved the dilemma; Virginia found shopping tiring and stupid,
Angela returned from her father's adventuring worn and bored.
Gradually the rule was formed that Angela accompanied her
mother and Virginia her father.

On such fortuities does life depend. Little Angela Murray, hurrying through Saturday morning's scrubbing of steps in order
that she might have her bath at one and be with her mother on
Chestnut Street at two, never realized that her mother took
her pleasure among all these pale people because it was there
that she happened to find it. It never occurred to her that the
delight which her mother obviously showed in meeting friends
on Sunday morning when the whole united Murray family
came out of church was the same as she showed on Chestnut
Street the previous Saturday, because she was finding the qualities which her heart craved, bustle, excitement and fashion. The
daughter could not guess that if the economic status or the
racial genius of coloured people had permitted them to run
modish hotels or vast and popular department stores her mother
would have been there. She drew for herself certain clearly
formed conclusions which her subconscious mind thus codified:
    First, that the great rewards of life—riches, glamour, pleasure,
—are for white-skinned people only. Secondly, that Junius and
Virginia were denied these privileges because they were dark;
here her reasoning bore at least an element of verisimilitude but
she missed the essential fact that her father and sister did not
care for this type of pleasure. The effect of her fallaciousness was
to cause her to feel a faint pity for her unfortunate relatives and
also to feel that coloured people were to be considered fortunate only in the proportion in which they measured up to the
physical standards of white people.
    One Saturday excursion left a far-reaching impression. Mrs.
Murray and Angela had spent a successful and interesting
afternoon. They had browsed among the contents of the small

exclusive shops in Walnut Street; they had had soda at Adams'
on Broad Street and they were standing finally in the portico of
the Walton Hotel deciding with fashionable and idle elegance
what they should do next. A thin stream of people constantly
passing threw an occasional glance at the quietly modish pair,
the well-dressed, assured woman and the refined and no less assured daughter. The door-man knew them; it was one of Mrs.
Murray's pleasures to proffer him a small tip, much appreciated
since it was uncalled for. This was the atmosphere which she
loved. Angela had put on her gloves and was waiting for her
mother, who was drawing on her own with great care, when she
glimpsed in the laughing, hurrying Saturday throng the figures
of her father and of Virginia. They were close enough for her
mother, who saw them too, to touch them by merely descending a few steps and stretching out her arm. In a second the pair
had vanished. Angela saw her mother's face change—with trepidation she thought. She remarked: "It's a good thing Papa
didn't see us, you'd have had to speak to him, wouldn't you?"
But her mother, giving her a distracted glance, made no reply.

That night, after the girls were in bed, Mattie, perched on
the arm of her husband's chair, told him about it. "I was at my
old game of playacting again to-day, June, passing you know,
and darling, you and Virginia went by within arm's reach and
we never spoke to you. I'm so ashamed."

But Junius consoled her. Long before their marriage he had
known of his Mattie's weakness and its essential harmlessness.
"My dear girl, I told you long ago that where no principle was
involved, your passing means nothing to me. It's just a little
joke; I don't think you'd be ashamed to acknowledge your old
husband anywhere if it were necessary."

"I'd do that if people were mistaking me for a queen," she
assured him fondly. But she was silent, not quite satisfied.
"After all," she said with her charming frankness, "it isn't you,
dear, who make me feel guilty. I really am ashamed to think
that I let Virginia pass by without a word. I think I should feel
very badly if she were to know it. I don't believe I'll ever let
myself be quite as silly as that again."

But of this determination Angela, dreaming excitedly of
Saturdays spent in turning her small olive face firmly away from
peering black countenances was, unhappily, unaware.

Chapter II

SATURDAY came to be the day of the week for Angela, but her sister Virginia preferred Sundays. She loved the atmosphere of golden sanctity which seemed to hover with a sweet glory about the stodgy, shabby little dwelling. Usually she came downstairs first so as to enjoy by herself the blessed "Sunday feeling" which, she used to declare, would have made it possible for her to recognize the day if she had awakened to it even in China. She was only twelve at this time, yet she had already developed a singular aptitude and liking for the care of the home, and this her mother gratefully fostered. Gradually the custom was formed of turning over to her small hands all the duties of Sunday morning; they were to her a ritual. First the kettle must be started boiling, then the pavement swept. Her father's paper must be carried up and left outside his door. Virginia found a nameless and sweet satisfaction in performing these services.

She prepared the Sunday breakfast which was always the same,—bacon and eggs, strong coffee with good cream for Junius, chocolate for the other three and muffins. After the kettle had boiled and the muffins were mixed it took exactly half an hour to complete preparations. Virginia always went about these matters in the same way. She set the muffins in the oven, pursing her lips and frowning a little just as she had seen her mother do; then she went to the foot of the narrow, enclosed staircase and called "hoo-hoo" with a soft rising inflection,—"last call to dinner," her father termed it. And finally, just for those last few minutes before the family descended she went into the box of a parlour and played hymns, old-fashioned and stately tunes,—"How firm a foundation", "The spacious firmament on high", "Am I a soldier of the Cross". Her father's inflexible bass, booming down the stairs, her mother's faint alto in thirds mingled with her own sweet treble; a shaft of sunlight, faint and watery in winter, strong and golden in summer, shimmering through the room in the morning dusk completed for the little girl a sensation of happiness which lay perilously near tears.

*

After breakfast came the bustle of preparing for church. Junius of course had come down in complete readiness; but the others must change their dresses; Virginia had mislaid her Sunday hair-ribbon again; Angela had discovered a rip in her best gloves and could not be induced to go down until it had been mended. "Wait for me just a minute, Jinny dear, I can't go out looking like this, can I?" She did not like going to church, at least not to their church, but she did care about her appearance and she liked the luxuriousness of being "dressed up" on two sucessive days. At last the little procession filed out, Mattie hoping that they would not be late, she did hate it so; Angela thinking that this was a stupid way to spend Sunday and wondering at just what period of one's life existence began to shape itself as *you* wanted it. Her father's thoughts were inchoate; expressed they would have revealed a patriarchal aspect almost biblical. He had been a poor boy, homeless, a nobody, yet he had contrived in his mid-forties to attain to the status of a respectable citizen, house-owner, a good provider. He possessed a charming wife and two fine daughters, and as was befitting he was accompanying them to the house of the Lord. As for Virginia, no one to see her in her little red hat and her mother's cut-over blue coat could have divined how near she was to bursting with happiness. Father, mother and children, well-dressed, well-fed, united, going to church on a beatiful Sunday morning; there was an immense cosmic rightness about all this which she sensed rather than realized. She envied no one the incident of finer clothes or a larger home; this unity was the core of happiness, all other satisfactions must radiate from this one; greater happiness could be only a matter of degree but never of essence. When she grew up she meant to live the same kind of life; she would marry a man exactly like her father and she would conduct her home exactly as did her mother. Only she would pray very hard every day for five children, two boys and two girls and then a last little one,—it was hard for her to decide whether this should be a boy or a girl,—which should stay small for a long, long time. And on Sundays they would all go to church.

Intent on her dreaming she rarely heard the sermon. It was different with the hymns, for they constituted the main part of the service for her father, and she meant to play them again for him later in the happy, golden afternoon or the grey dusk of early evening. But first there were acquaintances to greet, friends of her parents who called them by their first names and who, in speaking of Virginia and Angela still said: "And these are the babies; my, how they grow! It doesn't seem as though it could be you, Mattie Ford, grown up and with children!"

On Communion Sundays the service was very late, and Angela would grow restless and twist about in her seat, but the younger girl loved the sudden, mystic hush which seemed to descend on the congregation. Her mother's sweetly merry face took on a certain childish solemnity, her father's stern profile softened into beatific expectancy. In the exquisite diction of the sacramental service there were certain words, certain phrases that almost made the child faint; the minister had a faint burr in his voice and somehow this lent a peculiar underlying resonance to his intonation; he half spoke, half chanted and when, picking up the wafer he began "For in the night" and then broke it, Virginia could have cried out with the ecstasy which filled her. She felt that those who partook of the bread and wine were somehow transfigured; her mother and father wore an expression of ineffable content as they returned to their seats and there was one woman, a middle-aged, mischief making person, who returned from taking the sacrament, walking down the aisle, her hands clasped loosely in front of her and her face so absolutely uplifted that Virginia used to hasten to get within earshot of her after the church was dismissed, sure that her first words must savour of something mystic and holy. But her assumption proved always to be ill-founded.

The afternoon and the evening repeated the morning's charm but in a different key. Usually a few acquaintances dropped in; the parlour and dining-room were full for an hour or more of pleasant, harmless chatter. Mr. Henson, the policeman, a tall, yellow man with freckles on his nose and red "bad hair" would clap Mr. Murray on the back and exclaim "I tell you what, June,"—which always seemed to Virginia a remarkably daring way in which to address her tall, dignified father. Matthew Henson, a boy of sixteen, would inevitably be hovering about Angela who found him insufferably boresome and made no effort to hide her ennui. Mrs. Murray passed around rather hard cookies and delicious currant wine, talking stitches and patterns meanwhile with two or three friends of her youth with a frequent injection of "Mame, do you remember!"

Presently the house, emptied of all but the family, grew still again, dusk and the lamp light across the street alternately panelling the walls. Mrs. Murray murmured something about fixing a bite to eat, "I'll leave it in the kitchen if anybody wants it". Angela reflected aloud that she had still to get her Algebra or History or French as the case may be, but nobody moved. What they were really waiting for was for Virginia to start to play and finally she would cross the narrow absurdity of a room and stretching out her slim, brown hands would begin her version, a glorified one, of the hymns which they had sung in church that morning, and then the old favourites which she had played before breakfast. Even Angela, somewhat remote and difficult at first, fell into this evening mood and asked for a special tune or a repetition: "I like the way you play that, Jinny". For an hour or more they were as close and united as it is possible for a family to be.

At eight o'clock or thereabouts Junius said exactly as though it had not been in his thoughts all evening: "Play the 'Dying Christian', daughter". And Virginia, her treble sounding very childish and shrill against her father's deep, unyielding bass, began Pope's masterpiece on the death of a true believer. The magnificently solemn words: "Vital spark of heavenly flame", strangely appropriate minor music filled the little house with an awesome beauty which was almost palpable. It affected Angela so that in sheer self-defence she would go out in the kitchen and eat her share of the cold supper set by her mother. But Mattie, although she never sang this piece, remained while her husband and daughter sang on. Death triumphant and mighty had no fears for her. It was inevitable, she knew, but she would never have to face it alone. When her husband died, she would die too, she was sure of it; and if death came to her first it would be only a little while before Junius would be there stretching out his hand and guiding her through all the rough, strange places just as years ago, when he had been a coachman to the actress for whom she worked, he had stretched out his good, honest hand and had saved her from a dangerous and equivocal position. She wiped away happy and grateful tears.

"The world recedes, it disappears," sang Virginia. But it made no difference how far it drifted away as long as the four of them were together; and they would always be together, her father and mother and she and Angela. With her visual mind she saw them proceeding endlessly through space; there were her parents, arm in arm, and she and—but to-night and other nights she could not see Angela; it grieved her to lose sight thus of her sister, she knew she must be there, but grope as she might she could not find her. And then quite suddenly Angela was there again, but a different Angela, not quite the same as in the beginning of the picture.

And suddenly she realized that she was doing four things at once and each of them with all the intentness which she could muster; she was singing, she was playing, she was searching for Angela and she was grieving because Angela as she knew her was lost forever.

"Oh Death, oh Death, where is thy sting!" the hymn ended triumphantly,—she and the piano as usual came out a little ahead of Junius which was always funny. She said, "Where's Angela?" and knew what the answer would be. "I'm tired, mummy! I guess I'll go to bed."

"You ought to, you got up so early and you've been going all day."

Kissing her parents good-night she mounted the stairs languidly, her whole being pervaded with the fervid yet delicate rapture of the day.

Chapter III

MONDAY morning brought the return of the busy, happy week. It meant wash-day for Mattie, for she and Junius had never been able to raise their ménage to the status either of a maid or of putting out the wash. But this lack meant nothing to her,—she had been married fifteen years and still had the ability to enjoy the satisfaction of having a home in which she had full sway instead of being at the beck and call of others. She was old enough to remember a day when poverty for a coloured girl connoted one of three things: going out to service, working as ladies' maid, or taking a genteel but poorly paid position as seamstress with one of the families of the rich and great on Rittenhouse Square, out West Walnut Street or in one of the numerous impeccable, aristocratic suburbs of Philadelphia.

She had tried her hand at all three of these possibilities, had known what it meant to rise at five o'clock, start the laundry work for a patronizing indifferent family of people who spoke of her in her hearing as "the girl" or remarked of her in a slightly lower but still audible tone as being rather better than the usual run of niggers,—"She never steals, I'd trust her with anything and she isn't what you'd call lazy either." For this family she had prepared breakfast, gone back to her washing, served lunch, had taken down the clothes, sprinkled and folded them, had gone upstairs and made three beds, not including her own and then had returned to the kitchen to prepare dinner. At night she nodded over the dishes and finally stumbling up to the third floor fell into her unmade bed, sometimes not even fully undressed. And Tuesday morning she would begin on the long and tedious strain of ironing. For this she received four dollars a week with the privilege of every other Sunday and every Thursday off. But she could have no callers.

As a seamstress, life had been a little more endurable but more precarious. The wages were better while they lasted, she had a small but comfortable room; her meals were brought up to her on a tray and the young girls of the households in which she was employed treated her with a careless kindness which

448

while it still had its element of patronage was not offensive. But such families had a disconcerting habit of closing their households and departing for months at a time, and there was Mattie stranded and perilously trying to make ends meet by taking in sewing. But her clientèle was composed of girls as poor as she, who either did their own dressmaking or could afford to pay only the merest trifle for her really exquisite and meticulous work.

The situation with the actress had really been the best in many, in almost all, respects. But it presented its pitfalls. Mattie was young, pretty and innocent; the actress was young, beautiful and sophisticated. She had been married twice and had been the heroine of many affairs; maidenly modesty, virtue for its own sake, were qualities long since forgotten, high ideals and personal self-respect were too abstract for her slightly coarsened mind to visualize, and at any rate they were incomprehensible and even absurd in a servant, and in a coloured servant to boot. She knew that in spite of Mattie's white skin there was black blood in her veins; in fact she would not have taken the girl on had she not been coloured; all her servants must be coloured, for hers was a carelessly conducted household, and she felt dimly that all coloured people are thickly streaked with immorality. They were naturally loose, she reasoned, when she thought about it at all. "Look at the number of mixed bloods among them; look at Mattie herself for that matter, a perfectly white nigger if ever there was one. I'll bet her mother wasn't any better than she should be."

When the girl had come to her with tears in her eyes and begged her not to send her as messenger to the house of a certain Haynes Brokinaw, politician and well-known man about town, Madame had laughed out loud. "How ridiculous! He'll treat you all right. I should like to know what a girl like you expects. And anyway, if I don't care, why should you? Now run along with the note and don't bother me about this again. I hire you to do what I want, not to do as you want." She was not even jealous,—of a coloured working girl! And anyway, constancy was no virtue in her eyes; she did not possess it herself and she valued it little in others.

Mattie was in despair. She was receiving twenty-five dollars a month, her board, and a comfortable, pleasant room. She was seeing something of the world and learning of its amenities. It was during this period that she learned how very pleasant indeed life could be for a person possessing only a very little extra money and a white skin. But the special attraction which her present position held for her was that every day she had a certain amount of time to call her own, for she was Madame's personal servant; in no wise was she connected with the routine of keeping the house. If Madame elected to spend the whole day away from home, Mattie, once she had arranged for the evening toilette, was free to act and to go where she pleased.

And now here was this impasse looming up with Brokinaw. More than once Mattie had felt his covetous eyes on her; she had dreaded going to his rooms from the very beginning. She had even told his butler, "I'll be back in half an hour for the answer"; and she would wait in the great square hall as he had indicated for there she was sure that danger lurked. But the third time Brokinaw was standing in the hall. "Just come into my study," he told her, "while I read this and write the answer." And he had looked at her with his cold, green eyes and had asked her why she was so out of breath. "There's no need to rush so, child; stay here and rest. I'm in no hurry, I assure you. Are you really coloured? You know, I've seen lots of white girls not as pretty as you. Sit here and tell me all about your mother, —and your father. Do—do you remember him?" His whole bearing reeked with intention.

Within a week Madame was sending her again and she had suggested fearfully the new coachman. "No," said Madame. "It's Wednesday, his night off, and I wouldn't send him anyway; coachmen are too hard to keep nowadays; you're all getting so independent." Mattie had come down from her room and walked slowly, slowly to the corner where the new coachman, tall and black and grave, was just hailing a car. She ran to him and jerked down the arm which he had just lifted to seize the railing. "Oh, Mr. Murray," she stammered. He had been so astonished and so kind. Her halting explanation done, he took the note in silence and delivered it, and the next night and for many nights thereafter they walked through the silent, beautiful square, and Junius had told her haltingly and with fear that he loved her. She threw her arms about his neck: "And I love you too."

"You don't mind my being so dark then? Lots of coloured girls I know wouldn't look at a black man."

But it was partly on account of his colour that she loved him; in her eyes his colour meant safety. "Why should I mind?" she asked with one of her rare outbursts of bitterness, "my own colour has never brought me anything but insult and trouble."

The other servants, it appeared, had told him that sometimes she—he hesitated—"passed".

"Yes, yes, of course I do," she explained it eagerly, "but never to them. And anyway when I am alone what can I do? I can't label myself. And if I'm hungry or tired and I'm near a place where they don't want coloured people, why should I observe their silly old rules, rules that are unnatural and unjust,—because the world was made for everybody, wasn't it, Junius?"

She had told him then how hard and joyless her girlhood life had been,—she had known such dreadful poverty and she had been hard put to it to keep herself together. But since she had come to live with Madame Sylvio she had glimpsed, thanks to her mistress's careless kindness, something of the life of comparative ease and beauty and refinement which one could easily taste if he possessed just a modicum of extra money and the prerequisite of a white skin.

"I've only done it for fun but I won't do it any more if it displeases you. I'd much rather live in the smallest house in the world with you, Junius, than be wandering around as I have so often, lonely and unknown in hotels and restaurants." Her sweetness disarmed him. There was no reason in the world why she should give up her harmless pleasure unless, he added rather sternly, some genuine principle were involved.

It was the happiest moment of her life when Junius had gone to Madame and told her that both he and Mattie were leaving. "We are going to be married," he announced proudly. The actress had been sorry to lose her, and wanted to give her a hundred dollars, but the tall, black coachman would not let his wife accept it. "She is to have only what she earned," he said in stern refusal. He hated Madame Sylvio for having thrown the girl in the way of Haynes Brokinaw.

They had married and gone straight into the little house on Opal Street which later was to become their own. Mattie her husband considered a perfect woman, sweet, industrious, affectionate and illogical. But to her he was God.

When Angela and Virginia were little children and their mother used to read them fairy tales she would add to the ending, " And so they lived happily ever after, just like your father and me."

All this was passing happily through her mind on this Monday morning. Junius was working somewhere in the neighbourhood; his shop was down on Bainbridge Street, but he tried to devote Mondays and Tuesdays to work up town so that he could run in and help Mattie on these trying days. Before the advent of the washing machine he used to dart in and out two or three times in the course of a morning to lend a hand to the heavy sheets and the bed-spreads. Now those articles were taken care of in the laundry, but Junius still kept up the pleasant fiction.

Virginia attended school just around the corner, and presently she would come in too, not so much to get her own lunch as to prepare it for her mother. She possessed her father's attitude toward Mattie as someone who must be helped, indulged and protected. Moreover she had an unusually keen sense of gratitude toward her father and mother for their kindness and their unselfish ambitions for their children. Jinny never tired of hearing of the difficult childhood of her parents. She knew of no story quite so thrilling as the account of their early trials and difficulties. She thought it wonderfully sweet of them to plan, as they constantly did, better things for their daughters.

"My girls shall never come through my experiences," Mattie would say firmly. They were both to be school-teachers and independent.

It is true that neither of them felt any special leaning toward this calling. Angela frankly despised it, but she supposed she must make her living some way. The salary was fairly good—in fact, very good for a poor girl—and there would be the long summer vacation. At fourteen she knew already how much money she would save during those first two or three years and how she would spend those summer vacations. But although

she proffered this much information to her family she kept her
plans to herself. Mattie often pondered on this lack of openness
in her older daughter. Virginia was absolutely transparent. She
did not think she would care for teaching either, that is, not
for teaching in the ordinary sense. But she realized that for the
present that was the best profession which her parents could
have chosen for them. She would spend her summers learning
all she could about methods of teaching music.

"And a lot of good it will do you," Angela scoffed. "You
know perfectly well that there are no coloured teachers of
music in the public schools here in Philadelphia." But Jinny
thought it possible that there might be. "When Mamma was
coming along there were very few coloured teachers at all, and
now it looks as though there'd be plenty of chance for us. And
anyway you never know your luck."

By four o'clock the day's work was over and Mattie free to
do as she pleased. This was her idle hour. The girls would get
dinner, a Monday version of whatever the main course had
been the day before. Their mother was on no account to be
disturbed or importuned. To-day as usual she sat in the Morris
chair in the dining-room, dividing her time between the Sunday
paper and the girls' chatter. It was one of her most cherished
experiences,—this sense of a day's hard labour far behind her,
the happy voices of her girls, her joyous expectation of her
husband's home-coming. Usually the children made a game of
their preparations, recalling some nonsense of their early childhood days when it had been their delight to dress up as ladies.
Virginia would approach Angela: "Pardon me, is this Mrs.
Henrietta Jones?" And Angela, drawing herself up haughtily
would reply: "Er,—really you have the advantage of me." Then
Virginia: "Oh pardon! I thought you were Mrs. Jones and I
had heard my friend Mrs. Smith speak of you so often and
since you were in the neighbourhood and passing, I was going
to ask you in to have some ice-cream". The game of course
being that Angela should immediately drop her haughtiness
and proceed for the sake of the goodies to ingratiate herself
into her neighbour's esteem. It was a poor joke, long since
worn thin, but the two girls still used the greeting and for some
reason it had become part of the Monday ritual of preparing
the supper.

But to-night Angela's response lacked spontaneity. She was absorbed and reserved, even a little sulky. Deftly and swiftly she moved about her work, however, and no one who had not attended regularly on those Monday evening preparations could have guessed that there was anything on her mind other than complete absorption in the problem of cutting the bread or garnishing the warmed over roast beef. But Mattie was aware of the quality of brooding in her intense concentration. She had seen it before in her daughter but to-night, though to her practised eye it was more apparent than ever, she could not put her hand on it. Angela's response, if asked what was the matter, would be "Oh, nothing". It came to her suddenly that her older daughter was growing up; in a couple of months she would be fifteen. Children were often absorbed and moody when they were in their teens, too engaged in finding themselves to care about their effect on others. She must see to it that the girl had plenty of rest; perhaps school had been too strenuous for her to-day; she thought the high school programme very badly arranged, five hours one right after the other were much too long. "Angela, child, I think you'd better not be long out of bed to-night; you look very tired to me."

Angela nodded. But her father came in then and in the little hubbub that arose about his home-coming and the final preparations for supper her listlessness went without further remark.

Chapter IV

THE third storey front was Angela's bed-room. She was glad of its loneliness and security to-night,—even if her mother had not suggested her going to bed early she would have sought its shelter immediately after supper. Study for its own sake held no attractions for her; she did not care for any of her subjects really except Drawing and French. And when she was drawing she did not consider that she was studying, it was too naturally a means of self-expression. As for French, she did have to study that with great care, for languages did not come to her with any great readiness, but there was an element of fine lady-ism about the beautiful, logical tongue that made her in accordance with some secret subconscious ambition resolve to make it her own.

The other subjects, History, English, and Physical Geography, were not drudgery, for she had a fair enough mind; but then they were not attractive either, and she was lacking in Virginia's dogged resignation to unwelcome duties. Even when Jinny was a little girl she had been know to say manfully in the face of an uncongenial task: "Well I dotta det it done". Angela was not like that. But to-night she was concentrating with all her power on her work. During the day she had been badly hurt; she had received a wound whose depth and violence she would not reveal even to her parents,—because, and this only increased the pain, young as she was she knew that there was nothing they could do about it. There was nothing to be done but to get over it. Only she was not developed enough to state this stoicism to herself. She was like a little pet cat that had once formed part of their household; its leg had been badly torn by a passing dog, and the poor thing had dragged itself into the house and lain on its cushion patiently, waiting stolidly for this unfamiliar agony to subside. So Angela waited for the hurt in her mind to cease.

But across the history dates on the printed page and through stately lines of Lycidas she kept seeing Mary Hastings' accusing face, hearing Mary Hastings' accusing voice:

"Coloured! Angela, you never told me that you were coloured!"

And then her own voice in tragic but proud bewilderment. "Tell you that I was coloured! Why of course I never told you that I was coloured. Why should I?"

She had been so proud of Mary Hastings' friendship. In the dark and tortured spaces of her difficult life it had been a lovely, hidden refuge. It had been an experience so rarely sweet that she had hardly spoken of it even to Virginia. The other girls in her class had meant nothing to her. At least she had schooled herself to have them mean nothing. Some of them she had known since early childhood; they had lived in her neighbourhood and had gone to the graded schools with her. They had known that she was coloured, for they had seen her with Virginia, and sometimes her tall, black father had come to fetch her home on a rainy day. There had been pleasant enough contacts and intimacies; in the quiet of Jefferson Street they had played "The Farmer in the Dell", and "Here come three jolly, jolly sailor-boys"; dark retreats of the old market had afforded endless satisfaction for "Hide and Go Seek". She and those other children had gone shopping arm in arm for school supplies, threading their way in and out of the bustle and confusion that were Columbia Avenue.

As she grew older many of these intimacies lessened, in some cases ceased altogether. But she was never conscious of being left completely alone; there was always some one with whom to eat lunch or who was going her way after school. It was not until she reached the high school that she began to realize how solitary her life was becoming. There were no other coloured girls in her class but there had been only two or three during her school-life, and if there had been any she would not necessarily have confined herself to them; that this might be a good thing to do in sheer self-defence would hardly have occurred to her. But this problem did not confront her; what did confront her was that the very girls with whom she had grown up were evading her; when she went to the Assembly none of them sat next to her unless no other seat were vacant; little groups toward which she drifted during lunch, inexplicably dissolved to re-form in another portion of the room. Sometimes a girl in this new group threw her a backward glance charged either with a mean amusement or with annoyance.

Angela was proud; she did not need such a hint more than once, but she was bewildered and hurt. She took stories to school to read at recess, or wandered into the drawing laboratory and touched up her designs. Miss Barrington thought her an unusually industrious student.

And then in the middle of the term Mary Hastings had come, a slender, well-bred girl of fifteen. She was rather stupid in her work, in fact she shone in nothing but French and good manners. Undeniably she had an air, and her accent was remarkable. The other pupils, giggling, produced certain uncouth and unheard of sounds, but Mary said in French: "No, I have lent my knife to the brother-in-law of the gardener but here is my cane," quite as though the idiotic phrase were part of an imaginary conversation which she was conducting and appreciating. "She really knows what she's talking about," little Esther Bayliss commented, and added that Mary's family had lost some money and they had had to send her to public school. But it was some time before this knowledge, dispensed by Esther with mysterious yet absolute authenticity, became generally known. Meanwhile Mary was left to her own devices while the class with complete but tacit unanimity "tried her out". Mary, unaware of this, looked with her near-sighted, slightly supercilious gaze about the room at recess and seeing only one girl, and that girl Angela, who approached in dress, manner and deportment her own rather set ideas, had taken her lunch over to the other pupil's desk and said: "Come on, let's eat together while you tell me who everybody is."

Angela took the invitation as simply as the other had offered. "That little girl in the purplish dress is Esther Bayliss and the tall one in the thick glasses——"

Mary, sitting with her back to the feeding groups, never troubled to look around. "I don't mean the girls. I expect I'll know them soon enough when I get around to it. I mean the teachers. Do you have to dig for them?" She liked Angela and she showed it plainly and directly. Her home was in some remote fastness of West Philadelphia which she could reach with comparative swiftness by taking the car at Spring Garden Street. Instead she walked half way home with her new friend, up Seventeenth Street as far as Girard Avenue where, after a final exchange of school matters and farewells, she took the car, leaving Angela to her happy, satisfied thoughts. And presently she began to know more than happiness and satisfaction, she was knowing the extreme gratification of being the chosen companion of a popular and important girl, for Mary, although not quick at her studies, was a power in everything else. She dressed well, she had plenty of pocket money, she could play the latest marches in the gymnasium, she received a certain indefinable but flattering attention from the teachers, and she could make things "go". The school paper was moribund and Mary knew how to resuscitate it; she brought in advertisements from her father's business friends; she made her married sisters obtain subscriptions. Without being obtrusive or overbearing, without condescension and without toadying she was the leader of her class. And with it all she stuck to Angela. She accepted popularity because it was thrust upon her, but she was friendly with Angela because the latter suited her.

Angela was happy. She had a friend and the friendship brought her unexpected advantages. She was no longer left out of groups because there could be no class plans without Mary and Mary would remain nowhere for any length of time without Angela. So to save time and argument, and also to avoid offending the regent, Angela was always included. Not that she cared much about this, but she did like Mary; as is the way of a "fidus Achates", she gave her friendship whole-heartedly. And it was gratifying to be in the midst of things.

In April the school magazine announced a new departure. Henceforth the editorial staff was to be composed of two representatives from each class; of these one was to be the chief representative chosen by vote of the class, the other was to be assistant, selected by the chief. The chief representative, said the announcement pompously, would sit in at executive meetings and have a voice in the policy of the paper. The assistant would solicit and collect subscriptions, collect fees, receive and report complaints and in brief, said Esther Bayliss, "do all the dirty work". But she coveted the position and title for all that.

Angela's class held a brief meeting after school and elected Mary Hastings as representative without a dissenting vote.

"No," said Angela holding up a last rather grimy bit of paper. "Here is one for Esther Bayliss." Two or three of the girls giggled; everyone knew that she must have voted for herself; indeed it had been she who had insisted on taking a ballot rather than a vote by acclaim. Mary was already on her feet. She had been sure of the result of the election, would have been astonished indeed had it turned out any other way. "Well, girls," she began in her rather high, refined voice, "I wish to thank you for the—er—confidence you have bestowed, that is, placed in me and I'm sure you all know I'll do my best to keep the old paper going. And while I'm about it I might just as well announce that I'm choosing Angela Murray for my assistant."

There was a moment's silence. The girls who had thought about it at all had known that if Mary were elected, as assuredly she would be, this meant also the election of Angela. And those who had taken no thought saw no reason to object to her appointment. And anyway there was nothing to be done. But Esther Bayliss pushed forward: "I don't know how it is with the rest of you, but I should have to think twice before I'd trust my subscription money to a coloured girl."

Mary said in utter astonishment: "Coloured, why what are you talking about? Who's coloured?"

"Angela, Angela Murray, that's who's coloured. At least she used to be when we all went to school at Eighteenth and Oxford."

Mary said again: "Coloured!" And then, "Angela, you never told me you were coloured!"

Angela's voice was as amazed as her own: "Tell you that I was coloured! Why of course I never told you that I was coloured! Why should I?"

"There," said Esther, "see she never told Mary that she was coloured. What wouldn't she have done with our money!"

Angela had picked up her books and strolled out the door. But she flew down the north staircase and out the Brandywine Street entrance and so to Sixteenth Street where she would meet no one she knew, especially at this belated hour. At home there would be work to do, her lessons to get and the long, long hours of the night must pass before she would have to face again the hurt and humiliation of the classroom; before

she would have to steel her heart and her nerves to drop Mary
Hastings before Mary Hastings could drop her. No one, no
one, Mary least of all, should guess how completely she had
been wounded. Mary and her shrinking bewilderment! Mary
and her exclamation: "Coloured!" This was a curious business,
this colour. It was the one god apparently to whom you could
sacrifice everything. On account of it her mother had neglected
to greet her own husband on the street. Mary Hastings could
let it come between her and her friend.

In the morning she was at school early; the girls should all
see her there and their individual attitude should be her attitude. She would remember each one's greetings, would store
it away for future guidance. Some of the girls were especially
careful to speak to her, one or two gave her a meaning smile,
or so she took it, and turned away. Some did not speak at
all. When Mary Hastings came in Angela rose and sauntered
unseeing and unheeding deliberately past her through the
doorway, across the hall to Miss Barrington's laboratory. As
she returned she passed Mary's desk, and the girl lifted troubled
but not unfriendly eyes to meet her own; Angela met the
glance fully but without recognition. She thought to herself:
"Coloured! If they had said to me Mary Hastings is a voodoo,
I'd have answered, 'What of it? She's my friend.'"

Before June Mary Hastings came up to her and asked her to
wait after school. Angela who had been neither avoiding nor
seeking her gave a cool nod. They walked out of the French
classroom together. When they reached the corner Mary
spoke:

"Oh, Angela, let's be friends again. It doesn't really make
any difference. See, I don't care any more."

"But that's what I don't understand. Why should it have
made any difference in the first place? I'm just the same as I
was before you knew I was coloured and just the same afterwards. Why should it ever have made any difference at all?"

"I don't know, I'm sure. I was just surprised. It was all so
unexpected."

"What was unexpected?"

"Oh, I don't know. I can't explain it. But let's be friends."

"Well," said Angela slowly, "I'm willing, but I don't think it will ever be the same again."

It wasn't. Some element, spontaneity, trustfulness was lacking. Mary, who had never thought of speaking of colour, was suddenly conscious that here was a subject which she must not discuss. She was less frank, at times even restrained. Angela, too young to define her thoughts, yet felt vaguely: "She failed me once,—I was her friend,—yet she failed me for something with which I had nothing to do. She's just as likely to do it again. It's in her."

Definitely she said to herself, "Mary withdrew herself not because I was coloured but because she didn't know I was coloured. Therefore if she had never known I was coloured she would always have been my friend. We would have kept on having our good times together." And she began to wonder which was the more important, a patent insistence on the fact of colour or an acceptance of the good things of life which could come to you in America if either you were not coloured or the fact of your racial connections was not made known.

During the summer Mary Hastings' family, it appeared, recovered their fallen fortunes. At any rate she did not return to school in the fall and Angela never saw her again.

Chapter V

VIRGINIA came rushing in. "Angela, where's Mummy?"

"Out. What's all the excitement?"

"I've been appointed. Isn't it great? Won't Mother and Dad be delighted! Right at the beginning of the year too, so I won't have to wait. The official notice isn't out yet but I know it's all right. Miss Herren wants me to report tomorrow. Isn't it perfectly marvellous! Here I graduate from the Normal in June and in the second week of school in September I've got my perfectly good job. Darling child, it's very much better, as you may have heard me observe before, to be born lucky than rich. But I am lucky and I'll be rich too. Think of that salary for my very own! With both of us working, Mummy won't have to want for a thing, nor Father either. Mummy won't have to do a lick of work if she doesn't want to. Well, what have you got to say about it, old Rain-in-the-Face? Or perhaps this isn't Mrs. Henrietta Jones whom I'm addressing of?"

Angela giggled, then raised an imaginary lorgnette. "Er,—really I think you have the advantage of me. Well, I was thinking how fortunate you were to get your appointment right off the bat and how you'll hate it now that you have got it."

She herself, appointed two years previously, had had no such luck. Strictly speaking there are no coloured schools as such in Philadelphia. Yet, by an unwritten law, although coloured children may be taught by white teachers, white children must never receive knowledge at the hands of coloured instructors. As the number of coloured Normal School graduates is steadily increasing, the city gets around this difficulty by manning a school in a district thickly populated by Negroes, with a coloured principal and a coloured teaching force. Coloured children living in that district must thereupon attend that school. But no attention is paid to the white children who leave this same district for the next nearest white or "mixed" school.

Angela had been sixth on the list of coloured graduates. Five had been appointed, but there was no vacancy for her, and for several months she was idle with here and there a day, perhaps a week of substituting. She could not be appointed in any but

462

a coloured school, and she was not supposed to substitute in any but this kind of classroom. Then her father discovered that a young white woman was teaching in a coloured school. He made some searching inquiries and was met with the complacent rejoinder that as soon as a vacancy occurred in a white school, Miss McSweeney would be transferred there and his daughter could have her place.

Just as she had anticipated, Angela did not want the job after she received it. She had expected to loathe teaching little children and her expectation, it turned out, was perfectly well grounded. Perhaps she might like to teach drawing to grown-ups; she would certainly like to have a try at it. Meanwhile it was nice to be independent, to be holding a lady-like, respectable position so different from her mother's early days, to be able to have pretty clothes and to help with the house, in brief to be drawing an appreciably adequate and steady salary. For one thing it made it possible for her to take up work at the Philadelphia Academy of Fine Arts at Broad and Cherry.

Jinny was in excellent spirits at dinner. "Now, Mummy darling, you really shall walk in silk attire and siller hae to spare." Angela's appointment had done away with the drudgery of washday. "We'll get Hettie Daniels to come in Saturdays and clean up. I won't have to scrub the front steps any more and everything will be feasting and fun." Pushing aside her plate she rushed over to her father, climbed on his knee and flung her lovely bronze arms around his neck. She still adored him, still thought him the finest man in the world; she still wanted her husband to be just exactly like him; he would not be so tall nor would he be quite as dark. Matthew Henson was of only medium height and was a sort of reddish yellow and he distinctly was not as handsome as her father. Indeed Virginia thought, with a pang of shame at her disloyalty, that it would have been a fine thing if he could exchange his lighter skin for her father's colour if in so doing he might have gained her father's thick, coarsely grained but beautifully curling, open black hair. Matthew had inherited his father's thick, tight, "bad" hair. Only, thank heaven, it was darker.

Junius tucked his slender daughter back in the hollow of his arm.

"Well, baby, you want something off my plate?" As a child Virginia had been a notorious beggar.

"Darling! I was thinking that now you could buy Mr. Hallowell's car. He's got his eye on a Cadillac, Kate says, and he'd be willing to let Henry Ford go for a song."

Junius was pleased, but he thought he ought to protest. "Do I look as old as all that? I might be able to buy the actual car, now that my girls are getting so monied, but the upkeep, I understand, is pretty steep."

"Oh, nonsense," said Mattie. "Go on and get it, June. Think how nice it will be riding out North Broad Street in the evenings."

And Angela added kindly: "I think you owe it to yourself to get it, Dad. Jinny and I'll carry the house till you get it paid for."

"Well, there's no reason of course why I——" he corrected himself, "why we shouldn't have a car if we want it." He saw himself spending happy moments digging in the little car's inmost mysteries. He would buy new parts, change the engine perhaps, paint it and overhaul her generally. And he might just as well indulge himself. The little house was long since paid for; he was well insured, and his two daughters were grown up and taking care of themselves. He slid Jinny off his knee.

"I believe I'll run over to the Hallowells now and see what Tom'll take for that car. Catch him before he goes down town in it."

Virginia called after him. "Just think! Maybe this time next week you'll be going down town in it."

She was very happy. Life was turning out just right. She was young, she was twenty, she was about to earn her own living, —"to be about to live"—she said, happily quoting a Latin construction which had always intrigued her. Her mother would never have to work again; her father would have a Henry Ford; she herself would get a new, good music teacher and would also take up the study of methods at the University of Pennsylvania.

Angela could hear her downstairs talking to Matthew Henson whose ring she had just answered. "Only think, Matt, I've been appointed."

"Great!" said Matthew. "Is Angela in? Do you think she'd like to go to the movies with me to-night? She was too tired last time. Run up and ask her, there's a good girl."

Angela sighed. She didn't want to go out with Matthew; he wearied her so. And besides people always looked at her so strangely. She wished he would take it into his head to come and see Jinny.

Sunday was still a happy day. Already an air of prosperity, of having arrived beyond the striving point, had settled over the family. Mr. Murray's negotiations with Tom Hallowell had been most successful. The Ford, a little four-seater coupé, compact and sturdy, had changed hands. Its former owner came around on Sunday to give Junius a lesson. The entire household piled in, for both girls were possessed of the modern slenderness. They rode out Jefferson Street and far, far out Ridge Avenue to the Wissahickon and on to Chestnut Hill. From time to time, when the traffic was thin, Junius took the wheel, anticipating Tom's instructions with the readiness of the born mechanic. They came back laughing and happy and pardonably proud. The dense, tender glow of the late afternoon September sun flooded the little parlour, the dining-room was dusky and the kitchen was redolent of scents of ginger bread and spiced preserves. After supper there were no lessons to get. "It'll be years before I forget all that stuff I learned in practice school," said Jinny gaily.

Later on some boys came in; Matthew Henson inevitably, peering dissatisfied through the autumn gloom for Angela and immediately content when he saw her; Arthur Sawyer, who had just entered the School of Pedagogy and was a little ashamed of it, for he considered teaching work fit only for women. "But I've got to make a living somehow, ain't I? And I won't go into that post-office!"

"What's the matter with the post-office?" Henson asked indignantly. He had just been appointed. In reality he did not fancy the work himself, but he did not want it decried before Angela.

"Tell me what better or surer job is there for a coloured man in Philadelphia?"

"Nothing," said Sawyer promptly, "not a thing in the world

except school teaching. But that's just what I object to. I'm
sick of planning my life with regard to being coloured. I'm not
a bit ashamed of my race. I don't mind in the least that once
we were slaves. Every race in the world has at some time occupied a servile position. But I do mind having to take it into
consideration every time I want to eat outside of my home,
every time I enter a theatre, every time I think of a profession."

"But you do have to take it into consideration," said Jinny
softly. "At present it's one of the facts of our living, just as
lameness or near-sightedness might be for a white man."

The inevitable race discussion was on.

"Ah, but there you're all off, Miss Virginia." A tall, lanky,
rather supercilious youth spoke up from the corner. He had
been known to them all their lives as Franky Porter, but he
had taken lately to publishing poems in the Philadelphia
Tribunal which he signed F. Seymour Porter. "Really you're
all off, for you speak as though colour itself were a deformity.
Whereas, as Miss Angela being an artist knows, colour may
really be a very beautiful thing, mayn't it?"

"Oh don't drag me into your old discussion," Angela answered crossly. "I'm sick of this whole race business if you ask
me. And don't call me Miss Angela. Call me Angela as you've
all done all our lives or else call me Miss Murray. No, I don't
think being coloured in America is a beautiful thing. I think
it's nothing short of a curse."

"Well," said Porter slowly, "I think its being or not being a
curse rests with you. You've got to decide whether or not
you're going to let it interfere with personal development and
to that extent it may be harmful or it may be an incentive. I
take it that Sawyer here, who even when we were all kids always
wanted to be an engineer, will transmute his colour either into
a bane or a blessing according to whether he lets it make him
hide his natural tendencies under the bushel of school-teaching
or become an inspiration toward making him the very best
kind of engineer that there ever was so that people will just
have to take him for what he is and overlook the fact of colour."

"That's it," said Jinny. "You know, being coloured often
does spur you on."

"And that's what I object to," Angela answered perversely.
"I'm sick of this business of always being below or above a

certain norm. Doesn't anyone think that we have a right to be happy simply, naturally?"

Gradually they drifted into music. Virginia played a few popular songs and presently the old beautiful airs of all time, "Drink to me only with thine eyes" and "Sweet and Low". Arthur Sawyer had a soft, melting tenor and Angela a rather good alto; Virginia and the other boys carried the air while Junius boomed his deep, unyielding bass. The lovely melodies and the peace of the happy, tranquil household crept over them, and presently they exchanged farewells and the young men passed wearied and contented out into the dark confines of Opal Street. Angela and Mattie went upstairs, but Viginia and her father stayed below and sang very softly so as not to disturb the sleeping street; a few hymns and finally the majestic strains of "The Dying Christian" floated up. Mrs. Murray had complained of feeling tired. "I think I'll just lie a moment on your bed, Angela, until your father comes up." But her daughter noticed that she had not relaxed, instead she was straining forward a little and Angela realized that she was trying to catch every note of her husband's virile, hearty voice.

She said, "You heard what we were all talking about before the boys left. You and father don't ever bother to discuss such matters, do you?"

Her mother seemed to strain past the sound of her voice. "Not any more; oh, of course we used to talk about such things, but you get so taken up with the problem of living, just life itself you know, that by and by being coloured or not is just one thing more or less that you have to contend with. But of course there have been times when colour was the starting point of our discussions. I remember how when you and Jinny were little things and she was always running to the piano and you were scribbling all over the walls,—many's the time I've slapped your little fingers for that, Angela,—we used to spend half the night talking about you, your father and I. I wanted you to be great artists but Junius said: 'No, we'll give them a good, plain education and set them in the way of earning a sure and honest living; then if they've got it in them to travel over all the rocks that'll be in their way as coloured girls, they'll manage, never you fear.' And he was right." The music downstairs

ceased and she lay back, relaxed and drowsy. "Your father's always right."

Much of this was news to Angela, and she would have liked
to learn more about those early nocturnal discussions. But she
only said, smiling, "You're still crazy about father, aren't you,
darling?"

Her mother was wide awake in an instant. "Crazy! I'd give
my life for him!"

The Saturday excursions were long since a thing of the past;
Henry Ford had changed that. Also the extra work which the
girls had taken upon themselves in addition to their teaching,
—Angela at the Academy, Virginia at the University,—made
Saturday afternoon a too sorely needed period of relaxation to
be spent in the old familiar fashion. Still there were times when
Angela in search of a new frock or intent on the exploration of
a picture gallery asked her mother to accompany her. And at
such times the two indulged in their former custom of having
tea and a comfortable hour's chat in the luxurious comfort of
some exclusive tearoom or hotel. Mattie, older and not quite
so lightly stepping in these days of comparative ease as in those
other times when a week's arduous duties lay behind her, still
responded joyously to the call of fashion and grooming, the air
of "good living" which pervaded these places. Moreover she
herself was able to contribute to this atmosphere. Her daughters
insisted on presenting her with the graceful and dainty clothes
which she loved, and they were equally insistent on her wearing them. "No use hanging them in a closet," said Jinny
blithely. All her prophecies had come true—her mother had
the services of a maid whenever she needed them, she went
clad for the most part "in silk attire", and she had "siller to
spare" and to spend.

She was down town spending it now. The Ladies' Auxiliary
of her church was to give a reception after Lent, and Mattie
meant to hold her own with the best of them. "We're getting
to be old ladies," she said a bit wistfully, "but we'll make you
young ones look at us once or twice just the same." Angela replied that she was sure of that. "And I know one or two little
secrets for the complexion that will make it impossible for you
to call yourself old."

But those her mother knew already. However she expressed a willingness to accept Angela's offer. She loved to be fussed over, and of late Angela had shown a tendency to rival even Jinny in this particular. The older girl was beginning to lose some of her restlessness. Life was pretty hum-drum, but it was comfortable and pleasant; her family life was ideal and her time at the art school delightful. The instructor was interested in her progress, and one or two of the girls had shown a desire for real intimacy. These intimations she had not followed up very closely, but she was seeing enough of a larger, freer world to make her chafe less at the restrictions which somehow seemed to bind in her own group. As a result of even this slight satisfaction of her cravings, she was indulging less and less in brooding and introspection, although at no time was she able to adapt herself to living with the complete spontaneity so characteristic of Jinny.

But she was young, and life would somehow twist and shape itself to her subsconscious yearnings, just as it had done for her mother, she thought, following Mattie in and out of shops, delivering opinions and lending herself to all the exigencies which shopping imposed. It was not an occupation which she particularly enjoyed, but, like her mother, she adored the atmosphere and its accompaniment of well-dressed and luxuriously stationed women. No one could tell, no one would have thought for a moment that she and her mother had come from tiny Opal Street; no one could have dreamed of their racial connections. "And if Jinny were here," she thought, slowly selecting another cake, "she really would be just as capable of fitting into all this as mother and I; but they wouldn't let her light." And again she let herself dwell on the fallaciousness of a social system which stretched appearance so far beyond being.

From the tea-room they emerged into the damp greyness of the March afternoon. The streets were slushy and slimy; the sky above sodden and dull. Mattie shivered and thought of the Morris chair in the minute but cosy dining-room of her home. She wanted to go to the "Y" on Catherine Street and there were two calls to make far down Fifteenth. But at last all this was accomplished. "Now we'll get the next car and before you know it you'll be home."

"You look tired, Mother," said Angela.

"I am tired," she acknowledged, and, suddenly sagging against her daughter, lost consciousness. About them a small crowd formed, and a man passing in an automobile kindly drove the two women to a hospital in Broad Street two blocks away. It was a hospital to which no coloured woman would ever have been admitted except to char, but there was no such question to be raised in the case of this patient. "She'll be all right presently," the interne announced, "just a little fainting spell brought on by over-exertion. Was that your car you came in? It would be nice if you could have one to get her home in."

"Oh, but I can," and in a moment Angela had rushed to the telephone forgetting everything except that her father was in his shop to-day and therefore almost within reach and so was the car.

Not long after he came striding into the hospital, tall and black and rather shabby in his working clothes. He was greeted by the clerk with a rather hostile, "Yes, and what do you want?"

Angela, hastening across the lobby to him, halted at the intonation.

Junius was equal to the moment's demands. "I'm Mrs. Murray's chauffeur," he announced, hating the deception, but he would not have his wife bundled out too soon. "Is she very badly off, Miss Angela?"

His daughter hastened to reassure him. "No, she'll be down in a few minutes now."

"And meanwhile you can wait outside," said the attendant icily. She did not believe that black people were exactly human; there was no place for them in the scheme of life so far as she could see.

Junius withdrew, and in a half hour's time the young interne and the nurse came out supporting his wan wife. He sprang to the pavement: "Lean on me, Mrs. Murray."

But sobbing, she threw her arms about his neck. "Oh Junius, Junius!"

He lifted her then, drew back for Angela and mounting himself, drove away. The interne stepped back into the hospital raging about these damn white women and their nigger servants. Such women ought to be placed in a psycho-pathic ward and the niggers burned.

*

The girls got Mrs. Murray into the Morris chair and ran up-stairs for pillows and wraps. When they returned Junius was in the chair and Mrs. Murray in his arms. "Oh, June, dear June, such a service of love."

"Do you suppose she's going to die?" whispered Jinny, stricken. What, she wondered, would become of her father.

But in a few days Mattie was fully recovered and more happy than ever in the reflorescence of love and tenderness which had sprung up between herself and Junius. Only Junius was not so well. He had had a slight touch of grippe during the winter and the half hour's loitering in the treacherous March weather, before the hospital, had not served to improve it. He was hoarse and feverish, though this he did not immediately admit. But a tearing pain in his chest compelled him one morning to suggest the doctor. In a panic Mattie sent for him. Junius really ill! She had never seen him in anything but the pink of condition. The doctor reluctantly admitted pneumonia —"a severe case but I think we can pull him through."

He suffered terribly—Mattie suffered with him, never leav-ing his bedside. On the fifth day he was delirious. His wife thought, "Surely God isn't going to let him die without speak-ing to me again."

Toward evening he opened his eyes and saw her tender, stricken face. He smiled. "Dear Mattie," and then, "Jinny, I'd like to hear some music, 'Vital spark'——"

So his daughter went down to the little parlour and played and sang "The Dying Christian".

Angela thought, "Oh, isn't this terrible! Oh how can she?" Presently she called softly, "Jinny, Jinny come up."

Junius' hand was groping for Mattie's. She placed it in his. "Dear Mattie," he said, " Heaven opens on my eyes,——"

The house was still with the awful stillness that follows a fu-neral. All the bustle and hurry were over; the end, the fulfil-ment toward which the family had been striving for the last three days was accomplished. The baked funeral meats had been removed; Virginia had seen to that. Angela was up in her room, staring dry-eyed before her; she loved her father, but not even for him could she endure this aching, formless pain of bereavement. She kept saying to herself fiercely: "I must get over this, I can't stand this. I'll go away."

Mrs. Murray sat in the old Morris chair in the dining-room. She stroked its arms with her plump, worn fingers; she laid her face again and again on its shabby back. One knew that she was remembering a dark, loved cheek. Jinny said, "Come up-stairs and let me put you to bed, darling. You're going to sleep with me, you know. You're going to comfort your little girl, aren't you, Mummy?" Then as there was no response, "Darling, you'll make yourself ill."

Her mother sat up suddenly. "Yes, that's what I want to do. Oh, Jinny, do you think I can make myself ill enough to follow him soon? My daughter, try to forgive me, but I must go to him. I can't live without him. I don't deserve a daughter like you, but,—don't let them hold me back. I want to die, I must die. Say you forgive me,——"

"Darling," and it was as though her husband rather than her daughter spoke, "whatever you want is what I want." By a supreme effort she held back her tears, but it was years before she forgot the picture of her mother sitting back in the old Morris chair, composing herself for death.

Chapter VI

A T the Academy matters progressed smoothly without the flawing of a ripple. Angela looked forward to the hours which she spent there and honestly regretted their passage. Her fellow students and the instructors were more than cordial, there was an actual sense of camaraderie among them. She had not mentioned the fact of her Negro strain, indeed she had no occasion to, but she did not believe that this fact if known would cause any change in attitude. Artists were noted for their broad-mindedness. They were the first persons in the world to judge a person for his worth rather than by any hallmark. It is true that Miss Henderson, a young lady of undeniable colour, was not received with the same cordiality and attention which Angela was receiving, and this, too, despite the fact that the former's work showed undeniable talent, even originality. Angela thought that something in the young lady's personality precluded an approach to friendship; she seemed to be wary, almost offensively stand-offish. Certainly she never spoke unless spoken to; she had been known to spend a whole session without even glancing at a fellow student.

Angela herself had not arrived at any genuine intimacies. Two of the girls had asked her to their homes but she had always refused; such invitations would have to be returned with similar ones and the presence of Jinny would entail explanations. The invitation of Mr. Shields, the instructor, to have tea at his wife's at home was another matter and of this she gladly availed herself. She could not tell to just what end she was striving. She did not like teaching and longed to give it up. On the other hand she must make her living. Mr. Shields had suggested that she might be able to increase both her earning capacity and her enjoyments through a more practical application of her art. There were directorships of drawing in the public schools, positions in art schools and colleges, or, since Angela frankly acknowledged her unwillingness to instruct, there was such a thing as being buyer for the art section of a department store.

"And anyway," said Mrs. Shields, "you never know what may

be in store for you if you just have preparation." She and her
husband were both attracted to the pleasant-spoken, talented
girl. Angela possessed an undeniable air, and she dressed well,
even superlatively. Her parents' death had meant the possession of half the house and half of three thousand dollars' worth
of insurance. Her salary was adequate, her expenses light. Indeed even her present mode of living gave her little cause for
complaint except that her racial affiliations narrowed her confines. But she was restlessly conscious of a desire for broader
horizons. She confided something like this to her new friends.

"Perfectly natural," they agreed. "There's no telling where
your tastes and talents will lead you,—to Europe perhaps and
surely to the formation of new and interesting friendships.
You'll find artistic folk the broadest, most liberal people in the
world."

"There are possibilities of scholarships, too," Mr. Shields concluded more practically. The Academy offered a few in competition. But there were others more liberally endowed and
practically without restriction.

Sundays on Opal Street bore still their aspect of something different and special. Jinny sometimes went to church, sometimes
packed the car with a group of laughing girls of her age and
played at her father's old game of exploring. Angela preferred
to stay in the house. She liked to sleep late, get up for a leisurely
bath and a meticulous toilet. Afterwards she would turn over
her wardrobe, sorting and discarding; read the week's forecast
of theatres, concerts and exhibits. And finally she would begin
sketching, usually ending up with a new view of Hetty Daniels'
head.

Hetty, who lived with them now in the triple capacity, as she
saw it, of housekeeper, companion, and chaperone, loved to
pose. It satisfied some unquenchable vanity in her unloved,
empty existence. She could not conceive of being sketched because she was, in the artistic jargon, "interesting", "paintable",
or "difficult". Models, as she understood it, were chosen for
their beauty. Square and upright she sat, regaling Angela with
tales of the romantic adventures of some remote period which
was her youth. She could not be very old, the young girl
thought; indeed, from some of her dates she must have been at

least twelve years younger than her mother. Yet Mrs. Murray
had carried with her to the end some irrefragable quality of
girlishness which would keep her memory forever young.

Miss Daniels' great fetish was sex morality. "Them young
fellers was always 'round me thick ez bees; wasn't any night
they wasn't more fellows in my kitchen then you an' Jinny ever
has in yore parlour. But I never listened to none of the' talk,
jist held out agin 'em and kept my pearl of great price untar-
nished. I aimed then and I'm continual to aim to be a verjous
woman."

Her unslaked yearnings gleamed suddenly out of her eyes,
transforming her usually rather expressionless face into something wild and avid. The dark brown immobile mask of her
skin made an excellent foil for the vividness of an emotion
which was so apparent, so palpable that it seemed like something superimposed upon the background of her countenance.

"If I could just get that look for Mr. Shields," Angela said
half aloud to herself, "I bet I could get any of their old
scholarships. . . . So you had lots more beaux than we have,
Hetty? Well you wouldn't have to go far to outdo us there."

The same half dozen young men still visited the Murray
household on Sundays. None of them except Matthew Henson
came as a suitor; the others looked in partly from habit, partly,
Jinny used to say, for the sake of Hetty Daniels' good ginger
bread, but more than for any other reason for the sake of having a comfortable place in which to argue and someone with
whom to conduct the argument.

"They certainly do argue," Angela grumbled a little, but she
didn't care. Matthew was usually the leader in their illimitable
discussions, but she much preferred him at this than at his
clumsy and distasteful love-making. Of course she could go
out, but there was no place for her to visit and no companions
for her to visit with. If she made calls there would be merely a
replica of what she was finding in her own household. It was
true that in the ultra-modern set Sunday dancing was being
taken up. But she and Virginia did not fit in here any too well.
Her fancy envisaged a comfortable drawing-room (there *were*
folks who used that term), peopled with distinguished men
and women who did things, wrote and painted and acted,—
people with a broad, cultural background behind them, or,

lacking that, with the originality of thought and speech which
comes from failing, deliberately failing, to conform to the pattern. Somewhere, she supposed, there must be coloured people
like that. But she didn't know any of them. She knew there
were people right in Philadelphia who had left far, far behind
them the economic class to which her father and mother had
belonged. But their thoughts, their actions were still cramped
and confined; they were sitting in their new, even luxurious
quarters, still mental parvenus, still discussing the eternal race
question even as these boys here.

To-night they were hard at it again with a new phase which
Angela, who usually sat only half attentive in their midst, did
not remember ever having heard touched before. Seymour
Porter had started the ball by forcing their attention to one of
his poems. It was not a bad poem; as modern verse goes it possessed a touch distinctly above the mediocre.

"Why don't you stop that stuff and get down to brass tacks,
Porter?" Matthew snarled. "You'll be of much more service to
your race as a good dentist than as a half-baked poet." Henson
happened to know that the amount of study which the young
poet did at the University kept him just barely registered in the
dental college.

Porter ran his hand over his beautifully groomed hair. He
had worn a stocking cap in his room all the early part of the
day to enable him to perform this gesture without disaster. "There
you go, Henson,—service to the race and all the rest of it.
Doesn't it ever occur to you that the race is made up of individuals and you can't conserve the good of the whole unless
you establish that of each part? Is it better for me to be a first
rate dentist and be a cabined and confined personality or a
half-baked poet, as you'd call it, and be myself?"

Henson reasoned that a coloured American must take into
account that he is usually living in a hostile community. "If
you're only a half-baked poet they'll think that you're a representative of your race and that we're all equally no account.
But if you're a fine dentist, they won't think, it's true, that
we're all as skilled as you, but they will respect you and concede
that probably there're a few more like you. Inconsistent, but
that's the way they argue."

Arthur Sawyer objected to this constant yielding to an invisible censorship. "If you're coloured you've just got to straddle a bit; you've got to consider both racial and individual integrity. I've got to be sure of a living right now. So in order not to bring the charge of vagrancy against my family I'm going to teach until I've saved enough money to study engineering in comfort."

"And when you get through?" Matthew asked politely.

"When I get through, if this city has come to its senses, I'll get a big job with Baldwin. If not I'll go to South America and take out naturalization papers."

"But you can't do that," cried Jinny, "we'd need you more than ever if you had all that training. You know what I think? We've all of us got to make up our minds to the sacrifice of something. I mean something more than just the ordinary sacrifices in life, not so much for the sake of the next generation as for the sake of some principle, for the sake of some immaterial quality like pride or intense self-respect or even a saving complacency; a spiritual tonic which the race needs perhaps just as much as the body might need iron or whatever it does need to give the proper kind of resistance. There are some things which an individual might want, but which he'd just have to give up forever for the sake of the more important whole."

"It beats me," said Sawyer indulgently, "how a little thing like you can catch hold of such a big thought. I don't know about a man's giving up his heart's desire forever, though, just because he's coloured. That seems to me a pretty large order."

"Large order or not," Henson caught him up, "she comes mighty near being right. What do you think, Angela?"

"Just the same as I've always thought. I don't see any sense in living unless you're going to be happy."

Angela took the sketch of Hetty Daniels to school. "What an interesting type!" said Gertrude Quale, the girl next to her. "Such cosmic and tragic unhappiness in that face. What is she, not an American?"

"Oh yes she is. She's an old coloured woman who's worked in our family for years and she was born right here in Philadelphia."

"Oh coloured! Well, of course I suppose you would call her

an American though I never think of darkies as Americans.
Coloured,—yes that would account for that unhappiness in
her face. I suppose they all mind it awfully."

It was the afternoon for the life class. The model came in, a
short, rather slender young woman with a faintly pretty, shrew-
ish face full of a certain dark, mean character. Angela glanced
at her thoughtfully, full of pleasant anticipation. She liked to
work for character, preferred it even to beauty. The model
caught her eye; looked away and again turned her full gaze
upon her with an insistent, slightly incredulous stare. It was
Esther Bayliss who had once been in the High School with
Angela. She had left not long after Mary Hastings' return to
her boarding school.

Angela saw no reason why she should speak to her and presently, engrossed in the portrayal of the round, yet pointed little
face, forgot the girl's identity. But Esther kept her eyes fixed on
her former school-mate with a sort of intense, angry brooding
so absorbing that she forgot her pose and Mr. Shield spoke to
her two or three times. On the third occasion he said not
unkindly, "You'll have to hold your pose better than this, Miss
Bayliss, or we won't be able to keep you on."

"I don't want you to keep me on." She spoke with an amazing vindictiveness. "I haven't got to the point yet where I'm
going to lower myself to pose for a coloured girl."

He looked around the room in amazement; no, Miss
Henderson wasn't there, she never came to this class he remembered. "Well after that we couldn't keep you anyway.
We're not taking orders from our models. But there's no coloured girl here."

"Oh yes there is, unless she's changed her name." She
laughed spitefully. "Isn't that Angela Murray over there next
to that Jew girl?" In spite of himself, Shields nodded. "Well,
she's coloured though she wouldn't let you know. But I know.
I went to school with her in North Philadelphia. And I tell you
I wouldn't stay to pose for her not if you were to pay me ten
times what I'm getting. Sitting there drawing from me just as
though she were as good as a white girl!"

Astonished and disconcerted, he told his wife about it. "But
I can't think she's really coloured, Mabel. Why she looks and
acts just like a white girl. She dresses in better taste than any-

body in the room. But that little wretch of a model insisted that she was coloured."

"Well she just can't be. Do you suppose I don't know a coloured woman when I see one? I can tell 'em a mile off."

It seemed to him a vital and yet such a disgraceful matter. "If she is coloured she should have told me. I'd certainly like to know, but hang it all, I can't ask her, for suppose she should be white in spite of what that little beast of a model said?" He found her address in the registry and overcome one afternoon with shamed curiosity drove up to Opal Street and slowly past her house. Jinny was coming in from school and Hetty Daniels on her way to market greeted her on the lower step. Then Virginia put the key in the lock and passed inside. "She is coloured," he told his wife, "for no white girl in her senses would be rooming with coloured people."

"I should say not! Coloured, is she? Well, she shan't come here again, Henry."

Angela approached him after class on Saturday. "How is Mrs. Shields? I can't get out to see her this week but I'll be sure to run in next."

He blurted out miserably, "But, Miss Murray, you never told me that you were coloured."

She felt as though she were rehearsing a well-known part in a play. "Coloured! Of course I never told you that I was coloured. Why should I?"

But apparently there was some reason why she should tell it; she sat in her room in utter dejection trying to reason it out. Just as in the old days she had not discussed the matter with Jinny, for what could the latter do? She wondered if her mother had ever met with any such experiences. Was there something inherently wrong in "passing"?

Her mother had never seemed to consider it as anything but a lark. And on the one occasion, that terrible day in the hospital when passing or not passing might have meant the difference between good will and unpleasantness, her mother had deliberately given the whole show away. But her mother, she had long since begun to realize, had not considered this business of colour or the lack of it as pertaining intimately to her personal happiness. She was perfectly satisfied, absolutely content

whether she was part of that white world with Angela or up on
little Opal Street with her dark family and friends. Whereas it
seemed to Angela that all the things which she most wanted
were wrapped up with white people. All the good things were
theirs. Not, some coldly reasoning instinct within was saying,
because they were white. But because for the present they had
power and the badge of that power was whiteness, very like
the colours on the escutcheon of a powerful house. She possessed the badge, and unless there was someone to tell she
could possess the power for which it stood.

Hetty Daniels shrilled up: "Mr. Henson's down here to see
you."

Tiresome though his presence was, she almost welcomed
him to-night, and even accepted his eager invitation to go to
see a picture. "It's in a little gem of a theatre, Angela. You'll
like the surroundings almost as much as the picture, and that's
very good. Sawyer and I saw it about two weeks ago. I thought
then that I'd like to take you."

She knew that this was his indirect method of telling her that
they would meet with no difficulty in the matter of admission;
a comforting assurance, for Philadelphia theatres, as Angela
knew, could be very unpleasant to would-be coloured patrons.
Henson offered to telephone for a taxi while she was getting
on her street clothes, and she permitted the unnecessary extravagance, for she hated the conjectures on the faces of passengers in the street cars; conjectures, she felt in her sensitiveness,
which she could only set right by being unusually kind and
friendly in her manner to Henson. And this produced undesirable effects on him. She had gone out with him more often in
the Ford, which permitted a modicum of privacy. But Jinny
was off in the little car to-night.

At Broad and Ridge Avenue the taxi was held up; it was
twenty-five minutes after eight when they reached the theatre.
Matthew gave Angela a bill. "Do you mind getting the tickets
while I settle for the cab?" he asked nervously. He did not
want her to miss even the advertisements. This, he almost
prayed, would be a perfect night.

Cramming the change into his pocket, he rushed into the
lobby and joined Angela who, almost as excited as he, for she
liked a good picture, handed the tickets to the attendant. He

returned the stubs. "All right, good seats there to your left."
The theatre was only one storey. He glanced at Matthew.

"Here, here, where do you think you're going?"

Matthew answered unsuspecting: "It's all right. The young
lady gave you the tickets."

"Yes, but not for you; she can go in, but you can't." He
handed him the torn ticket, turned and took one of the stubs
from Angela, and thrust that in the young man's unwilling
hand. "Go over there and get your refund."

"But," said Matthew and Angela could feel his very manhood sickening under the silly humiliation of the moment,
"there must be some mistake. I sat in this same theatre less
than three weeks ago."

"Well, you won't sit in there to-night; the management's
changed hands since then, and we're not selling tickets to
coloured people." He glanced at Angela a little uncertainly.
"The young lady can come in——"

Angela threw her ticket on the floor. "Oh, come Matthew,
come."

Outside he said stiffly, "I'll get a taxi, we'll go somewhere
else."

"No, no! We wouldn't enjoy it. Let's go home and we don't
need a taxi. We can get the Sixteenth Street car right at the
corner."

She was very kind to him in the car; she was so sorry for
him, suddenly conscious of the pain which must be his at being
stripped before the girl he loved of his masculine right to protect, to appear the hero.

She let him open the two doors for her but stopped him in
the box of a hall. "I think I'll say good-night now, Matthew;
I'm more tired than I realized. But,—but it was an adventure,
wasn't it?"

His eyes adored her, his hand caught hers: "Angela, I'd have
given all I hope to possess to have been able to prevent it;
you know I never dreamed of letting you in for such humiliation. Oh how are we ever going to get this thing straight?"

"Well, it wasn't your fault." Unexpectedly she lifted her delicate face to his, so stricken and freckled and woebegone, and
kissed him; lifted her hand and actually stroked his reddish,
stiff, "bad" hair.

Like a man in a dream he walked down the street wondering how long it would be before they married.

Angela, waking in the middle of the night and reviewing to herself the events of the day, said aloud: "This is the end," and fell asleep again.

The little back room was still Jinny's, but Angela, in order to give the third storey front to Hetty Daniels, had moved into the room which had once been her mother's. She and Virginia had placed the respective head-boards of their narrow, virginal beds against the dividing wall so that they could lie in bed and talk to each other through the communicating door-way, their voices making a circuit from speaker to listener in what Jinny called a hairpin curve.

Angela called in as soon as she heard her sister moving, "Jinny, listen. I'm going away."

Her sister, still half asleep, lay intensely quiet for another second, trying to pick up the continuity of this dream. Then her senses came to her.

"What'd you say, Angela?"

"I said I was going away. I'm going to leave Philadelphia, give up school teaching, break away from our loving friends and acquaintances, and bust up the whole shooting match."

"Haven't gone crazy, have you?"

"No, I think I'm just beginning to come to my senses. I'm sick, sick, sick of seeing what I want dangled right before my eyes and then of having it snatched away from me and all of it through no fault of my own."

"Darling, you know I haven't the faintest idea of what you're driving at."

"Well, I'll tell you." Out came the whole story, an accumulation of the slights, real and fancied, which her colour had engendered throughout her lifetime; though even then she did not tell of that first hurt through Mary Hastings. That would always linger in some remote, impenetrable fastness of her mind, for wounded trust was there as well as wounded pride and love. "And these two last happenings with Matthew and Mr. Shields are just too much; besides they've shown me the way."

"Shown you what way?"

Virginia had arisen and thrown an old rose kimono around her. She had inherited her father's thick and rather coarsely waving black hair, enhanced by her mother's softness. She was slender, yet rounded; her cheeks were flushed with sleep and excitement. Her eyes shone. As she sat in the brilliant wrap, cross-legged at the foot of her sister's narrow bed, she made the latter think of a strikingly dainty, colourful robin.

"Well you see as long as the Shields thought I was white they were willing to help me to all the glories of the promised land. And the doorman last night,—he couldn't tell what I was, but he could tell about Matthew, so he put him out; just as the Shields are getting ready in another way to put me out. But as long as they didn't know it didn't matter. Which means it isn't being coloured that makes the difference, it's letting it be known. Do you see?

"So I've thought and thought. I guess really I've had it in my mind for a long time, but last night it seemed to stand right out in my consciousness. Why should I shut myself off from all the things I want most,—clever people, people who do things, Art,—" her voice spelt it with a capital,—"travel and a lot of things which are in the world for everybody really but which only white people, as far as I can see, get their hands on. I mean scholarships and special funds, patronage. Oh Jinny, you don't know, I don't think you can understand the things I want to see and know. You're not like me——".

"I don't know why I'm not," said Jinny looking more like a robin than ever. Her bright eyes dwelt on her sister. "After all, the same blood flows in my veins and in the same proportion. Sure you're not laying too much stress on something only temporarily inconvenient?"

"But it isn't temporarily inconvenient; it's happening to me every day. And it isn't as though it were something that I could help. Look how Mr. Shields stressed the fact that I hadn't told him I was coloured. And see how it changed his attitude toward me; you can't think how different his manner was. Yet as long as he didn't know, there was nothing he wasn't willing and glad, glad to do for me. Now he might be willing but he'll not be glad though I need his assistance more than some white girl who will find a dozen people to help her just because she is white." Some faint disapproval in her sister's face halted her for

a moment. "What's the matter? You certainly don't think I
ought to say first thing: 'I'm Angela Murray. I know I look white
but I'm coloured and expect to be treated accordingly!' Now
do you?"

"No," said Jinny, "of course that's absurd. Only I don't think
you ought to mind quite so hard when they do find out the
facts. It seems sort of an insult to yourself. And then, too, it
makes you lose a good chance to do something for—for all of
us who can't look like you but who really have the same combination of blood that you have."

"Oh that's some more of your and Matthew Henson's philosophy. Now be practical, Jinny; after all I am both white and
Negro and look white. Why shouldn't I declare for the one
that will bring me the greatest happiness, prosperity and respect?"

"No reason in the world except that since in this country
public opinion is against any infusion of black blood it would
seem an awfully decent thing to put yourself, even in the face
of appearances, on the side of black blood and say: 'Look here,
this is what a mixture of black and white really means!'"

Angela was silent and Virginia, feeling suddenly very young,
almost childish in the presence of this issue, took a turn about
the room. She halted beside her sister.

"Just what is it you want to do, Angela? Evidently you have
some plan."

She had. Her idea was to sell the house and to divide the
proceeds. With her share of this and her half of the insurance
she would go to New York or to Chicago, certainly to some
place where she could by no chance be known, and launch out
"into a freer, fuller life".

"And leave me!" said Jinny astonished. Somehow it had not
dawned on her that the two would actually separate. She did
not know what she had thought, but certainly not that. The
tears ran down her cheeks.

Angela, unable to endure either her own pain or the sight of
it in others, had all of a man's dislike for tears.

"Don't be absurd, Jinny! How could I live the way I want to
if you're with me. We'd keep on loving each other and seeing
one another from time to time, but we might just as well face
the facts. Some of those girls in the art school used to ask me

to their homes; it would have meant opportunity, a broader outlook, but I never dared accept because I knew I couldn't return the invitation."

Under that Jinny winced a little, but she spoke with spirit. "After that, Angela dear, I'm beginning to think that you *have* more white blood in your veins than I, and it was that extra amount which made it possible for you to make that remark." She trailed back to her room and when Hetty Daniels announced breakfast she found that a bad headache required a longer stay in bed.

For many years the memory of those next few weeks lingered in Virginia's mind beside that other tragic memory of her mother's deliberate submission to death. But Angela was almost tremulous with happiness and anticipation. Almost as though by magic her affairs were arranging themselves. She was to have the three thousand dollars and Jinny was to be the sole possessor of the house. Junius had paid far less than this sum for it, but it had undoubtedly increased in value. "It's a fair enough investment for you, Miss Virginia," Mr. Hallowell remarked gruffly. He had disapproved heartily of this summary division, would have disapproved more thoroughly and openly if he had had any idea of the reasons behind it. But the girls had told no one, not even him, of their plans. "Some sisters' quarrel, I suppose," he commented to his wife. "I've never seen any coloured people yet, relatives that is, who could stand the joint possession of a little money."

A late Easter was casting its charm over the city when Angela, trim, even elegant, in her conventional tailored suit, stood in the dining-room of the little house waiting for her taxi. She had burned her bridges behind her, had resigned from school, severed her connection with the Academy, and had permitted an impression to spread that she was going West to visit indefinitely a distant cousin of her mother's. In reality she was going to New York. She had covered her tracks very well, she thought; none of her friends was to see her off; indeed, none of them knew the exact hour of her departure. She was even leaving from the North Philadelphia station so that none of the porters of the main depôt, friends perhaps of the boys who came to her house, and, through some far flung communal instinct familiar to coloured people, acquainted with her by sight, would be able to tell of her going. Jinny, until she heard of this, had meant to accompany her to the station, but Angela's precaution palpably scotched this idea; she made no comment when Virginia announced that it would be impossible for her to see her sister off. An indefinable steeliness was creeping upon them.

Yet when the taxi stood rumbling and snorting outside, Angela, her heart suddenly mounting to her throat, her eyes smarting, put her arm tightly about her sister who clung to her frankly crying. But she only said: "Now, Jinny, there's nothing to cry about. You'll be coming to New York soon. First thing I know you'll be walking up to me: 'Pardon me! Isn't this Mrs. Henrietta Jones?'"

Virginia tried to laugh, "And you'll be saying: 'Really you have the advantage of me.' Oh, Angela, don't leave me!"

The cabby was honking impatiently. "I must, darling. Good-bye, Virginia. You'll hear from me right away."

She ran down the steps, glanced happily back. But her sister had already closed the door.

MARKET

Chapter I

FIFTH AVENUE is a canyon; its towering buildings dwarf the importance of the people hurrying through its narrow confines. But Fourteenth Street is a river, impersonally flowing, broad-bosomed, with strange and devious craft covering its expanse. To Angela the famous avenue seemed but one manifestation of living, but Fourteenth Street was the rendezvous of life itself. Here for those first few weeks after her arrival in New York she wandered, almost prowled, intent upon the jostling shops, the hurrying, pushing people, above all intent upon the faces of those people with their showings of grief, pride, gaiety, greed, joy, ambition, content. There was little enough of this last. These men and women were living at a sharper pitch of intensity than those she had observed in Philadelphia. The few coloured people whom she saw were different too; they possessed an independence of carriage, a purposefulness, an assurance in their manner that pleased her. But she could not see that any of these people, black or white, were any happier than those whom she had observed all her life.

But *she* was happier; she was living on the crest of a wave of excitement and satisfaction which would never wane, never break, never be spent. She was seeing the world, she was getting acquainted with life in her own way without restrictions or restraint; she was young, she was temporarily independent, she was intelligent, she was white. She remembered an expression "free, white and twenty-one",—this was what it meant then, this sense of owning the world, this realization that other things being equal, all things were possible. "If I were a man," she said, "I could be president", and laughed at herself for the "if" itself proclaimed a limitation. But that inconsistency bothered her little; she did not want to be a man. Power, greatness, authority, these were fitting and proper for men; but there were sweeter, more beautiful gifts for women, and power of a

487

certain kind too. Such a power she would like to exert in this
glittering new world, so full of mysteries and promise. If she
could afford it she would have a salon, a drawing-room where
men and women, not necessarily great, but real, alive, free, and
untrammelled in manner and thought, should come and pour
themselves out to her sympathy and magnetism. To accomplish
this she must have money and influence; indeed since she was so
young she would need even protection; perhaps it would be
better to marry . . . a white man. The thought came to her
suddenly out of the void; she had never thought of this possibility before. If she were to do this, do it suitably, then all that
richness, all that fullness of life which she so ardently craved
would be doubly hers. She knew that men had a better time of
it than women, coloured men than coloured women, white men
than white women. Not that she envied them. Only it would
be fun, great fun to capture power and protection in addition
to the freedom and independence which she had so long coveted and which now lay in her hand.

But, she smiled to herself, she had no way of approaching
these ends. She knew no one in New York; she could conceive
of no manner in which she was likely to form desirable acquaintances; at present her home consisted of the four walls of
the smallest room in Union Square Hotel. She had gone there
the second day after her arrival, having spent an expensive twenty-
four hours at the Astor. Later she came to realize that there
were infinitely cheaper habitations to be had, but she could
not tear herself away from Fourteenth Street. It was Spring,
and the Square was full of rusty specimens of mankind who sat
on the benches, as did Angela herself, for hours at a stretch, as
though they thought the invigorating air and the mellow sun
would work some magical burgeoning on their garments such
as was worked on the trees. But though these latter changed,
the garments changed not nor did their owners. They remained
the same, drooping, discouraged down and outers. "I am seeing life," thought Angela, "this is the way people live," and
never realized that some of these people looking curiously,
speculatively at her wondered what had been her portion to
bring her thus early to this unsavoury company.

"A great picture!" she thought. "I'll make a great picture of
these people some day and call them 'Fourteenth Street types'."

And suddenly a vast sadness invaded her; she wondered if there were people more alive, more sentient to the joy, the adventure of living, even than she, to whom she would also be a "type". But she could not believe this. She was at once almost irreconcilably too concentrated and too objective. Her living during these days was so intense, so almost solidified, as though her desire to live as she did and she herself were so one and the same thing that it would have been practically impossible for another onlooker like herself to insert the point of his discrimination into her firm panoply of satisfaction. So she continued to browse along her chosen thoroughfare, stopping most often in the Square or before a piano store on the same street. There was in this shop a player-piano which was usually in action, and as the front glass had been removed the increased clearness of the strains brought a steady, patient, apparently insatiable group of listeners to a standstill. They were mostly men, and as they were far less given, Angela observed, to concealing their feelings than women, it was easy to follow their emotional gamut. Jazz made them smile but with a certain wistfulness—if only they had time for dancing now, just now when the mood was on them! The young woman looking at the gathering of shabby pedestrians, worn business men and ruminative errand boys felt for them a pity not untinged with satisfaction. *She* had taken what she wanted while the mood was on her. Love songs, particularly those of the sorrowful ballad variety brought to these unmindful faces a strained regret. But there was one expression which Angela could only half interpret. It drifted on to those listening countenances usually at the playing of old Irish and Scottish tunes. She noticed then an acuter attitude of attention, the eyes took on a look of inwardness of utter remoteness. A passer-by engrossed in thought caught a strain and at once his gait and expression fell under the spell. The listeners might be as varied as fifteen people may be, yet for the moment they would be caught in a common, almost cosmic nostalgia. If the next piece were jazz, that particular crowd would disperse, its members going on their meditative ways, blessed or cursed with heaven knew what memories which must not be disturbed by the strident jangling of the latest popular song.

"Homesick," Angela used to say to herself. And she would feel so, too, though she hardly knew for what,—certainly not

for Philadelphia and that other life which now seemed so removed as to have been impossible. And she made notes in her
sketch book to enable her some day to make a great picture of
these "types" too.

Of course she was being unconscionably idle; but as her days
were filled to overflowing with the impact of new impressions,
this signified nothing. She could not guess what life would
bring her. For the moment it seemed to her both wise and
amusing to sit with idle hands and see what would happen. By
a not inexplicable turn of mind she took to going very frequently to the cinema where most things did happen. She
found herself studying the screen with a strained and ardent
intensity, losing the slight patronizing scepticism which had
once been hers with regard to the adventures of these shadowy
heroes and heroines; so utterly unforeseen a turn had her own
experiences taken. This time last year she had never dreamed
of, had hardly dared to long for a life as free and as full as hers
was now and was promising to be. Yet here she was on the
threshhold of a career totally different from anything that a
scenario writer could envisage. Oh yes, she knew that hundreds, indeed thousands of white coloured people "went over
to the other side", but that was just the point, she knew the
fact without knowing hitherto any of the possibilities of the
adventure. Already Philadelphia and her trials were receding
into the distance. Would these people, she wondered, glancing
about her in the soft gloom of the beautiful theatre, begrudge
her, if they knew, her cherished freedom and sense of unre-
straint? If she were to say to this next woman for instance,
"I'm coloured," would she show the occasional dog-in-the-
manger attitude of certain white Americans and refuse to sit by
her or make a complaint to the usher? But she had no intention of making such an announcement. So she spent many
happy, irresponsible, amused hours in the marvellous houses
on Broadway or in the dark commonplaceness of her beloved
Fourteenth Street. There was a theatre, too, on Seventh Avenue
just at the edge of the Village, which she came to frequent, not
so much for the sake of the plays, which were the same as elsewhere, as for the sake of the audience, a curiously intimate sort
of audience made of numerous still more intimate groups.

Their members seemed both purposeful and leisurely. When she came here her loneliness palled on her, however. All unaware her face took on the wistfulness of the men gazing in the music store. She wished she knew some of these pleasant people.

It came to her that she was neglecting her Art. "And it was for that that I broke away from everything and came to New York. I must hunt up some classes." This she felt was not quite true, then the real cause rushed up to the surface of her mind: "And perhaps I'll meet some people."

She enrolled in one of the art classes in Cooper Union. This, after all, she felt would be the real beginning of her adventure. For here she must make acquaintances and one of them, perhaps several, must produce some effect on her life, perhaps alter its whole tenor. And for the first time she would be seen, would be met against her new background or rather, against no background. No boyish stowaway on a ship had a greater exuberance in going forth to meet the unknown than had Angela as she entered her class that first afternoon. In the room were five people, working steadily and chatting in an extremely desultory way. The instructor, one of the five, motioned her to a seat whose position made her one of the group. He set up her easel and as she arranged her material she glanced shyly but keenly about her. For the first time she realized how lonely she had been. She thought with a joy which surprised herself: "Within a week I'll be chatting with them too; perhaps going to lunch or to tea with one of them." She arranged herself for a better view. The young woman nearest her, the possessor of a great mop of tawny hair and smiling clear, slate-grey eyes glanced up at her and nodded, "Am I in your way?" Except for her hair and eyes she was nondescript. A little beyond sat a coloured girl of medium height and build, very dark, very clean, very reserved. Angela, studying her with inner secret knowledge, could feel her constantly withdrawn from her companions. Her refinement was conspicuous but her reserve more so; when asked she passed and received erasers and other articles but she herself did no borrowing nor did she initiate any conversation. Her squarish head capped with a mass of unnaturally straight and unnaturally burnished hair possessed a kind of

ugly beauty. Angela could not tell whether her features were
good but blurred and blunted by the soft night of her skin or
really ugly with an ugliness lost and plunged in that skin's deep
concealment. Two students were still slightly behind her. She
wondered how she could best contrive to see them.

Someone said: "Hi, there! Miss New One, have *you* got a
decent eraser? all mine are on the blink." Not so sure whether
or not the term applied to herself she turned to meet the
singularly intent gaze of a slender girl with blue eyes, light
chestnut hair and cheeks fairly blazing with some unguessed
excitement. Angela smiled and offered her eraser.

"It ought to be decent, it's new."

"Yes, it's a very good one; many thanks. I'll try not to trouble
you again. My name's Paulette Lister, what's yours?"

"Angèle Mory." She had changed it thus slightly when she
came to New York. Some troubling sense of loyalty to her father and mother had made it impossible for her to do away
with it altogether.

"Mory," said a young man who had been working just
beyond Paulette; "that's Spanish. Are you by any chance?"

"I don't think so."

"He is," said Paulette. "His name is Anthony Cruz—isn't that
a lovely name? But he changed it to Cross because no American
would ever pronounce the z right, and he didn't want to be
taken for a widow's cruse."

"That's a shameful joke," said Cross, "but since I made it
up, I think you might give me a chance to spring it, Miss Lister.
A poor thing but mine own. You might have a heart."

"Get even with her, why don't you, by introducing her as
Miss Blister?" asked Angela, highly diverted by the foolish
talk.

Several people came in then, and she discovered that she
had been half an hour too early, the class was just beginning.
She glanced about at the newcomers, a beautiful Jewess with a
pearly skin and a head positively foaming with curls, a tall
Scandinavian, an obvious German, several more Americans.
Not one of them made the photograph on her mind equal to
those made by the coloured girl whose name, she learned, was
Rachel Powell, the slate-eyed Martha Burden, Paulette Lister

and Anthony Cross. Her prediction came true. With in a week she was on jestingly intimate terms with every one of them except Miss Powell, who lent her belongings, borrowed nothing, and spoke only when she was spoken to. At the end of ten days Miss Burden asked Angela to come and have lunch "at the same place where I go".

On an exquisite afternoon she went to Harlem. At One Hundred and Thirty-fifth Street she left the 'bus and walked through from Seventh Avenue to Lenox, then up to One Hundred and Forty-seventh Street and back down Seventh Avenue to One Hundred and Thirty-ninth Street, through this to Eighth Avenue and then weaving back and forth between the two Avenues through Thirty-eighth, Thirty-seventh down to One Hundred and Thirty-fifth Street to Eighth Avenue where she took the Elevated and went back to the New York which she knew.

But she was amazed and impressed at this bustling, frolicking, busy, laughing great city within a greater one. She had never seen coloured life so thick, so varied, so complete. Moreover, just as this city reproduced in microcosm all the important features of any metropolis, so undoubtedly life up here was just the same, she thought dimly, as life anywhere else. Not all these people, she realized, glancing keenly at the throngs of black and brown, yellow and white faces about her were servants or underlings or end men. She saw a beautiful woman all brown and red dressed as exquisitely as anyone she had seen on Fifth Avenue. A man's sharp, high-bred face etched itself on her memory,—the face of a professional man perhaps, —it might be an artist. She doubted that; he might of course be a musician, but it was unlikely that he would be her kind of an artist, for how could he exist? Ah, there lay the great difference. In all material, even in all practical things these two worlds were alike, but in the production, the fostering of those ultimate manifestations, this world was lacking, for its people were without the means or the leisure to support them and enjoy. And these were the manifestations which she craved, together with the freedom to enjoy them. No, she was not sorry that she had chosen as she had, even though she could now realize that life viewed from the angle of Opal and Jefferson

Streets in Philadelphia and that same life viewed from One
Hundred and Thirty-fifth Street and Seventh Avenue in New
York might present bewilderingly different facets.

Unquestionably there was something very fascinating, even
terrible, about this stream of life,—it seemed to her to run
thicker, more turgidly than that safe, sublimated existence in
which her new friends had their being. It was deeper, more
mightily moving even than the torrent of Fourteenth Street.
Undoubtedly just as these people,—for she already saw them
objectively, doubly so, once with her natural remoteness and
once with the remoteness of her new estate,—just as these
people could suffer more than others, just so they could enjoy
themselves more. She watched the moiling groups on Lenox
Avenue; the amazingly well-dressed and good-looking throngs
of young men on Seventh Avenue at One Hundred and Thirty-
seventh and Thirty-fifth Streets. They were gossiping, laughing, dickering, chaffing, combining the customs of the small
town with the astonishing cosmopolitanism of their clothes
and manners. Nowhere down town did she see life like this.
Oh, all this was fuller, richer, not finer but richer with the difference in quality that there is between velvet and silk. Harlem
was a great city, but after all it was a city within a city, and she
was glad, as she strained for last glimpses out of the lurching
"L" train, that she had cast in her lot with the dwellers outside
its dark and serried tents.

Chapter II

"WHERE do you live?" asked Paulette, "when you're not here at school?"

Angela blushed as she told her.

"In a hotel? In Union Square? Child, are you a millionaire? Where did you come from? Don't you care anything about the delights of home? Mr. Cross, come closer. Here is this poor child living benightedly in a hotel when she might have two rooms at least in the Village for almost the same price."

Mr. Cross came closer but without saying anything. He was really, Angela thought, a very serious, almost sad young man. He had never continued long the bantering line with which he had first made her acquaintance.

She explained that she had not known where to go. "Often I've thought of moving, and of course I'm spending too much money for what I get out of it,—I've the littlest room."

Paulette opened her eyes very wide which gave an onlooker the effect of seeing suddenly the blue sky very close at hand. Her cheeks took on a flaming tint. She was really a beautiful, even fascinating girl—or woman,—Angela never learned which, for she never knew her age. But her fascination did not rest on her looks, or at least it did not arise from that source; it was more the result of her manner. She was so alive, so intense, so interested, if she were interested, that all her nerves, her emotions even were enlisted to accomplish the end which she might have in view. And withal she possessed the simplicity of a child. There was an unsuspected strength about her also that was oddly at variance with the rather striking fragility of her appearance, the trustingness of her gaze, the limpid unaffectedness of her manner. Mr. Cross, Angela thought negligently, must be in love with her; he was usually at her side when they sketched. But later she came to see that there was nothing at all between these two except a certain friendly appreciation tempered by a wary kindness on the part of Mr. Cross and a negligent generosity on the part of Paulette.

She displayed no negligence of generosity in her desire and

eagerness to find Angela a suitable apartment. She did hold
out, however, with amazing frankness for one "not too near
me but also not too far away". But this pleased the girl, for she
had been afraid that Paulette would insist on offering to share
her own apartment and she would not have known how to refuse. She had the complete egoist's desire for solitude.

Paulette lived on Bank Street; she found for her new friend
"a duck,—just a duck,—no other word will describe it,—of an
apartment" on Jayne Street, two rooms, bath and kitchenette.
There was also a tiny balcony giving on a mews. It was more
than Angela should have afforded, but the ease with which her
affairs were working out gave her an assurance, almost an arrogance of confidence. Besides she planned to save by getting
her own meals. The place was already furnished, its former occupant was preparing to go to London for two or more years.

"Two years," Angela said gaily, "everything in the world can
happen to me in that time. Oh I wonder what will have happened; what I will be like!" And she prepared to move in her
slender store of possessions. Anthony, prompted, she suspected
by Paulette, offered rather shyly to help her. It was a rainy day,
there were several boxes after all, and taxis were scarce, though
finally he captured one for her and came riding back in triumph
with the driver. Afterwards a few books had to be arranged,
pictures must be hung. She had an inspiration.

"You tend to all this and I'll get you the best dinner you ever
tasted in your life." Memories of Monday night dinners on
Opal Street flooded her memory. She served homely, filling
dishes, "fit for a drayman," she teased him. There were corn-
beef hash, roasted sweet potatoes, corn pudding, and, regardless of the hour, muffins. After supper she refused to let him
help her with the dishes but had him rest in the big chair in the
living-room while she laughed and talked with him from
the kitchenette at a distance of two yards. Gradually, as he sat
there smoking, the sadness and strain faded out of his thin,
dark face, he laughed and jested like any other normal young
man. When he bade her good-bye he let his slow dark gaze
rest in hers for a long silent moment. She closed the door and
stood laughing, arranging her hair before the mirror.

"Of course he's loads better looking, but something about
him makes me think of Matthew Henson. But nothing doing,

young-fellow-me-lad. Spanish and I suppose terribly proud. I wonder what he'd say if he really knew?"

She was to go to Paulette's to dinner. "Just we two," stipulated Miss Lister. "Of course, I could have a gang of men, but I think it will be fun for us to get acquainted." Angela was pleased; she was very fond of Paulette, she liked for her generous, capable self. And she was not quite ready for meeting men. She must know something more about these people with whom she was spending her life. Anthony Cross had been affable enough, but she was not sure that he, with his curious sadness, his half-proud, half-sensitive tendency to withdrawal, were a fair enough type. However, in spite of Paulette's protestations, there were three young men standing in her large, dark living-room when Angela arrived.

"But you've got to go at once," said Paulette, laughing but firm; "here is my friend,—isn't she beautiful? We've too many things to discuss without being bothered by you."

"Paulette has these fits of cruelty," said one of the three, a short, stocky fellow with an ugly, sensitive face. "She'd have made a good Nero. But anyway I'm glad I stayed long enough to see you. Don't let her hide you from us altogether." Another man made a civil remark; the third one standing back in the gloomy room said nothing, but the girl caught the impression of tallness and blondness and of a pair of blue eyes which stared at her intently. She felt awkward and showed it.

"See, you've made her shy," said Paulette accusingly. "I won't bother introducing them, Angèle, you'll meet them all too soon." Laughing, protesting, the men filed out, and their unwilling hostess closed the door on them with sincere lack of regret. "Men," she mused candidly. "Of course we can't get along without them any more than they can without us, but I get tired of them,—they're nearly all animals. I'd rather have a good woman friend any day." She sighed with genuine sincerity. "Yet my place is always full of men. Would you rather have your chops rare or well done? I like mine cooked to a cinder." Angela preferred hers well done. "Stay here and look around; see if I have anything to amuse you." Catching up an apron she vanished into some smaller and darker retreat which she called her kitchen.

The apartment consisted of the whole floor of a house on Bank Street, dark and constantly within the sound of the opening front door and the noises of the street. "But you don't have the damned stairs when you come in late at night," Paulette explained. The front room was, Angela supposed, the bedroom, though the only reason for this supposition was the appearance of a dressing-table and a wide, flat divan about one foot and a half from the floor, covered with black or purple velvet. The dressing table was a good piece of mahogany, but the chairs were indifferently of the kitchen variety and of the sort which, magazines affirm, may be made out of a large packing box. In the living room, where the little table was set, the same anomaly prevailed; the china was fine, even dainty, but the glasses were thick and the plating had begun to wear off the silver ware. On the other hand the pictures were unusual, none of the stereotyped things; instead Angela remarked a good copy of Breughel's "Peasant Wedding", the head of Bernini and two etchings whose authors she did not know. The bookcase held two paper bound volumes of the poems of Béranger and Villon and a little black worn copy of Heine. But the other books were high-brow to the point of austerity: Ely, Shaw and Strindberg.

"Perhaps you'd like to wash your hands?" called Paulette. "There's a bathroom down the corridor there, you can't miss it. You may have some of my favourite lotion if you want it—up there on the shelf." Angela washed her hands and looked up for the lotion. Her eyes opened wide in amazement. Beside the bottle stood a man's shaving mug and brush and a case of razors.

The meal, "for you can't call it a dinner," the cook remarked candidly, was a success. The chops were tender though smoky; there were spinach, potatoes, tomato and lettuce salad, rolls, coffee and cheese. Its rugged quality surprised Angela not a little; it was more a meal for a working man than for a woman, above all, a woman of the faery quality of Paulette. "I get so tired," she said, lifting a huge mouthful, "if I don't eat heartily; besides it ruins my temper to go hungry." Her whole attitude toward the meal was so masculine and her appearance so daintily feminine that Angela burst out laughing, explaining with much amusement the cause of her merriment. "I hope you don't mind," she ended, "for of course you are conspicuously feminine. There's nothing of the man about you."

To her surprise Paulette resented this last statement. "There is a great deal of the man about me. I've learned that a woman is a fool who lets her femininity stand in the way of what she wants. I've made a philosophy of it. I see what I want; I use my wiles as a woman to get it, and I employ the qualities of men, tenacity and ruthlessness, to keep it. And when I'm through with it, I throw it away just as they do. Consequently I have no regrets and no encumbrances."

A packet of cigarettes lay open on the table and she motioned to her friend to have one. Angela refused, and sat watching her inhale in deep respirations; she had never seen a woman more completely at ease, more assuredly mistress of herself and of her fate. When they had begun eating Paulette had poured out two cocktails, tossing hers off immediately and finishing Angela's, too, when the latter, finding it too much like machine oil for her taste, had set it down scarcely diminished. "You'll get used to them if you go about with these men. You'll be drinking along with the rest of us."

She had practically no curiosity and on the other hand no reticences. And she had met with every conceivable experience, had visited France, Germany and Sweden; she was now contemplating a trip to Italy and might go to Russia; she would go now, in fact, if it were not that a friend of hers, Jack Hudson, was about to go there, too, and as she was on the verge of having an affair with him she thought she'd better wait. She didn't relish the prospect of such an event in a foreign land, it put you too much at the man's mercy. An affair, if you were going to have one, was much better conducted on your own *pied à terre*.

"An affair?" gasped Angela.

"Yes,—why, haven't you ever had a lover?"

"A lover?"

"Goodness me, are you a poll parrot? Why yes, a lover. I've had"—she hesitated before the other's complete amazement, —"I've had more than one, I can tell you."

"And you've no intention of marrying?"

"Oh I don't say that; but what's the use of tying yourself up now while you're young? And then, too, this way you don't always have them around your feet; you can always leave them or they'll leave you. But it's better for you to leave them first. It insures your pride." With her babyish face and her sweet, high voice she was like a child babbling precociously. Yet she seemed bathed in intensity. But later she began to talk of her books and of her pictures, of her work and on all these subjects she spoke with the same subdued excitement; her eyes flashed, her cheeks grew scarlet, all experience meant life to her in various manifestations. She had been on a newspaper, one of the New York dailies; she had done press-agenting. At present she was illustrating for a fashion magazine. There was no end to her versatilities.

Angela said she must go.

"But you'll come again soon, won't you, Angèle?"

A wistfulness crept into her voice. "I do so want a woman friend. When a woman really is your friend she's so dependable and she's not expecting anything in return." She saw her guest to the door. "We could have some wonderful times. Good-night, Angèle." Like a child she lifted her face to be kissed.

Angela's first thought as she walked down the dark street was for the unfamiliar name by which Paulette had called her. For though she had signed herself very often as Angèle, no one as yet used it. Her old familiar formula came to her: "I wonder what she would think if she knew." But of one thing she was sure: if Paulette had been in her place she would have acted in exactly the same way. "She would have seen what she wanted and would have taken it," she murmured and fell to thinking of the various confidences which Paulette had bestowed upon her,—though so frank and unreserved were her remarks that "confidences" was hardly the name to apply to them. Certainly, Angela thought, she was in a new world and with new people. Beyond question some of the coloured people of her acquaintance must have lived in a manner which would not bear inspection, but she could not think of one who would thus have discussed it calmly with either friend or stranger. Wondering what it would be like to conduct oneself absolutely according to one's own laws, she turned into the dark little vestibule on Jayne Street. As usual the Jewish girl who lived above her was standing blurred in the thick blackness of the hall, and as usual Angela did not realize this until, touching the button and turning on the light, she caught sight of Miss Salting straining her face upwards to receive her lover's kiss.

Chapter III

From the pinnacle of her satisfaction in her studies, in her new friends and in the joke which she was having upon custom and tradition she looked across the class-room at Miss Powell who preserved her attitude of dignified reserve. Angela thought she would try to break it down; on Wednesday she asked the coloured girl to have lunch with her and was pleased to have the invitation accepted. She had no intention of taking the girl up as a matter either of patronage or of loyalty. But she thought it would be nice to offer her the ordinary amenities which their common student life made natural and possible. Miss Powell it appeared ate generally in an Automat or in a cafeteria, but Angela knew of a nice tea-room. "It's rather arty, but they do serve a good meal and it's cheap." Unfortunately on Wednesday she had to leave before noon; she told Miss Powell to meet her at the little restaurant. "Go in and get a table and wait for me, but I'm sure I'll be there as soon as you will." After all she was late, but, what was worse, she found to her dismay that Miss Powell, instead of entering the tea-room, had been awaiting her across the street. There were no tables and the two had to wait almost fifteen minutes before being served.

"Why on earth didn't you go in?" asked Angela a trifle impatiently, "you could have held the table." Miss Powell answered imperturbably: "Because I didn't know how they would receive me if I went in by myself." Angela could not pretend to misunderstand her. "Oh, I think they would have been all right," she murmured blushing at her stupidity. How quickly she had forgotten those fears and uncertainties. She had never experienced this sort of difficulty herself, but the certainly knew of them from Virginia and others.

The lunch was not a particularly pleasant one. Either Miss Powell was actually dull or she had made a resolve never to let herself go in the presence of white people; perhaps she feared being misunderstood, perhaps she saw in such encounters a lurking attempt at sociological investigations; she would lend herself to no such procedure, that much was plain. Angela could feel her effort to charm, to invite confidence, glance upon and fall back from this impenetrable armour. She had been amazed to find both Paulette and Martha Burden already gaining their living by their sketches. Miss Burden indeed was a caricaturist of no mean local reputation; Anthony Cross was frankly a commercial artist, though he hoped some day to be a recognised painter of portraits. She was curious to learn of Miss Powell's prospects. Inquiry revealed that the young lady had one secret aspiration; to win or earn enough money to go to France and then after that, she said with sudden ardour, "anything could happen". To this end she had worked, saved, scraped, gone without pleasures and clothes. Her work was creditable, indeed above the average, but not sufficiently imbued, Angela thought, with the divine promise to warrant this sublimation of normal desires.

Miss Powell seemed to read her thought. "And then it gives me a chance to show America that one of us can stick; that we have some idea above the ordinary humdrum of existence."

She made no attempt to return the luncheon but she sent Angela one day a bunch of beautiful jonquils,—and made no further attempt at friendship. To one versed in the psychology of this proud, sensitive people the reason was perfectly plain. "You've been awfully nice to me and I appreciate it but don't think I'm going to thrust myself upon you. Your ways and mine lie along different paths."

Such contacts, such interpretations and investigations were making up her life, a life that for her was interesting and absorbing, but which had its perils and uncertainties. She had no purpose, for it was absurd for her, even with her ability, to consider Art an end. She was using it now deliberately, as she had always used it vaguely, to get in touch with interesting people and with a more attractive atmosphere. And she was spending money too fast; she had been in New York eight months, and she had already spent a thousand dollars. At this rate her little fortune which had seemed at first inexhaustible would last her less than two years; at best, eighteen months more. Then she must face,—what? Teaching again? Never, she'd had enough of that. Perhaps she could earn her living with her brush, doing menu cards, Christmas and birthday greetings, flowers,

Pierrots and Pierrettes on satin pillow tops. She did not relish that. True there were the specialities of Paulette and of Martha Burden, but she lacked the deft sureness of the one and the slightly mordant philosophy underlying the work of the other. Her own speciality she felt sure lay along the line of reproducing, of interpreting on a face the emotion which lay back of that expression. She thought of her Fourteenth Street "types", —that would be the sort of work which she would really enjoy, that and the depicting of the countenance of a purse-proud but lonely man, of the silken inanity of a society girl, of the smiling despair of a harlot. Even in her own mind she hesitated before the use of that terrible word, but association was teaching her to call a spade a spade.

Yes, she might do worse than follow the example of Mr. Cross and become a portrait painter. But somehow she did not want to have to do this; necessity would, she was sure, spoil her touch; besides, she hated the idea of the position in which she would be placed, fearfully placating and flattering possible patrons, hurrying through with an order because she needed the cheque, accepting patronage and condescension. No, she hoped to be sought after, to have the circumstances which would permit her to pick and choose, to refuse if the whim pleased her. It should mean something to be painted by "Mory". People would say, "I'm going to have my portrait done by 'Mory'". But all this would call for position, power, wealth. And again she said to herself . . . "I might marry—a white man. Marriage is the easiest way for a woman to get those things, and white men have them." But she knew only one white man, Anthony Cross, and he would never have those qualities, at feast not by his deliberate seeking. They might come eventually but only after long years. Long, long years of struggle with realities. There was a simple, genuine steadfastness in him that made her realize that he would seek for the expression of truth and of himself even at the cost of the trimmings of life. And she was ashamed, for she knew that for the vanities and gewgaws of a leisurely and irresponsible existence she would sacrifice her own talent, the integrity of her ability to interpret life, to write down a history with her brush.

*

Martha Burden was as strong and as pronounced a personage as Paulette; even stronger perhaps because she had the great gift of silence. Paulette, as Angela soon realized, lived in a state of constant defiance. "I don't care what people think," was her slogan; men and women appealed to her in proportion to the opposition which they, too, proclaimed for the established thing. Angela was surprised that she clung as persistently as she did to a friendship with a person as conventional and reactionary as herself. But Martha Burden was not like that. One could not tell whether or not she was thinking about other people's opinions. It was probable that the other people and their attitude never entered her mind. She was cool and slightly aloof, with the coolness and aloofness of her slaty eyes and her thick, tawny hair. Neither the slatiness nor the tawniness proclaimed warmth—only depth, depth and again depth. It was impossible to realize what she would be like if impassioned or deeply stirred to anger. There would probably be something implacable, god-like about her; she would be capable of a long, slow, steady burning of passion. Few men would love Martha though many might admire her. But a man once enchanted might easily die for her.

Angela liked her house with its simple elegance, its fine, soft curtains and steady, shaded glow of light that stood somehow for home. She liked her husband, Ladislas Starr, whom Martha produced without a shade of consciousness that this was the first intimation she had given of being married. They were strong individualists, molten and blended in a design which failed to obscure their emphatic personalities. Their apartment in the Village was large and neat and sunny; it bore no trace of palpable wealth, yet nothing conducing to comfort was lacking. Book-cases in the dining-room and living-room spilled over; the *Nation*, the *Mercury*, the *Crisis, a magazine of the darker races*, left on the broad arm of an easy chair, mutely invited; it was late autumn, almost winter, but there were jars of fresh flowers. The bedroom where Angela went to remove her wrap was dainty and restful.

The little gathering to which Martha had invited her was made up of members as strongly individual as the host and hostess. They were all specialists in their way, and specialists for the most part in some offshoot of a calling or movement which was itself already highly specialized. Martha presented a psychiatrist, a war correspondent,—"I'm that only when there is a war of course," he explained to Angela's openly respectful gaze, —a dramatist, a corporation lawyer, a white-faced, conspicuously beautiful poet with a long evasive Russian name, two press agents, a theatrical manager, an actress who played only Shakespeare rôles, a teacher of defective children and a medical student who had been a conscientious objector and had served a long time at Leavenworth. He lapsed constantly into a rapt self-communing from which he only roused himself to utter fiery tirades against the evils of society.

In spite of their highly specialised interests they were all possessed of a common ground of knowledge in which such subjects as Russia, Consumers' Leagues, and the coming presidential election figured most largely. There was much laughter and chaffing but no airiness, no persiflage. One of the press agents, Mrs. Cecil, entered upon a long discussion with the corporation lawyer on a Bill pending before Congress; she knew as much as he about the matter and held her own in a long and almost bitter argument which only the coming of refreshments broke up.

Just before the close of the argument two other young men had come in, but Angela never learned their vocation. Furthermore she was interested in observing the young teacher of defective children. She was coloured; small and well-built, exquisitely dressed, and of a beautiful tint, all bronze and soft red, "like Jinny" thought Angela, a little astonished to observe how the warmth of her appearance overshadowed or rather overshone everyone else in the room. The tawniness even of Miss Burden's hair went dead beside her. The only thing to cope with her richness was the classical beauty of the Russian poet's features. He seemed unable to keep his eyes away from her; was punctiliously attentive to her wants and leaned forward several times during the long political discussion to whisper low spoken and apparently amusing comments. The young woman, perfectly at ease in her deep chair, received his attentions with a slightly detached, amused objectivity; an objectivity which she had for everyone in the room including Angela at whom she had glanced once rather sharply. But the detachment of her manner was totally different from Miss Powell's sensitive dignity. Totally without self-consciousness she let her warm dark eyes travel from one face to another. She might have been saying: "How far you are away from the things that really matter, birth and death and hard, hard work!" The Russian poet must have realized this, for once Angela heard him say, leaning forward, "*You* think all this is futile, don't you?"

Martha motioned for her to wait a moment until most of the other guests had gone, then she came forward with one of the two young men who had come in without introduction. "This is Roger Fielding, he'll see you home."

He was tall and blond with deeply blue eyes which smiled on her as he said: "Would you like to walk or ride? It's raining a little."

Angela said she preferred to walk.

"All right then. Here, Starr, come across with that umbrella I lent you."

They went out into the thin, tingling rain of late Autumn. "I was surprised," said Roger, "to see you there with the high-brows. I didn't think you looked that way when I met you at Paulette's."

"We've met before? I'm—I'm sorry, but I don't seem to re-member you."

"No I don't suppose you would. Well, we didn't exactly meet; I saw you one day at Paulette's. That's why I came this evening, because I heard you'd be here and I'd get a chance to see you again; but I was surprised because you didn't seem like that mouthy bunch. They make me tired taking life so plaguey seriously. Martha and her old high-brows!" he ended ungratefully.

Angela, a little taken back with the frankness of his desire to meet her, said she hadn't thought they were serious.

"Not think them serious? Great Scott! what kind of talk are you used to? You look as though you'd just come out of a Sunday-school! Do you prefer bible texts?"

But she could not explain to him the picture which she saw in her mind of men and women at her father's home in Opal Street,—the men talking painfully of rents, of lynchings, of building and loan associations; the women of child-bearing and the sacrifices which must be made to put Gertie through school, to educate Howard. "I don't mean for any of my children to go through what I did." And in later years in her own first maturity, young Henson and Sawyer and the others in the tiny parlour talking of ideals and inevitable sacrifices for the race; the burnt-offering of individualism for some dimly glimpsed racial whole. This was seriousness, even sombreness, with a great sickening vital upthrust of reality. But these other topics, peaks of civilization superimposed upon peaks, she found, even though interesting, utterly futile.

They had reached the little hall now. "We must talk loud," she whispered.

"Why?" he asked, speaking obediently very loud indeed.

"Wait a minute; no, she's not there. The girl above me meets her young man here at night and just as sure as I forget her and come in quietly there they are in the midst of a kiss. I suspect she hates me."

In his young male sophistication he thought at first that this was a lead, but her air was so gay and so childishly guileless that he changed his opinion. "Though no girl in this day and time could be as simple and innocent as *she* looks."

But aloud he said, "Of course she doesn't hate you, nobody could do that. I assure you I don't."

She thought his gallantries very amusing. "Well, it relieves me to hear you say so; that'll keep me from worrying for one night at least." And withdrawing her hand from his retaining grasp, she ran upstairs.

A letter from Virginia lay inside the door. Getting ready for bed she read it in bits.

"Angela darling, wouldn't it be fun if I were to come to New York too? Of course you'd keep on living in your Village and I'd live in famous Harlem, but we'd both be in the same city, which is where two only sisters ought to be,—dumb I calls it to live apart the way we do. The man out at the U. of P. is crazy to have me take an exam. in music; it would be easy enough and much better pay than I get here. So there are two perfectly good reasons why I should come. He thinks I'll do him credit and I want to get away from this town."

Then between the lines the real reason betrayed itself:

"I do have such awful luck. Edna Brown had a party out in Merion not long ago and Matthew took me. And you know what riding in a train can do for me,—well that night of all nights I had to become car-sick. Matthew had been so nice. He came to see me the next morning, but, child, he's never been near me from that day to this. I suppose a man can't get over a girl's being such a sight as I was that night. Can't things be too hateful!"

Angela couldn't help murmuring: "Imagine anyone wanting old Matthew so badly that she's willing to break up her home to get over him. Now why couldn't he have liked her instead of me?"

And pondering on such mysteries she crept into bed. But she fell to thinking again about the evening she had spent with Martha and the people whom she had met. And again it seemed to her that they represented an almost alarmingly unnecessary class. If any great social cataclysm were to happen they would surely be the first to be swept out of the running. Only the real people could survive. Even Paulette's mode of living, it seemed to her, had something more forthright and vital.

Chapter IV

I N the morning she was awakened by the ringing of the tele-phone. The instrument was an extravagance, for, save for Anthony's, she received few calls and made practically none. But the woman from whom she had taken the apartment had persuaded her into keeping it. Still, as she had never indicted the change in ownership, its value was small. She lay there for a moment blinking drowsily in the thin but intensely gold sun-shine of December thinking that her ears were deceiving her.

Finally she reached out a rosy arm, curled it about the edge of the door jamb and, reaching the little table that stood in the other room just on the other side of the door, set the instrument up in her bed. The apartment was so small that almost every-thing was within arm's reach.

"Hello," she murmured sleepily.

"Oh, I thought you must be there; I said to myself: 'She couldn't have left home this early'. What time do you go to that famous drawing class of yours anyway?"

"I beg your pardon! Who is this speaking, please?"

"Why, Roger, of course,—Roger Fielding. Don't say you've forgotten me already. This is Angèle, isn't it?"

"Yes this is Angèle Mory speaking, Mr. Fielding."

"Did I offend your Highness, Miss Mory? Will you have lunch with me to-day and let me tell you how sorry I am?"

But she was lunching with Anthony. "I have an engagement."

"Of course you have. Well, will you have tea, dinner, supper to-day,—breakfast and all the other meals to-morrow and so on for a week? You might just as well say 'yes' because I'll pes-ter you till you do."

"I'm engaged for tea, too, but I'm not really as popular as I sound. That's my last engagement for this week; I'll be glad to have dinner with you."

"Right-oh! Now don't go back and finish up that beauty sleep, for if you're any more charming than you were last night I won't answer for myself. I'll be there at eight."

Inexperienced as she was, she was still able to recognize his method as a bit florid; she preferred, on the whole, Anthony's manner at lunch when he leaned forward and touching her hand very lightly said: "Isn't it great for us to be here! I'm so content, Angèle. Promise me you'll have lunch with me every day this week. I've had a streak of luck with my drawings."

She promised him, a little thrilled herself with his evident sincerity and with the niceness of the smile which so transfigured his dark, thin face, robbing it of its tenseness and strain.

Still something, some vanity, some vague premonition of adventure, led her to linger over her dressing for the dinner with Roger. There was never very much colour in her cheeks, but her skin was warm and white; there was vitality beneath her pallor; her hair was warm, too, long and thick and yet so fine that it gave her little head the effect of being surrounded by a nimbus of light; rather wayward, glancing, shifting light for there were little tendrils and wisps and curls in front and about the temples which no amount of coaxing could subdue. She touched up her mouth a little, not so much to redden it as to give a hint of the mondaine to her appearance. Her dress was flame-colour—Paulette had induced her to buy it,—of a plain, rather heavy beautiful glowing silk. The neck was high in back and girlishly modest in front. She had a string of good artificial pearls and two heavy silver bracelets. Thus she gave the effect of a flame herself; intense and opaque at the heart where her dress gleamed and shone, transparent and fragile where her white warm neck and face rose into the tenuous shadow of her hair. Her appearance excited herself.

Roger found her delightful. As to women he considered himself a connoisseur. This girl pleased him in many respects. She was young; she was, when lighted from within by some indescribable mechanism, even beautiful; she had charm and, what was for him even more important, she was puzzling. In repose, he noticed, studying her closely, her quiet look took on the resemblance of an arrested movement, a composure on tip-toe so to speak, as though she had been stopped in the swift transition from one mood to another. And back of that momentary cessation of action one could see a mind darting, quick, restless, indefatigable, observing, tabulating, perhaps even mocking. She had for him the quality of the foreigner, but she gave this quality an objectivity as though he were the stranger and she the well-known established personage taking note of his peculiarities and apparently boundlessly diverted by them.

But of all this Angela was absolutely unaware. No wonder she was puzzling to Roger, for, in addition to the excitement which she—a young woman in the high tide of her youth, her health, and her beauty—would be feeling at receiving in the proper setting the devotion and attention which all women crave, she was swimming in the flood of excitement created by her unique position. Stolen waters are the sweetest. And Angela never forgot that they were stolen. She thought: "Here I am having everything that a girl ought to have just because I had sense enough to suit my actions to my appearance." The realization, the secret fun bubbling back in some hidden recess of her heart, brought colour to her cheeks, a certain temerity to her manner. Roger pondered on this quality. If she were reckless!

The dinner was perfect; it was served with elegance and beauty. Indeed she was surprised at the surroundings, the grandeur even of the hotel to which he had brought her. She had no idea of his means, but had supposed that his circumstances were about those of her other new friends; probably he was better off than Anthony, whose poverty she instinctively sensed, and she judged that his income, whatever it might be, was not so perilous as Paulette's. But she would have put him on the same footing as the Starrs. This sort of expenditure, however, meant money, "unless he really does like me and is splurging this time just for me". The idea appealed to her vanity and gave her a sense of power; she looked at Roger with a warm smile. At once his intent, considering gaze filmed; he was already leaning toward her but he bent even farther across the perfect little table and asked in a low, eager tone: "Shall we stay here and dance or go to your house and talk and smoke a bit?"

"Oh we'll stay and dance; it would be so late by the time we get home that we'd only have a few minutes."

Presently the golden evening was over and they were in the vestibule at Jayne Street. Roger said very loudly: "Where's that push button?" Then lower: "Well, your young lovers aren't here to-night either. I'm beginning to think you made that story up, Angèle."

She assured him, laughing, that she had told the truth. "You come here some time and you'll see them for yourself." But she wished she could think of something more ordinary to say. His hands held hers very tightly; they were very strong and for the first time she noticed that the veins stood up on them like cords. She tried to pull her own away and he released them and, taking her key, turned the lock in the inner door, then stood looking down at her.

"Well I'm glad they're not here to-night to take their revenge." And as he handed her back the key he kissed her on the lips. His knowledge of women based on many, many such experiences, told him that her swift retreat was absolutely unfeigned.

As on a former occasion she stood, after she had gained her room, considering herself in the glass. She had been kissed only once before, by Matthew Henson, and that kiss had been neither as casual nor as disturbing as this. She was thrilled, excited, and vaguely displeased. "He is fresh, I'll say that for him." And subsiding into the easy chair she thought for a long time of Anthony Cross and his deep respectful ardour.

In the morning there were flowers.

From the class-room she went with Paulette to deliver the latter's sketches. "Have tea to-day with me; we'll blow ourselves at the Ritz. This is the only time in the month that I have any money, so we'll make the best of it."

Angela looked about the warm, luxurious room at the serene, luxurious women, the super-groomed, super-deferential, tremendously confident men. She sighed. "I love all this, love it."

Paulette, busy blowing smoke-rings, nodded. "I blew sixteen that time. Watch me do it again. There's nothing really to this kind of life, you know."

"Oh don't blow smoke-rings! It's the only thing in the world that can spoil your looks. What do you mean there's nothing to it?"

"Well for a day-in-and-day-out existence, it just doesn't do. It's too boring. It's fun for you and me to drift in here twice a year when we've just had a nice, fat cheque which we've got to spend. But there's nothing to it for every day; it's too much like reaching the harbour where you would be. The tumult and the shouting are all over. I'd rather live just above the danger line down on little old Bank Street, and think up a way to make five hundred dollars so I could go to the French Riviera second class and bum around those little towns, Villefranche, Beaulieu, Cagnes,—you must see them, Angèle—and have a spanking affair with a real man with honest to God blood in his veins than to sit here and drink tea and listen to the nothings of all these tame tigers, trying you out, seeing how much it will take to buy you."

Angela was bewildered by this outburst. "I thought you said you didn't like affairs unless you could conduct them in your own *pied à terre*."

"Did I? Well that was another time—not to-day. By the way, what would you say if I were to tell you that I'm going to Russia?"

She glanced at her friend with the bright shamelessness of a child, for she knew that Angela had heard of Jack Hudson's acceptance as newspaper correspondent in Moscow.

"I wouldn't say anything except that I'd much rather be here in the warmth and cleanliness of the Ritz than be in Moscow where I'm sure it will be cold and dirty."

"That's because you've never wanted anyone." Her face for a moment was all desire. Beautiful but terrible too. "She actually looks like Hetty Daniels," thought Angela in astonishment. Only, alas, there was no longer any beauty in Hetty's face.

"When you've set your heart on anybody or on anything there'll be no telling what you'll do, Angèle. For all your innocence you're as deep, you'll be as desperate as Martha Burden once you're started. I know your kind. Well, if you must play around in the Ritz, etcet., etcet., I'll tell Roger Fielding. He's a good squire and he can afford it."

"Why? Is he so rich?"

"Rich! If all the wealth that he—no, not he, but his father—if all the wealth that old man Fielding possesses were to be converted into silver dollars there wouldn't be space enough in this room, big as it is, to hold it."

Angela tried to envisage it. "And Roger, what does he do?"

"Spend it. What is there for him to do? Nothing except have a good time and keep in his father's good graces. His father's

some kind of a personage and all that, you know, crazy about
his name and his posterity. Roger doesn't dare get drunk and
lie in the gutter and he mustn't make a misalliance. Outside of
that the world's his oyster and he eats it every day. There's a
boy who gets everything he wants."

"What do you mean by a misalliance? He's not royalty."

"Spoken like a good American. No, he's not. But he mustn't
marry outside certain limits. No chorus girl romances for his
father. The old man wouldn't care a rap about money but he
would insist on blue blood and the Mayflower. The funny
thing is that Roger, for all his appearing so democratic, is that
way too. But of course he's been so run after the marvel is
that he's as unspoiled as he is. But it's the one thing I can't
stick in him. I don't mind a man's not marrying me; but I
can't forgive him if he thinks I'm not good enough to marry
him. Any woman is better than the best of men." Her face
took on its intense, burning expression; one would have said
she was consumed with excitement.

Angela nodded, only half-listening. Roger a multi-millionaire!
Roger who only two nights ago had kissed and mumbled her
fingers, his eyes avid and yet so humble and beseeching!

"One thing, if you do start playing around with Roger be
careful. He's a good bit of a rotter, and he doesn't care what he
says or spends to gain his ends." She laughed at the inquiry in
her friend's eyes. "No, I've never given Roger five minutes'
thought. But I know his kind. They're dangerous. It's wrong for
men to have both money and power; they're bound to make
some woman suffer. Come on up the Avenue with me and I'll
buy a hat. I can't wear this whang any longer. It's too small,
looks like a peanut on a barrel."

Angela was visual minded. She saw the days of the week, the
months of the year in little narrow divisions of space. She saw
the past years of her life falling into separate, uneven compartments whose ensemble made up her existence. Whenever she
looked back on this period from Christmas to Easter she saw a
bluish haze beginning in a white mist and flaming into something red and terrible; and across the bluish haze stretched the
name: Roger.

Roger! She had never seen anyone like him: so gay, so

beautiful, like a blond, glorious god, so overwhelming, so persistent. She had not liked him so much at first except as one
likes the sun or the sky or a singing bird, anything jolly and free.
There had been no touching points for their minds. He knew
nothing of life except what was pleasurable; it is true his idea of
the pleasurable did not always coincide with hers. He had no
fears, no restraints, no worries. Yes, he had one; he did not want
to offend his father. He wanted ardently and unswervingly his
father's money. He did not begrudge his senior a day, an hour,
a moment of life; about this he had a queer, unselfish sincerity.
The old financial war horse had made his fortune by hard labour and pitiless fighting. He had given Roger his being, the
entrée into a wonderful existence. Already he bestowed upon
him an annual sum which would have kept several families in
comfort. If Roger had cared to save for two years he need
never have asked his father for another cent. With any kind of
luck he could have built up for himself a second colossal fortune. But he did not care to do this. He did not wish his father
one instant's loss of life or of its enjoyment. But he did want final possession of those millions.

Angela liked him best when he talked about "my dad"; he
never mentioned the vastness of his wealth, but by now she
could not have helped guessing even without Paulette's aid
that he was a wealthy man. She would not take jewellery from
him, but there was a steady stream of flowers, fruit, candy, books,
fine copies of the old masters. She was afraid and ashamed to
express a longing in his presence. And with all this his steady,
constant attendance. And an odd watchfulness which she felt
but could not explain.

"He must love me," she said to herself, thinking of his caresses. She had been unable to keep him from kissing her. Her
uneasiness had amused and charmed him: he laughed at her
Puritanism, succeeded in shaming her out of it. "Child, where
have you lived? Why there's nothing in a kiss. If I didn't kiss
you I couldn't come to see you. And I have to see you, Angèle!"
His voice grew deep; the expression in his eyes made her own
falter.

Yet he did not ask her to marry him. "But I suppose it's because he can see I don't love him yet." And she wondered what
it would be like to love. Even Jinny knew more about this than

she, for she had felt, perhaps still did feel, a strong affection for Matthew Henson. Well, anyway, if they married she would probably come to love him; most women learned to love their husbands. At first after her conversation with Paulette about Roger she had rather expected a diminution at any time of his attentions, for after all she was unknown; from Roger's angle she would be more than outside the pale. But she was sure now that he loved and would want to marry her, for it never occurred to her that men bestowed attentions such as these on a passing fancy. She saw her life rounding out like a fairy tale. Poor, coloured—coloured in America; unknown, a nobody! And here at her hand was the forward thrust shadow of love and of great wealth. She would do lots of good among col-oured people; she would see that Miss Powell, for instance, had her scholarship. Oh she would hunt out girls and men like Seymour Porter,—she had almost forgotten his name,—or was it Arthur Sawyer?—and give them a taste of life in its fullness and beauty such as they had never dreamed of.

To-night she was to go out with Roger. She wore her flame-coloured dress again; a pretty green one was also hanging up in her closet, but she wore the flame one because it lighted her up from within—lighted not only her lovely, fine body but her mind too. Her satisfaction with her appearance let loose some inexplicable spring of gaiety and merriment and simplicity so that she seemed almost daring.

Roger, sitting opposite, tried to probe her mood, tried to gauge the invitation of her manner and its possibilities. She touched him once or twice, familiarly; he thought almost pos-sessively. She seemed to be within reach now if along with that accessibility she had recklessness. It was this attribute which for the first time to-night he thought to divine within her. If in addition to her insatiable interest in life—for she was always asking him about people and places,—she possessed this reck-lessness, then indeed he might put to her a proposal which had been hanging on his lips for weeks and months. Something in-nocent, pathetically untouched about her had hitherto kept him back. But if she had the requisite daring! They were din-ing in East Tenth Street in a small *café*—small contrasted with the Park Avenue Hotel to which he had first taken her. But about them stretched the glitter and perfection of crystal and

silver, of marvellous napery and of obsequious service. Everything, Angela thought, looking about her, was translated. The
slight odour of food was, she told Fielding, really an aroma:
the mineral water which he was drinking because he could not
help it and she because she could not learn to like wine, was
nectar; the bread, the fish, the courses were ambrosia. The
food, too, in general was to be spoken of as viands.

"Vittles, translated," she said laughing.

"And you, you, too, are translated. Angèle, you are wonderful, you are charming," his lips answered but his senses beat
and hammered. Intoxicated with the magic of the moment and
the surroundings, she turned her smiling countenance a little
nearer, and saw his face change, darken. A cloud over the sun.

"Excuse me," he said and walked hastily across the room
back of her. In astonishment she turned and looked after him.
At a table behind her three coloured people (under the direction of a puzzled and troubled waiter,) were about to take a
table. Roger went up and spoke to the headwaiter authorita-
tively, even angrily. The latter glanced about the room, nodded
obsequiously and crossing, addressed the little group. There
was a hasty, slightly acrid discussion. Then the three filed out,
past Angela's table this time, their heads high.

She turned back to her plate, her heart sick. For her the evening was ended. Roger came back, his face flushed, triumphant,
"Well I put a spoke in the wheel of those 'coons'! They forget
themselves so quickly, coming in here spoiling white people's
appetites. I told the manager if they brought one of their
damned suits I'd be responsible. I wasn't going to have them
here with you, Angèle. I could tell that night at Martha Burden's by the way you looked at that girl that you had no time
for darkies. I'll bet you'd never been that near to one before
in your life, had you? Wonder where Martha picked that
one up."

She was silent, lifeless. He went on recounting instances of
how effectively he had "spoked the wheel" of various coloured
people. He had blackballed Negroes in Harvard, aspirants for
small literary or honour societies. "I'd send 'em all back to
Africa if I could. There's been a darkey up in Harlem's got the
right idea, I understand; though he must be a low brute to
cave in on his race that way; of course it's merely a matter of

money with him. He'd betray them all for a few thousands. Gosh, if he could really pull it through I don't know but what I'd be willing to finance it."

To this tirade there were economic reasons to oppose, tenets of justice, high ideals of humanity. But she could think of none of them. Speechless, she listened to him, her appetite fled.

"What's the matter, Angèle? Did it make you sick to see them?"

"No, no not that. I—I don't mind them; you're mistaken about me and that girl at Martha Burden's. It's you, you're so violent. I didn't know you were that way!"

"And I've made you afraid of me? Oh, I don't want to do that." But he was flattered to think that he had affected her. "See here, let's get some air. I'll take you for a spin around the Park and then run you home."

But she did not want to go to the Park; she wanted to go home immediately. His little blue car was outside; in fifteen minutes they were at Jayne Street. She would not permit him to come inside, not even in the vestibule; she barely gave him her hand.

"But Angèle, you can't leave me like this; why what have I done? Did it frighten you because I swore a little? But I'd never swear at you. Don't go like this."

She was gone, leaving him staring and nonplussed on the sidewalk. Lighting a cigarette, he climbed back in his car. "Now what the devil!" He shifted his gears. "But she likes me. I'd have sworn she liked me to-night. Those damn niggers! I bet she's thinking about me this minute."

He would have lost his bet. She was thinking about the co-loured people.

She could visualize them all so plainly; she could interpret their changing expressions as completely as though those changes lay before her in a book. There were a girl and two men, one young, the other the father perhaps of either of the other two. The fatherly-looking person, for so her mind docketed him, bore an expression of readiness for any outcome whatever. She knew and understood the type. His experiences of surprises engendered by this thing called prejudice had been too vast for them to appear to him as surprises. If they were served this was

a lucky day; if not he would refuse to let the incident shake his
stout spirit.

It was to the young man and the girl that her interest went
winging. In the mirror behind Roger she had seen them entering the room and she had thought: "Oh, here are some of
them fighting it out again. O God! please let them be served,
please don't let their evening be spoiled." She was so happy
herself and she knew that the reception of fifty other *maîtres
d'hotel* could not atone for a rebuff at the beginning of the
game. The young fellow was nervous, his face tense,—thus
might he have looked going to meet the enemy's charge in the
recent Great War; but there the odds were even; here the cards
were already stacked against him. Presently his expression
would change for one of grimness, determination and despair.
Talk of a lawsuit would follow; apparently did follow; still a
lawsuit at best is a poor substitute for an evening's fun.

But the girl, the girl in whose shoes she herself might so easily have been! She was so clearly a nice girl, with all that the
phrase implies. To Angela watching her intently and yet with
the indifference of safety she recalled Virginia, so slender, so
appealing she was and so brave. So very brave! Ah, that courage! It affected at first a gay hardihood: "Oh I know it isn't
customary for people like us to come into this café, but everything is going to be all right." It met Angela's gaze with a
steadiness before which her own quailed, for she thought:
"Oh, poor thing! perhaps she thinks that I don't want her
either." And when the blow had fallen the courage had had to
be translated anew into a comforting assurance. "Don't worry
about me, Jimmy," the watching guest could just hear her.
"Indeed, indeed it won't spoil the evening, I should say not;
there're plenty of places where they'd be all right. We just happened to pick a lemon."

The three had filed out, their heads high, their gaze poised
and level. But the net result of the evening's adventure would
be an increased cynicism in the elderly man, a growing bitterness for the young fellow, and a new timidity in the girl, who,
even after they had passed into the street, could not relieve her
feelings, for she must comfort her baffled and goaded escort.

Angela wondered if she had been half as consoling to
Matthew Henson,—was it just a short year ago? And suddenly,

sitting immobile in her arm-chair, her evening cloak slipping unnoticed to the floor, triumph began to mount in her. Life could never cheat her as it had cheated that coloured girl this evening, as it had once cheated her in Philadephia with Matthew. She was free, free to taste life in all its fullness and sweetness, in all its minutest details. By exercising sufficient courage to employ the unique weapon which an accident of heredity had placed in her grasp she was able to master life. How she blessed her mother for showing her the way! In a country where colour or the lack of it meant the difference between freedom and fetters how lucky she was!

But, she told herself, she was through with Roger Fielding.

Chapter V

Now it was Spring, Spring in New York. Washington Square was a riot of greens that showed up bravely against the great red brick houses on its north side. The Arch viewed from Fifth Avenue seemed a gateway to Paradise. The long deep streets running the length of the city invited an exploration to the ends where pots of gold doubtless gleamed. On the short crosswise streets the April sun streamed in splendid banners of deep golden light.

In two weeks Angela had seen Roger only once. He telephoned every day, pleading, beseeching, entreating. On the one occasion when she did permit him to call there were almost tears in his eyes. "But, darling, what did I do? If you'd only tell me that. Perhaps I could explain away whatever it is that's come between us." But there was nothing to explain she told him gravely, it was just that he was harder, more cruel than she had expected; no, it wasn't the coloured people, she lied and felt her soul blushing, it was that now she knew him when he was angry or displeased, and she could see how ruthless, how determined he was to have things his way. His willingness to pay the costs of the possible lawsuit had filled her with a sharp fear. What could one do against a man, against a group of men such as he and his kind represented who would spend time and money to maintain a prejudice based on a silly, time-worn tradition?

Yet she found she did not want to lose sight of him completely. The care, the attention, the flattery with which he had surrounded her were beginning to produce their effect. In the beautiful but slightly wearying balminess of the Spring she missed the blue car which had been constantly at her call; eating a good but homely meal in her little living room with the cooking odours fairly overwhelming her from the kitchenette, she found herself longing unconsciously for the dainty food, the fresh Spring delicacies which she knew he would be only too glad to procure for her. Shamefacedly she had to acknowledge that the separation which she was so rigidly enforcing meant a difference in her tiny exchequer, for it had now been many months since she had regularly taken her main meal by herself and at her own expense.

To-day she was especially conscious of her dependence upon him, for she was to spend the afternoon in Van Cortlandt Park with Anthony. There had been talk of subways and the Elevated. Roger would have had the blue car at the door and she would have driven out of Jayne Street in state. Now it transpired that Anthony was to deliver some drawings to a man, a tricky customer, whom it was best to waylay if possible on Saturday afternoon. Much as he regretted it he would probably be a little late. Angela, therefore, to save time must meet him at Seventy-second Street. Roger would never have made a request like that; he would have brought his lawyer or his business man along in the car with him and, dismissing him with a curt "Well I'll see if I can finish this to-morrow," would have hastened to her with his best Walter Raleigh manner, and would have produced the cloak, too, if she would but say so. Perhaps she'd have to take him back. Doubtless later on she could manage his prejudices if only he would speak. But how was she to accomplish that?

Still it was lovely being here with Anthony in the park, so green and fresh, so new with the recurring newness of Spring. Anthony touched her hand and said as he had once before, "I'm so content to be with you, Angel. I may call you Angel, mayn't I? You are that to me, you know. Oh if you only knew how happy it makes me to be content, to be satisfied like this. I could get down on my knees and thank God for it like a little boy." He looked like a little boy as he said it. "Happiness is a hard thing to find and harder still to keep."

She asked him idly, "Haven't you always been happy?"

His face underwent a startling change. Not only did the old sadness and strain come back on it, but a great bitterness such as she had never before seen.

"No," he said slowly as though thinking through long years of his life. " I haven't been happy for years, not since I was a little boy. Never once have I been happy nor even at ease until I met you."

But she did not want him to find his happiness in her. That way would only lead to greater unhappiness for him. So she said, to change the subject: "Could you tell me about it?"

But there was nothing to tell, he assured her, his face growing darker, grimmer. "Only my father was killed when I was a
little boy, killed by his enemies. I've hated them ever since; I
never stopped hating them until I met you." But this was just
as dangerous a road as the other plus the possibilities of re-
opening old wounds. So she only shivered and said vaguely,
"Oh, that was terrible! Too terrible to talk about. I'm sorry,
Anthony!" And then as a last desperate topic: "Are you ever
going back to Brazil?" For she knew that he had come to the
United States from Rio de Janeiro. He had spent Christmas at
her house, and had shown her pictures of the great, beautiful
city and of his mother, a slender, dark-eyed woman with a perpetual sadness in her eyes.

The conversation languished, She thought: "It must be terrible to be a man and to have these secret hates and horrors
back of one." Some Spanish feud, a matter of hot blood and
ready knives, a sudden stroke, and then this deadly memory
for him.

"No," he said after a long pause. "I'm never going back to
Brazil. I couldn't." He turned to her suddenly. "Tell me, Angel,
what kind of girl are you, what do you think worth while?
Could you, for the sake of love, for the sake of being loyal to
the purposes and vows of someone you loved, bring yourself
to endure privation and hardship and misunderstanding, hardship that would be none the less hard because it really could be
avoided?"

She thought of her mother who had loved her father so
dearly, and of the wash-days which she had endured for him,
the long years of household routine before she and Jinny had
been old enough to help her first with their hands and then
with their earnings. She thought of the little, dark, shabby house,
of the made-over dresses and turned coats. And then she saw
Roger and his wealth and his golden recklessness, his golden
keys which could open the doors to beauty and ease and—
decency! Oh, it wasn't decent for women to have to scrub and
work and slave and bear children and sacrifice their looks and
their pretty hands,—she saw her mother's hands as they had always looked on wash day, they had a white, boiled appearance.
No, she would not fool herself nor Anthony. She was no senti-
mentalist. It was not likely that she, a girl who had left her little

sister and her home to go out to seek life and happiness, would
throw it over for poverty,—hardship. If a man loved a woman
how could he ask her that?

So she told him gently: "No, Anthony, I couldn't," and
watched the blood drain from his face and the old look of unhappiness drift into his eyes.

He answered inadequately. "No, of course you couldn't."
And turning over—he had been sitting on the grass at her feet
—he lay face downward on the scented turf. Presently he sat
up and giving her a singularly sweet but wistful smile, said: "I
almost touched happiness, Angèle. Did you by any chance ever
happen to read Browning's 'Two in the Roman Campagna'?"

But she had read very little poetry except what had been required in her High School work, and certainly not Browning.

He began to interpret the fragile, difficult beauty of the
poem with its light but sure touch on evanescent, indefinable
feeling. He quoted:

> "How is it under our control
> To love or not to love?"

And again:

> "Infinite yearning and the pang
> Of finite hearts that yearn."

They were silent for a long time. And again she wondered
how it would feel to love. He watched the sun drop suddenly
below some tree tops and rose to his feet shivering a little as
though its disappearance had made him immediately cold.

"'So the good moment goes.' Come, Angel, we'll have to
hasten. It's getting dark and it's a long walk to the subway."

The memory of the afternoon stayed by her, shrouding her
thoughts, clinging to them like a tenuous, adhering mantle.
But she said to herself: "There's no use thinking about that.
I'm not going to live that kind of life." And she knew she
wanted Roger and what he could give her and the light and
gladness which he always radiated. She wanted none of Anthony's poverty and privation and secret vows,—he meant, she
supposed, some promise to devote himself to REAL ART,—her
visual mind saw it in capitals. Well, she was sick of tragedy, she

belonged to a tragic race. "God knows it's time for one member of it to be having a little fun."

"Yes," she thought all through her class, painting furiously —for she had taken up her work in earnest since Christmas— "yes, I'll just make up my mind to it. I'll take Roger back and get married and settle down to a pleasant, safe, beautiful life." And useful. It should be very useful. Perhaps she'd win Roger around to helping coloured people. She'd look up all sorts of down-and-outers and give them a hand. And she'd help Anthony, at least she'd offer to help him; she didn't believe he would permit her.

Coming out of the building a thought occurred to her: "Take Roger back, but back to what? To his old status of admiring, familiar, generous friend? Just that and no more?" Here was her old problem again. She stopped short to consider it.

Martha Burden overtook her. "Planning the great masterpiece of the ages, Angèle? Better come along and work it out by my fireside. I can give you some tea. Are you coming?"

"Yes," said Angela, still absorbed.

"Well," said Martha after they had reached the house. "I've never seen any study as deep as that. Come out of it Angèle, you'll drown. You're not by any chance in love, are you?"

"No," she replied, "at least I don't know. But tell me, Martha, suppose—suppose I were in love with one of them, what do you do about it, how do you get them to propose?"

Martha lay back and laughed. "Such candour have I not met, no, not in all Flapperdom. Angèle, if I could answer that I'd be turning women away from my door and handing out my knowledge to the ones I did admit at a hundred dollars a throw."

"But there must be some way. Oh, of course, I know lots of them propose, but how do you get a proposal from the ones you want,—the,—the interesting ones?"

"You really want to know? The only answer I can give you is Humpty Dumpty's dictum to Alice about verbs and adjectives: 'It depends on which is the stronger." She interpreted for her young guest was clearly mystified. "It depends on (A) whether you are strong enough to make him like you more than you like him; (B) whether if you really do like him more than he does you you can conceal it. In other words, so far as liking is concerned you must always be ahead of the game, you must always like or appear to like him a little less than he does you. And you must make him want you. But you mustn't give. Oh yes, I know that men are always wanting women to give, but they don't want the women to want to give. They want to take,—or at any rate to compel the giving."

"It sounds very complicated, like some subtle game."

A deep febrile light came into Martha's eyes. "It is a game, and the hardest game in the world for a woman, but the most fascinating; the hardest in which to strike a happy medium. You see, you have to be careful not to withhold too much and yet to give very little. If we don't give enough we lose them. If we give too much we lose ourselves. Oh, Angèle, God doesn't like women."

"But," said Angela thinking of her own mother, "there are some women who give all and men like them the better for it."

"Oh, yes, that's true. Those are the blessed among women. They ought to get down on their knees every day and thank God for permitting them to be their normal selves and not having to play a game." For a moment her still, proud face broke into deeps of pain. "Oh, Angèle, think of loving and never, never being able to show it until you're asked for it; think of living a game every hour of your life!" Her face quivered back to its normal immobility.

Angela walked home through the purple twilight musing no longer on her own case but on this unexpected revelation. "Well," she said, "I certainly shouldn't like to love like that." She thought of Anthony: "A woman could be her true self with him." But she had given him up.

If the thing to do were to play a game she would play one. Indeed she rather enjoyed the prospect. She was playing a game now, a game against public tradition on the one hand and family instinct on the other; the stakes were happiness and excitement, and almost anyone looking at the tricks which she had already taken would prophesy that she would be the winner. She decided to follow all the rules as laid down by Martha Burden and to add any workable ideas of her own. When Roger called again she was still unable to see him, but her voice was a shade less curt over the telephone; she did not cut him off so abruptly. "I must not withhold too much," she reminded herself. He was quick to note the subtle change in intonation. "But you're going to let me come to see you soon, Angèle," he pleaded. "You wouldn't hold out this way against me forever. Say when I may come."

"Oh, one of these days; I must go now, Roger. Good-bye."

After the third call she let him come to spend Friday evening. She heard the blue car rumbling in the street and a few minutes later he came literally staggering into the living-room so laden was he with packages. Flowers, heaps of spring posies had come earlier in the day, lilacs, jonquils, narcissi. Now this evening there were books and candy, handkerchiefs,—"they were so dainty and they looked just like you," he said fearfully, for she had never taken an article of dress from him,—two pictures, a palette and some fine brushes and last a hamper of all sorts of delicacies. "I thought if you didn't mind we'd have supper here; it would be fun with just us two."

How much he pleased her he could not divine; it was the first time he had ever given a hint of any desire for sheer domesticity. Anthony had sought nothing better than to sit and smoke and watch her flitting about in her absurd red or violet apron. Matthew Henson had been speechless with ecstasy when on a winter night she had allowed him to come into the kitchen while she prepared for him a cup of cocoa. But Roger's palate had been so flattered by the concoctions of chefs famous in London, Paris and New York that he had set no store by her simple cooking. Indeed his inevitable comment had been: "Here, what do you want to get yourself all tired out for? Let's go to a restaurant. It's heaps less bother."

But to-night he, too, watched her with humble, delighted eyes. She realized that he was conscious of her every movement; once he tried to embrace her, but she whirled out of his reach without reproach but with decision. He subsided, too thankful to be once more in her presence to take any risks. And when he left he had kissed her hand.

She began going about with him again, but with condescension, with kindness. And with the new vision gained from her talk with Martha she could see his passion mounting. "Make him want you,"—that was the second rule. It was clear that he did, no man could be as persevering as this otherwise. Still he did not speak. They were to meet that afternoon in front of

the school to go "anywhere you want, dear, I'm yours to command". It was the first time that he had called for her at the
building, and she came out a little early, for she did not want
any of the three, Martha, Paulette, nor Anthony, to see whom
she was meeting. It would be better to walk to the corner, she
thought, they'd be just that much less likely to recognize him.
She heard footsteps hurrying behind her, heard her name and
turned to see Miss Powell, pleased and excited. She laid her
hand on Angela's arm but the latter shook her off. Roger must
not see her on familiar terms like this with a coloured girl
for she felt that the afternoon portended something and she
wanted no side issues. The coloured girl gave her a penetrating
glance; then her habitual reserve settled down blotting out the
eagerness, leaving her face blurred and heavy. "I beg your pardon, Miss Mory, I'm sure," she murmured and stepped out
into the tempestuous traffic of Fourth Avenue. Angela was
sorry; she would make it up to-morrow, she thought, but she
had not dismissed her a moment too soon for Roger came
rushing up, his car resplendent and resplendent himself in a
grey suit, soft grey hat and blue tie. Angela looked at him approvingly. "You look just like the men in the advertising pages
of the Saturday *Evening Post*," she said, and the fact that he did
not wince under the compliment proved the depth of his devotion, for every one of his outer garments, hat, shoes, and
suit, had been made to measure.

They went to Coney Island. "The ocean will be there, but
very few people and only a very few amusements," said Roger.
They had a delightful time; they were like school children, easily and frankly amused; they entered all the booths that were
open, ate pop-corn and hot dogs and other local dainties. And
presently they were flying home under the double line of trees
on Ocean Parkway and entering the bosky loveliness of Prospect Park. Roger slowed down a little.

"Oh," said Angela. "I love this car."

He bent toward her instantly. "Does it please you? Did you
miss it when you made me stay away from you?"

She was afraid she had made a mistake: "Yes, but that's not
why I let you come back."

"I know that. But you do like it, don't you, comfort and
beauty and dainty surroundings?"

"Yes," she said solemnly, "I love them all."

He was silent then for a long, long time, his face a little set, a worried line on his forehead.

"Well now what's he thinking about?" she asked herself, watching his hands and their clever manipulation of the steering wheel though his thoughts, she knew, were not on that.

He turned to her with an air of having made up his mind. "Angèle, I want you to promise to spend a day out riding with me pretty soon. I—I have something I want to say to you." He was a worldly young man about town but he was actually mopping his brow. "I've got to go south for a week for my father,—he owns some timber down there with which he used to supply saw-mills but since the damned niggers have started running north it's been something of a weight on his hands. He wants me to go down and see whether it's worth his while to hold on to it any longer. It's so rarely that he asks anything of me along a business line that I'd hate to refuse him. But I'll be back the morning of the twenty-sixth. I'll have to spend the afternoon and evening with him out on Long Island but on the twenty-seventh could you go out with me?"

She said as though all this preamble portended nothing: "I couldn't give you the whole day, but I'd go in the afternoon."

"Oh," his face fell a little. "Well, the afternoon then. Only of course we won't be able to go far out. Perhaps you'd like me to arrange a lunch and we'd go to one of the Parks, Central or the Bronx, or Van Cortlandt,——"

"No, not Van Cortlandt," she told him. That park was sacred to Anthony Cross.

"Well, wherever you say. We can settle it even that day. The main thing is that you'll go."

She said to herself. "Aren't men funny! He could have asked me five times over while he was making all these arrangements." But she was immensely relieved, even happy. She felt very kindly toward him; perhaps she was in love after all, only she was not the demonstrative kind. It was too late for him to come in, but they sat in the car in the dark security of Jayne Street and she let him take her in his arms and kiss her again and again. For the first time she returned his kisses.

*

Weary but triumphant she mounted the stairs almost stumbling from a sudden, overwhelming fatigue. She had been under a strain! But it was all over now; she had conquered, she had been the stronger. She had secured not only him but an assured future, wealth, protection, influence, even power. She herself was power,—like the women one reads about, like Cleopatra,—Cleopatra's African origin intrigued her, it was a fitting comparison. Smiling, she took the last steep stairs lightly, springily, suddenly reinvigorated.

As she opened the door a little heap of letters struck her foot. Switching on the light she sat in the easy chair and incuriously turned them over. They were bills for the most part, she had had to dress to keep herself dainty and desirable for Roger. At the bottom of the heap was a letter from Virginia. When she became Mrs. Roger Fielding she would never have to worry about a bill again; how she would laugh when she remembered the small amounts for which these called! Never again would she feel the slight quake of dismay which always overtook her when she saw she words: "Miss Angèle Mory in account with, ——" Outside of the regular monthly statement for gas she had never seen a bill in her father's house. Well, she'd have no difficulty in getting over her squeamish training.

Finally she opened Jinny's letter. Her sister had written:

"Angela I'm coming up for an exam on the twenty-eighth. I'll arrive on the twenty-sixth or I could come the day before. You'll meet me, won't you? I know where I'm going to stay,"— she gave an address on 139th Street—"but I don't know how to get there; I don't know your school hours, write and tell me so I can arrive when you're free. There's no reason why I should put you out."

So Virginia was really coming to try her luck in New York. It would be nice to have her so near. "Though I don't suppose we'll be seeing so much of each other," she thought, absently reaching for her schedule. "Less than ever now, for I suppose Roger and I will live in Long Island; yes, that would be much wiser. I'll wear a veil when I go to meet her, for those coloured porters stare at you so and they never forget you."

The twenty-seventh came on Thursday; she had classes in the morning; well, Jinny would be coming in the afternoon anyway, and after twelve she had,—Oh heavens that was *the* day, the day she was to go out with Roger, the day that he would put the great question. And she wrote to Virginia:

"Come the twenty-sixth, Honey, any time after four. I couldn't possibly meet you on the twenty-seventh. But the twenty-sixth is all right. Let me know when your train comes in and I'll be there. And welcome to our city."

Chapter VI

THE week was one of tumult, almost of agony. After all, matters were not completely settled, you never could tell. She would be glad when the twenty-seventh had come and gone, for then, then she would be rooted, fixed. She and Roger would marry immediately. But now he was so far away, in Georgia; she missed him and evidently he missed her for the first two days brought her long telegrams almost letters. "I can think of nothing but next Thursday, are you thinking of it too?" The third day brought a letter which said practically the same thing, adding, "Oh, Angèle; I wonder what you will say!"

"But he could ask me and find out," she said to herself and suddenly felt assured and triumphant. Every day thereafter brought her a letter reiterating this strain. "And I know how he hates to write!"

The letter on Wednesday read, "Darling, when you get this I'll actually be in New York; if I can I'll call you up but I'll have to rush like mad so as to be free for Thursday, so perhaps I can't manage."

She made up her mind not to answer the telephone even if it did ring, she would strike one last note of indifference though only she herself would be aware of it.

It was the day on which Jinny was to arrive. It would be fun to see her, talk to her, hear all the news about the queer, staid people whom she had left so far behind. Farther now than ever. Matthew Henson was still in the post-office, she knew. Arthur Sawyer was teaching at Sixteenth and Fitzwater; she could imagine the sick distaste that mantled his face every time he looked at the hideous, discoloured building. Porter had taken his degree in dentistry but he was not practising, on the contrary he was editing a small weekly, getting deeper, more and more hopelessly into debt she was sure. . . . It would be fun some day to send him a whopping cheque; after all, he had taken a chance just as she had; she recognized his revolt as akin to her own, only he had not had her luck. She must ask Jinny about all this.

It was too bad that she had to meet her sister,—but she

must. Just as likely as not she'd be car sick and then New York was terrifying for the first time to the stranger,—she had known an instant's sick dread herself that first day when she had stood alone and ignorant in the great rotunda of the station. But she was different from Jinny; nothing about life ever made her really afraid; she might hurt herself, suffer, meet disappointment, but life could not alarm her; she loved to come to grips with it, to force it to a standstill, to yield up its treasures. But Jinny although brave, had secret fears, she was really only a baby. Her little sister! For the first time in months she thought of her with a great surge of sisterly tenderness.

It was time to go. She wore her most unobtrusive clothes, a dark blue suit, a plain white silk shirt, a dark blue, bell-shaped hat—a *cloche*—small and fitting down close over her eyes. She pulled it down even farther and settled her modish veil well over the tip of her nose. It was one thing to walk about the Village with Miss Powell. There were practically no coloured people there. But this was different. Those curious porters should never be able to recognize her. Seymour Porter had worked among them one summer at Broad Street station in Philadelphia. He used to say: "They aren't really curious, you know, but their job makes them sick; so they're always hunting for the romance, for the adventure which for a day at least will take the curse off the monotonous obsequiousness of their lives."

She was sorry for them, but she could not permit them to remedy their existence at her expense.

In her last letter she had explained to Jinny about those two troublesome staircases which lead from the train level of the New York Pennsylvania Railroad station to the street level. "There's no use my trying to tell you which one to take in order to bring you up to the right hand or to the left hand side of the elevator because I never know myself. So all I can say, dear, is when you do get up to the elevator just stick to it and eventually I'll see you or you'll see me as I revolve around it. Don't you move, for it might turn out that we were both going in the same direction."

True to her own instructions, she was stationed between the

two staircases, jerking her neck now toward one staircase, now toward the other, stopping short to look at the elevator itself. She thrust up her veil to see better.

A man sprinted by in desperate haste, brushing so closely by her that the corner of his suit-case struck sharply on the thin inner curve of her knee.

"My goodness!" she exclaimed involuntarily.

For all his haste he was a gentleman, for he pulled of his hat, threw her a quick backward glance and began: "I beg your—why darling, darling, you don't mean to say you came to meet me!"

"Meet you! I thought you came in this morning." It was Roger, Roger and the sight of him made her stupid with fear.

He stooped and kissed her, tenderly, possessively. "I did,—oh Angela you *are* a beauty! Only a beauty can wear plain things like that. I did come in this morning but I'm trying to catch Kirby, my father's lawyer, he ought to be coming in from Newark just now and I thought I'd take him down to Long Island with me for the night. I've got a lot of documents for him here in this suitcase—that Georgia business was most complicated—that way I won't have to hunt him up in the morning and I'll have more time to—to arrange for our trip in the afternoon. What are you doing here?"

What was she doing there? Waiting for her sister Jinny who was coloured and who showed it. And Roger hated Negroes. She was lost, ruined, unless she could get rid of him. She told the first lie that came into her mind.

"I'm waiting for Paulette." All this could be fixed up with Paulette later. Miss Lister would think as little of deceiving a man, any man, as she would of squashing a mosquito. They were fair game and she would ask no questions.

His face clouded. "Can't say I'm so wild about your waiting for Paulette. Well we can wait together—is she coming up from Philadelphia? That train's bringing my man too from Newark." He had the male's terrible clarity of understanding for train connections.

"What time does your train go to Long Island? I thought you wanted to get the next one."

"Well, I'd like to but they're only half an hour apart. I can wait. Better the loss of an hour to-day than all of to-morrow morning. We can wait together; see the people are beginning to come up. I wish I could take you home but the minute he shows up I'll have to sprint with him."

"Now God be on my side," she prayed. Sometimes these trains were very long. If Mr. Kirby were in the first car and Jinny toward the end that would make all of ten minutes' difference. If only she hadn't given those explicit directions!

There was Jinny, her head suddenly emerging into view above the stairs. She saw Angela, waved her hand. In another moment she would be flinging her arms about her sister's neck; she would be kissing her and saying, "Oh, Angela, Angela darling!"

And Roger, who was no fool, would notice the name Angela—Angèle; he would know no coloured girl would make a mistake like this.

She closed her eyes in a momentary faintness, opened them again.

"What's the matter?" said Roger sharply, "are you sick?"

Jinny was beside her. Now, now the bolt would fall. She heard the gay, childish voice saying laughingly, assuredly:

"I beg your pardon, but isn't this Mrs. Henrietta Jones?"

Oh, God was good! Here was one chance if only Jinny would understand! In his astonishment Roger had turned from her to face the speaker. Angela, her eyes beseeching her sister's from under her close hat brim, could only stammer the old formula: "Really you have the advantage of me. No, I'm not Mrs. Jones."

Roger said rudely, "Of course she isn't Mrs. Jones. Come, Angèle." Putting his arm through hers he stooped for the suitcase.

But Jinny, after a second's bewildered but incredulous stare, was quicker even than they. Her slight figure, her head high, preceded them; vanished into a telephone booth.

Roger glared after her. "Well of all the damned cheek!"

For the first time in the pursuit of her chosen ends she began to waver. Surely no ambition, no pinnacle of safety was supposed to call for the sacrifice of a sister. She might be selfish,—oh, undoubtedly she had been selfish all these months to leave Jinny completely to herself—but she had never meant to be cruel. She tried to picture the tumult of emotions in her sister's mind, there must have been amazement,—oh she had seen it all on her face, the utter bewilderment, the incredulity and then the settling down on that face of a veil of dignity and pride—like a baby trying to harden mobile features. She was in her apartment again now, pacing the floor, wondering what to do. Already she had called up the house in 139th Street, it had taken her a half-hour to get the number for she did not know the householder's name and "Information" had been coy,—but Miss Murray had not arrived yet. Were they expecting her? Yes, Miss Murray had written to say that she would be there between six and seven; it was seven-thirty now and she had not appeared. Was there any message? "No, no!" Angela explained she would call again.

But where was Jinny? She couldn't be lost, after all she was grown-up and no fool, she could ask directons. Perhaps she had taken a cab and in the evening traffic had been delayed,—or had met with an accident. This thought sent Angela to the telephone again. There was no Miss Murray as yet. In her wanderings back and forth across the room she caught sight of herself in the mirror. Her face was flushed, her eyes shining with remorse and anxiety. Her vanity reminded her: "If Roger could just see me now". Roger and to-morrow! He would have to speak words of gold to atone for this breach which for his sake she had made in her sister's trust and affecton.

At the end of an hour she called again. Yes, Miss Murray had come in. So great was her relief that her knees sagged under her. Yes of course they would ask her to come to the telephone. After a long silence the voice rang again over the wire. "I didn't see her go out but she must have for she's not in her room."

"Oh all right," said Angela, "the main thing was to know that she was there." But she was astonished. Jinny's first night in New York and she was out already! She could not go to see her Thursday because of the engagement with Roger, but she'd make good the next day; she'd be there the first thing, Friday morning. Snatching up a sheet of note-paper she began a long letter full of apologies and excuses. "And I can't come to-morrow, darling, because as I told you I have a very important engagement, an engagement that means very much to me. Oh you'll understand when I tell you about it." She put a special delivery stamp on the letter.

Her relief at learning that Jinny was safe did not ease her guilty conscience. In a calmer mood she tried now to find excuses for herself, extenuating circumstances. As soon as Jinny understood all that was involved she would overlook it. After all, Jinny would want her to be happy. "And anyway," she thought to herself sulkily, "Mamma didn't speak to Papa that day that we were standing on the steps of the Hotel Walton." But she knew that the cases were not analogous; no principle was involved, her mother's silence had not exposed her husband to insult or contumely, whereas Roger's attitude to Virginia had been distinctly offensive. "And moreover," her thoughts continued with merciless clarity, "when a principle *was* at stake your mother never hesitated a moment to let those hospital attendants know of the true status of affairs. In fact she was not aware that she was taking any particular stand. Her husband was her husband and she was glad to acknowledge that relationship."

A sick distaste for her action, for her daily deception, for Roger and his prejudices arose within her. But with it came a dark anger against a country and a society which could create such an issue. And she thought: "If I had spoken to Jinny, had acknowledged her, what good would it have done me or her either? After it was all over she would have been exactly where she was before and I would have lost everything. And I do so want to be happy, to have a good time. At this very hour tomorrow I'll probably be one of the most envied girls in New York. And afterwards I can atone for it all. I'll be good to all sorts of people; I'll really help humanity, lots of coloured folks will be much better of on account of me. And if I had spoken to Jinny I could never have helped them at all." Once she murmured: "I'll help Jinny too, the darling! She shall have everything in the world she wants." But in her heart she knew already that Jinny would want nothing.

Chapter VII

T HURSDAY came and Thursday sped as Thursdays will. For
a long time Angela saw it as a little separate entity of time
shut away in some hidden compartment of her mind, a compartment whose door she dreaded to open.

On Friday she called up her sister early in the morning. "Is
that you, Jinny? Did you get my letter? Is it all right for me to
come up?"

"Yes," said Jinny noncommittally, to all questions, then laconically: "But you'd better come right away if you want to catch
me. I take the examination to-day and haven't much time."

Something in the matter-of-factness of her reply disconcerted Angela. Yet there certainly was no reason why her sister
should show any enthusiasm over seeing her. Only she did
want to see her, to talk to some one of her very own to-day.
She would like to burrow her head in Virginia's shoulder and
cry! But a mood such as Jinny's voice indicated did not invite
confidences.

A stout brown-skinned bustling woman suggesting immense
assurance and ability opened the door. "Miss Murray told me
that she was expecting someone. You're to go right on up. Her's
is the room right next to the third storey front."

"She was expecting someone." Evidently Virginia had been
discreet. This unexpected, unsought for carefulness carried a sting
with it.

"Hello," said Jinny, casually thrusting a dishevelled but picturesque head out of the door. "Can you find your way in?
This room's larger than any two we ever had at home, yet
already it looks like a ship at sea." She glanced about the disordered place. "I wonder if this is what they mean by 'shipshape'.
Here I'll hang up this suit, then you can sit down. Isn't it a
sweetie? Got it at Snellenburg's."

She had neither kissed nor offered to shake hands with her
sister, yet her manner was friendly enough, even cordial. "See
I've bobbed my hair," she went on. "Like it? I'm wild about it
even if it does take me forever to fix it." Standing before a mirror she began shaping the ends under with a curling iron.

539

Angela thought she had never seen any one so pretty and so colourful. Jinny had always shown a preference for high colours; to-day she was revelling in them; her slippers were high heeled small red mules; a deep green dressing-gown hung gracefully from her slim shoulders and from its open collar flamed the rose and gold of her smooth skin. Her eyes were bright and dancing. Her hair, black, alive and curling, ended in a thick velvety straightness like cut plush.

Angela said stiffly, "I hope I didn't get you up, telephoning so early."

Virginia smiled, flushing a little more deeply under the dark gold of her skin. "Oh dear no! I'd already had an earlier call than that this morning."

"You had!" exclaimed Angela, astonished. "I didn't know you knew anyone in New York." She remembered her sister's mysterious disappearance the first night of her arrival. "And see here, Jinny, I'm awfully sorry about what happened the other night. I wouldn't have had it happen for a great deal. I wish I could explain to you about it." How confidently she had counted on having marvellous news to tell Virginia and now how could she drag to the light yesterday's sorry memory? "But I called you up again and again and you hadn't arrived and then when they finally did tell me that you had come, it appeared that you had gone out. Where on earth did you go?"

Jenny began to laugh, to giggle in fact. For a moment she was the Virginia of her school days, rejoicing in some innocent mischief, full of it. "I wasn't out. There's a wash-room down the hall and I went there to wash my face,——" it clouded a moment. "And when I came back I walked as I thought into my room. Instead of that I had walked into the room of another lodger. And there he sat——"

"Oh," said Angela inattentively. "I'm glad you weren't out. I was quite worried. Listen, Virginia," she began desperately, "I know you think that what I did in the station the other day was unspeakable; it seems almost impossible for me to explain it to you. But that man with me was a very special friend,——"

"He must have been indeed," Jinny interrupted drily, "to make you cut your own sister." She was still apparently fooling with her hair, her head perched on one side, her eyes glued to the mirror. But she was not making much progress and her lips were trembling.

Angela proceeded unheeding, afraid to stop. "A special friend, and we had come to a very crucial point in our relationship. It was with him that I had the engagement yesterday."

"Well, what about it? Were you expecting him to ask you to marry him? Did he?"

"No," said Angela very low, "that's just what he didn't do though he,—he asked everything else."

Virginia, dropping the hair-brush, swung about sharply. "And you let him talk like that?"

"I couldn't help it once he had begun,—I was so taken by surprise, and, besides, I think that his ultimate intentions are all right."

"His ultimate intentions! Why, Angela what are you talking about? You know perfectly well what his ultimate intentions are. Isn't he a white man? Well, what kind of intentions would he have toward a coloured woman?"

"Simple! He doesn't know I'm coloured. And besides some of them are decent. You must remember that I know something about these people and you don't, you couldn't, living that humdrum little life of yours at home."

"I know enough about them and about men in general to recognize an insult when I hear one. Some men bear their character stamped right on their faces. Now this man into whose room I walked last night by mistake,——"

"I don't see how you can do very much talking walking into strange men's rooms at ten o'clock at night."

The triviality of the retort left Jinny dumb.

It was their first quarrel.

They sat in silence for a few minutes; for several minutes. Virginia, apparently completely composed, was letting the tendrils of her mind reach far, far out to the ultimate possibilities of this *impasse* in relationship between herself and her sister. She thought: "I really have lost her, she's really gone out of my ken just as I used to lose her years ago when father and I would be singing 'The Dying Christian'. I'm twenty-three years old and I'm really all alone in the world." Up to this time she had always felt she had Angela's greater age and supposedly greater

wisdom to fall back on, but she banished this conjecture forever. "Because if she could cut me when she hadn't seen me for
a year for the sake of a man who she must have known meant
to insult her, she certainly has no intention of openly acknowl-
edging me again. And I don't believe I want to be a sister in
secret. I hate this hole and corner business."

She saw again the scene in the station, herself at first so
serene, so self-assured, Angela's confused coldness, Roger's
insolence. Something hardened, grew cold within her. Even
his arrogance had failed to bring Angela to her senses, and
suddenly she remembered that it had been possible in slavery
times for white men and women to mistreat their mulatto relations, their own flesh and blood, selling them into deeper
slavery in the far South or standing by watching them beaten,
almost, if not completely, to death. Perhaps there was something fundamentally different between white and coloured blood
after all. Aloud she said: "You know before you went away that
Sunday morning you said that you and I were different.
Perhaps you're right, Angela; perhaps there is an extra infusion
of white blood in your veins which lets you see life at another
angle. If that's the case I have no right to judge you. You must
forgive my ignorant comments."

She began slipping into a ratine dress of old blue trimmed
with narrow collars and cuffs and a tiny belt of old rose. Above
the soft shades the bronze and black of her head etched themselves sharply; she might have been a dainty bird of Paradise
cast in a new arrangement of colours but her tender face was
set in strange and implacable lines.

Angela looked at her miserably. She had not known just
what, in her wounded pride and humiliation, she had expected
to gain from her sister, but certainly she had hoped for some
balm. And in any event not this cool aloofness. She had forgotten that her sister might be suffering from a wound as poignant
as her own. The year had made a greater breach than she had
anticipated; she had never been as outspoken, as frank with
Virginia as the latter had been with her, but there had always
been a common ground between them, a meeting place. In
the household Jinny had had something of a reputation for her
willingness to hear all sides of a story, to find an excuse or
make one.

An old aphorism of Hetty Daniels returned to her. "He who would have friends must show himself friendly." And she had done anything but that; she had neglected Jinny, had failed to answer her letters, had even planned,—was it only day before yesterday!—to see very little of her in what she had dreamed would be her new surroundings. Oh she had been shameful! But she would make it up to Jinny now—and then she could come to her at this, this crisis in her life which so frightened and attracted her. She was the more frightened because she felt that attraction. She would make her sister understand the desires and longings which had come to her in this strange, dear, free world, and then together they would map out a plan of action. Jinny might be a baby but she had strength. So much strength, said something within her, that just as likely as not she would say: "Let the whole thing go, Angela, Angela! You don't want to be even on the outskirts of a thing like this."

Before she could begin her overtures Jinny was speaking. "Listen, Angela, I've got to be going. I don't know when we'll be seeing each other again, and after what happened Wednesday you can hardly expect me to be looking you up, and as you doubtless are very busy you'd hardly be coming 'way up here. But there are one or two things I want to talk to you about. First about the house."

"About the house? Why it's yours. I've nothing more to do with it."

"I know, but I'm thinking of selling it. There is such a shortage of houses in Philadelphia just now; Mr. Hallowell says I can get at least twice as much as father paid for it. And in that case you've some more money coming to you."

If only she had known of this,—when?—twenty-four hours earlier, how differently she might have received Roger's proposition. If she had met Virginia Wednesday and had had the talk for which she had planned!

"Well of course it would be awfully nice to have some more money. But what I don't understand is how are you going to live? What are you going to do?"

"If I pass this examination I'm coming over here, my appointment would be only a matter of a few months. I'm sure of that. This is May and I'd only have to wait until September. Well, I wouldn't be working this summer anyway. And there's no way in the world which I could fail to pass. In fact I'm really thinking of taking a chance and coming over here to substitute. Mr. Holloster, the University of Pennsylvania man, has been investigating and he says there's plenty of work. And I guess I'm due to have a change; New York rather appeals to me. And there certainly is something about Harlem!" In spite of her careless manner Angela knew she was thinking about Matthew Henson. She stretched out her hand, pulled Jinny's head down on her shoulder. "Oh darling, don't worry about him. Matthew really wasn't the man for you."

"Well," said Virginia, "as long as I think he was, the fact that he wasn't doesn't make any real difference, does it? At least not at first. But I certainly shan't worry about it."

"No don't,—I,——" It was on the tip of her tongue to say "I know two or three nice young men whom you can play around with. I'll introduce you to them." But could she? Jinny understood her silence; smiled and nodded. "It's all right, honey, you can't do anything; you would if you could. We've just got to face the fact that you and I are two separate people and we've got to live our lives apart, not like the Siamese twins. And each of us will have to go her chosen way. After all each of us is seeking to get all she can out of life! and if you can get more out of it by being white, as you undoubtedly can, why, why shouldn't you? Only it seems to me that there are certain things in living that are more fundamental even than colour,— but I don't know. I'm all mixed up. But evidently you don't feel that way, and you're just as likely to be right as me."

"Jinny!"

"My dear, I'm not trying to reproach you. I'm trying to look at things without sentiment. After all, in a negative way, merely by saying nothing, you're disclaiming your black blood in a country where it is an inconvenience,—oh! there's not a doubt about that. You may be proud of it, you may be perfectly satisfied with it—I am—but it certainly can shut you out of things. So why shouldn't you disclaim a living manifestation of that blood?"

Before this cool logic Angela was silent. Virginia looked at her sister, a maternal look oddly apparent on her young face. When she was middle-aged she would be the embodiment of motherhood. How her children would love her!

"Angela, you'll be careful!"

"Yes; darling. Oh if only I could make you understand what it's all about."

"Yes, well, perhaps another time. I've got to fly now." She hesitated, took Angela by the arms and gazed into her eyes. "About this grand white party that you were in the station with. Are you awfully in love with him?"

"I'm not in love with him at all."

"Oh, pshaw!" said innocent Virginia, "you've got nothing to worry about! Why, what's all the shooting for?"

PLUM BUN

Chapter I

A NGELA wanted to ride downtown with her sister. "Perhaps I might bring you luck." But on this theme Jinny was adamant. "You'd be much more likely to bring yourself bad luck. No, there's no sense in taking a chance. I'll take the elevated; my landlady said it would drop me very near the school where I'm taking the examination. You go some other way." Down in the hall Mrs. Gloucester was busy dusting, her short bustling figure alive with housewifely ardour. Virginia paused near her and held out her hand to Angela. "Good-bye, Miss Mory," she said wickedly, "it was very kind of you to give me so much time. If you can ever tear yourself away from your beloved Village, come up and I'll try to show you Harlem. I don't think it's going to take me long to learn it."

Obediently Angela let her go her way and walking over to Seventh Avenue mounted the 'bus, smarting a little under Jinny's generous precautions. But presently she began to realize their value, for at One Hundred and Fourteenth Street Anthony Cross entered. He sat down beside her. "I never expected to see you in my neighbourhood."

"Oh is this where you live? I've often wondered."

"As it happens I've just come here, but I've lived practically all over New York." He was thin, restless, unhappy. His eyes dwelt ceaselessly on her face. She said a little nervously:

"It seems to me I hardly ever see you any more. What do you do with yourself?"

"Nothing that you would be interested in."

She did not dare make the obvious reply and after all, though she did like him very much, she was not interested in his actions. For a long moment she sought for some phrase which would express just the right combination of friendliness and indifference.

"It's been a long time since we've had lunch together; come

and have it to-day with me. You be my guest." She thought
of Jinny and the possible sale of the house. "I've just found out
that I'm going to get a rather decent amount of money, certainly enough to stand us for lunch."

"Thank you, I have an engagement; besides I don't want to
lunch with you in public."

This was dangerous ground. Flurried, she replied unwisely:
"All right, come in some time for tea; every once in a while I
make a batch of cookies; I made some a week ago. Next time I
feel the mood coming on me I'll send you a card and you can
come and eat them, hot and hot."

"You know you've no intention of doing any such thing.
Besides you don't know my address."

"An inconvenience which can certainly be rectified," she
laughed at him.

But he was in no laughing mood. "I've no cards with me, but
they wouldn't have the address anyway." He tore a piece of
paper out of his notebook, scribbled on it. "Here it is. I have
to get off now." He gave her a last despairing look. "Oh, Angel,
you know you're never going to send for me!"

The bit of paper clutched firmly in one hand, she arrived finally at her little apartment. Naturally of an orderly turn of
mind she looked about for her address book in which to write
the street and number. But some unexplained impulse led her
to smooth the paper out and place it in a corner of her desk.
That done she took off her hat and gloves, sat down in the
comfortable chair and prepared to face her thoughts.

Yesterday! Even now at a distance of twenty-four hours she
had not recovered her equilibrium. She was still stunned, still
unable to realize the happening of the day. Only she knew that
she had reached a milestone in her life; a possible turning
point. If she did not withdraw from her acquaintanceship with
Roger now, even though she committed no overt act she would
never be the same; she could never again face herself with the
old, unshaken pride and self-confidence. She would never be
the same to herself. If she withdrew, then indeed, indeed she
would be the same old Angela Murray, the same girl save for a
little sophistication that she had been before she left Philadelphia, only she would have started on an adventure and would

not have seen it to its finish, she would have come to grips
with life and would have laid down her arms at the first onslaught. Would she be a coward or a wise, wise woman? She
thought of two poems that she had read in "Hart's Class-
Book", an old, old book of her father's,—one of them ran:

> 'He either fears his fate too much
>   Or his deserts are small,
> Who dares not put it to the touch
>   For fear of losing all.'

The other was an odd mixture of shrewdness and cowardice:

> 'He who fights and runs away
>   Shall live to fight another day
> But he who is in battle slain
>   Has fallen ne'er to rise again.'

Were her deserts small or should she run away and come
back to fight another day when she was older, more experienced? More experienced! How was she to get that experience?
Already she was infinitely wiser, she would, if occasion required
it, exercise infinitely more wariness than she had yesterday with
Roger. Yet it was precisely because of that experience that she
would know how to meet, would even know when to expect
similar conditions.

She thought that she knew which verse she would follow if
she were Jinny, but, back once more in the assurance of her
own rooms, she knew that she did not want to be Jinny, that
she and Jinny were two vastly different persons. "But," she said
to herself, "if Jinny were as fair as I and yet herself and placed
in the same conditions as those in which I am placed her colour
would save her. It's a safeguard for Jinny; it's always been a
curse for me."

Roger had come for her in the blue car. There were a hamper
and two folding chairs and a rug stored away in it. It was a gorgeous day. "If we can," he said, "we'll picnic." He was extremely
handsome and extremely nervous. Angela was nervous too,
though she did not show it except in the loss of her colour. She
was rather plain to-day; to be so near the completion of her

goal and yet to have to wait these last few agonizing moments, perhaps hours, was deadly. They were rather silent for a while, Roger intent on his driving. Traffic in New York is a desperate strain at all hours, at eleven in the morning it is deadly; the huge leviathan of a city is breaking into the last of its stride. For a few hours it will proceed at a measured though never leisurely pace and then burst again into the mad rush of the homeward bound.

But at last they were out of the city limits and could talk. For the first time since she had known him he began to speak of his possessions. "Anything, anything that money can buy, Angèle, I can get and I can give." His voice was charged with intention. They were going in the direction of Forest Hills; he had a cottage out there, perhaps she would like to see it. And there was a grove not far away. "We'll picnic there," he said, "and—and talk." He certainly was nervous, Angela thought, and liked him the better for it.

The cottage or rather the house in Forest Hills was beautiful, absolutely a gem. And it was completely furnished with taste and marked daintiness. "What do you keep it furnished for?" asked Angela wondering. Roger murmured that it had been empty for a long time but he had seen this equipment and it had struck him that it was just the thing for this house so he had bought it; thereby insensibly reminding his companion again that he could afford to gratify any whim. They drove away from the exquisite little place in silence. Angela was inclined to be amused; surely no one could have asked for a better opening than that afforded by the house. What would make him talk, she wondered, and what, oh what would he say? Something far, far more romantic than poor Matthew Henson could ever have dreamed of,—yes and far, far less romantic, something subconscious prompted her, than Anthony Cross had said. Anthony with his poverty and honour and desperate vows!

They had reached the grove, they had spread the rug and a tablecloth; Roger had covered it with dainties. He would not let her lift a finger, she was the guest and he her humble servant. She looked at him smiling, still forming vague contrasts with him and Matthew and Anthony.

Roger dropped his sandwich, came and sat behind her. He

put his arm around her and shifted his shoulder so that her head lay against it.

"Don't look at me that way Angèle, Angèle! I can't stand it."

So it was actually coming. "How do you want me to look at you?"

He bent his head down to hers and kissed her. "Like this, like this! Oh Angèle, did you like the house?"

"Like it? I loved it."

"Darling, I had it done for you, you know. I thought you'd like it."

It seemed a strange thing to have done without consulting her, and anyway she did not want to live in a suburb. Opal Street had been suburb enough for her. She wanted, required, the noise and tumult of cities.

"I don't care for suburbs, Roger." How strange for him to talk about a place to live in and never a word of love!

"My dear girl, you don't have to live in a suburb if you don't want to. I've got a place, an apartment in Seventy-second Street, seven rooms; that would be enough for you and your maid, wouldn't it? I could have this furniture moved over there, or if you think it too cottagey, you could have new stuff altogether."

Seven rooms for three people! Why she wanted a drawing-room and a studio and where would he put his things? This sudden stinginess was quite inexplicable.

"But Roger, seven rooms wouldn't be big enough."

He laughed indulgently, his face radiant with relief and triumph. "So she wants a palace, does she? Well, she shall have it. A whole *ménage* if you want it, a place on Riverside Drive, servants and a car. Only somehow I hadn't thought of you as caring about that kind of thing. After that little hole in the wall you've been living in on Jayne Street I'd have expected you to find the place in Seventy-Second Street as large as you'd care for!"

A little hurt, she replied: "But I was thinking of you too. There wouldn't be room for your things. And I thought you'd want to go on living in the style you'd been used to." A sudden welcome explanation dawned on her rising fear. "Are you keeping this a secret from your father? Is that what's the trouble?"

Under his thin, bright skin he flushed. "Keeping what a secret from my father? What are you talking about, Angèle?"

She countered with his own question. "What are *you* talking
about, Roger?"

He tightened his arms about her, his voice stammered, his
eyes were bright and watchful. "I'm asking you to live in my
house, to live for me; to be my girl; to keep a love-nest where
I and only I may come." He smiled shamefacedly over the cheap
current phrase.

She pushed him away from her; her jaw fallen and slack but
her figure taut. Yet under her stunned bewilderment her mind
was racing. So this was her castle, her fortress of protection,
her refuge. And what answer should she make? Should she
strike him across his eager, half-shamed face, should she get up
and walk away, forbidding him to follow? Or should she stay
and hear it out? Stay and find out what this man was really like;
what depths were in him and, she supposed, in other men. But
especially in this man with his boyish, gallant air and his face as
guileless and as innocent apparently as her own.

That was what she hated in herself, she told that self fiercely,
shut up with her own thoughts the next afternoon in her room.
She hated herself for staying and listening. It had given him
courage to talk and talk. But what she most hated had been
the shrewdness, the practicality which lay beneath that resolve
to hear it out. She had thought of those bills; she had thought
of her poverty, of her helplessness, and she had thought too of
Martha Burden's dictum: "You must make him want you." Well
here was a way to make him want her and to turn that wanting
to account. "Don't," Martha said, "withhold too much. Give a
little." Suppose she gave him just the encouragement of listening to him, of showing him that she did like him a little; while
he meanwhile went on wanting, wanting—men paid a big price
for their desires. Her price would be marriage. It was a game,
she knew, which women played all over the world although it
had never occurred to her to play it; a dangerous game at which
some women burned their fingers. "Don't give too much,"
said Martha, "for then you lose yourself." Well, she would give
nothing and she would not burn her fingers. Oh, it would be a
great game.

Another element entered too. He had wounded her pride
and he should salve it. And the only unguent possible would
be a proposal of marriage. Oh if only she could be a girl in a
book and when he finally did ask her for her hand, she would
be able to tell him that she was going to marry someone else,
someone twice as eligible, twice as handsome, twice as wealthy.

Through all these racing thoughts penetrated the sound of
Roger's voice, pleading, persuasive, seductive. She was amazed
to find a certain shamefaced timidity creeping over her; yet it
was he who should have shown the shame. And she could not
understand either why she was unable to say plainly: "You say
you care for me, long for me so much, why don't you ask me
to come to you in the ordinary way?" But some pride either
unusually false or unusually fierce prevented her from doing
this. Undoubtedly Roger with his wealth, his looks and his
family connections had already been much sought after. He
knew he was an "eligible". Poor, unknown, stigmatized, if he
but knew it, as a member of the country's least recognized group
she could not bring herself to belong even in appearance to
that band of young women who so obviously seek a "good
match".

When he had paused a moment for breath she told him
sadly: "But, Roger, people don't do that kind of thing, not decent people."

"Angèle, you are such a child! This is exactly the kind of
thing people do do. And why not? Why must the world be let
in on the relationships of men and women? Some of the sweetest unions in history have been of this kind."

"For others perhaps, but not for me. Relationships of the
kind you describe don't exist among the people I know." She
was thinking of her parents, of the Hallowells, of the Hensons
whose lives were indeed like open books.

He looked at her curiously, "The people you know! Don't
tell me you haven't guessed about Paulette!"

She had forgotten about Paulette! "Yes I know about her.
She told me herself. I like her, she's been a mighty fine friend,
but, Roger, you surely don't want me to be like her."

"Of course I don't. It was precisely because you weren't like her that I became interested. You were such a babe in the woods. Anyone could see you'd had no experience with men."

This obvious lack of logic was too bewildering. She looked at him like the child which, in these matters, she really was. "But,—but Roger, mightn't that be a beginning of a life like Paulette's? What would become of me after we, you and I, had separated? Very often these things last only for a short time, don't they?"

"Not necessarily; certainly not between you and me. And I'd always take care of you, you'd be provided for." He could feel her gathering resentment. In desperation he played a cunning last card: "And besides who knows, something permanent may grow out of this. I'm not entirely my own master, Angèle."

Undoubtedly he was referring to his father whom he could not afford to offend. It never occurred to her that he might be lying, for why should he?

To all his arguments, all his half-promises and implications she returned a steady negative. As twilight came on she expressed a desire to go home; with the sunset her strength failed her; she felt beaten and weary. Her unsettled future, her hurt pride, her sudden set-to with the realities of the society in which she had been moving, bewildered and frightened her. Resentful, puzzled, introspective, she had no further words for Roger; it was impossible for him to persuade her to agree or to disagree with his arguments. During the long ride home she was resolutely mute.

Yet on the instant of entering Jayne Street she felt she could not endure spending the long evening hours by herself and she did not want to be alone with Roger. She communicated this distaste to him. While not dishevelled they were not presentable enough to invade the hotels farther uptown. But, anxious to please her, he told her they could go easily enough to one of the small cabarets in the Village. A few turns and windings and they were before a house in a dark side street knocking on its absurdly barred door, entering its black, myterious portals. In a room with a highly polished floor, a few tables and chairs, some rather bizarre curtains, five or six couples were sitting, among them Paulette, Jack Hudson, a tall, rather big, extremely

blonde girl whose name Angela learned was Carlotta Parks,
and a slender, black-avised man whose name she failed to
catch. Paulette hailed him uproariously; the blonde girl rose
and precipitately threw her arms about Fielding's neck.

"Roger!"

"Don't," he said rather crossly. "Hello, Jack." He nodded to
the dark man whom he seemed to know indifferently well.
"What have they got to eat here, you fellows? Miss Mory and
I are tired and hungry. We've been following the pike all day."
Miss Parks turned and gave Angela a long, considering look.

"Sit here," said Paulette, "there's plenty of room. Jack, you
order for them, the same things we've been having. You get
good cooking here." She was radiant with happiness and content. Under the influence of the good, stimulating food Angela
began to recover, to look around her.

Jack Hudson, a powerfully built bronze figure of a man,
beamed on Paulette, saying nothing and in his silence saying
everything. The dark man kept his eyes on Carlotta, who was
oblivious to everyone but Roger, clearly her friend of long
standing. She sat clasping one of his hands, her head almost upon
his shoulder. "Roger it's so good to see you again! I've thought
of you so often! I've been meaning to write to you; we're having
a big house party this summer. You must come! Dad's asking
up half of Washington; attachés, 'Prinzessen, Countessen and
serene English Altessen'; he'll come up for week-ends."

A member of the *haut monde*, evidently she was well-
connected, powerful, even rich. A girl of Roger's own set
amusing herself in this curious company. Angela felt her heart
contract with a sort of helpless jealousy.

The dark man, despairing of recapturing Carlotta's attention,
suddenly asked Angèle if she would care to dance. He was a
superb partner and for a moment or two, reinvigorated by the
food and the snappy music, she became absorbed in the
smooth, gliding motion and in her partner's pleasant conversation. Glancing over her shoulder she noted Carlotta still talking
to Roger. The latter, however, was plainly paying the girl no
attention. His eyes fixed on Angela, he was moodily following
her every motion, almost straining, she thought, to catch her
words. His eyes met hers and a long, long look passed between
them so fraught, it seemed to her, with a secret understanding

and sympathy, that her heart shook with a moment's secret wavering.

Her partner escorted her back to the table. Paulette, flushed and radiant, with the mien of a dishevelled baby, was holding forth while Hudson listened delightedly. As a *raconteuse* she had a faint, delicious malice which usually made any recital of her adventures absolutely irresistible. "Her name," she was saying loudly, regardless of possible listeners, "was Antoinette Spewer, and it seems she had it in for me from the very first. She told Sloane Corby she wanted to meet me and he invited both of us to lunch. When we got to the restaurant she was waiting for me in the lobby; Sloane introduced us and—she pulled a lorgnette on me,—a lorgnette on *me*!" She said it very much as a Westerner might speak of someone "pulling" a revolver. "But I fixed that. There were three or four people passing near us. I drew back until they were well within hearing range, and then I said to her: 'I beg pardon but what did you say your last name was?' Well, when a person's named Spewer she can't shout it across a hotel lobby! Oh, she came climbing down off her high horse; she respects me to this day, I tell you."

Roger rose. "We must be going; I can't let Miss Mory get too tired." He was all attention and courtesy. Miss Parks looked at her again, narrowing her eyes.

In the car Roger put his arm about her. "Angèle, when you were dancing with that fellow I couldn't stand it! And then you looked at me,—oh such a look! You were thinking about me, I felt it, I knew it."

Some treacherous barrier gave way within her "Yes, and I could tell you were thinking about me."

"Of course you could! And without a word! Oh, darling, darling, can't you see that's the way it would be? If you'd only take happiness with me there we would be with a secret bond, an invisible bond, existing for us alone and no one else in the world the wiser. But we should know and it would be all the sweeter for that secrecy."

Unwittingly he struck a responsive chord within her,— stolen waters were the sweetest, she of all people knew that.

Aloud she said: "Here we are, Roger. Some of the day has been wonderful; thank you for that."

"You can't go like this! You're going to let me see you again?

She knew she should have refused him, but again some treacherous impulse made her assent. He drove away, and, turning, she climbed the long, steep flights of stairs, bemused, thrilled, frightened, curious, the sense of adventure strong upon her. To-morrow she would see Jinny, her own sister, her own flesh and blood, one of her own people. Together they would thresh this thing out.

Chapter II

A CURIOUS period of duelling ensued. Roger was young, rich and idle. Nearly every wish he had ever known had been born within him only to be satisfied. He could not believe that he would fail in the pursuit of this baffling creature who had awakened within him an ardour and sincerity of feeling which surprised himself. The thought occurred to him more than once that it would have been a fine thing if this girl had been endowed with the name and standing and comparative wealth of—say Carlotta Parks,—but it never occurred to him to thwart in this matter the wishes of his father who would, he knew, insist immediately on a certified account of the pedigree, training and general fitness of any strange aspirant for his son's hand. Angela had had the good sense to be frank; she did not want to become immeshed in a tissue of lies whose relationship, whose sequence and interdependence she would be likely to forget. To Roger's few questions she had said quite truly that she was the daughter of "poor but proud parents";—they had laughed at the hackneyed phrase,—that her father had been a boss carpenter and that she had been educated in the ordinary public schools and for a time had been a school teacher. No one would ever try to substantiate these statements, for clearly the person to whom they applied would not be falsifying such a simple account. There would be no point in so doing. Her little deceits had all been negative, she had merely neglected to say that she had a brown sister and that her father had been black.

Roger found her unfathomable. His was the careless, unreasoned cynicism of the modern, worldly young man. He had truly, as he acknowledged, been attracted to Angela because of a certain incurious innocence of hers apparent in her observations and in her manner. He saw no reason why he should cherish that innocence. If questioned he would have answered: "She's got to learn about the world in which she lives sometime; she might just as well learn of it through me. And I'd always look out for her." In the back of his mind, for all his unassuming even simple attitude toward his wealth and power, lurked the conviction that that same wealth and power could heal any wound, atone for any loss. Still there were times when even he experienced a faint, inner qualm, when Angela would ask him: "But afterwards, what would become of me, Roger?" It was the only question he could not meet. Out of all his hosts of precedents from historical Antony and Cleopatra down to notorious affinities discovered through blatant newspaper "stories" he could find for this only a stammered "There's no need to worry about an afterwards, Angèle, for you and I would always be friends."

Their frequent meetings now were little more than a trial of strength. Young will and determination were pitted against young will and determination. On both the excitement of the chase was strong, but each was pursuing a different quarry. To all his protestations, arguments and demands, Angela returned an insistent: "What you are asking is impossible." Yet she either could not or would not drive him away, and gradually, though she had no intention of yielding to his wishes, her first attitude of shocked horror began to change.

For three months the conflict persisted. Roger interposed the discussion into every talk, on every occasion. Gradually it came to be the *raison d'être* of their constant comradeship. His arguments were varied and specious. "My dearest girl, think of a friendship in which two people would have every claim in the world upon each other and yet no claim. Think of giving all, not because you say to a minister 'I will', but from the generosity of a powerful affection. That is the very essence of free love. I give you my word that the happiest couples in the world are those who love without visible bonds. Such people are bound by the most durable ties. Theirs is a state of the closest because the freest, most elastic union in the world."

A singularly sweet and curious intimacy was growing up between them. Roger told Angela many anecdotes about his father and about his dead mother, whom he still loved, and for whom he even grieved in a pathetically boyish way. "She was so sweet to me, she loved me so. I'll never forget her. It's for her sake that I try to please my father, though Dad's some pumpkins on his own account." In turn she was falling into the habit of relating to him the little happenings of her every-day life, a life which she was beginning to realize must, in his eyes, mean the last word in the humdrum and the monotonous. And yet how full of adventure, of promise, even of mystery did it seem compared with Jinny's!

Roger had much intimate knowledge of people and told her many and dangerous secrets. "See how I trust you, Angèle; you might trust me a little!"

If his stories were true, certainly she might just as well trust him a great deal, for all her little world, judging it by the standards by which she was used to measuring people, was tumbling in ruins at her feet. If this were the way people lived then what availed any ideals? The world was made to take pleasure in; one gained nothing by exercising simple virtue, it was after all an extension of the old formula which she had thought out for herself many years ago. Roger spent most of his time with her, it seemed. Anything which she undertook to do delighted him. She would accept no money, no valuable presents. "And I can't keep going out with you to dinners and luncheons forever, Roger. It would be different if,—if we really meant anything to each other." He deliberately misunderstood her, "But nothing would give me more pleasure than for us to mean the world to one another." He sent her large hampers of fruit and even the more ordinary edibles; then he would tease her about being selfish. In order to get rid of the food she had asked him to lunch, to dinner, since nothing that she could say would make him desist from sending it.

Nothing gave her greater joy really than this playful housekeeping. She was very lonely; Jinny had her own happy interests; Anthony never came near her nor did she invite him to come; Martha Burden seemed engrossed in her own affairs, she was undergoing some secret strain that made her appear more remote, more strongly self-sufficient, more mysterious than ever. Paulette, making overt preparations to go to Russia with Hudson, was impossibly, hurtingly happy. Miss Powell,— but she could not get near her; the young coloured girl showed her the finest kind of courtesy, but it had about it a remote and frozen quality, unbreakable. However, Angela for the moment did not desire to break it; she must run no more risks with Roger, still she put Miss Powell on the list of those people whom she would some day aid,—when everything had turned out all right.

The result of this feeling of loneliness was, of course, to turn her more closely to Roger. He paid her the subtle compliment of appearing absolutely at home in her little apartment; he grew to like her plain, good cooking and the experiments which sometimes she made frankly for him. And afterwards as the fall closed in there were long, pleasant evenings before an open fire, or two or three last hours after a brisk spin in the park in the blue car. And gradually she had grown to accept and even inwardly to welcome his caresses. She perched with an air of great unconsciousness on the arm of the big chair in which he was sitting but the transition became constantly easier from the arm of the chair to his knee, to the steely embrace of his arm, to the sound of the hard beating of his heart, to his murmured: "This is where you belong, Angèle, Angèle." He seemed an anchor for her frail insecure bark of life.

It was at moments like these that he told her amazing things about their few common acquaintances. There was not much to say about Paulette. "I think," said Roger judicially, "that temperamentally she is a romantic adventurer. Something in her is constantly seeking a change but she will never be satisfied. She's a good sport, she takes as she gives, asking nothing permanent and promising nothing permanent." Angela thought it rather sad. But Roger dismissed the theme with the rather airy comment that there were women as there were men "like that". She wondered if he might not be a trifle callous.

More than once they had spoken of Martha Burden; Angela confessed herself tremendously intrigued by the latter, by that tense, brooding personality. She learned that Martha, made of the stuff which dies for causes, was constantly being torn between theory and practice.

"She's full," said Roger, "of the most high-falutin, advanced ideas. Oh I've known old Martha all my life, we were brought up together, it's through her really that I began to know the people in this part of town. She's always been a sort of sister. More than once I've had to yank her by the shoulders out of difficulties which she herself created. I made her marry Starr."

"Made her marry him,—didn't she want him?"

"Yes, she wanted him all right, but she doesn't believe in marriage. She's got the courage of her convictions, that girl. Why actually she lived with Starr two years while I was away doing

Europe. When I came back and found out what had happened I told Starr I'd beat him into pulp if he didn't turn around and make good."

"But why the violence? Didn't he want to?"

"Yes, only," he remembered suddenly his own hopes, "not every man is capable of appreciating a woman who breaks through the conventions for him. Some men mistake it for cheapness but others see it for what it is and love more deeply and gratefully." Softly, lingeringly he touched the soft hair shadowing her averted cheek. "I'm one of those others, Angèle."

She wanted to say: "But why shouldn't we marry? Why not make me safe as well as Martha?" But again her pride intervened. Instead she remarked that Martha did not seem always happy.

"No, well that's because she's got this fool idea of hers that now that they are bound the spontaneity is lacking. She wants to give without being obliged to give; to take because she chooses and not because she's supposed to. Oh she's as true as steel and the best fighter in a cause, but I've no doubt but that she leads old Starr a life with her temperament."

Angela thought that there were probably two sides to this possibility. A little breathlessly she asked Roger if he knew Anthony Cross.

"Cross, Cross! A sallow, rather thin fellow? I think I saw him once or twice at Paulette's. No, I don't really know him. A sullen, brooding sort of chap I should say. Frightfully self-absorbed and all that."

For some reason a little resentment sprang up in her. Anthony might brood, but his life had been lived on dark, troublesome lines that invited brooding; he had never known the broad, golden highway of Roger's existence. And anyway she did not believe, if Martha Burden had been Anthony's lifelong friend, almost his sister, that he would have told his sweetheart or his wife either of those difficult passages in her life. Well, she would have to teach Roger many things. Aloud she spoke of Carlotta Parks.

"She's an interesting type. Tell me about her."

But Roger said rather shortly that there was nothing to tell. "Just a good-hearted, high-spirited kid, that's all, who lets the whole world know her feelings."

*

According to Paulette there was more than this to be told about Miss Parks. "I don't know her myself, not being a member of that crowd. But I've always heard that she and Roger were childhood sweethearts, only they've just not pulled it off. Carlotta's family is as old as his. Her people have always been statesmen, her father's in the Senate. I don't think they have much money now. But the main thing is she pleases old man Fielding. Nothing would give him more pleasure than to see Carlotta Roger's wife. I may be mistaken, but I think nothing would give Carlotta more pleasure either."

"Doesn't he care for her?" Queer how her heart tightened, listening for the answer.

"Yes, but she likes him too much and shows it. So he thinks he doesn't want her. Roger will never want any woman who comes at his first call. Don't you hate that sort of man? They are really the easiest to catch; all you've got to do provided they're attracted at all, is to give one inviting glance and then keep steadily retreating. And they'll come—like Bo Peep's sheep. But I don't want a man like that; he'd cramp my style. His impudence, expecting a woman to repress or evoke her emotions just as he wants them! Hasn't a woman as much right to feel as a man and to feel first? Never mind, some woman is going to 'get' Roger yet. He doesn't think it possible because he has wealth and position. He'll be glad to come running to Carlotta then. I don't care very much for her,—she's a little too loud for me," objected the demure and conservative Miss Lister, "but I do think she likes Roger for himself and not for what he can give her!"

Undoubtedly this bit of knowledge lent a new aspect; the adventure began to take on fresh interest. Everything seemed to be playing into her hands. Roger's interest and longing were certainly undiminished. Martha Burden's advice, confirmed by Paulette's disclosure, was bound to bring results. She had only to "keep retreating".

But there was one enemy with whom she had never thought to reckon, she had never counted on the treachery of the forces of nature; she had never dreamed of the unaccountable weakening of those forces within. Her weapons were those furnished

by the conventions but her fight was against conditions; impulses, yearnings which antedated both those weapons and the
conventions which furnished them. Insensibly she began to
see in Roger something more than a golden way out of her
material difficulties; he was becoming more than a means
through which she should be admitted to the elect of the world
for whom all things are made. Before her eyes he was changing
to the one individual who was kindest, most thoughtful of her,
the one whose presence brought warmth and assurance.
Furthermore, his constant attention, flatteries and caresses
were producing their inevitable effect. She was naturally cold;
unlike Paulette, she was a woman who would experience the
grand passion only once, perhaps twice, in her life and she
would always have to be kindled from without; in the last analysis her purity was a matter not of morals, nor of religion, nor
of racial pride; it was a matter of fastidiousness. Bit by bit Roger
had forced his way closer and closer into the affairs of her life,
and his proximity had not offended that fastidiousness. Gradually his demands seemed to her to represent a very natural and
beautiful impulse; his arguments and illustrations began to
bear fruit; the conventions instead of showing in her eyes as
the codified wisdom based on the experiences of countless
generations of men and women, seemed to her prudish and
unnecessary. Finally her attitude reduced itself to this: she
would have none of the relationship which Roger urged so insistently, not because according to all the training which she
had ever received, it was unlawful, but because viewed in the
light of the great battle which she was waging for pleasure,
protection and power, it was inexpedient.

The summer and the early fall had passed. A cold, rainy autumn was closing in; the disagreeable weather made motoring
almost impossible. There were always the theatres and the cabarets, but Roger professed himself as happy nowhere else but at
her fireside. And she loved to have him there, tall and strong
and beautiful, sometimes radiant with hope, at others sulking
with the assurance of defeat. He came in one day ostensibly to
have tea with her; he had an important engagement for the
evening but he could not let the day pass without seeing her.
Angela was tired and a little dispirited. Jinny had sold the
house and had sent her twelve hundred dollars as her share,

but the original three thousand was almost dissipated. She must not touch this new gift from heaven; her goal was no nearer; the unwelcome possibility of teaching, on the contrary, was constantly before her. Moreover, she was at last realising the danger of this constant proximity, she was appalled by her thoughts and longings. Upon her a great fear was creeping not only of Roger but of herself.

Always watchful, he quickly divined her distrait mood, resolved to try its possibilities for himself. In a tense silence they drank their tea and sat gazing at the leaping, golden flames. The sullen night closed in. Angela reminded him presently that he must go but on he sat and on. At eight o'clock she reminded him again; he took out his watch and looked at it indifferently. "It's too late for me to keep it now, besides I don't want to go. Angèle be kind, don't send me away."

"But you've had no dinner."

"Nor you either. I'm like the beasts of the field keeping you like this. Shall we go out somewhere?" But she was languid; she did not want to stir from the warm hearth out into the chilly night.

"No, I don't want to go. But you go, Roger. I can find something here in the house for myself, but there's not a thing for you. I hate to be so inhospitable."

"Tell you what, suppose I go around to one of these *delicatessens* and get something. Too tired to fix up a picnic lunch?"

In half an hour he returned, soaked. "It's raining in torrents! Why I never saw such a night!" He shook himself, spattering rain-drops all over the tiny apartment.

"Roger! You'll have to take of your coat!"

He sat in his shirt-sleeves before the fire, his hair curling and damp, his head on his hand. He looked so like a little boy that her heart shook within her. Turning he caught the expression in her eyes, sprang towards her. "Angèle you know, you *know* you like me a little!"

"I like you a very great deal." He put his arm about her, kissed her; her very bones turned to water. She freed herself, finding an excuse to go into the kitchenette. But he came and stood towering over her in the doorway, his eyes on her every motion. They ate the meal, a good one, almost as silently as they had drunk the tea; a terrible awareness of each other's presence was upon them, the air was charged with passion. Outside the rain and wind beat and screamed.

"It's a terrible night," she said, but he made no reply. She said again, "Roger, it's getting late, you must go home." Very reluctantly then, his eyes still on hers, he rose to his feet, got into his overcoat and, hat in hand, stooped to kiss her good-night. His arm stole about her, holding her close against him. She could feel him trembling, she was trembling herself. Another second and the door had closed behind him.

Alone, she sat looking at the fire and thinking: "This is awful. I don't believe anything is going to come of this. I believe I'll send him a note to-morrow and tell him not to come any more."

Someone tapped on the door; astonished that a caller should appear at such an hour, but not afraid, she opened it. It was Roger. He came striding into the room, flinging off his wet coat, and yet almost simultaneously catching her up in his arms. "It's such a terrible night, Angèle; you can't send me out in it. Why should I go when the fire is here and you, so warm and soft and sweet!"

All her strength left her; she could not even struggle, could not speak. He swept her up in his arms, cradling her in them like a baby with her face beneath his own. "You know that we were meant for each other, that we belong to each other!"

A terrible lassitude enveloped her out of which she heard herself panting: "Roger, Roger let me go! Oh, Roger, must it be like this? Can't it be any other way?"

And from a great distance she heard his voice breaking, pleading, promising: "Everything will be all right, darling, darling. I swear it. Only trust me, trust me!"

Life rushed by on a great, surging tide. She could not tell whether she was utterly happy or utterly miserable. All that she could do was to feel; feel that she was Roger's totally. Her whole being turned toward him as a flower to the sun. Without him life meant nothing; with him it was everything. For the time being she was nothing but emotion; he was amazed himself at the depth of feeling which he had aroused in her.

Now for the first time she felt possessive; she found herself deeply interested in Roger's welfare because, she thought, he was

hers and she could not endure having a possession whose qualities were unknown. She was not curious about his money nor
his business affairs but she thirsted to know how his time away
from her was spent, whom he saw, what other places he frequented. Not that she begrudged him a moment away from
her side, but she must be able to account for that moment.

Yet if she felt possessive of him her feeling also recognized
his complete absorption of her, so completely, so exhaustively
did his life seem to envelop hers. For a while his wishes, his
pleasure were the end and aim of her existence; she told herself
with a slight tendency toward self-mockery that this was the
explanation of being, of her being; that men had other aims,
other uses but that the sole excuse for being a woman was to
be just that,—a woman. Forgotten were her ideals about her
Art; her ambition to hold a salon; her desire to help other
people; even her intention of marrying in order to secure her future. Only something quite outside herself, something watchful, proud, remote from the passion and rapture which flamed
within her, kept her free and independent. She would not accept money, she would not move to the apartment on Seventy-
second Street; she still refused gifts so ornate that they were
practically bribes. She made no explanations to Roger, but he
knew and she knew too that her surrender was made out of the
lavish fullness and generosity of her heart; there was no calculation back of it; if this were free love the freedom was the
quality to be stressed rather than the emotion.

Sometimes, in her inchoate, wordless intensity of feeling
which she took for happiness, she paused to take stock of that
other life, those other lives which once she had known; that
life which had been hers when she had first come to New York
before she had gone to Cooper Union, in those days when she
had patrolled Fourteenth Street and had sauntered through
Union Square. And that other life which she knew in Opal Street,
—æons ago, almost in another existence. She passed easily over
those first few months in New York because even then she had
been approaching a threshold, getting ready to enter on a new,
undreamed of phase of being. But sometimes at night she lay
for hours thinking over her restless, yearning childhood, her
fruitless days at the Academy, the abortive wooing of Matthew
Henson. The Hensons, the Hallowells, Hetty Daniels,—Jinny!

How far now she was beyond their pale! Before her rose the eager, starved face of Hetty Daniels; now she herself was cognizant of phases of life for which Hetty longed but so contemned. Angela could imagine the envy back of the tone in which Hetty, had she but known it, would have expressed her disapproval of her former charge's manner of living. "Mattie Murray's girl, Angela, has gone straight to the bad; she's living a life of sin with some man in New York." And then the final, blasting indictment. "He's a white man, too. Can you beat that?"

Chapter III

ROGER'S father, it appeared, had been greatly pleased with his son's management of the saw-mills in Georgia; as a result he was making more and more demands on his time. And the younger man half through pride, half through that steady determination never to offend his father, was always ready to do his bidding. Angela liked and appreciated her lover's filial attitude, but even in the period of her warmest interest she resented, secretly despised, this tendency to dependence. He was young, superbly trained; he had the gift of forming friendships whose strength rested on his own personality, yet he distrusted too much his own powers or else he was lazy— Angela could never determine which. During this phase of their acquaintanceship she was never sure that she loved him, but she was positive that if at this time he had been willing to fling aside his obsequious deference to his father's money and had said to her: "Angèle, if you'll help me, we'll build up a life, a fortune of our own," she would have adored him.

Her strong, independent nature, buffeted and sickened and strengthened by the constant attrition of colour prejudice, was unable to visualise or to pardon the frame of mind which kept Roger from joining battle with life when the odds were already so overwhelmingly in his favour. Alone, possessed of a handicap which if guessed at would have been as disabling as a game leg or an atrophied body, she had dared enter the lists. And she was well on the way to winning a victory. It was to cost her, she was beginning to realize, more than she had anticipated. But having entered she was not one to draw back,—unless indeed she changed her goal. Hers was a curious mixture of materialism and hedonism, and at this moment the latter quality was uppermost in her life. But she supposed that in some vague future she and Roger would marry. His ardour rendered her complacent.

But she was not conscious of any of these inner conflicts and criticisms; she was too happy. Now she was adopting a curious detachment toward life tempered by a faint cynicism,—a detachment which enabled her to say to herself: "Rules are for ordinary people but not for me." She remembered a verse from a poet, a coloured woman about whom she had often wondered. The lines ran:

"The strong demand, contend, prevail.
The beggar is a fool!"

She would never be a beggar. She would ask no further counsel nor advice of anyone. She had been lucky thus far in seeking advice only from Paulette and Martha Burden, two people of markedly independent methods of thought and action. They had never held her back. Now she would no longer consult even them. She would live her life as an individualist, to suit herself without regard for the conventions and established ways of life. Her native fastidiousness, she was sure, would keep her from becoming an offence in her own eyes.

In spite of her increasing self-confidence and self-sufficiency Roger's frequent absences left her lonely. Almost then, without any conscious planning on her part, she began to work at her art with growing vigour and interest. She was gaining in assurance; her technique showed an increased mastery, above all she had gained in the power to compose, a certain sympathy, a breadth of comprehension, the manifestation of that ability to interpret which she had long suspected lay within her, lent themselves to her hand. Mr. Paget, the instructor, spoke of her paintings with increased respect; the attention of visitors was directed thereto. Martha Burden and even Paulette, in the intervals of her ecstatic preparations, admitted her to the freemasonry of their own assured standing. Anthony Cross reminded her of the possibilities for American students at Fontainebleau. But she only smiled wisely; she would have no need of such study, but she hoped with all her heart that Miss Powell would be the recipient of a prize which would enable her to attend there.

"If she isn't," she promised herself, "I'll make Roger give her her expenses. I'd be willing to take the money from him for that."

To her great surprise her other interest besides her painting lay in visiting Jinny. If anyone had asked her if she were satisfied with her own life, her reply would have been an instant affirmative. But she did not want such a life for her sister. For

Virginia there must be no risks, no secrets, no irregularities.
Her efforts to find out how her sister spent her free hours
amazed herself; their fruitlessness filled her with a constant
irritation which Virginia showed no inclination to allay. The
younger girl had passed her examination and had been appointed; she was a successful and enthusiastic teacher; this much
Angela knew, but beyond this nothing. She gathered that
Virginia spent a good deal of time with a happy, intelligent,
rather independent group of young coloured men and women;
there was talk occasionally of the theatre, of a dance, of small
clubs, of hikes, of classes at Columbia or at New York City
College. Angela even met a gay, laughing party, consisting of
Virginia and her friends *en route* to Brooklyn, she had been
later informed briefly. The girls were bright birds of paradise,
the men, her artist's eye noted, were gay, vital fauns. In the
subway beside the laughing, happy groups, white faces showed
pale and bloodless, other coloured faces loomed dull and
hopeless. Angela began tardily to recognize that her sister had
made her way into that curious, limited, yet shifting class of
the "best" coloured people; the old Philadelphia phrase came
drifting back to her, "people that you know." She was amazed
at some of the names which Virginia let drop from her lips in
her infrequent and laconic descriptions of certain evenings
which she had spent in the home of Van Meier, a great coloured
American, a littérateur, a fearless and dauntless apostle of the
rights of man; his name was known, Martha Burden had assured her, on both sides of the water.

Such information she picked up as best she might for Virginia
vouchsafed nothing; nor did she, on the infrequent occasions
on which she ran across her sister, even appear to know her.
This Angela pointed out, was silly. "You might just as well speak,"
she told Jinny petulantly, remembering uncomfortably the occasion when she herself had cut her sister, an absolute stranger
in New York. "Plenty of white and coloured people are getting
to know each other and they always acknowledge the acquaintanceship. Why shouldn't we? No harm could come of it." But
in Virginia's cool opinion no good could come of it either.
Usually the younger girl preserved a discreet silence; whatever
resolves she might have made with regard to the rupture
between herself and her sister, she was certainly able to keep her

own counsel. It was impossible to glean from her perfect, slightly distrait manner any glimpse of her inner life and her intentions. Frequently she showed an intense preoccupation from which she awakened to let fall a remark which revealed to Angela a young girl's normal reactions to the life about her, pleasant, uneventful and tinged with a cool, serene happiness totally different from the hot, heady, turgid rapture which at present was Angela's life.

The Jewish girl, Rachel Salting, who lived on the floor above, took to calling on Angela. "We're young and here by ourselves," she said smiling, "it's stupid for us not to get acquainted, don't you think so?" Hers was a charming smile and a charming manner. Indeed she was a very pretty girl, Angela thought critically. Her skin was very, very pale, almost pearly, her hair jet black and curling, her eyes large and almond-shaped. Her figure was straight and slender but bore none the less some faint hint of an exotic voluptuousness. Her interests, she informed her new friend, were all with the stage, her ideal being Raquel Meller.

Angela welcomed her friendliness. A strange apathy, an unusual experience for her, had invaded her being; her painting claimed, it is true, a great deal of time and concentration; her hours with Virginia, while not always satisfactory, were at least absorbing; but for the first time in her knowledge, her whole life was hanging on the words, the moods, the actions of some one else—Roger. Without him she was quite lost; not only was she unable to order her days without him in mind, she was even unable to go in quest of new adventures in living as was once her wont. Consequently she received with outstretched arms anything beyond the ordinary which might break the threatening monotony of her life.

Rachel Salting was like a fresh breeze, a curious mixture of Jewish conservatism and modernity. Hers was a keen, clear mind, well trained in the New York schools and colleges with many branching interests. She spoke of psychiatry, housing problems, Zionism, child welfare, with a knowledge and zest which astounded Angela, whose training had been rather superficial and who had begun to adopt Paulette's cleverness and Martha Burden's slightly professional, didactic attitude toward things in general as norms for herself. Rachel, except when dwelling on the Jewish problem, seemed to have no particular views to set forth. Her discussions, based on her wide reading, were purely academic, she had no desire to proselyte, she was no reformer. She was merely a "nice", rather jolly, healthy young woman, an onlooker at life which she had to get through with and which she was finding for the moment at any rate, extremely pleasant.

She was very happy; happy like Virginia with a happiness vastly different from what Angela was calling by that name; a breathless, constant, smiling happiness, palpable, transparent, for all the world to see. Within a few weeks after their acquaintanceship had started, Rachel with smiles and blushes revealed her great secret. She was going to be married.

"To the very best man in the world, Angèle."

"Yes, I'm sure of it."

"He's very good-looking, tall,——"

"As though I didn't know that."

"How could you know?"

"Darling child, haven't I seen him, at least the outline of him, often enough in the hall when I'd come in and turn on that wretched light? I didn't think you'd ever forgive me for it. It did seem as though I were doing it on purpose."

"Oh, I knew you weren't. Then you have seen him?"

"Yes, he's tall and blond. Quite a nice foil for your darkness. See, I'm always the artist."

"Yes," Rachel said slowly, "he is blond."

Angela thought she detected a faint undertone of worry in her hitherto triumphant voice but decided that that was unlikely.

But Rachel confirmed this impression by her next words: "If only everything will turn out all right."

Angel's rather material mind prompted her to ask: "What's the matter, is he very poor?"

Rachel stared. "Poor? As though that mattered. Yes, he's poor, but I don't care about that."

"Well, if you don't care about that, what's the trouble then? He's free, white and twenty-one, isn't he?"

"Yes, yes, it's only—oh you wouldn't understand, you lucky girl! It's nothing you'd ever have to bother about. You see we've got to get our parents' consent first. We haven't spoken of it yet. When we do, I'm afraid there'll be a row."

Some ritual inherent in her racial connections, Angela decided, and asked no further questions. Indeed, she had small chance, for Rachel, once launched, had begun to expound her gospel of marriage. It was an old, old story. Angela could have closed her eyes and imagined her own mother rhapsodizing over her future with Junius. They would be poor, very poor at first but only at first, and they would not mind poverty a bit. It would be fun together. There were little frame houses in the Bronx that rented comparatively cheap. Perhaps Angela knew of them.

Angela shuddering inwardly, acknowledged that she had seen them, dull brown, high-shouldered affairs, perched perilously on stoops. The rooms would be small, square, ugly,——

Rachel would help her John in every way. They would economize. "I won't wash and iron, for that is heart-breaking work, and I want to keep myself dainty and pretty for him, so that when we do become better off he won't have to be ashamed of me. And all the time even in our hardest days I'll be trying my luck at play-writing." She spoke with the unquenchable ambition which was her racial dowry. "I'll be attending lectures and sitting up in the galleries of theatres where they have the most successful plays. And some day I'll land." Her fanciful imagination carried her years ahead. "On our First Night, Angela, you must be in our box and I'll have an ermine coat. Won't it be wonderful? But nothing will be more wonderful than those first few years when we'll be absolutely dependent on each other; I on what he makes, he on the way I run the home. That will be heaven."

Confidences such as these left Angela unmoved but considerably shaken. There must be something in the life of sacrifice, even drudgery which Rachel had depicted. Else why should so many otherwise sensible girls take the risk? But there, it was silly for her to dwell on such pictures and scenes. Such a life would never come to her. It was impossible to conceive of such a life with Roger. Yet there were times in her lonely room when she pondered long and deeply, drawing pictures. The time would be summer; she would be wearing a white dress, would be standing in the doorway of a house in the suburbs very,

very near New York. There'd be the best possible dinner on
the table. She did love to cook. And a tall, strong figure would
be hurrying up the walk: "I had the best luck to-day, Angèle,
and I brought you a present." And presently after dinner she
would take him upstairs to her little work-room and she'd draw
aside the curtain and show him a portrait of a well-known society woman. "She's so pleased with it; and she's going to get me
lots of orders,——" Somehow she was absolutely sure that the
fanciful figure was not Roger.

Her lover, back from a three weeks' trip to Chicago, dissipated
that sureness. He was glad, overwhelmingly glad to be back
and to see Angèle. He came to her apartment directly from the
train, not stopping even to report to his father. "I can see him
to-morrow. To-night is absolutely yours. What shall we do,
Angèle? We can go out to dinner and the theatre or run out to
the Country Club or stay here. What do you say?"

"We'll have to stay here, Roger; I'll fix up a gorgeous dinner,
better than anything you've had to eat in any of your old
hotels. But directly after, I'll have to cut and run because I
promised Martha Burden faithfully to go to a lecture with her
tonight."

"I never knew you to be interested in a lecture before."

She was worried and showed it. "But this is a different sort
of lecture. You know how crazy Martha is about race and social
movements. Well, Van Meier is to speak to-night and Martha
is determined that a lot of her friends shall hear him. I'm to go
with her and Ladislas."

"What's to keep me from going?"

"Nothing, only he's coloured, you know."

"Well, I suppose it won't rub off. I've heard of him. They say
he really has brains. I've never seen a nigger with any yet; so
this bids fair to be interesting. And, anyway, you don't think
I'm going to let my girl run off from me the very moment I
come home, do you? Suppose I have Reynolds bring the big
car here and we'll take Martha and Ladislas along and anyone
else she chooses to bring."

The lecture was held in Harlem in East One Hundred and
Thirty-fifth Street. The hall was packed, teeming with suppressed excitement and a certain surcharged atmosphere. Angela

radiant, calmed with the nearness and devotion of Roger, looked about her with keen, observing eyes. And again she sensed that fullness, richness, even thickness of life which she had felt on her first visit to Harlem. The stream of living ran almost molten; little waves of feeling played out from groups within the audience and beat against her consciousness and against that of her friends, only the latter were without her secret powers of interpretation. The occasion was clearly one of moment. "I'd come any distance to hear Van Meier speak," said a thin-faced dark young man behind them. "He always has something to say and he doesn't talk down to you. To hear him is like reading a classic, clear and beautiful and true."

Angela, revelling in types and marshalling bits of information which she had got from Virginia, was able to divide the groups. There sat the most advanced coloured Americans, beautifully dressed, beautifully trained, whimsical, humorous, bitter, impatiently responsible, yet still responsible. In one section loomed the dark, eager faces of West Indians, the formation of their features so markedly different from that of the ordinary American as to give them a wild, slightly feral aspect. These had come not because they were disciples of Van Meier but because they were earnest seekers after truth. But unfortunately their earnestness was slightly marred by a stubbornness and an unwillingness to admit conviction. Three or four coloured Americans, tall, dark, sleek young men sat within earshot, speaking with a curious didactic precision. "They're quoting all the sociologists in the world," Ladislas Starr told his little group in astonishment.

Martha, with her usual thoroughness, knew all about them. They were the editors of a small magazine whose chief bid to fame lay in the articles which they directed monthly against Van Meier; articles written occasionally in a spirit of mean jealousy but usually in an effort to gain a sort of inverted glory by carrying that great name on its pages.

Here and there a sprinkling of white faces showed up plainly, startlingly distinct patterns against a back-ground of patient, softly stolid black faces; faces beaten and fashioned by life into a mold of steady, rock-like endurance, of unshakable, unconquered faith. Angela had seen such faces before in the churches in Philadelphia; they brought back old pictures to her mind.

"There he is!" exclaimed Martha triumphantly. "That's Van

Meier! Isn't he wonderful?" Angela saw a man, bronze, not very tall but built with a beautiful symmetrical completeness, cross the platform and sit in the tall, deep chair next to the table of the presiding officer. He sat with a curious immobility, gazing straight before him like a statue of an East Indian idol. And indeed there was about him some strange quality which made one think of the East; a completeness, a superb lack of self-consciousness, an odd, arresting beauty wrought by the perfection of his fine, straight nose and his broad, scholarly forehead. One look, however casual, gave the beholder the assurance that here indeed was a man, fearless, dauntless, the captain of his fate.

He began to speak on a clear, deep, bell-like note. Angela thought she had never heard its equal for beauty, for resonance, for culture. And as the young man had said he did not talk down. His English was the carefully sifted language of the savant, his periods polished, almost poetical. He was noted on two continents for his sociological and economic contributions, but his subject was racial sacrifice. He urged the deliberate introduction of beauty and pleasure into the difficult life of the American Negro. These objects should be theirs both as racial heritage and as compensation. Yet for a time, for a long time, there would have to be sacrifices, many sacrifices made for the good of the whole. "Our case is unique," the beautiful, cultured voice intoned; "those of us who have forged forward, who have gained the front ranks in money and training, will not, are not able as yet to go our separate ways apart from the unwashed, untutored herd. We must still look back and render service to our less fortunate, weaker brethren. And the first step toward making this a workable attitude is the acquisition not so much of a racial love as a racial pride. A pride that enables us to find our own beautiful and praiseworthy, an intense chauvinism that is content with its own types, that finds completeness within its own group; that loves its own as the French love their country, because it is their own. Such a pride can accomplish the impossible." He quoted:

> "It is not courage, no, nor hate
> That lets us do the things we do;
> It's pride that bids the heart be great,—"

He sat down to a surge of applause that shook the building. Dark, drooping faces took on an expression of ecstatic uplift, it was as though they suddenly saw themselves, transformed by racial pride as princes in a strange land in temporary serfdom, princes whose children would know freedom.

Martha Burden and Ladislas went up to speak to him; they were old friends. Angela, with Roger, visibly impressed, stood on one side and waited. Paulette and Hudson came pushing through the crowd, the former flushed and excited. Little groups of coloured people stood about, some deeply content with a sort of vicarious pride, some arguing; Angela caught sight of Virginia standing with three young men and two girls. They were for the most part gesticulating, lost in a great excitement. But Jinny seemed listless and aloof; her childish face looked thin and more forlornly young than ever. Anthony Cross and a tall man of undeniably Spanish type passed the little party and spoke to one of the men, received introductions. Presently Cross, swinging about, caught sight of Angela and Roger. He bowed hastily, flushing; caught his companion's arm and walked hurriedly from the hall, his head very straight, his slender figure always so upright, so *élancé*, more erect than ever.

Presently Martha's party was all out on the sidewalk; Roger in fine spirits invited Paulette and Hudson to ride down town in his car. Paulette was bubbling over with excited admiration of Van Meier. "He isn't a man, he's a god," she proclaimed. "Did you ever see such a superb personality? He's not a magnificent coloured man, he's not 'just as good as a white man'; he is a man, just that; colour, race, conditions in his case are pure accidents, he over-rides them all with his ego. Made me feel like a worm too; I gave him my prettiest smile, grand white lady making up to an 'exceptional Negro' and he simply didn't see me; took my hand,—I did my best to make my grasp a clinging one—and he passed me right along disengaging himself as cool as a cucumber and making room for a lady of colour." She finished reflectively, " I wonder what he would be like alone."

"None of your nonsense, Paulette," said Roger frowning.

Hudson smiled. "Paulette's a mighty attractive little piece, I'll admit, but I'd back Van Meier against her every time; she'd present no temptation to him; the man's not only a prophet and the son of a prophet; he's pride incarnate."

Roger said meditatively, "I wonder what proportion of white blood he has in his veins. Of course that's where he gets his ability."

"You make me tired," said Martha. "Of course he doesn't get it from his white blood; he gets it from all his bloods. It's the mixture that makes him what he is. Otherwise all white people would be gods. It's the mixture and the endurance which he has learned from being coloured in America and the determination to see life without bitterness,——"

"Oh help, help," exclaimed Roger. "No more lectures to-night. Look, you're boring Angèle to death."

"Nothing of the kind," said Angela, "on the contrary I never was more interested in my life." And reaching back she gave Martha's hand a hearty squeeze.

Sometimes as on that first day at the art class, the five of them, Miss Powell, Paulette, Cross, Martha and Angela met before hours. Miss Powell as always was silent—she came solely for her work—but the others enjoyed a little preliminary chat. A week or so after the Van Meier lecture all but Paulette were gathered thus on an afternoon when she too came rushing in, starry eyed, flushed, consumed with laughter.

"I've played the biggest joke on myself," she announced, I've been to see Van Meier."

Martha was instant attention. "A joke on Van Meier?"

"No, on myself, I tell you."

It appeared that she had got Miss Powell to introduce her to one of the clerks in the great leader's office. Paulettte then with deliberate intention had asked the girl to lunch and afterwards had returned with her to the office expressing a desire to meet her employer. Van Meier had received her cordially enough but with the warning that he was very busy.

"So I told him that I wouldn't sit down, thinking of course he'd urge me to. But he just raised his eyebrows in the most quiz-zical way and said, 'Well?'

"Of course I couldn't let matters rest like that so I sat down and began talking to him, nothing much you know, just telling him how wonderful he was and letting him see that I'd be glad to know him better. You should have seen him looking at me and not saying a word. Presently he reached out his hand and touched a bell and Miss Thing-um-bob came in,—your friend, you know, Miss Powell. He looked at her and nodding toward me said: 'Take her away'. I never felt such small potatoes in my life. I tell you he's a personage. Wasn't it great?"

Martha replied crossly that the whole thing seemed to her in dreadfully poor taste, while Miss Powell, after one incredulous stare at the first speaker, applied herself more sedulously to her work. Even Anthony, shocked out of his habitual moroseness pronounced the proceedings "a bit thick, Miss Lister". Angela conscious of a swelling pride, stowed the incident away as a titbit for Virginia.

Chapter IV

LIFE had somehow come to a standstill; gone was its quality of high adventure and yet with the sense of tameness came no compensating note of assurance, of permanence. Angela pondered much about this; with her usual instinct for clarity, for a complete understanding of her own emotional life, she took to probing her inner consciousness. The fault, she decided, was bound up in her relationship with Roger. At present in a certain sense she might be said to be living for him; at least his was the figure about which her life resolved, revolved. Yet she no longer had the old, heady desire to feel herself completely his, to claim him as completely hers, neither for his wealth nor for the sense of security which he could afford nor for himself. For some reason he had lost his charm for her, much, she suspected, in the same way in which girls in the position which was hers, often lost their charm for their lovers.

And this realization instead of bringing to her a sense of relief, brought a certain real if somewhat fantastic shame. If there was to be no permanence in the relationship, if laying aside the question of marriage, it was to lack the dignity, the graciousness of an affair of long standing, of sympathy, of mutual need, then indeed according to the code of her childhood, according to every code of every phase of her development, she had allowed herself to drift into an inexcusably vulgar predicament. Even when her material safety and security were at stake and she had dreamed vaguely of yielding to Roger's entreaties to ensure that safety and security, there might have been some excuse. Life, she considered, came before creed or code or convention. Or if she had loved and there had been no other way she might have argued for this as the supreme experience of her life. But she was no longer conscious of striving for marriage with Roger; and as for love—she had known a feeling of gratitude, intense interest, even intense possessiveness for him but she did not believe she had ever known love.

But because of this mingling of shame and reproach she found herself consciously striving to keep their relations on the highest plane possible in the circumstances. She wished now

not so much that she had never left Jinny and the security of
their common home-life, as that the necessity for it had never
arisen. Now suddenly she found herself lonely, she had been in
New York nearly three years but not even yet had she struck
down deep into the lode of genuine friendship. Paulette was
kind and generous; she desired, she said, a close woman friend
but Paulette was still the adventuress. She was as likely to
change her vocation and her place of dwelling as she was to
change her lover. Martha Burden, at once more stable and
more comprehending in the conduct of a friendship once she
had elected for it, was, on the other hand, much more conservative in the expenditure of that friendliness; besides she was
by her very nature as reserved as Paulette was expansive, and
her native intenseness made it difficult for her to dwell very
long on the needs of anyone whose problems did not centre
around her own extremely fixed ideas and principles.

As for Anthony Cross,—by some curious, utterly inexplicable
revulsion of feeling, Angela could not bring herself to dwell
long on the possibilities of a friendship with him. Somehow it
seemed to her sacrilegious in her present condition to bring
the memory of that far-off day in Van Cortlandt Park back to
mind. As soon as his image arose she dismissed it, though there
were moments when it was impossible for his vision to come
before her without its instantly bringing to mind Rachel
Salting's notions of love and self-sacrifice. Well, such dreams
were not for her, she told herself impatiently. For her own
soul's integrity she must make the most of this state in which
she now found herself. Either she must effect through it a marriage whose excuse should be that of safety, assurance and a
resulting usefulness; or she must resolve it by patience, steadfastness and affection into a very apotheosis of "free love." Of
all possible *affaires du coeur* this must in semblance at any rate,
be the ultimate image desideration, the finest flower of chivalry
and devotion.

To this end she began then devoting herself again to the renewal
of that sense of possessiveness in Roger and his affairs which
had once been so spontaneous within her. But to this Roger
presented unexpected barriers; he grew restive under such manifestations; he who had once fought so bitterly against her

indifference resented with equal bitterness any showing of possessive interest. He wanted no claims upon him, he acknowledged none. Gradually his absences, which at first were due to
the business interests of his father, occurred for other reasons
or for none at all. Angela could not grasp this all at once; it was
impossible for her to conceive that kindness should create indifference; in spite of confirmatory stories which she had heard,
of books which she had read, she could not make herself
believe that devotion might sometimes beget ingratitude, loss
of appreciation. For if that were so then a successful relationship
between the sexes must depend wholly on the marriage tie without reference to compatibility of taste, training or ideals. This
she could scarcely credit. In some way she must be at fault.

No young wife in the first ardour of marriage could have
striven more than she to please Roger. She sought by reading
and outside questions to inform herself along the lines of Roger's
training—he was a mining engineer. His fondness for his father
prompted her to numerous inquiries about the interest and
pursuits of the older Fielding; she made suggestions for Roger's
leisure hours. But no matter how disinterested her attitude
and tone his response to all this was an increased sullenness,
remoteness, wariness. Roger was experienced in the wiles of
women; such interest could mean only one thing,—marriage.
Well, Angela might just as well learn that he had no thought,
had never had any thought, of marrying her or any other woman
so far removed from his father's ideas and requirements.

Still Angela, intent on her ideals, could not comprehend.
Things were not going well between them; affairs of this kind
were often short-lived, that had been one of her first objections
to the arrangement, but she had not dreamed that one withdrew when the other had committed no overt offence. She was
as charming, as attractive, as pretty as she had ever been and
far, far more kind and thoughtful. She had not changed, how
could it be possible that he should be different?

A week had gone by and he had not dropped in to see her.
Loneliness settled over her like a pall, frightening her seriously
because she was realizing that this time she was not missing
Roger so much as that a person for whom she had let slip the
ideals engendered by her mother's early teaching, a man for
whom she had betrayed and estranged her sister, was passing

out of her ken. She had rarely called him on the telephone but suddenly she started to do so. For three days the suave voice of his man, Reynolds, told her that Mr. Fielding was "out, m'm."

"But did you give him my message? Did you ask him to call me as soon as he came in?"

"Yes, m'm."

"And did he?"

"That I couldn't tell you, m'm."

She could not carry on such a conversation with a servant.

On the fifth day Roger appeared. She sprang toward him. "Oh Roger, I'm so glad to see you. Did Reynolds tell you I called? Why have you been so long coming?"

"I'd have been still longer if you hadn't stopped 'phoning. Now see here, Angèle, this has got to stop. I can't have women calling me up all hours of the day, making me ridiculous in the eyes of my servants. I don't like it, it's got to stop. Do you understand me?"

Surprised, bewildered, she could only stammer: "But you call me whenever you feel like it."

"Of course I do, that's different. I'm a man." He added a cruel afterword. "Perhaps you notice that I don't call you up as often as I used."

Her pride was in arms. More than once she thought of writing him a brief note telling him that so far as she was concerned their "affair" was ended. But a great stubbornness possessed her; she was curious to see how this sort of thing could terminate; she was eager to learn if all the advice which older women pour into the ears of growing girls could be as true as it was trite. Was it a fact that the conventions were more important than the fundamental impulses of life, than generosity, kindness, unselfishness? For whatever her original motives, her actual relationship with Fielding had called out the most unselfish qualities in her. And she began to see the conventions, the rules that govern life, in a new light; she realized suddenly that for all their granite-like coldness and precision they also represented fundamental facts; a sort of concentrated compendium of the art of living and therefore as much to be observed and respected as warm, vital impulses.

Towards Roger she felt no rancour, only an apathy incapable

of being dispersed. The conversation about the telephone left an effect all out of proportion to its actual importance; it represented for her the apparently unbridgeable difference between the sexes; everything was for men, but even the slightest privilege was to be denied to a woman unless the man chose to grant it. At least there were men who felt like that; not all men, she felt sure, could tolerate such an obviously unjust status. Without intent to punish, with no set purpose in her mind, simply because she was no longer interested, she began to neglect Roger. She no longer let other engagements go for him; she made no attempt to be punctual in keeping such engagements as they had already made; in his presence she was often absorbed, absentminded, lost in thought. She ceased asking him questions about his affairs.

Long before their quarrel they had accepted an invitation from Martha Burden to a small party. Angela was surprised that Roger should remember the occasion, but clearly he did; he was on hand at the correct date and hour and the two of them fared forth. During the brief journey he was courteous, even politely cordial, but the difference between his attitude and that of former days was very apparent. The party was of a more frivolous type than Martha usually sponsored, she was giving it for a young, fun-loving cousin of Ladislas; there was no general conversation, some singing, much dancing, much pairing off in couples. Carlotta Parks was present with Ralph Ashley, the slender, dark man who had appeared with Carlotta when Angela first met her. As soon as Roger appeared Carlotta came rushing toward him.

"I've been waiting for you!" She dragged at his hand and not unwillingly he suffered himself to be led to a small sofa. They chatted a few minutes; then danced; Roger simply must look at Martha's new etchings. The pair was inseparable for the evening. Try as she might Angela could discover no feeling of jealousy but her dignity was hurt. She could not have received less attention from her former lover if they had never met. At first she thought she would make up to Ashley but something malicious in Carlotta's glance deterred her. No, she was sick of men and their babyish, faithless ways; she did not care enough about Roger to play a game for him. So she sat quietly in a deep chair, smoking, dipping into the scattered piles of books which lent the apartment its air of cheerful disorder. Occasionally she chatted; Ladislas Starr perched on the arm of her chair and beguiled her with gay tales of his university days in pre-war Vienna.

But she would never endure such an indignity again. On the way home she was silent. Roger glanced at her curiously, raised his eyebrows when she asked him to come in. She began quietly: "Roger I'll never endure again the treatment——"

But he was ready, even eager for a quarrel. "It looks to me as though you were willing to endure anything. No woman with an ounce of pride would have stood for what you've been standing lately."

She said evenly: "You mean this is the end? We're through?"

"Well, what do you think about it? You certainly didn't expect it to last for ever."

His tone was unbelievably insulting. Eyeing him speculatively she replied: "No, of course I didn't expect it to last for ever, but I didn't think it would end like this. I don't see yet why it should."

The knowledge of his unpardonable manner lay heavy upon him, drove him to fresh indignity. "I suppose you thought some day I'd kiss your hand and say 'You've been very nice to me; I'll always remember you with affection and gratitude. Good-bye.'"

"Well, why shouldn't you have said that? Certainly I'd expected that much sooner than a scene of this sort. I never dreamed of letting myself in for this kind of thing."

Some ugly devil held him in its grasp. "You knew perfectly well what you were letting yourself in for. Any woman would know it."

She could only stare at him, his words echoing in her ears: "You knew perfectly well what you were letting yourself in for."

The phrase had the quality of a cosmic echo; perhaps men had been saying it to women since the beginning of time. Doubtless their biblical equivalent were the last words uttered by Abraham to Hagar before she fared forth into the wilderness.

Chapter V

LONG after Roger had left her she sat staring into the dark shadows of the room. For a long time the end, she knew, had been imminent; she had been curious to see how it would arrive, but the thought had never crossed her mind that it would come with harsh words and with vulgarity. The departure of Roger himself—she shut her hand and opened it—meant nothing; she had never loved, never felt for him one-tenth of the devotion which her mother had known for her father, of the spontaneous affection which Virginia had offered Matthew Henson. Even in these latter weeks when she had consciously striven to show him every possible kindness and attention she had done so for the selfish preservation of her ideals. Now she looked back on those first days of delight when his emotions and her own had met at full tide; when she dreamed that she alone of all people in the world was exempt from ordinary law. How, she wondered futilely, could she ever have suffered herself to be persuaded to tamper with the sacred mysteries of life? If she had held in her hand the golden key,—love! But to throw aside the fundamental laws of civilization for passion, for the hot-headed wilfulness of youth and to have it end like this, drably, vulgarly, almost in a brawl! How could she endure herself? And Roger and his promises of esteem and golden memories!

For a moment she hated him for his fine words and phrases, hated him for tricking her. No matter what she had said, how she had acted, he should have let her go. Better a wound to her passion than later this terrible gash in her proud assurance, this hurt in the core of herself. "God!" she said, raging in her tiny apartment as a tiger in a menagerie rages in its inadequate cage, "God, isn't there any place where man's responsibility to woman begins?"

But she had grown too much into the habit of deliberately ordering her life, of hewing her own path, of removing the difficulties that beset that path, to let herself be sickened, utterly prostrated by what had befallen her. Roger, her companion, had gone; she had been caught up in an inexcusably needless affair without the pretext of love. Thank God she had taken nothing from Roger; she had not sold herself; only bestowed that self foolishly, unworthily. However upset and harassed her mind might be it could not dwell too long on this loss of a lover. There were other problems to consider; for Roger's passing meant the vanishing of the last hope of the successful marriage which once she had so greatly craved. And even though she had not actively considered this for some time, yet as a remote possibility it had afforded a sense of security. Now that mirage was dispelled; she was brought with a sudden shock back to reality. No longer was it enough for her to plan how she could win to a pleasant and happy means of existence, she must be on the *qui vive* for the maintenance of that very existence itself. New York had literally swallowed her original three thousand dollars; part of Virginia's gift was also dissipated. Less than a thousand dollars stood between her and absolute penury. She could not envisage turning to Jinny; life which had seemed so promising, so golden, had failed to supply her with a single friend to whom she could turn in an hour of extremity.

Such thoughts as these left her panic-stricken, cold with fear. The spectre of possible want filled her dreams, haunted her waking hours, thrust aside the devastating shame of her affair with Roger to replace it with dread and apprehension. In her despair she turned more ardently than ever to her painting; already she was capable of doing outstanding work in portraiture, but she lacked *cachet*; she was absolutely unknown.

This condition of her mind affected her appearance; she began to husband her clothes, sadly conscious that she could not tell where others would come from. Her face lost its roundness, the white warmness of her skin remained but there were violet shadows under her eyes; her forehead showed faint lines; she was slightly shabby. Gradually the triumphant vividness so characteristic of Angèle Mory left her, she was like any one of a thousand other pitiful, frightened girls thronging New York. Miss Powell glanced at her and thought: "she looks unhappy, but how can she be when she has a chance at everything in the world just because she's white?"

Anthony marked her fading brightness; he would have liked to question her, comfort her, but where this girl was concerned the rôle of comforter was not for him. Only the instructor, Mr. Paget guessed at her extremity. He had seen too many students not to recognize the signs of poverty, of disaster in love, of despair at the tardy flowering of dexterity that had been mistaken for talent. Once after class he stopped Angela and asked her if she knew of anyone willing to furnish designs for a well-known journal of fashion.

"Not very stimulating work, but the pay is good and the firm reliable. Their last artist was with them eight years. If you know of anyone,——"

She interrupted: "I know of myself. Do you think they'd take me on?"

"I could recommend you. They applied to me, you see. Doubtless they'd take my suggestions into account."

He was very kind; made all the necessary arrangements. The firm received Angela gladly, offering her a fair salary for work that was a trifle narrow, a bit stultifying. But it opened up possibilities; there were new people to be met; perhaps she would make new friends, form ties which might be lasting.

"Oh," she said hopefully to herself, "life is wonderful! It's giving me a new deal and I'll begin all over again. I'm young and now I'm sophisticated; the world is wide, somewhere there's happiness and peace and a place for me. I'll find it."

But her hope, her sanguineness, were a little forced, her superb self-confidence perceptibly diminished. The radiance which once had so bathed every moment of her existence was fading gently, inexorably into the "light of common day".

HOME AGAIN

Chapter I

NEW YORK, it appeared, had two visages. It could offer an aspect radiant with promise or a countenance lowering and forbidding. With its flattering possibilities it could elevate to the seventh heaven, or lower to the depths of hell with its crushing negations. And loneliness! Loneliness such as that offered by the great, noisy city could never be imagined. To realize it one would have to experience it. Coming home from work Angela used to study the people on the trains, trying to divine what cause had engraved a given expression on their faces, particularly on the faces of young women. She picked out for herself four types, the happy, the indifferent, the preoccupied, the lonely. Doubtless her classification was imperfect, but she never failed, she thought, to recognize the signs of loneliness, a vacancy of expression, a listlessness, a faintly pervading despair. She remembered the people in Union Square on whom she had spied so blithely when she had first come to New York. Then she had thought of them as being "down and out", mere idlers, good for nothing. It had not occurred to her that their chief disaster might be loneliness. Her office was on Twenty-third Street and often at the noon-hour she walked down to the dingy Square and looked again in on the sprawling, half-recumbent, dejected figures. And between them and herself she was able to detect a terrifying relationship. She still carried her notebook, made sketches, sitting watching them and jotting down a line now and then when their vacant, staring eyes were not fixed upon her. Once she would not have cared if they had caught her; she would have said with a shrug: "Oh they wouldn't mind, they're too far gone for that." But since then her sympathy and knowledge had waxed. How fiercely she would have rebelled had anyone from a superior social plane taken her for copy!

In the evenings she worked at the idea of a picture which

she intended for a masterpiece. It was summer and the classes
at Cooper Union had been suspended. But she meant to return
in the fall, perhaps she would enter the scholarship contest and
if successful, go abroad. But the urge to wander was no longer
in the ascendant. The prospect of Europe did not seem as alluring now as the prospect of New York had appeared when
she lived in Philadelphia. It would be nice to stay put, rooted;
to have friends, experiences, memories.

Paulette, triumphant to the last, had left with Hudson for Russia. Martha and Ladislas were spending the summer with Martha's people on Long Island. Roger had dropped into the void,
but she could not make herself miss him; to her he was the
symbol of all that was most futile in her existence, she could
forgive neither him nor herself for their year of madness. If the
experience, she told herself, had ended—so-be-it—everything
ends. If it had faded into a golden glow with a wealth of memories, the promise of a friendship, she would have had no qualms;
but as matters had turned out it was an offence in her nostrils,
a great blot on the escutcheon of her fastidiousness.

She wished that Martha had asked her to spend week-ends
with her but the idea had apparently never crossed the latter's
mind. "Good-bye until fall," she had said gaily, "do you know,
I'm awfully glad to go home this time. I always have my old
room; it's like begining life all over again. Of course I wouldn't
give up New York but life seems so much more real and durable
down there. After all it's where my roots are."

Her roots! Angela echoed the expression to herself on a note
that was wholly envious. How marvellous to go back to parents,
relatives, friends with whom one had never lost touch! The
peace, the security, the companionableness of it! This was a
relationship which she had forfeited with everyone, even with
Jinny. And as for her other acquaintances in Philadelphia,
Henson, Butler, Kate and Agnes Hallowell, so completely, so
casually, without even a ripple had she dropped out of their
lives that it would have been impossible for her to re-establish
their old, easy footing even had she so desired.

Virginia, without making an effort, seemed overwhelmed,
almost swamped by friendships, pleasant intimacies, a thousand
charming interests. She and Sara Penton, another teacher, had

taken an apartment together, a three room affair on the top floor of a house on 139th Street, in "Striver's Row", explained Jinny. Whether or not the nickname was deserved, it seemed to Angela well worth an effort to live in this beautiful block with its tree-bordered pavements, its spacious houses, its gracious neighbourliness. A doctor and his wife occupied the first two floors; they were elderly, rather lonely people, for their two children had married and gone to other cities. They had practically adopted Virginia and Sara; nursing them when they had colds, indulgently advising them as to their callers. Mrs. Bradley, the doctor's wife, occasionally pressed a dress for them; on stormy days the doctor drove them in his car around to "Public School 89" where they both taught. Already the two girls were as full of intimacies, joyous reminiscences, common plans as though they had lived together for years. Secrets, nicknames, allusions, filled the atmosphere. Angela grew sick of the phrases: "Of course you don't understand that; just some nonsense and it would take too long to explain it. Besides you wouldn't know any of the people." Even so, unwelcome as the expression was, she did not hear it very often, for Jinny did not encourage her visits to the apartment even as much as to the boarding house.

"Sara will think it strange if you come too often."

"We might tell her," Angela rejoined, "and ask her to keep it a secret."

But Jinny opined coolly that that would never do; it was bad to entrust people with one's secrets. "If you can't keep them yourself, why should they?" she asked sagely. Her attitude showed no malice, only the complete acceptance of the stand which her sister had adopted years ago.

In her sequestered rooms in the Village lying in the summer heat unkempt and shorn of its glamour Angela pondered long and often on her present mode of living. Her life, she was pretty sure, could not go on indefinitely as it did now. Even if she herself made no effort it was unlikely that the loneliness could persist. Jinny, she shrewdly suspected, had known something of this horrible condition when she, the older sister had left her so ruthlessly to go off and play at adventure. This loneliness and her unfortunate affair with Henson had doubtless proved too much for her, and she had deliberately sought change and distraction elsewhere. There were depths upon depths of strength in Jinny and as much purpose and resource as one might require. Now here she was established in New York with friends, occupation, security, leading an utterly open life, no secrets, no subterfuges, no goals to be reached by devious ways.

Jinny had changed her life and been successful. Angela had changed hers and had found pain and unhappiness. Where did the fault lie? Not, certainly, in her determination to pass from one race to another. Her native good sense assured her that it would have been silly for her to keep on living as she had in Philadelphia, constantly, through no fault of her own, being placed in impossible positions, eternally being accused and hounded because she had failed to placard herself, forfeiting old friendships, driven fearfully to the establishing of new ones. No, the fault was not there. Perhaps it lay in her attitude toward her friends. Had she been too coldly deliberate in her use of them? Certainly she had planned to utilize her connection with Roger, but on this point she had no qualms; he had been paid in full for any advantages which she had meant to gain. She had not always been kind to Miss Powell, "but," she murmured to herself, "I was always as kind to her as I dared be in the circumstances and far, far more attentive than any of the others." As for Anthony, Paulette, and Martha, her slate was clear on their score. She was struck at this point to realize that during her stay of nearly three years these five were the only people to whom she could apply the term friends. Of these Roger had dropped out; Miss Powell was negative; Paulette had gone to Russia. There remained only Martha and Anthony. Martha was too intensely interested in the conduct of her own life in connection with Ladislas to make a friend, a satisfying, comfortable, intimate friend such as Sara Penton seemed to be with Virginia. There remained then only Anthony—yes, and her new acquaintance, Rachel Salting.

She began then in her loneliness to approach Rachel seeking for nothing other than those almost sisterly intimacies which spring up between solitary women cut off in big cities from their homes and from all the natural resources which add so much to the beauty and graciousness of young womanhood. "If anything comes out of this friendship to advance me in any way," she told herself solemnly, "it will happen just because it happens but I shall go into this with clean hands and a pure heart —merely because I like Rachel."

After the fever and fret of her acquaintanceship with Roger, the slight unwholesomeness attendant on Paulette, the didactic quality lurking in Martha's household, it was charming, even delicious to enter on a friendship with this simple, intelligent, enthusiastic girl. Rachel, for all her native endowment, her wide reading and her broad scholastic contacts, had the straightforward utter sincerity and simplicity of a child; at times Angela felt quite sophisticated, even blasé beside her. But in reality they were two children together; Angela's brief episode with Roger had left no trace on her moral nature; she was ashamed now of the affair with a healthy shame at its unworthiness; but beyond that she suffered from no morbidness. Her sum total of the knowledge of life had been increased; she saw men with a different eye, was able to differentiate between the attitudes underlying the pleasantries of the half dozen young men in her office; listening, laughing, weighing all their attentions, accepting none. In truth she had lost to a degree her taste for the current type of flirtations. She might marry some day but all that was still in the dim future. Meanwhile the present beckoned; materially she was once more secure, her itching ambition was temporarily lulled; she had a friend. It was just as well to let time slide by for a while.

The two girls spent their evenings together. Rachel's fiancé, John Adams, was a travelling salesman and nearly always out of town. When he was home Angela was careful to have an engagement, though Rachel assured her, laughing and sparkling, that the two were already so used to each other that a third person need not feel *de trop*. Occasionally the three of them went during the hot summer nights to Coney Island or Far Rockaway. But this jaunt took on the proportions more of an ordeal than a pleasure trip; so packed were the cars with helpless humanity, so crowded the beaches, so nightmarish the trip home. Fortunately Angela came face to face one day with Ralph Ashley, Carlotta's former friend. Low-spirited, lonely, distrait, he asked Angela eagerly to allow him to call occasionally. He seemed a rather bookish, serious young man who had failed to discover the possibilities of his inner resources. Without an acquaintance or a book he was helpless. Angela's self-reliance and cleverness seemed to offer a temporary harbour. Apparently with Carlotta out of town, he was at loose ends. By some tacit understanding he was taken into the little group and as he possessed a car which he was willing and eager to share the arrangement was a very happy one.

These were pleasant days. Long afterwards, Angela, looking back recalled them as among the happiest she had known in New York. In particular she liked the hours when she and Rachel were together busied with domestic, homely affairs. They advised each other on the subject of dress; Angela tried out new recipes. In the late evenings she worked on the sketches, recalling them from her note-book while Rachel, sitting side-wise in the big chair, her legs dangling comfortably over its arm, offered comments and suggestions. She had had "courses in art", and on a trip to France and Italy at the age of eighteen had visited the Louvre, the Pitti and Uffizi Galleries. All this lent a certain pithiness and authority to the criticisms which she poured forth for her friend's edification; her remarks rarely produced any effect on Angela, but both girls felt that Rachel's knowledge gave a certain effect of "atmosphere".

Usually Rachel's talk was on John and their approaching marriage, their unparalleled courtship. Many years later Angela could have related all the details of that simple, almost sylvan wooing, the growing awareness of the two lovers, their mutual fears and hopes, their questionings, assurances and their bliss-ful engagement. She knew to a penny what John made each week, how much he put by, the amount which thrifty Rachel felt must be in hand before they could marry. Once this recital, so unvarying, so persistent, would have bored her, but she was more sympathetic in these days; sometimes she found herself making suggestions, saving the house-wifely clippings culled from newspapers, proposing decorations for the interior of one of the ugly little houses on which Rachel had so inexplicably set her heart. She was a little older than her friend, she had had experience in keeping house and in shopping with her mother in those far-off days; she ventured occasionally to advise Rachel in her rare purchases very much as though the latter were her own sister instead of a chance acquaintance whom she had known less than a year.

It was a placid, almost ideal existence. Only one thread of worry ran through its fabric, the thought that Rachel and John would soon be marrying and again Angela would be left on the search for a new friend. With one of them in the Bronx and the other Greenwich Village, frequent communication would be physically impossible. But, curiously enough, whenever Angela lamented over this to her friend, a deep sombreness would descend on the latter; she would remark gloomily: "Time enough to worry about that; after all we might not get married. You never can tell." This was too enigmatic for Angela and finally she grew to look on it as a jest, a rather poor one but still a jest.

Chapter II

INTO the midst of this serenity came a bolt from the blue. Rachel, a librarian, was offered the position of head librarian in a far suburb of Brooklyn. Furthermore a wealthy woman from Butte, Montana, desiring to stay in New York for a few months and taking a fancy to the dinginess of Jayne Street and to the inconveniences of Rachel's apartment found she must live there and not otherwise. No other location in the whole great city would do; she was willing to sublet at any figure. Unwillingly Rachel named a price which she secretly considered in the nature of highway robbery, but none of this mattered to Mrs. Denver, who was used to paying for what she wanted. And Rachel could not refuse, for both offers meant a substantial increase in the nest-egg which was to furnish the little brown house in the Bronx. In reality it meant to her extraordinary, unhoped for luck whose only flaw consisted in the enforced separation from her new friend. But to Angela it brought the awfulness of a catastrophe, though not for one moment would she let her deep dismay be suspected. After her first involuntary exclamation of consternation she never faltered in her complete acquiesence in the plan. But at heart she was sick.

The sudden flitting entailed much work and bustle. Rachel was as untidy as Angela was neat; everything she possessed had to be collected separately; there were no stacks of carefully folded clothing to be lifted wholesale and placed in gaping trunks. To begin with the trunks themselves were filled with dubious odds and ends which required to be sorted, given or even thrown away. There was no question of abandoning the *débris*, for the apartment must be left habitable for Mrs. Denver.

A nightmare then of feverish packing ensued; hasty meals, general house-cleaning. In order to assuage the sinking of her heart Angela plunged into it with great ardour. But at night, weary as she would be from the extra activity of the day, she could not fight off the sick dismay which overflowed her in great, submerging waves. It seemed to her she could not again endure loneliness; she could never summon the strength to seek out new friends, to establish fresh intimacies. She was twenty-six years old and the fact that after having lived all those years she was still solitary appalled her. Perhaps some curse such as one reads of in mediæval legends had fallen upon her. "Perhaps I'm not meant to have friends," she told herself lying face downwards in her pillows on the sweltering June nights. And a great nostalgia for something real and permanent swept upon her; she wished she were either very, very young, safe and contented once more in the protection of her father's household or failing that, very, very old.

A nature as strong, as self-reliant as hers could not remain long submerged; she had seen too many bad beginnings convert themselves into good endings. One of her most valuable native endowments lay in her ability to set herself and her difficulties objectively before her own eyes; in this way she had solved more than one problem. On the long ride in the subway back from Brooklyn whither she had accompanied Rachel on the night of the latter's departure she resolved to pursue this course that very night. Mercifully the terrible heat had abated, a little breeze came sifting in her open windows, moving the white sash curtains, even agitating some papers on the table. Soberly she set about the business of getting supper. Once she thought of running up to Rachel's former apartment and proffering some hospitality to Mrs. Denver. Even if the rich new tenant should not accept she'd be pleased doubtless; sooner or later she would be offering a return of courtesies, a new friendship would spring up. Again there would be possibilities. But something in her rebelled against such a procedure; these intimacies based on the sliding foundation of chance sickened her; she would not lend herself to them—not ever again. From this day on she'd devote herself to the establishing of permanencies.

Supper over, the dishes cleared away, she sat down and prepared to think. Callers were unlikely; indeed there was no one to call, since Ashley was out of town for the week-end, but the pathos of this fact left her untouched. To-night she courted loneliness.

An oft heard remark of her mother's kept running through her mind: "You get so taken up with the problem of living, with just life itself, that by and by being coloured or not is just one thing more or less that you have to contend with." It had been a long time since she had thought about colour; at one time it had seemed to complicate her life immensely, now it seemed to her that it might be of very little importance. But her thoughts skirted the subject warily for she knew how immensely difficult living could be made by this matter of race. But that should take a secondary place; at present life, a method of living was the main thing, she must get that problem adjusted and first she must see what she wanted. Companionship was her chief demand. No more loneliness, not even if that were the road that led to the fulfilment of vast ambition, to the realization of the loftiest hopes. And for this she was willing to make sacrifices, let go if need be of her cherished independence, lead a double life, move among two sets of acquaintances.

For deep in her heart she realized the longing to cast in her lot once more with Virginia, her little sister whom she should never have left. Virginia, it is true, showed no particular longing for her; indeed she seemed hardly cognizant of her existence; but this attitude might be a forced one. She thought, "I didn't want her, the darling, and so she just made herself put me out of her life." Angela was well aware of the pluck, the indomitableness that lay beneath Jinny's babyish exterior, but there was a still deeper stratum of tenderness and love and loyalty which was the real Virginia. To this Angela would make her appeal; she would acknowledge her foolishness, her selfishness; she would bare her heart and crave her sister's forgiveness. And then they would live together, Jinny and she and Sara Penton if need be; what a joke it would all be on Sara! And once again she would know the bliss and happiness of a home and the stabilities of friendships culled from a certain definite class of people, not friendships resulting from mere chance. There would be blessed Sunday mornings and breakfasts, long walks; lovely evenings in the autumn to be filled with reminiscences drawn from these days of separation. How Virginia would open her eyes at her tales of Paulette and Martha! She would never mention Roger. And as for colour; when it seemed best to be coloured she would be coloured; when it was best to be white she would be that. The main thing was, she would know once more the joys of ordinary living, home, companionship, loyalty, security, the bliss of possessing and being possessed. And to think it was all possible and waiting for her; it was only a matter of a few hours, a few miles.

A great sense of peace, of exaltation descended upon her. Almost she could have said: "I will arise and go unto my father".

On Sunday accordingly she betook herself to her sister's apartment in 139th Street. Miss Penton, she thought, would be out; she had gathered from the girls' conversation many pointed references to Sara's great fondness, of late, for church, exceeded only by her interest in the choir. This interest in the choir was ardently encouraged by a member of that body who occasionally walked home with Sara in order more fully to discuss the art of music. Virginia no longer went to church; Sunday had become her "pick-up day", the one period in the week which she devoted to her correspondence, her clothes and to such mysterious rites of beautifying and revitalizing as lay back of her healthy, blooming exquisiteness. This would be the first time in many months that the sisters would have been alone together and it was with high hopes that Angela, mounting the brown stone steps and ringing the bell, asked for Virginia.

Her sister was in, but so was Sara, so was a third girl, a Miss Louise Andrews. The room was full of the atmosphere of the lightness, of the badinage, of the laughter which belong to the condition either of youth or of extreme happiness. In the middle of the room stood a large trunk from whose yawning interior Jinny lifted a glowing, smiling face. Angela was almost startled at the bright ecstasy which radiated from it. Sara Penton was engaged rather negligently in folding clothes; Miss Andrews perched in magnificent ease on the daybed, struck an occasional tune from a ukelele and issued commands which nobody heeded.

"Hello," said Virginia carelessly. "Can you get in? I was thinking of writing to you."

"Oh," Angela's hopes fluttered, fell, perished. "You're not going away?" Her heart echoed Jinny's old cry: "And leave me—when I'm all ready to come back to you, when I need you so terribly!"

But of all this Virginia was, of course, unaware. "Nothing

different," she said briskly. "I'm going away this very afternoon to Philadelphia, Merion, points south and west, going to stay with Eda Brown."

Angela was aghast. "I wanted to see you about something rather important, Virginia—at least," she added humbly, "important to me." Rather impatiently she glanced at the two girls hoping they would take the hint and leave them, but they had not even heard her, so engrossed were they in discussing the relative merits of one- and two-piece sports clothes.

Her sister was kind but not curious. "Unless it's got something to do with your soul's salvation I'm afraid it'll have to wait a bit," she said gaily. "I'm getting a two o'clock train and I must finish this trunk—Sara's such a poor packer or I'd leave it for her. As it is she's going to send it after me. Aren't you, darling?" Already Angela's request was forgotten. "After I finish this," the gay voice went on, "I've got some 'phoning to do and—oh a million things."

"Let me help you," said Angela suddenly inspired, "then we'll call a taxi and we can go down to the station together and we'll have a long talk so I can explain things."

Virginia was only half-attentive. "Miss Mory wants to go to the station with me," she said throwing a droll look at her friends. "Shall I take her along?" She vanished into the bedroom, Louise Andrews at her heels, both of them overwhelmed with laughter bubbling from some secret spring.

Cut and humiliated, Angela stood silent. Sara Penton who had been looking after the vanishing figures turned and caught her expression. "Don't mind her craziness. She's not responsible to-day."

She came closer. "For heaven's sake don't let on I told you; she's engaged."

This was news. "Engaged? To whom?"

"Oh somebody she's always been crazy about." The inevitable phrase followed: "You wouldn't know who he was."

Not know who he was, not know Matthew! She began to say "Why I knew him before Virginia," but remembering her rôle, a stupid and silly one now, caught herself, stood expectantly.

"So you see," Sara went on mysteriously, one eye on the bedroom, "you mustn't insist on going to the station with her; he's going to take her down."

"Why, is he here?"

"Came yesterday. We've been threatening all morning to butt in. That's the reason she spoke as she did about your going down. She expressed herself to us, you bet, but she probably wouldn't feel like doing that to you."

"Probably not," said Angela, her heart cold. Her little sister was engaged and she was learning of it from strangers. It was all she could do to hold back the tears. "But you've only yourself to blame," she reminded herself valiantly.

The two girls came back; Virginia still laughing but underneath the merriment Angela was able to detect a flurry of nervousness. After all, Jinny was just a child. And she was so happy, it would never do to mar that happiness by the introduction of the slightest gloom or discomfort. Her caller rose to her feet. "I guess I'll be going."

Virginia made no effort to detain her, but the glance which she turned on her sister was suddenly very sweet and friendly. "Here, I'll run down to the door with you. Sara, be a darling and pick out the best of those stockings for me, put in lots. You know how hard I am on them."

Out in the hall she flung an impulsive arm about her sister. "Oh, Angela, I'm so happy, so happy. I'm going to write you about it right away, you'll be so surprised." Astonishingly she gave the older girl a great hug, kissed her again and again.

"Oh," said Angela, the tears welling from her eyes, "Oh Jinny, you do forgive me, you do, you do? I'm so sorry about it all. I've been wretched for a long time. I thought I had lost you, Virginia."

"I know," said Jinny, "I'm a hard-hearted little wretch." She giggled through her own tears, wiped them away with the back of her childish bronze hand. "I was just putting you through; I knew you'd get sick of Miss Anne's folks and come back to me. Oh Angela, I've wanted you so. But it's all right now. I won't be back for ten weeks, but then we will talk! I've got the most marvellous plans for both of us—for all of us." She looked like a wise baby. "You'll get a letter from me in a few days telling you all about it. Angela, I'm so happy, but I must fly. Good-bye, darling."

They clung for a moment in the cool, dim depths of the wide hall.

*

Angela could have danced in the street. As it was she walked
gaily down Seventh Avenue to 110th Street and into the bosky
reaches of the park. Jinny had forgiven her. Jinny longed for
her, needed her; she had known all along that Angela was suffering, had deliberately punished her. Well, she was right, everything was right this glorious memorable day. She was to have
a sister again, some one of her own, she would know the joy
of sharing her little triumphs, her petty woes. Wise Jinny,
wonderful Jinny!

And beautiful Jinny, too, she thought. How lovely, how
dainty, how fresh and innocent her little sister seemed. This
brought her mind to Matthew and his great good fortune.
"I'd like to see him again," she mused, smiling mischievously.
"Doubtless he's forgotten me. It would be great fun to make
him remember." Only, of course, now he was Jinny's and she
would never get in the way of that darling. "Not even if he
were some one I really wanted with all my heart and soul. But
I'd never want Matthew." It would be fun, she thought, to see
him again. He would make a nice brother, so sturdy and kind
and reliable. She must be careful never to presume on that old
youthful admiration of his. Smiling and happy she reached her
house, actually skipped up the steps to her rooms. Her apartment no longer seemed lonely; it was not beautiful and bright
like Jinny's but it was snug and dainty. It would be fun to have
Virginia and Sara down; yes, and that new girl, that Miss Andrews, too. She didn't care what the other people in the house
thought. And the girls themselves, how astonished they would
be to learn the true state of affairs! Suddenly remembering
Mrs. Denver, she ran up to see her; that lady, in spite of her
wealth and means for self-indulgence, was palpably lonely. Angela cheered her up with mirthful accounts of her own first
days in New York; she'd been lonely too, she assured her
despondent hostess, sparkling and fascinating.

"I don't see how anybody with a disposition like yours could
ever be lonely," said Mrs. Denver enviously. She'd been perilously near tears all day.

Gone, gone was all the awful melancholy, the blueness that
had hung about her like a palpable cloud. She was young, fascinating; she was going to be happy,—again. *Again!* She

caught her breath at that. Oh, God was good! This feeling of lightness, of exaltation had been unknown to her so long; not since the days when she had first begun to go about with Roger had she felt so free, bird-like. In the evening Ralph Ashley came with his car and drove her halfway across Long Island, or so it seemed. They stopped at a gorgeous hotel and had a marvellous supper. Ashley was swept off his feet by her gay vitalness. In the doorway of the Jayne Street house she gave him her hand and a bewitching smile. "You can't imagine how much I've enjoyed myself. I'll always remember it." And she spoke sincerely, for soon this sort of thing would be far behind her.

"You're a witch," said Ashley, his voice shaking a little. "You can have this sort of thing whenever you want it and you know it. Be kind to me, Angèle. I'm not a bad fellow." Frightened, she pushed him away, ran in and slammed the door. No, no, no, her heart pounded. Roger had taught her an unforgettable lesson. Soon she'd be with Jinny and Matthew, safe, sheltered.

Chapter III

I N the middle of the night she found herself sitting up in
bed. A moment before she had been asleep, but a sudden
thought had pierced her consciousness so sharply that the
effect was that of an icy hand laid suddenly on her shoulder.
Jinny and Matthew marry—why, that meant—why, of course
it meant that they would have to live in Philadelphia. How
stupid she had been! And she couldn't go back there—never,
never. Not because of the difficulties which she had experienced
as a child; she was perfectly willing to cast in her lot again with
coloured people in New York. But that was different; there
were signal injustices here, too—oh, many, many of them—but
there were also signal opportunities. But Philadelphia with its
traditions of liberty and its actual economic and social slavery,
its iniquitous school system, its prejudiced theatres, its limited
offering of occupation! A great, searing hatred arose in her for
the huge, slumbering leviathan of a city which had hardly
moved a muscle in the last fifty years. So hide-bound were its
habits that deliberate insult could be offered to coloured people without causing the smallest ripple of condemnation or
even consternation in the complacent commonwealth. Virginia
in one of her expansive moments had told her of a letter received from Agnes Hallowell, now a graduate of the Women's
Medical College. Agnes was as fair as Angela, but she had
talked frankly, even with pride, of her racial connections. "I
had nothing to be ashamed of," Angela could imagine her saying, her cheeks flushing, her black eyes snapping. On her graduation she had applied for an internship at a great hospital for
the insane; a position greatly craved by ardent medical graduates because of the unusually large turnover of pathological
cases. But the man in charge of such appointments, looking
Agnes hard in the eye told her suavely that such a position
would never be given to her "not if you passed ahead of a thousand white candidates."

As for Angela, here was the old problem of possible loneliness back on her hands. Virginia, it was true, would hardly
marry at once, perhaps they would have a few happy months

together. But afterwards. . . . She lay there, wide awake now, very still, very straight in her narrow bed, watching the thick blackness grow thinner, less opaque. And suddenly as on a former occasion, she thought of marriage. Well, why not? She had thought of it once before as a source of relief from poverty, as a final barrier between herself and the wolves of prejudice; why not now as a means of avoiding loneliness? "I must look around me," her thoughts sped on, and she blushed and smiled in the darkness at the cold-bloodedness of such an idea. But, after all, that was what men said—and did. How often had she heard the expression—"he's ready to settle down, so he's looking around for a wife". If that were the procedure of men it should certainly be much more so the procedure of women since their fate was so much more deeply involved. The room was growing lighter; she could see the pictures a deeper blur against the faint blur of the wall. Her passing shame suddenly spent itself, for, after all, she knew practically no men. There was Ashley— but she was through with men of his type. The men in her office were nearly all impossible, but there were three, she told herself, coldly, unenthusiastic, who were not such terrible pills.

"But no," she said out loud. "I'd rather stay single and lonely, too, all my life than worry along with one of them. There must be someone else." And at once she thought of Anthony Cross. Of course there was Anthony. "I believe I've always had him in the back of my mind," she spoke again to the glimmering greyness. And turning on her pillow she fell, smiling, asleep.

Monday was a busy day; copy must be prepared for the engraver; proofs of the current edition of the magazine had to be checked up; some important French fashion plates for which she was responsible had temporarily disappeared and must be unearthed. At four-thirty she was free to take tea with Mrs. Denver, who immediately thereafter bore her off to a "movie" and dinner. Not until nine o'clock was she able to pursue her new train of thought. And even when she was at liberty to indulge in her habit of introspection she found herself experiencing a certain reluctance, an unexpected shyness. Time was needed to brood on this secret with its promise of happiness;

this means of salvation from the problems of loneliness and weakness which beset her. For since the departure of Roger she frequently felt herself less assured; it would be a relief to have some one on whom to lean; some one who would be glad to shield and advise her,—and love her! This last thought seemed to her marvellous. She said to herself again and again: "Anthony loves me, I know it. Think of it, he loves me!" Her face and neck were covered with blushes; she was like a young girl on the eve of falling in love, and indeed she herself was entering on that experience for the first time. From the very beginning she had liked Anthony, liked him as she had never liked Roger—for himself, for his sincerity, for his fierce pride, for his poverty, for his honest, frantic love. "And now," she said solemnly, "I believe I'm going to love him; I believe I love him already."

There were many things to be considered. His poverty,—but she no longer cared about that; insensibly her association with Rachel Salting, her knowledge of Rachel's plans and her high flouting of poverty had worked their influence. It would be fun, fun to begin at the beginning, to save and scrape and mend. Like Rachel she would do no washing and ironing, she would keep herself dainty and unworn, but everything else, everything else she would do. Cook—and she could cook; she had her blessed mother to thank for that. For a moment she was home again on Opal Street, getting Monday dinner, laughing with Virginia about Mrs. Henrietta Jones. There they were at the table, her pretty mother, her father with his fine, black face—his black face, she had forgotten that.

Colour,—here the old problem came up again. Restlessly she paced the room, a smouldering cigarette in her fingers. She rarely smoked but sometimes the insensate little cylinder gave her a sense of companionship. Colour, colour, she had forgotten it. Now what should she do,—tell Anthony? He was Spanish, she remembered, or no,—since he came from Brazil he was probably Portuguese, a member of a race devoid, notoriously devoid of prejudice against black blood. But Anthony had lived in America long enough to become inoculated; had he ever spoken about coloured people, had the subject ever come up? Wait a minute, there was Miss Powell; she remembered now that his conduct towards the young coloured woman had always been conspicuously correct; he had placed chairs for her, opened doors, set up easels; once the three of them had walked out of Cooper Union together and Anthony had carefully helped Miss Powell on a car, removing his hat with that slightly foreign gesture which she admired so much. And so far as she knew he had never used any of Roger's cruelly slighting expressions; the terms "coon", "nigger", "darky" had never crossed his lips. Clearly he had no conscious feeling against her people—"my people" she repeated, smiling, and wondered herself which people she meant, for she belonged to two races, and to one far more conspicuously than the other. Why, Anthony had even attended the Van Meier lecture. And she wondered what Van Meier would say if she presented her problem to him. He had no brief, she knew, against intermarriage, though, because of the high social forfeit levied, he did not advocate its practice in America. For a moment she considered going to him and asking his advice. But she was afraid that he would speak to her about racial pride and she did not want to think of that. Life, life was what she was struggling for, the right to live and be happy. And once more her mother's dictum flashed into her mind. "Life is more important than colour." This, she told herself, was an omen, her mother was watching over her, guiding her. And, burying her face in her hands, she fell on her knees and wept and prayed.

Virginia sent a gay missive: "As soon as you left that wretch of a Sara told me that she had let you in on the great news. I wish I'd known it, I'd have spoken to you about it there in the hall; only there was so much to explain. But now you know the main facts, and I can wait until I see you to tell you the rest. But isn't it all wonderful? Angela, I do believe I'm almost the happiest girl alive!

"It's too lovely here. Edna is very kind and you know I always did like Pennsylvania country. Matthew is out almost every day. He tells me it renews his youth to come and talk about old times,—anyone to hear us reminiscing, starting every other sentence with 'do you remember——?' would think that we averaged at least ninety years apiece. It won't pique your vanity, will it, if I tell you that he seems to have recovered entirely from his old crush on you? Maybe he was just in love with the family and didn't know it.

"We go into Philadelphia every day or two. The city has changed amazingly. But after the hit or miss method of New York society there is something very restful and safe about this tight organization of 'old Philadelphians'. In the short time I've been here I've met loads of first families, people whose names we only knew when we were children. But they all seem to remember father and mother; they all begin: 'My dear, I remember when Junius Murray——' I meet all these people, old and young, through Matthew, who seems to have become quite the beau here and goes everywhere. He really is different. Even his hair in some mysterious way is changed. Not that I ever minded; only he's so awfully nice that I just would like all the nice things of the world added unto him. We were talking the other day about the wedding, and I was thinking what a really distinguished appearance he would make. Dear old Matt, I'm glad I put off marriage until he could cut a fine figure. Write me, darling, if you feel like it, but don't expect to hear much from me. I'm so happy I can't keep still long enough to write. The minute I get back to New York though we'll have such a talk as never was."

Mrs. Denver was growing happier; New York was redeeming itself and revealing all the riches which she had suspected lay hidden in its warehouses. Through one letter of introduction forced into her unwilling hands by an officious acquaintance on her departure from Butte she had gained an *entrée* into that kindest and happiest of New York's varied groups, the band of writers, columnists, publishers and critics. The lady from the middle West had no literary pretensions herself, but she liked people who had them and lived up to them; she kept abreast of literary gossip, read *Vanity Fair*, the *New Yorker*, and *Mercury*. As she was fairly young, dainty, wealthy and generous and no grinder of axes, she was caught up and whirled right along into the galaxy of teas, luncheons, theatre parties and "barbecues" which formed the relaxations of this joyous crowd. Soon she was overwhelmed, with more invitations than she could accept; to those which she did consider she always couched her acceptance in the same terms. "Yes I'll come if I may bring my young friend, Angèle Mory, along with me. She's a painter whom you'll all be glad to know some day." Angela's chance kindness to her in her days of loneliness and boredom had not fallen on barren ground.

Now indeed Angela was far removed from the atmosphere which she had known in Greenwich Village; the slight bohemianism which she had there encountered was here replaced by a somewhat bourgeois but satisfying sophistication. These people saw the "Village" for what it was, a network of badly laid off streets with, for the most part, uncomfortable, not to say inconvenient dwellings inhabited by a handful of artists in the midst of a thousand *poseurs*. Her new friends were frankly interested in the goods of this world. They found money an imperative, the pre-eminent, concomitant of life; once obtained, they spent it on fine apartments, beautiful raiment, delicate viands, and trips to Paris and Vienna. Conversation with them was something more than an exchange of words; "quips and jests" passed among them, and, though flavoured with allusions to stage and book, so that Angela was at times hard put to it to follow the trend of the talk, she half suspected that she was in this company assisting more nearly at the restoration of a lost art than in any other circles in the world save in the corresponding society of London.

Once again her free hours could be filled to overflowing with attention, with gaiety, with intellectual excitement; it came to her one day that this was the atmosphere of which she once had dreamed. But she was not quite happy, her economic condition interfered here. Constantly she was receiving every conceivable manifestation of an uncalculating generosity at the hands not only of Mrs. Denver but of her new acquaintances. And she could make no adequate return; her little apartment had turned too shabby for her to have guests of this calibre, even in to tea. Her rich friend, making short shrift of such furniture as Rachel Salting had left behind, had transformed her dwelling into a marvel of luxury and elegance; tiny but beautiful. Mrs. Denver was the soul of real and delicate kindness but Angela could not accept favours indefinitely; besides she was afraid to become too used to this constant tide from a horn of plenty on which she had absolutely no claim. If there were any one thing

which the harsh experiences of these last three years had taught
her it was the impermanence of relationships; she must, she
felt, lay down and follow a method of living for herself which
could never betray her when the attention of the rich and great
should be withdrawn. Gradually she ceased accepting Mrs. Denver's invitations; she pleaded the necessity of outside work along
the lines of her employment; she was busy, too, on the portrait
of her mother, stimulating her vivid memory with an old faded
photograph. Her intention was to have it as a surprise for Virginia upon the latter's return.

But before withdrawing completely she made the acquaintance of a young married woman and her husband, a couple so
gifted, so genuine and sincere that she was unable to keep to the
letter her spartan promise of cutting herself entirely adrift from
this fascinating cross-section of New York society. The husband,
Walter Sandburg, was a playwright; his name was a household
word; the title of one or another of his dramas glittered on
Broadway every night. His wife, Elizabeth, reviewed books for
one of the great New York weeklies. Their charming apartment
in Fifty-fifth Street was the centre for many clever and captivating people. Between these two and Angela something of a real
friendship awakened; she was not ashamed to have them see
the shabbiness of her apartment. The luncheons to which she
treated Elizabeth in the Village tearooms and in apartment
stores brought as great satisfaction as the more elaborate meals
at the Algonquin, the favourite rendezvous of many of these
busy, happy, contented workers.

Ashley, too, had returned to a town still devoid of Carlotta,
and in his loneliness was again constantly seeking Angela. His
attitude was perfect; never by word or look did he revive the
unpleasant impression which he had once made; indeed, in a
sober, disillusioned sort of way, she was growing to like him
very much. He was shy, sensitive, sympathetic and miserably
lonely. It was not likely that his possessions were as fabulously
great as Roger's but it was certain that he belonged to Roger's
social group with all that such a ranking implies. But in spite of
this he was curiously diffident; lacking in pep, the girls in his
"set" coldly classified him, and let him alone. Outside his group
ambitious Amazons daubed him "easy" and made a mad rush
for him and his fabled millions. The two verdicts left him

ashamed and frightened; annually he withdrew farther and farther into his shell, emerging only in response to Carlotta's careless and occasional beckoning or to Angela's genuine and pre-occupied indifference.

But this was not her world; for years she had craved such a *milieu*, only to find herself, when once launched into it, outwardly perfectly at ease, inwardly perturbed and dismayed. Although she rarely thought of colour still she was conscious of living in an atmosphere of falseness, of tangled implications. She spoke often of Martha Burden and her husband; Walter Sandburg the playwright, knew Ladislas Starr; Elizabeth had met Paulette Lister in some field of newspaper activity, and Ashley of course had seen Roger in Angela's company. Behind these three or four names and the background which familiarity with them implied, she did not dare venture and in her gayest moments she was aware of the constant stirring within of a longing for someone real and permanent with whom she could share her life. She would, of course make up with Jinny, but Jinny was going to live in Philadelphia, where she herself would never sojourn again. That aftermath was the real consideration.

Her thoughts went constantly winging to Anthony; her determination became static. Saving only this invisible mixture of dark blood in her veins they, too, could meet on a par. They were both young, both gifted, ambitious, blessedly poor. Together they would climb to happier, sunnier heights. To be poor with Anthony; to struggle with him; to help him keep his secret vow; to win his surprised and generous approbation; finally to reach the point where she, too, could open her home to poor, unknown, struggling geniuses,—life could hold nothing more pleasing than these possibilities. And how kind she would be to these strangers! How much she hoped that among them there would be some girl struggling past the limitations of her heritage even as she herself had done. Through some secret, subtle bond of sympathy she would, she was sure, be able to recognize such a girl; and how she would help her and spur her on! To her communings she said humbly, "I am sure that this course will work out all right for me for see, I am planning chiefly for Anthony and for helpless, harassed people; hardly anything for myself but protection and love. I am willing to work for success and happiness." And even as she spoke she knew that the summit of her bliss would be reached in the days while she and Anthony were still poor and struggling and when she would be giving of her best to make things so.

Elizabeth Sandburg reminiscing about the early married days of herself and Walter gave a fillip to her thought. Said Elizabeth: "Walt and I were just as poor as we could be, we only made twenty dollars a week, and half of that went for a room in cheap hotel. Meals even at the punkest places were awfully expensive, and half the time I used to cook things over the gas-jet. I didn't know much about cooking, and I imagine the stuff was atrocious, but we didn't mind. There were we with no one to interfere with us; we had each other and we didn't give a damn."

Smiling, glowing, she gave Angela a commission to paint hers and her Walter's portraits. "We'll leave the price to you and if you really put the job over I'll get you a lot of other sitters. No, don't thank me. What are friends for? That's what I always say."

Chapter IV

SOMETIMES this thought confronted her: "Perhaps Anthony no longer needs me; has forgotten me." And at the bare idea her heart would contract with an actual, palpable movement. For by now he was representing not only surcease from loneliness but peace and security; a place not merely in society but in the world at large. Marriage appeared, too, in a different light. Until she had met Roger she had not thought much about the institution except as an adventure in romance or as a means to an end; in her case the method of achieving the kind of existence which once had been her ideal. But now she saw it as an end in itself; for women certainly; the only, the most desirable and natural end. From this state a gifted, an ambitious woman might reach forth and acquit herself well in any activity. But marriage must be there first, the foundation, the substratum. Of course there were undoubtedly women who, like men, took love and marriage as the sauce of existence and their intellectual interests as the main dish. Witness for instance, Paulette. Now that she came to think of it, Paulette might vary her lovers but she never varied in the manifestation of her restless, clever mental energy. At no time did she allow her "love-life", as the psycho-analyst termed it, to interfere with her mental interests. Indeed she made no scruple of furthering these same interests by her unusual and pervasive sex charm. But this was Paulette, a remarkable personage, a woman apart. But for most women there must be the safety, the assurance of relationship that marriage affords. Indeed, most women must be able to say as did men, "You are mine," not merely, "I am yours."

A certain scorching humility thrust itself upon her. In all her manifestations of human relationships, how selfish she had been! She had left Virginia, she had taken up with Roger to further her own interests. For a brief interval she had perhaps loved Roger with the tumultuous, heady passion of hot, untried youth. But again when, this subsiding, she had tried to introduce a note of idealism, it had been with the thought of saving her own soul. She thought of her day in the park with Anthony, his uncomplaining acceptance of her verdict; his wistfully grateful: "I almost touched happiness". How easily she might have made him happy if she had turned her thoughts to his needs. But she had never thought of that; she had been too intent always on happiness for herself. Her father, her mother and Jinny had always given and she had always taken. Why was that? Jinny had sighed: "Perhaps you *have* more white blood than Negro in your veins." Perhaps this selfishness was what the possession of white blood meant; the ultimate definition of Nordic Supremacy.

Then she remembered that Anthony was white and, bewildered, she ceased trying to cogitate, to unravel, decipher, evaluate. She was lonely, she loved. She meant to find a companion; she meant to be beloved.

She must act.

None of her new friends was acquainted with Anthony. Ralph Ashley in response to a tentative question could not recall ever having seen him. The time was August, consequently he could not be at the school. Telephone books revealed nothing. "Lost in a great city!" she told herself and smiled at the cheap novel flavour of the phrase. She sent her thoughts fluttering back to the last time she had really seen Anthony, to their last intimate conversation. They had met that day after she had cut Jinny; she remembered, smiling now in her superior knowledge, the slight panic which she had experienced at his finding her in a 'bus in Harlem. There had been some chaffing about tea and he had given her his address and she had put it,—where? It was not in her address book. A feverish search through her little desk revealed it in the pages of her prayer book, the one which she had used as a child. This she considered a good omen. The bit of paper was crinkled and blurred but she was able to make out an address on One Hundred and Fourteenth Street. Suppose he were no longer there! She could not brook the thought of another night of uncertainty; it was ten o'clock but she mounted a 'bus, rode up to One Hundred and Fourteenth and Seventh Avenue. Her heart beat so loudly as she turned the corner,—it seemed as though the inhabitants of the rather shabby block hearing that human dynamo would throng their windows. The street, like many others in New York, possessed the pseudo elegance and impressiveness which comes from an equipment of brown stone houses with their massive fronts, their ostentatious regularity and simplicity, but a second glance revealed its down-at-heel condition; gaping windows disclosed the pitiful smallness of the rooms that crouched behind the pretentious outsides. There was something faintly humorous, ironical, about being cooped up in these deceptive palaces; according to one's temperament one might laugh or weep at the thought of how these structures, the product of human energy could yet cramp, imprison, even ruin the very activity which had created them.

Angela found her number, mounted the steps, sought in the dim, square hall feverishly among the names in the bells. Sullivan, Brown, Hendrickson, Sanchez,—and underneath the name of Sanchez on the same card, five small, neat characters in Anthony's inimitably clear printing—Cross. She almost fainted with the relief of it. Her fingers stole to the bell,—perhaps her onetime fellow-student was up in his room now,—how strange that this bit of gutta percha and its attendant wires should bridge all the extent of time and space that had so long lain between them! But she could not push it; Anthony, she was sure, was real enough, close enough to the heart of living to refuse to be shocked by any mere breach of the conventionalities. Even so, however, to seek at eleven o'clock at night and without preliminary warning admission to the rooms of a man whom one has not noticed for a year, was, as he himself would have put it, "a bit thick".

The little note which she sent was a model of demureness and propriety. "Dear Anthony," it read, "Do you remember my promising to ask you in for tea the next time I made a batch of cookies? Well, to-morrow at 5.30 will be the next time. Do come!"

He had changed; her interested, searching eyes descried it in a moment. Always grave, always austere, always responsible, there was now in his manner an imponderable yet perceptible increment of each quality. But this was not all; his old familiar tortured look had left him; a peace, a quality of poise hovered about him, the composure which is achieved either by the attainment or by the relinquishment of the heart's desire. There is really very little difference, since each implies the cessation of effort.

All this passed rapidly through Angela's mind. Aloud she said: "How do, Anthony? you're really looking awfully well. It's nice to see you again."

"It's nice to see you," he replied. Certainly there was nothing remarkable about their conversation. After the bantering, the jests and allusions which she had been used to hearing at the Sandburgs,—compared with the snappy jargon of Mrs. Denver's "crowd" this was trivial, not to say banal. She burst out laughing. Anthony raised his eyebrows.

"What's so funny? Is it a secret joke?"

"No,—only I've been thinking hard about you for a long time." She made a daring stroke. "Presumably you've thought occasionally about me. Yet when we meet we sit up like a dandy and a dowager with white kid gloves on and exchange comments on our appearances. I suppose the next step in order would be to talk about the weather. Have you had much rain up in One Hundred and Fourteenth Street, Mr. Cross?"

Some of his poise forsook him. The pervasive peacefulness that sat so palpably upon him deserted him like a rended veil. "You've been thinking about me for a long time? Just how long?"

"I couldn't tell you when it began." She ventured another bold stroke. "But you've been in the back of my mind,—oh for ages, ages."

The poise, the composure, the peace were all fled now. Hastily, recklessly he set down his glass of tea, came and towered over her. She bit her lips to hide their trembling. Oh he was dear, dearer than she had ever imagined, so transparent, so honest. Who was she to deserve him?

His face quivered. He should never have come near this girl! As suddenly as he had left his chair he returned to it, settled himself comfortably and picked up his glass. "I've been away from you so long I had forgotten."

"Forgotten what?"

"Forgotten how dangerous you are. Forgotten how a woman like you plays with poor fools like me. Why did you send for me? To set me dancing once more to your tune?"

His bitterness surprised and frightened her. "Anthony, Anthony don't talk like that! I sent for you because I wanted to see you, wanted to talk to my old friend."

Appeased, he lounged back in the famous and unique easy chair, lit a cigarette. She brought out some of her sketches, displayed her note-book. He was especially interested in the "Fourteenth Street Types", was pleased with the portrait of her mother. "She doesn't look like you, though I can see you probably have her hair and that pearly tint of her skin. But you must have got your nose from your father. You know all the rest of your face," he dwelt on her features dreamily, "your lips, your eyes, your curly lashes are so deliciously feminine. But that straight nose of yours betokens strength." The faded, yet striking photograph lay within reach. He picked it up, studying it thoughtfully. "What a beautiful woman;—all woman I should say. Did she have much effect on your life?"

"N-no, I can't say she did." She remembered those Saturday excursions and their adventures in "passing", so harmless, yet so far-reaching. "Oh yes, in one respect she influenced me greatly, changed my whole life."

He nodded, gazing moodily at the picture. "My mother certainly affected me."

Angela started to say glibly, "She made you what you are to-day"; but a glance at his brooding countenance made her think better of it.

"What's this?" He had turned again to the sketch book and was poring upon a mass of lightly indicated figures passing apparently in review before the tall, cloaked form of a woman, thin to emaciation, her hands on her bony hips, slightly bent forward, laughing uproariously yet with a certain chilling malevolence. "I can't make it out."

With something shamefaced in her manner she took it from him. "I'm not sure yet whether I'll develop it. I,—it's an idea that has slowly taken possession of me since I've been in New York. The tall woman is Life and the idea is that she laughs at us; laughs at the poor people who fall into the traps which she sets for us."

Sorrow set its seal on his face as perceptibly as though it had been stamped there. He came closer. "You've found that out too? If I could have managed it you would never have known

it. I wanted so to keep it from you." His manner suddenly
changed. "I must go. This afternoon has been perfect; I can't
thank you enough,—but I'm not coming again."

"Not coming again! What nonsense! Why, why ever not?
Now, Anthony, don't begin that vow business. To-day has
been perfect, marvellous. You don't suppose I'm going to let
my friend go when I'm really just discovering him!"

Weakly he murmured that it was foolish for them to take up
each other's time; he was going away.

"All the more reason, then, why we should be seeing each
other."

His glance fell on the formless sketch. "If I could only get
one laugh on life. . . . When are you going to let me see
you again? I'm my own man just now; my time is at your
disposal."

The next afternoon they met outside her office building and
dined together. On Friday they sailed to the Atlantic High-
lands. Saturday, Sunday, Monday, Tuesday flashed by, meaning
nothing to either except for the few hours which they spent in
each other's company. Thursday was a slack day; she arranged
her work so as to be free for the afternoon, and they passed the
hurrying, glamorous hours in Van Cortlandt Park, laughing,
jesting, relating old dreams, relapsing into silences more intimate than talk, blissfully aware of each other's presence, still
more throbbingly aware of a conversation held in this very
Park years ago. Back again in the little hall on Jayne Street he
took her in his arms and kissed her slowly, with rapture, with
adoration and she returned his kisses. For a long time he held
her close against his pounding heart; she opened her languid
eyes to meet his burning gaze which she could feel rather than
see. Slowly he took her arms from his neck, let them drop.

"Angel, Angel, I shall love you always. Life cannot rob me of
that. Good-bye, my sweetest."

He was lost in the shadowy night.

The next day passed and the next. A week sped. Absolute silence. No sign of him by either word or line.

At the end of ten days, on a never to be forgotten Sunday afternoon, she went to see him. Without conscious volition on her
part she was one moment in her apartment on Jayne Street;

and at the end of an hour she was pressing a button above the name Cross in a hall on One Hundred and Fourteenth Street, hearing the door click, mounting the black well of a stair-way, tapping on a door bearing the legend "Studio".

A listless voice said "Come in."

Presently the rather tall, slender young man sitting in his shirt sleeves, his back toward her, staring dejectedly but earnestly at a picture on the table before him asked: "What can I do for you?"

The long and narrow room boasted a rather good parquet floor and a clean plain wall paper covered with unframed pictures and sketches. In one corner stood an easel; the furniture for the most part was plain but serviceable and comfortable, with the exception of an old-fashioned horse-hair sofa which Angela thought she had never seen equalled for its black shininess and its promise of stark discomfort.

On entering the apartment she had felt perturbed, but as soon as she saw Anthony and realized that the picture at which he was gazing was an unfinished sketch of herself, her worry fled. He had asked his question without turning, so she addressed his back:

"You can tell me where you found that terrible sofa; I had no idea there were any in existence. Thought they had died out with the Dodo."

The sound of her voice brought him to her side. "Angèle, tell me what are you doing here?"

She tried to keep the light touch: "Not until you have told me about the sofa." But his dark, tormented face and the strain under which she had been suffering for the past week broke down her defence. Swaying, she caught at his hand. "Anthony, Anthony, how could you?"

He put his arm about her and led her to the despised sofa; looked at her moodily. "Why did you come to see me, Angèle?"

Ordinarily she would have fenced, indulged in some fancy skirmishing; but this was no ordinary occasion; indeed in ordinary circumstances she would not have been here. She spoke gravely and proudly.

"Because I love you. Because I think you love me." A sudden terrible fear assailed her. "Oh, Anthony, don't tell me you were only playing!"

"With you? So little was I playing that the moment I began to suspect you cared,—and I never dreamed of it until that last day in the park,—I ran away from you. I knew you had so many resources; men will always adore you, want you, that I thought you'd soon forget; turn to someone else just as you had turned for a sudden whim to me from God knows how many admirers."

She shook her head, but she was frightened; some nameless fear knocking at her heart. "I turned to you from no one, Anthony. I've had only one 'admirer' as you call it in New York and I had long, long since ceased thinking of him. No, Anthony, I came to you because I needed you; you of all men in New York. I think in the world. And I thought you needed me."

They sat in silence on the terrible sofa. He seized her hand and covered it with kisses; started to take her in his arms, then let them fall in a hopeless gesture.

"It's no good, Angel; there's no use trying to buck fate. Life has caught us again. What you're talking about is absolutely impossible."

"What do you mean, impossible?" The little mute fear that had lain within her for a long time as a result of an earlier confidence of his bestirred itself, spoke.

"Anthony, those men, those enemies that killed your father, —did you kill one of them?" She had her arms about him. "You know it's nothing to me. Don't even tell me about it. Your past belongs to you; it's your future I'm interested in, that I want."

He pushed her from him, finally, even roughly. "No, I've never killed a man. Though I've wanted to. But I was a little boy when it all happened and afterwards I wouldn't go back because of my mother." He went over to a drawer and took out a revolver. "I've half a mind to kill myself now, now before I go mad thinking how I've broken my promise, broken it after all these years." He looked at her wistfully, yet implacably. "I wish that I had died long before it was given to me to see that beautiful, loving look on your face change into one of hatred and dread and anger."

She thought he must be raving; she tried to sooth him. "Never mind, Anthony; I don't care a rap about what you've done.

Only tell me why do you say everything's impossible for us? Why can't we mean everything to each other, be married——"

"Because I'm coloured." In her bewildered relief she fell away from him.

"Yes, that's right, you damned American! I'm not fit for you to touch now, am I? It was all right as long as you thought I was a murderer, a card sharp, a criminal, but the black blood in me is a bit too much, isn't it?" Beside himself he rushed to the windows, looked on the placid Sunday groups festooning the front steps of the brown stone houses. "What are you going to do, alarm the neighbourhood? Well, let me tell you, my girl, before they can get up here I'll be dead." His glance strayed to the revolver. "They'll never catch me as they did my father."

It was on the point of her tongue to tell him her great secret. Her heart within her bubbled with laughter to think how quickly she could put an end to this hysteria, how she could calm this black madness which so seethed within him, poisoning the very spring of his life. But his last words turned her thoughts to something else, to another need. How he must have suffered, loving a girl who he felt sure would betray him; yet scorning to keep up the subterfuge.

She said to him gently: "Anthony, did you think I would do that?"

His answer revealed the unspeakable depths of his acquaintance with prejudice; his incurable cynicism. "You're a white American. I know there's nothing too dastardly for them to attempt where colour is involved."

A fantastic notion seized her. Of course she would tell him that she was coloured, that she was willing to live with coloured people. And if he needed assurance of her love, how much more fully would he believe in her when she realized that not even for the sake of the conveniences to be had by passing would she keep her association with white people secret from him. But first she must try to restore his faith in human goodness. She said to him gently: "Tell me about it, Anthony."

And sitting there in the ugly, tidy room in the sunshot duskiness of the early summer evening, the half-subdued noises of the street mounting up to them, he told her his story. An old story it was, but in its new setting, coupled with the fact that

Angela for years had closed her mind to the penalty which men sometimes pay for being "different", it sounded like some unbelievable tale from the Inquisition.

His father, John Hall, of Georgia, had been a sailor and rover, but John's father was a well-known and capable farmer who had stayed in his little town and slowly amassed what seemed a fortune to the poor and mostly ignorant whites by whom he was surrounded. In the course of John's wanderings he had landed at Rio de Janeiro and he had met Maria Cruz, a Brazilian with the blood of many races in her veins. She herself was apparently white, but she looked with favour on the brown, stalwart sailor, thinking nothing of his colour, which was very much the same as that of her own father. The two married and went to many countries. But finally John, wearying of his aimless life, returned to his father, arriving a month before it was time to receive the old man's blessing and his property. Thence all his troubles. Certain white men in the neighbourhood had had their eyes turned greedily on old Anthony Hall's possessions. His son had been a wanderer for many years; doubtless he was dead. Certainly it was not expected that he would return after all these years to his native soil; most niggers leaving the South left for ever. They knew better than to return with their uppity ways.

Added to the signal injustice of John Hall's return and the disappointment caused thereby, was the iniquity of his marriage to a beautiful and apparently white wife. Little Anthony could remember his father's constant admonition to her never to leave the house; the latter had, in his sudden zeal for home, forgotten what a sojourn in Georgia could mean. But his memory was soon refreshed and he was making every effort to dispose of his new possessions without total loss. This required time and patience, but he hoped that only a few months need elapse before they might shake off the dust of this cursed hole for ever.

"Just a little patience, Maria," he told his lovely wife.

But she could not understand. True, she never ventured into the town, but an infrequent visit to the little store was imperative and she did not mind an occasional admiring glance. Indeed she attributed her husband's admonitions to his not unwelcome jealousy. Anthony, always a grave child, constituted himself her constant guardian; his father, he knew, had to be away in neighbouring townships where he was trying to put through his deal, so the little boy accompanied his silly trusting mother everywhere. When they passed a group of staring, mouthing men he contrived to hurt his finger or stub his toe so as to divert his mother's attention. In spite of his childish subterfuges, indeed because of them, his mother attracted the notice of Tom Haley, son of the magistrate. Anthony apparently had injured his hand and his beautiful mother, bending over it with great solicitude, made a picture too charming, too challenging to be overlooked. Haley stepped forward, actually touched his cap. "Can I do anything to help you, ma'am?" She looked at him with her lovely, melting eyes, spoke in her foreign liquid voice. He was sure he had made a conquest. Afterwards, chagrined by the gibes of the bystanders who jeered at him for his courtesy to a nigger wench "for that's all she is, John Hall's wife", he ground his heel in the red dust; he would show her a thing or two.

In the hot afternoon, awakened from her siesta by a sudden knock, she came to the door, greeted her admirer of the early morning. She was not quite pleased with the look in his eyes, but she could not suspect evil. Haley, who had done some wandering on his own account and had picked up a few words of Spanish, let fall an insulting phrase or two. Amazed and angry she struck him across his face. The boy, Anthony, uneasily watching, screamed; there was a sudden tumult of voices and Haley fled, forgetting for the moment that these were Negro voices and so need not be dreaded. An old coloured man, mumbling and groaning "Gawd forgive you, Honey; we'se done fer now" guided the child and the panic-stricken mother into the swamp. And lying there hidden at night they could see the sparks and flames rising from the house and buildings, which represented the labour of Anthony Hall's sixty years. In a sudden lull they caught the sounds of the pistol shots which riddled John Hall's body.

"Someone warned my father," said Anthony Cross wearily, "but he would go home. Besides, once back in town he would have been taken anyway, perhaps mobbed and burned in the public square. They let him get into his house; he washed and dressed himself for death. Before nightfall the mob came to teach this man their opinion of a nigger who hadn't taught his wife her duty toward white men. First they set fire to the house, then called him to the window. He stepped out on a little veranda; Haley opened fire. The body fell over the railing dead before it could touch the ground, murdered by the bullets from twenty pistols. Souvenir hunters cut off fingers, toes, his ears, —a friend of my grandfather found the body at night and buried it. They said it was unlike anything they had ever seen before, totally dehumanized. After I heard that story I was unable to sleep for nights on end. As for my mother,——' "

Angela pressed his head close against her shoulder. There were no words for a thing like this, only warm human contact.

He went on wanly. "As for my mother, she was like a madwoman. She has gone all the rest of her life haunted by a terrible fear."

"Of white people," Angela supplemented softly. "Yes, I can see how she would."

He glanced at her sombrely. "No, of coloured people. She believes that we, particularly the dark ones, are cursed, otherwise, why should we be so abused, so hounded. Two years after my father's death she married a white man, not an American— that was spared me,—but a German who, I believe, treats her very kindly. I was still a little boy but I begged and pleaded with her to leave the whole race alone; I told her she owed it to the memory of my father. But she only said women were poor, weak creatures; they must take protection where they could get it."

Horrified, mute with the tragedy of it all, she could only stare at him white-lipped.

"Don't ask me how I came up. Angèle, for a time I was nothing, worthless, only I have never denied my colour; I have always taken up with coloured causes. When I've had a special point to make I've allowed the world to think of me as it would but always before severing my connections I told of the black blood that was in my veins. And then it came to me that for my father's sake I would try to make something of myself. So I sloughed off my evil ways, they had been assumed only in bravado,—and came to New York where I've been living quietly, I hope usefully, keeping my bitterness within myself where it could harm no one but me.

"I made one vow and kept it,—never by any chance to allow myself to become entangled with white people; never to listen to their blandishments; always to hate them with a perfect hate. Then I met you and loved you and somehow healing began. I thought, if she loves me she'll be willing to hear me through. And if after she hears me she is willing to take me, black blood and all,—but mind," he interrupted himself fiercely, "I'm not ashamed of my blood. Sometimes I think it's the leaven that will purify this Nordic people of their cruelty and their savage lust of power."

She ignored this. "So you were always going to tell me."

"Tell you? Of course I would have told you. Oh, I'm a man, Angel, with a man's record. When I was a sailor,—there're some pages in my life I couldn't let your fingers touch. But *that* I'd have told you, it was too vital, too important. Not that I think it really means this mixture of blood, as life goes, as God meant the world to go. But here in America it could make or mar life. Of course I'd have told you."

Here was honour, here was a man! So would her father have been. Having found this comparison her mind sought no further.

A deep silence descended upon them; in his case the silence of exhaustion. But Angela was thinking of his tragic life and of how completely, how surprisingly she could change it. Smiling, she spoke to him of happiness, of the glorious future. "I've something amazing to tell you, but I won't spring it on you all at once. Can't we go out to Van Cortlandt Park to-morrow evening?"

He caught her hand. "No matter what in the goodness of your heart you may be planning, there is no future, none, none, Angel, for you and me. Don't deceive yourself,—nor me. When I'm with you I forget sometimes. But this afternoon has brought it all back to me. I'll never forget myself and my vow again."

A bell shrilled three, four times.

He looked about frowning. "That's Sanchez; he's forgotten his key again. My dear girl, my Angel, you must go,—and you must not, must not come back. Hurry, hurry! I don't want him to see you here." He guided her towards the door, stemming her protestations. "I'll write you at once, but you must go. God bless and keep you."

In another moment she was out in the dim hall, passing a dark, hurrying figure on the stairs. The heavy door swung silently behind her, thrusting her inexorably out into the engulfing summer night; the shabby pretentious house was again between her and Anthony with his tragic, searing past.

Chapter V

ALL the next day and the next she dwelt on Anthony's story; she tried to put herself in his place, to force herself into a dim realization of the dark chamber of torture in which his mind and thoughts had dwelt for so many years. And she had added her modicum of pain, had been so unsympathetic, so unyielding; in the midst of the dull suffering, the sickness of life to which perhaps his nerves had become accustomed she had managed to inject an extra pinprick of poignancy. Oh, she would reward him for that; she would brim his loveless, cheated existence with joy and sweetness; she would cajole him into forgetting that terrible past. Some day he should say to her: "You have brought me not merely new life, but life itself." Those former years should mean no more to him than its pre-natal existence means to a baby.

Her fancy dwelt on, toyed with all the sweet offices of love; the delicate bondage that could knit together two persons absolutely *en rapport*. At the cost of every ambition which she had ever known she would make him happy. After the manner of most men his work would probably be the greatest thing in the world to him. And he should be the greatest thing in the world to her. He should be her task, her "job", the fulfilment of her ambition. A phrase from the writings of Anatole France came drifting into her mind. "There is a technique of love." She would discover it, employ it, not go drifting haphazardly, carelessly into this relationship. And suddenly she saw her affair with Roger in a new light; she could forgive him, she could forgive herself for that hitherto unpardonable union if through it she had come one iota nearer to the understanding and the need of Anthony.

His silence—for although the middle of the week had passed she had received no letter,—worried her not one whit. In the course of time he would come to her, remembering her perfect sympathy of the Sunday before and thinking that this woman was the atonement for what he considered her race. And then she would surprise him, she would tell him the truth, she would make herself inexpressibly dearer and nearer to him when he

came to know that her sympathy and her tenderness were real,
fixed and lasting, because they were based and rooted in the
same blood, the same experiences, the same comprehension of
this far-reaching, stupid, terrible race problem. How inexpressibly happy, relieved and overwhelmed he would be! She would
live with him in Harlem, in Africa, anywhere, any place. She
would label herself, if he asked it; she would tell every member
of her little coterie of white friends about her mixed blood; she
would help him keep his vow and would glory in that keeping.
No sacrifice of the comforts which came to her from "passing",
of the assurance, even of the safety which the mere physical
fact of whiteness in America brings, would be too great for her.
She would withdraw where he withdrew, hate where he hated.

His letter which came on Thursday interrupted her thoughts,
her fine dreams of self-immolation which women so adore. It
was brief and stern, and read:

> "Angèle, don't think for one moment that I do not
> thank you for Sunday. . . . My heart is at your feet for
> what you revealed to me then. But you and I have noth-
> ing in common, have never had, and now can never have.
> More than race divides us. I think I shall go away. Mean-
> while you are to forget me; amuse yourself, beautiful,
> charming, magnetic Angel with the men of your own
> race and leave me to my own.
>
>   "ANTHONY."

It was such a strange letter; its coldness and finality struck a
chill to her heart. She looked at the lonely signature, "Anthony",
—just that, no word of love or affection. And the phrase: "More
than race divides us." Its hidden significance held a menace.

The letter was awaiting her return from work. She had come
in all glowing with the promise of the future as she conceived
it. And then here were these cold words killing her high hopes
as an icy blast kills the too trusting blossoms of early spring.
. . . Holding the letter she let her supper go untasted, unre-
garded, while she evolved some plan whereby she could see
Anthony, talk to him. The tone of his letter did not sound as
though he would yield to ordinary persuasion. And again in
the midst of her bewilderment and suffering she was struck

afresh with the difficulties inherent in womanhood in conducting the most ordinary and most vital affairs of life. She was still a little bruised in spirit that she had taken it upon herself to go to Anthony's rooms Sunday; it was a step she felt conventionally, whose justification lay only in its success. As long as she had considered it successful, she had been able to relegate it to the uttermost limbo of her self-consciousness. But now that it seemed to avail nothing it loomed up before her in all its social significance. She was that creature whom men, in their selfish fear, have contrived to paint as the least attractive of human kind,—"a girl who runs after men." It seemed to her that she could not stand the application of the phrase, no matter how unjustly, how inaptly used in her own case.

Looking for a word of encouragement she re-read the note. The expression "My heart is at your feet" brought some reassurance; she remembered, too, his very real emotion of Sunday, only a few days before. Men, real men, men like Anthony, do not change. No, she could not let him go without one last effort. She would go to Harlem once more to his house, she would see him, reassure him, allay his fears, quench his silly apprehensions of non-compatability. As soon as he knew that they were both coloured, he'd succumb. Now he was overwrought. It had never occurred to her before that she might be glad to be coloured. . . . She put on her hat, walked slowly out the door, said to herself with a strange foreboding: "When I see this room again, I'll either be very happy, or very, very sad. . . ." Her courage rose, braced her, but she was sick of being courageous, she wanted to be a beloved woman, dependent, fragile, sought for, feminine; after this last ordeal she would be "womanly" to the point of ineptitude. . . .

During the long ride her spirits rose a little. After all, his attitude was almost inevitable. He thought she belonged to a race which to him stood for treachery and cruelty; he had seen her with Roger, Roger, the rich, the gay; he saw her as caring only for wealth and pleasure. Of course in his eyes she was separated from him by race and by more than race.

For long years she was unable to reconstruct that scene; her mind was always too tired, too sore to re-enact it.

As in a dream she saw Anthony's set, stern face, heard his

firm, stern voice: "Angel-girl,—Angèle I told you not to come back. I told you it was all impossible."

She found herself clutching at his arm, blurting out the truth, forgetting all her elaborate plans, her carefully pre-concerted drama. "But, Anthony, Anthony, listen, everything's all right. I'm coloured; I've suffered too; nothing has to come between us."

For a moment off his guard he wavered. "Angèle, I didn't think you'd lie to me."

She was in tears, desperate. "I'm not lying, Anthony. It's perfectly true."

"I saw that picture of your mother, a white woman if I ever saw one,——"

"Yes, but a white coloured woman. My father was black, perfectly black and I have a sister, she's brown. My mother and I used to 'pass' sometimes just for the fun of it; she didn't mind being coloured. But I minded it terribly,—until very re-cently. So I left my home,—in Philadelphia,—and came here to live,—oh, going for white makes life so much easier. You know it, Anthony." His face wan and terrible frightened her. "It doesn't make you angry, does it? You've passed yourself, you told me you had. Oh Anthony, Anthony, don't look at me like that! What is it?"

She caught at his hand, following him as he withdrew to the shiny couch where they both sat breathless for a moment. "God!" he said suddenly; he raised his arms, beating the void like a madman. "You in your foolishness, I in my carelessness, 'passing, passing' and life sitting back laughing, splitting her sides at the joke of it. Oh, it was all right for you,—but I didn't care whether people thought I was white or coloured,—if we'd only known,——"

"What on earth are you talking about? It's all right now."

"It isn't all right; it's worse than ever." He caught her wrist. "Angel, you're sure you're not fooling me?"

"Of course I'm not. I have proof, I've a sister right here in New York; she's away just now. But when she comes back, I'll have you meet her. She is brown and lovely,—you'll want to paint her—don't you believe me, Anthony?"

"Oh yes, I believe you," he raised his arms again in a beautiful,

fluid gesture, let them fall. "Oh, damn life, damn it, I say
. . . isn't there any end to pain!"

Frightened, she got on her knees beside him. "Anthony, what's
the matter? Everything's going to be all right; we're going to
be happy."

"You may be. I'll never be happy. You were the woman I
wanted,—I thought you were white. For my father's sake I
couldn't marry a white girl. So I gave you up."

"And I wouldn't stay given up. See, here I am back again.
You'll never be able to send me away." Laughing but shame-
faced, she tried to thrust herself into his arms.

"No, Angel, no! You don't understand. There's, there's somebody else——"

She couldn't take it in. "Somebody else. You mean,—you're
married? Oh Anthony, you don't mean you're married!"

"No, of course not, of course not! But I'm engaged."

"Engaged, engaged and not to me,—to another girl? And
you kissed me, went around with me? I knew other men did
that, but I never thought that of you! I thought you were like
my father!" And she began to cry like a little girl.

Shame-faced, he looked on, jamming his hands tightly into
his pockets. "I never meant to harm you; I never thought until
that day in the park that you would care. And I cared so terribly! Think, I had given you up, Angèle,—I suppose that isn't your
name really, is it?—all of a sudden, you came walking back into
my life and I said, 'I'll have the laugh on this dammed mess
after all. I'll spend a few days with her, love her a little, just a
little. She'll never know, and I'll have a golden memory!' Oh, I
had it coming to me, Angel! But the minute I saw you were
beginning to care I broke off short."

A line from an old text was running through her head, rendering her speechless, inattentive. She was a little girl back in
the church again in Philadelphia; the minister was intoning
"All we like sheep have gone astray". He used to put the emphasis on the first word and Jinny and she would look at each
other and exchange meaning smiles; he was a West Indian and
West Indians had a way of misplacing the emphasis. The line
sounded so funny: "*All* we like sheep,——" but perhaps it
wasn't so funny after all; perhaps he had read it like that not

because he was a West Indian but because he knew life and human nature. Certainly *she* had gone astray,—with Roger. And now here was Anthony, Anthony who had always loved her so well. Yet in his background there was a girl and he was engaged.

This brought her to a consideration of the unknown fiancée, —her rival. Deliberately she chose the word, for she was not through yet. This unknown, unguessed at woman who had stolen in like a thief in the night. . . .

"Have you known her long?" she asked him sharply.

"Who? Oh my,—my friend. No, not as long as I've known you."

A newcomer, an upstart. Well at least she, Angela, had the advantage of precedence.

"She's coloured, of course?"

"Of course."

They sat in a weary silence. Suddenly he caught her in his arms and buried his head in her neck. A quick pang penetrated to the very core of her being. He must have been an adorable baby. . . . Anthony and babies!

"Now God, Life, whatever it is that has power, this time you must help me!" cried her heart. She spoke to him gently.

"Anthony, you know I love you. Do you still love me?"

"Always, always, Angel."

"Do you—Oh, Anthony, I don't deserve it, but do you by any chance worship me?"

"Yes, that's it, that's just it, I worship you. I adore you. You are God to me. Oh, Angèle, if you'd only let me know. But it's too late now."

"No, no don't say that, perhaps it isn't too late. It all depends on this. Do you worship *her*, Anthony?" He lifted his haggard face.

"No—but she worships *me*. I'm God to her do you see? If I fail her she won't say anything, she'll just fall back like a little weak kitten, like a lost sheep, like a baby. She'll die." He said as though unaware of his listener. "She's such a little thing. And sweet."

Angela said gently: "Tell me about her. Isn't it all very sudden? You said you hadn't known her long."

He began obediently. "It was not long after I—I lost you.

She came to me out of nowhere, came walking to me into my room by mistake; she didn't see me. And she put her head down on her hands and began to cry terribly. I had been crying too—in my heart, you understand,—and for a moment I thought she might be the echo of that cry, might be the cry itself. You see, I'd been drinking a little,—you were so far removed, white and all that sort of thing. I couldn't marry a white woman, you know, not a white American. I owed that to my father.

"But at last I saw it was a girl, a real girl and I went over to her and put my hand on her shoulder and said: 'Little girl, what's the matter?'

"And she lifted her head, still hidden in the crook of her arm, you know the way a child does and said: 'I've lost my sister'. At first I thought she meant lost in the street and I said "Well, come with me to the police station, I'll go with you, we'll give them a description and you'll find her again. People don't stay lost in this day and time'. I got her head on my shoulder, I almost took her on my knee, Angèle, she was so simple and forlorn. And presently she said: 'No, I don't mean lost that way; I mean she's left me, she doesn't want me any more. She wants other people'. And I've never been able to get anything else out of her. The next morning I called her up and somehow I got to seeing her, for her sake, you know. But afterwards when she grew happier,—she was so blithe, so lovely, so healing and blessed like the sun or a flower,—then I saw she was getting fond of me and I stayed away.

"Well, I ran across you and that Fielding fellow that night at the Van Meier lecture. And you were so happy and radiant, and Fielding so possessive,—damn him!—damn him!—he— you didn't let him hurt you Angèle?"

As though anything that had ever happened in her life could hurt her like this! She had never known what pain was before. White-lipped, she shook her head. "No, he didn't hurt me."

"Well, I went to see her the next day. She came into the room like a shadow,—I realized she was getting thin. She was kind and sweet and far-off; impalpable, tenuous and yet there. I could see she was dying for me. And all of a sudden it came to me how wonderful it would be to have someone care like that. I went to her; I took her in my arms and I said: 'Child,

child, I'm not bringing you a whole heart but could you love me?' You see I couldn't let her go after that."

"No," Angela's voice was dull, lifeless. "You couldn't. She'd die."

"Yes, that's it; that's just it. And I know you won't die, Angel."

"No, you're quite right. I won't die."

An icy hand was on her heart. At his first words: "She came walking into my room,——" an icy echo stirred a memory deep, deep within her inner consciousness. She heard Jinny saying: "I went walking into his room,——"

Something stricken, mortally stricken in her face fixed his attention. "Don't look like that, my girl, my dear Angel. . . . There are three of us in this terrible plight,—if I had only known. . . . I don't deserve the love of either of you but if one of you two must suffer it might as well be she as you. Come, we'll go away; even unhappiness, even remorse will mean something to us as long as we're together."

She shook her head. "No, that's impossible,—if it were someone else, I don't know, perhaps—I'm so sick of unhappiness, —maybe I'd take a chance. But in her case it's impossible."

He looked at her curiously. "What do you mean 'in her case'?"

"Isn't her name Virginia Murray?"

"Yes, yes! How did you guess it? Do you know her?"

"She's my sister. Angèle Mory,—Angela Murray, don't you see. It's the same name. And it's all my fault. I pushed her, sent her deliberately into your arms."

He could only stare.

"I'm the unkind sister who didn't want her. Oh, can't you understand? That night she came walking into your room by mistake it was because I had gone to the station to meet her and Roger Fielding came along. I didn't want him to know that I was coloured and I,—I didn't acknowledge her, I cut her."

"Oh," he said surprised and inadequate. "I don't see how you could have done that to a little girl like Virginia. Did she know New York?"

"No." She drooped visibly. Even the loss of him was nothing compared to this rebuke. There seemed nothing further to be said.

Presently he put his arm about her. "Poor Angèle. As though

you could foresee! It's what life does to us, leads us into pitfalls apparently so shallow, so harmless and when we turn around there we are, caught, fettered,——"

Her miserable eyes sought his. "I was sorry right away, Anthony. I tried my best to get in touch with her that very evening. But I couldn't find her;—already you see, life was getting even with me, she had strayed into your room."

He nodded. "Yes, I remember it all so plainly. I was getting ready to go out, was all prepared as a matter of fact. Indeed I moved that very night. But I loitered on and on, thinking of you.

"The worst of it is I'll always be thinking of you. Oh Angèle, what does it matter, what does anything matter if we just have each other? This damned business of colour, is it going to ruin all chances of happiness? I've known trouble, pain, terrible devastating pain all my life. You've suffered too. Together perhaps we could find peace. We'd go to your sister and explain. She is kind and sweet; surely she'd understand."

He put his arms about her and the two clung to each other, solemnly, desperately, like children.

"I'm sick of pain, too, Anthony, sick of longing and loneliness. You can't imagine how I've suffered from loneliness."

"Yes, yes I can. I guessed it. I used to watch you. I thought you were probably lonely inside, you were so different from Miss Lister and Mrs. Starr. Come away with me and we'll share our loneliness together, somewhere where we'll forget——"

"And Virginia? You said yourself she'd die,——"

"She's so young, she—she could get over it." But his tone was doubtful, wavering.

She tore herself from him. "No, I took her sister away from her; I won't take her lover. Kiss me good-bye, Anthony."

They sat on the hard sofa. "To think we should find one another only to lose each other! To think that everything, every single thing was all right for us but that we were kept apart by the stupidity of fate. I'd almost rather we'd never learned the truth. Put your dear arms about me closer, Angel, Angel. I want the warmth, the sweetness of you to penetrate into my heart. I want to keep it there forever. Darling, how can I let you go?"

She clung to him weeping, weeping with the heart-broken abandonment of a child.

A bell shrilled four times.

He jumped up. "It's Sanchez, he's forgotten his key; thank God he did forget it. My darling, you must go. But wait for me. I'll meet you,—we'll go to your house, we'll find a way. We can't part like this!" His breath was coming in short gasps; she could see little white lines deepening about his mouth, his nostrils. Fearfully she caught at her hat.

"God bless you; good-bye Anthony. I won't see you again."

Halfway down the black staircase she met the heedless Sanchez, tall, sallow, thin, glancing at her curiously with a slightly amused smile. Politely he stood aside to let her pass, one hand resting lightly against his hip. Something in his attitude made her think of her unfinished sketch of Life. Hysterical, beside herself, she rushed down the remaining steps afraid to look around lest she should see the thin dark figure in pursuit, lest her ears should catch the expansion of that faint meaning smile into a guffaw, uproarious, menacing.

Chapter VI

ONCE long ago in the old days in the house on Opal Street she had been taken mysteriously ill. As a matter of fact she had been coming down with that inglorious disease, the mumps. The expense of having a doctor was a consideration, and so for twenty-four hours she was the object of anxious solicitude for the whole house. Her mother had watched over her all night; her father came home twice in the day to see how she felt; Jinny had with some reluctance bestowed on her an oft-coveted, oft-refused doll. In the midst of all her childish pain and suffering she had realized that at least her agony was shared, that her tribulation was understood. But now she was ill with a sickness of the soul and there was no one with whom she could share her anguish.

For two days she lay in her little room; Mrs. Denver, happening in, showered upon her every attention. There was nothing, nothing that Angela could suggest, the little fluttering lady said sincerely, which she might not have. Angela wished that she would go away and leave her alone, but her experiences had rendered her highly sensitive to the needs of others; Mrs. Denver, for all her money, her lack of responsibility, her almost childish appetite for pleasure, was lonely too; waiting on the younger, less fortunate woman gave her a sense of being needed; she was pathetically glad when the girl expressed a desire for anything no matter how expensive or how trivial. Angela could not deprive her entirely of those doubtful pleasures. Still there were moments, of course, when even Mrs. Denver for all her kindly officiousness had to betake herself elsewhere and leave her willing patient to herself and her thoughts.

Minutely, bit by bit, in the long forty-eight hours she went over her life; was there anything, any over tact, any crime which she had committed and for which she might atone? She had been selfish, yes; but, said her reasoning and unwearied mind, "Everybody who survives at all is selfish, it is one of the prerequisites of survival." In "passing" from one race to the other she had done no harm to anyone. Indeed she had been forced to take this action. But she should not have forsaken Virginia.

Here at this point her brain, so clear and active along all other lines, invariably failed her. She could not tell what stand to take; so far as leaving Philadelphia was concerned she had left it to seek her fortune under more agreeable circumstances; if she had been a boy and had left home no one would have had a word of blame, it would have been the proper thing, to be expected and condoned. There remained then only the particular incident of her cutting Jinny on that memorable night in the station. That was the one really cruel and unjust action of her whole life.

"Granted," said something within her rooted either in extreme hard common sense or else in a vast sophistry, "granted, but does that carry with it as penalty the shattering of a whole life, or even the suffering of years? Certainly the punishment is far in excess of the crime." And it was then that she would lie back exhausted, hopeless, bewildered, unable to cope further with the myterious and apparently meaningless ferocity of life. For if this were a just penalty for one serious misdemeanour, what compensation should there not be for the years in which she had been a dutiful daughter, a loving sister? And suddenly she found herself envying people possessed of a blind religious faith, of the people who could bow the head submissively and whisper: "Thy will be done." For herself she could see how beaten and harried, one might subside into a sort of blind passivity, an acceptance of things as they are, but she would never be able to understand a force which gave one the imagination to paint a great desire, the tenacity to cling to it, the emotionalism to spend on its possible realization but which would then with a careless sweep of the hand wipe out the picture which the creature of its own endowment had created.

More than once the thought came to her of dying. But she hated to give up; something innate, something of the spirit stronger than her bodily will, set up a dogged fight, and she was too bruised and sore to combat it. "All right," she said to herself wearily, "I'll keep on living." She thought then of black people, of the race of her parents and of all the odds against living which a cruel, relentless fate had called on them to endure. And she saw them as a people powerfully, almost overwhelmingly endowed with the essence of life. They had to persist, had to survive because they did not know how to die.

*

Not because she felt like it, but because some day she must begin once more to take up the motions of life, she moved on the third day from her bed to the easy chair, sat there listless and motionless. To-morrow she would return to work,—to work and the sick agony of forcing her mind back from its dolorous, painful, vital thoughts to some consideration of the dull, uninteresting task in hand. God, how she hated that! She remembered studying her lessons as a girl; the intense absorption with which she used to concentrate. Sometimes she used to wonder: "Oh what will it be like when I am grown up; when I won't be studying lessons . . ." Well, this was what it was like. Or no, she was still studying with the same old absorption,—an absorption terribly, painfully concentrated,—the lessons set down by life. It was useless to revolve in her head the causes for her suffering, they were so trivial, so silly. She said to herself, "There is no sorrow in the world like my sorrow", and knew even as she said it that some one else, perhaps only in the next block, in the next house, was saying the same thing.

Mrs. Denver tapped lightly, opened the door, came in closing it mysteriously behind her.

"I've a great surprise for you." She went on with an old childish formula: "Will you have it now, or wait till you get it?"

Angela's features twisted into a wan smile. "I believe I'd better have it now. I'm beginning to think I don't care for surprises."

"You'll like this one." She went to the door and ushered in Rachel Salting.

"I know you two want to talk," Mrs. Denver called over her shoulder. "Cheer her up, Rachel, and I'll bring you both a fine spread in an hour or so." She closed the door carefully behind her.

Angela said, "What's the matter, Rachel?" She almost added, "I hardly knew you." For her friend's face was white and wan with grief and hopelessness; gone was all her dainty freshness, her pretty colour; indeed her eyes, dark, sunken, set in great pools of blackness, were the only note,—a terrible note,—of relief against that awful whiteness.

Angela felt her strength leaving her; she rose and tottered

back to the grateful security of her bed, lay down with an overwhelming sense of thankfulness for the asylum afforded her
sudden faintness. In a moment, partly recovered, she motioned
to Rachel to sit beside her.

"Oh," said Rachel, "you've been ill,—Mrs. Denver told me.
I ought not to come bothering you with my worries. Oh,
Angèle, I'm so wretched! Whatever shall I do?"

Her friend, watching her, was very gentle. "There're lots of
awful things that can happen. I know that, Rachel. Maybe your
trouble isn't so bad that it can't be helped. Have you told John
about it?" But even as she spoke she sensed that the difficulty
in some way concerned John. Her heart contracted at the
thought of the pain and suffering to be endured.

"Yes, John knows,—it's about him. Angèle, we can't marry."

"Can't marry. Why, is he,—it can't be that he's—involved
with some one else!"

A momentary indignation flashed into Rachel's face bringing back life and colour. For a small space she was the Rachel
Salting of the old happy days. "Involved with some one else!"
The indignation was replaced by utter despair. "How I wish he
were! That at least could be arranged. But this can never be altered. He,—I, our parents are dead set against it. Hadn't you
ever noticed, Angèle? He's a Gentile and I'm a Jew."

"But lots of Jews and Gentiles marry."

"Yes, I know. Only—he's a Catholic. But my parents are
orthodox—they will never consent to my marriage. My father
says he'd rather see me dead and my mother just sits and moans.
I kept it from her as long as I could,—I used to pray about it,
I thought God must let it turn out all right, John and I love
each other so. But I went up to Utica the other day, John went
with me, and we told them. My father drove him out of the
house; he said if I married him he'd curse me. I am afraid of
that curse. I can't go against them. Oh, Angèle, I wish I'd never
been born."

It was a delicate situation; Angela had to feel her way; she
could think of nothing but the trite and obvious. "After all,
Rachel, your parents have lived their lives; they have no business trying to live yours. Personally I think all this pother about
race and creed and colour, tommyrot. In your place I should

certainly follow my own wishes; John seems to be the man for you."

But Rachel weeping, imbued with the spirit of filial piety, thought it would be selfish.

"Certainly no more selfish than their attempt to regulate your life for you."

"But I'm afraid," said Rachel shivering, "of my father's curse." It was difficult for Angela to sympathize with an attitude so archaic; she was surprised to find it lurking at the bottom of her friend's well-trained intelligence.

"Love," she said musing to herself rather than to her friend, "is supposed to be the greatest thing in the world but look how we smother and confine it. Jews mustn't marry Catholics; white people mustn't marry coloured——"

"Oh well, of course not," Rachel interrupted in innocent surprise. "I wouldn't marry a nigger in any circumstances. Why, would you?"

But Angela's only answer was to turn and, burying her head in her pillow, to burst into unrestrained and bitter laughter. Rachel went flying to call Mrs. Denver.

"Oh come quick, come quick! Angèle's in hyterics. I haven't the ghost of an idea what to do for her!"

Once more the period of readjustment. Once more the determination to take life as she found it; bitter dose after sweet, bitter after sweet. But it seemed to her now that both sweetness and bitterness together with her high spirit for adventure lay behind her. How now was she to pass through the tepid, tasteless days of her future? She was not quite twenty-seven, and she found herself wondering what life would be like in ten, five, even one year's time. Changes did flow in upon one, she knew, but in her own case she had been so used herself to give the impetus to these changes. Now she could not envisage herself as making a move in any direction. With the new sullenness which seemed to be creeping upon her daily, she said "Whatever move I make is always wrong. Let life take care of itself." And she saw life, even her own life, as an entity quite outside her own ken and her own directing. She did not care greatly what happened; she would not, it was true, take her own life, but she would not care if she should die. Once if her mind had harboured such thoughts she would have felt an instant self-pity. "What a shame that I so young, so gifted, with spirits so high should meet with death!" But now her senses were blunting; so much pain and confusion had brought about their inevitable attrition. "I might just as well be unhappy, or meet death as anyone else," she told herself still with that mounting sullenness.

Mrs. Denver, the Sandburgs and Ashley were the only people who saw her. It did seem to Mrs. Denver that the girl's ready, merry manner was a little dimmed; if her own happy, sunny vocabulary had known the term she would have daubed her cynical. The quasi-intellectual atmosphere at the Sandburgs suited her to perfection; the faint bitterness which so constantly marred her speech was taken for sophistication, her frequent silences for profoundness; in a small way, aided by her extraordinary good looks and the slight mystery which always hung about her, she became quite a personage in their entourage; the Sandburgs considered her a splendid find and plumed themselves on having "brought her out".

The long golden summer, so beautiful with its promise of happiness, so sickening with its actuality of pain ripened into early, exquisite September. Virginia was home again; slightly more golden, very, very faintly plumper, like a ripening fruit perfected; brimming with happiness, excitement and the most complete content, Angela thought, that she had ever seen in her life.

Jinny sent for the older girl and the two sat on a Sunday morning, away from Sara Penton and the other too insistent friends, over on Riverside Drive looking out at the river winding purple and alluring in the soft autumn haze.

"Weren't you surprised?" asked Jinny. Laconically, Angela admitted to no slight amazement. She still loved her sister but more humbly, less achingly than before. Their lives, she thought now would never, could never touch and she was quite reconciled. Moreover, in some of Virginia's remarks there was the hint of the acceptance of such a condition. Something had brought an irrevocable separation. They would always view each other from the two sides of an abyss, narrow but deep, deep.

The younger girl prattled on. "I don't know whether Sara told you his name,—Anthony Cross? Isn't it a dear name?"

"Yes, it's a nice name, a beautiful name," said Angela heartily; when she had learned it was of no consequence. She added without enthusiasm that she knew him already; he had been a member of her class at Cooper Union.

"You don't talk as though you were very much taken with him," said Jinny, making a face. "But never mind, he suits me, no matter whom he doesn't suit." There was that in her countenance which made Angela realize and marvel again at the resoluteness of that firm young mind. No curse of parents could have kept Virginia from Anthony's arms. As long as Anthony loved her, was satisfied to have her love, no one could come between them. Only if he should fail her would she shrivel up and die.

On the heels of this thought Virginia made an astounding remark: "You know it's just perfect that I met Anthony; he's really been a rock in a weary land. Next to Matthew Henson he will, I'm sure, make me happier than any man in the world." Dreamily she added an afterthought: "And I'll make him happy too, but, oh, Angela, Angela, I always wanted to marry Matthew!"

The irony of that sent Angela home. Virginia wanting Matthew and marrying Anthony; Anthony wanting Angela and marrying Virginia. Herself wanting Anthony and marrying, wanting, no other; unable to think of, even to dream of another lover. The irony of it was so palpable, so ridiculously palpable that it put her in a better mood; life was bitter but it was amusingly bitter; if she could laugh at it she might be able to outwit it yet. The thought brought Anthony to mind: "If I could only get a laugh on life, Angèle!"

Sobered, she walked from the 'bus stop to Jayne Street. Halfway up the narrow, tortuous stair case she caught sight of a man climbing, climbing. He stopped outside her door. "Anthony?" she said to herself while her heart twisted with pain. "If it is Anthony,——" she breathed, and stopped. But something within her, vital, cruel, persistent, completed her thought. "If it is Anthony,—after what Virginia said this morning,—if he knew that he was not the first, that even as there had been one other there might still be others; that Virginia in her bright, hard, shallow youthfulness would not die any more than she had died over Matthew,—would console herself for the loss of Anthony even as she had consoled herself for the loss of Matthew!" But no, what Jinny had told her was in confidence, a confidence from sister to sister. She would never break faith with Jinny again; nor with herself.

"But Anthony," she said to herself in the few remaining seconds left on the staircase, "you were my first love and I think I was yours."

However, the man at the door was not Anthony; on the contrary he was, she thought, a complete stranger. But as he turned at her footsteps, she found herself looking into the blue eyes of Roger. Completely astounded, she greeted him, "You don't mean it's you, Roger?"

"Yes," he said humbly, shamefacedly, "aren't you going to let me in, Angèle?"

"Oh yes, of course, of course"; she found herself hoping that he would not stay long. She wanted to think and she would like to paint; that idea must have been in the back of her head ever since she had left Jinny. Hard on this thought came another. "Here's Roger. I never expected to see him in these rooms again; perhaps some day Anthony will come back. Oh, God, be kind!"

But she must tear her thoughts away from Anthony. She looked at Roger curiously, searchingly; in books the man who had treated his sweetheart unkindly often returned beaten, dejected, even poverty-stricken, but Roger, except for a slight hesitation in his manner, seemed as jaunty, as fortunate, as handsome as ever. He was even a trifle stouter.

Contrasting him with Anthony's hard-bitten leanness, she addressed him half absently. "I believe you're actually getting fat!"

His quick high flush revealed his instant sensitiveness to her criticism. But he was humble. "That's all right, Angèle. I deserve anything you choose to say if you'll just say it."

She was impervious to his mood, utterly indifferent, so indifferent that she was herself unaware of her manner. "Heavens,

I've sort of forgotten, but I don't remember your ever having been so eager for criticism heretofore!"

He caught at one phrase. "Forgotten! You don't mean to say you've forgotten the past and all that was once so dear to us?"

Impatience overwhelmed her. She wished he would go and leave her to her thoughts and to her picture; such a splendid idea had come to her; it was the first time for weeks that she had felt like working. Aware of the blessed narcotic value of interesting occupation, she looked forward to his departure with a sense of relief; even hoped with her next words to pre- cipitate it.

"Roger, you don't mean to say that you called on me on a hot September Sunday just to talk to me in that theatrical manner? I don't mind telling you I've a million things to do this afternoon; let's get down to bed rock so we can both be up and doing."

She had been sitting, almost lolling at ease in the big chair, not regarding him, absently twisting a scarf in her fingers. Now she glanced up and something in the hot blueness of his eyes brought her to an upright position, alert, attentive.

"Angèle, you've got to take me back."

"Back! I don't know what you're talking about. Between you and me there is no past, so don't mention it. If you've nothing better to say than that, you might as well get out."

He tried to possess himself of her hands but she shook him off, impatiently, angrily, with no pretence at feeling. "Go away, Roger. I don't want to be bothered with you!" This pinchbeck emotionalism after the reality of her feeling for Anthony, the sincerity of his feeling for her! "I won't have this sort of thing; if you won't go I will." She started for the door but he barred her way, suddenly straight and serious.

"No listen, Angèle, you must listen. I'm in earnest this time. You must forgive me for the past, for the things I said. Oh, I was unspeakable! But I had it in my head,—you don't know the things a man has borne in on him about designing women,—if he's got anything, family, money,——" she could see him striv- ing to hide his knowledge of his vast eligibility. "I thought you were trying to 'get' me, it made me suspicious, angry. I knew you were poor,——"

"And nobody! Oh say it, say it!"

"Well, I will say it. According to my father's standards, nobody. And when you began to take an interest in me, in my affairs,——"

"You thought I was trying to marry you. Well, at first I was. I was poor, I was nobody! I wanted to be rich, to be able to see the world, to help people. And then when you and I came so near to each other I didn't care about marriage at all—just about living! Oh, I suppose my attitude was perfectly pagan. I hadn't meant to drift into such a life, all my training was against it, you can't imagine how completely my training was against it. And then for a time I was happy. I'm afraid I didn't love you really, Roger, indeed I know now that in a sense I didn't love you, but somehow life seemed to focus into an absolute perfection. Then you became petulant, ugly, suspicious, afraid of my interest, of my tenderness. And I thought, 'I can't let this all end in a flame of ugliness; it must be possible for people to have been lovers and yet remain friends.' I tried so hard to keep things so that it would at least remain a pleasant memory. But you resented my efforts. What I can't understand is—why shouldn't I, if I wanted to, either try to marry you or to make an ideal thing of our relationship? Why is it that men like you resent an effort on our part to make our commerce decent? Well, it's all over now. . . . Theoretically 'free love' or whatever you choose to call it, is all right. Actually, it's all wrong. I don't want any such relationship with you or with any other man in this world. Marriage was good enough for my mother, it's good enough for me."

"There's nothing good enough for you, Angèle; but marriage is the best thing that I have to offer and I'm offering you just that. And it's precisely because you were honest and frank and decent and tried to keep our former relationship from deteriorating into sordidness that I am back."

Clearly she was staggered. Marriage with Roger meant protection, position, untold wealth, unlimited opportunities for doing good. Once how she would have leapt to such an offer!

"What's become of Carlotta?" she asked bluntly.

"She's on the eve of marrying Tom Estes, a fellow who was in college with me. He has heaps more money than I. Carlotta thought she'd better take him on."

"I see." She looked at him thoughtfully, then the remembrance of her great secret came to her, a secret which she could never share with Roger. No! No more complications and their consequent disaster! "No, no, we won't talk about it any more. What you want is impossible; you can't guess how completely impossible."

He strode toward her, seized her hands. "I'm in earnest, Angèle; you've no idea how tired I am of loneliness and uncertainty and,—and of seeking women; I want someone whom I can love and trust, whom I can teach to love me,—we could get married to-morrow. There's not an obstacle in our way."

His sincerity left her unmoved. "What would your father say?"

"Oh, we wouldn't be able to tell him yet; he'd never consent! Of course we'd have to keep things quiet, just ourselves and one or two friends, Martha and Ladislas perhaps, would be in the know."

More secrets! She pulled her hands away from him. "Oh Roger, Roger! I wouldn't consider it. No, when I marry I want a man, a man, a real one, someone not afraid to go on his own!" She actually pushed him toward the door. "Some people might revive dead ashes, but not you and I. . . . I'd never be able to trust you again and I'm sick of secrets and playing games with human relationships. I'm going to take my friendships straight hereafter. Please go. I've had a hard summer and I'm very tired. Besides I want to work."

Baffled, he looked at her, surprise and indignation struggling in his face. "Angèle, are you sure you know what you're doing? I've no intention of coming back, so you'd better take me now."

"Of course you're not coming back! I'm sure I wouldn't want you to; my decision is final." Not unsympathetically she laughed up into his doleful face, actually touched his cheek. "If you only knew how much you look like a cross baby!"

Her newly developed sympathy and understanding made her think of Ashley. Doubtless Carlotta's defection would hit him very hard. Her conjecture was correct although the effect of the blow was different from what she had anticipated. Ashley was not so perturbed over the actual loss of the girl as confirmed in his opinion that he was never going to be able to form and keep a lasting friendship. In spite of his wealth, his native timidity had always made him distrustful of himself with women of his own class; a veritable Tony Hardcastle, he spent a great deal of time with women whom he did not actually admire, whom indeed he disliked, because, he said to Angela wistfully, they were the only ones who took him seriously.

"No one but you and Carlotta have ever given me any consideration, have ever liked me for myself, Angèle."

They were seeing a great deal of each other; in a quiet, unemotional way they were developing a real friendship. Angela had taken up her painting again. She had re-entered the classes at Cooper Union and was working with great zest and absorption on a subject which she meant to enter in the competition for scholarships at the school at Fontainebleau. Ashley, who wrote some good verse in the recondite, falsely free style of the present day, fell into the habit of bringing his work down to her little living room, and in the long tender autumn evenings the two worked seriously, with concentration. Ashley had travelled widely and had seen a great deal of life, though usually from the sidelines; Angela for all her lack of wandering, "had lived deeply", he used to tell her, pondering on some bit of philosophy which she let fall based on the experiences of her difficult life.

"You know, in your way you're quite a wonder, Angèle; there's a mystery hanging about you; for all your good spirits, your sense of humour, you're like the Duse, you seem to move in an aura of suffering, of the pain which comes from too great sensitivity. And yet how can that be so? You're not old enough, you've had too few contacts to know how unspeakable life can be, how damnably she can get you in wrong,——"

An enigmatic smile settled on her face. "I don't know about life, Ralph? How do you think I got the idea for this masterpiece of mine?" She pointed to the painting on which she was then engaged.

"That's true, that's true. I've wondered often about that composition; lots of times I've meant to ask you how you came to evolve it. But keep your mystery to yourself, child; it adds to your charm."

About this she had her own ideas. Mystery might add to the charm of personality but it certainly could not be said to add to the charm of living. Once she thought that stolen waters

were sweetest, but now it was the unwinding road and the
open book that most intrigued.

Ashley, she found, for all his shyness, possessed very definite
ideas and convictions of his own, was absolutely unfettered in
his mode of thought, and quite unmoved by social traditions
and standards. An aristocrat if ever there were one, he believed
none the less in the essential quality of man and deplored the
economic conditions which so often tended to set up superficial and unreal barriers which make as well as separate the
classes.

With some trepidation Angela got him on the subject of colour. He considered prejudice the greatest blot on America's
shield. "We're wrong, all wrong about those people; after all
they did to make America habitable! Some day we're going to
wake up to our shame. I hope it won't be too late."

"But you wouldn't want your sister to marry a nigger!"

"I'm amazed, Angèle, at your using such a word as an exclusive term. I've known some fine coloured people. There're
hardly any of unmixed blood in the United States, so the term
Negro is usually a misnomer. I haven't a sister; if I had I'd
advise her against marriage with an American coloured man
because the social pressure here would probably be too great,
but that would be absolutely the only ground on which I'd object to it. And I can tell you this; I wouldn't care to marry a
woman from the Congo but if I met a coloured woman of my
own nationality, well-bred, beautiful, sympathetic, I wouldn't let
the fact of her mixed blood stand in my way, I can tell you."

A sort of secondary interest in living was creeping into to her
perspective. The high lights, the high peaks had faded from
her sight. She would never, she suspected, know such spontaneity of feeling and attitude again as she had felt toward both
Roger and Anthony. Nor would she again approach the experiences of existence with the same naïve expectation, the same
desire to see how things would turn out. Young as she was she
felt like a battle-scarred veteran who, worn out from his own
strenuous activities, was quite content to sit on the side-lines
gazing at all phases of warfare with an equal eye.

Although she no longer intended to cast in her lot with Virginia, she made no further effort to set up barriers between

herself and coloured people. Let the world take her as it would. If she were in Harlem, in company with Virginia and Sara Penton she went out to dinner, to the noisy, crowded, friendly "Y" dining-room, to "Gert's" tearoom, to the clean, inviting drug-store for rich "sundaes". Often, too, she went shopping with her sister and to the theatre; she had her meet Ashley and Martha. But she was careful in this company to avoid contact with people whose attitude on the race question was unknown, or definitely antagonistic.

Harlem intrigued her; it was a wonderful city; it represented, she felt, the last word in racial pride, integrity and even self-sacrifice. Here were people of a very high intellectual type, exponents of the realest and most essential refinement living cheek by jowl with coarse or ill-bred or even criminal, certainly indifferent, members of their race. Of course some of this propinquity was due to outer pressure, but there was present, too, a hidden consciousness of race-duty, a something which if translated said: "Perhaps you do pull me down a little from the height to which I have climbed. But on the other hand, perhaps, I'm helping you to rise."

There was a hair-dresser's establishment on 136th Street where Virginia used to have her beautiful hair treated; where Sara Penton, whose locks were of the same variety as Matthew's, used to repair to have their unruliness "pressed". Here on Saturdays Angela would accompany the girls and sit through the long process just to overhear the conversations, grave and gallant and gay, of these people whose blood she shared but whose disabilities by a lucky fluke she had been able to avoid. For, while she had been willing for the sake of Anthony to re-enlist in the struggles of this life, she had never closed her eyes to its disadvantages; to its limitedness! What a wealth of courage it took for these people to live! What high degree of humour, determination, steadfastness, undauntedness were not needed,—and poured forth! Maude, the proprietress of the business, for whom the establishment was laconically called "Maude's", was a slight, sweet-faced woman with a velvety seal-brown skin, a charming voice and an air of real refinement. She was from Texas, but had come to New York to seek her fortune, had travelled as ladies' maid in London and Paris, and was as thoroughly conversant with the arts of her calling as any hairdresser in the vicinity of the Rue de la Paix or on Fifth Avenue. A rare quality of hospitality emanated from her presence; her little shop was always full not only of patrons but of callers, visitors from "down home", actresses from the current coloured "show", flitting in like radiant birds of paradise with their rich brown skins, their exotic eyes and the gaily coloured clothing which an unconscious style had evolved just for them.

In this atmosphere, while there was no coarseness, there was no restriction; life in busy Harlem stopped here and yawned for a delicious moment before going on with its pressure and problems. A girl from Texas, visiting "the big town" for a few weeks took one last glance at her shapely, marvellously "treated" head, poised for a second before the glass and said simply, "Well, good-bye, Maude; I'm off for the backwoods, but I'll never forget Harlem." She passed out with the sinuous elegant carriage acquired in her few weeks' sojourn on Seventh Avenue.

A dark girl, immaculate in white from head to foot, asked: "What's she going back South for? Ain't she had enough of Texas *yet?*"

Maude replied that she had gone back there because of her property. "Her daddy owns most of the little town where they live."

"Child, ain't you learned that you don't *never* own no property in Texas as long as those white folks are down there too? Just let those Ku Kluxers get it into their heads that you've got something they want. She might just as well leave there first as last; she's bound to have to some day. I know it's more'n a notion to pull up stakes and start all over again in a strange town and a strange climate, but it's the difference between life and death. I know I done it and I don't expect ever to go back."

She was a frail woman, daintily dressed and shod. Her voice was soft and drawling. But Angela saw her sharply as the epitome of the iron and blood in a race which did not know how to let go of life.

MARKET IS DONE

Chapter I

THE eternal routine of life went on,—meals, slumber, talk, work—and all of it meaning nothing; a void starting nowhere and leading nowhither; a "getting through" with the days. Gradually however two points fixed themselves in her horizon, and about these her life revolved. One was her work, —her art. Every week found her spending three or four of its nights at her easel. She was feverishly anxious to win one of the prizes in the contest which would be held in May; if successful she would send in her application for registration in the Fountainebleau School of Fine Arts which was financed by Americans and established, so read the circular, "as a summer school for American architects, painters and sculptors". If she were successful in winning this, she would leave the United States for a year or two, thus assuring herself beyond question of a new deal of the cards. The tenacity with which she held to this plan frightened her a little until she found out that there were also possible funds from which she could, with the proper recommendation, borrow enough money to enable her to go abroad with the understanding that the refund was to be made by slow and easy payments. Ashley discovered this saving information, thus relieving her of the almost paralyzing fear which beset her from time to time. It both amused and saddened her to realize that her talent which she had once used as a blind to shield her real motives for breaking loose and coming to New York had now become the greatest, most real force in her life.

Miss Powell, with whom Angela in her new mood had arranged a successful truce, knew of her ambition, indeed shared it. If she herself should win a prize, that money, combined with some small savings of her own and used in connection with the special terms offered by the American Committee, would mean the fruition of her dearest dreams. All this she confided

to Angela on two Sunday mornings which the latter spent with
her in her rather compressed quarters up in 134th Street. A
dwelling house nearby had been converted into a place of worship for one of the special divisions of religious creed so dear
to coloured people's heart. Most of the service seemed to consist of singing, and so the several hours spent by the two girls
in earnest talk were punctuated by the outbursts of song issuing from the brazen-coated throats of the faithful.

The other point about which her thoughts centred was her
anomalous position. Yet that clear mind of hers warned her
again and again that there was nothing inherently wrong or mean
or shameful in the stand which she had taken. The method
thereof might come in perhaps for a little censure. But otherwise her harshest critics, if unbiased, could only say that instead
of sharing the burdens of her own group she had elected to
stray along a path where she personally could find the greatest
ease, comfort and expansion. She had long since given up the
search for happiness. But there were moments when a chance
discussion about coloured people couched in the peculiarly
brutal terms which white America affects in the discussion of
this problem made her blood boil, and she longed to confound
her *vis-à-vis* and his tacit assumption that she, being presumably a white woman, would hold the same views as he, with the
remark: "I'm one of them,—do you find me worthless or dishonest or offensive in any way?" Such a *dénouement* would have,
she felt, been a fine gesture. But life she knew had a way of allowing grand gestures to go unremarked and unrewarded.
Would it be worth while to throw away the benefits of casual
whiteness in America when no great issue was at stake? Would
it indeed be worth while to forfeit them when a great issue was
involved? Remembering the material age in which she lived
and the material nation of which she was a member, she was
doubtful. Her mother's old dictum recurred: "Life is more important than colour."

The years slipped by. Virginia seemed in no haste to marry.
Anthony whom Angela saw occasionally at the Art School
shared apparently in this cool deliberateness. Yet there was
nothing in his action or manner to make her feel that he was
anticipating a change. Rather, if she judged him correctly he,

like herself, tired of the snarl into which the three of them had
been drawn, had settled down to a resigned acceptance of fate.
If conceivable, he was quieter, more reserved than ever, yet ra-
diating a strange restfulness and the peace which comes from
surrender.

In May the prizes for the contest were announced. Angela
received the John T. Stewart Prize for her "Fourteenth Street
Types"; her extreme satisfaction was doubled by the knowledge that the Nehemiah Sloan Prize, of equal value, had been
awarded Miss Powell for her picture entitled "A Street in Harlem". The coloured girl was still difficult and reserved, but under
Angela's persistent efforts at friendship her frank and sympathetic interest and comprehension of her class-mate's difficulties, the latter had finally begun to thaw a little. They were not
planning to live together in France, their tastes were not sufficiently common for that closeness, but both were looking
forward to a year of pleasure, of inspiring work, to a life that
would be "different". Angela was relieved, but Miss Powell was
triumphant; not unpleasantly, she gave the impression of having
justified not only her calling but herself and, in a lesser degree,
her race. The self-consciousness of colour, racial responsibility,
lay, Angela had discovered, deep upon her.

The passage money to France was paid. Through the terms
offered by the committee of the School for Americans at
Fontainebleau, an appreciable saving had been effected. The girls
were to sail in June. As the time drew nearer Angela felt herself
becoming more and more enthusiastic. She had at first looked
upon her sojourn abroad as a heaven-sent break in the montony
and difficulties of her own personal problems, but lately, with
the involuntary reaction of youth, she was beginning to recover
her sense of embarking on a great adventure. Her spirits mounted
steadily.

One evening she went around to Martha Burden's to discuss
the trip; she wanted information about money, clothes, possible
tips.

"Everything you can think of, Martha," she said with something of her former vital manner. "This is an old story to you,
—you've been abroad so many times you ought to write an
encyclopædia on "What to take to Europe". I mean to follow

your advice blindly and the next time I see Miss Powell I'll pass it along to her."

"No need to," said Martha laconically and sombrely. "She isn't going."

"Not going! Why she was going two weeks ago."

"Yes, but she's not going this week nor any other week I'm afraid; at least not through the good offices of the American Committee for the Fontainebleau School of Fine Arts. They've returned her passage money. Didn't you know it? I thought everybody had heard of it."

Angela fought against a momentary nausea. "No, I didn't know it. I haven't seen her for ages. I'm so busy getting myself together. Martha, what's it all about? Is it because she's coloured? You don't mean it's because she's coloured?"

"Well, it is. They said they themselves were without prejudice, but that they were sure the enforced contact on the boat would be unpleasant to many of the students, garnered as they would be from all parts of the United States. Furthermore they couldn't help but think that such contact would be embarrassing to Miss Powell too. Oh, there's no end to the ridiculous piffle which they've written and said. I've had a little committee of students and instructors going about, trying to stir up public sentiment. Mr. Cross has been helping and Paget too. I wish Paulette were here; she'd get some yellow journal publicity. Van Meier has come out with some biting editorials; he's shown up a lot of their silly old letters. I shouldn't be surprised but what if we kept at it long enough we'd get somewhere."

She reflected a moment. "Funny thing is we're having such a hard time in making Miss Powell show any fight. I don't understand that girl."

Angela murmured that perhaps she had no hope of making an impression on prejudice. "It's so unreasonable and far-reaching. Maybe she doesn't want to sacrifice her peace of mind for what she considers a futile struggle."

"That's what Mr. Cross said. He's been wonderful to her and an indefatigable worker. Of course you'll be leaving soon since none of this touches you, but come into a committee meeting or two, won't you? We're meeting here. I'll give you a ring."

"Well," said Angela to herself that night after she had regained her room. "I wonder what I ought to do now?" Even yet she was receiving an occasional reporter; the pleasant little stir of publicity attendant on her prize had not yet died away. Suppose she sent for one of them and announced her unwillingness to accept the terms of the American Committee inasmuch as they had withdrawn their aid from Miss Powell. Suppose she should finish calmly: "I, too, am a Negro". What would happen? The withdrawal of the assistance without which her trip abroad, its hoped for healing, its broadening horizons would be impossible. Evidently, there was no end to the problems into which this matter of colour could involve one, some of them merely superficial, as in this instance, some of them gravely physical. Her head ached with the futility of trying to find a solution to these interminable puzzles.

As a child she and Jinny had been forbidden to read the five and ten cent literature of their day. But somehow a copy of a mystery story entitled "Who killed Dr. Cronlin?" found its way into their hands, a gruesome story all full of bearded men, hands preserved in alcohol, shadows on window curtains. Shivering with fascination, they had devoured it after midnight or early in the morning while their trusting parents still slumbered. Every page they hoped would disclose the mystery. But their patience went unrewarded for the last sentence of the last page still read: "Who killed Dr. Cronlin?"

Angela thought of it now, and smiled and sighed. "Just what is or is not ethical in this matter of colour?" she asked herself. And indeed it was a nice question. Study at Fontainebleau would have undoubtedly changed Miss Powell's attitude toward life forever. If she had received the just reward for her painstaking study, she would have reasoned that right does triumph in essentials. Moreover the inspiration might have brought out latent talent, new possibilities. Furthermore, granted that Miss Powell had lost out by a stroke of ill-fortune, did that necessarily call for Angela's loss? If so, to what end?

Unable to answer she fell asleep.

Absorbed in preparations she allowed two weeks to pass by, then, remembering Martha's invitation, she went again to the Starr household on an evening when the self-appointed committee was expected to meet. She found Anthony, Mr. Paget,

Ladislas and Martha present. The last was more perturbed than ever. Indeed an air of sombre discouragement lay over the whole company.

"Well," asked the newcomer, determined to appear at ease in spite of Anthony's propinquity, "how are things progressing?"

"Not at all," replied Mr. Paget. "Indeed we're about to give up the whole fight."

Ladislas with a sort of provoked amusement explained then that Miss Powell herself had thrown up the sponge. "She's not only withdrawn but she sends us word to-night that while she appreciates the fight we're making she'd rather we'd leave her name out of it."

"Did you ever hear anything to equal that?" snapped Martha crossly. I wonder if coloured people aren't natural born quitters. Sometimes I think I'll never raise another finger for them."

"You don't know what you're talking about," said Anthony hotly. "If you knew the ceaseless warfare which most coloured people wage, you'd understand that sometimes they have to stop their fight for the trimmings of life in order to hang on to the essentials which they've got to have and for which they must contend too every day just as hard as they did the first day. No, they're not quitters, they've merely learned to let go so they can conserve their strength for another bad day. I'm coloured and I know."

There was a moment's tense silence while the three white people stared speechless with surprise. Then Martha said in a still shocked voice: "Coloured! Why, I can't believe it. Why, you never told us you were coloured."

"Which is precisely why I'm telling you now," said Anthony, coldly rude. "So you won't be making off-hand judgments about us." He started toward the door. "Since the object for which this meeting has been called has become null and void I take it that we are automatically dismissed. Goodnight."

Martha hastened after him. "Oh, Mr. Cross, don't go like that. As though it made any difference! Why should this affect our very real regard for each other?"

"Why should it indeed?" he asked a trifle enigmatically. "I'm sure I hope it won't. But I must go." He left the room, Paget and Ladislas both hastening on his heels.

Martha stared helplessly after him. "I suppose I haven't said the right thing. But what could I do? I was so surprised!" She turned to Angela: "And I really can't get over his being coloured, can you?"

"No," said Angela solemnly, "I can't . . ." and surprised herself and Martha by bursting into a flood of tears.

For some reason the incident steadied her determination. Perhaps Anthony was the vicarious sacrifice, she told herself and knew even as she said it that the supposition was pure bunk. Anthony did not consider that he was making a sacrifice; his confession or rather his statement with regard to his blood had the significance of the action of a person who clears his room of rubbish. Anthony did not want his mental chamber strewn with the chaff of deception and confusion. He did not label himself, but on the other hand he indulged every now and then in a general house-cleaning because he would not have the actions of his life bemused and befuddled.

As for Angela she asked for nothing better than to put all the problems of colour and their attendant difficulties behind her. She could not meet those problems in their present form in Europe; literally in every sense she would begin life all over. In France or Italy she would speak of her strain of Negro blood and abide by whatever consequences such exposition would entail. But the consequences could not engender the pain and difficulties attendant upon them here.

Somewhat diffidently she began to consider the idea of going to see Miss Powell. The horns of her dilemma resolved themselves into an unwillingness to parade her own good fortune before her disappointed classmate and an equal unwillingness to depart for France, leaving behind only the cold sympathy of words on paper. And, too, something stronger, more insistent than the mere consideration of courtesy urged her on. After all, this girl was one of her own. A whim of fate had set their paths far apart but just the same they were more than "sisters under the skin." They were really closely connected in blood, in racial condition, in common suffering. Once again she thought of herself as she had years ago when she had seen the coloured girl refused service in the restaurant: "It might so easily have been Virginia."

Without announcement then she betook herself up town to

Harlem and found herself asking at the door of the girl's apartment if she might see Miss Powell. The mother whom Angela
had last seen so proud and happy received her with a note of
sullen bafflement which to the white girl's consciousness
connoted: "Easy enough for you, all safe and sound, high and
dry, to come and sympathize with my poor child." There was
no trace of gratitude or of appreciation of the spirit which had
inspired Angela to pay the visit.

To her inquiry Mrs. Powell rejoined: "Yes, I guess you c'n
see her. There're three or four other people in there now pes-
terin' her to death. I guess one mo' won't make no diffunce."

Down a long narrow hall she led her, past two rooms whose
dark interiors seemed Stygian in contrast with the bright sunlight which the visitor had just left. But the end of the hall
opened into a rather large, light, plain but comfortable dining-
room where Miss Powell sat entertaining, to Angela's astonishment, three or four people, all of them white. Her astonishment,
however, lessened when she perceived among them John
Banky, one of the reporters who had come rather often to
interview herself and her plans for France. All of them, she
judged angrily, were of his profession, hoping to wring their
half column out of Miss Powell's disappointment and embarrassment.

Angela thought she had never seen the girl one half so attractive and exotic. She was wearing a thin silk dress, plainly made
but of a flaming red from which the satin blackness of her neck
rose, a straight column topped by her squarish, somewhat
massive head. Her thin, rather flat dark lips brought into sharp
contrast the dazzling perfection of her teeth; her high cheek
bones showed a touch of red. To anyone whose ideals of beauty
were not already set and sharply limited, she must have made a
breathtaking appeal. As long as she sat quiescent in her rather
sulky reticence she made a marvellous figure of repose; focus-
sing all the attention of the little assemblage even as her dark
skin and hair drew into themselves and retained the brightness
which the sun, streaming through three windows, showered
upon her.

As soon as she spoke she lost, however, a little of this perfection. For though a quiet dignity persisted, there were pain and
bewilderment in her voice and the flat sombreness of utter

despair. Clearly she did not know how to get rid of the intrud-
ers, but she managed to maintain a poise and aloofness which
kept them at their distance. Surely, Angela thought, listening
to the stupid, almost impertinent questions put, these things
can mean nothing to them. But they kept on with their baiting
rather as a small boy keeps on tormenting a lonely and dispirited animal at the Zoo.

"We were having something of an academic discussion with
Miss Powell here," said Banky, turning to Angela. "This," he
informed his co-workers, "is Miss Mory, one of the prizewin-
ners of the Art Exhibit and a classmate of Miss Powell. I believe
Miss Powell was to cross with you,—as—er—your room-mate
did you say?"

"No," said Angela, flushing a little for Miss Powell, for she
thought she understood the double meaning of the question,
"we weren't intending to be room-mates. Though so far as I
am concerned," she heard herself, to her great surprise, saying:
"I'd have been very glad to share Miss Powell's state-room if
she had been willing." She wanted to get away from this aspect.
"What's this about an academic discussion?"

Miss Powell's husky, rather mutinous voice interrupted: "There
isn't any discussion, Miss Mory, academic or otherwise. It seems
Mr. Paget told these gentlemen and Miss Tilden here, that I
had withdrawn definitely from the fight to induce the Committee for the American Art School abroad to allow me to take
advantage of their arrangements. So they came up here to get
me to make a statement and I said I had none to make other
than that I was sick and tired of the whole business and I'd be
glad to let it drop."

"And I," said Miss Tilden, a rangy young lady wearing an
unbecoming grey dress and a peculiarly straight and hideous
bob, "asked her if she weren't really giving up the matter
because in her heart she knew she hadn't a leg to stand on."

Angela felt herself growing hot. Something within her urged
caution, but she answered defiantly: "What do you mean she
hasn't a leg to stand on?"

"Well, of course, this is awfully plain speaking and I hope
Miss Powell won't be offended," resumed Miss Tilden, showing only too plainly that she didn't care whether Miss Powell
were offended or not, "but after all we do know that a great

many people find the—er—Negroes objectionable and so of course no self-respecting one of them would go where she wasn't wanted."

Miss Powell's mother hovering indefinitely in the background, addressing no one in particular, opined that she did not know that "that there committee owned the boat. If her daughter could only afford it she'd show them how quickly she'd go where she wanted and not ask no one no favours either."

"Ah, but," said Miss Tilden judicially, "there's the fallacy. Something else is involved here. There's a social side to this matter, inherent if not expressed. And that *is* the question." She shook a thin bloodless finger at Miss Powell. "Back of most of the efforts which you people make to get into schools and clubs and restaurants and so on, isn't there really this desire for social equality? Come now, Miss Powell, be frank and tell me."

With such sharpness as to draw the attention of everyone in the room Angela said: "Come, Miss Tilden, that's unpardonable and you know it. Miss Powell hadn't a thought in mind about social equality. All she wanted was to get to France and to get there as cheaply as possible."

Banky, talking in a rather affected drawl, confirmed the last speaker. "I think, too, that's a bit too much, Miss Tilden. We've no right to interpret Miss Powell's ideas for her."

A short, red-faced young man intervened: "But just the same *isn't* that the question involved? Doesn't the whole matter resolve itself into this: Has Miss Powell or any other young coloured woman knowing conditions in America the right to thrust her company on a group of people with whom she could have nothing in common except her art? If she stops to think she must realize that not one of the prospective group of students who would be accompanying her on that ship would really welcome her presence. Here's Miss Mory, for instance, a fellow student. What more natural under other circumstances than that she should have made arrangements to travel with Miss Powell? She knows she has to share her cabin with some one. But no; such a thought apparently never entered her head. Why? The answer is obvious. Very well then. If she, knowing Miss Powell, feels this way, how much more would it be the feeling of total strangers?"

A sort of shocked silence fell upon the room. It was an

impossible situation. How, thought Angela desperately, knowing the two sides, could she ever explain to these smug, complacent people Miss Powell's ambition, her chilly pride, the remoteness with which she had treated her fellow-students, her only too obvious endeavour to share their training and not their friendship? Hastily, almost crudely, she tried to get something of this over, ashamed for herself, ashamed for Miss Powell whose anguished gaze begged for her silence.

At last the coloured girl spoke. "It's wonderful of you to take my part in this way, Miss Mory. I had no idea you understood so perfectly. But don't you see there's no use in trying to explain it? It's a thing which one either does see or doesn't see." She left her soft, full, dark gaze rest for a second on her auditors. "I'm afraid it is not in the power of these persons to grasp what you mean."

The stocky young man grew a little redder. "I think we do understand, Miss Powell. All that Miss Mory says simply confirms my first idea. For otherwise, understanding and sympathizing with you as she does, why has she, for instance, never made any very noticeable attempt to become your friend? Why shouldn't she have asked you to be her side-partner on this trip which I understand you're taking together? There would have been an unanswerable refutation for the committee's arguments. But no, she does nothing even though it means the thwarting for you of a life-time's ambition. Mind, I'm not blaming you, Miss Mory. You are acting in accordance with a natural law. I'm just trying to show Miss Powell here how inevitable the workings of such a law are."

It was foolish reasoning and fallacious, yet containing enough truth to make it sting. Some icy crust which had formed over Angela's heart shifted, wavered, broke and melted. Suddenly it seemed as though nothing in the world were so important as to allay the poignancy of Miss Powell's situation; for this, she determined quixotically, no price would be too dear. She said icily in tones which she had never heard herself use before: "It's true I've never taken any stand hitherto for Miss Powell for I never thought she needed it. But now that the question has come up I want to say that I'd be perfectly willing to share my stateroom with her and to give her as much of my company as she could stand. However, that's all out of the question now because Miss Powell isn't going to France on the American Committee Fund and I'm not going either." She stopped a second and added quietly: "And for the same reason."

Someone said in bewilderment: "What do you mean when you say you're not going? And for the same reason?"

"I mean that if Miss Powell isn't wanted, I'm not wanted either. You imply that she's not wanted because she's coloured. Well, I'm coloured too."

One of the men said under his breath, "God, what a scoop!" and reached for his hat. But Banky, his face set and white, held him back.

"I don't believe you know what you're saying, Miss Mory. But anyway, whether it's true or untrue, for God's sake take it back!"

His tone of horror added the last touch. Angela laughed in his face. "Take it back!" She could hardly contain herself. "Do you really think that being coloured is as awful as all that? Can't you see that to my way of thinking it's a great deal better to be coloured and to miss—oh—scholarships and honours and pre-ferments, than to be the contemptible things which you've all shown yourselves to be this morning? Coming here baiting this poor girl and her mother, thrusting your self-assurance down their throats, branding yourselves literally dogs in the manger?" She turned to the coloured girl's mother. "Mrs. Powell, you surely don't want these people here any longer. Have I your permission to show them out?" Crossing the room superbly she opened the door. "This way, please, and don't come back any more. You can rest assured we'll find a way to keep you out."

Silently the little line filed out. Only Miss Tilden, laying her hand on Angela's arm paused to say avidly: "You'll let me come to see you, surely? I can give you some fine publicity, only I must have more data. How about an exclusive interview?"

Angela said stonily: "Mrs. Powell will show you the front door." Then she and her former class-mate stood regarding each other. The dark girl crossed the room and caught her hands and kissed them. "Oh," she said, "it was magnificent—I never guessed it,—but you shouldn't have done it. It's all so unjust, so—silly—and so tiresome. You, of course, only get it when you bring it upon yourself. But I'm black and I've had it all my

life. You don't know the prizes within my grasp that have been
snatched away from me again because of colour." She turned
as her mother entered the room. "Mother, wasn't she magnificent?"

"She was a fool," Mrs. Powell replied shortly.

Her words brought the exalted Angela back to earth. "Yes,"
she said, smiling whimsically, "I am just that, a fool. I don't
know what possessed me. I'm poor, I was in distress; I wanted
a new deal. Now I don't know which way to turn for it. That
story will be all over New York by to-morrow morning." She
burst out laughing. "Think of my choosing four reporters
before whom to make my great confession!" Her hand sought
Miss Powell's. "Good-bye, both of you. Don't worry about
me. I never dreamed that anything like this could happen, but
the mere fact that is has shows that the truth was likely to come
out any day. So don't blame yourselves for it. Goodbye."

Banky was waiting for her in the vestibule downstairs. "I'm so
sorry about the whole damned business, Miss Mory," he said
decently. "It's a damned shame. If there's anything I can
do——"

Rather shortly she said there was nothing. "And you don't
need to worry. As I told you upstairs, being coloured isn't as
awful as all that. I'll get along." Ignoring his hand she passed
by him into the street. It was Saturday afternoon so there was
a chance of her finding Jinny at home.

"And if she isn't there I can wait," she told herself; and
thanked God in her heart for the stability implied in sister-
hood.

Jinny was home, mulling happily over the small affairs which
kept her a little girl. Her sister, looking at the serene loveliness
of her face, said irrelevantly: "You make me feel like an old
woman."

"Well," replied Jinny, "you certainly have the art of concealing time's ravages, for you not only look young but you have
the manner of someone who's just found a million dollars.
Come in and tell me about it."

"Found a million dollars! H'm, lost it I should say!" But a
sudden wave of relief and contentment broke over her. "Oh,
Jinny, tell me, have I been an utter fool! I've thrown away

every chance I've ever had in the world,—just for a whim." Suddenly close in the full tide of sisterliness, they sat facing each other on the comfortable couch while Angela told her story. "I hadn't the faintest idea in the world of telling it. I was thinking only the other day how lucky I was compared to Miss Powell, and the first thing I knew there it all came tripping off my tongue. But I had to do it. If you could just have seen those pigs of reporters and Miss Powell's face under their relentless probing. And old Mrs. Powell, helpless and grunting and sweating and thinking me a fool; she told me so, you know. . . . Why, Jinny, darling, you're not ever crying! Darling, there's nothing to cry about; what's the matter, Honey!"

"It's because you *are* a fool that I am crying," said Jinny sobbing and sniffling, her fingers in her eyes. "You're a fool and the darlingest girl that ever lived, and my own precious, lovely, wonderful sister back again. Oh, Angela, I'm so happy. Tell them to send you your passage money back; say you don't want anything from them that they don't want to give; let them go, let them all go except the ones who like you for yourself. And dearest, if you don't mind having to skimp a bit for a year or two and not spreading yourself as you planned, we'll get you off to Europe after all. You know I've got all my money from the house. I've never touched it. You can have as much of that as you want and pay me back later or not at all."

Laughing and crying, Angela told her that she couldn't think of it. "Keep your money for your marriage, Jinny. It'll be some time before—Anthony will make any real money, I imagine. But I will take your advice and go to Europe after all. All this stuff will be in the paper to-morrow, I suppose, so I'll write the American Committee people to-night. As for the prize money, if they want that back they can have it. But I don't think they will; nothing was said about Miss Powell's. That's a thousand dollars. I'll take that and go to Paris and live as long as I can. If I can't have the thousand I'll use the few hundreds that I have left and go anyway. And when I come back I'll go back to my old job or—go into the schools. But all that's a long way off and we don't know what might turn up."

There were one or two matters for immediate consideration. The encounter with the reporters had left Angela a little more shaken than was at first apparent. "I don't want to run into them again," she said ruefully. Her lease on the little apartment in Jayne Street had still a month to run. She would go down this very evening, get together her things, and return to Jinny, with whom she would live quietly until it was time for her to sail. Her mail she could leave with the janitor to be called for. Fortunately the furniture was not hers; there were only a few pictures to be removed. After all, she had very few friends to consider,—just the Sandburgs, Martha Burden, Mrs. Denver, Ralph Ashley and Rachel Salting.

"And I don't know what to do about them," she said, pondering. "After all, you can't write to people and say: 'Dear friend:—You've always thought I was white. But I'm not really. I'm coloured and I'm going back to my own folks to live.' Now can you? Oh, Jinny, Jinny, isn't it a great old world?"

In the end, after the story appeared, as it assuredly did, in the next morning's paper, she cut out and sent to each of her former friends copies of Miss Tilden's story whose headlines read: "Socially Ambitious Negress Confesses to Long Hoax."

With the exception of Banky's all the accounts took the unkindest attitude possible. The young Hungarian played up the element of self-sacrifice and the theory that blood after all was thicker than water. Angela guessed rightly that if he could have he would have preferred omitting it, and that he had only written it up to offset as far as possible the other accounts. Of the three other meanly insinuating stories Miss Tilden's was the silliest and most dangerous. She spoke of mixed blood as the curse of the country, a curse whose "insidiously concealed influence constantly threatens the wells of national race purity. Such incidents as these make one halt before he condemns the efforts of the Ku Klux Klan and its unceasing fight for 100 per cent. Americanism."

The immediate effect of this publicity was one which neither of the sisters had foreseen. When Angela reported for work on the following Monday morning she found a note on her desk asking her immediate appearance in the office. The president returning her good-morning with scant courtesy, showed her a clipping and asked if she were the Miss Mory of the story. Upon her assurance that she was none other, he handed her a month's salary in lieu of notice and asked her to consider her connection with the firm at an end.

"We have no place for deceit in an institution such as this," he said augustly.

The incident shook both girls to a degree. Virginia, particularly was rendered breathless by its cruel immediacy. Never before had she come so close to the special variation of prejudice manifested to people in Angela's position. That the president of the concern should attribute the girl's reticence on this subject to deceit seemed to her the last ounce of injustice. Angela herself was far less perturbed.

"I've seen too much of this sort of thing to feel it as you do, Virginia. Of course, as you see, there are all kinds of absurdities involved. In your case, showing colour as you do, you'd have been refused the job at the very outset. Perhaps they would have said that they had found coloured people incompetent or that other girls had a strong natural aversion toward working beside one of us. Now here I land the position, hold it long enough to prove ability and the girls work beside me and remain untainted. So evidently there's no blind inherent disgust to be overcome. Looking just the same as I've ever looked I let the fact of my Negro ancestry be known. Mind, I haven't changed the least bit, but immediately there's all this holding up of hands and the cry of deceit is raised. Some logic, that! It really would be awfully funny, you see, Jinny, if it couldn't be fraught with such disastrous consequences for people like, say, Miss Powell."

"Don't mention her," said Jinny vehemently. "If it hadn't been for her you wouldn't have been in all this trouble."

Angela smiled. "If it hadn't been for her, you and I probably never would have really found each other again. But you mustn't blame her. Sooner or later I'd have been admitting,— 'confessing', as the papers say,—my black blood. Not that I myself think it of such tremendous importance; in spite of my efforts to break away I really don't, Virginia. But because this country of ours makes it so important, against my own conviction I was beginning to feel as though I were laden down with a great secret. Yet when I begin to delve into it, the matter of blood seems nothing compared with individuality, character,

living. The truth of the matter is, the whole business was just
making me fagged to death."

She sat lost intently in thought. "All of the complications of
these last few years,—and you can't guess what complications
there have been, darling child,—have been based on this business of 'passing'. I understand why Miss Powell gave up the
uneven fight about her passage. Of course, in a way it would
have been a fine thing if she could have held on, but she was
perfectly justified in letting go so she could avoid still greater
bitterness and disappointment and so she could have something left in her to devote to her art. You can't fight and create
at the same time. And I understand, too, why your Anthony
bestirs himself every little while and makes *his* confession; simply so he won't have to be bothered with the trappings of pretence and watchfulness. I suppose he told you about that night
down at Martha Burden's?"

"Yes," said Jinny, sighing, "he has terrible ideals. There's something awfully lofty about Anthony. I wish he were more like
Matthew, comfortable and homey. Matt's got some ideals, too,
but he doesn't work them overtime. Anthony's a darling, two
darlings, but he's awfully, awfully what-do-you-call-it, ascetic. I
shouldn't be at all surprised but what he had a secret canker
eating at his heart."

Angela said rather sternly, "Look here, Jinny, I don't believe
you love him after all, do you?"

"Well now, when I get right down to it sometimes I think I
do. Sometimes I think I don't. Of course the truth of the matter is, I'd hardly have thought about Anthony or marriage
either just now, if I hadn't been so darn lonely. You know I'm
not like you, Angela. When we were children I was the one
who was going to have a career, and you were always going to
have a good time. Actually it's the other way round; you're the
one who's bound to have a career. You just gravitate to adventure. There's something so forceful and so strong about you
that you can't keep out of the battle. But, Angela, I want a
home,—with you if you could just stand still long enough, or
failing that, a home with husband and children and all that
goes with it. Of course I don't mind admitting that at any time
I'd have given up even you for Matthew. But next to being his
wife I'd rather live with you, and next to that I'd like to marry

Anthony. I don't like to be alone; for though I can fend for myself I don't want to."

Angela felt herself paling with the necessity of hiding her emotion. "So poor Anthony's only third in your life?"

"Yes, I'm afraid he is . . . Darling, what do you say to scallops for dinner? I feel like cooking to-day. Guess I'll hie me to market."

She left the room, and her sister turned to the large photograph of Cross which Virginia kept on the mantel. She put her fingers on the slight youthful hollows of his pictured cheeks, touched his pictured brow. "Oh Anthony, Anthony, is Life cheating you again? You'll always be first in my life, dearest."

Perhaps Virginia's diagnosis of her character was correct. At any rate she welcomed the present combination of difficulties through which she was now passing. Otherwise this last confession of Jinny's would have plunged her into fresh unhappiness. But she had many adjustments to make and to face. First of all there was her new status in the tiny circle in which she had moved. When at the end of two weeks she went down to her old apartment in Jayne Street to ask for her mail, she was, in spite of herself amazed and hurt to discover a chilled bewilderment, an aloofness, in the manner of Mrs. Denver, with whom she had a brief encounter. On the other hand there were a note and a calling card from Martha Burden, and some half dozen letters from Elizabeth and Walter Sandburg.

Martha's note ran: "Undoubtedly you and Mr. Cross are very fine people. But I don't believe I could stand another such shock very soon. Of course it was magnificent of you to act as you did. But oh, my dear, how quixotic. And after all *à quoi bon?* Will you come to see me as soon you get this, or send me word how I may see you? And Angèle, if you let all this nonsense interfere with your going to Europe I'll never forgive you. Ladislas and I have several thousand dollars stored away just begging to be put out at interest."

Elizabeth Sandburg said nothing about the matter, but Angela was able to read her knowledge between the lines. The kind-hearted couple could not sufficiently urge upon her their unchanging regard and friendship. "Why on earth don't you come and see us?" Elizabeth queried in her immense, wandering chirography, five words to a page. "You can't imagine how we miss you. Walter's actually getting off his feed. Do take a moment from whatever masterpiece you're composing and give us a week-end."

But from Rachel Salting and from Ashley not one single word!

Chapter II

MORE than ever her determination to sail became fixed. "Some people," she said to Jinny, "might think it the thing to stay here and fight things out. Martha, for instance, is keenly disappointed because I won't let the committee which had been working for Miss Powell take up my case. I suspect she thinks we're all quitters. But I know when I've had enough. I told her I wanted to spend my life doing something besides fighting. Moreover, the Committee, like myself, is pretty sick of the whole affair, though not for the same reason, and I think there'd be even less chance for a readjustment in my case than there was in Miss Powell's."

An interview with Clarke Otter, Chairman of the Advisory Board of the American Committee, had given her this impression. Mr. Otter's attitude betokened a curious admixture of resentment at what he seemed to consider her deceit in "passing" and exasperation at her having been quixotic enough to give the show away. "We think you are quite right in expressing your determination not to take advantage of the Committee's arrangements. It evidences a delicacy of feeling quite unusual in the circumstances." Angela was boiling with anger when she left.

A letter to the donor of the prize brought back the laconic answer that the writer was interested "not in Ethnology but in Art."

"I'd like to see that party," said Angela, reverting to the jargon of her youth. "I'll bet he's nowhere near as stodgy as he sounds. I shouldn't wonder but what he was just bubbling over with mirth at the silliness of it all."

Certainly she herself was bubbling over with mirth or with what served for that quality. Virginia could not remember ever having seen her in such high spirits, not since the days when they used to serve Monday's dinner for their mother and play at the *rôles* in which Mrs. Henrietta Jones had figured so largely. But Angela herself knew the shallowness of that mirth whose reality, Anthony, unable to remain for any length of time in her presence and yet somehow unable to stay away, sometimes suspected.

Her savings, alas! including the prize money, amounted roughly to 1,400 dollars. Anthony had urged her to make the passage second class on one of the large, comfortable boats. Then, if she proved herself a good sailor, she might come back third class.

"And anyway don't put by any more than enough for that," said Jinny maternally, "and if you need any extra money write to me and I'll send you all you want."

From stories told by former foreign students who had sometimes visited the Union it seemed as though she might stretch her remaining hundreds over a period of eight or nine months. "And by that time I'll have learned enough to know whether I'm to be an honest-to-God artist or a plain drawing teacher."

"I almost hope it will be the latter," said Jinny with a touching selfishness, "so you'll have to come back and live with us. Don't you hope so, Anthony?"

Angela could see him wince under the strain of her sister's artlessness. "Eight or nine months abroad ought to make a great difference in her life," he said with no particular relevance. "Indeed in the lives of all of us." Both he and Angela had only one thought these days, that the time for departure would have to arrive. Neither of them had envisaged the awfulness of this pull on their self-control.

Now there were only five days before her departure on Monday. She divided them among the Sandburgs, Anthony and Jinny who was coming down with a summer cold. On Saturday the thought came to her that she would like to see Philadelphia again; it was a thought so persistent that by nine o'clock she was in the train and by 11.15 she was preparing for bed in a small side-room in the Hotel Walton in the city of her birth. Smiling, she fell asleep vaguely soothed by the thought of being so close to all that had been once the scene of her steady, unchecked life.

The propinquity was to shake her more than she could dream.

In the morning she breakfasted in her room, then coming downstairs stood in the portico of the hotel drawing on her gloves as she had done so many years before when she had been a girl shopping with her mother. A flood of memories rushed over her, among them the memory of that day when her father and Virginia had passed them on the street and they had not spoken. How trivial the reason for not speaking seemed now! In later years she had cut Jinny for a reason equally trivial.

She walked up toward Sixteenth Street. It was Sunday and the beautiful melancholy of the day was settling on the quiet city. There was a freshness and a solemnity in the air as though even the atmosphere had been rarified and soothed. A sense of loneliness invaded her; this was the city of her birth, of her childhood and of most of her life. Yet there was no one, she felt, to whom she could turn this beautiful day for a welcome; old acquaintances might be mildly pleased, faintly curious at seeing her, but none of them would show any heart-warming gladness. She had left them so abruptly, so completely. Well, she must not think on these things. After all, in New York she had been lonely too.

The Sixteenth Street car set her down at Jefferson Street and slowly she traversed the three long blocks. Always quiet, always respectable, they were doubly so in the sanctity of Sunday morning. What a terrible day Sunday could be without friends, ties, home, family. Only five years ago, less than five years, she had had all the simple, stable fixtures of family life, the appetizing breakfast, the music, the church with its interesting, paintable types, long afternoons and evenings with visitors and discussions beating in the void. And Matthew Henson, would he, she wondered, give her welcome? But she thought that still she did not want to see him. She was not happy, but she was not through adventuring, through tasting life. And she knew that a life spent with Matthew Henson would mean a cessation of that. After all, was he, with his steadiness, his uprightness, his gift for responsibility any happier than she? She doubted it.

Oh, she hoped Sundays in Paris would be gay!

Opal Street came into her vision, a line, a mere shadow of a street falling upon the steadfastness of Jefferson. Her heart quickened, tears came into her eyes as she turned that corner which she had turned so often, that corner which she had once left behind her forever in order to taste and know life. In the hot July sun the street lay almost deserted. A young coloured man, immaculate in white shirt sleeves, slim and straight, bending in his doorway to pick up the bulky Sunday paper, straightened up to watch her advancing toward him. Just this side of

him stood her former home,—how tiny it was and yet how full
of secrets, of knowledge of joy, despair, suffering, futility—in
brief Life! She stood a few moments in front of it, just gazing,
but presently she went up and put her hand on the red brick,
wondering blindly if in some way the insensate thing might
not communicate with her through touch. A coloured woman
sitting in the window watching her rather sharply, came out
then and asked her suspiciously what she wanted.

"Nothing," Angela replied dully. "I just wanted to look at
the house."

"It isn't for sale, you know."

"No, no, of course not. I just wanted to look at it again. I
used to live here, you see. I wondered——" Even if she did get
permission to go inside, could she endure it? If she could just
stand once in that little back room and cry and cry—perhaps
her tears would flood away all that mass of regret and confusion and futile memories, and she could begin life all over with
a blank page. Thank God she was young! Suddenly it seemed
to her that entering the house once more, standing in that room
would be a complete panacea. Raising her eyes expectantly to
the woman's face she began: "Would you be so kind——?"

But the woman, throwing her a last suspicious look and
muttering that she was "nothing but poor white trash," turned
and, slamming the door behind her, entered the little square
parlour and pulled down the blinds.

The slim young man came running down the steet toward her.
Closer inspection revealed his ownership of a pleasant brown
freckled face topped by thick, soft, rather closely cropped dark-
red hair.

"Angela," he said timidly, and then with more assurance: "It
is Angela Murray."

She turned her stricken face toward him. "She wouldn't let
me in, Matthew. I'm going to France to-morrow and I thought
I'd like to see the old house. But she wouldn't let me look at it.
She called me,"—her voice broke with the injustice of it,—
"poor white trash."

"I know," he nodded gravely. "She'd do that kind of thing;
she doesn't understand, you see." He was leading her gently
toward his house. "I think you'd better come inside and rest a

moment. My father and mother have gone off for their annual trip to Bridgeton; mother was born there, you know. But you won't mind coming into the house of an old and tried friend."

"No," she said, conscious of an overwhelming fatigue and general sense of let-downness, "I should say I wouldn't." As they crossed the threshold she tried faintly to smile but the effort was too much for her and she burst into a flood of choking, strangling, noisy tears.

Matthew removed her hat and fanned her; brought her ice-water and a large soft handkerchief to replace her own sodden wisp. Through her tears she smiled at him, understanding as she did so, the reason for Virginia's insistence on his general niceness. He was still Matthew Henson, still freckled and brown, still capped with that thatch of thick bad hair. But care and hair-dressings and improved toilet methods and above all the emanation of a fine and generous spirit had metamorphosed him into someone still the old Matthew Henson and yet someone somehow translated into a quintessence of kindliness and gravity and comprehending.

She drank the water gratefully, took out her powder puff.

"I don't need to ask you how you are," he said, uttering a prayer of thanks for averted hysterics. "When a lady begins to powder her nose, she's bucking up all right. Want to tell me all about it?"

"There's nothing to tell. Only I wanted to see the house and suddenly found myself unexpectedly homesick, lonely, misunderstood. And when that woman refused me so cruelly, it was just too much." Her gaze wavered, her eyes filled again.

"Oh," he said in terror, "for God's sake don't cry again! I'll go over and give her a piece of my mind; I'll make her turn the whole house over to you. I'll bring you her head on a charger. Only 'dry those tears'." He took her handkerchief and dried them himself very, very gently.

She caught his hand. "Matthew, you're a dear."

He shrugged negligently, "You haven't always thought that."

This turn of affairs would never do. "What were you planning to do when I barged in? Getting ready to read your paper and be all homey and comfortable?"

"Yes, but I don't want to do that now. Tell you what, Angela, let's have a lark. Suppose we have dinner here? You get it.

Remember how it used to make me happy as a king in the old days if you'd just hand me a glass of water? You said you were sailing to-morrow; you must be all packed. What time do you have to be back? I'll put you on the train."

The idea enchanted her. "I'd love it! Matthew, what fun!" They found an apron of his mother's, and in the ice-box, cold roast beef, lettuce which Philadelphians call salad, beets and corn. "I'll make muffins," said Angela joyously, "and you take a dish after dinner and go out and get some ice-cream. Oh, Matthew, how it's all coming back to me! Do you still shop up here in the market?"

They ate the meal in the little dark cool dining-room, the counterpart of the dining-room in Junius Murray's one-time house across the way. But somehow its smallness was no longer irksome; rather it seemed a tiny island of protection reared out of and against an encroaching sea of troubles. In fancy she saw her father and mother almost a quarter of a century ago coming proudly to such a home, their little redoubt of refuge against the world. How beautiful such a life could be, shared with some one beloved,—with Anthony! Involuntarily she sighed.

Matthew studying her thoughtfully said: "You're dreaming, Angela. Tell me what it's all about."

"I was thinking what a little haven a house like this could be; what it must have meant to my mother. Funny how I almost pounded down the walls once upon a time trying to get away. Now I can't think of anything more marvellous than having such a place as this, here, there, anywhere, to return to."

Startled, he told her of his surprise at hearing such words from her. "If Virginia had said them I should think it perfectly natural; but I hadn't thought of you as being interested in home. How, by the way, is Virginia?"

"Perfect."

With a wistfulness which barely registered with her absorption, he queried: "I suppose she's tremendously happy?"

"Happy enough."

"A great girl, little Virginia." In his turn he fell to musing, roused himself. "You haven't told me of your adventures and your flight into the great world."

"There's not much to tell, Matthew. All I've seen and experienced has been the common fate of most people, a little sharpened, perhaps, a little vivified. Briefly, I've had a lot of fun and a measure of trouble. I've been stimulated by adventure; I've known suffering and love and pain."

"You're still surprising me. I didn't suppose a girl like you could know the meaning of pain." He gave her a twisted smile. "Though you certainly know how to cause it. Even yet I can get a pang which no other thought produces if I let my mind go back to those first few desperate days after you left me. Heavens, can't you suffer when you're young!"

She nodded, laid her hand on his. "Terribly. Remember, I was suffering too, Matthew, though for different causes. I was so pushed, so goaded . . . well, we won't talk about that any more . . . I hope you've got over all that feeling. Indeed, indeed I wasn't worth it. Do tell me you haven't let it harass you all these years."

His hand clasped hers lightly, then withdrew. "No I haven't. . . . The suddenness, the inevitableness of your departure checked me, pulled me up short. I suffered, oh damnably, but it was suffering with my eyes open. I knew then you weren't for me; that fundamentally we were too far apart. And eventually I got over it. Those days!" He smiled again wryly, recalling a memory. "But I went on suffering just the same, only in another way. I fell in love with Jinny."

Her heart in her breast stopped beating. "Matthew, you didn't! Why on earth didn't you ever say so?"

"I couldn't. She was such a child, you see; she made it so plain all the time that she looked on me as her sister's beau and therefore a kind of dependable brother. After you went I used to go to see her, take her about. Why she'd swing on my arm and hold up her face for a good-night kiss! Once, I remember, we had been out and she became car-sick,—poor little weak thing! She was so ashamed! Like a baby, you know, playing at being grown-up and then ashamed for reverting to babyhood. I went to see her the next day and she was so little and frail and confiding! I stayed away then for a long time and the next thing I knew she was going to New York. I misjudged you awfully then, Angela. You must forgive me. I thought you had pulled her away. I learned later that I was wrong, that you and she rarely saw each other in New York. Do you know why she left?"

There was her sister's pride to shield but her own need to succour; who could have dreamed of such a dilemma? "I can't betray Jinny," she said to herself and told him that while she personally had not influenced her sister the latter had had a very good reason for leaving Philadelphia.

"I suppose so. Certainly she left. But she'd write me, occasionally, letters just like her dear self, so frank and girlish and ingenuous and making it so damnably plain that any demonstration of love on my part was out of the question. I said to myself: 'I'm not going to wreck my whole life over those Murray girls'. And I let our friendship drift off into a nothingness. . . . Then she came to visit Edna Brown this summer. I fairly leaped out to Merion to see her. The moment I laid eyes on her I realized that she had developed, had become a woman. She was as always, kind and sweet, prettier, more alluring than ever. I thought I'd try my luck . . . and Edna told me she was engaged. What's the fellow like, Angela?"

"Very nice, very fine."

"Wild about her, I suppose?"

Desperately she looked at him. "He's a rather undemonstrative sort. I suppose he's wild enough. Only,—well they talk as though they had no intention of marrying for years and years and they both seem perfectly content with that arrangement."

He frowned incredulously. "What! If I thought they weren't in earnest!"

Impulsively she broke out: "Oh, Matthew, don't you know, —there's so much pain, such suffering in the world,—a man should never leave any stone unturned to achieve his ultimate happiness. Why don't you—write to Jinny, go to New York to see her?"

Under his freckles his brown skin paled. "You think there's a chance?"

"My dear, I wouldn't dare say. I know she likes you very, very much. And I don't think she regards you as a brother."

"Angela, you wouldn't fool me?"

"Why should I do that? And remember after all I'm giving you no assurance. I'm merely saying it's worth taking a chance.

Now let's see, we'll straighten up this place and then we must fly."

At the station she kissed him good-bye. "Anyway you're always a brother to me. Think of what I've told you, Matthew; act on it."

"I shall. Oh, Angela, suppose it should be that God sent you down here to-day?"

"Perhaps He did." They parted solemnly.

Three hours later found her entering her sister's apartment. Jinny, her cold raging, her eyes inflamed and weeping, greeted her plaintively. "Look at me, Angela. And you leaving tomorrow! I'll never be able to make that boat!" The telephone rang. "It's been ringing steadily for the last hour, somebody calling for you. Do answer it."

The message was from Ashley. He had been away in New Orleans. "And I came back and found that clipping. I knew you sent it. Girl, the way I've pursued you this day! Finally I caught up with Martha Burden, she told me where you were staying. May I come up? Be there in half an hour."

"Not to-night, Ralph. Would you like to come to the boat to-morrow?"

"So you're going anyhow? Bully! But not before I've seen you! Suppose I take you to the boat?"

"Awfully nice of you, but I'm going with my sister."

Here Jinny in a voice full of misplaced consonants told her she was going to do nothing of the sort. "With this cold!"

Angela spoke into the receiver again. "My sister says she isn't going, so I will fall back on you if I may." She hung up.

Virginia wanted to hear of the trip. The two sisters sat talking far into the night, but Angela said no word about Matthew.

Monday was a day of surprises. Martha and Ladislas Starr, unable to be on hand for the sailing of the boat, came up to the house to drive down town with the departing traveller. Secretly Angela was delighted with this arrangement, but it brought a scowl to Ashley's face.

Virginia, miserable with the wretchedness attendant on a summer cold, bore up bravely. "I don't mind letting you go like this from the house; but I couldn't stand the ship! Angela, you're not to worry about me one bit. Only come back to me,—happy. I know you will. Oh how different this is from that parting years ago in Philadelphia!"

"Yes," said Angela soberly. "Then I was to be physically ninety miles away from you, but we were really seas apart. Now —darling, three thousand miles are nothing when there is love and trust and understanding. And Jinny, listen! Life is full of surprises. If a chance for real happiness comes your way don't be afraid to grasp at it."

"Cryptic," wheezed Jinny, laughing. "I don't know what you're talking about, but I'll do my best to land any happiness that comes drifting toward me." They kissed each other gravely, almost coldly, without tears. But neither could trust herself to say the actual good-bye.

Angela was silent almost all the way down to the dock, answering her friends only in monosyllables. There, another surprise awaited her in the shape of Mrs. Denver, who remained, however, only for a few moments. "I couldn't stand having you go," she said pitifully, "without seeing you for one last time." And, folding the girl in a close embrace, she broke down and murmured sadly of a lost daughter who would have been "perhaps like you, dear, had she lived."

Elizabeth Sandburg, the gay, the complacent, the beloved of life, clung to her, weeping, "I can't bear to lose you, Angèle." Walter put his arm about her. "Kiss me, old girl. And mind, if you need anything, *anything*, you're to call on us. If you get sick we'll come over after you,—am I right, Lizzie?"

"Yes, of course, of course . . . and don't call me Lizzie. . . . Come away, can't you, and leave them a moment together. Don't you see Ashley glaring at you?"

They withdrew to a good point of vantage on the dock.

Angela, surprised and weeping, remembering both Mrs. Denver's words and the manifestations of kindness in her stateroom said: "They really did love me after all, didn't they?"

"Yes," said Ashley earnestly, "we all love you. I'm coming over to see you by and by, Angèle, may I? You know we've a lot of things to talk about, some things which you perhaps think mean a great deal to me but which in reality mean nothing. Then on the other hand there are some matters which actually do mean something to me but whose value to you I'm not sure of."

"Oh," she said, wiping her eyes and remembering her former secret. "You aren't coming over to ask me to marry you, are you? You don't have to do that. And anyway 'it is not now as it hath been before'. There's no longer a mystery about me, you know. So the real attraction's gone. Remember, I'm not expecting a thing of you, so please, please don't ask it. Ralph, I can't placard myself, and I suppose there will be lots of times when in spite of myself I'll be 'passing'. But I want you to know that from now on, so far as sides are concerned, I am on the coloured side. And I don't want you to come over on that side." She shook her head finally. "Too many complications even for you."

For though she knew he believed in his brave words, she was too sadly experienced to ask an American to put them to the test.

"All right," he said, smiling at her naïve assumptions. "I won't ask you to marry me,—at least not yet. But I'm coming over just the same. I don't suppose you've got a lien on Paris."

"Of course I haven't," she giggled a little. "You know perfectly well I want you to come." Her face suddenly became grave. "But if you do come you won't come to make love without meaning anything either, will you? I'd hate that between you and me."

"No," he said gently, instantly comprehending. "I won't do that either."

"You'll come as a friend?"

"Yes, as a friend."

A deck hand came up then and said civilly that in a few minutes they would be casting off and all visitors must go ashore.

Chapter III

A MONG her steamer-letters was a brief note from Anthony:

"Angela, my angel, my dear girl, good-bye. These last few weeks have heaven and hell. I couldn't bear to see you go,—so I've taken myself off for a few hours . . . don't think I'll neglect Jinny. I'll never do that. Am I right in supposing that you still care a little? Oh Angela, try to forget me,—but don't do it! I shall never forget you!"

There were letters and flowers from the Burdens, gifts of all sorts from Ashley and Mrs. Denver, a set of notes for each day out from Virginia. She read letters, examined her gifts and laid them aside. But all day long Anthony's note reposed on her heart; it lay at night beneath her head.

Paris at first charmed and wooed her. For a while it seemed to her that her old sense of joy in living for living's sake had returned to her. It was like those first few days which she had spent in exploring New York. She rode delightedly in the motor-buses on and on to the unknown, unpredictable terminus; she followed the winding Seine; crossing and re-crossing the bridges each with its distinctive characteristics. Back of the Panthéon, near the church of St. Geneviève she discovered a Russian restaurant where strange, exotic dishes were served by tall blond waiters in white, stiff Russian blouses. One day, wandering up the Boulevard du Mont Parnasse, she found at its juncture with the Boulevard Raspail the Café Dome, a student restaurant of which many returned students had spoken in the Art School in New York. On entering she was recognized almost immediately by Edith Martin, a girl who had studied with her in Philadelphia.

Miss Martin had lived in Paris two years; knew all the gossip and the characters of the Quarter; could give Angela points on pensions, cafés, tips and the Gallic disposition. On all these topics she poured out perpetually a flood of information, presented her friends, summoned the new comer constantly to her studio or camped uninvited in the other girl's tiny quarters at the Pension Franciana. There was no chance for actual physical loneliness, yet Angela thought after a few weeks of persistent comradeship that she had never felt so lonely in her life. For the first time in her adventuresome existence she was caught up in a tide of homesickness.

Then this passed too with the summer, and she found herself by the end of September engrossed in her work. She went to the Academy twice a day, immersed herself in the atmosphere of the Louvre and the gallery of the Luxembourg. It was hard work, but gradually she schooled herself to remember that this was her life, and that her aim, her one ambition, was to become an acknowledged, a significant painter of portraits. The instructor, renowned son of a still more renowned father, almost invariably praised her efforts.

With the coming of the fall the sense of adventure left her. Paris, so beautiful in the summer, so gay with its thronging thousands, its hosts bent on pleasure, took on another garb in the sullen greyness of late autumn. The tourists disappeared and the hard steady grind of labour, the intent application to the business of living, so noticeable in the French, took the place of a transient, careless freedom. Angela felt herself falling into line; but it was good discipline as she herself realized. Once or twice, in periods of utter loneliness or boredom, she let her mind dwell on her curiously thwarted and twisted life. But the ability for self-pity had vanished. She had known too many others whose lives lay equally remote from goals which had at first seemed so certain. For a period she had watched feverishly for the incoming of foreign mail, sure that some word must come from Virginia about Matthew, but the months crept sullenly by and Jinny's letters remained the same artless missives prattling of school-work, Anthony, Sara Penton, the movies and visits to Maude the inimitable.

"Of course not everything can come right," she told herself. Matthew evidently had, on second thought, deemed it wisest to consult the evidence of his own senses rather than be guided by the hints which in the nature of things she could offer only vaguely.

Within those six months she lost forever the blind optimism of youth. She did not write Anthony nor did she hear from him.

*

Christmas Eve day dawned or rather drifted greyly into the
beholder's perception out of the black mistiness of the murky
night. In spite of herself her spirits sank steadily. Virginia had
promised her a present,—"I've looked all over this whole town,"
she wrote, "to find you something good enough, something
absolutely perfect. Anthony's been helping me. And at last I've
found it. We've taken every possible precaution against the in-
terference of wind or rain or weather, and unless something
absolutely unpredictable intervenes, it will be there for you
Christmas Eve or possibly the day before. But remember, don't
open until Christmas."

But it was now six o'clock on Christmas Eve and no present
had come, no letter, no remembrance of any kind. "Oh," she
said to herself "what a fool I was to come so far away from
home!" For a moment she envisaged the possibility of throwing herself on the bed and sobbing her heart out. Instead she
remembered Edith Martin's invitation to make a night of it
over at her place, a night which was to include dancing and
chaffing, a trip just before midnight to hear Mass at St. Sulpice,
and a return to the studio for doubtless more dancing and jesting and laughter, and possibly drunkenness on the part of the
American male.

At ten o'clock as she stood in her tiny room rather sullenly
putting the last touches to her costume, the maid, Héloïse,
brought her a cable. It was a long message from Ashley wishing her health, happiness and offering to come over at a week's
notice. Somehow the bit of blue paper cheered her, easing her
taut nerves. "Of course they're thinking about me. I'll hear
from Jinny any moment; it's not her fault that the delivery is
late. I wonder what she sent me."

Returning at three o'clock Christmas morning from the
party she put her hand cautiously in the door to switch on the
light for fear that a package lay near the threshold, but there
was no package there. "Well, even if it were there I couldn't
open it," she murmured, "for I'm too sleepy." And indeed she
had drugged herself with dancing and gaiety into an overwhelming drowsiness. Barely able to toss aside her pretty dress,
she tumbled luxuriously into bed, grateful in the midst of her
somnolence for the fatigue which would make her forget. . . .

In what seemed to her less than an hour, she heard a tremendous knocking at the door.

"*Entrez*," she called sleepily and relapsed immediately into slumber. The door, as it happened, was unlocked; she had been too fatigued to think of it the night before. Heloise stuck in a tousled head. "My God," she told the cook afterwards, "such a time as I had to wake her! There she was asleep on both ears and the gentleman downstairs waiting!"

Angela finally opened bewildered eyes. "A gentleman," reiterated Héloise in her staccato tongue. "He awaits you below. He says he has a present which he must put into your own hands. Will Mademoiselle then descend or shall I tell him to come back?"

"Tell him to come back," she murmured, then opened her heavy eyes. "Is it really Christmas, Héloise? Where is the gentleman?"

"As though I had him there in my pocket," said Héloise later in her faithful report to the cook.

But finally the message penetrated. Grasping a robe and slippers, she half leaped, half fell down the little staircase and plunged into the five foot square drawing-room. Anthony sitting on the tremendously disproportionate tan and maroon sofa rose to meet her.

His eyes on her astonished countenance, he began searching about in his pockets, slapping his vest, pulling out keys and handkerchiefs. "There ought to be a tag on me somewhere," he remarked apologetically, "but anyhow Virginia and Matthew sent me with their love."

THE BLACKER THE BERRY

A NOVEL OF NEGRO LIFE

Wallace Thurman

To Ma Jack

The blacker the berry
The sweeter the juice . . .

   —Negro folk saying

My color shrouds me in . . . .

   —Countee Cullen

Contents

PART I — EMMA LOU — 693

PART II — HARLEM — 729

PART III — ALVA — 748

PART IV — RENT PARTY — 773

PART V — PYRRHIC VICTORY — 806

PART I

Emma Lou

ORE acutely than ever before Emma Lou began to feel
that her luscious black complexion was somewhat of a
liability, and that her marked color variation from the other
people in her environment was a decided curse. Not that she
minded being black, being a Negro necessitated having a colored skin, but she did mind being too black. She couldn't understand why such should be the case, couldn't comprehend
the cruelty of the natal attenders who had allowed her to be
dipped, as it were, in indigo ink when there were so many
more pleasing colors on nature's palette. Biologically, it wasn't
necessary either; her mother was quite fair, so was her mother's
mother, and her mother's brother, and her mother's brother's
son; but then none of them had had a black man for a father.
Why *had* her mother married a black man? Surely there had
been some eligible brown-skin men around. She didn't particularly desire to have had a "high yaller" father, but for her sake
certainly some more happy medium could have been found.

She wasn't the only person who regretted her darkness either. It was an acquired family characteristic, this moaning and
grieving over the color of her skin. Everything possible had
been done to alleviate the unhappy condition, every suggested
agent had been employed, but her skin, despite bleachings,
scourgings, and powderings, had remained black—fast black—
as nature had planned and effected.

She should have been born a boy, then color of skin wouldn't
have mattered so much, for wasn't her mother always saying
that a black boy could get along, but that a black girl would
never know anything but sorrow and disappointment? But she
wasn't a boy; she was a girl, and color did matter, mattered so
much that she would rather have missed receiving her high
school diploma than have to sit as she now sat, the only odd
and conspicuous figure on the auditorium platform of the
Boise high school. Why had she allowed them to place her in

693

the center of the first row, and why had they insisted upon her dressing entirely in white so that surrounded as she was by similarly attired pale-faced fellow graduates she resembled, not at all remotely, that comic picture her Uncle Joe had hung in his bedroom? The picture wherein the black, kinky head of a little red-lipped pickaninny lay like a fly in a pan of milk amid a white expanse of bedclothes.

But of course she couldn't have worn blue or black when the call was for the wearing of white, even if white was not complementary to her complexion. She would have been odd-looking anyway no matter what she wore and she would also have been conspicuous, for not only was she the only dark-skinned person on the platform, she was also the only Negro pupil in the entire school, and had been for the past four years. Well, thank goodness, the principal would soon be through with his monotonous farewell address, and she and the other members of her class would advance to the platform center as their names were called and receive the documents which would signify their unconditional release from public school.

As she thought of these things, Emma Lou glanced at those who sat to the right and to the left of her. She envied them their obvious elation, yet felt a strange sense of superiority because of her immunity for the moment from an ephemeral mob emotion. Get a diploma?—What did it mean to her? College?—Perhaps. A job?—Perhaps again. She was going to have a high school diploma, but it would mean nothing to her whatsoever. The tragedy of her life was that she was too black. Her face and not a slender roll of ribbon-bound parchment was to be her future identification tag in society. High school diploma indeed! What she needed was an efficient bleaching agent, a magic cream that would remove this unwelcome black mask from her face and make her more like her fellow men.

"Emma Lou Morgan."

She came to with a start. The principal had called her name and stood smiling down at her benevolently. Some one—she knew it was her Cousin Buddie, stupid imp—applauded, very faintly, very provokingly. Some one else snickered.

"Emma Lou Morgan."

The principal had called her name again, more sharply than before and his smile was less benevolent. The girl who sat to the left of her nudged her. There was nothing else for her to do but to get out of that anchoring chair and march forward to receive her diploma. But why did the people in the audience have to stare so? Didn't they all know that Emma Lou Morgan was Boise high school's only nigger student? Didn't they all know—but what was the use. She had to go get that diploma, so summoning her most insouciant manner, she advanced to the platform center, brought every muscle of her lithe limbs into play, haughtily extended her shiny black arm to receive the proffered diploma, bowed a chilly thanks, then holding her arms stiffly at her sides, insolently returned to her seat in that forboding white line, insolently returned once more to splotch its pale purity and to mock it with her dark, outlandish difference.

Emma Lou had been born in a semi-white world, totally surrounded by an all-white one, and those few dark elements that had forced their way in had either been shooed away or else greeted with derisive laughter. It was the custom always of those with whom she came into most frequent contact to ridicule or revile any black person or object. A black cat was a harbinger of bad luck, black crape was the insignia of mourning, and black people were either evil niggers with poisonous blue gums or else typical vaudeville darkies. It seemed as if the people in her world never went half-way in their recognition or reception of things black, for these things seemed always to call forth only the most extreme emotional reactions. They never provoked mere smiles or mere melancholy, rather they were the signal either for boisterous guffaws or pain-induced and tear-attended grief.

Emma Lou had been becoming increasingly aware of this for a long time, but her immature mind had never completely grasped its full, and to her, tragic significance. First there had been the case of her father, old black Jim Morgan they called him, and Emma Lou had often wondered why it was that he of all the people she heard discussed by her family should always be referred to as if his very blackness condemned him to receive no respect from his fellow men.

She had also began to wonder if it was because of his blackness that he had never been in evidence as far as she knew.

Inquiries netted very unsatisfactory answers. "Your father is no good." "He left your mother, deserted her shortly after you were born." And these statements were always prefixed or followed by some epithet such as "dirty black no-gooder" or "durn his onery black hide." There was in fact only one member of the family who did not speak of her father in this manner, and that was her Uncle Joe, who was also the only person in the family to whom she really felt akin, because he alone never seemed to regret, to bemoan, or to ridicule her blackness of skin. It was her grandmother who did all the regretting, her mother who did the bemoaning, her Cousin Buddie and her playmates, both white and colored, who did the ridiculing.

Emma Lou's maternal grandparents, Samuel and Maria Lightfoot, were both mulatto products of slave-day promiscuity between male masters and female chattel. Neither had been slaves, their own parents having been granted their freedom because of their rather close connections with the white branch of the family tree. These freedmen had migrated into Kansas with their children, and when these children had grown up they in turn had joined the westward-ho parade of that current era, and finally settled in Boise, Idaho.

Samuel and Maria, like many others of their kind and antecedents, had had only one compelling desire, which motivated their every activity and dictated their every thought. They wished to put as much physical and mental space between them and the former home of their parents as was possible. That was why they had left Kansas, for in Kansas there were too many reminders of that which their parents had escaped and from which they wished to flee. Kansas was too near the former slave belt, too accessible to disgruntled southerners, who, deprived of their slaves, were inculcated with an easily communicable virus, nigger hatred. Then, too, in Kansas all Negroes were considered as belonging to one class. It didn't matter if you and your parents had been freedmen before the Emancipation Proclamation, nor did it matter that you were almost three-quarters white. You were, nevertheless, classed with those hordes of hungry, ragged, ignorant black folk arriving from the South in such great numbers, packed like so many stampeding cattle in dirty, manure-littered box cars.

From all of this these maternal grandparents of Emma Lou

fled, fled to the Rocky Mountain states which were too far away for the recently freed slaves to reach, especially since most of them believed that the world ended just a few miles north of the Mason-Dixon line. Then, too, not only were the Rocky Mountain states beyond the reach of this raucous and smelly rabble of recently freed cotton pickers and plantation hands, but they were also peopled by pioneers, sturdy land and gold seekers from the East, marching westward, always westward in search of El Dorado, and being too busy in this respect to be violently aroused by problems of race unless economic factors precipitated matters.

So Samuel and Maria went into the fast farness of a little known Rocky Mountain territory and settled in Boise, at the time nothing more than a trading station for the Indians and whites, and a red light center for the cowboys and sheepherders and miners in the neighboring vicinity. Samuel went into the saloon business and grew prosperous. Maria raised a family and began to mother nuclear elements for a future select Negro social group.

There was of course in such a small and haphazardly populated community some social intermixture between whites and blacks. White and black gamblers rolled the dice together, played tricks on one another while dealing faro, and became allies in their attempts to outfigure the roulette wheel. White and black men amicably frequented the saloons and dancehalls together. White and black women leaned out of the doorways and windows of the jerry-built frame houses and log cabins of "Whore Row." White and black housewives gossiped over back fences and lent one another needed household commodities. But there was little social intercourse on a higher scale. Slue-foot Sal, the most popular high yaller on "Whore Row," might be a buddy to Irish Peg and Blond Liz, but Mrs. Amos James, whose husband owned the town's only drygoods store, could certainly not become too familiar with Mrs. Samuel Lightfoot, colored, whose husband owned a saloon. And it was not a matter of the difference in their respective husbands' businesses. Mrs. Amos James did associate with Mrs. Arthur Emory, white, whose husband also owned a saloon. It was purely a matter of color.

Emma Lou's grandmother then, holding herself aloof from

the inmates of "Whore Row," and not wishing to associate
with such as old Mammy Lewis' daughters, who did most of
the town wash, and others of their ilk, was forced to choose
her social equals slowly and carefully. This was hard, for there
were so few Negroes in Boise anyway that there wasn't much
cream to skim off. But as the years passed, others, who, like
Maria and her husband, were mulatto offsprings of mulatto
freedmen seeking a freer land, moved in, and were soon initi-
ated into what was later to be known as the blue vein circle, so
named because all of its members were fair-skinned enough for
their blood to be seen pulsing purple through the veins of their
wrists.

Emma Lou's grandmother was the founder and the acknowledged leader of Boise's blue veins, and she guarded its
exclusiveness passionately and jealously. Were they not a superior class? Were they not a very high type of Negro, comparable
to the persons of color group in the West Indies? And were
they not entitled, ipso facto, to more respect and opportunity
and social acceptance than the more pure blooded Negroes?
In their veins was some of the best blood of the South. They
were closely akin to the only true aristocrats in the United
States. Even the slave masters had been aware of and acknowledged in some measure their superiority. Having some of
Marse George's blood in their veins set them apart from ordinary Negroes at birth. These mulattoes as a rule were not ordered to work in the fields beneath the broiling sun at the urge
of a Simon Legree lash. They were saved and trained for the
more gentle jobs, saved and trained to be ladies' maids and
butlers. Therefore, let them continue this natural division of
Negro society. Let them also guard against unwelcome and
degenerating encroachments. Their motto must be "Whiter
and whiter every generation," until the grandchildren of the
blue veins could easily go over into the white race and become
assimilated so that problems of race would plague them no
more.

Maria had preached this doctrine to her two children, Jane
and Joe, throughout their apprentice years, and can therefore
be forgiven for having a physical collapse when they both, first
Joe, then Emma Lou's mother, married not mulattoes, but a
copper brown and a blue black. This had been somewhat of a

necessity, for, when the mating call had made itself heard to them, there had been no eligible blue veins around. Most of their youthful companions had been sent away to school or else to seek careers in eastern cities, and those few who had remained had already found their chosen life's companions. Maria had sensed that something of the kind might happen and had urged Samuel to send Jane and Joe away to some eastern boarding school, but Samuel had very stubbornly refused. He had his own notions of the sort of things one's children learned in boarding school, and of the greater opportunities they had to apply that learning. True, they might acquire the same knowledge in the public schools of Boise, but then there would be some limit to the extent to which they could apply this knowledge, seeing that they lived at home and perforce must submit to some parental supervision. A cot in the attic at home was to Samuel a much safer place for a growing child to sleep than an iron four poster in a boarding school dormitory.

So Samuel had remained adamant and the two carefully reared scions of Boise's first blue vein family had of necessity sought their mates among the lower orders. However, Joe's wife was not as undesirable as Emma Lou's father, for she was almost three-quarters Indian, and there was scant possibility that her children would have revolting dark skins, thick lips, spreading nostrils, and kinky hair. But in the case of Emma Lou's father, there were no such extenuating characteristics, for his physical properties undeniably stamped him as a full blooded Negro. In fact, it seemed as if he had come from one of the few families originally from Africa, who could not boast of having been seduced by some member of the southern aristocracy, or befriended by some member of a strolling band of Indians.

No one could understand why Emma Lou's mother had married Jim Morgan, least of all Jane herself. In fact she hadn't thought much about it until Emma Lou had been born. She had first met Jim at a church picnic, given in a woodlawn meadow on the outskirts of the city, and almost before she had realized what was happening she had found herself slipping away from home, night after night, to stroll down a well shaded street, known as Lover's Lane, with the man her mother had forbidden her to see. And it hadn't been long before they had decided that an elopement would be the only thing to assure themselves the pleasure of being together without worrying about Mama Lightfoot's wrath, talkative neighbors, prying town marshals, and grass stains.

Despite the rancor of her mother and the whispering of her mother's friends, Jane hadn't really found anything to regret in her choice of a husband until Emma Lou had been born. Then all the fears her mother had instilled in her about the penalties inflicted by society upon black Negroes, especially upon black Negro girls, came to the fore. She was abysmally stunned by the color of her child, for she had been certain that since she herself was so fair that her child could not possibly be as dark as its father. She had been certain that it would be a luscious admixture, a golden brown with all its mother's desirable facial features and its mother's hair. But she hadn't reckoned with nature's perversity, nor had she taken under consideration the inescapable fact that some of her ancestors too had been black, and that some of their color chromosomes were still imbedded within her. Emma Lou had been fortunate enough to have hair like her mother's, a thick, curly black mass of hair, rich and easily controlled, but she had also been unfortunate enough to have a face as black as her father's, and a nose which, while not exactly flat, was as distinctly negroid as her too thick lips.

Her birth had served no good purpose. It had driven her mother back to seek the confidence and aid of Maria, and it had given Maria the chance she had been seeking to break up the undesirable union of her daughter with what she termed an ordinary black nigger. But Jim's departure hadn't solved matters at all, rather it had complicated them, for although he was gone, his child remained, a tragic mistake which could not be stamped out or eradicated even after Jane, by getting a divorce from Jim and marrying a red-haired Irish Negro, had been accepted back into blue vein grace.

Emma Lou had always been the alien member of the family and of the family's social circle. Her grandmother, now a widow, made her feel it. Her mother made her feel it. And her Cousin Buddie made her feel it, to say nothing of the way she was regarded by outsiders. As early as she could remember, people had been saying to her mother, "What an extraordinarily black child! Where did you adopt it?" or else, "Such lovely unniggerish hair on such a niggerish-looking child." Some had even been facetious and made suggestions like, "Try some lye, Jane, it may eat it out. She can't look any worse."

Then her mother's re-marriage had brought another person into her life, a person destined to give her, while still a young child, much pain and unhappiness. Aloysius McNamara was his name. He was the bastard son of an Irish politician and a Negro washerwoman, and until he had been sent East to a parochial school, Aloysius, so named because that was his father's middle name, had always been known as Aloysius Washington, and the identity of his own father had never been revealed to him by his proud and humble mother. But since his father had been prevailed upon to pay for his education, Aloysius' mother thought it the proper time to tell her son his true origin and to let him assume his real name. She had hopes that away from his home town he might be able to pass for white and march unhindered by bars of color to fame and fortune.

But such was not to be the case, for Emma Lou's prospective stepfather was so conscious of the Negro blood in his veins and so bitter because of it, that he used up whatever talents he had groaning inwardly at capricious fate, and planning revenge upon the world at large, especially the black world. For it was Negroes and not whites whom he blamed for his own, to him, life's tragedy. He was not fair enough of skin, despite his mother's and his own hopes, to pass for white. There was a brownness in his skin, inherited from his mother, which immediately marked him out for what he was, despite the red hair and the Irish blue eyes. And his facial features had been modeled too generously. He was not thin lipped, nor were his nostrils as delicately chiseled as they might have been. He was a Negro. There was no getting around it, although he tried in every possible way to do so.

Finishing school, he had returned West for the express purpose of making his father accept him publicly and personally advance his career. He had wanted to be a lawyer and figured that his father's political pull was sufficiently strong to draw him beyond race barriers and set him as one apart. His father had not been entirely cold to these plans and proposals, but his father's wife had been. She didn't mind her husband giving this nigger bastard of his money, and receiving him in his home on rare and private occasions. She was trying to be liberal, but she wasn't going to have people point to her and say, "That's Boss McNamara's wife. Wonder if that nigger son is his'n or hers. They do say. . . ." So Aloysius had found himself shunted back into the black world he so despised. He couldn't be made to realize that being a Negro did not necessarily indicate that one must also be a ne'er-do-well. Had he been white, or so he said, he would have been a successful criminal lawyer, but being considered black it was impossible for him ever to be anything more advanced than a pullman car porter or a dining car waiter, and acting upon this premise, he hadn't tried to be anything else.

His only satisfaction in life was the pleasure he derived from insulting and ignoring the real blacks. Persons of color, mulattoes, were all right, but he couldn't stand detestable black Negroes. Unfortunately, Emma Lou fell into this latter class, and suffered at his hands accordingly, until he finally ran away from his wife, Emma Lou, Boise, Negroes, and all, ran away to Canada with Diamond Lil of "Whore Row."

Summer vacation was nearly over and it had not yet been decided what to do with Emma Lou now that she had graduated from high school. She herself gave no help nor offered any suggestions. As it was, she really did not care what became of her. After all it didn't seem to matter. There was no place in the world for a girl as black as she anyway. Her grandmother had assured her that she would never find a husband worth a dime, and her mother had said again and again, "Oh, if you had only been a boy!" until Emma Lou had often wondered why it was that people were not able to effect a change of sex or at least a change of complexion.

It was her Uncle Joe who finally prevailed upon her mother to send her to the University of Southern California in Los Angeles. There, he reasoned, she would find a larger and more intelligent social circle. In a city the size of Los Angeles there were Negroes of every class, color, and social position. Let Emma Lou go there where she would not be as far away from home as if she were to go to some eastern college.

Jane and Maria, while not agreeing entirely with what Joe

said, were nevertheless glad that at last something which seemed adequate and sensible could be done for Emma Lou. She was to take the four year college course, receive a bachelor degree in education, then go South to teach. That, they thought, was a promising future, and for once in the eighteen years of Emma Lou's life every one was satisfied in some measure. Even Emma Lou grew elated over the prospects of the trip. Her Uncle Joe's insistence upon the differences of social contacts in larger cities intrigued her. Perhaps he was right after all in continually reasserting to them that as long as one was a Negro, one's specific color had little to do with one's life. Salvation depended upon the individual. And he also told Emma Lou, during one of their usual private talks, that it was only in small cities one encountered stupid color prejudice such as she had encountered among the blue vein circle in her home town.

"People in large cities," he had said, "are broad. They do not have time to think of petty things. The people in Boise are fifty years behind the times, but you will find that Los Angeles is one of the world's greatest and most modern cities, and you will be happy there."

On arriving in Los Angeles, Emma Lou was so busy observing the colored inhabitants that she had little time to pay attention to other things. Palm trees and wild geraniums were pleasant to behold, and such strange phenomena as pepper trees and century plants had to be admired. They were very obvious and they were also strange and beautiful, but they impinged upon only a small corner of Emma Lou's consciousness. She was minutely aware of them, necessarily took them in while passing, viewing the totality without pondering over or lingering to praise their stylistic details. They were, in this instance, exquisite theatrical props, rendered insignificant by a more strange and a more beautiful human pageant. For to Emma Lou, who, in all her life, had never seen over five hundred Negroes, the spectacle presented by a community containing over fifty thousand, was sufficient to make relatively commonplace many more important and charming things than the far famed natural scenery of Southern California.

She had arrived in Los Angeles a week before registration day at the university, and had spent her time in being shown and seeing the city. But whenever these sightseeing excursions took her away from the sections where Negroes lived, she immediately lost all interest in what she was being shown. The Pacific Ocean in itself did not cause her heart beat to quicken, nor did the roaring of its waves find an emotional echo within her. But on coming upon Bruce's Beach for colored people near Redondo, or the little strip of sandied shore they had appropriated for themselves at Santa Monica, the Pacific Ocean became an intriguing something to contemplate as a background for their activities. Everything was interesting as it was patronized, reflected through, or acquired by Negroes.

Her Uncle Joe had been right. Here, in the colored social circles of Los Angeles, Emma Lou was certain that she would find many suitable companions, intelligent, broad-minded people of all complexions, intermixing and being too occupied otherwise to worry about either their own skin color or the skin color of those around them. Her Uncle Joe had said that Negroes were Negroes whether they happened to be yellow, brown, or black, and a conscious effort to eliminate the darker elements would neither prove or solve anything. There was nothing quite so silly as the creed of the blue veins: "Whiter and whiter, every generation. The nearer white you are the more white people will respect you. Therefore all light Negroes marry light Negroes. Continue to do so generation after generation, and eventually white people will accept this racially, bastard aristocracy, thus enabling those Negroes who really matter to escape the social and economic inferiority of the American Negro."

Such had been the credo of her grandmother and of her mother and of their small circle of friends in Boise. But Boise was a provincial town, given to the molding of provincial people with provincial minds. Boise was a backwoods town out of the main stream of modern thought and progress. Its people were cramped and narrow, their intellectual concepts stereotyped and static. Los Angeles was a happy contrast in all respects.

On registration day, Emma Lou rushed out to the campus of the University of Southern California one hour before the registrar's office was scheduled to open. She spent the time roaming around, familiarizing herself with the layout of the campus and learning the names of the various buildings, some old and vineclad, others new and shiny in the sun, and watching the crowds of laughing students, rushing to and fro, greeting one another and talking over their plans for the coming school year. But her main reason for such an early arrival on the campus had been to find some of her fellow Negro students. She had heard that there were to be quite a number enrolled, but in all her hour's stroll she saw not one, and finally somewhat disheartened she got into the line stretched out in front of the registrar's office, and, for the moment, became engrossed in becoming a college freshman.

All the while, though, she kept searching for a colored face, but it was not until she had been duly signed up as a student and sent in search of her advisor that she saw one. Then three colored girls had sauntered into the room where she was having a conference with her advisor, sauntered in, arms interlocked, greeted her advisor, then sauntered out again. Emma Lou had wanted to rush after them—to introduce herself, but of course it had been impossible under the circumstances. She had immediately taken a liking to all three, each of whom was what is known in the parlance of the black belt as high brown, with modishly-shingled bobbed hair and well formed bodies, fashionably attired in flashy sport garments. From then on Emma Lou paid little attention to the business of choosing subjects and class hours, so little attention in fact that the advisor thought her exceptionally tractable and somewhat dumb. But she liked students to come that way. It made the task of being advisor easy. One just made out the program to suit oneself, and had no tedious explanations to make as to why the student could not have such and such a subject at such and such an hour, and why such and such a professor's class was already full.

After her program had been made out, Emma Lou was directed to the bursar's office to pay her fees. While going down the stairs she almost bumped into two dark-brown-skinned boys, obviously brothers if not twins, arguing as to where they should go next. One insisted that they should go back to the registrar's office. The other was being equally insistent that they should go to the gymnasium and make an appointment for their required physical examination. Emma Lou boldly

stopped when she saw them, hoping they would speak, but
they merely glanced up at her and continued their argument,
bringing cards and pamphlets out of their pockets for reference
and guidance. Emma Lou wanted to introduce herself to them,
but she was too bashful to do so. She wasn't yet used to going
to school with other Negro students, and she wasn't exactly
certain how one went about becoming acquainted. But she finally decided that she had better let the advances come from
the others, especially if they were men. There was nothing forward about her, and since she was a stranger it was no more
than right that the old-timers should make her welcome. Still,
if these had been girls . . . , but they weren't, so she continued her way down the stairs.

In the bursar's office, she was somewhat overjoyed at first to
find that she had fallen into line behind another colored girl
who turned around immediately, and, after saying hello, announced in a loud, harsh voice:

"My feet are sure some tired!"

Emma Lou was so taken aback that she couldn't answer.
People in college didn't talk that way. But meanwhile the girl
was continuing:

"Ain't this registration a mess?"

Two white girls who had fallen into line behind Emma Lou
snickered. Emma Lou answered by shaking her head. The girl
continued:

"I've been standin' in line and climbin' stairs and talkin' and
a-signin' till I'm just 'bout done for."

"It is tiresome," Emma Lou returned softly, hoping the girl
would take a hint and lower her own strident voice. But she
didn't.

"Tiresome ain't no name for it," she declared more loudly
than ever before, then, "Is you a new student?"

"I am," answered Emma Lou, putting much emphasis on
the "I am."

She wanted the white people who were listening to know
that she knew her grammar if this other person didn't. "Is
you," indeed! If this girl was a specimen of the Negro students
with whom she was to associate, she most certainly did not
want to meet another one. But it couldn't be possible that all
of them—those three girls and those two boys for instance—

were like this girl. Emma Lou was unable to imagine how such a person had ever gotten out of high school. Where on earth could she have gone to high school? Surely not in the North. Then she must be a southerner. That's what she was, a southerner—Emma Lou curled her lips a little—no wonder the colored people in Boise spoke as they did about southern Negroes and wished that they would stay South. Imagine any one preparing to enter college saying "Is you," and, to make it worse, right before all these white people, these staring white people, so eager and ready to laugh. Emma Lou's face burned.

"Two mo', then I goes in my sock."

Emma Lou was almost at the place where she was ready to take even this statement literally, and was on the verge of leaving the line. Supposing this creature did "go in her sock!" God forbid!

"Wonder where all the spades keep themselves? I ain't seen but two 'sides you."

"I really do not know," Emma Lou returned precisely and chillily. She had no intentions of becoming friendly with this sort of person. Why she would be ashamed even to be seen on the street with her, dressed as she was in a red-striped sport suit, a white hat, and white shoes and stockings. Didn't she know that black people had to be careful about the colors they affected?

The girl had finally reached the bursar's window and was paying her fees, and loudly differing with the cashier about the total amount due.

"I tell you it ain't that much," she shouted through the window bars. "I figured it up myself before I left home."

The cashier obligingly turned to her adding machine and once more obtained the same total. When shown this, the girl merely grinned, examined the list closely, and said:

"I'm gonna' pay it, but I still think you're wrong."

Finally she moved away from the window, but not before she had turned to Emma Lou and said,

"You're next," and then proceeded to wait until Emma Lou had finished.

Emma Lou vainly sought some way to escape, but was unable to do so, and had no choice but to walk with the girl to the registrar's office where they had their cards stamped in return for the bursar's receipt. This done, they went onto the campus together. Hazel Mason was the girl's name. Emma Lou had fully expected it to be either Hyacinth or Geranium. Hazel was from Texas, Prairie Valley, Texas, and she told Emma Lou that her father, having become quite wealthy when oil had been found on his farm lands, had been enabled to realize two life ambitions—obtain a Packard touring car and send his only daughter to a "fust-class" white school.

Emma Lou had planned to loiter around the campus. She was still eager to become acquainted with the colored members of the student body, and this encounter with the crass and vulgar Hazel Mason had only made her the more eager. She resented being approached by any one so flagrantly inferior, any one so noticeably a typical southern darky, who had no business obtruding into the more refined scheme of things. Emma Lou planned to lose her unwelcome companion somewhere on the campus so that she could continue unhindered her quest for agreeable acquaintances.

But Hazel was as anxious to meet some one as was Emma Lou, and having found her was not going to let her get away without a struggle. She, too, was new to this environment and in a way was more lonely and eager for the companionship of her own kind than Emma Lou, for never before had she come into such close contact with so many whites. Her life had been spent only among Negroes. Her fellow pupils and teachers in school had always been colored, and as she confessed to Emma Lou, she couldn't get used "to all these white folks."

"Honey, I was just achin' to see a black face," she had said, and, though Emma Lou was experiencing the same ache, she found herself unable to sympathize with the other girl, for Emma Lou classified Hazel as a barbarian who had most certainly not come from a family of best people. No doubt her mother had been a washerwoman. No doubt she had innumerable relatives and friends all as ignorant and as ugly as she. There was no sense in any one having a face as ugly as Hazel's, and Emma Lou thanked her stars that though she was black, her skin was not rough and pimply, nor was her hair kinky, nor were her nostrils completely flattened out until they seemed to spread all over her face. No wonder people were prejudiced against dark skinned people when they were so ugly, so haphazard in their dress, and so boisterously mannered as was this present specimen. She herself was black, but nevertheless she had come from a good family, and she could easily take her place in a society of the right sort of people.

The two strolled along the lawn-bordered gravel path which led to a vine-covered building at the end of the campus. Hazel never ceased talking. She kept shouting at Emma Lou, shouting all sorts of personal intimacies as if she were desirous of the whole world hearing them. There was no necessity for her to talk so loudly, no necessity for her to afford every one on the crowded campus the chance to stare and laugh at them as they passed. Emma Lou had never before been so humiliated and so embarrassed. She felt that she must get away from her offensive companion. What did she care if she had to hurt her feelings to do so. The more insulting she could be now, the less friendly she would have to be in the future.

"Good-by," she said abruptly, "I must go home." With which she turned away and walked rapidly in the opposite direction. She had only gone a few steps when she was aware of the fact that the girl was following her. She quickened her pace, but the girl caught up with her and grabbing hold of Emma Lou's arm, shouted,

"Whoa there, Sally."

It seemed to Emma Lou as if every one on the campus was viewing and enjoying this minstrel-like performance. Angrily she tried to jerk away, but the girl held fast.

"Gal, you sure walk fast. I'm going your way. Come on, let me drive you home in my buggy."

And still holding on to Emma Lou's arm, she led the way to the side street where the students parked their cars. Emma Lou was powerless to resist. The girl didn't give her a chance, for she held tight, then immediately resumed the monologue which Emma Lou's attempted leave-taking had interrupted. They reached the street, Hazel still talking loudly, and making elaborate gestures with her free hand.

"Here we are," she shouted, and releasing Emma Lou's arm, salaamed before a sport model Stutz roadster. "Oscar," she continued, "meet the new girl friend. Pleased to meetcha, says he. Climb aboard."

And Emma Lou had climbed aboard, perplexed, chagrined,

thoroughly angry, and disgusted. What was this little black fool doing with a Stutz roadster? And of course, it would be painted red—Negroes always bedecked themselves and their belongings in ridiculously unbecoming colors and ornaments. It seemed to be a part of their primitive heritage which they did not seem to have sense enough to forget and deny. Black girl—white hat—red and white striped sport suit—white shoes and stockings—red roadster. The picture was complete. All Hazel needed to complete her circus-like appearance, thought Emma Lou, was to have some purple feathers stuck in her hat.

Still talking, the girl unlocked and proceeded to start the car. As she was backing it out of the narrow parking space, Emma Lou heard a chorus of semi-suppressed giggles from a neighboring automobile. In her anger she had failed to notice that there were people in the car parked next to the Stutz. But as Hazel expertly swung her machine around, Emma Lou caught a glimpse of them. They were all colored and they were all staring at her and at Hazel. She thought she recognized one of the girls as being one of the group she had seen earlier that morning, and she did recognize the two brothers she had passed on the stairs. And as the roadster sped away, their laughter echoed in her ears, although she hadn't actually heard it. But she had seen the strain in their faces, and she knew that as soon as she and Hazel were out of sight, they would give free rein to their suppressed mirth.

Although Emma Lou had finished registering, she returned to the university campus on the following morning in order to continue her quest for collegiate companions without the alarming and unwelcome presence of Hazel Mason. She didn't know whether to be sorry for the girl and try to help her or to be disgusted and avoid her. She didn't want to be intimately associated with any such vulgar person. It would damage her own position, cause her to be classified with some one who was in a class by herself, for Emma Lou was certain that there was not, and could not be, any one else in the university just like Hazel. But despite her vulgarity, the girl was not all bad. Her good nature was infectious, and Emma Lou had surmised from her monologue on the day before how utterly unselfish a person she could be and was. All of her store of the world's goods were at hand to be used and enjoyed by her friends. There was not, as she had said, "a selfish bone in her body." But even that did not alter the disgusting fact that she was not one who would be welcome by the "right sort of people." Her flamboyant style of dress, her loud voice, her raucous laughter, and her flagrant disregard or ignorance of English grammar seemed inexcusable to Emma Lou, who was unable to understand how such a person could stray so far from the environment in which she rightfully belonged to enter a first class university. Now Hazel, according to Emma Lou, was the type of Negro who should go to a Negro college. There were plenty of them in the South whose standard of scholarship was not beyond her ability. And then, in one of those schools, her darky-like clownishness would not have to be paraded in front of white people, thereby causing discomfort and embarrassment to others of her race, more civilized and circumspect than she.

The problem irritated Emma Lou. She didn't see why it had to be. She had looked forward so anxiously, and so happily to her introductory days on the campus, and now her first experience with one of her fellow colored students had been an unpleasant one. But she didn't intend to let that make her unhappy. She was determined to return to the campus alone, seek out other companions, see whether they accepted or ignored the offending Hazel, and govern herself accordingly.

It was early and there were few people on the campus. The grass was still wet from a heavy overnight dew, and the sun had not yet dispelled the coolness of the early morning. Emma Lou's dress was of thin material and she shivered as she walked or stood in the shade. She had no school business to attend to; there was nothing for her to do but to walk aimlessly about the campus.

In another hour, Emma Lou was pleased to see that the campus walks were becoming crowded, and that the side streets surrounding the campus were now heavy with student traffic. Things were beginning to awaken. Emma Lou became jubilant and walked with jaunty step from path to path, from building to building. It then occurred to her that she had been told that there were more Negro students enrolled in the School of Pharmacy than in any other department of the university, so finding the Pharmacy building she began to wander through its crowded hallways.

Almost immediately, she saw a group of five Negro students, three boys and two girls, standing near a water fountain. She was both excited and perplexed, excited over the fact that she was so close to those she wished to find, and perplexed because she did not know how to approach them. Had there been only one person standing there, the matter would have been comparatively easy. She could have approached with a smile and said, "Good morning." The person would have returned her greeting, and it would then have been a simple matter to get acquainted.

But five people in one bunch, all known to one another and all chatting intimately together!—it would seem too much like an intrusion to go bursting into their gathering—too forward and too vulgar. Then, there was nothing she could say after having said "good morning." One just didn't break into a group of five and say, "I'm Emma Lou Morgan, a new student, and I want to make friends with you." No, she couldn't do that. She would just smile as she passed, smile graciously and friendly. They would know that she was a stranger, and her smile would assure them that she was anxious to make friends, anxious to become a welcome addition to their group.

One of the group of five had sighted Emma Lou as soon as she had sighted them:

"Who's this?" queried Helen Wheaton, a senior in the College of Law.

"Some new 'pick,' I guess," answered Bob Armstrong, who was Helen's fiance and a senior in the School of Architecture.

"I bet she's going to take Pharmacy," whispered Amos Blaine.

"She's hottentot enough to take something," mumbled Tommy Brown. "Thank God, she won't be in any of our classes, eh Amos?"

Emma Lou was almost abreast of them now. They lowered their voices, and made a pretense of mumbled conversation among themselves. Only Verne Davis looked directly at her and it was she alone who returned Emma Lou's smile.

"Whatcha grinnin' at?" Bob chided Verne as Emma Lou passed out of earshot.

"At the little frosh, of course. She grinned at me. I couldn't stare at her without returning it."

"I don't see how anybody could even look at her without grinning."

"Oh, she's not so bad," said Verne.

"Well, she's bad enough."

"That makes two of them."

"Two of what, Amos?"

"Hottentots, Bob."

"Good grief," exclaimed Tommy, "why don't you recruit some good-looking co-eds out here?"

"We don't choose them," Helen returned.

"I'm going out to the Southern Branch where the sight of my fellow female students won't give me dyspepsia."

"Ta-ta, Amos," said Verne, "and you needn't bother to sit in my car any more if you think us so terrible." She and Helen walked away, leaving the boys to discuss the sad days which had fallen upon the campus.

Emma Lou, of course, knew nothing of all this. She had gone her way rejoicing. One of the students had noticed her, had returned her smile. This getting acquainted was going to be an easy matter after all. It was just necessary that she exercise a little patience. One couldn't expect people to fall all over one without some preliminary advances. True, she was a stranger, but she would show them in good time that she was worthy of their attention, that she was a good fellow and a well-bred individual quite prepared to be accepted by the best people.

She strolled out on to the campus again trying to find more prospective acquaintances. The sun was warm now, the grass dry, and the campus overcrowded. There was an infectious germ of youth and gladness abroad to which Emma Lou could not remain immune. Already she was certain that she felt the presence of that vague something known as "college spirit." It seemed to enter into her, to make her jubilant and set her every nerve tingling. This was no time for sobriety. It was the time for youth's blood to run hot, the time for love and sport and wholesome fun.

Then Emma Lou saw a solitary Negro girl seated on a stone bench. It did not take her a second to decide what to do. Here was her chance. She would make friends with this girl and should she happen to be a new student, they could become friends and together find their way into the inner circle of those colored students who really mattered.

Emma Lou was essentially a snob. She had absorbed this trait from the very people who had sought to exclude her from their presence. All of her life she had heard talk of "right sort of people," and of "the people who really mattered," and from these phrases she had formed a mental image of those to whom they applied. Hazel Mason most certainly could not be included in either of these categories. Hazel was just a vulgar little nigger from down South. It was her kind, who, when they came North, made it hard for the colored people already resident there. It was her kind who knew nothing of the social niceties or the polite conventions. In their own home they had been used only to coarse work and coarser manners. And they had been forbidden the chance to have intimate contact in schools and in public with white people from whom they might absorb some semblance of culture. When they did come North and get a chance to go to white schools, white theaters, and white libraries, they were too unused to them to appreciate what they were getting, and could be expected to continue their old way of life in an environment where such a way was decidedly out of place.

Emma Lou was determined to become associated only with those people who really mattered, northerners like herself or superior southerners, if there were any, who were different from whites only in so far as skin color was concerned. This girl, to whom she was now about to introduce herself, was the type she had in mind, genteel, well and tastily dressed, and not ugly.

"Good morning."

Alma Martin looked up from the book she was reading, gulped in surprise, then answered, "Good morning."

Emma Lou sat down on the bench. She was congeniality itself. "Are you a new student?" she inquired of the astonished Alma, who wasn't used to this sort of thing.

"No, I'm a 'soph'," then realizing she was expected to say more, "you're new, aren't you?"

"Oh yes," replied Emma Lou, her voice buoyant and glad. "This will be my first year."

"Do you think you will like it?"

"I'm just crazy about it already. You know," she advanced confidentially, "I've never gone to school with any colored people before."

"No?"

"No, and I am just dying to get acquainted with the colored students. Oh, my name's Emma Lou Morgan."

"And mine is Alma Martin."

They both laughed. There was a moment of silence. Alma looked at her wrist watch, then got up from the bench.

"I'm glad to have met you. I've got to see my advisor at ten-thirty. Good-by." And she moved away gracefully.

Emma Lou was having difficulty in keeping from clapping her hands. At last she had made some headway. She had met a second-year student, one who, from all appearances, was in the know, and, who, as they met from time to time, would see that she met others. In a short time Emma Lou felt that she would be in the whirl of things collegiate. She must write to her Uncle Joe immediately and let him know how well things were going. He had been right. This was the place for her to be. There had been no one in Boise worth considering. Here she was coming into contact with really superior people, intelligent, genteel, college-bred, all trying to advance themselves and their race, unconscious of intra-racial schisms, caused by differences in skin color.

She mustn't stop upon meeting one person. She must find others, so once more she began her quest and almost immediately met Verne and Helen strolling down one of the campus paths. She remembered Verne as the girl who had smiled at her. She observed her more closely, and admired her pleasant dark brown face, made doubly attractive by two evenly placed dimples and a pair of large, heavily-lidded, pitch black eyes. Emma Lou thought her to be much more attractive than the anemic-looking yellow girl with whom she was strolling. There was something about this second girl which made Emma Lou feel that she was not easy to approach.

"Good morning." Emma Lou had evolved a formula.

"Good morning," the two girls spoke in unison. Helen was about to walk on but Verne stopped.

"New student?" she asked.

"Yes, I am."

"So am I. I'm Verne Davis."

"I'm Emma Lou Morgan."

"And this is Helen Wheaton."

"Pleased to meet you, Miss Morgan."

"And I'm pleased to meet you, too, both of you," gushed Emma Lou. "You see, I'm from Boise, Idaho, and all through high school I was the only colored student."

"Is that so?" Helen inquired listlessly. Then turning to Verne said, "Better come on Verne if you are going to drive us out to the 'Branch'."

"All right. We've got to run along now. We'll see you again, Miss Morgan. Good-by."

"Good-by," said Emma Lou and stood watching them as they went on their way. Yes, college life was going to be the thing to bring her out, the turning point in her life. She would show the people back in Boise that she did not have to be a "no-gooder" as they claimed her father had been, just because she was black. She would show all of them that a dark skin girl could go as far in life as a fair skin one, and that she could have as much opportunity and as much happiness. What did the color of one's skin have to do with one's mentality or native ability? Nothing whatsoever. If a black boy could get along in the world, so could a black girl, and it would take her, Emma Lou Morgan, to prove it.

With which she set out to make still more acquaintances.

Two weeks of school had left Emma Lou's mind in a chaotic state. She was unable to draw any coherent conclusions from the jumble of new things she had experienced. In addition to her own social strivings, there had been the academic routine to which she had had to adapt herself. She had found it all bewildering and overpowering. The university was a huge business proposition and every one in it had jobs to perform. Its bigness awed her. Its blatant reality shocked her. There was nothing romantic about going to college. It was, indeed, a serious business. One went there with a purpose and had several other purposes inculcated into one after school began. This getting an education was stern and serious, regulated and systematized, dull and unemotional.

Besides being disappointed at the drabness and lack of romance in college routine, Emma Lou was also depressed by her inability to make much headway in the matter of becoming intimately associated with her colored campus mates. They were all polite enough. They all acknowledged their introductions to her and would speak whenever they passed her, but seldom did any of them stop for a chat, and when she joined the various groups which gathered on the campus lawn between classes, she always felt excluded and out of things because she found herself unable to participate in the general conversation. They talked of things about which she knew nothing, of parties and dances, and of people she did not know. They seemed to live a life off the campus to which she was not privy, and into which they did not seem particularly anxious to introduce her.

She wondered why she never knew of the parties they talked about, and why she never received invitations to any of their affairs. Perhaps it was because she was still new and comparatively unknown to them. She felt that she must not forget that most of them had known one another for a long period of time and that it was necessary for people who "belonged" to be wary of strangers. That was it. She was still a stranger, had only been among them for about two weeks. What did she expect? Why was she so impatient?

The thought of the color question presented itself to her time and time again, but she would always dismiss it from her mind. Verne Davis was dark and she was not excluded from the sacred inner circle. In fact, she was one of the most popular colored girls on the campus. The only thing that perplexed Emma Lou was that although Verne too was new to the group, had just recently moved into the city, and was also just beginning her first year at the University, she had not been kept at a distance or excluded from any of the major extra-collegiate activities. Emma Lou could not understand why there should be this difference in their social acceptance. She was certainly as good as Verne.

In time Emma Lou became certain that it was because of her intimacy with Hazel that the people on the campus she really wished to be friendly with paid her so little attention. Hazel was a veritable clown. She went scooting about the campus, cutting capers, playing the darky for the amused white students. Any time Hazel asked or answered a question in any of the lecture halls, there was certain to be laughter. She had a way of phrasing what she wished to say in a manner which was invariably laugh provoking. The very tone and quality of her voice designated her as a minstrel type. In the gymnasium she would do buck and wing dances and play low-down blues on the piano. She was a pariah among her own people because she did not seem to know, as they knew, that Negroes could not afford to be funny in front of white people even if that was their natural inclination. Negroes must always be sober and serious in order to impress white people with their adaptability and non-difference in all salient characteristics save skin color. All of the Negro students on the campus, except Emma Lou, laughed at her openly and called her Topsy. Emma Lou felt sorry for her although she, too, regretted her comic propensities and wished that she would be less the vaudevillian and more the college student.

Besides Hazel, there was only one other person on the campus who was friendly with Emma Lou. This was Grace Giles, also a black girl, who was registered in the School of Music. The building in which she had her classes was located some distance away, and Grace did not get over to the main campus grounds very often, but when she did, she always looked for Emma Lou and made welcome overtures of friendship. It was her second year in the university, and yet, she too seemed to be on the outside of things. She didn't seem to be invited to the parties and dances, nor was she a member of the Greek letter sorority which the colored girls had organized. Emma Lou asked her why.

"Have they pledged you?" was Grace Giles' answer.

"Why no."

"And they won't either."

"Why?" Emma Lou asked surprised.

"Because you are not a high brown or half-white."

Emma Lou had thought this too, but she had been loathe to believe it.

"You're silly, Grace. Why—Verne belongs."

"Yeah," Grace had sneered, "Verne, a bishop's daughter with plenty of coin and a big Buick. Why shouldn't they ask her?"

Emma Lou did not know what to make of this. She did not want to believe that the same color prejudice which existed among the blue veins in Boise also existed among the colored college students. Grace Giles was just hypersensitive. She wasn't taking into consideration the fact that she was not on the campus regularly and thus could not expect to be treated as if she were. Emma Lou fully believed that had Grace been a regularly enrolled student like herself, she would have found things different, and she was also certain that both she and Grace would be asked to join the sorority in due time.

But they weren't. Nor did an entire term in the school change things one whit. The Christmas holidays had come and gone and Emma Lou had not been invited to one of the many parties. She and Grace and Hazel bound themselves together and sought their extra-collegiate pleasures among people not on the campus. Hazel began to associate with a group of housemaids and mature youths who worked only when they had to, and played the pool rooms and the housemaids as long as they proved profitable. Hazel was a welcome addition to this particular group what with her car and her full pocketbook. She had never been proficient in her studies, had always found it impossible to keep pace with the other students, and, finally realizing that she did not belong and perhaps never would, had decided to "go to the devil," and be done with it.

It was not long before Hazel was absent from the campus more often than she was present. Going to cabarets and parties, and taking long drunken midnight drives made her more and more unwilling and unable to undertake the scholastic grind on the next morning. Just before the mid-term examinations, she was advised by the faculty to drop out of school until the next year, and to put herself in the hands of a tutor during the intervening period. It was evident that her background was not all that it should be; her preparatory work had not been sufficiently complete to enable her to continue in college. As it was, they told her, she was wasting her time. So Hazel disappeared from the campus and was said to have gone back to Texas. "Serves her right, glad she's gone," was the verdict of her colored campus fellows.

The Christmas holidays for Emma Lou were dull and uneventful. The people she lived with were rheumatic and not much given to yuletide festivities. It didn't seem like Christmas to Emma Lou anyway. There was no snow on the ground, and the sun was shining as brightly and as warmly as it had shone during the late summer and early autumn months. The wild geraniums still flourished, the orange trees were blossoming, and the whole southland seemed to be preparing for the annual New Year's Day Tournament of Roses parade in Pasadena.

Emma Lou received a few presents from home, and a Christmas greeting card from Grace Giles. That was all. On Christmas Day she and Grace attended church in the morning, and spent the afternoon at the home of one of Grace's friends. Emma Lou never liked the people to whom Grace introduced her. They were a dull, commonplace lot for the most part, people from Georgia, Grace's former home, untutored people who didn't really matter. Emma Lou borrowed a word from her grandmother and classified them as "fuddlers," because they seemed to fuddle everything—their language, their clothes, their attempts at politeness, and their efforts to appear more intelligent than they really were.

The holidays over, Emma Lou returned to school a little reluctantly. She wasn't particularly interested in her studies, but having nothing else to do kept up in them and made high grades. Meanwhile she had been introduced to a number of young men and gone out with them occasionally. They too were friends of Grace's and of the same caliber as Grace's other friends. There were no college boys among them except Joe Lane who was flunking out in the School of Dentistry. He did not interest Emma Lou. As it was with Joe, so it was with all the other boys. She invariably picked them to pieces when they took her out, and remained so impassive to their emotional advances that they were soon glad to be on their way and let her be. Emma Lou was determined not to go out of her class, determined either to associate with the "right sort of people" or else to remain to herself.

Had any one asked Emma Lou what she meant by the "right sort of people" she would have found herself at a loss for a comprehensive answer. She really didn't know. She had a vague idea that those people on the campus who practically ignored her were the only people with whom she should associate. These people, for the most part, were children of fairly well-to-do families from Louisiana, Texas and Georgia, who, having made nest eggs, had journeyed to the West for the same reasons that her grandparents at an earlier date had also journeyed West. They wanted to live where they would have greater freedom and greater opportunity for both their children and themselves. Then, too, the World War had given impetus to this westward movement. There was more industry in the West and thus more chances for money to be made, and more opportunities to invest this money profitably in property and progeny.

The greater number of them were either mulattoes or light brown in color. In their southern homes they had segregated themselves from their darker skinned brethren and they continued this practice in the North. They went to the Episcopal, Presbyterian, or Catholic churches, and though they were not as frankly organized into a blue vein society as were the Negroes of Boise, they nevertheless kept more or less to themselves. They were not insistent that their children get "whiter and whiter every generation", but they did want to keep their children and grandchildren from having dark complexions. A light brown was the favored color; it was therefore found expedient to exercise caution when it came to mating.

The people who, in Emma Lou's phrase, really mattered, the business men, the doctors, the lawyers, the dentists, the more moneyed pullman porters, hotel waiters, bank janitors, and majordomos, in fact all of the Negro leaders and members of the Negro upper class, were either light skinned themselves or else had light skinned wives. A wife of dark complexion was considered a handicap unless she was particularly charming, wealthy, or beautiful. An ordinary looking dark woman was no suitable mate for a Negro man of prominence. The college youths on whom the future of the race depended practiced this precept of their elders religiously. It was not the girls in the school who were prejudiced—they had no reason to be, but they knew full well that the boys with whom they wished to associate, their future husbands, would not tolerate a dark girl unless she had, like Verne, many things to compensate for her dark skin. Thus they did not encourage a friendship with some one whom they knew didn't belong. Thus they did not even pledge girls like Grace, Emma Lou, and Hazel into their sorority, for they knew that it would make them the more miserable to attain the threshold only to have the door shut in their faces.

Summer vacation time came and Emma Lou went back to Boise. She was thoroughly discouraged and depressed. She had been led to expect so much pleasure from her first year in college and in Los Angeles; but she had found that the people in large cities were after all no different from people in small cities. Her Uncle Joe had been wrong—her mother and grandmother had been right. There was no place in the world for a dark girl.

Being at home depressed her all the more. There was absolutely nothing for her to do nor any place for her to go. For a month or more she just lingered around the house, bored by her mother's constant and difficult attempts to be maternal, and irritated by her Cousin Buddy's freshness. Adolescent boys were such a nuisance. The only bright spot on the horizon was the Sunday School Union picnic scheduled to be held during the latter part of July. It was always the crowning social event of the summer season among the colored citizens of Boise. Both the Methodists and Baptists missions cooperated in this affair and had their numbers augmented by all the denominationally unattached members of the community. It was always a gala, democratic affair designed to provide a pleasant day in the out-of-doors. It was, besides the annual dance fostered by the local chapters of the Masons and the Elks, the only big community gathering to which the entire colored population of Boise looked forward.

Picnic day came, and Emma Lou accompanied her mother, her uncle, and her cousin to Bedney's Meadow, a green, heavily forested acre of park land, which lay on the outskirts of the city, surrounded on three sides by verdant foothills. The day went by pleasantly enough. There were the usually heavily laden wooden tables, to which all adjourned in the late afternoon, and there were foot races, games, and canoeing.

Emma Lou took part in all these activities and was surprised to find that she was having a good time. The company was congenial, and she found that since she had gone away to college she had become somewhat of a personage. Every one seemed to be going out of his way to be congenial to her. The blue veins did not rule this affair. They were, in fact, only a minority element, and, for one of the few times of the year, mingled freely and unostentatiously with their lower caste brethren.

All during the day, Emma Lou found herself paired off with a chap by the name of Weldon Taylor. In the evening they went for a stroll up the precipitous footpaths in the hills which grew up from the meadow. Weldon Taylor was a newcomer in the West trying to earn sufficient money to re-enter an eastern school and finish his medical education. Emma Lou rather liked him. She admired his tall, slender body, the deep burnish of his bronze colored skin, and his mass of black curly hair. Here, thought Emma Lou, is the type of man I like. Only she did wish that his skin had been colored light brown instead of dark brown. It was better if she was to marry that she did not get a dark skin mate. Her children must not suffer as she had and would suffer.

The two talked of commonplace things as they walked along, comparing notes on their school experiences, and talking of their professors and their courses of study. It was dusk now and the sun had disappeared behind the snow capped mountains. The sky was a colorful haze, a master artist's canvas on which the colors of day were slowly being dominated by the colors of night. Weldon drew Emma Lou off the little path they had been following, and led her to a huge bowlder which jutted out, elbow like, from the side of a hill, and which was hidden from the meadow below by clumps of bushes. They sat down, his arm slipped around her waist, and, as the darkness of night more and more conquered the evanescent light of day, their lips met, and Emma Lou grew lax in Weldon's arms. . . .

When they finally returned to the picnic grounds all had left save a few stragglers like themselves who had sauntered away from the main party. These made up a laughing, half-embarrassed group, who collected their baskets and reluctantly withdrew from the meadow to begin the long walk back to their homes. Emma Lou and Weldon soon managed to fall at the end of the procession, walking along slowly, his arm around her waist. Emma Lou felt an ecstasy surging through her at this moment greater than she had ever known before. This had been her first intimate sexual contact, her first awareness of the physical and emotional pleasures able to be enjoyed by two human beings, a woman and a man. She felt some magnetic force drawing her to this man walking by her side, which made her long to feel the pleasure of his body against hers, made her want to know once more the pleasure which had attended the union of their lips, the touching of their tongues. It was with a great effort that she walked along apparently calm, for inside she was seething. Her body had become a kennel for clashing, screaming compelling urges and desires. She loved this man. She had submitted herself to him, had gladly suffered momentary physical pain in order to be introduced into a new and incomparably satisfying paradise.

Not for one moment did Emma Lou consider regretting the loss of her virtue, not once did any of her mother's and grandmother's warnings and solicitations revive themselves and cause her conscience to plague her. She had finally found herself a mate; she had finally come to know the man she should love, some inescapable force had drawn them together, had made them feel from the first moment of their introduction that they belonged to one another, and that they were destined to explore nature's mysteries together. Life was not so cruel after all. There were some compensatory moments. Emma Lou believed that at last she had found happiness, that at last she had found her man.

Of course, she wasn't going back to school. She was going to stay in Boise, marry Weldon, and work with him until they should have sufficient money to go East, where he could re-enter medical school, and she could keep a home for him and spur him on. A glorious panorama of the future unrolled itself in her mind. There were no black spots in it, no shadows, nothing but luminous landscapes, ethereal in substance.

It was the way of Emma Lou always to create her worlds within her own mind without taking under consideration the fact that other people and other elements, not contained within herself, would also have to aid in their molding. She had lived to herself for so long, had been shut out from the stream of things in which she was interested for such a long period during the formative years of her life, that she considered her own imaginative powers omniscient. Thus she constructed a future world of love on one isolated experience, never thinking for the moment that the other party concerned might not be of the same mind. She had been lifted into a superlatively perfect emotional and physical state. It was unthinkable, incongruous, that Weldon, too, had not been similarly lifted. He had for the moment shared her ecstasy, therefore, according to Emma Lou's line of reasoning, he would as effectively share what she imagined would be the fruits of that ecstatic moment.

The next two weeks passed quickly and happily. Weldon called on her almost every night, took her for long walks, and thrilled her with his presence and his love making. Never before in her life had Emma Lou been so happy. She forgot all the sad past. Forgot what she had hitherto considered the tragedy of her birth, forgot the social isolation of her childhood and of her college days. What did being black, what did the antagonistic mental attitudes of the people who really mattered mean when she was in love? Her mother and her Uncle Joe were so amazed at the change in her that they became afraid, sensed danger, and began to be on the look-out for some untoward development; for hitherto Emma Lou had always been sullen and morose and impertinent to all around the house. She had always been the anti-social creature they had caused her to feel she was and, since she was made to feel that she was a misfit, she had encroached upon their family life and sociabilities only to the extent that being in the house made necessary. But now she was changed—she had become a vibrant, joyful being. There was always a smile on her face, always a note of joy in her voice as she spoke or sang. She even made herself agreeable to her Cousin Buddy, who in the past she had either ignored or else barely tolerated.

"She must be in love, Joe," her mother half whined.

"That's good," he answered laconically. "It probably won't last long. It will serve to take her mind off herself."

"But suppose she gets foolish?" Jane had insisted, remembering no doubt her own foolishness, during a like period of her own life, with Emma Lou's father.

"She'll take care of herself," Joe had returned with an assurance he did not feel. He, too, was worried, but he was also pleased at the change in Emma Lou. His only fear was that perhaps in the end she would make herself more miserable than she had ever been before. He did not know much about this Weldon fellow, who seemed to be a reliable enough chap, but no one had any way of discerning whether or no his intentions were entirely honorable. It was best, thought Joe, not to worry about such things. If, for the present, Emma Lou was more happy than she had ever been before, there would be time enough to worry about the future when its problems materialized.

"Don't you worry about Emma Lou. She's got sense."

"But, Joe, suppose she does forget herself with this man? He is studying to be a doctor and he may not want a wife, especially when. . . ."

"Damn it, Jane!" her brother snapped at her. "Do you think every one is like you? The boy seems to like her."

"Men like any one they can use, but you know as well as I that no professional man is going to marry a woman dark as Emma Lou."

"Men marry any one they love, just as you and I did."

"But I was foolish."

"Well?"

"That's right—Be unconcerned. That's right—Let her go to the devil. There's no hope for her anyway. Oh—why—why did I marry Jim Morgan?" and she had gone into the usual crying fit which inevitably followed this self-put question.

Then, without any warning, as if to put an end to all problems, Weldon decided to become a Pullman porter. He explained to Emma Lou that he could make more money on the railroad than he could as a hotel waiter in Boise. It was necessary for his future that he make as much money as possible in as short a time as possible. Emma Lou saw the logic of this and agreed that it was the best possible scheme, until she realized that it meant his going away from Boise, perhaps forever. Oakland, California, was to be his headquarters, and he, being a new man, would not have a regular run. It was possible that he might be sent to different sections of the country each and every time he made a trip. There was no way of his knowing before he reported for duty just where he might be sent. It might be Boise or Palm Beach or Albany or New Orleans. One never knew. That was the life of the road, and one had to accept it in order to make money.

It made Emma Lou shiver to hear him talk so dispassionately about the matter. There didn't seem to be the least note of regret in his voice, the least suggestion that he hated to leave her or that he would miss her, and, for the first time since the night of their physical union, Emma Lou began to realize that perhaps after all he did not feel toward her as she did toward him. He couldn't possibly love her as much as she loved him, and, at the same time, remain so unconcerned about having to part from her. There was something radically wrong here, something conclusive and unexpected which was going to hurt her, going to plunge her back into unhappiness once more. Then she realized that not once had he ever spoken of marriage or even hinted that their relationship would continue indefinitely. He had said that he loved her, he had treated her kindly, and had seemed as thrilled as she over their physical contacts. But now it seemed that since he was no longer going to be near her, no longer going to need her body, he had forgotten that he loved her. It was then that all the old preachments of her mother and grandmother were resurrected and began to swirl through her mind. Hadn't she been warned that men didn't marry black girls? Hadn't she been told that they would only use her for their sexual convenience? That was the case with Weldon! He hadn't cared about her in the first place. He had taken up with her only because he was a stranger in the town and lonesome for a companion, and she, like a damn fool, had submitted herself to him! And now that he was about to better his condition, about to go some place where he would have a wider circle of acquaintances, she was to be discarded and forgotten.

Thus Emma Lou reasoned to herself and grew bitter. It never occurred to her that the matter of her color had never once entered the mind of Weldon. Not once did she consider that he was acting toward her as he would have acted toward any girl under similar circumstances, whether her face had been white, yellow, brown, or black. Emma Lou did not understand that Weldon was just a selfish normal man and not a color prejudiced one, at least not while he was resident in a community where the girls were few, and there were none of his college friends about to tease him for liking "dark meat." She did not know that for over a year he had been traveling about from town to town, always seeking a place where money was more plentiful and more easily saved, and that in every town he had managed to find a girl, or girls, who made it possible for him to continue his grind without being totally deprived of pleasurable moments. To Emma Lou there could only be one reason for his not having loved her as she had loved him. She was a black girl and no professional man could afford to present such a wife in the best society. It was the tragic feature of her life once more asserting itself. There could be no happiness in life for any woman whose face was as black as hers.

Believing this more intensely than ever before Emma Lou yet felt that she must manage in some way to escape both home and school. That she must find happiness somewhere else. The idea her Uncle Joe had given her about the provinciality of people in small towns re-entered her mind. After all Los Angeles, too, was a small town mentally, peopled by mentally small southern Negroes. It was no better than Boise. She was now determined to go East where life was more cosmopolitan and people were more civilized. To this end she begged her mother and uncle to send her East to school.

"Can't you ever be satisfied?"

"Now Jane," Joe as usual was trying to keep the peace——

"Now Jane, nothing! I never saw such an ungrateful child."

"I'm not ungrateful. I'm just unhappy. I don't like that school. I don't want to go there any more."

"Well, you'll either go there or else stay home." Thus Jane ended the discussion and could not be persuaded to reopen it.

And rather than remain home Emma Lou returned to Los Angeles and spent another long miserable, uneventful year in the University of Southern California, drawing more and more within herself and becoming more and more bitter. When vacation time came again she got herself a job as maid in a theater, rather than return home, and studied stenography during her spare hours. School began again and Emma Lou re-entered with more determination than ever to escape should the chance present itself. It did, and once more Emma Lou fled into an unknown town to escape the haunting chimera of intra-racial color prejudice.

PART II

Harlem

EMMA LOU turned her face away from the wall, and quizzically squinted her dark, pea-like eyes at the recently closed door. Then, sitting upright, she strained her ears, trying to hear the familiar squeak of the impudent floor boards, as John tiptoed down the narrow hallway toward the outside door. Finally, after she had heard the closing click of the double-barrelled police lock, she climbed out of the bed, picked up a brush from the bureau and attempted to smooth the sensuous disorder of her hair. She had just recently had it bobbed, boyishly bobbed, because she thought this style narrowed and enhanced the fulsome lines of her facial features. She was always trying to emphasize those things about her that seemed, somehow, to atone for her despised darkness, and she never faced the mirror without speculating upon how good-looking she might have been had she not been so black.

Mechanically, she continued the brushing of her hair, stopping every once in a while to give it an affectionate caress. She was intensely in love with her hair, in love with its electric vibrancy and its unruly buoyance. Yet, this morning, she was irritated because it seemed so determined to remain disordered, so determined to remain a stubborn and unnecessary reminder of the night before. Why, she wondered, should one's physical properties always insist upon appearing awry after a night of stolen or forbidden pleasure? But not being anxious to find an answer, she dismissed the question from her mind, put on a stocking-cap, and jumped back into the bed.

She began to think about John, poor John who felt so hurt because she had told him that he could not spend any more days or nights with her. She wondered if she should pity him, for she was certain that he would miss the nights more than he would the days. Yet, she must not be too harsh in her conclusions, for, after all, there had only been two nights, which, she smiled to herself, was a pretty good record for a newcomer to

Harlem. She had been in New York now for five weeks, and it seemed like, well, just a few days. Five weeks—thirty-five days and thirty-five nights, and of these nights John had had two. And now he sulked because she would not promise him another; because she had, in fact, boldly told him that there could be no more between them. Mischievously, she wished now that she could have seen the expression on his face, when, after seeming moments of mutual ecstasy, she had made this cold, manifesto-like announcement. But the room had been dark, and so was John. Ugh!

She had only written home twice. This, of course, seemed quite all right to her. She was not concerned about any one there except her Uncle Joe, and she reasoned that since he was preparing to marry again, he would be far too busy to think much about her. All that worried her was the pitiful spectacle of her mother, her uncle, and her cousin trying to make up lies to tell inquiring friends. Well, she would write today, that is, if she did not start to work, and she must get up at eight o'clock—was the alarm set?—and hie herself to an employment agency. She had only thirty-five dollars left in the bank, and, unless it was replenished, she might have to rescind her avowals to John in order to get her room rent paid.

She must go to sleep for another hour, for she wished to look "pert" when she applied for a job, especially the kind of job she wanted, and she must get the kind of job she wanted in order to show those people in Boise and Los Angeles that she had been perfectly justified in leaving school, home, and all, to come to New York. They all wondered why she had come. So did she, now that she was here. But at the moment of leaving she would have gone any place to escape having to remain in that hateful Southern California college, or having to face the more dreaded alternative of returning home. Home? It had never been a home.

It did seem strange, this being in Harlem when only a few weeks before she had been over three thousand miles away. Time and distance—strange things, immutable, yet conquerable. But was time conquerable? Hadn't she read or heard somewhere that all things were subject to time, even God? Yet, once she was there and now she was here. But even at that she hadn't conquered time. What was that line in Cullen's verse, "I run, but Time's abreast with me?" She had only traversed space and defied distance. This suggested a more banal, if a less arduous thought tangent. She had defied more than distance, she had defied parental restraint—still there hadn't been much of that —friendly concern—there had been still less of that, and malicious, meddlesome gossip, of which there had been plenty. And she still found herself unable to understand why two sets of people in two entirely different communities should seemingly become almost hysterically excited because she, a woman of twenty-one, with three years' college training and ample sophistication in the ways of sex and self-support, had decided to take a job as an actress' maid in order to get to New York. They had never seemed interested in her before.

Now she wondered why had she been so painfully anxious to come to New York. She had given as a consoling reason to inquisitive friends and relatives, school. But she knew too well that she had no intentions of ever re-entering school. She had had enough of *that* school in Los Angeles, and her experiences there, more than anything else, had caused this foolhardy hegira to Harlem. She had been desperately driven to escape, and had she not escaped in this manner she might have done something else much more mad.

Emma Lou closed her eyes once more, and tried to sublimate her mental reverie into a sleep-inducing lullaby. Most of all, she wanted to sleep. One had to look "pert" when one sought a job, and she wondered if eight o'clock would find her looking any more "pert" than she did at this present moment. What had caused her to urge John to spend what she knew would be his last night with her when she was so determined to be at her best the following morning! O, what the hell was the use? She was going to sleep.

The alarm had not yet rung, but Emma Lou was awakened gradually by the sizzling and smell of fried and warmed-over breakfast, by the raucous early morning wranglings and window to window greetings, and by the almost constant squeak of those impudent hall floor boards as the various people in her apartment raced one another to the kitchen or to the bathroom or to the front door. How could Harlem be so happily busy, so alive and merry at eight o'clock. Eight o'clock? The alarm rang. Emma Lou scuttled out of the bed and put on her clothes.

An hour later, looking as "pert" as possible, she entered the first employment agency she came to on 135th Street, between Lenox and Seventh Avenues. It was her first visit to such an establishment and she was particularly eager to experience this phase of a working girl's life. Her first four weeks in Harlem had convinced her that jobs were easy to find, for she had noticed that there were three or four employment agencies to every block in business Harlem. Assuring herself in this way that she would experience little difficulty in obtaining a permanent and tasty position, Emma Lou had abruptly informed Mazelle Lindsay that she was leaving her employ.

"But, child," her employer had objected, "I feel responsible for you. Your—your mother! Don't be preposterous. How can you remain in New York alone?"

Emma Lou had smiled, asked for her money once more, closed her ears to all protest, bid the chagrined woman goodbye, and joyously loafed for a week.

Now, with only thirty-five dollars left in the bank, she thought that she had best find a job—find a job and then finish seeing New York. Of course she had seen much already. She had seen John—and he—oh, damn John, she wanted a job.

"What can I do for you?" the harassed woman at the desk was trying to be polite.

"I—I want a job." R-r-ring. The telephone insistently petitioned for attention, giving Emma Lou a moment of respite, while the machine-like woman wearily shouted monosyllabic answers into the instrument, and, at the same time, tried to hush the many loud-mouthed men and women in the room, all, it seemed, trying to out-talk one another. While waiting, Emma Lou surveyed her fellow job-seekers. Seedy lot, was her verdict. Perhaps I should have gone to a more high-toned place. Well, this will do for the moment.

"What kinda job d'ye want?"

"I prefer," Emma Lou had rehearsed these lines for a week, "a stenographic position in some colored business or professional office."

" 'Ny experience?"

"No, but I took two courses in business college, during school vacations. I have a certificate of competency."

" 'Ny reference?"

"No New York ones."

"Where'd ya work before?"

"I—I just came to the city."

"Where'd ya come . . . ?" R-r-ring. The telephone mercifully reiterated its insistent blare, and, for a moment, kept that pesky woman from droning out more insulting queries.

"Now," she had finished again, "where'd ya come from?"

"Los Angeles."

"Ummm. What other kind of work would ya take?"

"Anything congenial."

"Waal, what is that, dishwashing, day work, nurse girl?"

Didn't this damn woman know what congenial meant? And why should a Jewish woman be in charge of a Negro employment agency in Harlem?

"Waal, girlie, others waiting."

"I'll consider anything you may have on hand, if stenographic work is not available."

"Wanta work part-time?"

"I'd rather not."

"Awright. Sit down. I'll call you in a moment."

"What can I do for you, young man?" Emma Lou was dismissed.

She looked for a place to sit down, and, finding none, walked across the narrow room to the window, hoping to get a breath of fresh air, and at the same time an advantageous position from which to watch the drama of some one else playing the rôle of a job-seeker.

R-r-ring.

"Whadda want? Wait a minute. Oh, Sadie."

A heavy set, dark-brown-skinned woman, with full, flopping breasts, and extra wide buttocks, squirmed off a too narrow chair, and bashfully wobbled up to the desk.

"Wanta' go to a place on West End Avenue? Part-time cleaning, fifty cents an hour, nine rooms, yeah? All right? Hello, gotta girl on the way. 'Bye. Two and a half, Sadie. Here's the address. Run along now, don't idle."

R-r-ring. " 'Lo, yes. What? Come down to the office. I can't sell jobs over the wire."

Emma Lou began to see the humor in this sordid situation, began to see something extremely comic in all these plaintive, pitiful-appearing colored folk, some greasy, some neat, some fat, some slim, some brown, some black (why was there only one mulatto in this crowd?), boys and men, girls and women, all single-filing up to the desk, laconically answering laconic questions, impertinently put, showing thanks or sorrow or in-difference, as their cases warranted, paying off promptly, or else seeking credit, the while the Jewish overseer of the dirty, dingy office asserted and reasserted her superiority.

Some one on the outside pushed hard on the warped door. Protestingly it came open, and the small stuffy room was filled with the odor and presence of a stout, black lady dressed in a greasy gingham housedress, still damp in the front from splash-ing dishwater. On her head was a tight turban, too round for the rather long outlines of her head. Beneath this turban could be seen short and wiry strands of recently straightened hair. And her face! Emma Lou sought to observe it more closely, sought to fathom how so much grease could gather on one woman's face. But her head reeled. The room was vile with noise and heat and body-smells, and this woman——

"Hy, Rosie, yer late. Got a job for ya."

The greasy-faced black woman grinned broadly, licked her pork chop lips and, with a flourish, sat down in an empty chair beside the desk. Emma Lou stumbled over three pairs of num-ber ten shoes, pulled open the door and fled into the street.

She walked hurriedly for about twenty-five yards, then slowed down and tried to collect her wits. Telephone bells echoed in her ears. Sour smells infested her nostrils. She looked up and discovered that she had paused in front of two garbage cans, waiting on the curbstone for the scavenger's truck.

Irritated, she turned around and retraced her steps. There were few people on the street. The early morning work crowds had already been swallowed by the subway kiosks on Lenox Avenue, and it was too early for the afternoon idlers. Yet there was much activity, much passing to and fro. One Hundred and Thirty-Fifth Street, Emma Lou mumbled to herself as she strolled along. How she had longed to see it, and what a different thoroughfare she had imagined it to be! Her eyes sought the opposite side of the street and blinked at a line of monotonously regular fire-escape-decorated tenement buildings. She thanked whoever might be responsible for the architectural difference of the Y.M.C.A., for the streaming bit of Seventh Avenue near by, and for the arresting corner of the newly constructed teachers' college building, which dominated the hill three blocks away, and cast its shadows on the verdure of the terraced park beneath.

But she was looking for a job. Sour smells assailed her nostrils once more. Rasping voices. Pleading voices. Tired voices. Domineering voices. And the insistent ring of the telephone bell all re-echoed in her head and beat against her eardrums. She must have staggered, for a passing youth eyed her curiously, and shouted to no one in particular, "oh, *no*, now." Some one else laughed. They thought she was drunk. Tears blurred her eyes. She wanted to run, but resolutely she kept her steady, slow pace, lifted her head a little higher, and, seeing another employment agency, faltered for a moment, then went in.

This agency, like the first, occupied the ground floor front of a tenement house, three-quarters of the way between Lenox and Seventh Avenue. It was cagey and crowded, and there was a great conversational hubbub as Emma Lou entered. In the rear of the room was a door marked "private," to the left of this door was a desk, littered with papers and index cards, before which was a swivel chair. The rest of the room was lined with a miscellaneous assortment of chairs, three rows of them, tied together and trying to be precise despite their varying sizes and shapes. A single window looked out upon the street, and the Y.M.C.A. building opposite.

All of the chairs were occupied and three people stood lined up by the desk. Emma Lou fell in at the end of this line. There was nothing else to do. In fact, it was all she could do after entering. Not another person could have been squeezed into that room from the outside. This office too was noisy and hot and pregnant with clashing body smells. The buzzing electric fan, in a corner over the desk, with all its whirring, could not stir up a breeze.

The rear door opened. A slender, light-brown-skinned boy,

his high cheekbones decorated with blackheads, his slender form accentuated by a tight fitting jazz suit of the high-waist-line, one-button coat, bell-bottom trouser variety, emerged smiling broadly, cap in one hand, a slip of pink paper in the other. He elbowed his way to the outside door and was gone.

"Musta got a job," somebody commented. "It's about time," came from some one else, "he said he'd been sittin' here a week."

The rear door opened again and a lady with a youthful brown face and iron-gray hair sauntered in and sat down in the swivel chair before the desk. Immediately all talk in the outer office ceased. An air of anticipation seemed to pervade the room. All eyes were turned toward her.

For a moment she fingered a pack of red index cards, then, as if remembering something, turned around in her chair and called out:

"Mrs. Blake says for all elevator men to stick around."

There was a shuffling of feet and a settling back into chairs. Noticing this, Emma Lou counted six elevator men and wondered if she was right. Again the brown aristocrat with the tired voice spoke up:

"Day workers come back at one-thirty. Won't be nothing doin' 'til then."

Four women, all carrying newspaper packages, got out of their chairs, and edged their way toward the door, murmuring to one another as they went, "I ain't fixin' to come back."

"Ah, she keeps you hyar."

They were gone.

Two of the people standing in line sat down, the third approached the desk, Emma Lou close behind.

"I wantsa—"

"What kind of job do you want?"

Couldn't people ever finish what they had to say?

"Porter or dishwashing, lady."

"Are you registered with us?"

"No'm."

"Have a seat. I'll call you in a moment."

The boy looked frightened, but he found a seat and slid into it gratefully. Emma Lou approached the desk. The woman's cold eyes appraised her. She must have been pleased with what she saw for her eyes softened and her smile reappeared. Emma Lou smiled, too. Maybe she was "pert" after all. The tailored blue suit——

"What can I do for you?"

The voice with the smile wins. Emma Lou was encouraged.

"I would like stenographic work."

"Experienced?"

"Yes." It was so much easier to say than "no."

"Good."

Emma Lou held tightly to her under-arm bag.

"We have something that would just about suit you. Just a minute, and I'll let you see Mrs. Blake."

The chair squeaked and was eased of its burden. Emma Lou thought she heard a telephone ringing somewhere in the distance, or perhaps it was the clang of the street car that had just passed, heading for Seventh Avenue. The people in the room began talking again.

"Dat last job." "Boy, she was dressed right down to the bricks."

"And I told him. . . ." "Yeah, we went to see 'Flesh and the Devil'." "Some parteee." "I just been here a week."

Emma Lou's mind became jumbled with incoherent wisps of thought. Her left foot beat a nervous tattoo upon a sagging floor board. The door opened. The gray-haired lady with the smile in her voice beckoned, and Emma Lou walked into the private office of Mrs. Blake.

Four people in the room. The only window facing a brick wall on the outside. Two telephones, both busy. A good-looking young man, fingering papers in a filing cabinet, while he talked over one of the telephones. The lady from the outer office. Another lady, short and brown, like butterscotch, talking over a desk telephone and motioning for Emma Lou to sit down. Blur of high powered electric lights, brighter than daylight. The butterscotch lady hanging up the receiver.

"I'm through with you young man." Crisp tones. Metal, warm in spite of itself.

"Well, I ain't through with you." The fourth person was speaking. Emma Lou had hardly noticed him before. Sullen face. Dull black eyes in watery sockets. The nose flat, the lips thick and pouting. One hand clutching a derby, the other clenched, bearing down on the corner of the desk.

"I have no intention of arguing with you. I've said my say. Go on outside. When a cook's job comes in, you can have it. That's all I can do."

"No, it ain't all you can do."

"Well, I'm not going to give you your fee back."

The lady from the outside office returns to her post. The good-looking young man is at the telephone again.

"Why not, I'm entitled to it."

"No, you're not. I send you on a job, the man asks you to do something, you walk out, Mister Big I-am. Then, show up here two days later and want your fee back. No siree."

"I didn't walk out."

"The man says you did."

"Aw, sure, he'd say anything. I told him I came there to be a cook, not a waiter. I——"

"It was your place to do as he said, then, if not satisfied, to come here and tell me so."

"I am here."

"All right now. I'm tired of this. Take either of two courses— go on outside and wait until a job comes in or else go down to the license bureau and tell them your story. They'll investigate. If I'm right——"

"You know you ain't right."

"Not according to you, no, but by law, yes. That's all."

Telephone ringing. Warm metal whipping words into it. The good-looking young man yawning. He looks like a Y.M.C.A. secretary. The butterscotch woman speaking to Emma Lou:

"You're a stenographer?"

"Yes."

"I have a job in a real estate office, nice firm, nice people. Fill out this card. Here's a pen."

"Mrs. Blake, you know you ain't doin' right."

Why didn't this man either shut up or get out?

"I told you what to do. Now please do one or the other. You've taken up enough of my time. The license bureau——"

"You know I ain't goin' down there. I'd rather you keep the fee, if you think it will do you any good."

"I only keep what belongs to me. I've found out that's the best policy."

Why should they want three people for reference? Where had she worked before? Lies. Los Angeles was far away.

"Then, if a job comes in you'll give it to me?"

"That's what I've been trying to tell you."

"Awright." And finally he went out.

Mrs. Blake grinned across the desk at Emma Lou. "Your folks won't do, honey."

"Do you have many like that?"

The card was made out. Mrs. Blake had it in her hand. Telephones ringing, both at once. Loud talking in the outer office. Lies. Los Angeles was far away. I can bluff. Mrs. Blake had finished reading over the card.

"Just came to New York, eh?"

"Yes."

"Like it better than Los Angeles?"

The good-looking young man turned around and stared at her coldly. Now he did resemble a Y.M.C.A. secretary. The lady from the outer office came in again. There was a triple criss-cross conversation carried on. It ended. The short bob-haired butterscotch boss gave Emma Lou instructions and information about her prospective position. She was half heard. Sixteen dollars a week. Is that all? Work from nine to five. Address on card. Corner of 139th Street, left side of the avenue. Dismissal. Smiles and good luck. Pay the lady outside five dollars. Awkward, flustered moments. Then the entrance door and 135th Street once more. Emma Lou was on her way to get a job.

She walked briskly to the corner, crossed the street and turned north on Seventh Avenue. Her hopes were high, her mind a medley of pleasing mental images. She visualized herself trim and pert in her blue tailored suit being secretary to some well-groomed Negro business man. There had not been many such in the West, and she was eager to know and admire one. There would be other girls in the office, too, girls who, like herself, were college trained and reared in cultured homes, and through these fellow workers she would meet still other girls and men, get in with the right sort of people.

She continued day-dreaming as she went her way, being practical only at such fleeting moments when she would wonder,—would she be able to take dictation at the required rate of speed?—would her fingers be nimble enough on the keyboard of the typewriter? Oh, bother. It wouldn't take her over one day to adapt herself to her new job.

A street crossing. Traffic delayed her and she was conscious of a man, a blurred tan image, speaking to her. He was ignored. Everything was to be ignored save the address digits on the buildings. Everything was secondary to the business at hand. Let traffic pass, let men aching for flirtations speak, let Seventh Avenue be spangled with forenoon sunshine and shadow, and polka-dotted with still or moving human forms. She was going to have a job. The rest of the world could go to hell.

Emma Lou turned into a four-story brick building and sped up one flight of stairs. The rooms were not numbered and directing signs in the hallway only served to confuse. But Emma Lou was not to be delayed. She rushed back and forth from door to door on the first floor, then to the second, until she finally found the office she was looking for.

Angus and Brown were an old Harlem real estate firm. They had begun business during the first decade of the century, handling property for a while in New York's far-famed San Juan Hill district. When the Negro population had begun to need more and better homes, Angus and Brown had led the way in buying real estate in what was to be Negro Harlem. They had been fighters, unscrupulous and canny. They had revealed a perverse delight in seeing white people rush pell-mell from the neighborhood in which they obtained homes for their colored clients. They had bought three six-story tenement buildings on 140th Street, and, when the white tenants had been slow in moving, had personally dispossessed them, and, in addition, had helped their incoming Negro tenants fight fistic battles in the streets and hallways, and legal battles in the court.

Now they were a substantial firm, grown fat and satisfied. Junior real estate men got their business for them. They held the whip. Their activities were many and varied. Politics and fraternal activities occupied more of their time than did real estate. They had had their hectic days. Now they sat back and took it easy.

Emma Lou opened the door to their office, consisting of one

medium-sized outer room overlooking 139th Street and two cubby holes overlooking Seventh Avenue. There were two girls in the outer office. One was busy at a typewriter; the other was gazing over her desk through a window into the aristocratic tree-lined city lane of 139th Street. Both looked up expectantly. Emma Lou noticed the powdered smoothness of their fair skins and the marcelled waviness of their shingled brown hair. Were they sisters? Hardly, for their features were in no way similar. Yet that skin color and that brown hair——.

"Can I do something for you?" The idle one spoke, and the other ceased her peck-peck-pecking on the typewriter keys. Emma Lou was buoyant.

"I'm from Mrs. Blake's employment agency."

"Oh," from both. And they exchanged glances. Emma Lou thought she saw a quickly suppressed smile from the fairer of the two as she hastily resumed her typing. Then——

"Sit down a moment, won't you, please? Mr. Angus is out, but I'll inform Mr. Brown that you are here." She picked a powder puff from an open side drawer in her desk, patted her nose and cheeks, then got up and crossed the office to enter cubby hole number one. Emma Lou observed that she, too, looked "pert" in a trim, blue suit and high-heeled patent leather oxfords——

"Mr. Brown?" She had opened the door.

"Come in Grace. What is it?" The door was closed.

Emma Lou felt nervous. Something in the pit of her stomach seemed to flutter. Her pulse raced. Her eyes gleamed and a smile of anticipation spread over her face, despite her efforts to appear dignified and suave. The typist continued her work. From the cubby hole came a murmur of voices, one feminine and affected, the other masculine and coarse. Through the open window came direct sounds and vagrant echoes of traffic noises from Seventh Avenue. Now the two in the cubby hole were laughing, and the girl at the typewriter seemed to be smiling to herself as she worked.

What did this mean? Nothing, silly. Don't be so sensitive. Emma Lou's eyes sought the pictures on the wall. There was an early twentieth century photographic bust-portrait, encased in a bevelled glass frame, of a heavy-set good-looking, brown-skinned man. She admired his mustache. Men didn't seem to take pride in such hirsute embellishments now. Mustaches these days were abbreviated and limp. They no longer were virile enough to dominate and make a man's face appear more strong. Rather, they were only insignificant patches weakly keeping the nostrils from merging with the upper lip.

Emma Lou wondered if that was Mr. Brown. He had a brown face and wore a brown suit. No, maybe that was Mr. Angus, and perhaps that was Mr. Brown on the other side of the room, in the square, enlarged kodak print, a slender yellow man, standing beside a motor car, looking as if he wished to say, "Yeah, this is me and this is my car." She hoped he was Mr. Angus. She didn't like his name and since she was to see Mr. Brown first, she hoped he was the more flatteringly portrayed.

The door to the cubby hole opened and the girl Mr. Brown had called Grace, came out. The expression on her face was too business-like to be natural. It seemed as if it had been placed there for a purpose.

She walked toward Emma Lou, who got up and stood like a child, waiting for punishment and hoping all the while that it will dissipate itself in threats. The typewriter was stilled and Emma Lou could feel an extra pair of eyes looking at her. The girl drew close then spoke:

"I'm sorry, Miss. Mr. Brown says he has some one else in view for the job. We'll call the agency. Thank you for coming in."

Thank her for coming in? What could she say? What should she say? The girl was smiling at her, but Emma Lou noticed that her fair skin was flushed and that her eyes danced nervously. Could she be hoping that Emma Lou would hurry and depart? The door was near. It opened easily. The steps were steep. One went down slowly. Seventh Avenue was still spangled with forenoon sunshine and shadow. Its pavement was hard and hot. The windows in the buildings facing it, gleaming reflectors of the mounting sun.

Emma Lou returned to the employment agency. It was still crowded and more stuffy than ever. The sun had advanced high into the sky and it seemed to be centering its rays on that solitary defenseless window. There was still much conversation. There were still people crowded around the desk, still people in all the chairs, people and talk and heat and smells.

"Mrs. Blake is waiting for you," the gray-haired lady with the young face was unflustered and cool. Emma Lou went into the inner office. Mrs. Blake looked up quickly and forced a smile. The good-looking young man, more than ever resembling a Y.M.C.A. secretary, turned his back and fumbled with the card files. Mrs. Blake suggested that he leave the room. He did, beaming benevolently at Emma Lou as he went.

"I'm sorry," Mrs. Blake was very kind and womanly. "Mr. Brown called me. I didn't know he had some one else in mind. He hadn't told me."

"That's all right," replied Emma Lou briskly. "Have you something else?"

"Not now. Er-er. Have you had luncheon? It's early yet, I know, but I generally go about this time. Come along, won't you, I'd like to talk to you. I'll be ready in about thirty minutes if you don't mind the wait."

Emma Lou warmed to the idea. At that moment, she would have warmed toward any suggestion of friendliness. Here, perhaps, was a chance to make a welcome contact. She was lonesome and disappointed, so she readily assented and felt elated and superior as she walked out of the office with the "boss."

They went to Eddie's for luncheon. Eddie's was an elbow-shaped combination lunch-counter and dining room that embraced a United Cigar Store on the northeast corner of 135th Street and Seventh Avenue. Following Mrs. Blake's lead, Emma Lou ordered a full noontime dinner, and, flattered by Mrs. Blake's interest and congeniality, began to talk about herself. She told of her birthplace and her home life. She told of her high school days, spoke proudly of the fact that she had been the only Negro student and how she had graduated cum laude. Asked about her college years, she talked less freely. Mrs. Blake sensed a cue.

"Didn't you like college?"

"For a little while, yes."

"What made you dislike it? Surely not the studies?"

"No." She didn't care to discuss this. "I was lonesome, I guess."

"Weren't there any other colored boys and girls? I thought. . . ."

Emma Lou spoke curtly. "Oh, yes, quite a number, but I suppose I didn't mix well."

The waiter came to take the order for dessert, and Emma Lou seized upon the fact that Mrs. Blake ordered sliced oranges to talk about California's orange groves, California's sunshine—anything but the California college she had attended and from which she had fled. In vain did Mrs. Blake try to maneuver the conversation back to Emma Lou's college experiences. She would have none of it and Mrs. Blake was finally forced to give it up.

When they were finished, Mrs. Blake insisted upon taking the check. This done, she began to talk about jobs.

"You know, Miss Morgan, good jobs are rare. It is seldom I have anything to offer outside of the domestic field. Most Negro business offices are family affairs. They either get their help from within their own family group or from among their friends. Then, too," Emma Lou noticed that Mrs. Blake did not look directly at her, "lots of our Negro business men have a definite type of girl in mind and will not hire any other."

Emma Lou wondered what it was Mrs. Blake seemed to be holding back. She began again:

"My advice to you is that you enter Teachers' College and if you *will* stay in New York, get a job in the public school system. You can easily take a light job of some kind to support you through your course. Maybe with three years' college you won't need to go to training school. Why don't you find out about that? Now, if I were you. . . ." Mrs. Blake talked on, putting much emphasis on every "If I were you."

Emma Lou grew listless and antagonistic. She didn't like this little sawed-off woman as she was now, being business like and giving advice. She was glad when they finally left Eddie's, and more than glad to escape after having been admonished not to oversleep, "But be in my office, and I'll see what I can do for you, dearie, early in the morning. There's sure to be something."

Left to herself, Emma Lou strolled south on the west side of Seventh Avenue to 134th Street, then crossed over to the east side and turned north. She didn't know what to do. It was too late to consider visiting another employment agency, and, furthermore, she didn't have enough money left to pay another fee. Let jobs go until tomorrow, then she would return to Mrs. Blake's, ask for a return of her fee, and find some other

employment agency, a more imposing one, if possible. She had
had enough of those on 135th Street.

She didn't want to go home, either. Her room had no outside vista. If she sat in the solitary chair by the solitary window,
all she could see were other windows and brick walls and people
either mysteriously or brazenly moving about in the apartments across the court. There was no privacy there, little fresh
air, and no natural light after the sun began its downward
course. Then the apartment always smelled of frying fish or of
boiling cabbage. Her landlady seemed to alternate daily between these two foods. Fish smells and cabbage smells pervaded the long, dark hallway, swirled into the room when the
door was opened and perfumed one's clothes disagreeably.
Moreover, urinal and foecal smells surged upward from the
garbage-littered bottom of the court which her window faced.

If she went home, the landlady would eye her suspiciously
and ask, "Ain't you got a job yet?" then move away, shaking
her head and dipping into her snuff box. Occasionally, in moments of excitement, she spat on the floor. And the little fat
man who had the room next to Emma Lou's could be heard
coughing suggestively—tapping on the wall, and talking to
himself in terms of her. He had seen her slip John in last night.
He might be more bold now. He might even try—oh no he
wouldn't.

She was crossing 137th Street. She remembered this corner.
John had told her that he could always be found there after
work any spring or summer evening.

Emma Lou had met John on her first day in New York. He
was employed as a porter in the theatre where Mazelle Lindsay
was scheduled to perform, and, seeing a new maid on the
premises, had decided to "make" her. He had. Emma Lou had
not liked him particularly, but he had seemed New Yorkish and
genial. It was John who had found her her room. It was John
who had taught her how to find her way up and down town
on the subway and on the elevated. He had also conducted her
on a Cook's tour of Harlem, had strolled up and down Seventh
Avenue with her evenings after they had come uptown from
the theater. He had pointed out for her the Y.W.C.A. with its
imposing annex, the Emma Ranson House, and suggested that
she get a room there later on. He had taken her on a Sunday

to several of the Harlem motion picture and vaudeville theaters, and he had been as painstaking in pointing out the
churches as he had been lax in pointing out the cabarets.
Moreover, as they strolled Seventh Avenue, he had attempted
to give her all the "inside dope" on Harlem, had told her of
the "rent parties," of the "numbers," of "hot" men, of "sweetbacks," and other local phenomena.

Emma Lou was now passing a barber shop near 140th
Street. A group of men were standing there beneath a huge
white and black sign announcing, "Bobbing's, fifty cents; hair-
cuts, twenty-five cents." They were whistling at three school
girls, about fourteen or fifteen years of age, who were passing,
doing much switching and giggling. Emma Lou curled her
lips. Harlem streets presented many such scenes. She looked at
the men significantly, forgetting for the moment that it was
none of her business what they or the girls did. But they didn't
notice her. They were too busy having fun with those fresh little
chippies.

Emma Lou experienced a feeling of resentment, then, realizing how ridiculous it all was, smiled it away and began to
think of John once more. She wondered why she had submitted herself to him. Was it cold-blooded payment for his kind
chaperoning? Something like that. John wasn't her type. He
was too pudgy and dark, too obviously an ex-cotton-picker
from Georgia. He was unlettered and she couldn't stand for
that, for she liked intelligent-looking, slender, light-brown-
skinned men, like, well . . . like the one who was just passing.
She admired him boldly. He looked at her, then over her, and
passed on.

Seventh Avenue was becoming more crowded now. School
children were out for their lunch hour, corner loafers and pool-
hall loiterers were beginning to collect on their chosen spots.
Knots of people, of no particular designation, also stood around
talking, or just looking, and there were many pedestrians,
either impressing one as being in a great hurry, or else seeming
to have no place at all to go. Emma Lou was in this latter class.
By now she had reached 142nd Street and had decided to cross
over to the opposite side and walk south once more. Seventh
Avenue was a wide, well-paved, busy thoroughfare, with a long,
narrow, iron fenced-in parkway dividing the east side from the

west. Emma Lou liked Seventh Avenue. It was so active and alive, so different from Central Avenue, the dingy main street of the black belt of Los Angeles. At night it was glorious! Where else could one see so many different types of Negroes? Where else would one view such a heterogeneous ensemble of mellow colors, glorified by the night?

People passing by. Children playing. Dogs on leashes. Stray cats crouching by the sides of buildings. Men standing in groups or alone. Black men. Yellow men. Brown men. Emma Lou eyed them. They eyed her. There were a few remarks passed. She thought she got their import even though she could not hear what they were saying. She quickened her step and held her head higher. Be yourself, Emma Lou. Do you want to start picking men up off of the street?

The heat became more intense. Brisk walking made her perspire. Her underclothes grew sticky. Harlem heat was so muggy. She could feel the shine on her nose and it made her self-conscious. She remembered how the "Grace" in the office of Angus and Brown had so carefully powdered her skin before confronting her employer, and, as she remembered this, she looked up, and sure enough, here she was in front of the building she had sought so eagerly earlier that morning. Emma Lou drew closer to the building. She must get that shine off of her nose. It was bad enough to be black, too black, without having a shiny face to boot. She stopped in front of the tailor shop directly beneath the office of Angus and Brown, and, turning her back to the street, proceeded to powder her shiny member. Three noisy lads passed by. They saw Emma Lou and her reflection in the sunlit show window. The one closest to her cleared his throat and crooned out, loud enough for her to hear, "There's a girl for you, 'Fats.'" "Fats" was the one in the middle. He had a rotund form and a coffee-colored face. He was in his shirt sleeves and carried his coat on his arm. Bell bottom trousers hid all save the tips of his shiny tan shoes. "Fats" was looking at Emma Lou, too, but as he passed, he turned his eyes from her and broadcast a withering look at the lad who had spoken:

"Man, you know I don't haul no coal." There was loud laughter and the trio merrily clicked their metal-cornered heels on the sun-baked pavement as they moved away.

PART III

Alva

IT WAS nine o'clock. The alarm rang. Alva's roommate awoke
cursing.

"Why the hell don't you turn off that alarm?"

There was no response. The alarm continued to ring.

"Alva!" Braxton yelled into his sleeping roommate's ear,
"Turn off that clock. Wake up," he began shaking him, "Wake
up, damn you . . . ya dead?"

Alva slowly emerged from his stupor. Almost mechanically
he reached for the clock, dancing merrily on a chair close to
the bed, and, finding it, pushed the guilty lever back into the
silent zone. Braxton watched him disgustedly:

"Watcha gettin' up so early for? Don'tcha know this is Monday?"

"Shure, I know it's Monday, but I gotta go to Uncle's. The
landlord'll be here before eleven o'clock."

"Watcha gonna pawn?"

"My brown suit. I won't need it 'til next Sunday. You got your
rent?"

"I got four dollars," Braxton advanced slowly.

"Cantcha get the other two?"

Braxton grew apologetic and explanatory, "Not today . . .
ya . . . see. . . ."

"Aw, man, you make me sick."

Disgust overcoming his languor, Alva got out of the bed.
This was getting to be a regular Monday morning occurrence.
Braxton was always one, two or three dollars short of having
his required half of the rent, and Alva, who had rented the
room, always had to make it up. Luckily for Alva, both he and
the landlord were Elks. Fraternal brothers must stick together.
Thus it was an easy matter to pay the rent in installments. The
only difficulty being that it was happening rather frequently.
There is liable to be a limit even to a brother Elk's patience, especially where money is concerned.

Alva put on his dressing gown, and his house shoes, then went into the little alcove which was curtained off in the rear from the rest of the room. Jumbled together on the marble topped stationary washstand were a half dozen empty gin bottles bearing a pre-prohibition Gordon label, a similar number of empty ginger ale bottles, a cocktail shaker, and a medley of assorted cocktail, water, jelly and whiskey glasses, filled and surrounded by squeezed orange and lemon rinds. The little two-burner gas plate atop a wooden dry goods box was covered with dirty dishes, frying pan, egg shells, bacon rinds, and a dominating though lopsided tea kettle. Even Alva's trunk, which occupied half the entrance space between the alcove and the room, littered as it was with paper bags, cracker boxes and greasy paper plates, bore evidence of the orgy which the occupants of the room staged over every weekend.

Alva surveyed this rather intimate and familiar disorder, faltered a moment, started to call Braxton, then remembering previous Monday mornings set about his task alone. It was Braxton's custom never to arise before noon. Alva who worked as a presser in a costume house was forced to get up at seven o'clock on every week day save Monday when he was not required to report for work until twelve o'clock. His employers thus managed to accumulate several baskets of clothes from the sewing room before their pressers arrived. It was better to have them remain at home until this was done. Then you didn't have to pay them so much, and having let the sewing room get head start, there was never any chance for the pressing room to slow down.

Alva's mother had been an American mulatto, his father a Filipino. Alva himself was small in stature as his father had been, small and well developed with broad shoulders, narrow hips and firm well modeled limbs. His face was oval shaped and his features more oriental than Negroid. His skin was neither yellow nor brown but something in between, something warm, arresting and mellow with the faintest suggestion of a parchment tinge beneath, lending it individuality. His eyes were small, deep and slanting. His forehead high, hair sparse and finely textured.

The alcove finally straightened up, Alva dressed rather

hurriedly, and, taking a brown suit from the closet, made his regular Monday morning trip to the pawn shop.

Emma Lou finished rinsing out some silk stockings and sat down in a chair to reread a letter she had received from home that morning. It was about the third time she had gone over it. Her mother wanted her to come home. Evidently the home-town gossips were busy. No doubt they were saying, "Strange mother to let that gal stay in New York alone. She ain't goin' to school, either. Wonder what she's doin'?" Emma Lou read all this between the lines of what her mother had written. Jane Morgan was being tearful as usual. She loved to suffer, and being tearful seemed the easiest way to let the world know that one was suffering. Sob stuff, thought Emma Lou, and, tearing the letter up, threw it into the waste paper basket.

Emma Lou was now maid to Arline Strange, who was play-ing for the moment the part of a mulatto Carmen in an alleged melodrama of Negro life in Harlem. Having tried, for two weeks to locate what she termed "congenial work," Emma Lou had given up the idea and meekly returned to Mazelle Lindsay. She had found her old job satisfactorily filled, but Mazelle had been sympathetic and had arranged to place her with Arline Strange. Now her mother wanted her to come home. Let her want. She was of age, and supporting herself. Moreover, she felt that if it had not been for gossip her mother would never have thought of asking her to come home.

"Stop your mooning, dearie." Arline Strange had returned to her dressing room. Act One was over. The Negro Carmen had become the mistress of a wealthy European. She would now shed her gingham dress for an evening gown.

Mechanically, Emma Lou assisted Arline in making the change. She was unusually silent. It was noticed.

" 'Smatter, Louie. In love or something?"

Emma Lou smiled, "Only with myself."

"Then snap out of it. Remember, you're going cabareting with us tonight. This brother of mine from Chicago insists upon going to Harlem to check up on my performance. He'll enjoy himself more if you act as guide. Ever been to Small's?" Emma Lou shook her head. "I haven't been to any of the cabarets."

"What?" Arline was genuinely surprised. "You in Harlem and never been to a cabaret? Why I thought all colored people went."

Emma Lou bristled. White people were so stupid. "No," she said firmly. "All colored people don't go. Fact is, I've heard that most of the places are patronized almost solely by whites."

"Oh, yes, I knew that, I've been to Small's and Barron's and the Cotton Club, but I thought there were other places." She stopped talking, and spent the next few moments deepening the artificial duskiness of her skin. The gingham dress was now on its hanger. The evening gown clung glamorously to her voluptuous figure. "For God's sake, don't let on to my brother you ain't been to Small's before. Act like you know all about it. I'll see that he gives you a big tip." The call bell rang. Arline said "Damn," gave one last look into the mirror, then hurried back to the stage so that the curtain could go up on the cabaret scene in Act Two.

Emma Lou laid out the negligee outfit Arline would be killed in at the end of Act Three, and went downstairs to stand in the stage wings, a makeup box beneath her arm. She never tired of watching the so-called dramatic antics on the stage. She wondered if there were any Negroes of the type portrayed by Arline and her fellow performers. Perhaps there were, since there were any number of minor parts being played by real Negroes who acted much different from any Negroes she had ever known or seen. It all seemed to her like a mad caricature.

She watched for about the thirtieth time Arline acting the part of a Negro cabaret entertainer, and also for about the thirtieth time, came to the conclusion that Arline was being herself rather than the character she was supposed to be playing. From where she was standing in the wings she could see a small portion of the audience, and she watched their reaction. Their interest seemed genuine. Arline did have pep and personality, and the alleged Negro background was strident and kaleidoscopic, all of which no doubt made up for the inane plot and vulgar dialogue.

They entered Small's Paradise, Emma Lou, Arline and Arline's brother from Chicago. All the way uptown he had plied Emma Lou with questions concerning New York's Black Belt. He had reciprocated by relating how well he knew the Negro section of Chicago. Quite a personage around the Black and Tan cabarets there, it seemed. "But I never," he concluded as the taxi drew up to the curb in front of Small's, "have seen any black gal in Chicago act like Arline acts. She claims she is presenting a Harlem specie. So I am going to see for myself." And he chuckled all the time he was helping them out of the taxi and paying the fare. While they were checking their wraps in the foyer, the orchestra began playing. Through the open entrance way Emma Lou could see a hazy, dim-lighted room, walls and ceiling colorfully decorated, floor space jammed with tables and chairs and people. A heavy set mulatto in tuxedo, after asking how many were in their party, led them through a lane of tables around the squared off dance platform to a ringside seat on the far side of the cabaret.

Immediately they were seated, a waiter came to take their order.

"Three bottles of White Rock." The waiter nodded, twirled his tray on the tip of his fingers and skated away.

Emma Lou watched the dancers, and noticed immediately that in all that insensate crowd of dancing couples there were only a few Negroes.

"My God, such music. Let's dance, Arline," and off they went, leaving Emma Lou sitting alone. Somehow or other she felt frightened. Most of the tables around her were deserted, their tops littered with liquid-filled glasses, and bottles of ginger ale and White Rock. There was no liquor in sight, yet Emma Lou was aware of pungent alcoholic odors. Then she noticed a heavy-jowled white man with a flashlight walking among the empty tables and looking beneath them. He didn't seem to be finding anything. The music soon stopped. Arline and her brother returned to the table. He was feigning anxiety because he had not seen the type of character Arline claimed to be portraying, and loudly declared that he was disappointed.

"Why there ain't nothing here but white people. Is it always like this?"

Emma Lou said it was and turned to watch their waiter, who with two others had come dancing across the floor, holding aloft his tray, filled with bottles and glasses. Deftly, he maneuvered away from the other two and slid to their table, put down a bottle of White Rock and an ice-filled glass before each one, then, after flicking a stub check on to the table, rejoined his companions in a return trip across the dance floor.

Arline's brother produced a hip flask, and before Emma Lou could demur mixed her a highball. She didn't want to drink. She hadn't drunk before, but. . . .

"Here come the entertainers!" Emma Lou followed Arline's turn of the head to see two women, one light brown skin and slim, the other chocolate colored and fat, walking to the center of the dance floor.

The orchestra played the introduction and vamp to "Muddy Waters." The two entertainers swung their legs and arms in rhythmic unison, smiling broadly and rolling their eyes, first to the left and then to the right. Then they began to sing. Their voices were husky and strident, neither alto nor soprano. They muddled their words and seemed to impregnate the syncopated melody with physical content.

As they sang the chorus, they glided out among the tables, stopping at one, then at another, and another, singing all the time, their bodies undulating and provocative, occasionally giving just a promise of an obscene hip movement, while their arms waved and their fingers held tight to the dollar bills and silver coins placed in their palms by enthusiastic onlookers.

Emma Lou, all of her, watched and listened. As they approached her table, she sat as one mesmerized. Something in her seemed to be trying to give way. Her insides were stirred, and tingled. The two entertainers circled their table; Arline's brother held out a dollar bill. The fat, chocolate colored girl leaned over the table, her hand touched his, she exercised the muscles of her stomach, muttered a guttural "thank you" in between notes and moved away, moaning "Muddy Waters," rolling her eyes, shaking her hips.

Emma Lou had turned completely around in her chair, watching the progress of that wah-wahing, jello-like chocolate hulk, and her slim light brown skin companion. Finally they completed their rounds of the tables and returned to the dance floor. Red and blue spotlights played upon their dissimilar figures, the orchestra increased the tempo and lessened the intensity of its playing. The swaying entertainers pulled up their dresses, exposing lace trimmed stepins and an island of flesh. Their stockings were rolled down below their knees, their stepins discreetly short and delicate. Finally, they ceased their swaying and began to dance. They shimmied and whirled, charlestoned and black-bottomed. Their terpsichorean ensemble was melodramatic and absurd. Their execution easy and emphatic. Emma Lou forgot herself. She gaped, giggled and applauded like the rest of the audience, and only as they let their legs separate, preparatory to doing one final split to the floor, did Emma Lou come to herself long enough to wonder if the fat one could achieve it without seriously endangering those ever tightening stepins.

"Dam' good, I'll say," a slender white youth at the next table asseverated, as he lifted an amber filled glass to his lips.

Arline sighed. Her brother had begun to razz her. Emma Lou blinked guiltily as the lights were turned up. She had been immersed in something disturbingly pleasant. Idiot, she berated herself, just because you've had one drink and seen your first cabaret entertainer, must your mind and body feel all aflame?

Arline's brother was mixing another highball. All around, people were laughing. There was much more laughter than there was talk, much more gesticulating and ogling than the usual means of expression called for. Everything seemed unrestrained, abandoned. Yet, Emma Lou was conscious of a note of artificiality, the same as she felt when she watched Arline and her fellow performers cavorting on the stage in "Cabaret Gal." This entire scene seemed staged, they were in a theater, only the proscenium arch had been obliterated. At last the audience and the actors were as one.

A call to order on the snare drum. A brutal sliding trumpet call on the trombone, a running minor scale by the clarinet and piano, an umpah, umpah by the bass horn, a combination four measure moan and strum by the saxophone and banjo, then a melodic ensemble, and the orchestra was playing another dance tune. Masses of people jumbled up the three entrances to the dance square and with difficulty, singled out their mates and became closely allied partners. Inadvertently, Emma Lou looked at Arline's brother. He blushed, and appeared uncomfortable. She realized immediately what was on his mind. He didn't know whether or not to ask her to dance with him. The ethics of the case were complex. She was a Negro and hired maid. But was she a hired maid after hours, and in this environment? Emma Lou had difficulty in suppressing a smile, then she decided to end the suspense.

"Why don't you two dance. No need of letting the music go to waste."

Both Arline and her brother were obviously relieved, but as they got up Arline said, "Ain't much fun cuddling up to your own brother when there's music like this." But off they went, leaving Emma Lou alone and disturbed. John ought to be here, slipped out before she remembered that she didn't want John any more. Then she began to wish that John had introduced her to some more men. But he didn't know the kind of men she was interested in knowing. He only knew men and boys like himself, porters and janitors and chauffeurs and bootblacks. Imagine her, a college trained person, even if she hadn't finished her senior year, being satisfied with the company of such unintelligent servitors. How had she stood John so long with his constant of defense, "I ain't got much education, but I got mother wit." Mother wit! Creation of the unlettered, satisfying illusion to the dumb, ludicrous prop to the mentally unfit. Yes, he had mother wit all right.

Emma Lou looked around and noticed at a near-by table three young colored men, all in tuxedos, gazing at her and talking. She averted her glance and turned to watch the dancers. She thought she heard a burst of ribald laughter from the young men at the table. Then some one touched her on the shoulder, and she looked up into a smiling oriental-like face, neither brown nor yellow in color, but warm and pleasing beneath the soft lights, and, because of the smile, showing a gleaming row of small, even teeth, set off by a solitary gold incisor. The voice was persuasive and apologetic, "Would you care to dance with me?" The music had stopped, but there was promise of an encore. Emma Lou was confused, her mind blankly chaotic. She was expected to push back her chair and get up. She did. And, without saying a word, allowed herself to be maneuvered to the dance floor.

In a moment they were swallowed up in the jazz whirlpool. Long strides were impossible. There were too many other legs striding for free motion in that over populated area. He held her close to him; the contours of her body fitting his. The two highballs had made her giddy. She seemed to be glowing inside.

The soft lights and the music suggested abandon and intrigue. They said nothing to one another. She noticed that her partner's face seemed alive with some inner ecstasy. It must be the music, thought Emma Lou. Then she got a whiff of his liquor-laden breath.

After three encores, the clarinet shrilled out a combination of notes that seemed to say regretfully, "That's all." Brighter lights were switched on, and the milling couples merged into a struggling mass of individuals, laughing, talking, over-animated individuals, all trying to go in different directions, and getting a great deal of fun out of the resulting confusion. Emma Lou's partner held tightly to her arm, and pushed her through the insensate crowd to her table. Then he muttered a polite "thank you" and turned away. Emma Lou sat down. Arline and her brother looked at her and laughed. "Got a dance, eh Louie?" Emma Lou wondered if Arline was being malicious, and for an answer she only nodded her head and smiled, hoping all the while that her smile was properly enigmatic.

Arline's brother spoke up. "Whadda say we go. I've seen enough of this to know that Arline and her stage director are all wet." Their waiter was called, the check was paid, and they were on their way out. In spite of herself, Emma Lou glanced back to the table where her dancing partner was sitting. To her confusion, she noticed that he and his two friends were staring at her. One of them said something and made a wry face. Then they all laughed, uproariously and cruelly.

Alva had overslept. Braxton, who had stayed out the entire night, came in about eight o'clock, and excitedly interrupted his drunken slumber.

"Ain't you goin' to work?"

"Work?" Alva was alarmed. "What time is it?"

" 'Bout eight. Didn't you set the clock?"

"Sure, I did." Alva picked up the clock from the floor and examined the alarm dial. It had been set for ten o'clock instead of for six. He sulked for a moment, then attempted to shake off the impending mood of regretfulness and disgust for self.

"Aw, hell, what's the dif'. Call 'em up and tell 'em I'm sick.

There's a nickel somewhere in that change on the dresser."
Braxton had taken off his tuxedo coat and vest.

"If you're not goin' to work ever, you might as well quit. I
don't see no sense in working two days and laying off three."

"I'm goin' to quit the damn job anyway. I been working
steady now since last fall."

"I thought it was about time you quit." Braxton had stripped
off his white full dress shirt, put on his bathrobe, and started
out of the room, to go downstairs to the telephone. Alva
reached across the bed and pulled up the shade, blinked at the
inpouring daylight and lay himself back down, one arm thrown
across his forehead. He had slipped off into a state of semi-
consciousness again when Braxton returned.

"The girl said she'd tell the boss. Asked who I was as usual."
He went into the alcove to finish undressing, and put on his
pajamas. Alva looked up.

"You goin' to bed?"

"Yes, don't you think I want some sleep?"

"Thought you was goin' to look for a job?"

"I was, but I hadn't figured on staying out all night."

"Always some damn excuse. Where'd you go?"

"Down to Flo's."

"Who in the hell is Flo?"

"That little yaller broad I picked up at the cabaret last night."

"I thought she had a nigger with her."

"She did, but I jived her along, so she ditched him, and gave
me her address. I met her there later."

Braxton was now ready to get into the bed. All this time he
had been preparing himself in his usual bedtime manner. His
face had been cold-creamed, his hair greased and tightly covered by a silken stocking cap. This done, he climbed over Alva
and lay on top of the covers. They were silent for a moment,
then Braxton laughed softly to himself.

"Where'd *you* go last night?"

"Where'd I go?" Alva seemed surprised. "Why I came home,
where'd ya think I went?" Braxton laughed again.

"Oh, I thought maybe you'd really made a date with that
coal scuttle blond you danced with."

"Ya musta thought it."

"Well, ya seemed pretty sweet on her."

"Whaddaya mean, sweet? Just because I danced with her once. I took pity on her, cause she looked so lonesome with those ofays. Wonder who they was?"

"Oh, she probably works for them. It's good you danced with her. Nobody else would."

"I didn't see nothing wrong with her. She might have been a little dark."

"Little dark is right, and you know when they comes blacker'n me, they ain't got no go." Braxton was a reddish brown aristocrat, with clear-cut features and curly hair. His paternal grandfather had been an Iroquois Indian.

Emma Lou was very lonesome. She still knew no one save John, two or three of the Negro actors who worked on the stage with Arline, and a West Indian woman who lived in the same apartment with her. Occasionally John met her when she left the theater at night and escorted her to her apartment door. He repeatedly importuned her to be nice to him once more. Her only answer was a sigh or a smile.

The West Indian woman was employed as a stenographer in the office of a Harlem political sheet. She was shy and retiring, and not much given to making friends with American Negroes. So many of them had snubbed and pained her when she was newly emigrant from her home in Barbadoes, that she lumped them all together, just as they seemed to do her people. She would not take under consideration that Emma Lou was new to Harlem, and not even aware of the prejudice American-born Harlemites nursed for foreign-born ones. She remembered too vividly how, on ringing the bell of a house where there had been a vacancy sign in the window, a little girl had come to the door, and, in answer to a voice in the back asking, "Who is it, Cora?" had replied, "monkey chaser wants to see the room you got to rent." Jasmine Griffith was wary of all contact with American Negroes, for that had been only one of the many embittering incidents she had experienced.

Emma Lou liked Jasmine, but was conscious of the fact that she could never penetrate her stolid reserve. They often talked to one another when they met in the hallway, and sometimes they stopped in one another's rooms, but there was never any talk of going places together, never any informal revelations or intimacies.

The Negro actors in "Cabaret Gal" all felt themselves superior to Emma Lou, and she in turn felt superior to them. She was just a maid. They were just common stage folk. Once she had had an inspiration. She had heard that "Cabaret Gal" was liable to run for two years or more on Broadway before road shows were sent out. Without saying anything to Arline she had approached the stage director and asked him, in all secrecy, what her chances were of getting into the cabaret ensemble. She knew they paid well, and she speculated that two or three years in "Cabaret Gal" might lay the foundations for a future stage career.

"What the hell would Arline do," he laughed, "if she didn't have you to change her complexion before every performance?"

Emma Lou had smiled away this bit of persiflage and had reiterated her request in such a way that there was no mistaking her seriousness.

Sensing this, the director changed his mood, and admitted that even then two of the girls were dropping out of "Cabaret Gal" to sail for Europe with another show, booked for a season on the continent. But he hastened to tell her, as he saw her eyes brighten with anticipation:

"Well, you see, we worked out a color scheme that would be a complement to Arline's makeup. You've noticed, no doubt, that all of the girls are about one color, and. . . ."

Unable to stammer any more, he had hastened away, embarrassed.

Emma Lou hadn't noticed that all the girls were one color. In fact, she was certain they were not. She hastened to stand in the stage wings among them between scenes and observe their skin coloring. Despite many layers of liquid powder she could see that they were not all one color, but that they were either mulatto or light-brown skin. Their makeup and the lights gave them an appearance of sameness. She noticed that there were several black men in the ensemble, but that none of the women were dark. Then the breach between Emma Lou and the show people widened.

Emma Lou had had another inspiration. She had decided to move. Perhaps if she were to live with a homey type of family they could introduce her to "the right sort of people." She blamed her enforced isolation on the fact that she had made no worthwhile contacts. Mrs. Blake was a disagreeable remembrance. Since she came to think about it, Mrs. Blake had been distinctly patronizing like . . . like . . . her high school principal, or like Doris Garrett, the head of the only Negro sorority in the Southern California college she had attended. Doris Garrett had been very nice to all her colored schoolmates, but had seen to it that only those girls who were of a mulatto type were pledged for membership in the Greek letter society of which she was the head.

Emma Lou reasoned that she couldn't go on as she was, being alone and aching for congenial companionship. True, her job didn't allow her much spare time. She had to be at Arline's apartment at eleven every morning, but except on the two matinee days, she was free from two until seven-thirty P.M., when she had to be at the theater, and by eleven-thirty every night, she was in Harlem. Then she had all day Sunday to herself. Arline paid her a good salary, and she made tips from the first and second leads in the show, who used her spare moments. She had been working for six weeks now, and had saved one hundred dollars. She practically lived on her tips. Her salary was twenty-five dollars per week. Dinner was the only meal she had to pay for, and Arline gave her many clothes.

So Emma Lou began to think seriously of getting another room. She wanted more space and more air and more freedom from fish and cabbage smells. She had been in Harlem now for about fourteen weeks. Only fourteen weeks? The count stunned her. It seemed much longer. It was this rut she was in. Well, she would get out of it. Finding a room, a new room, would be the first step.

Emma Lou asked Jasmine how one went about it. Jasmine was noncommittal, and said she didn't know, but she had heard that *The Amsterdam News*, a Harlem Negro weekly, carried a large "Furnished rooms for rent" section. Emma Lou bought a copy of this paper, and, though attracted, did not stop to read the news columns under the streaming headlines to the effect "Headless Man Found In Trunk"; "Number Runner Given Sentence"; "Benefit Ball Huge Success"; but turned immediately to the advertising section.

There were many rooms advertised for rent, rooms of all sizes and for all prices, with all sorts of conveniences and inconveniences. Emma Lou was more bewildered than ever. Then, remembering that John had said that all the "dictys" lived between Seventh and Edgecombe Avenues on 136th, 137th, 138th and 139th Streets, decided to check off the places in these streets. John had also told her that "dictys" lived in the imposing apartment houses on Edgecombe, Bradhurst and St. Nicholas Avenues. "Dictys" were Harlem's high-toned people, folk listed in the local social register, as it were. But Emma Lou did not care to live in another apartment building. She preferred, or thought she would prefer, living in a private house where there would be fewer people and more privacy.

The first place Emma Lou approached had a double room for two girls, two men, or a couple. They thought their advertisement had said as much. It hadn't, but Emma Lou apologized, and left. The next three places were nice but exorbitant. Front rooms with two windows and a kitchenette, renting for twelve, fourteen and sixteen dollars a week. Emma Lou had planned to spend not more than eight or nine dollars at the most. The next place smelled far worse than her present home. The room was smaller and the rent higher. Emma Lou began to lose hope, then rallying, had gone to the last place on her list from *The Amsterdam News*. The landlady was the spinster type, garrulous and friendly. She had a high forehead, keen intellectual eyes, and a sharp profile. The room she showed to Emma Lou was both spacious and clean, and she only asked eight dollars and fifty cents per week for it.

After showing her the room, the landlady had invited Emma Lou downstairs to her parlor. Emma Lou found a place to sit down on a damask covered divan. There were many other seats in the room, but the landlady, *Miss* Carrington, as she had introduced herself, insisted upon sitting down beside her. They talked for about a half an hour, and in that time, being a successful "pumper," *Miss* Carrington had learned the history of Emma Lou's experiences in Harlem. Satisfied of her ground, she grew more familiar, placed her hand on Emma Lou's knee, then finally put her arm around her waist. Emma Lou felt uncomfortable. This sudden and unexpected intimacy disturbed her. The room was close and hot. Damask coverings seemed to be everywhere. Damask coverings and dull red draperies and mauve walls.

"Don't worry any more, dearie, I'll take care of you from now on," and she had tightened her arm around Emma Lou's waist, who, feeling more uncomfortable than ever, looked at her wrist watch.

"I must be going."

"Do you want the room?" There was a note of anxiety in her voice. "There are lots of nice girls living here. We call this the 'Old Maid's Home.' We have parties among ourselves, and just have a grand time. Talk about fun! I know you'd be happy here."

Emma Lou knew she would too, and said as much. Then hastily, she gave *Miss* Carrington a three dollar deposit on the room, and left . . . to continue her search for a new place to live.

There were no more places on her *Amsterdam News* list, so noticing "Vacancy" signs in windows along the various streets, Emma Lou decided to walk along and blindly choose a house. None of the houses in 137th Street impressed her, they were all too cold looking, and she was through with 136th Street. *Miss* Carrington lived there. She sauntered down the "L" trestled Eighth Avenue to 138th Street. Then she turned toward Seventh Avenue and strolled along slowly on the south side of the street. She chose the south side because she preferred the appearance of the red brick houses there to the green brick ones on the north side. After she had passed by three "Vacancy" signs, she decided to enter the very next house where such a sign was displayed.

Seeing one, she climbed the terraced stone stairs, rang the doorbell and waited expectantly. There was a long pause. She rang the bell again, and just as she relieved her pressure, the door was opened by a bedizened yellow woman with sand colored hair and deep set corn colored eyes. Emma Lou noted the incongruous thickness of her lips.

"How do you do. I . . . I . . . would like to see one of your rooms."

The woman eyed Emma Lou curiously and looked as if she were about to snort. Then slowly she began to close the door in the astonished girl's face. Emma Lou opened her mouth and tried to speak, but the woman forestalled her, saying testily in broken English:

"We have nothing here."

Persons of color didn't associate with blacks in the Caribbean Island she had come from.

From then on Emma Lou intensified her suffering, mulling over and magnifying each malignant experience. They grew within her and were nourished by constant introspection and livid reminiscences. Again, she stood upon the platform in the auditorium of the Boise high school. Again that first moment of realization and its attendant strictures were disinterred and revivified. She was black, too black, there was no getting around it. Her mother had thought so, and had often wished that she had been a boy. Black boys can make a go of it, but black girls. . . .

No one liked black anyway. . . .

Wanted: light colored girl to work as waitress in tea-room. . . .

Wanted: Nurse girl, light colored preferred (children are afraid of black folks). . . .

"I don' haul no coal. . . ."

"It's like this, Emma Lou, they don't want no dark girls in their sorority. They ain't pledged us, and we're the only two they ain't, and we're both black."

The ineluctability of raw experience! The muddy mirroring of life's perplexities. . . . Seeing everything in terms of self. . . . The spreading sensitiveness of an adder's sting.

"Mr. Brown has some one else in mind. . . ."

"We have nothing here. . . ."

She should have been a boy. A black boy could get along, but a black girl. . . .

Arline was leaving the cast of "Cabaret Gal" for two weeks. Her mother had died in Chicago. The Negro Carmen must be played by an understudy, a real mulatto this time, who, lacking Arline's poise and personality, nevertheless brought down the house because of the crude vividity of her performance. Emma Lou was asked to act as her maid while Arline was away. Indignantly, she had taken the alternative of a two weeks' vacation. Imagine her being maid for a *Negro* woman! It was unthinkable.

Left entirely to herself, she proceeded to make herself more miserable. Lying in bed late every morning, semi-conscious, body burning, mind disturbed by thoughts of sex. Never before had she experienced such physical longing. She often thought of John and at times was almost driven to slip him into her room once more. But John couldn't satisfy her. She felt that she wanted something more than just the mere physical relationship with some one whose body and body coloring were distasteful to her.

When she did decide to get up, she would spend an hour before her dresser mirror, playing with her hair, parting it on the right side, then on the left, then in the middle, brushing it straight back, or else teasing it with the comb, inducing it to crackle with electric energy. Then she would cover it with a cap, pin a towel around her shoulders, and begin to experiment with her complexion.

She had decided to bleach her skin as much as possible. She had bought many creams and skin preparations, and had tried to remember the various bleaching aids she had heard of throughout her life. She remembered having heard her grandmother speak of that "old fool, Carrie Campbell," who, already a fair mulatto, had wished to pass for white. To accomplish this she had taken arsenic wafers, which were guaranteed to increase the pallor of one's skin.

Emma Lou had obtained some of these arsenic wafers and eaten them, but they had only served to give her pains in the pit of her stomach. Next she determined upon a peroxide solution in addition to something which was known as Black and White Ointment. After she had been using these for about a month she thought that she could notice some change. But in reality the only effects were an increase in blackheads, irritating rashes, and a burning skin.

Meanwhile she found her thoughts straying often to the chap she had danced with in the cabaret. She was certain he lived in Harlem, and she was determined to find him. She took it for granted that he would remember her. So day after day, she strolled up and down Seventh Avenue from 125th to 145th Street, then crossed to Lenox Avenue and traversed the same distance.

He was her ideal. He looked like a college person. He dressed
well. His skin was such a warm and different color, and she
had been tantalized by the mysterious slant and deepness of
his oriental-like eyes.

After walking the streets like this the first few days of her vacation, she became aware of the futility of her task. She saw
many men on the street, many well dressed, seemingly cultured,
pleasingly colored men and boys. They seemed to congregate
in certain places, and stand there all the day. She found herself
wondering when and where they worked, and how they could
afford to dress so well. She began to admire their well formed
bodies and gloried in the way their trousers fit their shapely
limbs, and in the way they walked, bringing their heels down
so firmly and so noisily on the pavement. Rubber heels were
out of fashion. Hard heels, with metal heel plates were the
mode of the day. These corner loafers were so care-free, always
smiling, eyes always bright. She loved to hear them laugh, and
loved to watch them, when, without any seeming provocation,
they would cut a few dance steps or do a jig. It seemed as if
they either did this from sheer exuberance or else simply to relieve the monotony of standing still.

Of course, they noticed her as she passed and repassed day
after day. She eyed them boldly enough, but she was still too
self-conscious to broadcast an inviting look. She was too afraid
of public ridicule or a mass mocking. Ofttimes men spoke to
her, and tried to make advances, but they were never the kind
she preferred. She didn't like black men, and the others seemed
to keep their distance.

One day, tired of walking, she went into a motion picture
theater on the avenue. She had seen the feature picture before,
but was too lethargic and too uninterested in other things to
go some place else. In truth, there was no place else for her to
go. So she sat in the darkened theater, squirmed around in her
seat, and began to wonder just how many thousands of Negroes there were in Harlem. This theater was practically full,
even in mid-afternoon. The streets were crowded, other theaters were crowded, and then there must be many more at
home and at work. Emma Lou wondered what the population
of Negro Harlem was. She should have read that Harlem
number of the Survey Graphic issued two or three years ago.

But Harlem hadn't interested her then for she had had no idea at the time that she would ever come to Harlem.

Some one sat down beside her. She was too occupied with herself to notice who the person was. The feature picture was over and a comedy was being flashed on the screen. Emma Lou found herself laughing, and, finding something on the screen to interest her, squared herself in her seat. Then she felt a pressure on one of her legs, the warm fleshy pressure of another leg. Her first impulse was to change her position. Perhaps she had touched the person next to her. Perhaps it was an accident. She moved her leg a little, but she still felt the pressure. Maybe it wasn't an accident. Her heart beat fast, her limbs began to quiver. The leg which was pressed against hers had such a pleasant, warm, fleshy feeling. She stole a glance at the person who had sat down next to her. He smiled . . . an impudent boyish smile and pressed her leg the harder.

"Funny cuss, that guy," he was speaking to her.

Slap him in the face. Change your seat. Don't be an idiot. He has a nice smile. Look at him again.

"Did you see him in 'Long Pants'?"

He was leaning closer now, and Emma Lou took note of a teakwood tan hand resting on her knee. She took another look at him, and saw that he had curly hair. He leaned toward her, and she leaned toward him. Their shoulders touched, his hand reached for hers and stole it from her lap. She wished that the theater wasn't so dark. But if it hadn't been so dark this couldn't have happened. She wondered if his hair and eyes were brown or jet black.

The feature picture was being reeled off again. They were too busy talking to notice that. When it was half over, they left their seats together. Before they reached the street, Emma Lou handed him three dollars, and, leaving the theater, they went to an apartment house on 140th Street, off Lenox Avenue. Emma Lou waited downstairs in the dirty marble hallway where she was stifled by urinal smells and stared at by passing people, waited for about ten minutes, then, in answer to his call, climbed one flight of stairs, and was led into a well furnished, though dark, apartment.

His name was Jasper Crane. He was from Virginia. Living in Harlem with his brother, so he said. He had only been in New

York a month. Didn't have a job yet. His brother wasn't very nice to him. . . wanted to kick him out because he was jealous of him, thought his wife was more attentive than a sister-in-law should be. He asked Emma Lou to lend him five dollars. He said he wanted to buy a job. She did. And when he left her, he kissed her passionately and promised to meet her on the next day and to telephone her within an hour.

But he didn't telephone nor did Emma Lou ever see him again. The following day she waited for an hour and a half in the vicinity of that hallway where they were supposed to meet again. Then she went to the motion picture theater where they had met, and sat in the same seat in the same row so that he could find her. She sat there through two shows, then came back on the next day, and on the next. Meanwhile several other men approached her, a panting fat Jew, whom she reported to the usher, a hunchback, whom she pitied and then admired as he "made" the girl sitting on the other side of him; and there were several not very clean, trampy-looking men, but no Jasper.

He had asked her if she ever went to the Renaissance Casino, a public hall, where dances were held every night, so Emma Lou decided to go there on a Saturday, hoping to see him. She drew twenty-five dollars from the bank in order to buy a new dress, a very fine elaborate dress, which she got from a "hot" man, who had been recommended to her by Jasmine. "Hot" men sold supposedly stolen goods, thus enabling Harlem folk to dress well but cheaply. Then she spent the entire afternoon and evening preparing herself for the night, had her hair washed and marcelled, and her fingernails manicured.

Before putting on her dress she stood in front of her mirror for over an hour, fixing her face, drenching it with a peroxide solution, plastering it with a mudpack, massaging it with a bleaching ointment, and then, as a final touch, using much vanishing cream and powder. She even ate an arsenic wafer. The only visible effect of all this on her complexion was to give it an ugly purple tinge, but Emma Lou was certain that it made her skin less dark.

She hailed a taxi and went to the Renaissance Casino. She did feel foolish, going there without an escort, but the doorman didn't seem to notice. Perhaps it was all right. Perhaps it was customary for Harlem girls to go about unaccompanied.

She checked her wraps and wandered along the promenade that bordered the dance floor. It was early yet, just ten-thirty, and only a few couples were dancing. She found a chair, and tried to look as if she were waiting for some one. The orchestra stopped playing, people crowded past her. She liked the dance hall, liked its draped walls and ceilings, its harmonic color design and soft lights.

The music began again. She didn't see Jasper. A spindly legged yellow boy, awkward and bashful, asked her to dance with him. She did. The boy danced badly, but dancing with him was better than sitting there alone, looking foolish. She did wish that he would assume a more upright position and stop scrunching his shoulders. It seemed as if he were trying to bend both their backs to the breaking point. As they danced they talked about the music. He asked her did she have an escort. She said yes, and hurried to the ladies' room when the dance was over.

She didn't particularly like the looks of the crowd. It was well-behaved enough, but . . . well . . . one could see that they didn't belong to the cultured classes. They weren't the right sort of people. Maybe nice people didn't come here. Jasper hadn't been so nice. She wished she could see him, wouldn't she give him a piece of her mind?—And for the first time she really sensed the baseness of the trick he had played on her.

She walked out of the ladies' room and found herself again on the promenade. For a moment she stood there, watching the dancers. The floor was more crowded now, the dancers more numerous and gay. She watched them swirl and glide around the dance floor, and an intense longing for Jasper or John or any one welled up within her. It was terrible to be so alone, terrible to stand here and see other girls contentedly curled up in men's arms. She had been foolish to come, Jasper probably never came here. In truth he was no doubt far away from New York by now. What sense was there in her being here. She wasn't going to stay. She was going home, but before starting toward the check room, she took one more glance at the dancers and saw her cabaret dancing partner.

He was dancing with a slender brown-skin girl, his smile as ecstatic and intense as before. Emma Lou noted the pleasing

lines of his body encased in a form-fitting blue suit. Why didn't
he look her way?

"May I have this dance?" A well modulated deep voice. A
slender stripling, arrayed in brown, with a dark brown face. He
had dimples. They danced. Emma Lou was having difficulty in
keeping track of Alva. He seemed to be consciously striving to
elude her. He seemed to be deliberately darting in among clus-
ters of couples, where he would remain hidden for some time,
only to reappear far ahead or behind her.

Her partner was congenial. He introduced himself, but she
did not hear his name, for at that moment, Alva and his partner
glided close by. Emma Lou actually shoved the supple, slender
boy she was dancing with in Alva's direction. She mustn't lose
him this time. She must speak. They veered close to one another. They almost collided. Alva looked into her face. She
smiled and spoke. He acknowledged her salute, but stared at
her, frankly perplexed, and there was no recognition in his face
as he moved away, bending his head close to that of his partner,
the better to hear something she was asking him.

The slender brown boy clung to Emma Lou's arm, treated
her to a soda, and, at her request, piloted her around the promenade. She saw Alva sitting in a box in the balcony, and suggested to her companion that they parade around the balcony
for a while. He assented. He was lonesome too. First summer
in New York. Just graduated from Virginia Union University.
Going to Columbia School of Law next year. Nice boy, but no
appeal. Too—supple.

They passed by Alva's box. He wasn't there. Two other couples and the girl he had been dancing with were. Emma Lou
and her companion walked the length of the balcony, then retraced their steps just in time to see Alva coming around the
corner carrying a cup of water. She watched the rhythmic
swing of his legs, like symmetrical pendulums, perfectly shaped;
and she admired once more the intriguing lines of his body
and pleasing foreignness of his face. As they met, she smiled at
him. He was certain he did not know her but he stopped and
was polite, feeling that he must find out who she was and where
he had met her.

"How do you do?" Emma Lou held out her hand. He

shifted the cup of water from his right hand to his left. "I'm glad to see you again." They shook hands. His clasp was warm, his palm soft and sweaty. The supple lad stepped to one side. "I—I," Emma Lou was speaking now, "have often wondered if we would meet again." Alva wanted to laugh. He could not imagine who this girl with the purple-powdered skin was. Where had he seen her? She must be mistaking him for some one else. Well, he was game. He spoke sincerely:

"And I, too, have wanted to see you."

Emma Lou couldn't blush, but she almost blubbered with joy.

"Perhaps we'll have a dance together."

"My God," thought Alva, "she's a quick worker."

"Oh, certainly, where can I find you?"

"Downstairs on the promenade, near the center boxes."

"The one after this?" This seemed to be the easiest way out. He could easily dodge her later.

"Yes," and she moved away, the supple lad clinging to her arm again.

"Who's the 'spade,' Alva?" Geraldine had seen him stop to talk to her.

"Damned if I know."

"Aw, sure you know who she is. You danced with her at Small's." Braxton hadn't forgotten.

"Well, I never. Is that *it*?" Laughter all around as he told about their first meeting. But he didn't dodge her, for Geraldine and Braxton riled him with their pertinacious badinage. He felt that they were making more fun of him than of her, and to show them just how little he minded their kidding he stalked off to find her. She was waiting, the slim, brown stripling swaying beside her, importuning her not to wait longer. He didn't want to lose her. She didn't want to lose Alva, and was glad when they danced off together.

"Who's your boy friend?" Alva had fortified himself with gin. His breath smelled familiar.

"Just an acquaintance." She couldn't let him know she had come here unescorted. "I didn't think you'd remember me."

"Of course, I did; how could I forget you?" Smooth tongue, phrases with a double meaning.

"I didn't forget *you*." Emma Lou was being coy. "I have often looked for you."

Looked for him where? My God, what an impression he must have made! He wondered what he had said to her before. Plunge in boy, plunge! The blacker the berry—he chuckled to himself.

Orchestra playing "Blue Skies," as an especial favor to her. Alva telling her his name and giving her his card, and asking her to 'phone him some day. Alva close to her and being nice, his arms tightening about her. She would call him tomorrow. Ecstasy ended too soon. The music stopped. He thanked her for the dance and left her standing on the promenade by the side of the waiting slender stripling. She danced with him twice more, then let him take her home.

At ten the next morning Emma Lou called Alva. Braxton came to the telephone.

"Alva's gone to work; who is it?" People should have more sense than to call that early in the morning. He never got up until noon. Emma Lou was being apologetic.

"Could you tell me what time he will be in?"

" 'Bout six-thirty. Who shall I say called? This is his room-mate."

"Just . . . Oh . . . I'll call him later. Thank you."

Braxton swore. "Why in the hell does Alva give so many damn women his 'phone number?"

Six-thirty-five. His roommate had said about six-thirty. She called again. *He* came to the 'phone. She thought his voice was more harsh than usual.

"Oh, I'm all right, only tired."

"Did you work hard?"

"I always work hard."

"I . . . I . . . just thought I'd call."

"Glad you did, call me again some time. Good-bye"—said too quickly. No chance to say "When will I see you again?"

She went home, got into the bed and cried herself to sleep.

Arline returned two days ahead of schedule. Things settled back into routine. The brown stripling had taken Emma Lou out twice, but upon her refusal to submit herself to him, had gone away in a huff, and had not returned. She surmised that it was the first time he had made such a request of any one. He did it so ineptly. Work. Home. Walks. Theaters downtown during the afternoon, and thoughts of Alva. Finally, she just had to call him again. He came to the 'phone:

"Hello. Who? Emma Lou? Where have you been? I've been wondering where you were?"

She was shy, afraid she might be too bold. But Alva had had his usual three glasses of before-dinner gin. He helped her out.

"When can I see you, Sugar?"

Sugar! He had called her "sugar." She told him where she worked. He was to meet her after the theater that very night.

"How many nights a week you gonna have that little inkspitter up here?"

"Listen here, Brax, you have who you want up here, don't you?"

"That ain't it. I just don't like to see you tied up with a broad like that."

"Why not? She's just as good as the rest, and you know what they say, 'The blacker the berry, the sweeter the juice.'"

"The only thing a black woman is good for is to make money for a brown-skin papa."

"I guess I don't know that."

"Well," Braxton was satisfied now, "if that's the case. . . ."

He had faith in Alva's wisdom.

PART IV

Rent Party

SATURDAY evening. Alva had urged her to hurry uptown from work. He was going to take her on a party with some friends of his. This was the first time he had ever asked her to go to any sort of social affair with him. She had never met any of his friends save Braxton, who scarcely spoke to her, and never before had Alva suggested taking her to any sort of social gathering either public or semipublic. He often took her to various motion picture theaters, both downtown and in Harlem, and at least three nights a week he would call for her at the theater and escort her to Harlem. On these occasions they often went to Chinese restaurants or to ice cream parlors before going home. But usually they would go to City College Park, find an empty bench in a dark corner where they could sit and spoon before retiring either to her room or to Alva's.

Emma Lou had, long before this, suggested going to a dance or to a party, but Alva had always countered that he never attended such affairs during the summer months, that he stayed away from them for precisely the same reason that he stayed away from work, namely, because it was too hot. Dancing, said he, was a matter of calisthenics, and calisthenics were work. Therefore it, like any sort of physical exercise, was taboo during hot weather.

Alva sensed that sooner or later Emma Lou would become aware of his real reason for not taking her out among his friends. He realized that one as color-conscious as she appeared to be would, at some not so distant date, jump to what for him would be uncomfortable conclusions. He did not wish to risk losing her before the end of summer, but neither could he risk taking her out among his friends, for he knew too well that he would be derided for his unseemly preference for "dark meat," and told publicly without regard for her feelings, that "black cats must go."

Furthermore he always took Geraldine to parties and dances.

773

Geraldine with her olive colored skin and straight black hair. Geraldine, who of all the people he pretended to love, really inspired him emotionally as well as physically, the one person he conquested without thought of monetary gain. Yet he had to do something with Emma Lou, and release from the quandary presented itself from most unexpected quarters.

Quite accidentally, as things of the sort happen in Harlem with its complex but interdependable social structure, he had become acquainted with a young Negro writer, who had asked him to escort a group of young writers and artists to a house-rent party. Though they had heard much of this phenomenon, none had been on the inside of one, and because of their rather polished manners and exteriors, were afraid that they might not be admitted. Proletarian Negroes are as suspicious of their more sophisticated brethren as they are of white men, and resent as keenly their intrusions into their social world. Alva had consented to act as cicerone, and, realizing that these people would be more or less free from the color prejudice exhibited by his other friends, had decided to take Emma Lou along too. He was also aware of her intellectual pretensions, and felt that she would be especially pleased to meet recognized talents and outstanding personalities. She did not have to know that these were not his regular companions, and from then on she would have no reason to feel that he was ashamed to have her meet his friends.

Emma Lou could hardly attend to Arline's change of complexion and clothes between acts and scenes, so anxious was she to get to Alva's house and to the promised party. Her happiness was complete. She was certain now that Alva loved her, certain that he was not ashamed or even aware of her dusky complexion. She had felt from the first that he was superior to such inane truck, now she knew it. Alva loved her for herself alone, and loved her so much that he didn't mind her being a coal scuttle blond.

Sensing something unusual, Arline told Emma Lou that she would remove her own make-up after the performance, and let her have time to get dressed for the party. This she proceeded to do all through the evening, spending much time in front of the mirror at Arline's dressing table, manicuring her nails, marcelling her hair, and applying various creams and cosmetics to her face in order to make her despised darkness less obvious. Finally, she put on one of Arline's less pretentious afternoon frocks, and set out for Alva's house.

As she approached his room door, she heard much talk and laughter, moving her to halt and speculate whether or not she should go in. Even her unusual and high-tensioned jubilance was not powerful enough to overcome immediately her shyness and fears. Suppose these friends of Alva's would not take kindly to her? Suppose they were like Braxton, who invariably curled his lip when he saw her, and seldom spoke even as much as a word of greeting? Suppose they were like the people who used to attend her mother's and grandmother's teas, club meetings and receptions, dismissing her with—"It beats me how this child of yours looks so unlike the rest of you . . . Are you sure it isn't adopted." Or suppose they were like the college youth she had known in Southern California? No, that couldn't be. Alva would never invite her where she would not be welcome. These were his friends. And so was Braxton, but Alva said he was peculiar. There was no danger. Alva had invited her. She was here. Anyway she wasn't so black. Hadn't she artificially lightened her skin about four or five shades until she was almost brown? Certainly it was all right. She needn't be a foolish ninny all her life. Thus, reassured, she knocked on the door, and felt herself trembling with excitement and internal uncertainty as Alva let her in, took her hat and coat, and proceeded to introduce her to the people in the room.

"Miss Morgan, meet Mr. Tony Crews. You've probably seen his book of poems. He's the little jazz boy, you know."

Emma Lou bashfully touched the extended hand of the curly-headed poet. She had not seen or read his book, but she had often noticed his name in the newspapers and magazines. He was all that she had expected him to be except that he had pimples on his face. These didn't fit in with her mental picture.

"Miss Morgan, this is Cora Thurston. Maybe I should'a introduced you ladies first."

"I'm no lady, and I hope you're not either, Miss Morgan." She smiled, shook Emma Lou's hand, then turned away to continue her interrupted conversation with Tony Crews.

"Miss Morgan, meet . . . ," he paused, and addressed a tall, dark yellow youth stretched out on the floor, "What name you going by now?"

The boy looked up and smiled.

"Why, Paul, of course."

"All right then, Miss Morgan, this is Mr. Paul, he changes his name every season."

Emma Lou sought to observe this person more closely, and was shocked to see that his shirt was open at the neck and that he was sadly in need of a haircut and shave.

"Miss Morgan, meet Mr. Walter." A small slender dark youth with an infectious smile and small features. His face was familiar. Where had she seen him before?

"Now that you've met every one, sit down on the bed there beside Truman and have a drink. Go on with your talk folks," he urged as he went over to the dresser to fill a glass with a milk colored liquid. Cora Thurston spoke up in answer to Alva's adjuration:

"Guess there ain't much more to say. Makes me mad to discuss it anyhow."

"No need of getting mad at people like that," said Tony Crews simply and softly. "I think one should laugh at such stupidity."

"And ridicule it, too," came from the luxurious person sprawled over the floor, for he did impress Emma Lou as being luxurious, despite the fact that his suit was unpressed, and that he wore neither socks nor necktie. She noticed the many graceful gestures he made with his hands, but wondered why he kept twisting his lips to one side when he talked. Perhaps he was trying to mask the size of his mouth.

Truman was speaking now, "Ridicule will do no good, nor mere laughing at them. I admit those weapons are about the only ones an intelligent person would use, but one must also admit that they are rather futile."

"Why futile?" Paul queried indolently.

"They are futile," Truman continued, "because, well, those people cannot help being like they are—their environment has made them that way."

Miss Thurston muttered something. It sounded like "hooey," then held out an empty glass. "Give me some more firewater,

Alva." Alva hastened across the room and refilled her glass. Emma Lou wondered what they were talking about. Again Cora broke the silence, "You can't tell me they can't help it. They kick about white people, then commit the same crime."

There was a knock on the door, interrupting something Tony Crews was about to say. Alva went to the door.

"Hello, Ray." A tall, blond, fair-skinned youth entered. Emma Lou gasped, and was more bewildered than ever. All of this silly talk and drinking, and now—here was a white man!

"Hy, everybody. Jusas Chraust, I hope you saved me some liquor." Tony Crews held out his empty glass and said quietly, "We've had about umpteen already, so I doubt if there's any more left."

"You can't kid me, bo. I know Alva would save me a dram or two." Having taken off his hat and coat he squatted down on the floor beside Paul.

Truman turned to Emma Lou. "Oh, Ray, meet Miss Morgan. Mr. Jorgenson, Miss Morgan."

"Glad to know you; pardon my not getting up, won't you?" Emma Lou didn't know what to say, and couldn't think of anything appropriate, but since he was smiling, she tried to smile too, and nodded her head.

"What's the big powwow?" he asked. "All of you look so serious. Haven't you had enough liquor, or are you just trying to settle the ills of the universe?"

"Neither," said Paul. "They're just damning our 'pink niggers'."

Emma Lou was aghast. Such extraordinary people—saying "nigger" in front of a white man! Didn't they have any race pride or proper bringing up? Didn't they have any common sense?

"What've they done now?" Ray asked, reaching out to accept the glass Alva was handing him.

"No more than they've always done," Tony Crews answered. "Cora here just felt like being indignant, because she heard of a forthcoming wedding in Brooklyn to which the prospective bride and groom have announced they will *not* invite any dark people."

"Seriously now," Truman began. Ray interrupted him.

"Who in the hell wants to be serious?"

"As I was saying," Truman continued, "you can't blame light Negroes for being prejudiced against dark ones. All of you know that white is the symbol of everything pure and good, whether that everything be concrete or abstract. Ivory Soap is advertised as being ninety-nine and some fraction per cent pure, and Ivory Soap is white. Moreover, virtue and virginity are always represented as being clothed in white garments. Then, too, the God we, or rather most Negroes worship is a patriarchal white man, seated on a white throne, in a spotless white Heaven, radiant with white streets and white-apparelled angels eating white honey and drinking white milk."

"Listen to the boy rave. Give him another drink," Ray shouted, but Truman ignored him and went on, becoming more and more animated.

"We are all living in a totally white world, where all standards are the standards of the white man, and where almost invariably what the white man does is right, and what the black man does is wrong, unless it is precedented by something a white man has done."

"Which," Cora added scornfully, "makes it all right for light Negroes to discriminate against dark ones?"

"Not at all," Truman objected. "It merely explains, not justifies, the evil—or rather, the fact of intra-racial segregation. Mulattoes have always been accorded more consideration by white people than their darker brethren. They were made to feel superior even during slave days . . . made to feel proud, as Bud Fisher would say, that they were bastards. It was for the mulatto offspring of white masters and Negro slaves that the first schools for Negroes were organized, and say what you will, it is generally the Negro with a quantity of mixed blood in his veins who finds adaptation to a Nordic environment more easy than one of pure blood, which, of course, you will admit, is, to an American Negro, convenient if not virtuous."

"Does that justify their snobbishness and self-evaluated superiority?"

"No, Cora, it doesn't," returned Truman. "I'm not trying to excuse them. I'm merely trying to give what I believe to be an explanation of this thing. I have never been to Washington and only know what Paul and you have told me about conditions there, but they seem to be just about the same as conditions in

Los Angeles, Omaha, Chicago, and other cities in which I have
lived or visited. You see, people have to feel superior to something, and there is scant satisfaction in feeling superior to domestic animals or steel machines that one can train or utilize. It
is much more pleasing to pick out some individual or some
group of individuals on the same plane to feel superior to. This
is almost necessary when one is a member of a supposedly despised, mistreated minority group. Then consider that the mulatto is much nearer white than he is black, and is therefore
more liable to act like a white man than like a black one, although I cannot say that I see a great deal of difference in any
of their actions. They are human beings first and only white or
black incidentally."

Ray pursed up his lips and whistled.

"But you seem to forget," Tony Crews insisted, "that because a man is dark, it doesn't necessarily mean he is not of
mixed blood. Now look at. . . ."

"Yeah, let him look at you or at himself or at Cora," Paul interrupted. "There ain't no unmixed Negroes."

"But I haven't forgotten that," Truman said, ignoring the
note of finality in Paul's voice. "I merely took it for granted
that we were talking only about those Negroes who were light-
skinned."

"But all light-skinned Negroes aren't color struck or color
prejudiced," interjected Alva, who, up to this time, like Emma
Lou, had remained silent. This was, he thought, a strategic
moment for him to say something. He hoped Emma Lou
would get the full significance of this statement.

"True enough," Truman began again. "But I also took it for
granted that we were only talking about those who were. As I
said before, Negroes are, after all, human beings, and they are
subject to be influenced and controlled by the same forces and
factors that influence and control other human beings. In an
environment where there are so many color-prejudiced whites,
there are bound to be a number of color-prejudiced blacks.
Color prejudice and religion are akin in one respect. Some
folks have it and some don't, and the kernel that is responsible
for it is present in us all, which is to say, that potentially we are
all color-prejudiced as long as we remain in this environment.
For, as you know, prejudices are always caused by differences,

and the majority group sets the standard. Then, too, since black is the favorite color of vaudeville comedians and jokesters, and, conversely, as intimately associated with tragedy, it is no wonder that even the blackest individual will seek out some one more black than himself to laugh at."

"So saith the Lord," Tony answered soberly.

"And the Holy Ghost saith, let's have another drink."

"Happy thought, Ray," returned Cora. "Give us some more ice cream and gin, Alva."

Alva went into the alcove to prepare another concoction. Tony started the victrola. Truman turned to Emma Lou, who, all this while, had been sitting there with Alva's arm around her, every muscle in her body feeling as if it wanted to twitch, not knowing whether to be sad or to be angry. She couldn't comprehend all of this talk. She couldn't see how these people could sit down and so dispassionately discuss something that seemed particularly tragic to her. This fellow Truman, whom she was certain she knew, with all his hi-faluting talk, disgusted her immeasurably. She wasn't sure that they weren't all poking fun at her. Truman was speaking:

"Miss Morgan, didn't you attend school in Southern California?" Emma Lou at last realized where she had seen him before. So *this* was Truman Walter, the little "cock o' the walk," as they had called him on the campus. She answered him with difficulty, for there was a sob in her throat. "Yes, I did." Before Truman could say more to her, Ray called to him:

"Say, Bozo, what time are we going to the party? It's almost one o'clock now."

"Is it?" Alva seemed surprised. "But Aaron and Alta aren't here yet."

"They've been married just long enough to be late to everything."

"What do you say we go by and ring their bell?" Tony suggested, ignoring Paul's Greenwich Village wit.

" 'Sall right with me." Truman lifted his glass to his lips. "Then on to the house-rent party . . . on to the bawdy bowels of Beale Street!"

They drained their glasses and prepared to leave.

*

"Ahhhh, sock it." . . . "Ummmm" . . . Piano playing—slow, loud, and discordant, accompanied by the rhythmic sound of shuffling feet. Down a long, dark hallway to an inside room, lit by a solitary red bulb. "Oh, play it you dirty no-gooder." . . . A room full of dancing couples, scarcely moving their feet, arms completely encircling one another's bodies . . . cheeks being warmed by one another's breath . . . eyes closed . . . animal ecstasy agitating their perspiring faces. There was much panting, much hip movement, much shaking of the buttocks. . . . "Do it twice in the same place." . . . "Git off that dime." Now somebody was singing, "I ask you very confidentially. . . ." "Sing it man, sing it." . . . Piano treble moaning, bass rumbling like thunder. A swarm of people, motivating their bodies to express in suggestive movements the ultimate consummation of desire.

The music stopped, the room was suffocatingly hot, and Emma Lou was disturbingly dizzy. She clung fast to Alva, and let the room and its occupants whirl around her. Bodies and faces glided by. Leering faces and lewd bodies. Anxious faces and angular bodies. Sad faces and obese bodies. All mixed up together. She began to wonder how such a small room could hold so many people. "Oh, play it again . . ." She saw the pianist now, silhouetted against the dark mahogany piano, saw him bend his long, slick-haired head, until it hung low on his chest, then lift his hands high in the air, and as quickly let them descend upon the keyboard. There was one moment of cacophony, then the long, supple fingers evolved a slow, tantalizing melody out of the deafening chaos.

Every one began to dance again. Body called to body, and cemented themselves together, limbs lewdly intertwined. A couple there kissing, another couple dipping to the floor, and slowly shimmying, belly to belly, as they came back to an upright position. A slender dark girl with wild eyes and wilder hair stood in the center of the room, supported by the strong, lithe arms of a longshoreman. She bent her trunk backward, until her head hung below her waistline, and all the while she kept the lower portion of her body quivering like jello.

"She whips it to a jelly," the piano player was singing now, and banging on the keys with such might that an empty gin bottle on top of the piano seemed to be seized with the ague. "Oh, play it Mr. Charlie." Emma Lou grew limp in Alva's arms.

"What's the matter, honey, drunk?" She couldn't answer. The music augmented by the general atmosphere of the room and the liquor she had drunk had presumably created another person in her stead. She felt like flying into an emotional frenzy —felt like flinging her arms and legs in insane unison. She had become very fluid, very elastic, and all the while she was giving in more and more to the music and to the liquor and to the physical madness of the moment.

When the music finally stopped, Alva led Emma Lou to a settee by the window which his crowd had appropriated. Every one was exceedingly animated, but they all talked in hushed, almost reverential tones.

"Isn't this marvelous?" Truman's eyes were ablaze with interest and excitement. Even Tony Crews seemed unusually alert.

"It's the greatest I've seen yet," he exclaimed.

Alva seemed the most unemotional one in the crowd. Paul the most detached. "Look at 'em all watching Ray."

"Remember, Bo," Truman counselled him. "Tonight you're 'passing.' Here's a new wrinkle, white man 'passes' for Negro."

"Why not? Enough of you pass for white." They all laughed, then transferred their interest back to the party. Cora was speaking:

"Didya see that little girl in pink—the one with the scar on her face—dancing with that tall, lanky, one-armed man? Wasn't she throwing it up to him?"

"Yeah," Tony admitted, "but she didn't have anything on that little Mexican-looking girl. She musta been born in Cairo."

"Saay, but isn't that one bad looking darkey over there, two chairs to the left; is he gonna smother that woman?" Truman asked excitedly.

"I'd say she kinda liked it," Paul answered, then lit another cigarette.

"Do you know they have corn liquor in the kitchen? They serve it from a coffee pot." Aaron seemed proud of his discovery.

"Yes," said Alva, "and they got hoppin'-john out there too."

"What the hell is hoppin'-john?"

"Ray, I'm ashamed of you. Here you are passing for colored and don't know what hoppin'-john is!"

"Tell him, Cora, I don't know either."

"Another one of these foreigners." Cora looked at Truman disdainfully. "Hoppin'-john is black-eyed peas and rice. Didn't they ever have any out in Salt Lake City?"

"Have they any chitterlings?" Alta asked eagerly.

"No, Alta," Alva replied, dryly. "This isn't Kansas. They have got pig's feet though."

"Lead me to 'em," Aaron and Alta shouted in unison, and led the way to the kitchen. Emma Lou clung to Alva's arm and tried to remain behind. "Alva, I'm afraid."

"Afraid of what? Come on, snap out of it! You need another drink." He pulled her up from the settee and led her through the crowded room down the long narrow dark hallway to the more crowded kitchen.

When they returned to the room, the pianist was just preparing to play again. He was tall and slender, with extra long legs and arms, giving him the appearance of a scarecrow. His pants were tight in the waist and full in the legs. He wore no coat, and a blue silk shirt hung damply to his body. He acted as if he were king of the occasion, ruling all from his piano stool throne. He talked familiarly to every one in the room, called women from other men's arms, demanded drinks from any bottle he happened to see being passed around, laughed uproariously, and made many grotesque and ofttimes obscene gestures.

There were sounds of a scuffle in an adjoining room, and an excited voice exclaimed, "You goddam son-of-a-bitch, don't you catch my dice no more." The piano player banged on the keys and drowned out the reply, if there was one.

Emma Lou could not keep her eyes off the piano player. He was acting like a maniac, occasionally turning completely around on his stool, grimacing like a witch doctor, and letting his hands dawdle over the keyboard of the piano with an agonizing indolence, when compared to the extreme exertion to which he put the rest of his body. He was improvising. The melody of the piece he had started to play was merely a base for more bawdy variations. His left foot thumped on the floor in time with the music, while his right punished the piano's loud-pedal. Beads of perspiration gathered grease from his slicked-down hair, and rolled oleagenously down his face and neck, spotting the already damp baby-blue shirt, and streaking his already greasy black face with more shiny lanes.

A sailor lad suddenly ceased his impassioned hip movement and strode out of the room, pulling his partner behind him, pushing people out of the way as he went. The spontaneous moans and slangy ejaculations of the piano player and of the more articulate dancers became more regular, more like a chanted obligato to the music. This lasted for a couple of hours interrupted only by hectic intermissions. Then the dancers grew less violent in their movements, and though the piano player seemed never to tire there were fewer couples on the floor, and those left seemed less loathe to move their legs.

Eventually, the music stopped for a long interval, and there was a more concerted drive on the kitchen's corn liquor supply. Most of the private flasks and bottles were empty. There were more calls for food, too, and the crap game in the side room annexed more players and more kibitzers. Various men and women had disappeared altogether. Those who remained seemed worn and tired. There was much petty person to person badinage and many whispered consultations in corners. There was an argument in the hallway between the landlord and two couples, who wished to share one room without paying him more than the regulation three dollars required of one couple. Finally, Alva suggested that they leave. Emma Lou had drifted off into a state of semi-consciousness and was too near asleep or drunk to distinguish people or voices. All she knew was that she was being led out of that dreadful place, that the perturbing "pilgrimage to the proletariat's parlor social," as Truman had called it, was ended, and that she was in a taxicab, cuddled up in Alva's arms.

Emma Lou awoke with a headache. Some one was knocking at her door, but when she first awakened it had seemed as if the knocking was inside of her head. She pressed her fingers to her throbbing temples, and tried to become more conscious. The knock persisted and she finally realized that it was at her door rather than in her head. She called out, "Who is it?"

"It's me." Emma Lou was not far enough out of the fog to recognize who "me" was. It didn't seem important anyway, so without any more thought or action, she allowed herself to doze off again. Whoever was on the outside of the door banged the louder, and finally Emma Lou distinguished the voice of her landlady, calling, "Let me in, Miss Morgan, let me in." The voice grew more sharp . . . "Let me in," and then in an under-tone, "Must have some one in there." This last served to awaken Emma Lou more fully, and though every muscle in her body protested, she finally got out of the bed and went to the door. The lady entered precipitously, and pushing Emma Lou aside sniffed the air and looked around as if she expected to surprise some one, either squeezing under the bed or leaping through the window. After she had satisfied herself that there was no one else in the room, she turned on Emma Lou furiously:

"Miss Morgan, I wish to talk to you." Emma Lou closed the door and wearily sat down upon the bed. The wrinkled faced old woman glared at her and shifted the position of her snuff so she could talk more easily. "I won't have it, I tell you, I won't have it." Emma Lou tried hard to realize what it was she wouldn't have, and failing, she said nothing, just screwed up her eyes and tried to look sober.

"Do you hear me?" Emma Lou nodded. "I won't have it. When you moved in here I thought I made it clear that I was a respectable woman and that I kept a respectable house. Do you understand that now?" Emma Lou nodded again. There didn't seem to be anything else to do. "I'm glad you do. Then it won't be necessary for me to explain why I want my room."

Emma Lou unscrewed her eyes and opened her mouth. What was this woman talking about? "I don't think I under-stand."

The old lady was quick with her answer. "There ain't nothin' for you to understand, but that I want you to get out of my house. I don't have no such carryings-on around here. A drunken woman in my house at all hours in the morning, being carried in by a man! Well, you coulda knocked me over with a feather."

At last Emma Lou began to understand. Evidently the land-lady had seen her when she had come in, no doubt had seen Alva carry her to her room, and perhaps had listened outside the door. She was talking again:

"You must get out. Your week is up Wednesday. That gives

you three days to find another room, and I want you to act like a lady the rest of that time, too. The idea!" she sputtered, and stalked out of the room.

This is a pretty mess, thought Emma Lou. Yet she found herself unable to think or do anything about it. Her lethargic state worried her. Here she was about to be dispossessed by an irate landlady, and all she could do about it was sit on the side of her bed and think—maybe I ought to take a dose of salts. Momentarily, she had forgotten it was Sunday, and began to wonder how near time it was for her to go to work. She was surprised to discover that it was still early in the forenoon. She couldn't possibly have gone to bed before four-thirty or five, yet it seemed as if she had slept for hours. She felt like some one who had been under the influence of some sinister potion for a long period of time. Had she been drugged? Her head still throbbed, her insides burned, her tongue was swollen, her lips chapped and feverish. She began to deplore her physical condition, and even to berate herself and Alva for last night's debauchery.

Funny people, his friends. Come to think of it they were all very much different from any one else she had ever known. They were all so, so—she sought for a descriptive word, but could think of nothing save that revolting, "Oh, sock it," she had heard on first entering the apartment where the house-rent party had been held.

Then she began to wonder about her landlady's charges. There was no need arguing about the matter. She had wanted to move anyway. Maybe now she could go ahead and find a decent place in which to live. She had never had the nerve to begin another room hunting expedition after the last one. She shuddered as she thought about it, then climbed back into the bed. She could see no need in staying up so long as her head ached as it did. She wondered if Alva had made much noise in bringing her in, wondered how long he had stayed, and if he had had any trouble manipulating the double-barrelled police lock on the outside door. Harlem people were so careful about barricading themselves in. They all seemed to fortify themselves, not only against strangers, but against neighbors and friends as well.

And Alva? She had to admit that she was a trifle disappointed in him and in his friends. They certainly weren't what she could have called either intellectuals or respectable people. Whoever heard of decent folk attending such a lascivious festival? She remembered their enthusiastic comments and tried to comprehend just what it was that had intrigued and interested them. Looking for material, they had said. More than likely they were looking for liquor and a chance to be licentious.

Alva himself worried her a bit. She couldn't understand why gin seemed so indispensable to him. He always insisted that he had to have at least three drinks a day. Once she had urged him not to follow this program. Unprotestingly, he had come to her the following evening without the usual juniper berry smell on his breath, but he had been so disagreeable and had seemed so much like a worn out and dissipated person that she had never again suggested that he not have his usual quota of drinks. Then, too, she had discovered that he was much too lovable after having had his "evening drams" to be discouraged from taking them. Emma Lou had never met any one in her life who was as loving and kind to her as Alva. He seemed to anticipate her every mood and desire, and he was the most soothing and satisfying person with whom she had ever come into contact. He seldom riled her—seldom ruffled her feelings. He seemed to give in to her on every occasion, and was the most chivalrous escort imaginable. He was always courteous, polite and thoughtful of her comfort.

As yet she had been unable to become angry with him. Alva never argued or protested unduly. Although Emma Lou didn't realize it, he used more subtle methods. His means of remaining master of all situations were both tactful and sophisticated; for example, Emma Lou never realized just how she had first begun giving him money. Surely he hadn't asked her for it. It had just seemed the natural thing to do after a while, and she had done it, willingly and without question. The ethical side of their relationship never worried her. She was content and she was happy—at least she was in possession of something that seemed to bring her happiness. She seldom worried about Alva not being true to her, and if she questioned him about such matters, he would pretend not to hear her and change the conversation. The only visible physical reaction would be a slight narrowing of the eyes, as if he were trying not to wince from the pain of some inner hurt.

Once she had suggested marriage, and had been shocked when Alva told her that to him the marriage ceremony seemed a waste of time. He had already been married twice, and he hadn't even bothered to obtain a divorce from his first wife before acquiring number two. On hearing this, Emma Lou had urged him to tell her more about these marital experiments, and after a little coaxing, he had done so, very impassively and very sketchily, as if he were relating the experiences of another. He told her that he had really loved his first wife, but that she was such an essential polygamous female that he had been forced to abdicate and hand her over to the multitudes. According to Alva, she had been as vain as Braxton, and as fundamentally dependent upon flattery. She could do without three square meals a day, but she couldn't do without her contingent of mealy-mouthed admirers, all eager to outdo one another in the matter of compliments. One man could never have satisfied her, not that she was a nymphomaniac with abnormal physical appetites, but because she wanted attention, and the more men she had around her, the more attention she could receive. She hadn't been able to convince Alva, though, that her battalion of admirers were all of the platonic variety. "I know niggers too well," Alva had summed it up to Emma Lou, "so I told her she just must go, and she went."

"But," Emma Lou had queried when he had started to talk about something else, "what about your second wife?"

"Oh," he laughed, "well, I married her when I was drunk. She was an old woman about fifty. She kept me drunk from Sunday to Sunday. When I finally got sober she showed me the marriage license and I well nigh passed out again."

"But where is she?" Emma Lou had asked, "and how did they let you get married while you were drunk and already had a wife?"

Alva had shrugged his shoulders. "I don't know where she is. I ain't seen her since I left her room that day. I sent Braxton up there to talk to her. Seems like she'd been drunk too. So, it really didn't matter. And as for a divorce, I know plenty spades right here in Harlem get married any time they want to. Who in the hell's gonna take the trouble getting a divorce, when, if you must marry and already have a wife, you can get another without going through all that red tape?"

Emma Lou had had to admit that this sounded logical, if illegal. Yet she hadn't been convinced. "But," she had insisted, "don't they look you up and convict you of bigamy?"

"Hell, no. The only thing the law bothers niggers about is for stealing, murdering, or chasing white women, and as long as they don't steal from or murder ofays, the law ain't none too particular about bothering them. The only time they act about bigamy is when one of the wives squawk, and they hardly ever do that. They're only too glad to see the old man get married again—then they can do likewise, without spending lots of time on lawyers and courthouse red tape."

This, and other things which Emma Lou had elicited from Alva, had convinced her that he was undoubtedly the most interesting person she had ever met. What added to this was the strange fact that he seemed somewhat cultured despite his admitted unorganized and haphazard early training. On being questioned, he advanced the theory that perhaps this was due to his long period of service as waiter and valet to socially prominent white people. Many Negroes, he had explained, even of the "dicty" variety, had obtained their *savoir faire* and knowledge of the social niceties in this manner.

Emma Lou lay abed, remembering the many different conversations they had had together, most of which had taken place on a bench in City College Park, or in Alva's room. With enough gin for stimulation, Alva could tell many tales of his life and hold her spellbound with vivid descriptions of the various situations he had found himself in. He loved to reminisce, when he found a good listener, and Emma Lou loved to listen when she found a good talker. Alva often said that he wished some one would write a story of his life. Maybe that was why he cultivated an acquaintance with these writer people. . . . Then it seemed as if this one-sided conversational communion strengthened their physical bond. It made Emma Lou more palatable to Alva, and it made Alva a more glamorous figure to Emma Lou.

But here she was day dreaming, when she should be wondering where she was going to move. She couldn't possibly remain in this place, even if the old lady relented and decided to give her another chance to be respectable. Somehow or other she felt that she had been insulted, and for the first time, began to feel angry with the old snuff-chewing termagant.

Her head ached no longer, but her body was still lethargic. Alva, Alva, Alva. Could she think of nothing else? Supposing—she sat upright in the bed—supposing she and Alva were to live together. They might get a small apartment and be with one another entirely. Immediately she was all activity. The headache was forgotten. Out of bed, into her bathrobe, and down the hall to the bathroom. Even the quick shower seemed to be a slow, tedious process, and she was in such a hurry to hasten into the street and telephone Alva, in order to tell him of her new plans, that she almost forgot to make the very necessary and very customary application of bleaching cream to her face. As it was, she forgot to rinse her face and hands in lemon juice.

Alva had lost all patience with Braxton, and profanely told him so. No matter what his condition, Braxton would not work. He seemed to believe that because he was handsome, and because he was Braxton, he shouldn't have to work. He graced the world with his presence. Therefore, it should pay him. "A thing of beauty is joy forever," and should be sustained by a communal larder. Alva tried to show him that such a larder didn't exist, that one either worked or hustled.

But as Alva had explained to Emma Lou, Braxton wouldn't work, and as a hustler he was a distinct failure. He couldn't gamble successfully, he never had a chance to steal, and he always allowed his egotism to defeat his own ends when he tried to get money from women. He assumed that at a word from him, anybody's pocketbook should be at his disposal, and that his handsomeness and personality were a combination none could withstand. It is a platitude among sundry sects and individuals that as a person thinketh, so he is, but it was not within the power of Braxton's mortal body to become the being his imagination sought to create. He insisted, for instance, that he was a golden brown replica of Rudolph Valentino. Every picture he could find of the late lamented cinema sheik he pasted either on the wall or on some of his belongings. The only reason that likenesses of his idol did not decorate all the wall space was because Alva objected to this flapperish ritual. Braxton emulated his silver screen mentor in every way, watched his every gesture on the screen, then would stand in front of his mirror at home and practice Rudy's poses and facial expressions. Strange as it may seem, there was a certain likeness between the two, especially at such moments when Braxton would suddenly stand in the center of the floor and give a spontaneous impersonation of his Rudy making love or conquering enemies. Then, at all times, Braxton held his head as Rudy held his, and had even learned how to smile and how to use his eyes in the same captivating manner. But his charms were too obviously cultivated, and his technique too clumsy. He would attract almost any one to him, but they were sure to bolt away as suddenly as they had come. He could have, but he could not hold.

Now, as Alva told Emma Lou, this was a distinct handicap to one who wished to be a hustler, and live by one's wits off the bounty of others. And the competition was too keen in a place like Harlem, where the adaptability to city ways sometimes took strange and devious turns, for a bungler to have much success. Alva realized this, if Braxton didn't, and tried to tell him so, but Braxton wouldn't listen. He felt that Alva was merely being envious—the fact that Alva had more suits than he, and that Alva always had clean shirts, liquor money and room rent, and that Alva could continue to have these things, despite the fact that he had decided to quit work during the hot weather, meant nothing to Braxton at all. He had facial and physical perfection, a magnetic body and much sex appeal. Ergo, he was a master.

However, lean days were upon him. His mother and aunt had unexpectedly come to New York to help him celebrate the closing day of his freshman year at Columbia. His surprise at seeing them was nothing in comparison to their surprise in finding that their darling had not even started his freshman year. The aunt was stoic—"What could you expect of a child with all that wild Indian blood in him? Now, our people. . . ." She hadn't liked Braxton's father. His mother simply could not comprehend his duplicity. Such an unnecessarily cruel and deceptive performance was beyond her understanding. Had she been told that he was guilty of thievery, murder, or rape, she could have borne up and smiled through her tears in true maternal fashion, but that he could so completely fool her for nine months—incredible; preposterous! it just couldn't be!

She and her sister returned to Boston, telling every one there what a successful year their darling had had at Columbia, and telling Braxton before they left that he could not have another cent of their money that summer, that if he didn't enter Columbia in the fall . . . well, he was not yet of age. They made many vague threats; none so alarming, however, as the threat of a temporary, if not permanent, suspension of his allowance.

By pawning some of his suits, his watch, and diamond ring, he amassed a small stake and took to gambling. Unlucky at love, he should, so Alva said, have been lucky at cards, and was. But even a lucky man will suffer from lack of skill and foolhardiness. Braxton would gamble only with mature men who gathered in the police-protected clubs, rather than with young chaps like himself, who gathered in private places. He couldn't classify himself with the cheap or the lowly. If he was to gamble, he must gamble in a professional manner, with professional men. As in all other affairs, he had luck, but no skill and little sense. His little gambling stake lasted but a moment, flitted from him feverishly, and left him holding an empty purse.

Then he took to playing the "numbers," placing quarters and half dollars on a number compounded of three digits and anxiously perusing the daily clearing house reports to see whether or not he had chosen correctly. Alva, too, played the numbers consistently and somehow or other, managed to remain ahead of the game, but Braxton, as was to be expected, "hit" two or three times, then grew excited over his winnings and began to play two or three or even five dollars daily on one number. Such plunging, unattended by scientific observation or close calculation, put him so far behind the game that his winnings were soon dissipated and he had to stop playing altogether.

Alva had quit work for the summer. He contended that it was far too hot to stand over a steam pressing machine during the sultry summer months, and there was no other congenial work available. Being a bellhop in one of the few New York hotels where colored boys were used, called for too long hours and broken shifts. Then they didn't pay much money and he hated to work for tips. He certainly would not take an elevator job, paying only sixty or sixty-five dollars a month at the most, and making it necessary for him to work nights one week from six to eight, and days the next week, vice versa. Being an elevator operator in a loft building required too much skill, patience, and muscular activity. The same could be said of the shipping clerk positions, open in the various wholesale houses. He couldn't, of course, be expected to be a porter, and swing a mop. Bootblacking was not even to be considered. There was nothing left. He was unskilled, save as a presser. Once he had been apprenticed to a journeyman tailor, but he preferred to forget that.

No, there was nothing he could do, and there was no sense in working in the summer. He never had done it; at least, not since he had been living in New York—so he didn't see why he should do it now. Furthermore, his salary hardly paid his saloon bill, and since his board and room and laundry and clothes came from other sources, why not quit work altogether and develop these sources to their capacity output? Things looked much brighter this year than ever before. He had more clothes, he had "hit" the numbers more than ever, he had won a baseball pool of no mean value, and, in addition to Emma Lou, he had made many other profitable contacts during the spring and winter months. It was safe for him to loaf, but he couldn't carry Braxton, or rather, he wouldn't. Yet he liked him well enough not to kick him into the streets. Something, he told Emma Lou, should be done for him first, so Alva started doing things.

First, he got him a girl, or rather steered him in the direction of one who seemed to be a good bet. She was. And as usual, Braxton had little trouble in attracting her to him. She was a simple-minded over-sexed little being from a small town in Central Virginia, new to Harlem, and had hitherto always lived in her home town where she had been employed since her twelfth year as maid-of-all-work to a wealthy white family. For four years, she had been her master's concubine, and probably would have continued in that capacity for an unspecified length of time, had not the mistress of the house decided that after all it might not be good for her two adolescent sons to become aware of their father's philandering. She had had to accept it. Most of the women of her generation and in her circle had done likewise. But these were the post world war days of modernity . . . and, well, it just wasn't being done, what with the growing intelligence of the "darkies," and the increased sophistication of the children.

So Anise Hamilton had been surreptitiously shipped away to New York, and a new maid-of-all-work had mysteriously appeared in her place. The mistress had seen to it that this new maid was not as desirable as Anise, but a habit is a habit, and the master of the house was not the sort to substitute one habit for another. If anything, his wife had made herself more miserable by the change, since the last girl loved much better than she worked, while Anise had proved competent on both scores, thereby pleasing both master and mistress.

Anise had come to Harlem and deposited the money her former mistress had supplied her with in the postal savings. She wouldn't hear to placing it in any other depository. Banks had a curious and discomforting habit of closing their doors without warning, and without the foresight to provide their patrons with another nest egg. If banks in Virginia went broke, those in wicked New York would surely do so. Now, Uncle Sam had the whole country behind him, and everybody knew that the United States was the most wealthy of the world's nations. Therefore, what safer place than the post office for one's bank account?

Anise got a job, too, almost immediately. Her former mistress had given her a letter to a friend of hers on Park Avenue, and this friend had another friend who had a sister who wanted a stock girl in her exclusive modiste shop. Anise was the type to grace such an establishment as this person owned, just the right size to create a smart uniform for, and shapely enough to allow the creator of the uniform ample latitude for bizarre experimentation. Most important of all, her skin, the color of beaten brass with copper overtones, synchronized with the gray plaster walls, dark hardwood furniture and powder blue rugs on the Maison Quantrelle.

Anise soon had any number of "boy friends," with whom she had varying relations. But she willingly dropped them all for Braxton, and, simple village girl that she was, expected him to do likewise with his "girl friends." She had heard much about the "two-timing sugar daddies" in Harlem, and while she was well versed in the art herself, having never been particularly true to her male employer, she did think that this sort of thing was different, and that any time she was willing to play fair, her consort should do likewise.

Alva was proud of himself when he noticed how rapidly things progressed between Anise and Braxton. They were together constantly, and Anise, not unused to giving her home town "boy friends" some of "Mister Bossman's bounty," was soon slipping Braxton spare change to live on. Then she undertook to pay his half of the room rent, and finally, within three weeks, was, as Alva phrased it, "treating Braxton royally."

But as ever, he was insistent upon being perverse. His old swank and swagger was much in evidence. With most of his clothing out of the pawnshop, he attempted to dazzle the Avenue when he paraded its length, the alluring Anise, attired in clothes borrowed from her employer's stockroom, beside him. The bronze replica of Rudolph Valentino was, in the argot of Harlem's pool hall Johnnies, "out the barrel." The world was his. He had in it a bottle, and he need only make it secure by corking. But Braxton was never the person to make anything secure. He might manage to capture the entire universe, but he could never keep it pent up, for he would soon let it alone to look for two more like it. It was to be expected, then, that Braxton would lose his head. He did, deliberately and diabolically. Because Anise was so madly in love with him, he imagined that all other women should do as she had done, and how much more delightful and profitable it would be to have two or three Anises instead of one. So he began a crusade, spending much of Anise's money for campaign funds. Alva quarrelled, and Anise threatened, but Braxton continued to explore and expend.

Anise finally revolted when Braxton took another girl to a dance on her money. He had done this many times before, but she hadn't known about it. She wouldn't have known about it this time if he hadn't told her. He often did things like that. Thought it made him more desirable. Despite her simplemindedness, Anise had spunk. She didn't like to quarrel, but she wasn't going to let any one make a fool out of her, so, the next week after the heartbreaking incident, she had moved and left no forwarding address. It was presumed that she had gone downtown to live in the apartment of the woman for whom she worked. Braxton seemed unconcerned about her disappearance, and continued his peacock-like march for some time, with feathers unruffled, even by frequent trips to the pawnshop. But a peacock can hardly preen an unplumaged body, and, though Braxton continued to strut, in a few weeks after the break, he was only a sad semblance of his former self.

Alva nagged at him continually. "Damned if I'm going to carry you." Braxton would remain silent. "You're the most no-count nigger I know. If you can't do anything else, why in the hell don't you get a job?" "I don't see you working," Braxton would answer.

"And you don't see me starving, either," would be the come-back.

"Oh, jost 'cause you got that little black wench . . ."

"That's all right about the little black wench. She's forty with me, and I know how to treat her. I bet you couldn't get five cents out of her."

"I wouldn't try."

"Hell, if you tried it wouldn't make no difference. There's a gal ready to pay to have a man, and there are lots more like her. You couldn't even keep a good-looking gold mine like Anise. Wish I could find her."

Braxton would sulk a while, thinking that his silence would discourage Alva, but Alva was not to be shut up. He was truly outraged. He felt that he was being imposed upon, being used by some one who thought himself superior to him. He would admit that he wasn't as handsome as Braxton, but he certainly had more common sense. The next Monday Braxton moved.

Alva was to take Emma Lou to the midnight show at the La-fayette Theater. He met her as she left work and they had taken the subway uptown. On the train they began to talk, shouting into one another's ears, trying to make their voices heard above the roar of the underground tube.

"Do you like your new home?" Alva shouted. He hadn't seen her since she had moved two days before.

"It's nice," she admitted loudly, "but it would be nicer if I had you there with me."

He patted her hand and held it regardless of the onlooking crowd.

"Maybe so, sugar, but you wouldn't like me if you had to live with me all the time."

Emma Lou was aggrieved: "I don't see how you can say that. How do you know? That's what made me mad last Sunday."

Alva saw that Emma Lou was ready for argument and he had no intention of favoring her, or of discomfiting himself. He was even sorry that he said as much as he had when she had first broached the "living together" matter over the telephone on Sunday, calling him out of bed before noon while Geraldine was there too, looking, but not asking, for information. He smiled at her indulgently:

"If you say another word about it, I'll kiss you right here in the subway."

Emma Lou didn't put it beyond him so she could do nothing but smile and shut up. She rather liked him to talk to her that way. Alva was shouting into her ear again, telling her a scandalous tale he claimed to have heard while playing poker with some of the boys. He thus contrived to keep her entertained until they reached the 135th Street station where they finally emerged from beneath the pavement to mingle with the frowsy crowds of Harlem's Bowery, Lenox Avenue.

They made their way to the Lafayette, the Jew's gift of entertainment to Harlem colored folk. Each week the management of this theater presents a new musical revue of the three a day variety with motion pictures—all guaranteed to be from three to ten years old—sandwiched in between. On Friday nights there is a special midnight performance lasting from twelve o'clock until four or four-thirty the next morning, according to the stamina of the actors. The audience does not matter. It would as soon sit until noon the next day if the "high yaller" chorus girls would continue to undress, and the black face comedians would continue to tell stale jokes, just so long as there was a raucous blues singer thrown in every once in a while for vulgar variety.

Before Emma Lou and Alva could reach the entrance door, they had to struggle through a crowd of well dressed young men and boys, congregated on the sidewalk in front of the theater.

The midnight show at the Lafayette on Friday is quite a social
event among certain classes of Harlem folk, and, if one is a
sweetback or a man about town, one must be seen standing in
front of the theater, if not inside. It costs nothing to obstruct
the entrance way, and it adds much to one's prestige. Why, no
one knows.

Without untoward incident Emma Lou and Alva found the
seats he had reserved. There was much noise in the theater,
much passing to and fro, much stumbling down dark aisles.
People were always leaving their seats, admonishing their companions to hold them, and some one else was always taking
them despite the curt and sometimes belligerent, "This seat is
taken." Then, when the original occupant would return there
would be still another argument. This happened so frequently
that there seemed to be a continual wrangling automatically
staged in different parts of the auditorium. Then people were
always looking for some one or for something, always peering
into the darkness, emitting code whistles, and calling to Jane
or Jim or Pete or Bill. At the head of each aisle, both upstairs
and down, people were packed in a solid mass, a grumbling,
garrulous mass, elbowing their neighbors, cursing the management, and standing on tiptoe trying to find an empty, intact
seat—intact because every other seat in the theater seemed to
be broken. Hawkers went up and down the aisle shouting, "Ice
cream, peanuts, chewing gum or candy." People hissed at them
and ordered what they wanted. A sadly inadequate crew of
ushers inefficiently led people up one aisle and down another
trying to find their supposedly reserved seats; a lone fireman
strove valiantly to keep the aisles clear as the fire laws stipulated.
It was a most chaotic and confusing scene.

First, a movie was shown while the organ played mournful
jazz. About one o'clock the midnight revue went on. The curtain went up on the customary chorus ensemble singing the
customary, "Hello, we're glad to be here, we're going to please
you" opening song. This was followed by the usual song and
dance team, a blues singer, a lady Charleston dancer, and two
black faced comedians. Each would have his turn, then begin
all over again, aided frequently by the energetic and noisy chorus, which somehow managed to appear upon the stage almost

naked in the first scene, and keep getting more and more naked as the evening progressed.

Emma Lou had been to the Lafayette before with John and had been shocked by the scantily clad women and obscene skits. The only difference that she could see in this particular revue was that the performers were more bawdy and more boisterous. And she had never been in or seen such an audience. There was as much, if not more, activity in the orchestra and box seats than there was on the stage. It was hard to tell whether the cast was before or behind the proscenium arch. There seemed to be a veritable contest going on between the paid performers and their paying audience, and Emma Lou found the spontaneous monkey shines and utterances of those around her much more amusing than the stereotyped antics of the hired performers on the stage.

She was surprised to find that she was actually enjoying herself, yet she supposed that after the house-rent party she could stand anything. Imagine people opening their flats to the public and charging any one who had the price to pay twenty-five cents to enter? Imagine people going to such bedlam Bacchanals?

A new scene on the stage attracted her attention. A very colorfully dressed group of people had gathered for a party. Emma Lou immediately noticed that all the men were dark, and that all the women were either a very light brown or "high yaller." She turned to Alva:

"Don't they ever have anything else but fair chorus girls?"

Alva made a pretense of being very occupied with the business on the stage. Happily, at that moment, one of a pair of black faced comedians had set the audience in an uproar with a suggestive joke. After a moment Emma Lou found herself laughing too. The two comedians were funny, no matter how prejudiced one might be against unoriginality. There must be other potent elements to humor besides surprise. Then a very Topsy-like girl skated onto the stage to the tune of "Ireland must be heaven because my mother came from there." Besides being corked until her skin was jet black, the girl had on a wig of kinky hair. Her lips were painted red—their thickness exaggerated by the paint. Her coming created a stir. Every one concerned was indignant that something like her should crash their party. She attempted to attach herself to certain men in the crowd. The straight men spurned her merely by turning away. The comedians made a great fuss about it, pushing her from one to the other, and finally getting into a riotous argument because each accused the other of having invited her. It ended by them agreeing to toss her bodily off the stage to the orchestral accompaniment of "Bye, Bye, Blackbird," while the entire party loudly proclaimed that "Black cats must go."

Then followed the usual rigamarole carried on weekly at the Lafayette concerning the undesirability of black girls. Every one, that is, all the males, let it be known that high browns and "high yallers" were "forty" with them, but that. . . . They were interrupted by the re-entry of the little black girl riding a mule and singing mournfully as she was being thus transported across the stage:

> A yellow gal rides in a limousine,
> A brown-skin rides a Ford,
> A black gal rides an old jackass
> But she gets there, yes my Lord.

Emma Lou was burning up with indignation. So color-conscious had she become that any time some one mentioned or joked about skin color, she immediately imagined that they were referring to her. Now she even felt that all the people near by were looking at her and that their laughs were at her expense. She remained silent throughout the rest of the performance, averting her eyes from the stage and trying hard not to say anything to Alva before they left the theater. After what seemed an eternity, the finale screamed its good-bye at the audience, and Alva escorted her out into Seventh Avenue.

Alva was tired and thirsty. He had been up all night the night before at a party to which he had taken Geraldine, and he had had to get up unusually early on Friday morning in order to go after his laundry. Of course when he had arrived at Bobby's apartment where his laundry was being done, he found that his shirts were not yet ironed, so he had gone to bed there, with the result that he hadn't been able to go to sleep, nor had the shirts been ironed, but that was another matter.

"First time I ever went to a midnight show without something on my hip," he complained to Emma Lou as they crossed the taxi-infested street in order to escape the crowds leaving the theater and idling in front of it, even at four A.M. in the morning.

"Well," Emma Lou returned vehemently, "it's the last time I'll ever go to that place any kind of way."

Alva hadn't expected this. "What's the matter with you?"

"You're always taking me some place, or placing me in some position where I'll be insulted."

"Insulted?" This was far beyond Alva. Who on earth had insulted her and when. "But," he paused, then advanced cautiously, "Sugar, I don't know what you mean."

Emma Lou was ready for a quarrel. In fact she had been trying to pick one with him ever since the night she had gone to that house-rent party, and the landlady had asked her to move on the following day. Alva's curt refusal of her proposal that they live together had hurt her far more than he had imagined. Somehow or other he didn't think she could be so serious about the matter, especially upon such short notice. But Emma Lou had been so certain that he would be as excited over the suggestion as she had been that she hadn't considered meeting a definite refusal. Then the finding of a room had been irritating to contemplate. She couldn't have called it irritating of accomplishment because Alva had done that for her. She had told him on Sunday morning that she had to move and by Sunday night he had found a place for her. She had to admit that he had found an exceptionally nice place too. It was just two blocks from him, on 138th Street between Eighth Avenue and Edgecombe. It was near the elevated station, near the park, and cost only ten dollars and fifty cents per week for the room, kitchenette and private bath.

On top of his refusal to live with her, Alva had broken two dates with Emma Lou, claiming that he was playing poker. On one of these nights, after leaving work, Emma Lou had decided to walk past his house. Even at a distance she could see that there was a light in his room, and when she finally passed the house, she recognized Geraldine, the girl with whom she had seen Alva dancing at the Renaissance Casino, seated in the window. Angrily, she had gone home, determined to break with Alva on the morrow, and on reaching home had found a letter from her mother which had disturbed her even more. For a long time now her mother had been urging her to come home, and her Uncle Joe had even sent her word that he meant to forward a ticket at an early date. But Emma Lou had no intentions of going home. She was so obsessed with the idea that her mother didn't want her, and she was so incensed at the people with whom she knew she would be forced to associate, that she could consider her mother's hysterically-put request only as an insult. Thus, presuming, she had answered in kind, giving vent to her feelings about the matter. This disturbing letter was in answer to her own spleenic epistle, and what hurt her most was, not the sharp counsellings and verbose lamentations therein, but the concluding phrase, which read, "I don't see how the Lord could have given me such an evil, black hussy for a daughter."

The following morning she had telephoned Alva, determined to break with him, or at least make him believe she was about to break with him, but Alva had merely yawned and asked her not to be a goose. Could he help it if Braxton's girl chose to sit in his window? It was as much Braxton's room as it was his. True, Braxton wouldn't be there long, but while he was, he certainly should have full privileges. That had quieted Emma Lou then, but there was nothing that could quiet her now. She continued arguing as they walked toward 135th Street.

"You don't want to know what I mean."

"No, I guess not," Alva assented wearily, then quickened his pace. He didn't want to have a public scene with this black wench. But Emma Lou was not to be appeased.

"Well, you will know what I mean. First you take me out with a bunch of your supposedly high-toned friends, and sit silently by while they poke fun at me. Then you take me to a theater, where you know I'll have my feelings hurt." She stopped for breath. Alva filled in the gap.

"If you ask me," he said wearily, "I think you're full of stuff. Let's take a taxi. I'm too tired to walk." He hailed a taxi, pushed her into it, and gave the driver the address. Then he turned to Emma Lou, saying something which he regretted having said a moment later.

"How did my friends insult you?"

"You know how they insulted me, sitting up there making fun of me 'cause I'm black."

Alva laughed, something he also regretted later.

"That's right, laugh, and I suppose you laughed with them then, behind my back, and planned all that talk before I arrived."

Alva didn't answer and Emma Lou cried all the rest of the way home. Once there he tried to soothe her.

"Come on, Sugar, let Alva put you to bed."

But Emma Lou was not to be sugared so easily. She continued to cry. Alva sat down on the bed beside her.

"Snap out of it, won't you, Honey? You're just tired. Go to bed and get some sleep. You'll be all right tomorrow."

Emma Lou stopped her crying.

"I may be all right, but I'll never forget the way you've allowed me to be insulted in your presence."

This was beginning to get on Alva's nerves but he smiled at her indulgently:

"I suppose I should have gone down on the stage and biffed one of the comedians in the jaw?"

"No," snapped Emma Lou, realizing she was being ridiculous, "but you could've stopped your friends from poking fun at me."

"But, Sugar," this was growing tiresome. "How can you say they were making fun of you. It's beyond me."

"It wasn't beyond you when it started. I bet you told them about me before I came in, told them I was black. . . ."

"Nonsense, weren't some of them dark? I'm afraid," he advanced slowly, "that you are a trifle too color-conscious," he was glad he remembered that phrase.

Emma Lou flared up: "Color-conscious . . . who wouldn't be color-conscious when everywhere you go people are always talking about color. If it didn't make any difference they wouldn't talk about it, they wouldn't always be poking fun, and laughing and making jokes. . . ."

Alva interrupted her tirade. "You're being silly, Emma Lou. About three-quarters of the people at the Lafayette tonight were either dark brown or black, and here you are crying and fuming like a ninny over some reference made on the stage to a black person." He was disgusted now. He got up from the bed. Emma Lou looked up.

"But, Alva, you don't know."

"I do know," he spoke sharply for the first time, "that you're a damn fool. It's always color, color, color. If I speak to any of my friends on the street you always make some reference to their color and keep plaguing me with—'Don't you know nothing else but light-skinned people?' And you're always beefing about being black. Seems like to me you'd be proud of it. You're not the only black person in this world. There are gangs of them right here in Harlem, and I don't see them going around a-moanin' 'cause they ain't half white."

"I'm not moaning."

"Oh, yes you are. And a person like you is far worse than a hinkty yellow nigger. It's your kind helps make other people color-prejudiced."

"That's just what I'm saying; it's because of my color. . . ."

"Oh, go to hell!" And Alva rushed out of the room, slamming the door behind him.

Braxton had been gone a week. Alva, who had been out with Marie, the creole Lesbian, came home late, and, turning on the light, found Geraldine asleep in his bed. He was so surprised that he could do nothing for a moment but stand in the center of the room and look—first at Geraldine and then at her toilet articles spread over his dresser. He twisted his lips in a wry smile, muttered something to himself, then walked over to the bed and shook her.

"Geraldine, Geraldine," he called. She awoke quickly and smiled at him.

"Hello. What time is it?"

"Oh," he returned guardedly, "somewhere after three."

"Where've you been?"

"Playing poker."

"With whom?"

"Oh, the same gang. But what's the idea?"

Geraldine wrinkled her brow.

"The idea of what?"

"Of sorta taking possession?"

"Oh," she seemed enlightened, "I've moved to New York."

It was Alva's cue to register surprise.

"What's the matter? You and the old lady fall out?"

"Not at all."

"Does she know where you are?"

"She knows I'm in New York."

"You know what I mean. Does she know you're going to stay?"

"Certainly."

"But where are you going to live?"

"Here."

"Here?"

"Yes."

"But . . . but . . . well, what is this all about, anyhow?"

She sat up in the bed and regarded him for a moment, a light smile playing around her lips. Before she spoke she yawned; then in a cool, even tone of voice, announced "I'm going to have a baby."

"But," he began after a moment, "can't you—can't you . . . ?"

"I've tried everything and now it's too late. There's nothing to do but have it."

PART V

Pyrrhic Victory

It was two years later. "Cabaret Gal," which had been on the road for one year, had returned to New York and the company had been disbanded. Arline was preparing to go to Europe and had decided not to take a maid with her. However, she determined to get Emma Lou another job before she left. She inquired among her friends, but none of the active performers she knew seemed to be in the market for help, and it was only on the eve of sailing that she was able to place Emma Lou with Clere Sloane, a former stage beauty, who had married a famous American writer and retired from public life.

Emma Lou soon learned to like her new place. She was Clere's personal maid, and found it much less tiresome than being in the theater with Arline. Clere was less temperamental and less hurried. She led a rather leisurely life, and treated Emma Lou more as a companion than as a servant. Clere's husband, Campbell Kitchen, was very congenial and kind too, although Emma Lou, at first, seldom came into contact with him, for he and his wife practically led separate existences, meeting only at meals, or when they had guests, or when they both happened to arise at the same hour for breakfast. Occasionally, they attended the theater or a party together, and sometimes entertained, but usually they followed their own individual paths.

Campbell Kitchen, like many other white artists and intellectuals, had become interested in Harlem. The Negro and all things negroid had become a fad, and Harlem had become a shrine to which feverish pilgrimages were in order. Campbell Kitchen, along with Carl Van Vechten, was one of the leading spirits in this "Explore Harlem; Know the Negro" crusade. He, unlike many others, was quite sincere in his desire to exploit those things in Negro life which he presumed would eventually win for the Negro a more comfortable position in American life. It was he who first began the agitation in the higher places of journalism which gave impetus to the spiritual craze. It was he who ferreted out and gave publicity to many unknown blues singers. It was he who sponsored most of the younger Negro writers, personally carrying their work to publishers and editors. It wasn't his fault entirely that most of them were published before they had anything to say or before they knew how to say it. Rather it was the fault of the faddistic American public which followed the band wagon and kept clamoring for additional performances, not because of any manifested excellence, but rather because of their sensationalism and pseudo-barbaric *decor*.

Emma Lou had heard much of his activity, and had been surprised to find herself in his household. Recently he had written a book concerning Negro life in Harlem, a book calculated by its author to be a sincere presentation of those aspects of life in Harlem which had interested him. Campbell Kitchen belonged to the sophisticated school of modern American writers. His novels were more or less fantastic bits of realism, skipping lightly over the surfaces of life, and managing somehow to mirror depths through superficialities. His novel on Harlem had been a literary failure because the author presumed that its subject matter demanded serious treatment. Hence, he disregarded the traditions he had set up for himself in his other works, and produced an energetic and entertaining hodgepodge, where the bizarre was strangled by the sentimental, and the erotic clashed with the commonplace.

Negroes had not liked Campbell Kitchen's delineation of their life in the world's greatest colored city. They contended that, like "Nigger Heaven" by Carl Van Vechten, the book gave white people a wrong impression of Negroes, thus lessening their prospects of doing away with prejudice and race discrimination. From what she had heard, Emma Lou had expected to meet a sneering, obscene cynic, intent upon ravaging every Negro woman and insulting every Negro man, but he proved to be such an ordinary, harmless individual that she was won over to his side almost immediately.

Whenever they happened to meet, he would talk to her about her life in particular and Negro life in general. She had to admit that he knew much more about such matters than she or any other Negro she had ever met. And it was because of

one of these chance talks that she finally decided to follow Mrs.
Blake's advice and take the public school teachers' examination.

Two years had wrought little change in Emma Lou, although
much had happened to her. After that tearful night, when Alva
had sworn at her and stalked out of her room, she had somewhat taken stock of herself. She wondered if Alva had been
right in his allegations. Was she supersensitive about her color?
Did she encourage color prejudice among her own people,
simply by being so expectant of it? She tried hard to place the
blame on herself, but she couldn't seem to do it. She knew she
hadn't been color-conscious during her early childhood days;
that is, until she had had it called to her attention by her
mother or some of her mother's friends, who had all seemed to
take delight in marvelling, "What an extraordinarily black child!"
or "Such beautiful hair on such a black baby!"

Her mother had even hidden her away on occasions when
she was to have company, and her grandmother had been cruel
in always assailing Emma Lou's father, whose only crime seemed
to be that he had had a blue black skin. Then there had been
her childhood days when she had ventured forth into the
streets to play. All of her colored playmates had been mulattoes, and her white playmates had never ceased calling public
attention to her crow-like complexion. Consequently, she had
grown sensitive and had soon been driven to play by herself,
avoiding contact with other children as much as possible. Her
mother encouraged her in this, had even suggested that she
not attend certain parties because she might not have a good
time.

Then there had been the searing psychological effect of that
dreadful graduation night, and the lonely embittering three
years at college, all of which had tended to make her color
more and more a paramount issue and ill. It was neither fashionable nor good for a girl to be as dark as she, and to be, at
the same time, as untalented and undistinguished. Dark girls
could get along if they were exceptionally talented or handsome or wealthy, but she had nothing to recommend her, save
a beautiful head of hair. Despite the fact that she had managed
to lead her classes in school, she had to admit that mentally
she was merely mediocre and average. Now, had she been as

intelligent as Mamie Olds Bates, head of a Negro school in Florida, and president of a huge national association of colored women's clubs, her darkness would not have mattered. Or had she been as wealthy as Lillian Saunders, who had inherited the millions her mother had made producing hair straightening commodities, things might have been different; but here she was, commonplace and poor, ugly and undistinguished.

Emma Lou recalled all these things, while trying to fasten the blame for her extreme color-consciousness on herself as Alva had done, but she was unable to make a good case of it. Surely, it had not been her color-consciousness which had excluded her from the only Negro sorority in her college, nor had it been her color-consciousness that had caused her to spend such an isolated three years in Southern California. The people she naturally felt at home with had, somehow or other, managed to keep her at a distance. It was no fun going to social affairs and being neglected throughout the entire evening. There was no need in forcing one's self into a certain milieu only to be frozen out. Hence, she had stayed to herself, had had very few friends, and had become more and more resentful of her blackness of skin.

She had thought Harlem would be different, but things had seemed against her from the beginning, and she had continued to go down, down, down, until she had little respect left for herself.

She had been glad when the road show of "Cabaret Gal" had gone into the provinces. Maybe a year of travel would set her aright. She would return to Harlem with considerable money saved, move into the Y.W.C.A., try to obtain a more congenial position, and set about becoming respectable once more, set about coming into contact with the "right sort of people." She was certain that there were many colored boys and girls in Harlem with whom she could associate and become content. She didn't wish to chance herself again with a Jasper Crane or an Alva.

Yet, she still loved Alva, no matter how much she regretted it, loved him enough to keep trying to win him back, even after his disgust had driven him away from her. She sadly recalled how she had telephoned him repeatedly, and how he had hung up the receiver with the brief, cruel "I don't care to talk to you," and she recalled how, swallowing her pride, she had gone to his house the day before she had left New York. Alva had greeted her coolly, then politely informed her that he couldn't let her in, as he had other company.

This had made her ill, and for three days after "Cabaret Gal" opened in Philadelphia, she had confined herself to her hotel room and cried hysterically. When it was all over, she had felt much better. The outlet of tears had been good for her, but she had never ceased to long for Alva. He had been the only completely satisfying thing in her life, and it didn't seem possible for one who had pretended to love her as much as he, suddenly to become so completely indifferent. She measured everything by her own moods and reactions, translated everything into the language of Emma Lou, and variations bewildered her to the extent that she could not believe in their reality.

So, when the company had passed through New York on its way from Philadelphia to Boston, she had approached Alva's door once more. It had never occurred to her that any one save Alva would answer her knock, and the sight of Geraldine in a negligee had stunned her. She had hastened to apologize for knocking on the wrong door, and had turned completely away without asking for Alva, only to halt as if thunderstruck when she heard his voice, as Geraldine was closing the door, asking, "Who was it, Sugar?"

For a while, Alva had been content. He really loved Geraldine, or so he thought. To him she seemed eminently desirable in every respect, and now that she was about to bear him a child, well . . . he didn't yet know what they would do with it, but everything would work out as it should. He didn't even mind having to return to work, nor, for the moment, mind having to give less attention to the rest of his harem.

Of course, Geraldine's attachment of herself to him ruled Emma Lou out more definitely than it did any of his other "paying off" people. He had been thoroughly disgusted with her and had intended to relent only after she had been forced to chase him for a considerable length of time. But Geraldine's coming had changed things altogether. Alva knew when not to attempt something, and he knew very well that he could not toy with Emma Lou and live with Geraldine at the same time. Some of the others were different. He could explain Geraldine to them, and they would help him keep themselves secreted from her. But Emma Lou, never! She would be certain to take it all wrong.

The months passed; the baby was born. Both of the parents were bitterly disappointed by this sickly, little "ball of tainted suet," as Alva called it. It had a shrunken left arm and a deformed left foot. The doctor ordered oil massages. There was a chance that the infant's limbs could be shaped into some semblance of normality. Alva declared that it looked like an idiot. Geraldine had a struggle with herself, trying to keep from smothering it. She couldn't see why such a monstrosity should live. Perhaps as the years passed it would change. At any rate, she had lost her respect for Alva. There was no denying to her that had she mated with some one else, she might have given birth to a normal child. The pain she had experienced had shaken her. One sight of the baby and continual living with it and Alva in that one, now frowsy and odoriferous room, had completed her disillusionment. For one of the very few times in her life, she felt like doing something drastic.

Alva hardly ever came home. He had quit work once more and started running around as before, only he didn't tell her about it. He lied to her or else ignored her altogether. The baby now a year old was assuredly an idiot. It neither talked nor walked. Its head had grown out of all proportion to its body, and Geraldine felt that she could have stood its shrivelled arm and deformed foot, had it not been for its insanely large and vacant eyes which seemed never to close, and for the thick grinning lips, which always remained half open and through which came no translatable sounds.

Geraldine's mother was a pious woman, and, of course, denounced the parents for the condition of the child. Had they not lived in sin, this would not be. Had they married and lived respectably, God would not have punished them in this manner. According to her, the mere possession of a marriage license and an official religious sanction of their mating would have assured them a bouncing, healthy, normal child. She refused to take the infant. Her pastor had advised her not to, saying that the parents should be made to bear the burden they had brought upon themselves.

For once, neither Geraldine nor Alva knew what to do. They

couldn't keep on as they were now. Alva was drinking more and more. He was also becoming less interested in looking well. He didn't bother about his clothes as much as before, his almond shaped eyes became more narrow, and the gray parchment conquered the yellow in his skin and gave him a deathlike pallor. He hated that silent, staring idiot infant of his, and he had begun to hate its mother. He couldn't go into the room sober. Yet his drinking provided no escape. And though he was often tempted, he felt that he could not run away and leave Geraldine alone with the baby.

Then he began to need money. Geraldine couldn't work because some one had to look after the child. Alva wouldn't work now, and made no effort to come into contact with new "paying off" people. The old ones were not as numerous or as generous as formerly. Those who hadn't drifted away didn't care enough about the Alva of today to help support him, his wife and child. Luckily, though, about this time, he "hit" the numbers twice in one month, and both he and Geraldine borrowed some money on their insurance policies. They accrued almost a thousand dollars from these sources, but that wouldn't last forever, and the problem of what they were going to do with the child still remained unsolved.

Both wanted to kill it, and neither had the courage to mention the word "murder" to the other. Had they been able to discuss this thing frankly with one another, they could have seen to it that the child smothered itself or fell from the crib sometime during the night. No one would have questioned the accidental death of an idiot child. But they did not trust one another, and neither dared to do the deed alone. Then Geraldine became obsessed with the fear that Alva was planning to run away from her. She knew what this would mean and she had no idea of letting him do it. She realized that should she be left alone with the child it would mean that she would be burdened throughout the years it lived, forced to struggle and support herself and her charge. But were she to leave Alva, some more sensible plan would undoubtedly present itself. No one expected a father to tie himself to an infant, and if that infant happened to be ill and an idiot . . . well, there were any number of social agencies which would care for it. Assuredly, then she must get away first. But where to go?

She was stumped again and forced to linger, fearing all the while that Alva would fail to return home once he left. She tried desperately to reintroduce a note of intimacy into their relationship, tried repeatedly to make herself less repellent to him, and, at the same time, discipline her own self so that she would not communicate her apprehensions to him. She hired the little girl who lived in the next room to take charge of the child, bought it a store of toys and went out to find a job. This being done, she insisted that Alva begin taking her out once again. He acquiesced. He wasn't interested one way or the other as long as he could go to bed drunk every night and keep a bottle of gin by his bedside.

Neither, though, seemed interested in what they were doing. Both were feverishly apprehensive at all times. They quarrelled frequently, but would hasten to make amends to one another, so afraid were they that the first one to become angry might make a bolt for freedom. Alva drank more and more. Geraldine worked, saved and schemed, always planning and praying that she would be able to get away first.

Then Alva was taken ill. His liquor-burned stomach refused to retain food. The doctor ordered him not to drink any more bootleg beverages. Alva shrugged his shoulders, left the doctor's office and sought out his favorite speakeasy.

Emma Lou was busy, and being busy, had had less time to think about herself than ever before. Thus, she was less distraught and much less dissatisfied with herself and with life. She was taking some courses in education in the afternoon classes at City College, preparatory to taking the next public school teacher's examination. She still had her position in the household of Campbell Kitchen, a position she had begun to enjoy and appreciate more and more as the master of the house evinced an interest in her and became her counsellor and friend. He encouraged her to read and opened his library to her. Ofttimes he gave her tickets to musical concerts or to the theater, and suggested means of meeting what she called "the right sort of people."

She had moved meanwhile into the Y.W.C.A. There she had met many young girls like herself, alone and unattached in New York, and she had soon found herself moving in a different world altogether. She even had a pal, Gwendolyn Johnson, a likable, light-brown-skinned girl, who had the room next to hers. Gwendolyn had been in New York only a few months. She had just recently graduated from Howard University, and was also planning to teach school in New York City. She and Emma Lou became fast friends and went everywhere together. It was with Gwendolyn that Emma Lou shared the tickets Campbell Kitchen gave her. Then on Sundays they would attend church. At first they attended a different church every Sunday, but finally took to attending St. Marks A.M.E. Church on St. Nicholas Avenue regularly.

This was one of the largest and most high-toned churches in Harlem. Emma Lou liked to go there, and both she and Gwendolyn enjoyed sitting in the congregation, observing the fine clothes and triumphal entries of its members. Then, too, they soon became interested in the various organizations which the church sponsored for young people. They attended the meetings of a literary society every Thursday evening, and joined the young people's bible class which met every Tuesday evening. In this way, they came into contact with many young folk, and were often invited to parties and dances.

Gwendolyn helped Emma Lou with her courses in education and the two obtained and studied copies of questions which had been asked in previous examinations. Gwendolyn sympathized with Emma Lou's color hyper-sensitivity and tried hard to make her forget it. In order to gain her point, she thought it necessary to down light people, and with this in mind, ofttimes told Emma Lou many derogatory tales about the mulattoes in the social and scholastic life at Howard University in Washington, D.C. The color question had never been of much moment to Gwendolyn. Being the color she was, she had never suffered. In Charleston, the mulattoes had their own churches and their own social life and mingled with darker Negroes only when the jim crow law or racial discrimination left them no other alternative. Gwendolyn's mother had belonged to one of these "persons of color" families, but she hadn't seen much in it all. What if she was better than the little black girl who lived around the corner? Didn't they both have to attend the same colored school, and didn't they both have to ride in the same section of the street car, and were not they both subject

to be called nigger by the poor white trash who lived in the adjacent block?

She had thought her relatives and associates all a little silly,
especially when they had objected to her marrying a man just
two or three shades darker than herself. She felt that this was
carrying things too far even in ancient Charleston where customs, houses and people all seemed antique and far removed
from the present. Stubbornly she had married the man of her
choice, and had exulted when her daughter had been nearer
the richer color of her father than the washed-out color of herself. Gwendolyn's father had died while she was in college, and
her mother had begun teaching in a South Carolina Negro industrial school, but she insisted that Gwendolyn must finish
her education and seek her career in the North.

Gwendolyn's mother had always preached for complete tolerance in matters of skin color. So afraid was she that her
daughter would develop a "pink" complex that she wilfully
discouraged her associating with light people and persistently
encouraged her to choose her friends from among the darker
elements of the race. And she insisted that Gwendolyn must
marry a dark brown man so that her children would be real
Negroes. So thoroughly had this become inculcated into her,
that Gwendolyn often snubbed light people, and invariably, in
accordance with her mother's sermonisings, chose dark-skinned
friends and beaux. Like her mother, Gwendolyn, was very exercised over the matter of intra-racial segregation and attempted to combat it verbally as well as actively.

When she and Emma Lou began going around together,
trying to find a church to attend regularly, she had immediately
black-balled the Episcopal Church, for she knew that most of
its members were "pinks," and despite the fact that a number
of dark-skinned West Indians, former members of the Church
of England, had forced their way in, Gwendolyn knew that the
Episcopal Church in Harlem, as in most Negro communities, was dedicated primarily to the salvation of light-skinned
Negroes.

But Gwendolyn was a poor psychologist. She didn't realize
that Emma Lou was possessed of a perverse bitterness and that
she idolized the thing one would naturally expect her to hate.
Gwendolyn was certain that Emma Lou hated "yaller" niggers

as she called them. She didn't appreciate the fact that Emma
Lou hated her own color and envied the more mellow complexions. Gwendolyn's continual damnation of "pinks" only
irritated Emma Lou and made her more impatient with her own
blackness, for, in damning them, Gwendolyn also enshrined
them for Emma Lou, who wasn't the least bit anxious to be
classified with persons who needed a champion.

However, for the time being, Emma Lou was more free than
ever from tortuous periods of self-pity and hatred. In her present field of activity, the question of color seldom introduced
itself except as Gwendolyn introduced it, which she did continually, even to the extent of giving lectures on race purity
and the superiority of unmixed racial types. Emma Lou would
listen attentively, but all the while she was observing Gwendolyn's light-brown skin, and wishing to herself that it were possible for her and Gwendolyn to effect a change in complexions,
since Gwendolyn considered a black skin so desirable.

They both had beaux, young men whom they had met at the
various church meetings and socials. Gwendolyn insisted that
they snub the "high yallers" and continually was going into
ecstasies over the browns and blacks they conquested. Emma
Lou couldn't get excited over any of them. They all seemed so
young and so pallid. Their air of being all-wise amused her, their
affected church purity and wholesomeness, largely a verbal matter, tired her. Their world was so small—church, school, home,
mother, father, parties, future. She invariably compared them
to Alva and made herself laugh by classifying them as a litter of
sick puppies. Alva was a bulldog and a healthy one at that. Yet
these sick puppies, as she called them, were the next generation
of Negro leaders, the next generation of respectable society
folk. They had a future; Alva merely lived for no purpose whatsoever except for the pleasure he could squeeze out of each
living moment. He didn't construct anything; the litter of pups
would, or at least they would be credited with constructing
something whether they did or not. She found herself strangely
uninterested in anything they might construct. She didn't see
that it would make much difference in the world whether they
did or did not. Months of sophisticated reading under Campbell Kitchen's tutelage had cultivated the seeds of pessimism
experience had sown. Life was all a bad dream recurrent in

essentials. Every dog had his day and every dog died. These priggish little respectable persons she now knew and associated with seemed infinitely inferior to her. They were all hypocritical and colorless. They committed what they called sin in the same colorless way they served God, family, and race. None of them had the fire and gusto of Alva, nor his light-heartedness. At last she had met the "right sort of people" and found them to be quite wrong.

However, she quelled her growing dissatisfaction and immersed herself in her work. Campbell Kitchen had told her again and again that economic independence was the solution to almost any problem. When she found herself a well-paying position she need not worry more. Everything else would follow and she would find herself among the pursued instead of among the pursuers. This was the gospel she now adhered to and placed faith in. She studied hard, finished her courses at Teachers College, took and passed the school board examination, and mechanically followed Gwendolyn about, pretending to share her enthusiasms and hatreds. All would soon come to the desired end. Her doctrine of pessimism was weakened by the optimism the future seemed to promise. She had even become somewhat interested in one of the young men she had met at St. Mark's. Gwendolyn discouraged this interest. "Why, Emma Lou, he's one of them yaller niggers; you don't want to get mixed up with him."

Though meaning well, she did not know that it was precisely because he was one of those "yaller niggers" that Emma Lou liked him.

Emma Lou and her new "yaller nigger," Benson Brown, were returning from church on a Tuesday evening where they had attended a Young People's Bible Class. It was a beautiful early fall night, warm and moonlit, and they had left the church early, intent upon slipping away from Gwendolyn, and taking a walk before they parted for the night. Emma Lou had no reason for liking Benson save that she was flattered that a man as light as he should find himself attracted to her. It always gave her a thrill to stroll into church or down Seventh Avenue with him. And she loved to show him off in the reception room of the Y.W.C.A. True, he was almost as colorless and uninteresting to her as the rest of the crowd with whom she now associated, but he had a fair skin and he didn't seem to mind her darkness. Then, it did her good to show Gwendolyn that she, Emma Lou, could get a yellow-skinned man. She always felt that the reason Gwendolyn insisted upon her going with a dark-skinned man was because she secretly considered it unlikely for her to get a light one.

Benson was a negative personality. His father was an ex-preacher turned Pullman porter because, since prohibition times, he could make more money on the Pullman cars than he could in the pulpit. His mother was an active church worker and club woman, "one of the pillars of the community," the current pastor at their church had called her. Benson himself was in college, studying business methods and administration. It had taken him six years to finish high school, and it promised to take him much longer to finish college. He had a placid, ineffectual dirty yellow face, topped by red mariney hair, and studded with gray eyes. He was as ugly as he was stupid, and he had been as glad to have Emma Lou interested in him as she had been glad to attract him. She actually seemed to take him seriously, while every one else more or less laughed at him. Already he was planning to quit school, go to work, and marry her; and Emma Lou, while not anticipating any such sudden consummation, remained blind to everything save his color and the attention he paid to her.

Benson had suggested their walk and Emma Lou had chosen Seventh Avenue in preference to some of the more quiet side streets. She still loved to promenade up and down Harlem's main thoroughfare. As usual on a warm night, it was crowded. Street speakers and their audiences monopolized the corners. Pedestrians and loiterers monopolized all of the remaining sidewalk space. The street was jammed with traffic. Emma Lou was more convinced than ever that there was nothing like it anywhere. She tried to formulate some of her impressions and attempted to convey them to Benson, but he couldn't see anything unusual or novel or interesting in a "lot of niggers hanging out here to be seen." Then, Seventh Avenue wasn't so much. What about Broadway or Fifth Avenue downtown where the white folks gathered and strolled. Now those were the streets, Seventh Avenue, Harlem's Seventh Avenue, didn't enter into it.

Emma Lou didn't feel like arguing. She walked along in silence, holding tightly to Benson's arm and wondering whether or not Alva was somewhere on Seventh Avenue. Strange she had never seen him. Perhaps he had gone away. Benson wished to stop in order to listen to one of the street speakers who, he informed Emma Lou, was mighty smart. It seemed that he was the self-styled mayor of Harlem, and his spiel nightly was concerning the fact that Harlem Negroes depended upon white people for most of their commodities instead of opening food and dress commissaries of their own. He lamented the fact that there were no Negro store owners, and regretted that wealthy Negroes did not invest their money in first class butcher shops, grocery stores, et cetera. Then, he perorated, the Jews, who now grew rich off their Negro trade, would be forced out, and the money Negroes spent would benefit Negroes alone.

Emma Lou knew that this was just the sort of thing that Benson liked to hear. She had to tug hard on his arm to make him remain on the edge of the crowd, so that she could see the passing crowds rather than center her attention on the speaker. In watching, Emma Lou saw a familiar figure approach, a very trim, well garbed figure, alert and swaggering. It was Braxton. She didn't know whether to speak to him or not. She wasn't sure that he would acknowledge her salute should she address him, yet here was her chance to get news of Alva, and she felt that she might risk being snubbed. It would be worth it. He drew near. He was alone, and, as he passed, she reached out her arm and touched him on the sleeve. He stopped, looked down at her and frowned.

"Braxton," she spoke quickly, "pardon me for stopping you, but I thought you might tell me where Alva is."

"I guess he's at the same place," he answered curtly, then moved away. Emma Lou bowed her head shamefacedly as Benson turned toward her long enough to ask who it was she had spoken to. She mumbled something about an old friend, then suggested that they go home. She was tired. Benson agreed reluctantly and they turned toward the Y.W.C.A.

A taxi driver had brought Alva home from a saloon where he had collapsed from cramps in the stomach. That had been on a Monday. The doctor had come and diagnosed his case. He was in a serious condition, his stomach lining was practically eaten away and his entire body wrecked from physical excess. Unless he took a complete rest and abstained from drinking liquor and all other forms of dissipation, there could be no hope of recovery. This hadn't worried Alva very much. He chafed at having to remain in bed, but the possibility of death didn't worry him. Life owed him very little, he told Geraldine. He was content to let the devil take his due. But Geraldine was quite worried about the whole matter. Should Alva die or even be an invalid for any lengthy period, it would mean that she alone would have the burden of their misshapen child. She didn't want that burden. In fact, she was determined not to have it. And neither did she intend to nurse Alva.

On the Friday morning after the Monday Alva had been taken ill, Geraldine left for work as was her custom. But she did not come back that night. Every morning during that week she had taken away a bundle of this and a bundle of that until she had managed to get away most of her clothes. She had saved enough money out of her earnings to pay her fare to Chicago. She had chosen Chicago because a man who was interested in her lived there. She had written to him. He had been glad to hear from her. He ran a buffet flat. He needed some one like her to act as hostess. Leaving her little bundles at a girl friend's day after day and packing them away in a second hand trunk, she had planned to leave the moment she received her pay on Saturday. She had intended going home on Friday night, but at the last moment she had faltered and reasoned that as long as she was away and only had twenty-four hours more in New York she might as well make her disappearance then. If she went back she might betray herself or else become soft-hearted and remain.

Alva was not very surprised when she failed to return home from work that Friday. The woman in the next room kept coming in at fifteen-minute intervals after five-thirty inquiring: "Hasn't your wife come in yet?" She wanted to get rid of the child which was left in her care daily. She had her own work to do, her own husband and child's dinner to prepare; and, furthermore, she wasn't being paid to keep the child both day and night. People shouldn't have children unless they intended taking care of them. Finally Alva told her to bring the baby back to his room . . . his wife would be in soon. But he knew full well that Geraldine was not coming back. Hell of a mess. He was unable to work, would probably have to remain in bed another week, perhaps two. His money was about gone, and now Geraldine was not there to pay the rent out of her earnings. Damn. What to do . . . what to do? He couldn't keep the child. If he put it in a home they would expect him to contribute to its support. It was too bad that he didn't know some one to leave this child of his with as his mother had done in his case. He began to wish for a drink.

Hours passed. Finally the lady came into the room again to see if he or the baby wanted anything. She knew Geraldine had not come in yet. The partition between the two rooms was so thin that the people in one were privy to everything the people in the other did or said. Alva told her his wife must have gone to see her sick mother in Long Island. He asked her to take care of the baby for him. He would pay her for her extra trouble. The whole situation offered her much pleasure. She went away radiant, eager to tell the other lodgers in the house her version of what had happened.

Alva got up and paced the room. He felt that he could no longer remain flat on his back. His stomach ached, but it also craved for alcoholic stimulant. So did his brain and nervous system in general. Inadvertently, in one of his trips across the room, he looked into the dresser mirror. What he saw there halted his pacing. Surely that wan, dissipated, bloated face did not belong to him. Perhaps he needed a shave. He set about ridding himself of a week's growth of beard, but being shaved only made his face look more like the face of a corpse. It was liquor he needed. He wished to hell some one would come along and get him some. But no one came. He went back to bed, his eyes fixed on the clock, watching its hands approach midnight. Five minutes to go. . . . There was a knock on the door. Eagerly he sat up in the bed and shouted, "Come in."

But he was by no means expecting or prepared to see Emma Lou.

Emma Lou's room in the Y.W.C.A. at three o'clock that same morning. Emma Lou busy packing her clothes. Gwendolyn in negligee, hair disarrayed, eyes sleepy, yet angry:

"You mean you're going over there to live with that man?"

"Why not? I love him."

Gwendolyn stared hard at Emma Lou. "But don't you understand he's just tryin' to find some one to take care of that brat of his? Don't be silly, Emma Lou. He doesn't really care for you. If he did, he never would have deserted you as you once told me he did, or have subjected you to all those insults. And . . . he isn't your type of man. Why, he's nothing but a . . ."

"Will you mind tending to your own business, Gwendolyn," her purple powdered skin was streaked with tears.

"But what about your appointment?"

"I shall take it."

"What!" She forgot her weariness. "You mean to say you're going to teach school and live with that man, too? Ain't you got no regard for your reputation? I wouldn't ruin myself for no yaller nigger. Here you're doing just what folks say a black gal always does. Where is your intelligence and pride? I'm through with you, Emma Lou. There's probably something in this stuff about black people being different and more low than other colored people. You're just a common ordinary nigger! God, how I despise you!" And she had rushed out of the room, leaving Emma Lou dazed by the suddenness and wrath of her tirade.

Emma Lou was busier than she had ever been before in her life. She had finally received her appointment and was teaching in one of the public schools in Harlem. Doing this in addition to nursing Alva and Alva Junior, and keeping house for them in Alva's same old room. Within six months she had managed to make little Alva Junior take on some of the physical aspects of a normal child. His little legs were in braces, being straightened. Twice a week she took him to the clinic where he had violet ray sun baths and oil massages. His little body had begun to fill out and simultaneously it seemed as if his head was decreasing in size. There was only one feature which remained unchanged; his abnormally large eyes still retained their insane stare. They appeared frozen and terrified as if their owner was gazing upon some horrible, yet fascinating object or occurrence. The doctor said that this would disappear in time.

During those six months there had been a steady change in Alva Senior, too. At first he had been as loving and kind to Emma Lou as he had been during the first days of their relationship. Then, as he got better and began living his old life again, he more and more relegated her to the position of a hired nurse girl. He was scarcely civil to her. He seldom came home except to eat and get some pocket change. When he did come home nights, he was usually drunk, so drunk that his companions would have to bring him home, and she would have to undress him and put him to bed. Since his illness, he could not stand as much liquor as before. His stomach refused to retain it, and his legs refused to remain steady.

Emma Lou began to loathe him, yet ached for his physical nearness. She was lonesome again, cooped up in that solitary room with only Alva Junior for company. She had lost track of all her old friends, and, despite her new field of endeavor, she had made no intimate contacts. Her fellow colored teachers were congenial enough, but they didn't seem any more inclined to accept her socially than did her fellow white teachers. There seemed to be some question about her antecedents. She didn't belong to any of the collegiate groups around Harlem. She didn't seem to be identified with any one who mattered. They wondered how she had managed to get into the school system.

Of course Emma Lou made little effort to make friends among them. She didn't know how. She was too shy to make an approach and too suspicious to thaw out immediately when some one approached her. The first thing she noticed was that most of the colored teachers who taught in her school were lighter colored than she. The darkest was a pleasing brown. And she had noticed them putting their heads together when she first came around. She imagined that they were discussing her. And several times upon passing groups of them, she imagined that she was being pointed out. In most cases what she thought was true, but she was being discussed and pointed out, not because of her dark skin, but because of the obvious traces of an excess of rouge and powder which she insisted upon using.

It had been suggested, in a private council among the Negro members of the teaching staff, that some one speak to Emma Lou about this rather ludicrous habit of making up. But no one had the nerve. She appeared so distant and so ready to take offense at the slightest suggestion even of friendship that they were wary of her. But after she began to be a standard joke among the pupils and among the white teachers, they finally decided to send her an anonymous note, suggesting that she use fewer aids to the complexion. Emma Lou, on receiving the note, at first thought that it was the work of some practical joker. It never occurred to her that the note told the truth and that she looked twice as bad with paint and powder as she would without it. She interpreted it as being a means of making fun of her because she was darker than any one of the other colored girls. She grew more haughty, more acid, and more distant than ever. She never spoke to any one except as a matter of business. Then she discovered that her pupils had nicknamed her . . . "Blacker'n me."

What made her still more miserable was the gossip and comments of the woman in the next room. Lying in bed nights or else sitting at her table preparing her lesson plans, she could hear her telling every one who chanced in——

"You know that fellow in the next room? Well, let me tell you. His wife left him, yes-sireee, left him flat on his back in the bed, him and the baby, too. Yes, she did. Walked out of here just as big as you please to go to work one morning and she ain't come back yet. Then up comes this little black wench. I heard her when she knocked on the door that very night his wife left. At first he was mighty s'prised to see her, then started laying it on, kissed her and hugged her, a-tellin' her how much he loved her, and she crying like a fool all the time. I never heard the likes of it in my life. The next morning in she moves an' she's been here ever since. And you oughter see how she carries on over that child, just as loving, like as if she was his own mother. An' now that she's here an' workin' an' that nigger's well again, what does he do but go out an' get drunk worse than he uster with his wife. Would you believe it? Stays away three and four nights a week, while she hustles out of here an' makes time every morning. . . ."

On hearing this for about the twentieth time, Emma Lou determined to herself that she was not going to hear it again. (She had also planned to ask for a transfer to a new school, one on the east side in the Italian section where she would not have to associate with so many other colored teachers.) Alva hadn't been home for four nights. She picked Alva Junior from out his crib and pulled off his nightgown, letting him lie naked in her lap. She loved to fondle his warm, mellow-colored body, loved to caress his little crooked limbs after the braces had been removed. She wondered what would become of him. Obviously she couldn't remain living with Alva, and she certainly couldn't keep Alva Junior forever. Suppose those evil school teachers should find out how she was living and report it to the school authorities? Was she morally fit to be teaching youth? She remembered her last conversation with Gwendolyn.

For the first time now she also saw how Alva had used her during both periods of their relationship. She also realized that she had been nothing more than a commercial proposition to him at all times. He didn't care for dark women either. He had never taken her among his friends, never given any signs to the public that she was his girl. And now when he came home with some of his boy friends, he always introduced her as Alva Junior's mammy. That's what she was, Alva Junior's mammy, and a typical black mammy at that.

Campbell Kitchen had told her that when she found economic independence, everything else would come. Well now that she had economic independence she found herself more enslaved and more miserable than ever. She wondered what he thought of her. She had never tried to get in touch with him since she had left the Y.W.C.A., and had never let him know of her whereabouts, had just quit communicating with him as unceremoniously as she had quit the Y.W.C.A. No doubt Gwendolyn had told him the whole sordid tale. She could never face him again unless she had made some effort to reclaim herself. Well, that's what she was going to do. Reclaim herself. She didn't care what became of Alva Junior. Let Alva and that yellow slut of a wife of his worry about their own piece of tainted suet.

She was leaving. She was going back to the Y.W.C.A., back to St. Mark's A.M.E. Church, back to Gwendolyn, back to Benson. She wouldn't stay here and have that child grow up to call her "black mammy." Just because she was black was no reason why she was going to let some yellow nigger use her. At once she was all activity. Putting Alva Jr.'s nightgown on, she laid him back into his crib and left him there crying while she packed her trunk and suitcase. Then, asking the woman in the next room to watch him until she returned, she put on her hat and coat and started for the Y.W.C.A., making plans for the future as she went.

Halfway there she decided to telephone Benson. It had been seven months now since she had seen him, seven months since, without a word of warning or without leaving a message, she had disappeared, telling only Gwendolyn where she was going. While waiting for the operator to establish connections, she recalled the conversation she and Gwendolyn had had at the time, recalled Gwendolyn's horror and disgust on hearing what Emma Lou planned doing, recalled . . . some one was answering the 'phone. She asked for Benson, and in a moment heard his familiar:

"Hello."

"Hello, Benson, this is Emma Lou." There was complete silence for a moment, then:

"Emma Lou?" he dinned into her ear. "Well, where have you been. Gwennie and I have been trying to find you."

This warmed her heart; coming back was not going to be so difficult after all.

"You did?"

"Why, yes. We wanted to invite you to our wedding."

The receiver fell from her hand. For a moment she stood like one stunned, unable to move. She could hear Benson on the other end of the wire clicking the receiver and shouting "Hello, Hello," then the final clicking of the receiver as he hung up, followed by a deadened . . . "operator" . . . "operator" from central.

Somehow or other she managed to get hold of the receiver and replace it in the hook. Then she left the telephone booth and made her way out of the drugstore into the street. Seventh Avenue as usual was alive and crowded. It was an early spring evening and far too warm for people to remain cooped up in stuffy apartments. Seventh Avenue was the gorge into which Harlem cliff dwellers crowded to promenade. It was heavy laden, full of life and color, vibrant and leisurely. But for the first time since her arrival in Harlem, Emma Lou was impervious to all this. For the moment she hardly realized where she was. Only the constant jostling and the raucous ensemble of street noises served to bring her out of her daze.

Gwendolyn and Benson married. "What do you want to waste your time with that yaller nigger for? I wouldn't marry a yaller nigger."

"Blacker'n me" . . . "Why don't you take a hint and stop plastering your face with so much rouge and powder."

Emma Lou stumbled down Seventh Avenue, not knowing where she was going. She noted that she was at 135th Street. It was easy to tell this particular corner. It was called the campus. All the college boys hung out there when the weather permitted, obstructing the traffic and eyeing the passersby professionally. She turned west on 135th Street. She wanted quiet. Seventh Avenue was too noisy and too alive and too happy. How could the world be happy when she felt like she did? There was no place for her in the world. She was too black, black is a portent of evil, black is a sign of bad luck.

> "A yaller gal rides in a limousine
> A brown-skin does the same;
> A black gal rides in a rickety Ford,
> But she gets there, yes, my Lord."

"Alva Jr's black mammy." "Low down common nigger." "Jes' crazy 'bout that little yaller brat."

She looked up and saw a Western Union office sign shining above a lighted doorway. For a moment she stood still, repeating over and over to herself Western Union, Western Union, as if to understand its meaning. People turned to stare at her as they passed. They even stopped and looked up into the air trying to see what was attracting her attention, and, seeing nothing, would shrug their shoulders and continue on their way. The Western Union sign suggested only one thing to Emma Lou and that was home. For the moment she was ready to rush into the office and send a wire to her Uncle Joe, asking for a ticket, and thus be able to escape the whole damn mess. But she immediately saw that going home would mean beginning her life all over again, mean flying from one degree of unhappiness into another probably much more intense and tragic than the present one. She had once fled to Los Angeles to escape Boise, then fled to Harlem to escape Los Angeles, but these mere geographical flights had not solved her problems in the past, and a further flight back to where her life had begun, although facile of accomplishment, was too futile to merit consideration.

Rationalizing thus, she moved away from in front of the Western Union office and started toward the park two blocks away. She felt that it was necessary that she do something about herself and her life and do it immediately. Campbell Kitchen had said that every one must find salvation within one's self, that no one in life need be a total misfit, and that there was some niche for every peg, whether that peg be round or square. If this were true then surely she could find hers even at this late date. But then hadn't she exhausted all possibilities? Hadn't she explored every province of life and everywhere met the same problem? It was easy for Campbell Kitchen or for Gwendolyn to say what they would do had they been she, for they were looking at her problem in the abstract, while to her it was an empirical reality. What could they know of the adjustment proceedings necessary to make her life more full and more happy? What could they know of her heartaches?

She trudged on, absolutely oblivious to the people she passed or to the noise and bustle of the street. For the first time in her life she felt that she must definitely come to some conclusion about her life and govern herself accordingly. After all she wasn't the only black girl alive. There were thousands on thousands, who, like her, were plain, untalented, ordinary, and who, unlike herself, seemed to live in some degree of comfort. Was she alone to blame for her unhappiness? Although this had been suggested to her by others, she had been too obtuse to accept it. She had ever been eager to shift the entire blame on others when no doubt she herself was the major criminal.

But having arrived at this—what did it solve or promise for the future? After all it was not the abstractions of her case which at the present moment most needed elucidation. She could strive for a change of mental attitudes later. What she needed to do now was to accept her black skin as being real and unchangeable, to realize that certain things were, had been, and would be, and with this in mind begin life anew, always fighting, not so much for acceptance by other people, but for acceptance of herself by herself. In the future she would be eminently selfish. If people came into her life—well and good. If they didn't—she would live anyway, seeking to find herself and achieving meanwhile economic and mental independence. Then possibly, as Campbell Kitchen had said, life would open up for her, for it seemed as if its doors yielded more easily to the casual, self-centered individual than to the ranting, praying pilgrim. After all it was the end that mattered, and one only wasted time and strength seeking facile open-sesame means instead of pushing along a more difficult and direct path.

By now Emma Lou had reached St. Nicholas Avenue and was about to cross over into the park when she heard the chimes of a clock and was reminded of the hour. It was growing late—too late for her to wander in the park alone where she knew she would be approached either by some persistent male or an insulting park policeman. Wearily she started towards home, realizing that it was necessary for her to get some rest in order to be able to be in her class room on the next morning. She mustn't jeopardize her job, for it was partially through the money she was earning from it that she would be able to find her place in life. She was tired of running up blind alleys all of which seemed to converge and lead her ultimately to the same blank wall. Her motto from now on would be "find —not seek." All things were at one's finger-tips. Life was most kind to those who were judicious in their selections, and she, weakling that she now realized she was, had not been a connoisseur.

As she drew nearer home she felt certain that should she attempt to spend another night with Alva and his child, she would surely smother to death during the night. And even though she felt this, she also knew within herself that no matter how much at the present moment she pretended to hate Alva that he had only to make the proper advances in order to win her to him again. Yet she also knew that she must leave him if she was to make her self-proposed adjustment—leave him now even if she should be weak enough to return at some not so distant date. She was determined to fight against Alva's influence over her, fight even though she lost, for she reasoned that even in losing she would win a pyrrhic victory and thus make her life less difficult in the future, for having learned to fight future battles would be easy.

She tried to convince herself that it would not be necessary for her to have any more Jasper Cranes or Alvas in her life. To assure herself of this she intended to look John up on the morrow and if he were willing let him re-enter her life. It was clear to her now what a complete fool she had been. It was clear to her at last that she had exercised the same discrimination against her men and the people she wished for friends that they had exercised against her—and with less reason. It served her right that Jasper Crane had fooled her as he did. It served her right that Alva had used her once for the money she could give him and again as a black mammy for his child. That was the price she had had to pay for getting what she thought she wanted. But now she intended to balance things. Life after all was a give and take affair. Why should she give important things and receive nothing in return?

She was in front of the house now and looking up saw that all the lights in her room were lit. And as she climbed the stairs she could hear a drunken chorus of raucous masculine laughter. Alva had come home meanwhile, drunk of course and accompanied by the usual drunken crowd. Emma Lou started to turn back, to flee into the street—anywhere to escape being precipitated into another sordid situation, but remembering that this was to be her last night there, and that the new day would find her beginning a new life, she subdued her flight impulse and without knocking threw open the door and walked into the room. She saw the usual and expected sight: Alva, face a death mask, sitting on the bed embracing an effeminate boy whom she knew as Bobbie, and who drew hurriedly away from Alva as he saw her. There were four other boys in the room, all in varied states of drunkenness—all laughing boisterously at some obscene witticism. Emma Lou suppressed a shudder and calmly said "Hello Alva"—The room grew silent. They all seemed shocked and surprised by her sudden appearance. Alva did not answer her greeting but instead turned to Bobbie and asked him for another drink. Bobbie fumbled nervously at his hip pocket and finally produced a flask which he handed to Alva. Emma Lou stood at the door and watched Alva drink the liquor Bobbie had given him. Every one else in the room watched her. For the moment she did not know what to say or what to do. Obviously she couldn't continue standing there by the door nor could she leave and let them feel that she had been completely put to rout.

Alva handed the flask back to Bobbie, who got up from the bed and said something about leaving. The others in the room also got up and began staggering around looking for their hats. Emma Lou thought for a moment that she was going to win without any further struggle, but she had not reckoned with Alva who, meanwhile, had sufficiently emerged from his stupor to realize that his friends were about to go.

"What the hell's the matter with you," he shouted up at Bobbie, and without waiting for an answer reached out for Bobbie's arm and jerked him back down on the bed.

"Now stay there till I tell you to get up."

The others in the room had now found their hats and started toward the door, eager to escape. Emma Lou crossed the room to where Alva was sitting and said, "You might make less noise, the baby's asleep."

The four boys had by this time opened the door and staggered out into the hallway. Bobbie edged nervously away from Alva, who leered up at Emma Lou and snarled "If you don't like it—"

For the moment Emma Lou did not know what to do. Her first impulse was to strike him, but she was restrained because underneath the loathsome beast that he now was, she saw the Alva who had first attracted her to him, the Alva she had always loved. She suddenly felt an immense compassion for him and had difficulty in stifling an unwelcome urge to take him into her arms. Tears came into her eyes, and for a moment it seemed as if all her rationalization would go for naught. Then once more she saw Alva, not as he had been, but as he was now, a drunken, drooling libertine, struggling to keep the embarrassed Bobbie in a vile embrace. Something snapped within her. The tears in her eyes receded, her features grew set, and she felt herself hardening inside. Then, without saying a word, she resolutely turned away, went into the alcove, pulled her suitcases down from the shelf in the clothes-closet, and, to the blasphemous accompaniment of Alva berating Bobbie for wishing to leave, finished packing her clothes, not stopping even when Alva Junior's cries deafened her, and caused the people in the next room to stir uneasily.

CHRONOLOGY

BIOGRAPHICAL NOTES

NOTE ON THE TEXTS

NOTES

Chronology

1919   February 17: Returning veterans of the Fifteenth Regiment of New York's National Guard march triumphally through Harlem. February 19–21: While the Paris Peace Conference is taking place, W.E.B. Du Bois organizes Pan-African Conference in Paris, attended by fifty-seven delegates from the United States, the West Indies, Europe, and Africa; conference calls for acknowledgment and protection of the rights of Africans under colonial rule. March: Release of *The Homesteader*, directed and produced by self-published novelist and entrepreneur Oscar Micheaux, first feature-length film by an African American. May: Hair-care entrepreneur Madam C. J. Walker dies at her estate in Irvington, New York; her daughter A'Lelia Walker assumes control of the Madam C.J. Walker Manufacturing Company. May–October: In what becomes known as "the Red Summer," racial conflicts boil over in the wake of the return of African American veterans; incidents of racial violence erupt across the United States, including outbreaks in Charleston, South Carolina; Longview, Texas; Omaha; Washington, D.C.; Chicago; Knoxville; and Elaine, Arkansas. June: Marcus Garvey establishes his Black Star Line (the shipping concern will operate until 1922). July: Claude McKay's poem "If We Must Die," written in response to the summer of violence, appears in Max Eastman's magazine *The Liberator*. September: Jessie Redmon Fauset joins staff of *The Crisis*, the literary magazine of the NAACP founded in 1910, as literary editor.

1920   January: *The Brownie's Book*, a magazine for African American children, founded by W.E.B. Du Bois with Jessie Redmon Fauset and Augustus Dill, begins its run of twenty-four issues. Oscar Micheaux releases the anti-lynching film, *Within Our Gates*, an answer both to D. W. Griffith's inflammatory *The Birth of a Nation* (1915) and the Red Summer of 1919. April: In an article in *The Crisis*, W.E.B. Du Bois writes: "A renaissance of American Negro literature is due." August: The Universal Negro Improvement Association (UNIA), founded by Jamaican immigrant and Pan-Africanist Marcus Garvey, holds its first convention at Madison Square Garden in New York City, attended by some 25,000 delegates. November: James Weldon Johnson becomes executive secretary (and first black officer) of the NAACP. Mamie Smith's "Crazy Blues" is released by Okeh Records. Eugene O'Neill's *The Emperor Jones*, starring Charles Gilpin, opens at the Provincetown Playhouse in Greenwich Village.

Books

W.E.B. Du Bois: *Darkwater: Voices from Within the Veil* (Harcourt, Brace & Howe)

Claude McKay: *Spring in New Hampshire and Other Poems* (Grant Richards)

1921   February: Max Eastman invites Claude McKay, just returned from England, to become associate editor of *The Liberator*. March: Harry Pace forms Black Swan Phonograph Company, one of the first black-owned record companies in Harlem; its most successful recording artist is Ethel Waters. May: *Shuffle Along*, a pioneering all–African American production, with book by Flournoy Miller and Aubrey Lyles and music and lyrics by Eubie Blake and Noble Sissle, opens on Broadway and becomes a hit. It showcases such stars as Florence Mills and Josephine Baker. June: Langston Hughes publishes his poem "The Negro Speaks of Rivers" in *The Crisis*. August–September: Exhibit of African American art at the 135th Street branch of the New York Public Library, including work by Henry Ossawa Tanner, Meta Fuller, and Laura Wheeler Waring. December: René Maran, a native of Martinique, becomes the first black recipient of the Prix Goncourt, for his novel *Batouala*; soon translated into English, it will be widely discussed in the African American press.

1922   January: The Dyer Anti-Lynching Bill is passed by the House of Representatives; it is subsequently blocked in the Senate. Spring: *Birthright*, novel of African American life by the white novelist T. S. Stribling, is published by Century Publications. (Oscar Micheaux will make two films based on the book, in 1924 and 1938.) White real estate magnate William E. Harmon establishes the Harmon Foundation to advance African American achievements.

Books

Georgia Douglas Johnson: *Bronze* (B. J. Brimmer)

James Weldon Johnson, editor: *The Book of American Negro Poetry* (Harcourt, Brace)

Claude McKay: *Harlem Shadows* (Harcourt, Brace; expanded version of *Spring in New Hampshire*)
T. S. Stribling: *Birthright* (Century)

1923   January: *Opportunity: A Journal of Negro Life*, published by the National Urban League and edited by sociologist Charles S. Johnson, is founded. Claude McKay addresses the Fourth Congress of the Third International in Moscow. February: Bessie Smith's "Downhearted Blues" (written and originally recorded by Alberta Hunter) is released by Columbia Records and sells nearly a million copies within six months. May: Willis Richardson's *The Chip Woman*, produced by the National Ethiopian Art Players, becomes the first serious play by an African American playwright to open on Broadway. June: Marcus Garvey receives a five-year sentence for mail fraud. December: Tenor Roland Hayes, having won acclaim in London as a singer of classical music, gives a concert of lieder and spirituals at Town Hall in New York. *The Messenger*, founded in 1917 by Asa Philip Randolph and Chandler Owen as a black trade unionist magazine with socialist sympathies, begins publishing more literary material under editorial guidance of George S. Schuyler and Theophilus Lewis.

Books
Marcus Garvey: *Philosophy and Opinion of Marcus Garvey* (Universal Publishing House)
Jean Toomer: *Cane* (Boni & Liveright)

1924   March: The Civic Club dinner, held in honor of Jessie Redmon Fauset on publishing her first novel *There Is Confusion*, is sponsored by *Opportunity* and Charles S. Johnson. Those in attendance include Alain Locke, W.E.B. Du Bois, Countee Cullen, Eric Walrond, Gwendolyn Bennett, and such representatives of the New York publishing world as Alfred A. Knopf and Horace Liveright. (In retrospect the occasion is often taken to mark the beginning of the Harlem Renaissance.) May: W.E.B. Du Bois attacks Marcus Garvey in *The Crisis* article "A Lunatic or a Traitor." Eugene O'Neill's play *All God's Chillun Got Wings*, starring Paul Robeson and controversial for its theme of miscegenation, opens. Autumn: Countee Cullen is the first recipient of Witter Bynner Poetry Competition. September: René Maran publishes poems by Countee Cullen, Langston Hughes, Claude McKay, and Jean Toomer in his Paris newspaper, *Les Continents.* Louis Armstrong comes to New York from Chicago to join Fletcher Henderson's band at the Roseland Ballroom.

Books

W.E.B. Du Bois: *The Gift of Black Folk: The Negroes in the Making of America* (Stratford)

Jessie Redmon Fauset: *There Is Confusion* (Boni & Liveright)

Walter White: *The Fire in the Flint* (Knopf)

1925   February: After his appeals are denied, Marcus Garvey begins serving his sentence for mail fraud at Atlanta Federal Penitentiary. March: Howard Philosophy Professor Alain Locke edits a special issue of *The Survey Graphic* titled "Harlem: Mecca of the New Negro"; in November *The New Negro*, an expanded book version, is published by Albert and Charles Boni. The volume features six pages of painter Aaron Douglas's African-inspired illustrations, and includes writing by Jean Toomer, Rudolph Fisher, Zora Neale Hurston, Eric Walrond, Countee Cullen, James Weldon Johnson, Langston Hughes, Georgia Douglas Johnson, Richard Bruce Nugent, Anne Spencer, Claude McKay, Jessie Redmon Fauset, Arthur Schomburg, Charles S. Johnson, W.E.B. Du Bois, and E. Franklin Frazier. May: *Opportunity* holds its first awards dinner, recognizing, among others, Langston Hughes ("The Weary Blues," first prize), Countee Cullen, Zora Neale Hurston, Eric Walrond, and Sterling Brown. Paul Robeson appears at Greenwich Village Theatre in a concert entirely devoted to spirituals, accompanied by Lawrence Brown. August: A. Phillip Randolph organizes the Brotherhood of Sleeping Car Porters. October: The American Negro Labor Congress is founded in Chicago. November: First prize of *The Crisis* awards goes to poet Countee Cullen. Paul Robeson stars in Oscar Micheaux's film *Body and Soul.* December: Marita Bonner publishes essay "On Being Young—A Woman—And Colored" in *The Crisis*, about the predicament and possibilities of the educated black woman.

Books

Countee Cullen: *Color* (Harper)

James Weldon Johnson and J. Rosamond Johnson, editors: *The Book of American Negro Spirituals* (Viking Press)

Alain Locke, editor: *The New Negro: An Interpretation* (Albert and Charles Boni)

1926   January: The Harmon Foundation announces its first awards for artistic achievement by African Americans. Palmer Hayden, a World War I veteran and menial laborer, wins the gold medal for painting. February: Jessie Redmon Fauset steps down as editor of *The Crisis*. The play *Lulu Belle*, starring Lenore Ulric in blackface as well as the African American actress Edna Thomas, opens to great success on Broadway; it helps create a vogue of whites frequenting Harlem nightspots. March: The Savoy Ballroom opens on Lenox Avenue between 140th and 141st Streets. June: Successive issues of *The Nation* feature Langston Hughes's "The Negro Artist and the Racial Mountain" and George S. Schuyler's "The Negro-Art Hokum." July: W.E.B. Du Bois founds Krigwa Players, Harlem theater group devoted to plays depicting African American life. August: Carl Van Vechten, white novelist and close friend to many Negro Renaissance figures, publishes his roman à clef, *Nigger Heaven*, with Knopf. Although many of his friends—including James Weldon Johnson, Nella Larsen, and Langston Hughes—are supportive, the book is widely disliked by African American readers, and notably condemned by W.E.B. Du Bois. October: Arthur Schomburg's collection of thousands of books, manuscripts, and artworks is purchased for the New York Public Library by the Carnegie Corporation; it will form the basis of what will become the Schomburg Center for Research in Black Culture. November: *Fire!!*, a journal edited by Wallace Thurman, makes its sole appearance. Contributors include Langston Hughes, Zora Neale Hurston, and Gwendolyn Bennett, among others. "Smoke, Lilies and Jade," a short story by Richard Bruce Nugent published in *Fire!!*, shocks many by its delineation of a homosexual liaison as well as by Nugent's suggestive line drawings. Most copies are accidentally destroyed in a fire. December: Countee Cullen begins contributing a column, "The Dark Tower," to *Opportunity*. (It will run until September 1928.)

Books

W. C. Handy, editor: *Blues: An Anthology* (Boni & Boni)
Langston Hughes: *The Weary Blues* (Knopf)
Alain Locke, editor: *Four Negro Poets* (Simon & Schuster)

Carl Van Vechten: *Nigger Heaven* (Knopf)

Eric Walrond: *Tropic Death* (Boni & Liveright; story collection)

Walter White: *Flight* (Knopf)

1927   July: Ethel Waters stars on Broadway in the revue *Africana*. August: Rudolph Fisher's essay "The Caucasian Storms Harlem" is published in *The American Mercury*. September: James Weldon Johnson's *The Autobiography of an Ex-Colored Man*, first published anonymously in 1912, is republished by Knopf. October: A'Lelia Walker, cosmetics heiress and Harlem socialite, opens The Dark Tower, a tearoom intended as a cultural gathering place, at her home on West 130th Street: "We dedicate this tower to the aesthetes. That cultural group of young Negro writers, sculptors, painters, music artists, composers, and their friends." The Theatre Guild production of DuBose Heyward's play *Porgy*, with an African American cast, opens to great success. December: Marcus Garvey, pardoned by Calvin Coolidge after serving more than half of five-year sentence for mail fraud, is deported. Duke Ellington and his orchestra begin what will prove a years-long engagement at the Cotton Club of Harlem.

Books

Countee Cullen: *Copper Sun* (Harper)

Countee Cullen, editor: *Caroling Dusk: An Anthology of Verse by Negro Poets* (Harper)

Langston Hughes: *Fine Clothes to the Jew* (Knopf)

Charles S. Johnson, editor: *Ebony and Topaz* (Journal of Negro Life/National Urban League)

James Weldon Johnson: *God's Trombones: Seven Negro Sermons in Verse* (Knopf)

Alain Locke and Montgomery Gregory, editors: *Plays of Negro Life* (Harper)

1928   January: The first Harmon Foundation art exhibition opens at New York's International House. April 9: Countee Cullen marries Nina Yolande, daughter of W.E.B. Du Bois; the wedding is a major social event, attended by thousands of people. (The marriage breaks up several months later.) May: Bill "Bojangles" Robinson appears on Broadway in the revue *Blackbirds of 1928*. June: *The Messenger* ceases publication when the Brotherhood of Sleeping Car Porters can no longer financially support the journal. November:

Wallace Thurman publishes the first and only issue of the magazine *Harlem: A Forum of Negro Life*.

Books

W.E.B. Du Bois: *Dark Princess: A Romance* (Harcourt, Brace)

Jessie Redmon Fauset: *Plum Bun* (Frederick Stokes)

Rudolph Fisher: *The Walls of Jericho* (Knopf)

Georgia Douglas Johnson: *An Autumn Love Cycle* (Harold Vinal)

Nella Larsen: *Quicksand* (Knopf)

Claude McKay: *Home to Harlem* (Harper)

1929   February: *Harlem*, co-authored by Wallace Thurman and William Rapp, opens on Broadway to mixed reviews. Archibald Motley, Jr. wins gold medal for painting from the Harmon Foundation. October 29: The New York stock market plunges, eliminating much of the funding powering "New Negro" literature and arts.

Books

Countee Cullen: *The Black Christ and Other Poems* (Harper)

Nella Larsen: *Passing* (Knopf)

Claude McKay: *Banjo: A Story Without a Plot* (Harper)

Wallace Thurman: *The Blacker the Berry* (Macaulay)

Walter White: *Rope and Faggot: A Biography of Judge Lynch* (Knopf)

1930   February: *The Green Pastures*, a play by Marc Connelly, based on Roark Bradford's *Ol' Man Adam an' His Chillun* (1928), opens on Broadway with an all-black cast; it will be one of the most successful plays of its era. July: The Nation of Islam, colloquially known as the Black Muslims, founded by W. D. Fard in Detroit at the Islam Temple. Dancer and anthropology student Katharine Dunham founds Ballet Nègre in Chicago. James Weldon Johnson publishes a limited edition of "Saint Peter Relates an Incident of the Resurrection Day," a poem protesting the insulting treatment accorded to African American Gold Star Mothers visiting American cemeteries in Europe.

Books

Langston Hughes: *Not Without Laughter* (Macmillan)

Charles S. Johnson: *The Negro in American Civilization: A Study of Negro Life and Race Relations* (Henry Holt)

James Weldon Johnson: *Black Manhattan* (Knopf)

James Weldon Johnson: *Saint Peter Relates an Incident of the Resurrection Day* (Viking Press)

1931   April–July: The "Scottsboro Boys," a group of young African American men accused of raping two white women, are tried and convicted; a massive, lengthy, and only partly successful campaign to free them begins. Sculptor Augusta Savage, whose real-life rebuff by the white art establishment becomes part of the back story for *Plum Bun*, establishes the Savage Studio of Arts and Crafts in Harlem.

Books

Arna Bontemps: *God Sends Sunday* (Harcourt, Brace)
Sterling Brown: *Outline for the Study of Poetry of American Negroes* (Harcourt, Brace)
Countee Cullen: *One Way to Heaven* (Harper)
Jessie Redmon Fauset: *The Chinaberry Tree* (Frederick Stokes)
Langston Hughes: *Dear Lovely Death* (Troutbeck Press)
George S. Schuyler: *Black No More* (Macaulay)
Jean Toomer: *Essentials: Definitions and Aphorisms* (Lakeside Press)

1932   June: Langston Hughes, Dorothy West, Louise Thompson, and more than a dozen other African Americans travel to the Soviet Union to film *Black and White*, a movie about American racism. (Due to shifting Soviet policies, the movie will never be made.)

Books

Sterling Brown: *Southern Road* (Harcourt, Brace)
Rudolph Fisher: *The Conjure-Man Dies* (Covici-Friede)
Langston Hughes: *The Dream Keeper* (Knopf)
Claude McKay: *Gingertown* (Harper; story collection)
George S. Schuyler: *Slaves Today* (Brewer, Warren, and Putnam)
Wallace Thurman: *Infants of the Spring* (Macaulay)
Wallace Thurman and Abraham Furman: *Interne* (Macaulay)

1933   **Books**

Jessie Redmon Fauset: *Comedy: American Style* (Frederick A. Stokes)
James Weldon Johnson: *Along This Way* (Knopf)

Alain Locke: *The Negro in America* (American Library Association)

Claude McKay: *Banana Bottom* (Harper)

1934   January: The Apollo Theater opens. February: *Negro*, an anthology of work by and about African Americans, edited by Nancy Cunard, is published by Wishart in London. March: Dorothy West founds the magazine *Challenge*. May: W.E.B. Du Bois resigns from the NAACP; he is replaced as editor of *The Crisis* by Roy Wilkins. November: Aaron Douglas completes *Aspects of Negro Life*, four murals commissioned by the New York Public Library. December: Wallace Thurman and Rudolph Fisher die within days of one another. Richard Wright writes the initial draft of his first novel, *Lawd Today*, published posthumously in 1963. M. B. Tolson completes sequence of poems *A Gallery of Harlem Portraits*, published posthumously in 1979.

Books

Langston Hughes: *The Ways of White Folks* (Knopf; story collection)

Zora Neale Hurston: *Jonah's Gourd Vine* (Lippincott)

James Weldon Johnson: *Negro Americans, What Now?* (Viking Press)

1935   March 19: A riot sparked by rumors of white violence against a Puerto Rican youth results in three African American deaths and millions of dollars in damage to white-owned properties. April: In "Harlem Runs Wild," published in *The Nation*, Claude McKay asserts that the riot is "the gesture of despair of a bewildered, baffled, and disillusioned people." The Works Progress Administration (WPA) established by U.S. President Franklin Delano Roosevelt; writers and artists who will eventually find employment under its aegis include Richard Wright, Ralph Ellison, Dorothy West, Margaret Walker, Augusta Savage, Romare Bearden, and Jacob Lawrence. October: Langston Hughes's play *Mulatto* and George Gershwin's opera *Porgy and Bess* open on Broadway.

Books

Countee Cullen: *The Medea and Some Poems* (Harper)

Frank Marshall Davis: *Black Man's Verse* (Black Cat Press)

W.E.B. Du Bois: *Black Reconstruction in America, 1860–1880* (Harcourt, Brace)

Zora Neale Hurston: *Mules and Men* (Lippincott)
James Weldon Johnson: *Saint Peter Relates an Incident: Selected Poems* (Viking Press)

1936   February: The National Negro Congress, representing some 600 organizations, holds its first meeting in Chicago. June: Mary McLeod Bethune is appointed Director of the Division of Negro Affairs of the National Youth Administration, becoming the highest-ranking African American official of the Roosevelt administration.

Books
Arna Bontemps: *Black Thunder* (Macmillan)
Alain Locke: *Negro Art—Past and Present* (Associates in Negro Folk Education)
Alain Locke: *The Negro and His Music* (Associates in Negro Folk Education)

Biographical Notes

Jean Toomer   Born Nathan Pinchback Toomer on December 26, 1899, in Washington, D.C., the only son of Nathan Eugene Toomer, a Georgia planter who had been born into slavery, and Nina Pinchback, the daughter of P.B.S. Pinchback, a Louisiana politician who during Reconstruction served as the state's lieutenant governor (and briefly as acting governor) and was elected to the U.S. Senate in 1873 but did not serve owing to the contestation of his election. Toomer's parents were of mixed race and, like Toomer, very light-skinned. His parents separated when he was very young; he grew up in the household of his maternal grandfather. Most, if not all, of his early years were spent in Washington, D.C.; he later commented that he did not really live in an African American neighborhood until he was a teenager. Following a short residence in upstate New York with his mother and her second husband, Toomer returned to Washington following her death in 1909 and graduated in 1914 from the elite all-black M Street School (renamed Paul Laurence Dunbar High School in 1916). Toomer enrolled in classes at a variety of schools, including the University of Wisconsin, the Massachusetts College of Agriculture, the American College of Physical Training (Chicago), the University of Chicago, the City College of New York, and New York University, but did not earn an undergraduate degree. He changed his name to Jean Toomer and in his early twenties lived in Greenwich Village where he met writers including Van Wyck Brooks and Witter Bynner, and formed a close friendship with Waldo Frank. In the fall of 1921 he took a temporary teaching job at an agricultural school in Sparta, Georgia, an experience that became the basis for much of *Cane*, a fusion of fiction, poetry, and drama that was published by Boni and Liveright in 1923. His poetry and prose appeared in magazines such as *Broom*, *The Liberator*, *Nomad*, and *The Little Review*, and *Cane* upon publication received wide critical acclaim. Toomer became interested in the mystical ideas of George Ivanovich Gurdjieff; in January 1924 in New York he met A. R. Orage, an English disciple of Gurdjieff, and spent that summer at Gurdjieff's Institute for the Harmonious Development of Man at Fontainebleau, France. Returning to America, he conducted Gurdjieff workshops in New York, Chicago, and Portage, Wisconsin. He married the writer Margery Latimer in 1931, and their marriage led to a national anti-miscegenation scandal when reported on by *Time*. (At the time of the marriage Toomer issued a statement in which he wrote: "There is a new race in America. I am a member of this new race. It is neither white nor black nor in-between. It is the American race [. . .].") Latimer died the following year as a result of giving birth to their daughter Margery. Toomer married Marjorie Content in 1934, and thereafter settled permanently in Doylestown, Pennsylvania. After the appearance of *Cane* he continued to publish poems and prose pieces in magazines, but did not widely circulate much of the writing—including novels, stories, poetry, and plays—composed during that period. *Essentials: Definitions and Aphorisms* and *A Fiction and Some Facts*, small privately printed volumes, appeared in 1931, and the long poem "The Blue Horizon," a meditation on a raceless America on which he had begun work in the early 1920s, was published in the poetry anthology *The New Caravan* in 1936. He traveled to India in 1939. He joined the Religious Society of Friends (Quakers) in 1940. In later years he published *An Interpretation of Friends Worship* (1947) and *The Flavor of Man* (1949). His writings were collected posthumously in *The Wayward and the Seeking: A Collection of Writings by Jean Toomer* (1980) and *The Collected Poems of Jean Toomer* (1988). Toomer was in poor health in his last decades; he died March 30, 1967, in Doylestown.

Claude McKay   Born Festus Claudius McKay on September 15, 1889, in Sunny Ville, Jamaica, last of eleven children of the relatively prosperous farmers Thomas Francis McKay and Hannah Ann Edwards McKay. Around 1897 he went to live with his eldest brother, Uriah Theodore (U'Theo), a teacher, who was entrusted with his education. During a brief period of apprenticeship to a local craftsman, McKay met Walter Jekyll, an English scholar and folklorist resident in Jamaica who encouraged his literary ambitions. In 1911 McKay joined the Jamaican constabulary, leaving the force after a year. His first two books, *Songs of Jamaica* and *Constab Ballads*, collections of poetry mostly written in local Jamaican vernacular, were published in 1912. McKay moved to the United States in the summer of 1912 to attend the Tuskegee Institute in Alabama; he transferred to Kansas State University, where he studied for nearly two years but did not complete a degree. (Of his first encounter with white American racial attitudes he later wrote: "I had heard of prejudice in America but never dreamed of it being so intensely bitter.") After moving to New York City in 1914, McKay was briefly married to Eulalie Imelda Edwards, whom he had known in Jamaica, and for a short time he ran a restaurant in Brooklyn. His wife returned to Jamaica after six months; there she gave birth to their daughter Ruth, who never met her father. McKay never remarried and is thought to have been romantically involved with both men and women. On his move to Harlem, which was his base from 1917 to 1919, he later wrote: "Harlem was my first positive reaction to American life . . . After two years in the blue-sky-law desert of Kansas, it was like entering a paradise of my own people." He worked initially at a variety of jobs before settling into longer-term employment as a dining-car waiter on the Pennsylvania Railroad. His poetry appeared in *Seven Arts* in 1917 and (following a friendly meeting with editor Frank Harris) in *Pearson's Magazine* in 1918. He became involved in radical political circles, forming a friendship with the black socialist leader Hubert H. Harrison and joining the IWW (International Workers of the World), as well as Cyril Briggs's semi-secret radical organization the African Blood Brotherhood, in 1919. (Within the next few years, in all likelihood, he joined the American Communist Party, then functioning as an illegal underground organi-zation.) After publishing a poem in *The Liberator* he became friendly with the magazine's editor Max Eastman and his sister Crystal East-man; in July 1919 *The Liberator* published a spread of seven poems by McKay, including the sonnet "If We Must Die," written in response to the racial violence of the Red Summer of 1919. With the help of some British admirers, he traveled to London, where he lived from the fall of 1919 to the end of 1920. He became involved with Sylvia Pankurst's Workers' Socialist Federation and eventually became a staff member of her magazine *The Workers' Dreadnought*. The critic C. K. Ogden published a large selection of McKay's poetry in *Cambridge Magazine* and arranged for the publication of the poetry collection *Spring in New Hampshire*. Disillusioned by what he considered the problematic racial attitudes of many on the English left, and embroiled in the in-ternal politics of the WSF, McKay decided to return to New York. Upon his return he was invited by Max Eastman to become associate editor of *The Liberator* along with Floyd Dell and Robert Minor; sub-sequently Dell and Minor were replaced by Michael Gold. Internal tensions at the magazine led McKay to resign his editorship in August 1922, leaving Gold, a more orthodox Communist, as sole editor. *Harlem Shadows*, a poetry collection incorporating all the poems from *Spring in New Hampshire* along with much other work, appeared in 1922. With the help of a fund-raising campaign, McKay traveled to the Soviet Union in September 1922. Working as a stoker on his way across the Atlantic, he stopped in London and Berlin before traveling to Moscow, where he attended the Fourth Congress of the Third Inter-national despite initial opposition from a dominant faction in the American Communist Party. In a speech before the Congress, McKay was critical of unexamined racial prejudice on the part of white Ameri-can radicals; during the conference he also met with Leon Trotsky. He remained in Russia for another six months, meeting a number of liter-ary figures including Boris Pilnyak, Yevgeny Zamyatin, and Vladimir

Mayakovsky and publishing articles in the Soviet press which he re-
worked into the study *The Negroes in America*, published in Russian
in 1923. Afterward he settled mostly in France, spending a great deal
of time in Marseilles and Toulon, and with periods of residence in
Spain and Morocco. He destroyed his novel "Color Scheme" after it
was rejected by a number of publishers. His first published novel,
Home to Harlem (1928), was a commercial success, although it met
with much negative criticism in the African American press. McKay
subsequently published a second novel describing the port life of
Marseilles, *Banjo: A Story Without a Plot* (1929), *Gingertown* (1932),
a collection of stories, and *Banana Bottom* (1933), a novel set in Jamaica; another novel, "The Jungle and the Bottoms" (later retitled
"Romance in Marseilles") remained unpublished. He left France in
1930 and began a three-year residence in Morocco. His essay "A Negro Writer to His Critics" appeared in the New York *Herald Tribune*
in 1932. He returned to the United States in January 1934, settling in
Harlem. He began publishing journalism in *The Nation*, including
"Harlem Runs Wild," an account of the Harlem riots of March 19,
1935; found employment with the Federal Writers' Project; and published a memoir, *A Long Way from Home* (1937), and the study *Harlem:
Negro Metropolis* (1940). His attempts to establish a Negro Authors'
Guild ended in failure. Having suffered from ill health for years, he
suffered a major collapse in 1942, followed by a debilitating stroke the
next year, and received assistance from Friendship House, a Catholic
lay organization. He published no further books, although his essays
and poetry continued to appear in *The New Leader*, *The Nation*, *The
Amsterdam News*, and other periodicals. McKay converted to Catholi-
cism a few years before his death in Chicago, where he worked for the
National Catholic Youth Organization. He died on May 22, 1948.

Nella Larsen   Born Nellie Walker in Chicago on April 13, 1891, the
daughter of Peter Walker, a cook from the Danish West Indies (now
U.S. Virgin Islands), and Mary Hansen, a Danish immigrant. (There
are no documents to establish whether her parents were legally married.) Her father apparently died or left the family when she was very
young, and her mother married Peter Larsen, also of Scandinavian
ancestry, and had a daughter, Anna, with him. Anna was considered
white, and Nella would subsequently feel alienated from the family as
the one dark daughter. For several years in her childhood (probably
between 1895 and 1898) Larsen lived in Denmark with her mother
and half-sister. On returning to the United States, Larsen attended
Fisk University's high school in Nashville. After leaving Fisk—she
may have been expelled as a result of her protest against Fisk's dress
code—she traveled again to Denmark, remaining there until 1912 and

by her own account auditing courses at the University of Copenhagen. Subsequently Larsen studied nursing in New York City at Lincoln Hospital and later worked at Tuskegee Hospital and for the New York City Health Department. Larsen married physicist Elmer S. Imes in May 1919 and within three years had left nursing and begun a brief career as a librarian in the New York Public Library system, including the Children's Room at the 135th Street branch. Larsen's first publication, an article on Danish children's games, appeared in *The Brownie's Book*, a magazine for African American children published under the auspices of the NAACP's *The Crisis*. With her husband Larsen led an active social life in New York, where her friends in cultural and literary circles included Walter White and James Weldon Johnson; she became particularly close to Carl Van Vechten. Her novels *Quicksand* (1928) and *Passing* (1929) were published by Alfred A. Knopf and attracted considerable praise, including laudatory reviews by W.E.B. Du Bois; she became the first black woman to win the Guggenheim Fellowship (1930). She was accused of plagiarism when resemblances were detected between her short story "Sanctuary" (1930) and an earlier story by the English writer Sheila Kaye-Smith. Her husband joined the faculty of Fisk, where he began an affair with Edith Gilbert, the school's white director of publicity and finances. Larsen traveled alone to Europe on her Guggenheim Fellowship, staying in Spain and France and completing a novel ("Mirage"), which was rejected by Knopf. (This and other unpublished work by Larsen does not survive in manuscript.) After returning to America she lived for a time with her husband at Fisk, although the two led separate lives; they were divorced in 1933. In later life Larsen distanced herself from most of her friends, some of whom later suggested she may have battled problems with alcohol or drugs. She returned to professional nursing in 1944, working at Gouverneur Hospital on New York's Lower East Side. In 1961 Larsen began working as night supervisor in the psychiatric ward of Metropolitan Hospital, where she remained employed until her death on March 30, 1964.

Jessie Redmon Fauset   Born Jessie Redmon Fauset in Camden County, New Jersey, near Philadelphia, on April 27, 1882, the seventh child of African Methodist Episcopal minister Redmon Fauset and Annie Seamon Fauset, who died when Fauset was still a young girl. After her father's remarriage to Bella Huff, Fauset moved to Philadelphia, where she attended the predominantly white Philadelphia High School for Girls. Having been denied admission to Bryn Mawr on the basis of race, she attended Cornell University, 1901–05, and received an undergraduate degree in classical languages; she was also the first African American female Phi Beta Kappa key holder. She began corresponding with W.E.B. Du Bois in 1903, and with his help secured a summer teaching position at Fisk University in 1904. After graduating from Cornell, and unable to find employment in Philadelphia's segregated high school system, she taught for fourteen years at M Street High School (renamed Paul Laurence Dunbar High School in 1916) in Washington, D.C., the educational home of the District of Columbia's black elite. Fauset earned a master's degree in French at the University of Pennsylvania in 1919. That same year Du Bois offered her the opportunity to move to New York City as literary editor of the NAACP publication *The Crisis*, to which she had been contributing articles, stories, and poems since 1912. As editor she encouraged the work of Jean Toomer, Claude McKay, Langston Hughes, Nella Larsen, Countee Cullen, George S. Schuyler, and other emerging African American writers. With fellow *Crisis* staff member Augustus Granville Dill, Fauset edited the NAACP's children's publication, *The Brownie's Book*, 1920–21. She continued to contribute prolifically to *The Crisis*; her essay "The Gift of Laughter" was included in Alain Locke's anthology *The New Negro* (1925); and her Sunday teas and literary soirées became gathering places for writers and intellectuals. (Langston Hughes would comment about these occasions: "A good time was shared by talking literature and reading poetry aloud and perhaps enjoying some conversation in French. White people were seldom present unless they were very distinguished white people, because Jessie Fauset did not feel like opening her home to mere sightseers, or faddists momentarily in love with Negro life.") In 1921 she attended the Second Pan-African Congress in Brussels as a delegate of the Delta Sigma Theta sorority. The publication of her first novel, *There Is Confusion*, by Boni and Liveright was celebrated by a dinner at the Civic Club on March 21, 1924, widely attended by African American writers and by representatives of mainstream publishing houses, and was afterward taken as an inaugural event of the Harlem Renaissance. She traveled again in Europe, 1924–25. A second novel, *Plum Bun* (1928), was followed by *The Chinaberry Tree* (1931) and *Comedy: American Style* (1933), all published by Frederick A. Stokes. Fauset left *The Crisis* in 1927 and returned to teaching at New York City's De Witt Clinton High School (where she may have taught the young James Baldwin). In 1929 she married Herbert Harris, an insurance agent. She gave up teaching in 1944 and moved with her husband to Montclair, New Jersey; she had little involvement in literary circles in her later years. After her husband's death in 1958 she moved to Philadelphia, where she died on April 30, 1961.

Wallace Thurman   Born August 16, 1902, in Salt Lake City, Utah, the son of Beulah Jackson and Oscar Thurman, and raised by his mother and grandmother in Utah, his parents having divorced in the year of Thurman's birth. His mother was married at least six times; his father he scarcely knew in his adult years except for an encounter in 1929. His maternal grandmother, Emma Jackson ("Ma Jack"), kept a tavern and engaged in bootlegging activities at various times. A voracious reader at an early age, Thurman briefly attended high school in Omaha, Nebraska, where he had gone with his mother, before returning to Salt Lake City where he graduated from West Salt Lake High School. He spent two years as a pre-med student at the University of Utah; after a hiatus, he enrolled in 1922 in the journalism program at the University of Southern California, apparently dropping out after a semester. After leaving school he was employed as associate editor at the Los Angeles newspaper *The Pacific Defender*. He also worked as a postal clerk, forming a friendship with fellow postal worker Arna Bontemps. Thurman founded *The Outlet*, described by him as "the first western Negro literary magazine," of which he published six issues (no copies are known to have survived). After the failure of the magazine he moved to New York, arriving in Harlem in the fall of 1925 and renewing his friendship with Bontemps, who found him a room in the same boarding house where he was staying. Plagued by ill health, Thurman supported himself with difficulty. (In a 1928 letter to Claude McKay, he wrote: "I came to Harlem knowing one individual. Since then I have struggled and starved and had a hell of a good time generally.") Along with Nella Larsen, Aaron Douglas, and other Harlem writers and artists he attended Jean Toomer's workshop on Gurdjieff's teachings. Theophilus Lewis, for whose short-lived magazine *The Looking Glass* Thurman had worked as writer and editorial assistant, found Thurman an editorial position at *The Messenger*, to which he also contributed articles and reviews. He played the leading role in editing the literary journal *Fire!!* (1926), whose other editors were Langston Hughes, Zora Neale Hurston, Richard Bruce Nugent, Gwendolyn Bennett, John P. Davis, and Aaron Douglas. Only one issue appeared, in November 1926; it was controversial, due in part to the sexual frankness of Nugent's "Smoke, Lilies and Jade" and Thurman's story "Cordelia the Crude." The print run was almost completely destroyed in an apartment fire, and Thurman bore most of the burden of the magazine's considerable financial losses. Also in November 1926 Thurman moved into an apartment at 267 West 136th Street (nicknamed "Niggeratti Manor"), which he shared with the artist and writer Richard Bruce Nugent and which became a social center frequented by Hughes, Hurston, Dorothy West, and others. Another journal launched by Thurman in 1928, *Harlem: A Journal of Negro Life*, published only a single issue. His article "Negro Life in New York's Harlem" was published in the Haldeman-Julius Little

Blue Book series in 1928. In August 1928 he married Louise Thompson but the marriage broke up within months (or perhaps weeks); Thompson would later remark of Thurman that "he took nothing seriously. He laughed about everything. He would often threaten to commit suicide but you knew he would never try it. And he would never admit he was a homosexual." He worked as an editor at Macfadden Publishers and contributed stories to *True Story* under pseudonyms. His novel *The Blacker the Berry* was published by the Macaulay Company in February 1929. The same month, his play *Harlem: A Melodrama of Negro Life in Harlem*, written in collaboration with the white playwright William Jourdan Rapp and based on Thurman's story "Cordelia the Crude," opened on Broadway and ran for ninety-three performances. Thurman began to spend much time outside of New York City, returning to Salt Lake City and later staying in Los Angeles and the Long Island home of Theophilus Lewis. He finished a collection of essays, "Aunt Hagar's Children," which was not published in his lifetime. A second novel, *Infants of the Spring*, containing thinly veiled portraits of himself and many of his artistic colleagues, was published by Macaulay in 1932. He was hired as a reader and subsequently as editor at Macaulay. *The Interne*, a novel based on a play by Thurman and co-written with Abraham Furman, was published in 1932. Furman subsequently introduced Thurman to the independent film producer Brian Foy; Thurman went to Hollywood in February 1934 and wrote the stories for two low-budget films, *Tomorrow's Children* and *High School Girl*. He returned to New York in poor health, exacerbated by heavy drinking, and following a diagnosis of acute tuberculosis entered City Hospital on Welfare Island. He died there on December 22, 1934.

Note on the Texts

This volume collects five novels—*Cane* (1923), by Jean Toomer; *Home to Harlem* (1928), by Claude McKay; *Quicksand* (1928), by Nella Larsen; *Plum Bun* (1928), by Jessie Redmon Fauset; and *The Blacker the Berry* (1929), by Wallace Thurman—associated with what has come to be known as the Harlem Renaissance, a period of great creativity and change in African American cultural life, with its epicenter in New York's Harlem neighborhood. A companion volume in The Library of America series, *Harlem Renaissance: Four Novels of the 1930s*, includes four later novels: *Not Without Laughter* (1930), by Langston Hughes; *Black No More* (1931), by George S. Schuyler; *The Conjure-Man Dies* (1932), by Rudolph Fisher; and *Black Thunder* (1936), by Arna Bontemps. The texts of all of these novels have been taken from the first printings of the first editions.

Cane. By Jean Toomer's own account in *The Wayward and the Seeking* (1980), his posthumously published autobiographical writings, he began the poems, sketches, and short stories later gathered in *Cane* at the end of November 1921, "on the train coming north" after a stint during the fall as temporary principal of a school in rural Sparta, Georgia. He had in fact already written one story subsequently adapted in *Cane*, "Georgia Night," sending it to *The Liberator* while still in Sparta. But back in Washington, D.C., Toomer intensified his literary efforts. By March 24, 1922, he was able to report, in a letter to Waldo Frank: "I have thrown my energies into writing. I have written any number of poems, several sketches in play form, and one long piece which I call a Play in Three Acts." Frank—the established writer of the pair, whom Toomer had met in 1920—encouraged Toomer to send his work, and having read it responded with enthusiasm. He immediately suggested that Toomer submit "some of the shorter things" to the *Dial* and *Broom*, and he followed up on April 25, 1922, with a detailed critical evaluation of Toomer's manuscripts. He faulted "Natalie Mann," a play Toomer did not ultimately include in *Cane*, and praised "Kabnis" in particular, while suggesting changes: "I wonder if you would not have done better in a freer form of narrative, in which your dialog, which has no kinship with the theatric, might have thrived more successfully." Toomer accepted almost all of Frank's advice and began revising. He also announced a plan for a book in a letter to Frank on July 19: "I've had the impulse to collect my sketches and poems under

the title perhaps of CANE. Such pieces as Karintha, Carma, Avey, and
Kabnis (revised) coming under the sub head of Cane Stalks and Choruses. Poems under the sub head of Leaves and Syrup Songs. And my
vignettes, of which I have any number, under Leaf Traceries in Washington." The two corresponded extensively about each other's work
in July and August, and in September and October they traveled together to Spartanburg, South Carolina, where Frank, then working
on his novel *Holiday* (1923), hoped to get a firsthand sense of the
South. Returning from Spartanburg, Toomer wrote "Box Seat," "Theater," and "Blood-Burning Moon"; on December 12, he sent Frank a
completed draft of *Cane*. Boni & Liveright, to whom Frank had already recommended the book, decided to accept *Cane* for publication
around the end of the year. Frank reread Toomer's manuscript before
meeting with Horace Liveright on January 8, 1923, and suggested
further revisions. He hoped Toomer might cut several poems ("Something Is Melting Down in Washington," "Tell Me," "Glaciers of
Dusk," and "Prayer") and revise the story "Box Seat." Toomer argued
that "Prayer" was important to the integrity of his work but he yielded
on the other poems and sent Frank additional ones, giving him the
authority to choose which, if any, to add. He rearranged the book's
parts and revised "Box Seat," about which the two had especially corresponded. Toomer sent his revised manuscript to Horace Liveright
on February 27. Both Toomer and Frank read proofs (Frank arguing,
for one, for the retention of Toomer's irregular two- and three-dot el-
lipses). *Cane* was published by Boni & Liveright in September 1923.

Many of the poems, sketches, and stories gathered in *Cane* were
published in magazines between April 1922 and September 1923. The
following is a list of these periodical appearances, in the order in
which Toomer's works were ultimately published in *Cane*:

Karintha: *Broom*, January 1923
November Cotton Flower: *The Nomad*, Summer 1923
Becky: *The Liberator*, October 1922
Face: *Modern Review*, January 1923 (with "Conversion" and "Portrait
     in Georgia," one of three "Georgia Portraits")
Carma: *The Liberator*, September 1922
Song of the Son: *The Crisis*, April 1922
Georgia Dusk: *The Liberator*, September 1922
Fern: *The Little Review*, Autumn 1922
Esther: *Modern Review*, January 1923
Conversion: *Modern Review*, January 1923
Portrait in Georgia: *Modern Review*, January 1923
Blood-Burning Moon: *Prairie*, March–April 1923
Seventh Street: *Broom*, December 1922

Storm Ending: *Double Dealer*, September 1922
Her Lips Are Copper Wire: *S4N*, May–August 1923
Calling Jesus: *Double Dealer*, September 1922 (as "Nora")
Harvest Song: *Double Dealer*, December 1922
Kabnis: *Broom*, August 1923 (section I); *Broom*, September 1923
    (section V)

To varying degrees, Toomer revised most of these individual works
before he gathered them in *Cane*, and (along with Frank) he retained
considerable control over the form in which they finally appeared.
Boni & Liveright reprinted *Cane* once, in 1927, without altering the
text; another reprint (New York: University Place Press) was published
in 1951. The present volume prints the text of the 1923 Boni & Liveright first printing.

Home to Harlem. Claude McKay began his first novel, *Home to
Harlem*, on the suggestion of William Aspinwall Bradley, an American
literary agent based in Paris. Toward the end of 1926, Bradley visited
McKay in Cap d'Antibes, where McKay was staying with his friend
Max Eastman. Bradley conveyed the good news that Harper &
Brothers in New York would be willing to publish a collection of sto-
ries that McKay had recently completed. But a novel, they felt—as
McKay recalled in his 1937 memoir *A Long Way from Home*—would
bring him "more prestige and remuneration than a book of short sto-
ries." McKay and Bradley agreed that "Home to Harlem," a story
McKay had written in 1925, would work well at greater length, and
McKay quickly began expanding it. In February 1927, he told Bradley
that he had finished two chapters: "I am having a picnic doing it.
Everything is clear and I see through the whole story to the end."
Bradley, in the meantime, retrieved a copy of the story "Home to
Harlem" from the magazine *Opportunity*, to which McKay had sent it
for a 1926 competition and which he feared might publish it. McKay
finished the novel by May and sent Bradley the final chapters. By early
December, having "fled to Marseilles," he was correcting proofs.
    During the writing of *Home to Harlem* McKay had expressed a de-
sire to avoid any confrontation over potentially objectionable content
and a willingness to be edited, but in the end he was happy, he wrote
Bradley, that Harper & Brothers had not "chopped it up" as he feared
they might. Eugene Saxton, his editor at the firm, had changed only
occasional words and phrases, McKay reported. No manuscripts or
other prepublication versions of the novel are now known to be extant, so further detail about Saxton's revisions is unavailable. Harper
& Brothers published the novel in early March 1928; in April, McKay
wrote Bradley: "I see *Home to Harlem* like an impudent dog has

[moved] right in among the best sellers in New York." The firm reprinted the novel at least eleven times in 1928 and 1929, without altering the text; it was not subsequently republished until after McKay's death. The present volume prints the text of the 1928 Harper & Brothers first printing.

Quicksand. In early drafts, Nella Larsen's *Quicksand* was titled "Cloudy Amber." In July 1926, when she had half-completed the novel, she discussed potential publishers with her friend Carl Van Vechten; at Van Vechten's suggestion, she decided it ought to go first to Alfred A. Knopf rather than to Albert and Charles Boni, a less prestigious firm then advertising a $1000 prize for the best novel "about Negro life and written by a Negro." In November 1926, as she was finishing "Cloudy Amber," Larsen met Walter White—novelist and then assistant secretary of the NAACP—at a party hosted by Knopf senior editor Harry Block. White offered the assistance of his secretary, Carrie Overton, in typing Larsen's manuscript. Larsen gave Van Vechten a copy of "Cloudy Amber" on December 4, 1926; "read this after dinner & find it in many ways remarkable," he noted in his daybook. Van Vechten responded promptly and in detail, suggesting that she lengthen the novel and change its title and offering to take the novel personally to Knopf (his own publisher, with whom he had considerable influence). Larsen took Van Vechten's advice. In March 1927, Knopf accepted her revised *Quicksand* and returned an edited manuscript. She made final revisions and sent the manuscript back to Knopf to be typeset, receiving her first copies of the book about a year later. *Quicksand* was officially published on March 31, 1928 and was not reprinted during her lifetime. The present volume prints the text of the first Knopf edition.

Plum Bun. Jessie Redmon Fauset began her second novel, *Plum Bun*, during the summer of 1924, just a few months after Boni & Liveright had published her first, *There Is Confusion*. On October 8 she wrote to Langston Hughes from Paris: "I like the stuff of my next novel—I have a good title for it too—but I am troubled as I have never been before with form. Somehow I've never thought much about form except for verse. But now I think I am over zealous—I write and destroy and smoke and get nervous." By the next fall she had finished a draft of the novel, titled "Market." She shared this version with W.E.B. Du Bois, whose unpublished response was dated September 10, 1925, and submitted her manuscript to Boni & Liveright. On October 21, 1925, she wrote to Carl Van Vechten in the hope that he might help her to find a new publisher for "Market": "Mr. Liveright has rejected the book and it is now being read by the Viking Press. I know that you are acquainted with members of that firm and if you can help me in this case I should certainly appreciate it." But Viking, too, decided not to publish the book. It would be three years before the novel finally appeared in print, under the title *Plum Bun*. No manuscript versions of the novel are known to be extant, and the extent to which Fauset may have revised "Market" in the interim is uncertain. Her agent, Brandt & Brandt, finally placed the novel with the London firm of Elkin Mathews & Marrot, which published it in October 1928. Early the next year the novel was released in the United States by the New York firm of Frederick A. Stokes, in the form of the British sheets with the Stokes imprint on the title page. Stokes subsequently had the text reset, and by April 1929 the publisher was able to call its current printing the "third"; but this American setting, which repeats the British spellings, introduced new errors into the text and contains no changes that can be considered authorial. *Plum Bun* did not appear in print again during Fauset's lifetime. The text in the present volume follows the 1928 Elkin Mathews & Marrot edition.

The Blacker the Berry. Relatively little evidence has survived about the composition and textual history of *The Blacker the Berry*, Wallace Thurman's first novel. On April 22, 1927, Thurman's friend Harold Jackman reported in a letter to Countee Cullen that Thurman had finished a novel; about a month later, in an undated letter to Langston Hughes, Thurman wrote that he had sent the novel to Doubleday. In another undated letter to Hughes (January 1928?) Thurman gave an update: "The novel is about re-written." By April 22, 1928, he had shown the novel to Jackman (who called it "very good" in a letter to Claude McKay). Doubleday evidently decided not to accept the novel; instead, it was published by the Macaulay Company in New York on February 1, 1929. *The Blacker the Berry* was not reprinted during Thurman's lifetime. The text in the present volume has been taken from the 1929 Macaulay first edition.

This volume presents the texts of the editions chosen for inclusion here but does not attempt to reproduce every feature of their typographic design. The texts are reprinted without change, except for the correction of typographical errors. Spelling, punctuation, and capitalization are often expressive features, and they are not altered, even when inconsistent or irregular. The following is a list of typographical errors corrected, cited by page and line number: 36.18, at thought; 51.6, overhead; 87.22, me.'; 6 104.13, home.'; 107.35, Otherwise. . ."; 123.21, do think; 127.21, her She; 151.17, cabarets a; 176.17, dearie.'; 201.14, and was; 204.22, burninshed; 209.23, hynotize; 236.8, News,; 246.16–17, on shopping; 247.27, with powder; 267.28, overwhem; 275.32, Telli me; 281.30, exhibtion; 301.37, mouth;; 308.27, complicated.; 310.13, Money,; 312.6, enentirely; 316.6, twenty odd; 330.5, She; 330.16, a well; 347.10, she was; 350.17, as welfare; 363.13, Fisher,; 370.25, Kirkplads; 373.2–3, Amielenborg; 377.21, "Helios"; 381.29, Konigen's; 416.35–36, dusting mending; 428.14, Huh! she; 452.32, fimly; 466.7, profession.; 475.28, argue;; 484.19, "Look; 484.20, means!"; 485.27–28, Angela trim; 488.23, Hotel She; 506.11, whch; 511.37, tabulating; 514.12, on your; 516.9, he did; 518.21, filled; 519.25, her car; 525.1, happiness would; 530.37–38, again again; 563.3, conventions,; 575.23, married; 578.36, 'Well'?"; 586.29, herself "God!"; 590.15, sobeit; 608.36, glaxy; 614.11–12, bewildered; she; 616.20, Mr Cross; 617.23, glibly;; 618.26, ago Back; 620.32, revolver "I've; 623.31, swamp And; 631.12, understand There's; 631.28, memory! Oh; 640.4, her.'; 641.30, years'; 642.11–12, sunny, vocabulary; 644.8, herself,; 651.17, week's; 653.22–23, presumbably; 662.7, herself ashamed; 674.23, nothing with; 675.40, Let's; 675.40, you; 683.31, Movies; 707.21, redstripped; 713.11, good-loking; 734.24, Yer; 735.3, fire-escape decorated; 750.27, one; 751.4, "No" she; 753.15, inpregnate; 759.3, Gal,"; 770.13, "She's; 790.7, Supposing she; 820.6, but possibility; 821.38, Geraldine; 822.3, Geraldine; 822.30, Junior,; 823.15, Junior,.

Notes

In the notes below, the reference numbers denote page and line of the present volume; the line count includes titles and headings but not blank lines. No note is made for material found in standard desk-reference works. For additional information and references to other studies, see Wayne F. Cooper, *Claude McKay: Rebel Sojourner in the Harlem Renaissance* (Baton Rouge: Louisiana State University Press, 1987); Thadious M. Davis, *Nella Larsen, Novelist of the Harlem Renaissance: A Woman's Life Unveiled* (Baton Rouge: Louisiana State University Press, 1994); Geneviève Fabre and Michel Feith, eds., *Jean Toomer and the Harlem Renaissance* (New Brunswick, New Jersey: Rutgers University Press, 2001); Brent Hayes Edwards, *The Practice of Diaspora: Literature, Translation, and the Rise of Black Internationalism* (Cambridge, Massachusetts: Harvard University Press, 2003); Nathan Irvin Huggins, *Harlem Renaissance* (New York: Oxford University Press, 1971); George Hutchinson, *In Search of Nella Larsen: A Biography of the Color Line* (Cambridge, Massachusetts: Harvard University Press, 2006); George Hutchinson, ed., *The Cambridge Companion to the Harlem Renaissance* (Cambridge, United Kingdom: Cambridge University Press, 2007); David Levering Lewis, *When Harlem Was in Vogue* (New York: Alfred A. Knopf, 1980); Nellie Y. McKay, *Jean Toomer, Artist: A Study of His Literary Life and Work, 1894–1936* (Chapel Hill: University of North Carolina Press, 1984); Jacquelyn Y. McLendon, *The Politics of Color in the Fiction of Jessie Fauset and Nella Larsen* (Charlottesville: University Press of Virginia, 1995); Eleonore van Notten, *Wallace Thurman's Harlem Renaissance* (Amsterdam: Rodopi, 1994); Kathleen Pfeiffer, ed., *Brother Mine: The Correspondence of Jean Toomer and Waldo Frank* (Champaign: University of Illinois Press, 2010); Charles Scruggs and Lee Vandemarr, *Jean Toomer and the Terrors of American History* (Philadelphia: University of Pennsylvania Press, 1998); Amritjit Singh and Daniel M. Scott III, eds., *The Collected Writings of Wallace Thurman: A Harlem Renaissance Reader* (New Brunswick, New Jersey: Rutgers University Press, 2003); Carolyn Wedin Sylvander, *Jessie Redmon Fauset, Black American Writer* (Troy, New York: Whitston Publishing, 1981); and Steven Watson, *The Harlem Renaissance: Hub of African-American Culture, 1920–1930* (New York: Pantheon, 1995).

CANE

1.1   CANE]   The first edition of *Cane* included the following foreword by
Waldo Frank (1889–1967), author of *Our America* (1919), *City Block* (1922),
and many other works, with whom Toomer had collaborated closely while
writing the novel:

> Reading this book, I had the vision of a land, heretofore sunk in the
> mists of muteness, suddenly rising up into the eminence of song. Innu-
> merable books have been written about the South; some good books
> have been written in the South. This book *is* the South. I do not mean
> that *Cane* covers the South or is the South's full voice. Merely this: a
> poet has arisen among our American youth who has known how to
> turn the essences and materials of his Southland into the essences and
> materials of literature. A poet has arisen in that land who writes, not as
> a Southerner, not as a rebel against Southerners, not as a Negro, not as
> apologist or priest or critic: who writes as a *poet*. The fashioning of
> beauty is ever foremost in his inspiration: not forcedly but simply, and
> because these ultimate aspects of his world are to him more real than
> all its specific problems. He has made songs and lovely stories of his
> land . . . not of its yesterday, but of its immediate life. And that has
> been enough.
>
> How rare this is will be clear to those who have followed with con-
> cern the struggle of the South toward literary expression, and the par-
> ticular trial of that portion of its folk whose skin is dark. The gifted
> Negro has been too often thwarted from becoming a poet because his
> world was forever forcing him to recollect that he was a Negro. The
> artist must lose such lesser identities in the great well of life. The En-
> glish poet is not forever protesting and recalling that he is English. It is
> so natural and easy for him to be English that he can sing as a man. The
> French novelist is not forever noting: "This is French." It is so atmo-
> spheric for him to be French, that he can devote himself to saying:
> "This is human." This is an imperative condition for the creating of
> deep art. The whole will and mind of the creator must go below the
> surfaces of race. And this has been an almost impossible condition for
> the American Negro to achieve, forced every moment of his life into a
> specific and superficial plane of consciousness.
>
> The first negative significance of *Cane* is that this so natural and re-
> strictive state of mind is completely lacking. For Toomer, the Southland
> is not a problem to be solved; it is a field of loveliness to be sung: the
> Georgia Negro is not a downtrodden soul to be uplifted; he is material
> for gorgeous painting: the segregated self-conscious brown belt of
> Washington is not a topic to be discussed and exposed; it is a subject of
> beauty and of drama, worthy of creation in literary form.
>
> It seems to me, therefore, that this is a first book in more ways than
> one. It is a harbinger of the South's literary maturity: of its emergence
> from the obsession put upon its minds by the unending racial crisis—an

obsession from which writers have made their indirect escape through sentimentalism, exoticism, polemic, "problem" fiction, and moral melodrama. It marks the dawn of direct and unafraid creation. And, as the initial work of a man of twenty-seven, it is the harbinger of a literary force of whose incalculable future I believe no reader of this book will be in doubt.

How typical is *Cane* of the South's still virgin soil and of its pressing seeds! and the book's chaos of verse, tale, drama, its rhythmic rolling shift from lyrism to narrative, from mystery to intimate pathos! But read the book through and you will see a complex and significant form take substance from its chaos. Part One is the primitive and evanescent black world of Georgia. Part Two is the threshing and suffering brown world of Washington, lifted by opportunity and contact into the anguish of self-conscious struggle. Part Three is Georgia again . . . the invasion into this black womb of the ferment seed: the neurotic, educated, spiritually stirring Negro. As a broad form this is superb, and the very looseness and unexpected waves of the book's parts make *Cane* still more *South*, still more of an æsthetic equivalent of the land.

What a land it is! What an Æschylean beauty to its fateful problem! Those of you who love our South will find here some of your love. Those of you who know it not will perhaps begin to understand what a warm splendor is at last at dawn.

> A feast of moon and men and barking hounds,
> An orgy for some genius of the South
> With bloodshot eyes and cane-lipped scented mouth
> Surprised in making folk-songs. . . .

So, in his still sometimes clumsy stride (for Toomer is finally a poet in prose) the author gives you an inkling of his revelation. An individual force, wise enough to drink humbly at this great spring of his land . . . such is the first impression of Jean Toomer. But beyond this wisdom and this power (which shows itself perhaps most splendidly in his complete freedom from the sense of persecution), there rises a figure more significant: the artist, hard, self-immolating, the artist who is not interested in races, whose domain is Life. The book's final Part is no longer "promise"; it is achievement. It is no mere dawn: it is a bit of the full morning. These materials . . . the ancient black man, mute, inaccessible, and yet so mystically close to the new tumultuous members of his race, the simple slave Past, the shredding Negro Present, the iridescent passionate dream of the To-morrow . . . are made and measured by a craftsman into an unforgettable music. The notes of his counterpoint are particular, the themes are of intimate connection with us Americans. But the result is that abstract and absolute thing called Art.

4.1   ⌒]   The curved lines reproduced here and on pages 45 and 92 have been taken from the first edition of *Cane* (1923). Toomer himself suggested they be added. "Between each of the three sections, a curve," he wrote Waldo Frank in a letter of December 12, 1922, having just sent a completed draft of the book. "These, to vaguely indicate the design." His letter begins:

> My brother!
>   CANE is on its way to you!
>   For two weeks I have worked steadily at it. The book is done. From three angles, CANE'S design is a circle. Aesthetically, from simple forms to complex ones, and back to simple forms. Regionally, from the South up into the North, and back into the South again. From the point of view of the spiritual entity behind the work, the curve really starts with Bona and Paul (awakening), plunges into Kabnis, emerges in Karintha etc. swings upward into Theatre and Box Seat, and ends (pauses) in Harvest Song.
>   Whew!

11.29   hant]   Haunt, ghost.

15.20   mazda]   Electric light bulbs. (From "Mazda," a trademark used as a generic term.)

53.9   normal school]   Teachers' college.

59.34   Dictie]   African American slang: snobbish, high class.

64.6   eoho]   Toomer's rendition of a call or exclamation.

92.2   Waldo Frank]   See note 1.1.

103.21   Mame Lamkins]   See Walter White, "The Work of the Mob," *The Crisis*, September 1918, and Stephen Graham, *Children of the Slaves* (London: Macmillan, 1920) on the lynching of Mary Turner, Toomer's source for the story of Mame Lamkins.

HOME TO HARLEM

136.2   *Louise Bryant*]   Bryant (1885–1936), American-born author of *Six Red Months in Russia* (1918) and *Mirrors of Moscow* (1923), had helped McKay financially, enabling him to travel to the south of France after a bout of influenza in 1923–24, and worked with him to find a publisher for a collection of short stories, one of which was expanded as *Home to Harlem*.

140.30–31   Bal Musette]   A dance hall, usually featuring accordion music.

141.25–26   Limehouse]   A port district of London.

148.5   *maisons closes.*]   Brothels.

148.6   apaches]   Ruffians or thugs (from the "Apaches," a turn-of-the-century Parisian street gang).

150.4   dickty]   See note 59.34.

152.2   sweetmen]   Ladies' men or pimps, who lived off women's money.

168.31   f.o.c.]   Free of charge.

169.5–6   Thomas Nelson Page's . . . Cohen's porter]   Page (1853–1922) was the author, among other works, of *In Ole Virginia* (1887), a collection of plantation stories in negro dialect; Cohen (1891–1959) published over 200 magazine stories featuring the "porter-philosopher" Epic Peters, some of them later collected in *Epic Peters, Pullman Porter* (1930).

170.17–19   Jack Johnson . . . Madame Walker.]   Jack Johnson (1878–1946), the first African American heavyweight boxing world champion; James Reese Europe (1881–1919), bandleader and composer; Ada Overton Walker (1880–1914), vaudeville performer; Charles "Buddy" Gilmore (fl. c. 1905–1925), drummer for dancers Vernon Castle (1887–1918) and Irene Castle (1893–1969), who introduced the "Castle Walk" around 1912; Madam C. J. Walker (1867–1919), wealthy hair-care entrepreneur.

170.28   Bert Williams and Walker]   Egbert Williams (1874–1922) and George Walker (1873–1911) performed together as Williams & Walker, a vaudeville comedy duo.

173.7   'Tickling Blues']   Probably the "Tickling Blues" (1928) by Julia Johnson (fl. 1920s).

180.31   coon-can]   Conquian, an early form of the card game Rummy.

181.9   Virginia Dare]   A popular brand of sweet white wine produced by Garrett and Company, originally from North Carolina scuppernong grapes and ater flavored California grapes. During Prohibition the wine was de-alcoholized.

181.12   White Rock]   A brand of soda water.

184.15   jippi-jappa hat]   A panama hat, woven from palm straw.

200.13   Code Napoleon]   The French civil code introduced in 1804 under Napoleon Bonaparte.

202.4   those wonderful pagan verses]   The Biblical Song of Songs, sometimes interpreted as an account of a relationship between King Solomon and the Queen of Sheba.

203.21   Dr. Frank Crane.]   Crane (1861–1928), a Presbyterian minister, columnist, public speaker, and advocate of positive thinking, was the author of the ten-volume *Four Minute Essays* (1919) and *Everyday Wisdom* (1927).

211.21   *Et l'âme . . . l'air.*]   From the poem "L'Ideal" (1865) by Sully Prudhomme (1839–1907).

245.1   Henri Barbusse's *Le Feu*]   *Under Fire* (1916), novel based on the World War I experiences of Henri Barbusse (1873–1935).

250.27   p-i.]   Pimp.

263.13   A.B.S.]   Able seaman, a rank in the merchant marine.

285.17–19   Bert Williams . . . Cole and Johnson.]   For Bert Williams
and George Walker, see note 170.28; for Aida Overton Walker (as she was
sometimes billed), see note 170.17–19. Anita Patti Brown (c. 1882–1950) was a
noted soprano; Robert Allen Cole (1868–1911), along with John Rosamond
Johnson (1873–1954) and his brother James Weldon Johnson (1871–1939), wrote
and performed as "Cole and Johnson" and "Cole and the Johnson Brothers."

QUICKSAND

298.1   E. S. I.]   Elmer S. Imes (1883–1941), Larsen's husband until 1933.

299.1–5   My old man . . . HUGHES]   From Langston Hughes' poem
"Cross," first published in The Crisis in 1925 and collected in The Weary Blues
(1926).

302.13   Marmaduke Pickthall's Saïd the Fisherman.]   A popular picaresque
novel (1903) set in London and the Levant.

303.12–13   hewers of wood . . . water]   See Joshua 9:21.

342.22   Duncan Phyfe]   Phyfe (1768–1854) was a noted early American
furniture designer.

346.33–34   Pavlova . . . Robeson.]   Anna Pavlova (1881–1931), a Russian
prima ballerina; Florence Mills (1896–1927), an African American singer and
dancer who starred in Shuffle Along (1921) and other revues; John McCormack
(1884–1945), an Irish tenor; Taylor Gordon (1893–1971), African American
tenor and vaudeville performer; Walter Hampden (1879–1955), a white actor
and theater manager; Paul Robeson (1898–1976), celebrated actor and
bass-baritone.

347.5–6   Ibsen's remark]   Larsen borrows from Books in General (1919), by
the English critic Sir John Collings Squire (1884–1958), writing under the
pseudonym Solomon Eagle: "As Ibsen used so often to remark, there is a great
deal wrong with the drains; but after all there are other parts of the edifice."

349.35–36   the Garvey movement.]   Jamaican-born Marcus Garvey (1887–
1940) founded the Universal Negro Improvement Association in 1914, the
newspaper The Negro World in 1918, and the Black Star Line, a shipping company, in 1919. A stirring orator, he encouraged racial pride and a return to African roots; his organization acquired a large following and spread to many
countries. In 1925, he was convicted of mail fraud and in 1927 he was deported
to Jamaica.

372.11   "The far-off interest of tears."]   From Tennyson's In Memoriam
A.H.H. (1850), canto I.

377.19–20   Danish melodies of Gade and Heise.]   Niels Wilhelm Gade
(1817–1890) and Peter Heise (1830–1879).

377.21   Nielsen's 'Helios'] The *Helios Overture* (1903), a short orchestral work by Danish composer Carl August Nielsen (1865–1931).

379.28–29   "Everybody Gives Me Good Advice."] A 1906 "comic coon song" with words by Alfred Bryan (1871–1958) and music by James Kendis (1883–1946) and Herman Paley (1879–1955).

381.29   Kongens Nytorv] Kongens Nytorv (Danish: King's New Square), a central square in Copenhagen often used for exhibitions.

406.35–36   *Showers of . . . blessings*] See Ezekiel 34:26 for the source of this text, on which several hymns have been based.

427.35–428.13   Anatole France . . . call him to mind."] See "The Procurator of Judea," a story about early Christians, in *Mother of Pearl* (1908), by Anatole France (1844–1924).

431.13   Houbigant] French perfume manufacturer, founded in 1775.

PLUM BUN

433.4–7   *"To Market . . . is done."*] Traditional English nursery rhyme.

445.34   "bad hair"] Hard-to-straighten, closely curled hair.

455.35   Lycidas] Elegy by John Milton (1608–1674), first published in 1638.

463.20   and siller hae] And silver have: see "The Siller Croun" (c. 1788) by Susanna Blamire (1747–1794), the "muse of Cumberland"; the poem was later set to music (c. 1800) by Joseph Haydn (1732–1809).

548.4–15   two poems . . . again.'] See John S. Hart's *Class Book of Poetry, Consisting of Selections from Distinguished English and American Poets*, first published in 1845. The first poem is from "I'll Never Love Thee More," an English song often attributed to and perhaps adapted by James Graham, 1st Marquess of Montrose (1612–1650); the second is from Oliver Goldsmith's 1762 revision, in an anthology titled *The Art of Poetry on a New Plan*, of Samuel Butler's *Hudibras* (1663–78).

569.1–5   a verse from a poet . . . fool!"] See "The Suppliant," from the book *Bronze* (1922), by Georgia Douglas Johnson (c. 1880–1966).

571.18–19   Raquel Meller] Meller (1888–1962), a Spanish singer and actress, performed in New York to considerable acclaim beginning in 1926.

576.37–39   "It is not courage . . . great,—"] See "To Lucasta on Going to the War—for the Fourth Time," from *Fairies and Fusiliers* (1918), by Robert Graves (1895–1985), as misquoted in the opening editorial of *The Crisis*, March 1919.

648.3   Tony Hardcastle] Tony Lumpkin, son of Mrs. Hardcastle in the play *She Stoops to Conquer* (1773), by Oliver Goldsmith (1728–1774).

648.25   the Duse]   Eleonora Duse (1858–1924), Italian actress.

655.5–14   "Not going . . . because she's coloured?"]   Fauset's account of Rachel Powell's career closely parallels the story of Augusta Savage (1892–1962), an African American sculpture student and a recent graduate of Cooper Union who, in a widely publicized incident in 1923, was denied the scholarship she had won to the Fontainebleau School of Fine Arts because of her race.

656.18   "Who killed Dr. Cronlin?"]   See *Who Killed Dr. Cronin; or, At Work on the Great Chicago Mystery* (1889), by Old Cap Lee, number 341 in the New York Detective Library series, published in Chicago by Frank Tousey. "Old Cap Lee" was a house name used for many of the firm's detective and mystery stories.

THE BLACKER THE BERRY

688.1   *To Ma Jack*]   Emma Ellen Jackson (1862–c. 1940), Thurman's maternal grandmother, with whom he lived for considerable periods during his childhood and adolescence.

689.4–5   My color . . . *Cullen*]   See the opening lines of "The Shroud of Color" (1924), a poem by Countee Cullen (1903–1946).

698.27   Simon Legree]   A cruel plantation master in the novel *Uncle Tom's Cabin* (1852), by Harriet Beecher Stowe (1811–1896).

730.40–731.1   that line in Cullen's . . . abreast with me?"]   See "To You Who Read My Book," the opening poem in Countee Cullen's *Color* (1925).

737.21–22   'Flesh and the Devil']   Film (1926) directed by Clarence Brown, starring Greta Garbo, John Gilbert, and Lars Hanson.

740.23–24   San Juan Hill district.]   A mainly African American neighborhood on Manhattan's West Side that has been described as a "proto-Harlem"; it was largely razed during the 1960s.

746.6–7   "hot" men, of "sweetbacks,"]   "'Hot men' sell 'hot stuff,'" Thurman wrote in his 1927 essay "Negro Life in New York's Harlem"; "which when translated from Harlemese into English, means merchandise supposedly obtained illegally and sold on the q.t. far below par." A sweetback, as he defined the term in his 1929 glossary "Harlemese," is "a colored gigolo, or man who lived off women." See also note 152.2.

765.39–40   that Harlem . . . Survey Graphic]   The March 1925 issue of *Survey Graphic*—published in book form as *The New Negro* (1925)—focused on "Harlem: Mecca of the New Negro." It included "Enter the New Negro," by Alain Locke, "The Making of Harlem," by James Weldon Johnson, "The South Lingers On," by Rudolph Fisher, and "The Black Man Brings His Gifts," by W.E.B. Du Bois, among other items.

766.20 'Long Pants'] 1927 film directed by Frank Capra and starring comedian Harry Langdon.

771.7 "Blue Skies,"] Popular 1926 song by Irving Berlin (1888–1989).

778.27 Bud Fisher] The physician and novelist Rudolph Fisher (1897–1934), nicknamed "Bud."

799.35–36 "Ireland must be . . . there."] Popular 1916 song with lyrics by Joseph McCarthy (1885–1943) and Howard Johnson (1887–1941), and music by Fred Fisher (1875–1942).

800.17–20 A yellow gal rides . . . my Lord.] Thurman's version of a blues set piece. A similar lyric by Henry Thomas (1874–c. 1950) was recorded in 1929 as "Charmin' Betsy."

807.29 "Nigger Heaven" . . . Van Vechten] Controversial roman à clef (1926) by white novelist Carl Van Vechten (1880–1964).

THE LIBRARY OF AMERICA SERIES

The Library of America fosters appreciation and pride in America's literary heritage by publishing, and keeping permanently in print, authoritative editions of America's best and most significant writing. An independent nonprofit organization, it was founded in 1979 with seed funding from the National Endowment for the Humanities and the Ford Foundation.

1. Herman Melville: *Typee, Omoo, Mardi*
2. Nathaniel Hawthorne: *Tales and Sketches*
3. Walt Whitman: *Poetry and Prose*
4. Harriet Beecher Stowe: *Three Novels*
5. Mark Twain: *Mississippi Writings*
6. Jack London: *Novels and Stories*
7. Jack London: *Novels and Social Writings*
8. William Dean Howells: *Novels 1875–1886*
9. Herman Melville: *Redburn, White-Jacket, Moby-Dick*
10. Nathaniel Hawthorne: *Collected Novels*
11. Francis Parkman: *France and England in North America*, vol. I
12. Francis Parkman: *France and England in North America*, vol. II
13. Henry James: *Novels 1871–1880*
14. Henry Adams: *Novels, Mont Saint Michel, The Education*
15. Ralph Waldo Emerson: *Essays and Lectures*
16. Washington Irving: *History, Tales and Sketches*
17. Thomas Jefferson: *Writings*
18. Stephen Crane: *Prose and Poetry*
19. Edgar Allan Poe: *Poetry and Tales*
20. Edgar Allan Poe: *Essays and Reviews*
21. Mark Twain: *The Innocents Abroad, Roughing It*
22. Henry James: *Literary Criticism: Essays, American & English Writers*
23. Henry James: *Literary Criticism: European Writers & The Prefaces*
24. Herman Melville: *Pierre, Israel Potter, The Confidence-Man, Tales & Billy Budd*
25. William Faulkner: *Novels 1930–1935*
26. James Fenimore Cooper: *The Leatherstocking Tales*, vol. I
27. James Fenimore Cooper: *The Leatherstocking Tales*, vol. II
28. Henry David Thoreau: *A Week, Walden, The Maine Woods, Cape Cod*
29. Henry James: *Novels 1881–1886*
30. Edith Wharton: *Novels*
31. Henry Adams: *History of the U.S. during the Administrations of Jefferson*
32. Henry Adams: *History of the U.S. during the Administrations of Madison*
33. Frank Norris: *Novels and Essays*
34. W.E.B. Du Bois: *Writings*
35. Willa Cather: *Early Novels and Stories*
36. Theodore Dreiser: *Sister Carrie, Jennie Gerhardt, Twelve Men*
37a. Benjamin Franklin: *Silence Dogood, The Busy-Body, & Early Writings*
37b. Benjamin Franklin: *Autobiography, Poor Richard, & Later Writings*
38. William James: *Writings 1902–1910*
39. Flannery O'Connor: *Collected Works*
40. Eugene O'Neill: *Complete Plays 1913–1920*
41. Eugene O'Neill: *Complete Plays 1920–1931*
42. Eugene O'Neill: *Complete Plays 1932–1943*
43. Henry James: *Novels 1886–1890*
44. William Dean Howells: *Novels 1886–1888*
45. Abraham Lincoln: *Speeches and Writings 1832–1858*
46. Abraham Lincoln: *Speeches and Writings 1859–1865*
47. Edith Wharton: *Novellas and Other Writings*
48. William Faulkner: *Novels 1936–1940*
49. Willa Cather: *Later Novels*
50. Ulysses S. Grant: *Memoirs and Selected Letters*
51. William Tecumseh Sherman: *Memoirs*
52. Washington Irving: *Bracebridge Hall, Tales of a Traveller, The Alhambra*
53. Francis Parkman: *The Oregon Trail, The Conspiracy of Pontiac*
54. James Fenimore Cooper: *Sea Tales: The Pilot, The Red Rover*
55. Richard Wright: *Early Works*
56. Richard Wright: *Later Works*
57. Willa Cather: *Stories, Poems, and Other Writings*
58. William James: *Writings 1878–1899*
59. Sinclair Lewis: *Main Street & Babbitt*
60. Mark Twain: *Collected Tales, Sketches, Speeches, & Essays 1852–1890*
61. Mark Twain: *Collected Tales, Sketches, Speeches, & Essays 1891–1910*
62. *The Debate on the Constitution: Part One*
63. *The Debate on the Constitution: Part Two*
64. Henry James: *Collected Travel Writings: Great Britain & America*
65. Henry James: *Collected Travel Writings: The Continent*

66. *American Poetry: The Nineteenth Century*, Vol. 1
67. *American Poetry: The Nineteenth Century*, Vol. 2
68. Frederick Douglass: *Autobiographies*
69. Sarah Orne Jewett: *Novels and Stories*
70. Ralph Waldo Emerson: *Collected Poems and Translations*
71. Mark Twain: *Historical Romances*
72. John Steinbeck: *Novels and Stories 1932–1937*
73. William Faulkner: *Novels 1942–1954*
74. Zora Neale Hurston: *Novels and Stories*
75. Zora Neale Hurston: *Folklore, Memoirs, and Other Writings*
76. Thomas Paine: *Collected Writings*
77. *Reporting World War II: American Journalism 1938–1944*
78. *Reporting World War II: American Journalism 1944–1946*
79. Raymond Chandler: *Stories and Early Novels*
80. Raymond Chandler: *Later Novels and Other Writings*
81. Robert Frost: *Collected Poems, Prose, & Plays*
82. Henry James: *Complete Stories 1892–1898*
83. Henry James: *Complete Stories 1898–1910*
84. William Bartram: *Travels and Other Writings*
85. John Dos Passos: *U.S.A.*
86. John Steinbeck: *The Grapes of Wrath and Other Writings 1936–1941*
87. Vladimir Nabokov: *Novels and Memoirs 1941–1951*
88. Vladimir Nabokov: *Novels 1955–1962*
89. Vladimir Nabokov: *Novels 1969–1974*
90. James Thurber: *Writings and Drawings*
91. George Washington: *Writings*
92. John Muir: *Nature Writings*
93. Nathanael West: *Novels and Other Writings*
94. *Crime Novels: American Noir of the 1930s and 40s*
95. *Crime Novels: American Noir of the 1950s*
96. Wallace Stevens: *Collected Poetry and Prose*
97. James Baldwin: *Early Novels and Stories*
98. James Baldwin: *Collected Essays*
99. Gertrude Stein: *Writings 1903–1932*
100. Gertrude Stein: *Writings 1932–1946*
101. Eudora Welty: *Complete Novels*
102. Eudora Welty: *Stories, Essays, & Memoir*
103. Charles Brockden Brown: *Three Gothic Novels*
104. *Reporting Vietnam: American Journalism 1959–1969*
105. *Reporting Vietnam: American Journalism 1969–1975*
106. Henry James: *Complete Stories 1874–1884*
107. Henry James: *Complete Stories 1884–1891*
108. *American Sermons: The Pilgrims to Martin Luther King Jr.*
109. James Madison: *Writings*
110. Dashiell Hammett: *Complete Novels*
111. Henry James: *Complete Stories 1864–1874*
112. William Faulkner: *Novels 1957–1962*
113. John James Audubon: *Writings & Drawings*
114. *Slave Narratives*
115. *American Poetry: The Twentieth Century*, Vol. 1
116. *American Poetry: The Twentieth Century*, Vol. 2
117. F. Scott Fitzgerald: *Novels and Stories 1920–1922*
118. Henry Wadsworth Longfellow: *Poems and Other Writings*
119. Tennessee Williams: *Plays 1937–1955*
120. Tennessee Williams: *Plays 1957–1980*
121. Edith Wharton: *Collected Stories 1891–1910*
122. Edith Wharton: *Collected Stories 1911–1937*
123. *The American Revolution: Writings from the War of Independence*
124. Henry David Thoreau: *Collected Essays and Poems*
125. Dashiell Hammett: *Crime Stories and Other Writings*
126. Dawn Powell: *Novels 1930–1942*
127. Dawn Powell: *Novels 1944–1962*
128. Carson McCullers: *Complete Novels*
129. Alexander Hamilton: *Writings*
130. Mark Twain: *The Gilded Age and Later Novels*
131. Charles W. Chesnutt: *Stories, Novels, and Essays*
132. John Steinbeck: *Novels 1942–1952*
133. Sinclair Lewis: *Arrowsmith, Elmer Gantry, Dodsworth*
134. Paul Bowles: *The Sheltering Sky, Let It Come Down, The Spider's House*
135. Paul Bowles: *Collected Stories & Later Writings*
136. Kate Chopin: *Complete Novels & Stories*
137. *Reporting Civil Rights: American Journalism 1941–1963*
138. *Reporting Civil Rights: American Journalism 1963–1973*
139. Henry James: *Novels 1896–1899*
140. Theodore Dreiser: *An American Tragedy*
141. Saul Bellow: *Novels 1944–1953*
142. John Dos Passos: *Novels 1920–1925*
143. John Dos Passos: *Travel Books and Other Writings*

144. Ezra Pound: *Poems and Translations*
145. James Weldon Johnson: *Writings*
146. Washington Irving: *Three Western Narratives*
147. Alexis de Tocqueville: *Democracy in America*
148. James T. Farrell: *Studs Lonigan: A Trilogy*
149. Isaac Bashevis Singer: *Collected Stories I*
150. Isaac Bashevis Singer: *Collected Stories II*
151. Isaac Bashevis Singer: *Collected Stories III*
152. Kaufman & Co.: *Broadway Comedies*
153. Theodore Roosevelt: *The Rough Riders, An Autobiography*
154. Theodore Roosevelt: *Letters and Speeches*
155. H. P. Lovecraft: *Tales*
156. Louisa May Alcott: *Little Women, Little Men, Jo's Boys*
157. Philip Roth: *Novels & Stories 1959–1962*
158. Philip Roth: *Novels 1967–1972*
159. James Agee: *Let Us Now Praise Famous Men, A Death in the Family*
160. James Agee: *Film Writing & Selected Journalism*
161. Richard Henry Dana, Jr.: *Two Years Before the Mast & Other Voyages*
162. Henry James: *Novels 1901–1902*
163. Arthur Miller: *Collected Plays 1944–1961*
164. William Faulkner: *Novels 1926–1929*
165. Philip Roth: *Novels 1973–1977*
166. *American Speeches: Part One*
167. *American Speeches: Part Two*
168. Hart Crane: *Complete Poems & Selected Letters*
169. Saul Bellow: *Novels 1956–1964*
170. John Steinbeck: *Travels with Charley and Later Novels*
171. Capt. John Smith: *Writings with Other Narratives*
172. Thornton Wilder: *Collected Plays & Writings on Theater*
173. Philip K. Dick: *Four Novels of the 1960s*
174. Jack Kerouac: *Road Novels 1957–1960*
175. Philip Roth: *Zuckerman Bound*
176. Edmund Wilson: *Literary Essays & Reviews of the 1920s & 30s*
177. Edmund Wilson: *Literary Essays & Reviews of the 1930s & 40s*
178. *American Poetry: The 17th & 18th Centuries*
179. William Maxwell: *Early Novels & Stories*
180. Elizabeth Bishop: *Poems, Prose, & Letters*
181. A. J. Liebling: *World War II Writings*
182s. *American Earth: Environmental Writing Since Thoreau*
183. Philip K. Dick: *Five Novels of the 1960s & 70s*

184. William Maxwell: *Later Novels & Stories*
185. Philip Roth: *Novels & Other Narratives 1986–1991*
186. Katherine Anne Porter: *Collected Stories & Other Writings*
187. John Ashbery: *Collected Poems 1956–1987*
188. John Cheever: *Collected Stories & Other Writings*
189. John Cheever: *Complete Novels*
190. Lafcadio Hearn: *American Writings*
191. A. J. Liebling: *The Sweet Science & Other Writings*
192s. *The Lincoln Anthology: Great Writers on His Life and Legacy from 1860 to Now*
193. Philip K. Dick: *VALIS & Later Novels*
194. Thornton Wilder: *The Bridge of San Luis Rey and Other Novels 1926–1948*
195. Raymond Carver: *Collected Stories*
196. *American Fantastic Tales: Terror and the Uncanny from Poe to the Pulps*
197. *American Fantastic Tales: Terror and the Uncanny from the 1940s to Now*
198. John Marshall: *Writings*
199s. *The Mark Twain Anthology: Great Writers on His Life and Works*
200. Mark Twain: *A Tramp Abroad, Following the Equator, Other Travels*
201. Ralph Waldo Emerson: *Selected Journals 1820–1842*
202. Ralph Waldo Emerson: *Selected Journals 1841–1877*
203. *The American Stage: Writing on Theater from Washington Irving to Tony Kushner*
204. Shirley Jackson: *Novels & Stories*
205. Philip Roth: *Novels 1993–1995*
206. H. L. Mencken: *Prejudices: First, Second, and Third Series*
207. H. L. Mencken: *Prejudices: Fourth, Fifth, and Sixth Series*
208. John Kenneth Galbraith: *The Affluent Society and Other Writings 1952–1967*
209. Saul Bellow: *Novels 1970–1982*
210. Lynd Ward: *Gods' Man, Madman's Drum, Wild Pilgrimage*
211. Lynd Ward: *Prelude to a Million Years, Song Without Words, Vertigo*
212. The Civil War: *The First Year Told by Those Who Lived It*
213. John Adams: *Revolutionary Writings 1755–1775*
214. John Adams: *Revolutionary Writings 1775–1783*
215. Henry James: *Novels 1903–1911*
216. Kurt Vonnegut: *Novels & Stories 1963–1973*
217. *Harlem Renaissance: Five Novels of the 1920s*

218. *Harlem Renaissance: Four Novels of the 1930s*
219. Ambrose Bierce: *The Devil's Dictionary, Tales, & Memoirs*
220. Philip Roth: *The American Trilogy 1997–2000*

To subscribe to the series or to order individual copies, please visit www.loa.org or call (800) 964.5778.

*This book is set in 10 point Linotron Galliard,
a face designed for photocomposition by Matthew Carter
and based on the sixteenth-century face Granjon. The paper
is acid-free lightweight opaque and meets the requirements
for permanence of the American National Standards Institute.
The binding material is Brillianta, a woven rayon cloth made
by Van Heek-Scholco Textielfabrieken, Holland. Composition by Dedicated Book Services. Printing by
Malloy Incorporated. Binding by Dekker Book-
binding. Designed by Bruce Campbell.*